McDougal Littell

THE LANGUAGE OF
Literature

ANNOTATED TEACHER'S EDITION

GRADE 6

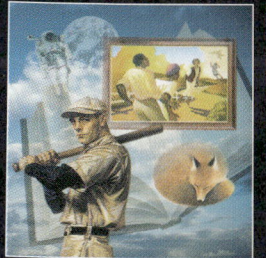 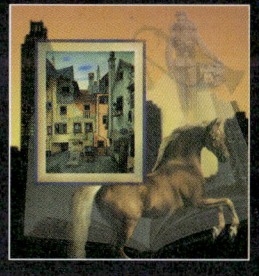  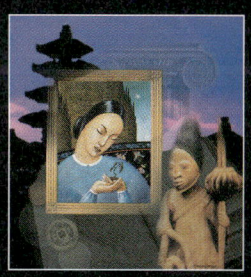  

WARNING: No part of this book may be reproduced or transmitted in any form or by any means, electronic or mechanical, including photocopying and recording, or by any information storage and retrieval system, without prior written permission of McDougal Littell Inc. unless such copying is expressly permitted by federal copyright law. Address inquiries to Manager, Rights and Permissions, McDougal Littell Inc., P.O. Box 1667, Evanston, IL 60204.

ISBN: 0-395-73708-7

Copyright © 1997 by McDougal Littell Inc. All rights reserved.

Printed in the United States of America.

2 3 4 5 6 7 8 9 - DWO - 01 00 99 98 97

Table of Contents

Telling Our Story
What Is *The Language of Literature?* T4
Program Authors and Consultants T5

Overview
Core Components T6
Resource Materials T8
Integrated Technology T8
Assessment Package T9
Access for Students Acquiring English T9

A Closer Look

TEACHING LITERATURE
The Literature Lesson: Pupil's Edition T10
The Literature Lesson: Resource Materials T12

INTEGRATING LANGUAGE AND WRITING SKILLS
The Writing Workshops: Pupil's Edition T14
Writing and Language: Resource Materials T17
Special Features of the Pupil's Edition T18

THE TEACHER'S EDITION
Unit Support T20
Selection and Writing Workshop Support T22

ASSESSMENT
Assessment Resources T24

Advice from the Experts
Practical suggestions for planning your school year

Planning Your Year T26
Developing a Classroom Profile: Multimodal Learners ... T28
Developing a Classroom Profile: Students Acquiring English ... T29
Planning Your Instruction T30
Setting Up Your Classroom T32
New Technology and the English Classroom T34
Preparing for Assessment T36
Making Connections T39

Annotated Student Text

Additional Unit Resources
Unit 1 Resources 17a
Unit 2 Resources 149a
Unit 3 Resources 255a
Unit 4 Resources 387a
Unit 5 Resources 517a
Unit 6 Resources 633a

THE LANGUAGE OF LITERATURE

Telling Our Story

What Is *The Language of Literature?*

Is it a literature anthology? an integrated language arts series? a new approach to teaching and learning? *The Language of Literature* is all of these things—and much, much more.

CLASSIC STORIES, FRESH VOICES, AND NEW PERSPECTIVES

The powerful mix of selections in *The Language of Literature* reflects the exciting nature of our own society:

- Classic and contemporary literature
- Multicultural perspectives
- A mix of genres
- Authentic readings in a variety of media.

A PROGRAM, NOT A BOOK

The Language of Literature is not simply an anthology with a collection of "extras." It is a seamlessly integrated program that links a student book to comprehensive lesson support; mini-lessons in writing, language, and communication; innovative technology; and access for students with special needs.

AN INTEGRATED APPROACH TO LANGUAGE

The selections in *The Language of Literature* become the springboard to a rich mix of language experiences:

- Writing workshops
- Grammar and vocabulary instruction
- Oral communication activities
- Critical viewing and listening
- Research skills
- Visual and media literacy

A WAY TO MAKE STUDENTS CARE

A strong student-centered approach acknowledges the differences among readers and the experiences they bring to a literary selection or writing experience. Responding options, multimodal activities, access materials for all students, and strategies for using media and technology ensure that students learn in a way that matches their individual learning styles.

A NEW WAY OF SEEING

A striking art program is only the beginning of the series' attention to visual and media literacy. Special activities and features throughout the program teach students that reading literature can be the first step toward reading the people and the world around them.

A SPRINGBOARD TO THE WORLD

Every prereading page, response section, and writing workshop provides meaningful activities and thoughtful connections that link the literature to students' own lives, to other curriculum areas, to their family and community, to other cultures, and to the situations and issues they confront every day in the "real world."

A PARTNER IN TECHNOLOGY

A rich videodisc treasury of images, audio and electronic libraries, Internet connections, and the unique Writing Coach software all support the literature and activities in this series. In addition, lessons in the pupil book model the use of technology to access information, network with others, and produce creative multimedia projects.

A WAY TO CONNECT AND REFLECT

Perhaps most importantly, *The Language of Literature* provides a way for students to connect the literature to the often confusing situations they encounter on the pathway from childhood to adulthood. The thoughtfully chosen selections, carefully crafted themes, and rich variety of learning options connect to students' lives and allow them to reflect on how universal certain experiences are.

Program Authors and Consultants

Arthur N. Applebee Professor of Education, State University of New York at Albany; Director, Center for the Learning and Teaching of Literature; Senior Fellow, Center for Writing and Literacy

Andrea B. Bermúdez Professor of Studies in Language and Culture; Director, Research Center for Language and Culture; Chair, Foundations and Professional Studies, University of Houston-Clear Lake

Sheridan Blau Senior Lecturer in English and Education and former Director of Composition, University of California at Santa Barbara; Director, South Coast Writing Project; Director, Literature Institute for Teachers; Vice President, National Council of Teachers of English

Rebekah Caplan Coordinator, English Language Arts K-12, Oakland Unified School District, Oakland, California; Teacher-Consultant, Bay Area Writing Project, University of California at Berkeley; served on the California State English Assessment Development Team for Language Arts

Franchelle S. Dorn Professor of Drama, Howard University, Washington, D.C.; Adjunct Professor, Graduate School of Opera, University of Maryland, College Park, Maryland; Co-founder of The Shakespeare Acting Conservatory, Washington, D.C.

Peter Elbow Professor of English, University of Massachusetts at Amherst; Fellow, Bard Center for Writing and Thinking

Susan Hynds Professor and Director of English Education, Syracuse University, Syracuse, New York

Judith A. Langer Professor of Education, State University of New York at Albany; Co-director, Center for the Learning and Teaching of Literature; Senior Fellow, Center for Writing and Literacy

James Marshall Professor of English and English Education, University of Iowa, Iowa City

THE LANGUAGE OF LITERATURE TEACHER'S EDITION **T5**

THE LANGUAGE OF LITERATURE
Overview

Core Components

The Language of Literature is a seamlessly integrated program that provides teachers with a common-sense system for teaching literature, language, and communication skills. The components described on these pages—the core elements of the program—provide teachers and students with all of the materials they need in a flexible, customizable format. (For more information on each element, please see pages T10 to T25.)

ANNOTATED TEACHER'S EDITION

This comprehensive book provides all of the material you require for a successful teaching experience.

- Unit Content Overview and Planning Charts
- Student Projects
- Professional Enrichment Pages
- Family and Community Involvement
- Annotations for Literature Selections and Writing Workshops
- Bar Codes to LaserLinks
- Recommended Resources

PUPIL EDITION

A rich mix of classic, contemporary and multicultural literature is the starting point from which your class begins its exploration of a world of ideas and experiences. Writing Workshops in each unit continue this exploration, moving students from the literature to interactions with real-world communication and technology.

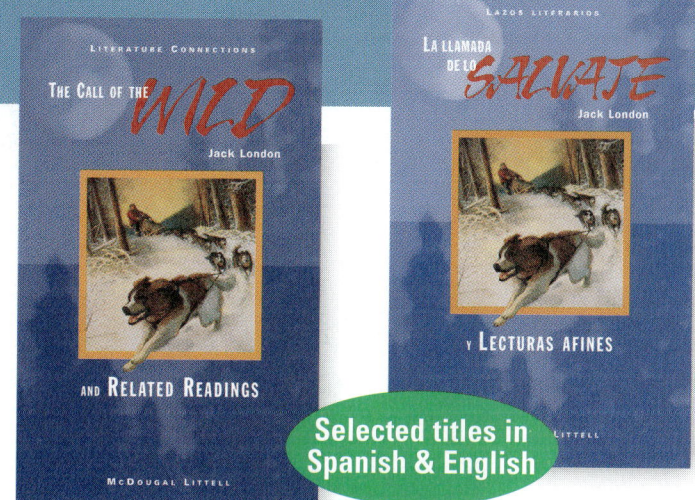

Selected titles in Spanish & English

LITERATURE CONNECTIONS

Unique to *The Language of Literature*, these stand-alone books allow you to decide which plays and novels to include in your literature class. Each longer work is accompanied by several related readings that extend the subject or theme.

SourceBook Provides you with all the information and student support materials you will need to present fresh and effective lessons.

Spanish Editions Selected titles are also available in Spanish, with corresponding Spanish SourceBook pages.

OVERVIEW
(CONTINUED)

Resource Materials

UNIT RESOURCE BOOK Organized by unit and selection, these copymasters provide you with a variety of ways to build and reinforce student skills in reading comprehension, spelling, vocabulary, and writing.

GRAMMAR MINI-LESSONS WRITING MINI-LESSONS These transparency packs allow teachers to identify areas where students need help, and to teach exactly what is needed when it is needed. Corresponding grammar exercise sheets ensure that students get the practice they need on key areas of language and usage.

**LASERLINKS**
A treasury of full-motion video, photographs, and fine art, this videodisc provides the following program support:

- Selection Support: Historical and Cultural Background
- Author Interviews
- Writing Springboards
- Visual Vocabulary
- Art Galleries
- Storytelling

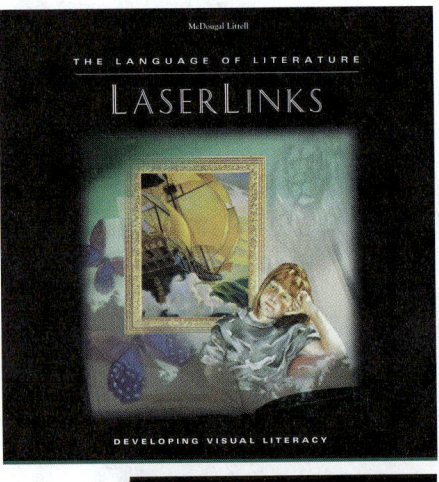

Integrated Technology

 **INTERNET CONNECTIONS** Program-related information can be accessed through the McDougal Littell home page at http://www.hmco.com/mcdougal

 **WRITING COACH**
A comprehensive word processing program with a unique, multi-column format and on-line writing support, the Writing Coach is a powerful tool for collaborative writing, peer response, and evaluation.

 **AUDIO LIBRARY** These tapes contain professional recordings of nearly every selection in the anthology. The performances can be used to enhance the literature or to provide support for less proficient readers.

T8 THE LANGUAGE OF LITERATURE **TEACHER'S EDITION**

Assessment Package

TEACHER'S GUIDE TO ASSESSMENT AND PORTFOLIO USE This guide describes the types and uses of assessment and includes guidesheets, assessment forms, and checklists.

FORMAL ASSESSMENT This booklet contains selection and unit tests, writing assessment materials, and standardized test practice.

ALTERNATIVE ASSESSMENT With these materials—modeled on the authentic assessment materials used in many states and districts across the country—you can evaluate the processes students use as they read and write, as well as the products they create.

Access for Students Acquiring English

TEACHER'S SOURCEBOOK FOR LANGUAGE DEVELOPMENT A teacher handbook that includes teaching strategies and techniques.

TRANSLATIONS IN SPANISH A separate anthology that includes Spanish translations of one selection per unit.

RELATED READINGS Literature that is tied thematically to *The Language of Literature* units. Available in Spanish, Vietnamese, Cantonese, Cambodian, and Hmong.

SELECTION SUMMARIES Summaries of the literature in five languages: Spanish, Vietnamese, Cantonese, Cambodian, and Hmong.

READING AND WRITING SUPPORT Practice activities that support every literature selection and guidesheets for Writing Workshops

FAMILY AND COMMUNITY INVOLVEMENT Available in six languages, these pages allow students to extend unit activities outside the classroom.

LITERATURE CONNECTIONS Spanish translations of selected titles for grades 6-12.

AUDIO LIBRARY These professional recordings may be used as support for Students Acquiring English

LASERLINKS A separate Spanish audio track and Spanish language captions allow students full access to the resources on these videodiscs.

T9

A CLOSER LOOK
Teaching Literature

The Literature Lesson: Pupil Edition

Each literature lesson is divided into three sections: Previewing, the literature selection itself, and Responding Options. This student-centered lesson offers a wide range and choice of activities.

PREVIEWING

Personal Connection Helps students explore prior experience and knowledge about topics covered in the selection.

Historical (Biographical, Cultural, Literary, Geographical, Scientific, etc.) Connection Provides important background information relevant to the selection.

Reading Connection Presents direct instruction in a reading skill designed to improve comprehension of the selection.

Writing Connection Serves as an alternative to the Reading Connection. Allows students to explore selection-related topics through writing.

Graphic Organizer Helps students explore new topics and structure their thinking.

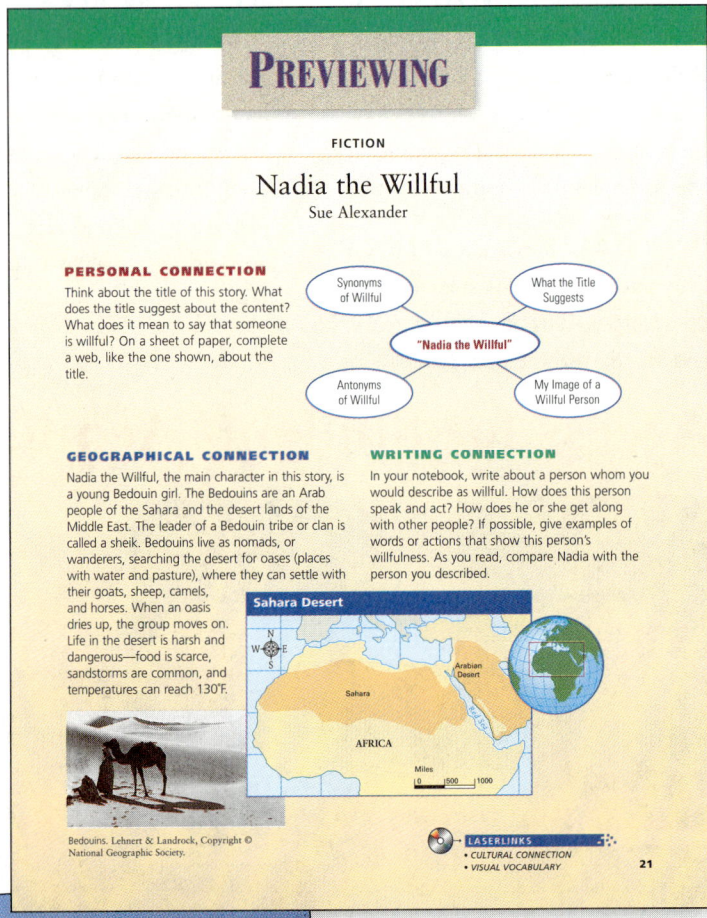

In the land of the drifting sands where the Bedouin move their tents to follow the fertile grasses, there lived a girl whose stubbornness and flashing temper caused her to be known throughout the desert as Nadia the Willful.

Nadia's father, the sheik Tarik, whose kindness and graciousness caused his name to be praised in every tent, did not know what to do with his willful daughter.

Only Hamed, the eldest of Nadia's six brothers and Tarik's favorite son, could calm Nadia's temper when it flashed.

THE SELECTION
The finest literature offerings. Represented are traditional and contemporary pieces, familiar and new voices.

Natural and thematic connections. Selections are organized thematically and, where appropriate, chronologically.

Attractive, engaging design. Helps entice and motivate students.

Active reading questions. Provided as appropriate within selections to help students with comprehension of more challenging pieces.

RESPONDING OPTIONS

From Personal Response to Critical Analysis Invites student-centered discussion with the response-based approach made famous by McDougal Littell. Includes questions that help students relate the literature to their own lives.

Another Pathway Offers an alternative to typical classroom discussion. Generates full exploration of major issues in the selection.

Literary Concepts Introduces or reviews major literary terms and applies them to the selection just read.

Quickwrites Give students several innovative ways of responding to what they have read through writing.

Alternative Activities Offer opportunities to respond to their reading through multimodal activities.

Words to Know Reinforces vocabulary introduced in the selection with motivating exercises.

Author Biography Makes the authors come to life with interesting, student-friendly information. Includes listings of other works by the authors.

ADDITIONAL RESPONDING OPTIONS

Critic's Corner Gives critical commentary on an author or piece of literature and asks students to respond.

Literary Links Asks students to make connection between selection just read and another selection read at an earlier point in the book.

The Writer's Style Asks students to engage in analysis of style by focusing on stylistic traits of author being studied.

Across the Curriculum Provides cross-curricular activities that invite students to go beyond the selection to investigate new areas of study.

Art Connection Asks students to reflect on a work of fine art included in the selection.

TEACHING LITERATURE
(CONTINUED)

The Literature Lesson: Resource Materials

The literature in the Pupil's Edition is reinforced and extended by the following teaching tools for students' own use.

UNIT RESOURCE BOOK
Worksheets and tests provide support for all literature selections.

- **Strategic Reading: Literature Worksheets** reinforce reading strategies and extend the understanding of literary elements.
- **Reading SkillBuilders**
- **Vocabulary SkillBuilders**
- **Spelling SkillBuilders**
- **Selection and Unit Tests** stimulate higher order thinking skills as they assess understanding of selections, literary terms, and language skills.
- **Family and Community Involvement** Worksheets connect unit themes to students' world. A separate booklet provides these same worksheets in five languages: Spanish, Vietnamese, Cantonese, Cambodian, and Hmong.

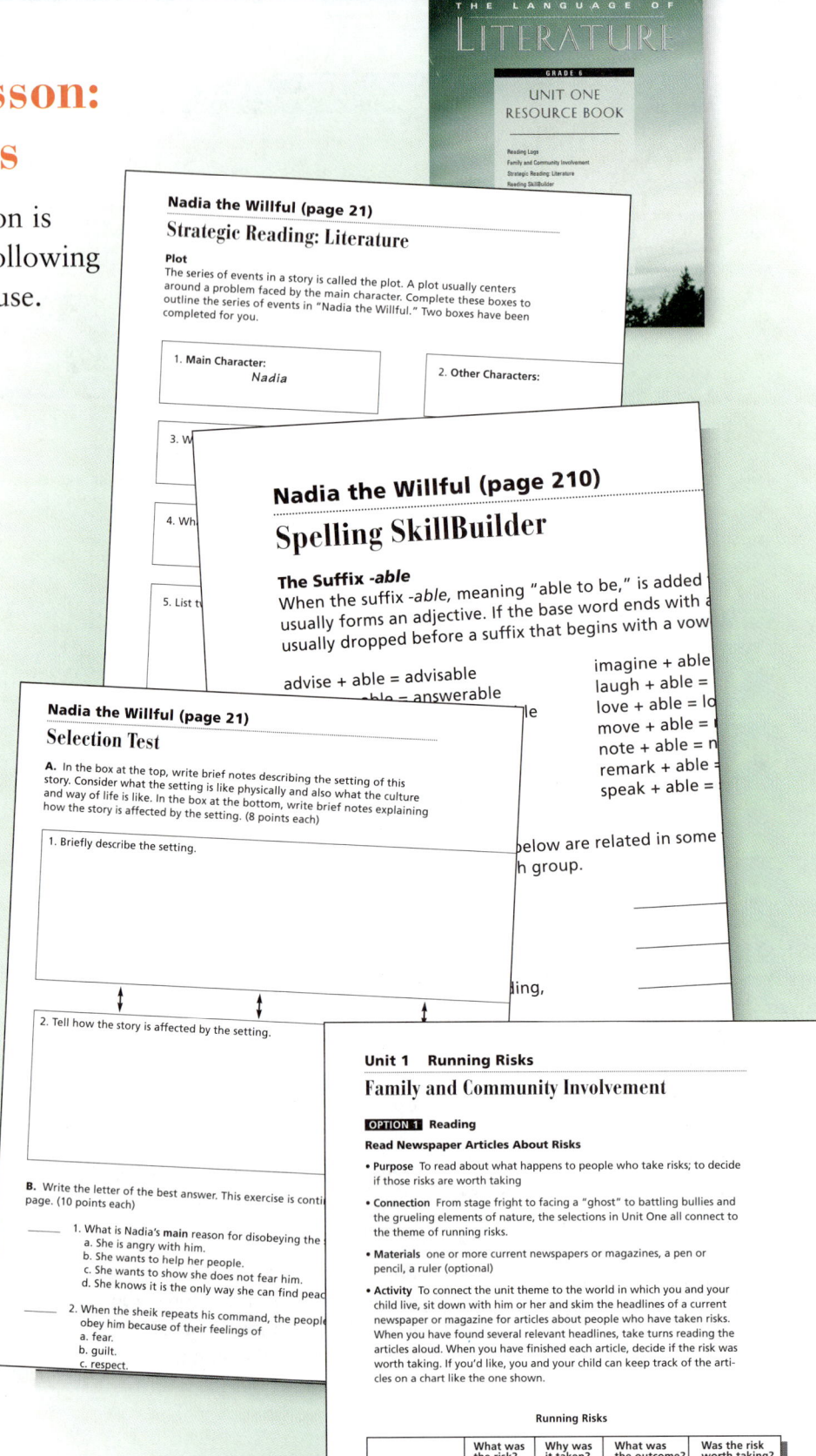

T12 THE LANGUAGE OF LITERATURE TEACHER'S EDITION

LASERLINKS

A Level One videodisc program that enhances the literature curriculum, develops visual literacy, and helps students explore and interact with the literature.

- Provides historical and cultural background to strengthen interdisciplinary connections
- Helps build students' vocabulary through the Visual Vocabulary feature
- Contains author interviews
- Includes images that stimulate writing
- Presents storyteller in action

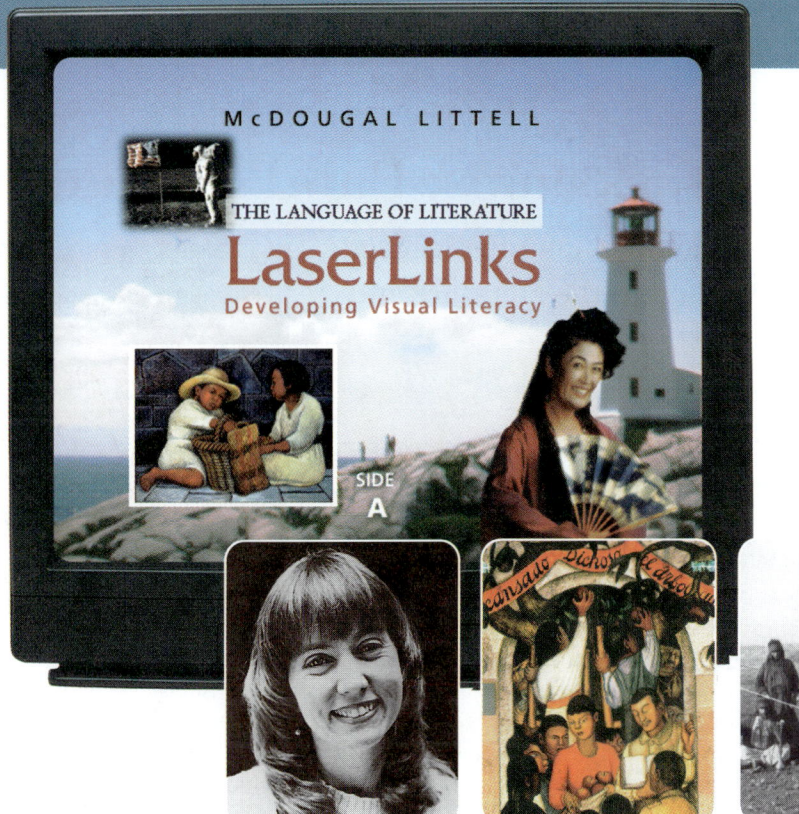

AUDIO LIBRARY

Recordings of almost all selections in each anthology. Provides easy listening, enhances and enriches students' literary experience, and helps students develop strategies for critical listening.

INTERNET CONNECTIONS

The following resources can be accessed through the McDougal Littell home page at http://www.hmco.com/mcdougal

- Literature selection support
- Links to professional materials and organizations
- Teacher discussion groups and bulletin boards

THE LANGUAGE OF LITERATURE TEACHER'S EDITION **T13**

A CLOSER LOOK

Integrating Language and Writing Skills

The Writing Workshops: Pupil Edition

Paired writing workshops in each unit offer students two distinct ways to respond to the literature and make "real world" connections.

WRITING ABOUT LITERATURE
This workshop appears as a set of three related lessons.

- **The Writer's Style** lesson focuses on a writing skill such as sentence variety or elaboration. Literary excerpts and a real-world model show the technique in context.

- **The Guided Assignment** invites students to explore the literature through both creative and analytical writing.

- **Complete Writing Process.** Provides advice for each stage of the writing process, from prewriting to publication and reflection.

- **Student models.** Illustrate the process and choices of another student writer.

- **Peer response questions and Standards for Evaluation.** Help students assess and revise their writing.

- **Skills Instruction.** Grammar in Context and Grammar Skillbuilders teach grammar concepts that relate to the writing.

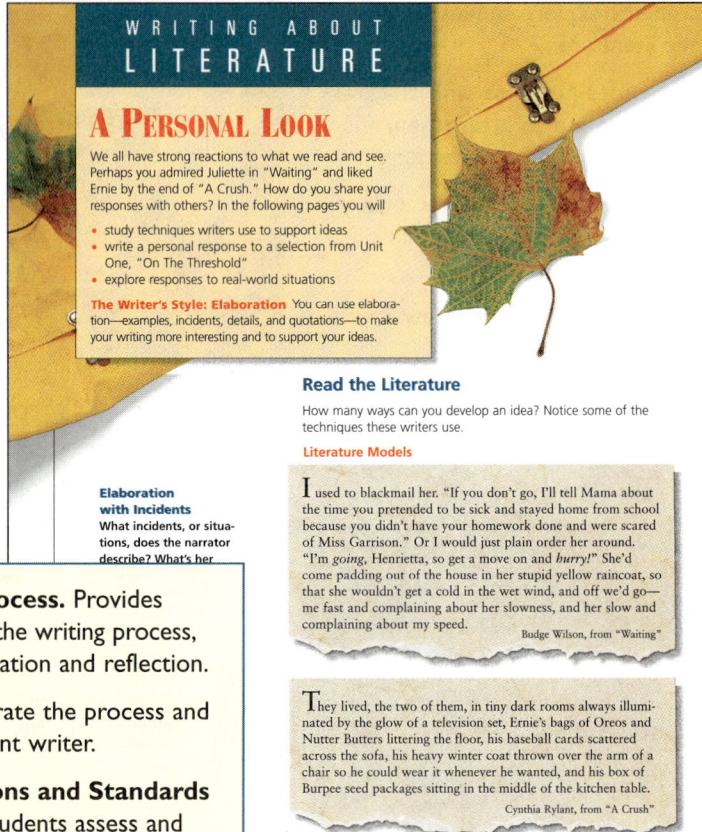

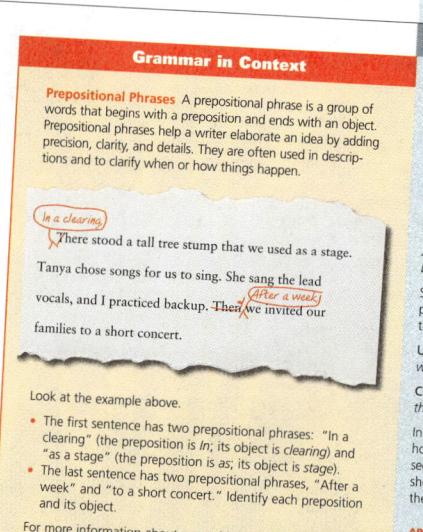

- **Reading the World** builds visual literacy and shows students how the same skills they have just used to analyze and write about literature can also be used to observe, interpret, and understand the world around them.

WRITING FROM EXPERIENCE

The second writing workshop invites students to extend the unit theme by creating products for real purposes and real audiences in situations they encounter in the world around them.

Primary source materials. Magazine and newspaper articles, photographs, charts, and graphs provide a springboard to writing while building critical thinking and media literacy skills.

Oral communication and research skills. Used during prewriting as students gather information. Students are also encouraged to use technology—from CD-ROMs to on-line services—to access information.

Alternative forms of publishing. Visual, oral, and electronic products are suggested and modeled.

T15

INTEGRATING LANGUAGE AND WRITING SKILLS
(CONTINUED)

SCOPE AND SEQUENCE OF WRITING INSTRUCTION

The writing workshops in *The Language of Literature* grow in sophistication as your students do, providing a rich variety of writing assignments that become more challenging in every grade. In the following chart, blue dots indicate the Writing About Literature workshops, and red dots indicate the Writing from Experience workshops. The number following each assignment represents the unit in which it appears.

Writing Strands	Grade 6	Grade 7	Grade 8
Firsthand and Expressive	• Personal Response / 1* • Anecdote / 1	• Personal Response / 1 • First Hand Narrative / 1	• Firsthand Narrative / 1 • Personal Response / 4
Narrative and Literary	• Character Sketch / 2 • Fill in the Blanks / 4 • Writing in Kind: Poem / 5	• Short Story / 2 • Creative Response: Extending story / 4 • Writing in Kind: Fable / 6	• Creative Response: Change story element / 1 • Short Story / 2 • Creative Response: Scene from play / 6
Informative Exposition	• Interpretive: Analyze passage / 2 • Analysis: Plot devices / 3 • Problem-solution / 3 • Compare-contrast / 4 • Critical: Evaluating the message / 6	• Analysis: Imagery / 2 • Interpretive: Answering big question / 3 • Definition: Abstract idea / 3 • Critical: Review (poetry) / 5 • Compare-contrast / 6	• Interpretive: Finding the message / 2 • Critical: Evaluating ideas / 3 • Problem-solution / 3 • Eyewitness / 4 • Analysis: Poetry / 5
Persuasion	• Opinion / 5	• Opinion / 5	• Persuasive Essay / 5
Report	• I-Search / 6	• Report / 4	• Report / 6

*Denotes unit number

Writing and Language: Resource Materials

MINI-LESSONS

The unique mini-lesson transparency packs in *The Language of Literature* allow you to decide what your students need to learn and when they need to learn it.

- **Writing Mini-Lessons.** Cover skills ranging from unity and coherence to voice and style.
- **Grammar Mini-Lessons with Copy Masters.** Provide instruction on the most common usage problems faced by writers.

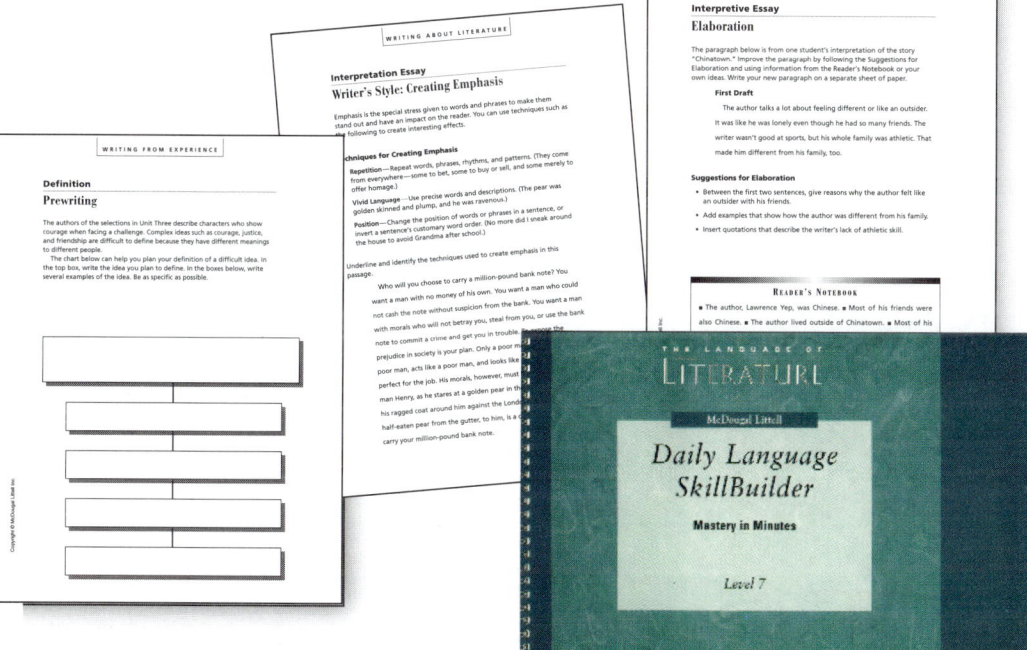

UNIT RESOURCE BOOK

In addition to support for the literature selections, the Unit Resource Book provides comprehensive practice and support for each stage of the writing process. Copymasters include the following:

Writer's Style Worksheet
Prewriting Worksheet
Elaboration Practice
Peer Response Guide
Revising and Proofreading Practice
Complete Student Model
Rubrics for Evaluation

DAILY LANGUAGE SKILLBUILDER

Through daily exercises, this product integrates grammar, proofreading, and punctuation skills with literature-based content

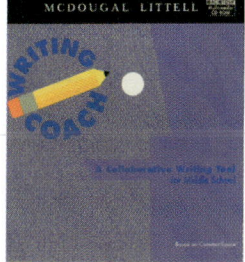

WRITING COACH
Collaborative Writing Software
This interactive, multimedia writing program on CD-ROM guides students through the writing process in a collaborative environment.

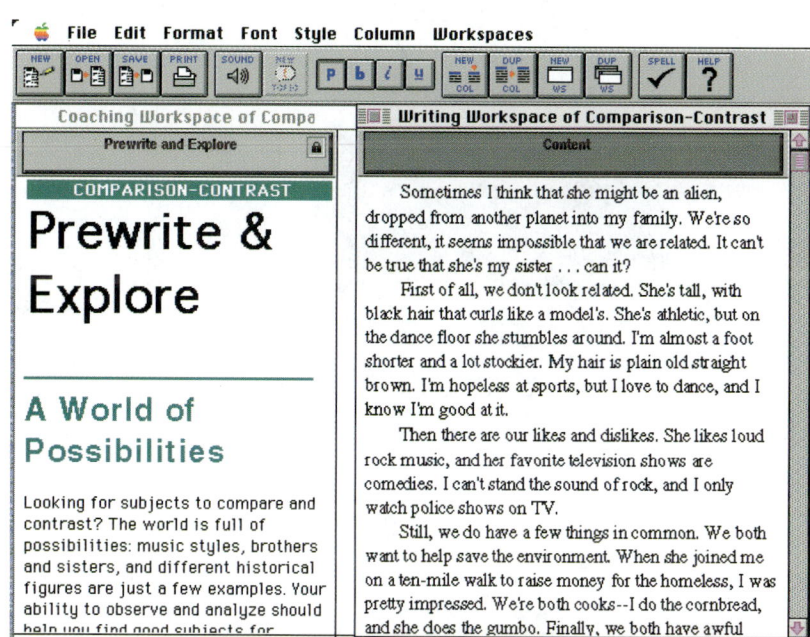

T17

A CLOSER LOOK

Special Features of the Pupil Edition

This book contains a wealth of special features to help enrich each student's learning experience.

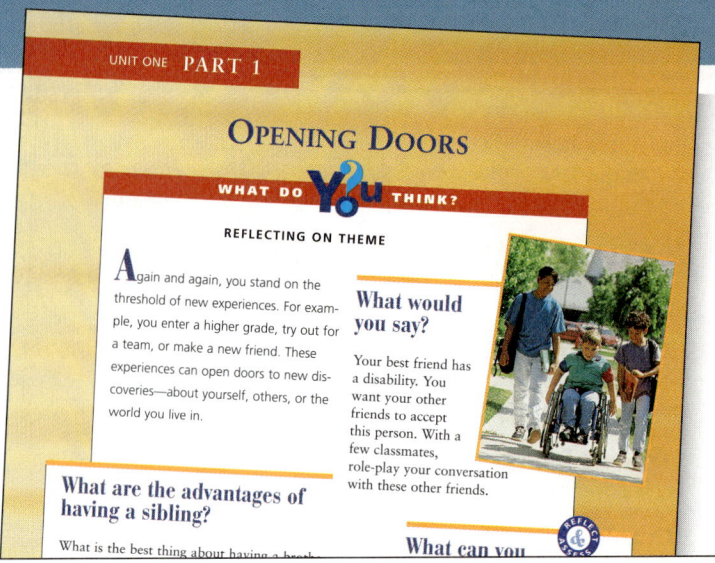

WHAT DO YOU THINK?
Motivating activities at the beginning of each unit part that help introduce students to the theme they are about to encounter in the next grouping of selections.

STRATEGIES FOR READING
Shows students how active readers read—what they think about as they read and how they make connections between the text and real-world experiences. Model provides thoughts and comments of two students engaged in the following active reading strategies:

- Question
- Connect
- Predict
- Clarify
- Evaluate

FOCUS ON FICTION/ NONFICTION/POETRY/DRAMA
Helps introduce and reinforce basic knowledge of literary elements. Also includes strategies used when reading a particular genre. Feature provides students with a strong foundation for the reading of literature.

T18

THE ORAL TRADITION

Celebrates storytelling in an entire unit devoted to folk tales from around the world. The featured storyteller also appears on LaserLinks. Activity-based response options throughout the unit tie to other curriculum areas.

REFLECT & ASSESS

Features end-of-unit activities that help students review and reflect upon what they have learned in the course of a unit. Includes options for:

- Reflecting on Theme
- Reviewing Literary Concepts
- Portfolio Building

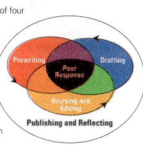

STUDENT HANDBOOKS

- Reading Terms and Literary Concepts
- Writing Handbook
- Multimedia Handbook
- Grammar Handbook

T19

A CLOSER LOOK

The Teacher's Edition

Unit Support

Special pages in the Teacher's Edition provide professional enrichment and help you plan your lessons, organize necessary materials, and carry out unit-related projects.

SKILLS TRACE

Allows you to see at a glance the scope and sequence of reading, writing, speaking, listening, viewing, study, research, grammar, spelling, and literary skills taught within each part of a unit. Also tracks the teaching of vocabulary words and the type and frequency of multimodal activities.

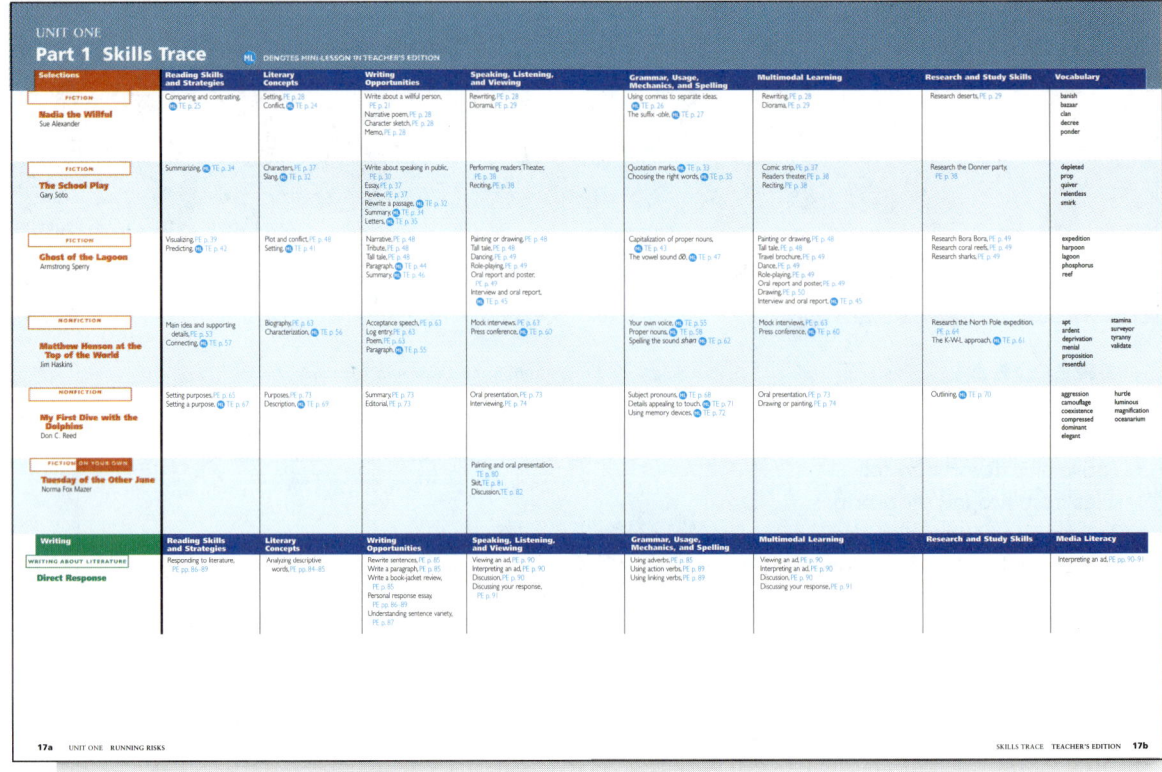

RECOMMENDED RESOURCES

Invaluable listings of unit-specific resources for both you and your students. Includes titles of novels and plays, cross-curricular readings, and media resources. Helps you extend and enrich the curriculum and enrich yourself professionally as well.

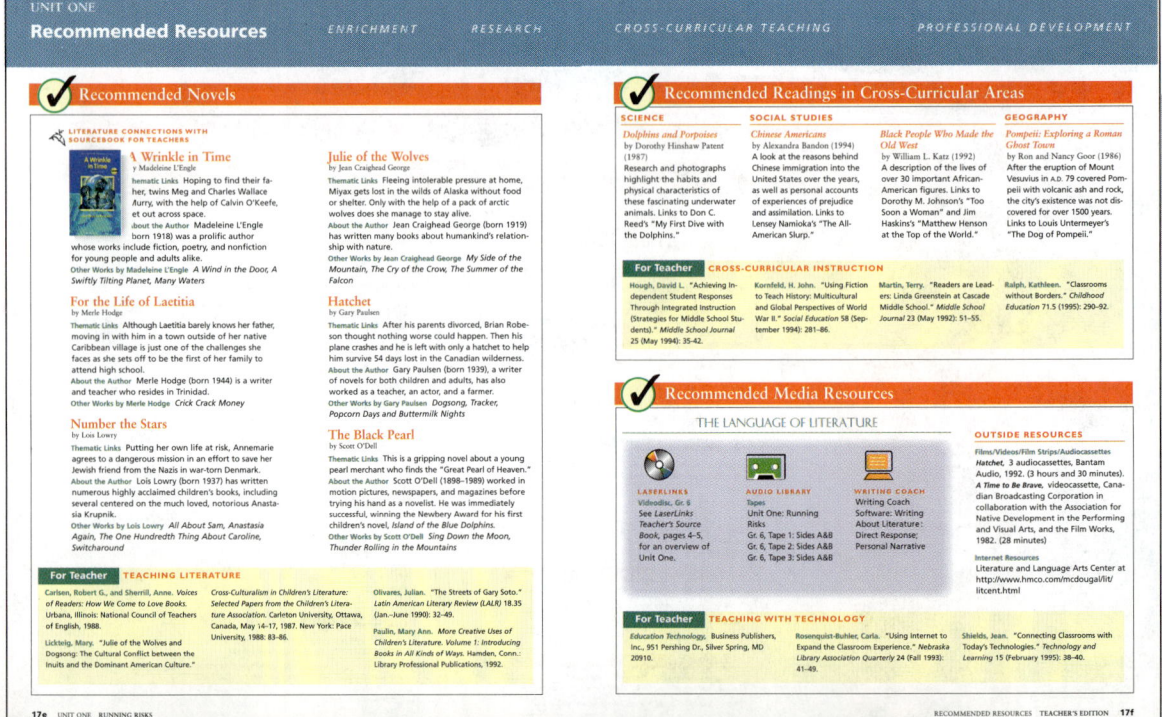

T20

PROFESSIONAL ENRICHMENT

Articles that give practical ideas for teaching literature and writing. Topics relate to unit content.

FAMILY AND COMMUNITY INVOLVEMENT

Activities designed to involve parents and other family members and to foster students' interaction with other people in their communities. Corresponding worksheets are provided.

COOPERATIVE PROJECT

Content-related projects for teachers interested in cooperative learning. Includes suggestions for how to assign and manage the projects and tells how connections might be made to other curriculum areas. Two different projects are included for each unit.

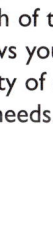

LESSON PLANNER

Helps you plan your lessons by indicating approximate length of time for each task. Allows you to accommodate a variety of classroom situations and needs.

TEACHERS EDITION
(CONTINUED)

Selection and Writing Workshop Support

The Annotated Teacher's Edition of *The Language of Literature* is a professional sourcebook designed to promote effective and efficient teaching. Each page contains features that allow you to take students into, through, and beyond the literature.

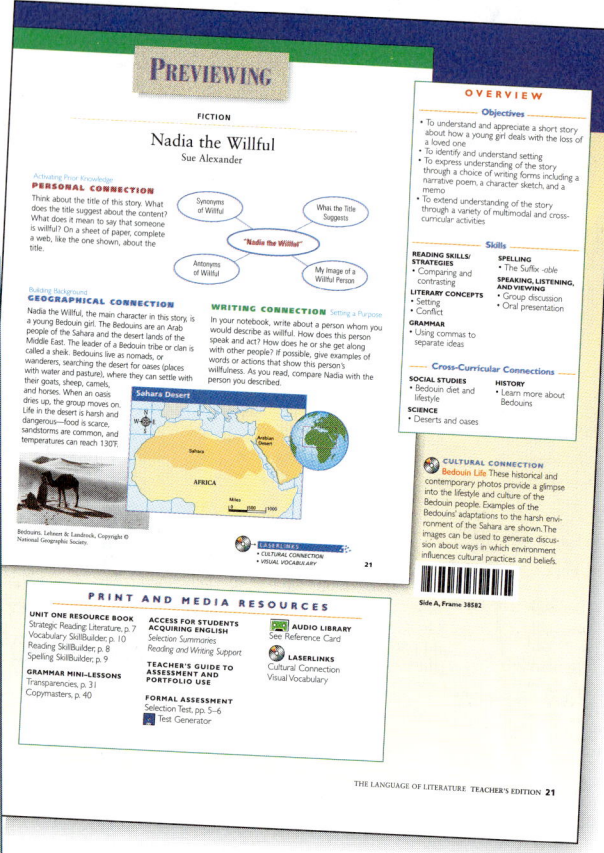

SELECTION ANNOTATIONS

Notes on literary concepts and critical thinking skills appear with each selection and its corresponding activity pages. Also included are the following features.

- **Overview** Lists objectives, key skills, and cross-curricular connections
- **Print and Media Resources**
- **Selection Summary**
- **LaserLinks bar codes**
- **Words to Know**
- **Art Notes**
- **Customizing for**
  - multiple learning styles
  - students acquiring English
  - gifted and talented students
  - less-proficient readers

- **Activities** Suggestions for whole class, small group, and individual activities
- **Mini-Lessons** Provided for grammar, spelling, reading, genre, writing, and a number of other subjects
- **Active Reading Questions**
- **Comprehension Check**
- **Assessment Options**
- **Links Across the Curriculum**
- **Links to** *The Writer's Craft*
- **Activity Support and Answer Keys**

T22

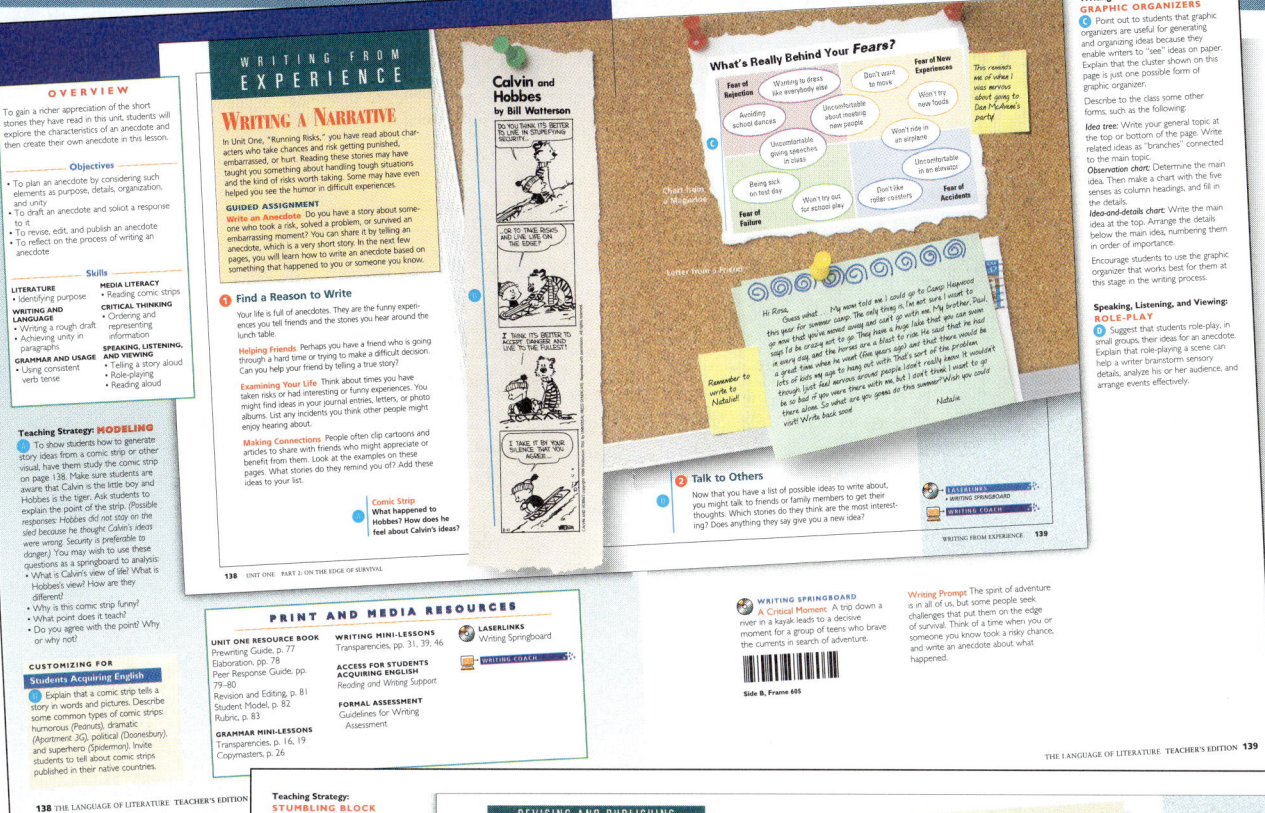

WORKSHOP ANNOTATIONS

The Teacher's Edition notes for the Writing Workshops provide support similar to that provided for each literary selection. In addition, Writing Workshops contain the following:

- **Writing Springboards** Provides writing ideas from LaserLinks.
- **Modeling** Gives suggestions for using both literary models and student writing models.
- **SkillBuilder Mini-Lesson Support**
- **Visual and Media Literacy Features**
- **Research Skills**
- **Oral Communication**
- **Rubrics**
- **Standards for Evaluation**

T23

A CLOSER LOOK
Assessment

Assessment Resources

The Language of Literature provides you with material that allows you to customize assessment to best fit the activities and structure of your particular classroom. With options for formal, informal, and alternative assessment, these resources provide you with all the support you need.

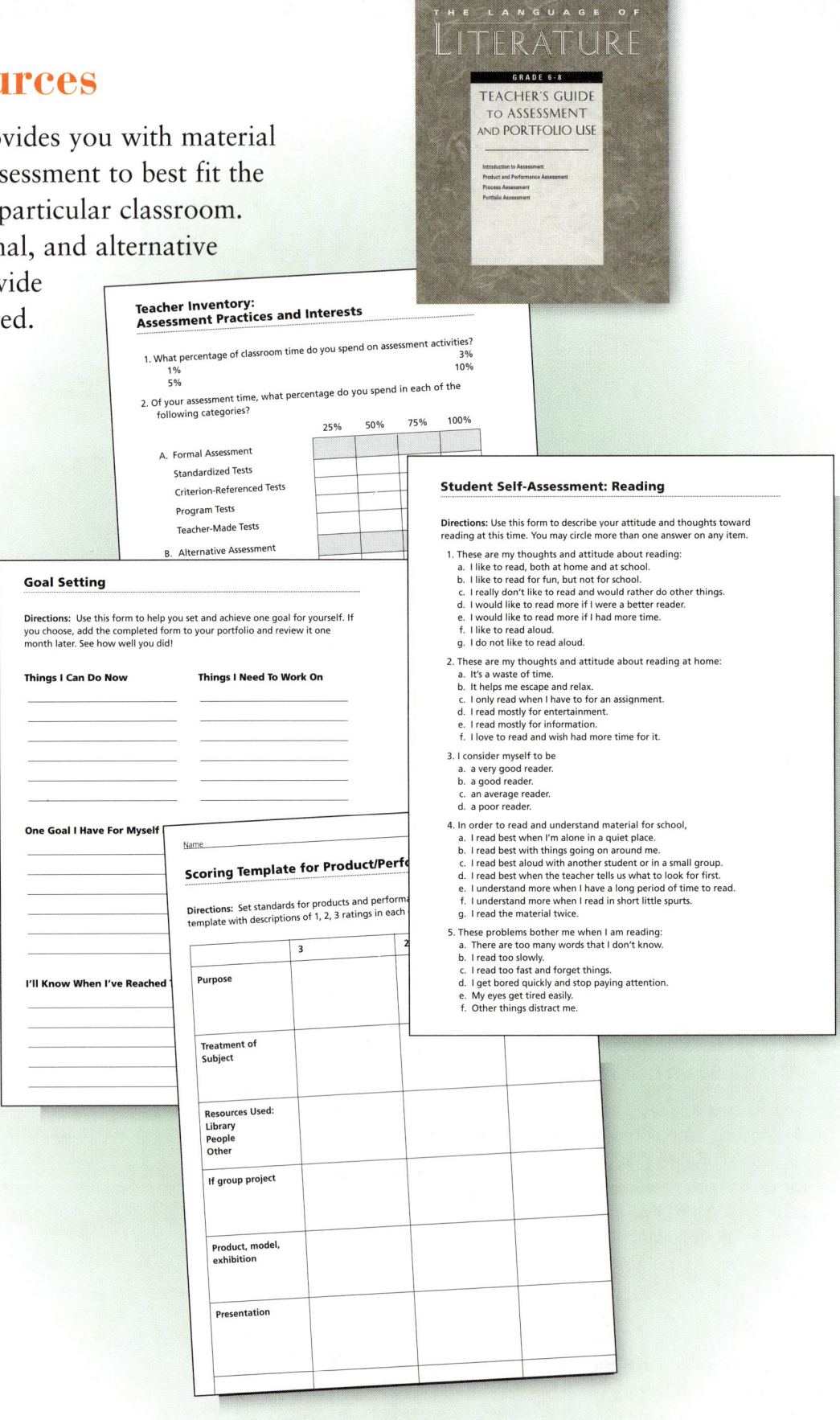

TEACHER'S GUIDE TO ASSESSMENT AND PORTFOLIO USE

This Teacher's Guide

- provides information on different types and forms of assessment: formal selection and unit tests, portfolio building, authentic assessment, reading notebooks, self-assessment, group and project assessment, and more

- helps you decide which assessment types you wish to use and explains how to implement those approaches

- provides forms and checklists that can be used to give shape to assessment choices

T24 THE LANGUAGE OF LITERATURE TEACHER'S EDITION

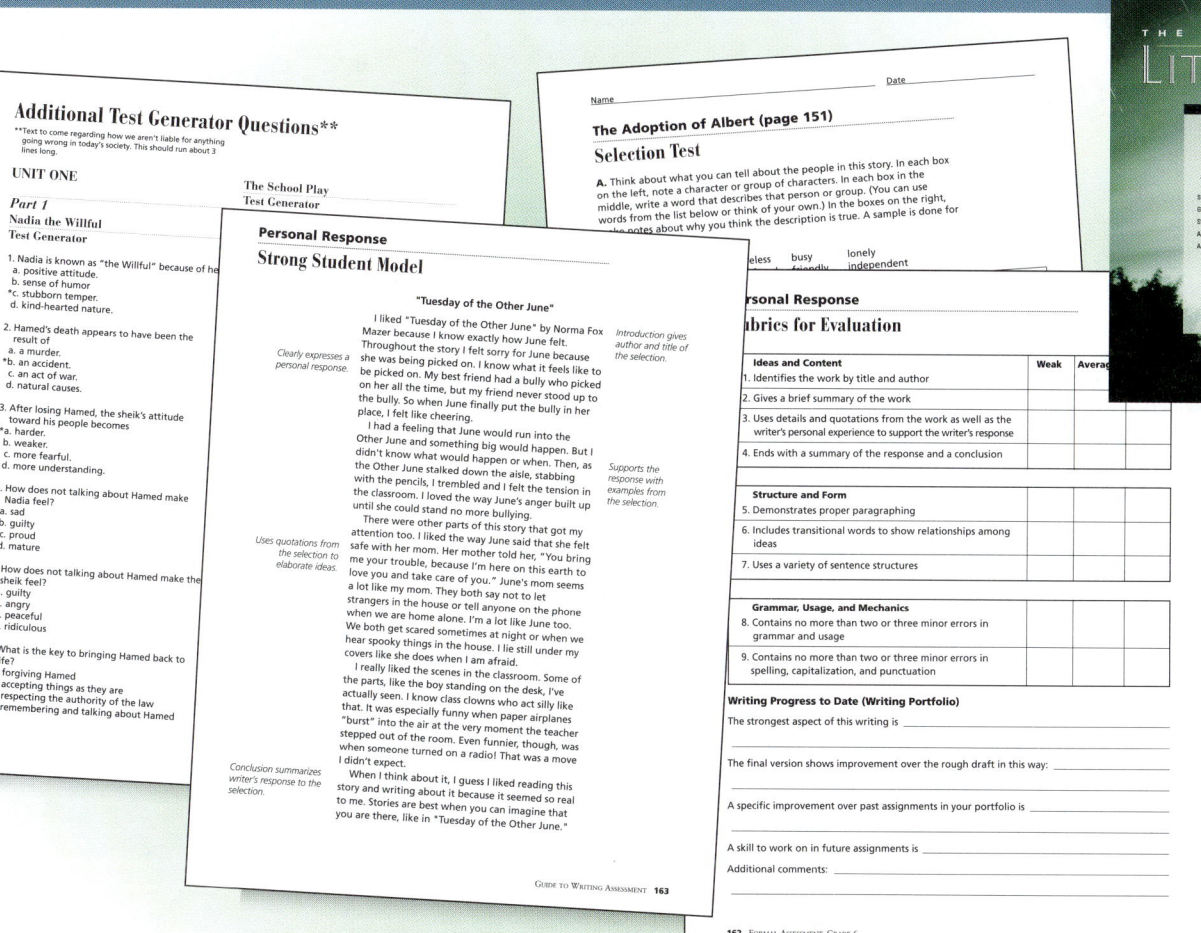

FORMAL ASSESSMENT

The formal assessment booklet contains everything you will need for efficient assessment of students' skills in reading literature and in writing.

- Selection and Unit Tests
- Writing Prompts
- Scoring rubrics and sample papers
- Standardized Test Practice

A test generator is also available to help you customize assessment.

ALTERNATIVE ASSESSMENT

These assessments integrate all of the language arts processes and are modeled on authentic assessment materials used in many states across the country.

- **Unit Integrated Assessments** are completed over two days and are based on the On Your Own selections in the student book. Prereading activities and post-reading response and discussion lead to in-depth writing options.

- The **End-of-Year Integrated Assessment** includes a reader and a Student Response Booklet. It is completed over several days and requires students to respond to three or more related selections.

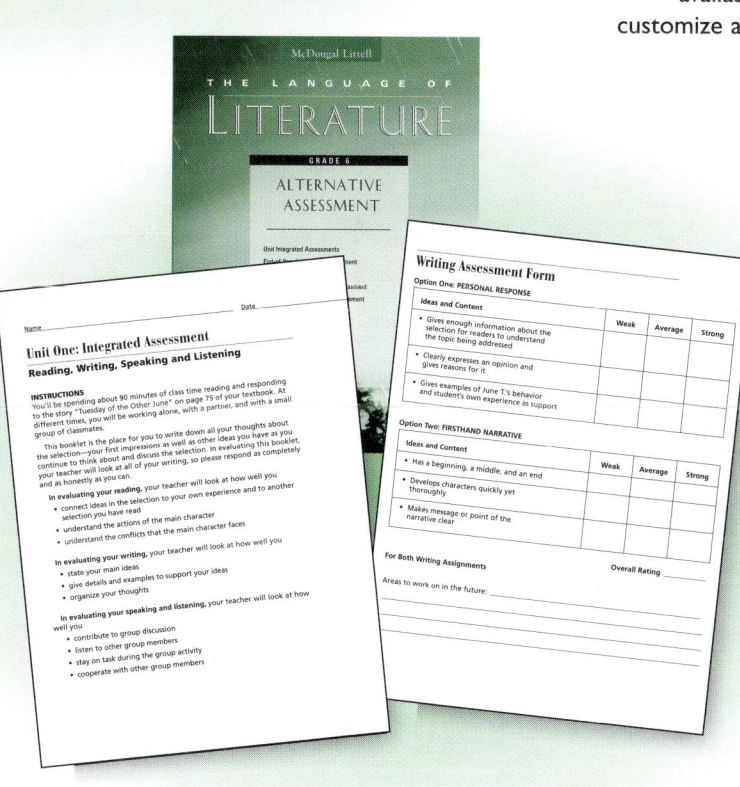

THE LANGUAGE OF LITERATURE Teacher's Edition **T25**

GETTING STARTED . . .
Advice from the Experts

Planning YOUR YEAR

Every new school year requires much planning. The information and advice on these pages comes from the consultants on *The Language of Literature* and is designed to help you bring some of your plans into focus. (You may want to copy the pages and keep them in your lesson planner for easy reference.) As you begin your planning, here's a list of questions to consider. Their answers and some additional information can be found on the pages cited.

Developing a Classroom Profile   See pages T28–T29.

✔ **Who are my students?**

- ☐ What can I learn about my students from previous teachers, students, records, and portfolios—and how can I best use this information?
- ☐ What are my students' preferred learning styles, and how can I best accommodate them?
- ☐ If I have students who are not proficient in English, what will their needs be?
- ☐ Are there any other special needs represented in my class?
- ☐ What adjustments do I need to make due to tracking, mainstreaming, and other situations?

Planning My Instruction   See pages T30–T31.

✔ **What do I want to teach?**

- ☐ What are the requirements of my school, district, and state?
- ☐ What are my personal preferences?
- ☐ What are my students' preferences?
- ☐ How can I use both classic literature and young-adult literature to reflect the needs and interests of my students?
- ☐ What mix of stories, poetry, essays, and novels do I want to teach?
- ☐ How can I effectively combine writing, language, and communication skills?
- ☐ Do I want to teach a research paper and/or other longer projects?

✔ **How much collaborating do I want to do with other teachers?**

- ☐ To plan thematic units and/or projects
- ☐ To coordinate instruction

✔ **What mix of instructional styles do I want to use?**

- ☐ Lectures
- ☐ Cooperative/collaborative work
- ☐ Writing workshops/peer response groups

✔ **How will I organize the content?**

- ☐ By genre or mode
- ☐ By theme

Setting Up My Classroom   See pages T32–T33.

✔ **How will I organize my classroom?**

- ☐ In rows of desks
- ☐ With tables and chairs
- ☐ In paired-seating arrangements
- ☐ In cooperative learning groups
- ☐ In stations or centers

Taking Advantage of Technology   See pages T34–T35.

✔ **How large a role will technology play in my classroom?**

- ☐ What technological resources do I have at my disposal?
- ☐ For what purpose or purposes do I want to use them?
- ☐ How can I best set up my classroom or use a lab to take advantage of these resources?

Preparing for Assessment   See pages T36–T38.

✔ **What types of assessment do I want to use or prepare for?**

Do I want to use one or more of the following:

- ☐ Portfolios, journals, and/or logs
- ☐ Process assessment
- ☐ Product assessment
- ☐ Peer and self-assessment
- ☐ My own observations
- ☐ Tests from *The Language of Literature*
- ☐ District- or state-mandated tests
- ☐ Standardized tests

Planning Connections   See pages T39–T40.

✔ **What kinds of connections do I want to make outside the classroom?**

- ☐ To other curriculum areas
- ☐ To other classrooms or schools
- ☐ To my students' parents
- ☐ To the community
- ☐ To the world

DEVELOPING A Classroom PROFILE

> To avoid misunderstanding, it is critical that teachers disregard the assumption that all students have the same, or similar, frames of reference or perceptions about the world.
>
> Andrea Bermúdez
> Professor of Studies in Language and Culture, University of Houston-Clear Lake

UNDERSTANDING LEARNING STYLES

Your students are all unique. They have different sets of characteristics, abilities, and needs. It should not be surprising, therefore, to learn that they have different learning styles as well. This theory gained acceptance in the early 1980s, due in large part to the research of Harvard psychologist Howard Gardner. Gardner recognizes seven types of intelligences: linguistic, logical-mathematical, spatial, musical, bodily-kinesthetic, interpersonal, and intrapersonal. He claims that everyone has all seven of these intelligences, but in different proportions.

Understanding your students' intelligences, or learning styles, will help you teach them more effectively. How can you tell which learning style or styles your students favor? As you consider each of your students, asking yourself these questions will help.

Does the student . . .	Then he or she is mostly a . . .	So try these activities and assignments:
☐ Have good verbal skills? think in words? have highly developed auditory skills? like to read and write?	Linguistic Learner	Creative writing; essays; debates and speeches; oral reports; dramatic readings and performances; storytelling; joke, pun, and riddle telling
☐ Think conceptually? think and reason in a highly abstract and logical way?	Logical-Mathematical Learner	Graphic organizers; charts, graphs, and time lines; coded messages; prediction exercises; models; computer projects; science experiments
☐ Think in visual images and pictures? enjoy drawing, designing, building, daydreaming, inventing?	Spatial Learner	Drawings and paintings; comic strips; maps and flow charts; dioramas, displays, and murals; collages; drawing games; photography activities
☐ Have a sensitivity to music, nonverbal sounds, and rhythm? enjoy singing, playing, and listening to and moving to music?	Musical Learner	Interpretive dances; musical plays and compositions; rap songs, jingles, and melodies; rhyming games; playing a musical instrument
☐ Process knowledge through bodily sensations? have exceptional fine-motor coordination? communicate through body language?	Bodily-Kinesthetic Learner	Demonstration speeches; experiments; using gestures, facial expressions, and pantomime; impersonations; role-playing
☐ Understand other people? organize, communicate, and socialize well?	Interpersonal Learner	Discussions; cooperative and collaborative projects; peer coaching; conducting interviews; simulation activities; human graphs
☐ Prefer working alone? seem intuitive, independent, private, and self-motivated?	Intrapersonal Learner	Response journals, dialogue journals, learning logs; observations; photo essays; autobiographical stories; written reports

A PROFILE OF THE STUDENT ACQUIRING ENGLISH

Culturally and linguistically diverse students bring to the classroom a wealth of experiences that can enrich the learning environment of all your students. Developing multicultural sensitivity involves (a) acceptance of each student's circumstances, (b) a genuine search for information about his or her background and prior knowledge, (c) an updated bank of teaching strategies, and (d) a desire to find the best options for each student.

The Student Acquiring English

- generally focuses attention on style, not content
- is often unaware of learning strategies that could facilitate comprehension
- may become disorderly and disobedient due to an inability to relate to the learning environment
- often does not make eye contact when addressing others
- may seem to have difficulty meeting deadlines
- may not seem to understand classroom "rules"
- generally shows a different speaking and listening style
- may organize thoughts in a pattern that does not correspond to the expected linear-sequential pattern characteristic of standard English communication
- may exhibit an external locus of control, seeming overly dependent on teachers or peers for validation of responses

Common Problem Areas

The following problem areas pose special challenges to students acquiring English as they try to read and understand information.

Vocabulary Difficulty

If the student has no prior experience with the words appearing in a selection, the normal links between certain concepts and their labels will not occur. Problems often arise when a selection contains the following:

- low frequency words
- idiomatic or dialectal expressions
- jargon

Unfamiliar Content

The student may misunderstand the message in what he or she is reading if not given the proper context. This often happens as a result of the following:

- a lack of prior experience with the context
- ideas expressed in an unfamiliar or abstract way
- ideas expressed being of an unfamiliar culture

Grammatical Features of the Selection

Comprehension problems arise when the student encounters the following:

- dialectal forms
- outdated grammatical forms
- unusual word order

Effective Teaching and Learning Strategies

These instructional strategies have been shown to be successful when used with students acquiring English.

Cognitive Mapping

- Many SAE students, however, may organize and categorize information differently than English speakers would. Instruction in cognitive mapping can enable students to integrate previous experience with new knowledge.

An Integrated Approach

- The integrated approach to learning is particularly successful with students acquiring English. Students learn about reading and writing while listening, they learn about writing from reading, and they gain insights into reading from writing. Any strategy or approach based on dissecting language and mutually exclusive components jeopardizes second-language acquisition by not drawing on the prior knowledge and strengths of the learner.

Cooperative Learning

- Cooperative learning is a generic term that refers to a variety of approaches to integrating students into group activities where each participant is responsible for contributing to group outcomes and products. Cooperative learning strategies significantly improve students' achievement and productivity for a wide range of subjects and grade levels. This approach also improves self-esteem and respect for others. For more detailed information, see the *Teacher's SourceBook for Language Development*.

Planning YOUR INSTRUCTION

Just as your students all have their own preferred learning styles, you have your own preferred teaching styles. Understanding when and where your most comfortable style really works—and when another method would reach your goals and the goals of your students more effectively—will help you plan just the right type of instruction for every situation.

Here are some questions to ask yourself as you make decisions about your instruction:

- ☐ What is my objective for the lesson . . . today, this week, this month, this term?
- ☐ What is my time frame . . . 45 minutes, 90 minutes, three class periods, longer?
- ☐ Who are my students (refer to your classroom profiles, pages T28 and T29)?
- ☐ What teaching styles am I most comfortable with?
- ☐ What additional teaching techniques would be effective with these students and this material?

Consider these options . . .

WHOLE-CLASS INSTRUCTION

Lecture

EXAMPLES:
- ☐ Introducing a new unit of study
- ☐ Providing instruction for a project
- ☐ Introducing grammatical principles or definitions of literary elements

Teacher-led Discussion

EXAMPLES:
- ☐ Exploring students' ideas about and responses to literature selections and themes
- ☐ Examining complex issues and problems

Viewing

EXAMPLES:
- ☐ Viewing a filmstrip or a videotape
- ☐ Watching demonstrations, performances, and project presentations

COLLABORATIVE LEARNING

Pairs or Partners

EXAMPLES:
- ☐ Sharing responses to literature
- ☐ Interviewing and reciprocal questioning
- ☐ Brainstorming for project or writing ideas
- ☐ Peer tutoring
- ☐ Writing workshops

Small Groups (3-8 students)

EXAMPLES:
- ☐ Discussing literature or other topics
- ☐ Planning and problem-solving activities
- ☐ Writing workshops
- ☐ Cooperative work on reports, projects, and presentations
- ☐ Cooperative planning and producing of larger projects such as plays, panel discussions or debates, and videotapes

INDEPENDENT LEARNING

Students Working Individually

EXAMPLES:
- ☐ Independent reading and writing
- ☐ Drawing, painting, and collages
- ☐ Listening to audiotapes

. . . for meeting these instructional goals . . .	. . . with these guidelines and cautions:
☐ Developing critical listening and note-taking skills ☐ Providing unknown historical or cultural background ☐ Introducing new concepts or skills	☐ Lectures appeal to linguistic learners with highly developed auditory skills. Other students may tune you out because this style lacks interactivity. ☐ Lectures are most effective if no longer than 20 minutes. Research shows that immediately after a 10-minute presentation, average adult listeners retain less than 50% of what they hear—and 48 hours later, they recall only 25%.
☐ Developing critical listening, responding, and conversational skills ☐ Introducing or reviewing skills	☐ Not all students are comfortable speaking in front of their peers. Highly verbal students can drown out students who favor other learning styles. ☐ When you lead the discussion, students may tend to direct their comments to you rather than to other students. Encourage students to speak directly to one another as well as to you.
☐ Supporting and improving visual literacy ☐ Developing evaluative skills ☐ Encouraging appreciation for music, art, and various kinds of performances	☐ Although viewing is a comfortable activity for most students, it's essentially passive. You'll want to choose occasions carefully. ☐ To help students remain focused, agree on goals ahead of time and provide standards and forms for evaluating what students are watching.
☐ Reinforcing cooperative learning skills ☐ Providing support for students acquiring English ☐ Encouraging peer feedback for writing	☐ It's important to cultivate a classroom atmosphere of support and trust so that pair interactions are effective and productive. ☐ You may want to pair students differently for different purposes. Strong students may be paired with weaker students, native English speakers with students acquiring English, talkative students with more reserved students, and so on.
☐ Developing problem-solving skills ☐ Encouraging peer feedback for writing ☐ Reinforcing cooperative learning skills ☐ Providing opportunities for students to explore various points of view ☐ Improving social skills and promoting self-esteem in students of all abilities	☐ Some students will lean too hard on other members of the group. Both groups and individual students need to be accountable. ☐ Some students can get lost in the shuffle of a larger group. Individual students should have specific responsibilities. ☐ Group size can be determined by the task. Small groups are appropriate for sharing personal writing and receiving individual attention; larger groups are effective when the task is large or complex. ☐ The "jigsaw" method may be useful for groups working on complex tasks. The group divides the assignment into pieces and assigns each student a piece. Then students work together to meld the pieces into a coherent whole.
☐ Providing opportunities for reflection and self-assessment ☐ Providing support for students acquiring English	☐ Individual learning tasks require a quiet classroom atmosphere. Highly developed interpersonal learners may distract other students. ☐ Using independent learning too frequently can hinder students' development of collaborative and cooperative skills.

THE LANGUAGE OF LITERATURE TEACHER'S EDITION

Setting Up YOUR CLASSROOM

Are you planning to try some new instructional approaches this year? If so, you also may want to consider some new classroom setups. Moving away from the traditional arrangement of desks in rows will provide you and your students a welcome change—and will be more conducive to different teaching and learning situations. Here are a few pointers:

If you teach in the same room all day, the ideas on these pages will provide ways to set up your room for a variety of purposes.

If you switch rooms, team teach, or share your room, you can find an arrangement that best meets everyone's needs. Some options:

☐ One arrangement that works for everyone

☐ Different classrooms for different purposes

☐ A resource room or common area that could be used for specific types of activities

Before you arrange your classroom, draw a scale floor plan of it. Then add furniture and design a setting that will best accommodate your instructional plans.

When you have your floor plan firmed up, post lists of procedures in the different areas of your classroom. Encourage students to add new procedures as needs arise in the future.

Don't be afraid to experiment with different arrangements throughout the year. You may find that some arrangements work better than others for specific projects or assignments.

> *The ideal literature classroom is a literary community where students... have room to respond, interpret, think critically, and contrast their ideas with those of other readers.*
>
> Judith Langer and Arthur Applebee
> Professors of Education,
> State University of New York at Albany

A LOOK AT THREE CLASSROOM SETUPS
Lectures and Demonstrations

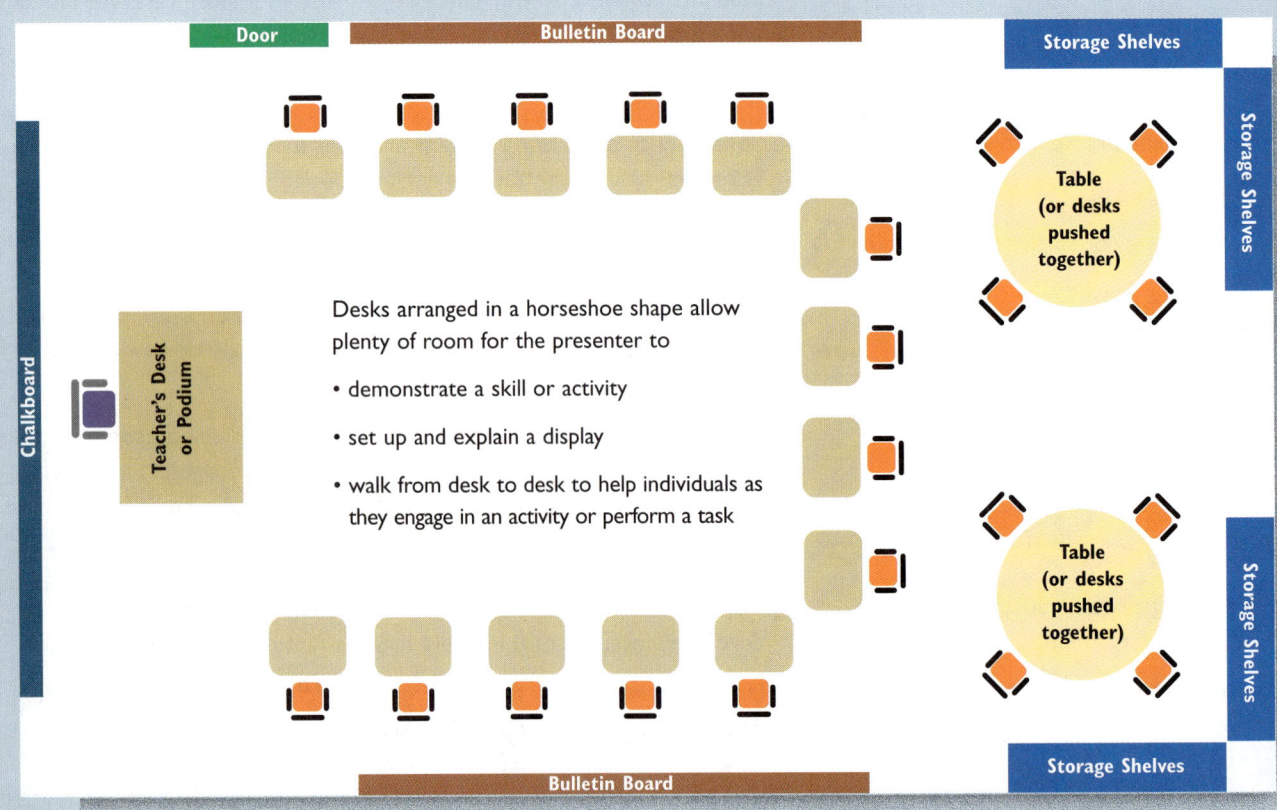

Desks arranged in a horseshoe shape allow plenty of room for the presenter to

- demonstrate a skill or activity
- set up and explain a display
- walk from desk to desk to help individuals as they engage in an activity or perform a task

T32 THE LANGUAGE OF LITERATURE TEACHER'S EDITION

Peer Tutoring & Cooperative Learning

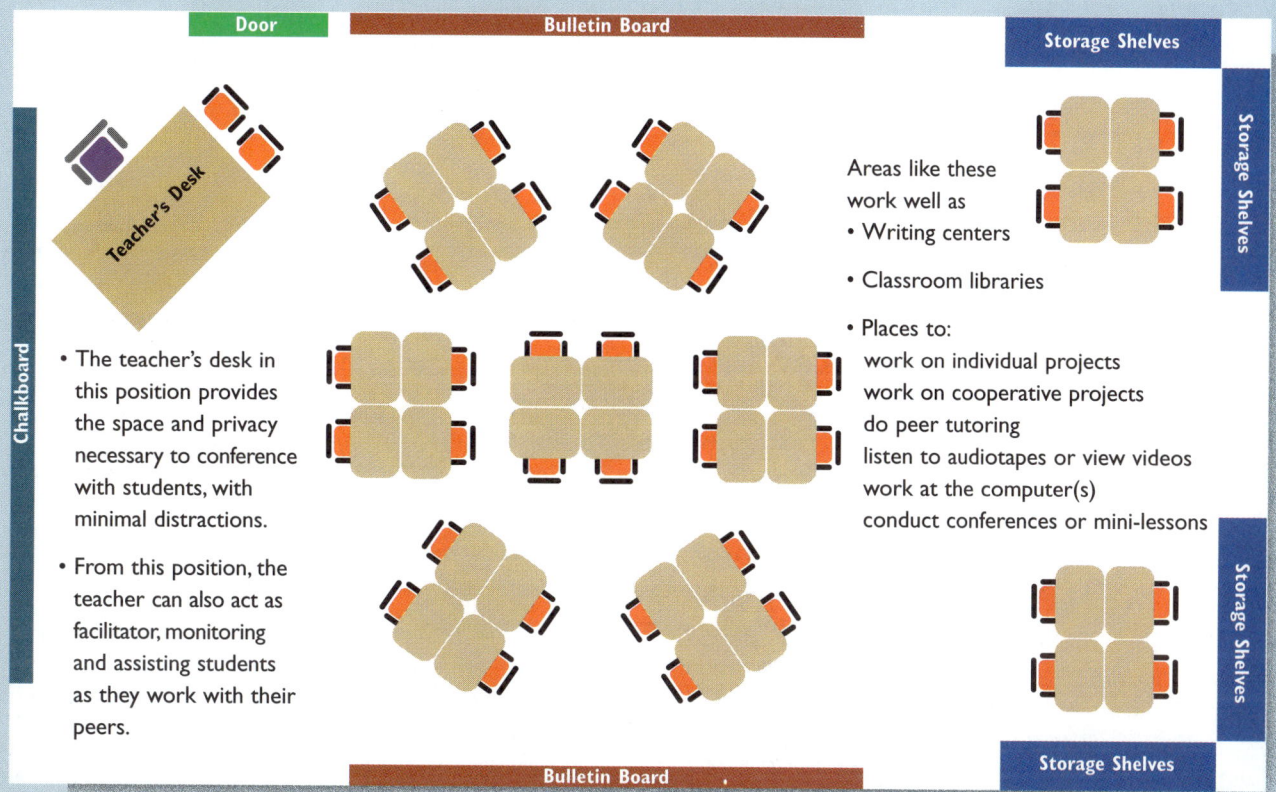

Work Stations

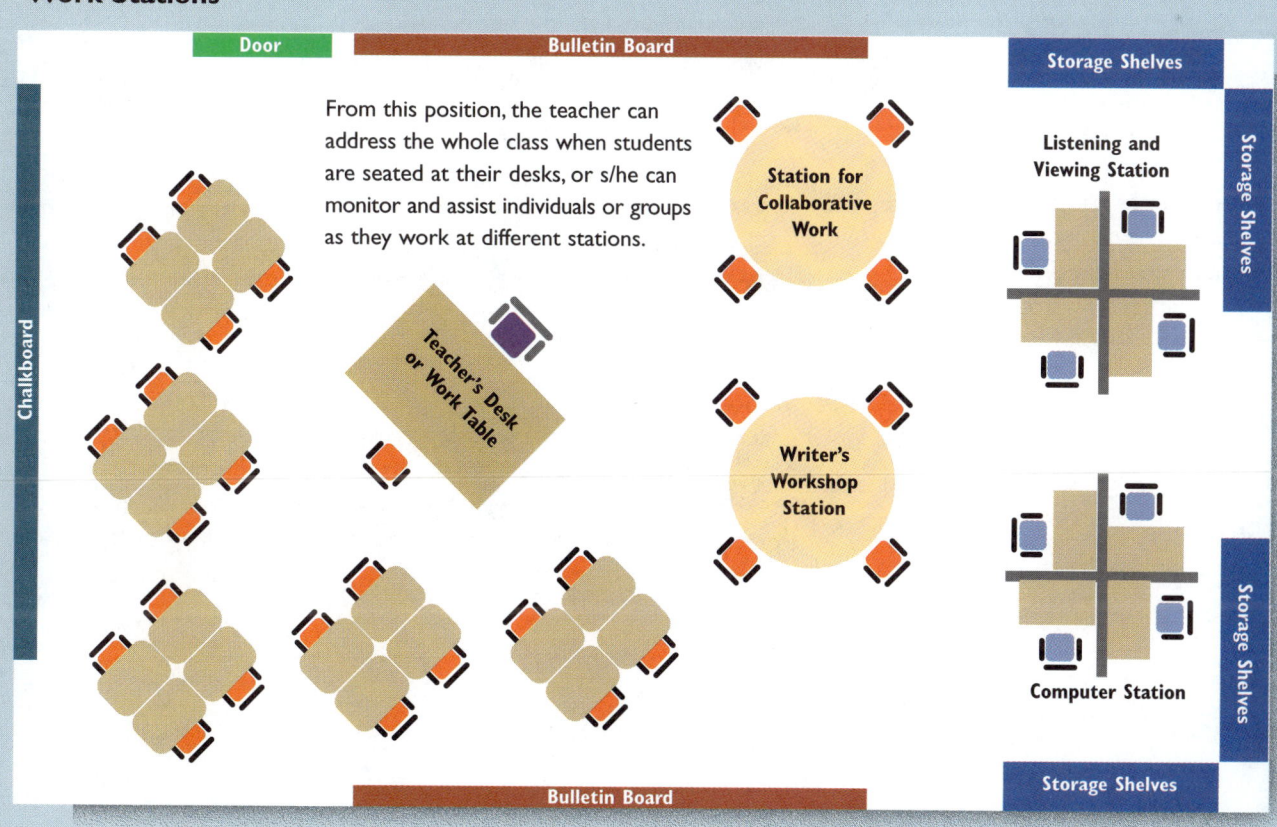

NEW Technology AND THE ENGLISH CLASSROOM

> Technology enables students to become active participants in their own learning.
>
> Jeffrey N. Golub
> Assistant Professor of English Education, University of South Florida, Tampa

The idea of using technology as part of your instructional plan is not simply the latest passing fad. Instead, it reflects continuing revelations about what is worth knowing and how students learn. For this reason, it promises to change the nature of classroom instruction.

Why is technology so important? Primarily because the use of computers is not a "spectator sport." Rather, computers require users to do the work themselves instead of passively sitting back and watching or listening to someone else—typically a teacher—dispense information. Thus, using technology enables students to become active participants in their own learning. Similarly, the teacher's role changes to that of a "designer" and "director"—one who *designs* innovative and worthwhile instructional activities and then *directs* students as they work through these activities.

Let's look for a moment at how technology is being used in English classrooms across the country.

Bringing Literature to Life

Teachers are always striving to make connections between literature and students' lives by providing "real-world" relevance in the form of historical and biographical information, cross-curricular ties, and connections to current issues. Recordings and films have always been the primary resources used to achieve this goal, but more recent technology—such as laser discs and CD-ROMs—is providing teachers with new worlds of information to draw from.

Taking the Fear Out of Writing

In probably their most familiar function, computers offer terrific opportunities for writing because (1) they provide students with more efficient and effective means of drafting, revising, editing, and publishing their writing efforts, and (2) they allow new kinds of opportunities for peer response, collaboration, and sharing.

More Enthusiastic Writers Research has shown repeatedly that students tend to be more fluent and less inhibited when they work at computers: the many editing features and on-line resources make revision easy. In addition, publishing programs allow students to create products far more exciting than words on paper have ever been. Computers can also make portfolio building simpler and cleaner: journal entries, drafts and revisions, and finished products are easy to store, categorize, and retrieve on computers or disks.

Easier Collaboration. If you have access to a writing lab, you will find that, with readily available software programs and by networking, or linking, the computers, students can be more easily encouraged to collaborate on their planning and writing efforts. When students can compose and comment on-screen they often become much more articulate and less reserved.

Making Connections

One of the most commonly heard complaints among teachers is that they seldom have a chance to network with each other and share ideas. Through the wonders of the Internet, this problem has all but disappeared. Education sites exist where teachers can find information ranging from developments in state assessments to projects that have worked well in other classrooms. Through the Internet, teachers can also set up classroom exchanges with other schools across the country, allow their students to go on electronic field trips, and plan interactions between the class and famous authors, scientists, and other professionals.

Developing Information Literacy

The use of technology in the English classroom enables teachers to help their students develop what will become one of the most basic skills needed for the 21st-century—media and information literacy. Students need to learn how to access information from a wide variety of both print and electronic sources; how to select appropriate information from the vast array of available resources; how to analyze and evaluate information that they read, see, and hear daily; and how to communicate their conclusions and insights clearly, completely, ethically, and persuasively. In particular, the growth of telecommunications opportunities in the form of information webs presents students with the opportunity to actively seek pertinent information and to engage in the processes of selection, analysis, and evaluation.

Conclusion These are just some of the ways in which technology can make learning happen for your students. But they help demonstrate that, if used creatively, technology can bring new excitement and levels of success to any English classroom—even while helping us achieve the same goals we have always had: to make our students solid readers, thinkers, and communicators.

Technology	Uses in the English Classroom	*The Language of Literature*
Videodisc A 12-inch disc, used with a videodisc player, that can store thousands of still images as well as full-motion video. Images can be accessed immediately through the use of bar codes.	• To provide background information and cross-curricular connections for selection enrichment • For presenting real-world situations and images that can be used as writing springboards • To bring movies, archival material, and recordings of live performances into the classroom • To teach visual literacy	**LASERLINKS** Support for lessons in the student book, including • Author and Selection Background • Visual Vocabulary • Professional Storyteller • Writing Springboards
Floppy Disks and CD-ROM'S Both are information storage devices that can hold text, still images, and full-motion video. Compact discs, however, are able to store encyclopedic amounts of information.	• As sources of additional or enhanced selections • As a reference tool: encyclopedias, atlases, and almanacs are all available in CD-ROM form • For writing: publishing software, image banks, and word processing programs all enhance student writing	**THE ELECTRONIC LIBRARY** Additional classic selections to expand program options **WRITING COACH** Special word processing program with on-line writing tips and handbooks, multiple text columns for revision and peer response, and a multimedia Idea Generator
Internet/ World Wide Web/ On-line Services A connected system of on-line computer networks through which mail and data can be transferred.	• To obtain additional information on a selection, author, or topic • To teach information-access skills • To gather professional materials, project ideas, research articles • To network with other teachers and set up classroom exchanges • To interact with authors, public figures, scientists, and other professionals	**THE MCDOUGAL LITTELL HOME PAGE** Can be accessed on the World Wide Web at http://www.hmco.com/mcdougal and contains the following resources: • Internet links for specific selections in *The Language of Literature* • Teacher discussion groups/ bulletin boards • Links to professional organizations • Guest speakers

PREPARING FOR Assessment

The word *assessment* conjures up many different images and raises just as many questions in teachers' minds. Although assessment options are often categorized as either formal or alternative, assessment activities usually embrace qualities of both kinds. Most teachers use a combination of many types of assessment in determining what a student knows or is able to do. The overview on these three pages will introduce you to the types of assessment used in *The Language of Literature* and will help you decide which ones you might want to try with your students this year. (For teacher resources and information on implementing these types of assessment, see the following three booklets: *Teacher's Guide to Assessment and Portfolio Use, Formal Assessment,* and *Alternative Assessment.*)

WHAT TYPES OF ASSESSMENT ARE THERE?

TYPES OF ASSESSMENT

FORMAL — Asks "What do you know?"

PURPOSES
Usually paper-and-pencil tests; helps teachers
- measure students' achievement against students in their own class, district, state, or country
- report students' achievement to parents and administrators
- make appropriate instructional and grouping decisions

FORMATS
Test formats are commonly
- true-false
- multiple choice
- matching
- essay
- standardized
- norm-referenced
- criterion-referenced
- objective

ALTERNATIVE — Asks "What can you do?"

PURPOSES
Usually tasks that emulate real-life situations; helps teachers
- get a broad picture of each student as a problem solver, critical thinker, and acquirer of knowledge
- measure student growth over time

TASKS
Tasks are commonly
- authentic
- products or performances
- processes

T36 THE LANGUAGE OF LITERATURE TEACHER'S EDITION

WHAT FORMS CAN ALTERNATIVE ASSESSMENT TAKE?

For more information on implementing these types of assessment, see the *Teacher's Guide to Assessment and Portfolio Use*.

> Portfolios offer one of the best vehicles for classroom-based assessment because they typically contain a variety of student work and they make it easy to separate evaluation from the process of instruction.
>
> Judith Langer and Arthur Applebee
> Professors of Education, State University of New York at Albany

✓ Product and Performance Assessment

- Requires students to produce tangible products or create performances that demonstrate their understanding of skills and concepts
- Focuses teacher's attention on the end product rather than on the processes, behaviors, or strategies students used to create it
- Is based on judgment and observation guided by criteria

TYPES OF EVALUATION CRITERIA USED
Can include rubrics, formal scales and checklists, and peer and self-evaluations

POSSIBLE PRODUCTS
- scripts, dialogues
- audiotapes, videotapes
- charts, maps, graphs
- games, puzzles
- puppet shows
- plays, skits, talent shows
- interviews, debates
- role-playing
- dances
- mock trials
- cooking or sports demonstrations
- recipes, menus
- children's books
- museum exhibits
- research papers
- inventions
- book or movie reviews
- questionnaires, surveys
- print or TV ads
- poems, riddles, jokes
- time capsules
- awards
- oral histories
- murals, collages
- computer programs
- scale models, dioramas
- essays, editorials
- family trees

✓ Portfolio Assessment

- Is a purposeful collection of student work that exhibits overall efforts, progress, and achievement over time in one or more areas of the curriculum
- Is a combination of process and product assessment, with a strong measure of self-evaluation and self-reflection

TYPES OF EVALUATION CRITERIA USED
Can include inventories, conference notes, rubrics, formal scales and checklists, anecdotal records, observations, and peer evaluations

POSSIBLE PRODUCTS TO INCLUDE IN THE PORTFOLIO
- interest inventories
- outlines
- written assignments
- videotapes
- reading records
- audiotapes
- performance plans
- photographs
- logs
- sketches or drawings
- journal entries
- works in progress
- textbook tasks
- research findings
- reports
- book reports or reviews
- project evaluations
- standardized tests

✓ Process Assessment

- Requires students to demonstrate or share their processes, behaviors, strategies, and critical thinking abilities as they work to understand skills and concepts
- Focuses teacher's attention on student processes, behaviors, and strategies rather than on the final results
- Is based on judgment and observation guided by criteria

TYPES OF EVALUATION CRITERIA USED
Can include rubrics, formal scales and checklists, anecdotal records, observations, and self- and peer evaluations

POSSIBLE PROCESSES
While the evaluator observes students' abilities to apply higher-order thinking skills during certain processes, he or she focuses on the following:

- the use of reading strategies to develop interpretations of a text
- behavior during peer review
- evidence of investment in a task
- the ability to work in a collaborative group
- drafts created while writing an essay
- the ability to participate in class discussions
- the use of conferences to refine work
- evolving personal criteria and standards

THE LANGUAGE OF LITERATURE TEACHER'S EDITION T37

> *If criteria for evaluation are consistent with those stressed during instruction, and if response is shared between student and teacher, assessment can become an effective complement to any learning situation.*
>
> Judith Langer and Arthur Applebee
> Professors of Education, State University of New York at Albany

HOW CAN I PREPARE MY STUDENTS FOR THESE TYPES OF ASSESSMENT?

A major difference between formal assessment and alternative assessment is what you choose to assess and how you choose to assess it. Alternative assessment is a natural outgrowth and extension of classroom practices. Therefore, it is important to establish an effective learning—and testing—environment right away. Following are a few pointers to help you get started.

✔ Establish an environment based on trust.

Because alternative assessment makes students much more in charge of their own learning, and much more responsible for demonstrating their learning in a variety of ways, it is important to establish a classroom environment that is based on trust. Many of the activities students will be engaging in will be unfamiliar to them—and to you. Let them see that you are right in there with them, taking risks and trying new experiences. Help them understand that it's all right to try and fail—even seemingly unsuccessful experiences bring about growth and learning.

✔ Establish a tone of reflection and self-evaluation.

At the beginning of the year, ask your students to write letters describing themselves as readers, writers, and classroom participants. Also have them describe what they hope to accomplish during the coming year. Have them keep their letters in their notebooks, journals, or portfolios; encourage them to reread the letters regularly. Reflecting on their performance will help them acknowledge and evaluate their growth over the year. It will also help them see that learning and evaluating are ongoing and ever-changing processes.

✔ Help your students set goals and make commitments.

In order to grow as learners, your students must become actively involved in setting goals and making commitments. Their goals can be for a day, a week, a project, or the year; but whatever their duration, encourage students to consider their strengths and limitations so that the goals they set will be realistic.

✔ Help students view assessment in a new light.

One of the best things you can do for your students is help them break away from the notion that a "test" is something to study for the night before and then to forget. Help them see that alternative assessment involves a demonstration of what they know at a particular moment, but that what they know is bound to keep changing as new knowledge builds on old.

✔ Help your students discover their individual learning styles and preferences.

Chances are, most of your students are not fully aware of their own learning styles and preferences. Why not help them recognize which tasks and situations suit them best and help them learn more effectively? (See page T28.) After all, the better your students understand themselves, the better you'll understand how to teach and assess them.

✔ Encourage peer review as a regular part of the assessment process.

Sometimes it's easier for students to "get inside the minds" of their peers. And sometimes it's easier for them to take instruction or criticism from their peers. This is an excellent strategy, as long as growth and learning are taking place.

✔ Help your students learn to operate independently of you.

As students get comfortable with their learning environment, they'll probably want to do more and more without your help. Try to provide as many opportunities as possible for them to develop into independent learners—you'll be doing one of the best things you can do to prepare them for life in the real world!

✔ Improve and increase your own assessment tools.

As an evaluator, your goal should be to get as broad a view as possible of each of your students. Increasing your ability to provide situations in which you can observe your students will help you get more complete pictures of them. It will also help you learn more about yourself!

MAKING Connections

The Language of Literature bases all of its instruction on a "connected" approach to learning. On every page—from the Previewing pages to the Writing Workshops and Reading the World feature— students are encouraged to find the links between the literature, other subject areas, their own lives, and the world around them.

Of course, there are always more connections to be made, and certain themes and selections are particularly rich with possibilities. When you identify a selection or idea that you feel might have particular interest for your students, you may want to involve the class, as well as other teachers, in expanding the lesson into a more customized exploration. The following chart describes one way to accomplish this.

STEP 1 What Will We Explore?

As a class, or in small groups, have students ask questions such as the following:

- What really excited me or fascinated me about this selection?
- What questions did I have as I read this?
- What didn't I understand?
- What would I like to find out more about?
- What people, experiences, issues, or situations did this remind me of that might be interesting to explore?

TIP: Clustering, discussion, brainstorming, freewriting, and notebooks and logs are among the methods that can be used to generate ideas.

STEP 2 What Skills or Information Will We Need?

Once the questions are in place, have students identify the skills needed to find the answers. For example, the story "The Circuit" might prompt questions about the life of the migrant worker. Will students need certain map-reading or geographical skills to learn the answers? Would information about farming or economics be important?

STEP 3 What Resources Will We Use?

At this point, students can be encouraged to plan the kinds of resources they might use to continue their exploration. Remind them of the following possibilities:

- print resources
- interviews
- surveys and questionnaires
- CD-ROM
- the Internet and other on-line resources

TIP: This is also the point at which you might collaborate with other teachers to take advantage of team teaching and block scheduling to coordinate overlapping topics. Classroom exchanges within or between schools may also be useful to arrange at this point. Technology can provide exciting options for networking as well.

STEP 4 How Will the Results Be Shared?

The methods for sharing information will be as varied as the projects themselves. Following are just a few of the possibilities students might consider:

- essays
- photo journals
- dramas
- videos
- speeches
- oral histories
- paintings
- music
- multimedia
- panel
- fairs
- community program

See page T40 for an example of the explorations generated from the selection "The Moustache."

> Teachers need to help their students feel integral and involved in their community and the larger world.
>
> Susan Hynds
> Professor of English Education,
> Syracuse University, Syracuse, New York

A SAMPLE PLANNING MAP

Below is an example of the different explorations that were generated from one story by a teacher following the approach outlined on page T39.

SELECTION: "THE MOUSTACHE"

SUMMARY: a boy gains a new understanding of his grandmother when he visits her in a nursing home.

COMMUNITY
- Visit a nursing home/hospital
- Write a letter to the American Association of Retired Persons (AARP)
- Plan community involvement doing volunteer work with the elderly, in nursing homes or hospitals

FIRSTHAND EXPERIENCE
- Interview an elderly member of your own family
- Create a family history

WORLD
- Study the representation of the elderly in our media
- Observe and discuss social attitudes toward elderly
- Carry out survey on attitudes to elderly (Internet, print)
- Interview care worker
- Research legislation regarding the elderly

CROSS-CURRICULAR LINKS
- Math: Plot the changes in life expectancy over the past century
- Social studies: Discuss the effect of the Great Depression on society
- Art: Consider the portrayal of the elderly in fine art

T40 THE LANGUAGE OF LITERATURE TEACHER'S EDITION

McDougal Littell

THE LANGUAGE OF
LITERATURE

McDougal Littell

THE LANGUAGE OF
LITERATURE

Arthur N. Applebee
Andrea B. Bermúdez
Sheridan Blau
Rebekah Caplan
Franchelle Dorn
Peter Elbow
Susan Hynds
Judith A. Langer
James Marshall

McDougal Littell
A HOUGHTON MIFFLIN COMPANY

Evanston, Illinois ▪ Boston ▪ Dallas

Acknowledgments

Unit One

Ruth Cohen, Inc.: "The All-American Slurp" by Lensey Namioka, from *Visions*, edited by Don Gallo. All rights reserved by Lensey Namioka.

Alfred A. Knopf, Inc.: *Nadia the Willful* by Sue Alexander; Copyright © 1983 by Sue Alexander. Reprinted by arrangement with Alfred A. Knopf, Inc.

Harcourt Brace & Company: "Primer Lesson," from *Slabs of the Sunburnt West* by Carl Sandburg; Copyright 1922 by Harcourt Brace & Company and renewed 1950 by Carl Sandburg. Reprinted and recorded by permission of Harcourt Brace & Company.

Delacorte Press: "The School Play" by Gary Soto, from *Funny You Should Ask*, edited by David Gale; Copyright © 1992 by Gary Soto. Reprinted by permission of Delacorte Press, a division of Bantam Doubleday Dell Publishing Group, Inc.

Scott Meredith Literary Agency: "Ghost of the Lagoon" by Armstrong Sperry. Reprinted by permission of the author and the author's agents, Scott Meredith Literary Agency, L.P., 845 Third Avenue, New York, NY 10022.

Walker and Company: "Matthew Henson at the Top of the World," from *Against All Opposition: Black Explorers in America* by Jim Haskins; Reprinted by permission of Walker and Company, 435 Hudson Street, New York, NY 10014. All rights reserved.

Continued on page 872

Cover Art

Background photo: Skyline with trees, Copyright © Y. Watabe/Photonica. **Painting of Ship:** Illustration by Lee Christiansen. **Girl:** Copyright © Joyce Stiglich. **Book:** Photo by Alan Shortall. **Butterflies and frame:** Photos by Sharon Hoogstraten.

Warning: No part of this work may be reproduced or transmitted in any form or by any means, electronic or mechanical, including photocopying and recording, or by any information storage or retrieval system without prior written permission of McDougal Littell Inc. unless such copying is expressly permitted by federal copyright law. With the exception of non-for-profit transcription in Braille, McDougal Littell Inc. is not authorized to grant permission for further uses of copyrighted selections reprinted in this text without the permission of their owners. Permission must be obtained from the individual copyright owners as identified herein. Address inquiries to Manager, Rights and Permissions, McDougal Littell Inc., P.O. Box 1667, Evanston, IL 60204.

ISBN 0-395-73701-X

Copyright © 1997 by McDougal Littell Inc. All rights reserved. Printed in the United States of America.

3 4 5 6 7 8 9 – DWO – 02 01 00 99 98 97

Senior Consultants

The senior consultants guided the conceptual development for *The Language of Literature* series. They participated actively in shaping prototype materials for major components, and they reviewed completed prototypes and/or completed units to ensure consistency with current research and the philosophy of the series.

Arthur N. Applebee Professor of Education, State University of New York at Albany; Director, Center for the Learning and Teaching of Literature; Senior Fellow, Center for Writing and Literacy

Andrea B. Bermúdez Professor of Studies in Language and Culture; Director, Research Center for Language and Culture; Chair, Foundations and Professional Studies, University of Houston-Clear Lake

Sheridan Blau Senior Lecturer in English and Education and former Director of Composition, University of California at Santa Barbara; Director, South Coast Writing Project; Director, Literature Institute for Teachers; Vice President, National Council of Teachers of English

Rebekah Caplan Coordinator, English Language Arts K-12, Oakland Unified School District, Oakland, California; Teacher-Consultant, Bay Area Writing Project, University of California at Berkeley; served on the California State English Assessment Development Team for Language Arts

Franchelle Dorn Professor of Drama, Howard University, Washington, D.C.; Adjunct Professor, Graduate School of Opera, University of Maryland, College Park, Maryland; Co-founder of The Shakespeare Acting Conservatory, Washington, D.C.

Peter Elbow Professor of English, University of Massachusetts at Amherst; Fellow, Bard Center for Writing and Thinking

Susan Hynds Professor and Director of English Education, Syracuse University, Syracuse, New York

Judith A. Langer Professor of Education, State University of New York at Albany; Co-director, Center for the Learning and Teaching of Literature; Senior Fellow, Center for Writing and Literacy

James Marshall Professor of English and English Education, University of Iowa, Iowa City

Contributing Consultants

Tommy Boley Associate Professor of English, University of Texas at El Paso

Jeffrey N. Golub Assistant Professor of English Education, University of South Florida, Tampa

William L. McBride Reading and Curriculum Specialist; former middle and high school English instructor

Multicultural Advisory Board

The multicultural advisors reviewed literature selections for appropriate content and made suggestions for teaching lessons in a multicultural classroom.

Dr. Joyce M. Bell, Chairperson, English Department, Townview Magnet Center, Dallas, Texas

Dr. Eugenia W. Collier, author; lecturer; Chairperson, Department of English and Language Arts; teacher of Creative Writing and American Literature, Morgan State University, Maryland

Kathleen S. Fowler, President, Palm Beach County Council of Teachers of English, Boca Raton Middle School, Boca Raton, Florida

Noreen M. Rodriguez, Trainer for Hillsborough County School District's Staff Development Division, independent consultant, Gaither High School, Tampa, Florida

Michelle Dixon Thompson, Seabreeze High School, Daytona Beach, Florida

Teacher Review Panels

The following educators provided ongoing review during the development of the tables of contents, lesson design, and key components of the program.

CALIFORNIA

Steve Bass, 8th Grade Team Leader, Meadowbrook Middle School, Ponway Unified School District

Cynthia Brickey, 8th Grade Academic Block Teacher, Kastner Intermediate School, Clovis Unified School District

Karen Buxton, English Department Chairperson, Winston Churchill Middle School, San Juan School District

continued on page 881

Manuscript Reviewers

The following educators reviewed prototype lessons and tables of contents during the development of *The Language of Literature* program.

William A. Battaglia, Herman Intermediate School, San Jose, California

Hugh Delle Broadway, McCullough High School, The Woodlands, Texas

Robert M. Bucan, National Mine Middle School, Ishpeming, Michigan

Ann E. Clayton, Department Chair for Language Arts, Rockway Middle School, Miami, Florida

Linda C. Dahl, National Mine Middle School, Ishpeming, Michigan

Shirley Herzog, Reading Department Coordinator, Fairfield Middle School, Fairfield, Ohio

continued on page 882

Student Board

The student board members read and evaluated selections to assess their appeal for sixth-grade students.

Ted Burke, East Aurora Middle School, East Aurora, New York

Ian Graham, Churchill Road Elementary School, McLean, Virginia

Melissa Hall, Frenship Intermediate School, Wolfforth, Texas

Stephanie Liberati, Hampton Middle School, Allison Park, Pennsylvania

Bridget McGuire, St. John of the Cross, Western Springs, Illinois

Eileen Pablos-Velez, Henry H. Filer Middle School, Hialeah, Florida

Nicole Putnam, Rockway Middle School, Miami, Florida

Eli Shlaes, Davidson Middle School, San Rafael, California

Theresa Sullivan, St. Ann's School, Wilmington, Delaware

Christine Tran, Foothill Middle School, Walnut Creek, California

Alexis Wong, Foothill Middle School, Walnut Creek, California

THE LANGUAGE OF LITERATURE TEACHER'S EDITION **vii**

The Language of Literature

CORE COMPONENTS

Student Anthology
A rich mix of classic and contemporary literature

& Literature Connections
Longer works with related readings

FREE!
Choose from a variety of *Literature Connections* titles when you adopt *The Language of Literature* from McDougal Littell
Call 800-323-5435 for details

Literature Connections

Each hardback volume contains

- Novel or Play
- Related Readings—poems, stories, plays, and articles that provide new perspectives on the longer works
- Teacher's SourceBook filled with background information and activities

Additional Literature Connections such as:

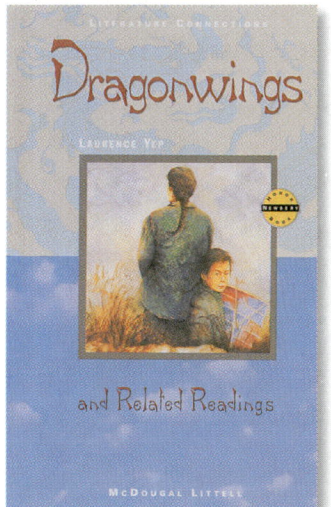

Dragonwings
by Laurence Yep
and Related Readings

The Flying Machine / PLAY
Ray Bradbury

Crazy Boys / POEM
Beverly McLoughland

The Skydivers / POEM
Joseph Colin Murphy

'The Chinese Must Go' / ESSAY
Bernard A. Weisberger

Ginger for the Heart / SHORT STORY
Paul Yee

The Story of an Eyewitness / ARTICLE
Jack London

Across Five Aprils
Irene Hunt

The Call of the Wild*
Jack London

The Clay Marble
Minfong Ho

The Contender
Robert Lipsyte

The Diary of Anne Frank
Frances Goodrich and Albert Hackett

Dogsong
Gary Paulsen

Dragonwings
Laurence Yep

The Giver
Lois Lowry

The Glory Field
Walter Dean Myers

The House of Dies Drear
Virginia Hamilton

I, Juan de Pareja*
Elizabeth Borton de Treviño

Johnny Tremain
Esther Forbes

Maniac Magee
Jerry Spinelli

Nothing but the Truth
Avi

Roll of Thunder, Hear My Cry*
Mildred D. Taylor

So Far from the Bamboo Grove
Yoko Kawashima Watkins

Tuck Everlasting*
Natalie Babbitt

Where the Red Fern Grows
Wilson Rawls

The Witch of Blackbird Pond
Elizabeth George Speare

A Wrinkle in Time
Madeleine L'Engle

*A Spanish version is also available.

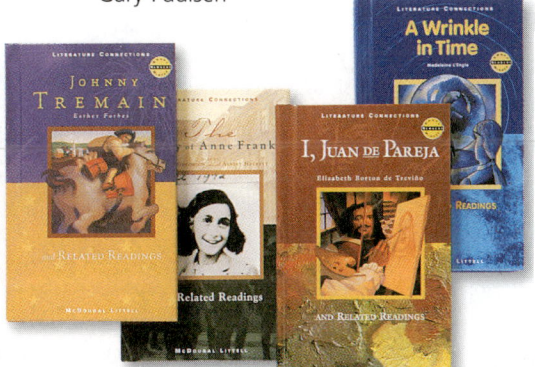
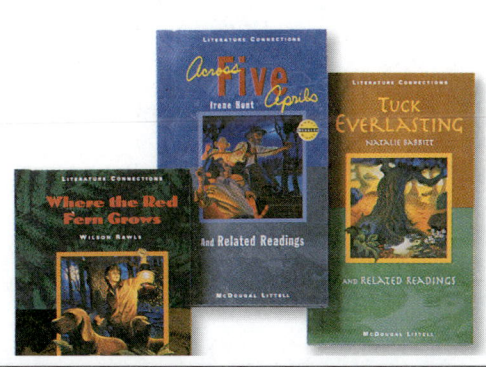

THE LANGUAGE OF LITERATURE TEACHER'S EDITION ix

UNIT ONE *Running Risks* — 16

Learning the Language of Literature 1
   ▸ Strategies for Reading 5
   READING MODEL: **The All-American Slurp** by Lensey Namioka 6

Part 1 Seizing the Moment

WHAT DO YOU THINK? Reflecting on Theme   18

▸ FOCUS ON FICTION: Reading Strategies 19

Sue Alexander	**Nadia the Willful**	FICTION	21
Carl Sandburg	**Primer Lesson** / LITERARY INSIGHT	POETRY	27
Gary Soto	**The School Play**	FICTION	30
Armstrong Sperry	**Ghost of the Lagoon**	FICTION	39

▸ FOCUS ON NONFICTION: Reading Strategies 51

Jim Haskins	**Matthew Henson at the Top of the World**	NONFICTION	53
	HISTORICAL INSIGHT / Early Explorers		
Don C. Reed	**My First Dive with the Dolphins**	NONFICTION	65
Norma Fox Mazer	**Tuesday of the Other June**		
	ON YOUR OWN / ASSESSMENT OPTION	FICTION	75
Eve Merriam	**Mean Song** / LITERARY INSIGHT	POETRY	83

WRITING ABOUT LITERATURE   Direct Response

Writer's Style: Descriptive Words 84
Guided Assignment: Write a Personal Response 86
Grammar in Context: Action Verbs 89
   SKILLBUILDERS: Using Adverbs, Understanding Sentence Variety, Using Linking Verbs

READING THE WORLD: VISUAL LITERACY 90
  Responding to Ads
  SKILLBUILDER: Analyzing Your Response

Part 2 On the Edge of Survival

	WHAT DO YOU THINK? Reflecting on Theme		92
Dorothy M. Johnson	**Too Soon a Woman**	FICTION	93
Rosemary and Stephen Vincent Benét	**Western Wagons** / LITERARY INSIGHT	POETRY	99
	▸ FOCUS ON POETRY: Reading Strategies		102
Lewis Carroll	**The Walrus and the Carpenter**	POETRY	104
Maya Angelou	**Life Doesn't Frighten Me**	POETRY	110
Abiodun Oyewole	**Another Mountain**	POETRY	110
Gary Paulsen	*from* **Woodsong**	NONFICTION	117
Louis Untermeyer	**The Dog of Pompeii**	FICTION	124
	HISTORICAL INSIGHT / Pompeii		134

WRITING FROM EXPERIENCE   Firsthand and Expressive Writing

Guided Assignment: Write an Anecdote 138
Prewriting: Planning Your Anecdote
Drafting: Writing It All Down
Revising and Publishing: Polishing Your Anecdote
  SKILLBUILDERS: Ordering and Representing Information, Achieving Unity in Paragraphs, Using Consistent Verb Tense

UNIT REVIEW: REFLECT & ASSESS 146

ACROSS TIME AND PLACE: The Oral Tradition
For more stories related to the unit theme, see page 638.

UNIT TWO *The Need to Belong* — 148

Part 1 Finding a Special Place

WHAT DO YOU THINK? Reflecting on Theme 150

Barbara Robinson	**The Adoption of Albert**	FICTION	151
Robert Service	**The Cremation of Sam McGee**	POETRY	161
Laurence Yep	**Chinatown,** *from* **The Lost Garden**	NONFICTION	170
Bashō, Issa, and Raymond R. Patterson	**Three Haiku**	POETRY	180
Myron Levoy	**Aaron's Gift**	FICTION	184
Norma Landa Flores	**Street Corner Flight** / LITERARY INSIGHT	POETRY	193
Shel Silverstein (REFLECT & ASSESS)	**Where the Sidewalk Ends**	POETRY	197
Mary Howitt	**The Spider and the Fly**	POETRY	198
Charles Reznikoff	**Two girls of twelve or so at a table**	POETRY	201
N. Scott Momaday	**New World**	POETRY	202
Rachel Field	**Something Told the Wild Geese**	POETRY	205

ON YOUR OWN / ASSESSMENT OPTION

WRITING ABOUT LITERATURE   Interpretation

Writer's Style: Main Idea and Details 206
Guided Assignment: Interpret a Passage 208
Grammar in Context: Sentence Fragments 211
  SKILLBUILDERS: Using Dashes, Using Quotations, Understanding Parts of Speech

READING THE WORLD: VISUAL LITERACY 212
  What's the Big Idea?
  SKILLBUILDER: Drawing Conclusions

Part 2 Tests of Endurance

WHAT DO YOU THINK? Reflecting on Theme ... 214

Yoshiko Uchida	**Oh Broom, Get to Work**	NONFICTION	215
James Berry	**It Seems I Test People**	POETRY	223
Jean Little	**Growing Pains**	POETRY	223
H. M. Hoover	**The Mushroom**	NONFICTION	228

▸ Reading Strategies: Chronological Order
HISTORICAL INSIGHT / The Survival of the Mushroom

Michael Anthony	**Cricket in the Road**	FICTION	237
Eleanor Farjeon	**The Quarrel** / LITERARY INSIGHT	POETRY	240

WRITING FROM EXPERIENCE — Narrative and Literary Writing
Guided Assignment: Write a Character Sketch. ... 244
Prewriting: Making Observations
Drafting: Getting Your Ideas Down
Revising and Publishing: Finishing Your Sketch
SKILLBUILDERS: Using Sensory Details, Varying Your Sentences, Using Action Verbs

UNIT REVIEW: REFLECT & ASSESS ... 252

ACROSS TIME AND PLACE: The Oral Tradition
For more stories related to the unit theme, see page 660.

xiii

UNIT THREE *A Sense of Fairness* 254

Part 1 Coping with Injustice

WHAT DO YOU THINK? Reflecting on Theme 256

Walter Dean Myers	**Abd al-Rahman Ibrahima,** *from* **Now Is Your Time!**	NONFICTION	257
Dudley Randall	**Ancestors** / LITERARY INSIGHT	POETRY	267
Sandra Cisneros	**Eleven**	FICTION	271
T. Ernesto Bethancourt	**User Friendly**	FICTION	277

▶ Reading Strategies: Specialized Vocabulary

William Saroyan   **The Summer of the Beautiful White Horse** .... FICTION 291
HISTORICAL INSIGHT / The Empire of the Armenians

REFLECT & ASSESS   Susan Haven   **Thanksgiving in Polynesia**
ON YOUR OWN / ASSESSMENT OPTION .... FICTION 302

> **WRITING ABOUT LITERATURE** Analysis
>
> **Writer's Style:** Dialogue 310
> **Guided Assignment:** Write a Plot Analysis 312
> **Grammar in Context:** Coordinating Conjunctions 315
> SKILLBUILDERS: Using Quotation Marks, Writing a Summary, Using Commas with Conjunctions

READING THE WORLD: VISUAL LITERACY 316
What Happens Next?
SKILLBUILDER: Predicting Outcomes

Part 2 Facing the Consequences

WHAT DO YOU THINK? Reflecting on Theme 318

Isaac Bashevis Singer	**Shrewd Todie and Lyzer the Miser** .... FICTION 319
	HISTORICAL INSIGHT / The Rabbi in the Community
Patricia and Fredrick McKissack	*from* **A Long Hard Journey** .... NONFICTION 329
Theodore Roethke	**Night Journey** / LITERARY INSIGHT .... POETRY 338
John Greenleaf Whittier	**Barbara Frietchie** .... POETRY 341
Jacqueline Balcells	**The Enchanted Raisin** .... FICTION 346
	▶ FOCUS ON DRAMA: Reading Strategies 357
Les Crutchfield, based on a story by Martin Storm	**A Shipment of Mute Fate** .... DRAMA 359

WRITING FROM EXPERIENCE | Informative Exposition

Guided Assignment: Write a Problem-Solution Essay 376
Prewriting: Gathering Information
Drafting: Getting Your Ideas Down
Revising and Publishing: Polishing Your Draft
SKILLBUILDERS: Conducting an Interview, Elaborating on Ideas, Using Pronouns Correctly

UNIT REVIEW: REFLECT & ASSESS 384

ACROSS TIME AND PLACE: The Oral Tradition
For more stories related to the unit theme, see page 682.

xv

THE LANGUAGE OF LITERATURE TEACHER'S EDITION **XV**

UNIT FOUR *Proving Ground* — 386

Part 1 Showing Your True Colors

WHAT DO YOU THINK? Reflecting on Theme — 388

Author	Selection	Genre	Page
Elizabeth Borton de Treviño	**The Secret of the Wall**	FICTION	389
Pat Cummings	from **Talking with Artists**	NONFICTION	406
Paul Engle	**Water Color** / LITERARY INSIGHT	FICTION	411
Gish Jen	**The White Umbrella**	FICTION	414
Dorthi Charles	**Concrete Cat**	POETRY	424
John Ciardi	**Chang McTang McQuarter Cat**	POETRY	424
Alvin Schwartz	from **Gold and Silver, Silver and Gold**	NONFICTION	430

▶ Reading Strategies: Problem Solving
HISTORICAL INSIGHT / The History of Piracy

Bill Littlefield — from **Champions**
ON YOUR OWN / ASSESSMENT OPTION . . . . NONFICTION 441

WRITING ABOUT LITERATURE — Creative Response

Writer's Style: Show, Don't Tell 448
Guided Assignment: Fill In the Blanks 450
Grammar in Context: Prepositional Phrases 453

SKILLBUILDERS: Understanding Complex Subjects and Predicates, Using Time-Order Transition Words, Understanding Objects of Prepositions

READING THE WORLD: VISUAL LITERACY 454
What on Earth?
SKILLBUILDER: Formulating Questions

xvi THE LANGUAGE OF LITERATURE TEACHER'S EDITION

Part 2 Taking Necessary Steps

WHAT DO YOU THINK? Reflecting on Theme 456

Luther Standing Bear	**At Last I Kill a Buffalo**	NONFICTION	457
Vachel Lindsay	**The Flower-Fed Buffaloes** / LITERARY INSIGHT	POETRY	467
Anne Terry White	**Tutankhamen,** from **Lost Worlds**	NONFICTION	470
	HISTORICAL INSIGHT / The Boy Pharaoh		
Shiro Murano	**Pole Vault**	POETRY	480
May Swenson	**Analysis of Baseball**	POETRY	480
Mary O'Hara	**My Friend Flicka**	FICTION	486

WRITING FROM EXPERIENCE Informative Exposition

Guided Assignment: Write a Compare-Contrast Essay 506
Prewriting: Working Through Ideas
Drafting: Thinking on the Page
Revising and Publishing: Putting It All Together
  SKILLBUILDERS: Using Graphic Organizers, Using Transitions, Using Comparatives and Superlatives

UNIT REVIEW: REFLECT & ASSESS 514

ACROSS TIME AND PLACE: The Oral Tradition
For more stories related to the unit theme, see page 708.

UNIT FIVE The Pursuit of a Goal — 516

Part 1 Facing Inner Fears

WHAT DO YOU THINK? Reflecting on Theme 518

Elizabeth Ellis	**Flowers and Freckle Cream**	FICTION	519
Pat Mora	**Same Song** / LITERARY INSIGHT	POETRY	523
Daniel Cohen	**The First Emperor,** from **The Tomb Robbers**	NONFICTION	526

▶ Reading Strategies: Techniques of SQ3R
HISTORICAL INSIGHT / The Emperor

Lilian Moore	**Message from a Caterpillar**	POETRY	537
Paul Fleischman	**Chrysalis Diary**	POETRY	537
Francisco Jiménez	**The Circuit**	FICTION	545
Lucille Clifton	**the 1st** / LITERARY INSIGHT	POETRY	552
Kristin Hunter	**The Scribe**		

ON YOUR OWN / ASSESSMENT OPTION .... FICTION 555

WRITING ABOUT LITERATURE — Creative Response

Writer's Style: Sensory Language 562
Guided Assignment: Write a Poem 564
Grammar in Context: Inverted Sentences 567
SKILLBUILDERS: Using Compound Sentences, Using Sound Devices, Understanding Subject-Verb Agreement

READING THE WORLD: VISUAL LITERACY 568
Hidden Values
SKILLBUILDER: Looking Beyond Appearances

xviii

Part 2 Reluctant Heroes

WHAT DO YOU THINK? Reflecting on Theme 570

J. R. R. Tolkien, dramatized by Patricia Gray
The Hobbit .... DRAMA 571
HISTORICAL INSIGHT / Dragon Friends and Foes

WRITING FROM EXPERIENCE Persuasion

Guided Assignment: Write an Opinion Essay 622
Prewriting: Finding a Focus
Drafting: Pulling It Together
Revising and Publishing: Adding Final Touches
SKILLBUILDERS: Separating Fact from Opinion, Using Precise Language, Using Active Voice

UNIT REVIEW: REFLECT & ASSESS 630

ACROSS TIME AND PLACE: The Oral Tradition
For more stories related to the unit theme, see page 728.

UNIT SIX Across Time and Place: The Oral Tradition 632

STORYTELLERS PAST AND PRESENT 634
KEEPING THE PAST ALIVE 636

Links to Unit One
retold by Jane Yolen
retold by Diane Wolkstein
retold by Julius Lester

Running Risks 638
Wings .... GREEK MYTH 640
The Red Lion .... ANCIENT PERSIAN TALE 649
Why Monkeys Live in Trees .... AFRICAN FOLK TALE 654
CROSS-CURRICULAR PROJECTS 658

Links to Unit Two
as told by
Dang Manh Kha
to Ann Nolan Clark

by Lynn Joseph
retold by Pura Belpré

The Need to Belong 660
In the Land of Small Dragon ... VIETNAMESE FOLK TALE 662

The Bamboo Beads .... TRINIDADIAN FOLK TALE 670
The Legend of the
Hummingbird .... PUERTO-RICAN LEGEND 676
CROSS-CURRICULAR PROJECTS 680

Links to Unit Three
retold by Fan Kissen
retold by Ricardo E. Alegría
retold by Victor Montejo

A Sense of Fairness 682
Damon and Pythias: A Drama .. GREEK LEGEND 684
The Three Wishes .... PUERTO-RICAN FOLK TALE 691
The Disobedient Child .... GUATEMALAN FABLE 694
CROSS-CURRICULAR PROJECTS 698

WRITING ABOUT LITERATURE | Criticism

Writer's Style: Sentence Composing 700
Guided Assignment: Evaluate the Lesson of a Story 702
Grammar in Context: Compound Subjects and Predicates 705
SKILLBUILDERS: Understanding Pronouns and Their Antecedents, Organizing Your Review, Making Compound Subjects and Verbs Agree

READING THE WORLD: VISUAL LITERACY 706
Believe It or Not
SKILLBUILDER: Evaluating the Message

Links to Unit Four	**Proving Ground**		708
retold by Olivia E. Coolidge	**Arachne**	GREEK MYTH	710
retold by Claus Stamm	**Three Strong Women**	JAPANESE TALL TALE	715
retold by Joseph Bruchac	**The White Buffalo Calf Woman and the Sacred Pipe**	LAKOTA SIOUX LEGEND	723
	CROSS-CURRICULAR PROJECTS		726
Links to Unit Five	**The Pursuit of a Goal**		728
retold by Carol Kendall and Yao-Wen Li	**The Living Kuan-yin**	CHINESE FOLK TALE	730
retold by Robert D. San Souci	**Sister Fox and Brother Coyote**	MEXICAN-AMERICAN FOLK TALE	735
retold by The Brothers Grimm	**King Thrushbeard**	GERMAN FOLK TALE	741
	CROSS-CURRICULAR PROJECTS		746

WRITING ABOUT LITERATURE | Report

Guided Assignment: Write an I-Search Report............................. 748
Prewriting: Researching Your Topic
Drafting: Sharing Your Experience
Revising and Publishing: Pulling It All Together
 SKILLBUILDERS: Taking Notes, Outlining Your Ideas, Creating a List of Sources

UNIT REVIEW: REFLECT AND ASSESS 756

Selections by Genre, Writing Workshops

Short Story
The All-American Slurp	6
Nadia the Willful	21
The School Play	30
Ghost of the Lagoon	39
Tuesday of the Other June	75
Too Soon a Woman	93
The Dog of Pompeii	124
The Adoption of Albert	151
Aaron's Gift	184
Cricket in the Road	237
Eleven	271
User Friendly	277
The Summer of the Beautiful White Horse	291
Thanksgiving in Polynesia	302
Shrewd Todie and Lyzer the Miser	320
The Enchanted Raisin	346
The Secret of the Wall	389
The White Umbrella	414
My Friend Flicka	486
Flowers and Freckle Cream	519
The Circuit	545
The Scribe	555

Nonfiction
Matthew Henson at the Top of the World	53
My First Dive with the Dolphins	65
from *Woodsong*	117
Chinatown, from *The Lost Garden*	170
Oh Broom, Get to Work	215
The Mushroom	228
Abd al-Rahman Ibrahima, from *Now Is Your Time!*	257
from *A Long Hard Journey*	329
from *Talking with Artists*	406
from *Gold and Silver, Silver and Gold*	430
from *Champions*	441
At Last I Kill a Buffalo	457
Tutankhamen, from *Lost Worlds*	470
The First Emperor, from *The Tomb Robbers*	526

Drama
A Shipment of Mute Fate	359
The Hobbit	571

Poetry
Primer Lesson	27
Mean Song	83
Western Wagons	99
The Walrus and the Carpenter	104
Life Doesn't Frighten Me	110
Another Mountain	110
The Cremation of Sam McGee	161
Three Haiku	180
Street Corner Flight	193
Where the Sidewalk Ends	197
The Spider and the Fly	198
Two girls of twelve or so at a table	201
New World	202
Something Told the Wild Geese	205
It Seems I Test People	223
Growing Pains	223
The Quarrel	240
Barbara Frietchie	341
Night Journey	338

Water Color	.411
Concrete Cat	.424
Chang McTang McQuarter Cat	.424
The Flower-Fed Buffaloes	.467
Pole Vault	.480
Analysis of Baseball	.480
Same Song	.523
Message from a Caterpillar	.537
Chrysalis Diary	.537
The First	.552

The Oral Tradition
Myths, Legends, Folk Tales, and Fables

Wings	.640
The Red Lion	.649
Why Monkeys Live in Trees	.654
In the Land of Small Dragon	.662
The Bamboo Beads	.670
The Legend of the Hummingbird	.676
Damon and Pythias: A Drama	.684
The Three Wishes	.691
The Disobedient Child	.694
Arachne	.710
Three Strong Women	.715
The White Buffalo Calf Woman and the Sacred Pipe	.723
The Living Kuan-yin	.730
Sister Fox and Brother Coyote	.735
King Thrushbeard	.741

Writing About Literature

Direct Response	.84
Interpretation	.206
Analysis	.310
Creative Response	.448
Creative Response	.562
Criticism	.700

Writing from Experience

Firsthand and Expressive Writing	.138
Narrative and Literary Writing	.244
Informative Exposition	.376
Informative Exposition	.506
Persuasion	.622
Report	.748

Reading the World: Visual Literacy

Responding to Ads	.90
What's the Big Idea?	.212
What Happens Next?	.316
What on Earth?	.454
Hidden Values	.568
Believe It or Not	.706

LEARNING THE LANGUAGE OF LITERATURE

Objectives

Designed to help students realize that their encounters with the literature in this book will challenge them to discover new ways of reading, learning and understanding, this section has the following purposes:
- To involve students in an activity that will help them perceive the study of literature in a new way
- To help students discover how literature connects to their own lives and the world around them
- To introduce students to the parts of the book
- To familiarize students with the tools necessary for learning, such as a reading log, a notebook, and strategies for reading
- To provide a model of real students using reading strategies to become involved with literature

LEARNING THE LANGUAGE OF LITERATURE

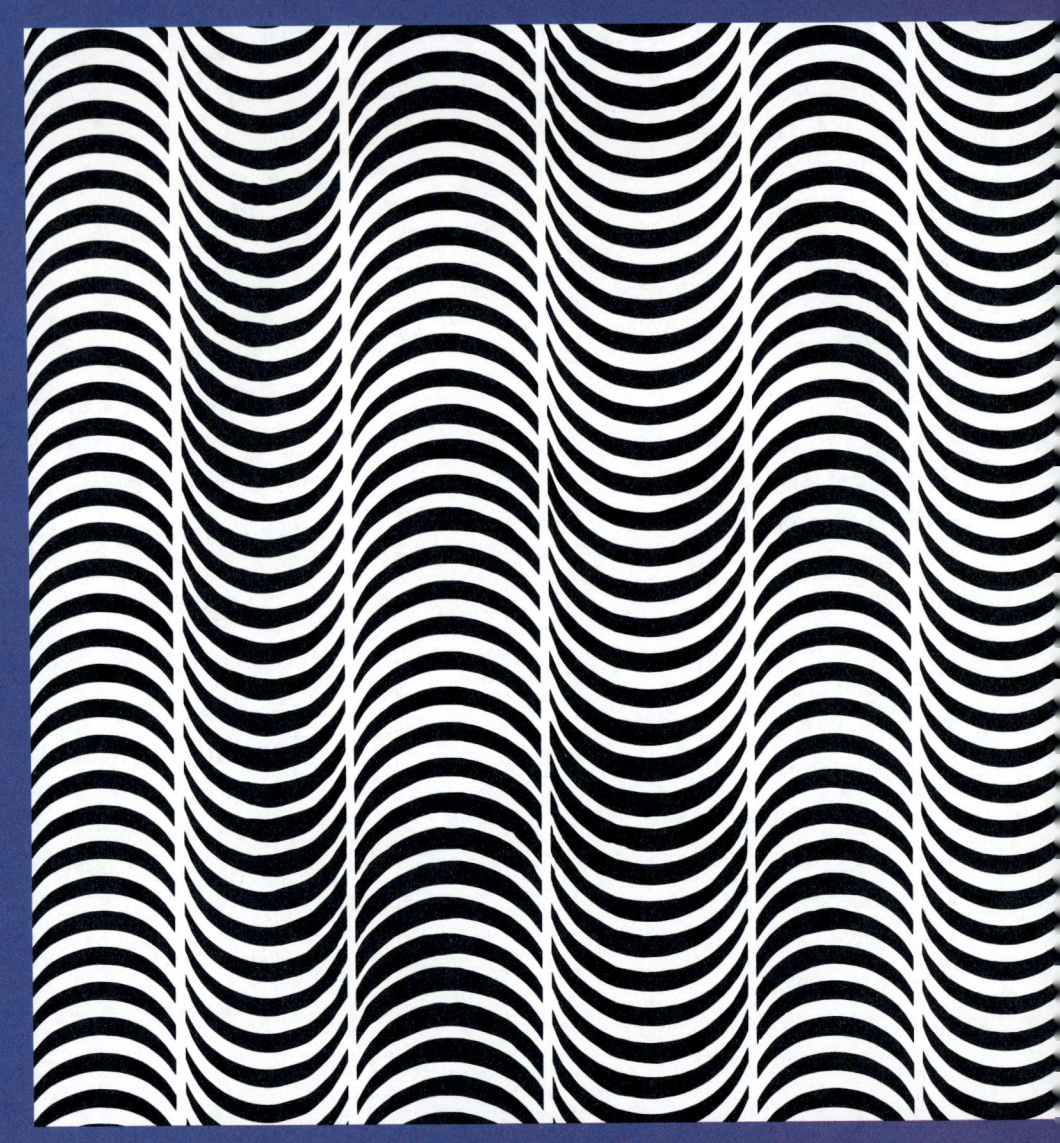

Can You Read Between the Lines?

Take a quick glance at the picture on the left and then look away. What did you see? Now, look again. Do you see anything else this time? There's more to this picture than meets the eye!

LOOK AGAIN

With a partner, take turns trying to see a second picture hidden in the pattern. Follow these steps.

1. What new ways of looking at the picture can you think of? What happens when you squint at the picture? What happens when you look at it from different angles? when you look at it up close? when you move it away?

2. Keep looking at the pattern until you see a hidden picture. Note how long it took you to see it.

3. Describe to your partner the picture you see.

4. Close your book to hide the pattern. Wait a minute or two.

5. Open the book again. How long did it take you to see the hidden picture this time?

6. If you have trouble finding the hidden picture, ask your partner for pointers and keep trying.

CONNECT TO LITERATURE

To see the hidden picture, you had to find a way to look at more than just the lines. In the same way, understanding literature involves more than just looking at words on a page. You have to learn to read between the lines. The more you think about what you read, the more you'll notice. Turn the page to see what you might find in literature.

Look Again

It may be necessary for students to view this pattern from a distance in order to discern the image. Most students will see a face in the pattern, although the specific characteristics of the face may vary. You may wish to have students draw or sketch the face that they see in the pattern and compare their perceptions of the face with those of others in the class. If any students are having difficulty finding a hidden picture in the pattern, encourage volunteers to help them "see" the picture by tracing with a finger the outline of the hidden face.

Connect to Literature

Encourage students to understand the reason for this activity by stressing the idea that reading literature is similar to looking at this pattern. In other words, understanding and appreciating literature involves looking beyond the obvious, or "reading between the lines," to make new discoveries.

What Can You Find in Literature?

These two pages are designed both to extend the explanation of literature that was introduced in the opening activity, and to provide an overview of the pupil book for students.

You can help students work through this page by first generating a class discussion. Ask students to describe how literature currently affects their lives.

- What does the word *literature* mean to you?
- What kinds of literature do you like to read? Why?
- Do you think studying literature is important? Why or why not?
- Do you think literature, or the study of literature, can affect people's lives? How?
- Have you ever read something that helped you think new thoughts and form new ideas or that affected your emotions strongly?

What Can You Find in Literature?

Pick up your book. What's inside? Stories? Poems? An essay or two? But wait—there's so much more! This year, you will look beyond the words on a page to discover a world of ideas and images. What do you think might be hiding between the lines of literature?

EXCITING PLACES

How would you like to visit an ancient Roman city, search for a pharaoh's tomb in the Valley of the Kings, or journey to the top of the world? The **literature selections** you'll read this year will take you to those places and more. For example, the excerpt from *Gold and Silver, Silver and Gold*, on page 430, will place you on the deck of a pirate ship.

YOUR PERSONALITY

Your reactions to literature can reveal sides of yourself you've never seen before. The **Previewing** pages before each selection let you explore your ideas about a subject and also provide you with background information. For example, on page 93 you examine the hardships of frontier life before you read "Too Soon a Woman" by Dorothy M. Johnson. The **Responding** pages after a selection help you further explore and gain a deeper understanding of what you've read. To glimpse some responding activities, turn to page 100.

2 LEARNING THE LANGUAGE OF LITERATURE

STRONG IDEAS

The **Writing About Literature** workshops will help you sift through literature's many layers to discover new ideas and to share your discoveries with others. Some of your discoveries will be surprising or confusing, but the workshop on page 206 can help you find meaning in what you've read. The **Writing from Experience** workshops help you find connections between unit themes and your own life. For example, after you have explored right and wrong in Unit Three, you will write about a problem that concerns you and come up with a solution.

SURPRISING CONNECTIONS

As you discover new people and exciting places in the stories you read, you'll be amazed at the connections they have to your own life and to the world around you. The **Reading the World** feature will show you how to apply the skills you use when reading literature to everyday situations. As an example, the lesson on page 90 invites you to examine how and why you respond to advertising.

Illustration Copyright ©
CSA Archive.

LEARNING THE LANGUAGE OF LITERATURE   **3**

You may wish to have students read these two pages on their own, with a partner, or as a class. Encourage students to turn to the specific pages and examples suggested. Also suggest that they write down any comments or questions they think of while reading. Once students have read the two pages, discuss the questions they have recorded and ask them if their expectations about the book or the study of literature have changed. (For further information about each of the book sections that are mentioned, please turn to pages T10–T11, T14–T15, and T22–T23 at the front of this Teacher's Edition.)

THE LANGUAGE OF LITERATURE **TEACHER'S EDITION** **3**

MULTIPLE PATHWAYS
Help students to understand the concept of multiple pathways by engaging them in the following activity. Have students imagine that they are going to take a trip across the country, from the east coast to the west coast. Ask them to identify as many forms of transportation as possible that they could use and to identify the differences among the forms of transportation. Make sure students understand that the end result with each form of transportation is the same—it's the means by which they get to their destination that differs. Tell students that learning is similar to traveling. There are many ways to learn, all of which involve different strategies and experiences.

PORTFOLIO
Students will use their portfolios to file the work they will carry out in the projects and activities throughout the book. You can determine the way in which students use their portfolios. For instance, you may wish to have students include not only their completed work, but also outlines, drafts, and revisions. These portfolios can also be used to help students reflect on and assess what they learned from these projects.

NOTEBOOK
Students will use their notebooks to record their responses to and notes for some items on the Previewing and Responding pages. At various times, you may wish to have students use their notes to help them participate in paired or group discussions. You also may wish to return to these previewing notes after students have finished reading a selection to allow them to reflect and assess whether any of their thoughts have changed.

READING LOG
Students will use their reading logs to record their thoughts and responses while reading. At times, students will be responding to questions incorporated in the selections, but they should also be encouraged to record their ideas and questions whenever they read independently.

You can use these three tools in any number of ways that best suit the needs of your class. Refer to the *Teacher's Guide to Assessment and Portfolio Use* for more information on using these tools, and to the *Unit Resource Book* for copymasters of different examples of reading logs.

How Can You Keep What You Find?

You've seen some of the wonderful things you can discover in literature. Now it's time to get acquainted with several different ways that you can make your discoveries your own.

MULTIPLE PATHWAYS
How do you learn best? Do you prefer working alone or with others? Do you like writing, talking, acting, or drawing? This book offers you many choices that allow you to tailor learning experiences to your own strengths. In addition, you'll collaborate with classmates to share ideas, improve your writing, and make connections to other subject areas. You may even use a computer in the process. Technological tools such as the LaserLinks and the Writing Coach offer you even more learning options.

PORTFOLIO
Many artists, photographers, designers, and writers keep samples of their work in a portfolio that they show to others. You, too, will be collecting your work in a portfolio throughout the year. Your portfolio may include writing samples, records of activities, and artwork. You probably won't put all your work in your portfolio—just carefully chosen pieces. Discuss with your teacher the kind of portfolio you will be keeping this year. Suggestions for using your portfolio appear throughout this book.

Notebook

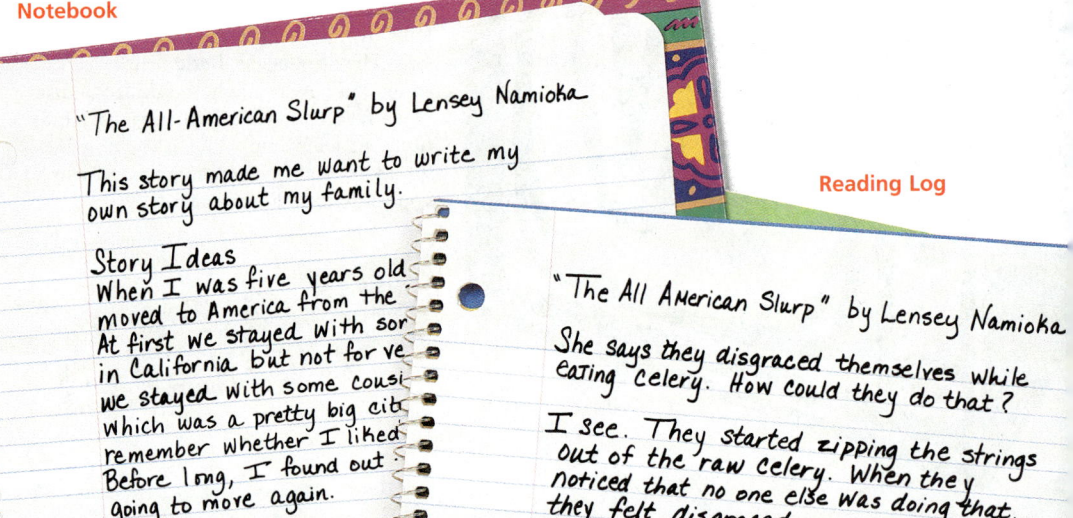

Reading Log

4 THE LANGUAGE OF LITERATURE TEACHER'S EDITION

...k on the selection, the final p...
...scribes the meaning of the whole story.
"At first, I wasn't sure exactly what the story was about. The writer talks a lot about Chinatown and about the different streets, ills, and other parts of town. Some of the stories he tells are unny. So I thought maybe this story was supposed to be funny. When I reread the story, I discovered that the writer talks a lot about feeling different or like an outsider. He was Chinese, but he didn't live in Chinatown or speak Chinese like all his friends. It was like he was lonely even though he had all these friends. The writer wasn't good at sports, either, so he was different from his family too.
When the writer talks about his singing adventure, he sets us up because we think it's a funny scene. But then he starts talking about his deep feelings. He says, "But the experience cured me of wanting to dress up and be something else." In this passage

Portfolio

NOTEBOOK

Choose any type of notebook to dedicate to your study of literature. Divide the notebook into three parts. Use the first section before reading, while reading, and after you have read a selection. Jot down ideas and thoughts, describe personal experiences, and take notes about the selection. Also include any charts, diagrams, and drawings that help you connect your reading to your life. The second section will be for your reading log, which is described below. Use the third section as a writer's notebook to record ideas and inspirations that you might want to use later in your writing.

READING LOG

In your reading log you will record a special kind of response to literature—your direct comments as you read a selection. The reading strategies detailed at the right will help you think about what you read. Experiment with recording your own comments as you read. You will find specific opportunities to use your reading log throughout this book.

Strategies for Reading

Reading is not a spectator sport. To get the most out of literature, you must think about what you read. The strategies below describe the kinds of thinking that active readers do as they read. You can use these strategies, too.

QUESTION

Question what's happening while you read. Searching for reasons behind events and characters' feelings can help you feel more involved in what you're reading. Make notes about confusing words or statements, but don't worry if you don't understand everything. As you read further, you'll probably begin to see things more clearly.

CONNECT

Connect personally with what you're reading. Think of similarities between the descriptions in the selection and what you have personally experienced, heard about, or read about.

PREDICT

Try to figure out what will happen next and how the selection might end. Then read on to see if you made a good guess.

CLARIFY

Stop occasionally to review what you understand so far, and expect to have your understanding change and develop as you read on. Also, watch for answers to questions you had earlier.

EVALUATE

Form opinions about what you read, both while you're reading and after you've finished. Make judgments about the information and develop your own ideas about events.

Now turn the page to see how two student readers put these strategies to work.

LEARNING THE LANGUAGE OF LITERATURE

Strategies for Reading

Ask volunteers to talk about a time they read a very exciting story. Ask students to describe their reading experiences of being actively involved in the story. Tell students that when they are involved in reading they are probably using some of the strategies described on this page. Explain that these strategies are ways that active readers get more pleasure and understanding from what they read and that using these strategies can make reading easier and more enjoyable.

Invite students to read aloud and discuss the descriptions of the strategies for reading on this page. Ask students to share occasions when they have used these strategies. Explain that the model they are about to read shows what some readers thought as they were reading the story. Suggest that they cover the remarks in the margin while they read each page; then they can go back and compare their thoughts with the printed ones. Stress that these readers' thoughts are not "right" answers but rather a set of possible active responses.

READING MODEL
Objectives

This model can be used in several ways:

- You may wish to have students cover the sidebar notes and read "The All-American Slurp" as they practice recording their thoughts in a reading log. Afterwards, students can compare their responses to those of other classmates and to the student readers to illustrate how different readers respond to the same selection.

- You might read the selection aloud, pausing to have students record their ideas and reactions. You may wish to read aloud and have students take turns role-playing Jay's and Tiffany's responses.

READING MODEL

While reading the story "The All-American Slurp," two sixth-grade students spoke their thoughts out loud. The thoughts of Tiffany Providence and Jay Pepitone appear alongside the story to illustrate how active readers think as they read. After each comment, a label identifies the reading strategy or strategies that the comment reflects. You'll see that no two readers think alike. The ways in how they respond and use reading strategies vary widely. To get the most from this model, first read the story yourself and respond to it in your own way. Then read the responses of Tiffany and Jay, and compare them with your own.

The All-American SLURP
By Lensey Namioka

6 READING MODEL

6 THE LANGUAGE OF LITERATURE TEACHER'S EDITION

The first time our family was invited out to dinner in America, we disgraced ourselves while eating celery. We had emigrated to this country from China, and during our early days here we had a hard time with American table manners.

In China we never ate celery raw, or any other kind of vegetable raw. We always had to disinfect the vegetables in boiling water first. When we were presented with our first relish tray, the raw celery caught us unprepared.

We had been invited to dinner by our neighbors, the Gleasons. After arriving at the house, we shook hands with our hosts and packed ourselves into a sofa. As our family of four sat stiffly in a row, my younger brother and I stole glances at our parents for a clue as to what to do next.

Tiffany: "Stole glances"? I guess that means they looked at each other when the others weren't looking.
CLARIFYING

Mrs. Gleason offered the relish tray to Mother. The tray looked pretty, with its tiny red radishes, curly sticks of carrots, and long, slender stalks of pale green celery. "Do try some of the celery, Mrs. Lin," she said. "It's from a local farmer, and it's sweet."

Mother picked up one of the green stalks, and Father followed suit. Then I picked up a stalk, and my brother did too. So there we sat, each with a stalk of celery in our right hand.

Jay: This doesn't make sense to me: "Father followed suit." How does that fit in?
QUESTIONING

Mrs. Gleason kept smiling. "Would you like to try some of the dip, Mrs. Lin? It's my own recipe: sour cream and onion flakes, with a dash of Tabasco sauce."

Most Chinese don't care for dairy products, and in those days I wasn't even ready to drink fresh milk. Sour cream sounded perfectly revolting. Our family shook our heads in unison.

Jay: Don't know what that word means. I think it means ... like ... "together" because it says "Our family...."
CLARIFYING

Mrs. Gleason went off with the relish tray to the other guests, and we carefully watched to see what they did. Everyone seemed to eat the raw vegetables quite happily.

Mother took a bite of her celery. *Crunch.* "It's not bad!" she whispered.

Father took a bite of his celery. *Crunch.* "Yes, it is good," he said, looking surprised.

I took a bite, and then my brother. *Crunch, crunch.* It was more than good; it was delicious. Raw celery has a slight sparkle, a zingy taste that you don't get in cooked celery. When Mrs. Gleason came around with the relish tray, we each took another stalk of celery, except my brother. He took two.

Tiffany: How come they didn't eat raw vegetables?
QUESTIONING

There was only one problem: long strings ran through the length of the stalk, and they got caught in my teeth. When I help my mother in the kitchen, I always pull the strings out before slicing celery.

THE ALL-AMERICAN SLURP **7**

A Unfamiliar words and phrases can be stumbling blocks to a reader's understanding of a selection. Often the meaning of an unfamiliar word or phrase can be inferred from context clues. Tiffany isn't sure what "stolen glances" means, but she makes an attempt to clarify its meaning.

B Jay isn't sure what "Father followed suit" means, and he notes his question. However, he moves along, knowing that he can come back later to figure it out if he needs to do so. While questions about the meaning of words and phrases often don't need to be answered exactly, students should learn to judge whether they are making sense of the story as a whole and to recognize when vocabulary help is essential to their understanding.

C Again, Jay is confused about the meaning of a word. He uses context clues in the sentence to help clarify possible meanings for the word unison. Using context clues to clarify unfamiliar words or phrases is an important reading strategy.

D Tiffany seems to have missed the narrator's earlier comment about her family never eating celery raw in China. Her question reflects an attempt to understand why the characters are responding the way they are.

THE LANGUAGE OF LITERATURE **TEACHER'S EDITION** **7**

E Again, Tiffany questions a passage in the selection that she finds confusing. Her questioning may be a result of her missing the earlier information about the family being from China and not eating celery raw. Students should be encouraged to make inferences based on information they already know in order to answer their questions as they read.

F Readers often recognize situations in stories that remind them of personal experiences and concerns. Such prior knowledge can add depth and richness to a reader's understanding of a selection. Here, Jay connects the selection to his own experience by noting something that he does as a dinner guest.

G Tiffany wonders if she missed some information while reading or if this information has not yet been stated. Students should be encouraged to learn when to stop and reread for important information and when to read ahead for more information.

H Jay records his thoughts about information not stated in the passage. Because this information is not central to his understanding of the selection, he notes his questions and continues reading. Students should be encouraged to keep track of their questions and to return to those left unanswered at the end of a selection.

E *Tiffany:* Why would they pull out the little strings in the celery?
QUESTIONING

F *Jay:* Whenever I eat at anybody else's house, I eat slower than I usually do. That way, I can make sure nothing flies out of my mouth and I don't make any noise while I'm chewing.
CONNECTING

G *Tiffany:* Was the brother's name mentioned before?
QUESTIONING

H *Jay:* I wonder why he didn't learn to play baseball in China. I wonder if they don't have it there.
QUESTIONING

8 READING MODEL

I pulled the strings out of my stalk. *Z-z-zip, z-z-zip.* My brother followed suit. *Z-z-zip, z-z-zip, z-z-zip.* To my left, my parents were taking care of their own stalks. *Z-z-zip, z-z-zip, z-z-zip.*

Suddenly I realized that there was dead silence except for our zipping. Looking up, I saw that the eyes of everyone in the room were on our family. Mr. and Mrs. Gleason, their daughter Meg, who was my friend, and their neighbors the Badels—they were all staring at us as we busily pulled the strings of our celery.

That wasn't the end of it. Mrs. Gleason announced that dinner was served and invited us to the dining table. It was lavishly covered with platters of food, but we couldn't see any chairs around the table. So we helpfully carried over some dining chairs and sat down. All the other guests just stood there.

Mrs. Gleason bent down and whispered to us, "This is a buffet dinner. You help yourselves to some food and eat it in the living room."

Our family beat a retreat back to the sofa as if chased by enemy soldiers. For the rest of the evening, too mortified to go back to the dining table, I nursed a bit of potato salad on my plate.

Next day Meg and I got on the school bus together. I wasn't sure how she would feel about me after the spectacle our family made at the party. But she was just the same as usual, and the only reference she made to the party was, "Hope you and your folks got enough to eat last night. You certainly didn't take very much. Mom never tries to figure out how much food to prepare. She just puts everything on the table and hopes for the best."

I began to relax. The Gleasons' dinner party wasn't so different from a Chinese meal after all. My mother also puts everything on the table and hopes for the best.

Meg was the first friend I had made after we came to America. I eventually got acquainted with a few other kids in school, but Meg was still the only real friend I had.

My brother didn't have any problems making friends. He spent all his time with some boys who were teaching him baseball, and in no time he could speak English much faster than I could—not better, but faster.

I worried more about making mistakes, and I spoke carefully, making sure I could say everything right before opening my mouth. At least I had a better accent than my parents, who never really got rid of their Chinese accent, even years later. My parents had both studied English in school before coming to America, but what they had studied was mostly written English, not spoken.

Father's approach to English was a scientific one. Since Chinese verbs have no tense, he was fascinated by the way English verbs changed form according to whether they were in the present, past imperfect, perfect, pluperfect, future, or future perfect tense. He was always making diagrams of verbs and their inflections, and he looked for opportunities to show off his mastery of the pluperfect and future perfect tenses, his two favorites. "I shall have finished my project by Monday," he would say smugly.

Mother's approach was to memorize lists of polite phrases that would cover all possible social situations. She was constantly muttering things like "I'm fine, thank you. And you?" Once she accidentally stepped on someone's foot and hurriedly blurted, "Oh, that's quite all right!" Embarrassed by her slip, she resolved to do better next time. So when someone stepped on her foot, she cried, "You're welcome!"

In our own different ways, we made progress in learning English. But I had another worry, and that was my appearance. My brother didn't have to worry, since Mother bought him blue jeans for school, and he dressed like all the other boys. But she insisted that girls had to wear skirts. By the time she saw that Meg and the other girls were wearing jeans, it was too late. My school clothes were bought already, and we didn't have money left to buy new outfits for me. We had too many other things to buy first, like furniture, pots, and pans.

The first time I visited Meg's house, she took me upstairs to her room, and I wound up trying on her clothes. We were pretty much the same size, since Meg was shorter and thinner than average. Maybe that's how we became friends in the first place. Wearing Meg's jeans and T-shirt, I looked at myself in the mirror. I could almost pass for an American—from the back, anyway. At least the kids in school wouldn't stop and stare at me in the hallways, which was what they did when they saw me in my white blouse and navy blue skirt that went a couple of inches below the knees.

When Meg came to my house, I invited her to try on my

Jay: This is kind of funny—that she stepped on someone's foot and said "That's quite all right!" Same with saying "You're welcome!"
EVALUATING

THE ALL-AMERICAN SLURP **9**

> The opinions that readers form when evaluating a story are often based on personal judgments. Jay makes a judgment about the mother's character and her behavior. In this selection, students' judgments about the ways in which the author uses humorous details and descriptions can lead to an interesting class discussion.

J Jay uses his personal knowledge in order to make a judgment about the setting of the story. Readers often use their judgments about a story's setting in order to enrich their understanding and appreciation of events in a story.

K Tiffany contemplates information not stated directly in the passage. While certain information may not be crucial to a reader's understanding of the story, students should be encouraged to ask questions in order to sustain interest in what they read.

L Tiffany's comment about the jeans indicates her growing involvement in the story. Students should be encouraged to form opinions about what they read in order to develop their own ideas about characters and events.

M Jay "reads between the lines" in order to clarify information in the passage. He is able to infer that the family will be getting a car based on the information about the father's taking driving lessons. Readers often enrich their understanding of a story by inferring information not stated directly from details in a passage.

N Again, Jay uses details in the passage to make inferences and form opinions about what he is reading.

J *Jay:* The setting …the time must be pretty far back from when I was born because they didn't have a car.
EVALUATING

K *Tiffany:* Was she wearing a dress while riding a bike?
QUESTIONING

L *Tiffany:* Her mother finally got her a pair of jeans!
EVALUATING

M *Jay:* Father started taking driving lessons, so I guess that means they'll get a car.
CLARIFYING

N *Jay:* Maybe they live in the city, because they're going to a big, expensive restaurant with all the waiters dressed in suits.

10 READING MODEL

Chinese dresses, the ones with a high collar and slits up the sides. Meg's eyes were bright as she looked at herself in the mirror. She struck several sultry poses, and we nearly fell over laughing.

The dinner party at the Gleasons' didn't stop my growing friendship with Meg. Things were getting better for me in other ways too. Mother finally bought me some jeans at the end of the month, when Father got his paycheck. She wasn't in any hurry about buying them at first, until I worked on her. This is what I did. Since we didn't have a car in those days, I often ran down to the neighborhood store to pick up things for her. The groceries cost less at a big supermarket, but the closest one was many blocks away. One day, when she ran out of flour, I offered to borrow a bike from our neighbor's son and buy a ten-pound bag of flour at the big supermarket. I mounted the boy's bike and waved to Mother. "I'll be back in five minutes!"

Before I started pedaling, I heard her voice behind me. "You can't go out in public like that! People can see all the way up to your thighs!"

"I'm sorry," I said innocently. "I thought you were in a hurry to get the flour." For dinner we were going to have pot-stickers (fried Chinese dumplings), and we needed a lot of flour.

"Couldn't you borrow a girl's bicycle?" complained Mother. "That way your skirt won't be pushed up."

"There aren't too many of those around," I said. "Almost all the girls wear jeans while riding a bike, so they don't see any point buying a girl's bike."

We didn't eat pot-stickers that evening, and Mother was thoughtful. Next day we took the bus downtown, and she bought me a pair of jeans. In the same week, my brother made the baseball team of his junior high school, Father started taking driving lessons, and Mother discovered rummage sales. We soon got all the furniture we needed, plus a dart board and a 1,000-piece jigsaw puzzle (fourteen hours later, we discovered that it was a 999-piece jigsaw puzzle). There was hope that the Lins might become a normal American family after all.

Then came our dinner at the Lakeview Restaurant.

The Lakeview was an expensive restaurant, one of those places where a headwaiter dressed in tails conducted you to your seat, and the only light came from candles and flaming desserts. In one corner of the room a lady harpist played tinkling melodies.

Father wanted to celebrate, because he had just been promoted.

A Kitchen on the Eve of a Festival, Zhou Jihe. Courtesy of Foreign Languages Press, Beijing, China.

Art Note

A Kitchen on the Eve of a Festival by Zhou Jihe The "flat" look of this painting results from the artist's presentation of multiple perspectives, a common practice within Asian art. Objects in this kitchen scene can be "viewed" from a variety of positions; there is no single point of view presented. An analogy can be made relating the artist's use of perspective and the multiple perspectives readers will have of the same literary work.

Reading the Art *How would you describe the painting's style? How are objects in the painting presented? Would you describe this painting as realistic? Why or why not?*

⓪ Again, Jay notes an unfamiliar word without interrupting his reading. Students should be encouraged to record unfamiliar words or phrases they encounter as they read. Students may choose to look up the word in a dictionary during or after reading. Encourage students to read the selection a second time after defining unfamiliar vocabulary.

⓪ Jay: Systematic—*here's another word I don't know.*
QUESTIONING

He worked for an electronics company, and after his English started improving, his superiors decided to appoint him to a position more suited to his training. The promotion not only brought a higher salary but was also a tremendous boost to his pride.

Up to then we had eaten only in Chinese restaurants. Although my brother and I were becoming fond of hamburgers, my parents didn't care much for Western food, other than chow mein.

But this was a special occasion, and Father asked his coworkers to recommend a really elegant restaurant. So there we were at the Lakeview, stumbling after the headwaiter in the murky dining room.

At our table we were handed our menus, and they were so big that to read mine I almost had to stand up again. But why bother? It was mostly in French, anyway.

Father, being an engineer, was always systematic. He took out a pocket French dictionary. "They told me that most of the items would be in French, so I came prepared." He even had a pocket flashlight, the size of a marking pen. While Mother held the flashlight over the menu, he looked up the items that were in French.

"*Pâté en croûte*," he muttered. "Let's see . . . *pâté* is paste . . . *croûte* is crust . . . hmm . . . a paste in crust."

The waiter stood looking patient. I squirmed and died at least fifty times.

At long last Father gave up. "Why don't we just order four complete dinners at random?" he suggested.

"Isn't that risky?" asked Mother. "The French eat some rather peculiar things, I've heard."

"A Chinese can eat anything a Frenchman can eat," Father declared.

The soup arrived in a plate. How do you get soup up from a plate? I glanced at the other diners, but the ones at the nearby

12 READING MODEL

tables were not on their soup course, while the more distant ones were invisible in the darkness.

Fortunately my parents had studied books on Western etiquette before they came to America. "Tilt your plate," whispered my mother. "It's easier to spoon the soup up that way."

She was right. Tilting the plate did the trick. But the etiquette book didn't say anything about what you did after the soup reached your lips. As any respectable Chinese knows, the correct way to eat your soup is to slurp. This helps to cool the liquid and prevent you from burning your lips. It also shows your appreciation.

We showed our appreciation. *Shloop*, went my father. *Shloop*, went my mother. *Shloop, shloop*, went my brother, who was the hungriest.

The lady harpist stopped playing to take a rest. And in the silence, our family's consumption of soup suddenly seemed unnaturally loud. You know how it sounds on a rocky beach when the tide goes out and the water drains from all those little pools? They go *shloop, shloop, shloop*. That was the Lin family, eating soup.

At the next table a waiter was pouring wine. When a large *shloop* reached him, he froze. The bottle continued to pour, and red wine flooded the tabletop and into the lap of a customer. Even the customer didn't notice anything at first, being also hypnotized by the *shloop, shloop, shloop*.

It was too much. "I need to go to the toilet," I mumbled, jumping to my feet. A waiter, sensing my urgency, quickly directed me to the ladies' room.

I splashed cold water on my burning face, and as I dried myself with a paper towel, I stared into the mirror. In this perfumed ladies' room, with its pink-and-silver wallpaper and marbled sinks, I looked completely out of place. What was I doing here? What was our family doing in the Lakeview Restaurant? In America?

The door to the ladies' room opened. A woman came in and glanced curiously at me. I retreated into one of the toilet cubicles and latched the door.

Time passed—maybe half an hour, maybe an hour. Then I heard the door open again, and my mother's voice. "Are you in there? You're not sick, are you?"

There was real concern in her voice. A girl can't leave her family just because they slurp their soup. Besides, the toilet cubicle had a few drawbacks as a permanent residence. "I'm all right," I said, undoing the latch.

Mother didn't tell me how the rest of the dinner went, and I

Tiffany: Her parents studied Western what?
QUESTIONING (P)

Jay: Here's another word I don't know—etiquette—but I think it means "manners" because they're telling her it's easier to spoon the soup that way.
CLARIFYING (Q)

Jay: They're all going to start slurping the soup, and everyone's going to stop eating and look at them.
PREDICTING (R)

Jay: That's what I would do!
CONNECTING (S)

Tiffany: The narrator stayed in the bathroom all through dinnertime!
CLARIFYING (T)

THE ALL-AMERICAN SLURP 13

(P) Tiffany notes her confusion with an unfamiliar word and continues to read uninterrupted.

(Q) Jay notes an unfamiliar word, but he relies on context clues in the next sentence to clarify the meaning of the word.

(R) Readers often make predictions as they read about what will happen next in a selection. Based on information he has previously learned in the selection about the characters, Jay makes a prediction about what he thinks will occur next. Jay will then continue reading to see if his prediction is correct.

(S) As he did earlier, Jay relates an event in the passage with his own experiences to enrich his understanding of the narrator's actions.

(T) Tiffany uses details from the passage to infer that the narrator has stayed in the bathroom during dinner. These kinds of inferences can help readers to clarify characters' actions and behaviors in a story.

U At this point in the story, Jay evaluates the narrator's actions and forms an opinion about her by imagining himself in her position. Students should be aware that readers often use more than one reading strategy to enrich their understanding of characters and events in a story.

V Again, Tiffany uses details in the passage to make inferences about the narrator's parents and their feelings toward their daughter. Readers often must make inferences in order to clarify their understanding of relationships among characters.

W Jay's question reflects his understanding of the central conflict faced by the narrator of the story. This question, if left unanswered by students at the end of the story, provides a good starting point for a class discussion about the conflicts faced by the characters in the story as well as the selection's overall theme.

X Here Jay connects the story to his own life by articulating his disgust for a particular kind of food. Jay's choice of words in his reaction, however, does reflect a lack of cultural sensitivity. You may wish to point out to students that Jay might have connected this passage to his own experiences by wondering if he would have been able to eat a type of food not common in his culture or by imagining a food commonly found in American cuisine that others might not find appealing.

Y Again, based on the information Jay already knows from the selection, he makes a prediction about what might happen next in the story. An active reader often makes note of his or her predictions and reads on to see if the predictions are correct. Note that this prediction, while logical, is not correct. Students will find they often have to revise their predictions as they read.

U **Jay:** I don't think I'd be able to really forget about something like that.
CONNECTING/EVALUATING

V **Tiffany:** The narrator's parents called her a stupid girl but were really proud of her.
CLARIFYING

W **Jay:** Why does this girl care so much about her family becoming Americanized if they're Chinese? Why doesn't she care about her culture?
QUESTIONING

X **Jay:** Chicken gizzards—that sounds disgusting!
CONNECTING

Y **Jay:** I wonder if they're going to try to have the Gleasons—who had them over to their dinner party—do something stupid or embarrassing to get back at them.
PREDICTING

14   READING MODEL

---

didn't want to know. In the weeks following, I managed to push the whole thing into the back of my mind, where it jumped out at me only a few times a day. Even now, I turn hot all over when I think of the Lakeview Restaurant.

But by the time we had been in this country for three months, our family was definitely making progress toward becoming Americanized. I remember my parents' first PTA meeting. Father wore a neat suit and tie, and Mother put on her first pair of high heels. She stumbled only once. They met my homeroom teacher and beamed as she told them that I would make honor roll soon at the rate I was going. Of course Chinese etiquette forced Father to say that I was a very stupid girl and Mother to protest that the teacher was showing favoritism toward me. But I could tell they were both very proud.

The day came when my parents announced that they wanted to give a dinner party. We had invited Chinese friends to eat with us before, but this dinner was going to be different. In addition to a Chinese-American family, we were going to invite the Gleasons.

"Gee, I can hardly wait to have dinner at your house," Meg said to me. "I just *love* Chinese food."

That was a relief. Mother was a good cook, but I wasn't sure if people who ate sour cream would also eat chicken gizzards stewed in soy sauce.

Mother decided not to take a chance with chicken gizzards. Since we had Western guests, she set the table with large dinner plates, which we never used in Chinese meals. In fact we didn't use individual plates at all but picked up food from the platters in the middle of the table and brought it directly to our rice bowls. Following the practice of Chinese-American restaurants, Mother also placed large serving spoons on the platters.

The dinner started well. Mrs. Gleason exclaimed at the beautifully arranged dishes of food: the colorful candied fruit in the sweet-and-sour pork dish, the noodle-thin shreds of chicken meat stir-fried with tiny peas, and the glistening pink prawns in a ginger sauce.

At first I was too busy enjoying my food to notice how the guests were doing. But soon I remembered my duties. Sometimes guests were too polite to help themselves, and you had to serve them with more food.

I glanced at Meg, to see if she needed more food, and my eyes nearly popped out at the sight of her plate. It was piled with food:

---

14 THE LANGUAGE OF LITERATURE TEACHER'S EDITION

the sweet-and-sour meat pushed right against the chicken shreds, and the chicken sauce ran into the prawns. She had been taking food from a second dish before she finished eating her helping from the first!

Horrified, I turned to look at Mrs. Gleason. She was dumping rice out of her bowl and putting it on her dinner plate. Then she ladled prawns and gravy on top of the rice and mixed everything together, the way you mix sand, gravel, and cement to make concrete.

I couldn't bear to look any longer, and I turned to Mr. Gleason. He was chasing a pea around his plate. Several times he got it to the edge, but when he tried to pick it up with his chopsticks, it rolled back toward the center of the plate again. Finally he put down his chopsticks and picked up the pea with his fingers. He really did! A grown man!

All of us, our family and the Chinese guests, stopped eating to watch the activities of the Gleasons. I wanted to giggle. Then I caught my mother's eyes on me. She frowned and shook her head slightly, and I understood the message: the Gleasons were not used to Chinese ways, and they were just coping the best they could. For some reason I thought of celery strings.

When the main courses were finished, Mother brought out a platter of fruit. "I hope you weren't expecting a sweet dessert," she said. "Since the Chinese don't eat dessert, I didn't think to prepare any."

"Oh, I couldn't possibly eat dessert!" cried Mrs. Gleason. "I'm simply stuffed!"

Meg had different ideas. When the table was cleared, she announced that she and I were going for a walk. "I don't know about you, but I feel like dessert," she told me, when we were outside. "Come on; there's a Dairy Queen down the street. I could use a big chocolate milk shake!"

Although I didn't really want anything more to eat, I insisted on paying for the milk shakes. After all, I was still hostess.

Meg got her large chocolate milk shake, and I had a small one. Even so, she was finishing hers while I was only half done. Toward the end she pulled hard on her straws and went *shloop,* shloop.

"Do you always slurp when you eat a milk shake?" I asked, before I could stop myself.

Meg grinned. "Sure. All Americans slurp."

Tiffany: The narrator's mother is trying to make their company feel comfortable.
CLARIFYING/EVALUATING — **Z**

Tiffany: The Gleasons eat a lot!
EVALUATING — **AA**

Jay: The same things are happening to the Gleasons that happened to the Lins. Meg probably wanted to laugh at the girl just like she wants to laugh at Meg now.
EVALUATING — **BB**

Tiffany: So the Chinese and the Americans have something in common—slurping.
EVALUATING — **CC**

Jay: I like this. It was pretty funny in some parts.
EVALUATING — **DD**

THE ALL-AMERICAN SLURP **15**

Z Tiffany clarifies this event in the story by using details from the passage to make inferences about what is going on. She forms an opinion of the narrator's mother based on this inference.

AA As an active reader, Tiffany pays attention to characters and events in the story. She then is able to make a quick judgment about the Gleasons based on their actions in this passage.

BB Jay by this time has a good sense of the story's main theme and forms an opinion about the events in the passage based on what he has carefully read.

CC Tiffany develops her own ideas about the characters and events in the story based on what she has read. She is able to draw parallels between the Chinese and American families which lead her to reflect on the story's main theme.

DD Jay has finished reading the selection and forms an opinion of the entire story. His evaluation also reflects on the author's use of humor to generate interest in the story.

BIOGRAPHY

LENSEY NAMIOKA

Lensey Namioka (1929–) was born in Beijing, China. She began her career as a math instructor. Namioka is the author of travel books and articles, as well as numerous books for young people. Married to a Japanese mathematician and the mother of two daughters, Namioka says, "For my writings I draw heavily on my Chinese cultural heritage and on my husband's Japanese cultural heritage. My involvement with Japan started many years before my marriage, since my mother spent many years in Japan."

UNIT ONE

UNIT THEMES

Unit One

Running Risks In this unit, students will read selections that explore risks people take in life in order to achieve something. The unit contains two parts: Part 1, "Seizing the Moment," and Part 2, "On the Edge of Survival." Selections in both parts contribute to the unit theme by detailing how various characters respond to the physical and emotional challenges they face.

Part 1

Seizing the Moment Selections in Part 1 emphasize characters' responses to various difficulties, such as the loss of a loved one in "Nadia the Willful" and the challenge of remembering a speaking part in "The School Play."

Part 2

On the Edge of Survival Selections in Part 2 emphasize characters' experiences with life-threatening challenges, such as frontier life in "Too Soon a Woman" and an unexpected confrontation with a wild bear in the excerpt from *Woodsong*.

Links to Unit Six
The Oral Tradition Unit Six contains literature from the oral tradition that connects with the themes in Unit One. You may wish to begin or end Unit One by using the following selections from Unit Six that relate to the theme "Running Risks":
- "Wings," p. 640
- "The Red Lion," p. 649
- "Why Monkeys Live in Trees," p. 654

UNIT ONE

RUNNING Risks

Only
those
who
dare
to
fail
greatly
can
ever
achieve
greatly.

Robert F. Kennedy
U.S. Senator
1925–1968

It's All Relative (1995),
Brad Holland. Copyright ©
1995 Brad Holland.

Art Note

It's All Relative by Brad Holland
Reading the Art What effect does the abstract background surrounding the solitary figure in the painting have on you? Why do you think the artist might have chosen to paint the background in this way? What does this background represent to you?

Exploring Theme

To help students explore the connections between the art, the quotation, and the unit theme, have them consider the following questions:

1. What meaning does the title of this unit suggest to you? *(Possible responses: In life, people must confront personal challenges and difficulties head-on, even in the face of danger. One must be prepared to take risks.)*

2. In what way do you think the quotation relates to the theme "Running Risks"? *(Possible responses: The quotation expresses the idea that a person must take risks and face challenges—even with the possibility of failure—in order to achieve something. One can succeed in life only if he or she takes risks.)*

3. How do you think the art relates to the unit theme? *(Possible responses: The solitary figure is shown momentarily balanced, surrounded by a seemingly dangerous environment. The tightrope is not continuous, and it appears as if there is no rope for the figure's next step. The painting suggests the risks and challenges people face in life's journey.)*

4. What kinds of stories do you expect to read in this unit? *(Possible responses: This unit will contain stories about risks and challenges people face in life and the various ways in which people deal with these risks and challenges. This unit will have exciting tales of danger and adventure.)*

5. In what ways do the unit theme, the quotation, and the art connect with your own experiences? Discuss a personal experience in which you felt like a tightrope walker facing a difficult challenge. What did you learn from the experience? *(Responses will vary.)*

THE LANGUAGE OF LITERATURE TEACHER'S EDITION **17**

UNIT ONE
Part 1 Skills Trace

(ML) DENOTES MINI-LESSON IN TEACHER'S EDITION

Selections	Reading Skills and Strategies	Literary Concepts	Writing Opportunities	Speaking, Listening, and Viewing
FICTION **Nadia the Willful** Sue Alexander	Comparing and contrasting, (ML) TE p. 25	Setting, PE p. 28 Conflict, (ML) TE p. 24	Write about a willful person, PE p. 21 Narrative poem, PE p. 28 Character sketch, PE p. 28 Memo, PE p. 28	Rewriting, PE p. 28 Diorama, PE p. 29
FICTION **The School Play** Gary Soto	Summarizing, (ML) TE p. 34	Characters, PE p. 37 Slang, (ML) TE p. 32	Write about speaking in public, PE p. 30 Essay, PE p. 37 Review, PE p. 37 Rewrite a passage, (ML) TE p. 32 Summary, (ML) TE p. 34 Letters, (ML) TE p. 35	Performing readers Theater, PE p. 38 Reciting, PE p. 38
FICTION **Ghost of the Lagoon** Armstrong Sperry	Visualizing, PE p. 39 Predicting, (ML) TE p. 42	Plot and conflict, PE p. 48 Setting, (ML) TE p. 41	Narrative, PE p. 48 Tribute, PE p. 48 Tall tale, PE p. 48 Paragraph, (ML) TE p. 44 Summary, (ML) TE p. 46	Painting or drawing, PE p. 48 Tall tale, PE p. 48 Dancing, PE p. 49 Role-playing, PE p. 49 Oral report and poster, PE p. 49 Interview and oral report, (ML) TE p. 45
NONFICTION **Matthew Henson at the Top of the World** Jim Haskins	Main idea and supporting details, PE p. 53 Connecting, (ML) TE p. 57	Biography, PE p. 63 Characterization, (ML) TE p. 56	Acceptance speech, PE p. 63 Log entry, PE p. 63 Poem, PE p. 63 Paragraph, (ML) TE p. 55	Mock interviews, PE p. 63 Press conference, (ML) TE p. 60
NONFICTION **My First Dive with the Dolphins** Don C. Reed	Setting purposes, PE p. 65 Setting a purpose, (ML) TE p. 67	Purposes, PE p. 73 Description, (ML) TE p. 69	Summary, PE p. 73 Editorial, PE p. 73	Oral presentation, PE p. 73 Interviewing, PE p. 74
FICTION ON YOUR OWN **Tuesday of the Other June** Norma Fox Mazer				Painting and oral presentation, TE p. 80 Skit, TE p. 81 Discussion, TE p. 82

Writing	Reading Skills and Strategies	Literary Concepts	Writing Opportunities	Speaking, Listening, and Viewing
WRITING ABOUT LITERATURE **Direct Response**	Responding to literature, PE pp. 86–89	Analyzing descriptive words, PE pp. 84–85	Rewrite sentences, PE p. 85 Write a paragraph, PE p. 85 Write a book-jacket review, PE p. 85 Personal response essay, PE pp. 86–89 Understanding sentence variety, PE p. 87	Viewing an ad, PE p. 90 Interpreting an ad, PE p. 90 Discussion, PE p. 90 Discussing your response, PE p. 91

17a UNIT ONE RUNNING RISKS

Grammar, Usage, Mechanics, and Spelling	Multimodal Learning	Research and Study Skills	Vocabulary
Using commas to separate ideas, ML TE p. 26 The suffix -able, ML TE p. 27	Rewriting, PE p. 28 Diorama, PE p. 29	Research deserts, PE p. 29	banish bazaar clan decree ponder
Quotation marks, ML TE p. 33 Choosing the right words, ML TE p. 35	Comic strip, PE p. 37 Readers theater, PE p. 38 Reciting, PE p. 38	Research the Donner party, PE p. 38	depleted prop quiver relentless smirk
Capitalization of proper nouns, ML TE p. 43 The vowel sound $\overline{oo}$, ML TE p. 47	Painting or drawing, PE p. 48 Tall tale, PE p. 48 Travel brochure, PE p. 49 Dance, PE p. 49 Role-playing, PE p. 49 Oral report and poster, PE p. 49 Drawing, PE p. 50 Interview and oral report, ML TE p. 45	Research Bora Bora, PE p. 49 Research coral reefs, PE p. 49 Research sharks, PE p. 49	expedition harpoon lagoon phosphorus reef
Your own voice, ML TE p. 55 Proper nouns, ML TE p. 58 Spelling the sound shən ML TE p. 62	Mock interviews, PE p. 63 Press conference, ML TE p. 60	Research the North Pole expedition, PE p. 64 The K-W-L approach, ML TE p. 61	apt stamina ardent surveyor deprivation tyranny menial validate proposition resentful
Subject pronouns, ML TE p. 68 Details appealing to touch, ML TE p. 71 Using memory devices, ML TE p. 72	Oral presentation, PE p. 73 Drawing or painting, PE p. 74	Outlining, ML TE p. 70	aggression hurtle camouflage luminous coexistence magnification compressed oceanarium dominant elegant

Grammar, Usage, Mechanics, and Spelling	Multimodal Learning	Research and Study Skills	Media Literacy
Using adverbs, PE p. 85 Using action verbs, PE p. 89 Using linking verbs, PE p. 89	Viewing an ad, PE p. 90 Interpreting an ad, PE p. 90 Discussion, PE p. 90 Discussing your response, PE p. 91		Interpreting an ad, PE pp. 90–91

UNIT ONE
Part 2 Skills Trace

ML DENOTES MINI-LESSON IN TEACHER'S EDITION

Selections	Reading Skills and Strategies	Literary Concepts	Writing Opportunities	Speaking, Listening, and Viewing
FICTION **Too Soon a Woman** Dorothy M. Johnson	Visualizing, ML TE p. 96	Theme, PE p. 100 Plot, ML TE p. 98	Comparison, PE p. 93 Summary, PE p. 100 Diary entry, PE p. 100 Wedding announcement, PE p. 100 Description, PE p. 101	Summarizing, PE p. 100 Performing Readers Theater, PE p. 101 Listing, PE p. 101
POETRY **The Walrus and the Carpenter** Lewis Carroll	Understanding narrative poetry, PE p. 104	Rhyme and rhythm, PE p. 108	Speech, PE p. 108 Wanted poster, PE p. 108 Rewrite the ending, ML TE p. 107	Oral reading, PE p. 109 Oral reading, ML TE p. 105
POETRY **Life Doesn't Frighten Me** Maya Angelou **Another Mountain** Abiodun Oyewole		Speaker and tone, PE p. 110 Free verse, PE p. 115 Rhyme, PE p. 115 Rhythm, ML TE p. 112	Award nomination, PE p. 115 Profile, PE p. 115	Dramatic reading, PE p. 115 Music, PE p. 116 Music, ML TE p. 114
NONFICTION from **Woodsong** Gary Paulsen	Making predictions, PE p. 117 Predicting, ML TE p. 120	Autobiography, PE p. 122 Author's purpose, ML TE p. 121	Poem, PE p. 122 Rewrite a scene, PE p. 122	Debating, PE p. 122
FICTION **The Dog of Pompeii** Louis Untermeyer	Reading historical fiction, PE p. 124 Connecting, ML TE p. 127	Conflict, PE p. 135 Setting, PE p. 135 Sensory details, ML TE p. 131	Account, PE p. 135 Eyewitness account, PE p. 135	Performing a scene, PE p. 135 Oral presentation, PE p. 136 Poster, PE p. 136 Press conference, ML TE p. 128 Reading aloud, ML TE pp. 129, 131

Writing	Reading Skills and Strategies	Literary Concepts	Writing Opportunities	Speaking, Listening, and Viewing
WRITING FROM EXPERIENCE **Firsthand and Expressive Writing**	Setting a purpose, PE p. 140	Main idea and details, PE pp. 140–41 Characters, PE p. 141 Details, PE p. 143	Writing an anecdote, PE pp. 138–45 Story map, PE p. 141 Drafting, PE pp. 142–43 Revising and publishing, PE pp. 144–45	Telling an anecdote, PE p. 141 Comic strip, PE p. 145

Grammar, Usage, Mechanics, and Spelling	Multimodal Learning	Research and Study Skills	Vocabulary
Adjectives, ML TE p. 95 Special endings: the suffix -ing, ML TE p. 99	Summary, PE p. 100 Readers Theater, PE p. 101 Sketch, ML TE p. 96	Research the westward movement, PE p. 101	anxiety endure grudging savoring sedately
	Oral reading, PE p. 109 Illustrations, PE p. 109	Research oysters, PE p. 109	
Choosing the right word, ML TE p. 111	Dramatic reading, PE p. 115 Collage, PE p. 116 Music, PE p. 116 Music, ML TE p. 114	Research Jean-Michel Basquiat and Keith Haring, ML TE p. 113	
Commas in a series, ML TE p. 119	Debate, PE p. 122	Research bears, PE p. 123	menace novelty predator rummaging scavenging
Details appealing to hearing, ML TE p. 129 Prepositional phrases, ML TE p. 132 Spelling words with suffixes, ML TE p. 134	Perform a scene, PE p. 135 Oral presentation, PE p. 136 Poster, PE p. 136 Three-dimensional scene, PE p. 136 Picture, PE p. 137 Press conference, ML TE p. 128 Reading aloud, ML TE pp. 129, 131	Research volcanoes, PE p. 136 Using reference books/Research Mount Vesuvius, ML TE p. 133	dislodging eruption restore shrine vapor

Grammar, Usage, Mechanics, and Spelling	Multimodal Learning	Research and Study Skills	Media Literacy
Ordering and representing information, PE p. 141 Achieving unity in paragraphs, PE p. 143 Using consistent verb tense, PE p. 145	Analyzing journals, letters, and photographs, PE pp. 138–39 Interpreting comic strips and magazine illustrations, PE pp. 138–39 Telling an anecdote, PE p. 141 Comic strip, PE p. 145		Analyzing journals, letters, and photographs, PE pp. 138–39 Interpreting comic strips and magazine illustrations, PE pp. 138–39

UNIT ONE
Recommended Resources

ENRICHMENT   RESEARCH

✓ Recommended Novels

 LITERATURE CONNECTIONS WITH SOURCEBOOK FOR TEACHERS

A Wrinkle in Time
by Madeleine L'Engle

Thematic Links Hoping to find their father, twins Meg and Charles Wallace Murry, with the help of Calvin O'Keefe, set out across space.
About the Author Madeleine L'Engle (born 1918) was a prolific author whose works include fiction, poetry, and nonfiction for young people and adults alike.
Other Works by Madeleine L'Engle *A Wind in the Door, A Swiftly Tilting Planet, Many Waters*

For the Life of Laetitia
by Merle Hodge

Thematic Links Although Laetitia barely knows her father, moving in with him in a town outside of her native Caribbean village is just one of the challenges she faces as she sets off to be the first of her family to attend high school.
About the Author Merle Hodge (born 1944) is a writer and teacher who resides in Trinidad.
Other Works by Merle Hodge *Crick Crack Money*

Number the Stars
by Lois Lowry

Thematic Links Putting her own life at risk, Annemarie agrees to a dangerous mission in an effort to save her Jewish friend from the Nazis in war-torn Denmark.
About the Author Lois Lowry (born 1937) has written numerous highly acclaimed children's books, including several centered on the much loved, notorious Anastasia Krupnik.
Other Works by Lois Lowry *All About Sam, Anastasia Again, The One Hundredth Thing About Caroline, Switcharound*

Julie of the Wolves
by Jean Craighead George

Thematic Links Fleeing intolerable pressure at home, Miyax gets lost in the wilds of Alaska without food or shelter. Only with the help of a pack of arctic wolves does she manage to stay alive.
About the Author Jean Craighead George (born 1919) has written many books about humankind's relationship with nature.
Other Works by Jean Craighead George *My Side of the Mountain, The Cry of the Crow, The Summer of the Falcon*

Hatchet
by Gary Paulsen

Thematic Links After his parents divorced, Brian Robeson thought nothing worse could happen. Then his plane crashes and he is left with only a hatchet to help him survive 54 days lost in the Canadian wilderness.
About the Author Gary Paulsen (born 1939), a writer of novels for both children and adults, has also worked as a teacher, an actor, and a farmer.
Other Works by Gary Paulsen *Dogsong, Tracker, Popcorn Days and Buttermilk Nights*

The Black Pearl
by Scott O'Dell

Thematic Links This is a gripping novel about a young pearl merchant who finds the "Great Pearl of Heaven."
About the Author Scott O'Dell (1898–1989) worked in motion pictures, newspapers, and magazines before trying his hand as a novelist. He was immediately successful, winning the Newbery Award for his first children's novel, *Island of the Blue Dolphins*.
Other Works by Scott O'Dell *Sing Down the Moon, Thunder Rolling in the Mountains*

For Teacher | **TEACHING LITERATURE**

Carlsen, Robert G., and Sherrill, Anne. *Voices of Readers: How We Come to Love Books.* Urbana, Illinois: National Council of Teachers of English, 1988.

Lickteig, Mary. "Julie of the Wolves and Dogsong: The Cultural Conflict between the Inuits and the Dominant American Culture."

Cross-Culturalism in Children's Literature: Selected Papers from the Children's Literature Association. Carleton University, Ottawa, Canada, May 14–17, 1987. New York: Pace University, 1988: 83–86.

Olivares, Julian. "The Streets of Gary Soto." *Latin American Literary Review (LALR)* 18.35 (Jan.–June 1990): 32–49.

Paulin, Mary Ann. *More Creative Uses of Children's Literature. Volume 1: Introducing Books in All Kinds of Ways.* Hamden, Conn.: Library Professional Publications, 1992.

CROSS-CURRICULAR TEACHING   PROFESSIONAL DEVELOPMENT

Recommended Readings in Cross-Curricular Areas

SCIENCE

Dolphins and Porpoises
by Dorothy Hinshaw Patent (1987)
Research and photographs highlight the habits and physical characteristics of these fascinating underwater animals. Links to Don C. Reed's "My First Dive with the Dolphins."

SOCIAL STUDIES

Chinese Americans
by Alexandra Bandon (1994)
A look at the reasons behind Chinese immigration into the United States over the years, as well as personal accounts of experiences of prejudice and assimilation. Links to Lensey Namioka's "The All-American Slurp."

Black People Who Made the Old West
by William L. Katz (1992)
A description of the lives of over 30 important African-American figures. Links to Dorothy M. Johnson's "Too Soon a Woman" and Jim Haskins's "Matthew Henson at the Top of the World."

GEOGRAPHY

Pompeii: Exploring a Roman Ghost Town
by Ron and Nancy Goor (1986)
After the eruption of Mount Vesuvius in A.D. 79 covered Pompeii with volcanic ash and rock, the city's existence was not discovered for over 1500 years. Links to Louis Untermeyer's "The Dog of Pompeii."

For Teacher — CROSS-CURRICULAR INSTRUCTION

Hough, David L. "Achieving Independent Student Responses Through Integrated Instruction (Strategies for Middle School Students)." *Middle School Journal* 25 (May 1994): 35–42.

Kornfeld, H. John. "Using Fiction to Teach History: Multicultural and Global Perspectives of World War II." *Social Education* 58 (September 1994): 281–86.

Martin, Terry. "Readers are Leaders: Linda Greenstein at Cascade Middle School." *Middle School Journal* 23 (May 1992): 51–55.

Ralph, Kathleen. "Classrooms without Borders." *Childhood Education* 71.5 (1995): 290–92.

Recommended Media Resources

THE LANGUAGE OF LITERATURE

LASERLINKS
Videodisc, Gr. 6
See *LaserLinks Teacher's Source Book*, pages 4–5, for an overview of Unit One.

AUDIO LIBRARY
Tapes
Unit One: Running Risks
Gr. 6, Tape 1: Sides A&B
Gr. 6, Tape 2: Sides A&B
Gr. 6, Tape 3: Sides A&B

WRITING COACH
Writing Coach Software: Writing About Literature: Direct Response; Personal Narrative

OUTSIDE RESOURCES

Films/Videos/Film Strips/Audiocassettes
Hatchet, 3 audiocassettes, Bantam Audio, 1992. (3 hours and 30 minutes).
A Time to Be Brave, videocassette, Canadian Broadcasting Corporation in collaboration with the Association for Native Development in the Performing and Visual Arts, and the Film Works, 1982. (28 minutes)

Internet Resources
Literature and Language Arts Center at http://www.hmco.com/mcdougal/lit/litcent.html

For Teacher — TEACHING WITH TECHNOLOGY

Education Technology, Business Publishers, Inc., 951 Pershing Dr., Silver Spring, MD 20910.

Rosenquist-Buhler, Carla. "Using Internet to Expand the Classroom Experience." *Nebraska Library Association Quarterly* 24 (Fall 1993): 41–49.

Shields, Jean. "Connecting Classrooms with Today's Technologies." *Technology and Learning* 15 (February 1995): 38–40.

UNIT ONE
Professional Enrichment

Staging a Readers Theater

"The play's the thing!" Shakespeare proclaimed in Hamlet nearly four hundred years ago.

Everyone loves a play—even the most bashful students. Creative dramatics can bring new excitement to the classroom. A Readers Theater is ideally suited to introduce your sixth graders to the drama of drama!

Explain to the class that a Readers Theater is one kind of dramatic performance. In a Readers Theater, actors and actresses stand on a bare stage and hold scripts. They must keep the audience's attention without props, scenery, or costumes. Readers Theater is ideally suited to a classroom dramatic performance precisely because so little technical preparation is required.

Start by selecting a piece of literature—it can be a story students are already familiar with, one of the plays in this book (see *A Shipment of Mute Fate* and *The Hobbit*), or a literary selection, easily adapted to dramatic performance, such as "The School Play." Then use the following techniques to stage a Readers Theater adaptation of the work.

STAGECRAFT
- Readers should step forward as they make "entrances" and step back for "exits."
- Have the main characters walk in and around the other characters.
- Use "freezes" to end scenes.
- Instruct actors to focus their delivery out toward the audience rather than toward other characters.

PREPARATION
Nothing succeeds like preparation! Explore with the class the importance of complete and thorough preparation for a successful Readers Theater. Try these ideas:
- Set aside time for students to read their material aloud several times before the actual performance.
- Students should rehearse with their groups as well as on their own. Encourage students to meet with their groups on their free time, perhaps before or after class.
- Make sure students know how to pronounce any difficult or foreign words.
- Be sure that students understand all the words. They cannot correctly interpret what they don't understand.
- Explain to the performers that they should pay special attention to the key points in their performance, such as excitement, tension, or flashes of humor in the script.
- Show students how to mark their scripts to cue places that require special emphasis and body language. Students can use a pencil, highlight marker, or pen to mark their cues.

PROJECTION
Help students learn to speak up. Remind them that they should not shout, but aim their voice outward, to the very back of the room. Show them how to hold their head and their script up, rather than down, as they read. Good posture will improve voice projection.

VOICE CONTROL
Explain how the voice can be used as an instrument to express the nuances of the script. Model the process by reading part of the script to the class. For example, to emphasize humor, readers can increase the volume of their voice. To show tension, they can raise the volume and then lower it.

MOVEMENT
Guide students to use their whole body to express the character's personality. Their hands and face can be used to express emotion. Body language, including posture and movements, can also express emotion. Point out how posture also affects voice—both its tone and its volume.

CONCLUSION
When students are ready to stage their Readers Theater performance, consider inviting another class to be part of the audience. All that hard work and preparation shouldn't go unnoticed!

Related Reading

 Childress, Alice. *When the Rattlesnake Sounds.* New York: Coward, 1975.

 Davis, Ossie. *Escape to Freedom: A Play about Young Frederick Douglass.* New York: Viking, 1978.

 Kamerman, Sylvia. ed. *Space and Science Fiction Plays for Young People.* Boston, MA: Plays, 1987.

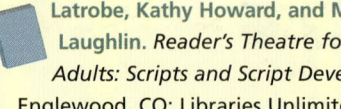 Latrobe, Kathy Howard, and Mildred Knight Laughlin. *Reader's Theatre for Young Adults: Scripts and Script Development.* Englewood, CO: Libraries Unlimited, Inc., 1989.

Family and Community Involvement

Family

From experiencing stage fright to facing a "ghost" to battling bullies and the grueling elements of nature, all of the selections in Unit One connect to the theme of taking risks.

The Unit One Resource Book copymasters listed below provide activities that students can take home and complete with a parent or other family member.

OPTION 1: READ NEWSPAPER ARTICLES

- **Connection** All of the selections in Unit One illustrate the theme of running risks.
- **Activity** *Copymaster, page 4* Students and family members skim newspapers or magazines for articles about people who have taken risks. After they have taken turns reading the articles aloud, they decide if the risk was worth taking. A chart is provided for keeping track of the articles.

OPTION 2: WRITE AN ADVICE COLUMN

- **Connection** In both "The School Play" and "Tuesday of the Other June," the main characters must decide how to deal with bullies.
- **Activity** *Copymaster, page 5* Students and family members write advice-column questions and answers on the topic of bullies and how to handle them.

OPTION 3: WATCH A DOCUMENTARY

- **Connection** In "My Dive With the Dolphins," the author takes a risk and finds out many things about dolphins that he never knew before.
- **Activity** *Copymaster, page 6* Students and family members view a documentary on dolphins as a way of preparing students to read "My Dive With the Dolphins." A KWL chart is provided.

Community

OPTION 1

- **Connection** The selections in Unit One all illustrate the theme of running risks.
- **Activity** Have the class interview a psychologist to discuss personality types and why some people are more prone to take risks than other people are.

OPTION 2

- **Connection** The main character in "Nadia the Willful" is a young Bedouin girl who lives in the Middle East. She risks going against her family's beliefs as she grieves the loss of her brother.
- **Activity** Have the class interview a grief counselor to discuss the ways people deal with a death in the family.

OPTION 3

- **Connection** "The Walrus and the Carpenter" is a classic poem by Lewis Carroll; "Mean Song" and "Life Doesn't Frighten Me" are poems by two popular contemporary poets. All the poems deal with risk-taking.
- **Activity** Stage a "poetry slam." Invite a local poet to read poems to the class, and then ask members of the class to share poems that they have written.

OPTION 4

- **Connection** *Woodsong* is an account of Gary Paulsen's experiences in the wilderness of Minnesota and Alaska.
- **Activity** Have the class interview a scouting leader to discuss the risks involved in camping in the wild, as well as how to camp without leaving a trace.

PROFESSIONAL ENRICHMENT, FAMILY AND COMMUNITY INVOLVEMENT   TEACHER'S EDITION   **17h**

UNIT ONE
Part 1 Cooperative Project

A Survival Board Game

Overview

Students will research board games and create their own board game with a survival theme.

PROJECT AT A GLANCE

The selections in Unit One, Part 1 have a common theme of survival, whether in terms of life and death or just surviving life's smaller troubles and indignities. For this project, students will pool their knowledge, experiences, and imaginations to create a playable board game that involves difficulties that must be overcome to win the game. Students will work in small groups to decide on a setting for the game, write rules, and illustrate a game board. Games may later be exchanged for examination as well as individual play or tournament play.

OBJECTIVES
- To research and analyze current board games
- To develop a board game with a survival theme that fits a targeted audience
- To write a complete set of game rules
- To work cooperatively to create a board game prototype

SUGGESTED GROUP SIZE
4–6 students per group

MATERIALS
- Commercial board games for examination
- Large sheet of poster board for each group
- Small objects (buttons, coins, bottle caps) for use as markers
- Spinners or number cubes
- Art and office supplies (paper, glue, markers, pencils, rulers, index cards)

1 Getting Started

Arranging the Project
Gather all the necessary materials. The commercial board games should represent a variety of age levels and should include some popular games as well as some obscure ones. These may be set up on the side of the classroom or passed around the class.

You also will need a wide range of art or office supplies, as individual games will require different materials. Some items, such as markers and index cards, should be available in large quantities. Encourage the students to make sketches of the game on scratch paper before committing it to the poster board.

Arranging for Construction
You may want to make arrangements with school officials for the students to work in an area such as the cafeteria or art room that has large tables that seat several students and accommodate large amounts of materials. A certain level of noise will prevail, so take this into account when looking for a suitable place to work.

If you cannot make such arrangements, you may want to allow students to push desks together in the classroom to provide an adequate work surface.

2 Creating the Board Games

Introducing the Project
Explain that students will be working in small groups to create and produce a board game prototype based on a survival theme. The games should be interesting, colorful, fun, and playable. Games should be directed at a particular group or age level, and students should select a game environment appropriate for that group. Complete game rules covering every possible situation should be written in clear, easy-to-understand language.

To get the ball rolling, you might ask students to find the conflict in a few popular TV shows and describe how the characters managed to overcome or survive each situation. The discussion can continue on into personal experiences and those found in well-known fairy tales, fables, and children's stories. Use this discussion as a springboard to discuss possible settings for the games.

Group Investigations
Divide students into groups of four to six. The groups will work together to gather information on board games. Groups should visit stores that sell board games and interview the store managers. They should find out which games are popular and which are failures, what age groups are targeted, what settings are represented, and the level of difficulty for each game. Interviews may also be conducted among friends and family as to favorite board games and the reasons they enjoy them. As students are gathering information, meet briefly with each group to check on its progress.

Creating a Project Description
After students have gathered information and done some preliminary planning, each group should prepare a one-page description of its board game. This not only solidifies the project in the minds of students but also can alert you to possible duplication and impractical points of the games. Discuss the plans with each group to clarify any hazy points.

OPTION 1: A LIFE-SIZE GAME
Have groups create a life-size game in which students act as markers. Arrange for a life-size game board to be laid out in an available area of the school (playground, gym, cafeteria, stage) where the game can be played by the entire class, divided into teams. Ask students to create a game that is challenging and amusing, and that also can be set up and taken down easily and quickly without permanent markings or damage to the area.

OPTION 2: LUCK AND SKILL
Ask students to examine commercial board games to determine whether winning is primarily dependent on luck or skill. Have half the teams focus their games on winning by luck and the other half focus on skill.

OPTION 3: ADVERTISING A GAME
Ask groups to devise and execute a complete advertising campaign for their board game. Music, ad copy, and video presentations can all be considered.

 ## Sharing the Games

The project should culminate in a Game Day where school administrators, families, or students from other classes examine, judge, or play the board games. Elimination tournament play might be arranged in which players advance as they win, until there is one ultimate winner. If more than one class in your school is participating in this project, you might ask a panel of "experts" to judge the games based on appeal, playability, level appropriateness, and ease of play.

 ## Assessing the Project

The following rubric can be used for group or individual assessment

3 Full Accomplishment Students followed directions and produced a board game that has a survival theme and is colorful, easy to play, and appropriate for the age/level indicated.

2 Substantial Accomplishment Students produced a board game, but rules are incomplete, or the survival theme is not evident, or the game is inappropriate for the indicated age/level.

1 Little or Partial Accomplishment Students produced a board game that is incomplete or does not fulfill the requirements of the assignment.

For the Portfolio
Keep the board games in your classroom or in the school library for future reference and use. Include a copy of your written assessment in each group member's personal portfolio. At the end of the year, games may be returned to the students or donated to eldercare facilities, day-care centers, or shelters.

Note: For other assessment options, see the *Teacher's Guide to Assessment and Portfolio Use.*

Cross-Curricular Options

SOCIAL STUDIES

Have students research a particular location in your city, state, country, or the world in which to base their game. The game should reflect some of the unique qualities of the location. As an option, assign a particular historical period in which the games are to be set.

ART
Allow students to design and execute small clay sculptures (animals, figures, geometric designs, appropriate items) for use as markers for the game.

LANGUAGE ARTS
Have students write short stories, giving the fictional account of a "trip" through the game board as seen through the eyes of one of the markers.

Resources

Super-Colossal Book of Puzzles, Tricks and Games by Sheila Anne Barry provides examples of an assortment of games, activities, and puzzles.

Make Your Own Chess Set by David Carroll gives instructions for constructing 23 different types of chess sets; also gives a history for each chess piece.

UNIT ONE
Part 1 Lesson Planner

TIME ALLOTMENTS SHOWN ARE APPROXIMATE. DEPENDING ON YOUR GOALS AND THE NEEDS OF YOUR STUDENTS, YOU MAY WISH TO ALLOW MORE OR LESS TIME FOR CERTAIN PORTIONS OF THE LESSON.

Table of Contents	Discussion	Previewing the Selection	Reading the Selection
PART OPENER SEIZING THE MOMENT What Do You Think? page 18	**20 MINUTES** • Reflect on the part theme		
GENRE LESSON Focus on Fiction page 19	**20 MINUTES** • Discuss characteristics of fiction • Discuss strategies for reading fiction		
SELECTION Nadia the Willful page 22 AVERAGE		**20 MINUTES** • PERSONAL CONNECTION • GEOGRAPHICAL CONNECTION • WRITING CONNECTION	**15 MINUTES** • Introduce vocabulary • Read pp. 22–27 (6 pp.)
SELECTION The School Play page 31 EASY		**20 MINUTES** • PERSONAL CONNECTION • HISTORICAL CONNECTION • WRITING CONNECTION	**20 MINUTES** • Introduce vocabulary • Read pp. 31–36 (6 pp.)
SELECTION Ghost of the Lagoon page 40 AVERAGE		**15 MINUTES** • PERSONAL CONNECTION • GEOGRAPHICAL CONNECTION • READING CONNECTION: Visualizing	**40 MINUTES** • Introduce vocabulary • Read pp. 40–47 (8 pp.)
GENRE LESSON Focus on Nonfiction page 51	**20 MINUTES** • Discuss characteristics of nonfiction • Discuss strategies for reading nonfiction		
SELECTION Matthew Henson at the Top of the World page 54 AVERAGE		**15 MINUTES** • PERSONAL CONNECTION • GEOGRAPHICAL CONNECTION • READING CONNECTION: Main idea and supporting details	**50 MINUTES** • Introduce vocabulary • Read pp. 54–62 (9 pp.)
SELECTION My First Dive with the Dolphins page 66 AVERAGE		**20 MINUTES** • PERSONAL CONNECTION • SCIENCE CONNECTION • READING CONNECTION: Setting purposes	**40 MINUTES** • Introduce vocabulary • Read pp. 66–72 (7 pp.)
FICTION ON YOUR OWN Tuesday of the Other June page 75 EASY			**40 MINUTES** • Read pp. 75–83 (9 pp.)

Writing	Writer's Style	Prewriting	Drafting and Revising
WRITING ABOUT LITERATURE Direct Response	**30 MINUTES**	**20 MINUTES**	**75 MINUTES**

Time estimates assume in-class work. You may wish to assign some of these stages as homework.

Responding to the Selection

FROM PERSONAL RESPONSE TO CRITICAL ANALYSIS	OR	ANOTHER PATHWAY	LITERARY CONCEPTS	QUICKWRITES
		40 MINUTES		
• Discussion questions	OR	• Rewrite a section	• Setting	• Narrative poem • Character sketch • Memo
		40 MINUTES		
• Discussion questions	OR	• Comic strip	• Characters	• Essay • Review
		50 MINUTES		
• Discussion questions	OR	• Paint or draw a picture	• Plot and conflict	• Narrative • Tribute • Tall tale
		50 MINUTES		
• Discussion questions	OR	• Mock Interview	• Biography	• Acceptance speech • Log entry • Poem
		50 MINUTES		
• Discussion questions	OR	• Chart and oral presentation	• Purposes	• Summary • Editorial

Extension Activities

- ALTERNATIVE ACTIVITIES
- LITERARY LINKS
- CRITIC'S CORNER
- THE WRITER'S STYLE
- ACROSS THE CURRICULUM
- ART CONNECTION
- WORDS TO KNOW
- BIOGRAPHY

40 MINUTES — ✓ SCIENCE ✓ ✓

60 MINUTES — ✓ HISTORY ✓ ✓

50 MINUTES — ✓ ✓ SCIENCE ✓ ✓ ✓

40 MINUTES — ✓ SOCIAL STUDIES ✓ ✓

50 MINUTES — ✓ ✓ ✓

Publishing and Reflecting — 30 MINUTES

Grammar in Context — 10 MINUTES

Reading the World — 30 MINUTES

LESSON PLANNER TEACHER'S EDITION **17I**

PART 1

WHAT DO YOU THINK?

Objectives

The activities on this page can be used to
- introduce the Part 1 theme, "Seizing the Moment," since each activity is connected to one or more of the selections in Part 1
- create materials for students' personal portfolios that they can later reconsider or revise
- build an understanding of theme that can be reviewed and revised as students progress through the unit

Which is toughest?
Suggest to students that they compare the three situations and order them from easiest to most difficult before they create their rating scale. (See "Ghost of the Lagoon," p. 39.)

Who can handle the pressure?
Encourage students to list important details about the people they will be role-playing so that they can refer to this information during the discussion. In addition, ask students to think about the ways in which different kinds of pressure motivate people to "seize the moment." (See "Matthew Henson at the Top of the World," p. 53, and "My First Dive with the Dolphins," p. 65.)

What's your next move?
Once groups have created a list of problems and obstacles, instruct them to determine the objectives of their board game—for example, whether there will be a final winner—and to devise the rules of play. (See "The School Play," p. 30, and "Tuesday of the Other June," p. 75.)

What makes a decision good or bad?
Encourage partners to discuss the effects of their quick decisions as well as the reasons why they made the decisions they did. (See "Nadia the Willful," p. 21.)

UNIT ONE **PART 1**

SEIZING THE MOMENT

WHAT DO YOU THINK?

REFLECTING ON THEME

In as little time as an instant, it is possible to take a step or make a decision that has long-lasting effects. Use an activity on this page to explore what it is like to act under pressure. Take notes of your thoughts and ideas. You can compare them later with the thoughts of the characters in Part 1 as they attempt to "seize the moment."

Which is toughest?

In your notebook, create a scale like the one shown here. Use the scale to show how you would rate the difficulty of each of these situations.

- You are purposely shoved by another student.
- You want to tell someone that you really like him or her.
- You fail a math test and now must work with a tutor.

Easy ←――――→ Difficult

Who can handle the pressure?

In old newspapers or magazines, find articles about people acting under pressure. Then, in a small group, take the roles of these people. In the style of a TV talk show, discuss people who have "seized a moment." After the discussion, list the personal traits that are common to all the guests.

What's your next move?

With a group of classmates, brainstorm some kinds of problems and obstacles that young people face every day. Then create a board game called "A Day in My Life." Be sure that the game represents daily problems and offers options for solutions.

What makes a decision good or bad?

Recall a decision you made quickly, without thinking about the possible results. Create a diagram similar to the one shown. Would you make the same choice again? Talk about it with a partner.

Problem	
Decision I Made	
Pros	Cons
Conclusions	

18

Across the Curriculum

History Invite students to research historical figures who have acted under pressure to make long-lasting or groundbreaking decisions. Have students write brief research papers that detail the contributions of the people who "seized the moment." Students can share their findings in a class presentation.

COMMUNITY OUTREACH

To encourage students to think more deeply about the theme "Seizing the Moment," invite individuals from your local community to speak to the class about decision-making processes that greatly affect the community. These individual might be school board officials, local politicians, court or law enforcement officials, or health care officials. Encourage students to generate a list of thought-provoking questions to ask these individuals prior to their appearance.

18 THE LANGUAGE OF LITERATURE TEACHER'S EDITION

Focus on Fiction

When you read a story, you are reading a work of fiction. **Fiction** is writing that comes from an author's imagination. Although the author makes the story up, he or she might base it on real events.

Fiction writers write short stories and novels. A **short story** usually revolves around a single idea and is short enough to be read at one sitting. The fiction selections that you will read in this book are short stories. A **novel** is much longer and more complex.

Fiction writing contains four main elements: **character, setting, plot,** and **theme.** In some stories, all four elements are well developed. In other cases, an author may decide to focus on only one or two elements.

CHARACTER Characters are the people, animals, or imaginary creatures that take part in the action of a story. Usually, a short story centers on events in the life of one person, animal, or creature. This is the story's **main character.**

Generally, there are also one or more **minor characters** in the story. Minor characters sometimes provide part of the background for the story. More often, however, minor characters interact with the main character and with one another. Their words and actions help to move the plot along.

SETTING A story's setting is the time and place in which the action of the story happens. The time may be in the past, the present, or the future; in daytime or in the night; at any season. The place where the story's action occurs may be imaginary or real.

PLOT The sequence of events in a story is called the story's plot. The plot is the writer's blueprint for what happens, when it happens, and to whom it happens. One event causes another, which causes another, and so on until the end of the story.

Generally, a plot is built around a **conflict**—a problem or struggle involving two or more opposing forces. Conflicts can range from life-or-death struggles to disagreements between friends.

Although the development of each plot is different, traditional works of fiction generally follow a pattern that includes the following stages:

Exposition Exposition sets the stage for a story. Characters are introduced, the setting is described, and the conflict begins to unfold.

FOCUS ON FICTION **19**

FOCUS ON FICTION

This feature defines *fiction* and provides an explanation of the terms used to discuss it. It also introduces students to the conventions of the genre and suggests strategies for reading fiction. The terms introduced here are covered in depth in the fictional selections that follow.

Objectives

- To understand and appreciate fiction
- To understand the elements of fiction: character, setting, plot, and theme
- To develop effective strategies for reading fiction

Teaching Strategies: ELEMENTS OF FICTION

Character Invite the class to brainstorm a list of well-known fictional characters from novels, short stories, movies, and television. List all the characters on the chalkboard. Then have volunteers categorize them as main characters or minor characters. You may wish to use a chart such as the one shown to record students' responses.

Main Characters	Minor Characters

Setting Have students describe the classroom setting. To spark ideas, use a web like the one shown:

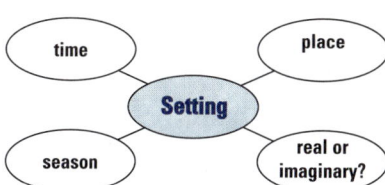

Plot Explain that just as architects draw blueprints before something is built, writers also make plans for the framework of their story. This plan is called a plot. A plot has a beginning, middle, and end. Have the class discuss the progression of plot in a familiar story. Then ask students to describe how the plot would be affected if a particular event had not occurred.

THE LANGUAGE OF LITERATURE **TEACHER'S EDITION** **19**

Theme Invite students to share some important life lessons they have learned, such as "Treat others as you wish to be treated" and "Honesty is the best policy." Explain that such messages about life are often what authors of fiction present in their stories as themes. Point out that a theme of a story can be understood by considering its characters, setting, and plot.

Reading Strategies: MODELING

Invite volunteers to read aloud the Strategies for Reading Fiction. Tell students they will be using these strategies as they read "Nadia the Willful" on page 21 and other examples of fiction throughout the book. Then model the strategies as students read "Nadia the Willful." You may wish to use the models provided or create your own.

- **Preview** *"From the title, I expect this story is about a stubborn girl. Words like* Sheik *and* desert *lead me to think the story is set in the Middle East."*
- **Visualize** *"I imagine the desert where Nadia lives is dry and hot and that there is a lot of sand blowing in the wind."*
- **Connect** *"I have also been called stubborn by others in the past when I have stood up for something I really believed in."*
- **Question** *"Why does Tarik not let anyone speak Hamed's name?"*
- **Predict** *"I think Nadia will cause trouble for herself by speaking Hamed's name."*
- **Build** *"From the story's title, I expected Nadia to be a spoiled, disobedient girl. But now I realize that Nadia is not stubborn in a negative way, as people think. She wants so much to keep the memory of her brother alive."*
- **Evaluate** *"I especially like the way characters are portrayed in this story. Nadia is a strong character who teaches her father a very valuable lesson."*
- **Discuss** Invite students to generate a short set of questions or opinions of the characters and story that they can discuss with a partner.

Complications As the story continues, the plot gets more complex. The characters struggle to find solutions to the conflict, and suspense and a feeling of excitement and energy build.

Climax The climax is the point of greatest interest or suspense in the story. It is the turning point, when the action reaches a peak and the outcome of the conflict is decided. The climax may occur because of a decision the characters reach or because of a discovery or an event that changes the situation. The climax usually results in a change in the characters or a solution to the problem.

Resolution The resolution usually occurs at the conclusion of the story. Loose ends are tied up, and the story ends.

THEME The theme of a story is the main message the writer conveys to the reader. This message might be a lesson about life or a belief about people and their actions. In most cases, the theme is not stated directly; it is like a hidden message that the reader must decode. As you discuss literature, however, you will find that different readers can discover different themes in the same story. The following suggestions will help you unlock a theme:

- Review what happened to the main character. Did he or she change during the story? What did he or she learn about life?
- Skim the story for key phrases and sentences—statements that go beyond the action of the story to say something important about life or people.
- Think about the story's title. Does it have a special meaning that could lead you to the main idea of the work?

STRATEGIES FOR READING FICTION

To really "get inside" a story, try the following strategies:

- **Preview the story.** Before you read, look at the title and the pictures. Skim through the pages and read some words here and there.
- **Visualize what you are reading.** Can you picture a similar place in your mind? Is the action easy to imagine?
- **Make connections.** Do any of the characters have thoughts or experiences that you have had? Does the story remind you of an event or a person you've heard of or read about?
- **Question as you read.** The events, characters, and ideas in the story ought to make sense to you. "Why is the door unlocked?" "Why is she so rude?" Asking good questions as you read is at the heart of good reading.
- **Make predictions.** During your reading, stop occasionally to predict what might happen next and how you think the story will end.
- **Build on your knowledge.** Let your thoughts change and grow as you learn more about the characters and events in the story.
- **Evaluate the story.** Think about your feelings about the characters and their actions. Also consider how well the author is telling his or her story.
- **Discuss the story.** When you have finished reading, talk about the story with someone else.

Remember, a story never tells you everything; it leaves room for your own ideas. After you read a story, you are left with first impressions, but you need to be able to elaborate and explain them on the basis of the story itself, your own experiences, and other stories you have read.

PREVIEWING

FICTION

Nadia the Willful
Sue Alexander

Activating Prior Knowledge
PERSONAL CONNECTION
Think about the title of this story. What does the title suggest about the content? What does it mean to say that someone is willful? On a sheet of paper, complete a web, like the one shown, about the title.

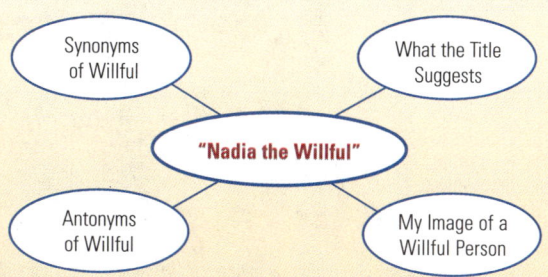

Building Background
GEOGRAPHICAL CONNECTION
Nadia the Willful, the main character in this story, is a young Bedouin girl. The Bedouins are an Arab people of the Sahara and the desert lands of the Middle East. The leader of a Bedouin tribe or clan is called a sheik. Bedouins live as nomads, or wanderers, searching the desert for oases (places with water and pasture), where they can settle with their goats, sheep, camels, and horses. When an oasis dries up, the group moves on. Life in the desert is harsh and dangerous—food is scarce, sandstorms are common, and temperatures can reach 130°F.

WRITING CONNECTION *Setting a Purpose*
In your notebook, write about a person whom you would describe as willful. How does this person speak and act? How does he or she get along with other people? If possible, give examples of words or actions that show this person's willfulness. As you read, compare Nadia with the person you described.

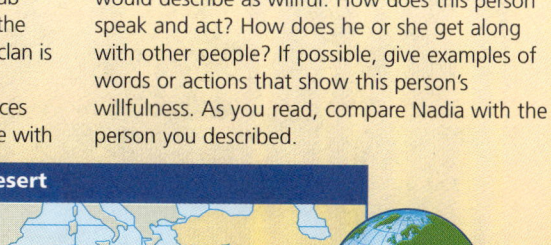

Bedouins. Lehnert & Landrock, Copyright © National Geographic Society.

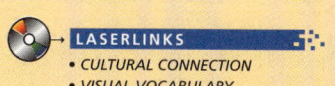

LASERLINKS
- CULTURAL CONNECTION
- VISUAL VOCABULARY

21

OVERVIEW

Objectives
- To understand and appreciate a short story about how a young girl deals with the loss of a loved one
- To identify and understand setting
- To express understanding of the story through a choice of writing forms including a narrative poem, a character sketch, and a memo
- To extend understanding of the story through a variety of multimodal and cross-curricular activities

Skills

READING SKILLS/ STRATEGIES
- Comparing and contrasting

LITERARY CONCEPTS
- Setting
- Conflict

GRAMMAR
- Using commas to separate ideas

SPELLING
- The Suffix -able

SPEAKING, LISTENING, AND VIEWING
- Group discussion
- Oral presentation

Cross-Curricular Connections

SOCIAL STUDIES
- Bedouin diet and lifestyle

SCIENCE
- Deserts and oases

HISTORY
- Learn more about Bedouins

 **CULTURAL CONNECTION**
Bedouin Life These historical and contemporary photos provide a glimpse into the lifestyle and culture of the Bedouin people. Examples of the Bedouins' adaptations to the harsh environment of the Sahara are shown. The images can be used to generate discussion about ways in which environment influences cultural practices and beliefs.

Side A, Frame 38582

PRINT AND MEDIA RESOURCES

UNIT ONE RESOURCE BOOK
Strategic Reading: Literature, p. 7
Vocabulary SkillBuilder, p. 10
Reading SkillBuilder, p. 8
Spelling SkillBuilder, p. 9

GRAMMAR MINI–LESSONS
Transparencies, p. 31
Copymasters, p. 40

ACCESS FOR STUDENTS ACQUIRING ENGLISH
Selection Summaries
Reading and Writing Support

TEACHER'S GUIDE TO ASSESSMENT AND PORTFOLIO USE

FORMAL ASSESSMENT
Selection Test, pp. 5–6
 Test Generator

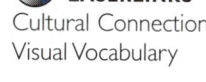 **AUDIO LIBRARY**
See Reference Card

LASERLINKS
Cultural Connection
Visual Vocabulary

THE LANGUAGE OF LITERATURE **TEACHER'S EDITION** 21

SUMMARY

Nadia's stubbornness and quick temper have earned her the nickname Nadia the Willful in her Bedouin community. (The Bedouin are a nomadic people of North Africa and the Middle East.) When Nadia's temper flares, only her oldest brother, Hamed, can tease her into a good humor. Hamed disappears in the desert, however, and Nadia's father, the sheik Tarik, is so sad that he forbids anyone to speak Hamed's name. Despite the sheik's commands, Nadia begins talking about Hamed as a way of coping with her memories and grief. Others follow her example, until one day Tarik overhears a shepherd speaking of Hamed and cruelly banishes him. The fearful Bedouin now turn away from Nadia's memories. Unable to bear the silence, she confronts her father and restores his fading memories by telling him stories about Hamed. Recognizing her understanding—and now wiser himself—Tarik renames his daughter Nadia the Wise.

Thematic Link: *Seizing the Moment*
Only by seizing the moment and breaking the silence imposed by her father can Nadia begin to feel peace and accept her brother's death.

Art Note

***Bedouins* by John Singer Sargent** John Singer Sargent (1856–1925) is chiefly known as a painter of high-society portraits. He also traveled widely, however, and often recorded his experiences in his paintings. *Bedouins,* painted in about 1905 or 1906, shows a Bedouin man and woman, members of one of the wandering tribes of Arabs. Sargent's use of spare strokes and various shades of blue and brown suggests the shimmering atmosphere of the Bedouins' desert home.

Reading the Art *What do you think is the relationship between the Bedouins in the portrait? Do you picture Nadia as being like these people? If not, how does your image of her differ?*

Bedouins (about 1905–1906), John Singer Sargent. Watercolor, 18″ × 12″, The Brooklyn Museum, New York. Purchased by special subscription (09.814).

22

WORDS TO KNOW

banish (băn′ĭsh) *v.* to send away; exile (p. 26)
bazaar (bə-zär′) *n.* in Middle Eastern countries, an outdoor market of small shops (p. 24)
clan (klăn) *n.* a family group or tribe (p. 24)
decree (dĭ-krē′) *n.* an official order (p. 24)
ponder (pŏn′dər) *v.* to think about carefully (p. 27)

 VISUAL VOCABULARY

• **bazaar** (bə-zär′)   • **sheik** (shēk)
• **oasis** (ō-ā′sĭs)   • **stallion** (stăl′yən)

Side A, Frame 38589

22 THE LANGUAGE OF LITERATURE TEACHER'S EDITION

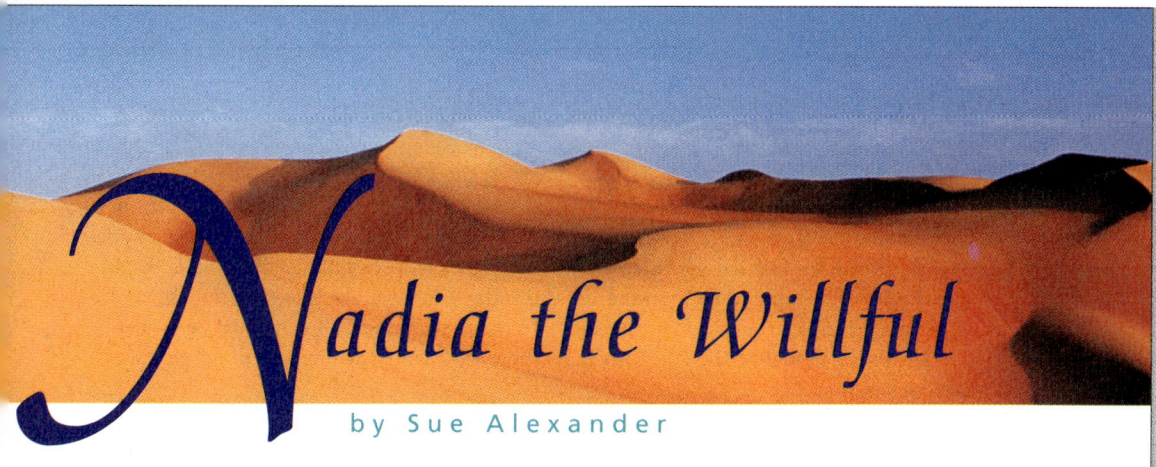

Nadia the Willful

by Sue Alexander

In the land of the drifting sands where the Bedouin move their tents to follow the fertile grasses, there lived a girl whose stubbornness and flashing temper caused her to be known throughout the desert as Nadia the Willful.

Nadia's father, the sheik Tarik, whose kindness and graciousness caused his name to be praised in every tent, did not know what to do with his willful daughter.

Only Hamed, the eldest of Nadia's six brothers and Tarik's favorite son, could calm Nadia's temper when it flashed.

NADIA THE WILLFUL 23

 Multicultural Perspectives

REMEMBERING THE DEAD Tell students that different cultures respond to death in different ways. In some cultures, before a person is buried, people hold a wake, a gathering of relatives and friends to honor the person who died. Jewish people observe shiva, a seven-day mourning period that follows a funeral. During shiva, friends and relatives visit the children, spouse, or parents of the person who died, bringing food and keeping the mourners company. Ask students to discuss how their family mourns the death of a loved one.

THE LANGUAGE OF LITERATURE TEACHER'S EDITION 23

CUSTOMIZING FOR
Gifted and Talented Students

Ask students to use a diagram similar to the one shown to list traits that describe Tarik at the points of the story indicated.

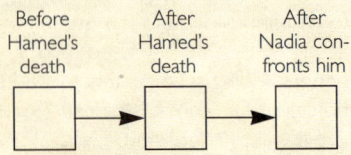

Before Hamed's death → After Hamed's death → After Nadia confronts him

Possible responses:
- Before Hamed's death: kind, gracious, good leader
- After Hamed's death: harsh, cold, sad
- After Nadia confronts him: grateful, relieved, wiser, kind once again

Critical Thinking: SYNTHESIZING

B Have students analyze Nadia's first response to Hamed's death. Ask them if they think that Nadia's response is consistent with what they know of her character thus far. *(Possible response: Since earlier in the story Nadia is described as stubborn and quick-tempered, it makes sense that she would at first scream, cry, and refuse to accept his death.)*

STRATEGIC READING FOR
Less-Proficient Readers

C Ask the following questions to be sure that students understand what has happened in the story so far.

- Why is Nadia called "willful"? *(She is stubborn and quick-tempered.)* **Noting Relevant Details**
- What has happened to Hamed? *(He has disappeared into the desert.)* **Drawing Conclusions**

Set a Purpose Have students read on to find out how Nadia and other members of the tribe react to Tarik's decree.

Use the UNIT ONE RESOURCE BOOK, pp. 7–8, for guidance in reading the selection.

Literary Concept: CONFLICT

D Ask students to describe the internal struggle Nadia is experiencing and how that struggle is affecting her. *(Possible response: Nadia wants to speak of Hamed, but she is not allowed to; this makes her unhappy and angry.)*

"Oh, angry one," he would say, "shall we see how long you can stay that way?" And he would laugh and tease and pull at her dark hair until she laughed back. Then she would follow Hamed wherever he led.

One day before dawn, Hamed mounted his father's great white stallion and rode to the west to seek new grazing ground for the sheep. Nadia stood with her father at the edge of the oasis and watched him go.

Hamed did not return.

Nadia rode behind her father as he traveled across the desert from oasis to oasis, seeking Hamed.

Shepherds told them of seeing a great white stallion fleeing before the pillars of wind that stirred the sand. And they said that the horse carried no rider.

Passing merchants, their camels laden with spices and sweets for the bazaar, told of the emptiness of the desert they had crossed.

Tribesmen, strangers, everyone whom Tarik asked, sighed and gazed into the desert, saying, "Such is the will of Allah."[1]

At last Tarik knew in his heart that his favorite son, Hamed, had been claimed, as other Bedouin before him, by the drifting sands. And he told Nadia what he knew—that Hamed was dead.

B Nadia screamed and wept and stamped the sand, crying, "Not even Allah will take Hamed from me!" until her father could bear no more and sternly bade her to silence.

Nadia's grief knew no bounds. She walked blindly through the oasis, neither seeing nor hearing those who would console her. And Tarik was silent. For days he sat inside his tent, speaking not at all and barely tasting the meals set before him.

Then, on the seventh day, Tarik came out of his tent. He called all his people to him, and when they were assembled, he spoke. "From this day forward," he said, "let no one utter Hamed's name. Punishment shall be swift for those who would remind me of what I have lost." **C**

Each memory brought Hamed's name to Nadia's lips.

Hamed's mother wept at the decree. The people of the clan looked at one another uneasily. All could see the hardness that had settled on the sheik's face and the coldness in his eyes, and so they said nothing. But they obeyed.

Nadia, too, did as her father decreed, though each day held something to remind her of Hamed. As she passed her brothers at play, she remembered games Hamed had taught her. As she walked by the women weaving patches for the tents and heard them talking and laughing, she remembered tales Hamed had told her and how they had made her laugh. And as she watched the shepherds with their flock, she remembered the little black lamb Hamed had loved.

Each memory brought Hamed's name to Nadia's lips, but she stilled the sound. And each time that she did so, her unhappiness grew until, finally, she could no longer contain it. She wept and raged at anyone and anything that crossed her path. Soon everyone at the **D**

---
1. **Allah** (äl′ə): the name for God in the Islamic religion.

WORDS TO KNOW	
bazaar (bə-zär′)	*n.* in Middle Eastern countries, an outdoor market of small shops
decree (dĭ-krē′)	*n.* an official order
clan (klăn)	*n.* a family group or tribe

24

Mini-Lesson Literary Concepts

CONFLICT Inform students that in a work of literature a conflict is a struggle between opposing forces. A struggle between a character and an outside force, such as society, nature, or another character, is an external conflict. A struggle within a character's mind is an internal conflict. An internal conflict often occurs when a character has to make a difficult decision or deal with conflicting feelings.

Application Have students think about the different conflicts in "Nadia the Willful." For example, they might refer to the passage highlighted above for an example of conflict between Nadia and her father. Ask students to discuss whether they think this is an example of an internal or external conflict. Then have them try to identify other conflicts in the selection and whether the conflicts are internal or external.

24 THE LANGUAGE OF LITERATURE **TEACHER'S EDITION**

La caravane [The caravan] (1880), Alexandre-Gabriel Decamps. Louvre, Paris. Giraudon/Art Resource, New York.

Art Note

La caravane by Alexandre-Gabriel Decamps Alexandre-Gabriel Decamps experimented with the contrasts between light and shade (a painting technique called chiaroscuro) in an attempt to capture visual contrasts as they appear in nature. *La caravane* is an example of his efforts to convey the play of light and shadow in the desert during the early morning or early evening hours.

Reading the Art *What do you think it would be like to live in a region such as the one portrayed in the painting? Does the painting seem to be a realistic portrayal of the way Nadia and her clan live?*

CUSTOMIZING FOR
Multiple Learning Styles

E **Spatial or Graphic Learners** Have students compare the art on this page with the events that have taken place in the story so far. Ask them to discuss what events they think the art might represent.

Active Reading: EVALUATE

F Have students evaluate Nadia's response to her brother's game. Is speaking Hamed's name a wise thing for Nadia to do? Why or why not? If students need help, share the following thought process with them:

Think-Aloud Model *Speaking Hamed's name might be good because Nadia needs to release her grief and frustration. Also, since she was so close to Hamed, it would help her remember him. However, I think speaking Hamed's name could also be bad, because it goes against Tarik's wishes.*

Literary Concept: CONFLICT

G Have students note the conflict between Nadia and her mother as well as the effect Nadia has on the other members of her clan. What is the cause of this conflict? *(Possible response: Although Nadia wants to speak about Hamed, her mother and other members of the clan are afraid to listen and speak because the sheik has forbidden it.)*

---

oasis fled at her approach. And she was more lonely than she had ever been before.

One day, as Nadia passed the place where her brothers were playing, she stopped to watch them. They were playing one of the games that Hamed had taught her. But they were playing it wrong.

Without thinking, Nadia called out to them. "That is not the way! Hamed said that first you jump this way and then you jump back!"

Her brothers stopped their game and looked around in fear. Had Tarik heard Nadia say Hamed's name? But the sheik was nowhere to be seen.

"Teach us, Nadia, as our brother taught you," said her smallest brother.

And so she did. Then she told them of other games and how Hamed had taught her to play them. And as she spoke of Hamed, she felt an easing of the hurt within her.

So she went on speaking of him.

She went to where the women sat at their loom and spoke of Hamed. She told them tales that Hamed had told her. And she told how he had made her laugh as he was telling them.

At first the women were afraid to listen to the willful girl and covered their ears, but after a time, they listened and laughed with her.

"Remember your father's promise of punishment!" Nadia's mother warned when she heard Nadia speaking of Hamed. "Cease, I implore you!"

Nadia knew that her mother had reason to be afraid, for Tarik, in his grief and bitterness, had grown quick-tempered and sharp of tongue. But she did not know how to tell her mother that speaking of Hamed eased the pain she felt, and so she said only, "I will speak of my brother! I will!" And she ran away from the sound of her mother's voice.

NADIA THE WILLFUL 25

Mini-Lesson — Reading Skills/Strategies

COMPARING AND CONTRASTING Explain to students that comparing and contrasting are skills that good readers use when they point out the similarities and differences between two or more characters or objects in a selection. Tell students that using this skill helps give them a broader understanding of what they are reading.

Application Ask students to think about the different characters' reactions to Hamed's death. Encourage them to record their findings in a chart like the one shown. Encourage them to consider the possible reasons for any differences.

Reteaching/Reinforcement
• Unit One Resource Book, p. 8

Character	Nadia	Nadia's mother	Tarik	Tribespeople
Reaction	sad but wanting to talk about and remember her brother	sad and silent	angry and wanting to forget about Hamed	afraid to speak of Hamed because of Tarik's anger

THE LANGUAGE OF LITERATURE TEACHER'S EDITION 25

Linking to Social Studies

H Explain to students that traditional nomadic Bedouins generally live in tents. Their diet includes meat and dairy products produced from their livestock, as well as rice and dates. During the past 50 years, some Middle Eastern nations have given Bedouins land on which to settle, which has led many of them to give up their nomadic lifestyle and live in one place.

Literary Concept: CONFLICT

I Invite students to discuss the conflict between Nadia and Tarik. Ask them to determine the cause. *(Possible response: An external conflict exists between Nadia and her father because he forbids anyone to speak Hamed's name. Nadia needs to speak Hamed's name aloud to keep his memory alive.)*

Critical Thinking: SPECULATING

J Ask students why Nadia accuses her father of stealing Hamed from her. *(Possible response: Nadia feels that Tarik, by forbidding her to speak about Hamed, is causing her to forget her brother.)*

She went to where the shepherds tended the flock and spoke of Hamed. The shepherds ran from her in fear and hid behind the sheep. But Nadia went on speaking. She told of Hamed's love for the little black lamb and how he had taught it to leap at his whistle. Soon the shepherds left off their hiding and came to listen. Then they told their own stories of Hamed and the little black lamb.

The more Nadia spoke of Hamed, the clearer his face became in her mind. She could see his smile and the light in his eyes. She could hear his voice. And the clearer Hamed's voice and face became, the less Nadia hurt inside and the less her temper flashed. At last, she was filled with peace.

But her mother was still afraid for her willful daughter. Again and again she sought to quiet Nadia so that Tarik's bitterness would not be turned against her. And again and again Nadia tossed her head and went on speaking of Hamed.

Soon, all who listened could see Hamed's face clearly before them.

One day, the youngest shepherd came to Nadia's tent, calling, "Come, Nadia! See Hamed's black lamb; it has grown so big and strong!"

But it was not Nadia who came out of the tent.

It was Tarik.

On the sheik's face was a look more fierce than that of a desert hawk, and when he spoke, his words were as sharp as a scimitar.[2]

"I have forbidden my son's name to be said. And I promised punishment to whoever disobeyed my command. So shall it be. Before the sun sets and the moon casts its first shadow on the sand, you will be gone from this oasis—never to return."

"No!" cried Nadia, hearing her father's words.

"I have spoken!" roared the sheik. "It shall be done!"

Trembling, the shepherd went to gather his possessions.

And the rest of the clan looked at one another uneasily and muttered among themselves.

In the hours that followed, fear of being <u>banished</u> to the desert made everyone turn away from Nadia as she tried to tell them of Hamed and the things he had done and said.

And the less she was listened to, the less she was able to recall Hamed's face and voice. And the less she recalled, the more her temper raged within her, destroying the peace she had found.

"I have spoken!" roared the sheik. "It shall be done!"

By evening, she could stand it no longer. She went to where her father sat, staring into the desert, and stood before him.

"You will not rob me of my brother Hamed!" she cried, stamping her foot. "I will not let you!"

Tarik looked at her, his eyes colder than the desert night.

But before he could utter a word, Nadia spoke again. "Can you recall Hamed's face? Can you still hear his voice?"

---

2. **scimitar** (sĭm′ĭ-tər): a curved sword.

WORDS TO KNOW
banish (băn′ĭsh) *v.* to send away; exile

26

Mini-Lesson ✏ Grammar

USING COMMAS TO SEPARATE IDEAS

Explain to students that commas can help readers avoid confusion by separating words or ideas. Commas are often used to separate three or more items in a series or to join two independent clauses with a conjunction.

Application Ask students to explain the use of commas in the sentence on page 27. *(to separate items in a series of three or more)*

Then copy the sentences shown on the chalkboard, omitting the commas, and have students suggest the correct location of commas.

Reteaching/Reinforcement
- *Grammar Handbook*, anthology, pp. 847–848
- *Grammar Mini-Lessons*, copymasters, p. 40, transparencies, p. 31

Commas That Separate Ideas, p. 574

Examples:

Tarik, Nadia, and Nadia's mother missed Hamed.

Tarik felt sad about Hamed's death, but he did not show his feelings.

Tarik started in surprise, and his answer seemed to come unbidden to his lips. "No, I cannot! Day after day I have sat in this spot where I last saw Hamed, trying to remember the look, the sound, the happiness that was my beloved son—but I cannot."

And he wept.

Nadia's tone became gentle. "There is a way, honored father," she said. "Listen."

And she began to speak of Hamed. She told of walks she and Hamed had taken and of talks they had had. She told how he had taught her games, told her tales, and calmed her when she was angry. She told many things that she remembered, some happy and some sad.

 And when she was done with the telling, she said gently, "Can you not recall him now, Father? Can you not see his face? Can you not hear his voice?"

Tarik nodded through his tears, and for the first time since Hamed had been gone, he smiled.

"Now you see," Nadia said, her tone more gentle than the softest of the desert breezes, "there is a way that Hamed can be with us still."

The sheik pondered what Nadia had said. After a long time, he spoke, and the sharpness was gone from his voice.

"Tell my people to come before me, Nadia," he said. "I have something to say to them."

When all were assembled, Tarik said, "From this day forward, let my daughter Nadia be known not as willful but as wise. And let her name be praised in every tent, for she has given me back my beloved son."

And so it was. The shepherd returned to his flock, kindness and graciousness returned to the oasis, and Nadia's name was praised in every tent. And Hamed lived again—in the hearts of all who remembered him. ❖

LITERARY INSIGHT

✳ PRIMER LESSON ✳

BY CARL SANDBURG

Look out how you use proud words.
When you let proud words go, it is
   not easy to call them back.
They wear long boots, hard boots; they
   walk off proud; they can't hear you
   calling—
Look out how you use proud words.

WORDS TO KNOW
ponder (pŏn'dər) v. to think about carefully

27

CUSTOMIZING FOR
Students Acquiring English

1. Explain that the idiom *day after day* means "for many days."

2. Help students understand that Nadia is not speaking literally of Hamed when she asks Tarik, "Can you not see his face? Can you not hear his voice?"

STRATEGIC READING FOR
Less-Proficient Readers

K Have students summarize the events following Tarik's decree. *(Nadia disobeys her father in order to remember Hamed. Tarik becomes very angry. This leads Nadia to confront her father and to teach him the importance of speaking about Hamed.)* **Summarizing**

CUSTOMIZING FOR
Gifted and Talented Students

L Ask students if they believe that Nadia has become any less willful. *(Possible responses: No, Nadia is still willful; her willfulness is what forced Tarik to reconsider his actions and to recognize her wisdom. Yes, she is now able to communicate her viewpoint to Tarik with gentle words.)*

COMPREHENSION CHECK
1. How does Nadia react at first to the news of her brother's death? *(She screams and weeps and will not let anyone console her.)*
2. What does Tarik decree? *(No one may speak the name Hamed.)*
3. Why does Nadia like to talk about Hamed? *(She talks about Hamed because it relieves her grief to keep his memory alive.)*
4. At the end of the story, what does sheik Tarik want Nadia to be called? *(Wise, not Willful)*

LITERARY INSIGHT

According to the poem, what can be the result of using "proud words"? *(They cannot be taken back.)*

CARL SANDBURG

Carl Sandburg (1878–1967) is best known for his award-winning works of poetry and historical prose.

Mini-Lesson Spelling

THE SUFFIX -ABLE The suffix *-able* is commonly added to words to form adjectives meaning "able to be." If the base word ends with a silent *e*, the *e* is usually dropped before a suffix that begins with a vowel.

Example: value + able = valuable

Words from the selection with the suffix *-able*

answerable   bearable
approachable ponderable
movable   lovable

Application Have students add the suffix *-able* to the following words.

1. remark *(remarkable)*   5. endure *(endurable)*
2. imagine *(imaginable)*   6. question *(questionable)*
3. comfort *(comfortable)* 7. advise *(advisable)*
4. note *(notable)*   8. punish *(punishable)*

Ask students to think of other words that fit this pattern and to write the words in their personal word lists.

Reteaching/Reinforcement
• *Unit One Resource Book,* p. 9

THE LANGUAGE OF LITERATURE TEACHER'S EDITION **27**

From Personal Response to Critical Analysis

1. Responses will vary.
2. Students who think that Nadia deserves to be called willful may say that she insists on saying and doing as she pleases. Students who disagree may note that she is honest about her feelings.
3. Possible response: At first Nadia is very stubborn about her attitude. Over time, she learns to accept her brother's death and to confront Tarik in a calm and receptive way. In doing so, she becomes peaceful and wise.
4. Some students may suggest that Nadia changes Tarik's mind because she is stubborn and refuses to back down; others may point out that Nadia shows Tarik that silence does not erase grief and that remembering Hamed is both good and comforting.
5. Possible response: Nadia's willful behavior and quick temper could result in her saying things out of stubbornness or pride, rather than saying what she means. Sandburg's poem could be taken as a warning to Nadia to try to be less willful and more thoughtful.
6. Student responses will vary.

Another Pathway

Cooperative Learning Students should begin by deciding what part of the story they plan to rewrite and whether they are going to rewrite it from Nadia's or Tarik's point of view. In each group, one student may record the ideas and decisions, while another student organizes and edits the ideas to ensure that they make sense and reflect the decisions made by the group. A third student should help check the group's version for clarity. Another student should read the group's story to the class.

Rubric

3 Full Accomplishment Students successfully collaborate on a story that reflects the plot and characterization of the original selection.

2 Substantial Accomplishment Some students are not encouraged to participate or are left without roles. Story is missing key plot or character elements.

1 Little or Partial Accomplishment Story is strongly influenced by one or two members of the group or does not correlate well with plot and characterization of original version.

RESPONDING OPTIONS

FROM PERSONAL RESPONSE TO CRITICAL ANALYSIS

REFLECT
1. What were your thoughts about Nadia as you finished reading? Write about her in your notebook.

RETHINK
Close Textual Reading
2. Think about the word web and notebook entry about willfulness that you made for the Personal Connection on page 21. In your opinion, does Nadia deserve to be called willful? Explain.
3. How does Nadia change across time, and why?
4. Nadia's father promises to punish anyone who speaks Hamed's name. Why do you think Nadia is able to change her father's mind?
   Consider
   • Nadia's character
   • the effect of grief on her father

RELATE
5. Read "Primer Lesson" on page 27. What connections do you see between Sandburg's warning about "proud words" and Nadia the Willful?
6. Nadia and Tarik have different ways of reacting to death. Do their actions bring to mind any feelings or experiences of grief and death that you know about or have read about?

LITERARY CONCEPTS

The **setting** of a story is the time and place in which the events of the story happen. Skim the story and make a list of details about the setting. What role does the setting play in this story? How important is the setting?

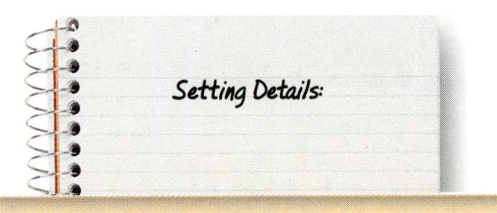
Setting Details:

Multimodal Learning
ANOTHER PATHWAY

Cooperative Learning
What if this story were told by Nadia or by Tarik? With a small group, choose what you consider the most important section of the story. Then rewrite that section, telling it from either Nadia's or Tarik's point of view. Share your version with the class.

QUICKWRITES

1. Compose a **narrative poem** that tells the events of this story. (For a description of narrative poetry, see page 104.)
2. Prepare a **character sketch** that would help an actor playing Tarik in a film version of "Nadia the Willful" to understand Tarik's character.
3. Imagine you are the set designer for the film version of the story. Write a **memo** to the director, describing the setting that you want to create. In your memo use details that you gathered for the Literary Concepts activity.

📁 **PORTFOLIO** Save your writing. You may want to use it later as a springboard to a piece for your portfolio.

28 UNIT ONE PART 1: SEIZING THE MOMENT

Literary Concepts

Have students form small groups to compare their lists of details. Encourage them to discuss their responses to the questions about setting. You may wish to refer students to the following lines from the selection:
• Page 23—"In the land of the drifting sands where the Bedouin move their tents to follow the fertile grasses"
• Page 24—"Tarik knew in his heart that his favorite son, Hamed, had been claimed, as other Bedouin before him, by the drifting sands."

QuickWrites

1. Encourage students to make a list of the most important events and characters in the story.
2. Suggest that students review the story and make a list of details describing Tarik's character.
3. Stress that students' memos should be brief and emphasize only those details of the setting that they think are most important.

The Writer's Craft

Writing a Poem, pp. 84–88
Describing People and Places, pp. 50–61
Letter Form, p. 609

28 THE LANGUAGE OF LITERATURE TEACHER'S EDITION

Multimodal Learning

ALTERNATIVE ACTIVITIES

Make a desert **diorama.** Cut a small square opening in one side of a shoebox. Using sand, sandpaper, paint, and other materials, create the setting of the story inside the shoebox. Then make paper figures of the characters and their animals to position within the scene. View the scene from the top or through the opening.

ACROSS THE CURRICULUM

Science Find out how deserts and oases form and change. Present your information to the class in an oral report.

WORDS TO KNOW

Review the Words to Know in the boxes at the bottom of the selection pages. Write the word most closely related to the idea of each sentence.

1. The sheik was angered by the theft of the horses and commanded that anyone found stealing a horse be put to death.
2. The marketplace was packed with every imaginable item—blankets, saddles, robes of woven cloth, and even wooden toys for children.
3. Looking out at the horizon, Hamed sat and thought of the extraordinary size of the hot and silent desert.
4. They camped at the oasis, all of the families of the tribe sleeping in tents and cooking food for one another over open fires.
5. There was no way he could survive in the desert alone, but he had no choice because the tribe would not let him live among them any longer.

SUE ALEXANDER

At the age of eight, Sue Alexander began writing stories for her friends. She says, "At that time I was small for my age (I still am) and very clumsy. So clumsy, in fact, that none of my classmates wanted me on their teams at recess time." One day Alexander spent recess time telling a made-up story to someone else who was not playing. Before her story was finished, all the rest of the class had come to listen. This incident sparked her love of storytelling.

Alexander says she would not trade writing for any other profession because writing satisfies her

1933–

sense of fun and her need to share. Her fantasy stories all begin the same way—with how she feels about something. She writes for young people because she likes to excite their imaginations.

Alexander's short stories have been published in *My Weekly Reader* and other magazines for younger readers. The book publication of *Nadia the Willful* won many honors, including one from the American Library Association in 1983.

OTHER WORKS *World Famous Muriel, Lila on the Landing, There's More—Much More* Extended Reading

NADIA THE WILLFUL **29**

Across the Curriculum

Science *Cooperative Learning* You may wish to have students work in small groups to complete the activity concerning deserts and oases. You may want to have each group assign work based on finding information, organizing the information for presentation, preparing any visual aids (for example, maps or charts), and presenting the group's work to the class. Encourage one student to organize and keep track of the group's individual assignments and collected information. The report may be divided into smaller sections that different members can orally present.

ADDITIONAL SUGGESTION

History *Learn More About Bedouins* Have interested students research the life of Bedouins. Students should consider some of the following questions: What is the history of Bedouins? When did they start living in the desert? Why do they move from place to place? How have their movements or style of living changed over time?

SUE ALEXANDER

When asked why she writes for young people, Sue Alexander replied, "Because they have imaginations that soar, touched off by a word, a phrase, an image . . . a condition I share. To be able to provide a spark for this process gives me the greatest personal joy." The picture book *Nadia the Willful* was named the American Library Association Booklist Children's Reviewer's Choice in 1983 and the Child Study Association Children's Book of the Year in 1984.

Alternative Activities

Have students draw a sketch or plan of their diorama before they start constructing it. If students are unsure of details of the setting, suggest that they refer to their list of details about setting from the Literary Concepts exercise on page 28. Encourage them to include only the most important parts of the setting, so that the scene they create is recognizable.

Words to Know

1. decree
2. bazaar
3. ponder
4. clan
5. banish

Reteaching/Reinforcement
• *Unit One Resource Book*, p. 10

THE LANGUAGE OF LITERATURE TEACHER'S EDITION **29**

OVERVIEW

Objectives

- To understand and appreciate a short story about a boy's first role in a play
- To identify and understand characters
- To express understanding of the story through a choice of writing forms, including an essay and a theater review
- To extend understanding of the story through a variety of multimodal and cross-curricular activities

Skills

READING SKILLS/ STRATEGIES
- Summarizing

THE WRITER'S STYLE
- Choosing the right words

GRAMMAR
- Quotation marks

LITERARY CONCEPTS
- Characters
- Slang

GENRE STUDY
- Fiction: short story

SPEAKING, LISTENING, AND VIEWING
- Group discussion
- Oral presentation

Cross-Curricular Connections

SOCIAL STUDIES
- Survivors

SCIENCE
- Starvation

HISTORY
- Donner party

HISTORICAL CONNECTION
Westward Ho! These images illustrate the conditions pioneers endured as they journeyed through the Sierra Nevada in the 1800s.

Side A, Frame 38594

PREVIEWING

FICTION

The School Play
Gary Soto

PERSONAL CONNECTION *Activating Prior Knowledge*

You stand backstage, listening closely to the lines the actors on the stage are speaking, waiting to make your entrance. Suddenly a hand touches your shoulder, and someone whispers, "You're on!" Think back to your own experiences of performing in public or giving oral reports in school. With your classmates, discuss what you remember most about rehearsing, performing, and receiving an audience's reaction.

HISTORICAL CONNECTION *Building Background*

In "The School Play," a class is preparing to perform *The Last Stand,* a play based on a tragic incident in America's past. In 1846, a group of 82 pioneers from Illinois and nearby states, led by George and Jacob Donner, set out for California in covered wagons. When trying to cross the Sierra Nevada mountain range in eastern California, they became snowbound in the pass through the mountains. More fierce weather swept in, and the travelers ran out of food. Many began dying of starvation. In their desperation, some of the remaining members of the party resorted to eating the bodies of the dead to survive. Only 47 of the pioneers made it through that grim winter. Donner Pass is now a national landmark, and accounts of what took place there continue to fascinate people.

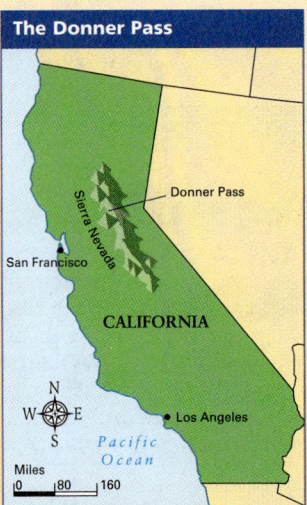

WRITING CONNECTION *Setting a Purpose*

Many people feel nervous about speaking or performing in public. In fact, public speaking is often at or near the top of people's lists of personal fears. In your notebook, write about why this might be true and whether people should find speaking in public so frightening. As you read, think about how the characters in this story illustrate your ideas.

30 UNIT ONE PART 1: SEIZING THE MOMENT

• HISTORICAL CONNECTION

PRINT AND MEDIA RESOURCES

UNIT ONE RESOURCE BOOK
Strategic Reading: Literature, p. 13
Vocabulary SkillBuilder, p. 15
Reading SkillBuilder, p. 14

GRAMMAR MINI-LESSONS
Transparencies, p. 33
Copymasters, p. 42

WRITING MINI-LESSONS
Transparencies, p. 36

ACCESS FOR STUDENTS ACQUIRING ENGLISH
Selection Summaries
Reading and Writing Support

FORMAL ASSESSMENT
Selection Test, pp. 7–8
Test Generator

 **AUDIO LIBRARY**
See Reference Card

 **LASERLINKS**
Historical Connection
Author Background

30 THE LANGUAGE OF LITERATURE TEACHER'S EDITION

THE SCHOOL PLAY
BY GARY SOTO

In the school play at the end of his sixth-grade year, all Robert Suarez had to remember to say was, "Nothing's wrong. I can see," to a pioneer woman, who was really Belinda Lopez. Instead of a pioneer woman, Belinda was one of the toughest girls since the beginning of the world. She was known to slap boys and grind their faces into the grass so that they bit into chunks of wormy earth. More than once Robert had witnessed Belinda staring down the janitor's pit bull, who licked his frothing chops but didn't dare mess with her.

The class rehearsed for three weeks, at first without costumes. Early one morning Mrs. Bunnin wobbled into the classroom lugging a large cardboard box. She wiped her brow and said, "Thanks for the help, Robert."

Robert was at his desk scribbling a ballpoint tattoo that spelled DUDE on the tops of his knuckles. He looked up and stared, blinking at his teacher. "Oh, did you need some help?" he asked.

She rolled her eyes at him and told him to stop writing on his skin. "You'll look like a criminal," she scolded.

Robert stuffed his hands into his pockets as he rose from his seat. "What's in the box?" he asked.

She muttered under her breath. She popped open the taped top and brought out skirts, hats, snowshoes, scarves, and vests. She tossed Robert a red beard, which he held up to his face, thinking it made him look handsome.

"I like it," Robert said. He sneezed and ran his hand across his moist nose.

His classmates were coming into the classroom and looked at Robert in awe. "That's bad," Ruben said. "What do I get?"

Mrs. Bunnin threw him a wrinkled shirt. Ruben raised it to his chest and said, "My dad could wear this. Can I give it to him after the play is done?"

Mrs. Bunnin turned away in silence. Most of the actors didn't have speaking

"NOTHING'S WRONG. I CAN SEE."

WORDS TO KNOW

depleted (dĭ-plē′tĭd) *adj.* emptied; drained
deplete *v.* (p. 33)
prop (prŏp) *n.* an object an actor uses in a play (p. 33)
quiver (kwĭv′ər) *v.* to shake with a rapid trembling movement (p. 33)
relentless (rĭ-lĕnt′lĭs) *adj.* refusing to stop or give up (p. 33)
smirk (smûrk) *v.* to smile in an insulting, self-satisfied manner (p. 33)

Art Note

The Old and the New Year by Pablo Picasso Pablo Picasso (1881–1973) enjoyed a prolific career that spanned most of the 20th century and consisted of painting, sculpture, drawing, graphics, and ceramics. *The Old and the New Year* (1953), a product of Picasso's later career, illustrates the artist's ongoing fascination with what he saw as the universal child in all humans. The extravagant lines and bright colors of the painting express a sense of playfulness and childlike qualities, while the mask suggests the possibility of returning to childhood.

Reading the Art Based on what you have read of the selection, do you think that this painting accurately reflects the feeling of the story? If not, what kind of art do you think would be more fitting for the story?

CUSTOMIZING FOR
Gifted and Talented Students

Encourage them to find, as they read the selection, passages that show the ways Robert uses his imagination to visualize certain situations. Ask them to explain what Robert is trying to describe.

Possible responses:

- Page 31—"Belinda staring down the janitor's pit bull"; shows how tough Belinda was

- Page 34—"could wrestle the assassins and be on television"; shows Robert as the president's bodyguard

The Old and the New Year (1953), Pablo Picasso. Musée d'Art et d'Histoire, St. Denis, France. Giraudon/Art Resource, New York. © Copyright 1996 Artists Rights Society, New York/SPADEM, Paris.

32

Mini-Lesson — Literary Concepts

SLANG Remind students that slang is very informal, everyday speech, not the standard version of a language. Slang is usually spoken by a particular group of people at a particular time, such as teenagers when they are alone together. Many slang terms are either made-up words or existing words that have taken on new meanings.

Application Begin by having students identify and discuss how they use slang. Ask them under what circumstances they use slang words and phrases and why they use them. Then have them think about the different uses of slang that appear in "The School Play." For example, have them refer to the passages  on page 31. Ask them to identify slang that appears in the passages. Then ask them to rewrite the passages, using more formal language. Have students compare their version with the original.

32 THE LANGUAGE OF LITERATURE TEACHER'S EDITION

parts. They just got cutout crepe-paper snowflakes to pin to their shirts or crepe-paper leaves to wear.

During the blizzard in which Robert delivered his line, Belinda asked, "Is there something wrong with your eyes?" Robert looked at the audience, which at the moment was a classroom of empty chairs, a dented world globe that had been dropped by almost everyone, one limp flag, one wastebasket, and a picture of George Washington, whose eyes followed you around the room when you got up to sharpen your pencil. Robert answered, "Nothing's wrong. I can see."

Mrs. Bunnin, biting on the end of her pencil, said, "Louder, both of you."

Belinda stepped up, nostrils flaring so that the shadows on her nose quivered, and said louder, "Sucka, is there something wrong with your eyeballs?"

"Nothing's wrong. I can see."

"Louder! Make sure the audience can hear you," Mrs. Bunnin directed. She tapped her pencil hard against the desk. She scolded, "Robert, I'm not going to tell you again to quit fooling with the beard."

"It's itchy."

"We can't do anything about that. Actors need props. You're an actor. Now try again."

Robert and Belinda stood center stage as they waited for Mrs. Bunnin to call "Action!" When she did, Belinda approached Robert slowly. "Sucka face, is there anything wrong with your mug?" Belinda asked. Her eyes were squinted in anger. For a moment Robert saw his head grinding into the playground grass.

"Nothing's wrong. I can see."

"NOTHING'S WRONG. I CAN SEE."

Robert giggled behind his red beard. Belinda popped her gum and smirked. She stood with her hands on her hips.

"What? What did you say?" Mrs. Bunnin asked, pulling off her glasses. "Are you chewing gum, Belinda?"

"No, Mrs. Bunnin," Belinda lied. "I just forgot my lines."

Belinda turned to face the snowflake boys clumped together in the back. She rolled out her tongue, on which rested a ball of gray gum, depleted of sweetness under her relentless chomp. She whispered "sucka" and giggled so that her nose quivered dark shadows.

The play, *The Last Stand*, was about the Donner party just before they got hungry and started eating each other. Everyone who scored at least twelve out of fifteen on their spelling tests got to say at least one line. Everyone else had to stand and be trees or snowflakes.

Mrs. Bunnin wanted the play to be a success. She couldn't risk having kids with bad memories on stage. The nonspeaking trees and snowflakes stood humming snow flurries, blistering wind, and hail, which they produced by clacking their teeth.

Robert's mother was proud of him because he was living up to the legend of Robert De Niro,[1] for whom he was named. Over dinner he said, "Nothing's wrong. I can see," when his brother asked him to pass the dishtowel,

---

1. **Robert De Niro** (də nîr′ō): a well-known American movie actor.

WORDS TO KNOW

quiver (kwĭv′ər) *v.* to shake with a rapid trembling movement
prop (prŏp) *n.* an object an actor uses in a play
smirk (smûrk) *v.* to smile in an insulting, self-satisfied manner
depleted (dĭ-plē′tĭd) *adj.* emptied; drained **deplete** *v.*
relentless (rĭ-lĕnt′lĭs) *adj.* refusing to stop or give up

33

Mini-Lesson Grammar

QUOTATION MARKS Tell students that when they write a person's exact words, they are writing a quotation. Quotation marks are always placed before and after the direct quotation.

Using the highlighted passage above, point out that commas are used to set off explanatory words from direct quotations. In the first sentence, the explanatory words Robert said come before the quotation; therefore, a comma is placed after the last explanatory word.

Application Write the following sentences on the chalkboard. Have students provide the correct placement of quotation marks and commas.

1. She wiped her brow and said Thanks for the help, Robert. *(She wiped her brow and said, "Thanks for the help, Robert.")*
2. I won't Robert said as he walked away. *("I won't," Robert said as he walked away.)*

Reteaching/Reinforcement
- *Grammar Handbook*, anthology p. 851
- *Grammar Mini-Lessons* copymasters, p. 42, transparencies, p. 33

Other Uses for Commas, p. 578
Quotation Marks, pp. 586–588

Active Reading: CLARIFY

A Ask students to clarify what Robert means when he refers to the audience as "a classroom of empty chairs…" *(Possible responses: Robert is emphasizing the emptiness of the room; he imagines that his audience is made up of all the things in the room.)*

STRATEGIC READING FOR
Less-Proficient Readers

B Be sure that students understand who the main characters are and what they are going to do. Ask the following questions:

- Why is Robert nervous? *(He is afraid that he will forget his lines in the school play.)* Summarizing
- Why is Robert in the play? *(Mrs. Bunnin, his teacher, is making him perform.)* Making Inferences

Set a Purpose Ask students to pay special attention to details about Robert's friends and family and about the school play as they read the next section.

Linking to Science

 C Human beings can die of exposure to the cold in a few hours and of thirst in a few days, but they can survive without food for weeks.

CUSTOMIZING FOR
Multiple Learning Styles

D **Musical Learners** Ask students to review the description of the sounds made by the characters attempting to impersonate snow, wind, and hail. Have volunteers work in a group to perform their own version of the sounds of a snowstorm.

Critical Thinking: ANALYZING

E Ask students why the sentences "Nothing's wrong. I can see." are repeated throughout the selection. *(Possible responses: The sentences are repeated as many times as Robert says them; the sentences are repeated to emphasize Robert's repeated attempts to remember the lines; the sentences are repeated to give the readers a sense of the importance of these lines in Robert's life.)*

Literary Concept: SLANG

F Have students note Robert's use of the word *buck* to refer to the dollar bill he finds. Ask them to identify some other slang words used to refer to money. *(Possible responses: loot, dead presidents, dinero, greenbacks)*

CUSTOMIZING FOR
Students Acquiring English

2 If some students do not know what an enchilada is, you may want to have Hispanic students describe it. Explain that "with the works" means "with many toppings" and ask students what their favorite toppings are.

STRATEGIC READING FOR
Less-Proficient Readers

G Ask students to describe the subject of the school play. *(The school play is about the Donner party.)* **Noting Relevant Details**

Then have them explain how Robert acts with his family and friends. *(He repeats his lines from the play as a way of communicating with his family and his friend, David.)* **Making Generalizations**

Set a Purpose As students read further, they should pay attention to how Robert performs his lines in the play.

---

their communal napkin. His sister said, "It's your turn to do dishes," and he said, "Nothing's wrong. I can see." His dog, Queenie, begged him for more than water and a dog biscuit. He touched his dog's own hairy beard and said, "Nothing's wrong. I can see."

One warm spring night, Robert lay on his back in the backyard, counting shooting stars. He was up to three when David, a friend who was really his brother's friend, hopped the fence and asked, "What's the matter with you?"

"Nothing's wrong. I can see," Robert answered. He sat up, feeling good because the line came naturally, without much thought. He leaned back on his elbow and asked David what he wanted to be when he grew up.

"I don't know yet," David said, plucking at the grass. "Maybe a fighter pilot. What do you want to be?"

"I want to guard the president. I could wrestle the assassins and be on television. But I'd pin those dudes, and people would say, 'That's him, our hero.'" David plucked at a stalk of grass and thought deeply.

Robert thought of telling David that he really wanted to be someone with a supergreat memory, who could recall facts that most people thought were unimportant. He didn't know if there was such a job, but he thought it would be great to sit at home by the telephone waiting for scientists to call him and ask hard questions.

The three weeks passed quickly. The day before the play, Robert felt happy as he walked home from school with no homework. As he turned onto his street, he found a dollar floating over the currents of wind.

"A buck," he screamed to himself. He snapped it up and looked for others. But he didn't find any more. It was his lucky day,

though. At recess he had hit a home run on a fluke bunt—a fluke because the catcher had kicked the ball, another player had thrown it into center field, and the pitcher wasn't looking when Robert slowed down at third, then burst home with dust flying behind him.

That night, it was his sister's turn to do the dishes. They had eaten enchiladas with the works, so she slaved with suds up to her elbows. Robert bathed in bubble bath, the suds peaked high like the Donner Pass. He thought about how full he was and how those poor people had had nothing to eat but snow. I can live on nothing, he thought and whistled like wind through a mountain pass, raking flat the suds with his palm.

The next day, after lunch, he was ready for the play, red beard in hand and his one line trembling on his lips. Classes herded into the auditorium. As the actors dressed and argued about stepping on each other's feet, Robert stood near a cardboard barrel full of toys, whispering over and over to himself, "Nothing's wrong. I can see." He was hot, itchy, and confused when he tied on the beard. He sneezed when a strand of the beard entered his nostril. He said louder, "Nothing's wrong. I can see," but the words seemed to get caught in the beard. "Nothing, no, no. I can see great," he said louder, then under his breath because the words seemed wrong. "Nothing's wrong, can't you see? Nothing's wrong. I can see you." Worried, he approached Belinda and asked if she remembered his line. Balling her hand into a fist, Belinda warned, "Sucka, I'm gonna bury your ugly face in the ground if you mess up."

"I won't," Robert said as he walked away. He bit a nail and looked into the barrel of

> "NOTHING'S WRONG. I CAN SEE."

34 UNIT ONE PART 1: SEIZING THE MOMENT

Mini-Lesson | Reading Skills/Strategies

SUMMARIZING Explain to students that effective readers use certain skills as they read. Good readers use summarizing skills when they tell briefly, in their own words, the main idea of a piece of writing. Point out that when readers summarize, they condense their ideas or those of the writer into precise statements. They omit, or remove, any details that are unimportant.

Application Encourage students to record, as they read the selection, the story's main ideas and most important details in their notebooks. Then ask them to write one or two paragraphs summarizing the story. Discuss the differences between summaries to ensure that students understand how to condense ideas into clear and concise sentences.

Reteaching/Reinforcement
• *Unit One Resource Book,* p. 14

toys. A clown's mask stared back at him. He prayed that his line would come back to him. He would hate to disappoint his teacher and didn't like the thought of his face being rubbed into spiky grass.

The curtain parted slightly, and the principal came out smiling onto the stage. She said some words about pioneer history and then, stern faced, warned the audience not to scrape the chairs on the just-waxed floor. The principal then introduced Mrs. Bunnin, who told the audience about how they had rehearsed for weeks.

Meanwhile, the class stood quietly in place with lunchtime spaghetti on their breath. They were ready. Belinda had swallowed her gum because she knew this was for real. The

Closing Scene (1963), David Hockney. Oil on canvas, 48" × 48", © David Hockney.

THE SCHOOL PLAY **35**

Active Reading: PREDICT

H Have students note Robert's trouble with his beard and remembering his lines. Ask them to predict what will happen. You may wish to use the following model to give them ideas of how to put into words what they might be thinking about.

Think-Aloud Model *I really think that Robert is going to get stage fright and forget his lines. He already seems so nervous, and the play hasn't even begun yet! Belinda is no help either. Instead of helping him, she just threatens him and adds to pressure. It definitely looks like he will mess up.*

Critical Thinking: SPECULATING

I Have students speculate on what is meant by "lunchtime spaghetti on their breath." *(Possible responses: The play was taking place after lunch; the students were served spaghetti for lunch; their breath smelled like spaghetti.)*

Art Note

Closing Scene by David Hockney
David Hockney is a British artist known for his photography and painting. During the 1960s and 1970s, he used his paintings to explore his fascination with the theater. *Closing Scene* is an example of Hockney's interest in the theater and, in particular, with the theater curtain, which he saw as having a link to the artist's canvas.

Reading the Art Does the presence of the performer peeking out from behind the curtain suggest a sense of anticipation for an upcoming performance? If so, do you think that feeling is similar to the sense of anticipation felt by Robert?

Mini-Lesson The Writer's Style

CHOOSING THE RIGHT WORDS
Remind students that standard English follows the rules of grammar and usage. However, language can be formal or informal; for example, the use of contractions is an example of informal language. Some slang is so informal that it is considered to be nonstandard. Point out to students that throughout this selection, Soto uses informal English and slang. He has chosen to do so because this is appropriate for his audience and for his type of writing; it effectively communicates Robert's thoughts and experiences.

Application Have students study the chart for the differences between formal and informal language. Then have them write two versions of a letter describing Robert's experiences with Belinda: one to a close friend and one to Mrs. Bunnin.

Reteaching/Reinforcement
- *Writing Handbook*, anthology, pp. 772–773
- *Writing Mini-Lessons* transparencies, p. 36

Levels of Languages, pp. 274–275

	Formal	Informal
Characteristics	advanced vocabulary and long sentences	simple vocabulary and short sentences
Type of writing	report, business letter, speech	friendly letter, note to best friend
Tone	serious	casual

THE LANGUAGE OF LITERATURE **TEACHER'S EDITION 35**

Active Reading: EVALUATE

J Have students discuss their opinions of Alfonso's view that the Donner party would feel sorry for what they had done.

CUSTOMIZING FOR
Gifted and Talented Students

K Ask students why Belinda acts the way she does. Do they think it's because she is as tough as Robert says and is not afraid of disobeying her teacher? Or do they think that Belinda likes the attention she receives from other students? Challenge students to debate possible motives for Belinda's behavior.

Literary Concept: SLANG

L Ask students what Alfonso means by "suck it up in bad times." *(Possible responses: You have to suffer through the bad times to get to the good; you have to be tough during hard times.)*

STRATEGIC READING FOR
Less-Proficient Readers

M Have students explain what happens during the play. *(Robert succeeds in saying his lines, but not in the correct order. Belinda only pinches him rather than hitting him, and Mrs. Bunnin thinks that his performance was "almost perfect.")* Summarizing

---

COMPREHENSION CHECK

1. To whom did Robert have to recite his lines in the school play? *(Belinda Lopez, one of the toughest girls in the class)*
2. What was the play about? *(the Donner party)*
3. Why does Robert repeat his lines again and again? *(He's afraid he's going to forget them.)*
4. What happened during the play? *(Robert spoke the words in the wrong order.)*

EDITOR'S NOTE With the permission of the author or copyright holder, and in accordance with certain state and district guidelines, brand names have been deleted to avoid inadvertent endorsement of a product.

---

snowflakes clumped together and began howling.

Robert retied his beard. Belinda, smoothing her skirt, looked at him and said, "If you know what's good for you, you'd better do it right." Robert grew nervous when the curtain parted and his classmates who were assigned to do snow, wind, and hail broke into song.

Alfonso stepped forward with his narrative about a blot on American history that would live with us forever. He looked at the audience, lost for a minute. He continued by saying that if the Donner party could come back, hungry from not eating for over a hundred years, they would be sorry for what they had done.

The play began with some boys in snowshoes shuffling around the stage, muttering that the blizzard would cut them off from civilization. They looked up, held out their hands, and said in unison, "Snow." One stepped center stage and said, "I wish I had never left the prairie." Another one said, "California is just over there." He pointed, and some of the first graders looked in the direction of the piano.

"What are we going to do?" one kid asked, brushing pretend snow off his vest.

"I'm getting pretty hungry," another said, rubbing her stomach.

The audience seemed to be following the play. A ribbon of sweat ran down Robert's face. When his scene came up, he staggered to center stage and dropped to the floor, just as Mrs. Bunnin had said, just as he had seen Robert De Niro do in that movie about a boxer. Belinda, bending over with an "Oh, my," yanked him up so hard that something clicked in his elbow. She boomed, "Is there anything wrong with your eyes?"

Robert rubbed his elbow, then his eyes, and said, "I can see nothing wrong. Wrong is nothing, I can see."

"How are we going to get through?" she boomed, wringing her hands together at the audience, some of whom had their mouths taped shut because they were known talkers. "My husband needs a doctor." The drama advanced through snow, wind, and hail that sounded like chattering teeth.

Belinda turned to Robert and muttered, "You mess-up. You're gonna hate life."

But Robert thought he'd done okay. At least, he reasoned to himself, I got the words right. Just not in the right order.

With his part of the play done, he joined the snowflakes and trees, chattering his teeth the loudest. He howled wind like a baying hound and snapped his fingers furiously in a snow flurry. He trembled from the cold.

The play ended with Alfonso saying that if they came back to life, the Donner party would be sorry for eating each other. "It's just not right," he argued. "You gotta suck it up in bad times."

Robert figured that Alfonso was right. He remembered how one day his sister had locked him in the closet and he didn't eat or drink for five hours. When he got out, he hit his sister, but not so hard as to leave a bruise. He then ate three sandwiches and felt a whole lot better.

The cast then paraded up the aisle into the audience. Belinda pinched Robert hard, but only once because she was thinking that it could have been worse. As he passed a smiling and relieved Mrs. Bunnin, she patted Robert's shoulder and said, "Almost perfect."

Robert was happy. He'd made it through without passing out from fear. Now the first and second graders were looking at him and clapping. He was sure everyone wondered who the actor was behind that smooth voice and red, red beard. ❖

"NOTHING'S WRONG. I CAN SEE."

36 UNIT ONE PART 1: SEIZING THE MOMENT

Mini-Lesson Genre Study

FICTION Remind students that fiction is literature that tells about imaginary people, places, or events. Fiction can take the form of both short stories and novels. "The School Play," like Sue Alexander's "Nadia the Willful," is an example of a **short story**—a work of fiction that can generally be read in one sitting. Short stories have characters, plot, setting, and theme, as do most other works of fiction. The plot of the story usually involves one main conflict or situation.

Application Have students copy the web on this page into their notebooks. Ask them to refer to it to identify the different aspects of "The School Play."

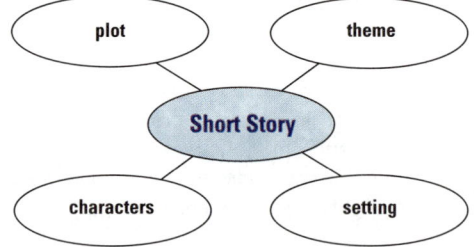

36 THE LANGUAGE OF LITERATURE TEACHER'S EDITION

RESPONDING OPTIONS

FROM PERSONAL RESPONSE TO CRITICAL ANALYSIS

REFLECT
1. In your notebook or on a sheet of paper, describe your impressions of the characters in this story.

RETHINK
2. What is your opinion about the way Robert delivers his lines?

3. Near the end of *The Last Stand*, Alfonso, the narrator, says, "You gotta suck it up in bad times." How well do you think Robert lives up to that statement?

Close Textual Reading
Consider
- how he behaves at home
- what happens to him the day before the performance
- how he behaves backstage just before the play begins

4. In your opinion, does Belinda Lopez take her part in the play as seriously as Robert does? Use evidence from the story to support your answer.

Thematic Link
5. What effects might Robert's acting experience have on the way he faces risks or challenges in the future? Explain.

RELATE
6. Stage fright strikes many people who run the risk of speaking or performing in public. With a partner or a small group of classmates, discuss the ideas about public speaking that you wrote for the Writing Connection on page 30 and some useful ways of dealing with this fear.

Multimodal Learning
ANOTHER PATHWAY

Draw a comic strip to illustrate the events in "The School Play." You can use actual lines from the story in the characters' speech balloons. Draw as many frames as necessary to show the major events in the story. Be sure that you present them in the order in which they occur.

QUICKWRITES

1. What if tryouts were announced for an all-school play in Robert's school? Do you think Robert would try out for a part? Draft an **essay** explaining your answer.

2. Pretend you are a critic for the school newspaper, seeing the performance of *The Last Stand*. What are your reactions to the acting, the costumes, and the set? Use your imagination and information from the story to write a **review** of the performance.

📁 **PORTFOLIO** *Save your writing. You may want to use it later as a springboard to a piece for your portfolio.*

LITERARY CONCEPTS

The people, animals, or imaginary creatures that take part in the action of a story are called **characters.** Usually a story has one main character, who is the focus of the action, and a number of minor characters. Identify the main character of "The School Play" and explain how he or she is the focus of the action. Then list a few of the minor characters and explain their importance to the story. Compare your list with a classmate's list.

THE SCHOOL PLAY 37

From Personal Response to Critical Analysis

1. Encourage students to refer to specific events in the story to illustrate their impressions.
2. Possible responses: Some students may agree that Robert's performance was "almost perfect." Other students might say that Robert's performance was not good enough and that it detracted from the play.
3. Possible responses: Some students may say that Robert succeeds in living up to that statement because he memorized and performed his lines even though he was nervous. Others may point out that Robert's behavior was affected by his nervousness.
4. Possible responses: Some students may say that Belinda takes her part in the play more seriously than Robert does because she continually threatens to harm Robert if he doesn't do a good job. Others may feel that Robert's desire to do well and his nervousness indicate how seriously he takes his part in the play.
5. Possible response: Robert's experiences teach him that there is nothing to be feared in facing challenges or risks. He learns that the consequences of messing up are not as bad as he imagined.
6. Responses will vary.

Another Pathway
Cooperative Learning Have students work with partners. In each pair, one student can be the designated illustrator, and the other can be responsible for writing the lines from the story in the speech balloons. Students should agree on and prepare a plan, outline the events they wish to include, and make sure that the events are in the right order.

Rubric
3 Full Accomplishment Students have successfully collaborated on a comic strip that reflects the major events and main characters.
2 Substantial Accomplishment Story correlates fairly well with plot and characterization of original version. Illustrations lack organization.
1 Little or Partial Accomplishment Comic strip shows lack of collaboration and does not relate to original events or characters.

Literary Concepts
Students should recognize that the main character in the story is Robert, and that events in the story are told from his perspective. The minor characters might include Belinda, Mrs. Bunnin, and David. You may wish to refer students to the following excerpts from the selection and ask them to list the character, his or her relationship to Robert, and what part he or she plays in the story.
- Page 31—"Belinda was one of the toughest girls since the beginning of the world."
- Page 34—"David plucked at a stalk of grass and thought deeply."

QuickWrites
1. Encourage students to list all the instances from the story of Robert's thoughts on performing in the school play. Then ask them to formulate outlines that list their opinions and to provide examples from the story to support the opinions.
2. Have students refer to The Writer's Style Mini-Lesson on Choosing the Right Words (page 35). Ask them to decide whether their reviews should be written in formal or informal language.

📁 **The Writer's Craft**
Personal Response, pp. 142–155

THE LANGUAGE OF LITERATURE TEACHER'S EDITION 37

Words to Know

Exercise A
1. Incorrect
2. Correct
3. Incorrect
4. Incorrect
5. Incorrect

Exercise B
Students may need a demonstration of a *quiver* and a *smirk* before beginning this exercise.

Reteaching/Reinforcement
• Unit One Resource Book, p. 15

Across the Curriculum

History *Cooperative Learning*
Encourage one or two students to organize and track the individual assignments and collected information. You may want to assign work based on finding information and organizing the information for display. You may also have spatial learners choose and prepare any visuals that the class wants to include.

ADDITIONAL SUGGESTION

Social Studies *Survivors* Students interested in the Donner party's struggle to survive may enjoy researching other real-life incidents of people surviving against great odds. Encourage students to use a variety of media resources: first-person narratives, documentary films and videos, newspapers, and TV news.

Gary Soto

On the quality of his writing, Soto has observed, "I think I'm very childlike, and I often write youthful poems. It's sort of a silly act, writing itself.... I like the youth in my poetry, sort of a craziness. For me that's really important. I don't want to take a dreary look at the world."

AUTHOR BACKGROUND
Gary Soto In this interview, the author Gary Soto tells of the influences that led him into the world of poetry.

Side A, Frame 744

ACROSS THE CURRICULUM

History As a class, research the Donner party. Some students might investigate the preparations pioneers made before starting their journey. Others might focus on the writings of such pioneers or the attempts to rescue the Donner party. Use the information you gather to set up a display for your classroom.

Multimodal Learning

ALTERNATIVE ACTIVITIES

Cooperative Learning In a **Readers Theater** production, performers present a work of literature by reading it aloud, almost as if it were the script of a play. Form teams to plan a Readers Theater production of "The School Play," with each team working on a specific part of the story. Teams should decide how to make the performance work as theater. For example, is a narrator needed? Should parts be deleted or rearranged? Present your finished production to another class.

WORDS TO KNOW

EXERCISE A Decide whether the boldfaced Word to Know is used correctly in each sentence below. On your paper, write *Correct* or *Incorrect*. Explain why the incorrectly used words are wrong.

1. We could hear the confident actor's voice **quiver** as he spoke.
2. Seeing her archenemy forget her lines during the performance caused one student to **smirk**.
3. Pioneers used **props** to hold up their wagons.
4. If the supply of artificial snowflakes is **depleted**, the snowflakes are plentiful.
5. A **relentless** round of applause ends quickly.

EXERCISE B "Nothing's wrong. I can see," are the lines Robert speaks again and again in "The School Play." Now *you're* on. Taking turns with a partner, recite Robert's lines in the following ways:

1. Speak the lines with a **quiver** in your voice.
2. **Smirk** as you speak the lines.

GARY SOTO

1952–

Recalling his school days, Gary Soto says, "I was no good at school. I could not sing, do art, or figure out math problems. I was deathly scared of the stage, yet jealous when my friends got up on the stage and sang with gusto." He later graduated *magna cum laude*—with high honors—from California State University. Soto is now a teacher of English and Chicano studies at the University of California, Berkeley.

A native of Fresno, California, Soto writes about the experiences of Mexican Americans. He first became known as a poet, having become drawn to poetry during his college years. His first book, *The Elements of San Joaquin,* consisted of poems dealing with memories of his childhood. This work won the U.S. Award of the International Poetry Forum. Other poetry collections followed, including *The Tale of Sunlight, Where Sparrows Work Hard,* and *Black Hair.*

Among young readers, Soto is best known for his short story collections, which have been praised for their fresh, childlike quality.

OTHER WORKS *Local News, Neighborhood Odes, Baseball in April and Other Stories, A Summer Life*

Extended Reading

• AUTHOR BACKGROUND

38 UNIT ONE PART 1: SEIZING THE MOMENT

Alternative Activities

Have the class as a whole devise an overall plan for their production, breaking down the story into parts, deciding whether to delete parts of the story, assessing whether a narrator is needed, and discussing whether any other decisions should be made to give the production uniformity. Then have the students work in small groups. Encourage groups to further divide their story part into smaller parts and roles for each group member. Remind groups that each member should have an assignment. Give students time to rehearse their roles. Have students get suggestions from other groups before they present the production to another classroom.

PREVIEWING

FICTION

Ghost of the Lagoon
Armstrong Sperry

PERSONAL CONNECTION *Activating Prior Knowledge*

Think of someone you know or have read about who has been courageous, who has taken risks. Describe what he or she did and why. Compare this person's experience with the experience of Mako, the main character in this story.

GEOGRAPHICAL CONNECTION *Building Background*

This story of danger and courage is set on Bora Bora, a small volcanic island in the southern Pacific Ocean. Ancient volcanoes on the island form many high peaks, making the land rough and mountainous. Bora Bora is surrounded by coral reefs, underwater ridges of stone produced by colonies of small animals. Bora Bora also has a large lagoon on its western side. A lagoon is a shallow body of water separated from the sea by sandbars or reefs.

The Polynesians who live on the island grow coconuts, sugar cane, rice, and tropical fruits, such as oranges and bananas. The islanders also collect mother-of-pearl, the shiny inner layer of some mollusk shells, and use this to make decorative objects. The islanders often use canoes to travel from one part of the island to another, because it is faster to travel by canoe than it is to walk.

READING CONNECTION *Active Reading*

Visualizing When you visualize something, you use your imagination to form a picture of it in your mind. To appreciate the elements of danger and suspense in "Ghost of the Lagoon," try to visualize the setting and the action as the author describes them. Imagine seeing the green water of the lagoon and the darkness of the night on Bora Bora.

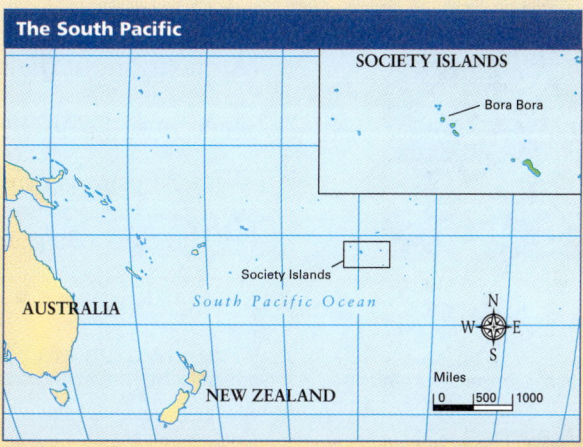

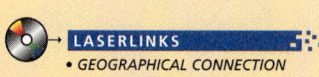
• GEOGRAPHICAL CONNECTION

GHOST OF THE LAGOON **39**

OVERVIEW

Objectives
- To understand and appreciate a classic short story about a life-or-death struggle
- To enrich reading by visualizing
- To identify and understand conflict as an element of plot
- To express understanding of the story through a choice of writing forms, including a narrative, a tribute, and a tall tale
- To extend understanding of the story through a variety of multimodal and cross-curricular activities

Skills

READING SKILLS/ STRATEGIES
- Visualizing
- Predicting

LITERARY CONCEPTS
- Plot
- Conflict
- Setting

THE WRITER'S STYLE
- Details appealing to sight

GRAMMAR
- Capitalization of proper nouns

SPELLING
- The vowel sound o͞o

SPEAKING, LISTENING, AND VIEWING
- Oral history
- Group discussion
- Oral presentation

Cross-Curricular Connections

SCIENCE
- Phosphorus
- Coral Reefs
- Sharks

GEOGRAPHY
- Tahiti
- South Seas cruise

 **GEOGRAPHICAL CONNECTION**
Polynesia "Ghost of the Lagoon" is set in the tropical Pacific, among the islands known as Polynesia. These images will help students understand the geography of Polynesia, as well as the kinds of boats and housing used by Polynesians.

Side A, Frame 38602

PRINT AND MEDIA RESOURCES

UNIT ONE RESOURCE BOOK
Strategic Reading: Literature, p. 19
Vocabulary SkillBuilder, p. 22
Reading SkillBuilder, p. 20
Spelling SkillBuilder, p. 21

GRAMMAR MINI–LESSONS
Transparencies, p. 25
Copymasters, p. 33

WRITING MINI–LESSONS
Transparencies, p. 38

ACCESS FOR STUDENTS ACQUIRING ENGLISH
Selection Summaries
Reading and Writing Support

FORMAL ASSESSMENT
Selection Test, pp. 9–10
 Test Generator

 **AUDIO LIBRARY**
See Reference Card

LASERLINKS
Geographical Connection
Science Connection
Art Gallery

THE LANGUAGE OF LITERATURE TEACHER'S EDITION **39**

Ghost of the Lagoon

by Armstrong Sperry

© Cheryl Cooper 1995

SUMMARY

Growing up on the island of Bora Bora, Mako has heard many legends about Tupa, the "white ghost of the lagoon." But the most haunting tale of all is the one Mako's grandfather tells about Tupa's killing of Mako's father. Mako swears that he will get even with Tupa someday, not realizing how soon his chance will come. The next afternoon, Mako and his dog, Afa, journey by canoe across the lagoon to collect fruit from a small island. It is nearly nightfall when Mako begins to paddle homeward. As he passes the coral reef where Tupa is supposed to live, a glowing white fin surfaces. It is Tupa, the great white shark, who begins to circle the boat. When Afa accidentally falls from the canoe, the shark charges. Putting all fear aside, Mako rescues his dog by killing the shark with a spear, then returns home a hero.

Thematic Link: *Seizing the Moment*
When his dog is threatened by Tupa, the great white shark, Mako risks his life and seizes the moment to rid Bora Bora of the ghost of the lagoon.

CUSTOMIZING FOR
Students Acquiring English

- Use **ACCESS FOR STUDENTS ACQUIRING ENGLISH,** *Reading and Writing Support.*
- If any students are from the Pacific Islands or other island cultures, ask them to contribute background information about the setting and any other information they believe to be appropriate.

STRATEGIC READING FOR
Less-Proficient Readers

Set a Purpose To draw students into the selection, have them sketch the lagoon described in the passage highlighted on page 40. Then ask them to read on to learn more about Mako and his family.

Use **UNIT ONE RESOURCE BOOK,** pp. 19–20, for guidance in reading the selection.

The island of Bora Bora, where Mako lived, is far away in the South Pacific. It is not a large island—you can paddle around it in a single day—but the main body of it rises straight out of the sea, very high into the air, like a castle. Waterfalls trail down the faces of the cliffs. As you look upward, you see wild goats leaping from crag to crag.

WORDS TO KNOW

expedition (ĕk'spĭ-dĭsh'ən) *n.* a journey with a goal or purpose (p. 44)
harpoon (här-pōōn') *n.* a spearlike weapon used to hunt large fish (p. 41)
lagoon (lə-gōōn') *n.* a shallow body of water separated from a sea by sandbars or coral reefs (p. 41)
phosphorus (fŏs'fər-əs) *n.* a substance that glows with a yellowish or white light (p. 45)
reef (rēf) *n.* a ridge of rocks, sand, or coral near the surface of water (p. 41)

40 THE LANGUAGE OF LITERATURE TEACHER'S EDITION

Mako had been born on the very edge of the sea, and most of his waking hours were spent in the waters of the lagoon, which was nearly enclosed by the two outstretched arms of the island. He was very clever with his hands; he had made a harpoon that was as straight as an arrow and tipped with five pointed iron spears. He had made a canoe, hollowing it out of a tree. It wasn't a very big canoe—only a little longer than his own height. It had an outrigger, a sort of balancing pole, fastened to one side to keep the boat from tipping over. The canoe was just large enough to hold Mako and his little dog, Afa. They were great companions, these two.

One evening Mako lay stretched at full length on the pandanus mats, listening to Grandfather's voice. Overhead, stars shone in the dark sky. From far off came the thunder of the surf on the reef.

The old man was speaking of Tupa, the ghost of the lagoon. Ever since the boy could remember, he had heard tales of this terrible monster. Frightened fishermen, returning from the reef at midnight, spoke of the ghost. Over the evening fires, old men told endless tales about the monster.

Tupa seemed to think the lagoon of Bora Bora belonged to him. The natives left presents of food for him out on the reef: a dead goat, a chicken, or a pig. The presents

WORDS TO KNOW
lagoon (lə-gōōn′) *n.* a shallow body of water separated from a sea by sandbars or coral reefs
harpoon (här-pōōn′) *n.* a spearlike weapon used to hunt large fish
reef (rēf) *n.* a ridge of rocks, sand, or coral near the surface of water

CUSTOMIZING FOR
Gifted and Talented Students
Point out the title of the story. Have students discuss circumstances in which an event or person can become legendary. If necessary, explain that a legend is a story about a real person or event, that it is handed down from generation to generation, and that it is believed to be untrue by some people. How might the passage of time and generations of retelling affect the truth?

Literary Concept: SETTING
A Have students note that Mako lives by the sea. Ask them to suggest things they would like to do and see in the seaside setting as it has been described up to this point. (*Possible responses: boating, exploring, swimming, hiking, climbing, observing animals, hunting, or fishing.*)

CUSTOMIZING FOR
Multiple Learning Styles
B Spatial or Graphic Learners
Have students create drawings of Mako's canoe based on the way it is described in the story. Explain that an outrigger is a bar that is parallel to and connected to one side of the boat to provide support, like training wheels on a bicycle. Encourage them to include Mako and Afa in the sketch in order to indicate the scale.

Active Reading: EVALUATE
C Point out to students that Tupa is referred to as both a "ghost" and a "monster." Ask them to discuss what they think Tupa really is. (*Possible responses: a ghost; something from the sea that scares people; a fish; a monster*)

Mini-Lesson   Literary Concepts

REVIEWING SETTING Remind students that the setting is the time and the place in which the story happens. The time may be past, present, or future. The place can be real or imaginary. Also point out that in some stories the setting may not be clearly defined, whereas in other stories, such as "Nadia the Willful," the setting plays an important role.

Application Invite students to think about the importance of the setting in "Ghost of the Lagoon." For example, direct them to the passage highlighted on page 40 for a description of the setting. Ask students to make a list of other details of the setting from the story. Then have them discuss whether they think the setting plays an important role in "Ghost of the Lagoon."

THE LANGUAGE OF LITERATURE TEACHER'S EDITION **41**

Art Note

Tahitian Woman and Boy by Paul Gauguin Paul Gauguin (1848–1903) was a French artist who was fascinated by the island of Tahiti. In its people he saw communal values and a closer understanding of nature, which he felt sharply contrasted with the values of the French people. Gauguin enhanced his realistic paintings with his imagination and often used colors symbolically in order to communicate what he saw as the spiritual nature of tribal life.

Reading the Art *Why do you think Gauguin chose to use such bright and bold colors? How do you think the people depicted in this painting differ from the people Gauguin encountered during his early career as a banker in Paris?*

Linking to Geography

 Tahiti, located in the South Pacific, is the largest of the Society Islands, the same island group to which Bora Bora belongs. Formerly a French colony, Tahiti now is part of French Polynesia. Tahiti is located approximately 200 miles southeast of Bora Bora and is a much larger island, measuring 388 square miles to Bora Bora's 15 square miles.

Tahitian Woman and Boy (1889), Paul Gauguin. Oil on canvas, 37¼″ × 24¼″, Norton Simon Art Foundation, Pasadena, California. Gift of Mr. Norton Simon, 1976.

42 UNIT ONE PART 1: SEIZING THE MOMENT

Mini-Lesson  Reading Skills/Strategies

ACTIVE READING: PREDICTING Explain to students that active readers use certain strategies as they read. Readers use predicting strategies when trying to figure out what will happen next in a story and how the selection might end.

Application Encourage students to record their predictions, as they read the selection, in a chart like the one shown. Remind them to include the actual events of the story as well as their predictions.

Reteaching/Reinforcement
• *Unit One Resource Book*, p. 20

Situation	Prediction	Actual Event
Mako imagines meeting Tupa.	Mako will meet Tupa.	Mako meets Tupa.
Mako will have to decide whether to fight.	Mako will let Tupa go.	Mako kills Tupa.

42 THE LANGUAGE OF LITERATURE TEACHER'S EDITION

always disappeared mysteriously, but everyone felt sure that it was Tupa who carried them away. Still, in spite of all this food, the nets of the fishermen were torn during the night, the fish stolen. What an appetite Tupa seemed to have!

Not many people had ever seen the ghost of the lagoon. Grandfather was one of the few who had.

"What does he really look like, Grandfather?" the boy asked, for the hundredth time.

The old man shook his head solemnly. The light from the cook fire glistened on his white hair. "Tupa lives in the great caves of the reef. He is longer than this house. There is a sail on his back, not large but terrible to see, for it burns with a white fire. Once, when I was fishing beyond the reef at night, I saw him come up right under another canoe—"

"What happened then?" Mako asked. He half rose on one elbow. This was a story he had not heard before.

The old man's voice dropped to a whisper. "Tupa dragged the canoe right under the water—and the water boiled with white flame. The three fishermen in it were never seen again. Fine swimmers they were, too."

Grandfather shook his head. "It is bad fortune even to speak of Tupa. There is evil in his very name."

"But King Opu Nui has offered a reward for his capture," the boy pointed out.

"Thirty acres of fine coconut land, and a sailing canoe as well," said the old man. "But who ever heard of laying hands on a ghost?"

Mako's eyes glistened. "Thirty acres of land and a sailing canoe. How I should love to win that reward!"

Grandfather nodded, but Mako's mother scolded her son for such foolish talk. "Be quiet now, son, and go to sleep. Grandfather has told you that it is bad fortune to speak of Tupa. Alas, how well we have learned that lesson! Your father—" She stopped herself.

"What of my father?" the boy asked quickly. And now he sat up straight on the mats.

"Tell him, Grandfather," his mother whispered.

The old man cleared his throat and poked at the fire. A little shower of sparks whirled up into the darkness.

"Your father," he explained gently, "was one of the three fishermen in the canoe that Tupa destroyed." His words fell upon the air like stones dropped into a deep well.

Mako shivered. He brushed back the hair from his damp forehead. Then he squared his shoulders and cried fiercely, "I shall slay Tupa and win the king's reward!" He rose to his knees, his slim body tense, his eyes flashing in the firelight.

"Hush!" his mother said. "Go to sleep now. Enough of such foolish talk. Would you bring trouble upon us all?"

Mako lay down again upon the mats. He rolled over on his side and closed his eyes, but sleep was long in coming.

The palm trees whispered above the dark lagoon, and far out on the reef the sea thundered.

The boy was slow to wake up the next morning. The ghost of Tupa had played through his dreams, making him restless. And so it was almost noon before Mako sat up on the mats and stretched himself. He called Afa, and the boy and his dog ran down to the lagoon for their morning swim.

GHOST OF THE LAGOON 43

Mini-Lesson  Grammar

CAPITALIZATION OF PROPER NOUNS
Remind students that a proper noun names a specific person, place, or thing. A proper noun may be made up of one or more words. All important words should be capitalized in proper nouns, for example, Bora Bora. Write the following examples on the chalkboard to emphasize the difference between proper and common nouns. Explain that common nouns refer to general—not specific—persons, places, or things.

Application Invite students to find the proper nouns in the passage  on page 43. (*Grandfather, Tupa, King Opu Nui, Mako*) Then write the following sentences on the board and ask students which words should be capitalized.
1. tupa seemed to think the Lagoon of bora bora belonged to him. (*Tupa seemed to think the lagoon of Bora Bora belonged to him.*)
2. i shall slay tupa! (*I shall slay Tupa!*)

Reteaching/Reinforcement
- *Grammar Handbook*, anthology pp. 839–841
- *Grammar Mini-Lessons* copymasters, p. 33, transparencies, p. 25

The Writer's Craft
Proper Names and Proper Adjectives, pp. 548–549

Common Nouns	Proper Nouns
island	Bora Bora
dog	Afa
boy	Mako

CUSTOMIZING FOR
Multiple Learning Styles

H **Intrapersonal Learners** Ask students to record their opinions of Mako in their notebooks. Have them consider Mako's response to learning about how his father died as well as his ability to run errands for his mother.

CUSTOMIZING FOR
Students Acquiring English

3 The word *bow* has several meanings, but is used here to mean "the front of a boat."

4 Ask students to try to figure out the meaning of "times without number." *(too many times to count)*

STRATEGIC READING FOR
Less-Proficient Readers

I Ask students to describe what Mako learned from his grandfather's story and what he vowed on hearing it. *(Mako's father was one of three fishermen killed by Tupa. Mako vowed to kill Tupa.)* **Noting Sequence of Events**

Set a Purpose Tell students to pay special attention to details of the setting as they read.

Literary Concept: PLOT

J Explain to students that the large initial letter marks a division in the organization of the story. Information given up to this point will lead to further action. Ask students to recall in general terms what has happened so far. *(The scene has been set; the tales told; the reward stated; a promise made; an expedition undertaken.)*

When they returned to the house, wide-awake and hungry, Mako's mother had food ready and waiting.

"These are the last of our bananas," she told him. "I wish you would paddle out to the reef this afternoon and bring back a new bunch."

The boy agreed eagerly. Nothing pleased him more than such an errand, which would take him to a little island on the outer reef, half a mile from shore. It was one of Mako's favorite playgrounds, and there bananas and oranges grew in great plenty.

"Come, Afa," he called, gulping the last mouthful. "We're going on an expedition." He picked up his long-bladed knife and seized his spear. A minute later, he dashed across the white sand, where his canoe was drawn up beyond the water's reach.

Afa barked at his heels. He was all white except for a black spot over each eye. Wherever Mako went, there went Afa also. Now the little dog leaped into the bow of the canoe, his tail wagging with delight. The boy shoved the canoe into the water and climbed aboard. Then, picking up his paddle, he thrust it into the water. The canoe shot ahead. Its sharp bow cut through the green water of the lagoon like a knife through cheese. And so clear was the water that Mako could see the coral gardens, forty feet below him, growing in the sand. The shadow of the canoe moved over them.

A school of fish swept by like silver arrows. He saw scarlet rock cod with ruby eyes and the head of a conger eel peering out from a cavern in the coral. The boy thought suddenly of Tupa, ghost of the lagoon. On such a bright day it was hard to believe in ghosts of any sort. The fierce sunlight drove away all thought of them. Perhaps ghosts were only old men's stories, anyway!

Mako's eyes came to rest upon his spear—the spear that he had made with his own hands—the spear that was as straight and true as an arrow. He remembered his vow of the night before. Could a ghost be killed with a spear? Some night, when all the village was sleeping, Mako swore to himself that he would find out! He would paddle out to the reef and challenge Tupa! Perhaps tonight. Why not? He caught his breath at the thought. A shiver ran down his back. His hands were tense on the paddle.

> **Perhaps ghosts were only old men's stories, anyway!**

As the canoe drew away from shore, the boy saw the coral reef that, above all others, had always interested him. It was of white coral—a long slim shape that rose slightly above the surface of the water. It looked very much like a shark. There was a ridge on the back that the boy could pretend was a dorsal fin, while up near one end were two dark holes that looked like eyes!

Times without number the boy had practiced spearing this make-believe shark, aiming always for the eyes, the most vulnerable spot. So true and straight had his aim become that the spear would pass right into the eyeholes without even touching the sides of the coral. Mako had named the coral reef Tupa.

This morning, as he paddled past it, he shook his fist and called, "Ho, Mister Tupa! Just wait till I get my bananas. When I come back, I'll make short work of you!"

Afa followed his master's words with a sharp bark. He knew Mako was excited about something.

WORDS TO KNOW
expedition (ĕk′spĭ-dĭsh′ən) *n.* a journey with a goal or purpose

44

 **Mini-Lesson**   **The Writer's Style**

Sight Words			
Fast Movements	**Slow Movements**	**Appearance**	**Shapes**
scamper	crawl	spotted	wavy
trot	drag	striped	flat
spring	sneak	shiny	round
dash	waddle	freckled	lean
zoom	saunter	glowing	skinny
dive	plod	bright	ruffled

DETAILS APPEALING TO SIGHT
Point out to students that good writers are also good observers. They look at the world around them and write details that paint vivid pictures in readers' minds. When writers want readers to "see" or visualize a scene, they often use sight words to describe a scene more vividly.

Application Invite students to find examples of sight words in the highlighted passage. Then refer them to the list of sight words at left and have them use words from the list to write a short paragraph describing Afa playing on the beach.

Reteaching/Reinforcement
- Writing Handbook, anthology pp. 784–785
- *Writing Mini-Lessons* transparencies, p. 38

Appealing to the Senses, pp. 266–275

The bow of the canoe touched the sand of the little island where the bananas grew. Afa leaped ashore and ran barking into the jungle, now on this trail, now on that. Clouds of sea birds whirled from their nests into the air with angry cries.

Mako climbed into the shallow water, waded ashore, and pulled his canoe up on the beach. Then, picking up his banana knife, he followed Afa. In the jungle the light was so dense and green that the boy felt as if he were moving underwater. Ferns grew higher than his head. The branches of the trees formed a green roof over him. A flock of parakeets fled on swift wings. Somewhere a wild pig crashed through the undergrowth while Afa dashed away in pursuit. Mako paused anxiously. Armed only with his banana knife, he had no desire to meet the wild pig. The pig, it seemed, had no desire to meet him, either.

Then, ahead of him, the boy saw the broad green blades of a banana tree. A bunch of bananas, golden ripe, was growing out of the top.

At the foot of the tree he made a nest of soft leaves for the bunch to fall upon. In this way the fruit wouldn't be crushed. Then with a swift slash of his blade he cut the stem. The bananas fell to the earth with a dull thud. He found two more bunches.

Then he thought, "I might as well get some oranges while I'm here. Those little rusty ones are sweeter than any that grow on Bora Bora."

So he set about making a net out of palm leaves to carry the oranges. As he worked, his swift fingers moving in and out among the strong green leaves, he could hear Afa's excited barks off in the jungle. That was just like Afa, always barking at something: a bird, a fish, a wild pig. He never caught anything, either. Still, no boy ever had a finer companion.

The palm net took longer to make than Mako had realized. By the time it was finished and filled with oranges, the jungle was dark and gloomy. Night comes quickly and without warning in the islands of the tropics.

Mako carried the fruit down to the shore and loaded it into the canoe. Then he whistled to Afa. The dog came bounding out of the bush, wagging his tail.

"Hurry!" Mako scolded. "We won't be home before the dark comes."

The little dog leaped into the bow of the canoe, and Mako came aboard. Night seemed to rise up from the surface of the water and swallow them. On the distant shore of Bora Bora, cook fires were being lighted. The first star twinkled just over the dark mountains. Mako dug his paddle into the water, and the canoe leaped ahead.

The dark water was alive with phosphorus. The bow of the canoe seemed to cut through a pale liquid fire. Each dip of the paddle trailed streamers of light. As the canoe approached the coral reef, the boy called, "Ho, Tupa! It's too late tonight to teach you your lesson. But I'll come back tomorrow." The coral shark glistened in the darkness.

And then, suddenly, Mako's breath caught in his throat. His hands felt weak. Just beyond the fin of the coral Tupa, there was another fin—a huge one. It had never been there before. And—could he believe his eyes? It was moving.

The boy stopped paddling. He dashed his hand across his eyes. Afa began to bark furiously. The great white fin, shaped like a small sail, glowed with phosphorescent light. Then Mako knew. Here was Tupa—the real Tupa—ghost of the lagoon!

WORDS TO KNOW
phosphorus (fŏs′fər-əs) *n.* a substance that glows with a yellowish or white light

---

Mini-Lesson: Speaking,  Listening, and Viewing

ORAL HISTORY Explain to students that oral history is different from written history because it is communicated through speaking rather than writing. Oral histories, like the stories Grandfather tells Mako in "Ghost of the Lagoon," are an important way that people, families, and entire societies pass on knowledge and traditions from generation to generation. By passing on such memories, people can communicate shared experiences and ways of viewing the world.

Application Have students choose a friend or family member to interview for an oral history. Then have the class brainstorm a list of possible questions to ask the people they are interviewing. Questions could include: What were things like when you were my age? What did you think of school? Can you remember a person or thing that frightened you? After students have interviewed their subjects, have them prepare an oral presentation for the class.

Active Reading: CONNECT

K Have students discuss how they relate to their own pets. Students should compare their observations of their pets' behavior with the description of Afa.

Linking to Science

L The word *phosphorus* comes from a Greek word meaning "bringer of light." The element, white phosphorus, is very flammable and can ignite spontaneously. Small sea creatures that give off light are described as phosphorescent. A shark does not give off light but may be illuminated by nearby phosphorescent creatures.

CUSTOMIZING FOR
Multiple Learning Styles

M Interpersonal Learners Take this opportunity to divide the class into small groups. Have groups make predictions about what they think is moving and what will happen next. Then have volunteers present their predictions to the class.

STRATEGIC READING FOR
Less-Proficient Readers

N Make sure that students have noted relevant details of the setting and plot.

- What object does Mako refer to as Tupa? *(a coral reef he passes on the way to get bananas)* Drawing Conclusions
- Why were Mako and Afa in a rush to leave the island? *(It was getting dark.)* Summarizing

Set a Purpose Encourage students to read on to find out if Mako meets Tupa.

CUSTOMIZING FOR
Students Acquiring English

5 Help students understand that "his voice died in his throat" is an example of personification, a figure of speech that assigns human traits to an object or a concept. Make sure students understand that Mako isn't able to cry out because he is so frightened.

Critical Thinking: ANALYZING

O Ask students why Mako gets angry and grabs Afa. *(Possible responses: Mako grabs Afa out of nervousness and fear; Mako grabs Afa because he is mad at the dog for misbehaving.)*

Active Reading: PREDICT

P Ask students to predict what they think is going to happen to Mako and Afa. Have them write their predictions in their notebooks.

Literary Concept: CONFLICT

Q Remind students that a conflict is a struggle between opposing forces. Ask them to identify the opposing forces here. *(Possible response: Mako and Tupa are attacking each other.)*

STRATEGIC READING FOR
Less-Proficient Readers

R Ask students to summarize what happens when Mako meets Tupa. *(Mako is afraid when he first sees Tupa, but he quickly regains his courage when Afa falls out of the canoe and is being charged by Tupa. Mako fights with and eventually kills Tupa, and Afa is saved.)*
Summarizing

---

5 His knees felt weak. He tried to cry out, but his voice died in his throat. The great shark was circling slowly around the canoe. With each circle, it moved closer and closer. Now the boy could see the phosphorescent glow of the great shark's sides. As it moved in closer, he saw the yellow eyes, the gill slits in its throat.

O Afa leaped from one side of the canoe to the other. In sudden anger Mako leaned forward to grab the dog and shake him soundly. Afa wriggled out of his grasp as Mako tried to catch him, and the shift in weight tipped the canoe on one side. The outrigger rose from the water. In another second they would be overboard. The boy threw his weight over quickly to balance the canoe, but with a loud splash Afa fell over into the dark water.

Mako stared after him in dismay. The little dog, instead of swimming back to the canoe, had headed for the distant shore. And there was the great white shark—very near.

"Afa! Afa! Come back! Come quickly!" Mako shouted.

P The little dog turned back toward the canoe. He was swimming with all his strength. Mako leaned forward. Could Afa make it? Swiftly the boy seized his spear. Bracing himself, he stood upright. There was no weakness in him now. His dog, his companion, was in danger of instant death.

Afa was swimming desperately to reach the canoe. The white shark had paused in his circling to gather speed for the attack. Mako raised his arm, took aim. In that instant the shark charged. Mako's arm flashed forward. All his strength was behind that thrust. The spear drove straight and true, right into the great shark's eye. Mad with pain and rage, Tupa whipped about, lashing the water in fury.

One flip of that tail could overturn the canoe.

The canoe rocked back and forth. Mako struggled to keep his balance as he drew back the spear by the cord fastened to his wrist.

He bent over to seize Afa and drag him aboard. Then he stood up, not a moment too soon. Once again the shark charged. Once again Mako threw his spear, this time at the other eye. The spear found its mark. Blinded and weak from loss of blood, Tupa rolled to the surface, turned slightly on his side. Was he dead?

Q

Mako knew how clever sharks could be, and he was taking no chances. Scarcely daring to breathe, he paddled toward the still body. He saw the faintest motion of the great tail. The shark was still alive. The boy knew that one flip of that tail could overturn the canoe and send him and Afa into the water, where Tupa could destroy them.

Swiftly, yet calmly, Mako stood upright and braced himself firmly. Then, murmuring a silent prayer to the shark god, he threw his spear for the last time. Downward, swift as sound, the spear plunged into a white shoulder.

Peering over the side of the canoe, Mako could see the great fish turn over far below the surface. Then slowly, slowly, the great shark rose to the surface of the lagoon. There he floated, half on one side.

Tupa was dead. **R**

Mako flung back his head and shouted for joy. Hitching a strong line about the shark's tail, the boy began to paddle toward the shore of Bora Bora. The dorsal fin, burning with the white fire of phosphorus, trailed after the canoe.

Men were running down the beaches of Bora Bora, shouting as they leaped into their

46 UNIT ONE PART 1: SEIZING THE MOMENT

Assessment Option

INFORMAL ASSESSMENT You can informally assess students' understanding of the selection and their ability to summarize by having them act out the following scenario:

Pretend that you are visiting your friend Mako on Bora Bora during the time that this story takes place. You decide to write a letter to your family explaining what has happened. You keep your letter brief, because stationery is expensive in Bora Bora. What can you tell your family?

Have students provide written summaries.

Rubric

3 Full Accomplishment Students provide clear and concise summaries. Plot and characters are accurately described.

2 Substantial Accomplishment Students describe most events and characters in the selection. Summaries may not be clear or concise.

1 Little or Partial Accomplishment Students omit parts of the plot or order events incorrectly. There are incorrect references to characters.

canoes and put out across the lagoon. Their cries reached the boy's ears across the water.

"It is Tupa—ghost of the lagoon," he heard them shout. "Mako has killed him!"

That night, as the tired boy lay on the pandanus mats listening to the distant thunder of the sea, he heard Grandfather singing a new song. It was the song which would be sung the next day at the feast which King Opu Nui would give in Mako's honor. The boy saw his mother bending over the cook fire. The stars leaned close, winking like friendly eyes. Grandfather's voice reached him now from a great distance, "Thirty acres of land and a sailing canoe. . . ." ❖

Tahitian Landscape (1891), Paul Gauguin. The Minneapolis Institute of Arts.

GHOST OF THE LAGOON 47

STRATEGIC READING FOR
Less-Proficient Readers

S Have students explain what happens to Mako. *(Mako and Afa return home and await the feast King Opu Nui is giving in Mako's honor. Mako also prepares to receive the king's reward: 30 acres and a canoe.)* Summarizing/Making Inferences

CUSTOMIZING FOR
Gifted and Talented Students

Ask students to compare the legendary "ghost" with the real shark. What did each look like? How did each act? What details about the ghost were enhanced by the tale-tellers?

Art Note

Tahitian Landscape by Paul Gauguin Gauguin was intrigued by the play of colors and shapes that he saw in the landscape of Tahiti. In *Tahitian Landscape*, he uses simple shapes and vivid colors to portray an island paradise.

Reading the Art *Compare the images in this painting with the impressions you have of Mako's island home after having read the selection. Is this how you pictured Bora Bora?*

COMPREHENSION CHECK
1. Where does Mako live? *(on Bora Bora, an island in the South Pacific)*
2. Who is Tupa? *(Grandfather called him the ghost of the lagoon; he was a huge shark.)*
3. What does Grandfather tell Mako? *(what Tupa looks like and that Tupa killed Mako's father)*
4. What happens when Mako returns from collecting bananas? *(He encounters, fights, and kills Tupa.)*
5. What is Mako's reward? *(30 acres and a canoe)*

Mini-Lesson  Spelling

THE VOWEL SOUND o͞o Tell students that the vowel sound o͞o is most frequently spelled *oo* but that it is sometimes spelled *-ue* or *-ew*. Demonstrate the sound with these examples from the selection.

lagoon   harpoon   food

Point out to students that not all words containing *oo*—for example, *look* and *stood*—are pronounced with the vowel sound o͞o. Remind them to pronounce words carefully when trying to spell them.

Application Read the following words to the class. Have students write each word using the correct spelling of the vowel sound o͞o.

1. spoon
2. brew
3. chew
4. loot
5. sue
6. coo
7. issue
8. stew
9. moon
10. cartoon

Ask students to think of other words with the o͞o sound and to write them in their personal word lists.

Reteaching/Reinforcement
• *Unit One Resource Book*, p. 21

From Personal Response to Critical Analysis

1. Accept all reasonable responses.
2. Possible responses: Mako became frightened when he saw Tupa; Mako was excited at the chance to kill the shark.
3. Possible responses: Saving Afa was the most important thing on Mako's mind; Mako had practiced spearing the reef; Mako wanted to avenge his father's death.
4. Possible responses: Mako would still have tried to kill Tupa to avenge his father's death; Mako was too frightened of Tupa to try to kill him.
5. Possible responses: The risk Mako runs is necessary to save Afa, his best friend; it was unnecessary for Mako to risk his life for a dog.
6. Responses will vary.

Another Pathway

Students should reread the story, paying special attention to details of the setting and plot. Also encourage them to refer to the lists of details of the setting that they made for the Literary Concept Mini-Lesson on page 41.

Rubric

3 Full Accomplishment Drawing clearly reflects an understanding of setting. Chronology of events is correct.

2 Substantial Accomplishment Drawing is missing key details from the setting. Mako's path is either missing events or events are not in correct order.

1 Little or Partial Accomplishment Most key details of the setting are missing from drawing. Key events are missing and are in wrong order.

RESPONDING OPTIONS

FROM PERSONAL RESPONSE TO CRITICAL ANALYSIS

REFLECT
1. What was your reaction as you read this story? Briefly describe your thoughts in your notebook.

RETHINK
2. How do you think Mako felt when he realized Tupa was swimming toward him?
3. Why do you think Mako is able to defeat Tupa?
4. What if Mako's dog were not in danger? Do you think Mako still would have tried to kill Tupa?

Consider
Close Textual Reading
- Mako's reaction when he learns how his father died
- Mako's desire for thirty acres and a canoe
- the last sentence of the story

5. In your opinion, is the risk Mako runs necessary? Why or why not?

RELATE
6. Do you think that in the same situation you would act as courageously as Mako does? In what kind of situation would you take such a big risk?

Thematic Link

Multimodal Learning
ANOTHER PATHWAY

Paint or draw a picture of Mako's village, the lagoon, and the little island on the outer reef. When you have completed the picture, draw on it the path you imagine Mako traveled during the events of the story. Display your painting in the classroom.

QUICKWRITES

1. Imagine that Mako is now an old man. Write a **narrative** account, from Mako's point of view, relating the story of his battle with Tupa.
2. Reread the last four paragraphs of the story. Write the **tribute** that King Opu Nui might give Mako at the feast. Which of Mako's accomplishments and traits will he mention in his tribute?
3. Create your own **tall tale** about Tupa the shark. Look through the story to find details about Tupa's appearance and behavior. Tell your tale to a partner.

📁 **PORTFOLIO** Save your writing. You may want to use it later as a springboard to a piece for your portfolio.

LITERARY CONCEPTS

The **plot** of a story is the writer's plan for what happens, when it happens, and to whom it happens. In a story plot, one event causes another, which causes another, and so on until the end of the story. Generally, a plot is built around a **conflict**—a problem or struggle involving two or more opposing forces. Describe the conflict in "Ghost of the Lagoon."

Character ⚡ Source of Conflict

48 UNIT ONE PART 1: SEIZING THE MOMENT

Literary Concepts

Have students form small groups to answer the following questions.

- Why does Mako promise to slay the "ghost of the lagoon"?
- How does Mako meet Tupa?
- What happens when Afa falls overboard?
- Why does King Opu Nui give Mako 30 acres and a canoe?

Use this discussion as a springboard into a whole-class examination of the conflict in "Ghost of the Lagoon."

QuickWrites

1. Have students create a timeline of the story's events before writing their narratives.
2. Before students write the tribute, have them brainstorm a list of Mako's accomplishments.
3. Explain to students that tall tales use exaggeration. Encourage them to exaggerate or embellish their details.

The Writer's Craft

Narrative and Literary Writing, pp. 71–88

Multimodal Learning

ALTERNATIVE ACTIVITIES

1. Create a **travel brochure** advertising Bora Bora. Use details from the story as well as information from a library or a travel bureau to describe the island's tourist attractions and history. Include pictures or your own drawings, and use persuasive writing to make your readers want to visit the island.

2. Create a **dance** that celebrates Mako's courage in facing and defeating Tupa.

3. **Cooperative Learning** With two partners, assign the roles of Mako, his father, and his grandfather. Based on details from the story as well as inferences you can make, role-play a **scene** in which the three discuss life on Bora Bora, the legend of Tupa, and the way that Tupa has affected each of their lives. What might Mako like to say to his father, given the chance? Present your scene to the class.

ACROSS THE CURRICULUM

Science
1. Investigate coral reefs. How are they formed? What are they composed of? Where are they found? Save the information you find in a notebook or computer document. Keep your reference file at hand to expand it with other entries in the future.

2. Find out more about sharks—the various kinds, their behavior, and the environments in which they live. Share your information in an oral report, illustrating it with a chart or a poster.

CRITIC'S CORNER

Theresa Sullivan, a member of the student board that reviewed the stories in this book, says, "I liked how this story was scary and not scary at the same time." Do you agree with her comment? Explain.

ART CONNECTION

A student of the now-beloved Impressionist painters, Paul Gauguin was a French artist who lived and worked in the last half of the nineteenth century. Shortly after resigning as a Paris stockbroker to devote himself to painting, Gauguin received money from the French government to visit Tahiti and paint Tahitian customs. However, Gauguin fell in love with Tahiti and returned to the tropics, where he spent the last several years of his life. In *Tahitian Woman and Boy* on page 42, Gauguin's brilliant colors and strong lines reveal his view of the Tahitian people as simple and unspoiled by civilization. How well do you think the images in this painting fit the characters of Mako and his mother?

Detail of *Tahitian Woman and Boy* (1889), Paul Gauguin. Oil on canvas, 37 ¼" × 24 ¼", Norton Simon Art Foundation, Pasadena, California. Gift of Mr. Norton Simon, 1976.

GHOST OF THE LAGOON **49**

Across the Curriculum

Science

1. Encourage students to consult reference books for material on coral reefs and the Pacific Ocean. Suggest that they create different sections (or files, if using a computer) for different parts of their research. For example, they can label one section "Reef Formation" or "Reef Locations," and another "Reef Flora and Fauna." Also suggest that students keep detailed notes on any reefs that they find particularly interesting, such as the Great Barrier Reef in Australia.

2. Have students work in small groups. You may want to have different group members concentrate on specific topics such as shark types, behavior, and environment. Depending on group size, one or two students should prepare visual aids for the class presentation. Have one student from each group act as the recorder of all decisions and information gathered by group members. Have groups elect one or more members to present their findings to the class.

ADDITIONAL SUGGESTION

Geography *South Seas Cruise* Remind students that the South Pacific contains many islands in addition to Bora Bora. Suggest that interested students find out more about the South Pacific. Have them research the area, plan a cruise route, and present their findings to the class. Encourage them to include detailed maps.

Art Connection

Accept all reasonable responses based on details or inferences from the story.

SCIENCE CONNECTION

Shark Studies Our understanding of sharks has grown as a result of the many dangerous hours biologists have spent observing them in their underwater habitat. Some of the methods scientists use to study these marine carnivores are shown here.

Side A, Frame 38609

Alternative Activities

1. Encourage students to become familiar with the language used in travel brochures. If possible, they should try to gather travel brochures describing Bora Bora or any other tropical island. As students plan their travel brochures, encourage them to pay special attention to the language they use to describe the chosen island. You may want to refer them to the Mini-Lesson on The Writer's Style (page 44) to review how to choose the right words.

2. Have students work in small groups to collaborate on their dance presentations. Group members should brainstorm ideas about choreography. Encourage students to use music and costumes in their performance.

3. Ask students to collaborate on the script that they will role-play for the class. Have them review the passage, taking note of the details given about Mako, his father, and his grandfather. Remind them to choose language that clearly reflects the personalities of the different characters. Encourage them to use costumes and settings (if possible) when presenting their scene to the class.

THE LANGUAGE OF LITERATURE **TEACHER'S EDITION** **49**

Words to Know

Exercise A
1. reef
2. phosphorus
3. lagoon
4. expedition
5. harpoon

The boxed letters form the word *courage*.

Exercise B
Drawings will vary.

Reteaching/Reinforcement
- *Unit One Resource Book,* p. 22

ARMSTRONG SPERRY

Armstrong Sperry was educated at the Yale School of Fine Art and the New York Art Students League before studying art in Paris. He started his career in publishing as an illustrator before combining his artistic talent with writing children's books. He has illustrated almost all of his numerous books and stories.

ART GALLERY
Gauguin on Polynesia The work of the French artist Paul Gauguin (1848–1903) is characterized by simple forms and brilliant colors. Several of his Polynesian paintings are shown here.

Side A, Frame 38615

WORDS TO KNOW

EXERCISE A Review the Words to Know in the boxes at the bottom of the selection pages. Copy the blanks below on a separate sheet of paper, and fill in the correct vocabulary words.

1. a ridge of rocks or coral near the surface of water
   r e e f
2. a glowing substance
   p h o s p h o r u s
3. a shallow body of water enclosed by a reef
   l a g o o n
4. a journey with a definite objective
   e x p e d i t i o n
5. a spearlike weapon used to hunt large fish
   h a r p o o n

Now use the letters in the boxes to complete the word below, which means "an ability to face danger and confront challenges."
   c o u r a g e

EXERCISE B Draw a picture to illustrate each of the Words to Know. Use labels and definitions to explain your drawings.

ARMSTRONG SPERRY

1892–1976

Armstrong Sperry once said that a writer "should tell his story clearly, in a supple prose that leaves his reader—young or old—wondering, 'What happens next?'" Sperry had an advantage for writing stories with exciting plots—he traveled widely in Europe, North America, and the West Indies and made use of what he saw. Inspired by his grandfather's stories of visits to the South Pacific, Sperry spent two years in French Polynesia. There he learned French and Tahitian and gathered information for a number of his books.

Sperry's talent for writing adventure stories set in exotic places led to the success of his book *Call It Courage.* This novel, based on a legend of the South Pacific, was awarded the Newbery Medal in 1941. Sperry's *The Rain Forest* received the Boys Clubs of America Junior Book Award in 1949.

Eventually, Sperry settled down, spending most of his time at his home in New Hampshire. He did not, however, lose his love of travel; throughout his life he continued to make voyages to far-off places.

OTHER WORKS *Lost Lagoon: A Pacific Adventure, Storm Canvas, Hull-Down for Action, No Brighter Glory, Black Falcon*

LASERLINKS
- SCIENCE CONNECTION
- ART GALLERY

50 UNIT ONE PART 1: SEIZING THE MOMENT

WHAT DO YOU THINK?
Reflecting on Theme

Mako fought Tupa without thinking about the possible risks. Have students review the diagram for the activity on page 18 about a quick decision they had made. Ask them to compare their thoughts before reading with their thoughts now. Ask them if they would come to the same conclusions. If their conclusions are different, invite students to draw another diagram.

FOCUS ON NONFICTION

Whereas some readers enjoy getting lost in the imaginary world of fiction, others prefer to read about real life. **Nonfiction** is writing about real people, places, and events.

There are two broad categories of nonfiction. One category, called **informative nonfiction,** is mainly written to provide factual information. Nonfiction of this type includes science and history books, encyclopedias, pamphlets, and most of the articles in magazines and newspapers. The main purpose of this material is to inform.

The other category of nonfiction is called **literary nonfiction** because it is written to be read and experienced in much the same way as fiction. However, literary nonfiction differs from fiction in that it deals with real people rather than fictional characters and with settings and plots that are not imagined but are actual places and true events.

The types of literary nonfiction you will read in this book are **autobiographies, biographies,** and **essays.**

AUTOBIOGRAPHY An autobiography is the true story of a person's life, told by that person. It is almost always written from the first-person point of view. Among the autobiographical writings you will read in this book are excerpts from *Woodsong* and *The Lost Garden.*

An autobiography is usually book length because it covers a long period of the writer's life. However, there are shorter types of autobiographical writing, such as **journals, diaries,** and **memoirs.**

BIOGRAPHY A biography is the true story of a person's life, told by someone else. The writer, or **biographer,** interviews the subject if possible and also researches the person's life by reading letters, books, diaries, and any other information he or she can find. A short biography of the African-American explorer Matthew Henson is included in this book. As you will see, biographies and autobiographies often contain many of the elements that fiction contains, such as character, setting, and plot.

FOCUS ON NONFICTION 51

FOCUS ON NONFICTION

This feature defines *nonfiction* and provides an explanation of the terms used to discuss it. It also introduces students to the conventions of the genre and suggests strategies for reading nonfiction. The terms introduced here are covered in depth in the nonfiction selections that follow.

Objectives

- To understand and appreciate nonfiction
- To recognize categories of nonfiction: autobiography, biography, and essay
- To develop effective strategies for reading nonfiction

Teaching Strategies:
CATEGORIES OF NONFICTION

Autobiography Invite a volunteer to read this paragraph to the class. Ask students if they have ever kept a journal or a diary about their daily activities. Explain that this is a common form of autobiographical writing. Then create a web showing the characteristics of autobiography. Here is a sample web:

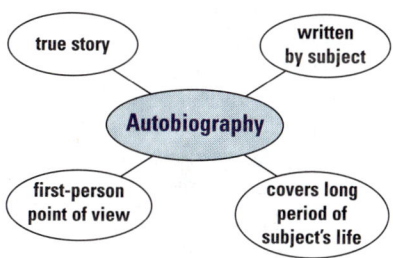

Biography Have students work in small groups to make a chart or a Venn diagram comparing and contrasting autobiography and biography.

THE LANGUAGE OF LITERATURE TEACHER'S EDITION 51

Essay Discuss with the class the different purposes an essay can have: to persuade, to entertain, to explain, to describe, or to express personal feelings.

Reading Strategies: MODELING

Invite volunteers to read aloud the Strategies for Reading Nonfiction. Tell students they will be using these strategies as they read "Matthew Henson at the Top of the World" on page 53 and other nonfiction selections throughout the book. Then model the strategies as students read "Matthew Henson at the Top of the World." You may wish to use the models provided or create your own.

- **Preview the selection** *"This looks like the story of someone who was part of a group of explorers in the Arctic."*
- **Figure out the organization** *"Most of the selection is organized chronologically. The author usually starts paragraphs and sections with a historical date."*
- **Separate facts and opinions** *"Most of the descriptions of what happened on a particular date are factual. The author's comment on page 56 that Matthew Henson was lucky is an opinion."*
- **Question the material** *"If Henson sought adventure, what else could he have done beside working on a ship? Why didn't Peary speak up on Henson's behalf when he wasn't awarded a gold medal?"*
- **Stop now and then** *"I wonder what kinds of exploration Henson will experience with Peary?"*
- **Build on your understanding** *"I was surprised to learn that even though Henson was invaluable to Peary and very well liked by him, he didn't get the recognition he deserved."*
- **Evaluate what you read** *"The author presents a great deal of interesting information. It might be worthwhile at some point to take a closer look at the facts he presents."*

ESSAY An essay is a short piece of nonfiction that deals with one subject. Essays are often found in newspapers and magazines. The writer might share an opinion, try to entertain or persuade the reader, or simply describe an incident that has special significance. Essays that explain how the author feels about a subject are called **informal essays** or **personal essays.** In this book, the selection "The Mushroom" is an example of an informal essay. Formal essays are rarely about personal subjects. They are usually scholarly and are generally not found in literature textbooks.

STRATEGIES FOR READING NONFICTION

Nonfiction can be read as literature or as a source of information. The nonfiction you will read in this book has been included because of its literary quality. As you read, try to step into and enjoy the true stories and opinions the authors have to share.

Use the following strategies when you read nonfiction:

- **Preview the selection.** Before you read, look at the title, pictures or diagrams, and any subtitles or terms in boldface or italic type. All of these will give you an idea of what the selection is about.
- **Figure out the organization.** If the work is a biography or autobiography, the organization is probably chronological—that is, events are told in the order they happened. Other selections may be organized around ideas the author wants to discuss.
- **Separate facts and opinions.** Facts are statements that can be proved, such as "There are several excerpts from autobiographies in this book." Opinions are statements that cannot be proved. They simply express a person's beliefs, such as "The excerpt from *Woodsong* is the best example of autobiography in this book." Writers sometimes present opinions as if they were facts. Be sure you can tell the difference.
- **Question the material.** As you read, ask yourself questions like these: "Why did things happen the way they did?" "How did people feel?" "What is the writer's opinion?" Try to decide whether you share the writer's opinion or have different ideas on the subject.
- **Stop now and then.** During your reading, pause in order to try to predict what will come next. Sometimes you will be surprised by what happens or by what an author has to say about an issue.
- **Build on your understanding.** Add new information to what you have already learned, and see if your ideas and opinions change.
- **Evaluate what you read.** Evaluation should be an ongoing process, not just something that you do after you finish reading. Remember, too, that evaluation involves more than deciding that a selection is good or bad. Form opinions about the people, events, and ideas that are presented. Decide whether you like the way the piece was written.

Finally, it is important to recognize that your understanding of a selection does not end when you stop reading. As you think more about what you have read and discuss it with others, you will find that your understanding continues to grow.

PREVIEWING

NONFICTION

Matthew Henson at the Top of the World
Jim Haskins

PERSONAL CONNECTION *Activating Prior Knowledge*

What images come to mind when you think of the word *explorer*? What character traits do you think a person needs to be an explorer? On the chalkboard or on a sheet of paper, copy and fill in a chart like the one shown, working either on your own or with your classmates.

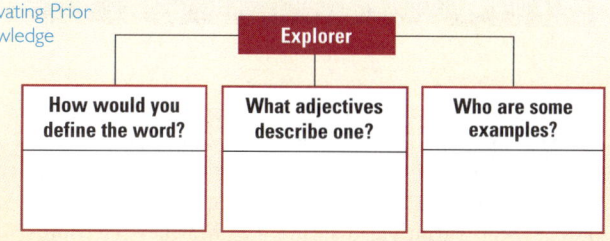

GEOGRAPHICAL CONNECTION *Building Background*

The selection you are about to read describes the adventurous life of the African-American explorer Matthew Henson. In 1908, Henson joined Commander Robert E. Peary of the U.S. Navy on one of the greatest quests of the 20th century. Their goal was to be the first men to reach the North Pole.

The geographic North Pole lies in the Arctic Ocean at the northern end of the axis on which the earth revolves. There is no land at the North Pole, but for most of the year the ocean is frozen solid, providing a surface for travel by dogsled.

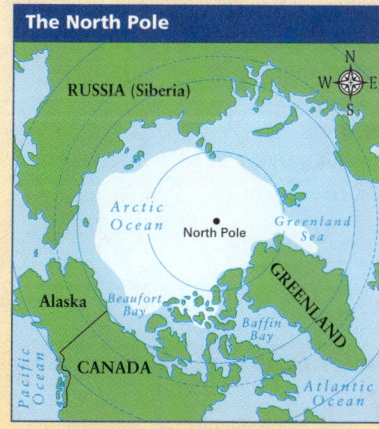

READING CONNECTION *Active Reading/ Setting a Purpose*

Main Idea and Supporting Details
In nonfiction, it is possible to figure out the author's most important points by identifying the topic or main idea of each paragraph. In searching for the main idea, you should read the entire paragraph, because the main idea may be stated at the beginning, the middle or the end. The other sentences in the paragraph give supporting details, additional information about the main idea. As you read this selection about two Arctic explorers, jot down a list in your reading log of the character traits these explorers displayed. Note supporting details for each of these traits.

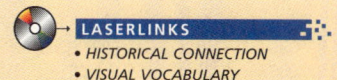
- HISTORICAL CONNECTION
- VISUAL VOCABULARY

53

OVERVIEW

Objectives

- To understand and appreciate a biographical account of Matthew Henson
- To enrich reading by using active reading strategies
- To identify and understand the biographical form
- To appreciate the use of diaries and letters
- To express understanding of the story through a choice of writing forms, including an acceptance speech, a log entry, and a poem
- To extend understanding of the story through a variety of multimodal and cross-curricular activities

Skills

READING SKILLS/ STRATEGIES
- Connecting

THE WRITER'S STYLE
- Your own voice

GRAMMAR
- More proper nouns

LITERARY CONCEPTS
- Biography
- Characterization

SPELLING
- The sound shən

GENRE STUDY
- Nonfiction

SPEAKING, LISTENING, AND VIEWING
- Press conference
- Group discussion
- Oral presentation

Cross-Curricular Connections

SCIENCE
- Ice

HISTORY
- The Civil War
- Reconstruction

GEOGRAPHY
- Panama Canal

SOCIAL STUDIES
- Eskimos
- Peary's claim

 HISTORICAL CONNECTION
The Peary-Henson Polar Expedition Matthew Henson and the other Arctic explorers of his day endured some of the harshest conditions on earth in their efforts to reach the North Pole. These photographs document some of the experiences of the members of the expedition.

Side A, Frame 38622

PRINT AND MEDIA RESOURCES

UNIT ONE RESOURCE BOOK
Strategic Reading: Literature, p. 25
Vocabulary SkillBuilder, p. 28
Reading SkillBuilder, p. 26
Spelling SkillBuilder, p. 27

GRAMMAR MINI–LESSONS
Transparencies, pp. 26, 27
Copymasters, pp. 33, 34

ACCESS FOR STUDENTS ACQUIRING ENGLISH
Selection Summaries
Reading and Writing Support

FORMAL ASSESSMENT
Selection Test, pp. 11–12
 Test Generator

 **AUDIO LIBRARY**
See Reference Card

 **LASERLINKS**
Historical Connection
Visual Vocabulary
Art Gallery

INTERNET RESOURCES
McDougal Littell Literature Center at http://www.hmco.com/mcdougal/lit

THE LANGUAGE OF LITERATURE TEACHER'S EDITION 53

SUMMARY

Born in 1866, Matthew Henson grew up with a hunger for adventure. He had a hard childhood and went to school for only a few years. At the age of 14 he became a cabin boy on a ship and began exploring the world. In 1887 he signed on as the servant of Robert E. Peary, a naval officer and explorer. Four years later, Henson and Peary sailed off to the first of their five expeditions to the Arctic. The fifth expedition, in 1908, had as its goal the North Pole, which had never been reached before. Seven explorers and 41 Eskimos began the grueling Arctic journey. Frostbite, exhaustion, and death reduced the party until only Peary, Henson, and 4 Eskimos remained. On April 6, 1908, Peary believed that the group had reached the North Pole, and he asked Henson to place the U.S. flag on the spot. Upon his return to the United States, Peary became a hero for his achievement; but because Henson was African American, his own contribution was not honored until much later.

Thematic Link: *Seizing the Moment*
Seizing the opportunity for adventure, Matthew Henson becomes one of the first people ever to reach the North Pole.

CUSTOMIZING FOR
Students Acquiring English

- Use **ACCESS FOR STUDENTS ACQUIRING ENGLISH,** *Reading and Writing Support.*
- Students may benefit from background information about the history of the United States during the late 1800s. They may need help understanding references to slavery, the Ku Klux Klan, and Reconstruction.

STRATEGIC READING FOR
Less-Proficient Readers

Set a Purpose To encourage students to become interested in the selection, have them describe what they think the North Pole is like. Then have them read to find out about Matthew Henson's childhood.

Use **UNIT ONE RESOURCE BOOK,** pp. 25–26, for guidance in reading the selection.

54

MATTHEW HENSON AT THE
TOP OF THE WORLD

by Jim Haskins

While the explorers of the American West faced many dangers in their travels, at least game and water were usually plentiful; and if winter with its cold and snow overtook them, they could, in time, expect warmth and spring. For Matthew Henson, in his explorations with Robert Peary at the North Pole, this was hardly the case. In many ways, to forge ahead into the icy Arctic took far greater <u>stamina</u> and courage than did the earlier explorers' travels, and Henson possessed such hardiness. As Donald MacMillan, a member of the expedition, was later to write: "Peary knew Matt Henson's real worth. . . . Highly respected by the Eskimos,[1] he was easily the most popular man on board ship. . . . Henson . . . was of more real value to our Commander than [expedition members] Bartlett, Marvin, Borup, Goodsell and myself all put together. Matthew Henson went to the Pole with Peary because he was a better man than any one of us."

Matthew Henson was born on August 8, 1866, in Charles County, Maryland, some forty-four miles south of Washington, D.C. His parents were poor, free tenant

---
1. **Eskimos:** a term used throughout this account to refer to the native peoples of the Arctic; the Eskimos of Greenland, such as those who traveled on Peary's expeditions, call themselves Inuit, as do the Eskimos of Canada.

WORDS TO KNOW
stamina (stăm′ə-nə) *n.* the strength to withstand hardship

54

WORDS TO KNOW

apt (ăpt) *adj.* quick to learn or understand (p. 58)
ardent (är′dnt) *adj.* full of enthusiasm or devotion (p. 58)
deprivation (dĕp′rə-vā′shən) *n.* a lack of what is needed for survival or comfort (p. 56)
menial (mē′nē-əl) *adj.* fit for a servant (p. 57)
proposition (prŏp′ə-zĭsh′ən) *n.* a plan offered for acceptance (p. 58)
resentful (rĭ-zĕnt′fəl) *adj.* angry due to a feeling of being treated unfairly (p. 57)
stamina (stăm′ə-nə) *n.* the strength to withstand hardship (p. 54)
surveyor (sər-vā′ər) *n.* a person who determines land boundaries by measuring angles and distances (p. 57)
tyranny (tĭr′ə-nē) *n.* an extremely harsh or unjust government or authority (p. 57)
validate (văl′ĭ-dāt′) *v.* to show to be correct (p. 61)

 VISUAL VOCABULARY

- **sledge** (slĕj)   • **surveyor** (sər-vā′ər)

Side A, Frame 38629

Matthew Henson in animal furs that protected him from the extreme Arctic cold. The Bettmann Archive.

MATTHEW HENSON AT THE TOP OF THE WORLD   55

CUSTOMIZING FOR
Gifted and Talented Students

Have students think about the hardships in Henson's life as they read the selection. Ask them to find passages that reveal how these hardships may have contributed to his determination to succeed.

Possible responses:

- *Page 56*—"Alone, homeless, and penniless, Matthew was forced to fend for himself." At the age of 13, Henson was already relying solely on himself for support.

- *Page 57*—"As soon as he was able, Matthew left the ship in Canada and made his way back to the United States. . . ." Even though he did not know what awaited him, Henson left a secure job for the unknown of the United States.

- *Page 60*—"So Matthew Henson described the grueling journey." The extreme conditions inspired Henson and Peary to continue.

- *Page 61*—"Because Henson was black, his contributions to the expedition were not recognized for many years." Henson would have to fight to be recognized as Peary's partner.

CUSTOMIZING FOR
Students Acquiring English

Ⓘ Explain that *hardly* is a negative word meaning "not at all."

CUSTOMIZING FOR
Multiple Learning Styles

Ⓐ **Spatial or Graphic Learners** Have students study the photograph of Henson on this page. Ask them what impression of this man they get from the photograph. Does this impression agree with the description of his characteristics given in the first paragraph?

Mini-Lesson  The Writer's Style

YOUR OWN VOICE Explain to students that when they write, each of them has his or her own special way of choosing words and putting them together. This special way is called a voice. Point out that writers sometimes use big, important-sounding words and long, complicated sentences to make their writing effective. Often, though, this results in writing that sounds strained and unnatural. Encourage students to use language that comes easily and naturally to them and explain that this will also make writing assignments much easier.

Application After many grueling hardships, Henson and Peary finally reached the North Pole. Have students write a paragraph describing how they would respond to this event if they were Henson. Have students pair up and exchange paragraphs. Partners should read and analyze each other's paragraphs, checking for the writer's use of a natural voice.

Reteaching/Reinforcement
- Writing Handbook, anthology pp. 784–785

The Writer's Craft
Appealing to the Senses, pp. 266–275

THE LANGUAGE OF LITERATURE TEACHER'S EDITION   **55**

Linking to History

B The Civil War began in 1861 and was fought between the North (Union) and the South (Confederacy). Ostensibly caused by bitter divisions over slavery, the Civil War also had deep-rooted political and economic causes.

Active Reading: EVALUATE

C Invite students to discuss how Lemuel Henson might have felt when he had to send his son away. *(Possible response: It was difficult for Matthew's father to send Matthew to stay with his uncle.)*

STRATEGIC READING FOR
Less-Proficient Readers

D Have students summarize the events of Matthew's early childhood. *(Matthew was born in Maryland. When he was seven, his mother died, and his father, unable to support him, sent Matthew to live with his uncle. Later, his uncle could no longer support him, so Matthew worked in a restaurant. He soon decided to become a sailor and left the restaurant to find work on a ship.)*
Summarizing

Set a Purpose Have students continue reading to find out what happens when Matthew finds work as a sailor.

Active Reading: QUESTION

E Encourage students to raise questions about the main idea in this paragraph. *(The main idea is that Henson wanted adventure and decided to seek it on a ship.)*

CUSTOMIZING FOR
Students Acquiring English

2 Show students that they can guess the meaning of unfamiliar words from their context. Ask them to find another expression that means the same as *took the boy under his wing.* (took care of him)

B farmers[2] who barely eked a living from the sandy soil. The Civil War had ended the year before Matthew was born, bringing with it a great deal of bitterness on the part of former slave-owners. One manifestation of this hostility was the terrorist activity on the part of the Ku Klux Klan[3] in Maryland. Many free and newly freed blacks had suffered at the hands of this band of night riders.[4] Matthew's father, Lemuel Henson, felt it was only a matter of time before the Klan turned its vengeful eyes on his family. That, and the fact that by farming he was barely able to support them, caused him to decide to move north to Washington, D.C.

C At first things went well for the Henson family, but then Matthew's mother died and his father found himself unable to care for Matthew. The seven-year-old boy was sent to live with his uncle, a kindly man who welcomed him and enrolled him in the N Street School. Six years later, however, another blow fell; his uncle himself fell upon hard times and could no longer support Matthew. The boy couldn't return to his father, because Lemuel had recently died. Alone, homeless, and penniless, Matthew was forced to fend for himself.

Matthew Henson was a bright boy and a hard worker, although he had only a sixth-grade education. Calling upon his own resourcefulness, he found a job as a dishwasher in a small restaurant owned by a woman named Janey Moore. When Janey discovered that Matthew had no place to stay, she fixed a cot for him in the kitchen; Matthew had found a home again.

Matthew Henson didn't want to spend his life waiting on people and washing dishes, however, no matter how kind Janey was. He had seen enough of the world through his schoolbooks to want more, to want adventure. This desire was reinforced by the men who frequented the restaurant—sailors from many ports, who spun tales of life on the ocean and of strange and wonderful places. As Henson listened, wide-eyed, to their stories, he decided, as had so many boys before him, that the life of a sailor with its adventures and dangers was for him. Having made up his mind, the fourteen-year-old packed up what little he owned, bade good-bye to Janey, and was off to Baltimore to find a ship. **D**

QUESTION
E What is the main idea of the paragraph you have just read?
Using a Reading Log

Although Matthew Henson's early life seems harsh, in many ways he was very lucky. When he arrived in Baltimore, he signed on as a cabin boy on the *Katie Hines*, the master of which was a Captain Childs. For many sailors at that time, life at sea was brutal and filled with hard work, deprivation, and a "taste of the cat": whipping. The captains of many vessels were petty despots, ruling with an iron hand and having little regard for a seaman's health or safety. Matthew was fortunate to find just the opposite in Childs.

Captain Childs took the boy under his wing. Although Matthew of course had to do the work he was assigned, Captain Childs took a fatherly interest in him. Having an excellent private library on the ship, the captain saw to

---

2. **tenant farmers:** people who farm land rented from others.
3. **Ku Klux Klan** (kōō′ klŭks klăn′): a secret society, organized in the South after the Civil War, that used terrorism to reassert the power of whites.
4. **night riders:** mounted and usually masked white men who committed acts of terror against African Americans during the period following the Civil War.

WORDS TO KNOW
deprivation (dĕp′rə-vā′shən) *n.* a lack of what is needed for survival or comfort

---

Mini-Lesson Literary Concepts

CHARACTERIZATION Remind students that characterization is the way a writer creates and develops a character's personality. Writers develop characters in four basic ways:

1. through physical description of the character
2. through the character's thoughts, speech, and actions
3. through the thoughts, speech, and actions of other characters
4. through direct comments on a character's nature

Application Invite students to think about the different techniques Jim Haskins uses to describe the characters in "Matthew Henson at the Top of the World." You may want to refer them to the passage highlighted on page 56 for a description of Captain Childs. Then encourage students to record characterization in a chart like the one shown as they read the selection. Show students the first entry as an example.

Character	How Developed	Observations
Captain Childs	direct comments	Captain Childs was a kind and thoughtful man.

---

56 THE LANGUAGE OF LITERATURE TEACHER'S EDITION

Matthew's education, insisting that he read widely in geography, history, mathematics, and literature while they were at sea.

The years on the *Katie Hines* were good ones for Matthew Henson. During that time he saw China, Japan, the Philippines, France, Africa, and southern Russia; he sailed through the Arctic to Murmansk. But in 1885 it all ended; Captain Childs fell ill and died at sea. Unable to face staying on the *Katie Hines* under a new skipper, Matthew left the ship at Baltimore and found a place on a fishing schooner bound for Newfoundland.

Now, for the first time, Henson encountered the kind of unthinking cruelty and <u>tyranny</u> so often found on ships at that time. The ship was filthy, the crew surly and <u>resentful</u> of their black shipmate, and the captain a dictator. As soon as he was able, Matthew left the ship in Canada and made his way back to the United States, finally arriving in Washington, D.C., only to find that things there had changed during the years he had been at sea.

Opportunities for blacks had been limited when Henson had left Washington in 1871, but by the time he returned they were almost nonexistent. Post–Civil War reconstruction had failed, bringing with its failure a great deal of bitter resentment toward blacks. Jobs were scarce, and the few available were <u>menial</u> ones. Matthew finally found a job as a stock clerk in a clothing and hat store, B. H. Steinmetz and Sons, bitterly wondering if this was how he was to spend the rest of his life. But his luck was still holding.

Steinmetz recognized that Matthew Henson was bright and hard working. One day Lieu-

A sextant (center) and other navigational instruments of Robert Peary. Victor R. Boswell, Jr., © National Geographic Society.

tenant Robert E. Peary, a young navy officer, walked into the store, looking for tropical hats. After being shown a number of hats, Peary unexpectedly offered Henson a job as his personal servant. Steinmetz had recommended him, Peary said, but the job wouldn't be easy. He was bound for Nicaragua to head an engineering survey team. Would Matthew be willing to put up with the discomforts and hazards of such a trip? Thinking of the adventure and opportunities offered, Henson eagerly said yes, little realizing that a partnership had just been formed that would span years and be filled with exploration, danger, and fame.

Robert E. Peary was born in Cresson, Pennsylvania, in 1856 but was raised in Maine, where his mother had returned after his father's death in 1859. After graduating from Bowdoin College, Peary worked as a <u>surveyor</u> for four years and in 1881 joined the navy's corps of civil engineers. One result of his travels for the navy

---

WORDS TO KNOW

tyranny (tĭr′ə-nē) *n.* an extremely harsh or unjust government or authority
resentful (rĭ-zĕnt′fəl) *adj.* angry due to a feeling of being treated unfairly.
menial (mē′nē-əl) *adj.* fit for a servant
surveyor (sər-vā′ər) *n.* a person who determines land boundaries by measuring angles and distances

57

Mini-Lesson  Reading Skills/Strategies

ACTIVE READING: CONNECT Explain to students that active readers use certain strategies as they read. Readers use connecting strategies when they try to think of similarities between what is described in the text and what they have experienced, heard about, or read about.

Application Encourage students to record their connections in their notebooks as they read the selection. If students have trouble thinking of connections, have them reread the description of Henson's relationship with Childs. Ask students if they have ever had a friend or relative who acted as their mentor. If possible, have students compare their connections with classmates.

Reteaching/Reinforcement
• *Unit One Resource Book*, p. 26

Critical Thinking: SPECULATING

F Ask students if they think that Henson would have had a more positive experience on the fishing schooner if he had not been African American. *(Possible responses: Yes, it was because of his race that the crew was surly and resentful toward him; No, the captain was cruel to all the crew.)*

Active Reading: CONNECT

G Have students discuss their opinions of Henson's response to the situation on the schooner. Ask them if they would have acted in the same manner. If not, how would they have dealt with the situation? You may want to share the following thought process with them.

Think-Aloud Model *I think Henson did the right thing by leaving the ship as soon as he did. Since the captain was cruel and the crew surly toward him, it seems as though he had very few options.*

Linking to History

 H Reconstruction, which lasted from the end of the Civil War through 1877, was the attempt to reorganize and reintegrate the South back into the Union. It was a period marked by the struggles between different political parties and between the president and Congress.

STRATEGIC READING FOR
Less-Proficient Readers

I Ask the following questions to make sure that students understand the events that have taken place up to this point.

• What happened when Henson went to Baltimore to get a job on a ship? *(He found a job on the* Katie Hines.*)* **Summarizing**

• Why did Henson leave the *Katie Hines*? *(Captain Childs died.)* **Noting Sequence of Events**

• For what did position did Peary initially hire Henson? *(his personal servant)* **Noting Relevant Details**

Set a Purpose Invite students to continue reading to find out what happens to Henson when he works with Peary.

THE LANGUAGE OF LITERATURE TEACHER'S EDITION **57**

Literary Concept:
CHARACTERIZATION

J Ask students to describe which of Peary's qualities Henson was drawn to. *(Possible responses: Peary's ambition, goals, interest in adventure, desire to make history)*

Linking to Geography

K The Panama Canal was built by the United States between 1904 and 1914. The canal links the Atlantic and Pacific oceans via the Caribbean Sea in the east and the Gulf of Panama in the west. The canal was owned and operated by the United States until 1978 when the Panama Canal Treaty was ratified, guaranteeing Panamanian control by the year 2000.

Critical Thinking: ANALYZING

L Ask students to explain why they think Henson was willing to accompany Peary even without pay. *(Henson was so excited about the prospect of exploring the Arctic that money did not matter.)*

Active Reading: CLARIFY

M To help students identify the main idea, have them characterize each sentence as being general or detailed. Students should see that the detailed sentences all support the main idea stated in the first sentence.

CUSTOMIZING FOR
Students Acquiring English

3 You may want to point out that *colored* was used in the past to refer to African Americans, but it is now considered to be derogatory.

STRATEGIC READING FOR
Less-Proficient Readers

N Ask students to summarize the relationship between Henson and Peary. *(Henson starts out as Peary's personal servant. Peary then asks Henson to accompany him on an expedition to the Arctic. During this first expedition, Peary learns how valuable Henson is to him.)*
Summarizing

Set a Purpose Encourage students to continue reading to find out what happens during the 1908 expedition to the North Pole.

---

and of his reading was an <u>ardent</u> desire for adventure. "I shall not be satisfied," Peary wrote to his mother, "until my name is known from one end of the earth to the other." This was a goal Matthew Henson could understand. As he later said, "I recognized in [Peary] the qualities that made me willing to engage myself in his service." In November 1887, Henson and Peary set sail for Nicaragua, along with forty-five other engineers and a hundred black Jamaicans.

Peary's job was to study the feasibility[5] of digging a canal across Nicaragua (that canal that would later be dug across the Isthmus of Panama).[6] The survey took until June of 1888, when the surveying party headed back to the United States. Henson knew he had done a good job for Peary, but even as they started north, Peary said nothing to him about continuing on as his servant. It was a great surprise, then, when one day Peary approached Henson with a <u>proposition</u>. He wanted to try to raise money for an expedition to the Arctic, and he wanted Henson to accompany him. Henson quickly accepted, saying he would go whether Peary could pay him or not.

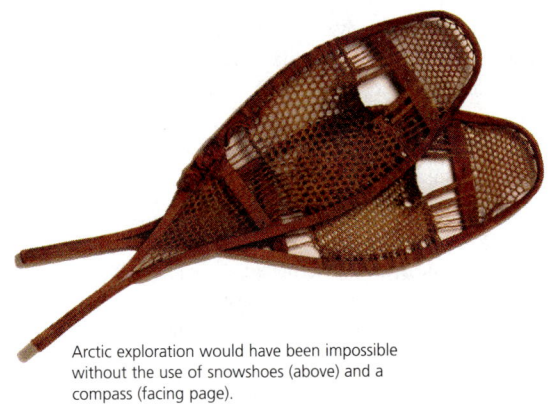

Arctic exploration would have been impossible without the use of snowshoes (above) and a compass (facing page).

"It was in June, 1891, that I started on my first trip to the Arctic regions, as a member of what was known as the 'North Greenland Expedition,'" Matthew Henson later wrote. So began the first of five expeditions on which Henson would accompany Peary.

CLARIFY
Does the main idea appear at the beginning, the middle, or the end of this paragraph?
Using a Reading Log

During this first trip to Greenland, on a ship named *Kite*, Peary discovered how valuable Henson was to any expedition. He reported that Henson was able to establish "a friendly relationship with the Eskimos, who believed him to be somehow related to them because of his brown skin. . . ." Peary's expedition was also greatly aided by Henson's expert handling of the Eskimos, dogs, and equipment. Henson also hunted with the Eskimos for meat for the expedition and cooked under the supervision of Josephine Peary, Robert's wife. On the expedition's return to New York, September 24, 1892, Peary wrote, "Henson, my faithful colored boy, a hard worker and <u>apt</u> at anything, . . . showed himself . . . the equal of others in the party."

This first expedition to the Arctic led to several others, but it was with the 1905 expedition that Peary first tried to find that mystical point, the North Pole, the sole goal of the 1908 expedition.

On July 6, 1908, the *Roosevelt* sailed from New York City. Aboard it were the supplies and men for an expedition to reach the North Pole. Accompanying Peary were Captain Robert

---

5. **feasibility** (fē′zə-bĭl′ĭ-tē): possibility of being completed successfully.
6. **Isthmus** (ĭs′məs) **of Panama**: a narrow strip of land connecting the North and South American continents.

WORDS TO KNOW
ardent (är′dnt) *adj.* full of enthusiasm or devotion
proposition (prŏp′ə-zĭsh′ən) *n.* a plan offered for acceptance
apt (ăpt) *adj.* quick to learn or understand

58

Mini-Lesson Grammar

MORE PROPER NOUNS Remind students that a proper noun names a specific person, place, or thing. Use the following list of guidelines.

1. particular places and things, including the names of cities, states, countries, and streets
2. months, days, holidays, and historical events
3. religions, nationalities, and languages
4. words referring to religious gods and scriptures
5. clubs, organizations, and business firms

Application Invite students to find the proper nouns in the passage  on pages 58–59. (*Roosevelt, New York City, North Pole, Peary, Captain Robert Bartlett, Ross Marvin, George Borup, Yale, Donald MacMillan, J. W. Goodsell, Matthew Henson, Greenland, Eskimos*) Then have them explain why each noun is capitalized.

Reteaching/Reinforcement
- *Grammar Handbook*, anthology pp. 839–842
- *Grammar Mini-Lessons* copymasters, pp. 33, 34, transparencies, pp. 26, 27

The Writer's Craft

More Proper Nouns, pp. 552–555

---

58 THE LANGUAGE OF LITERATURE TEACHER'S EDITION

Bartlett and Ross Marvin, who had been with Peary on earlier expeditions; George Borup, a young graduate from Yale and the youngest member of the group; Donald MacMillan, a teacher; and a doctor, J. W. Goodsell. And, of course, Matthew Henson. In Greenland the group was joined by forty-one Eskimos and 246 dogs, plus the supplies. "The ship," Henson wrote, "is now in a most perfect state of dirtiness." On September 5, the *Roosevelt* arrived at Cape Sheridan, and the group began preparing for their journey, moving supplies north to Cape Columbia by dog sled to establish a base camp. Peary named the camp Crane City in honor of Zenas Crane, who had contributed $10,000 to the expedition.

"IT WAS IN JUNE, 1891, THAT I STARTED ON MY FIRST TRIP TO THE ARCTIC REGIONS, AS A MEMBER OF WHAT WAS KNOWN AS THE 'NORTH GREENLAND EXPEDITION.'"

The plan was to have two men, Bartlett and Borup, go ahead of the rest of the group to cut a trail stretching from the base camp to the North Pole. On February 28, the two men set out, and on March 1, the remainder of the expedition started north, following the trail Bartlett and Borup had cut the day before. At first, trouble seemed to plague them. On the first day, three of the sledges[7] broke, Henson's among them. Fortunately, Henson was able to repair them, despite the fact that it was nearly 50 degrees below zero.

As the days passed, further trouble came the way of the expedition. Several times they encountered leads—open channels of water—and were forced to wait until the ice closed over before proceeding. On March 14, Peary decided to send Donald MacMillan and Dr. Goodsell back to the base camp. MacMillan could hardly walk, because he had frozen a heel when his foot had slipped into one of the leads. Dr. Goodsell was exhausted. As the expedition went on, more men were sent back due to exhaustion and frostbite. George Borup was sent back on March 20, and, on the 26th, so was Ross Marvin.

Although the expedition had encountered problems with subzero temperatures, with open water, and in handling the dogs, they had had no real injuries. On Ross Marvin's return trip to the base camp, however, he met with tragedy. On his journey, Marvin was accompanied by two Eskimos. He told them that he would go ahead to scout the trail. About an hour later, the Eskimos came upon a hole in the ice; floating in it was Marvin's coat. Marvin had gone through thin ice and, unable to save himself, had drowned or frozen. The Peary expedition had suffered its first—and fortunately its last—fatality.

By April 1, Peary had sent back all of the original expedition except for four Eskimos and Matthew Henson. When Bartlett, the last man to be sent back, asked Peary why he didn't also send Henson, Peary replied, "I can't get along without him." The remnant of the original group pushed on.

---

7. **sledges:** sleds pulled by dogs.

Active Reading: QUESTION

S Take this opportunity to discuss what questions or comments students have at this point in the selection. Have them write in their notebooks all questions and answers discussed.

Critical Thinking: ANALYZING

T Ask students to explain why Peary placed part of the American flag and two letters into the glass jar that he left at the pole. *(Possible response: Peary wanted to record the expedition's discovery.)* Have students explain what meaning they see in Peary's gesture. *(Possible responses: Peary wanted the world to know that his expedition had made it to the pole first. Peary wanted to claim the land for the United States. There was no real meaning to what Peary did; it was simply a symbolic gesture, similar to the actions of the first astronauts on the moon.)*

STRATEGIC READING FOR
Less-Proficient Readers

U Ask students to explain what the expedition does once it reaches the North Pole. *(Once the expedition reached the North Pole, Henson planted the American flag. Then Peary left a glass jar containing part of the flag and two letters describing the expedition and claiming land for the United States.)*
Summarizing/Noting Sequence of Events

Set a Purpose Have students read to find out what happens to Henson following the expedition.

We had been travelling eighteen to twenty hours out of every twenty-four. Man, that was killing work! Forced marches all the time. From all our other expeditions we had found out that we couldn't carry food for more than fifty days, fifty-five at a pinch. . . .

We used to travel by night and sleep in the warmest part of the day. I was ahead most of the time with two of the Eskimos.

So Matthew Henson described the grueling journey. Finally, on the morning of April 6, Peary called a halt. Henson wrote: "I was driving ahead and was swinging around to the right. . . . The Commander, who was about 50 feet behind me, called to me and said we would go into camp. . . ." In fact, both Henson and Peary felt they might have reached the Pole already. That day, Peary took readings with a sextant[8] and determined that they were within three miles of the Pole. Later he sledged ten miles north and found he was traveling south; to return to camp, Peary would have to return north and then head south in another direction—something that could only happen at the North Pole. To be absolutely sure, the next day Peary again took readings from solar observations. It was the North Pole, he was sure.

On that day Robert Peary had Matthew Henson plant the American flag at the North Pole. Peary then cut a piece from the flag and placed it and two letters in a glass jar that he left at the Pole. The letters read:

90 N. Lat., North Pole
April 6, 1909

Arrived here today, 27 marches from C. Columbia.
I have with me 5 men, Matthew Henson, colored, Ootah, Egingwah, Seegloo, and Ooqueah, Eskimos; 5 sledges and 38 dogs. My ship, the S.S. Roosevelt, is in winter quarters at Cape Sheridan, 90 miles east of Columbia.
The expedition under my command which has succeeded in reaching the Pole is under the auspices of the Peary Arctic Club of New York City, and has been fitted out and sent north by members and friends of the Club for the purpose of securing this geographical prize, if possible, for the honor and prestige of the United States of America.
The officers of the Club are Thomas H. Hubbard of New York, President; Zenas Crane, of Mass., Vice-president; Herbert L. Bridgman, of New York, Secretary and Treasurer.
I start back for Cape Columbia tomorrow.
Robert E. Peary
United States Navy

90 N. Lat., North Pole
April 6, 1909

I have today hoisted the national ensign of the United States of America at this place, which my observations indicate to be the North Polar axis of the earth, and have formally taken possession of the entire region, and adjacent, for and in the name of the President of the United States of America.
I leave this record and United States flag in possession.
Robert E. Peary
United States Navy

Having accomplished their goal, the small group set out on the return journey. It was, Matthew Henson wrote, "17 days of haste, toil, and misery. . . . We crossed lead after lead, sometimes like a bareback rider in the circus, balancing on cake after cake of ice." Finally they reached the *Roosevelt*, where they

---
8. **sextant:** an instrument used to measure the positions of heavenly bodies.

60 UNIT ONE PART 1: SEIZING THE MOMENT

Mini-Lesson: Speaking, Listening, and Viewing

PRESS CONFERENCE Explain to students that a press conference is called when someone has an important announcement to make. Students have probably seen press conferences on television. Most press conferences include time for questions from reporters.

Application Have students work in groups to plan a press conference in which Peary announces that he has reached the North Pole. Have one group of students plan Peary's statement and elect one member of the group to portray Peary. The group may decide if other members of the expedition will speak. Another group of students should portray members of the press and plan questions to ask.

60 THE LANGUAGE OF LITERATURE TEACHER'S EDITION

Robert Peary (second from right) and Henson (far right) on board ship with other members of an expedition, 1909. Culver Pictures.

could rest and eat well at last. The Pole had been conquered!

During the return trip to New York City, Henson became increasingly puzzled by Peary's behavior. "Not once in [three weeks]," Henson wrote, "did he speak a word to me. Then he . . . ordered me to get to work. Not a word about the North Pole or anything connected with it." Even when the *Roosevelt* docked in New York in September of 1909, Peary remained withdrawn and silent, saying little to the press and quickly withdrawing to his home in Maine.

The ostensible[9] reason for his silence was that when the group returned to New York, they learned that Dr. Frederick A. Cook was claiming that *he* had gone to the North Pole—and done so before Peary reached it. Peary told his friends that he wished to wait for his own proofs to be validated by the scientific societies before he spoke. He felt sure that Cook would not be able to present the kinds of evidence that he could present, and so it proved.

On December 15, Peary was declared the first to reach the North Pole; Cook could not present adequate evidence that he had made the discovery. Peary and Bartlett were awarded gold medals by the National Geographic Society; Henson was not. Because Henson was black, his contributions to the expedition were not recognized for many years.

After 1909, Henson worked in a variety of jobs. For a while, he was a parking-garage

---

9. **ostensible** (ŏ-stĕn′sə-bəl): claimed, but not necessarily true.

WORDS
TO
KNOW

validate (văl′ĭ-dāt′) *v.* to show to be correct

CUSTOMIZING FOR
Gifted and Talented Students

Have students discuss Henson's belated recognition for his part in Peary's expedition. Ask them if it was an insult to Henson that he had to wait so long for acknowledgment or if he should have been satisfied that he was finally recognized. Challenge students to debate the possibility of an experience like Henson's happening today.

COMPREHENSION CHECK

1. What was Henson's first job? *(working in a restaurant in Washington, D.C.)*
2. Why did he leave this job? *(He wanted to become a sailor, so he left to find work on a ship.)*
3. How does Henson meet Peary? *(Peary came into the store where Henson was working as a stock clerk.)*
4. What was Henson's first job with Peary? *(He was Peary's personal servant during a trip to Nicaragua.)*
5. What did Henson and Peary accomplish in 1909? *(They reached the North Pole.)*
6. Why wasn't Henson honored for his contributions to the expedition? *(because he was African American)*

HISTORICAL INSIGHT

1. Why do you think people risk their lives to explore new lands? *(Possible responses: fame; adventure; chance for better living conditions; pride of discovery)*
2. How might the experiences of the Eskimos compare with Henson's experiences? *(Possible responses: They all risked their lives during the expedition; the Eskimos, like Henson, were not recognized, because of their race.)*

---

attendant in Brooklyn, and at the age of forty-six, he became a clerk in the U.S. customshouse in Lower Manhattan. In the meantime, friends tried again and again to have his contributions to the expedition recognized. At last, in 1937, nearly thirty years after the expedition, he was invited to join the Explorers Club in New York, and in 1944, Congress authorized a medal for all of the men on the expedition, including Matthew Henson.

After his death in New York City on March 9, 1955, another lasting tribute was made to Henson's endeavors. In 1961, his home state of Maryland placed a bronze tablet in memory of him in the state house. It reads, in part:

MATTHEW ALEXANDER HENSON
Co-discoverer of the North Pole
with Admiral Robert Edwin Peary
April 6, 1909

Son of Maryland, exemplification of courage, fortitude, and patriotism, whose valiant deeds of noble devotion under the command of Admiral Robert Edwin Peary, in pioneer Arctic exploration and discovery, established everlasting prestige and glory for his state and country

HISTORICAL INSIGHT

Early Explorers

Since prehistoric times people have had an urge to explore the unknown. The Eskimos who assisted Matthew Henson and Robert Peary called themselves Inuit. They were descendants of the people who first migrated to and explored the Americas between 20,000 and 40,000 years ago.

During the most recent ice age affecting North America, which ended about 10,000 years ago, the formation of glaciers helped open up areas for exploration. The levels of the world's oceans dropped because much of the earth's water was frozen. Natural land bridges appeared in places once covered by water. One such bridge connected Asia with the Americas across what is now called the Bering Strait. This bridge allowed the Asian ancestors of the Eskimos to follow the mammals they hunted into new lands and to colonize the northern part of North America.

The Eskimos spread from the northeastern tip of Russia across Alaska and northern Canada to Greenland. Today there are about 120,000 Eskimos in these regions.

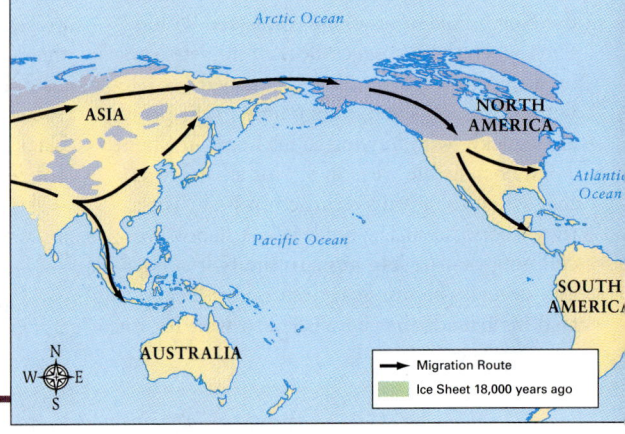

62 UNIT ONE PART 1: SEIZING THE MOMENT

Mini-Lesson · Spelling

SPELLING THE SOUND *shən* Explain to students that the sound *shən* is usually spelled *tion*. Write the following examples on the chalkboard. Encourage students to pronounce words carefully so that they spell them correctly.

deprivation   motivation
proposition   humiliation
expedition

Application Read the following words to the class. Have students write each word using the correct form of the sound *shən*.

1. contribution
2. observation
3. conjunction
4. violation
5. connection
6. selection
7. education
8. reconstruction
9. negotiation
10. graduation

Ask students to think of other words with the *shən* sound and to write them in their personal word lists.

Reteaching/Reinforcement
• *Unit One Resource Book*, p. 27

62 THE LANGUAGE OF LITERATURE TEACHER'S EDITION

RESPONDING OPTIONS

FROM PERSONAL RESPONSE TO CRITICAL ANALYSIS

REFLECT 1. How did reading about the events of Matthew Henson's life affect you? In your notebook, write about what impressed you the most. Then compare your ideas with those of your classmates.

RETHINK 2. How would you describe the relationship between Peary and Henson?
Consider
Close textual reading
- any traits the explorers had in common
- their years of taking risks together
- the descriptions of the men in each other's writings
- Peary's behavior after conquering the North Pole

3. If Robert Peary had asked Matthew Henson to accompany him on another expedition after 1909, do you think Henson would have accepted? Why or why not?

4. Look back at the adjectives you wrote for the Personal Connection on page 53. Which words best describe Matthew Henson? Compare your choices with your classmates' choices.

RELATE 5. What personal qualities of Matthew Henson do
Thematic Link you think would be useful for people venturing today into the unexplored regions of the world or into outer space? Explain your answer.

Multimodal Learning
ANOTHER PATHWAY
Cooperative Learning
In small groups prepare mock interviews of Peary and Henson after the expedition's arrival in New York City in 1909. Share your interviews with the class.

QUICKWRITES

1. In 1937, Matthew Henson was invited to join the Explorers Club in New York. Write the **acceptance speech** he might have given to that group.

2. Imagine that you are either Henson or Peary and write a **log entry** for one day of the three-week period after their arrival at the North Pole.

3. Throughout history there have been many "unsung," or uncelebrated, heroes. Write a **poem** that celebrates Matthew Henson and other heroes like him.

📁 **PORTFOLIO** *Save your writing. You may want to use it later as a springboard to a piece for your portfolio.*

LITERARY CONCEPTS

A **biography** is a true account of a person's life, written by another person. The writer looks at all of the facts that are available about the subject and decides what information to include in the biography. What kinds of research do you think Jim Haskins might have done to find out about Matthew Henson's role as co-discoverer of the North Pole?

MATTHEW HENSON AT THE TOP OF THE WORLD 63

From Personal Response to Critical Analysis

1. Encourage students to refer to the lists of characters traits they made for the Personal Connection on page 53.
2. Possible responses: Henson and Peary had similar values and goals—because of this, they respected each other; Peary's behavior after finding the North Pole was insulting and disrespectful toward Henson; the men could never be close because Henson was Peary's employee.
3. Possible responses: Yes, because Henson wanted to go on expeditions for the adventure. No, since Henson was not recognized as part of the expedition, he would not risk his life again.
4. Possible responses: brave, fearless, capable, friendly, loyal, adventurous, curious
5. Possible response: The qualities would be bravery and a sense of adventure. Without these qualities, Henson would have never had the desire to explore the world.

Another Pathway

Cooperative Learning Have students brainstorm questions and answers for the interview session. Then have them decide on the roles each will be playing. Each group should assign one student to be the interviewer and the other members to portray various characters from the selection. Remind students that characters' answers should be representative of the way the characters are portrayed in the selection.

Rubric
3 Full Accomplishment Group works well together and indicates an organized delineation of roles. Interviews show an understanding of events and characterization.
2 Substantial Accomplishment Group members less clear on defined roles. Some members interrupt or contradict others during presentation. Interviews indicate a misunderstanding of events or characters.
1 Little or Partial Accomplishment Group does not function well together. Interview questions and answers misrepresent events or characterization. Key characters are missing.

Literary Concepts

Students should recognize that Haskins might have used Henson's personal letters, journals, or diaries, as well as secondary sources such as encyclopedias and other materials.

QuickWrites

1. Have students base the tone of Henson's acceptance speech on their lists of personality traits from the Personal Connection on page 53.
2. Remind students to use sensory details and first-person point of view in their log entries. Encourage them to visualize the setting and the people of the selection.
3. Have students concentrate on the aspects that they believe make Henson a hero. Encourage them to incorporate these traits into their poems.

📁 The Writer's Craft

Personal Writing, p. 28–39
Personal Narrative, pp. 72–83
Writing a Poem, pp. 84–88

THE LANGUAGE OF LITERATURE TEACHER'S EDITION 63

Words to Know

1. tyranny
2. deprivation
3. resentful
4. surveyor
5. ardent
6. proposition
7. stamina
8. apt
9. validate
10. menial

Reteaching/Reinforcement
- *Unit One Resource Book*, p. 28

Across the Curriculum

Social Studies *Cooperative Learning* Have students brainstorm how they would like to approach their research and ask them to assign specific roles according to area of research. In each group, one student should also be assigned to record the plans, members' roles, and information found. Encourage students to consult a variety of reference books and stress that they look at recent sources of information.

ADDITIONAL SUGGESTION
Social Studies *Eskimos* Encourage partners or small groups to research and prepare a classroom display on the history and lifestyle of Eskimos. Remind students that their display should offer brief descriptions of Eskimo life and history and that they should support this information with detailed visual aids. Have students assign group work according to either research and visual roles, or according to subject headings that they create.

ART GALLERY
Eskimo and Inuit Art The art of Arctic peoples is strongly influenced by the artists' close relationship with their environment. These works show some of the materials used by Eskimo and Inuit artists.

Side A, Frame 38632

JIM HASKINS

In addition to being a respected writer of children's literature, Jim Haskins writes books for adults. His adult literature includes a number of biographies of famous African-American performers, such as Nat King Cole, Richard Pryor, and Scott Joplin. Haskins's novel, *The Cotton Club*, was the inspiration for Francis Ford Coppola's 1984 film of the same name.

THE WRITER'S STYLE

Haskins uses excerpts from diaries and letters in his biography of Henson. With a partner, choose a quotation from a diary or a letter in this selection. What effect do the personal words have on you, and why do you think Haskins includes them?

Multimodal Learning
ACROSS THE CURRICULUM

 Social Studies *Cooperative Learning* Robert Peary's claim to be the first to reach the North Pole was challenged as recently as 1989. Matthew Henson's role has also been questioned—did he actually plant the U.S. flag at the North Pole? Work with a small group of classmates to plan, research, and present a **status report** on the expedition. How have more-recent explorers attempted to prove or disprove the evidence for Peary's claim?

Important African-American figures in history, politics, entertainment, and sports have been the subjects of Jim Haskins's books. All of his works are nonfiction because Haskins has always preferred true stories to made-up ones. He has said, "It seems to me that the more you know about the real world, the better off you are."

Although Haskins learned to read early in his childhood, the public library in his Alabama hometown did not welcome black children. He stayed home and learned to rely on his family's encyclopedia. Explaining why African-Americans have usually been his subjects, he says, "I want children today, black and white, to be able to find books about black people and black history in case they want to read them." Haskins has written over 100 books, which have received a number of citations and awards, including the Coretta Scott King Award.

OTHER WORKS *The March on Washington*, *Against All Opposition: Black Explorers in America*, *Outward Dreams: Black Inventors and Their Inventions*

Extended Reading

WORDS TO KNOW

Review the Words to Know in the boxes at the bottom of the selection pages. On your paper, write the word that is closest in meaning to the italicized word or phrase in each sentence.

1. Matthew experienced the *extremely harsh and unjust treatment* that many blacks endured after the Civil War.
2. For many sailors in the 1800s, life at sea was filled with hard work and *lack of comforts*.
3. The presence of their black shipmate made some crew members *full of angry feelings*.
4. Peary worked as a *person who measures boundaries*.
5. Both Robert Peary and Matthew Henson felt an *enthusiastic* desire for adventure.
6. Peary had a *plan* for an expedition to the Arctic.
7. The Inuit admired Matthew's *endurance* in dealing with the Arctic region's cruel weather.
8. Peary described Matthew as a "hard worker" who was *"quick to learn."*
9. After returning from the North Pole, Peary had to wait for scientific societies to *show the correctness* of his proofs.
10. Once Matthew Henson's adventurous travels ended, only *poor, low-paying* jobs were available.

JIM HASKINS

1941–

• ART GALLERY

64 UNIT ONE PART 1: SEIZING THE MOMENT

Mini-Lesson — The Writer's Style

Invite students to review the Writer's Style Mini-Lesson on Your Own Voice on page 55. Encourage students to identify the personal words that are included in their chosen passage. Have partners compile lists of what the words mean to them. Then have them suggest possible explanations for Haskins's choices. Partners should compare their findings with other groups that studied similar quotations.

PREVIEWING

NONFICTION

My First Dive with the Dolphins
Don C. Reed

PERSONAL CONNECTION *Activating Prior Knowledge*
Think of encounters you have had with animals, perhaps in a zoo, in an aquarium, or even in your own backyard. Do these animals have personalities? Share your experiences with your classmates.

SCIENCE CONNECTION *Building Background*
In the selection you are about to read, the writer Don C. Reed describes his first encounter with dolphins. Marine dolphins are sea mammals closely related to whales and porpoises. Scientists rank dolphins among the most intelligent of animals, along with chimpanzees and dogs. Research has focused on dolphins' use of echolocation, a natural sound wave system with which they identify and locate underwater objects. Scientists are also studying how dolphins communicate among themselves by using series of whistles and clicks called phonations.

READING CONNECTION *Active Reading/Setting a Purpose*
Setting Purposes In this selection Reed is surprised by the differences in personalities among the dolphins he meets. Before reading, record what you already know about dolphins and what you want to know in a chart like the one shown. As you read, think about the surprising things that happen to Reed and the surprising things that you learn about dolphins.

What I (We) Know	What I (We) Want to Learn	What I (We) Learned
1. Marine dolphins are sea mammals closely related to whales and porpoises.		

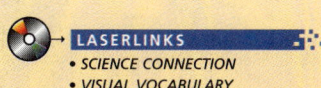
LASERLINKS
- SCIENCE CONNECTION
- VISUAL VOCABULARY

65

OVERVIEW

Objectives
- To understand and appreciate an autobiographical account of the author's first experience with dolphins
- To identify and understand author's purpose
- To express understanding of the selection through a choice of writing forms, including a summary, an editorial, and a diary entry
- To extend understanding of the selection through a variety of multimodal and cross-curricular activities

Skills

READING SKILLS/STRATEGIES
- Setting purposes

THE WRITER'S STYLE
- Details appealing to touch

GRAMMAR
- Subject pronouns

LITERARY CONCEPTS
- Author's purpose
- Description

SPELLING
- Using memory devices

STUDY SKILLS
- Outlining

SPEAKING, LISTENING, AND VIEWING
- Group discussion
- Oral presentation

Cross-Curricular Connections

SCIENCE
- Algae

SOCIAL STUDIES
- Oceanariums

GEOGRAPHY
- Dolphin homes

 **SCIENCE CONNECTION**
Talking with Dolphins Dolphins come to life in this film about research into dolphin communication. The intelligence and friendliness of these marine mammals have fascinated human beings for many centuries.

Side A, Frame 3231

PRINT AND MEDIA RESOURCES

UNIT ONE RESOURCE BOOK
Strategic Reading: Literature, p. 31
Vocabulary SkillBuilder, p. 34
Reading SkillBuilder, p. 32
Spelling SkillBuilder, p. 33

GRAMMAR MINI–LESSONS
Transparencies, p. 10
Copymasters, p. 12

WRITING MINI–LESSONS
Transparencies, p. 38

ACCESS FOR STUDENTS ACQUIRING ENGLISH
Selection Summaries
Reading and Writing Support

FORMAL ASSESSMENT
Selection Test, pp. 13–14
 Test Generator

 AUDIO LIBRARY
See Reference Card

 **LASERLINKS**
Science Connection
Art Gallery
Visual Vocabulary

INTERNET RESOURCES
McDougal Littell Literature Center at http://www.hmco.com/mcdougal/lit

THE LANGUAGE OF LITERATURE TEACHER'S EDITION **65**

SUMMARY

Don C. Reed includes many facts about dolphins in his account of his first day as a scuba diver at an oceanarium. When Reed nervously descends into the dolphin tank to clean it, the dolphins introduce themselves to him one by one. First comes Arnie, the troublemaker, who tries to scare Reed with a mock charge. Next comes gentle Ernestine, who allows him to stroke her side and pulls him on a dazzling underwater ride. Finally, Reed meets Lucky, the scarred and intelligent leader of the dolphins, who instantly commands the author's respect.

Thematic Link: *Seizing the Moment*
On his first dive with the dolphins, Don C. Reed seizes the moment and hitches a ride that changes his view of the underwater world.

CUSTOMIZING FOR
Students Acquiring English

- Use **ACCESS FOR STUDENTS ACQUIRING ENGLISH,** *Reading and Writing Support.*
- Except for unfamiliar vocabulary, this nonfiction selection should not present many comprehension problems. Because even native English speakers will be unfamiliar with much of the technical vocabulary, use this selection to build reading confidence in students acquiring English.

STRATEGIC READING FOR
Less-Proficient Readers

Set a Purpose To engage students in the selection, ask them to describe what they think swimming with dolphins might be like. Then have them read further to discover Don C. Reed's first thoughts about being in a tank full of dolphins.

Use **UNIT ONE RESOURCE BOOK,** pp. 31–32, for guidance in reading the selection.

MY FIRST DIVE with the Dolphins

by Don C. Reed

WORDS TO KNOW

aggression (ə-grĕsh′ən) *n.* threatening behavior; hostility (p. 70)
camouflage (kăm′ə-fläzh′) *n.* a disguise produced by blending in with the surroundings (p. 67)
coexistence (kō′ĭg-zĭs′təns) *n.* a state of living together in peace (p. 68)
compressed (kəm-prĕst′) *adj.* under greater than normal pressure **compress** *v.* (p. 67)
dominant (dŏm′ə-nənt) *adj.* having the most influence; controlling all others (p. 72)
elegant (ĕl′ĭ-gənt) *adj.* beautiful in shape or style (p. 71)
hurtle (hûr′tl) *v.* to move with great speed (p. 69)
luminous (lōō′mə-nəs) *adj.* full of light (p. 71)

magnification (măg′nə-fĭ-kā′shən) *n.* the causing of objects to appear enlarged (p. 68)
oceanarium (ō′shə-nâr′ē-əm) *n.* a large aquarium for the study and display of marine life (p. 67)

 VISUAL VOCABULARY

- **algae** (ăl′jē)
- **camouflage** (kăm′ə-fläzh′)
- **oceanarium** (ō′shə-nâr′ē-əm)
- **sonar** (sō′när′)

Side A, Frame 38637

66

 I stood on a narrow, red-painted stage above half a million gallons of cold salt water.

A wave slashed foam onto the stage and across my bare feet. I had a black rubber wet suit on but neither a hood nor "booties," those heavy neoprene[1] shoes that divers take for granted nowadays. It didn't occur to me to ask the other divers why we had neither foot nor head protection. I wore what the other folks wore. I wasn't about to complain: if the other divers had jumped off the edge in their underwear, I would have just shrugged and done the same.

That cold, windy March day in 1972 was my first day of work as a professional scuba diver for Marine World, soon to become Marine World/Africa USA, an oceanarium-zoo in northern California. I didn't let on how strange everything felt. I was only six months out of deep-sea-diving school and had almost no idea of what to expect.

The hard rubber mouthpiece still felt foreign clenched between my teeth. It seemed clumsy to breathe through my mouth instead of my nose. Each breath had to be "asked for," pulled in by a conscious lifting of the chest, creating a vacuum to suck in the compressed air.

Not wanting to dangle my legs in the water, I stood awkwardly on one foot at a time as I fumbled into the big, floppy swim fins.

As I pulled the black plastic mask over my face, the strap tugged at my hair. When I opened my eyes, my field of vision was narrowed by the mask. It was like staring through a section of pipe.

I took one giant step forward and fell . . . into another world.

I heard the crash of the surface as it broke apart and thumped shut above me; I felt the massage of pressure and the cold water rushing down my neck and spine. Air bubbles slid ticklingly up my face, heading for the surface, while I headed the opposite way, falling, dragged down by the heavy lead work belt around my waist. **A**

As the bubbles of my entry cleared, my vision returned. My fin tips folded softly underneath me as I landed on the green, algae-covered[2] floor. **B**

Oddly, I didn't spot the dolphins right away. Perhaps their dark/light camouflage patterns broke up their outlines. Then, all at once, there they

---

1. **neoprene** (nē′ə-prēn′): a weather-resistant synthetic rubber.
2. **algae-covered** (ăl′jē-kŭv′ərd): covered with algae, tiny plantlike organisms that grow in water.

WORDS TO KNOW
oceanarium (ō′shə-nâr′ē-əm) *n.* a large aquarium for the study and display of marine life
compressed (kəm-prĕst′) *adj.* under greater than normal pressure **compress** *v.*
camouflage (kăm′ə-fläzh′) *n.* a disguise produced by blending in with the surroundings

67

CUSTOMIZING FOR
Gifted and Talented Students
Tell students to note, as they read the selection, what Reed tells himself in order to overcome his fears and to explain the cause of his anxiety.

Possible responses:
- Page 68—"It's only the magnification down here, I told myself."/The dolphins' size is larger than expected.
- Page 68—"I reminded myself they were not sharks."/The dolphins seem more threatening than friendly.
- Page 70—"Hold still; don't do anything to make him think you want to fight."/Arnie is trying to intimidate Reed by swimming toward him at a high speed.
- Page 72—"Why fight it? I thought, dropping my scrub brush."/Ernestine's offers to tow Reed are too tempting to pass up.

Literary Concept: DESCRIPTION

A Have students note the details Reed uses to describe what it feels like to dive into the water. Encourage them to look for details that appeal to the senses. (Possible responses: "crash of the surface"; "thumped"; "massage of pressure"; "cold water rushing"; "slid ticklingly up my face"; "dragged down")

Linking to Science

 B Algae are a diversified group of plantlike organisms that live mostly in water. The algae in the sea comprise one of the world's most important sources of oxygen.

Mini-Lesson   Reading Skills/Strategies

ACTIVE READING: SETTING PURPOSES
Explain that the strategy of questioning plays an important role in setting purposes. Readers who ask questions as they read will become more involved in what they are reading. Encourage students to make notes—mental or written—as they read. Such notes might concern words or statements that interest or confuse them. Remind students that a confusing point may become clearer as they continue reading.

Application This activity might be done as an alternative to using the KWL chart presented in the Reading Connection on page 65. Encourage students to add their questions to a chart similar to the one shown, while they are reading. If time allows, have them share any unanswered questions with classmates.

Reteaching/Reinforcement
- *Unit One Resource Book*, p. 32

What is happening?	How does the character feel?	What do I think?	Possible Answer
Reed is about to dive into the dolphin tank.	He seems to be afraid.	Why is he doing it if he is afraid?	It's something he has always wanted to do.

THE LANGUAGE OF LITERATURE TEACHER'S EDITION **67**

Literary Concept:
CHARACTERIZATION

C Ask students how Reed describes the size of the dolphins. *(Possible responses: He says that they were bigger than he thought; he compares them to a professional wrestler or a football player.)*

Active Reading: PREDICT

D Have students predict whether Arnie will try to scare Reed. If so, have them predict how Reed will respond to the dolphin.

CUSTOMIZING FOR
Students Acquiring English

I Point out to students that Lassie (a dog) and Flipper (a dolphin) were stars of popular TV shows in the 1960s. Explain that *man's best friend* is an idiomatic expression referring to dogs.

STRATEGIC READING FOR
Less-Proficient Readers

E Ask the following questions to make sure students understand who the characters are and what they are doing by this point in the selection.

- Who is telling the story? *(Don C. Reed, the author)* Drawing Conclusions
- What is the difference between Spock and Arnie? *(Spock is expected not to bother Reed, but Arnie might give him trouble.)* Comparing and Contrasting

Set a Purpose Encourage students to continue reading to find out how Reed behaves during his first encounter with a dolphin.

Critical Thinking: CLASSIFYING

F Ask students to discuss the differences between dolphins and sharks. *(Possible responses: Dolphins use their teeth for fishing, not for ripping flesh. Dolphins are mammals, sharks are fish.)*

Subject Pronoun	
I	you
he	she
it	we
they	

C were—and so much *bigger* than I had expected. It's only the magnification down here, I told myself, a trick of underwater light. But I knew they weighed between 300 and 400 pounds each, as much as a giant professional wrestler or the biggest lineman on a football team.

I tried to remember the one-minute human-dolphin coexistence lesson that head diver Ted Pintarelli had given me.

"Spock—that's the one with the hole in his fin—he won't bother you. Neither will Delbert: he's got a shark scar on his belly that makes him easy to spot. The smallest one's Ernestine; she's okay. Lucky is king bull, the toughest dolphin in the tank. You'll recognize *him* right away: there's a purple spot on his cheek, and he's big and all scarred up from fights, and . . . well, you'll know him!

D "But Arnie, he's the one who'll give you trouble. He thinks he's bad, and he likes to try and scare new guys in the tank. Like he might swim fast at you or something. Just hold still if he does. Don't let him chase you out of the tank, or he'll make a game out of it, and you'll never get any work done. Don't look scared. He'll leave you alone . . . most of the time, anyway," the muscular, red-faced diver had added with a grin.

I had always thought of dolphins as sweet and gentle, like Flipper on the old TV show, who was sort of an oceangoing Lassie, man's best friend in the sea. Now I tried to figure out which one was Arnie. He was supposed to have a lower jaw shaped like a hook, whatever that meant. But it was no use: I couldn't tell the dolphins apart. They all looked like trouble to me. **E**

As the streamlined but massive gray creatures cruised around me, I reminded myself they were not sharks. Their eighty-eight white, needlelike teeth, which I could see so clearly, were meant for snagging swift herring on the run, not for ripping out a twenty-pound mouthful of flesh, as a white shark's teeth were. Dolphins were mammals, not fish, and the reason for the up-and-down motion of their tails was to bring them back up to the air. **F**

> "But Arnie, he's the one who'll give you trouble. . . . He likes to try and scare new guys in the tank."

Some said dolphins were smart like people. Certainly dolphins could do things with sonar[3] that we humans couldn't match. In one experiment I read about, dolphins were able to distinguish between two types of identical-looking plastic-coated wire—one with a lead core, the other with a copper core—just by sending their special clicking sounds inside them.

Well, I wasn't getting a whole lot of work done this way. In the distance I could see the three other divers, already lying down on the floor, their scrub brushes busy. As it was for them, cleaning algae off the underwater floors and walls and windows would be 95 percent of my job. The other 5 percent, the head diver **G** had promised, would be magic.

None of the divers had air tanks. Each diver breathed through a thin yellow air hose leading up to the surface, where it was plugged into a brass outlet on an air compressor. I

---

3. **sonar** (sō'när'): detection of objects by reflected sound waves.

WORDS TO KNOW
magnification (măg'nə-fĭ-kā'shən) *n.* the causing of objects to appear enlarged
coexistence (kō'ĭg-zĭs'təns) *n.* a state of living together in peace

68

 Mini-Lesson

SUBJECT PRONOUNS Explain to students that a subject pronoun can take the place of a noun that is the subject of a sentence. Subject pronouns also can be used after linking verbs. The following rules apply to the use of subject pronouns:

Use subject pronouns as the subject of a verb: <u>He</u> won't bother you.

Use subject pronouns as part of compound subjects: Ted and <u>he</u> went diving.

Use subject pronouns after linking verbs, such as *is*: A tough dolphin is <u>he</u>.

Application Have students choose the correct subject pronouns for the following sentences.

1. Spock and (she, her) hurtled toward Reed. *(she)*
2. The dolphin that swam past Reed is (he, him). *(he)*
3. Arnie and (I, me) did not get along. *(I)*

Reteaching/Reinforcement
- *Grammar Handbook*, anthology pp. 824–825
- *Grammar Mini-Lessons* copymasters, p. 12, transparencies, p. 10

The Writer's Craft
Using Subject Pronouns, pp. 440–441

---

68 THE LANGUAGE OF LITERATURE TEACHER'S EDITION

H noticed the strange shape of the bubbles as they left my regulator and wobbled to the surface. They were not round but dome-shaped, flat on the bottom, and they changed as they rose toward the mirrorlike surface twenty feet above.

In my hand was a short iron-handled scrub brush. I held it in the special way Ted had shown me.

"If you hold it the regular way, like a hairbrush, you can't get anything but wrist power behind it," Ted said. "But upside-down, the bristles are next to your palm, and you get your whole body into it. Switch hands every ten or twelve brush strokes, too, so you won't have to stop and rest."

Lying down in a sort of pushup position, I took an experimental scrub stroke at the floor. The brush was neither motorized nor self-operational. My tentative push did not accomplish much. Some scratches appeared in the green algae; that was all. The stuff clung like paint!

The algae has to be taken off, or it grows thicker and thicker and finally rots, breaking off at the roots, clouding the water, clogging the filtration system, and plugging up the windows. There are chemical ways to kill algae, of course, but these cannot be used because they are harmful to the dolphins' eyes.

I So we divers scrubbed. Algae was our job security!

I turned the brush on edge, so that the stroke it made would be one inch wide instead of six, and leaned all my shoulder strength behind the stroke. Now the brush bit. There. I had a one-by-twelve-inch piece of clean white floor. Just eleven more strokes and I'd have one whole square foot finished. And since the tank was 60 by 80 feet, that meant there were only 4,799 more square feet to go. **J**

Suddenly a blur of movement caught my eye. A dolphin was <u>hurtling</u> toward me. Although it was closing the distance between us unbelievably fast, I saw it as if it were in slow motion.

© Al Giddings/The Image Bank

WORDS TO KNOW
hurtle (hûr′tl) *v.* to move with great speed

69

Critical Thinking: HYPOTHESIZING

G Ask students to discuss what they think the head diver, Pintarelli, meant by "magic." *(Possible response: Most of the job would be routine and boring, but a small part would be wonderful and exciting.)*

Linking to Science

 **H** The regulator is attached to the diver's mouthpiece. It contains valves that control, or regulate, the flow of air from the supply tube into the diver's mouth as well as the flow of exhaled air into the water.

Active Reading: CLARIFY

I Have students clarify what Reed means when he states that "algae was our job security!" If students are having problems, you may wish to use the following model to give them ideas of what they might be thinking about.

Think-Aloud Model *Reading this statement led me to look back at page 68, to find Reed's statement that 95 percent of his job is scraping the algae off the inside of the tank. I think the narrator means that as long as there is algae to remove, he and all the other divers will have jobs.*

CUSTOMIZING FOR
Multiple Learning Styles

J **Logical-Mathematical Learners** Ask students to use Reed's formula to calculate the number of brush strokes it would take to clean the following floor sizes:

50 feet × 100 feet *(5,000 square feet = 60,000 brush strokes)*

150 feet × 150 feet *(22,500 square feet = 270,000 brush strokes)*

100 feet × 120 feet *(12,000 square feet = 144,000 brush strokes)*

Mini-Lesson  Literary Concepts

REVIEWING DESCRIPTION Remind students that a writer uses description to create a picture of a scene, an event, or a character. Writers choose details carefully to create descriptions. These details, sometimes called sensory details, usually appeal to a reader's sense of sight, sound, smell, touch, or taste.

Application Invite students to copy the web from this page into their notebooks, and encourage them to refer to it as they read the selection. Ask them to think about the different details used to describe the characters, scenes, and events in "My First Dive with the Dolphins." For example, refer them to the highlighted description above of the bubbles from Reed's air hose.

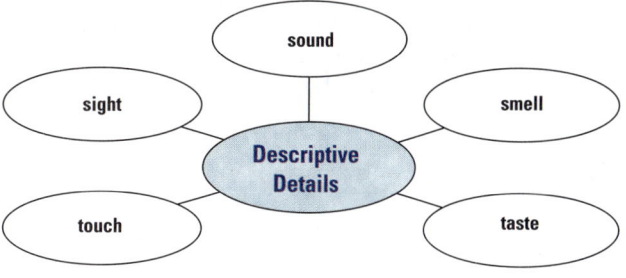

THE LANGUAGE OF LITERATURE TEACHER'S EDITION **69**

Literary Concept: DESCRIPTION

K Ask students why Reed describes Arnie's approach in such detail. *(Possible responses: to show Arnie's movements from Reed's point of view; to show the strong effect Arnie's actions have on him at that moment.)*

CUSTOMIZING FOR
Students Acquiring English

2 Point out that *Whooosh* and *klonk* are examples of onomatopoeia, words that imitate sounds. Encourage students to say these words with correct pronunciation and appropriate intonation.

CUSTOMIZING FOR
Multiple Learning Styles

L Bodily-Kinesthetic Learners
Have interested volunteers form a group to act out Arnie's attack. Encourage them to include the other dolphins and divers in their skit.

Literary Concept:
AUTHOR'S PURPOSE

M Ask students whether the narrator's encounter with Arnie is entertaining or informative? *(Possible responses: It is informative because Reed shows how a dolphin behaves and how it looks up close. It is entertaining because Reed uses interesting details that paint clear pictures of the encounter.)*

STRATEGIC READING FOR
Less-Proficient Readers

N Ask students to describe what Reed was doing before Arnie charged at him. *(Reed was scrubbing the algae off the inside of the tank before Arnie's charge.)* Noting Sequence of Events

Set a Purpose Have students pay close attention to the differences among the dolphins as students read the next section.

© Norbert Wu/Tony Stone Images

The dolphin's lower jaw hooked over its top one: it was Arnie. His head moved up and down violently, and his tail moved so fast that a trail of bubbles formed behind it. As the dolphin charged, I heard a roar of cavitation[4] as the very water tore, breaking into hydrogen and oxygen.

I didn't even have time to flinch properly. It was easy to do just what Ted recommended. I froze.

I knew that if the dolphin ran into me at that speed, whatever he hit would be broken. This was how dolphins were able to kill sharks: they smashed their insides with a high-speed ram.

Whooosh! I felt rather than heard a wash of water like a great wind. I saw the dolphin's stomach—he had a bellybutton! —then the animal turned like a veering jet.

But not to go away. No more than six feet from me, he stopped. I saw his narrow face, saw his jaws move, heard the *klonk* that I knew signaled aggression. His white teeth gleamed, sharp and clean as if they had been brushed. But dolphins do not fight seriously with their teeth.

In a motion so fast my mind had to reconstruct it afterward, the gristly ridge on the underside of the dolphin's tail flukes suddenly appeared right before my face. It was as if a baseball bat had been swung at my head—and stopped an inch before my face caved in.

Again I did nothing, but not through courage. My reflexes are slow. I had time to tell myself, Hold still; don't do anything to make him think you want to fight. I also had time to feel a wave of anger at this huge animal for picking on me for no reason at all.

Then another dolphin, heavy-bodied with a purple spot on the left side of his beak, eased into my vision, and Arnie casually swam off with him.

When my heart and breathing rates returned to relative normality, I went back to my work. I scrubbed and watched, and watched and scrubbed. My shoulders began to feel pumped full of blood, as they do in weightlifting workouts.

---

4. **cavitation** (kăv′ĭ-tā′shən): sudden formation of bubbles in a liquid by an object moving rapidly through it.

| WORDS TO KNOW | **aggression** (ə-grĕsh′ən) *n.* threatening behavior; hostility |

70

Mini-Lesson Study Skills

OUTLINING Tell students that making an outline is a helpful way to organize information, particularly the notes they take in class and as they read. Outlines show the main points and the smaller details of a topic. Point out that in a topic outline the main points and subpoints can be written in words or phrases. Roman numerals indicate the main points, capital letters show the subpoints, and Arabic numerals indicate the details.

Application One of the Alternative Activities on page 74 offers students the opportunity to research dolphins. Encourage students to organize their notes on one of these subjects into an outline.

70 THE LANGUAGE OF LITERATURE **TEACHER'S EDITION**

Suddenly something shining caught my attention. I turned my head, and the whirring roar of the regulator seemed to disappear.

In stillness like the hush in a cathedral, I saw the smallest dolphin move her head just slightly, and from the back of her neck something silvery emerged, as if she were manufacturing a halo.

Naah. Yes! There it was: a glistening, gleaming, silver bubble ring, rising. The dolphin flexed her neck again, and another ring emerged, rising faster, so that it joined its <u>luminous</u> relation and they merged, becoming first a figure eight and then a larger single circle, a Hula-Hoop of light.

After I'd spent nearly two hours in the water, the scrubbed-off algae was rising in darkening clouds, like night closing in.

I kept switching the brush back and forth, from hand to hand, trying not to think about Arnie. Long ago, in India, there was a saying that you should not worry about tigers, lest you bring one to you by the thought.

Still, I couldn't help wondering where he was. My head began to shift back and forth more rapidly as I tried to see but couldn't.

Just then, something touched me!

I rolled, ready to fight, and looked into the red-brown eye and the face of . . . whom?

It was definitely not the hook jaw of Arnie, and the purple spot of Lucky's cheek was not there. Spock was supposed to have a hole in his left pec fin, while Delbert had a shark scar. This must be Ernestine.

I told myself she wasn't really smiling: that happy look was just an accident of jaw formation, indicating nothing more than lines of bone and muscle. But looking at her made me feel happy just the same.

She was so beautiful. From a distance, the dolphins had looked simple, uncomplicated. But up close, everything about Ernestine was astonishing. The black pupil in the center of her red-brown eye seemed to radiate emotion. Six inches back from the eye was a fold of skin with an opening the size of a pinhole in it, the opening to her ear. Even the dolphin's skin was special: not perfectly smooth but textured with the tiniest of lines and colored with subtle gray patterns that were perfectly matched and fitted together, like the interlocking feathers on a hawk.

She had pectoral (chest) fins to steer with, tail flukes for power, and a blowhole at the back of her head that could release breath at 200 miles per hour, punching a hole in the ocean spray so the dolphin could inhale relatively dry air and not drown in a storm. From the shape of her beak—the reason for the name "bottlenose"—to the <u>elegant</u> flare of her tail flukes, she was a creature of wonder. I felt I could study her for a thousand years and not see everything.

> She was so beautiful. . . .
> Up close, everything about
> Ernestine was astonishing.

Ernestine nuzzled in beside me and laid her pectoral fin on my back.

This amazed me. A big animal I had never met before, and it swam up and touched me!

I couldn't resist her. Without conscious thought, my hand reached up and stroked her side. It felt smooth, soft, and firm, like the inside surface of a hard-boiled egg.

Suddenly the dolphin rolled, bringing the fin on her back into my hand. Then she took off.

WORDS TO KNOW
luminous (lōō'mə-nəs) *adj.* full of light
elegant (ĕl'ĭ-gənt) *adj.* beautiful in shape or style

71

Literary Concept: DESCRIPTION

O Have students indicate which words in this passage paint clear pictures in their minds of the scene. *(Possible responses: gleaming, silver, luminous, figure eight, circle, light)*

Critical Thinking: SYNTHESIZING

P Ask students what the saying about tigers has to do with Reed's present situation. *(Possible response: Reed recalls the saying as a way of helping him to put Arnie out of his mind.)*

STRATEGIC READING FOR Less-Proficient Readers

Q Ask students to explain the differences between Reed's encounter with Arnie and his encounter with Ernestine. *(Reed first meets Arnie when the dolphin charges at him. Reed's first encounter with Ernestine involves watching her make air bubble rings.)*
Summarizing/Noting Relevant Details

Set a Purpose Ask students to find out Reed's reaction to his next encounter with Ernestine as they continue reading.

CUSTOMIZING FOR Multiple Learning Styles

R **Spatial or Graphic Learners** Take this opportunity to have students make detailed sketches of Ernestine based on Reed's description of her appearance. You may want to display students' sketches in the classroom.

Mini-Lesson The Writer's Style

DETAILS APPEALING TO TOUCH Help students understand that throughout this selection, Reed uses specific sensory details to make his descriptions vivid. One of the senses Reed appeals to is touch. For example, refer students to the passage highlighted at the right. By using specific details related to touch *(smooth, soft, firm)*, Reed helps readers imagine what he feels as he touches Ernestine.

Application Encourage students to refer to the chart of touch words as they read the selection and to record in their notebooks any other touch words they find.

Reteaching/Reinforcement
• *Writer's Handbook,* anthology pp. 784–785
• *Writing Mini-Lessons* transparencies, p. 38

 The Writer's Craft
Appealing to the Senses, pp. 266–273

Touch Words		
cool	damp	slippery
icy	rough	smooth
waxy	furry	mushy

THE LANGUAGE OF LITERATURE TEACHER'S EDITION **71**

Critical Thinking: ANALYZING

S Have students discuss what comparisons Reed is making when he describes how it feels to be towed by Ernestine. *(Reed thinks that he is clumsy on land, but he feels graceful when he is swimming like a dolphin.)*

Literary Concept:
AUTHOR'S PURPOSE

T Ask students whether Reed's purpose in referring to Lucky in so many different ways is to entertain, to inform, or to persuade readers. *(Possible responses: Reed's purpose is to entertain readers by presenting a vivid description of an interesting subject. Reed's purpose is to inform readers about what a dolphin that behaves like Lucky is called.)*

STRATEGIC READING FOR
Less-Proficient Readers

U Have students give their opinions of Reed's future relationship with the dolphins. *(Possible responses: The fact that Lucky leaves Reed alone suggests that Reed is being accepted by the dolphins.)* Summarizing/Making Inferences

---

CUSTOMIZING FOR
Gifted and Talented Students

Have students discuss whether dolphins are as intelligent as humans. Challenge students to debate whether a dolphin's behavior is due mostly to training or to its own intelligence.

COMPREHENSION CHECK

1. Where is Reed at the time of this account? *(in the dolphin tank at Marine World)*
2. Why is he there? *(He has a job as a professional scuba diver, cleaning algae from the dolphin tank.)*
3. Of the dolphins in the tank, which were the ones to look out for? *(Lucky and Arnie)*
4. What does Arnie do when he spots Reed? *(He charges him.)*
5. How does Lucky react to Reed's presence? *(Lucky faces the narrator for a moment, appearing to discourage him from getting too friendly with Ernestine, then he leaves Reed alone.)*

he suddenness of the motion frightened me, and instantly I straightened my fingers, releasing the loose grip I had held so as not to make her feel restrained. Had I offended her?

But she turned and came back, rolling again to place her dorsal fin (the one on her back) in my right hand.

Why fight it? I thought, dropping my scrub brush.

This time, when Ernestine took off, I went along.

I left my human clumsiness behind. For glorious seconds I knew what it was to be the swiftest swimmer in the sea. She towed me, and I tried not to get in the way. I was conscious of my body's shape as an obstruction and tried to narrow myself.

We soared. The water rushed past my face and swirled around my body, and I felt the streaking lines of speed.

Klonk! At the sound, Ernestine flicked out and away from my hand and was gone in an instant. I hung in the water, becoming a sluggish human once again.

Before me "stood" a gray-white dolphin giant. There was no question as to his identity. I knew it was Lucky even before I saw the scars on his face and neck and shoulders and the dark spot on the left side of his jaw.

The <u>dominant</u> dolphin lowered his head slowly. Again I heard the noise of irritation, threat, or challenge, and for an instant I thought he would give me trouble for getting too friendly with Ernestine. But the *klonk*ing sound was softer now, as if the point had already been made.

I was in the presence of a leader. Whether I labeled him "alpha male" or "dominant dolphin bull" or "king among his own kind" made no difference. This chunk of sea was Lucky's territory, and he was very definitely in charge.

There was depth to Lucky, and intelligence. It was an intelligence different from my own, perhaps, but certainly deserving of respect. He looked like he knew how to live and how to die, like an Apache[5] chieftain living in the wild, who would find hardship and danger at every turn and was content that it should be so.

I was in the presence of a leader.

I did not understand all this at once, of course. I had no words to express what I felt then. There were only raw emotions, ideas, possibilities. My brain felt staggered, like a computer with information overload.

Trying to show neither fear nor aggression (and certainly not disrespect!), I let myself drift down, settling slowly back to the floor of the tank, to my dropped scrub brush, to my work.

Lucky only watched me go and made no move to follow. ❖

---
5. **Apache** (ə-păch′ē): belonging to a Native American people of the southwestern United States and northern Mexico.

WORDS TO KNOW
dominant (dŏm′ə-nənt) *adj.* having the most influence; controlling all others

---

Mini-Lesson Spelling

USING MEMORY DEVICES Remind students that becoming a good speller requires planning and practice. Point out that by learning some spelling tips and basic rules, they can improve their spelling. One tip is to invent memory devices to remember the spelling of difficult words. Share the following examples based on the Words to Know for this selection.

camou<u>flage</u>   The <u>flag</u> was blowing in the wind.

coex<u>ist</u>ence   There were <u>ten</u> dolphins in the tank.

agg<u>res</u>sion   The <u>egg</u> salad stain ruined her dre<u>ss</u>.

Application Have students write the following words in their personal word lists and ask them to invent memory devices for each one.

1. oceanarium
2. cavitation
3. embarrass
4. definitely
5. massive
6. sonar
7. magnification
8. occasion
9. luminous
10. oxygen

Reteaching/Reinforcement
• Unit One Resource Book, p. 33

---

72 THE LANGUAGE OF LITERATURE TEACHER'S EDITION

RESPONDING OPTIONS

FROM PERSONAL RESPONSE TO CRITICAL ANALYSIS

REFLECT 1. How did you react to the experiences described in the selection? Write down your thoughts in your notebook.

RETHINK 2. How do you think Lucky treated Don C. Reed when he entered the tank the next day? Give reasons for your answer.

3. What personality trait or traits does Reed have that you think would be helpful in working with dolphins?
Consider
Close textual reading
- Reed's reaction to the diving gear he received
- how he dealt with the job of removing algae
- his reactions to Arnie, Ernestine, and Lucky

4. The head diver told Reed that 95 percent of his job would be the cleaning of algae and 5 percent would be "magic." What was magical about Reed's job?

5. How do you think Reed feels during his first day on the job?

RELATE 6. On the basis of what you learned from the selection, would you want a job like the author's? Explain.

Multimodal Learning
ANOTHER PATHWAY

Create a chart with five columns, and label each one with a dolphin's name. Refer to Ted Pintarelli's descriptions of each dolphin's characteristics and to the author's own observations. List the personality traits of each dolphin in the appropriate column. Then compare and contrast the dolphins in an oral presentation for the class.

QUICKWRITES

1. In the last column of the chart you created for the Reading Connection on page 65, record any new ideas you learned about dolphins. Write a brief **summary** of what you learned, and explain what piece of information was the most surprising to you.

2. Should dolphins be held in captivity? Consider both the advantages for scientific research and the arguments against holding any wild animals captive. Choose one side of the issue, and write an **editorial** that expresses your opinion.

📁 **PORTFOLIO** *Save your writing. You may want to use it later as a springboard to a piece for your portfolio.*

LITERARY CONCEPTS

Authors write for four main reasons, or **purposes**: to entertain, to inform, to express opinions, and to persuade. A writer may combine two or three purposes in one piece of writing, but one purpose is usually the most important. What purposes do you think Don C. Reed had in mind when he wrote about his first dive? Which of these purposes do you think was most important to him? Explain.

Author's Purpose
- to entertain
- to inform
- to express opinions
- to persuade

MY FIRST DIVE WITH THE DOLPHINS **73**

From Personal Response to Critical Analysis

1. Responses will vary.
2. Possible responses: Lucky probably would be less wary of Reed since Reed presented no threat to him; just because Lucky was not aggressive on Reed's first day in the tank does not mean that he won't be aggressive when Reed returns.
3. Some students might suggest that Reed's enthusiasm is his most helpful trait. Because Reed is willing to do a good job and to make contact with dolphins, he is willing to do the tiring work and deal with a degree of risk.
4. Possible responses: Simply being in a tank with dolphins is "magic"; being in actual contact with the dolphins is "magic."
5. Possible responses: Reed has brief moments of fear; however, his basic feelings range from excitement to a sense of wonder and respect.
6. Responses will vary.

Another Pathway

Cooperative Learning Have students work independently on their lists of personality traits. Then ask them to work with partners to compare their lists. Have them brainstorm a list of comparisons and contrasts for each personality trait. For their oral presentations, one partner can present the comparisons and the other the contrasts.

Rubric

3 Full Accomplishment Partners collaborate on detailed list of similarities and differences. Student lists of traits are well organized and show attention to detail.

2 Substantial Accomplishment Partners illustrate less ability to collaborate on their presentations. Students either omit traits or offer less-detailed lists.

1 Little or Partial Accomplishment Partners show lack of ability to work together in a constructive manner. Student lists omit characters.

Literary Concepts

Have students work in small groups to decide on Reed's possible purposes for writing this selection. Then have them refer to the selection and list examples of each of the purposes. Ask groups to review their lists to decide which of the purposes they believe is the most important to Reed. Then have them brainstorm possible reasons for their findings. Groups should compare their findings with another group.

The Writer's Craft
Goals and Audience, pp. 211–213

QuickWrites

1. Have students review all of the columns from their charts on page 65. Encourage them to explain which new information was surprising and why.
2. Have students make a list of both the advantages and disadvantages of keeping animals in captivity. Remind them that, for an editorial, they should present their ideas convincingly by supporting their opinions.

THE LANGUAGE OF LITERATURE TEACHER'S EDITION **73**

Words to Know

1. oceanarium
2. compressed
3. coexistence
4. camouflage
5. magnification
6. aggression
7. luminous
8. elegant
9. dominant
10. hurtle

Reteaching/Reinforcement
• *Unit One Resource Book*, p. 34

Across the Curriculum

Social Studies *Cooperative Learning Oceanariums* Oceanariums differ from facility to facility and are different from zoos and aquariums. Have students form small groups to research the differences among oceanariums. The following questions may help students get started. Do these facilities have different philosophies about the study of marine life? What are the differences in the range of animals these facilities choose? Where do they obtain their animals? Do the facilities use animals for entertainment or educational purposes?

Geography *Dolphin Homes* Students can form pairs to research the areas of the world with dolphin populations. Have them create a map of the world indicating the locations of dolphin populations. Pairs can present their maps and explain to the class where and why dolphins inhabit certain areas.

Don C. Reed

The author views his writing as a way to "help the world." As he states, "I want my writing to be a positive force. I will not write empty entertainment. I want my stuff to have . . . value ."

ART GALLERY
Dolphins in History The relationship between human beings and dolphins is well documented in the art of ancient Greece and other civilizations of the past. Depictions of dolphins in various media—including frescoes, mosaics, and pottery—are shown here.

Side A, Frame 38642

Multimodal Learning

ALTERNATIVE ACTIVITIES

1. Reed says, "I took one giant step forward and fell . . . into another world." Which of his descriptions helped you experience the feeling of being underwater? Draw or paint a **scene** from the selection that inspires you.

2. **Cooperative Learning** Working with others, arrange an on-line interview with a representative of an oceanarium or a seaquarium to find out about others' direct experiences with dolphins. Prepare questions in advance, and present your information in an **interview report** to your class.

WORDS TO KNOW

Review the Words to Know in the boxes at the bottom of the selection pages. On your paper, write the vocabulary word that best completes each sentence.

1. The dolphins lived in a large outdoor _____.
2. The divers used air hoses rather than tanks as their source of _____ air.
3. Ted gave the author a short lesson in human-dolphin _____.
4. Dolphins are not easy to see underwater because of the _____ provided by their coloring.
5. The water in the tank produced a _____ of objects, making them appear larger.
6. An angry dolphin makes a special sound that is a sign of _____.
7. The smallest dolphin, Ernestine, created silvery, _____ rings in the water.
8. The narrator described the _____ flare of the dolphin's fluke.
9. Ted described Lucky as the largest, most aggressive, and _____ dolphin in the tank.
10. One dolphin, Arnie, liked to scare new divers and would _____ through the water toward them.

74 UNIT ONE PART 1: SEIZING THE MOMENT

DON C. REED

1945–

Don C. Reed began his career as a scuba diver in 1972, at Marine World near San Francisco, California. The seaquarium later became Marine World/Africa USA, an oceanarium-zoo, and moved to Vallejo, California. Reed spent 15 years there, eventually becoming head diver.

Reed has described himself as someone who tries to "listen" to what an animal is thinking. Although not a scientist, he believes that human beings and sea animals can coexist and that they can communicate their thoughts to each other by means of a yet-to-be discovered form of extrasensory perception. Reed's experiences over a 15-year period with a variety of sea creatures have provided the material for several articles and books. He has written for the magazines *Oceans* and *Highlights for Children*. "My First Dive with the Dolphins" is an excerpt from his book *The Dolphins and Me*.

OTHER WORKS *Notes from an Underwater Zoo, Sevengill: The Shark and Me, The Kraken* Extended Readin

LASERLINKS
• ART GALLERY

Alternative Activities

1. Remind students that when choosing from Reed's descriptions they should pay special attention to sensory details, especially those related to sight. Have students make a list of details from their chosen description prior to drawing. Have students compare drawings with the rest of the class.

2. Encourage students to review their list from the Personal Connection charts on page 65. Have them note any unanswered questions they have and incorporate them into their list of interview questions. Suggest that students find a partner to help present the interview results to the class.

THE LANGUAGE OF LITERATURE **TEACHER'S EDITION**

ON YOUR OWN

Tuesday of the Other June

by Norma Fox Mazer

"Be good, be good, be good, be good, my Junie," my mother sang as she combed my hair; a song, a story, a croon, a plea. "It's just you and me, two women alone in the world, June darling of my heart; we have enough troubles getting by, we surely don't need a single one more, so you keep your sweet self out of fighting and all that bad stuff. People can be little-hearted, but turn the other cheek, smile at the world, and the world'll surely smile back."

TUESDAY OF THE OTHER JUNE   **75**

OBJECTIVES

- To promote independent active reading
- To apply and practice skills learned in previous selections
- To provide an opportunity to assess students' performance through an alternative assessment instrument

Reading Pathways

- Invite students to read the selection aloud in small groups.
- Have volunteers give a dramatic reading of the poem on page 83.
- Have students read independently and record in their notebooks how they feel as they read about June M.'s treatment of June T., and June T.'s response.
- Evaluate how well students can read, interpret, discuss, and write about the selection on their own by using the Integrated Assessment for Unit One, located in the Alternative Assessment booklet. Administer the assessment at the end of the unit after students have read all the selections and completed all the writing that was assigned. Set aside two class periods, or about two hours, for the assessment.

PRINT AND MEDIA RESOURCES

UNIT ONE RESOURCE BOOK
Strategic Reading: Literature, p. 37

FORMAL ASSESSMENT
Selection Test, pp. 15–16
Part Test, pp. 17–18
  Test Generator

ALTERNATIVE ASSESSMENT
Unit One Integrated Assessment, pp. 1–6

ACCESS FOR STUDENTS ACQUIRING ENGLISH
Selection Summaries

  AUDIO LIBRARY
See Reference Card

THE LANGUAGE OF LITERATURE TEACHER'S EDITION **75**

SUMMARY

June feels safe in her life with her loving mother—until the Tuesday she starts a swimming class and meets a bully who is also named June. The Other June ridicules her and bruises her with punches, turning her weeks into miserable countdowns toward "Awfulday." After the last swimming class, June believes that she is finally free of the Other June's insults. But when June and her mother move to another part of town, she discovers that there is no escape, for the Other June is a classmate in her new school. Faced with being bullied every day, June desperately faces her attacker in class. "No. No. No. No more," she declares, taking the Other June by surprise. The Other June backs away, and June knows that her days as a victim are over.

Thematic Link: *Seizing the Moment* A young girl named June, who has endured a measure of private torment, seizes the opportunity to stand up to a bully she calls "the Other June."

Art Note

The Case for More School Days by C. F. Payne C. F. Payne uses realism combined with distortion to make a point about the girl in this painting. The focus is the expression on the girl's face, which seems to be a mixture of disgust and sarcasm.

Reading the Art Why do you think this piece was chosen as an illustration for "Tuesday of the Other June"? Is this how you picture the other June?

We stood in front of the mirror as she combed my hair, combed and brushed and smoothed. Her head came just above mine; she said when I grew another inch, she'd stand on a stool to brush my hair. "I'm not giving up this pleasure!" And she laughed her long honey laugh.

My mother was April, my grandmother had been May, I was June. "And someday," said my mother, "you'll have a daughter of your own. What will you name her?"

"January!" I'd yell when I was little. "February! No, November!" My mother laughed her honey laugh. She had little emerald eyes that warmed me like the sun.

Every day when I went to school, she went to work. "Sometimes I stop what I'm doing," she said, "lay down my tools, and stop everything, because all I can think about is you. Wondering what you're doing and if you need me. Now, Junie, if anyone ever bothers you—"

"—I walk away, run away, come on home as fast as my feet will take me," I recited.

"Yes. You come to me. You just bring me your trouble, because I'm here on this earth to love you and take care of you."

I was safe with her. Still, sometimes I woke up at night and heard footsteps slowly creeping up the stairs. It wasn't my mother, she was asleep in the bed across the room, so it was robbers, thieves, and murderers, creeping slowly . . . slowly . . . slowly toward my bed.

I stuffed my hand into my mouth. If I screamed and woke her, she'd be tired at work tomorrow. The robbers and thieves filled the warm darkness and slipped across the floor more quietly than cats. Rigid under the covers, I stared at the shifting dark and bit my knuckles and never knew when I fell asleep again.

In the morning we sang in the kitchen. "Bill Grogan's goat! Was feelin' fine! Ate three red shirts, right off the line!" I made sandwiches for our lunches, she made pancakes for breakfast, but all she ate was one pancake and a cup of coffee. "Gotta fly, can't be late."

I wanted to be rich and take care of her. She worked too hard; her pretty hair had gray in it

The Case for More School Days, C. F. Payne. First appeared in *The Atlantic Monthly*.

76 UNIT ONE PART 1: SEIZING THE MOMENT

that she joked about. "Someday," I said, "I'll buy you a real house, and you'll never work in a pot factory again."

"Such delicious plans," she said. She checked the windows to see if they were locked. "Do you have your key?"

I lifted it from the chain around my neck.

"And you'll come right home from school and—"

"—I won't light fires or let strangers into the house, and I won't tell anyone on the phone that I'm here alone," I finished for her.

"I know, I'm just your old worrywart mother." She kissed me twice, once on each cheek. "But you are my June, my only June, the only June."

She was wrong; there was another June. I met her when we stood next to each other at the edge of the pool the first day of swimming class in the Community Center.

"What's your name?" She had a deep growly voice.

"June. What's yours?"

She stared at me. "June."

"We have the same name."

"No we don't. June is my name, and I don't give you permission to use it. Your name is Fish Eyes." She pinched me hard. "Got it, Fish Eyes?"

The next Tuesday, the Other June again stood next to me at the edge of the pool. "What's your name?"

"June."

"Wrong. Your—name—is—Fish—Eyes."

"June."

"Fish Eyes, you are really stupid." She shoved me into the pool.

The swimming teacher looked up, frowning, from her chart. "No one in the water yet."

Later, in the locker room, I dressed quickly and wrapped my wet suit in the towel. The Other June pulled on her jeans. "You guys see that bathing suit Fish Eyes was wearing? Her mother found it in a trash can."

"She did not!"

The Other June grabbed my fingers and twisted. "Where'd she find your bathing suit?"

"She bought it, let me go."

"Poor little stupid Fish Eyes is crying. Oh, boo hoo hoo, poor little Fish Eyes."

"Your name is Fish Eyes." She pinched me hard.

After that, everyone called me Fish Eyes. And every Tuesday, wherever I was, there was also the Other June—at the edge of the pool, in the pool, in the locker room. In the water, she swam alongside me, blowing and huffing, knocking into me. In the locker room, she stepped on my feet, pinched my arms, hid my blouse, and knotted my braids together. She had large square teeth; she was shorter than I was, but heavier, with bigger bones and square hands. If I met her outside on the street, carrying her bathing suit and towel, she'd walk toward me, smiling a square, friendly smile. "Oh well, if it isn't Fish Eyes." Then she'd punch me, blam! her whole solid weight hitting me.

I didn't know what to do about her. She was training me like a dog. After a few weeks of this, she only had to look at me, only had to growl, "I'm going to get you, Fish Eyes," for my heart to slink like a whipped dog down into my stomach. My arms were covered with bruises. When my mother noticed, I made up a story about tripping on the sidewalk.

My weeks were no longer Tuesday, Wednesday, Thursday, and so on. Tuesday was

TUESDAY OF THE OTHER JUNE 77

Awfulday. Wednesday was Badday. (The Tuesday bad feelings were still there.) Thursday was Betterday, and Friday was Safeday. Saturday was Goodday, but Sunday was Toosoonday, and Monday—Monday was nothing but the day before Awfulday.

I tried to slow down time. Especially on the weekends, I stayed close by my mother, doing everything with her, shopping, cooking, cleaning, going to the laundromat. "Aw, sweetie, go play with your friends."

"Junie, listen to this. We're moving!"

"No, I'd rather be with you." I wouldn't look at the clock or listen to the radio (they were always telling you the date and the time). I did special magic things to keep the day from going away, rapping my knuckles six times on the bathroom door six times a day and never, ever touching the chipped place on my bureau. But always I woke up to the day before Tuesday, and always, no matter how many times I circled the worn spot in the living-room rug or counted twenty-five cracks in the ceiling, Monday disappeared and once again it was Tuesday.

The Other June got bored with calling me Fish Eyes. Buffalo Brain came next, but as soon as everyone knew that, she renamed me Turkey Nose.

Now at night it wasn't robbers creeping up the stairs, but the Other June, coming to torment me. When I finally fell asleep, I dreamed of kicking her, punching, biting, pinching. In the morning I remembered my dreams and felt brave and strong. And then I remembered all the things my mother had taught me and told me.

Be good, be good, be good; it's just us two women alone in the world. . . . Oh, but if it weren't, if my father wasn't long gone, if we'd had someone else to fall back on, if my mother's mother and daddy weren't dead all these years, if my father's daddy wanted to know us instead of being glad to forget us— oh, then I would have punched the Other June with a frisky heart, I would have grabbed her arm at poolside and bitten her like the dog she had made of me.

One night, when my mother came home from work, she said, "Junie, listen to this. We're moving!"

Alaska, I thought. Florida. Arizona. Someplace far away and wonderful, someplace without the Other June.

"Wait till you hear this deal. We are going to be caretakers, trouble-shooters for an eight-family apartment building. Fifty-six Blue Hill Street. Not janitors; we don't do any of the heavy work. April and June, Trouble-shooters, Incorporated. If a tenant has a complaint or a problem, she comes to us and we either take care of it or call the janitor for service. And for that little bit of work, we get to live rent free!" She swept me around in a dance. "Okay? You like it? I do!"

So. Not anywhere else, really. All the same, maybe too far to go to swimming class? "Can we move right away? Today?"

"Gimme a break, sweetie. We've got to pack, do a thousand things. I've got to line up someone with a truck to help us. Six weeks, Saturday the fifteenth." She circled it on the calendar. It was the Saturday after the last day of swimming class.

Soon, we had boxes lying everywhere, filled with clothes and towels and glasses wrapped in newspaper. Bit by bit, we cleared the rooms,

78 UNIT ONE PART 1: SEIZING THE MOMENT

Multicultural Perspectives

BREAKFAST June and her mother enjoy pancakes, hot cocoa, corn muffins, and cinnamon toast for breakfast. America's rich heritage was created in part by immigrants, who brought their own versions of these food to their new land and made them part of the whole. For example, the Germans who came here called pancakes *pfannkuchen;* to Russians, they were *blini;* French immigrants called them *crêpes;* Jewish people from Europe, *blintzes.* Chocolate comes from cacao beans, which were cultivated by the Mayan Indians of Central America and the Aztec Indians of Mexico. When Spain conquered Mexico in the 16th century, cacao beans were brought to Spain. From there the popularity of hot cocoa spread internationally, eventually coming back to the United States, along with sugar and spice. Corn muffins, which probably originated with Native Americans, remain a staple in Southern cooking.

© Bradley Clark.

OPTION 1

Individual Activity
PAINTING PORTRAITS

Using information from the selection, have students paint or draw portraits of the two Junes or find magazine photographs of people who students think resemble the characters. Have them write captions or make an oral presentation explaining the resemblance.

Teacher's Role Direct students to reread the story to find specific details that support their idea of what each June looks like.

Rubric

3 Full Accomplishment Students create realistic portraits, supported by details from the selection, of the two Junes.

2 Substantial Accomplishment Students create realistic portraits, but the portraits are not supported by details from the selection.

1 Little or Partial Accomplishment Students' portraits show that they have not understood or reflected on the appearance of the two Junes.

---

leaving only what we needed right now. The dining-room table staggered on a bunched-up rug, our bureaus inched toward the front door like patient cows. On the calendar in the kitchen, my mother marked off the days until we moved, but the only days I thought about were Tuesdays—Awfuldays. Nothing else was real except the too fast passing of time, moving toward each Tuesday . . . away from Tuesday . . . toward Tuesday. . . .

And it seemed to me that this would go on forever, that Tuesdays would come forever and I would be forever trapped by the side of the pool, the Other June whispering Buffalo Brain Fish Eyes Turkey Nose into my ear, while she ground her elbow into my side and smiled her square smile at the swimming teacher.

No more swimming class. No more Awfuldays. . . . No more Tuesdays.

And then it ended. It was the last day of swimming class. The last Tuesday. We had all passed our tests, and, as if in celebration, the Other June only pinched me twice. "And now," our swimming teacher said, "all of you are ready for the Advanced Class, which starts in just one month. I have a sign-up slip here. Please put your name down before you leave." Everyone but me crowded around. I went to the locker room and pulled on my clothes as fast as possible. The Other June burst through the door just as I was leaving. "Goodbye," I yelled, "good riddance to bad trash!" Before she could pinch me again, I ran past her and then ran all the way home, singing, "Goodbye. . . goodbye . . . goodbye, good riddance to bad trash!"

Later, my mother carefully untied the blue ribbon around my swimming class diploma. "Look at this! Well, isn't this wonderful! You are on your way, you might turn into an Olympic swimmer, you never know what life will bring."

"I don't want to take more lessons."

"Oh, sweetie, it's great to be a good swimmer." But then, looking into my face, she said, "No, no, no, don't worry, you don't have to."

The next morning, I woke up hungry for the first time in weeks. No more swimming class. No more Baddays and Awfuldays. No more Tuesdays of the Other June. In the kitchen, I made hot cocoa to go with my mother's corn muffins. "It's Wednesday, Mom," I said, stirring the cocoa. "My favorite day."

"Since when?"

"Since this morning." I turned on the radio so I could hear the announcer tell the time, the temperature, and the day.

Thursday for breakfast I made cinnamon toast, Friday my mother made pancakes, and on Saturday, before we moved, we ate the last slices of bread and cleaned out the peanut butter jar.

"Some breakfast," Tilly said. "Hello, you must be June." She shook my hand. She was a friend of my mother's from work; she wore big hoop earrings, sandals, and a skirt as dazzling as a rainbow. She came in a truck with John to help us move our things.

John shouted cheerfully at me, "So you're moving." An enormous man with a face covered with little brown bumps. Was he afraid his voice wouldn't travel the distance from his mouth to my ear? "You looking at my moles?" he shouted, and he heaved our big green flowered chair down the stairs. "Don't worry, they don't bite. Ha, ha, ha!" Behind him came my mother and Tilly balancing a bureau between them, and behind them I carried a lamp and the round, flowered Mexican tray that was my mother's favorite. She had found it at a garage sale and said it was as close to foreign travel as we would ever get.

The night before, we had loaded our car, stuffing in bags and boxes until there was barely room for the two of us. But it was only when we were in the car, when we drove past Abdo's Grocery, where they always gave us credit, when I turned for a last look at our street—it was only then that I understood we were truly going to live somewhere else, in another apartment, in another place mysteriously called Blue Hill Street.

Tilly's truck followed our car.

"Oh, I'm so excited," my mother said. She laughed. "You'd think we were going across the country."

Our old car wheezed up a long, steep hill. Blue Hill Street. I looked from one side to the other, trying to see everything.

My mother drove over the crest of the hill. "And now—ta da!—our new home."

"Which house? Which one?" I looked out the window and what I saw was the Other June. She was sprawled on the stoop of a pink house, lounging back on her elbows, legs outspread, her jaws working on a wad of gum. I slid down into the seat, but it was too late. I was sure she had seen me.

My mother turned into a driveway next to a big white building with a tiny porch. She leaned on the steering wheel. "See that window there, that's our living-room window . . . and that one over there, that's your bedroom. . . ."

We went into the house, down a dim, cool hall. In our new apartment, the wooden floors clicked under our shoes, and my mother showed me everything. Her voice echoed in the empty rooms. I followed her around in a daze.

Had I imagined seeing the Other June? Maybe I'd seen another girl who looked like her. A double. That could happen.

"Ho yo, where do you want this chair?" John appeared in the doorway. We brought in boxes and bags and beds and stopped only to eat pizza and drink orange juice from the carton.

"June's so quiet, do you think she'll adjust all right?" I heard Tilly say to my mother.

"Oh, definitely. She'll make a wonderful adjustment. She's just getting used to things."

But I thought that if the Other June lived on the same street as I did, I would never get used to things.

That night I slept in my own bed, with my own pillow and blanket, but with floors that creaked in strange voices and walls with cracks I didn't recognize. I didn't feel either happy or unhappy. It was as if I were waiting for something.

Monday, when the principal of Blue Hill Street School left me in Mr. Morrisey's classroom, I knew what I'd been waiting for. In that room full of strange kids, there was one person I knew. She smiled her square smile, raised her hand, and said, "She can sit next to me, Mr. Morrisey."

"Very nice of you, June M. OK, June T., take your seat. I'll try not to get you two Junes mixed up."

I sat down next to her. She pinched my arm. "Good riddance to bad trash," she mocked.

I was back in the Tuesday swimming class, only now it was worse, because every day would be Awfulday. The pinching had already started. Soon, I knew, on the playground and in the halls, kids would pass me, grinning. "Hiya, Fish Eyes."

The Other June followed me around during recess that day, droning in my ear, "You are

TUESDAY OF THE OTHER JUNE **81**

OPTION 2

Cooperative Learning
CREATE A SKIT
Have students work in small groups to create a skit of June's first two days at Blue Hill Street School. If possible, allow students to videotape their skits and invite the rest of the class to review them.

Teacher's Role Be sure that each group member has an active role. An elaborator can help the group construct a skit that elaborates on what they learned in the selection. A generator can come up with additional questions beyond the first thoughts elicited in group discussion. A checker of understanding can ensure that all group members understand the selection, the skit, and their role in the production.

Rubric
3 Full Accomplishment Groups create skits that are entertaining and that accurately reflect what the selection says about June's first two days at Blue Hill Street School.

2 Substantial Accomplishment Groups create skits that hang together but do not reflect full understanding of the story.

1 Little or Partial Accomplishment Groups create skits that misinterpret the action or characters of the story.

THE LANGUAGE OF LITERATURE **TEACHER'S EDITION** **81**

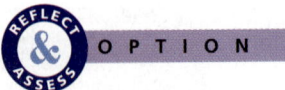

OPTION 3

Class Discussion
SHARING IDEAS

After students have read the selection, engage them in a whole-class discussion of the following questions:

1. At the end of the story, June T. changes her behavior. In your opinion, what causes her to do this? *(Possible responses: She is tired of being bullied; the other June has pushed June T. one step too far.)*
2. Why do you think June doesn't fight back physically when the other June acts like a bully? *(Possible responses: She listens to her mother's advice; she doesn't think that she could possibly win against the other June, who is shorter but heavier.)*
3. Why do you think June T. doesn't tell anyone about her problem? *(Possible responses: She wants to solve her problem herself; she doesn't want to upset or worry her mother.)*
4. What kind of person do you think the other June is? *(Possible responses: She is mean and strong. When she is confronted, however, she loses her confidence. She squawks, turns red, and backs down.)*

Teacher's Role As students share their impressions of the two Junes, prompt them to support their views by citing specific events or details from the selection.

---

my slave, you must do everything I say, I am your master, say it, say, 'Yes, master, you are my master.'"

I pressed my lips together, clapped my hands over my ears, but without hope. Wasn't it only a matter of time before I said the hateful words?

"How was school?" my mother said that night.

"OK."

She put a pile of towels in a bureau drawer. "Try not to be sad about missing your old friends, sweetie; there'll be new ones."

The next morning, the Other June was waiting for me when I left the house. "Did your mother get you that blouse in the garbage dump?" She butted me, shoving me against a tree. "Don't you speak anymore, Fish Eyes?" Grabbing my chin in her hands, she pried open my mouth. "Oh, ha ha, I thought you lost your tongue."

We went on to school. I sank down into my seat, my head on my arms. "June T., are you all right?" Mr. Morrisey asked. I nodded. My head was almost too heavy to lift.

The Other June went to the pencil sharpener. Round and round she whirled the handle. Walking back, looking at me, she held the three sharp pencils like three little knives.

Someone knocked on the door. Mr. Morrisey went out into the hall. Paper planes burst into the air, flying from desk to desk. Someone turned on a transistor radio. And the Other June, coming closer, smiled and licked her lips like a cat sleepily preparing to gulp down a mouse.

I remembered my dream of kicking her, punching, biting her like a dog.

Then my mother spoke quickly in my ear: Turn the other cheek, my Junie; smile at the world, and the world'll surely smile back.

But I had turned the other cheek and it was slapped. I had smiled and the world hadn't smiled back. I couldn't run home as fast as my feet would take me. I had to stay in school—and in school there was the Other June. Every morning, there would be the Other June, and every afternoon, and every day, all day, there would be the Other June.

She frisked down the aisle, stabbing the pencils in the air toward me. A boy stood up on his desk and bowed. "My fans," he said, "I greet you." My arm twitched and throbbed, as if the Other June's pencils had already poked through the skin. She came closer, smiling her Tuesday smile.

"No," I whispered, "no." The word took wings and flew me to my feet, in front of the Other June. "Noooooo." It flew out of my mouth into her surprised face.

The boy on the desk turned toward us. "You said something, my devoted fans?"

"No," I said to the Other June. "Oh, no! No. No. No. No more." I pushed away the hand that held the pencils.

The Other June's eyes opened, popped wide like the eyes of somebody in a cartoon. It made me laugh. The boy on the desk laughed, and then the other kids were laughing, too.

"No," I said again, because it felt so good to say it. "No, no, no, no." I leaned toward the Other June, put my finger against her chest. Her cheeks turned red, she squawked something—it sounded like "Eeeraaghyou!"—and she stepped back. She stepped away from me.

The door banged, the airplanes disappeared, and Mr. Morrisey walked to his desk. "OK. OK. Let's get back to work. Kevin Clark, how about it?" Kevin jumped off the desk, and Mr. Morrisey picked up a piece of chalk. "All right, class—" He stopped and looked at me and the Other June. "You two Junes, what's going on there?"

I tried it again. My finger against her chest. Then the words. "No—more." And she stepped back another step. I sat down at my desk.

"June M.," Mr. Morrisey said.

She turned around, staring at him with that big-eyed cartoon look. After a moment she sat down at her desk with a loud slapping sound.

Even Mr. Morrisey laughed.

And sitting at my desk, twirling my braids, I knew this was the last Tuesday of the Other June. ❖

LITERARY INSIGHT

MEAN SONG
by Eve Merriam

Snickles and podes,
Ribble and grodes:
That's what I wish you.

A nox in the groot,
A root in the stoot
And a gock in the forbeshaw, too.

Keep out of sight
For fear that I might
Glom you a gravely snave.

Don't show your face
Around any place
Or you'll get one flack snack in the bave.

LITERARY INSIGHT

1. What do you think the poem has in common with the story? *(Possible responses: Both are about child enemies; the poem says what June T. would like to have said to the other June.)*
2. How can you make sense of a poem with so many made-up words? *(Possible responses: By the words' sounds. Nox sounds like a punch. Glom also sounds like something menacing that you would want to avoid receiving.)*

Eve Merriam Eve Merriam once said she hadn't consciously decided to be a poet. Rather, the rhythm of poetry had so entranced her that she was compelled to write poems. Merriam's many volumes of juvenile verse include *There Is No Rhyme for Silver*, *A Sky Full of Poems*, and *You'll Be Good and I'll Be Night: Jump on the Bed Poems*. "Whatever you do," she once advised, "find ways to read poetry. Eat it, drink it, enjoy it, and share it."

NORMA FOX MAZER

1931–

Norma Fox Mazer believes stories are a way to understand the world and the people in it. She says that readers of fiction "will find a world where people face troubles but act to help themselves."

Mazer's interest in writing started in high school when she was editor of her school paper and a correspondent for her town's newspaper. After a year at college, she married the novelist Harry Mazer. For ten years, she and her husband struggled to write while raising their four children. Today she is a widely recognized and prize-winning writer of fiction for young adults.

Mazer lives in New York but spends her summers in Canada, where she does without electricity, telephones, newspapers, radios, or indoor plumbing. About her writing, Mazer says, "I seem to deal in the ordinary, the everyday, the real. I should like in my writing to give meaning and emotion to ordinary moments. In my books and stories I want people to eat chocolate pudding, break a dish, yawn, look in a store window, wear socks with holes in them." Readers can encounter many of Mazer's true-to-life characters in works like *After the Rain*, a Newbery Honor book.

OTHER WORKS *Three Sisters*; *The Solid Gold Kids*; *Bright Days, Stupid Nights*; *C, My Name Is Cal*; *D, My Name Is Danita*

NORMA FOX MAZER

Working-class family settings are important to Norma Fox Mazer. Her father drove a delivery truck, and her mother worked in clothing stores. Later in her writing career, Mazer collaborated with her husband, Harry Mazer, on *The Solid Gold Kid*, *Heartbeat*, and *Bright Days, Stupid Nights*.

OVERVIEW

In the Guided Assignment for this section, students will write a personal response essay. By exploring how they feel and what they think about a story, students learn to support their ideas with examples and to keep their readers in mind. The Writer's Style will help students understand the importance of using specific nouns, precise verbs, and vivid adjectives to make their writing interesting and clear. In Reading the World, students will explore how they respond to advertisements.

Objectives

- To understand how authors use descriptive words effectively
- To catch readers' attention through the use of adverbs
- To write a personal response to a work of literature
- To analyze real-world images

Skills

LITERATURE
- Identifying and analyzing creative words

GRAMMAR AND USAGE
- Using adverbs
- Understanding sentence variety
- Using linking verbs

MEDIA LITERACY
- Responding to advertisements

CRITICAL THINKING
- Analyzing your response
- Making judgments
- Analyzing

SPEAKING, LISTENING, AND VIEWING
- Group collaboration
- Peer response
- Group evaluation and discussion

Teaching Strategy: MODELING
In the following models, precise language is used to provoke particular responses in the reader. Carefully chosen verbs, adjectives, and other descriptive words can enhance all student writing.

A Mazer Possible responses: Descriptive words include *knocking, trampled on, squeezed, hid,* and *knotted.* Students may suggest other words such as *bumping, trampled, squeezed, took,* and *tied* or other synonyms.

B Sperry Possible responses: Descriptive words include *swept, silver arrows, scarlet,* and *ruby.* They help you see what is happening by adding color and specificity to the action and objects in the scene.

WRITING ABOUT LITERATURE

TAKING IT PERSONALLY

You are unique. Nobody sees the world or responds to it quite like you. This is true whether you are looking at a photograph, watching a baseball game, or reading a story. On the following pages, you'll explore the way you respond. You will

- see how authors choose words to stir a response in their readers
- write a personal response to a story or poem
- discover how your response differs from others' responses in real-life situations

Writer's Style: Descriptive Words Writers choose words that capture readers' attention. Specific nouns, precise verbs, and vivid adjectives help "show" readers what an author means.

Read the Literature

The writers of these passages have carefully chosen their words to create certain responses in their readers.

Literature Models

A Precise Verbs
Which words describe how mean the Other June is? What other words might work as well?

> In the water, she swam alongside me, blowing and huffing, knocking into me. In the locker room, she stepped on my feet, pinched my arms, hid my blouse, and knotted my braids together. She had large square teeth; she was shorter than I was, but heavier, with bigger bones and square hands.
>
> Norma Fox Mazer
> from "Tuesday of the Other June"

B Vivid Adjectives
Which words help the author describe the scene? How do these words help you "see" what is happening?

> A school of fish swept by like silver arrows. He saw scarlet rock cod with ruby eyes and the head of a conger eel peering out from a cavern in the coral.
>
> Armstrong Sperry
> from "Ghost of the Lagoon"

84 UNIT ONE PART 1: SEIZING THE MOMENT

PRINT AND MEDIA RESOURCES

UNIT ONE RESOURCE BOOK
The Writer's Style, p. 41
Prewriting Guide, p. 42
Elaboration, p. 43
Peer Response Guide, pp. 44–45
Revising and Proofreading, p. 46

GRAMMAR MINI-LESSONS
Transparencies, p. 17
Copymasters, p. 19

WRITING MINI-LESSONS
Transparencies, pp. 40, 41, 42

ACCESS FOR STUDENTS ACQUIRING ENGLISH
Reading and Writing Support

FORMAL ASSESSMENT
Guidelines for Writing Assessment

WRITING COACH

Connect to Life

Take a close look at the words this magazine writer uses. Then think about how the special words you notice make you feel about the passage.

Magazine Article

> Ok, boardheads, listen up. There's a nuclear wind blowing, and the wave you just caught—this huge, rolling wall of water—is now rumbling 20 feet below your head. You're hanging in midair, upside down and bat-style, your feet strapped to the sailboard above. Gulp. Now what?
>
> Laura Hilgers
> from "Irie Man"
> *Outside Kids,* Summer 1993

Creative Words Which words in this passage seem unusual or interesting? Whom is the writer writing to? How can you tell?

Try Your Hand: Choosing the Right Word

1. **Vivid Words** Rewrite the following sentences, using descriptive words to catch your readers' attention.
   - Mako watched the shark move.
   - Mako could see stars and hear thunder.
   - Afa went through the jungle and barked at animals.

2. **You Are There** With a small group, write a collaborative paragraph describing a funny, exciting, or special classroom event or situation. Remember, you want your readers to feel as though they are at the event.

3. **You Have to Read This!** A book-jacket review is a short summary or descriptive review that tries to hook people into reading the book. Write a book-jacket review for one of the selections in this unit. Try to make your review as eye-catching and descriptive as possible.

SkillBuilder

GRAMMAR FROM WRITING

Using Adverbs

An adverb modifies a verb, an adjective, or another adverb. You can use an adverb to tell *how, when, where,* or *to what extent.* Notice how Armstrong Sperry uses adverbs to add details that make this scene interesting:

> Swiftly, yet calmly, Mako stood upright and braced himself firmly. Then, murmuring a silent prayer to the shark god, he threw his spear for the last time.

APPLYING WHAT YOU'VE LEARNED

Add adverbs and other precise words to make these sentences more descriptive and interesting.

1. The crowd clapped when Mako fought the paper shark.
2. The stage sets looked good, and the water moved.
3. Lisa was Tupa, which we thought was funny.

HANDBOOKS

For more information on adverbs, see page 830 of the Grammar Handbook. For more information on word choice and elaboration, see page 783 of the Writing Handbook.

WRITING ABOUT LITERATURE 85

Critical Thinking:
MAKING JUDGMENTS

E Explain to students that although it is good to have immediate like-or-dislike reactions to movies, music, and stories, it is even better to tell others *how* they felt and *why* they liked or disliked something. Challenge students to make judgments about what they read by looking at their responses to particular aspects of the selection, such as the writer's use of descriptive words.

Teaching Strategy:
STUMBLING BLOCK

F Assure students that whatever selection they choose is acceptable. However, emphasize that they should try to choose a selection which evoked a strong personal response. Encourage them to reread the selection before focusing their response.

Writing Skill: POINT OF VIEW

G Freewrite to Discover provides an opportunity for students to gather information and explore what they think. Suggest that students think of the part or parts of the story that affected them the most as they freewrite. Guide them to explore all their reactions and how they came to think of their ideas.

WRITING ABOUT LITERATURE

Personal Response

E Have you ever watched a movie with a friend and discovered that the two of you had very different reactions to it? People respond to movies, music, and stories in very different ways. Sharing your reactions to a story is natural and fun.

GUIDED ASSIGNMENT

Write a Personal Response On the next few pages, you'll explore what you think and feel about a story by writing a personal response essay. In your essay, you may describe your thoughts and feelings about the story, about a certain character, or about the author's technique.

❶ Prewrite and Explore

Since you'll be writing a personal response essay, you need to think about the selections that made a strong impression on you.

F Consider looking at your QuickWrites or your reading log for help in choosing the selection you'll respond to.

FOCUSING YOUR RESPONSE

The following questions might help you reflect on the selection you choose:

- Which parts of the story made me take notice? Which were confusing? Which seemed important?
- Which parts of the story reminded me of my own life?
- What was my overall impression of the story?

❷ Freewrite to Discover

At first, you might not be sure exactly why or how a story affected you. To discover what you think, try freewriting about the story. Another possibility is to sketch the most memorable scene in the story and then write about it. The sketch and freewriting on these pages show how one student explored a story.

G

Student's Sketch

86 UNIT ONE PART 1: SEIZING THE MOMENT

86 THE LANGUAGE OF LITERATURE **TEACHER'S EDITION**

Student's Freewriting

I liked "Tuesday of the Other June" because I don't like bullies. The Other June was mean so it was cool when she was put in her place.

I like swimming, and there was a lot of swimming in the story. The story reminded me of my friend Rachel. She was picked on by a bully. But she didn't stand up for herself because she was too scared.

I think I'm most interested in this story because I know how June felt.

I should probably focus on the scene that I liked best—maybe use quotes from the story, too.

The characters seem real to me. It's like they could be actual kids in my class. I liked it when June stood up for herself. And the boy who stood up on his desk was hilarious. I saw that happen last year.

Now that you have explored your reaction a little, ask yourself the following questions:

- What affected me the most in this selection?
- Why did I feel the way I did?

3 Draft and Share

In writing a personal response essay, there are no right or wrong responses. However, supporting your responses with reasons and examples from the story and from your life will help readers understand your reactions. Pick out the details in the story, such as specific examples or quotations, that caused you to respond. You can use these to support your ideas. Remember that most essays have an introduction, a body, and a conclusion. When you've finished, ask a classmate to read your essay and give you suggestions.

 **PEER RESPONSE**

- What feelings came out strongest in my response essay?
- What story details can I add to support my response and help readers understand it?

SkillBuilder

 WRITER'S CRAFT

Understanding Sentence Variety

Writing can be boring if you write every sentence the same way. Changing the length and structure of your sentences will make your writing more interesting. For example, see how Armstrong Sperry changes the structure and length of his sentences in this passage from "Ghost of the Lagoon":

Then, picking up his paddle, he thrust it into the water. The canoe shot ahead. Its sharp bow cut through the green water of the lagoon like a knife through cheese.

Shorter sentences, like the sentence "The canoe shot ahead," can emphasize action or make powerful statements. Longer, complex sentences help prevent choppiness and can be used to add details.

APPLYING WHAT YOU'VE LEARNED
After you've drafted your ideas, carefully reread your sentences. You may want to rewrite some sentences to add variety and interest.

WRITING ABOUT LITERATURE **87**

Teaching Strategy: MODELING

H Point out to students some aspects of the freewriting examples. Show how students can note their initial reaction to the story—whether they like it or dislike it. However, encourage them to add reasons for their reactions. Students can also compare the story's action to their own experiences.

Writing Skill: ELABORATION

I Many students will choose examples in selections that contain precise or vivid language. Remind them that such verbs, adjectives, and adverbs are persuasive and that authors use them to create certain responses in their readers. Encourage students to quote words and phrases to support their own reactions to their chosen story.

Teaching Strategy: USING SKILLBUILDER

J You can help students to vary their sentences by teaching the SkillBuilder on Understanding Sentence Variety at this time. It will help students understand that varying sentence length and structure can make their writing more interesting.

 SkillBuilder — **WRITER'S CRAFT**

UNDERSTANDING SENTENCE VARIETY
Students can work together or in groups to practice creating sentence variety. Have them choose passages from selections and note the sentence variety authors employ. Ask them to discuss the effect of short and long sentences. Then challenge students to rewrite the passage, changing the length of sentences. Short sentences can be combined, and long ones can be divided. Ask them how the new sentences they have created affect the passage.

Application Student rewrites will vary. Check for variety of sentence lengths, for short and long sentences used effectively, and that sentence fragments and run-ons have been avoided.

Additional Suggestions Have small groups of students rewrite this long sentence in short and long units:

When the main character realizes what is going on and is shocked at first, she decides to take action by running straight toward the bull.

Reteaching/Reinforcement
- *Writing Mini-Lessons* transparencies, pp. 40, 41, 42

 **The Writer's Craft**

Sentence Combining, pp. 286–291

THE LANGUAGE OF LITERATURE **TEACHER'S EDITION** **87**

Critical Thinking: ANALYZING

K To aim for accuracy, diversity in language, and sentence variety in their personal responses, students should look at their word choices, make sure their draft accurately reflects their thoughts, and include enough examples and details as support.

Teaching Strategy: MANAGING THE PAPER LOAD

L Have students keep folders containing clearly dated and labelled stages of their project. Not only will students find it a useful means of organization, but you may find that it helps to manage the amounts of paper being produced.

Teaching Strategy: MODELING

M Discuss with students how this sample meets the Standards for Evaluation. Show how the writer integrates the author's name and the title of the work into the opening sentence. Also point out the writer's reaction in the opening paragraph and its accompanying explanation. In the second paragraph, the vivid and accurate words capture the excitement and tension that the writer felt.

Standards for Evaluation

Ideas and Content
- identifies the work by title and author
- gives a brief summary of the work as well as the writer's personal experience to support the writer's response
- ends with a summary of the response and a conclusion

Structure and Form
- demonstrates proper paragraphing
- includes transitional words to show relationships among ideas
- uses a variety of sentence structures

Grammar, Usage, and Mechanics
- contains no more than two or three minor errors in grammar and usage
- contains no more than two or three minor errors in spelling, capitalization, and punctuation

---

WRITING ABOUT LITERATURE

4 Revise and Edit

As you edit your draft, remember to make your introduction at least one paragraph and to start a new paragraph for each new idea. Also be sure to support each of your ideas with specific details from the story. After you have finished your draft, reflect on how well you presented your ideas and what you learned about writing a personal response.

Student Model

"Tuesday of the Other June"

I liked "Tuesday of the Other June" by Norma Fox Mazer because I know exactly how June felt. Throughout the story I felt sorry for June because she was being picked on. I know what it feels like to be picked on. My best friend had a bully who picked on her all the time, but my friend never stood up to the bully. So when June finally put the bully in her place, I felt like cheering.

How does the introduction explain the writer's response to the story?

How do references to specific scenes in the story clarify the writer's response?

I had a feeling that June would run into the Other June and something big would happen. But I didn't know what would happen or when. Then, as the Other June stalked down the aisle, stabbing with the pencils, I trembled and I felt the tension in the classroom. I loved the way June's anger built up until she could stand no more bullying.

Standards for Evaluation

A personal response
- gives the author and title of the work
- includes enough information about the work for readers unfamiliar with it to understand the response
- clearly expresses a response and gives reasons for it
- ends with a summary of the response and an overall conclusion

88 UNIT ONE PART 1: SEIZING THE MOMENT

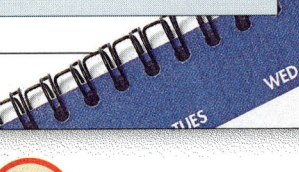

Assessment ✓ Option

SELF-ASSESSMENT To help students assess their own writing, have them ask themselves the following questions:
- *Have I included in my introduction how I felt?*
- *Did I explain enough of the story for my readers?*
- *Is my choice of words vivid and interesting?*
- *Can I add more vivid details to describe more accurately my reaction to the story?*
- *Is there a summary or close to my essay?*

88 THE LANGUAGE OF LITERATURE TEACHER'S EDITION

Grammar in Context

Action Verbs Using action verbs will make your writing more precise and interesting, helping readers to understand your personal response better. Some action verbs, such as *paddle* and *swim*, describe action you can see. Other action verbs, such as *enjoy* and *wish*, tell about action you cannot see.

> Then, as the Other June was walking down the aisle, *stalked* *stabbing* with the pencils, I was nervous and I was feeling the *trembled* *felt* tension in the classroom. I loved the way June's anger was building until she could stand no more bullying. *built up*

Notice how the revised version is more detailed and interesting. The action verbs help to express the writer's emotions and ideas vividly so that readers can better understand and appreciate the response.

Try Your Hand: Using Action Verbs

On a separate sheet of paper, revise the following paragraph, choosing stronger, more precise action verbs:

> Cobwebs and dust were on the book in front of me. I could barely read the title: *Woodsong*. I got the dirt off the book and began to read. I had the book for hours and never put it down. *Woodsong* was good and it was exciting. When I was done, I gave the book to my best friend.

SkillBuilder

 GRAMMAR FROM WRITING

Using Linking Verbs

Some verbs do not show action. They tell what something is, or they link the subject with one or more words in the predicate. Such verbs are called linking verbs. These are the most common linking verbs.

am	are	were	being
is	was	be	been

- The shark *was* a whitish color.
- The story *is* very suspenseful.
- I *am* eager to visit Bora Bora.

These are some other familiar linking verbs.

look	appear	become	taste
feel	sound	remain	smell

APPLYING WHAT YOU'VE LEARNED
Number a separate sheet of paper 1–5. After each number, write a linking verb that completes each sentence.

1. The next story _____ "Ghost of the Lagoon."
2. Some students _____ excited as they read.
3. As exciting as this story is, most students _____ calm.
4. It has _____ an all-time favorite for many students.
5. Most students _____ satisfied with the ending.

WRITING ABOUT LITERATURE **89**

Teaching Strategy:
USING THE SKILLBUILDER

You can help students to understand the difference between action and linking verbs by teaching the SkillBuilder on Using Linking Verbs at this time.

CUSTOMIZING FOR
Students Acquiring English

Students with less range of vocabulary may have difficulty recognizing other verbs. Encourage them to use a dictionary or thesaurus or to work with a partner to look for vivid and accurate words.

Try Your Hand

Responses will vary. Here is a sample:

Cobwebs and dust thickly covered the book in front of me. I could barely make out the title: *Woodsong*. I brushed the dirt off the book and began to read. I was glued to the book for hours and could not put it down. *Woodsong* gripped me with excitement. When I had finally finished, I presented the book to my best friend.

 SkillBuilder **GRAMMAR FROM WRITING**

USING LINKING VERBS Remind students that a predicate tells something about the subject. Point out that the predicates in the three examples shown begin with the verbs.

Application Possible responses:
1. *is* or *was*
2. *are, were, look, feel, appear,* or *become*
3. *are, were, look, feel, appear,* or *remain*
4. *been, become*
5. *are, were, look, feel, appear, sound,* or *remain*

Additional Suggestions You may wish to add these sentences to the exercise:

1. Most students can _____ and _____ the various sensory details.
2. Also, they _____ what the characters go through.
3. It _____ worthwhile reading—better than TV!

Reteaching/Reinforcement
- *Grammar Mini-Lessons* transparencies, p. 17

 **The Writer's Craft**

Kinds of Verbs, pp. 396–397

THE LANGUAGE OF LITERATURE TEACHER'S EDITION **89**

READING THE WORLD

On pages 84–89, students responded to a work of literature. In this lesson, students respond to ads. They learn that effective language can be used for a variety of purposes. Through studying the language used in advertisements, students also learn the importance of keeping readers in mind.

Critical Thinking: ANALYZING

P Draw students' attention to the language used to describe each animal, usually a mix of facts and emotional language. Ask them to specify whether it is the dog itself, the facts about the dog, or their emotional response to the words that make the ad effective.

Media Literacy: INTERPRETING AN ADVERTISEMENT

Q Students should note that the advertisements all are about dogs; however, the dogs are all different. Also, some students may notice that the type of person who might purchase each dog is indicated by the ads themselves. For instance, the beagle may go to a family, whereas the German shepherd would be more likely to go to someone who wants it for work or breeding. The precision of the language and the emotional appeal of the ads make them effective.

Speaking, Listening, and Viewing: GROUP DISCUSSION

R Reasons why students responded to one ad and not another will vary. Students may be responding to their purpose for owning a dog or what they know about the breeds. Point out how the language in the ads informs their opinions. The SkillBuilder about Analyzing Your Response draws attention to the language of advertisements.

READING THE WORLD

Responding to Ads

Authors of literature aren't the only writers who try to get a response out of you. People who write advertisements, billboards, magazine articles, and even classified ads, try to get you to respond in specific ways.

View Read the circled ads on this page. In your notebook, describe what the ads are about. Which ad would you be most likely to respond to? Why?

Interpret Think about what these ads have in common. How and why are they different? What makes each ad effective or ineffective?

Discuss Get together with a small group of classmates, and take turns discussing which ads got your attention and why. Talk about how and why people might respond differently to the ads. Then refer to the SkillBuilder at the right for help with analyzing your responses.

90 THE LANGUAGE OF LITERATURE TEACHER'S EDITION

SkillBuilder

CRITICAL THINKING

Analyzing Your Response

You know that some words make you respond in certain ways. Advertisers know this as well. Advertisers write ads for a specific audience. By carefully choosing words that appeal to that audience, ad writers can create the responses they want. For example, how might an advertiser write a commercial for a new kids' cereal? What words might an advertiser use to sell an adult cereal? Why might the writers use different words in each case?

Sometimes advertisers use words that create emotional responses. Emotions such as love, anger, jealousy, and happiness can be very powerful. When looking at ads, it is a good idea to make sure you don't let an emotional response get in the way of sound judgment.

APPLYING WHAT YOU'VE LEARNED

With a small group, write a list of familiar advertisements. Discuss what makes the advertisements memorable. You may want to talk about whether the advertisements appeal to your emotions and how that changes your response to the ads.

READING THE WORLD 91

SkillBuilder CRITICAL THINKING

ANALYZING YOUR RESPONSE A useful concept for students to understand is that of a language community. Readers join an author in a community if they like, identify with, or respond emotionally to the author's language. In the case of an advertisement, this means the seller has appealed to a specifically targeted audience, which might then buy the product.

Application Student advertisements will vary. Here are some items they may want to advertise: schoolbags, compact disks, houses, books, and computer games. Point out to groups that they do not have to write complete sentences and that space is often limited in advertisements.

THE LANGUAGE OF LITERATURE TEACHER'S EDITION 91

UNIT ONE
Part 2 Lesson Planner

TIME ALLOTMENTS SHOWN ARE APPROXIMATE. DEPENDING ON YOUR GOALS AND THE NEEDS OF YOUR STUDENTS, YOU MAY WISH TO ALLOW MORE OR LESS TIME FOR CERTAIN PORTIONS OF THE LESSON.

Table of Contents	Discussion	Previewing the Selection	Reading the Selection
PART OPENER ON THE EDGE OF SURVIVAL What Do You Think? page 92	**20 MINUTES** • Reflect on the part theme		
SELECTION Too Soon a Woman page 94 AVERAGE		**15 MINUTES** • PERSONAL CONNECTION • HISTORICAL CONNECTION • WRITING CONNECTION	**20 MINUTES** • Introduce vocabulary • Read pp. 94–99 (6 pp.)
GENRE LESSON Focus on Poetry page 102	**20 MINUTES** • Discuss characteristics of poetry • Discuss strategies for reading poetry		
SELECTION The Walrus and the Carpenter page 105 CHALLENGING		**15 MINUTES** • PERSONAL CONNECTION • BIOGRAPHICAL CONNECTION • READING CONNECTION: Understanding narrative poetry	**10 MINUTES** • Read pp. 105–07 (3 pp.)
SELECTION Life Doesn't Frighten Me Another Mountain page 111 AVERAGE		**15 MINUTES** • PERSONAL CONNECTION • LITERARY CONNECTION • WRITING CONNECTION	**A 10 MINUTES** • Read pp. 111–14 (4 pp.)
SELECTION from Woodsong page 118 AVERAGE		**20 MINUTES** • PERSONAL CONNECTION • GEOGRAPHICAL CONNECTION • READING CONNECTION: Making predictions	**15 MINUTES** • Introduce vocabulary • Read pp. 118–21 (4 pp.)
SELECTION The Dog of Pompeii page 125 AVERAGE		**15 MINUTES** • PERSONAL CONNECTION • HISTORICAL CONNECTION • READING CONNECTION: Reading historical fiction	**45 MINUTES** • Introduce vocabulary • Read pp. 125–34 (10 pp.)
Writing	**Exploring Topics**	**Prewriting**	**Drafting and Revising**
WRITING FROM EXPERIENCE Firsthand and Expressive Writing	**20 MINUTES**	**25 MINUTES**	**75 MINUTES**

Time estimates assume in-class work. You may wish to assign some of these stages as homework.

Responding to the Selection

FROM PERSONAL RESPONSE TO CRITICAL ANALYSIS	OR	ANOTHER PATHWAY	LITERARY CONCEPTS	QUICKWRITES
		40 MINUTES		
• Discussion questions	OR	• Chart and summary	• Theme	• Diary entry • Wedding announcement
		30 MINUTES		
• Discussion questions	OR	• Sensory-image chart	• Rhyme and rhythm	• Speech • Wanted poster
		30 MINUTES		
• Discussion questions	OR	• Dramatic reading	• Free verse and rhyme	
		30 MINUTES		
• Discussion questions	OR	• Debate	• Autobiography	• Poem • Scene
		50 MINUTES		
• Discussion questions	OR	• Create and perform a scene	• Conflict and setting	• Account • Eyewitness account

Extension Activities

- ALTERNATIVE ACTIVITIES
- LITERARY LINKS
- CRITIC'S CORNER
- THE WRITER'S STYLE
- ACROSS THE CURRICULUM
- ART CONNECTION
- WORDS TO KNOW
- BIOGRAPHY

50 MINUTES — ✔ ✔ — SOCIAL STUDIES — ✔ ✔

40 MINUTES — ✔ — ✔ SCIENCE — — ✔

40 MINUTES — ✔ ✔ ✔ — — ✔

20 MINUTES — — — SCIENCE ✔ ✔

40 MINUTES — ✔ ✔ — SCIENCE ✔ ✔

Publishing and Reflecting

30 MINUTES

Grammar in Context

Reading the World

LESSON PLANNER TEACHER'S EDITION **91b**

UNIT ONE
Part 2 Cooperative Project

Safety Matters

Overview

Students create a public service poster that is appropriate for display in their school.

PROJECT AT A GLANCE
The selections in Unit One, Part 2 reflect the universal need to feel safe. Examples of physical, mental, and emotional safety are shown in the stories and poems. For this project, students will select an aspect of safety that they feel is important in their lives and will create a public service message that draws attention to the matter. Students will work in small groups to create a poster they feel "gets the message across" to the other students. The posters can be displayed in the school halls or lobby.

OBJECTIVES
- To learn about factors that affect the safety of students
- To plan and execute a public service poster that draws attention to a particular safety matter
- To understand the effect of public service messages and how advertising affects behavior

SUGGESTED GROUP SIZE
4 students per group

MATERIALS
- Selection of magazines for examination
- One sheet of poster board per group
- Art materials (markers, pencils, paints, scissors, glue)

 Getting Started

Arranging the Project
Before students begin working on their posters, gather a large selection of magazines that contain public service messages. Any message is acceptable, so outdated magazines are fine. Schedule a reasonable amount of time for students to examine the magazines.

Make arrangements with the school administration to display the completed posters. This could be coordinated with a school Safety Day or in time for parent-teacher conferences.

Arranging the Poster Making
If your school has an art room, you may want to schedule time in that room for the actual artistic work. You also may be able to make arrangements with the art teacher to help students. By doing so, you can turn this into a cooperative art-literature project. As always, allow time for cleaning up.

2 Creating the Posters

Introducing the Project
Explain that students will be working in small groups to plan and create a poster that delivers a public safety message appropriate for the students in their school. Ask students to examine the magazines and note the public safety messages they contain. Such messages can be compared and contrasted. Allow students to comment on the effect—and the effectiveness—of the advertisement. Does it grab their attention? Is the message clear and persuasive? How does it involve safety?

Further discussion can center on billboard, radio, and TV public safety messages. Which are most effective? Which are least effective? Do celebrities influence how students feel about the message in general? Are colors influential? Does the length of the text or choice of words affect the message?

Tell students to try to create an effective poster that reflects a matter of concern to students in the school. You might hold a brief discussion during which students brainstorm a list of relevant issues that would be suitable for their posters.

Group Investigations
Divide students into groups of four. Each group will work to identify an appropriate area of concern in their school and develop a way to call it to the attention of their peers. Encourage students to talk to other classes to pinpoint a common safety concern. Information gathered in these informal interviews should be coordinated and used as a basis for a decision on the topic of the poster. Ask students to report to you periodically so you can keep track of their progress.

Creating a Project Description
After students have investigated public safety messages and surveyed their fellow students, they should submit a one-page description of their project. This should include the selected topic and a brief description of the proposed poster. This will help you avoid duplication of efforts and keep goals realistic. Confer with each group about their plans for the poster.

OPTION 1: VIDEO MESSAGES If your school has video equipment available, some groups could make a video of their message, complete with music, if appropriate. Set a specific time limit for each message (15 to 30 seconds is generally adequate). Students can show the videos in a school assembly. Have groups write a brief explanation of what times and channels they would like to see their messages on if they were actually shown on TV.

OPTION 2: RADIO MESSAGES Students can design and create messages for broadcast over the school's intercom system. Sound effects can be used to enhance the messages. Even if you do not have access to audio recording equipment, students can "submit" their messages from behind a sheet hung in the classroom, to create the feel of a simple audio message.

3 Sharing the Posters

This project should culminate in a public display of the posters. Invite an art teacher from another school to judge the posters, both on their artistic merit and on how well the message is conveyed. You might be able to display the posters in categories and to award ribbons or prizes in each category.

You also could invite the rest of the students to vote for their favorite posters. The winners may be displayed in a prominent place in the school for a few weeks after the general display has ended.

Assessing the Project

The following rubric can be used for group or individual assessment.

3 Full Accomplishment Students produced a meaningful, artistic poster (or video or radio message) on a subject appropriate to the lives of the students at the school.

2 Substantial Accomplishment Students' posters are complete, but artistic effort is minimal or the message is not appropriate to the lives of the students in the school.

1 Little or Partial Accomplishment Students' posters are incomplete or do not fulfill the requirements of the assignment.

For the Portfolio
If possible, take snapshots of each poster to include in students' portfolios. Include a copy of your written assessment of the group's work in each individual portfolio. Posters may be donated to a local shopping center or other public building.

Note: For other assessment options, see the *Teacher's Guide to Assessment and Portfolio Use.*

Cross-Curricular Options

PHYSICAL EDUCATION
Have students focus on a particular sport and select a safety message specifically for that sport. Those unfamiliar with the sport will need to investigate the rules and regulations, and possibly interview some players or the gym teacher before composing their safety message.

MUSIC
Students can write a public safety message jingle. They may compose an original score or write new lyrics for an existing melody. Credit should be given if using a copyrighted tune. The jingles may be recorded and played over the school's public address system.

SOCIAL STUDIES

Students should focus their public safety messages on a specific historical era. They will need to determine what safety concerns were prominent in the time period and select an appropriate medium with which to deliver the message.

Resources

Portable Video: A Production Guide for Young People by John LeBaron and Philip Miller provides a step-by-step guide to video production.

You'll Survive! by Fred Powledge gives tips to young people on how to survive common problems of adolescence.

Sports Medicine by Edward Edelson discusses how to prevent, diagnose, and treat a variety of sports injuries.

PART 2

WHAT DO YOU THINK?
Objectives

The activities on this page can be used to
- introduce the Part 2 theme, "On the Edge of Survival," since each activity is connected to one or more of the selections in Part 2
- create materials for students' personal portfolios that they can later reconsider or revise
- build an understanding of theme that can be reviewed and revised as students progress through the unit

How would you deal with danger?
Encourage students to think about any personal experiences they may have had with a natural disaster and to recall how they reacted. Students might also reflect on stories they may have read or heard concerning people caught in similar situations. You might wish to have students organize their list of alternatives in order of importance. (See "The Walrus and the Carpenter," p. 104; the excerpt from *Woodsong*, p. 117; and "The Dog of Pompeii," p. 124.)

Can you picture this?
Suggest that group members first brainstorm a list of important details about the event they wish to represent. Encourage students to use a variety of media. For instance, students may include illustrations from newspapers or magazines to represent aspects of the event they choose. Point out that their mural could be a chronological representation of the event. (See "Too Soon a Woman," p. 93.)

Who lives "on the edge"?
Suggest that students keep their designs simple. Encourage them to think about images, designs, and slogans that succinctly capture the spirit of their chosen person. (See the poems "Life Doesn't Frighten Me" and "Another Mountain," p. 110.)

UNIT ONE **PART 2**

ON THE EDGE OF SURVIVAL

WHAT DO YOU THINK?

REFLECTING ON THEME

In Part 2 of this unit, characters respond to a wide range of risky situations. Try out an activity on this page to share your ideas about what it takes to survive. Keep your notebook at hand to record your impressions, questions, and conclusions.

Can you picture this?

Recall a dangerous event or a heroic rescue that you have heard about. With two or three other students, paint or draw a mural that illustrates what happened. If necessary, add captions to explain parts of the mural. Display your mural for the class.

Who lives "on the edge"?

Some people seem to be constantly on the go, seeking new experiences and adventures. Design a T-shirt for one of those people—someone you either know or have read about. Include a statement or motto that could apply to the person.

How would you deal with danger?

Imagine that you are caught in a flash flood or another natural disaster that occurs with little warning. What will you do? Use a chart like the one shown to evaluate your alternatives. Add more if you need to. Share your chart with a classmate.

Looking back

Has there been any change in your ideas about what you find most challenging? Work with a partner to list more challenging situations—some that you have experienced and some that you read about in the selections in Part 1. Discuss how you would rank these situations now.

92

Looking Back
To help students brainstorm a list of more challenging situations, have them consider the following questions:
- Did any of the selections in Part 1 affect your ideas about the challenges that people face in life? If so, how?
- Are there any situations or experiences in your life that you would consider to be challenging now that you have read the selections in Part 1? What are they?
- What are some of the categories by which you could classify these challenging situations?

PARENTAL INVOLVEMENT
Invite students to interview a parent or another family member about a risky or dangerous situation he or she once faced. You may wish to have students work together to generate a list of thought-provoking questions before they conduct their interviews. The interview should elicit an account of the dangerous situation, of how the family member reacted, and of the outcome of the situation. Students can share their interviews in a class presentation.

PREVIEWING

FICTION

Too Soon a Woman
Dorothy M. Johnson

PERSONAL CONNECTION *Activating Prior Knowledge*

What do you know about the hardships that Western pioneers faced? Brainstorm a list of these problems and then, in a chart like the one shown here, group the problems under the headings "Weather," "Food," "Transportation," and "Other."

Problems of the Pioneers			
Weather	Food	Transportation	Other

HISTORICAL CONNECTION *Building Background*

In 1775, Daniel Boone and other woodsmen cut a trail through the Appalachian Mountains. This trail, the Wilderness Road, was the main route used by early pioneers who wanted to travel west. During the next 140 years, trails were pushed farther west as pioneers settled the Great Plains, the Rocky Mountains, and the land beyond the Rockies. Between 1840 and 1870, more than 350,000 pioneers suffered great hardships in migrating westward.

Individuals who farmed pieces of land on which they stayed were called homesteaders. Some homesteaders lived on the land they first settled. Others, like the family in this story, moved even farther west.

WRITING CONNECTION *Setting a Purpose*

Successful pioneers were strong, resourceful people who had to overcome many hardships in their search for land—from hostile climates to loneliness and poverty. As you read this story, compare the hardships and challenges faced by pioneers with those faced by people today. Take notes in your notebook or on a sheet of paper.

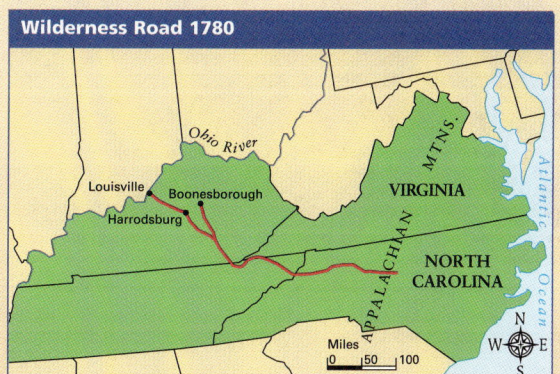
Wilderness Road 1780

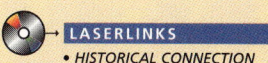
• HISTORICAL CONNECTION

TOO SOON A WOMAN 93

OVERVIEW

Objectives

- To understand and appreciate a work of historical fiction that shows the hardships faced by pioneers
- To examine the theme of a story
- To express understanding of the story through a choice of writing forms, including a journal entry and a newspaper announcement
- To extend understanding of the story through a variety of multimodal and cross-curricular activities

Skills

READING SKILLS/STRATEGIES
- Visualizing

LITERARY CONCEPTS
- Plot
- Theme

GRAMMAR
- Adjectives

SPELLING
- Special endings: the suffix -ing

SPEAKING, LISTENING, AND VIEWING
- Group discussion
- Oral presentation

Cross-Curricular Connections

SCIENCE
- Mushrooms

MATH
- Using a map scale

SOCIAL STUDIES
- Firsthand accounts of westward expansion

HISTORICAL CONNECTION
The Wilderness Road The pioneers who traveled west in 1775 were determined to cut a trail through the Appalachian Mountains. The settlers who followed had to endure many hardships to reach the Great Plains and the lands beyond. The historical images shown here document their journey.

Side A, Frame 38649

PRINT AND MEDIA RESOURCES

UNIT ONE RESOURCE BOOK
Strategic Reading: Literature, p. 51
Vocabulary SkillBuilder, p. 54
Reading SkillBuilder, p. 52
Spelling SkillBuilder, p. 53

GRAMMAR MINI-LESSONS
Transparencies, p. 12
Copymasters, p. 19

ACCESS FOR STUDENTS ACQUIRING ENGLISH
Selection Summaries
Reading and Writing Support

FORMAL ASSESSMENT
Selection Test, pp. 19–20
 Test Generator

 **AUDIO LIBRARY**
See Reference Card

 **LASERLINKS**
Historical Connection
Contemporary Connection

THE LANGUAGE OF LITERATURE TEACHER'S EDITION **93**

SUMMARY

The 11-year-old narrator tells of his westward trek with his widowed father and his sisters. The pioneer family travels by open wagon over prairies and mountains, with food growing scarcer each day. Pa grudgingly allows a young woman named Mary to join them. Needing to search for food, Pa settles the children in an abandoned cabin and leaves Mary in charge. He is gone longer than planned; in his absence, the family's horse runs away and the food runs out. In the woods Mary finds an enormous mushroom, which may be poisonous. She refuses to let the children eat it until she has tested a slice herself. The mushroom is not poisonous, and it nourishes the children until their father returns with a horse and supplies. At the end of the story, we learn that the heroic Mary will marry the father and become a stepmother to the children.

Thematic Link: *On the Edge of Survival* A pioneer family struggles to overcome harsh conditions in the wilderness.

Art Note

***The Gamekeeper's Daughter* by E. A. Walton** This portrait of a young woman is one of many portraits that the Scottish painter E. A. Walton produced. The informality of the pose and the strong arrangement of colors and tones give the painting its strength and power.

Reading the Art *Focus for a moment on the woman's downcast eyes and her facial expression. What kind of mood do they suggest? Are there other aspects of the painting that help to convey that mood?*

CUSTOMIZING FOR
Students Acquiring English

- Use **ACCESS FOR STUDENTS ACQUIRING ENGLISH,** *Reading and Writing Support.*

- There is a great deal of colloquial English in this selection. Encourage students to use context clues to figure out the meanings of phrases such as *prid'near out of grub, clean out of money, leave me be,* and *all-fired hungry.*

The Gamekeeper's Daughter (1886), E. A. Walton. Glasgow Museums: Art Gallery and Museum, Kelvingrove, Scotland.

WORDS TO KNOW

anxiety (ăng-zī′ĭ-tē) *n.* eager, nervous desire (p. 99)

endure (ĕn-dŏŏr′) *v.* to bear patiently (p. 97)

grudging (grŭj′ĭng) *adj.* given with reluctance **grudge** *v.* (p. 96)

savoring (sā′vər-ĭng) *adj.* appreciating fully; enjoying **savor** *v.* (p. 98)

sedately (sĭ-dāt′lē) *adv.* in a calm, dignified way (p. 99)

94 THE LANGUAGE OF LITERATURE TEACHER'S EDITION

Too Soon a Woman

by Dorothy M. Johnson

We left the home place behind, mile by slow mile, heading for the mountains, across the prairie where the wind blew forever.

At first there were four of us with the one-horse wagon and its skimpy load. Pa and I walked, because I was a big boy of eleven. My two little sisters romped and trotted until they got tired and had to be boosted up into the wagon bed.

That was no covered Conestoga, like Pa's folks came west in, but just an old farm wagon, drawn by one weary horse, creaking and rumbling westward to the mountains, toward the little woods town where Pa thought he had an old uncle who owned a little two-bit sawmill.

Two weeks we had been moving when we picked up Mary, who had run away from somewhere that she wouldn't tell. Pa didn't want her along, but she stood up to him with no fear in her voice.

"I'd rather go with a family and look after kids," she said, "but I ain't going back. If you won't take me, I'll travel with any wagon that will."

Pa scowled at her, and her wide blue eyes stared back.

"How old are you?" he demanded.

"Eighteen," she said. "There's teamsters come this way sometimes. I'd rather go with you folks. But I won't go back."

"We're prid'near out of grub," my father told her. "We're clean out of money. I got all I can handle without taking anybody else." He turned away as if he hated the sight of her. "You'll have to walk," he said.

So she went along with us and looked after the little girls, but Pa wouldn't talk to her.

Mini-Lesson Grammar

ADJECTIVES Point out to students that an adjective is a word that modifies, or describes, a noun or pronoun; that an adjective can come before or after the word it modifies; and that when two or more adjectives modify the same word, they are often separated with commas. Write the two sentences at the right on the chalkboard to demonstrate how adjectives can be used to modify words.

Application Have students identify at least five adjectives in the passage  above. *(covered, old, farm, drawn, one, weary, creaking, rumbling, little, woods, two-bit)*

Reteaching/Reinforcement
- *Grammar Handbook*, anthology p. 830
- *Grammar Mini-Lessons* copymasters p. 19, transparencies p. 12

📖 **The Writer's Craft**
What Are Adjectives? pp. 460–461

A bull charged around the arena.

An angry bull charged around the hot, dusty arena.

STRATEGIC READING FOR
Less-Proficient Readers

Have students make a list of any images of pioneer life and westward expansion they have encountered in books, films, or TV shows.

Set a Purpose Ask students to determine, as they read, the specific hardships facing the pioneer family in the story.

Use **UNIT ONE RESOURCE BOOK**, pp. 51–52, for guidance in reading the selection.

CUSTOMIZING FOR
Gifted and Talented Students

Have students pay attention to the dialogue as they read the selection. Ask them to describe the way the characters speak and to cite examples. Ask, Why might the author have written dialogue in this way? Is this how people in the Old West would have spoken?

Students' examples of dialogue representing the speech of the Old West may include the following:

- Page 96—"You're my pardner... but it might be she's got more brains. You mind what she says."
- Page 96—"If you get too all-fired hungry, butcher the horse. It'll be better than starvin'."
- Page 97—"I don't set up to know all about everything, like some people."

CUSTOMIZING FOR
Multiple Learning Styles

Ⓐ Spatial or Graphic Learners Have students relate the portrait by E. A. Walton to their impressions of Mary so far. Ask them to discuss whether the portrait captures any of Mary's qualities as revealed in the opening of the story.

Active Reading: EVALUATE

B Have students speculate why the homesteaders are described as "scared and desperate." *(Possible response: It has been raining, and the homesteaders' crops are spoiled and rotten. They are scared and desperate because of a severe lack of food.)*

CUSTOMIZING FOR
Students Acquiring English

I Point out that *grades* in this sentence refers to steep slopes in the mountain roads.

Literary Concept: PLOT

C Ask students to discuss why Pa's leaving is an important event in the plot. *(Possible response: Even though he thinks of his son as his partner, Pa decides to leave Mary in charge because she is older. This decision creates the possibility that Mary and the narrator may come into conflict and that dangerous situations may occur without the head of the family's being present to decide what to do.)*

STRATEGIC READING FOR
Less-Proficient Readers

D Ask students to list the different kinds of hardships faced by the family up to this point. *(There is a lack of food—crops in the area have been spoiled by heavy rains, and Pa's hunting and fishing have met with little success. There is a lack of shelter—the narrator has had to rig a makeshift tent to protect the family's cooking fire from the rain. There are transportation problems—the old horse cannot pull the wagon up the rutted roads in the mountains.)* **Noting Relevant Details**

Set a Purpose Ask students to read on to find out what Mary does when she finds something the children might eat.

On the prairie, the wind blew. But in the mountains, there was rain. When we stopped at little timber claims along the way, the homesteaders said it had rained all summer. Crops among the blackened stumps were rotted and spoiled. There was no cheer anywhere and little hospitality. The people we talked to were past worrying. They were scared and desperate.

So was Pa. He traveled twice as far each day as the wagon. He ranged through the woods with his rifle, but he never saw game. He had been depending on venison, but we never got any except as a grudging gift from the homesteaders.

He brought in a porcupine once; that was fat meat and good. Mary roasted it in chunks over the fire, half crying with the smoke. Pa and I rigged up the tarp sheet for a shelter to keep the rain from putting the fire clean out.

The porcupine was long gone, except for some of the tried-out fat that Mary had saved, when we came to an old, empty cabin. Pa said we'd have to stop. The horse was wore out, couldn't pull anymore up those grades on the deep-rutted roads in the mountains.

At the cabin, at least there was shelter. We had a few potatoes left and some corn meal. There was a creek that probably had fish in it, if a person could catch them. Pa tried it for half a day before he gave up. To this day I don't care for fishing. I remember my father's sunken eyes in his gaunt, grim face.

He took Mary and me outside the cabin to talk. Rain dripped on us from branches overhead.

"I think I know where we are," he said. "I calculate to get to old John's and back in about four days. There'll be grub in the town, and they'll let me have some whether old John's still there or not."

He looked at me. "You do like she tells you," he warned. It was the first time he had admitted Mary was on earth since we picked her up two weeks before.

"You're my pardner," he said to me, "but it might be she's got more brains. You mind what she says."

He burst out with bitterness, "There ain't anything good left in the world, or people to care if you live or die. But I'll get grub in the town and come back with it."

He took a deep breath and added, "If you get too all-fired hungry, butcher the horse. It'll be better than starvin'."

He kissed the little girls good-bye and plodded off through the woods with one blanket and the rifle.

The cabin was moldy and had no floor. We kept a fire going under a hole in the roof, so it was full of blinding smoke, but we had to keep the fire so as to dry out the wood.

The third night, we lost the horse. A bear scared him. We heard the racket, and Mary and I ran out, but we couldn't see anything in the pitch dark.

In gray daylight I went looking for him, and I must have walked fifteen miles. It seemed like I had to have that horse at the cabin when Pa came or he'd whip me. I got plumb lost two or three times and thought maybe I was going to die there alone and nobody would ever know it, but I found the way back to the clearing.

That was the fourth day, and Pa didn't come. That was the day we ate up the last of the grub.

The fifth day, Mary went looking for the horse. My sisters whimpered, huddled in a quilt by the fire, because they were scared and hungry.

| WORDS TO KNOW | **grudging** (grŭj´ĭng) *adj.* given with reluctance **grudge** *v.* |

96

Mini-Lesson — **Reading Skills/Strategies**

VISUALIZING Remind students that forming a mental picture based on a written description is called visualizing and that sensory details—those that convey sensations of sight, sound, touch, taste, and smell—help readers to visualize the characters, settings, and events in a work of literature.

Application Have students discuss the sensory details that appear in the passage highlighted above.

Ask how these details help them visualize the setting of the cabin. As students discuss their ideas, encourage them to categorize the details as sights, smells, sounds, and so on. After discussing the sensory details they used to visualize the setting, students may want to sketch the interior of the cabin.

Reteaching/Reinforcement
• *Unit One Resource Book,* p. 52

96 THE LANGUAGE OF LITERATURE TEACHER'S EDITION

I never did get dried out, always having to bring in more damp wood and going out to yell to see if Mary would hear me and not get lost. But I couldn't cry like the little girls did, because I was a big boy, eleven years old.

It was near dark when there was an answer to my yelling, and Mary came into the clearing.

Mary didn't have the horse—we never saw hide nor hair of that old horse again—but she was carrying something big and white that looked like a pumpkin with no color to it.

She didn't say anything, just looked around and saw Pa wasn't there yet, at the end of the fifth day.

"What's that thing?" my sister Elizabeth demanded.

"Mushroom," Mary answered. "I bet it hefts ten pounds."

"What are you going to do with it now?" I sneered. "Play football here?"

"Eat it—maybe," she said, putting it in a corner. Her wet hair hung over her shoulders. She huddled by the fire.

That was the day we ate up the last of the grub.

My sister Sarah began to whimper again. "I'm hungry!" she kept saying.

"Mushrooms ain't good eating," I said. "They can kill you."

"Maybe," Mary answered. "Maybe they can. I don't set up to know all about everything, like some people."

"What's that mark on your shoulder?" I asked her. "You tore your dress on the brush."

"What do you think it is?" she said, her head bowed in the smoke.

"Looks like scars," I guessed.

"'Tis scars. They whipped me. Now mind your own business. I want to think."

Elizabeth whimpered, "Why don't Pa come back?"

"He's coming," Mary promised. "Can't come in the dark. Your pa'll take care of you soon's he can."

She got up and rummaged around in the grub box.

"Nothing there but empty dishes," I growled. "If there was anything, we'd know it."

Mary stood up. She was holding the can with the porcupine grease.

"I'm going to have something to eat," she said coolly. "You kids can't have any yet. And I don't want any squalling, mind."

It was a cruel thing, what she did then. She sliced that big, solid mushroom and heated grease in a pan.

The smell of it brought the little girls out of their quilt, but she told them to go back in so fierce a voice that they obeyed. They cried to break your heart.

I didn't cry. I watched, hating her.

I <u>endured</u> the smell of the mushroom frying as long as I could. Then I said, "Give me some."

"Tomorrow," Mary answered. "Tomorrow, maybe. But not tonight." She turned to me with a sharp command: "Don't bother me! Just leave me be."

She knelt there by the fire and finished frying the slice of mushroom.

If I'd had Pa's rifle, I'd have been willing to kill her right then and there.

She didn't eat right away. She looked at the brown, fried slice for a while and said, "By tomorrow morning, I guess you can tell whether you want any."

WORDS TO KNOW
endure (ĕn-do͝or´) *v.* to bear patiently

97

Literary Concept: PLOT

H Ask students why Mary's talk with the narrator is an important moment in the plot. *(Possible response: Mary implies that if the mushroom is poisonous, she will die and the narrator will have to take charge of the situation and care for his little sisters by himself.)*

CUSTOMIZING FOR
Gifted and Talented Students

I Encourage students to put themselves in the narrator's place, imagining that they awaken to find that Mary has died from eating the mushroom. What would they do? Have students discuss the possible results of Mary's death and write a suitable ending to the story.

CUSTOMIZING FOR
Students Acquiring English

4 Make sure that students understand the reference to Gethsemane—in the Bible, the place where the disciples Peter, James, and John fell asleep while Jesus prayed on the night before his death (Mark 14:32–38). The narrator is comparing his vigil with Mary to that night. Discuss why the comparison is or is not appropriate.

© Bob Crofut.

The little girls stared at her as she ate. Sarah was chewing an old leather glove.

When Mary crawled into the quilts with them, they moved away as far as they could get.

I was so scared that my stomach heaved, empty as it was.

Mary didn't stay in the quilts long. She took a drink out of the water bucket and sat down by the fire and looked through the smoke at me.

She said in a low voice, "I don't know how it will be if it's poison. Just do the best you can with the girls. Because your pa will come back, you know. . . . You better go to bed, I'm going to sit up."

And so would you sit up. If it might be your last night on earth and the pain of death might seize you at any moment, you would sit up by the smoky fire, wide-awake, remembering whatever you had to remember, savoring life.

We sat in silence after the girls had gone to sleep. Once I asked, "How long does it take?"

"I never heard," she answered. "Don't think about it."

I slept after a while, with my chin on my chest. Maybe Peter dozed that way at Gethsemane as the Lord knelt praying.

Mary's moving around brought me wide-awake. The black of night was fading.

"I guess it's all right," Mary said. "I'd be able to tell by now, wouldn't I?"

I answered gruffly, "I don't know."

Mary stood in the doorway for a while, looking out at the dripping world as if she found

> **WORDS TO KNOW**
> **savoring** (sā′vər-ĭng) *adj.* appreciating fully; enjoying **savor** *v.*

98

Mini-Lesson  **Literary Concept**

1. Mary eats the mushroom.
2. Mary stays with Pa.
3. The horse runs away.
4. The family arrives at the cabin.
5. Mary meets the family.
6. The children eat the mushroom.

REVIEWING PLOT Help students recall that the series of events in a story is called the story's plot and that a plot usually features a conflict or a problem faced by the main character. Remind them that the actions taken to solve the problem build toward the story's climax, or turning point, after which the problem is solved and the story ends.

Application On the chalkboard, list these five events from the story. Have students work in pairs to arrange the events in chronological order. Then have them identify the events that constitute the conflict, the turning point, and the solution of the problem. *(5, 4, 3 [conflict], 1 [turning point], 6 [solution], 2)*

it beautiful. Then she fried slices of the mushroom while the little girls danced with <u>anxiety</u>.

We feasted, we three, my sisters and I, until Mary ruled, "That'll hold you," and would not cook any more. She didn't touch any of the mushroom herself.

That was a strange day in the moldy cabin. Mary laughed and was gay; she told stories, and we played "Who's Got the Thimble?" with a pine cone.

In the afternoon we heard a shout, and my sisters screamed, and I ran ahead of them across the clearing.

The rain had stopped. My father came plunging out of the woods leading a packhorse —and well I remember the treasures of food in that pack.

He glanced at us anxiously as he tore at the ropes that bound the pack.

"Where's the other one?" he demanded.

Mary came out of the cabin then, walking <u>sedately</u>. As she came toward us, the sun began to shine.

My stepmother was a wonderful woman. ❖

STRATEGIC READING FOR
Less-Proficient Readers

J Ask students to explain what happens after Mary eats the mushroom. *(Possible response: She survives and lets the children eat some of the mushroom. After she knows that the children have food and are safe, her mood changes. Mary tells stories and the children play games until their father returns.)* **Relating Cause and Effect**

COMPREHENSION CHECK

1. Who is the narrator of the story? *(an 11-year-old boy traveling west with his father and two sisters)*
2. How do the narrator's feelings toward Mary change during the course of the story? *(At first he ignores her. When his father chooses her to be in charge of the family, he appears to be jealous. Later, he begins to hate her, because she does not immediately share food that he and his sisters desperately need. At the end of the story, he realizes that she is a wonderful person.)*

LITERARY INSIGHT

Western Wagons
by Rosemary and Stephen Vincent Benét

They went with axe and rifle, when the trail was still to blaze,
They went with wife and children, in the prairie-schooner days,
With banjo and with frying pan—Susanna, don't you cry!
For I'm off to California to get rich out there or die!

We've broken land and cleared it, but we're tired of where we are.
They say that wild Nebraska is a better place by far.
There's gold in far Wyoming, there's black earth in Ioway,
So pack up the kids and blankets, for we're moving out today!

The cowards never started and the weak died on the road,
And all across the continent the endless campfires glowed.
We'd taken land and settled—but a traveler passed by—
And we're going West tomorrow—Lordy, never ask us why!

We're going West tomorrow, where the promises can't fail.
O'er the hills in legions, boys, and crowd the dusty trail!
We shall starve and freeze and suffer. We shall die, and tame the lands.
But we're going West tomorrow, with our fortune in our hands.

WORDS TO KNOW

anxiety (ăng-zī′ĭ-tē) *n.* eager, nervous desire
sedately (sĭ-dāt′lē) *adv.* in a calm, dignified way

99

LITERARY INSIGHT

1. According to the poem, why did people travel west? *(to find gold or to farm the land)*
2. How do the experiences of the family in "Too Soon a Woman" relate to this poem? *(Like the settlers in the poem, Pa is traveling west to make a better life for his family. Both in the story and in the poem, the travelers experience many hardships, such as starvation and suffering, along the way.)*

Rosemary and Stephen Vincent Benét This husband and wife often combined their writing talents. He was a Pulitzer Prize–winning author of poetry, fiction, drama, and even operas. She was working as a journalist in Paris when she met her husband.

Mini-Lesson Spelling

SPECIAL ENDINGS: THE SUFFIX -ING
Remind students that there are rules for adding -ing to verbs: for many verbs, simply add -ing, but for verbs that end in e, drop the final e before adding -ing.

Application Have students write each verb with the suffix -ing.

1. care
2. yell
3. catch
4. love
5. drive
6. sing
7. play
8. cry

Ask students to look for more words that fit this pattern and to write them in their personal word lists.

Reteaching/Reinforcement
• Unit One Resource Book, p. 53

```
grudge + ing  =  grudging
savor + ing   =  savoring
move + ing    =  moving
carry + ing   =  carrying
hold + ing    =  holding
fade + ing    =  fading
```

From Personal Response to Critical Analysis

1. Some students will say that the last sentence did surprise them, because the boy is hostile toward Mary throughout much of the story. Others will say that they were not surprised, because Mary proved herself to be a good "mother" by risking her own life for the children's safety.

2. Students may say that Mary is independent, tough, and caring. After running away from a harmful situation and traveling west on her own, she cares for the children in an unselfish and heroic way.

3. Responses will vary. Be sure that students explain their answers.

4. Pa seems to be a tough and very sad person. Because of the hardships facing his family, he seems to think that nothing in life is good. His acceptance of Mary, however, suggests that he recognizes her goodness.

5. Students may say that because Mary assumes responsibilities that women her age normally didn't have to, she is forced to become a woman earlier than she should.

6. Some students may say that although the specific situations are not the same, parents still face hardships and challenges in trying to raise and support their children. Others may say that because of modern conveniences, people do not have to face the same kinds of hardships today.

Another Pathway

Make sure that students note all of the problems facing the family in the story, that they are able to determine the category into which each problem falls, and that they are able to summarize the information they have learned. (*Possible responses: Weather—rain; Food—severe hunger; Transportation—horse unable to make it up steep inclines*)

Rubric

3 Full Accomplishment Students accurately identify the hardships facing the family and summarize the information concisely.

2 Substantial Accomplishment Students accurately identify most of the hardships and summarize the information adequately.

1 Little or Partial Accomplishment Students have difficulty in recognizing hardships in the story and in summarizing the information.

RESPONDING OPTIONS

FROM PERSONAL RESPONSE TO CRITICAL ANALYSIS

REFLECT 1. Did the last sentence of the story surprise you? Why or why not?

RETHINK 2. What is your opinion of Mary's character?
Consider
- *Close Textual Reading* what you know and can guess about Mary's past
- ways in which her past affects her present actions and attitudes
- whether she acts heroically

3. Would you eat the mushroom if you were in Mary's place? Explain your answer.

4. What can you understand about Pa from his actions and words?
Consider
- *Close Textual Reading* his comment "There ain't anything good left in the world, or people to care if you live or die"
- the fact that he eventually marries Mary

Thematic Link 5. How well do you think the title "Too Soon a Woman" fits this story? Explain your opinion.

RELATE 6. How do the hardships and challenges that pioneers faced compare with the hardships people face today?

LITERARY CONCEPTS

The **theme** of a story is a message the writer presents to the reader. A theme might be a lesson about life or a belief about people and their actions. An author rarely states a theme directly; usually the reader must infer, or figure out, the theme after reading the story carefully. What might be the theme of this story? If you have difficulty figuring it out, think about the following:

- What does the title tell you? (See question 5 under "From Personal Response to Critical Analysis.")
- What does the main character learn?
- How does the main character change?

100   UNIT ONE   PART 2: ON THE EDGE OF SURVIVAL

ANOTHER PATHWAY

Look back at the chart you made before reading "Too Soon a Woman." Add information on the problems the pioneers in this story faced. Use the chart to write a summary of the information you learned, then share your summary with other members of your class.

QUICKWRITES

1. Mary and the younger children face possible starvation. Write a **diary entry** that the narrator might have made at his darkest moment.

2. Pa asks Mary to become his wife and she accepts! Write a **wedding announcement** for the *Pioneer Times*.

📁 **PORTFOLIO** *Save your writing. You may want to use it later as a springboard to a piece for your portfolio.*

Literary Concepts

Have students work in small groups to determine the theme of the story. In each group, one student should act as facilitator to make sure all group members participate in the discussion, and another should record the group's ideas. When students are finished, have each group discuss their interpretation of the theme with another group.

QuickWrites

1. Encourage students to try to make the mood of their journal entry match the narrator's feelings at a particular moment in the story. Refer students to the selection for information about the way the narrator acts and thinks.

2. Encourage students to include in their announcement a summary of how the couple met. They might also discuss the personal characteristics that drew Pa and Mary together. Encourage them to write in the style of a newspaper article.

The Writer's Craft

Personal Voice, pp. 276–277
Report of Information, pp. 166–179

---

100   THE LANGUAGE OF LITERATURE TEACHER'S EDITION

ACROSS THE CURRICULUM

Cooperative Learning Social Studies To find out more about what happened during the westward movement, read some diaries or other accounts written by settlers. Create a Readers Theater presentation of several of these accounts. For more information on Readers Theater, see page 38.

ALTERNATIVE ACTIVITIES

Imagine that you are a member of a pioneer family about to travel more than a thousand miles to a new homestead. You have a horse and a wagon, and you may bring 300 pounds of supplies with you. Work with a small group of classmates to compile a **list** of supplies you will need during the journey. To remind you of the hardships you may face on your trip, consult the charts that the group members made for the Personal Connection on page 93. When you finish, compare your group's list with the lists that other groups have made.

Supplies we will need:
- *rope 10 lbs*
- *flour 5 lbs*

LITERARY LINKS

Compare and contrast Mary with Nadia in "Nadia the Willful" (page 21). Would you describe Mary as willful? In what ways are the two characters similar? different?

• CONTEMPORARY CONNECTION

WORDS TO KNOW

EXERCISE A Write an answer to each of the following questions.

1. Is a person filled with **anxiety** confident, nervous, calm, or happy?
2. If you **savor** a memory, are you forgetting, understanding, enjoying, or denying it?
3. Is a **grudging** smile the same as or the opposite of a wholehearted one?
4. Would someone be more likely to walk **sedately** in church, in a soccer game, or on the way home from school?
5. Which is a synonym of **endure**—believe, urge, tolerate, or blossom?

EXERCISE B Imagine that you are a child in a pioneer family that has halted on its westward trek. Night is falling, and you are asked to gather kindling for the campfire. Use three of the vocabulary words to describe how you would go about your task.

DOROTHY M. JOHNSON

1905–1984

Dorothy M. Johnson was an award-winning writer of Western stories and an honorary member of Montana's Blackfoot tribe, who gave her the name Kills-Both-Places. In such books as *Warrior for a Lost Nation* (a biography of Sitting Bull) and *Buffalo Woman*, Johnson demonstrated her understanding of Native Americans. At various times a magazine editor, a news editor, and a professor of journalism, she wrote many stories and articles and more than 15 books.

OTHER WORKS *The Hanging Tree, The Man Who Shot Liberty Valance, A Man Called Horse* Extended Reading

TOO SOON A WOMAN **101**

Literary Links

Possible responses: Both Mary and Nadia are strong-minded, independent, and willing to stand up for themselves. Mary takes charge of the children and decides not to let them eat the mushroom until she knows it is safe; Nadia speaks of her dead brother in spite of her father's orders, because she knows it is important to remember Hamed. Mary differs from Nadia in being less quick-tempered and angry.

Alternative Activities

Have students think about the hardships they might face in order to determine what supplies—such as food, clothing, shelter, and fuel—would be most important. If they need to make room for important items, ask them which of their choices they think they could live without.

Across the Curriculum

Social Studies *Cooperative Learning* You may wish to have students work in small groups to find out more about pioneer life. If you assign one diary or account to each group, one group member can research the account, another can create a summary, and the others can collaborate on the Readers Theater presentation.

ADDITIONAL SUGGESTION

 **Math** *How Far Did They Go?* The Wilderness Road was the main route used by the earliest pioneers and settlers traveling west. Have students look at the map of the Wilderness Road on page 93 and use the scale to determine its approximate length in miles.

CONTEMPORARY CONNECTION
Wilderness Skills For the millions of vacationers and adventurers who visit the great outdoors each year, wilderness skills can be a key to enjoyment—even to survival. A basic knowledge of such skills will help students understand the experiences of the characters in the selection.

Side A, Frame 38655

Words to Know

Exercise A
1. nervous
2. enjoying it
3. the opposite
4. in church
5. tolerate

Exercise B
Possible response: It was getting very dark, and I was filled with **anxiety** as I went looking for wood. Because of my fear, I could not walk **sedately** through the forest. Instead, I walked quickly, **savoring** the thought of being able to sit by a warm fire when I returned.

Reteaching/Reinforcement
Unit One Resource Book, p. 54

DOROTHY M. JOHNSON

The Man Who Shot Liberty Valance was made into a classic 1962 movie starring James Stewart and John Wayne. *A Man Called Horse*, about an Englishman captured by Indians in the 1800s, was the basis of a 1970 film version and its two sequels.

THE LANGUAGE OF LITERATURE TEACHER'S EDITION **101**

FOCUS ON POETRY

This feature defines *poetry* and provides an explanation of the terms used to discuss it. It also introduces students to the conventions of the genre and suggests strategies for reading poetry. The terms introduced here are covered in depth in the poems that follow.

Objectives

- To understand and appreciate poetry
- To understand the elements of poetry: form, sound, imagery, figurative language, and theme
- To develop effective strategies for reading poetry

Teaching Strategies: ELEMENTS OF POETRY

Form Have students look through the book to discover the different forms that poems can take. Point out the poem with the most unusual form, "Concrete Cat," which appears on page 425.

Sound Select a poem from this unit that has a strong rhyme and rhythm and read it aloud to the class.

Rhyme/Rhythm Select two volunteers to read aloud the lines from "Life Doesn't Frighten Me." The first reader should use his or her voice to stress the rhyme; the second reader should emphasize the rhythm.

Repetition Have students cite their own examples from familiar poetry, nursery rhymes, or song lyrics.

Imagery Have students analyze these images by identifying the senses to which they appeal. Students can show their results on a chart like the one shown.

Image	Sense(s)
concrete barrio	sight, touch

FOCUS ON POETRY

Poetry is the most compact form of literature. In a poem all kinds of ideas, feelings, and sounds are packed into a few carefully chosen words. The look, sounds, and language of a poem all work together to create a total effect.

FORM The way a poem looks—its arrangement on the page—is its **form**. Poetry is written in **lines**, which may or may not be sentences. Sometimes the lines are divided into groups called **stanzas**. Remember that poets choose arrangements of words and lines deliberately. The form of a poem can add to its meaning.

SOUND Most poems are meant to be read aloud. Therefore, poets choose and arrange words to create the sounds they want listeners to hear. There are many techniques that poets can use to control the sounds of their poems. Three of these are described below.

Rhyme Words that end with the same sounds are said to rhyme. Many poems contain rhyming words at the ends of the lines. Look for the rhymes in these lines from "Life Doesn't Frighten Me" by Maya Angelou on page 111:

> Shadows on the wall
> Noises down the hall
> Life doesn't frighten me at all

Rhythm A poem's rhythm is sometimes called its beat. The rhythm is the pattern of stressed and unstressed syllables—the word parts that are read with more and less emphasis—in the poem's lines. Listen for the stressed (´) and unstressed (˘) syllables in these lines from "The Walrus and the Carpenter" on page 105:

> The sĕa wăs wét as wét could bé,
> The sánds wĕre drý ăs drý.

Poems that do not have a regular rhythm—that sound more like conversation—are called free verse. "Another Mountain" on page 114 is an example of **free verse**.

Repetition A poet may choose to repeat sounds, words, phrases, or whole lines in a poem. Repetition helps the poet emphasize an idea or create a certain feeling.

IMAGERY Imagery involves words and phrases that appeal to the five senses. A poet may use imagery to create a picture in the reader's mind or to remind the reader of a familiar sensation. An example of imagery is contained in the opening lines of the poem "Street Corner Flight" by Norma Landa Flores on page 193:

102 UNIT ONE PART 2: ON THE EDGE OF SURVIVAL

From this side . . .
  of their concrete barrio
    two small boys hold
      fat white pigeons
trapped in their trembling hands.

FIGURATIVE LANGUAGE Poets use figurative language when they choose words and phrases that help readers see ordinary things in new ways. Such words and phrases are called **figures of speech.** Three figures of speech are explained below.

Simile A comparison that contains the word *like* or *as* is called a simile. The simile in these lines from "Barbara Frietchie" on page 342 compares the orchards around the town of Frederick to the garden of Eden:

> The clustered spires of Frederick stand
> Green-walled by the hills of Maryland.
> Round about them orchards sweep,
> Apple and peach trees fruited deep,
> Fair as the garden of the Lord
> To the eyes of the famished rebel horde …

Metaphor A comparison that does not contain the word *like* or *as* is called a metaphor.

Personification When a poet describes an animal or object as if it were human or had human qualities, the poet is using personification. In "Primer Lesson" by Carl Sandburg on page 27, proud words are presented as if they had a will of their own:

> They wear long boots, hard boots; they walk off proud; they can't hear you calling—

THEME All the poetic elements you have read about help poets establish their poems' themes. Just as in fiction, a poem's theme is a message about life that it conveys.

STRATEGIES FOR READING POETRY

- **Preview the poem.** Notice the poem's form: what shape it has on the page, how long it is, how long its lines are, and whether the lines are divided into stanzas.
- **Read the poem aloud.** Pause at the end of each complete thought, not necessarily at the end of each line. Look for end punctuation to help you find where each thought ends. As you read, listen for rhymes and rhythm and for the overall sound of the words in the poem.
- **Visualize the images.** In your mind's eye, picture the images and comparisons you find in the poem. Do the images remind you of feelings or experiences you have had?
- **Think about the words and phrases.** Allow yourself to wonder about any phrases or words that seem to stand out. Think about what that choice of those words adds to the poem.
- **Try to figure out the poem's theme.** Ask yourself, What's the point of this poem? What message is the poet trying to send or help me understand?
- **Let your understanding grow.** When you finish reading, you are left with first impressions of the poem. Over time, your rereadings of the poem, your discussions in class, and the other poetry you read will add to your understanding.
- **Allow yourself to enjoy the poem.** You may connect with the poem because it expresses feelings that you have felt or shows you the world through different eyes.

Figurative Language Ask students to speculate why poets find figurative language especially useful. Then discuss each of the following types of figurative language.
- **Simile** Invite students to brainstorm a list of similes that complete the phrase:
  "Friendship is like a(n) _____."
- **Metaphor** Have students omit the word *like* from their phrases to change their similes into metaphors.
- **Personification** To help students define personification, point out that it contains the word *person*.

Theme Have students explain the theme of "Barbara Frietchie" on page 342 in their own words.

Reading Strategies: MODELING
Invite volunteers to read aloud the Strategies for Reading Poetry. Tell students they will be using these strategies as they read "The Walrus and the Carpenter" on page 104 and other poems throughout the book. Then model the strategies as students read "The Walrus and the Carpenter." You may wish to use the models provided or create your own.
- **Preview** *"The poem is somewhat long and is divided into even stanzas."*
- **Read the poem aloud** *"I know that I should pause after* be *in line 13 and come to a full stop after* dry *in line 14. Also, the end of every other line in the poem rhymes."*
- **Visualize** *"I picture both the sun and moon in the sky at the same time, which is not something I usually see."*
- **Think about words and phrases** *"Many of the words and phrases are formal in style but their meanings are nonsensical. This combination adds to the humorous tone of the poem."*
- **Theme** *"This poem is humorous and not meant to be taken seriously. However, looking at what happens in the poem from the point of view of one of the oysters, I would say that the theme might be to be more careful and not trust strangers too easily."*
- **Let your understanding grow** Have students read the poem again and discuss what new impressions they have.
- **Allow yourself to enjoy the poem** *"This poem was pleasant to read because of its regular pattern of rhythm and rhyme as well as its humorous tone."*

OVERVIEW

Objectives

- To understand and appreciate a narrative poem that tells a humorous story
- To examine rhyme and rhythm in a poem
- To understand a poet's use of inverted word order
- To express understanding of the selection through a choice of writing forms, including a speech
- To extend understanding of the poem through a variety of multimodal and cross-curricular activities

Skills

LITERARY CONCEPTS
- Rhyme
- Rhythm

GENRE STUDY
- Poetry: narrative poetry

SPEAKING, LISTENING, AND VIEWING
- Oral interpretation
- Group discussion
- Oral presentation

Cross-Curricular Connections

SCIENCE
- Oysters

MATH
- Addition and division

 BIOGRAPHICAL CONNECTION

Lewis Carroll Many of the characters in Lewis Carroll's entertaining stories were based on people he knew. These historical images give readers a glimpse into his world.

Side A, Frame 38661

ALTERNATIVE
Previewing

Students can choose partners and discuss practical jokes that have been played on them.

Personal Connection

Discussion Prompts *Think of a time someone tricked you or played a practical joke on you. Describe what happened. Then listen as your partner tells his or her story. The following questions might help you get started:*

- Who played the trick on you?
- What was the trick?
- Did you think it was funny at the time? Why or why not?
- Do you still feel the same way about it?
- Could you or someone else have been harmed as a result of the trick?

As you read "The Walrus and the Carpenter," notice the trick that is played on the oysters.

PREVIEWING

POETRY

The Walrus and the Carpenter
Lewis Carroll

PERSONAL CONNECTION *Activating Prior Knowledge/Setting a Purpose*

Have you ever been tricked into doing something? How were you fooled? In your notebook, write about this experience. Watch for who gets tricked in this poem and what happens as a result.

BIOGRAPHICAL CONNECTION *Building Background*

Lewis Carroll was the author of the famous fantasy novel *Alice's Adventures in Wonderland* and its sequel *Through the Looking Glass,* in which "The Walrus and the Carpenter" appears. In *Through the Looking Glass* everything seems backward or absurd. For example, Alice must walk away from a place in order to reach it and must run fast in order to remain where she is.

Carroll enjoyed tricks and puns and nonsense. He wrote the Alice tales to amuse a ten-year-old friend, Alice Liddell. In Carroll's day, English schoolchildren were often asked to memorize long, boring poems that were intended to teach proper morals and behavior. Carroll made fun of this practice in "The Walrus and the Carpenter."

READING CONNECTION *Active Reading*

Understanding Narrative Poetry A poem that tells a story is called a narrative poem. Like works of prose fiction, narrative poems have characters, settings, plots, and sometimes dialogue. They also have many of the elements of poetry described on pages 102–103. "The Walrus and the Carpenter" is a narrative poem; it tells the story of a trick two characters play on some unfortunate young oysters. Read the poem as you would a story, pausing not at the end of each line but at the end of each sentence.

This illustration of Alice was created in 1865 by Sir John Tenniel, the first and most famous illustrator of *Alice's Adventures in Wonderland.*

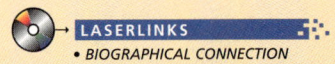
• BIOGRAPHICAL CONNECTION

104 UNIT ONE PART 2: ON THE EDGE OF SURVIVAL

PRINT AND MEDIA RESOURCES

UNIT ONE RESOURCE BOOK
Strategic Reading: Literature, p. 57

ACCESS FOR STUDENTS ACQUIRING ENGLISH
Selection Summaries
Reading and Writing Support

FORMAL ASSESSMENT
Selection Test, p. 21
 Test Generator

 **AUDIO LIBRARY**
See Reference Card

 **LASERLINKS**
Biographical Connection
Art Gallery

---

104 THE LANGUAGE OF LITERATURE TEACHER'S EDITION

The Walrus and the Carpenter
by Lewis Carroll

The sun was shining on the sea,
    Shining with all his might:
He did his very best to make
    The billows[1] smooth and bright—
5 And this was odd, because it was
    The middle of the night.

The moon was shining sulkily,[2]
    Because she thought the sun
Had got no business to be there
10   After the day was done—
"It's very rude of him," she said,
    "To come and spoil the fun!"

The sea was wet as wet could be,
    The sands were dry as dry.
15 You could not see a cloud because
    No cloud was in the sky:
No birds were flying overhead—
    There were no birds to fly.

The Walrus and the Carpenter
20   Were walking close at hand:
They wept like anything to see
    Such quantities of sand:
"If this were only cleared away,"
    They said, "it *would* be grand!"

25 "If seven maids with seven mops
    Swept it for half a year,
Do you suppose," the Walrus said,
    "That they could get it clear?"
"I doubt it," said the Carpenter,
30   And shed a bitter tear.

"O Oysters, come and walk with us!"
    The Walrus did beseech.
"A pleasant walk, a pleasant talk,
    Along the briny beach:
35 We cannot do with more than four,
    To give a hand to each."

---

1. **billows:** large waves.
2. **sulkily** (sŭl′kĭ-lē): in a gloomy, pouting way.

CUSTOMIZING FOR
Gifted and Talented Students

Suggest that students point out examples of foreshadowing—clues to what will eventually happen to the oysters—as they read the poem.

Possible responses:
- *Lines 39–42*—The oldest oyster won't go with the walrus.
- *Lines 77–78*—The walrus's words can be interpreted two ways: they might mean that the oysters will join the walrus and the carpenter for a meal, or they might mean that the oysters will be the meal.

Art Note

Illustration for "The Walrus and the Carpenter" by Peter Newell
Peter Newell was a popular illustrator of the late 19th and early 20th centuries. His work frequently appeared in magazines and children's publications. This illustration for "The Walrus and the Carpenter" was published in 1902.

Reading the Art *What are some of the ways in which the artist has made the walrus and the carpenter amusing?*

Critical Thinking:
ANALYZING

B Ask students to infer what the eldest oyster's response to the walrus suggests about that oyster's character. *(Possible response: He winks, which may mean that he is aware a trick is being played. He seems to be wise, and he probably knows from experience that he should be cautious.)*

STRATEGIC READING FOR
Less-Proficient Readers

C To be sure students are able to follow the poem, ask them how the young oysters respond when the walrus asks them to join him and the carpenter in a walk. *(They excitedly follow the pair.)* **Noting Sequence of Events**

Set a Purpose As students read, they should look for the outcome of the oysters' decision to follow the walrus and the carpenter.

Illustration by Peter Newell, 1902. Photo © 1995 Nawrocki Stock Photo, Inc./Historical. All rights reserved.

106 UNIT ONE PART 2: ON THE EDGE OF SURVIVAL

Mini-Lesson — Genre Study

POETRY On the chalkboard, draw the chart shown here. Use it to explain the following characteristics of **narrative poetry:**
- It has a setting, characters, and a plot.
- It often contains rhyme, rhythm, imagery, and figurative language.

Application Have students copy the chart in their notebooks. Then ask them to refer to it as they look for each characteristic in "The Walrus and the Carpenter." You may want to assign each characteristic to a different group of students and have the groups share their findings.

> **Narrative Poetry**
>
> | "Story" Characteristics | "Poetry" Characteristics |
> |---|---|
> | setting | rhyme |
> | characters | rhythm |
> | plot | imagery |
> | figurative language | |

106 THE LANGUAGE OF LITERATURE **TEACHER'S EDITION**

The eldest Oyster looked at him,
   But never a word he said:
The eldest Oyster winked his eye,
   And shook his heavy head—
Meaning to say he did not choose
   To leave the oyster-bed.

But four young Oysters hurried up,
   All eager for the treat:
Their coats were brushed, their faces washed,
   Their shoes were clean and neat—
And this was odd, because, you know,
   They hadn't any feet.

Four other Oysters followed them,
   And yet another four;
And thick and fast they came at last,
   And more, and more, and more—
All hopping through the frothy waves,
   And scrambling to the shore.

The Walrus and the Carpenter
   Walked on a mile or so,
And then they rested on a rock
   Conveniently low:
And all the little Oysters stood
   And waited in a row.

"The time has come," the Walrus said,
   "To talk of many things:
Of shoes—and ships—and sealing-wax—
   Of cabbages—and kings—
And why the sea is boiling hot—
   And whether pigs have wings."

"But wait a bit," the Oysters cried,
   "Before we have our chat;
For some of us are out of breath,
   And all of us are fat!"
"No hurry!" said the Carpenter.
   They thanked him much for that.

"A loaf of bread," the Walrus said,
   "Is what we chiefly need:
Pepper and vinegar besides
   Are very good indeed—
Now, if you're ready, Oysters dear,
   We can begin to feed."

"But not on us!" the Oysters cried,
   Turning a little blue.
"After such kindness, that would be
   A dismal³ thing to do!"
"The night is fine," the Walrus said.
   "Do you admire the view?

"It was so kind of you to come!
   And you are very nice!"
The Carpenter said nothing but
   "Cut us another slice.
I wish you were not quite so deaf—
   I've had to ask you twice!"

"It seems a shame," the Walrus said,
   "To play them such a trick.
After we've brought them out so far,
   And made them trot so quick!"
The Carpenter said nothing but
   "The butter's spread too thick!"

"I weep for you," the Walrus said:
   "I deeply sympathize."
With sobs and tears he sorted out
   Those of the largest size,
Holding his pocket-handkerchief
   Before his streaming eyes.

"O Oysters," said the Carpenter,
   "You've had a pleasant run!
Shall we be trotting home again?"
   But answer came there none—
And this was scarcely odd, because
   They'd eaten every one.

---

3. **dismal** (dĭz′məl): miserable; depressing.

THE WALRUS AND THE CARPENTER **107**

From Personal Response to Critical Analysis

1. Accept all reasonable responses.
2. Possible responses: I like these lines because the walrus mentions items that don't seem to have anything in common; I don't like these lines because they don't make any sense to me. Students may cite the walrus's conversations with the oysters as enjoyable.
3. Possible response: The eldest oyster knows what the walrus is up to because he has had other encounters with walruses. The younger oysters, however, don't suspect that they are going to be eaten.
4. Possible responses: Yes, because the walrus cries for them; no, because the poem is humorous, not serious.
5. Accept all reasonable responses.

Another Pathway

Cooperative Learning Have students design and create their sensory-image charts in groups of five or six. The members of each group should brainstorm examples of images in the poem to fill in their chart. One member can be assigned to encourage each student in the group to participate, and another can act as a recorder. If a group has difficulty providing examples, assign one person to act as a generator of further ideas.

Rubric

3 Full Accomplishment Students create detailed charts that accurately relate the poem's imagery to the five senses.

2 Substantial Accomplishment Students create less-detailed charts, mismatching some of the poem's imagery with the senses.

1 Little or Partial Accomplishment Students have difficulty creating charts and are unable to select relevant imagery.

RESPONDING OPTIONS

FROM PERSONAL RESPONSE TO CRITICAL ANALYSIS

REFLECT
1. What was your reaction to this poem and to the trick that is played on the oysters?

RETHINK
2. The best-known lines in this poem are

"The time has come," the Walrus said,
"To talk of many things:
Of shoes—and ships—and sealing wax—
Of cabbages—and kings—"

Explain why you like (or dislike) these lines. Which other lines of the poem do you particularly enjoy?

Thematic Link 3. The eldest oyster refuses the walrus's invitation, but the younger oysters accept it. Why?

Close Textual Link 4. Do you think that the poet intends for you to feel sorry for the oysters? Back up your opinion with evidence from the poem.

RELATE 5. Think of a time when you or your friends played a trick on someone, or when you had a trick played on you. What were the consequences?

LITERARY CONCEPTS

Rhyme is a repetition of the same sounds at the ends of words. Note the rhyme in these lines from Henry Wadsworth Longfellow's poem "Paul Revere's Ride":

Listen, my children, and you shall *hear*
Of the midnight ride of Paul Re*vere* …

Rhythm is the pattern of strong beats you hear when you read a poem aloud. Some poems have an even, regular beat that produces a musical sound. In other poems, the rhythm sounds more like conversation. Read "The Walrus and the Carpenter" aloud, then use adjectives to describe its rhymes and its rhythm.

Multimodal Learning
ANOTHER PATHWAY

Make a sensory-image chart with the names of the five senses as headings. Under each heading, list appropriate images from the poem. Which of the senses is not referred to in the poem?

QUICKWRITES

1. Suppose that one of the oysters wants to avoid being eaten. Help the oyster by writing an eloquent **speech** that might persuade the walrus and the carpenter to spare him or her.

2. Make a **wanted poster** for the walrus and the carpenter so that they can be captured and punished for the crime they committed against the poor, pitiful oysters. Be sure to describe the two criminals thoroughly.

📁 **PORTFOLIO** *Save your writing. You may want to use it later as a springboard to a piece for your portfolio.*

108   UNIT ONE   PART 2: ON THE EDGE OF SURVIVAL

Literary Concepts

Divide the class into two groups—one to deal with rhyme and one to deal with rhythm. Each group should designate a facilitator and a recorder. Have students reread the poem, looking for specific examples of rhyme and rhythm and describing each with an adjective or two. They might use charts like this to record their findings.

Rhyme	Adjectives
dry, sky, fly	short, common
beseech, beach, each	unusual

Rhythm	Adjectives
You could not see a cloud because/ No cloud was in the sky:	regular, almost singsong

QuickWrites

1. Encourage students to appeal to emotion as well as to reason and ethics. Help them include specific details and examples that might convince the walrus and the carpenter to spare the oyster.

2. Remind students to refer to the illustration as well as the words to gather details about how the walrus and the carpenter look. Encourage them to use words and phrases from the poem in their posters.

Organizing Details, pp. 217–221

108 THE LANGUAGE OF LITERATURE TEACHER'S EDITION

Multimodal Learning
ALTERNATIVE ACTIVITIES

1. **Cooperative Learning** With a group of classmates, prepare an **oral reading** of this poem. Decide on proper tones of voice for the narrator and each of the characters. Emphasize the rhymes and rhythm of the poem and observe all punctuation marks.

2. Imagine that you have been asked to illustrate a new edition of "The Walrus and the Carpenter." Rewrite the poem on a large sheet of paper, and draw or paint **illustrations** for it. Try to reveal the humor of the poem.

ACROSS THE CURRICULUM

Science You know that, despite the descriptions in this poem, real oysters don't have coats, faces, or feet. But what else do you know about oysters? Why are they called bivalves? How are they different from clams? Exchange information about oysters with a small group of classmates. Then look up oysters in a print or CD-ROM encyclopedia or in some other reference work. Share your information with the class in an oral report.

clam

oyster

THE WRITER'S STYLE

Line 106 of this poem is "But answer came there none—." Have you ever heard anyone speak this way? When people speak, they usually say the subject before the verb. Poets, however, sometimes reverse, or invert, the usual order of words to emphasize a particular word or phrase or to preserve a poem's rhymes and rhythm. Rewrite line 106 in subject-verb order. Then find other inverted lines in the poem. Why do you think Carroll might have written inverted lines in this poem?

LEWIS CARROLL

"Lewis Carroll" was the pen name of Charles Lutwidge Dodgson, an English mathematician. The eldest son in a family of 13, Dodgson was a creative child who made pets of snails and worms and invented games for his brothers and sisters. Although brilliant, Carroll was shy and stammered in the presence of adults. In the company of children, however, he became a witty, affectionate storyteller.

Carroll would send children letters barely the size of a postage stamp or ones written in reverse to be read in a mirror. He might begin a letter with "CLD

1832–1898

[his initials], Uncle loving your," and end it with "Nelly dear my." In one of his letters, he wrote what some say is the core of his belief: "One of the deep secrets of life . . . is that all this is really worth the doing, is what we do for others."

Some say Carroll never grew up. Perhaps he didn't. Upon his death at the age of 65, the doctor attending him told his sisters, "How wonderfully young your brother looks!"

OTHER WORKS *Alice's Adventures in Wonderland, Through the Looking Glass* Extended Reading

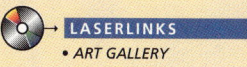
• ART GALLERY

THE WALRUS AND THE CARPENTER 109

Across the Curriculum

Science *Cooperative Learning* Divide the class into groups of four or five. You may want to have the members of each group divide up the reference materials, with each student checking one source. Each group can elect a facilitator to direct the other students in their research and a recorder to write up the group's results.

ADDITIONAL SUGGESTION

Math *Planning Dinner!* Have students discuss why the walrus and the carpenter could hold hands with only four oysters. The poem also suggests that the oysters that followed were in groups of four. Ask students, If the walrus and the carpenter plan on consuming 100 oysters each, how many groups of 4 oysters should they get to accompany them on their beach walk? *(100 + 100 = 200; 200 ÷ 4 = 50)*

LEWIS CARROLL

Besides being a mathematician and author, Lewis Carroll was an extremely accomplished portrait photographer. His two imaginative masterpieces— *Alice's Adventures in Wonderland* and *Through the Looking Glass*—have been popular with both children and adults ever since their publication more than 100 years ago.

ART GALLERY

Arthur Rackham's Illustrations from Alice in Wonderland Illustrations for *Alice in Wonderland* are often as fanciful as the stories themselves. These wonderful color pictures from *Alice in Wonderland* bring the story to life.

Side A, Frame 38665

The Writer's Style

To help students understand how inversions of word order help Carroll maintain the poem's rhythm and rhyme scheme, encourage students to read aloud each stanza in which they find an inversion. For more information about how poetry is written, refer students to The Writer's Craft pp. 84–87.

Alternative Activities

1. To practice capturing the appropriate tone and rhythm, students can tape-record their interpretations and then play them back.

2. Encourage students to experiment with a variety of media—such as crayons, paint, and pen and ink—as they create their illustrations. Suggest that they review the poem for specific details that support their interpretations of the characters and setting. If necessary, remind students that artists often evoke humor by means of exaggeration.

OVERVIEW

Objectives

- To understand and appreciate contemporary poetry about life's fears and challenges
- To examine free verse
- To understand and appreciate unconventional grammar in poetry
- To express understanding of the poems through a choice of writing forms, including an award nomination and a magazine profile
- To extend understanding of the poems through a variety of multimodal activities

Skills

WRITER'S STYLE
- Choosing the right word
- Unusual punctuation and capitalization

LITERARY CONCEPTS
- Free verse
- Rhythm
- Rhyme

SPEAKING, LISTENING, AND VIEWING
- Music
- Group discussion
- Oral presentation

ALTERNATIVE

Previewing

Have students, instead of making charts, work in groups of four or five to discuss the qualities a person needs to face life's fears and challenges.

Writing Connection

Discussion Prompts *Think about the qualities a person needs in order to deal with life's fears and challenges. Share your ideas with the other members of your group. The following questions might help you get started:*

- Whom do you know or know of that has had to face a serious problem?
- What was the problem?
- How did the person handle it?
- What qualities did the person have that helped him or her to deal with the problem?

LITERARY CONNECTION

Imagination and Tone Photographers and illustrators communicate with others through their art. The tones of their works are determined by the ways in which they see the world. These compelling and diverse images can be used in a discussion of how the imagination of a viewer and the tone of an image interact to generate meaning and emotion.

Side A, Frame 38674

110 THE LANGUAGE OF LITERATURE TEACHER'S EDITION

PREVIEWING

POETRY

Life Doesn't Frighten Me
Maya Angelou
(mī′ə ăn′jə-lō′)

Another Mountain
Abiodun Oyewole
(ä′bē-ō-dōōn′ ō′yā-wō′lä)

PERSONAL CONNECTION *Activating Prior Knowledge*

Think about a time when you tried to overcome one of your fears. If you succeeded, what qualities helped you succeed? If you didn't succeed, what qualities caused you to fail?

LITERARY CONNECTION

In a poem, the **speaker** is the voice that talks to the reader. The speakers of the two poems you are about to read face different kinds of fears and challenges. The poems therefore have slightly different tones. **Tone** is determined by the attitude a writer, in this case a poet, has toward his or her subject. The tone of a poem might be humorous, serious, angry, or sentimental. In these poems, the writers reveal their attitudes through their choice of words and through repetition of certain words and phrases.

WRITING CONNECTION *Setting a Purpose*

In a chart like the one shown here, list the qualities that a person needs in order to face life's fears and challenges. As you read the poems, decide whether the speakers have these qualities.

Qualities	Speaker of "Life Doesn't Frighten Me"	Speaker of "Another Mountain"

110   UNIT ONE   PART 2: ON THE EDGE OF SURVIVAL

- LITERARY CONNECTION

PRINT AND MEDIA RESOURCES

UNIT ONE RESOURCE BOOK
Strategic Reading: Literature, p. 61

WRITING MINI–LESSONS
Transparencies, p. 36

ACCESS FOR STUDENTS ACQUIRING ENGLISH
Selection Summaries
Reading and Writing Support

FORMAL ASSESSMENT
Selection Test, p. 23
Test Generator

AUDIO LIBRARY
See Reference Card

LASERLINKS
Literary Connection

Life Doesn't Frighten Me

by Maya Angelou

Shadows on the wall
Noises down the hall
Life doesn't frighten me at all
Bad dogs barking loud
5   Big ghosts in a cloud
Life doesn't frighten me at all.

Mean old Mother Goose
Lions on the loose
They don't frighten me at all
10 Dragons breathing flame
On my counterpane[1]
That doesn't frighten me at all,

I go boo
Make them shoo
15 I make fun
Way they run
I won't cry
So they fly
I just smile
20 They go wild
Life doesn't frighten me at all.

---
1. **counterpane** (koun′tər-pān′): bedspread.

LIFE DOESN'T FRIGHTEN ME   **111**

Mini-Lesson Writer's Style

CHOOSING THE RIGHT WORD Remind students that writers use different kinds of English for different purposes. **Standard English** is language that follows the rules of grammar and usage. **Nonstandard English** does not conform to the rules of grammar and usage.

Application Instruct students to look at the stanza highlighted above. Engage them in a discussion by asking them to identify the kinds of language in the stanza and to tell how they arrived at their decisions. Ask whether students feel nonstandard English to be appropriate in this situation. Have them discuss how elements of the poem (for example, its rhythm and rhyme scheme) might be affected if the poet followed the traditional rules of grammar and usage.

Reteaching/Reinforcement
- Writing Handbook, anthology pp. 772–773
- Writing Mini-Lessons transparencies, p. 36

 **The Writer's Craft**
Levels of Language, pp. 274–275

Thematic Link: *On the Edge of Survival*
These poems explore the struggle to survive despite fears and difficulties in life.

CUSTOMIZING FOR
Students Acquiring English
- Use **ACCESS FOR STUDENTS ACQUIRING ENGLISH**, *Reading and Writing Support*.
- Help students to appreciate the qualities of free verse. The vocabulary in these poems is not particularly difficult, so students should enjoy their rhythms and sounds.

STRATEGIC READING FOR
Less-Proficient Readers

Ask students to discuss some of their fears. Have them brainstorm ways of expressing and describing the fears.

Set a Purpose Have students pay attention, as they read, to the fears mentioned in "Life Doesn't Frighten Me" and the way the poet describes them.

Use **UNIT ONE RESOURCE BOOK**, page 61, for guidance in reading the selection.

Active Reading: PREDICT

A Ask students to predict, on the basis of the title, what the poem will be about. *(Possible response: The poem will be about the speaker's courage and determination to live her life without fear.)*

Literary Concept:
ALLITERATION

B Inform students that alliteration is a repetition of consonant sounds at the beginning of words. Have students identify the alliterating sounds in these lines. *(Bad dogs barking loud / Big ghosts in a cloud)* Ask them to describe the effect of the alliteration.

CUSTOMIZING FOR
Multiple Learning Styles

C Spatial or Graphic Learners
Encourage students to draw self-portraits, imagining themselves to have the attitude expressed by the speaker in this stanza.

THE LANGUAGE OF LITERATURE **TEACHER'S EDITION**   **111**

CUSTOMIZING FOR
Gifted and Talented Students

Ask students to think about the tone of the poem and their own feelings about overcoming fear. Then have each student write a stanza about something that he or she thinks is frightening. Be sure students' stanzas reproduce the poem's defiant tone and its "... doesn't frighten me at all" refrain.

Literary Concept: FREE VERSE

D Tell students that free verse is written like conversation, without a regular pattern of rhyme, rhythm, or line length. Ask how this stanza is both like and unlike free verse. *(The lines are of different lengths, and it sounds like conversation, but there is a pattern of rhyming words at the end of the lines.)*

STRATEGIC READING FOR
Less-Proficient Readers

E To be sure students understand the poem, ask them how the poet deals with her fears. *(She scares them away, laughs at them, and refuses to let them make her cry.)* **Restating**

Set a Purpose Have students pay attention, as they read "Another Mountain," to the poet's struggles and the way he describes them.

Literary Concept: REFRAIN

F Explain to students that a word, phrase, line, or group of lines repeated regularly in a poem is called a refrain. Ask them to identify the refrain in this poem and to describe its effect. *(Possible response: "Life doesn't frighten me at all," with some variations, is the refrain. Each time the speaker mentions something fearful, she repeats the refrain as if to convince herself that she is not scared.)*

Tough guys in a fight
All alone at night
Life doesn't frighten me at all.

25 Panthers in the park
Strangers in the dark
No, they don't frighten me at all.

D That new classroom where
Boys all pull my hair
30 (Kissy little girls
With their hair in curls)
They don't frighten me at all.

Don't show me frogs and snakes
And listen for my scream,
35 If I'm afraid at all
It's only in my dreams.

I've got a magic charm
That I keep up my sleeve,
I can walk the ocean floor
E 40 And never have to breathe.

Life doesn't frighten me at all
Not at all
Not at all.
F Life doesn't frighten me at all.

112 UNIT ONE PART 2: ON THE EDGE OF SURVIVAL

Mini-Lesson Literary Concept

RHYTHM Explain to students that a pattern of stressed and unstressed syllables in a poem is called a rhythm and that a poem with a very regular rhythm sounds like a song with a strong beat or a jump-rope rhyme.

Application Have students work in groups of three, each taking one or two stanzas of the poem and clapping or tapping out the rhythm as one person reads the passage aloud. One group member can circle the stressed syllables on a copy of the poem.

112 THE LANGUAGE OF LITERATURE TEACHER'S EDITION

Art Note

***Boy and Dog in a Johnnypump* by Jean-Michel Basquiat** The graffiti artist Jean-Michel Basquiat was one of the best-known Hispanic–African-American artists of the 1980s. This painting is from his early period (1980–1982), in which he often depicted skeleton-like figures reflecting his obsession with death.

Reading the Art *How does Basquiat represent the boy and the dog? Which parts of the boy and the dog are identifiable? Which parts have been transformed by the artist? How does the style of the painting affect the mood it conveys?*

From Personal Response to Critical Analysis

1. Possible response: The speaker seems to be a strong-minded person who has the determination and drive needed to face and overcome her fears.
2. Possible responses: The speaker's methods are effective, because people can face their fears by realizing what they are afraid of and believing that they have the power to overcome the fears. The speaker's methods may not be effective, because sometimes just claiming not to be afraid does not make fears go away.
3. Possible responses: The speaker is probably as fearless as she says she is, because she is a strong person determined to overcome her fears. The speaker is probably not as fearless as she says she is, because she keeps repeating "Life doesn't frighten me" as if to convince herself that she is not afraid.
4. Accept all reasonable responses.

Boy and Dog in a Johnnypump (1982), Jean-Michel Basquiat. Galerie Bischofberger, Zurich, Switzerland. Copyright © 1995 Artists Rights Society, New York/ADAGP, Paris.

FROM PERSONAL RESPONSE TO CRITICAL ANALYSIS

REFLECT 1. What are your impressions of the speaker of this poem? Describe your impressions in your notebook or on a sheet of paper.

RETHINK 2. Do the speaker's methods of taking charge seem effective to you? Why or why not?

3. Do you think the speaker is as fearless as she says she is? Explain your ideas.
   Consider
   Close Textual Reading
   • your feelings about overcoming fear
   • the tone of the poem

4. How do the qualities shown by the speaker compare with the qualities you have shown in facing your own fears?

LIFE DOESN'T FRIGHTEN ME   113

Multicultural Perspectives

GRAFFITI "ART" The term *graffiti*—from the plural form of the Italian word *graffito* ("a scratching or scribbling")—refers to designs scratched or painted on walls or other public surfaces. The making of graffiti is often regarded as an act of vandalism rather than of artistic creation. In the 1980s, however, urban American graffiti artists rose to prominence in the art world.

Application Students may research the lives and works of Jean-Michel Basquiat and Keith Haring. Both began as graffiti artists in New York City in the early 1980s and eventually became artistic celebrities. Have students analyze the works of these artists and consider how their simple, lively styles reflect their beginnings as "outlaw artists." Students might also debate the question, Is graffiti art, or is it lawlessness?

THE LANGUAGE OF LITERATURE TEACHER'S EDITION   113

CUSTOMIZING FOR
Students Acquiring English

1. Ask students to suggest a synonym of *weary*. (tired)
2. You may want to point out that in these lines the wind is treated as a person giving advice.

Critical Thinking: ANALYZING

G Remind students that poets' words are often not to be understood literally. Ask them what they think the poet is referring to here. *(The storm, the earth's rocking, and the avalanche of clouds represent the challenges and difficulties the speaker faces in life. The speaker's need to climb the mountain before these things occur represents a need to overcome these challenges before they threaten the speaker's life and smother the speaker's soul.)*

Art Note

My Front Yard, Summer by Georgia O'Keeffe The American painter Georgia O'Keeffe (1887–1986) usually chose subjects derived from nature. This particular landscape reflects the atmosphere and scenery of the Southwestern desert.

Reading the Art How can you tell that this painting shows a summertime landscape? Use details from the painting to support your answer.

COMPREHENSION CHECK

1. In "Life Doesn't Frighten Me," where does the speaker admit to being afraid? *(in her dreams)*
2. What are some examples of free verse in "Life Doesn't Frighten Me"? *(Possible response: the lines that don't rhyme exactly, such as "I just smile / They go wild" or those in the seventh and eighth stanzas)*
3. In "Another Mountain," what does the wind warn the speaker about? *(The wind warns the speaker about resting too long in a peace without struggle.)*
4. What does the mountain in "Another Mountain" stand for? *(Possible responses: a challenge, an obstacle, a prejudice, a struggle)*

My Front Yard, Summer (1941), Georgia O'Keeffe.
© 1996 The Georgia O'Keeffe Foundation/Artists Rights Society, New York. Photo by Malcolm Varon, New York, © 1994.

Another MOUNTAIN
by Abiodun Oyewole

Sometimes there's a mountain
that I must climb
even after I've climbed one already
But my legs are tired now
5   and my arms need a rest
my mind is too weary right now |1|
But I must climb before the storm comes
before the earth rocks
and an avalanche of clouds buries me |G|
10 and smothers my soul
And so I prepare myself for another climb
Another Mountain
and I tell myself it is nothing
it is just some more dirt and stone
15 and every now and then I should reach
another plateau and enjoy the view
of the trees and the flowers below
And I am young enough to climb
and strong enough to make it to any top
20 You see the wind has warned me |2|
about settling too long
about peace without struggle
The wind has warned me
and taught me how to fly
25 But my wings only work
After I've climbed a mountain

114 UNIT ONE PART 2: ON THE EDGE OF SURVIVAL

Mini-Lesson: Speaking,  Listening, and Viewing

MUSIC Explain to students that a tone poem (or symphonic poem) is a work in which a composer uses musical notes to express an experience, just as a poet uses words.

Application Have students listen to a recording of Richard Strauss's tone poem *An Alpine Symphony.* This work is a musical representation of the experience of climbing a mountain. Ask students to write down, as they listen, their ideas about what the various parts of the music represent. If program notes are available, they can be used to help students interpret particular passages.

114 THE LANGUAGE OF LITERATURE TEACHER'S EDITION

RESPONDING OPTIONS

FROM PERSONAL RESPONSE TO CRITICAL ANALYSIS

REFLECT 1. What is your image of the mountain described in "Another Mountain"? In your notebook, draw a picture of the mountain.

RETHINK 2. What might the last two lines, "But my wings only work / After I've climbed a mountain," mean?

3. What comparison does the speaker make throughout the poem? Is it an effective comparison? Why or why not?

RELATE
Thematic Link
4. Which of these two poems do you think has more to say about how a person should respond to the fears and challenges of life? Explain your choice.

Multimodal Learning
ANOTHER PATHWAY

Work with a partner, each of you preparing one of these poems for a dramatic reading for your class. Before you make your presentations, practice reciting the poems for each other. Speak slowly and keep your words clear and distinct.

LITERARY CONCEPTS

Poetry with no regular pattern of rhyme, rhythm, or line length is called **free verse**. Free verse often sounds like conversation. Writing free verse allows a poet to emphasize or concentrate on images and ideas rather than rhymes. Read "Another Mountain" aloud as naturally as possible. Do you think free verse is a good way of presenting the ideas in the poem? Why or why not?

CONCEPT REVIEW: Rhyme As you know, words that end with the same sounds are said to rhyme. Poems often contain rhyming words at the ends of lines. How do the rhymes in "Life Doesn't Frighten Me" add to your enjoyment of the poem?

QUICKWRITES

1. Imagine that each year a Try, Try Again Award is presented to individuals who show determination. Write an **award nomination** for the speaker of "Another Mountain."

2. Suppose you are asked to contribute to a magazine article about how young people deal with fears and challenges. Write a short **profile** of the speaker of "Life Doesn't Frighten Me."

📁 **PORTFOLIO** Save your writing. You may want to use it later as a springboard to a piece for your portfolio.

LIFE DOESN'T FRIGHTEN ME/ANOTHER MOUNTAIN **115**

From Personal Response to Critical Analysis

1. Drawings will vary. Make sure that students draw on the poem's details and imagery in creating their drawings.
2. Most students will respond that the speaker thinks that the knowledge and power to succeed and be happy in life come from encountering obstacles and struggling to overcome them.
3. Students should recognize that throughout the poem the speaker compares overcoming life's obstacles to climbing a mountain. Some students will say that the comparison is effective because the speaker carefully expresses the ways in which trying to deal with a hardship or an obstacle is like trying to conquer a mountain—sometimes life tires you, but you need determination to achieve freedom. Others may not agree, saying that the speaker simplifies the struggles and obstacles that people face in their lives.
4. Responses will vary. Make sure that students adequately support their opinions with information from the poems and from their own experience.

Another Pathway

Make sure that students familiarize themselves with the poems before presenting their dramatic readings. Encourage each student to identify the mood and tone of his or her poem and to read in a way that conveys the mood and tone.

Literary Concepts

Divide the class into groups of three or four and have each group write a short poem in free verse. In each group, one student can act as facilitator to organize the work and encourage the group members, and another can act as recorder, taking notes while the other students brainstorm ideas for the poem. All students in the group should participate in brainstorming and in writing the poem. If groups need to review the concept of free verse, refer them to the selections.

Concept Review Rhyme Students may respond that the rhymes make the poem sound like a chant, a cheer, or a nursery rhyme.

QuickWrites

1. Have students reread the poem before writing their nominations, looking for details that can be used to support their points.
2. Have students reread the poem before beginning to write their profiles, paying attention to details that reveal important information about the speaker. Encourage them to write in the style of a magazine profile.

📘 **The Writer's Craft**

Organizing Details, pp. 217–221

THE LANGUAGE OF LITERATURE TEACHER'S EDITION **115**

The Writer's Style

Students' opinions of the poet's style will vary. Encourage them to think about the reasons the poet may have had for writing as she did. Ask students to think, as they rewrite the lines, about how their changes affect the rhythm and the flow of words.

MAYA ANGELOU

Maya Angelou is considered by many to be one of the most important voices in contemporary African-American literature. In addition to her numerous literary awards, she has received honorary degrees from Smith College, Mills College, and Lawrence University. Recordings of her poetry are available for all to hear.

ABIODUN OYEWOLE

The Last Poets group was formed in 1969. Their spoken-word performances were part of a long tradition of African storytelling. Today, the Last Poets are considered pioneers of rap music.

Multimodal Learning

ALTERNATIVE ACTIVITIES

1. Create a **collage** to illustrate either poem, using drawings or magazine pictures.
2. What **music** would you use to accompany a reading of "Life Doesn't Frighten Me" or "Another Mountain"? Find recorded music, or create your own music, to match the mood of one of the poems.

THE WRITER'S STYLE

Reread "Another Mountain," paying attention to the lack of punctuation and the unusual use of capital letters. Does the poet's style help or hinder your understanding of the ideas in the poem? Rewrite several lines, adding standard capitalization and punctuation. How do the changes alter the effect of the poem?

CRITIC'S CORNER

Someone once said that Maya Angelou's poetry "strives to make us more aware of what each of us can endure, fail at, and still survive." How might this statement apply to the speaker of "Life Doesn't Frighten Me"?

MAYA ANGELOU

1928–

The life of Maya Angelou reflects her belief that "all things are possible for a human being, and I don't think there's anything in the world I can't do." Angelou grew up in the racially divided town of Stamps, Arkansas, with her brother and her grandmother. In 1940, she moved away from home and finished high school. Over the next three decades, Angelou worked at various times as a dancer, a singer, a composer, a stage and screen performer, a playwright, a poet, an editor, and a teacher.

I Know Why the Caged Bird Sings, her first autobiographical work, earned a National Book Award nomination in 1970. Angelou is best known for this book and has continued her life story in several other books. A collection of her poems received a Pulitzer Prize nomination in 1972. In 1993, she accepted an invitation to read an original poem at President Clinton's inauguration.

OTHER WORKS *Singin' and Swingin' and Gettin' Merry Like Christmas, And Still I Rise, The Complete Collected Poems of Maya Angelou* Extended Reading

ABIODUN OYEWOLE

The poetry of Abiodun Oyewole reflects the poet's deep commitment to young people, his sensitivity to the cultural heritage of African Americans, and his love of life. When asked what advice he would give young people about the challenges or fears they might encounter, he responds, "I'd say that every cloud has a silver lining, which sounds like a cliché but works as a rule. I do live by that."

Born in Cincinnati, Ohio, Oyewole has lived most of his life in New York City. During the 1960s, he was a member of a group of New York street poets called the Last Poets. Today, he works as a creative-writing consultant for the New York City Public Schools. He has also created plays and songs and has led a jazz group called Griot (named for a type of African storyteller).

Alternative Activities

1. Before students begin the activity, have each student reread the poem he or she has chosen to illustrate. Encourage students to make lists of imagery and details that they want to include in their collages. The lists will assist them in making drawings or selecting images.
2. Before students attempt to select music, have them reread the poems. Encourage them to list the imagery and ideas in the poems that are reflected in their choices of music.

PREVIEWING

NONFICTION

from Woodsong
Gary Paulsen

PERSONAL CONNECTION *Activating Prior Knowledge/Setting a Purpose*

The selection you are about to read is about someone who lives in the wilderness in Minnesota. Wild animals, such as bears, are a part of this writer's everyday experience. With a small group of classmates, discuss what you know about animals in the wild. Make a web like the one shown here. Use the suggested topics in the smaller circles as discussion starters.

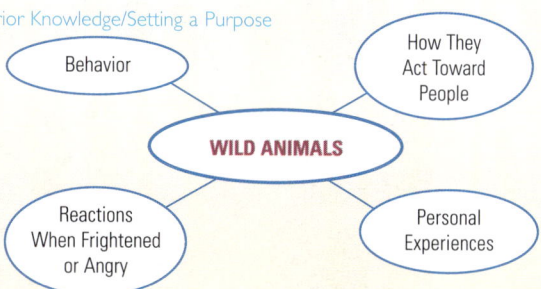

GEOGRAPHICAL CONNECTION *Building Background*

Thick forests once covered 70 percent of Minnesota. Today forests cover only about 35 percent of the state. Minnesota's most spectacular woods can be found in the 3-million-acre Superior National Forest, north of Lake Superior. The northern and northeastern sections of the state are the most rugged, with thousands of square miles of unbroken wilderness. In this region, people are scarce but wild animals are plentiful. One of the few states where timber wolves still roam free, Minnesota is also home to white-tailed deer, beavers, moose, and black bears.

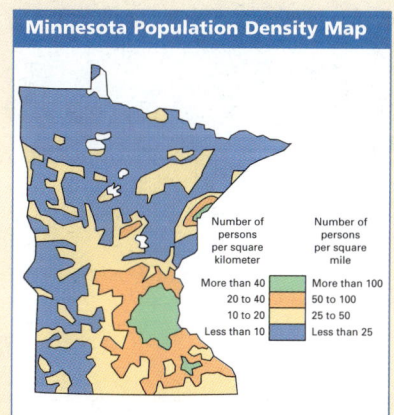

READING CONNECTION *Active Reading*

Making Predictions In both fiction and nonfiction, it is possible to find clues that will help you predict what is going to happen next. In this account of wilderness life, you will be reading about interactions between human beings and animals. To make predictions as you read, think about the facts in the selection and about what you already know. Decide where the events are leading, and predict the next logical step. To help you practice this reading strategy, questions have been inserted at two points in the selection. When you come to a question, pause and jot down your prediction in your reading log. Then read on to see what happens. Check your predictions after you finish the selection.

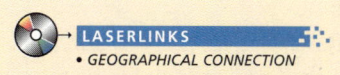
• GEOGRAPHICAL CONNECTION   117

OVERVIEW

Objectives

- To understand and appreciate an autobiographical work dealing with interactions between human beings and animals
- To enrich reading by using the active-reading strategy of predicting
- To express understanding of the selection through a choice of writing forms, including a poem and a rewriting of a scene
- To extend understanding of the selection through a variety of multimodal and cross-curricular activities

Skills

READING SKILLS/STRATEGIES
• Predicting

LITERARY CONCEPTS
• Autobiography
• Author's purpose

GRAMMAR
• Commas in series

SPEAKING, LISTENING, AND VIEWING
• Group discussion
• Oral presentation

Cross-Curricular Connections

SCIENCE
• Garbage-disposal methods
• Bears

GEOGRAPHY
• Making a map

GEOGRAPHICAL CONNECTION
Wild Minnesota The state of Minnesota still contains millions of acres of wilderness. These images will help students to understand the geography and extent of these wilderness areas and to identify some of the native flora and fauna. You may wish to use the images to prompt a discussion about human impact on the environment.

Side A, Frame 38679

PRINT AND MEDIA RESOURCES

UNIT ONE RESOURCE BOOK
Strategic Reading: Literature, p. 65
Vocabulary SkillBuilder, p. 67
Reading SkillBuilder, p. 66

GRAMMAR MINI–LESSONS
Transparencies, p. 31
Copymasters, p. 40

ACCESS FOR STUDENTS ACQUIRING ENGLISH
Selection Summaries
Reading and Writing Support

FORMAL ASSESSMENT
Selection Test, pp. 25–26
 Test Generator

 **AUDIO LIBRARY**
See Reference Card

LASERLINKS
Geographical Connection
Science Connection

THE LANGUAGE OF LITERATURE TEACHER'S EDITION **117**

SUMMARY

So many bears search for food outside Gary Paulsen's Minnesota cabin that he gives them nicknames and treats them like pets. One day, as Paulsen is burning trash that includes food scraps, the smell attracts a male bear nicknamed Scarhead. In his eagerness to get at the food, Scarhead rips up the structure where the trash is burned. When Paulsen angrily and unthinkingly tosses a stick at Scarhead, the bear turns on him. Paulsen, knowing that the creature can kill him with one blow, waits helplessly while Scarhead decides his fate. The bear chooses not to attack, and Paulsen hurries to get his rifle. He is about to shoot Scarhead—and then he realizes that the bear not only has spared his life but has reminded him to respect his fellow animals. Humbled and wiser, Paulsen puts the gun away.

Thematic Link: *On the Edge of Survival* A man faces unexpected danger as an angry bear confronts him.

CUSTOMIZING FOR
Students Acquiring English

- Use **ACCESS FOR STUDENTS ACQUIRING ENGLISH,** *Reading and Writing Support.*
- You may wish to discuss with them the kinds of wildlife, plants, and weather found in the Minnesota setting.

STRATEGIC READING FOR
Less-Proficient Readers

Have students write about situations that they feel taught them valuable lessons. Have them relate their experiences to Paulsen's experience as they read.

Set a Purpose Have students think, as they read, about the animals that are attracted to Paulsen's cabin and the reasons for their attraction.

Use **UNIT ONE RESOURCE BOOK,** pp. 65–66, for guidance in reading the selection.

FROM WOODSONG

Wabana-Wagamuman [Bear in the forest] (1989), Tom Uttech. Oil on canvas, courtesy of Struve Gallery, Chicago.

BY GARY PAULSEN

WORDS TO KNOW

menace (měn'ĭs) *n.* a possible danger; threat (p. 121)

novelty (nŏv'əl-tē) *n.* something new and unusual (p. 120)

predator (prĕd'ə-tər) *n.* an animal that hunts other animals for food (p. 119)

rummaging (rŭm'ĭ-jĭng) *adj.* searching thoroughly **rummage** *v.* (p. 121)

scavenging (skăv'ən-jĭng) *adj.* searching for discarded scraps **scavenge** *v.* (p. 119)

In Woodsong *Gary Paulsen describes his life as a trapper in the woods of northern Minnesota. He lived with his wife, Ruth, and his son, James, in a small cabin that did not have plumbing or electricity. At the time, Paulsen was not writing stories but simply learning the ways of the woods. This episode describes one of the lessons he learned.*

We have bear trouble. Because we feed processed meat to the dogs, there is always the smell of meat over the kennel. In the summer it can be a bit high[1] because the dogs like to "save" their food sometimes for a day or two or four—burying it to dig up later. We live on the edge of wilderness, and consequently the meat smell brings any number of visitors from the woods.

Skunks abound, and foxes and coyotes and wolves and weasels—all predators. We once had an eagle live over the kennel for more than a week, scavenging from the dogs, and a crazy group of ravens has pretty much taken over the puppy pen. Ravens are protected by the state, and they seem to know it. When I walk toward the puppy pen with the buckets of meat, it's a tossup to see who gets it—the pups or the birds. They have actually pecked the puppies away from the food pans until they have gone through and taken what they want.

Spring, when the bears come, is the worst. They have been in hibernation through the winter, and they are hungry beyond caution. The meat smell draws them like flies, and we frequently have two or three around the kennel at the same time. Typically they do not bother us much—although my wife had a bear chase her from the garden to the house one morning—but they do bother the dogs.

---

1. **it can be a bit high:** the smell can be rather strong.

WORDS TO KNOW
predator (prĕd′ə-tər) *n.* an animal that hunts other animals for food
scavenging (skăv′ən-jĭng) *adj.* searching for discarded scraps **scavenge** *v.*

119

Art Note

Wabana-Wagamuman by Tom Uttech
Tom Uttech's haunting woodland paintings are inspired by the wilderness regions of North America. The title of this painting is in the Chippewa (or Ojibwa) language.

Reading the Art What mood is conveyed by this painting? How do the colors, the textures, and the arrangement of the objects contribute to the mood?

CUSTOMIZING FOR
Gifted and Talented Students

Have students look for phrases set off by dashes in the selection. Ask them to explain why they think Paulsen includes each phrase.

Possible responses:

- Page 119—"Skunks abound, and foxes and coyotes and wolves and weasels—all predators." Paulsen is making it clear that these are examples of the wild animals that are attracted by the smell of meat.

- Page 121—"... and without thinking—because I was so used to him—I picked up a stick ..." In describing an action, Paulsen inserts a phrase that explains the reason for the action.

Literary Concept:
CAUSE AND EFFECT

A Have students rephrase this statement of a cause-and-effect relationship, using a different word in place of *consequently*. (Possible responses: <u>Because</u> we live on the edge of wilderness, the meat smell brings any number of visitors from the woods. We live on the edge of wilderness, <u>so</u> the meat smell brings any number of visitors from the woods.)

CUSTOMIZING FOR
Multiple Learning Styles

B **Spatial or Graphic Learners** Have students draw or paint some of the details of the setting described here.

CUSTOMIZING FOR
Students Acquiring English

1 Make sure students realize that here the word *pen* refers to a small enclosure for domestic animals.

2 Ask students to interpret the expression "it's a tossup." (*The pups get the meat half the time, and the birds get it half the time.*)

Mini-Lesson Grammar

COMMAS IN A SERIES Point out to students that a comma tells readers to pause, thus preventing the readers from running together words or ideas that should be kept separate. Tell them that in a series of three or more items, a comma is placed after each item except the last.

Application Have students place commas correctly in the following sentences.
1. At the grocery store, I bought lettuce tomatoes peppers and onions.
2. We saw seals swimming monkeys climbing and elephants bathing at the zoo.
3. In order to get to the cabin, they had to take a cab catch a bus ride on a ferry and walk a mile.

Reteaching/Reinforcement
- *Grammar Handbook,* anthology pp. 847–848
- *Grammar Mini-Lessons,* copymasters, p. 40, transparencies, p. 31

The Writer's Craft
Commas That Separate Ideas, p. 574

THE LANGUAGE OF LITERATURE **TEACHER'S EDITION** 119

Critical Thinking: ANALYZING

C Ask students why Paulsen may have chosen to set this sentence fragment off as a separate paragraph. *(Possible response: to call attention to the fragment and create a dramatic effect)*

CUSTOMIZING FOR
Students Acquiring English

3 Explain that the author deliberately uses an incomplete sentence here to heighten the impact of his words and to create suspense. You may want to ask students to rephrase the fragment as a complete sentence. *(That was a major mistake.)*

4 Explain that *snuff* is a slang word meaning "to kill."

Active Reading: PREDICT

D Ask students to predict what mistake the narrator will make. *(Possible response: Paulsen will let down his guard around a bear and get into trouble.)*

Linking to Science

E Point out that the events Paulsen recounts take place at a time before concern about air pollution led to prohibitions against burning garbage. Briefly discuss with students some garbage-disposal methods that are alternatives to burning or dumping. Ask which of these methods might be environmentally safe and practical for a family in an isolated wilderness area.

STRATEGIC READING FOR
Less-Proficient Readers

F Ask students these questions to make sure that they are following the story:

• Why do the bears come to Paulsen's yard? *(They are attracted by the smell of the meat that Paulsen feeds his dogs and by the smell of burning trash.)* Restating

• Why are the bears attracted by the burning trash? *(Some of the trash is paper that has been used to wrap food, and the bears have learned that where there is burning trash, there is often food.)* Making Inferences

Set a Purpose Have students read on to find out what happens when Scarhead makes another appearance.

They are so big and strong that the dogs fear them, and the bears trade on this fear to get their food. It's common to see them scare a dog into his house and take his food. Twice we have had dogs killed by rough bear swats that broke their necks—and the bears took their food.

We have evolved[2] an uneasy peace with them, but there is the problem of familiarity. The first time you see a bear in the kennel it is a novelty, but when the same ones are there day after day, you wind up naming some of them (old Notch-Ear, Billy-Jo, etc.). There gets to be a too-relaxed attitude. We started to treat them like pets.

3 A major mistake.

> **PREDICT**
> What mistake do you think the narrator makes?
> *Using a Reading Log*

There was a large male around the kennel for a week or so. He had a white streak across his head, which I guessed was a wound scar from some hunter—bear hunting is allowed here. He wasn't all that bad, so we didn't mind him. He would frighten the dogs and take their hidden stashes now and then, but he didn't harm them, and we became accustomed to him hanging around. We called him Scarhead, and now and again we would joke about him as if he were one of the yard animals.

At this time we had three cats, forty-two dogs, fifteen or twenty chickens, eight ducks, nineteen large white geese, a few banty hens, ten fryers which we'd raised from chicks and **4** couldn't (as my wife put it) "snuff and eat," and six woods-wise goats.

The bears, strangely, didn't bother any of the yard animals. There must have been a rule, or some order to the way they lived, because they would hit the kennel and steal from the dogs but leave the chickens and goats and other yard stock completely alone—although you would have had a hard time convincing the goats of this fact. The goats spent a great deal of time with their back hair up, whuffing and blowing snot at the bears—and at the dogs, who would *gladly* have eaten them. The goats never really believed in the truce.

There is not a dump or landfill to take our trash to, and so we separate it—organic, inorganic[3]—and deal with it ourselves. We burn the paper in a screened enclosure, and it is fairly efficient; but it's impossible to get all the food particles off wrapping paper, so when it's burned, the food particles burn with it.

And give off a burnt food smell.

And nothing draws bears like burning food. It must be that they have learned to understand human dumps—where they spend a great deal of time foraging. And they learn amazingly fast. In Alaska, for instance, the bears already know that the sound of a moose hunter's hunt means there will be a fresh gut pile when the hunter cleans the moose. They come at a run when they hear the shot. It's often a close race to see if the hunter will get to the moose before the bears take it away....

Because we're on the south edge of the wilderness area, we try to wait until there is a northerly breeze before we burn, so the food smell will carry south, but it doesn't always help. Sometimes bears, wolves, and other predators are already south, working the sheep farms down where it is more settled—they take a terrible toll[4] of sheep—and we catch them on the way back through.

---

2. **evolved** (ĭ-vŏlvd´): developed by a series of small changes.
3. **organic** (ôr-găn´ĭk), **inorganic** (ĭn´ôr-găn´ĭk): on the one hand, things made of plant or animal material; and on the other, things made of material that has never been alive.
4. **take a terrible toll:** destroy a large number.

WORDS TO KNOW
novelty (nŏv´əl-tē) *n.* something new and unusual

120

Mini-Lesson — **Reading Skills/Strategies**

ACTIVE READING: PREDICT Remind students that predicting is using what they already know to guess what might happen in the future. Tell them that as good readers read a story, they gather information and combine it with what they know from their own experience to predict what might happen next.

Application Ask students to look at the passage highlighted on page 121 and to predict what will happen to Paulsen. Have them discuss what information from the passage and from their own experience they used to make their predictions. Then invite them to indicate other points in the selection where they make predictions about what will happen.

Reteaching/Reinforcement
• *Unit One Resource Book,* p. 66

---

120 THE LANGUAGE OF LITERATURE TEACHER'S EDITION

That's what happened one July morning.

Scarhead had been gone for two or three days, and the breeze was right, so I went to burn the trash. I fired it off and went back into the house for a moment—not more than two minutes. When I came back out, Scarhead was in the burn area. His tracks (directly through the tomatoes in the garden) showed he'd come from the south.

He was having a grand time. The fire didn't bother him. He was trying to reach a paw in around the edges of flame to get at whatever smelled so good. He had torn things apart quite a bit—ripped one side off the burn enclosure—and I was having a bad day, and it made me mad.

I was standing across the burning fire from him, and without thinking—because I was so used to him—I picked up a stick, threw it at him, and yelled, "Get out of here."

I have made many mistakes in my life, and will probably make many more, but I hope never to throw a stick at a bear again.

In one rolling motion—the muscles seemed to move within the skin so fast that I couldn't take half a breath—he turned and came for me. Close. I could smell his breath and see the red around the sides of his eyes. Close on me he stopped and raised on his back legs and hung over me, his forelegs and paws hanging down, weaving back and forth gently as he took his time and decided whether or not to tear my head off.

I could not move, would not have time to react. I knew I had nothing to say about it. One blow would break my neck. Whether I lived or died depended on him, on his thinking, on his ideas about me—whether I was worth the bother or not.

I did not think then.

Looking back on it, I don't remember having one coherent[5] thought when it was happening. All I knew was terrible menace. His eyes looked very small as he studied me. He looked down on me for what seemed hours. I did not move, did not breathe, did not think or do anything.

And he lowered.

Perhaps I was not worth the trouble. He lowered slowly and turned back to the trash, and I walked backward halfway to the house and then ran—anger growing now—and took the rifle from the gun rack by the door and came back out.

PREDICT
What will the narrator do next?
Using a Reading Log

He was still there, rummaging through the trash. I worked the bolt and fed a cartridge in and aimed at the place where you kill bears and began to squeeze. In raw anger, I began to take up the four pounds of pull necessary to send death into him.

And stopped.

Kill him for what?

That thought crept in.

Kill him for what?

For not killing me? For letting me know it is wrong to throw sticks at four-hundred-pound bears? For not hurting me, for not killing me, I should kill him? I lowered the rifle and ejected the shell and put the gun away. I hope Scarhead is still alive. For what he taught me, I hope he lives long and is very happy, because I learned then—looking up at him while he made up his mind whether or not to end me—that when it is all boiled down, I am nothing more and nothing less than any other animal in the woods. ❖

---

5. **coherent** (kō-hîr′ənt): clear; logical.

WORDS TO KNOW
menace (mĕn′ĭs) *n.* a possible danger; threat
rummaging (rŭm′ĭ-jĭng) *adj.* searching thoroughly **rummage** *v.*

121

Mini-Lesson Literary Concept

AUTHOR'S PURPOSE On the chalkboard, draw the web shown at the right, and use it to remind students that authors write for four main reasons: to entertain, to inform, to express their opinions, and to persuade readers to do or believe something. Tell students that although a writer may have more than one purpose for writing a work, one of the purposes is usually the most important.

Application Ask students what they think were Paulsen's purposes for writing about his encounter with Scarhead. Have them discuss which purpose seems to be most important and why it is the most important one.

STRATEGIC READING FOR
Less-Proficient Readers

G Ask students to summarize the reasons why Scarhead makes Paulsen mad. *(Possible response: On what Paulsen calls "a bad day," he discovers that Scarhead not only has come back but has trampled the tomato plants and ripped off a side of the burn enclosure.)*
Summarizing

Active Reading: PREDICT

H Ask students to predict what the narrator will do next. *(Possible responses: The narrator is going to shoot the bear with the gun he has just brought outside. The narrator will not shoot the bear; he is angry, but he will calm down.)*

CUSTOMIZING FOR
Gifted and Talented Students

Have students discuss whether, in their opinion, human beings have the right to serve their own needs and interests by building homes in wilderness areas.

COMPREHENSION CHECK
1. Why is the smell of meat around Paulsen's cabin so strong in the summer? *(The dogs like to bury the meat and save it for later.)*
2. According to Paulsen, why is familiarity with the bears a problem? *(He becomes too relaxed around them and begins treating them as if they were pets.)*
3. Why does Paulsen wait until there is a northerly breeze before he burns his trash? *(Paulsen lives on the south edge of the wilderness area. He waits for a northerly breeze so that the food smell from the burning trash will be carried southward, away from most of the scavenging animals.)*
4. After Scarhead decides not to attack Paulsen, what does Paulsen want to do? *(kill the bear)*
5. What lesson does Paulsen learn from this experience? *(He realizes that he is nothing more and nothing less than any other animal.)*

EDITOR'S NOTE *With the permission of the author or copyright holder, a deletion was made because it refers to a section of Woodsong not excerpted here.*

THE LANGUAGE OF LITERATURE TEACHER'S EDITION **121**

From Personal Response to Critical Analysis

1. Accept all reasonable responses.
2. Possible responses: He is a person close to nature; he sometimes acts impulsively; he is very observant and thoughtful; he respects animals and doesn't think he is any better than they are.
3. Students will have predicted either that Paulsen would shoot Scarhead or that he would not shoot the bear.
4. Most students will say they learned that the risks of interactions with wild animals make living in the wilderness dangerous and that wild animals need to be left alone as much as possible.
5. Possible responses: Wild animals sometimes attack people, pets, and farm animals; eat crops; destroy property; and spread disease. People can build fences, set humane traps, and learn ways of adjusting to the presence of animals.

Another Pathway

Cooperative Learning Encourage students to form small groups to debate this issue. Make sure that they support their opinions with information from the selection and from personal experience.

Rubric

3 Full Accomplishment Students are able to express their opinions clearly and support the opinions adequately.

2 Substantial Accomplishment Students are able to express their opinions somewhat clearly and provide some support for the opinions.

1 Little or Partial Accomplishment Students have difficulty expressing their opinions and are unable to support the opinions.

RESPONDING OPTIONS

FROM PERSONAL RESPONSE TO CRITICAL ANALYSIS

REFLECT 1. Write three words that describe this selection. Compare your words with those of a classmate.

RETHINK 2. What kind of person is Gary Paulsen?
Consider
Close Textual Reading
- his observations about the animals around the kennel
- his feelings and actions toward the bear
- his comments about himself and about the lesson he learned

3. Look at the predictions you made for the Reading Connection on page 117. What did you think would happen when Paulsen faced Scarhead with his rifle? How accurate was your prediction?

4. How did reading Paulsen's account affect your impressions of living in the wilderness and of animals in the wild?

RELATE 5. Animals such as deer, skunks, woodchucks, rats, and pigeons often cause problems for humans. Discuss some unwanted-wildlife problems that you know about. What might be done to solve these problems?

Multimodal Learning
ANOTHER PATHWAY
Cooperative Learning
This selection ends with Paulsen saying, "I am nothing more and nothing less than any other animal in the woods." Debate the truth of this statement with a group of classmates.

QUICKWRITES

1. Think over Paulsen's experiences, as well as any wilderness experiences of your own. Create a **poem** that describes the risks a person runs in the wilderness.

2. Rewrite the trash-burning **scene** from the bear's point of view. Use details from the story and your own imagination to describe what Scarhead thinks and feels during his encounter with Paulsen.

📁 **PORTFOLIO** Save your writing. You may want to use it later as a springboard to a piece for your portfolio.

LITERARY CONCEPTS

An **autobiography** is a writer's account of his or her own life. It is almost always told from a first-person point of view, with the pronouns *I, we, me,* and *us.* Because an autobiography is written about a real person and real events, it is a form of nonfiction. An autobiography can provide information only the writer knows. From reading this selection, what do you learn about Paulsen that you might not have learned if someone else had told his story?

122 UNIT ONE PART 2: ON THE EDGE OF SURVIVAL

Literary Concepts

Have students write short autobiographical essays about experiences of theirs. Remind them that an autobiography includes information that only the writer knows, such as his or her thoughts and feelings about particular subjects or events. Make sure that students write from the first-person point of view and that they consistently use first-person pronouns. If you wish to extend the activity, encourage students to present their autobiographical essays to the class.

QuickWrites

1. Instruct students to plan their poems by listing the specific images and ideas they want to communicate through their writing. Remind them that poems do not have to include rhymes.
2. Have students reread the scene before writing their bear's-eye view accounts, trying to imagine Scarhead's feelings and thoughts. Make sure that their accounts are written from the first-person point of view.

 **The Writer's Craft**

Writing a Poem, pp. 84–88
Personal Narrative, pp. 72–83

122 THE LANGUAGE OF LITERATURE TEACHER'S EDITION

ACROSS THE CURRICULUM

Science Skim the selection and list all the details Gary Paulsen includes about bears. Then do research to find out more about the biological family called *Ursidae*. Does Scarhead demonstrate typical bear behavior? Is Paulsen's portrayal accurate? Record your information either on paper or as a computer document. Make it available in a reference file that you and others can use.

WORDS TO KNOW

EXERCISE A On your paper, write the letter of the phrase that best completes each sentence below.

1. A **predator** usually eats (a) grass and fruits (b) vegetables (c) other animals.
2. You would most likely find bears **scavenging** in (a) a garbage pile (b) a stream (c) a cave.
3. An animal that is a **menace** to humans is (a) dangerous (b) harmless (c) helpful.
4. A polar bear would be a **novelty** in (a) Alaska (b) a zoo (c) Africa.
5. If a bear were **rummaging** through your campsite, it would (a) make a mess (b) only circle your campfire (c) leave no trace of its presence.

EXERCISE B Copy and fill in the chart below to analyze the word *predator*. Do the same with *menace* or *novelty*.

Definition of *Predator*	Examples of Predators	Use of *Predator* in Selection	Synonym of *Predator*

GARY PAULSEN

1939–

Besides being a writer, Gary Paulsen has been a soldier, an animal trapper, and a rancher. As a trapper for the state of Minnesota, Paulsen was given four sled dogs to help him with his work. The time he spent with the dogs convinced him that he could no longer kill animals. His experiences motivated him to write *Woodsong* and the novels *Dogsong* and *Hatchet*, Newbery Honor Books. In 1990, his novel *The Winter Room* was also a Newbery Honor Book.

Because Paulsen's father was an army officer, his family moved frequently when he was a young boy. "School was a nightmare because I was unbelievably shy, and terrible at sports," he recalls. Paulsen was introduced to books by a friendly librarian who gave him his first library card. "She didn't care if I looked right, wore the right clothes, dated the right girls, was popular at sports—none of those prejudices existed in the public library." Paulsen read everything "as though I had been dying of thirst and the librarian had handed me a five-gallon bucket of water. I drank and drank."

As a writer, he has satisfied both young and adult readers, publishing more than 40 books, 200 articles, and 2 plays.

OTHER WORKS *Dogteam, Winterdance: The Fine Madness of Running the Iditarod, Tracker, The Cookcamp, The Island, Sisters/Hermanas* Extended Reading

• SCIENCE CONNECTION

WOODSONG 123

Alternative Activities

Have students research the constellations Ursa Major and Ursa Minor to find out how the constellations got their names and where they can be found in the sky.

Across the Curriculum

Science *Cooperative Learning* Have students work in groups of three or four to research bears. You may want to have each group research the habitat, behavior, diet, and other characteristics of a different species of bear. The groups can give class presentations to share their findings.

ADDITIONAL SUGGESTION

 **Geography** *Make a Map!* Have students create maps of the setting described in the selection, including the house, the garden, the yard, and the burn enclosure. Encourage them to reread the selection to gather information about the locations of these sites.

Words to Know

Exercise A
1. c   4. c
2. a   5. a
3. a

Exercise B
Answers will vary. Make sure students correctly define each word and locate its use in the selection.

Reteaching/Reinforcement
• *Unit One Resource Book*, p. 67

GARY PAULSEN

"I write because it's all I can do," Paulsen claims. "I've tried to do something else and I cannot, and have to come back to writing, though I often hate it—hate it and love it.... I write because it's all there is."

SCIENCE CONNECTION

Black Bear Research So many black bears roam the wilderness areas of Minnesota that researchers have plenty of opportunity to study them. These images show some of the ways in which researchers study the black bear in its natural habitat.

Side A, Frame 38687

THE LANGUAGE OF LITERATURE TEACHER'S EDITION 123

OVERVIEW

Objectives

- To understand and appreciate a work of historical fiction dealing with the disaster in ancient Pompeii
- To understand techniques authors use in writing historical fiction
- To examine external conflict and setting
- To express understanding of the story through a choice of writing forms, including an account from a character's point of view and an eyewitness account
- To extend understanding of the story through a variety of multimodal and cross-curricular activities

Skills

READING SKILLS/STRATEGIES
- Connecting

LITERARY CONCEPTS
- Conflict
- Setting
- Sensory details

GENRE STUDY
- Fiction: historical fiction

WRITER'S STYLE
- Details appealing to hearing

GRAMMAR
- Prepositional phrases

SPELLING
- Spelling words with suffixes

STUDY SKILLS
- Using reference books

SPEAKING, LISTENING, AND VIEWING
- Press conference
- Group discussion
- Oral presentation

Cross-Curricular Connections

SCIENCE
- Volcanoes
- Barometers
- Biological clock

SOCIAL STUDIES
- Mythology
- Celebrating with fireworks

HISTORICAL CONNECTION

The Eruption of Mount Vesuvius

Ancient Pompeii comes to life in this film, which tells the story of the city's burial beneath the ash of Vesuvius in A.D. 79.

Side A, Frame 4706

PREVIEWING

FICTION

The Dog of Pompeii
Louis Untermeyer

PERSONAL CONNECTION — Activating Prior Knowledge/Setting a Purpose

Has a destructive natural force—such as a brushfire, a tornado, or a flood—ever affected your community? Think about natural disasters you have experienced or heard about. How did people respond to the emergencies? How did people survive? Share memories and reflections with other members of your class. Then, as you read this story, compare those experiences with the experiences of the citizens of Pompeii when Vesuvius erupts.

HISTORICAL CONNECTION — Building Background

In A.D. 79, the volcanic mountain Vesuvius suddenly erupted. It poured tons of burning lava and ashes over the countryside and buried Pompeii, a nearby city, under 12 to 15 feet of ash and cinders. In 1748, a peasant digging in a vineyard in southern Italy struck a buried wall. The excavations that followed uncovered Pompeii. The remains of the city, well preserved by the ashes, present a clear picture of what life was like in the ancient Roman Empire. We now know how people dressed, how children were taught, and even how foods were prepared.

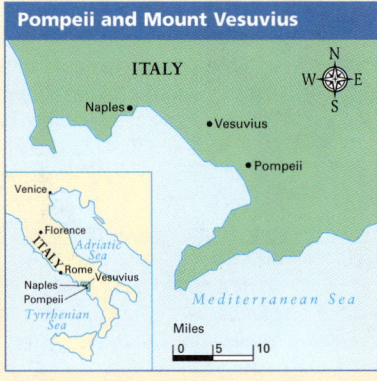

Pompeii and Mount Vesuvius

READING CONNECTION — Active Read

Reading Historical Fiction Writing in which a particular period of history is brought to life through an author's imagination is called historical fiction. The author usually blends factual information about the time, the place, and historical persons with imaginary characters, dialogue, and plot developments. From such writing you learn not only facts and figures about historical events but also the feelings people may have had about the events, as in this story about the eruption of Mount Vesuvius.

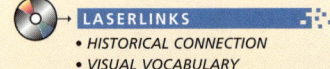
- HISTORICAL CONNECTION
- VISUAL VOCABULARY

124 UNIT ONE PART 2: ON THE EDGE OF SURVIVAL

PRINT AND MEDIA RESOURCES

UNIT ONE RESOURCE BOOK
Strategic Reading: Literature, p. 71
Vocabulary SkillBuilder, p. 74
Reading SkillBuilder, p. 72
Spelling SkillBuilder, p. 73

GRAMMAR MINI-LESSONS
Transparencies, p. 41

WRITING MINI-LESSONS
Transparencies, p. 38

ACCESS FOR STUDENTS ACQUIRING ENGLISH
Selection Summaries
Reading and Writing Support

FORMAL ASSESSMENT
Part Test, pp. 29–30
Selection Test, pp. 27–28
 Test Generator

 **AUDIO LIBRARY**
See Reference Card

 **LASERLINKS**
Historical Connection
Visual Vocabulary

 **INTERNET RESOURCES**
McDougal Littell Literature Center at http://www.hmco.com/mcdougal/lit

124 THE LANGUAGE OF LITERATURE TEACHER'S EDITION

THE DOG OF POMPEII

by Louis Untermeyer

Tito and his dog Bimbo lived (if you could call it living) under the wall where it joined the inner gate. They really didn't live there; they just slept there. They lived anywhere. Pompeii was one of the gayest of the old Latin towns, but although Tito was never an unhappy boy, he was not exactly a merry one. The streets were always lively with shining chariots and bright red trappings; the open-air

Cave Canem [Beware of dog], Roman Mosaic. Museo Archeologico Nazionale, Naples, Italy. Scala/Art Resource, New York.

SUMMARY

In the ancient Roman city of Pompeii, the blind boy Tito and his dog Bimbo live a simple life together. Three times a day, Bimbo slips away to steal raisin cakes and scraps of food for them to live on. Together they roam Pompeii, exploring its smells and sounds. One night the city's people are especially merry as they celebrate the birthday of the Roman emperor. Afterward Tito sleeps soundly, exhausted from the excitement. Early the next morning his dog pulls him awake and drags him toward the Forum. The ground trembles, and volcanic ash fills the air—the nearby volcano Mount Vesuvius is erupting! Pompeiians crowd the street as buildings burn and pumice falls. Confused and frightened, Tito tries to head to the center of town, but Bimbo forces him toward the sea. There someone lifts Tito safely into a boat, leaving Bimbo behind in the commotion. Centuries later, scientists find the skeleton of a dog in a Pompeiian bakery, a raisin cake still in its mouth.

Thematic Link: *On the Edge of Survival*
A blind boy and his dog attempt to escape violent destruction.

CUSTOMIZING FOR
Students Acquiring English

- Use **ACCESS FOR STUDENTS ACQUIRING ENGLISH**, *Reading and Writing Support*.
- Be prepared to offer background information on the ancient Roman Empire.

STRATEGIC READING FOR
Less-Proficient Readers

Set a Purpose Have students read to find out about Tito's relationship with his dog, Bimbo.

Use **UNIT ONE RESOURCE BOOK**, pp. 71–72, for guidance in reading the selection.

Art Note

Cave Canem In Pompeii, homeowners warned off robbers by placing mosaics like this one at the entrance of their houses. On some of these mosaics, the words *Cave canem* (kä′wā kä′něm), meaning "Beware of the dog," appear.

Reading the Art Even without seeing a "Beware of the dog" message, how can you tell that this mosaic serves as a warning to visitors and intruders? What is it about the way the dog is represented that tells you to be careful?

WORDS TO KNOW

dislodging (dĭs-lŏj′ĭng) *adj.* moving from a settled position **dislodge** *v.* (p. 131)
eruption (ĭ-rŭp′shən) *n.* an outburst or throwing forth of lava, water, steam, and other materials (p. 129)
restore (rĭ-stôr′) *v.* to bring back to an original condition (p. 134)
shrine (shrīn) *n.* a place of worship (p. 128)
vapor (vā′pər) *n.* fumes, mist, or smoke (p. 133)

VISUAL VOCABULARY
- **cameo** (kăm′ē-ō′)
- **Jupiter** (jōō′pĭ-tər)
- **mosaics** (mō-zā′ĭks)
- **promenade** (prŏm′ə-nād′)
- **villa** (vĭl′ə)

Side A, Frame 38694

THE LANGUAGE OF LITERATURE **TEACHER'S EDITION** 125

CUSTOMIZING FOR
Gifted and Talented Students

Encourage students to think about Tito's blindness as they read the selection. Ask them to consider whether the condition is represented as an obstacle or handicap and what advantages it might have. Have them cite details from the story to support their opinions.

Possible responses:

- Page 126—Tito relies a great deal on Bimbo to supply food; his blindness might therefore be considered a handicap.
- Page 127—Tito can hear and smell things that people with sight do not notice; his blindness therefore has some advantages.

Literary Concept: NARRATOR

A Remind students that a narrator is a person who tells a story. Ask them whether the narrator of "The Dog of Pompeii" is a character in the story or an outside voice created by the author. Have them explain how they know. *(Possible response: The narrator of this story is an outside voice created by the author. He or she tells the story about Tito and Bimbo but does not interact with characters in the story.)*

Active Reading: EVALUATE

B Ask students why it is Bimbo's business to "sleep lightly with one ear open and muscles ready for action." *(Possible response: Tito relies on Bimbo for protection, so Bimbo must be ready to deal with unexpected situations.)*

STRATEGIC READING FOR
Less-Proficient Readers

C To be sure students understand the relationship between Tito and Bimbo, ask them how Bimbo cares for Tito. *(Three times a day, Bimbo steals raisin cakes and scraps of food for Tito to eat.)* Summarizing

Set a Purpose Have students pay attention, as they read, to Tito's experiences while walking around the city.

---

theaters rocked with laughing crowds; sham battles and athletic sports were free for the asking in the great stadium. Once a year the Caesar[1] visited the pleasure city, and the fireworks lasted for days; the sacrifices[2] in the forum were better than a show. But Tito saw none of these things. He was blind—had been blind from birth. He was known to everyone in the poorer quarters. But no one could say how old he was; no one remembered his parents; no one could tell where he came from. Bimbo was another mystery. As long as people could remember seeing Tito—about twelve or thirteen years—they had seen Bimbo. Bimbo had never left his side. He was not only dog but nurse, pillow, playmate, mother, and father to Tito.

A Did I say Bimbo never left his master? (Perhaps I had better say comrade, for if anyone was the master, it was Bimbo.) I was wrong. Bimbo did trust Tito alone exactly three times a day. It was a fixed routine, a custom understood between boy and dog since the beginning of their friendship, and the way it worked was this: Early in the morning, shortly after dawn, while Tito was still dreaming, Bimbo would disappear. When Tito woke, Bimbo would be sitting quietly at his side, his ears cocked, his stump of a tail tapping the ground, and a fresh-baked bread—more like a large round roll—at his feet. Tito would stretch himself; Bimbo would yawn; then they would breakfast. At noon, no matter where they happened to be, Bimbo would put his paw on Tito's knee, and the two of them would return to the inner gate. Tito would curl up in the corner (almost like a dog) and go to sleep, while Bimbo, looking quite important (almost like a boy), would disappear again. In half an hour he'd be back with their lunch. Sometimes it would be a piece of fruit or a scrap of meat; often it was nothing but a dry crust. But sometimes there would be one of those flat, rich cakes, sprinkled with raisins and sugar, that Tito liked so much. At suppertime the same thing happened, although there was a little less of everything, for things were hard to snatch in the evening with the streets full of people. Besides, Bimbo didn't approve of too much food before going to sleep. A heavy supper made boys too restless and dogs too stodgy—and it was the business of a dog to sleep lightly with one ear open and muscles ready for action. **B**

> THERE WAS PLENTY OF EVERYTHING IN POMPEII IF YOU KNEW WHERE TO FIND IT—AND IF YOU HAD A DOG LIKE BIMBO.

But whether there was much or little, hot or cold, fresh or dry, food was always there. Tito never asked where it came from, and Bimbo never told him. There was plenty of rainwater in the hollows of soft stones; the old egg-woman at the corner sometimes gave him a cupful of strong goat's milk; in the grape season the fat winemaker let him have drippings of the mild juice. So there was no danger of going hungry or thirsty. There was plenty of everything in Pompeii if you knew where to find it—and if you had a dog like Bimbo. **C**

As I said before, Tito was not the merriest boy in Pompeii. He could not romp with the other youngsters and play hare and hounds and I spy and follow-your-master and ball-against-the-building and

---
1. **the Caesar** (sē′zər): the Roman emperor.
2. **sacrifices**: offerings of animals or objects to the gods.

126   UNIT ONE   PART 2: ON THE EDGE OF SURVIVAL

Mini-Lesson   Genre Study

FICTION Remind students that fiction is literature that tells about imaginary people, places, or events. Then tell them that when a writer does not make up the entire story but bases all or part of it on real people or events, the result is known as **historical fiction**.

Application Have students create a chart in which they list elements of the story that they think are imaginary and elements that they think are based on real people, places, and events. You can copy the chart at the right on the chalkboard to help students begin the activity.

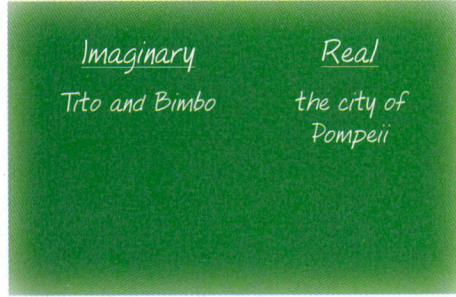

Imaginary	Real
Tito and Bimbo	the city of Pompeii

126   THE LANGUAGE OF LITERATURE   TEACHER'S EDITION

jackstones and kings and robbers with them. But that did not make him sorry for himself. If he could not see the sights that delighted the lads of Pompeii, he could hear and smell things they never noticed. He could really see more with his ears and nose than they could with their eyes. When he and Bimbo went out walking, he knew just where they were going and exactly what was happening.

"Ah," he'd sniff and say as they passed a handsome villa, "Glaucus Pansa is giving a grand dinner tonight. They're going to have three kinds of bread, and roast pigling, and stuffed goose, and a great stew—I think bear stew—and a fig pie." And Bimbo would note that this would be a good place to visit tomorrow.

Or, "H'm," Tito would murmur, half through his lips, half through his nostrils. "The wife of Marcus Lucretius is expecting her

The Sorceress and the Traveler. Mosaic from Pompeii, House of the Dioscuri. Museo Archeologico Nazionale, Naples, Italy. Scala/Art Resource New York.

THE DOG OF POMPEII 127

Critical Thinking: ANALYZING

D Ask students what they think the narrator means when he says that Tito can "see" more with his ears and nose than others can with their eyes. (*Possible response: Because Tito is blind, he must rely on sounds and smells for information that others get through their sight. His senses of smell and hearing are more sensitive than other people's, so he can experience things that other people cannot.*)

CUSTOMIZING FOR
Multiple Learning Styles

E **Bodily-Kinesthetic Learners** Have students wear blindfolds to pretend that they, like Tito, cannot see. Encourage them to try to identify classmates by their voices. You might also have students bring in various objects to be identified by touch or smell.

CUSTOMIZING FOR
Students Acquiring English

1 Point out that the suffix *-ling* means "small," so a pigling is a small pig. Ask students what the more common word *duckling* means.

2 Be sure students understand that *h'm* represents a sound Tito makes when he is thinking. Model the appropriate intonation and facial expression.

 **Mini-Lesson** — **Reading Skills/Strategies**

ACTIVE READING: CONNECTING Remind students that active readers use certain strategies as they read and that connecting is a strategy that involves relating the content of a literary work to what one already knows.

Application Ask students the following questions to assist them in understanding the strategy of connecting. You may want them to answer the questions in a classroom discussion, or you may prefer to make this a short writing activity.
• Have you ever known a pet or another animal who exhibited humanlike intelligence?
• In what ways was the animal similar to or different from Bimbo?

Reteaching/Reinforcement
• *Unit One Resource Book,* p. 72

THE LANGUAGE OF LITERATURE **TEACHER'S EDITION** 127

CUSTOMIZING FOR
Students Acquiring English

3 *Mm-m* is another representation of a sound—this time the sound Tito makes to indicate his appreciation of the smell of food. Model the appropriate intonation of *mm-m* and of the exclamation "What good things they have in the macellum today!"

Linking to Social Studies

 Inform students that in Greek and Roman mythology various gods and goddesses were believed to influence events in nature, like the weather. For instance, in Roman mythology, the god Neptune produced earthquakes and Jupiter caused lightning and thunder.

STRATEGIC READING FOR
Less-Proficient Readers

G To be sure that students are following the story up to this point, ask the following questions:

- How does Tito know that the tragic poet is ill? *(He can smell the smoke fumes being used to cure the poet's fever.)* **Noting Relevant Details**

- Why is there scarcely a building in Pompeii that is older than Tito? *(Most of the city's buildings were destroyed during an earthquake when Tito was about a year old. New buildings had to be built to replace them.)* **Making Inferences**

Set a Purpose Have students read on to find out about the debate on earthquakes that Tito hears in the public square and about the city's celebration of Caesar's birthday.

---

mother. She's shaking out every piece of goods in the house; she's going to use the best clothes—the ones she's been keeping in pine needles and camphor³—and there's an extra girl in the kitchen. Come, Bimbo, let's get out of the dust!"

Or, as they passed a small but elegant dwelling opposite the public baths, "Too bad! The tragic poet is ill again. It must be a bad fever this time, for they're trying smoke fumes instead of medicine. Whew! I'm glad I'm not a tragic poet!"

Or, as they neared the forum, "Mm-m! What good things they have in the macellum today!" (It really was a sort of butcher-grocer-marketplace, but Tito didn't know any better. He called it the macellum.) "Dates from Africa, and salt oysters from sea caves, and cuttlefish, and new honey, and sweet onions, and—ugh!—water-buffalo steaks. Come, let's see what's what in the forum." And Bimbo, just as curious as his comrade, hurried on. Being a dog, he trusted his ears and nose (like Tito) more than his eyes. And so the two of them entered the center of Pompeii.

The forum was the part of the town to which everybody came at least once during each day. It was the central square, and everything happened here. There were no private houses; all was public—the chief temples, the gold and red bazaars, the silk shops, the town hall, the booths belonging to the weavers and jewel merchants, the wealthy woolen market, the shrine of the household gods. Everything glittered here. The buildings looked as if they were new—which, in a sense, they were. The earthquake of twelve years ago had brought down all the old structures, and since the citizens of Pompeii were ambitious to rival Naples and even Rome, they had seized the opportunity to rebuild the whole town. And they had done it all within a dozen years. There was scarcely a building that was older than Tito.

Tito had heard a great deal about the earthquake, though being about a year old at the time, he could scarcely remember it. This particular quake had been a light one—as earthquakes go. The weaker houses had been shaken down; parts of the outworn wall had been wrecked; but there was little loss of life, and the brilliant new Pompeii had taken the place of the old. No one knew what caused these earthquakes. Records showed they had happened in the neighborhood since the beginning of time. Sailors said that it was to teach the lazy city folk a lesson and make them appreciate those who risked the dangers of the sea to bring them luxuries and protect their town from invaders. The priests said that the gods took this way of showing their anger to those who refused to worship properly and who failed to bring enough sacrifices to the altars and (though they didn't say it in so many words) presents to the priests. The tradesmen said that the foreign merchants had corrupted the ground and it was no longer safe to traffic in imported goods that came from strange places and carried a curse with them. Everyone had a different explanation—and everyone's explanation was louder and sillier than his neighbor's.

They were talking about it this afternoon as Tito and Bimbo came out of the side street into the public square. The forum was the

---

3. **camphor** (kăm′fər): a strong-smelling substance used as a moth repellent.

WORDS TO KNOW
shrine (shrīn) *n.* a place of worship

128

Mini-Lesson: Speaking, Listening, and Viewing

PRESS CONFERENCE Tell students that a press conference is a meeting called when someone wants to make an important announcement to reporters—for example, the President may call a press conference to announce a major appointment or to explain an important decision, and a corporation may call a press conference to announce a merger.

Application Divide the class into two groups: reporters and Pompeiian town officials. Have students hold a mock press conference in which the town officials release a statement about the impending eruption of Mount Vesuvius. Students who are reporters should be prepared to ask questions of the town officials so that they can present information about the situation to the public.

128 THE LANGUAGE OF LITERATURE TEACHER'S EDITION

favorite promenade[4] for rich and poor. What with the priests arguing with the politicians, servants doing the day's shopping, tradesmen crying their wares, women displaying the latest fashions from Greece and Egypt, children playing hide-and-seek among the marble columns, knots of soldiers, sailors, peasants from the provinces[5]—to say nothing of those who merely came to lounge and look on—the square was crowded to its last inch. His ears even more than his nose guided Tito to the place where the talk was loudest. It was in front of the shrine of the household gods that, naturally enough, the householders were arguing.

"I tell you," rumbled a voice which Tito recognized as bath master Rufus's, "there won't be another earthquake in my lifetime or yours. There may be a tremble or two, but earthquakes, like lightnings, never strike twice in the same place."

"Do they not?" asked a thin voice Tito had never heard. It had a high, sharp ring to it, and Tito knew it as the accent of a stranger. "How about the two towns of Sicily that have been ruined three times within fifteen years by the eruptions of Mount Etna? And were they not warned? And does that column of smoke above Vesuvius mean nothing?"

"That?" Tito could hear the grunt with which one question answered another. "That's always there. We use it for our weather guide. When the smoke stands up straight, we know we'll have fair weather; when it flattens out, it's sure to be foggy; when it drifts to the east—"

"Yes, yes," cut in the edged voice. "I've heard about your mountain barometer. But the column of smoke seems hundreds of feet higher than usual, and it's thickening and spreading like a shadowy tree. They say in Naples—"

"Oh, Naples!" Tito knew this voice by the little squeak that went with it. It was Attilio, the cameo[6] cutter. "*They* talk while we suffer. Little help we got from them last time. Naples commits the crimes, and Pompeii pays the price. It's become a proverb with us. Let them mind their own business."

"Yes," grumbled Rufus, "and others, too."

"Very well, my confident friends," responded the thin voice, which now sounded curiously flat. "We also have a proverb—and it is this: Those who will not listen to men must be taught by the gods. I say no more. But I leave a last warning. Remember the holy ones. Look to your temples. And when the smoke tree above Vesuvius grows to the shape of an umbrella pine, look to your lives."

Tito could hear the air whistle as the speaker drew his toga about him, and the quick shuffle of feet told him the stranger had gone.

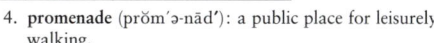

IT WAS THE CENTRAL SQUARE, AND EVERYTHING HAPPENED HERE. . . . EVERYTHING GLITTERED HERE.

---

4. **promenade** (prŏm´ə-nād´): a public place for leisurely walking.
5. **provinces:** areas of a country that are far from the capital.
6. **cameo** (kăm´ē-ō´): a gem or shell with a picture carved on it.

WORDS TO KNOW
eruption (ĭ-rŭp´shən) *n.* an outburst or throwing forth of lava, water, steam, and other materials

129

Literary Concept: DESCRIPTION

H Remind students that a description is a "word picture" of a scene, an event, or a character. Ask them to identify the details the author uses to create his description of the public square. *(Possible responses: sounds of priests arguing with politicians and of tradesmen crying their wares; images of finely dressed women, children playing hide-and-seek, and crowds of soldiers, sailors, and peasants)*

Active Reading: SUMMARIZE

I Ask students to summarize what Tito overhears the stranger saying about earthquakes and volcanoes. If they need help, share the following thought processes with them.

Think-Aloud Model *In what I've just read, the stranger is involved in a debate about earthquakes and volcanic eruptions with a few people in the public square. It seems to me that everyone seems to have a different opinion about why and when these things occur. The stranger says that earthquakes and volcanic eruptions are the gods' way of teaching people a lesson. He seems to think that the gods cause these disasters to punish people.*

Linking to Science

J Barometers are instruments that measure atmospheric pressure. Meteorologists use them in forecasting the weather. For instance, a decrease in atmospheric pressure is often a sign that rainy weather is on the way.

Active Reading: PREDICT

K Ask students to predict what might happen because of the increase in the amount of smoke coming out of Vesuvius. *(Possible response: The increase in the amount of smoke coming out of the volcano might indicate that there will be an eruption.)*

Mini-Lesson Writer's Style

DETAILS APPEALING TO HEARING
Remind students that all writers search for precise words to describe details—for example, the writer of this story uses precise words to describe the sounds Tito hears in the public square. Tell them that good readers will "listen" carefully to imagine these sounds.

Application Have students reread page 129, paying careful attention to the words used to describe the various voices that Tito hears in the public square. Have them discuss what kinds of voices these words suggest. You might also encourage volunteers to read the dialogue aloud, mimicking the voices in accordance with the descriptions.

Reteaching/Reinforcement
• *Writing Handbook*, anthology pp. 784–785
• *Writing Mini-Lessons* transparencies, p. 38

 The Writer's Craft

Appealing to the Senses, pp. 266–275

THE LANGUAGE OF LITERATURE TEACHER'S EDITION **129**

STRATEGIC READING FOR
Less-Proficient Readers

L To be sure students understand what is happening in the story, ask them what activities Tito attends on Caesar's birthday. *(a play in the uncovered theater and a mock naval battle)*
Summarizing

Set a Purpose Instruct students to pay attention, as they read, to what happens during the volcanic eruption.

Critical Thinking: ANALYZING

M Ask students what impressions they have of Tito's dreams and whether they think the description of the dreams serves any particular function. *(Possible response: Tito's dreams are very frightening and may be a warning about a volcanic eruption.)*

Literary Concept: SENSORY DETAILS

N Have students identify the five senses as you list them on the chalkboard. Explain that authors use sensory details to make characters and events seem more vivid to readers. Then ask students to identify the sensory details in the author's description of Tito's experience. *(Possible responses: The air is hot and heavy; Tito can taste it in his mouth; the air is like a warm powder that stings his nostrils and burns his eyes.)*

CUSTOMIZING FOR
Students Acquiring English

4 Point out that the suffix *-less* means "without" and ask students for a synonym of *sightless*. *(blind)*

"Now what," said the cameo cutter, "did he mean by that?"

"I wonder," grunted Rufus. "I wonder."

Tito wondered, too. And Bimbo, his head at a thoughtful angle, looked as if he had been doing a heavy piece of pondering. By nightfall the argument had been forgotten. If the smoke had increased, no one saw it in the dark. Besides, it was Caesar's birthday, and the town was in holiday mood. Tito and Bimbo were among the merrymakers, dodging the charioteers who shouted at them. A dozen times they almost upset baskets of sweets and jars of Vesuvian wine, said to be as fiery as the streams inside the volcano, and a dozen times they were cursed and cuffed. But Tito never missed his footing. He was thankful for his keen ears and quick instinct—most thankful of all for Bimbo.

They visited the uncovered theater, and though Tito could not see the faces of the actors, he could follow the play better than most of the audience, for their attention wandered—they were distracted by the scenery, the costumes, the by-play, even by themselves—while Tito's whole attention was centered in what he heard. Then to the city walls, where the people of Pompeii watched a mock naval battle in which the city was attacked by the sea and saved after thousands of flaming arrows had been exchanged and countless colored torches had been burned. Though the thrill of flaring ships and lighted skies was lost to Tito, the shouts and cheers excited him as much as any, and he cried out with the loudest of them.

The next morning there were *two* of the beloved raisin and sugar cakes for his breakfast. Bimbo was unusually active and thumped his bit of a tail until Tito was afraid he would wear it out. The boy could not imagine whether Bimbo was urging him to some sort of game or was trying to tell him something. After a while, he ceased to notice Bimbo. He felt drowsy. Last night's late hours had tired him. Besides, there was a heavy mist in the air—no, a thick fog rather than a mist—a fog that got into his throat and scraped it and made him cough. He walked as far as the marine gate[7] to get a breath of the sea. But the blanket of haze had spread all over the bay, and even the salt air seemed smoky.

He went to bed before dusk and slept. But he did not sleep well. He had too many dreams—dreams of ships lurching in the forum, of losing his way in a screaming crowd, of armies marching across his chest, of being pulled over every rough pavement of Pompeii.

He woke early. Or, rather, he was pulled awake. Bimbo was doing the pulling. The dog had dragged Tito to his feet and was urging the boy along. Somewhere. Where, Tito did not know. His feet stumbled uncertainly; he was still half asleep. For a while he noticed nothing except the fact that it was hard to breathe. The air was hot. And heavy. So heavy that he could taste it. The air, it seemed, had turned to powder, a warm powder that stung his nostrils and burned his sightless eyes.

Then he began to hear sounds. Peculiar sounds. Like animals under the earth. Hissings and groanings and muffled cries that a dying

> THE NOISES CAME FROM UNDERNEATH. HE NOT ONLY HEARD THEM—HE COULD FEEL THEM.

---
7. **marine gate:** a gate in the city wall, leading to the sea.

130 UNIT ONE PART 2: ON THE EDGE OF SURVIVAL

Multicultural Perspectives

CELEBRATING WITH FIREWORKS This story mentions that fireworks are set off during Caesar's visits to Pompeii (p. 126). Students may be interested to discover that a number of holidays besides the familiar Fourth of July are celebrated with fireworks. For example, Chinese New Year celebrations feature colorful parades and many, many fireworks.

Mount Vesuvius in Eruption (1817), Joseph Mallord William Turner, R.A., 1775–1851. Yale Center for British Art, New Haven, Connecticut, Paul Mellon Collection.

creature might make <u>dislodging</u> the stones of his underground cave. There was no doubt of it now. The noises came from underneath. He not only heard them—he could feel them. The earth twitched; the twitching changed to an uneven shrugging of the soil. Then, as Bimbo half pulled, half coaxed him across, the ground jerked away from his feet and he was thrown against a stone fountain.

The water—hot water—splashing in his face revived him. He got to his feet, Bimbo steadying him, helping him on again. The noises grew louder; they came closer. The cries were even more animal-like than before, but now they came from human throats. A few people, quicker of foot and more hurried by fear, began to rush by. A family or two—then a section—then, it seemed, an army broken out of bounds. Tito, bewildered though he was, could recognize Rufus as he bellowed past him, like a water buffalo gone mad. Time was lost in a nightmare.

It was then the crashing began. First a sharp crackling, like a monstrous snapping of twigs; then a roar like the fall of a whole forest of trees; then an explosion that tore earth and

WORDS TO KNOW
dislodging (dĭs-lŏj′ĭng) *adj.* moving from a settled position **dislodge** *v.*

131

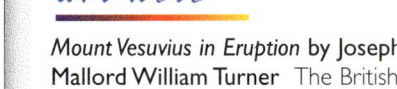

Art Note

***Mount Vesuvius in Eruption* by Joseph Mallord William Turner** The British artist J. M. W. Turner ranks among the greatest of all landscape painters. He liked to paint epic scenes of natural catastrophe, of which this painting is a prime example. Turner is noted for his dramatic use of color and composition as well as his powerfully impressionistic style.

Reading the Art Imagine that you are looking at this painting and Tito is with you. How would you describe the painting to him?

Literary Concept:
FIGURATIVE LANGUAGE

O Ask students what the author compares the sounds coming from beneath the earth to. Have them describe the effect of this comparison. (*Possible response: He compares them to the groanings and muffled cries that a dying creature might make as it squirms in its underground cave. The comparison creates an eerie and frightening mood.*)

Active Reading: CONNECT

P Have students recall personal experiences in which time seemed to "stand still" and relate those experiences to Tito's experience in the selection. Ask students whether their experiences help them to identify with Tito.

Mini-Lesson Literary Concept

REVIEWING SENSORY DETAILS Remind students that words and phrases that help readers to see, hear, taste, smell, and feel what a writer is describing are called sensory details.

Application Have students review the passage from the last paragraph on page 130 to the end of the first paragraph on page 132. Ask them to identify the sensory details the author uses and the sense to which each appeals. Invite one student to read the passage aloud so that students can better appreciate the effects of the sensory details.

THE LANGUAGE OF LITERATURE TEACHER'S EDITION **131**

Active Reading: CONNECT

Q Ask students to describe situations in which they did not know the exact time but were able to guess the approximate time. Have them describe how they made their guesses. Again, ask whether their experiences help them to identify with Tito.

Linking to Science

R A biological clock is an internal timing mechanism that controls certain functions and rhythms of a living organism. The regular alternation of day and night helps to keep people's internal clocks synchronized and running properly, but our internal clocks can nevertheless be affected in a variety of ways. For example, flying long distances in planes can cause people's biological clocks to become confused, creating the sensation commonly known as jet lag.

Literary Concept:
FIGURATIVE LANGUAGE

S Point out to students that the author uses a simile *(containing the word like)* here, comparing the earth's movements during the eruption to the wriggling of a caught snake. Have students write their own similes to convey the "wriggling" of the earth.

The volcanic ash that covered victims of the Pompeii disaster hardened over time. Archaeologists used the resulting "shells" as molds for body casts.© Krafft/Explorer, Photo Researchers.

sky. The heavens, though Tito could not see them, were shot through with continual flickerings of fire. Lightnings above were answered by thunders beneath. A house fell. Then another. By a miracle the two companions had escaped the dangerous side streets and were in a more open space. It was the forum. They rested here awhile—how long he did not know.

Tito had no idea of the time of day. He could *feel* it was black—an unnatural blackness. Something inside—perhaps the lack of breakfast and lunch—told him it was past noon. But it didn't matter. Nothing seemed to matter. He was getting drowsy, too drowsy to walk. But walk he must. He knew it. And Bimbo knew it; the sharp tugs told him so. Nor was it a moment too soon. The sacred ground of the forum was safe no longer. It was beginning to rock, then to pitch, then to split. As they stumbled out of the square, the earth wriggled like a caught snake, and all the columns of the temple of Jupiter[8] came down. It was the end of the world—or so it seemed.

To walk was not enough now. They must run. Tito was too frightened to know what to do or where to go. He had lost all sense of direction. He started to go back to the inner gate; but Bimbo, straining his back to the last inch, almost pulled his clothes from him. What did the creature want? Had the dog gone mad?

Then, suddenly, he understood. Bimbo was telling him the way out—urging him there.

---

8. **Jupiter:** the supreme god in Roman mythology.

132 UNIT ONE PART 2: ON THE EDGE OF SURVIVAL

Mini-Lesson  Grammar

PREPOSITIONAL PHRASES Inform students that a prepositional phrase is a group of words that begins with a preposition and ends with the preposition's object. Tell them that writers often use prepositional phrases to add details to stories. Then write these sentences on the chalkboard to demonstrate how details can be added to a sentence.

Application Invite students to find at least four prepositional phrases on page 132. *(with continual flickerings, of fire, by thunders, by a miracle, in a more open space, of the time, of day, of breakfast and lunch, of the forum, out of the square, like a caught snake, of the temple, of Jupiter, of the world, of direction, to the inner gate, to the last inch, from him)*

Reteaching/Reinforcement
• *Grammar Mini-Lessons* transparencies, p. 41

 **The Writer's Craft**

Using Prepositional Phrases, p. 506

> The dog stared at me.
>
> The dog stared at me <u>through the fog</u>.
>
> The dog stared at me <u>through the thick, gray fog</u>.

132 THE LANGUAGE OF LITERATURE TEACHER'S EDITION

The sea gate, of course. The sea gate—and then the sea. Far from falling buildings, heaving ground. He turned, Bimbo guiding him across open pits and dangerous pools of bubbling mud, away from buildings that had caught fire and were dropping their burning beams. Tito could no longer tell whether the noises were made by the shrieking sky or the agonized people. He and Bimbo ran on—the only silent beings in a howling world.

New dangers threatened. All Pompeii seemed to be thronging toward the marine gate; and, squeezing among the crowds, there was the chance of being trampled to death. But the chance had to be taken. It was growing harder and harder to breathe. What air there was choked him. It was all dust now—dust and pebbles, pebbles as large as beans. They fell on his head, his hands—pumice[9] stones from the black heart of Vesuvius. The mountain was turning itself inside out. Tito remembered a phrase that the stranger had said in the forum two days ago: "Those who will not listen to men must be taught by the gods." The people of Pompeii had refused to heed the warnings; they were being taught now—if it was not too late.

Suddenly it seemed too late for Tito. The red hot ashes blistered his skin; the stinging vapors tore his throat. He could not go on. He staggered toward a small tree at the side of the road and fell. In a moment Bimbo was beside him. He coaxed. But there was no answer. He licked Tito's hands, his feet, his face. The boy did not stir. Then Bimbo did the last thing he could—the last thing he wanted to do. He bit his comrade, bit deep in the arm. With a cry of pain, Tito jumped to his feet, Bimbo after him. Tito was in despair, but Bimbo was determined. He drove the boy on, snapping at his heels, worrying his way through the crowd; barking, baring his teeth, heedless of kicks or falling stones. Sick with hunger, half dead with fear and sulphur[10] fumes, Tito pounded on, pursued by Bimbo. How long he never knew. At last he staggered through the marine gate and felt soft sand under him. Then Tito fainted. . . .

Someone was dashing seawater over him. Someone was carrying him toward a boat.

"Bimbo," he called. And then louder, "Bimbo!" But Bimbo had disappeared.

Voices jarred against each other. "Hurry—hurry!" "To the boats!" "Can't you see the child's frightened and starving!" "He keeps calling for someone!" "Poor boy, he's out of his mind." "Here, child—take this!"

They tucked him in among them. The oarlocks creaked; the oars splashed; the boat rode over toppling waves. Tito was safe. But he wept continually.

"Bimbo!" he wailed. "Bimbo! Bimbo!"

He could not be comforted.

> ALL POMPEII SEEMED TO BE THRONGING TOWARD THE MARINE GATE . . . . THERE WAS THE CHANCE OF BEING TRAMPLED TO DEATH.

---

9. **pumice** (pŭm'ĭs): a light rock formed from lava
10. **sulphur** (sŭl'fər): a pale yellow chemical element that produces a choking fume when burned

WORDS TO KNOW
vapor (vā'pər) *n.* fumes, mist, or smoke

133

Mini-Lesson Study Skills

USING REFERENCE BOOKS Emphasize the usefulness of encyclopedias by modeling how to use the "See also . . ." cross-references at the end of entries to find information about related topics.

Application Have students use an encyclopedia to research Mount Vesuvius. Ask them to write short summaries of the information they find and to list the topics they looked up during their research.

STRATEGIC READING FOR Less-Proficient Readers

T Ask students whether they think Tito could find his way to the sea gate without Bimbo. *(Possible response: No, because he has lost his sense of direction and because he needs Bimbo to guide him around the fires and open pits.)* **Drawing Conclusions**

Set a Purpose Instruct students to read on to find out what happens to Tito and Bimbo as the story concludes.

Literary Concept: SENSORY DETAILS

U Ask students what sensory details the authors uses here and what sense or senses they appeal to. *(Possible response: "The red hot ashes blistered his skin; the stinging vapors tore his throat"—touch)*

Critical Thinking: MAKING JUDGMENTS

V Ask students whether they would be angry with Bimbo if they were in Tito's place. Have them support their answers. *(Some students will say that they would not be angry with Bimbo, because Bimbo has no other way to wake Tito up. Others will say that they would be angry with Bimbo, because the bite is painful and there may be other ways to alert Tito.)*

STRATEGIC READING FOR
Less-Proficient Readers

W To be sure that students have been able to follow the story, ask the following questions:

- What happens to Bimbo? *(He is buried in ash during the eruption and discovered 1,800 years later by scientists.)* **Summarizing**

- Why do you think the dog is found with a raisin cake in his mouth? *(He was trying to get something for Tito to eat when he died.)* **Making Inferences**

CUSTOMIZING FOR
Gifted and Talented Students

Remind students that animals are commonly depicted in fiction as faithful companions and helpers. Encourage them to recall other works that deal with similar adventures *(for example, Lassie, Old Yeller, The Incredible Journey, and the many nonfiction works of Gary Paulsen).* Then ask students to discuss some of the themes expressed in these stories. You might prompt them by suggesting the theme of loyalty.

COMPREHENSION CHECK

1. Who are the main characters in this story? *(a blind boy named Tito and his dog, Bimbo)*
2. How does Tito get the food he eats? *(Bimbo steals raisin cakes and scraps of food three times a day.)*
3. Why does the volcanic eruption take most Pompeiians by surprise? *(They don't believe that the increase of smoke from Vesuvius is a sign of a coming eruption. They are so used to the mountain's presence that they pay no attention to it.)*
4. How do some people manage to escape from Pompeii? *(by boarding boats and going out to sea)*

Eighteen hundred years passed. Scientists were restoring the ancient city; excavators were working their way through the stones and trash that had buried the entire town. Much had already be brought to light—statues, bronze instrument bright mosaics,[11] household articles; even delicate paintings had been preserved by the fall of ashes that had taken over two thousand lives. Columns were dug up, and the forum was beginning to emerge.

It was at a place where the ruins lay deepest that the director paused.

"Come here," he called to his assistant. "I think we've discovered the remains of a building in good shape. Here are four huge millstones that were most likely turned by slaves or mules—and here is a whole wall standing with shelves inside it. Why! It must have been a bakery. And here's a curious thing. What do you think I found under this heap where the ashes were thickest? The skeleton of a dog!"

"Amazing!" gasped his assistant. "You'd think a dog would have had sense enough to run away at the time. And what is that flat thing he's holding between his teeth? It can't be a stone."

"No. It must have come from this bakery. You know it looks to me like some sort of cake hardened with the years. And, bless me, if those little black pebbles aren't raisins. A raisin cake almost two thousand years old! I wonder what made him want it at such a moment."

"I wonder," murmured the assistant. ❖ **W**

Petrified bread from Pompeii. Museo Archeologico Nazionale, Naples, Italy. Alinari/Art Resource, New York

---

11. **mosaics** (mō-zā′ĭks): pictures or designs made by setting small colored stones or tiles into surfaces

HISTORICAL INSIGHT

In A.D. 62, seventeen years before Vesuvius erupted, a strong earthquake had damaged Pompeii and the neighboring city of Herculaneum. Scientists now believe Vesuvius was trying to erupt then but people did not understand the warning.

The blast that occurred in A.D. 79 was as strong as a nuclear explosion, and ten times more powerful than the 1980 eruption of Mount St. Helens in the state of Washington. Out of the estimated population of 20,000, nearly 2,000 were killed, many of them trapped in their homes. Other victims died at the sea gate, where they were hoping to escape by boat. Later eruptions continued to cover the ruins, and Pompeii lay undisturbed under the lava deposits for almost 1,700 years.

WORDS TO KNOW
restore (rĭ-stôr′) *v.* to bring back to an original condition

134

Mini-Lesson  Spelling

When suffix begins with vowel:	When suffix begins with consonant:
restore + able = restorable	hate + ful = hateful
dislodge + ing = dislodging	excite + ment = excitement
Exceptions:	**Exceptions:**
dye + ing = dyeing	true + ly = truly
courage + ous = courageous	argue + ment = argument

SPELLING WORDS WITH SUFFIXES

Remind students that when a suffix is added to a word that ends in silent e, the e is dropped if the suffix begins with a vowel but is kept if the suffix begins with a consonant.

Application Have students write the word produced by adding each suffix.

1. hate + ing
2. peace + ful
3. irritate + ing
4. blame + less
5. chime + ing
6. inflate + able
7. taste + ful
8. advise + able
9. strange + ly
10. amuse + ment

Ask students to look through the selection for more words that fit this pattern and to write them in their personal word lists.

Reteaching/Reinforcement
- *Unit One Resource Book,* p. 73

134 THE LANGUAGE OF LITERATURE TEACHER'S EDITION

RESPONDING OPTIONS

FROM PERSONAL RESPONSE TO CRITICAL ANALYSIS

REFLECT 1. How did you feel after reading this story? Share your thoughts with another student.

RETHINK 2. Do you think Bimbo is a realistic character? Defend your answer with evidence from the story.
   Consider
   Close Textual Reading
   - Bimbo's role in Tito's everyday life
   - how Bimbo responds to the volcanic eruption

   3. What do you think Louis Untermeyer's purpose was in ending the story of the Pompeii disaster 1800 years later?

   4. What did you learn about Vesuvius and Pompeii that you didn't know before? What would you like to learn more about?

RELATE 5. Compare the Pompeii citizens' response to the earthquake with responses to similar events that you have experienced or heard about.

Multimodal Learning
ANOTHER PATHWAY
Cooperative Learning
With a group of classmates, use the information in the story to create and act out a scene about some citizens of Pompeii who are trapped in the disaster. End the scene with a tableau—a moment in which all the performers freeze in position.

QUICKWRITES

1. Write an **account** of the final day in Pompeii from Tito's point of view, using only his sensory impressions of hearing, tasting, smelling, and feeling.

2. Naples and Pompeii lie on opposite sides of a large bay. Imagine that you are safely in Naples on the day Vesuvius erupts in A.D. 79. Write an **eyewitness account** of what you see happening to Pompeii.

📁 **PORTFOLIO** *Save your writing. You may want to use it later as a springboard to a piece for your portfolio.*

LITERARY CONCEPTS

A **conflict** is a struggle between opposing forces. There are two main kinds of conflicts in stories: external and internal. An **external conflict** is a struggle between a character and an outside force, such as another character or nature. For example, in the excerpt from *Woodsong*, Gary Paulsen faces an external conflict with a bear. What is the external conflict faced by Tito and Bimbo in "The Dog of Pompeii"?

CONCEPT REVIEW: Setting This story's setting—the time and place in which the events occur—plays an important role in the story. What words or phrases helped you to visualize ancient Pompeii clearly?

THE DOG OF POMPEII   135

Art Connection

Students can use graph paper to help them plan their mosaics, shading squares with colored pencils to produce their designs.

Across the Curriculum

Science *Cooperative Learning* Have students work in small groups to research volcanoes. You may want to assign a particular volcano to each group, who can then work collaboratively to research that volcano and to prepare the presentation or cutaway model.

ADDITIONAL SUGGESTION

Science *Make an Erupting Volcano!* Students can follow these directions to make an "active volcano":

1. Sculpt a volcano out of clay. Make a depression at the top to represent the crater.
2. Place a small amount of baking soda in the crater, then pour in a small amount of vinegar. Watch the volcano "explode." Red food coloring can be added to make the erupting mixture look like lava.

ART CONNECTION

In ancient Rome, mosaics like the one of the dog on page 125 often depicted scenes of daily life. Using small pieces of colored paper, design a mosaic that illustrates a scene from the story.

Multimodal Learning
ALTERNATIVE ACTIVITIES

1. A stranger in the forum says, "Those who will not listen to men must be taught by the gods." Think of other proverbs or sayings based on the events in the story and display them on a **poster** with illustrations.

2. Use modeling clay and other appropriate materials to create a three-dimensional **scene** from the ruined city of Pompeii. Refer to details in the selection as well as the photographs that accompany it for ideas.

CRITIC'S CORNER

One critic believes that the role of historical fiction is to help students explore the "similarities and differences in people from other times and places." Think about what you learn in "The Dog of Pompeii" about Tito and the other characters mentioned, and about life in the city of Pompeii. What similarities and differences do you see between life in ancient Rome and life at the end of the 20th century? What aspects of Tito and other characters do you think might be shared by people today?

ACROSS THE CURRICULUM

Science Find out more about volcanoes. Where are they located? How are they formed? Why do they erupt? Research some of the most destructive volcanic eruptions, such as those of Krakatau, El Chichón, and Mount Etna. Prepare a comparison chart to summarize your information, and use it in a presentation to the class. If you prefer, construct a three-dimensional cutaway model of a volcano, labeling the magma, the rock layers, the lava tube or conduit, and the crater. Use your model in an oral presentation about how a volcano erupts.

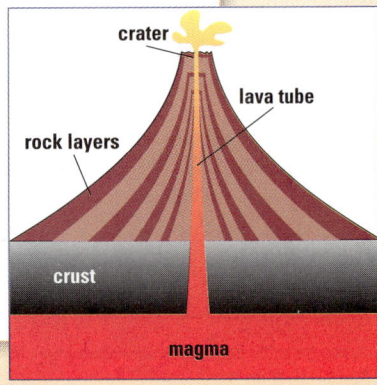

136 UNIT ONE PART 2: ON THE EDGE OF SURVIVAL

Alternative Activities

1. Have students begin by brainstorming a list of familiar sayings that can be related to the events in the story, such as "A dog is man's best friend." When each student has selected several sayings, have students think about images from the story that might make good illustrations for their posters. For instance, a drawing of Bimbo bringing a raisin cake to Tito could be used to illustrate the saying quoted above.

2. Before students begin to model their scenes, encourage them to skim the selection for possible settings to re-create. Instruct them to use the story's sensory details to assist them in planning their scenes. Make sure that students do not select settings that are too complicated to re-create adequately.

WORDS TO KNOW

EXERCISE A Identify each pair of words as synonyms or antonyms. On your paper, write *S* for *Synonyms* or *A* for *Antonyms*.

1. vapor—fume
2. restore—destroy
3. eruption—outbreak
4. shrine—temple
5. dislodging—replacing

EXERCISE B For one of the vocabulary words, create a picture that communicates the word's meaning.

LOUIS UNTERMEYER

1885–1977

As a boy, Louis Untermeyer disliked school but read constantly. He created bedtime stories for his brother Martin, later recalling, "Fantasy was the most important part of my boyhood—at least it is the only part I remember. My soul . . . was far away, sailing the blue Vesuvian bay. . . ."

While working successfully in the jewelry business for more than 20 years, Untermeyer spent much of his free time writing poems. After publishing a book of poems, he had difficulty seeing himself as anything other than a poet. He made the decision to devote all his time to writing.

Untermeyer earned a name for himself as a poet, critic, and novelist. He is best known, however, as a collector and editor of major poetry collections, many of which have been used to teach the art of poetry. He produced 56 collections and is credited with introducing the works of Robert Frost to a large audience. For about 25 years, Louis Untermeyer served as chairman of the Pulitzer Prize Poetry Jury.

OTHER WORKS *The Magic Circle: Stories and People in Poetry*, *The Wonderful Adventures of Paul Bunyan*, *The World's Great Stories: Fifty-Five Legends That Live Forever*, *The Donkey of God*, *Cat o' Nine Tales*, *The Paths of Poetry: Twenty-Five Poets and Their Poems* Extended Reading

THE DOG OF POMPEII 137

Words to Know

Exercise A
1. synonyms
2. antonyms
3. synonyms
4. synonyms
5. antonyms

Exercise B
Make sure that students' pictures adequately communicate the meanings of the chosen words.

Reteaching/Reinforcement
- *Unit One Resource Book*, p. 74

LOUIS UNTERMEYER

A storyteller at an early age, Louis Untermeyer talked himself and his brother Martin to sleep at night by reciting fantastic tales of his own creation. His interest in poetry resulted in friendships with some of this century's greatest writers, including Robert Frost and Ezra Pound.

WHAT DO YOU THINK?
Reflecting on Theme

Have students work in small groups to add characters and selected scenes from "The Dog of Pompeii" to their murals illustrating dangerous events. Remind them to include captions that explain what is happening in the scenes.

OVERVIEW

To gain a richer appreciation of the short stories they have read in this unit, students will explore the characteristics of an anecdote and then create their own anecdote in this lesson.

Objectives

- To plan an anecdote by considering such elements as purpose, details, organization, and unity
- To draft an anecdote and solicit a response to it
- To revise, edit, and publish an anecdote
- To reflect on the process of writing an anecdote

Skills

LITERATURE
- Identifying purpose

WRITING AND LANGUAGE
- Writing a rough draft
- Achieving unity in paragraphs

GRAMMAR AND USAGE
- Using consistent verb tense

MEDIA LITERACY
- Reading comic strips

CRITICAL THINKING
- Ordering and representing information

SPEAKING, LISTENING, AND VIEWING
- Telling a story aloud
- Role-playing
- Reading aloud

Teaching Strategy: MODELING

A To show students how to generate story ideas from a comic strip or other visual, have them study the comic strip on page 138. Make sure students are aware that Calvin is the little boy and Hobbes is the tiger. Ask students to explain the point of the strip. *(Possible responses: Hobbes did not stay on the sled because he thought Calvin's ideas were wrong. Security is preferable to danger.)* You may wish to use these questions as a springboard to analysis:

- What is Calvin's view of life? What is Hobbes's view? How are they different?
- Why is this comic strip funny?
- What point does it teach?
- Do you agree with the point? Why or why not?

CUSTOMIZING FOR
Students Acquiring English

B Explain that a comic strip tells a story in words and pictures. Describe some common types of comic strips: humorous *(Peanuts),* dramatic *(Apartment 3G),* political *(Doonesbury),* and superhero *(Spiderman).* Invite students to tell about comic strips published in their native countries.

WRITING FROM EXPERIENCE

WRITING A NARRATIVE

In Unit One, "Running Risks," you have read about characters who take chances and risk getting punished, embarrassed, or hurt. Reading these stories may have taught you something about handling tough situations and the kind of risks worth taking. Some may have even helped you see the humor in difficult experiences.

GUIDED ASSIGNMENT
Write an Anecdote Do you have a story about someone who took a risk, solved a problem, or survived an embarrassing moment? You can share it by telling an anecdote, which is a very short story. In the next few pages, you will learn how to write an anecdote based on something that happened to you or someone you know.

❶ Find a Reason to Write

Your life is full of anecdotes. They are the funny experiences you tell friends and the stories you hear around the lunch table.

Helping Friends Perhaps you have a friend who is going through a hard time or trying to make a difficult decision. Can you help your friend by telling a true story?

Examining Your Life Think about times you have taken risks or had interesting or funny experiences. You might find ideas in your journal entries, letters, or photo albums. List any incidents you think other people might enjoy hearing about.

Making Connections People often clip cartoons and articles to share with friends who might appreciate or benefit from them. Look at the examples on these pages. What stories do they remind you of? Add these ideas to your list.

Comic Strip
What happened to Hobbes? How does he feel about Calvin's ideas?

138 UNIT ONE PART 2: ON THE EDGE OF SURVIVAL

Calvin and Hobbes
by Bill Watterson

PRINT AND MEDIA RESOURCES

UNIT ONE RESOURCE BOOK
Prewriting Guide, p. 77
Elaboration, pp. 78
Peer Response Guide, pp. 79–80
Revision and Editing, p. 81
Student Model, p. 82
Rubric, p. 83

GRAMMAR MINI-LESSONS
Transparencies, p. 16, 19
Copymasters, p. 26

WRITING MINI-LESSONS
Transparencies, pp. 31, 39, 46

ACCESS FOR STUDENTS ACQUIRING ENGLISH
Reading and Writing Support

FORMAL ASSESSMENT
Guidelines for Writing Assessment

LASERLINKS
Writing Springboard

138 THE LANGUAGE OF LITERATURE TEACHER'S EDITION

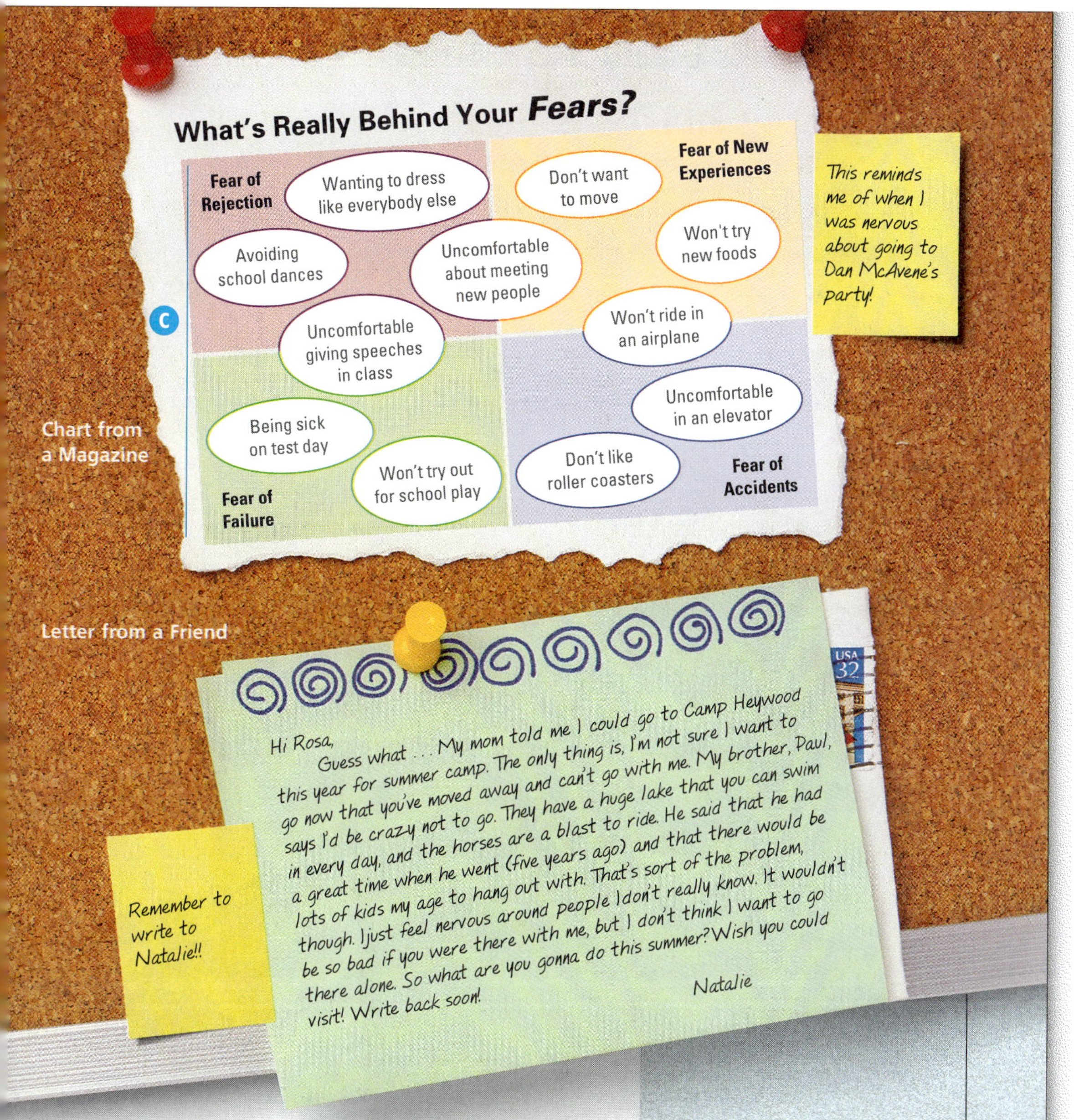

Chart from a Magazine

What's Really Behind Your Fears?

Fear of Rejection
- Wanting to dress like everybody else
- Avoiding school dances
- Uncomfortable giving speeches in class

Fear of New Experiences
- Don't want to move
- Won't try new foods
- Uncomfortable about meeting new people

Fear of Failure
- Being sick on test day
- Won't try out for school play

Fear of Accidents
- Won't ride in an airplane
- Uncomfortable in an elevator
- Don't like roller coasters

This reminds me of when I was nervous about going to Dan McAvene's party!

Letter from a Friend

Remember to write to Natalie!!

Hi Rosa,
 Guess what... My mom told me I could go to Camp Heywood this year for summer camp. The only thing is, I'm not sure I want to go now that you've moved away and can't go with me. My brother, Paul, says I'd be crazy not to go. They have a huge lake that you can swim in every day, and the horses are a blast to ride. He said that he had a great time when he went (five years ago) and that there would be lots of kids my age to hang out with. That's sort of the problem, though. I just feel nervous around people I don't really know. It wouldn't be so bad if you were there with me, but I don't think I want to go there alone. So what are you gonna do this summer? Wish you could visit! Write back soon!
 Natalie

② Talk to Others

Now that you have a list of possible ideas to write about, you might talk to friends or family members to get their thoughts. Which stories do they think are the most interesting? Does anything they say give you a new idea?

LASERLINKS
• WRITING SPRINGBOARD

WRITING COACH

WRITING FROM EXPERIENCE 139

Writing Skill: USING GRAPHIC ORGANIZERS

C Point out to students that graphic organizers are useful for generating and organizing ideas because they enable writers to "see" ideas on paper. Explain that the cluster shown on this page is just one possible form of graphic organizer.

Describe to the class some other forms, such as the following:

Idea tree: Write your general topic at the top or bottom of the page. Write related ideas as "branches" connected to the main topic.

Observation chart: Determine the main idea. Then make a chart with the five senses as column headings, and fill in the details.

Idea-and-details chart: Write the main idea at the top. Arrange the details below the main idea, numbering them in order of importance.

Encourage students to use the graphic organizer that works best for them at this stage in the writing process.

Speaking, Listening, and Viewing: ROLE-PLAY

D Suggest that students role-play, in small groups, their ideas for an anecdote. Explain that role-playing a scene can help a writer brainstorm sensory details, analyze his or her audience, and arrange events effectively.

WRITING SPRINGBOARD
A Critical Moment A trip down a river in a kayak leads to a decisive moment for a group of teens who brave the currents in search of adventure.

Side B, Frame 605

Writing Prompt The spirit of adventure is in all of us, but some people seek challenges that put them on the edge of survival. Think of a time when you or someone you know took a risky chance, and write an anecdote about what happened.

THE LANGUAGE OF LITERATURE TEACHER'S EDITION 139

CUSTOMIZING FOR
Less-Proficient Writers

E Some writers find choosing a story the most difficult part of the writing process. Without assistance, they may choose a story that lacks a point or that is overly familiar. Arrange students in small groups so that they may help one another select a story topic. Suggest that group members choose stories that offer fresh insights, rich details, or enjoyable punch lines. Check each student's work to make sure that the final choice is suitable.

Teaching Strategy:
STUMBLING BLOCK

F The concept of purpose often presents difficulty for student writers. Remind the class that purpose is the general reason for writing. On the board or using an overhead projector, list the four main purposes for writing: to express an opinion, to entertain, to inform, and to persuade. Discuss each purpose, and make sure that students can distinguish among them. Explain that some pieces of writing have a single purpose, whereas others have more than one purpose. Categorize each example given here by relating it to one of the four purposes. For example, the purpose of "a funny thing that happened" is to entertain. The purpose of "a lesson you've learned" is to inform. Then briefly review the selections in this unit, and ask volunteers to identify the author's purpose for each.

PREWRITING

Planning Your Anecdote

Zeroing In on the Story You now have a list of ideas for an anecdote. The steps below will help you choose one idea and write about it.

❶ Choose a Story

Look at the ideas you wrote down, and think about each incident. Would it be interesting to people? What would they get out of it? Choose the event that will make the best story.

❷ Focus on Your Purpose

What is the main point of your anecdote? Write down what you think is most important about the event. It might be a funny thing that happened, a lesson you've learned, or an important realization about yourself or someone else.

❸ Gather Details

Try to remember the details of your experience and your feelings at the time. Who was there? What were people wearing? Was there special music playing? Was the weather important?

Student's Ideas

- Joining the baseball team though I had never played before; became friends with Maria
- The costume party where I fooled everybody
- Being the only girl invited to Dan McAvene's birthday party
- Climbing to the top of the Blue Ridge Mountains last summer on vacation
- The time I told Bubba to stop picking on Tanya

Mini-Lesson: Speaking, Listening, and Viewing

MAKING A STORYBOARD Explain to students that a storyboard is a graphic representation of the events in a story, arranged in chronological order. A storyboard shows only the main events and only brief portions of dialogue. Point out that a storyboard is much like the comic strip students examined on page 138. Tell students that making a storyboard can help them to gather details and to focus on their purpose for writing.

Application Invite students to work in pairs to make storyboards for their anecdotes. Tell them that the storyboard should have at least six panels and should roughly depict the main events in the writer's anecdote. Then invite the pairs to discuss their storyboards, using these discussion prompts:
- What is my purpose?
- What additional details do I need?
- What details are unrelated to the purpose?

4 Tell Your Story Aloud

You might practice telling your anecdote to some friends before you write it down. They may have questions about details that are important to the story. As you tell your anecdote, notice what makes your friends laugh or what surprises them. You might take notes on their reactions, as one student did in the example below.

Student's Story Notes

> Things I learned when I told my story to Phil
> - He didn't get why I went to the party if I didn't feel well. (Explain that Mom made me.)
> - He thought the part about Dan's mom was boring, but it's really important so I have to think of a way to liven it up.
> - He asked me what I got Dan for a gift. (not really important to include)

5 Think About the Parts of an Anecdote

Anecdotes have certain features in common.

- They are brief and keep to the point by including only important details and events.
- Most start with a lively description, a curious fact, or the point the writer wants to illustrate.
- Characters are developed quickly yet thoroughly.
- A humorous anecdote usually ends with a punch line. In an anecdote that is meant to be helpful, the ending may repeat the message.

With these things in mind, think about how you will begin and end your anecdote and what details you will include. The SkillBuilder offers tips for organizing your story idea.

SkillBuilder

 CRITICAL THINKING

Ordering and Representing Information

Many writers find it helpful to sketch a plan before they start writing. A story map can help keep you focused on the important parts of your story. You might start by stating the point of your anecdote.

Point: to show that sometimes it's worth trying things that seem scary

↓

I was nervous about going to Dan's all-boy party.

↓

I decided to go, but when I got there, I felt out of place.

↓

I talked to Dan's mom.

↓

She thought up a fun game for everyone.

THINK & PLAN

Reflecting on Your Ideas

1. Did your friends react to your anecdote the way you wanted? How might you change it to get the reaction you want?
2. Do you still think readers will enjoy your story? Why or why not?

WRITING FROM EXPERIENCE **141**

SkillBuilder CRITICAL THINKING

ORDERING AND REPRESENTING INFORMATION Remind students that since an anecdote is a brief story, their story map should not have more than a few steps. Arrange students in pairs, and have the partners help each other limit their anecdotes to key events. Have them arrange each other's details on a time line to make sure the stories proceed logically.

Application Suggest that, where necessary, students add, delete, or rearrange events in order to make their anecdotes more effective. Also suggest that they expand key events and downplay minor ones.

Writing Skill: USING SENSORY LANGUAGE

G Remind students that sensory language refers to words and phrases that appeal to sight, taste, touch, hearing, and smell. Explore with the class how sensory details help readers imagine a scene much more effectively. Then discuss how writers sometimes include sufficient visual details but neglect to use details that appeal to the other four senses. Encourage students to tap into the other senses as they tell their stories. Suggest that they also use metaphors, similes, and hyperbole to bring in vivid sensory language.

Teaching Strategy: STUMBLING BLOCK

H Student writers often have difficulty shaping their details to their purpose and often are reluctant to adapt the truth to make a more effective story. Explain to students that good writers are like good storytellers: they adapt the details to their audience and purpose. Be sure students understand that they have "creative license" to revise the literal truth, changing details about time, place, and characters.

THE LANGUAGE OF LITERATURE **TEACHER'S EDITION** **141**

Writing Skill:
USING THE COMPUTER

I. Invite students to use a computer for drafting. Remind them that the purpose of drafting is to get ideas down on paper. Suggest that students, as they input their ideas, boldface a few key words in each idea. Tell them that at a later stage, these boldfaced terms will make it easier to see which ideas are relevant and which are not.

Point out the suggestions for revisions that the student writer has added to her rough draft. Guide students to use The Writing Coach, which provides them with the opportunity to make similar comments on their drafts.

Teaching Strategy:
STUMBLING BLOCK

J. It can be particularly difficult for writers to move from prewriting to drafting. Dealing with writer's block is no small matter for students—or for teachers. Inform students that even professional writers sometimes have difficulty getting started. Explain that many writers devise ways of overcoming the problem, including such rituals as sharpening pencils, making a cup of tea, and arranging the window shades. Invite students to share methods of overcoming writer's block that work for them.

Teaching Strategy: MANAGING THE PAPER LOAD

Feedback can be crucial during the drafting process. You may wish to respond to students' work on-line. Since keyboarding is often easier and faster than handwriting, you will be able to respond to more student papers in greater depth. Keyboarded comments will also be easier for students to read.

DRAFTING

Writing It All Down

Shaping Your Anecdote Once you have completed your story map or list of events, you can start to write your anecdote. You may write it all out from beginning to end or start with the scene you like best. Different methods work for different people. Just let your ideas flow!

1 Write a Rough Draft

Don't worry about making your anecdote look or sound perfect right away; you can fix it later. For now, just get your ideas written down. Include details as they come to you. (See the SkillBuilder for tips on using details.)

Student's Rough Draft

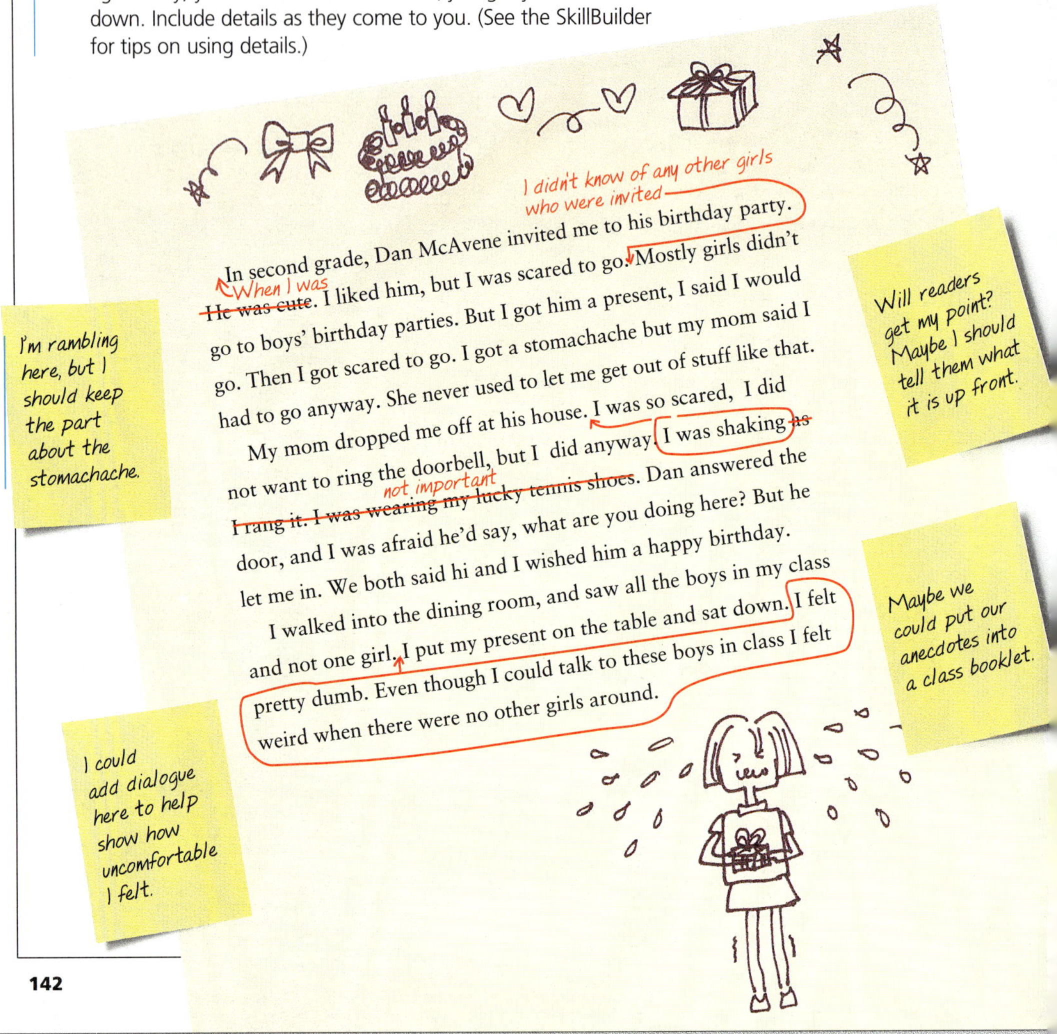

> In second grade, Dan McAvene invited me to his birthday party. ~~He was cute~~ *When I was* . I liked him, but I was scared to go. Mostly girls didn't go to boys' birthday parties. But I got him a present, I said I would go. Then I got scared to go. I got a stomachache but my mom said I had to go anyway. She never used to let me get out of stuff like that.
> My mom dropped me off at his house. I was so scared, I did not want to ring the doorbell, but I did anyway. I was shaking ~~as~~ *not important* I rang it. I was wearing my lucky tennis shoes. Dan answered the door, and I was afraid he'd say, what are you doing here? But he let me in. We both said hi and I wished him a happy birthday. I walked into the dining room, and saw all the boys in my class and not one girl. I put my present on the table and sat down. I felt pretty dumb. Even though I could talk to these boys in class I felt weird when there were no other girls around.

I didn't know of any other girls who were invited

I'm rambling here, but I should keep the part about the stomachache.

Will readers get my point? Maybe I should tell them what it is up front.

Maybe we could put our anecdotes into a class booklet.

I could add dialogue here to help show how uncomfortable I felt.

142

 WRITING SPRINGBOARD
Parents' War Stories Kahui—a teenage Cambodian immigrant living in California—recalls her arrival in the United States when she was four years old. She also describes her mother's tales about their escape from their war-torn homeland.

Side B, Frame 2844

Writing Prompt Because Kahui's language, customs, and experiences were different from those of her classmates, she felt scared and shy when she started school in the United States. Using her story as a guide, write about one of your experiences of starting something new.

142 THE LANGUAGE OF LITERATURE TEACHER'S EDITION

❷ Play with Language

The way your anecdote will sound depends on who your audience is. Think about how your language might change if you used your anecdote in the following ways:

- in a letter to a close friend
- to make a point at the beginning of a speech
- as an example within a news article
- to reveal something about a character in a story

You might experiment by writing a paragraph of your anecdote in a few different ways. The example below shows how one student reworked her first paragraph for a different audience.

Student's Second Version

> You think what you did took guts? Did I ever tell you about the time in second grade when Dan McAvene invited me to his birthday party? He was such a babe! I had this feeling I was the only girl he invited, but I told him I'd go. Of course, on the day of the party I was soooo nervous I got a stomachache. And you <u>know</u> my mom wouldn't let me get out of going!

PEER RESPONSE

Do you think your story is just about ready? Only a reader can tell you for sure. Ask a friend to read your draft, then have him or her answer questions like the following:

- Did the beginning of my anecdote grab your attention? If not, what could I do to make it more interesting?
- Do I have enough details? Are there unimportant details I should get rid of?
- What did you think of the punch line or message? How could I improve the ending?
- What was your favorite part? What made you laugh or made you think?

SkillBuilder

WRITER'S CRAFT

Achieving Unity in Paragraphs

Details are necessary to support your story ideas and help readers understand what is going on. However, unimportant or misplaced details can confuse and even bore your readers. If a detail does not add important information, leave it out.

APPLYING WHAT YOU'VE LEARNED
Which detail is not necessary in the paragraph below? Why?

I was worried about taking the test. Instead of studying the night before, I had watched TV. I ate popcorn while I watched. As Mr. Simon passed out the tests, I began to feel hot and dizzy. When he put mine in front of me, I just stared at it.

WRITING HANDBOOK

For more help with paragraphs, see the Writing Handbook, page 779.

RETHINK & EVALUATE

Preparing to Revise

1. Is it clear to your reader why this experience was important to you? How could you make your point better?
2. Whom would you like to read your anecdote? How can you change the language to make it work for your readers?

WRITING FROM EXPERIENCE 143

CUSTOMIZING FOR Students Acquiring English

 Adjusting the diction in a piece of writing in order to suit a particular audience is especially challenging for students acquiring because they are often not comfortable with English idiom, slang, jargon, connotation, and denotation. Pair these students with native English-speakers to complete this part of the writing process. Help partners work together equally by encouraging the students acquiring English to reframe, in their native language, troublesome parts of their draft before they revise it in English.

Speaking, Listening, and Viewing: READING ALOUD

Have partners read each other's draft aloud. This will enable the writers to more easily recognize problems with plot, awkward lapses in diction, and ineffective punch lines. Tell students that many writers read their work aloud, even if nobody is there to listen, in order to "hear" any problems and to identify parts that need revision.

SkillBuilder — WRITER'S CRAFT

ACHIEVING UNITY IN PARAGRAPHS Give students these guidelines for achieving unity in a paragraph:
1. State the main idea in a topic sentence.
2. Make sure all the other sentences develop the main idea.
3. Make sure that every sentence directly relates to the main idea.
4. Start a new paragraph each time you begin a new main idea.

Application "I ate popcorn while I watched" is off the topic and does not belong in the paragraph.

Additional Suggestions Have students identify unnecessary information in the following paragraph:

I had very little time to pack for my trip. I decided to use a large suitcase so I could pack several sweaters. My red sweater is my favorite. I packed some jeans, and then I threw in a few sets of sweats. I almost forgot socks, but I remembered them when I packed my sneakers. I really should buy a new pair of sneakers.

Reteaching/Reinforcement
- Writing Handbook, anthology p. 780
- *Writing Mini-Lessons* transparencies, p. 31

Narrative Writing, pp. 70–83

Teaching Strategy:
STUMBLING BLOCK

M Some students are unwilling to revise their work. Other students—those who are never satisfied with their work—may over-revise or may even not hand the work in. To relieve some of the tension these students feel, tell them that you will consider their paper as "a work in progress," even the final version. Eventually, they will be able to let go of their writing with less anxiety.

Teaching Strategy: MODELING

N Explore with students how this model meets the Standards for Evaluation on page 145. For example, point out that the story has an intriguing beginning that grabs the reader's attention and that the characters are developed quickly yet completely—readers get to know Dan as well as the narrator. Students should see that the point of the story is directly stated in the first sentence: "It's good to face the things that make you nervous." You might also point out that the writer could have included some additional details—mentioning, for example, sweating hands or nervous acts such as hair twirling.

REVISING AND PUBLISHING

Polishing Your Anecdote

Putting On the Finishing Touches You have the details and events of your anecdote on paper. Now it's time to make sure that your writing is clean and your story well told. The guidelines on these pages will help you finish your anecdote.

1 Revise and Edit

When you work on a story for a long time, it may be hard for you to see it clearly. Try taking a break and coming back to your anecdote when you can look at it with a fresh eye.

- Review the notes you wrote after telling your story to a friend. Do you think your written version is as enjoyable as the one you told your friend aloud?
- Use the Standards for Evaluation and the Editing Checklist to be sure you have used relevant details and kept the verb tense consistent.
- See how one student revised her writing for a class booklet of anecdotes.

What point is the writer making by telling this anecdote?

What other details might the writer have included to show how uncomfortable she was?

Student's Final Draft

Facing My Fears

I think it's good to face the things that make you nervous. Sometimes things aren't as bad as you thought they would be. When I was in second grade, I was invited to an all-boys birthday party. I didn't like the idea of being the only girl, but I liked Dan and said I would go. On the day of the party I got a stomachache because I was so nervous. My mom told me I had to go anyway.

I was shaking when she dropped me off. Dan answered the doorbell and said, "Hi. Come on in," as if I was just another guy. I swallowed hard and told him "Happy Birthday." He led me into the dining room, where I saw all the boys in my class. I took a deep breath, put my present on the table, and sat down.

I still felt a little weird, even after we ate the cake—but Dan's mom had an idea. We all went outside for a game. Suddenly, something landed on my head and I was all wet. A water balloon fight had started! At first I almost ran out of the yard, but then I stopped. I took a deep breath, grabbed a balloon, and threw it at Dan as hard as I could. All the boys grinned and cheered, even Dan.

144

144 THE LANGUAGE OF LITERATURE TEACHER'S EDITION

Student's Comic Strip

2 Share Your Work

If you publish your anecdote for a different reader, how might you change the form? The student who wrote the sample anecdote told her younger sister her story, using a comic strip. Part of it is shown above. She made the writing simpler and used pictures to get her message across. Why would this format be best for a very young reader?

What other forms might work well with the story you chose to tell? Consider sharing your anecdote, using one or more of the ideas presented in this lesson.

Standards for Evaluation

An anecdote
- is brief and includes only the important details
- has a beginning that grabs readers' attention or states the point the story will make
- develops the characters quickly yet thoroughly
- ends with a punch line or a message

SkillBuilder

 **GRAMMAR FROM WRITING**

Using Consistent Verb Tense
Read the following sentence. What problem do you see?

I gave him the bat and he walks up to the plate.

Gave is past tense, but *walks* is present tense. Anecdotes are usually told in the past tense. Be sure your verbs are all in the same tense so that your readers will not be confused.

GRAMMAR HANDBOOK

For more help with verb tense, see pages 835 of the Grammar Handbook.

Editing Checklist Use the following questions to help you revise your draft.

- Are my sentences complete?
- Is the verb tense consistent?
- Have I punctuated dialogue correctly?

REFLECT & ASSESS

Evaluating the Experience

1. How did writing about the experience help you to understand the event better?
2. Why is an anecdote a good way to make a point?

PORTFOLIO What other ideas do you have for anecdotes? Include them in your portfolio.

WRITING FROM EXPERIENCE 145

Speaking, Listening, and Viewing: COLLABORATIVE OPPORTUNITY

O Invite students to get together as a group to offer support and helpful comments to one another. Guide students to share what they discovered as they wrote. Have students use these discussion prompts:
- How did you find an anecdote to write about?
- Which writing techniques did you find the most useful? Why?
- What was the hardest part of this kind of writing?
- What part of this assignment did you like best?

Teaching Strategy: MANAGING THE PAPER LOAD

P To reduce grading time, try reading students' papers quickly for enjoyment and then respond by using √+, √, or √− rather than formal letter or number grades.

PORTFOLIO

Invite students to select the writing pieces they wish to include in their portfolio. In completing the activities of the Reflect & Assess feature of Unit One (pages 146–147), students may look again at these pieces. Suggest that students include drafts as well as final products in their portfolios. Encourage them to include at least one piece from each major genre.

Standards for Evaluation

Have students review their anecdote for the following:

Ideas and Content
- draws readers in with an interesting introduction
- tells an engaging story with a beginning, middle, and end
- develops characters quickly, yet thoroughly
- makes a point at the end

Structure and Form
- uses chronological order effectively
- uses transitions to make the order of events clear
- uses a variety of sentence structures

Grammar, Usage, and Mechanics
- contains no more than two or three minor errors in grammar and usage
- contains no more than two or three minor errors in spelling, capitalization, and punctuation

---

SkillBuilder GRAMMAR FROM WRITING

USING CONSISTENT VERB TENSE Remind students that switching tenses makes their writing hard to understand. Explain that a writer's choice of tense depends on the effect he or she wishes to achieve. The present tense gives writing a sense of immediacy, a "you are there" feeling. The past tense, in contrast, conveys a sense of authenticity, since the event is now part of history.

Application Have students revise the following paragraph so that all verbs are in either the present tense or the past tense:

I woke up early and realize it isn't a school day. I wanted to go back to sleep, but the dog licks my face and kept me awake. I get up, eat breakfast, and went outside to play fetch with the dog.

Reteaching/Reinforcement
- *Grammar Mini-Lessons* copymasters, p. 26, transparencies, pp. 16, 19

THE LANGUAGE OF LITERATURE Teacher's Edition 145

UNIT REVIEW

This feature allows students to reflect on what they have learned in Unit One and to assess how well they understand what they have learned. This feature provides students with multiple opportunities for self-assessment, although you may wish to use some of the activities to informally assess specific skills such as speaking and listening or cooperative work.

Objectives

- To allow students to reflect on and assess their understanding of theme
- To allow students to reflect on and assess their understanding of literary concepts such as setting and character
- To provide students with the opportunity to assess and build their portfolios

REFLECTING ON THEME

OPTION 1

Have students write short summaries for each of the selections in which they describe how each character was daring. Students can use this information when ranking the characters and writing their nomination speeches. Make sure students support their choices with details from the particular selection.

OPTION 2

Encourage groups to work together to list "high" or dramatic moments that would translate well into a tableau. When a part is chosen, they can plan pantomime scene-setting. Before students begin their discussions, you might have them work together to generate a list of future risky situations that they can assess.

OPTION 3

You may wish to bring in some examples of mobiles to help students with their own designs. Remind students that mobiles require the hanging shapes to be balanced; they will need to test and rearrange their mobiles as they work.

Self-Assessment

Encourage students to respond to real-life risky situations in their assessments. Have them think about risky situations they may have faced in the past and how they might have dealt with them differently if they had first read these selections.

REFLECT & ASSESS

UNIT ONE: RUNNING RISKS

In this unit, characters run risks by speaking out, by facing unexpected challenges, and by struggling with the forces of nature. What did their experiences teach you? What kinds of adventures do you enjoy as a reader and a writer? Explore these questions by completing one or more of the options in each of the following sections.

REFLECTING ON THEME

OPTION 1 Comparing the Daring Many of the characters in Unit One, "Running Risks," react to dangerous situations. Which five characters or real-life people in the selections do you think were especially daring? Rank them in order, from 1 (the most daring) to 5 (the least daring). Write a brief speech to nominate your number one choice for a medal, giving reasons why he or she deserves it.

OPTION 2 Freeze! With two classmates, choose a risky moment from a selection to act out in tableau. Pantomime briefly to establish the scene. Then freeze in position at the most exciting part of the action. Join other groups in a presentation of tableaus. Afterwards, discuss how reading about these moments has affected the way you would handle risky situations in the future.

OPTION 3 Moving Thoughts Work with a partner to make a mobile of words or phrases that describe the risk takers in this unit. First, brainstorm the personal traits common to those people. Then write the traits on shapes of colored paper. Use the shapes, as well as pictures you draw, to make the mobile.

Self-Assessment: After thinking about the risks taken in the selections, what do you think is the best way to deal with a risky situation? In your notebook, write a few paragraphs about what you have learned. Support your ideas by referring to specific selections or individuals in the unit.

REVIEWING LITERARY CONCEPTS

OPTION 1 Thinking About Setting The events described in this unit occur in different time periods and in places all over the world. Make a "setting dial" like the one shown. With a partner, take turns rotating the top circle to match a selection's title with its setting, and discuss how the setting affected the action of that selection. Which setting presented individuals with the most exciting risks? Which settings were presented with details that seemed to put you in the middle of the selections' action? Then move the circle to mix the titles and settings. Discuss how the selections' events or outcome might be different in the new settings.

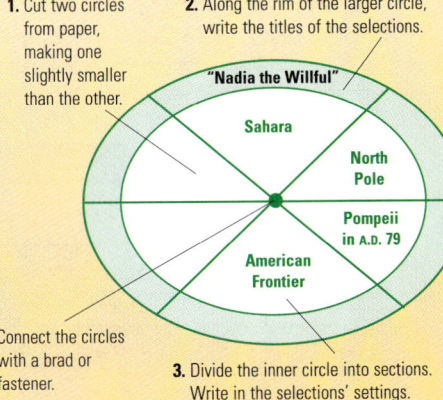

1. Cut two circles from paper, making one slightly smaller than the other.
2. Along the rim of the larger circle, write the titles of the selections.
3. Divide the inner circle into sections. Write in the selections' settings.
4. Connect the circles with a brad or fastener.

"Nadia the Willful" • Sahara • North Pole • Pompeii in A.D. 79 • American Frontier

146 UNIT ONE: RUNNING RISKS

OPTION 2 **Looking at Character** Recall that the most important characters in stories are called main characters and that less important characters are called minor characters. Make "character webs" for four of this unit's selections. In each, show the main character surrounded by three minor characters. (Part of a web for "Ghost of the Lagoon" is shown here.) Then, with a group of classmates, discuss the relationships between the characters. How do the decisions that the main characters make affect their relationships with minor characters?

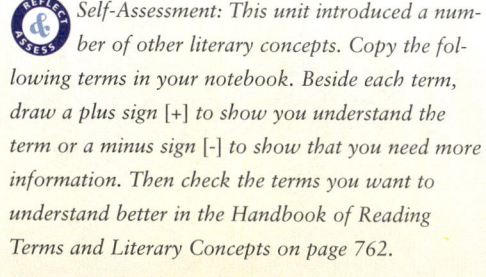

 Self-Assessment: This unit introduced a number of other literary concepts. Copy the following terms in your notebook. Beside each term, draw a plus sign [+] to show you understand the term or a minus sign [–] to show that you need more information. Then check the terms you want to understand better in the Handbook of Reading Terms and Literary Concepts on page 762.

author's purpose	biography	plot
autobiography	conflict	rhythm
	free verse	theme

PORTFOLIO BUILDING

- **QuickWrites** Was it easy or difficult for you to do the QuickWrites assignments that asked you to write as characters would? From your responses to those assignments, pick the two that you think are best. Explain in a short cover note why you think you did so well. Add your responses and the note to your portfolio.

- **Writing About Literature** You recently had the chance to write a personal response to a story. Imagine that the author of the story has asked you to suggest ways of changing it. Would you add a new character? Would you make the ending different? Attach a description of your suggested changes to the personal response you wrote.

- **Writing from Experience** When you wrote your anecdote, you described an interesting experience that you had. If you were to have the same experience again, would you do anything differently? How might you change your actions? Include your thoughts with your anecdote if you choose to keep it in your portfolio.

- **Personal Choice** Begin an "oral log" of your reactions to your work. Look back through your work for the Personal Connections, the Writing Connections, and the Another Pathway assignments, as well as the evaluations of all the other projects you completed in this unit. As you do so, dictate your comments into a tape recorder. (If you don't have one, you can simply write your comments on paper). Also comment on any projects and writing you have done on your own. Tell what you think you've done successfully and what you would redo if you could. Add the audiotape (or the written comments) to your portfolio.

 Self-Assessment: At this point, it's probably easy for you to review the pieces in your portfolio. Do so briefly. What kinds of writing or activities do you want to do again soon? Make a note to yourself.

SETTING GOALS

While completing the reading and writing activities in this unit, you probably spotted areas you need to develop. Look back through your portfolio, worksheets, and notebook. Think about what you'd like to explore further in your reading and writing for the next unit. Then copy and complete these statements:
I'd like to read more selections that _____.
I'd like to write more _____.

REFLECT & ASSESS **147**

SETTING GOALS

In order to help students set future goals, suggest that they jot down notes about the areas they want to develop and learn more about as they review their portfolios, worksheets, and notebooks. Have them use their notes to complete the statements. After students complete the next unit, they can return to these statements to check whether they are making progress in achieving their goals.

REVIEWING LITERARY CONCEPTS

OPTION 1

As partners engage in their discussions, they can write down their impressions of how the setting affects the action of the selection for each of the possible setting-title combinations. Encourage partners to share some of their impressions with the class.

OPTION 2

Have groups write down their impressions of how the decisions of the main character affect his or her relationship with minor characters. Invite students to devise ways in which this information can be incorporated into their character webs.

Self-Assessment For terms that students want to understand better, have them write, in their own words, a definition for each term after checking in the Handbook. Then have students apply each term to a selection they have read. For instance, a student can briefly describe the conflict facing a character in a particular selection or identify a selection's theme or genre.

PORTFOLIO BUILDING

You may wish to help students choose or modify options for them that best suit the goals you have established for the class. Encourage students to incorporate in their portfolios drafts in addition to final products so they can reflect on and assess their development and progress.

Self-Assessment In addition, you may want to have students consider which types of writing they felt most comfortable with and which types they would like to have more practice with. Students can create a chart that lists each type of writing and rates their abilities for each.

THE LANGUAGE OF LITERATURE **TEACHER'S EDITION** **147**

UNIT TWO

UNIT THEMES

Unit Two

The Need to Belong In this unit, students will read selections that explore the sense of belonging that most people want to experience—the need to be accepted by others and the need to be part of something important. The unit contains two parts: Part 1, "Finding a Special Place," and Part 2, "Tests of Endurance." Selections in both parts contribute to the unit theme by detailing the special places that various characters seek in their quest to belong and by revealing the struggles involved in this quest.

Part 1

Finding a Special Place Selections in Part 1 explore the special places that some characters have found and the places that other characters seek in their attempt to belong. For example, in "Chinatown" from *The Lost Garden,* Laurence Yep is an outsider in two worlds and must find the special place that is a balance between the two.

Part 2

Tests of Endurance Selections in Part 2 emphasize the struggles and conflicts that the characters face in order to fulfill their need to belong, such as the dispute a young boy has with his friends in "Cricket in the Road."

Links to Unit Six

The Oral Tradition Unit Six contains literature from the oral tradition that connects with the themes in Unit Two. You may wish to begin or end Unit Two by using the following selections from Unit Six that relate to the theme "The Need to Belong":
- "In the Land of Small Dragon," p. 662
- "The Bamboo Beads," p. 670
- "The Legend of the Hummingbird," p. 676

UNIT TWO

The Need to Belong

A place belongs forever to whomever claims it hardest.

JOAN DIDION
American writer

Swinger in Summer Shade (1981), Maud Gatewood. Acrylic on canvas, 60" × 72", courtesy of Somerhill Gallery, Chapel Hill, North Carolina.

148

148 THE LANGUAGE OF LITERATURE TEACHER'S EDITION

Art Note

Swinger in Summer Shade by Maud Gatewood

Reading the Art *How does the artist create a strong contrast between sun and shade on the canvas? How would you describe the effect of this contrast on the viewer?*

Exploring Theme

To help students explore the connections between the art, the quotation, and the unit theme, have them consider the following questions:

1. What does the phrase "the need to belong" mean to you? *(Possible responses: It means that people want to be accepted by others or to be a part of something that they think is special, such as a school group or a country. Everyone wants to be independent, but most people also want to feel needed by other people, to have a place where they fit in and feel special.)*

2. Do you agree with Joan Didion's statement? Why or why not? *(Possible responses: Students who do not agree may say that it depends on what Didion means by "place," that is, that there are other things that determine to whom a place belongs besides whoever claims it the most. Students who agree may say that whoever expresses the strongest desire for something will most likely end up being able to call it his or hers.)*

3. In what ways do you think the painting represents the idea of needing to belong? *(Possible responses: Many children think that swings are special places where they can go to be by themselves. The image of a girl swinging in a shady, quiet place is a good example of what it can be like to belong somewhere.)*

4. What kinds of stories do you think you will read in this unit? *(Possible response: stories about different people who are seeking a special place where they can feel like they belong)*

5. Discuss one of your own experiences of needing to belong. Do you have somewhere special where you feel you belong? Is there a special place where you would like to belong? *(Responses will vary.)*

UNIT TWO
Part 1 Skills Trace

ML DENOTES MINI-LESSON IN TEACHER'S EDITION

Selections	Reading Skills and Strategies	Literary Concepts	Writing Opportunities	Speaking, Listening, and Viewing
FICTION **The Adoption of Albert** Barbara Robinson	Using a reading log, PE p. 151 Using a reading log, **ML** TE p. 157	Tone, PE p. 159 Narrator, **ML** TE p. 156	Retelling from a new point of view, PE p. 159 Science report, PE p. 159 Script, PE p. 159 Family newsletter, PE p. 160 Write a new version, **ML** TE p. 156	Visual presentation, PE p. 160 Reading aloud, **ML** TE pp. 154, 156
POETRY **The Cremation of Sam McGee** Robert Service	Mood, PE p. 161	End rhyme and internal rhyme, PE p. 168 Rhythm, PE p. 168 Alliteration, **ML** TE p. 166	Condolence letter, PE p. 168 Narrative poem, PE p. 168 Details appealing to touch, **ML** TE p. 163 Poem, **ML** TE p. 166	Oral reading, PE p. 168 Oral report, PE p. 169 Directions and map, **ML** TE p. 162 Speech or essay, **ML** TE p. 164
NONFICTION **Chinatown from The Lost Garden** Laurence Yep	Distinguishing fact and opinion, **ML** TE p. 175	Memoir, PE p. 178 Setting, PE p. 178 Theme, **ML** TE p. 174	List and diagram, PE p. 170 Prediction, PE p. 178 Dialogue, PE p. 178 Rewriting, **ML** TE p. 172	Diagram and discussion, PE p. 179 Reading aloud, **ML** TE p. 172 Group presentation, **ML** TE p. 174
POETRY **Three Haiku** Bashō, Issa, and Raymond R. Patterson	Visualizing, PE p. 180	Imagery, PE p. 182	Explanation, PE p. 182 Personal essay, PE p. 182 Haiku, PE p. 182 Haiku, **ML** TE p. 181	
FICTION **Aaron's Gift** Myron Levoy	Predicting, PE p. 184 Predicting, **ML** TE p. 191	Characterization, PE p. 195 Theme, PE p. 195 Conflict, **ML** TE p. 189	Prediction, PE p. 194 Diary entry, PE p. 194 Dialogue, **ML** TE p. 187 Rewriting, **ML** TE p. 190	Debate, PE p. 195 Chart, PE p. 195 Body movements, PE p. 196 Pantomime, **ML** TE p. 188 Group presentation, **ML** TE p. 189
POETRY ON YOUR OWN **Where the Sidewalk Ends** Shel Silverstein **The Spider and the Fly** Mary Howitt **Two girls of twelve or so at a table** Charles Reznikoff **New World** N. Scott Momaday **Something Told the Wild Geese** Rachel Field				Interviewing, TE p. 203 Discussion, TE p. 205
Writing	**Reading Skills and Strategies**	**Literary Concepts**	**Writing Opportunities**	**Speaking, Listening, and Viewing**
WRITING ABOUT LITERATURE **Interpretation**	Analyzing main idea and details, PE pp. 206–07 Responding to literature, PE pp. 208–11	Analyzing main idea and details, PE pp. 206–07	Revise sentences, PE p. 207 Write a statement and examples, PE p. 207 Revise your writing, PE p. 207 Interpretation, PE pp. 208–11	Viewing a stage set, PE p. 212 Interpreting a stage set, PE p. 212 Discussion, PE p. 212 Discussing settings, PE p. 213

Grammar, Usage, Mechanics, and Spelling	Multimodal Learning	Research and Study Skills	Vocabulary
Main and helping verbs, ML TE p. 154 Combining sentences, ML TE p. 155 Spelling with the prefix re-, ML TE p. 158	Comic strip, PE p. 160 Visual presentation, PE p. 160 Reading aloud, ML TE pp. 154, 156	Research worms, PE p. 160	reunion
	Oral reading, PE p. 168 Draw or paint a scene, PE p. 169 Oral report, PE p. 169 Directions and map, ML TE p. 162 Speech or essay, ML TE p. 164	Research the Klondike gold rush, PE p. 169 Research the aurora borealis, PE p. 169	
Voice, ML TE p. 172 Pronouns and antecedents, ML TE p. 176 Compound words, ML TE p. 177	Draw a map, PE pp. 170, 178 Collage, PE p. 179 Chart, PE p. 179 Diagram and discussion, PE p. 179 Reading aloud, ML TE p. 172 Group presentation, ML TE p. 174		stereotype
Word choice, ML TE p. 181			
Direct objects of main verbs, ML TE p. 186 Using dialogue, ML TE p. 187 Final y words and suffixes, ML TE p. 193	Story map, PE p. 194 Debate, PE p. 195 Street map, PE p. 195 Chart, PE p. 195 Body movements, PE p. 196 Pantomime, ML TE p. 188 Group presentation, ML TE p. 189	Research pogroms, PE p. 195 Research pigeons, PE p. 195 Research New York City, PE p. 195	frenzied mascot stoop tenement thrash
	Interviews, TE p. 203 Diorama, TE p. 204 Discussion, TE p. 205		

Grammar, Usage, Mechanics, and Spelling	Multimodal Learning	Research and Study Skills	Media Literacy
Using dashes, PE p. 207 Using quotations, PE p. 209 Sentence fragments, PE p. 211 Understanding parts of speech, PE p. 211	Viewing a stage set, PE p. 212 Interpreting a stage set, PE p. 212 Discussing, PE p. 212 Discussing settings, PE p. 213		Interpreting an advertisement, PE p. 207

SKILLS TRACE TEACHER'S EDITION **149b**

UNIT TWO
Part 2 Skills Trace

ML DENOTES MINI-LESSON IN TEACHER'S EDITION

Selections	Reading Skills and Strategies	Literary Concepts	Writing Opportunities	Speaking, Listening, and Viewing
NONFICTION **Oh Broom, Get to Work** Yoshiko Uchida	Evaluating, ML TE p. 217	Anecdote, PE p. 221 Theme, ML TE p. 218	Write about a topic, PE p. 215 List of rules, PE p. 221 Diary entry, PE p. 221	Acting out a scene, PE p. 222
POETRY **It Seems I Test People** James Berry **Growing Pains** Jean Little	Reading poetry orally, PE p. 223	Simile, PE p. 226	Character sketch, PE p. 226 Advice column, PE p. 226 Rewrite lines, PE p. 227	Reading aloud, PE p. 223 Role-playing, PE p. 226 Reading aloud, ML TE p. 225
NONFICTION **The Mushroom** H.M. Hoover	Chronological order, PE p. 229 Chronological order, ML TE p. 230	Essay, PE p. 235	Tabloid-newspaper account, PE p. 235 Science fiction story, PE p. 235 Eyewitness account, PE p. 235 Summary, ML TE p. 232	Role-playing, PE p. 235 Oral reading, PE p. 236 Oral report, PE p. 236 Pencil game, PE p. 236
FICTION **Cricket in the Road** Michael Anthony	Understanding dialogue, PE p. 237	Internal and external conflict, PE p. 242	Description of experiences, PE p. 237 Dialogue, PE p. 241 Diary entry, PE p. 241 Poem, PE p. 241	Chart, PE p. 241 Song, PE p. 242

Writing	Reading Skills and Strategies	Literary Concepts	Writing Opportunities	Speaking, Listening, and Viewing
WRITING FROM EXPERIENCE **Narrative and Literary Writing**	Making inferences, PE p. 245 Visualizing, PE p. 249	Character, PE pp. 246, 248 Point of view, PE p. 247	Writing a character sketch, PE pp. 244–51 Drafting, PE pp. 248–49 Using sensory details, PE p. 247 Varying sentences, PE p. 249 Revising and publishing, PE pp. 250–51 Profile, PE p. 251	Interviewing, PE p. 246 Slide show, PE p. 251 Skit, PE p. 251 Photo essay, PE p. 251 Profile, PE p. 251

Grammar, Usage, Mechanics, and Spelling	Multimodal Learning	Research and Study Skills	Vocabulary
Common and proper nouns, ML TE p. 219 The suffix -ous, ML TE p. 220	Chart, PE p. 221 Display, PE p. 222 Act out a scene, PE p. 222	Research lacquer ware, PE p. 222	audacious indifferent deprive intrusion devise laden dispense pious dread pompous
	Reading aloud, PE p. 223 Role-playing, PE p. 226 Create a dance, PE p. 227 Draw a portrait, PE p. 227 Reading aloud, ML TE p. 225		
Types of verbs, ML TE p. 233 The suffix -ly, ML TE p. 234	Role-playing, PE p. 235 Oral reading, PE p. 236 Oral report, PE p. 236 Pencil game, PE p. 236	Research mushrooms, PE p. 236	consume debris exceed infinite mortally
Prepositional phrases, ML TE p. 239 Silent letters, ML TE p. 240	Chart, PE p. 241 Travel brochure, PE p. 242 Poster or brochure, PE p. 242 Song, PE p. 242	Research Trinidad, PE p. 242 Research cricket, PE p. 242	dumbfounded fume peal torrent tumult

Grammar, Usage, Mechanics, and Spelling	Multimodal Learning	Research and Study Skills	Media Literacy
Using sensory details, PE p. 247 Show, don't tell, PE p. 249 Varying sentences, PE p. 249 Using action verbs, PE p. 251	Analyzing an advice column, PE p. 244 Interpreting a biography, PE p. 245 Analyzing photographs and yearbooks, PE p. 246 Interview, PE p. 246 Slide show, PE p. 251 Skit, PE p. 251 Photo essay, PE p. 251 Profile, PE p. 251	Research a character, PE p. 246	Analyzing an advice column, PE p. 244 Interpreting a biography, PE p. 245 Analyzing photographs and yearbooks, PE p. 246

SKILLS TRACE   TEACHER'S EDITION   **149d**

UNIT TWO
Recommended Resources

ENRICHMENT   RESEARCH

Recommended Novels

 **LITERATURE CONNECTIONS WITH SOURCEBOOK FOR TEACHERS**

Maniac Magee
by Jerry Spinelli

Thematic Links In the home of the Beale family, runaway Jeffrey "Maniac" Magee finds the love and guidance that for most of his life has been out of reach.
About the Author Jerry Spinelli (born 1941) has tackled a wide range of issues in his work, from peer pressure to racism. He received the *Boston Globe-Horn* Book Award in 1990 and the Newbery Medal in 1991 for *Maniac Magee*.
Other Works by Jerry Spinelli *Crash, There's a Girl in My Hammerlock, Space Station Seventh Grade*

The Secret Garden
by Frances Hodgson Burnett

Thematic Links A secret garden brings magic, health, and happiness to a young orphan girl and her sickly cousin.
About the Author Frances Hodgson Burnett (1849–1924) loved gardens and got her inspiration for *The Secret Garden* from her garden in England, which contained 300 rose bushes. Wrote Burnett, "When you have a garden, you have a future."
Other Works by Frances Hodgson Burnett *A Little Princess, Little Lord Fauntleroy*

Letter from Rifka
by Karen Hesse

Thematic Links Rifka, a 12-year-old Russian Jew, shows extraordinary strength and enduring courage as her trip to America takes longer and longer due to unpleasant and sometimes life-threatening obstacles.
About the Author Karen Hesse (born 1952) has won numerous awards for this work, including the National Jewish Book award.
Other Works by Karen Hesse *Lester's Dog, Poppy's Chair, Wish on a Unicorn*

Away is a Strange Place to Be
by H. M. Hoover

Thematic Links Feeling at home among aliens is not easy for Abby and Brian, who have been kidnapped and turned into slaves in an artificial world in the year 2349.
About the Author H. M. Hoover (born 1935) is a writer of science fiction books for children. She weaves adventure, as well as social science and technology into her novels.
Other Works by H.M. Hoover *The Dawn Palace: The Story of Medea, The Shepherd Moon, The Bell Tree*

In the Year of the Boar and Jackie Robinson
by Betty Bao Lord

Thematic Links Moving to New York from China in 1947, Shirley faces cultural obstacles but eventually learns to fit in when she becomes an avid Dodgers and Jackie Robinson fan.
About the Author Betty Bao Lord (born 1938) writes novels that focus on Chinese culture, inside both China and the United States.
Other Works by Betty Bao Lord *Spring Moon, Eighth Moon*

Missing May
by Cynthia Rylant

Thematic Links Summer, a displaced orphan, learns the importance of family as she and her uncle help each other come to terms with the death of her aunt.
About the Author Cynthia Rylant (born 1954) grew up in West Virginia. Her interests include whale watching, Woody Allen films, and *Calvin and Hobbes*.
Other Works by Cynthia Rylant *A Couple of Kooks, Soda Jerk, Children of Christmas, Waiting to Waltz: A Childhood*

For Teacher — TEACHING LITERATURE

Cai, Mingshui. "A Balanced View of Acculturation: Comments on Laurence Yep's Three Novels." *Children's Literature in Education.* 23 (June 1992): 107–118.

White, Brian. "Preparing Middle School Students to Respond to Literature. (Using Autobiographical Writing Before Reading)." *Middle School Journal* 24 (Sept 1992): 21–23.

Wiencek, Joyce and John F. O'Flahavan. "From Teacher-led to Peer Discussions About Literature: Suggestions About Making the Shift." *Language Arts* 71.7 (Nov 1994): 488–498.

CROSS-CURRICULAR TEACHING   PROFESSIONAL DEVELOPMENT

Recommended Readings in Cross-Curricular Areas

SOCIAL STUDIES

Teenage Refugees from China Speak Out
by Colleen She (1990)
Chinese adolescents talk frankly about adapting to life in the United States. Links to Laurence Yep's *The Lost Garden*.

Out of the Gang
by Keith Elliot (1992)
An ex-gang member from Brooklyn talks about gang life and the importance of seeing yourself as an individual. Links to *Aaron's Gift*.

City Kids Speak on Prejudice
by CityKids Publishing Committee (1994)
This collection explores the concept of "safe space." Links to "Oh Broom, Get to Work" and *The Lost Garden*.

GEOGRAPHY

Trinidad and Tobago
by Patricia R. Urosevich (1988)
The cultural, economic, historic, and topographic details of Trinidad and Tobago are described. Links to Michael Anthony's *Cricket in the Road*.

For Teacher — CROSS-CURRICULAR INSTRUCTION

Lappas, Catherine. "Building Multicultural Bridges with Literature." *Readerly/Writerly Texts: Essays on Literature, Literary/Textual Criticism, and Pedagogy (RWT)*, 1.2 (Spring-Summer 1994)

Smith, J. Lea and Holly A. Johnson. "Dreaming of America: Weaving Literature into Middle-School Social Studies." *The Social Studies 86* (Mar./Apr. 1995): 60–68.

Steele, Anitra T. "Beyond Food, Festivals, and Folklore." *Wilson Library Bulletin 69* (January 1995): 60–61.

Van Ausdall, Barbara Wass. "Books Offer Entry into Understanding Cultures." *Educational Leadership 51* (May 1994): 32–35.

Recommended Media Resources

THE LANGUAGE OF LITERATURE

LASERLINKS
Videodisc, Gr. 6
See *LaserLinks Teacher's Source Book*, pages 20–21, for overview of Unit Two.

AUDIO LIBRARY
Tapes
Unit Two:
The Need To Belong
Gr. 6, Tape 4: Side A & B
Gr. 6, Tape 5: Side A & B

WRITING COACH
Writing Coach Software: Writing About Literature: Interpretive Response; Personal Narrative

OUTSIDE RESOURCES

Films/Videos/Film Strips/Audiocassettes
American Eyes. 1 videocassette, Cynthia A. Cherbak Productions, Inc.; San Diego: Media Guild, 1991. (30 minutes)
Meet the Newbery Author: Cynthia Rylant. 1 videocassette, Niles Siegel Productions in association with Macmillan/McGraw-Hill Company; an American School Publishers production. Chicago: American School Publishers, 1990. (20 minutes)

Internet Resources
Literature and Language Arts Center at http://www.hmco.com/mcdougal/lit/litcent.html

For Teacher — TEACHING WITH TECHNOLOGY

Bender, Robert M. "Creating Communities on the Internet: Electronic Discussion Lists in the Classroom." *Computers in Libraries* 15 (May 1995): 38–43.

Educational Technology. Educational Technology Publications, Inc., 720 Palisade Avenue, Englewood Cliffs, NJ 07632.

Vidor, Constance. "Show Students How to Use Telecommunications to Select Books." *School Library Media Activities Monthly* 11 (January 1995): 43+

UNIT TWO
Professional Enrichment

Reading and Writing Poetry

How many of us can confess that we didn't like poetry when we were kids? Poetry was unpleasant because we didn't understand it. Who wanted to work at "solving" a poem?

Besides, poetry didn't seem to have anything to do with our lives. Most likely, all of us are living proof that people can learn to appreciate poetry later in life and wind up falling in love with it—but we don't need to take that chance with our students! Here's how to help young readers appreciate the pleasures of poetry from the start.

Sixth graders need the opportunity to see that poetry isn't around just to frustrate them! Instead they must understand that poetry can enthrall, mimic, and mesmerize. It can also describe, portray, argue, express, explore, prod, and please. Sixth graders must realize that poetry isn't about puzzles; it's about power. Poetry captures life in all its glory. Good poetry uses imagery, figures of speech, structure, and sound to tell us more about ourselves and how we live.

How can you make reading and writing poetry matter to your students? Start by making it an important part of your classroom all the time. Start by reading poems aloud to your students. Read a poem that appeals to you, for your enthusiasm will be contagious.

In *Side by Side*, Nancie Atwell explains how she helps students learn to interpret a poem. After reading one of her favorite poems aloud, she explains, "why I had chosen to read [that] poem—what in the work had spoken to me. I pointed out things I had noticed about the poem on my first and second and third and fourth readings. Most importantly, I asked them what they thought of the poem and why, or what they had learned about how it might be written. I learned to demystify the process of reading a poem so that my students might see how a reader could relish unraveling the difficulties of poetry."

While your students are getting to know poetry, you must give them a chance to write their own. To do that, create a classroom environment that supports experimentation and sharing. The following are some suggestions for helping sixth graders enjoy reading and writing poetry.

- Give students a number of different poems to explore. Allow them to decide which poems they would like to read.
- Introduce poetry by using poems written by writers whose prose works students already know. Bridging prose and poetry this way helps students make connections between the known and the unknown. This can help demystify poetry.
- Urge students to first enjoy a poem, then analyze it.
- Show students how to ignore the line breaks and look for the punctuation as they read poetry. This will help improve understanding.
- A good way to understand more about a poem is to rewrite it in your own words. Encourage students to use this technique. Have them notice which lines are most difficult to rewrite and how their versions differ from the original and from each other's.
- Sixth graders, aware of their lack of experience, tend to skip unclear passages rather than question them. Encourage students to work in small groups to clarify confusing lines in a poem.
- To reinforce the concept that personal responses are the building blocks of interpretation, you may wish to have students interpret one of the pieces of fine art in their textbook as a poem. Have students begin by noting how they feel as they look at the artwork. Then lead them in a discussion of the ways in which the artist evokes these feelings, such as color, shape, and form. Finally, have students write their poems about the picture.
- Write your own poetry while students are writing theirs.
- Share your verse with the class. Students will be less likely to be afraid of sharing their efforts if they know that you are not afraid of sharing yours.
- Because interpreting poetry is highly subjective, you may wish to limit your assessment to structural elements.

Related Reading

 Janeczko, Paul B, sel. *The Place My Words Are Looking For: What Poets Say About and Through Their Work.* New York: Bradbury, 1990.

 Peck, Richard, ed. *Pictures That Storm Inside My Head: Poems for the Inner You.* New York: Avon, 1976.

 Untermeyer, Louis ed. *Rainbow in the Sky: Golden Anniversary Edition.* New York: Harcourt, 1985.

 Viorst, Judith. *If I Were in Charge of the World and Other Worries: Poems for Children and Their Parents.* New York: Macmillan, 1984.

Family and Community Involvement

Family

From feeling like an outsider to overcoming a conflict and learning a lesson about friendship, all of the selections in Unit Two connect to the theme of the need to belong. By completing some of the following activities, your students, their families, and other community members can make important connections outside the classroom as they explore real-life examples of the need to belong.

The following Copymasters for Unit Two provide activities that students can complete with a family member.

OPTION 1: DESIGN A COLLAGE OF A SPECIAL PLACE

- **Connection** Many of the selections in Unit Two deal with people's attempts to find a place that is special to them and where they feel they can belong.
- **Activity** *Copymaster, page 1* Students and family members design collages that express students' feelings about a place that is special to them.

OPTION 2: INTERVIEW AN IMMIGRANT

- **Connection** In "Chinatown," Lawrence Yep describes his difficult experiences as a child of an immigrant family.
- **Activity** *Copy Master, page 2* Students interview a family member or a friend of the family who has immigrated to the United States to find out about their experiences of trying to fit into a new culture.

OPTION 3: WRITE AND RECITE A POEM

- **Connection** In many of the selections in Unit Two, characters must face personal struggles and undergo tests of endurance to see if they have what it takes to meet the challenge.
- **Activity** *Copymaster, page 3* Students work with family members to write a short poem that explores a personal struggle they have experienced, as well as their thoughts about that struggle.

Community

OPTION 1

- **Connection** Many of the selections in Unit Two deal with characters who must undergo tests of endurance in order to face certain challenges.
- **Activity** Invite a volunteer from a local homeless shelter to discuss the day-to-day difficulties and struggles of trying to survive on the streets. You also may wish to have students volunteer some of their spare time at a local shelter.

OPTION 2

- **Connection** The main character in "Aaron's Gift" is a young boy who runs into trouble with a local gang of boys.
- **Activity** Invite a school counselor to discuss with students ways to stay out of gangs. You may also wish to have boys and girls who were previously members of gangs speak with students.

OPTION 3

- **Connection** The three haiku in Part 1 of this unit explore the beauty of nature.
- **Activity** Plan a field trip to a Japanese museum or to a botanical garden to explore the ways in which nature inspires poetry like haiku.

UNIT TWO
Part 1 Cooperative Project

Making an Area Special

Overview

Students will find a place in the community they can adopt and help improve.

PROJECT AT A GLANCE

The selections in Unit Two, Part 1 center on people's need to feel at home and happy in a place. For this project, students will find a place in the community they would like to adopt as their own and work together to make improvements to that place. They will create a plan of work, involve other members of the community to help, and analyze the results. The project might end with a tour of all the selected sights, but the real culmination of the project is a better community for all and a sense of pride for participating students.

OBJECTIVES

- To find a place in the community that can be adapted to the needs of students and the community
- To create a plan that tells specifically what needs to be done to improve the selected place
- To work cooperatively with others in the community

SUGGESTED GROUP SIZE
4–6 students per group

MATERIALS
Will vary

1 Getting Started

Arranging the Project
You may want to coordinate the project with other teachers who are doing the same activity. You might be able to combine classes, giving students a chance to work with different partners.

You might want to spend a little time canvassing the neighborhood for likely areas students can adopt. This will give you an idea of what is available as well as how many students would be needed for each area. For instance, you might create a larger work force for a 3-acre vacant lot than for a small park.

This is also the time to check with owners of the property or with local authorities to receive approval.

Arranging for Work
Since the actual work will most likely be done after school or on weekends, you might enlist the aid of parents and fellow teachers to act as supervisors for the projects. At least one adult should be present at all times.

Area merchants might be willing to donate garbage bags, paint, or other items students need for their project. You can leave the solicitation up to students, or contact merchants directly yourself. Stress to students that this should be a very low budget project, and they should concentrate on how their labor, not money, can make a difference.

2 Creating a Special Area

Introducing the Project
Explain that students will be working in groups to find an area of the community they can adopt and make their "special" place. Ideas include cleaning up a vacant lot, cleaning up land adjacent to a highway, planting grass in a park, or planting flowers around light poles. In any case, they should try to create a place they can feel proud of.

Many states now have an "Adopt a Highway" program, in which volunteers clean up the sides of the road a few times a year. In exchange for their labor, the state erects a sign giving public credit to the volunteers. Discuss how this can create a sense of pride for the volunteers. Also discuss whether or not students feel that a public sign is really necessary for promoting a sense of pride.

Group Investigations
Divide students into groups of four to six students (more if you have located a large project area). Groups should agree on a place, brainstorm ideas of what improvements are necessary, and decide how to accomplish these improvements. Students should be encouraged to discuss the project with others who are not involved to get outsiders' ideas, too. Periodic meetings of the entire class can be used to exchange these ideas.

Creating a Project Description
After students have gathered information and done some preliminary planning, each group should prepare a one-page description of its project. This will help you keep track of groups' intentions and make sure plans are not impractical. Meet with each group to review or clarify the plans before allowing students to implement them. If possible, take a "before" photo of each area.

OPTION 1: A SPECIAL PUBLIC ROOM
Students can find a room in a community building (YMCA, library, town hall, church) to adopt. Have students explain the project to and receive permission from those in charge before proceeding.

OPTION 2: A SPECIAL SCHOOLROOM
Students can find a room in the school to adopt, even if the adoption is not permanent. This might be coordinated with another school project, such as decorating for a dance or Parents' Day.

OPTION 3: A SPECIAL PARK Ask students to imagine that a specific building is being torn down. Groups should brainstorm a plan of what they would like to do in that space to make it their own special area. Since this is an optional paper project, encourage students to be creative, perhaps allowing them an unlimited budget.

3 Sharing the Special Places

If possible, arrange for a bus tour or walking tour so the entire class can see all the projects. If not, take photos of each area so students can see the results of the endeavors as the projects are being discussed in class. Invite school officials, property owners, and city officials to accompany you on the tour. You may also ask groups to prepare a brief self-assessment of the project. If applicable, encourage students to continue maintaining and improving their special places.

 Assessing the Project

The following rubric can be used for group or individual assessment

3 Full Accomplishment Students followed directions and created and/or improved an area to make it their special place.

2 Substantial Accomplishment Students produced a plan but did not effectively follow through or did not make improvements to the area.

1 Little or Partial Accomplishment Students' plan and area are incomplete or do not fulfill the requirements of the assignment.

For the Portfolio
Any "before" and "after" photos you took can be made into a display to show the entire school. Keep these for future reference. Include a copy of your written assessment as well as any self-assessments done by students in students' portfolios.

Note: For other assessment options, see the *Teacher's Guide to Assessment and Portfolio Use.*

Cross-Curricular Options

ART
Students can "decorate" a special room by finding furniture in magazines, creating a floor plan, selecting colors and fabrics, and making a final drawing of the room. Encourage them to visit an interior decorating shop or the decorating area of a department store. They can talk to the personnel and get ideas.

MATH

Ask students to find the total cost of making the area the way they imagine it. Square yardage can be figured for grass seed, square footage for paint, and lumber lengths for any structures desired. The cost of each item should be found by "shopping" in catalogs or surveying stores, and the total cost of the project calculated.

HEALTH AND SAFETY
Ask groups to select a place that needs safety improvements. All hazards should be listed, as well as suggestions as to how to remedy such hazards. Safety measures that are practical and inexpensive might be implemented by groups.

Resources

Wastes by Christina G. Miller and Louise A. Berry discusses the disposal problems of household wastes and garbage.

Coastal Rescue: Preserving Our Seashores by Christina B. Miller and Louise A. Berry describes the pollution of U.S. coastlines and how to stop it.

Cities Under Stress by Kathlyn Gay investigates urban problems such as crime, pollution, poor sewage systems, and bad highways.

COOPERATIVE PROJECT TEACHER'S EDITION **149j**

UNIT TWO
Part 1 Lesson Planner

TIME ALLOTMENTS SHOWN ARE APPROXIMATE. DEPENDING ON YOUR GOALS AND THE NEEDS OF YOUR STUDENTS, YOU MAY WISH TO ALLOW MORE OR LESS TIME FOR CERTAIN PORTIONS OF THE LESSON.

Table of Contents	Discussion	Previewing the Selection	Reading the Selection
PART OPENER **FINDING A SPECIAL PLACE** What Do You Think? page 150	**20 MINUTES** • Reflect on the part theme		
SELECTION **The Adoption of Albert** page 152 EASY		**15 MINUTES** • PERSONAL CONNECTION • CULTURAL CONNECTION • READING CONNECTION: Using a reading log	**40 MINUTES** • Read pp. 152–58 (7 pp.)
SELECTION **The Cremation of Sam McGee** page 162 CHALLENGING		**15 MINUTES** • PERSONAL CONNECTION • GEOGRAPHICAL CONNECTION • READING CONNECTION: Mood	**20 MINUTES** • Read pp. 162–67 (6 pp.)
SELECTION **Chinatown from The Lost Garden** page 171 AVERAGE		**20 MINUTES** • PERSONAL CONNECTION • HISTORICAL CONNECTION • WRITING CONNECTION	**40 MINUTES** • Introduce vocabulary • Read pp. 171–77 (7 pp.)
SELECTIONS **Three Haiku** page 181 CHALLENGING		**15 MINUTES** • PERSONAL CONNECTION • LITERARY CONNECTION • READING CONNECTION: Visualizing	**5 MINUTES** • Read pp. 181 (1 p.)
SELECTION **Aaron's Gift** page 185 CHALLENGING		**15 MINUTES** • PERSONAL CONNECTION • GEOGRAPHICAL CONNECTION • READING CONNECTION: Predicting	**40 MINUTES** • Introduce vocabulary • Read pp. 185–93 (9 pp.)
POETRY ON YOUR OWN **Where the Sidewalk Ends** page 197 AVERAGE **The Spider and the Fly** page 198 AVERAGE **Two girls of twelve or so at a table** page 201 AVERAGE **New World** page 203 AVERAGE **Something Told the Wild Geese** page 205 AVERAGE			**15 MINUTES** • Read pp. 197–205 (9 pp.)
Writing	**Writer's Style**	**Prewriting**	**Drafting and Revising**
WRITING ABOUT LITERATURE **Interpretive Response***	**25 MINUTES**	**20 MINUTES**	**70 MINUTES**

* Time estimates assume in-class work. You may wish to assign some of these stages as homework.

149k   UNIT TWO   THE NEED TO BELONG

Responding to the Selection

FROM PERSONAL RESPONSE TO CRITICAL ANALYSIS	OR	ANOTHER PATHWAY	LITERARY CONCEPTS	QUICKWRITES
40 MINUTES				
• Discussion questions	OR	• Retell a section	• Tone	• Science report • Script
40 MINUTES				
• Discussion questions	OR	• Oral reading	• Rhyme and rhythm	• Condolence letter • Narrative poem
40 MINUTES				
• Discussion questions	OR	• Draw a map	• Memoir and setting	• Prediction • Dialogue
20 MINUTES				
• Discussion questions	OR	• Explanation	• Imagery	• Personal essay • Haiku
30 MINUTES				
• Discussion questions	OR	• Story map	• Characterization and theme	• Prediction • Diary entry

Extension Activities

• ALTERNATIVE ACTIVITIES • LITERARY LINKS • CRITIC'S CORNER • THE WRITER'S STYLE • ACROSS THE CURRICULUM • ART CONNECTION • WORDS TO KNOW • BIOGRAPHY

	Alt. Act.	Lit. Links	Critic's	Writer's Style	Across Curriculum	Art	Words	Bio.
40 MINUTES	✔	✔			SCIENCE		✔	✔
40 MINUTES	✔	✔			SCIENCE			✔
40 MINUTES	✔	✔					✔	✔
10 MINUTES						✔		✔
40 MINUTES	✔	✔			SOCIAL STUDIES		✔	✔
								✔

Publishing and Reflecting — 30 MINUTES
Grammar in Context — 10 MINUTES
Reading the World — 30 MINUTES

LESSON PLANNER TEACHER'S EDITION

PART 1

WHAT DO YOU THINK?
Objectives

The activities on this page can be used to
- introduce the Part 1 theme, "Finding a Special Place," since each activity is connected to one or more of the selections in Part 1
- create materials for students' personal portfolios that they can later reconsider or revise
- build an understanding of theme that can be reviewed and revised as students progress through the unit

How do you see your special place?
Encourage students to begin by writing down details about what makes their place special—details they can then incorporate in their drawings or paintings. (See "The Cremation of Sam McGee," p. 161, and "Three Haiku," p. 180.)

Who affects your sense of belonging?
Tell students to begin by listing qualities about themselves and about the individuals they chose. Students can then use this information as they fill in their Venn diagrams. (See "Aaron's Gift," p. 184.)

What makes you *you*?
To help students rate themselves, have them make a list for each quality. They might tell, for instance, in how many different ways they are "Dreamy" or "Practical." You may wish to have the class work together to create additional scales, ones based on other personality traits. (See "Chinatown" from *The Lost Garden*, p. 170.)

How about this sticky situation?
Ask students to base their skits on their own experiences if they have ever been in this situation. Encourage partners to sketch outlines for their skits before writing them. (See "The Adoption of Albert," p. 151.)

UNIT TWO **PART 1**

FINDING A SPECIAL PLACE

WHAT DO  THINK?

REFLECTING ON THEME

Is a special place a specific spot? Or can a special place simply be a sense of belonging—being part of something that matters to you? Use the activities on this page to examine what it means to have a special place. As you read the selections in Part 1, watch for similarities between you and the characters.

How do you see your special place?
Draw or paint a picture of your special place. Present your artwork with the work of other classmates in a bulletin-board display.

Who affects your sense of belonging?

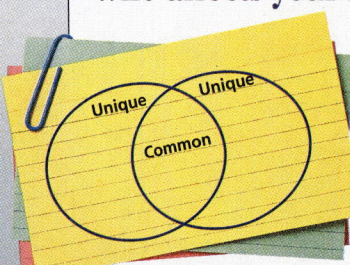

Think of one person—a close friend or a relative—who provides you with a feeling of belonging. Use this diagram to compare and contrast your qualities. Where the circles overlap, write the qualities that you share. In the larger sections, write the qualities that are unique to each of you.

How about this sticky situation?
Imagine you're in a shopping mall when a person runs up and happily throws his or her arms around you. You don't recognize the face—but the person obviously knows you. With a partner, create brief skits showing ways you could handle the situation.

What makes you *you*?
What words do people use to describe you? How would you describe yourself? In your notebook, copy the scales shown, and mark each horizontal line with an **X** to indicate where you think your personality falls. What kind of picture does this give you of yourself?

```
Dreamy ————— Practical
Follower ————— Leader
Cautious ————— Adventurous
Quiet ————— Outspoken
```

150

Across the Curriculum

 Social Studies Explain to students that assimilation often occurs when the members of an immigrant group or community desire to become part of the prevailing culture in terms of customs and viewpoints. Have students work in small groups to research the topic of immigration and assimilation in the United States. Students might focus on one particular immigrant community and examine its changing cultural history. Encourage groups to consider both the positive and the negative effects of assimilation.

PARENTAL INVOLVEMENT
Have students work with their parents or other relatives to create a collage that represents their ideas of "home." Ask students to consider what "home" means to them and whether it refers only to the place where one grows up or whether it can mean different things to different people. Students and their parents can look for pictures or draw illustrations that capture their ideas of "home" and then can assemble these images in their collage.

150 THE LANGUAGE OF LITERATURE TEACHER'S EDITION

PREVIEWING

FICTION

The Adoption of Albert
Barbara Robinson

PERSONAL CONNECTION *Activating Prior Knowledge*

The story you are about to read involves events that take place as part of a family reunion. Have you ever attended a family reunion? If so, describe in your notebook the family reunion and your attitude toward it. If not, describe what you imagine a family reunion would be like.

CULTURAL CONNECTION *Building Background*

Maintaining communication in families is not easy, especially when family members live far apart. A growing number of families plan extended family reunions to keep in touch and create new memories. According to Edith Wagner, editor of *Reunions* magazine, as many as 200,000 families plan reunions each year. "It used to be so simple because everyone lived close by," says Wagner. "Now it's a job to get a family together."

READING CONNECTION *Active Reading/Setting a Purpose*

Using a Reading Log The reading strategies introduced on page 5 and summarized in the chart shown here are based on the kinds of connections active readers make when they read. You can use your Reading Log to help you practice these strategies as you sort through the sequence of events in this story. As you read, record your questions and ideas about characters and events in the story. Also record any new thoughts you may have about family reunions. After you finish reading, discuss your questions and thoughts with your classmates.

Reading Log Strategies	
Questioning	Ask questions about the events and characters in the story.
Connecting	Think of similarities between events in the story and your own experiences.
Predicting	Predict what might happen next and how the story might end.
Clarifying	Stop at times for a quick review of what you understand so far.
Evaluating	Form opinions about the story.

THE ADOPTION OF ALBERT **151**

OVERVIEW

Objectives

- To understand and appreciate a humorous short story about a family
- To enrich reading by using active reading strategies
- To examine tone
- To express understanding of the story through a choice of writing forms, including a science report and a TV script
- To extend understanding of the story through a variety of multimodal and cross-curricular activities

Skills

READING SKILLS/STRATEGIES
- Using a reading log

LITERARY CONCEPTS
- Tone
- Narrator

THE WRITER'S STYLE
- Combining sentences

GRAMMAR
- Main and helping verbs

SPELLING
- Spelling with the prefix *re-*

SPEAKING, LISTENING, AND VIEWING
- Group discussion
- Oral presentation

Cross-Curricular Connections

SOCIAL STUDIES
- Family trees

SCIENCE
- Earthworms

ALTERNATIVE
Previewing

Instead of writing about a family reunion, students can choose a partner and discuss the topic.

Personal Connection

Discussion Prompts *Describe a family reunion you have attended or what you imagine the experience would be like. The following questions might help you get started:*

- Where was the family reunion held?
- Who attended the reunion?
- What was your favorite moment of the reunion?

As you read "The Adoption of Albert," pay attention to the family reunion that is held and what is going on behind all the activity.

PRINT AND MEDIA RESOURCES

UNIT TWO RESOURCE BOOK
Strategic Reading: Literature, p. 4
Reading SkillBuilder, p. 5
Spelling SkillBuilder, p. 6

GRAMMAR MINI-LESSONS
Transparencies, p. 16
Copymasters, p. 24

WRITING MINI-LESSONS
Transparencies, pp. 40, 41

ACCESS FOR STUDENTS ACQUIRING ENGLISH
Selection Summaries
Reading and Writing Support

TEACHER'S GUIDE TO ASSESSMENT AND PORTFOLIO USE

FORMAL ASSESSMENT
Selection Test, pp. 31–32
 Test Generator

AUDIO LIBRARY
See Reference Card

THE LANGUAGE OF LITERATURE TEACHER'S EDITION **151**

The Adoption of Albert

by Barbara Robinson

SUMMARY

Eleven-year-old Louis brings his new friend Albert home during preparations for a family reunion. Amid all the activity, nobody pays much attention when Albert stays overnight. This leaves the boys plenty of time to pursue a new interest: cutting up live earthworms, stuffing the parts in dirt-filled coffee cans, and waiting for them to regenerate. Albert does not appear to be interested in returning home, and he happily takes part in Louis's family reunion. Just as Louis's mother starts wondering exactly who Albert is and where he lives, Aunt Rhoda recognizes him as a passenger in a traffic accident she recently witnessed. Louis's father locates Albert's worried parents at the police station. Albert and his parents are reunited, and all ends happily—except for a little mix-up involving earthworm parts and coffee.

Thematic Link: *Finding a Special Place*
In this story, a young boy tries to find a new place to live until he is identified and reunited with his parents.

CUSTOMIZING FOR
Students Acquiring English

- Use **ACCESS FOR STUDENTS ACQUIRING ENGLISH,** *Reading and Writing Support.*
- You may want to use this story and the Cultural Connection on page 151 to spark an oral or written discussion of family customs in cultures the students are familiar with.

STRATEGIC READING FOR
Less-Proficient Readers

Ask students to remember when they made a new friend. Have them discuss how they met this friend and how the friendship developed.

Set a Purpose Have students read to find out who Albert is.

Use **UNIT TWO RESOURCE BOOK,** pp. 4–5, for guidance in reading the selection.

There were so many children in our neighborhood that my mother was never surprised to find unfamiliar ones in the house, or in the backyard, or in my room, or in Louis's room.

"Well, who's this?" she would say, and she would then go on to connect that child with whatever house or family he belonged to.

But when Louis showed up with his new friend Albert, Mother had other things on her mind: the family <u>reunion</u>, which was two days away; the distant cousin who would be staying at our house; most of all, my Aunt Rhoda's famous Family Reunion cake, which, in Aunt Rhoda's absence, Mother felt obliged to provide.

Aunt Rhoda's absence, and the reason for it, were both first-time events: She had never before missed a family reunion, and neither she nor anyone else had ever before been called into court to testify about anything. Aunt Rhoda was to testify about an

WORDS TO KNOW
reunion (rē-yōōn′yən) *n.* a gathering of the members of a group who have been separated

152

WORDS TO KNOW

reunion (rē-yōōn′yĕn) *n.* a bringing together of people again after a period of separation (p. 152)

---

152 THE LANGUAGE OF LITERATURE TEACHER'S EDITION

Long Weekend (1990), Brian Jones. Courtesy Nancy Poole's Studio, Toronto, Canada.

Art Note

Long Weekend by Brian Jones
Brian Jones (1950–) is a Canadian painter whose work often centers on domestic scenes. Some of his paintings represent actual memories of his childhood; all present familiar images of family life. As with *Long Weekend*, the figures in his paintings are highly stylized and exaggerated to express movement and emotion.

Reading the Art What in this scene is familiar to you? How do the style and exaggeration of figures in this scene express movement and emotion? What kinds of emotions do you think are being expressed?

CUSTOMIZING FOR
Gifted and Talented Students

As students read the selection, have them look for ways the author develops Albert's personality in the story through description, dialogue, and actions.

(Possible responses: Albert is described as a shy, small, quiet boy. His dialogue and actions also reveal that he is quiet, because he never really tells anyone who he is or why he is there. He seems like a mysterious character because he never speaks up and lets others know why he isn't at his own house. For instance, when the family picture is being taken, Frank refers to Albert as Clyde's son, and Albert never contradicts this. His mysterious quality is also created by thoughts and dialogue of other characters, such as Mary Elizabeth, who constantly says that she doesn't know what he's doing there.)

Multicultural Perspectives

FAMILY Different cultures have different ideas about what makes a family. Besides the traditional American nuclear family (mother, father, and children), there are many types of family arrangements. For example, in Polynesian (South Pacific) culture the family is a much bigger group. It includes children, parents, grandparents, aunts, uncles, and cousins often living together. The grandparents have as important a role in raising the children as do the parents. In Polynesia, the boundary between one's immediate and extended family is less important than it is in other cultures. In such a culture, family reunions are unheard of, because the family is always together!

Literary Concept: NARRATOR

A Ask students to tell what they can infer about the narrator of this paragraph and discuss how they reached their decisions. *(The narrator is a character in the story; he or she is a member of the family preparing for the reunion. You can tell that this person is the narrator because the author uses the word I, writing the story from the first-person point of view.)* Make sure students realize that the narrator's gender is not yet mentioned. As an additional exercise, ask students to look at column 1 on page 155 and find where the name of the narrator is first revealed.

CUSTOMIZING FOR
Multiple Learning Styles

B Logical-Mathematical Learners Invite students to think of ways Louis could more accurately measure the lengths of his earthworms. Some students may have ideas about devices Louis could use to measure them.

Active Reading: PREDICT

C Have students predict what could happen to the earthworms. *(Possible response: I think there may be some undivided earthworms in the coffee cans that will escape and wiggle into another room.)*

---

automobile accident she had witnessed—the only automobile accident in local memory, my father said, that did not involve Aunt Mildred.

All in all, it was a complicated time for Mother—cake, cousins, company—and when Louis appeared at the kitchen door and said, "This is Albert," she was too distracted to ask her usual questions.

> "The tail ends grow new heads, and the head ends grow new tails."

Nor did she ask them at suppertime. By then she was up to her elbows in cake batter and left the three of us to eat alone with my father, who also didn't know Albert, but assumed that everyone else did.

A I didn't know Albert either, but there was no reason I should. He was Louis's friend, he was Louis's age, he even looked a lot like Louis— small and quiet and solemn—and it didn't occur to me to find out any more about him. I did ask, "Where do you live, Albert?"; and when he said, "Here," I just thought he meant here in the neighborhood instead of someplace else.

Mother thought the same thing. "Where does that little boy live?" she asked me the next morning, and I said, "Here," and she said, "I wonder which house?"

Albert had spent the night, and there was a note propped against the cereal box: *Albert and I have gone to dig worms.*

Louis had been collecting worms all summer and measuring them to see how long a worm

got to be before it died. "I think that's what kills them," he said. "I think they die of length."

So far his longest worm was between four inches and four and a half inches. All his worms were between one size and another because they wouldn't hold still. "It's really hard," he said. "I have to stretch them out and measure them at the same time, and if I'm not careful they come apart."

"Oh, Louis," I said, "that's awful! What do you do then?"

He shrugged. "I bury the pieces. What else can I do?"

Of course, most kids wouldn't even do that, but Louis was neater than most kids.

It was late afternoon when he and Albert came back, and they had big news. They also had two coffee cans full of worm parts.

"I thought you buried them," I said.

"I didn't have to! Albert says . . . Albert says . . ." I had never seen Louis so pleased and excited. "Tell her what you said."

"It doesn't kill them," Albert said. "The tail ends grow new heads, and the head ends grow new tails." **B**

I looked in the coffee cans, but I couldn't tell the difference between head and tails. Louis said he couldn't tell the difference either. "But it doesn't matter," he said, "because the worms can. *They* know. We're going to keep them, and watch them grow, and measure them . . . and maybe name them."

"They're no trouble," Albert said. "They just eat dirt. We've got some." He held up another coffee can.

They took all three coffee cans up to Louis's room, and this worried me a lot because I knew I would have to sleep in Louis's room when everybody came for the family reunion. **C**

My father said he was always astonished

154 UNIT TWO PART 1: FINDING A SPECIAL PLACE

Mini-Lesson  Grammar

> Louis's mother is preparing for the family reunion.
>
> They <u>did</u> not know who Albert was.

MAIN AND HELPING VERBS Tell students that many verbs are single words. Often, however, a verb is made up of two or more words. When this happens, the last word is the main verb, and the other words are helping verbs. Forms of the verbs *be, have,* and *do* are the most common helping verbs. Write the first example to the left on the chalkboard to demonstrate. Then remind students that the main verb and its helping verbs are not always together. Write the next example on the chalkboard to demonstrate.

Application Refer students to the passage highlighted above. Ask students to identify all the main verbs and their helping verbs. Have them rewrite these sentences, underlining the main verbs twice and the helping verbs once. Read the passage aloud, pausing after each sentence to discuss its verb usage.

Reteaching/Reinforcement
• *Grammar Handbook,* anthology pp. 835–836
• *Grammar Mini-Lessons* copymasters, p. 24; transparencies, p. 16

 The Writer's Craft
Main Verbs and Helping Verbs, pp. 399–400

154 THE LANGUAGE OF LITERATURE **TEACHER'S EDITION**

that there was anybody left to *come* to the family reunion. "Your whole family is already here," he told Mother, "living around the corner, or three streets away, or on the other side of town."

"Not everybody," Mother said. "There's Virginia and Evelyn and Clyde . . ." She reeled off the names—cousins, mostly, whom we knew only from Christmas cards, and from their annual appearance at the reunion.

Some, in fact, had already appeared and were upstairs unpacking their suitcases. Mother, who was busy catching up on their news and shuffling food around in the refrigerator and getting out all the dishes and silverware, either didn't realize that Albert was still with us or just didn't remember that she had ever seen him in the first place.

My father had gone off to borrow picnic tables for the next day, and since I didn't want to sit around and watch worms grow, I went next door to play with my friend Maxine Slocum and forgot all about Albert.

That night when I took my sleeping bag into Louis's room, he was already asleep in a mound of bedclothes . . . and there was another mound of bedclothes beside him.

"Louis." I shook him awake. "Who is that?"

"It's Albert," he said.

"Why doesn't he go home?"

Louis looked surprised. "He *is* home. He's going to live here now. Remember? He told you. . . . Don't worry, Mary Elizabeth," he added. "You'll like Albert."

"I already like Albert," I said, "but I don't think he can live here. I think he has to live with his parents."

"He doesn't want to," Louis said. "He even told them so. He told them, 'I don't want to live with you anymore,' and they said, 'All right, Albert, you just go and live someplace else.'"

I had never heard of such a thing, except when my friend Wanda McCall baptized the hamsters with her mother's French perfume. The house smelled wonderful, but all the hamsters got sick and so did Mrs. McCall, and Mr. McCall gave Wanda two dollars and told her to get lost. But he didn't mean forever.

Neither had Albert's parents, I decided. They would probably call tomorrow and tell him to come home.

"Louis." I shook him again. "Where are the worms?"

"They aren't worms yet," he reminded me. "The cans are in the closet."

I didn't think either half of a worm could go very far, but I put my sleeping bag on the other side of the room anyway, just in case.

When I woke up the next morning Louis and Albert were gone, but they had made the bed and folded up their clothes and left a note that said, *We'll be back for the picnic.* Please don't move the worms. There was a P.S.: *Tell the lady cousin in the purple underwear that I'm sorry. I didn't know she was in there.* Then there was another P.S.: *It was really Albert, but pretend it was me and tell her I'm sorry. Or if you don't want to, just find out who she is and I'll tell her.*

That was nice of Louis, I thought, but I really didn't want to ask around about everyone's underwear.

"I guess not," Louis said later. "It's okay. . . . Albert felt bad about it, that's all."

"Where is Albert?" I asked.

"Over there." Louis pointed to where Mother's brother Frank was taking pictures with his new camera.

"You'll have to get closer together," we

THE ADOPTION OF ALBERT   155

Art Note

The Last Picnic by Brian Jones Like *Long Weekend*, this painting is representative of Jones's distinctive stylization and exaggeration of figures engaged in familiar domestic activities. Note, however, that the background remains realistic in its details.

Reading the Art Why do you think the title of this painting is *Last Picnic*? What details in the painting support the meaning of the title?

Critical Thinking: ANALYZE

F Ask students why they think Albert is worried and might want to go with Louis to move the cans. *(Possible response: All of Louis's relatives are talking about Albert as if he were Clyde's son. He might be feeling uncomfortable, and so he probably wants to leave before they find out who he is.)*

CUSTOMIZING FOR
Students Acquiring English

I Have students note that the words in quotation marks are part of Aunt Rhoda's "new vocabulary" relating to her experiences at the courthouse and the police station. Explain that "the litigants" are people involved in a lawsuit, and "ID's" are identification. "Mug shots" can be figured out from context further on.

Literary Concept: NARRATOR

G Ask students to discuss whether the narrator in this passage is a character in the story or an outside voice. *(Possible response: Mary Elizabeth, the narrator, is telling the reader what people are saying, but she's not speaking, so it seems like an outside observer is telling the story.)*

---

heard him say, "and put Clyde's boy in front of you, Blanche."

"Who is Clyde's boy?" Louis asked me.

"I think it's Albert," I said. "He's the only boy there."

I was right. "Looks just *like* Clyde," we heard Aunt Blanche say.

F I thought Albert looked a little worried, but Louis said he was just worried about the worms. "We're going to move them someplace else," he said. "Albert thinks they might get out and crawl around—especially the head parts, Albert said, because they could see where they were going."

That made me shiver, so I hoped they would put them somewhere up high.

By then Aunt Rhoda had arrived, to everyone's surprise. She never did get to testify, she said, because "the litigants" had to go to the police station to look at "mug shots" and "supply ID's." Aunt Rhoda had picked up a whole new vocabulary.

"Mug shots?" my father said. "ID's? Now, what does that mean? This was a traffic accident, not a holdup."

"I don't know," Mother told him. "Rhoda just said they had to study mug shots of children."

"There is no such thing as mug shots of children. Mug shots are of criminals. Rhoda's got it all wrong." He went to question Aunt Rhoda further and stumbled into the one event he always tried to avoid: the big family photograph, with everyone in it.

The Last Picnic (1993), Brian Jones. Courtesy Nancy Poole's Studio, Toronto, Canada.

Uncle Frank had set up a different camera and lined everybody up, but he was missing some people: my parents, Aunt Mildred . . . "And Louis," he said. "And Clyde's boy. Clyde, where's your boy?"

Clyde looked surprised. "He's in the army."

"I mean the little one."

"Looks just like you," Aunt Blanche put in.

"He doesn't look one bit like me," Clyde said. "He looks like his mother."

"No," Aunt Blanche said stubbornly. "He looks like you."

Clyde was stubborn too. "How do you know what he looks like, Blanche? You haven't seen him in six years!"

"I saw him fifteen minutes ago!"

"Who?" my father said, arriving on the scene with Mother.

G

156   UNIT TWO   PART 1: FINDING A SPECIAL PLACE

Mini-Lesson  Literary Concepts

REVIEWING NARRATOR Tell students that the person who tells a story is called the narrator. In some stories the narrator is a character who takes part in the action and is identified as the first-person "I." At other times the narrator is an outside voice created by the author. In choosing a narrator the author determines the amount and kind of information the reader is given.

Application Encourage students to think about how and why the story would be different with an outside voice telling the events. Have students write a short version of the selection in which an outside observer is the narrator. Ask students to think about what aspects of the story would be the same and what aspects would have to be changed if none of the characters in the story narrated the events. Invite volunteers to read their rewritten stories to the class.

156 THE LANGUAGE OF LITERATURE TEACHER'S EDITION

"They're talking about Albert," I said. "Louis's friend Albert."

"Albert!" Mother looked amazed. "Is that little boy here again?"

"He never left," I said.

So I was sent to get Albert and find out where he lived, while Mother explained to everybody who he was (which was hard, because she didn't *know* who he was) and my father pressed Aunt Rhoda for more details about her experiences in court—fearful, he later said, that she had wandered into the wrong courtroom and the wrong trial and was now mixed up with a bunch of criminals.

I found Louis crawling around the floor of his room. "We dropped some of a worm," he said, "but only one, and I'll find it. We took the rest of them out of the closet."

"Mother wants to know where Albert lives," I told him.

"You mean . . . besides here?" Louis was being stubborn too, just like Aunt Blanche and Clyde. "I don't know."

"Well, what's Albert's name?"

"You mean . . . besides Albert? I'll ask him."

"But, Louis—don't you know?"

"I only met him day before yesterday," Louis said. "He was sitting on the curb outside the model-airplane store, after his parents told him to go live someplace else. He didn't know anyplace else, so I told him he could live here. And after that, all we talked about was worms."

Albert didn't know where he lived either. "I can't remember," he said. "We haven't lived there long enough for me to remember. I think it's the name of a tree."

Albert was right. He lived on Catalpa Street, and his name was Henderson. But it was Aunt Rhoda, of all people, who supplied the information, while Louis and Albert were upstairs looking for the missing worm.

Aunt Rhoda recognized Albert in the picture because, when she witnessed the automobile accident, she had also witnessed Albert in one of the cars with his parents—the very same people, she said, who were at this moment examining mug shots at the police station.

"Isn't it a small world!" Aunt Rhoda said . . . and everyone agreed, except my father.

He had assumed, all along, that Mother knew who Albert was and knew where Albert came from. "And I suppose," he said, "that Albert is staying with us now because his parents have to be in court—but didn't the Hendersons mention *why* they had to be in court?"

"I don't know the Hendersons," Mother said.

"Well, did Albert . . ."

"I don't know Albert either." Mother was getting testy under all this cross-examination. "Obviously, Louis said it would be all right for Albert to stay here—and it *is* all right," she said. "Those poor people have enough trouble. That's the least we can do for them."

In the meantime Louis and Albert came downstairs—"We found the worm," Louis assured me—went to get more fried chicken and potato salad, and ran into Aunt Rhoda, who said she was certainly surprised to see Albert again and to see him *here*.

"I live here," Albert said.

"Oh, no," Aunt Rhoda laughed. "You live on Catalpa Street."

"Not anymore," Albert said.

Of course Aunt Rhoda reported this to Mother, who was by then completely mystified

THE ADOPTION OF ALBERT 157

Mini-Lesson — Reading Skills/Strategies

ACTIVE READING: USING A READING LOG Remind students that active readers use strategies as they read. Have volunteers define the strategies of questioning, connecting, predicting, clarifying, and evaluating. If necessary, refer students to the chart for the Reading Connection on page 151.

Application Have students review the questions they recorded about this story's characters and events. Ask them if their questions were answered as they read. Have students record their questions and answers in a chart like the one shown. If students still have unanswered questions, invite them to read the story once more for possible answers.

Reteaching/Reinforcement
Unit Two Resource Book, p. 5

Question	Answer
Why is Albert living with Louis?	He has left home and meets Louis, who says Albert could live with him.

Linking to Social Studies

Many families find it interesting and helpful to make and maintain a family tree. This graphically sets down a family's history through the generations. Special symbols may designate adoptive, foster, or step relationships. The tree may help young people grasp visually where they fit in and to whom they are related. It may be illustrated by photos or drawings and may be framed, kept in a special place (such as a Bible), or photocopied for family members. Encourage students who have family trees to bring them to class.

Active Reading: CONNECT

Ask students to discuss what they would have done if they had been in Louis's place.

CUSTOMIZING FOR
Students Acquiring English

Explain that the idiom *of all people* suggests that it is unlikely and surprising that Aunt Rhoda would know Albert's name and address.

STRATEGIC READING FOR
Less-Proficient Readers

Ask students the following questions to help guide them through the reading:

- How did Albert end up living at Louis's house? *(Louis tells his sister that he met Albert outside the model-airplane store. Albert said he had no place to live and Louis invited him to live with his family.)* Summarizing

- Whose son do some family members think Albert is? *(Clyde's)* Noting Relevant Details

- Why does Aunt Rhoda begin using a lot of police terms? *(She has been to court as a witness and seems to have picked up some of the phrases used by the police.)* Making Inferences

Set a Purpose Have students read to find out what happens when Louis's family figures out who Albert actually is.

THE LANGUAGE OF LITERATURE TEACHER'S EDITION 157

STRATEGIC READING FOR
Less-Proficient Readers

K Ask students the following questions to help them review the story:

- What happens when Louis's family finds out who Albert is? *(Once they realize Albert isn't a family member, they reunite him with his parents.)* **Summarizing**

- Why does Aunt Rhoda recognize Albert? *(During the accident she witnessed, she saw Albert in a car with his parents.)* **Noting Relevant Details**

- Why would Albert still be lonely and sad if Louis hadn't met him? *(Albert's mother says that he doesn't know any other children and that he has no one to play with.)* **Drawing Conclusions**

CUSTOMIZING FOR
Gifted and Talented Students

Ask students how the author maintains a humorous tone throughout the story, despite the fact that the main idea of the story, a runaway child, is somber and tragic. Have students discuss how the story might have been different if the author had not used a humorous tone in describing the events.

COMPREHENSION CHECK

1. How would you describe Albert's character? *(He is a shy, quiet, lonely boy who is very interested in earthworms, is adaptable to a situation, and seems to have a tendency to get himself into trouble.)*

2. Why doesn't Louis's mother find out who Albert is when he first comes over to her house? *(She is busy preparing for the family reunion and is distracted.)*

3. Why had Aunt Rhoda been in court? *(She had witnessed an automobile accident and had to testify.)*

4. What happens to the can of worms at the end of the story? *(Aunt Rhoda makes coffee for everyone and mistakes the can of worms for a can of coffee.)*

---

about Albert and pretty fed up with all the sketchy bits and pieces of news about him. She left Aunt Rhoda to cut the Family Reunion cake and make the coffee, and went off to find Louis. My father, having also concluded that Louis was the key to it all, had done the same thing.

Between them, they quickly figured out that Louis did not know the Hendersons and that he barely knew Albert . . . and that Albert had left home and was prepared to live with us forever.

My father called the police station, where the Hendersons were indeed studying pictures of missing children and supplying information about their own missing child . . . and in no time they arrived at our house and were reunited with Albert.

> **"In my house," she said, "if a can says coffee, that's what's in it."**

This was exactly the kind of happy ending my mother loved best—even Albert seemed happy to be back with his family.

"Well, now he has a friend," Mrs. Henderson said, beaming at Louis. "That was the trouble. He didn't know anyone, didn't have anyone to play with or talk to. Thank goodness for you, Louis!"

The Hendersons obviously saw Louis as the hero of it all, which exasperated my father.

"I don't know why you're so grumpy," Mother said. "Just suppose Louis hadn't come along and found Albert outside the airplane store—then what?"

"Then Albert would have gone home where he belonged," my father said, "and none of this would have happened."

"Exactly!" Mother said. "And he would still be a lonely, unhappy little boy . . . way over there on Catalpa Street."

She invited the Hendersons to stay for cake and coffee and to meet all the relatives. Aunt Rhoda said she couldn't meet them officially, or talk to them, because of being a witness, but she waved to them from the back porch, and Mrs. Henderson waved back and called to her, "Your cake recipe is wonderful!"

"Have some coffee," Mother said. "It's Rhoda's coffee, too."

Aunt Rhoda said later that it was pretty silly to call it *her* coffee just because she'd made it, and she also said that she didn't feel one bit responsible for what had happened.

"In my house," she said, "if a can says coffee, that's what's in it, and it wouldn't occur to me to look."

Mother said, in all fairness, it wouldn't occur to her to look either. . . . "Except, of course, I don't keep my coffee on that high shelf, so I might have looked."

My father, who had been the first one to sip the coffee—and, therefore, the *only* one to sip the coffee—said he wished *someone* had looked.

"Was it the can full of dirt?" I asked Louis, and he shook his head no.

"Oh, I'm sorry, Louis," I said, "but you and Albert can get some more worms."

"And it was only the tail ends, anyway," Albert said . . . although I hadn't really wanted to know that. ❖

K

158 UNIT TWO PART 1: FINDING A SPECIAL PLACE

Mini-Lesson  Spelling

SPELLING WITH THE PREFIX RE- Tell students that the prefix *re-* means "again." When adding the prefix *re-* to a base word, you do not change the spelling of the base word—even if the base word begins with a vowel. Make sure students understand that not all words beginning with *re-* contain a prefix. There must be a base word that can stand alone in order for *re-* to be a prefix.

re + union = **reunion**

Application Have students write each word using the prefix *re-*.

1. call
2. produce
3. construct
4. view
5. apply
6. stock
7. introduce
8. instate
9. condition
10. examine

Reteaching/Reinforcement
- *Unit Two Resource Book*, p. 6

RESPONDING OPTIONS

FROM PERSONAL RESPONSE TO CRITICAL ANALYSIS

REFLECT
1. With a few classmates, role-play the scene of the story that you think is the funniest.

RETHINK
2. How would you describe Louis's family?
   Consider
   Close Textual Reading
   - the way they interact
   - their reactions to Albert
   - their preparation for the family reunion
   - their attitude toward visitors

3. Were you surprised by the reaction of Albert's parents when they finally discover him at Louis's house? Why or why not?

4. How did this story affect your attitude toward family reunions?

RELATE
5. Not every family is able to organize and attend an annual reunion. How important do you think it is for families to keep in touch?

LITERARY CONCEPTS

Tone is a writer's expression of his or her attitude toward a subject. For example, a work's tone might be amused, outraged, or neutral. Tone is often revealed by the writer's style. Describe the tone of "The Adoption of Albert" and explain why Barbara Robinson might have chosen to express that attitude toward her subject.

LITERARY LINKS

Compare and contrast the type of humor Barbara Robinson uses in this story with the type that Gary Soto uses in "The School Play" (page 30). How is Louis in this story similar to and different from Robert in "The School Play"?

Multimodal Learning
ANOTHER PATHWAY

What if this story were told from Albert's point of view, or that of any character other than Mary Elizabeth? Choose a section of the story and retell it from the point of view of Albert or another character of your choice. How does the change in perspective affect your understanding of the story?

QUICKWRITES

1. Louis is very excited to find out something new about worms. Write a **science report** that Louis might have written for school the day after Albert's visit.

2. What if "The Adoption of Albert" were the first episode of a TV sitcom? Improvise a **script** that follows the general outline of the story.

📁 **PORTFOLIO** *Save your writing. You may want to use it later as a springboard to a piece for your portfolio.*

THE ADOPTION OF ALBERT **159**

From Personal Response to Critical Analysis

1. Make sure students reread the scene and pay attention to the characters' personalities.
2. Possible responses: Louis's family seems to be very caring, friendly, and warm. Louis's family is also very funny, especially in the way they deal and interact with their relatives.
3. Some students will say they were surprised because Albert's parents didn't seem upset or angry with him. Other students will say that they were not surprised because Albert's parents were glad to find Albert safe.
4. Responses will vary.
5. Many students may say that it is very important because one's family is an important source of love and support. Others may say that some family members don't get along with one another and have no desire to keep in touch.

Literary Links

Both short stories take a humorous attitude toward a potentially serious subject. In "The School Play," the humor comes from the way the author describes the events. In "The Adoption of Albert," much of the humor comes from the characters' dialogue and actions.

While Louis and Robert are both confident young boys, they also make mistakes—Robert forgets his lines in the school play, and Louis puts his can of worms in a risky place.

Another Pathway

Have students work in pairs to select a new narrator. Have partners engage in an imaginary dialogue. One can play their chosen narrator, and the other can play an outsider asking questions. Encourage students to incorporate the narrator's responses and personality in their retelling.

Rubric
- **3 Full Accomplishment** Retelling describes events accurately and captures the personality of the narrator.
- **2 Substantial Accomplishment** Some events are missing or inadequately described. The style does not reflect all aspects of the narrator's personality.
- **1 Little or Partial Accomplishment** Few events are described accurately, and little of the narrator's personality comes through.

Literary Concepts

Have students work with partners to list two or three examples from the story in which the author's tone toward her subject is apparent. Ask students to support their responses. For example, students might point to Robinson's use of dialogue to show how miscommunication among family members can sometimes be funny. Her humorous tone throughout helps show why Albert, an only child, might want to stay with Louis's family.

QuickWrites

1. Remind students to write the report from Louis's point of view. Students may want to reread the selection, reviewing events involving worms. Ask students to think about the way Louis might write, as well as the points he might cover in his report.
2. Encourage students to match the author's attitude toward the subject matter and to write in the style of a TV script, using mostly dialogue and action.

The Writer's Craft

Report of Information, pp. 166–179
Using Dialogue, pp. 278–280

THE LANGUAGE OF LITERATURE TEACHER'S EDITION **159**

Across the Curriculum

Science *Cooperative Learning* Divide students into small groups to research the topic. One student in each group should act as facilitator to organize the group and to make sure that everyone is participating. Another student should be chosen as scribe to record the group's ideas and research. Groups can use illustrated encyclopedias, dictionaries, or documentary videos for visual resources. Have each group elect one or more presenters.

Words to Know

Root Word: *occupied*, which means having one's attention or energies taken up

PREOCCUPIED, which means already engaged or interested in something

Prefix and/or Suffix: *pre-*, which means before or in advance

Mary Elizabeth's mother is preoccupied.

Multimodal Learning
ALTERNATIVE ACTIVITIES

1. Choose an episode from the story, and draw a **comic strip** of the events in the episode. Use some of the author's actual words and try to match the tone of your comic strip to the tone of the story.
2. Create a humorous **family newsletter** describing the events that occur before and during the family reunion. Write it from the point of view of any character you choose.

ACROSS THE CURRICULUM

Science Cooperative Learning Work with a group to complete the research begun by Louis and Albert. How long *do* worms get? Can worm parts grow new heads or tails? Do worms really "die of length"? Present your information to the class in a visual format, using poster board, schematic diagrams, and three-dimensional models.

WORDS TO KNOW

WORDPLAY
Understanding the parts of words—roots, prefixes, and suffixes—can help you figure out, or infer, the words' meanings. Study the word map for the vocabulary word *reunion,* shown here. Then make your own word map for the word *preoccupied,* using a dictionary if necessary. Which character in this story would you describe as preoccupied?

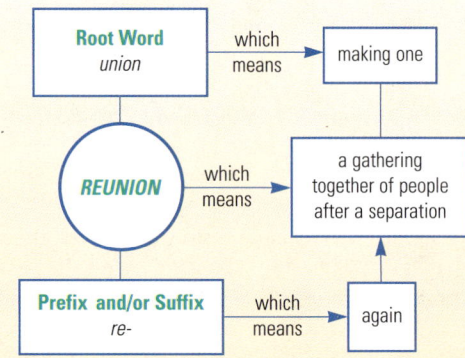

BARBARA ROBINSON

"The Adoption of Albert" is one of ten humorous stories about Louis Lawson and his family in Barbara Robinson's *My Brother Louis Measures Worms and Other Louis Stories,* published in 1988. Another of Robinson's popular books, *The Best Christmas Pageant Ever,* describes the misadventures of the Herdman children—"absolutely the worst kids in the history of the world"—who decide to take over the annual church Christmas pageant. That book received an award from the American Library Association and was produced as a television film in 1983.

Robinson says, "Each book that I have written for boys and girls is also a book I have written for myself . . . since, if I don't find the story exciting or interesting or funny, if I don't enjoy the characters or care what happens to them, I don't think boys and girls will either." She adds, "Since I don't plan my books in outline form, I am often in the position of the reader, asking 'What's going to happen next?'"

What does Barbara Robinson like to read? Her "all-time favorite book" is Robert Louis Stevenson's *Treasure Island*. Extended Reading
OTHER WORKS *Across from Indian Shore; Trace Through the Forest; The Fattest Bear in the First Grade; Temporary Times, Temporary Places*

160 UNIT TWO PART 1: FINDING A SPECIAL PLACE

Alternative Activities

1. Encourage students to choose an episode that they will be able to represent in a comic strip without too much difficulty. Suggest that students choose an episode that contains dialogue to make the comic strip more interesting and humorous. Students should first outline the events and sketch ideas for possible illustrations.
2. Have students first create an outline for the events they wish to cover in their newsletter. Make sure students write consistently from the point of view of their chosen characters and that they write in the style of a family newsletter. Encourage students to keep the tone informal and humorous.

PREVIEWING

POETRY

The Cremation of Sam McGee
Robert Service

PERSONAL CONNECTION Activating Prior Knowledge/Setting a Purpose

"The Cremation of Sam McGee" is a poem about friendship and a challenge that a person faces for the sake of friendship. Have you ever given your word that you would help a friend in need? Did you succeed in keeping your promise? Draw a promise-and-outcome graphic like the one shown here, and fill it in with an account of your experience.

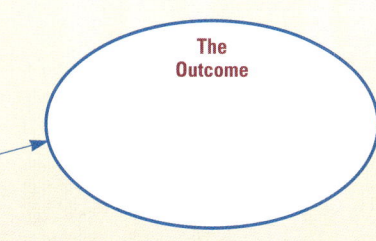

GEOGRAPHICAL CONNECTION Building Background

The narrator of this poem is a gold miner, and the poem's setting is the Yukon Territory. The Yukon Territory is located in the northwestern corner of Canada, with Alaska to the west and the Arctic Ocean to the north. This area is known for its long, dark, extremely cold winters. The average January temperature at Dawson in the Yukon Territory is −16°F. In the late 1800s, many people risked their lives in the icy Yukon, searching for gold near the Klondike River.

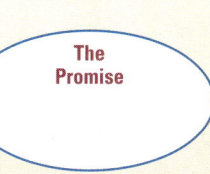

READING CONNECTION Active Reading

Mood A feeling that a writer wants readers to get while reading his or her work is called a **mood.** Writers choose words carefully to create moods. For example, in the first stanza of "The Cremation of Sam McGee," the words *strange, secret tales,* and *queer sights* create an eerie mood. As you read this poem about friendship and loyalty, pay attention to how you are feeling and to the words that help to create that mood.

• GEOGRAPHICAL CONNECTION

OVERVIEW

Objectives
- To understand and appreciate a narrative poem about keeping a promise
- To examine end and internal rhyme
- To express understanding of the poem through a choice of writing forms, including a condolence letter and a narrative poem
- To extend understanding of the poem through a variety of multimodal and cross-curricular activities

Skills

LITERARY CONCEPTS
- Rhyme
- Alliteration

THE WRITER'S STYLE
- Details appealing to touch

SPEAKING, LISTENING, AND VIEWING
- Directions
- Group discussion
- Oral presentation

Cross-Curricular Connections

HISTORY
- Dog sledding

SOCIAL STUDIES
- Yukon territory

SCIENCE
- Aurora borealis

GEOGRAPHICAL CONNECTION
The Yukon Territory The environment of the Yukon Territory is a harsh one, with severe winter conditions. These photos show some of the Yukon's geographical features, as well as gold miners who endured life there.

Side A, Frame 38700

PRINT AND MEDIA RESOURCES

UNIT TWO RESOURCE BOOK
Strategic Reading: Literature, p. 9

WRITING MINI–LESSONS
Transparencies, p. 38

ACCESS FOR STUDENTS ACQUIRING ENGLISH
Selection Summaries
Reading and Writing Support

FORMAL ASSESSMENT
Selection Test, pp. 33–34
 Test Generator

AUDIO LIBRARY
See Reference Card

LASERLINKS
Geographical Connection
Science Connection

INTERNET RESOURCES
McDougal Littell Literature Center at http://www.hmco.com/mcdougal/lit

THE LANGUAGE OF LITERATURE TEACHER'S EDITION **161**

SUMMARY

The poem tells about two gold miners traveling by dogsled through Alaska during a cold winter. One of them, Sam McGee, is from the warm state of Tennessee and finds it hard to stand the cold. He convinces the second man (the narrator) to promise to cremate him if he dies. Indeed, the next day Sam dies of the cold. To keep his promise, the narrator continues his journey with Sam's body in his sled. Finally, he comes across an abandoned ship, and he decides to use its furnace to burn Sam's body. He stuffs the body along with some coal into the furnace, lights a fire, and closes the door. Finally the narrator believes that the job must be finished. He decides to peek inside the furnace and is astonished to see Sam smiling at him. Sam tells him to close the door because this is the first time he has been warm since he left Tennessee. The narrator declares that this was the queerest thing he had ever seen in the Far North, where strange things commonly occur.

Thematic Link: *Finding a Special Place*
In this poem, a man must brave the elements and keep a promise to a dying man as he searches for a special place.

STRATEGIC READING FOR
Less-Proficient Readers

Ask students to think about an experience they shared with a friend that tested their friendship, such as an argument. Have students discuss the situation, what they did during the experience, and the outcome of the situation.

Set a Purpose Have students read to find out who Cap and Sam are and why they are in the Arctic.

UNIT TWO RESOURCE BOOK, p. 9, provides guidance in reading the selection.

The Cremation of Sam McGee
by Robert Service

There are strange things done in the midnight sun
   By the men who moil for gold;
The Arctic trails have their secret tales
   That would make your blood run cold;
5 *The Northern Lights have seen queer sights,*
   But the queerest they ever did see
Was that night on the marge of Lake Lebarge
   I cremated Sam McGee.

2 moil: work very hard.

7 marge: edge.

Dawn over the Yukon from *The Cremation of Sam McGee* by Robert Service and illustrated by Ted Harrison. Used by permission of Kids Can Press, Ltd., Toronto. Illustration Copyright © 1986 by Ted Harrison.

162

Mini-Lesson: Speaking, Listening, and Viewing

DIRECTIONS Paying attention to directions given orally is an important skill. Students need to listen for two kinds of details. First, they should listen for what must be done. Second, they should listen for the order in which steps must be done.

Application Have students pretend that they run an inn near the site where Cap cremated Sam McGee. The site is now a tourist attraction, and, as the innkeeper, they must give visitors directions to get there. Students should write a brief set of their own directions, noting various markers along the way to help the tourists. When completed, read a few of these directions aloud to the class. Ask students to pay attention to the directions to see if they can remember them—otherwise they will get lost and die in the frozen Arctic. Test students' listening abilities by asking them to sketch a map that details the directions.

162 THE LANGUAGE OF LITERATURE TEACHER'S EDITION

Now Sam McGee was from Tennessee,
   where the cotton blooms and blows.
Why he left his home in the South to roam
   'round the Pole, God only knows.
He was always cold, but the land of gold
   seemed to hold him like a spell;
Though he'd often say in his homely way
   that "he'd sooner live in hell."

On a Christmas Day we were mushing our way
   over the Dawson trail.
Talk of your cold! through the parka's fold
   it stabbed like a driven nail.
If our eyes we'd close, then the lashes froze
   till sometimes we couldn't see;
It wasn't much fun, but the only one
   to whimper was Sam McGee.

And that very night, as we lay packed tight
   in our robes beneath the snow,
And the dogs were fed, and the stars o'erhead
   were dancing heel and toe,
He turned to me, and "Cap," says he,
   "I'll cash in this trip, I guess;
And if I do, I'm asking that you
   won't refuse my last request."

Well, he seemed so low that I couldn't say no;
   then he says with a sort of moan:
"It's the cursèd cold, and it's got right hold
   till I'm chilled clean through to the bone.
Yet 'tain't being dead—it's my awful dread
   of the icy grave that pains;
So I want you to swear that, foul or fair,
   you'll cremate my last remains."

17 **mushing:** driving dogsleds.
18 **Dawson trail:** a route in the Yukon Territory of Canada.

THE CREMATION OF SAM MCGEE **163**

Mini-Lesson The Writer's Style

DETAILS APPEALING TO TOUCH Remind students that good writers appeal to a combination of senses to make their descriptions vivid. One of the senses writers appeal to is touch, to help the reader imagine what the object being described feels like. Refer students to the lines highlighted to show how Service uses imaginative sensory details to evoke the feelings of being cold.

Application Have students use details appealing to touch as they write a short description of traveling in a cold climate. Before students begin writing, encourage them to brainstorm a list of aspects of the cold dealing with the sense of touch. Then have them think of imaginative ways to describe these details.

Reteaching/Reinforcement
• Writing Handbook, anthology pp. 784–785
• *Writing Mini-Lessons* transparencies, p. 38

 **The Writer's Craft**
Appealing to the Senses, pp. 266–275

CUSTOMIZING FOR
Gifted and Talented Students

Ask students to discuss the poet's use of imagery and sensory details to contrast cold and heat throughout the poem. Have students identify examples and discuss the effects of this contrast.

Possible responses:

• Page 163—"He was always cold" and "'he'd sooner live in hell.'" Feeling as he does, Sam is totally out of place in an Arctic setting.

• Page 163—"my awful dread of the icy grave" and "cremate my last remains." Sam McGee hates the cold so much that he wishes to avoid it even in death.

• Page 164—"by the lone firelight" and "to the homeless snows"; the relative warmth of the fire is contrasted with the stark cold of the region.

• Page 166—"It was icy cold, but the hot sweat rolled down my cheeks…" The contrast between hot and cold reflects Cap's inner conflict about fulfilling his promise.

Literary Concept: RHYME

A Ask students to identify both internal and end rhyme in this stanza. *(internal: McGee/Tennessee, home/roam, cold/gold, say/way. end: blows/knows, spell/hell)*

CUSTOMIZING FOR
Students Acquiring English

1 Point out that the apostrophe before *'round* replaces the missing letter *a*. The word *around* is abbreviated to fit the rhythm of the poem. Ask students to find another example on page 163 of a word abbreviated for rhythm. *(o'erhead, line 27)*

2 Explain that the colloquial phrase *cash in* means "die."

Literary Concept: ALLITERATION

B Ask students to identify examples of alliteration in these lines. *(seemed so low that I couldn't say no; he says with a sort of moan; cursèd cold)*

Active Reading: CLARIFY

C Ask students what Sam's last request is and why he makes it. *(Sam wants to be cremated. He hates the cold so much that he refuses to be buried in it.)*

THE LANGUAGE OF LITERATURE TEACHER'S EDITION **163**

Active Reading: CLARIFY

D Ask students what has happened to Sam McGee. *(Possible response: He froze to death.)*

Literary Concept: RHYME

E Ask students what the poet does to sentence structure in order to create both end and internal rhyme. Have students point out examples from the stanza to back up their responses. *(Possible response: The poet uses short phrases and leaves out certain words. For example, in the lines "With a corpse half hid that I couldn't get rid, / because of a promise given," the poet does not say "rid of" because "of" wouldn't create internal rhyme with "hid.")*

STRATEGIC READING FOR
Less-Proficient Readers

F Ask students the following questions to help guide them through the poem:

- Who are the main characters of the poem? *(Sam McGee and Cap)* **Restating**
- Why are they in the Arctic? *(to search for gold)* **Noting Relevant Details**
- Why does Sam McGee not like the Arctic? *(He is from a warm place—Tennessee—and is not used to the cold.)* **Making Inferences**
- What does the speaker promise Sam McGee? *(He promises he will cremate Sam McGee when he dies.)* **Noting Relevant Details**

Set a Purpose Have students read to find out what happens after Sam McGee dies.

CUSTOMIZING FOR
Students Acquiring English

3 Make sure that students understand that *mad* here means "insane."

A pal's last need is a thing to heed,
   so I swore I would not fail;
And we started on at the streak of dawn;
   but God! he looked ghastly pale.
45 He crouched on the sleigh, and he raved all day
   of his home in Tennessee;
And before nightfall a corpse was all
   that was left of Sam McGee.

There wasn't a breath in that land of death,
50   and I hurried, horror-driven,
With a corpse half hid that I couldn't get rid,
   because of a promise given;
It was lashed to the sleigh, and it seemed to say:
   "You may tax your brawn and brains,
55 But you promised true, and it's up to you
   to cremate those last remains."

Now a promise made is a debt unpaid,
   and the trail has its own stern code.
In the days to come, though my lips were dumb,
60   in my heart how I cursed that load.
In the long, long night, by the lone firelight,
   while the huskies, round in a ring,
Howled out their woes to the homeless snows
   —O God! how I loathed the thing.

65 And every day that quiet clay
   seemed to heavy and heavier grow;
And on I went, though the dogs were spent
   and the grub was getting low;
The trail was bad, and I felt half mad,
70   but I swore I would not give in;
And I'd often sing to the hateful thing,
   and it hearkened with a grin.

Till I came to the marge of Lake Lebarge,
   and a derelict there lay;
75 It was jammed in the ice, but I saw in a trice
   it was called the "Alice May."
And I looked at it, and I thought a bit,
   and I looked at my frozen chum;
Then "Here," said I, with a sudden cry,
80   "is my cre-ma-tor-eum."

74 derelict: an abandoned ship.

164 UNIT TWO PART 1: FINDING A SPECIAL PLACE

Assessment Option

SELF-ASSESSMENT Students can assess how well they understand the selection by reversing the main premise of the poem. Write the following on the board:

Imagine that Sam McGee is a prospector from the Yukon exploring Tennessee. Instead of craving the warmth of Tennessee, Sam longs for the coldness of the North.

Have students describe how the poem would be different based on this new premise. Students can explain the differences in a brief informative speech or in a three- to four-paragraph comparison/contrast essay. Remind students to consider such elements as conflict and characterization as well as plot and theme.

To help students assess their own work, have them respond to the following questions:
- What did you enjoy about this activity?
- What did you find difficult about this activity?
- Did this activity help you to understand the selection in new ways? How?

Ice Fog over the Lake from *The Cremation of Sam McGee* by Robert Service and illustrated by Ted Harrison. Used by permission of Kids Can Press, Ltd., Toronto. Illustration Copyright © 1986 by Ted Harrison.

THE CREMATION OF SAM MCGEE 165

Critical Thinking: ANALYZE

G Ask students why they think the poet spells out "cre-ma-tor-eum" in this way. *(Possible response: By spelling the word this way, the poet emphasizes its pronunciation and makes the end rhyme "chum," "-eum" more apparent.)*

Literary Concept:
ALLITERATION

H Ask students to identify the alliteration in these four lines. *(Then I made a hike, for I didn't like to hear him sizzle so; / And the heavens scowled, and the huskies / howled, and the wind began to blow.)*

Linking to History

 **I** A dogsled is drawn by a team of dogs, usually over ice and snow. The breed of dog commonly used to pull the sled is the husky. Probably originating in Siberia and brought around 1000 A.D. to Arctic North America by Thule people (Eskimo), the dogsled is used primarily by Arctic peoples for long-distance transportation.

Active Reading: CLARIFY

J Ask students at what time of day the narrator again ventured near the makeshift crematorium. *(Possible response: It was night, because the narrator says that the stars were out in the sky.)*

CUSTOMIZING FOR
Multiple Learning Styles

K **Graphic Learners** Invite students to draw or sketch a picture that illustrates this stanza. Encourage students to incorporate into their illustration sensory details and imagery used by the poet.

STRATEGIC READING FOR
Less-Proficient Readers

L Check students' understanding by asking these questions.

- What happens after Sam dies? *(The narrator goes looking for wood to cremate Sam.)* **Summarizing**
- How does the narrator cremate Sam McGee? *(He takes wood from the cabin of the ship, lights a fire under the boiler, and puts Sam's body in.)* **Summarizing**
- What does the narrator find when he looks in the furnace? *(Sam sitting in the furnace with a smile on his face, looking cool and calm)* **Noting Relevant Details**

Some planks I tore from the cabin floor,
    and I lit the boiler fire;
Some coal I found that was lying around,
    and I heaped the fuel higher;
85 The flames just soared, and the furnace roared
    —such a blaze you seldom see,
And I burrowed a hole in the glowing coal,
    and I stuffed in Sam McGee.

H Then I made a hike, for I didn't like
90   to hear him sizzle so;
And the heavens scowled, and the huskies howled, **I**
    and the wind began to blow.
It was icy cold, but the hot sweat rolled
    down my cheeks, and I don't know why;
95 And the greasy smoke in an inky cloak
    went streaking down the sky.

I do not know how long in the snow
    I wrestled with grisly fear;
J But the stars came out and they danced about
100   ere again I ventured near;
I was sick with dread, but I bravely said:
    "I'll just take a peep inside.
I guess he's cooked, and it's time I looked"; . . .
    Then the door I opened wide.

105 And there sat Sam, looking cool and calm,
    in the heart of the furnace roar;
And he wore a smile you could see a mile,
K   and he said: "Please close that door.
It's fine in here, but I greatly fear
110   you'll let in the cold and storm—
Since I left Plumtree, down in Tennessee,
    it's the first time I've been warm."

There are strange things done in the midnight sun
    By the men who moil for gold;
115 *The Arctic trails have their secret tales*
    That would make your blood run cold;
The Northern Lights have seen queer sights,
    But the queerest they ever did see
Was that night on the marge of Lake Lebarge
L 120   *I cremated Sam McGee.*

100 **ere** (âr): before.

Mini-Lesson   **Literary Concepts**

REVIEWING ALLITERATION Remind students that the repeating of consonant sounds at the beginning of two or more words is called alliteration. Poets use alliteration to emphasize certain words. Alliteration also can add a musical or rhythmic beat to a work. Refer students to the stanzas marked on page 163 and above for specific examples of alliteration in the poem.

Application Have students write a short poem about eating ice cream that uses alliteration. Before students begin writing their alliterative poems, encourage them to brainstorm a list of images that create the feeling or sensation of eating ice cream. Have them close their eyes and visualize small details of this simple act. Then have students examine their list for connections where they can use alliteration.

The Boilers from *The Cremation of Sam McGee* by Robert Service and illustrated by Ted Harrison. Used by permission of Kids Can Press, Ltd., Toronto. Illustration Copyright © 1986 by Ted Harrison.

CUSTOMIZING FOR
Gifted and Talented Students
Have students relate a situation in which they were held to a difficult promise they had made and how they handled the experience. Ask them to discuss if they think there are situations in which promises can be broken. Encourage students to refer to the poem in their discussion.

COMPREHENSION CHECK
1. Why are Cap and Sam McGee in the Arctic? *(They are mining for gold.)*
2. Why does Cap agree to keep the promise? *("A Promise made is a debt unpaid"; It's the law of the trail to keep one's promises.)*
3. How does Cap carry out his promise? *(He sets Sam McGee's corpse on fire in the furnace of an abandoned ship.)*
4. What does Cap discover after he carries out his promise? *(Sam McGee comes back to life.)*

From Personal Response to Critical Analysis

1. Responses will vary.
2. Possible response: The narrator says that the trail has its own strict code that he must live by, so he feels a strong obligation to honor the promise.
3. Possible responses: Even though the narrator is scared, he is very loyal and trustworthy because he keeps his promise to Sam McGee. He shows determination and resolve in keeping his promise, even though he is tired and wants to leave the body behind.
4. Possible responses: The mood at the end of the poem is different from the mood at the beginning because readers know all the events that occurred in between; the mood at the end is the same. The poet uses the stanza to end the poem in the same, mysterious way in which he had started it.
5. Most students will say that people should try as much as possible to keep a promise, unless their safety or well-being is put in danger.

Another Pathway

Cooperative Learning Before the groups present their oral readings of the poem, encourage them to practice by rereading the poem. Each group should divide the poem so that all students in the group can take a turn to read. Make sure students practice tapping out the rhythm before reading the poem to the class.

Rubric

3 Full Accomplishment Reading shows appropriate division of tasks and an accurate presentation of the poem's rhythm.

2 Substantial Accomplishment Tasks are unevenly divided, and tapping patterns are somewhat irregular.

1 Little or Partial Accomplishment Some students participate much more than others. The tapping shows little or none of the poem's rhythm.

RESPONDING OPTIONS

FROM PERSONAL RESPONSE TO CRITICAL ANALYSIS

REFLECT
1. List the images in "The Cremation of Sam McGee" that stand out in your mind.

RETHINK
2. Why do you think the speaker of the poem feels such a strong obligation to honor Sam McGee's last request?
3. What words would you use to describe the narrator of this poem? Use evidence from the poem to support your answer.
4. The words in the first and last stanzas of the poem are the same. Do you think that these stanzas create the same mood or different moods? Explain your opinion.

RELATE
5. How far do you think someone should go to keep a promise?

Multimodal Learning
ANOTHER PATHWAY

Cooperative Learning
With a group of classmates, present an oral reading of "The Cremation of Sam McGee." Experiment with using found objects, like pencils and rulers, to tap out the rhythm of the poem as you read it. Perform the reading for the class and see how the sounds affect the mood of the poem.

LITERARY CONCEPTS

Rhyme that occurs at the ends of lines is called **end rhyme**. Rhyme within a line is called **internal rhyme**. The following lines show both internal and end rhyme:

> There are strange things done in the midnight sun
>   By the men who moil for gold;
> The Arctic trails have their secret tales
>   That would make your blood run cold;

Find another example of end rhyme and of internal rhyme in the poem.

CONCEPT REVIEW: Rhythm As you know, a poem's beat is called its rhythm. A poet will often structure the rhythm of a poem to make readers feel a certain mood, or emotion. What mood does the rhythm of "The Cremation of Sam McGee" create?

QUICKWRITES

1. Often, after a person dies, people send letters expressing their sadness and regret to that person's family members and friends. These letters are known as condolence letters. Compose a **condolence letter** that the poem's speaker might write to Sam McGee's family and friends in Tennessee.

2. Write your own humorous **narrative poem** about the climate that you find the least comfortable.

📁 **PORTFOLIO** Save your writing. You may want to use it later as a springboard to a piece for your portfolio.

168   UNIT TWO   PART 1: FINDING A SPECIAL PLACE

Literary Concepts

Examples of rhymes will vary. If necessary, review the marked stanzas on pages 163–164. Students may say that the poem's rhythm evokes a mood of eerie suspense.

Divide students into small groups and have each group cooperatively write a short narrative poem relating a fantastic tale of travel. The poem should use both end and internal rhyme. When the poems are finished, have one volunteer from each group read its poem aloud. Ask students in the audience to point out examples of end and internal rhyme in the poems and to discuss the effect of each poem's rhythm.

QuickWrites

1. Before students begin writing, encourage them to think about what the narrator might want to say about Sam in the letter. Make sure students write in the style of a condolence letter and that they stress the narrator's sadness over Sam's death.

2. Before students begin, encourage them to brainstorm a list of things about the climate they find the least comfortable. Encourage students to use sensory details and imagery that communicate their experiences in the particular climate.

 The Writer's Craft

Personal Writing, pp. 28–39
Writing a Poem, pp. 84–88

Multimodal Learning
ALTERNATIVE ACTIVITIES

1. Reread the poem and jot down details and descriptions that create vivid pictures in your mind. Then draw or paint a **scene** from the poem.
2. Research the Klondike gold rush of the late 1800s. Who were the miners who poured into the Yukon in hopes of striking it rich? Where did they come from? What tools did they use? Prepare an **oral report** for your class. Illustrate your report with pictures and maps.

LITERARY LINKS
Compare this poem with the narrative poem "The Walrus and the Carpenter" (page 104). List at least three ways in which the poems are alike.

ACROSS THE CURRICULUM
 Science Research information about the aurora borealis, or northern lights. Where do most auroras occur? How does solar energy contribute to their formation? Present your findings in a chart that illustrates how auroras come about.

Usually green in color, an aurora can also streak the sky in red or purple.

ROBERT SERVICE

1874–1958

According to Robert Service, his classic narrative poem was "the result of an accident." He explained that he was at a party where a miner told a far-fetched story about a man who cremated his friend. Service left the party and immediately started writing the poem in his mind. When he woke up the next day, he wrote it all down from memory, and it quickly became a success. In fact, many people who have studied this poem have enjoyed it so much that they have memorized stanzas or even the entire poem.

Sam McGee was the name of a real person, a customer at the Bank of Commerce where Service worked. The *Alice May* was based on a real boat (the *Olive May*) abandoned on Lake Laberge in the Yukon.

Service was born in England, grew up in Scotland, and moved to the Yukon when he was in his 20s. He worked as a bank teller but wrote poems about the miners and the lumberjacks of Canada. When he became a popular writer, he quit his job at the bank and wrote full-time. In addition to "The Cremation of Sam McGee," Service wrote another famous narrative poem, "The Shooting of Dan McGrew."

When Service was in his 30s, he moved to Europe and continued to write poems and novels. He also served as an ambulance driver during World War I. He lived for many years far from the Yukon, in Paris, where he died in 1958.

OTHER WORKS *The Spell of the Yukon, The Trail of '98* Extended Reading

• SCIENCE CONNECTION

THE CREMATION OF SAM MCGEE 169

Alternative Activities
1. Encourage students to select a passage from the poem that uses sensory details and vivid imagery. Have students create a list of details and images from the passage to be included in their illustrations. Encourage students to use a variety of media, such as crayons, paint, markers, and pen and ink.
2. Students can complete the activity cooperatively. Divide students into small groups to carry out research of the Klondike gold rush. A facilitator can oversee the research and make sure all students participate. Another student can be the group's recorder, and another can prepare the research information for the oral report. Finally, one student should present the group's findings to the class.

Literary Links
Possible responses: Both poems have rhyme, rhythm, and stanzas. Both poems are humorous and tell a fantastic tale.

Across the Curriculum
Science *Cooperative Learning* Divide students into small groups to carry out research on the aurora borealis. In addition to the questions mentioned, students might research myths associated with the aurora borealis, when and how scientists began to study it, and any other information they feel is important to understanding the northern lights.

ADDITIONAL SUGGESTION
 **Social Studies** *Explore the Yukon* Remind students that the poem is set in the Yukon Territory in Canada. Have students research the history of this area, including its original inhabitants and their cultures. Students can also research the contemporary inhabitants of the area and how their cultures have changed over time.

ROBERT SERVICE
Robert Service thought up this poem on a night when the moon was bright. The brightness of the moon inspired the first line of the poem. From that point on, Service composed line after line in his mind, though he did not write them down until the next morning. Although the man who told Service the story of the cremated miner went into bankruptcy, the poem based on the story brought Service great success and fame.

SCIENCE CONNECTION
The Northern Lights Bands or sheets of light—called the aurora borealis, or northern lights—are sometimes visible in the night skies of the world's northern regions. This film shows the phenomenon and explains its causes.

Side A, Frame 6724

THE LANGUAGE OF LITERATURE **Teacher's Edition** 169

OVERVIEW

Objectives

- To understand and appreciate an autobiographical excerpt about a Chinese-American boy's experiences growing up
- To examine a memoir
- To express understanding of the selection through a choice of writing forms, including a prediction and an imaginary dialogue
- To extend understanding of the selection through a variety of multimodal and cross-curricular activities

Skills

READING SKILLS/ STRATEGIES
- Distinguishing fact and opinion

LITERARY CONCEPTS
- Memoir
- Theme

THE WRITER'S STYLE
- Voice

GRAMMAR
- Pronouns and antecedents

SPELLING
- Compound words

SPEAKING, LISTENING, AND VIEWING
- Group discussion
- Oral presentation

Cross-Curricular Connections

SCIENCE
- Organ transplants

SOCIAL STUDIES
- Chinese dialects
- Chinatown

HISTORY
- Fair Housing Laws

HISTORICAL CONNECTION
Historical Chinatowns Some Chinese immigrants became merchants after their arrival in the United States. These vintage historical images will give students a glimpse into the life of such immigrants during the first half of the 20th century.

Side A, Frame 38707

CULTURAL CONNECTION
Memories of China Chinatowns are rich in expressions of Chinese culture and rituals. These contemporary images can prompt a discussion of how culture influenced the creation of this memoir.

Side A, Frame 38713

PREVIEWING

NONFICTION

Chinatown from The Lost Garden
Laurence Yep

PERSONAL CONNECTION *Activating Prior Knowledge*

In the selection you are about to read, a boy describes the culture and community in which he grew up. What are the characteristics of your neighborhood or community? Think about how you would describe your community to a stranger. Are the boundaries limited to an apartment building, to one block, to several blocks, or to a subdivision? What are your connections to the different parts of your neighborhood? Draw a simple map of your community, like the one shown here. Label the parts of the community that you are connected to, and indicate how you are connected to them. As you read, compare your community to the one described by Laurence Yep. *Setting a Purpose*

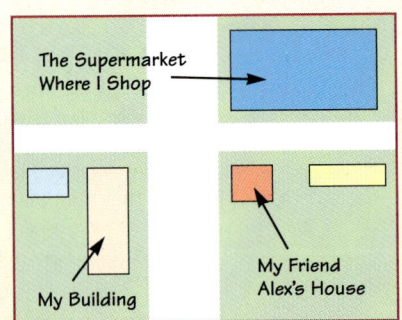

Building Background

HISTORICAL CONNECTION

In the 1800s the Chinese population in California rose dramatically. The gold rush of 1848 drew thousands of Chinese immigrants to San Francisco. In the 1860s, many Chinese laborers came to work for the Central Pacific Railroad Company. As the Chinese population grew, many people began to view the new Chinese Americans as an economic burden. Laws were passed restricting Chinese immigration. Other laws isolated Chinese Americans in communities called Chinatowns.

Not until the 1960s were immigration laws changed to end discrimination based on race. Fair housing laws were passed that allowed the Chinese Americans to live where they wished.

WRITING CONNECTION

Everyone is someone's son or daughter. Who else are you? A Boy Scout or Girl Scout? A student at a particular school? A regular basketball player at a local park? A member of a youth group at a church, a synagogue, or a temple? In your notebook, list the different roles you play in your community. Use the map you drew for the Personal Connection to get started. Then, to record your roles, create a diagram like the one shown. In your notebook, explain which role you find most challenging.

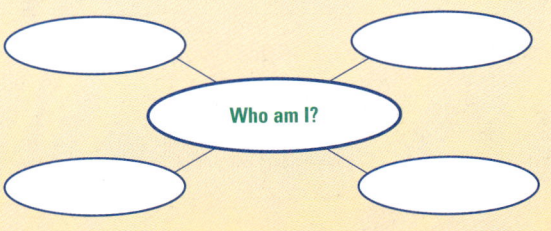

LASERLINKS
- CULTURAL CONNECTION
- HISTORICAL CONNECTION

170 UNIT TWO PART 1: FINDING A SPECIAL PLACE

PRINT AND MEDIA RESOURCES

UNIT TWO RESOURCE BOOK
Strategic Reading: Literature, p. 13
Reading SkillBuilder, p. 14
Spelling SkillBuilder, p. 15

GRAMMAR MINI-LESSONS
Transparencies, pp. 10–11
Copymasters, pp. 15–16

WRITING MINI-LESSONS
Transparencies, p. 36

ACCESS FOR STUDENTS ACQUIRING ENGLISH
Selection Summaries
Reading and Writing Support

FORMAL ASSESSMENT
Selection Test, pp. 35–36
 Test Generator

 **AUDIO LIBRARY**
See Reference Card

LASERLINKS
Historical Connection
Cultural Connection
Author Background

INTERNET RESOURCES
McDougal Littell Literature Center at http://www.hmco.com/mcdougal/lit

170 THE LANGUAGE OF LITERATURE TEACHER'S EDITION

Chinatown

from *The Lost Garden*

by Laurence Yep

Celebration, Chinatown (1940), Dong Kingman.
Private collection.

CHINATOWN **171**

SUMMARY

In this autobiographical selection, Laurence Yep tells of his boyhood memories of San Francisco's Chinatown. Although the young Yep lives outside Chinatown, he spends much of his time exploring its streets. Because of unfair housing laws, most Asian Americans are forced to live in Chinatown, separated from the "rich white world" that lies just beyond its boundaries. Yep has a glimpse of that world when he accompanies a friend on his Nob Hill paper route. Among Yep's classmates at a Catholic school in Chinatown is a social misfit named Paul, who claims that his damaged eyes has been replaced with a donated eye from a rich white person. Across the street from the school is the Chinese Playground, where the unathletic Yep performs disastrously in school sports. Yep sometimes feels like an outsider among his friends because he does not speak Chinese and has different ways of playing schoolyard games. All this makes him wonder about his true identity and about the contradictions in his life.

Thematic Link: *Finding a Special Place*
An Asian-American author recounts a past full of contradiction and confusion as he attempts to find his place in the world.

Art Note

***Celebration, Chinatown* by Dong Kingman** Dong Kingman (1911–) is a Chinese-American watercolor artist and educator. His paintings and murals are in numerous collections in the United States and Hong Kong. His art appeared in the movie *Flower Drum Song*.

Reading the Art Describe the setting of this art. What details give you clues about its setting? Do you think the scene depicts the past, present, or future? How do you know?

WORDS TO KNOW

stereotype (stĕr′ē-ə-tīp′) *n.* a mental picture or idea about a type of person held in common opinion or judgment by others (p. 172)

CUSTOMIZING FOR
Students Acquiring English

- Use **ACCESS FOR STUDENTS ACQUIRING ENGLISH,** *Reading and Writing Support.*

- This story is about a community of people of Chinese ancestry living in San Francisco. Invite students who have experiences of being inside or outside of an ethnic community to compare and contrast their stories with the narrator's.

THE LANGUAGE OF LITERATURE TEACHER'S EDITION **171**

STRATEGIC READING FOR
Less-Proficient Readers

Ask students to write a brief account of a situation in which they thought they did not fit in or were out of place.

Set a Purpose Have students read to find out about the community Yep grew up in.

Use **UNIT TWO RESOURCE BOOK**, pp. 13–14, for guidance in reading the selection.

Active Reading: PREDICT

A Ask students to predict what the rest of the selection will be about. Encourage students to think about what the author means by "the pieces of the puzzle" if they need help in determining the context of their predictions. *(Students should predict that the selection will be about the author's attempt to explore Chinatown and search his cultural heritage for answers.)*

CUSTOMIZING FOR
Multiple Learning Styles

B **Linguistic Learners** Point out to students that the author describes plant life outside Chinatown as being a shade of green that is "alive." Have students create a list of sensory details about things that are this shade of green.

Literary Concept: THEME

C Ask students to discuss what theme or message the author is presenting in his description of Chinatown and its surrounding area. *(Possible response: The author talks about the boundary between Chinatown and the wealthier, white neighborhoods that surround it. This brings up the theme of being different and the effects of people drawing lines to separate themselves.)*

Critical Thinking: ANALYZE

D Ask students why the author refers to the Stockton tunnel as "the symbolic end to Chinatown." *(Possible response: The tunnel through the hill both links and separates two different, self-contained areas: Chinatown and the wealthy, white neighborhood downtown. Even though the tunnel links these two areas, they are very different; so the tunnel symbolically separates the two places.)*

This selection is a chapter from Laurence Yep's memoir The Lost Garden. *Yep grew up as a Chinese American in an African-American neighborhood of San Francisco. He attended school in Chinatown, although he did not speak or understand Chinese. His lack of knowledge of Chinese, among other things, made him an outsider in Chinatown—sometimes even among his friends.*

A If Uncle Francis and other members of our family left Chinatown to explore America, my experience was the reverse because I was always going into Chinatown to explore the streets and perhaps find the key to the pieces of the puzzle. But the search only seemed to increase the number of pieces.

When I was a boy, Chinatown was much more like a small town than it is now. It was small not only in terms of population but in physical area as well. Its boundaries were pretty well set by Pacific Avenue on the north next to the Italian neighborhood of North Beach, Kearny Street on the east, Sacramento Street on the south, and Stockton Street on the west—an area only of a few city blocks.

There is a stereotype that the Chinese lived in Chinatown because they wanted to. The fact was that before the fair housing laws[1] they often had no choice.

B For years there was a little cottage on an ivy-covered hill in the southwest corner of Chinatown just above the Stockton tunnel. There was—and still is—very little plant life in Chinatown, so the only color green I saw was the paint on my school. The kind of green that is alive—lawns, bushes, and trees—was something I had to leave Chinatown to see, except for that ivy-covered slope. On windy days, the ivy itself would stir and move like a living sea; and overlooking the ivy was a cottage that was charm itself. However, as much as I admired the house—on occasion I was disloyal enough to the Pearl Apartments to want to live in it—I knew it wasn't for us. My Auntie Mary had once tried to rent it and had been refused because she was Chinese.

Out of some forty-five or so students in my class, I was one of the few who lived outside of Chinatown. Now, thanks to the fair housing laws that were passed in the 1960s, almost none of my former classmates live there; and Chinatown itself has spilled out of its traditional boundaries. **C**

There is a stereotype that the Chinese lived in Chinatown because they wanted to.

When I was a boy, though, we could see the results of white money and power on three sides of us. To the east we could stare up at the high-rise office buildings of the business district; and to the west, up the steep streets, were the fancy hotels of Nob Hill.[2] Southward lay downtown and the fancy department stores.

Grant Avenue led directly to downtown; but for years I always thought of the Stockton tunnel as the symbolic end to Chinatown. When it had been cut right through a hill, my **D**

---

1. **fair housing laws:** the civil rights acts of 1964 and 1968, which outlawed racial discrimination in the sale and rental of property, private as well as public.
2. **Nob Hill:** a wealthy neighborhood in northeastern San Francisco. It adjoins Chinatown and is noted for its large luxury hotels, such as the Fairmont and the Mark Hopkins.

WORDS TO KNOW
stereotype (stĕr′ē-ə-tīp′) *n.* a fixed idea, especially an idea about how a person should look or act

172

Mini-Lesson The Writer's Style

VOICE Ask students if, when they call a friend on the phone, they announce who's calling. Most students will say no; friends recognize the sound of each other's voice as well as the way each puts words together. Writers are recognizable in a similar way. Every writer has a special way of choosing words and putting them together. It's called a writing voice.

Application Refer students to the highlighted passage above. Ask them to rewrite this passage using their own writing voice. When students are done with the activity, invite volunteers to read their rewritten passages to the class. Encourage students to discuss the differences among the various rewritten passages and the original. Ask students to try to identify those elements that make each writer's voice unique. For example, have them look at how different writers describe Chinatown's plant life.

Reteaching/Reinforcement
• Writing Handbook, anthology pp. 788–789
• *Writing Mini-Lessons* transparencies, p. 36

Personal Voice, pp. 276–277

---

172 THE LANGUAGE OF LITERATURE TEACHER'S EDITION

Detail. Young Chinese Americans enjoy a view of San Francisco Bay and the Bay Bridge (upper right).
Courtesy California Historical Society, San Francisco.

CHINATOWN 173

CUSTOMIZING FOR
Gifted and Talented Students

As students read the selection, ask them to discuss how the author sees Chinatown as different from the surrounding white community and how he sees himself as different from the Chinese community to which he looks for identification. Ask students to think about where this puts the author in terms of these different communities. *(Possible responses: The surrounding neighborhoods are wealthier; mostly white people live there. There are fancy hotels with plush carpets and ornate chandeliers, big office buildings, fancy department stores, and green trees, plants, and bushes. In Chinatown, there are mostly working-class Chinese families living in projects or tenement buildings. Yep also mentions that there is very little green plant life in Chinatown. The author also feels separated from the Chinese community, because he doesn't speak Chinese and doesn't know how to play some of the games that the other children play. He also is not good at sports, unlike the rest of his family. This seems to place the author between the two communities. He doesn't fully fit into either one, so he ends up feeling lost somewhere in the middle.)*

Multicultural Perspectives

GAMES PEOPLE PLAY Dominoes is the name of various games played with small rectangular tiles (also called dominoes) made of wood, ivory, bone, or plastic. The face of each tile is divided in half, and each half either is marked with dots (called pips) or is blank. Dominoes are thought to have been brought from China to Italy in the 14th century.

Mancala, or wari, is a strategic game that originated in ancient Egypt and now is played throughout Africa. Players have a number of pebbles that are distributed in a series of pockets around the playing board. At each move, the player must make estimates requiring numerical skill and good judgment in order to go "out" before an opponent does.

THE LANGUAGE OF LITERATURE **TEACHER'S EDITION** 173

CUSTOMIZING FOR
Students Acquiring English

1 Make sure that students know what a paper route is and that it is a typical early morning or after-school job for many young people in the United States.

2 Point out that the word *accidentally* is in quotation marks because the narrator feels that it isn't truthful.

Literary Concept: MEMOIR

E Have students identify the clues in the sentence that confirm that this is an account of Yep's own experiences. *(He says that he remembers the nun asking students to act as Paul's special friends.)*

STRATEGIC READING FOR
Less-Proficient Readers

F Make sure students understand Yep's descriptions of Chinatown and the surrounding neighborhoods by asking the following questions:

- Who tried to rent the cottage on the hill, and why was she not allowed to? *(Yep's Aunt Mary tried to rent the cottage but was refused because she was Chinese.)* **Noting Relevant Details**

- Why are the concrete hallways in the back of the hotel on Nob Hill as bleak as the ones in the Chinatown housing projects? *(Only the hotel workers use the area in the back. Guests wouldn't normally be in this area, so it doesn't have to look as nice as the rest of the hotel.)* **Making Inferences**

Set a Purpose As students read, have them pay attention to Yep's experiences with physical education while in school.

Critical Thinking: ANALYZE

G Ask students why Paul would announce to everyone that the world looked the same through either of his eyes. *(Possible response: Many people feel that a person of a different race is different. Paul's announcement shows that your eyes work the same way no matter what race you are.)*

---

father and his young friends had held foot races through it after midnight, hooting and hollering so that the echoes seemed to be the cheers of a huge crowd. The rich white world began just on the other side of the tunnel.

There were also invisible barriers that separated the wealthy whites from the Chinese who cleaned their apartments or waited on their tables. The Chinese could see and even touch the good life; but they could not join in.

The world looked just the same whether it was a Chinese eye or an American one.

One of my classmates, Harold, had a paper route on Nob Hill. I still find it hard to believe that, up hills that angled some forty degrees or so, he carried a kind of poncho loaded with papers in front and back. But he did that every afternoon. Once I went along with him; and I followed him into one of the fanciest hotels on Nob Hill, past the elaborately uniformed doorman, over the plush carpets, under the ornate chandeliers, and around in back, down concrete hallways as bleak as the ones in the Chinatown housing projects that were painted a cheap, gaudy yellow—a shade which my friend referred to as "landlord yellow." Harold would deliver the afternoon newspapers to the laundrymen and other workers. And with my friend that day, I wandered all around the roots of that palatial dream of wealth.

When the poncho was flat, my friend and I returned to his tenement apartment where there was only one toilet to a floor; and the toilet lacked both a door and toilet paper. When you went, you brought in your own toilet paper. Nothing could be done about the door except changing your attitude about privacy.

Many of my schoolmates lived in the Chinatown projects, and I wasn't sure if life was any better in them than life in the projects near our store. Another newspaper carrier named Paul lived there. As the oldest boy, Paul was expected to look after his younger brothers and sisters while his parents worked—a common practice among many Chinese families. However, as a result, Paul had failed to develop many social skills let alone improve his English. I remember the nun sending him out on an errand and then asking the rest of the class to act as his special friend—which was easy for her to say because she was an adult.

As far as I knew, he hung around with his own group in the projects rather than with anyone from school. His group, though, must have been pretty rough because one of them threw a knife that "accidentally" hit Paul in the eye. Fortunately, there was a charity that arranged an operation; and he was given a new eye from someone who had recently died.

We never knew the identity of the donor, but Paul amused himself by claiming it was a rich white. First, he would clap a hand over his new eye and roll his remaining Chinese eye around. Then he would put his hand over his old one and gaze around elaborately with his new American eye. And then he would announce to us that the world looked just the same whether it was a Chinese eye or an American eye.

Paul had shot up early and was a giant compared to the rest of us. When he ran, he looked like an ostrich with arms. He would kick out his legs explosively while his arms flailed the air, so it was hard not to laugh; but we didn't because he was also immensely strong.

174 UNIT TWO PART 1: FINDING A SPECIAL PLACE

Mini-Lesson Literary Concepts

REVIEWING THEME Remind students that a theme is the message about life or human nature that the writer presents to the reader. Some themes are stated directly. Most often, however, the reader must figure out a theme. Any lessons learned by the main character can be clues to the theme.

Application Have students work in groups of four or five to determine the theme of this selection. Ask groups to review the selection together and jot down any specific passages or examples that help reveal the theme. For example, ask students why Yep compares and contrasts Chinatown and Nob Hill in such detail. When groups have completed the activity, they can present their ideas to the class. One student in each group should act as facilitator, another as recorder, and another as presenter.

The playground at St. Mary's was only a concrete basketball court below. Up above, there was a kind of patio between the convent and the school where the younger children could play. However, the nuns were so worried about our knocking one another down that they forbade us to run during recess. About the only thing we could play under those conditions was a kind of slow-motion tag.

At noon, we could go across the street to the Chinese Playground—the playground where my father had once been the director. In those days, it consisted of levels. The first level near the alley that became known as Hang Ah Alley was a volleyball and a tennis court. Down the steps was the next level with a sandbox (which was usually full of fleas), a small director's building, a Ping-Pong table, an area covered by tan bark that housed a slide, a set of bars, and a set of swings and other simple equipment. The level next to the Chinese Baptist church was the basketball court. We had Physical Education once a week there. The playground director taught the boys, and I suppose the nun handled the girls. Sometimes it was calisthenics; other times it was baseball played with a tennis ball on the tennis court. There was no pitcher. Rather, the "batter" threw up the ball and hit it with his fist. Because of his size and added arm strength from his own paper route, Paul could hit a home run almost every time, sending the tennis ball flying over the high wire mesh fence.

However, my experience was frequently the reverse. Because the present director knew that my father had once been the director of the playground, he was always urging me on to one disaster after another.

The worst happened when he wasn't present, though. In third grade, we had a very sweet nun, Sister Bridget, who used to play kickball with us. Kickball was like baseball except that the pitcher bowled a ball the size of a basketball over the ground and the "batter" kicked it. One time someone kicked a ball so that it rolled foul. Retrieving it, I threw it to sister; but as fate would have it, she had turned her head right at that moment to look at something else. I wound up hitting her in the head; and though there was no physical harm, I broke her glasses. Even though my parents paid for replacements, the rest of my class treated me as if I were taboo for striking a nun. I learned what it meant to be shunned and to be invisible.

The only sport that I was remotely good at was football.

The experience also reinforced my belief that I was terrible at sports. Despite all the practice and coaching from my father, I was hopeless when it came to catching any ball in any shape or size. Nor could I dribble a basketball, even though my father sometimes kept me practicing in the little courtyard until it was almost too dark to see.

The only sport that I was remotely good at was football. Having worked and lifted crates in the store made me fairly strong. As a result, I was a good lineman at blocking and rushing—like my hero, Leo Nomellini. However, I was still hopeless at catching a pass. I still remember one game where I dropped three touchdown passes in a row. I was so bad that our opponents stopped covering me. Our quarterback, unable to resist a wide-open target, persisted in throwing to me—and I dropped yet a fourth pass that could have been a touchdown.

CHINATOWN **175**

Active Reading: CONNECT

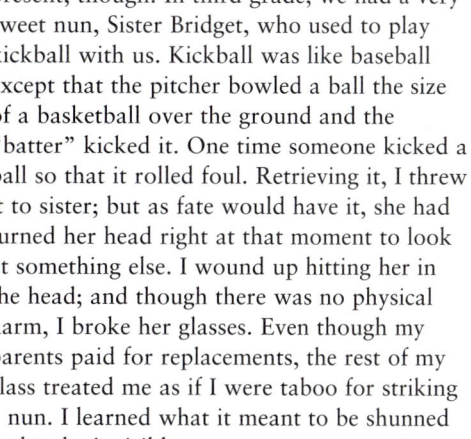 Ask students to think about Yep's experience of hitting the nun with the ball. Then ask if they have ever accidentally done something harmful. Have students recall how they felt about themselves after the experience.

Literary Concept: MEMOIR

 Have students discuss how Yep's account of the accident might have been different if an observer had been telling the story. (*An observer probably would not have known Yep's emotions and so would not have described his feeling shunned and invisible after the experience.*)

CUSTOMIZING FOR
Students Acquiring English

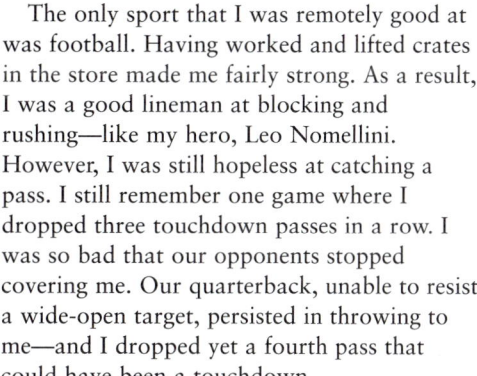 Make sure that students know that *taboo* means "forbidden." After Yep accidentally hit the nun, other children didn't want to be around him, as if he were an outcast.

Critical Thinking: HYPOTHESIZING

 Have students speculate why else Yep felt disgraceful for not excelling at sports, besides the fact that everyone in his family was athletic. (*Possible response: Boys are expected to be good athletes and often feel pressure to excel at sports.*)

Mini-Lesson — Reading Skills/Strategies

DISTINGUISHING FACT AND OPINION
Use the first highlighted example to illustrate that a fact is a statement that can be proved. In contrast, an opinion is a statement that expresses a person's feelings or beliefs, such as in the second highlighted example. Opinions cannot be proved.

Application Explain to students that a memoir often contains both facts and opinions because the author relates factual events in the past but also expresses his or her feelings about these events. Have students make a chart with the headings "Facts" and "Opinions." Instruct students to list five statements from the selection that are facts and five that are opinions. Make sure students are able to support their choices.

Reteaching/Reinforcement
• *Unit Two Resource Book*, p. 14

THE LANGUAGE OF LITERATURE **TEACHER'S EDITION** **175**

STRATEGIC READING FOR
Less-Proficient Readers

K Ask students to summarize the "disasters" Yep experienced during physical-education classes while growing up. *(Once he threw a ball and hit Sister Bridget in the head. He wasn't good at catching balls and could not dribble a basketball. He was a good lineman in football but could not catch any passes. During one football game, he even dropped four touchdown passes.)*
Summarizing

Set a Purpose As students read, have them note the ways Yep felt like an outsider growing up in the Chinese community.

Linking to Social Studies

 **L** The Chinese language consists of more than 50 dialects, but 7 predominate: Mandarin, Wu, Min, Kejia, Yue, Gan (or Kan), and Xiang (or Hsiang). Of these 7 dialects, by far the most common is Mandarin, spoken by at least 63 percent of China's population.

Literary Concept: THEME

M Ask students to discuss why the incidents Yep describes make him feel separated from Harold. *(Although the boys are friends, Yep does not have as strong a tie to his Chinese heritage as Harold does.)*

Detail. Chinese-American children reading with their teacher. Courtesy California Historical Society, San Francisco.

The fact that my whole family was athletic only added to my disgrace. My father had played both basketball and football. My mother had also played basketball as well as being a track star, winning gold medals at the Chinese Olympics—a track event held for Chinese Americans. My brother was also excellent at basketball as well as bowling. Even worse, my father had coached championship teams when he had been a director at Chinese Playground—the very site of most of my failures. I often felt as if I were a major disappointment to my family.

K

176 UNIT TWO PART 1: FINDING A SPECIAL PLACE

Moreover, my lack of Chinese made me an outsider in Chinatown—sometimes even among my friends. Since it was a Catholic school taught by nuns, my friends would always tell dirty jokes in Chinese so the nuns wouldn't understand. However, neither did I, so I missed out on a good deal of humor when I was a boy. What Chinese I did pick up was the Chinese that got spoken in the playground—mostly insults and vulgar names.

L

There were times even with a good friend like Harold when I felt different. Though Harold and I would go see American war movies, he could also open up a closet and show me the exotic Chinese weapons his father, a gardener, would fashion in his spare time, and I could sense a gulf between my experience and that of Harold. It was as if we belonged to two different worlds.

M

Even my friends' games and entertainments in Chinatown could sometimes take their own different spin. They weren't quite like the games I saw American boys playing on television or read about in Homer Price. Handball was played with the all-purpose tennis ball against a brick wall in the courtyard.

Nor do I remember anyone ever drawing a circle with chalk and shooting marbles in the American way. Instead, someone would set up marbles on one side of the basketball court at

---

Mini-Lesson Grammar

PRONOUNS AND ANTECEDENTS
Write the sentences to the left on the chalkboard and invite a volunteer to read both. Explain that the words *his, he,* and *it* are pronouns. Pronouns take their meaning from the words they replace. Now explain that the word a pronoun stands for is the antecedent of the pronoun. In the examples, *Harold* is the antecedent of the pronouns *his* and *he. Book* is the antecedent of *it.* Usually a pronoun appears after its antecedent in a sentence. However, sometimes a pronoun and its antecedent may appear in separate sentences.

Application Refer students to the highlighted passage above and ask them to list as many pronouns and their antecedents as possible. Then read aloud the paragraph, pausing after each sentence to note any pronouns and antecedents. After completing the paragraph, discuss with students which pronouns or antecedents were difficult to identify and why.

Reteaching/Reinforcement
- Grammar Handbook, anthology pp. 826–828
- *Grammar Mini-Lessons* copymasters, pp. 15–16; transparencies, pp. 10–11

Pronouns and Antecedents, pp. 436–437

Harold made Harold's own flip book so Harold could play with the book.

Harold made his own flip book so he could play with it.

176 THE LANGUAGE OF LITERATURE TEACHER'S EDITION

St. Mary's and invite the others to try to hit them. If they did, they got the marbles. If they didn't, the boy would quickly snatch up their shooters. The ideal spot, of course, was where irregularities in the paving created bumps or dips to protect the owner's marbles. At times, one edge of the courtyard would resemble a bazaar with different boys trying to entice shooters to try their particular setup with various shouted jingles.

Other times, they would set up baseball or football cards. Trading cards weren't meant to be collector's items but were used like marbles. In the case of cards, the shooter would send a card flying with a flick of the wrist. Mint cards[3] did not always fly the truest; and certain cards with the right bends and folds became deadly treasures.

But that sense of being different became sharpest the time I was asked to sing. Our school had a quartet that they sent around to build goodwill. The two girls and two boys dressed up in outfits that were meant to be Chinese: the girls in colored silk pajamas and headdresses with pom-poms, the boys in robes with black vests and caps topped by red knobs.

How could I pretend to be somebody else when I didn't even know who I was?

However, one day in December, one of the boys took sick, so the nuns chose me to take his place. Musical ability was not a consideration; the fit of the costume was the important thing. We were brought to sing before a group of elderly people. I can remember following a cowboy with an accordion and a cowgirl with a short, spangled skirt who sang Christmas carols with a country twang.

Then we were ushered out on the small stage and I could look out at the sea of elderly faces. I think they were quite charmed with the costumed Chinese children. Opening their mouths, the others began to sing in Chinese. Now during all this, no one had bothered to find out if I could sing, let alone sing in Chinese. I recognized the tune as "Silent Night" but the words were all in Chinese. I tried to fake it, but I was always one note and one pretend-syllable behind the others. Then they swung into "It Came Upon a Midnight Clear." This time they sang in English, so I tried to sing along and ranged all over the musical scale except the notes I was supposed to be singing. Finally, one of the girls elbowed me in the ribs and from the side of her mouth, she whispered fiercely, "Just mouth the words."

Up until then I had enjoyed putting on costumes and even had a variety of hats, including cowboy and Robin Hood outfits as well as a French Foreign Legion hat and a Roman helmet; but the experience cured me of wanting to dress up and be something else. How could I pretend to be somebody else when I didn't even know who I was?

In trying to find solutions, I had created more pieces to the puzzle: the athlete's son who was not an athlete, the boy who got "A's" in Chinese school without learning Chinese, the boy who could sing neither in key nor in Chinese with everyone else. ❖

---

3. **mint cards:** freshly unwrapped trading cards, not yet damaged by handling.

CHINATOWN 177

Literary Concept: THEME

N Have students discuss what they think Yep means when he asks this question. (Yep feels he doesn't fit into any community. He doesn't know where he fits in, so he doesn't really know who he is.)

CUSTOMIZING FOR
Students Acquiring English

4 If your school does not use a letter grading system, make sure that students understand that an A is the highest possible grade.

STRATEGIC READING FOR
Less-Proficient Readers

O Ask students how the games the other children played made Yep feel. (The toys and objects that the children played with were familiar to Yep, but they played with them differently. This made Yep feel like an outsider.) **Making Generalizations**

CUSTOMIZING FOR
Gifted and Talented Students

Have students discuss why people often are uncomfortable being different. Ask students to think about their own experiences of being different and relate them to Yep's.

COMPREHENSION CHECK

1. According to Yep, what stereotype did people have about the Chinese? (They lived in Chinatown because they wanted to, not because they were forced to.)
2. How did Yep feel about his athletic abilities as a child? (He was ashamed because he did not excel at sports.)
3. Why was it difficult for Yep to perform in the school quartet? (He couldn't carry a tune and wasn't able to sing in Chinese.)
4. Does Yep feel that while growing up he was able to find the key to the pieces of the puzzle he mentions at the beginning? (No, he feels that he created more pieces to the puzzle in the end.)

Mini-Lesson Spelling

COMPOUND WORDS Explain to students that compound words are formed by joining two words together.

stereo + type = stereotype
down + town = downtown
land + lord = landlord
play + ground = playground
basket + ball = basketball

Application Ask students to identify at least five more compound words from the selection. Have students write each word and divide it into its smaller words. As an additional activity, have students define each word and then define the compound word in order to see how the meanings of both words are used to form a new word. Ask students to look for more compound words in their own writing and in things that they read and to write them in their personal word lists.

Reteaching/Reinforcement
• *Unit Two Resource Book,* p. 15

THE LANGUAGE OF LITERATURE TEACHER'S EDITION 177

From Personal Response to Critical Analysis

1. Responses will vary.
2. Most students will say that the puzzle Yep is trying to solve has to do with finding out who he is and where he fits in.
3. Some students may suggest that he could have learned more about his Chinese heritage, for instance by studying the language.
4. Responses will vary. Some students may stress that it is important to know about where you came from and to belong to a community of people who share a similar cultural background. Other students may say that it is very important to know about and understand your origins and heritage even if you live among people who are different from you.

Literary Link

Have students compare and contrast Yep as a child with Albert in "The Adoption of Albert." Ask students to think about how each character feels or behaves in his individual situation. (Both boys are outsiders. Yep does not fit in with his community. Albert does not belong to Louis's family, but he does not want to be with his own family.)

Another Pathway

Cooperative Learning Divide students into small groups. One student should be the facilitator and make sure that all members in the group are given a chance to participate in the activity. Another student can record the group's ideas. Another student can be put in charge of drawing the map. Encourage students to reread the selection for help in understanding the geography of the spaces Yep describes. Students should also pay attention to the details Yep uses to describe the various neighborhoods, buildings, and spaces.

Rubric

3 Full Accomplishment Students work cooperatively to produce an accurate map.
2 Substantial Accomplishment A few details are misplaced or missing from the map.
1 Little or Partial Accomplishment Students do not share the work evenly. Many details are missing from the map.

RESPONDING OPTIONS

FROM PERSONAL RESPONSE TO CRITICAL ANALYSIS

REFLECT 1. What do you think of this account of Laurence Yep's childhood experiences in Chinatown? Describe your thoughts in your notebook or on a sheet of paper.

RETHINK 2. Yep says, "In trying to find solutions, I had created more pieces to the puzzle." How would you describe the puzzle he is trying to solve?
Consider
Close Textual Reading
- the community in which he lives
- his parents' expectations
- the language barrier

Thematic Link 3. What are some ways in which Yep might have handled his problem of being divided between the Chinese and non-Chinese communities?

RELATE 4. Growing up in San Francisco, Laurence Yep longed to fit into the culture in which he lived. Later, however, he learned to appreciate his Chinese heritage. Explain how important you think it is to know about and understand your origins and heritage.

Multimodal Learning
ANOTHER PATHWAY
Cooperative Learning
Work with a group of classmates to draw a map showing the places that Laurence Yep describes—Nob Hill, Chinatown, St. Mary's School, the Chinese Playground, and the neighborhood in which he lived. Locate Yep and his friends Paul and Harold on the map.

LITERARY CONCEPTS

A **memoir** is a writer's account of his or her personal experiences. It is almost always told from the first-person point of view. Because a memoir is written about real people and real events, it is a type of nonfiction. It can provide information only the writer knows. What do you learn about Laurence Yep that you might not have learned if someone else had told his story?

CONCEPT REVIEW: Setting Yep provides numerous details to describe the various parts of San Francisco. Find a passage in the selection that you think is especially effective in helping you imagine the setting.

QUICKWRITES

1. Using what you have learned about Paul's and Harold's personalities, write a **prediction** of what will happen to them in future years.
2. Write an imaginary **dialogue** between Yep as a young man and Yep as an older man. In the younger Yep's speeches, include questions and comments about the confusion of living in two worlds. For the older Yep, compose words of advice.

📁 **PORTFOLIO** Save your writing. You may want to use it later as a springboard to a piece for your portfolio.

178 UNIT TWO PART 1: FINDING A SPECIAL PLACE

Literary Concepts

Encourage students to reread the selection, paying attention to places where Yep reveals his private emotions and feelings. Students should understand that if the story had been told by someone else, the reader would not know as much about Yep's feelings of not belonging.

Concept Review Have students skim the selection to locate passages that describe various aspects of San Francisco. The opening paragraphs of the story provide many geographical details.

QuickWrites

1. Ask students to reread page 174. For help in writing their predictions, students should take note of the details Yep uses to describe the boys. Remind students that they will be predicting what will happen, so they should use the future tense.
2. Encourage students to think about the questions the younger Yep might have, based on his personality in the selection, and how the older Yep might respond to these questions. Make sure that students write in proper dialogue form.

The Writer's Craft

Examining a Paragraph, pp. 222–224
Quotation Marks, pp. 586–587

178 THE LANGUAGE OF LITERATURE TEACHER'S EDITION

Multimodal Learning
ALTERNATIVE ACTIVITIES

1. Look back at the diagram you created for the Writing Connection. Create a **collage** of objects and pictures that illustrate your roles. You might use photographs, parts of toys or household objects, old report cards, ribbons, and pins. You can also include drawings and magazine pictures.

2. Yep mentions that children in Chinatown played marbles in a way different from the way American children played. Prepare a **chart** explaining how to play marbles in one of the two ways.

CRITIC'S CORNER

A British author once described writers of memoirs as "drawing themselves with a pen." Do you think that statement applies to Yep's writing in this memoir? Why or why not?

WORDS TO KNOW

WORDPLAY Review page 172 and locate the word **stereotype.** Use a dictionary to find out what the word means and what part of speech it is in the sentence where it occurs. Then copy and complete the diagram below. Share and discuss your diagram with a small group of classmates.

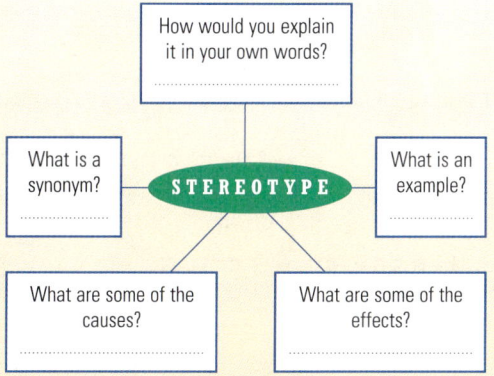

LAURENCE YEP

Laurence Yep began writing while in high school, when a teacher promised an A to any student who published an article in a national magazine. He earned the A by writing a science-fiction story that he sold for a penny per word.

Yep's first book, *Sweetwater*, published five years later, is also science fiction. It revolves around a young man who belongs to a minority group of transplanted aliens on another planet. Yep writes, "Probably the reason that much of my writing has found its way to a teenage audience is that I'm always pursuing the theme of being an outsider—an alien—and

1948–

many teenagers feel they're aliens."

Yep spent six years researching Chinese-American history before he wrote *Dragonwings*, a fictionalized account of the first aircraft flight on the West Coast, in 1909. The novel blends Chinese folklore, myths, and legends with historical facts about the flight, Chinatown, and the San Francisco earthquake of 1906. *Dragonwings* has received 15 awards, including selection as a Newbery Honor Book.

OTHER WORKS *Sweetwater, Dragonwings, Child of the Owl, Sea Glass, Dragon of the Lost Sea, The Serpent's Children, Dragon Steel, The Star Fisher*

Extended Reading

• AUTHOR BACKGROUND

CHINATOWN 179

Across the Curriculum

Social Studies Have students research Chinatowns in cities other than San Francisco. For example, students can find out the populations of Chinatowns in such cities as New York, Boston, and Philadelphia, as well as the history of such communities. Encourage students to draw maps that detail the specific Chinatown they are researching.

History Have students research the history of fair housing laws. Students should address issues such as who was affected by housing discrimination before the laws were passed; how the laws came about; and how the laws affected society after they were passed. Many municipalities have housing authorities or departments, which may serve as a useful resource.

Words to Know

Diagrams will vary. Make sure students are able to define *stereotype* in their own words before completing the rest of the diagram.

Laurence Yep A third-generation Chinese American, Laurence Yep sharpened his understanding of Chinese traditions and ideas through reading. Many of his books, including *Child of the Owl* and *Sea Glass*, often focus on characters caught between two cultures.

Yep has taught at various schools, including the University of California at Berkeley, where he was a writer in residence.

AUTHOR BACKGROUND
Laurence Yep In this interview, the author speaks about his career and about the influence of culture on his writing.

Side A, Frame 8091

Alternative Activities

1. Before students begin making their collages, encourage them to think about the roles they play and what images and pictures best represent these roles.

2. Have students reread the passage about marbles in the selection, and ask them to pay attention to how the different games are played. Before students make their charts, encourage them to write a brief summary of each game.

THE LANGUAGE OF LITERATURE TEACHER'S EDITION 179

OVERVIEW

Objectives
- To understand and appreciate haiku
- To examine the use of imagery
- To express understanding of the poems through a choice of writing forms, including a personal essay and a haiku
- To extend understanding of the poems through a variety of multimodal and cross-curricular activities

Skills

LITERARY CONCEPT
- Imagery

THE WRITER'S STYLE
- Word choice

SPEAKING, LISTENING, AND VIEWING
- Group discussion
- Oral presentation

Cross-Curricular Connections

HISTORY
- Development of haiku

MATH
- Counting syllables

ALTERNATIVE
Previewing
Instead of writing about an object in the classroom, students can choose partners and discuss the topic.

Personal Connection
Discussion Prompts *Choose an object in the classroom. Examine it and discuss with a partner some words that describe the object.*

Thematic Link: *Finding a Special Place* In these haiku, poets fleetingly describe and capture special moments from a particular point of view.

LITERARY CONNECTION
Haiku Traditional haiku deal with aspects of nature, particularly with the seasons. This group of images shows the kinds of settings that have inspired haiku poets, along with the instruments they use in their craft.

Side A, Frame 38720

CULTURAL CONNECTION
The Culture of Japan In this film, views of Japan are accompanied by traditional Japanese music. You may wish to use the film to prompt discussion about various aspects of Japanese culture.

Side A, Frame 12205

180 THE LANGUAGE OF LITERATURE TEACHER'S EDITION

PREVIEWING

POETRY

Three Haiku
Bashō, Issa, and Raymond R. Patterson

PERSONAL CONNECTION *Activating Prior Knowledge/Setting a Purpose*

The unusual poems you are about to read capture moments that have been meaningful to three poets. Choose an object in the room and try to observe it as though you were seeing it for the first time. On a piece of paper, write the name of the object and five words that describe what it looks like or what you notice about it that you have overlooked before.

LITERARY CONNECTION *Building Background*

Haiku are three-line, unrhymed poems of a type originally developed in Japan. In Japanese haiku, the first and third lines contain five syllables, and the second line contains seven syllables. (Haiku written in English or translated into English do not always fit this formula.) With only a few carefully chosen words, a haiku captures and conveys a single small moment, feeling, or object.

READING CONNECTION *Active Read*

Visualizing As you read these haiku, try to visualize, or form mental pictures of, the images in them. Reread each haiku a few times to visualize the image clearly and to experience the moment the poet presents.

Structure of Haiku

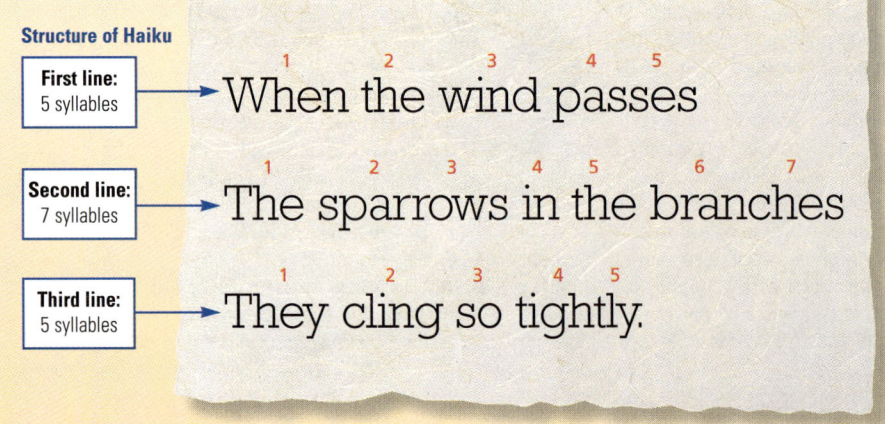

First line: 5 syllables — When the wind passes
Second line: 7 syllables — The sparrows in the branches
Third line: 5 syllables — They cling so tightly.

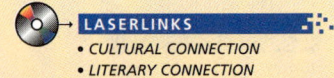
- CULTURAL CONNECTION
- LITERARY CONNECTION

180 UNIT TWO PART 1: FINDING A SPECIAL PLACE

PRINT AND MEDIA RESOURCES

UNIT TWO RESOURCE BOOK
Strategic Reading: Literature, p. 19

WRITING MINI-LESSONS
Transparencies, p. 38

ACCESS FOR STUDENTS ACQUIRING ENGLISH
Reading and Writing Support

FORMAL ASSESSMENT
Selection Test, p. 37
Test Generator

 **AUDIO LIBRARY**
See Reference Card

 **LASERLINKS**
Cultural Connection
Literary Connection

Three Haiku

On sweet plum blossoms
The sun rises suddenly.
Look, a mountain path!

BY BASHŌ

Beautiful, seen through holes
Made in a paper screen:
The Milky Way.

BY ISSA

Glory, Glory . . .
Across Grandmother's knees
A kindly sun
Laid a yellow quilt.

BY RAYMOND R. PATTERSON

Incense wrapper (Edo period, Japan; 17th–18th centuries) attributed to Ogata Korin, 1658–1716. Wrapper mounted on hanging scroll, ink and color on gold-ground paper, 33 × 24.1 cm, The Art Institute of Chicago, Russell Tyson Purchase Fund (1966.470). Photograph © 1994, The Art Institute of Chicago, all rights reserved.

Art Note

***Incense Wrapper* attributed to Ogata Korin** Ogata Korin (1658–1716) was the son of an important Japanese textile-making family. This incense wrapper depicts morning glories by using a mix of opaque pigment with translucent black-ink wash on gold paper. Ogata Korin's work influenced a number of artists and began a tradition that embodied a highly decorative style.

Reading the Art *How is the image on this incense wrapper like a haiku?*

Literary Concept: RHYTHM

A Ask students to tap out the rhythm of each haiku. Have students discuss how the rhythm of the haiku affects the imagery presented in each poem.

CUSTOMIZING FOR
Multiple Learning Styles

B **Spatial or Graphic Learners** Invite students to draw or sketch the images created in their minds by this haiku.

Critical Thinking: ANALYZE

C Have students discuss why they think these specific details have been chosen by the poet in writing the haiku.

Active Reading: CONNECT

D Ask students if this haiku brings to mind similar feelings or experiences. Have them relate the feelings or their impressions of the experience.

CUSTOMIZING FOR
Gifted and Talented Students

Ask students how accurate and successful they think a haiku can be at capturing a fleeting impression or feeling. Have students discuss and give examples of experiences that are difficult to put into words.

Mini-Lesson  The Writer's Style

WORD CHOICE Tell students that word choice is especially important to haiku poets because they use so few words.

Application Ask students to write three different haiku that describe the same subject. Write the information to the right on the chalkboard.

Reteaching/Reinforcement
- Writing Handbook, anthology p. 778
- Writing Mini-Lessons transparencies, p. 38

Writing a Poem, pp. 84–88

1. **Look inside your head** Close your eyes and try to focus your thoughts inward. What images and ideas come to mind?

2. **Explore ideas** Write words or sketch images that occur to you. Look for these details:

Sensory images What do you see, hear, smell, taste, and touch when you think of your subject?

Words and phrases What words, phrases, or sounds remind you of your subject?

Comparisons Is your subject like anything else? Look for comparisons.

THE LANGUAGE OF LITERATURE TEACHER'S EDITION **181**

From Personal Response to Critical Analysis

1. Responses will vary.
2. Some students will say rereading the haiku affected their appreciation of it because they focused on slightly different details of the imagery each time. Some students may say that the haiku evoked different feelings or experiences each time they read it. Other students will say rereading the haiku did not affect their appreciation of it because the haiku is so short and tries to capture a very small impression or feeling that does not change.
3. Possible responses: A haiku poet probably pays attention to tiny details and notices things that other people do not. Haiku poets have a good command of language because they know how to describe private feelings in a few words.
4. Responses will vary.

Literary Links

Ask students to compare and contrast the use of imagery in one of the haiku with that in a free-verse poem such as "Life Doesn't Frighten Me" or "Another Mountain." *(Possible response: The free-verse poems are longer, so there is room for many images, which combine to support the writer's theme. A haiku focuses on a single image.)*

Another Pathway

Encourage students to reread each haiku and jot down the images, feelings, and ideas communicated by the poem. Have students think of feelings or experiences similar to the messages the haiku are communicating. You may wish to divide the class into small groups so students can discuss their responses to the haiku.

Rubric

3 Full Accomplishment Students clearly relate the poems to specific experiences or feelings.

2 Substantial Accomplishment Students relate some of the poems to their experiences.

1 Little or Partial Accomplishment Students are unable to comprehend the poems and have difficulty relating them to their own lives.

RESPONDING OPTIONS

FROM PERSONAL RESPONSE TO CRITICAL ANALYSIS

REFLECT 1. What thoughts were in your mind after you read the three haiku? Jot down your thoughts in your notebook.

RETHINK 2. Did reading the haiku by Issa more than once affect your appreciation of the image it presents? Explain why or why not.

3. On the basis of your reading of these haiku, describe the kind of person you imagine a haiku poet to be.

RELATE 4. Which haiku best helps you to visualize or experience a moment of being in a special place? Why?

Multimodal Learning
ANOTHER PATHWAY

Haiku poets often use images of simple things to suggest truths about the world. Explain the message each poem conveys to you. Compare your response with the responses of your classmates.

LITERARY CONCEPTS

Imagery refers to the use of words that appeal to the five senses: sight, hearing, touch, taste, and smell. Most poetic images appeal to the sense of sight; they help readers "see" things in their mind. Which words in the three haiku appeal to the senses? Make a chart like the one shown here to record what you find.

Haiku By	Image(s)	Sense(s) Appealed To

ART CONNECTION

Incense Wrapper on page 181 is probably the creation of the Japanese artist Ogata Korin (1658–1716). This wrapper—in itself a useful object—was made by painting on thick gold paper. The contrast of the wrapper's beauty with its simple function suggests the idea that the material things of this world pass away quickly. How might this idea also be suggested by the images presented in haiku?

182 UNIT TWO PART 1: FINDING A SPECIAL PLACE

QUICKWRITES

1. Write a **personal essay** about an aspect of the natural world that is described in one of the haiku. Be sure to express your feelings about the subject in your essay.

2. Cut index cards into thirds and write the words of all three haiku on separate cards. (Omit the articles *a*, *an*, and *the*.) Then turn the cards over and choose ten at random. Use the words on the cards, along with a few of your own, to write a **haiku**.

📁 **PORTFOLIO** Save your writing. You may want to use it later as a springboard to a piece for your portfolio.

Literary Concepts

Remind students that a haiku seeks to capture a single image with just a few words. Students might say that all three haiku use words appealing to the sense of sight *(look, seen)*. Some might also identify words appealing to touch *(the sun as a quilt)*, taste *(sweet)*, or smell *(sweet plum blossoms)*.

QuickWrites

1. Have students reread their chosen haiku to determine the aspect of the natural world depicted in it. Encourage students to think about why their choice depicts an important aspect of the natural world and how it makes them feel.
2. Have students first create word webs out of the randomly chosen words. Ask students to think of ways these words are related and how they might be used together.

The Writer's Craft

Personal Response, pp. 142–155
Writing a Poem, pp. 84–88

BASHŌ

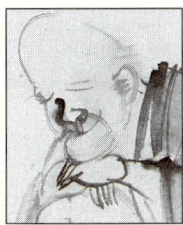
1644–1694

Bashō is considered one of Japan's greatest poets. Early in his life, he went to work for a noble family and became the companion of the family's son. When the son died, Bashō was greatly upset. He left the family's service and became a wandering poet, teaching haiku to make a living.

One day, according to legend, Bashō was out with some students. One of them suddenly announced that he had thought of a poem: "Pluck off the wings of a bright red dragonfly and there a pepper pod will be." Bashō informed the student that he would never be a poet. A poet, according to Bashō, would have created this image: "Add but the wings to a bright red pepper pod and there a dragonfly will be." Whether or not the story is true, it reflects a sympathy that, along with his superb skill as a poet, has made Bashō a major figure in Japanese and world literature.

ISSA

1763–1827

Issa, born Kobayashi Nobuyuki, led a life full of poverty, illness, and tragedy. His mother died when he was three. When his father remarried, his stepmother was so unkind to the boy that he left home for Edo (now Tokyo) at the age of 13 to find work. There he studied haiku, decided to live as a poet, and took the pen name Issa (meaning "cup of tea"). In 1814 he married a woman named Kiku. The couple had five children, all of whom died as infants. Kiku herself died in 1823.

Issa's troubles helped him understand the struggles of the weak and led him to feel tenderness and compassion toward all living things, no matter how small or insignificant. Perhaps the compassionate voice of his poetry is the reason Issa remains one of Japan's best-loved poets.

RAYMOND R. PATTERSON

Raymond R. Patterson (1929–) was born in New York City. After finishing college, he worked as a children's supervisor at Youth House for Boys in New York City. He also taught English at Benedict College in Columbia, South Carolina, and in New York City public schools. From 1960 to 1962, he wrote a weekly column on African-American history, "From Our Past."

In 1968 Patterson became a lecturer in English at City College in New York and director of Black Poets Reading, Inc. He received a Borestone Mountain poetry award in 1950 and a National Endowment for the Arts discovery grant for 1969–1970. Patterson's *Twenty-Six Ways of Looking at a Black Man and Other Poems* was published in 1969.

Alternative Activities

1. Invite students to create a collage for one of the haiku. Students should find images from magazines and newspapers, as well as use their own drawings and sketches. Encourage students to make a list of imagery and details from the haiku that they wish to include in their collages.
2. Ask students what kinds of music they would pick to go along with these haiku. Ask students to find recorded music or to make their own music to match the impressions evoked by the haiku.

Art Connection

Discuss with students the fleeting images captured by the haiku. Some students may say that these images are seen and then are gone as quickly as a wrapper is thrown away. Other students may say that the wrapper will be forgotten but the images described in the haiku will be remembered.

Across the Curriculum

History *Cooperative Learning* Divide the class into small groups of three or four. Have groups research the history of haiku as an art form in Japan. Students should find out how this form of poetry came into being, identify some of the major figures in the development of haiku, and discover how the popularity of the form spread outside Japan. Groups can present their findings to the class.

Math *Counting Syllables* Have students examine different poetic forms—haiku, sonnet, and free verse, for instance—and calculate the number of syllables in each line, stanza, and poem. Students can create charts that detail and compare their calculations for each type of poem.

BASHŌ

Born Matsuo Munefusa, Bashō had no source of income except for his art. He frequently taught students and judged poetry contests. He traveled extensively and wrote records of his trips, the most famous of which is *The Narrow Road of the Interior* (1702).

ISSA

During especially difficult periods of his youth, Issa would flee to the outdoors—especially to the groves of great chestnut and pine trees that stood in his village. Thus, as a child he learned to associate the natural world with freedom, imagination, and possibility.

RAYMOND R. PATTERSON

Patterson's most popular work, *Riot Rimes U.S.A.*, is an 85-poem sequence that depicts the Harlem riot of 1965. The poems in this sequence are alternately humorous and ironic. They offer a first-person perspective on an event that Patterson believes to be the high point of the African-American experience in America.

OVERVIEW

Objectives

- To understand and appreciate a short story about a young boy who learns the true meaning of giving a gift
- To enrich reading by using active reading strategies
- To examine characterization
- To express understanding of the story through a choice of writing forms, including a prediction and a diary entry
- To extend understanding of the story through a variety of multimodal and cross-curricular activities

Skills

READING SKILLS/ STRATEGIES
- Predicting

LITERARY CONCEPTS
- Characterization
- Theme
- Conflict

THE WRITER'S STYLE
- Using dialogue

GRAMMAR
- Direct objects of verbs

SPELLING
- Final y words and suffixes

SPEAKING, LISTENING, AND VIEWING
- Pantomime
- Group discussion
- Oral presentation

Cross-Curricular Connections

SOCIAL STUDIES
- Czar Alexander III

SCIENCE
- Carrier pigeons

HISTORY
- Roller-skating
- Immigration
- Pogroms

HISTORICAL CONNECTION

The Cossacks During the late 1900s, Cossacks engaged in widespread brutality against Jewish communities in the Russian Empire. While members of the Russian upper class danced in ballrooms, regiments of Cossacks carried out pogroms ordered by the czar. You may wish to use these historical images to begin a discussion about the influence of these events on Aaron's actions in the story.

Side A, Frame 38726

Art Note

Autumn by Craig McPherson Born and educated in Kansas, McPherson (1948-) moved to New York City in 1975, and the city soon became a recurring subject in his art.

Reading the Art Given the absence of vegetation, what other elements of the painting help you to identify the season in which this cityscape is depicted?

PREVIEWING

FICTION

Aaron's Gift
Myron Levoy

PERSONAL CONNECTION Activating Prior Knowledge

Some gifts carry a big price tag, while others—like the one in this story—are priceless. In your notebook or on a sheet of paper, write about the best gift you ever gave or received. What made that gift so special?

GEOGRAPHICAL CONNECTION Building Background

In this story, one character's ideas about gifts are strongly influenced by her childhood in a Jewish village in the Ukraine. Although now an independent country of eastern Europe, during the late 19th century this area was part of the Russian Empire. The brutal leader of the Russian Empire was Czar Alexander the Third. At that time, Jews in the Ukraine lived in constant fear of Cossacks—soldiers loyal to the czar (emperor). These soldiers frequently attacked Jewish communities in raids known as pogroms. While Alexander the Third was czar, thousands of Jews left the Ukraine and came to the United States.

184 • LASERLINKS • HISTORICAL CONNECTION

READING CONNECTION Active Reading

Predicting Before you even begin reading, you can try to predict what a story will be about. For example, on the basis of the title of this story, the information in the Geographical Connection, and the illustrations throughout the story, you might try predicting what Aaron's gift will be.

When you read a story, guessing what will happen next keeps you involved in the action. As you read this story, you will come across a question that asks you to predict what the main character will do next. Look for other points where you might predict what will happen. Write your predictions in your Reading Log. Then read on to see where the action takes you and to learn whether your predictions turn out to be true.

Setting Purpo

My Predictions
Aaron will fix the pigeon's wing.
Aaron will ask to keep Pidge.

PRINT AND MEDIA RESOURCES

UNIT TWO RESOURCE BOOK
Strategic Reading: Literature, p. 23
Vocabulary SkillBuilder, p. 26
Reading SkillBuilder, p. 24
Spelling SkillBuilder, p. 25

WRITING MINI-LESSONS
Transparencies, p. 48

ACCESS FOR STUDENTS ACQUIRING ENGLISH
Selection Summaries
Reading and Writing Support

FORMAL ASSESSMENT
Selection Test, pp. 39–40
Test Generator

 **AUDIO LIBRARY**
See Reference Card

 **LASERLINKS**
Historical Connection

184 THE LANGUAGE OF LITERATURE TEACHER'S EDITION

Aaron's Gift
by Myron Levoy

Detail of *Autumn* (1980–1981), Craig McPherson. Oil on canvas, 54″ × 48″, Museum of the City of New York (83.4), Gift of the American Institute of Arts and Letters.

SUMMARY

While roller-skating in the park, Aaron Kandel finds a pigeon with a broken wing. Aaron brings "Pidge" home, certain that his bird-loving Ukrainian grandmother will be pleased. As Pidge's wing heals, Aaron begins training him to be a carrier pigeon. When some neighborhood toughs hear about the pigeon, they offer to let Aaron join their gang if he will let them use Pidge as their mascot. When Aaron appears at the gang meeting, the boys build a fire and try to throw his bird into it. Aaron rescues Pidge, but the bird flies away during the struggle. Aaron is heartbroken, because he has planned to give Pidge to his grandmother for her 60th birthday, believing that the pigeon would replace the beloved pet goat she had as a girl in the Ukraine—a goat that was cruelly killed. Aaron runs home and tearfully tells his family about his own encounter with cruelty and about the loss of his grandmother's gift. Instead of being disappointed, Aaron's grandmother tells him that he has given her a greater gift than the pigeon. Aaron later understands that he has given the gift of freedom both to Pidge and to the goat that it represents.

Thematic Link: *Finding a Special Place* Caring for an injured pigeon enables a young boy to understand his family's place in history.

CUSTOMIZING FOR
Students Acquiring English

- Use **ACCESS FOR STUDENTS ACQUIRING ENGLISH**, *Reading and Writing Support.*
- This story relates a Jewish grandmother's experiences in the anti-Semitic Ukraine. You may want to ask students to talk or write about the experiences of their immigrant relatives.

STRATEGIC READING FOR
Less-Proficient Readers

Ask students to tell about a relative with whom they share a special bond.

Set a Purpose Have students read to find out what Aaron finds while roller-skating in the park.

Use **UNIT TWO RESOURCE BOOK**, pp. 23–24, for guidance in reading the selection.

WORDS TO KNOW

frenzied (frĕn′zēd) *adj.* wild; frantic (p. 186)
mascot (măs′kŏt′) *n.* a person, an animal, or an object believed to bring good luck, especially one kept as the symbol of an organization such as a sports team (p. 188)
stoop (stōōp) *n.* a small porch outside the door to a building (p. 187)
tenement (tĕn′ə-mənt) *n.* an apartment building in a run-down, crowded city area (p. 192)
thrashing (thrăsh′ĭng) *n.* moving wildly **thrash** *v.* (p. 186)

CUSTOMIZING FOR
Gifted and Talented Students

As students read, have them discuss the significance of the parallel between the story about Aaron and the story about his grandmother. How are the two stories similar? What purpose do these parallel stories serve?

(Both stories are concerned with the experiences of young children who must deal with the loss of a pet. The parallel stories strengthen the bond between Aaron and his grandmother and explain why Aaron decides to give Pidge to his grandmother as a birthday present.)

CUSTOMIZING FOR
Students Acquiring English

I Ask students to guess the meaning of *Class A*, using the surrounding contextual clues.

Linking to History

A The first roller skates were made in Holland early in the 18th century. They were modeled after ice skates, with the wheels in one row. In the United States, conventional skates with two sets of wheels side by side were introduced about 100 years later. In 1884 the invention of the ball-bearing wheel advanced the popularity of roller-skating. In the late 1970s, in-line skates, with the wheels in one row, were introduced as another refinement of roller skates. Their popularity has increased dramatically in the 1990s.

CUSTOMIZING FOR
Multiple Learning Styles

B Bodily-Kinesthetic Learners
Have students volunteer to act out the movements of the injured pigeon.

Active Reading: PREDICT

C Encourage students to suggest reasons why Aaron caught the pigeon. Then have them debate the merits of each idea.

Luckily, Aaron hadn't eaten the cookies.

He broke a cookie into small crumbs and tossed some toward the pigeon.

The pigeon spotted the cookie crumbs.

It folded its wings as best it could.

---

186 THE LANGUAGE OF LITERATURE TEACHER'S EDITION

A Aaron Kandel had come to Tompkins Square Park to roller-skate, for the streets near Second Avenue were always too crowded with children and peddlers and old ladies and baby buggies. Though few children had bicycles in those days, almost every child owned a pair of roller skates. And Aaron was, it must be said, a Class A, triple-fantastic roller skater.

Aaron skated back and forth on the wide walkway of the park, pretending he was an aviator in an air race zooming around pylons,[1] which were actually two lampposts. During his third lap around the racecourse, he noticed a pigeon on the grass, behaving very strangely. Aaron skated to the line of benches, then climbed over onto the lawn.

B The pigeon was trying to fly, but all it could manage was to flutter and turn round and round in a large circle, as if it were performing a <u>frenzied</u> dance. The left wing was only half open and was beating in a clumsy, jerking fashion; it was clearly broken.

Luckily, Aaron hadn't eaten the cookies he'd stuffed into his pocket before he'd gone clacking down the three flights of stairs from his apartment, his skates already on. He broke a cookie into small crumbs and tossed some toward the pigeon. "Here pidge, here pidge," he called. The pigeon spotted the cookie crumbs and, after a moment, stopped <u>thrashing</u> about. It folded its wings as best it could, but the broken wing still stuck half out. Then it strutted over to the crumbs, its head bobbing forth-back, forth-back, as if it were marching a little in front of the rest of the body—perfectly normal, except for that half-open wing which seemed to make the bird stagger sideways every so often.

The pigeon began eating the crumbs as Aaron quickly unbuttoned his shirt and pulled it off. Very slowly, he edged toward the bird, making little kissing sounds like the ones he heard his grandmother make when she fed the sparrows on the back fire escape.

Then suddenly Aaron plunged. The shirt, in both hands, came down like a torn parachute. The pigeon beat its wings, but Aaron held the shirt to the ground, and the bird couldn't escape. Aaron felt under the shirt, gently, and gently took hold of the wounded pigeon.

"Yes, yes, pidge," he said, very softly. "There's a good boy. Good pigeon, good."

"That's your new name. Pidge."

C PREDICT
What will Aaron do with the pigeon?
Using a Reading Log

The pigeon struggled in his hands, but little by little Aaron managed to soothe it. "Good boy, pidge. That's your new name. Pidge. I'm gonna take you home, Pidge. Yes, yes, *ssh*. Good boy. I'm gonna fix you up. Easy, Pidge, easy does it. Easy, boy."

Aaron squeezed through an opening between the row of benches and skated slowly out of the park, while holding the pigeon carefully with both hands as if it were one of his mother's rare, precious cups from the old country. How fast the pigeon's heart was beating! Was he afraid? Or did all pigeons' hearts beat fast?

---
1. **pylons** (pī′lŏnz′): towers marking turning points for airplanes in a race.

| WORDS TO KNOW | **frenzied** (frĕn′zēd) *adj.* wildly excited; frantic
thrashing (thrăsh′ĭng) *n.* moving wildly **thrash** *v.* |

Mini-Lesson Grammar

DIRECT OBJECTS OF MAIN VERBS Tell students that a direct object is the noun or pronoun that receives the action of the verb in a sentence. Only action verbs can have direct objects. To find the direct object in a sentence, first find the main verb. Then ask *whom* or *what* after the verb. The word in the sentence that answers the question is the direct object. If no word answers the question, there is no direct object. Refer students to the highlighted passage above and write the sentences to the left on the chalkboard.

Application Ask students to copy the following sentences and to underline each verb once and the direct object twice.
1. Grandmother fed the birds in the yard.
2. Aaron found sticks to make a splint.
3. How did Aaron catch the bird?

Reteaching/Reinforcement

 The Writer's Craft

Direct Objects of Verbs, pp. 403–404

Bobby (1939), Jack Humphrey. Collection of John Corey.

It was fortunate that Aaron was an excellent skater, for he had to skate six blocks to his apartment, over broken pavement and sudden gratings and curbs and cobblestones. But when he reached home, he asked Noreen Callahan, who was playing on the stoop, to take off his skates for him. He would not chance going up three flights on roller skates this time.

"Is he sick?" asked Noreen.

"Broken wing," said Aaron. "I'm gonna fix him up and make him into a carrier pigeon[2] or something."

"Can I watch?" asked Noreen.

"Watch what?"

"The operation. I'm gonna be a nurse when I grow up."

"OK," said Aaron. "You can even help. You can help hold him while I fix him up."

Aaron wasn't quite certain what his mother would say about his newfound pet, but he was pretty sure he knew what his grandmother would think. His grandmother had lived with them ever since his grandfather had died three years ago. And she fed the sparrows and jays and crows and robins on the back fire escape with every spare crumb she could find. In fact, Aaron noticed that she sometimes created crumbs where they didn't exist, by squeezing and tearing pieces of her breakfast roll when his mother wasn't looking.

Aaron didn't really understand his grandmother, for he often saw her by the window having long conversations with the birds, telling them about her days as a little girl in the Ukraine. And once he saw her take her mirror from her handbag and hold it out toward the birds. She told Aaron that she wanted them to see how beautiful they were. Very strange. But Aaron did know that she would love Pidge, because she loved everything.

---

2. **carrier pigeon:** a pigeon trained to carry messages from place to place.

WORDS TO KNOW
stoop (stoōp) *n.* a small porch outside the main door of a building

187

Linking to Science

F The carrier (or homing) pigeon is known for its remarkable ability to return to its home roost. Carrier pigeons have been used to send messages for nearly 2,000 years; even during the two world wars, many communications corps used carrier pigeons to send important messages. Today homing pigeons are still kept by thousands of racing enthusiasts and are entered in races. The average homing pigeon can fly at a speed of 45 miles per hour.

Critical Thinking: SPECULATE

G Ask students to speculate why Aaron has such a strong need to belong to the gang. *(Possible responses: Aaron may not have many friends, so "joining the gang" may have an appealing association. Aaron also may be looking for acceptance and approval from older boys, which he thinks he can get if he joins the gang.)*

Literary Concept: CONFLICT

H Ask students to summarize the conflict in this scene. *(Possible response: Aaron is in conflict with his mother. He wants to join a club of older boys, but she demands that he stay away from them.)*

To his surprise, his mother said he could keep the pigeon, temporarily, because it was sick, and we were all strangers in the land of Egypt,[3] and it might not be bad for Aaron to have a pet. *Temporarily.*

The wing was surprisingly easy to fix, for the break showed clearly and Pidge was remarkably patient and still, as if he knew he was being helped. Or perhaps he was just exhausted from all the thrashing about he had done. Two Popsicle sticks served as splints, and strips from an old undershirt were used to tie them in place. Another strip held the wing to the bird's body.

Aaron's father arrived home and stared at the pigeon. Aaron waited for the expected storm. But instead, Mr. Kandel asked, "Who *did* this?"

"Me," said Aaron. "And Noreen Callahan."

"Sophie!" he called to his wife. "Did you see this! Ten years old and it's better than Dr. Belasco could do. He's a genius!"

F As the days passed, Aaron began training Pidge to be a carrier pigeon. He tied a little cardboard tube to Pidge's left leg and stuck tiny rolled-up sheets of paper with secret messages into it: THE ENEMY IS ATTACKING AT DAWN. Or: THE GUNS ARE HIDDEN IN THE TRUNK OF THE CAR. Or: VINCENT DEMARCO IS A BRITISH SPY. Then Aaron would set Pidge down at one end of the living room and put some popcorn at the other end. And Pidge would waddle slowly across the room, cooing softly, while the ends of his bandages trailed along the floor.

At the other end of the room, one of Aaron's friends would take out the message, stick a new one in, turn Pidge around, and aim him at the popcorn that Aaron put down on his side of the room.

And Pidge grew fat and contented on all the popcorn and crumbs and corn and crackers and Aaron's grandmother's breakfast rolls.

Aaron had told all the children about Pidge, but he only let his very best friends come up and play carrier pigeon with him. But telling everyone had been a mistake. A group of older boys from down the block had a club—Aaron's mother called it a gang—and Aaron had longed to join as he had never longed for anything else. To be with them and share their secrets, the secrets of older boys. To be able to enter their clubhouse shack on the empty lot on the next street. To know the password and swear the secret oath. To belong.

About a month after Aaron had brought the pigeon home, Carl, the gang leader, walked over to Aaron in the street and told him he could be a member if he'd bring the pigeon down to be the club <u>mascot</u>. Aaron couldn't believe it; he immediately raced home to get Pidge. But his mother told Aaron to stay away from those boys, or else. And Aaron, miserable, argued with his mother and pleaded and cried and coaxed. It was no use. Not with those boys. No.

---

3. **we were all . . . Egypt:** a reference to the biblical command to the Hebrews "Love ye therefore the stranger: for ye were strangers in the land of Egypt" (Deuteronomy 10:19).

WORDS TO KNOW

mascot (măs′kŏt′) *n.* a person, an animal, or an object that is believed to bring good luck, especially one serving as the symbol of an organization (such as a sports team)

188

Mini-Lesson: Speaking, Listening, and Viewing

PANTOMIME Explain to students that pantomime is a form of acting without words. Because the actors have no dialogue, they must tell a story using only gestures, movements, and facial expressions.

Application Have students work in small groups to present a pantomime of a scene from the story. The scene in which Aaron teaches Pidge to be a carrier pigeon or the one in which Aaron argues with his mother are two possibilities.

---

188 THE LANGUAGE OF LITERATURE TEACHER'S EDITION

Aaron's mother tried to change the subject. She told him that it would soon be his grandmother's sixtieth birthday, a very special birthday indeed, and all the family from Brooklyn and the East Side would be coming to their apartment for a dinner and celebration. Would Aaron try to build something or make something for Grandma? A present made with his own hands would be nice. A decorated box for her hairpins or a crayon picture for her room or anything he liked.

In a flash Aaron knew what to give her: Pidge! Pidge would be her present! Pidge with his wing healed, who might be able to carry messages for her to the doctor or his Aunt Rachel or other people his grandmother seemed to go to a lot. It would be a surprise for everyone. And Pidge would make up for what had happened to Grandma when she'd been a little girl in the Ukraine, wherever that was.

Often, in the evening, Aaron's grandmother would talk about the old days long ago in the Ukraine, in the same way that she talked to the birds on the back fire escape. She had lived in a village near a place called Kishinev[4] with hundreds of other poor peasant families like her own. Things hadn't been too bad under someone called Czar Alexander the Second,[5] whom Aaron always pictured as a tall, handsome man in a gold uniform. But Alexander the Second was assassinated, and Alexander the Third,[6] whom Aaron pictured as an ugly man in a black cape, became the czar. And the Jewish people of the Ukraine had no peace anymore.

One day, a thundering of horses was heard coming toward the village from the direction of Kishinev. "The Cossacks! The Cossacks!" someone had shouted. The czar's horsemen! Quickly, quickly, everyone in Aaron's grandmother's family had climbed down to the cellar through a little trap door hidden under a mat in the big central room of their shack. But his grandmother's pet goat, whom she'd loved as much as Aaron loved Pidge and more, had to be left above, because if it had made a sound in the cellar, they would never have lived to see the next morning. They all hid under the wood in the woodbin and waited, hardly breathing.

Suddenly, from above, they heard shouts and calls and screams at a distance. And then the noise was in their house. Boots pounding on the floor, and everything breaking and crashing overhead. The smell of smoke and the shouts of a dozen men.

The terror went on for an hour, and then the sound of horses' hooves faded into the distance. They waited another hour to make sure, and then the father went up out of the cellar and the rest of the family followed. The door to the house had been torn from its hinges, and every piece of furniture was broken. Every window, every dish, every stitch of clothing was totally destroyed, and one wall had been completely bashed in. And on the floor was the goat, lying quietly. Aaron's grandmother, who was just a little girl of eight at the time, had wept over the goat all day and all night and could not be consoled.

> In a flash Aaron knew what to give her.

---

4. **Kishinev** (kĭsh′ə-nĕf′): a city (known today as Chisinau) that is now the capital of the country of Moldova.
5. **Czar Alexander the Second:** emperor of Russia from 1855 to 1881.
6. **Alexander the Third:** emperor of Russia from 1881 to 1894.

AARON'S GIFT **189**

Mini-Lesson — Literary Concepts

REVIEWING CONFLICT Remind students that a struggle between opposing forces is called a conflict. The struggle faced by a character creates the conflict that is important to every story. Conflict may be external or internal. External conflict occurs between a character and an outside force, such as society, nature, or even another character. Internal conflict is a struggle within one character's mind. An internal conflict occurs when a character has to make a difficult decision or deal with opposing ideas.

Application Divide students into small groups to identify the conflicts that occur in the story and to determine whether the conflicts are external or internal. One student in each group should act as facilitator to make sure all members of the group participate in the discussion. Another student should act as recorder. After students complete their discussion, one student in each group should present the group's ideas to the class.

Active Reading: CLARIFY

I Ask students why a pigeon would be a good gift for Aaron's grandmother. *(Possible responses: The pigeon would be a good gift because Aaron's grandmother seems to be very fond of birds; Aaron imagines she could use Pidge to carry messages; the gift would make up for what happened to Grandma as a little girl.)*

STRATEGIC READING FOR
Less-Proficient Readers

J Ask students the following questions to help guide them through the reading:

- After Aaron fixes the pigeon's broken wing, what does he do with the bird? *(He trains it to be a carrier pigeon by attaching secret messages to the bird's leg and coaxing it across the room with popcorn.)* Summarizing
- Why does Aaron want so badly to join Carl's gang? *He wants to belong to a group, to share their secrets, use their clubhouse, and know their special password and oath.)* Noting Relevant Details

Set a Purpose Have students read to find out about the grandmother's experiences as a little girl in the Ukraine.

Critical Thinking: ANALYZE

K Ask students to describe the shift in setting and why they think this shift occurs. *(The story shifts from present-day New York to a Ukrainian village in the past when Aaron's grandmother was a little girl. This shift occurs in order to tell a story about Aaron's grandmother.)*

Literary Concept: SENSORY DETAILS

L Ask students to identify the sensory details used in this section and to describe the effect of these details. *(Shouts and calls and screams at a distance, boots pounding, everything breaking and crashing, the smell of smoke, shouts of a dozen men, sound of horses' hooves fading into the distance. These details support the quality of terror in this scene.)*

THE LANGUAGE OF LITERATURE TEACHER'S EDITION **189**

Art Note

Backyards, Brooklyn **by Ogden Pleissner**
As a boy growing up in Brooklyn, Ogden Pleissner (1905–1938) drew constantly. After finishing art school in 1929, he lived and worked in a studio at 186 Washington Park, where he painted *Backyards, Brooklyn*. After the painting was completed, it was quickly purchased by the Metropolitan Museum of Art in New York City.

Reading the Art What kind of neighborhood is depicted in this painting? What details in the painting support your impressions of this neighborhood?

Active Reading: CLARIFY

M Ask students to describe what happened to Aaron's grandmother. (*She was the victim of an attack by Cossack soldiers. As she and her family hid in their cellar, the soldiers destroyed everything in their house, including her pet goat.*)

Linking to History

 **N** Among the most infamous pogroms were those at Kiev and more than 200 other sites, mostly in the Ukraine, in 1881; at Kishinev in 1903; and at Odessa, Yekaterinoslav, and hundreds of other places in 1905. The worst pogroms took place during the violent periods of the Russian revolutions and civil war (1917–1921), in which more than 60,000 Jews were killed.

Critical Thinking: ANALYZE

O Ask students why this sentence is in italics. (*Possible responses: The sentence is in italics to show that Aaron is thinking. Also, Aaron is addressing the pigeon's wing, and the author draws attention to this by putting it in italics.*)

CUSTOMIZING FOR
Students Acquiring English

3 Point out that Carl uses ungrammatical (*We got*) and informal (*kinda*) language when talking to Aaron. Ask students how this affects their perception of Carl.

Backyards, Brooklyn (1932), Ogden Minton Pleissner. Oil on canvas, 24″ × 30 ⅛″, The Metropolitan Museum of Art, New York. Arthur Hoppock Hearn Fund, 1932 (32.80.2). All rights reserved, The Metropolitan Museum of Art.

M **CLARIFY**
What happened to Aaron's grandmother?
Using a Reading Log

N

But they had been lucky. For other houses had been burned to the ground. And everywhere, not goats alone, nor sheep, but men and women and children lay quietly on the ground. The word for this sort of massacre, Aaron had learned, was *pogrom*. It had been a pogrom. And the men on the horses were Cossacks. Hated word. Cossacks.

And so Pidge would replace that goat of long ago. A pigeon on Second Avenue where no one needed trap doors or secret escape passages or woodpiles to hide under. A pigeon for his grandmother's sixtieth birthday. *Oh wing, heal quickly so my grandmother can send you flying to everywhere she wants!* **O**

But a few days later, Aaron met Carl in the street again. And Carl told Aaron that there was going to be a meeting that afternoon in which a map was going to be drawn up to show where a secret treasure lay buried on the empty lot. "Bring the pigeon and you can come into the shack. We got a badge for you. A new kinda membership badge with a secret code on the back." **3**

190 UNIT TWO PART 1: FINDING A SPECIAL PLACE

Assessment ✓ Option

INFORMAL ASSESSMENT You can informally assess students' understanding of the selection and their ability to comprehend characterization by setting up the following activity: *Pretend that you are Aaron's grandmother. Rewrite the story from her point of view. Make sure you pay attention to and use details about her character from the selection in your version.*

Rubric

3 Full Accomplishment Students rewrite the story from the grandmother's point of view using details about her character from the selection and present the grandmother in a manner consistent with her character.

2 Substantial Accomplishment Students rewrite the story from the grandmother's point of view using adequate details from the selection and present the grandmother in a manner that is somewhat consistent with her character.

1 Little or Partial Accomplishment Students have difficulty rewriting the story from the grandmother's point of view, have trouble using details from the selection, and present the grandmother in a manner inconsistent with her character.

190 THE LANGUAGE OF LITERATURE TEACHER'S EDITION

Aaron ran home, his heart pounding almost as fast as the pigeon's. He took Pidge in his hands and carried him out the door while his mother was busy in the kitchen making stuffed cabbage, his father's favorite dish. And by the time he reached the street, Aaron had decided to take the bandages off. Pidge would look like a real pigeon again, and none of the older boys would laugh or call him a bundle of rags.

Gently, gently he removed the bandages and the splints and put them in his pocket in case he should need them again. But Pidge seemed to hold his wing properly in place.

When he reached the empty lot, Aaron walked up to the shack, then hesitated. Four bigger boys were there. After a moment, Carl came out and commanded Aaron to hand Pidge over.

"Be careful," said Aaron. "I just took the bandages off."

"Oh sure, don't worry," said Carl. By now Pidge was used to people holding him, and he remained calm in Carl's hands.

"OK," said Carl. "Give him the badge." And one of the older boys handed Aaron his badge with the code on the back. "Now light the fire," said Carl.

"What . . . what fire?" asked Aaron.

"The fire. You'll see," Carl answered.

"You didn't say nothing about a fire," said Aaron. "You didn't say nothing to—"

"Hey!" said Carl. "I'm the leader here. And you don't talk unless I tell you that you have p'mission. Light the fire, Al."

The boy named Al went out to the side of the shack, where some wood and cardboard and old newspapers had been piled into a huge mound. He struck a match and held it to the newspapers.

"OK," said Carl. "Let's get 'er good and hot. Blow on it. Everybody blow."

Aaron's eyes stung from the smoke, but he blew alongside the others, going from side to side as the smoke shifted toward them and away.

"Let's fan it," said Al.

In a few minutes, the fire was crackling and glowing with a bright yellow-orange flame.

"Get me the rope," said Carl.

One of the boys brought Carl some cord and Carl, without a word, wound it twice around the pigeon, so that its wings were tight against its body.

"What . . . what are you *doing!*" shouted Aaron. "You're hurting his wing!"

"Don't worry about his wing," said Carl. "We're gonna throw him into the fire. And when we do, we're gonna swear an oath of loyalty to—"

"No! *No!*" shouted Aaron, moving toward Carl.

"Grab him!" called Carl. "Don't let him get the pigeon!"

But Aaron had leaped right across the fire at Carl, taking him completely by surprise. He threw Carl back against the shack and hit out at his face with both fists. Carl slid down to the ground, and the pigeon rolled out of his hands. Aaron scooped up the pigeon and ran, pretending he was on roller skates so that he would go faster and faster. And as he ran across the lot he pulled the cord off Pidge and tried to find a place, *any* place, to hide him.

Gently, gently he removed the bandages.

PREDICT

What will happen to Pidge?
Using a Reading Log

AARON'S GIFT **191**

Mini-Lesson Literary Concepts

ACTIVE READING: PREDICTING Remind students that predicting means guessing what might happen in the future on the basis of what you already know. Good readers gather information as they read. They combine that information with their own experiences to predict what might happen next in a story.

Application Instruct students to look at the two highlighted passages above. Ask them what they predicted would happen to Aaron and Pidge while reading these parts of the story. Make sure students identify the information they used to make this prediction, whether from the story or from their own experiences. Have students construct a chart like the one shown and fill in the information they used in making their predictions.

Reteaching/Reinforcement
• *Unit Two Resource Book,* p. 24

Prediction	Information from Story	Information from Experience

THE LANGUAGE OF LITERATURE **TEACHER'S EDITION 191**

STRATEGIC READING FOR
Less-Proficient Readers

P Ask students the following questions to help guide them through the reading:
• Where did Aaron's grandmother live when she was a little girl? *(in a village near Kishinev in the Ukraine)* Noting Relevant Details
• Why is the passage about Aaron's grandmother and her goat included in the story? *(to explain one reason why Aaron wants to give her the pigeon as a birthday present)* Making Inferences

Set a Purpose Have students read to find out what happens to Aaron and Pidge.

Active Reading: EVALUATE

Q Ask students to explain why Aaron hands Pidge over to Carl even though he is very concerned to protect the bird. *(If Aaron doesn't give Pidge to Carl, he cannot join the club and get the badge.)*

Active Reading: PREDICT

R Ask student what they think will happen to Pidge. *(Carl will try to hurt Pidge; Carl will use Pidge to force Aaron to do something he will not want to do.)*

Literary Concept: CONFLICT

S Ask students to summarize Aaron's conflict in this scene. *(Aaron is in conflict with the gang because they want to kill the defenseless pigeon. The conflict is intensified because Aaron wants to give the pigeon to his grandmother.)*

Critical Thinking:
MAKING JUDGMENTS

T Ask students if they agree or disagree with Aaron's comparing the boys to the Cossacks. *(Possible responses: I agree with Aaron because the boys are behaving in a violent and destructive manner like the Cossacks; they are trying to kill the pigeon, just as the Cossacks killed the grandmother's goat. I disagree with Aaron, because they are not inflicting violence on thousands of people with government support, as the Cossacks did.)*

Active Reading: CONNECT

U Have volunteers tell about a situation in which they came home to their family after a frightening or upsetting experience. Ask students to discuss what they thought, and how others reacted to them.

STRATEGIC READING FOR
Less-Proficient Readers

V Ask students the following questions to guide them in reviewing the reading:

- What do the older boys want to do with Pidge? *(They want to throw him into the fire as part of a ceremony to swear an oath of loyalty.)* **Noting Relevant Details**

- What happens to Pidge? *(He slips from Aaron's hands and manages to fly toward the park.)* **Summarizing**

But the boys were on top of him, and the pigeon slipped from Aaron's hands.

"Get him!" shouted Carl.

Aaron thought of the worst, the most horrible thing he could shout at the boys. "Cossacks!" he screamed. "You're all Cossacks!"

Two boys held Aaron back while the others tried to catch the pigeon. Pidge fluttered along the ground just out of reach, skittering one way and then the other. Then the boys came at him from two directions. But suddenly Pidge beat his wings in rhythm, and rose up, up, over the roof of the nearest tenement, up over Second Avenue toward the park.

With the pigeon gone, the boys turned toward Aaron and tackled him to the ground and punched him and tore his clothes and punched him some more. Aaron twisted and turned and kicked and punched back, shouting "Cossacks! Cossacks!" And somehow the word gave him the strength to tear away from them.

When Aaron reached home, he tried to go past the kitchen quickly so his mother wouldn't see his bloody face and torn clothing. But it was no use; his father was home from work early that night and was seated in the living room. In a moment Aaron was surrounded by his mother, father, and grandmother, and in another moment he had told them everything that had happened, the words tumbling out between his broken sobs. Told them of the present he had planned, of the pigeon for a goat, of the gang, of the badge with the secret code on the back, of the shack, and the fire, and the pigeon's flight over the tenement roof.

And Aaron's grandmother kissed him and thanked him for his present which was even better than the pigeon.

"What present?" asked Aaron, trying to stop the series of sobs.

And his grandmother opened her pocketbook and handed Aaron her mirror and asked him to look. But all Aaron saw was his dirty, bruised face and his torn shirt.

Aaron thought he understood, and then, again, he thought he didn't. How could she be so happy when there really was no present? And why pretend that there was?

Later that night, just before he fell asleep, Aaron tried to imagine what his grandmother might have done with the pigeon. She would have fed it, and she certainly would have talked to it, as she did to all the birds, and . . . and then she would have let it go free. Yes, of course. Pidge's flight to freedom must have been the gift that had made his grandmother so happy. Her goat has escaped from the Cossacks at last, Aaron thought, half dreaming. And he fell asleep with a smile. ❖

> *Pidge beat his wings in rhythm, and rose.*

WORDS TO KNOW
tenement (tĕn′ə-mənt) *n.* a rundown apartment building

192

Multicultural Perspectives

Between 1880 and 1920, nearly 2.5 million Jewish people immigrated to the United States from a variety of eastern European countries. Many of these immigrants settled in industrial cities in the East—such as Boston, New York, and Philadelphia—and the Midwest. However, by 1920 most Americans were convinced that there were too many immigrants. Opposition to Jewish immigrants from Eastern Europe resulted in the passage in 1924 of a law that put a sharp limit on the number of immigrants permitted to come to the United States. This law also established national quotas aimed at reducing immigration from southern and eastern European countries on the grounds that such immigrants were not as likely to make good Americans as those from northern and western Europe. Asians had already been excluded in 1917.

192 THE LANGUAGE OF LITERATURE TEACHER'S EDITION

LITERARY INSIGHT

Street Corner Flight

BY NORMA LANDA FLORES

From this side . . .
   of their concrete barrio[1]
     two small boys hold
       fat white pigeons
trapped in their trembling hands.

Then,
  gently,
    not disturbing
      their powers of flight,
        release them
into the air.

They were free
  to glide above
    rushing traffic
      soar beyond
        labyrinths[2] of
food stamps . . . loneliness . . . and want.

They were free
  to fly
    toward the other side . . .
a world away.

---

1. **barrio** (bä′rē-ō′): a city neighborhood where many Spanish-speaking people live.
2. **labyrinths** (lăb′ə-rĭnths′): mazes.

CUSTOMIZING FOR
Gifted and Talented Students

Have students locate two places in the story where Aaron's grandmother uses a mirror. Ask students to comment on the similarity and meaning of the two examples and how their meaning connects to the main idea of the story.

COMPREHENSION CHECK

1. What does Aaron notice about the pigeon he finds in the park? *(It has a broken wing.)*
2. How does Aaron get Pidge to walk across the room while training it to be a carrier pigeon? *(He puts popcorn on the other side of the room to tempt the pigeon.)*
3. Why does Aaron want to give the pigeon to his grandmother for her birthday? *(to replace her goat that was killed in a pogrom when she was a girl)*
4. How does the pigeon escape danger? *(It flies away over the tenement buildings toward the park.)*

LITERARY INSIGHT

1. What basic theme is shared by both the main selection and the Insight poem? *(Both concern young people and birds seeking freedom in city neighborhoods.)*
2. What might the birds' flight symbolize? *(Possible responses: hope and freedom—if the birds can escape, perhaps the boys can as well.)*
3. Whom do you think "they" refers to in lines 12 and 18? *(The pigeons that are actually flying above the city. The word also seems to refer to the boys, who, through the birds, can symbolically fly to a world beyond the barrio.)*

Norma Landa Flores A native of Los Angeles, Norma Landa Flores (1937–) believes that words, both spoken and written, have the power to help individuals rise above difficult circumstances. While corresponding with Gwendolyn Brooks, a poet she greatly admired, Flores realized that she could make use of all the elements of her ancestry and her life. Of that period Flores says she learned to "take gifts from the past to survive in the present."

Mini-Lesson Spelling

FINAL Y WORDS AND SUFFIXES Point out to students that when a suffix is added to many words ending in *y*, the *y* is changed to *i* or *ie* before the suffix is added.

frenzy + ed = frenzied

lady + s = ladies

Application Have students add suffixes to the following words.
1. clumsy + ness
2. buggy + s
3. lucky + ly
4. spy + ed
5. carry + er
6. sixty + eth
7. bury + ed
8. lonely + ness
9. temporary + ly
10. country + s
11. worry + ed
12. happy + er

Ask students to look, in their own writing and in things that they read, for more words that fit this pattern. Have them add these words to their personal word lists.

Reteaching/Reinforcement
- *Unit Two Resource Book*, p. 25

THE LANGUAGE OF LITERATURE **TEACHER'S EDITION** 193

From Personal Response to Critical Analysis

1. Encourage students to use details from the story in their picture.
2. Most students will say that giving Pidge his freedom was Aaron's gift to his grandmother. Some will also say that Aaron's bravery and determination to save Pidge's life is his gift.
3. Possible responses: Aaron is a caring, thoughtful boy. He fixes Pidge's broken wing, plans to give his grandmother the best gift he can think of, and shares an important task with Noreen. He respects the members of his family, except in going against his mother's advice about the gang. His desire to join the gang is not a negative one, since he wants to feel accepted and liked by the older boys.
4. Students' responses will vary, depending on the gift they wrote about.
5. Possible responses: The poem deals with two boys releasing pigeons to freedom, much like Aaron. The idea of freedom, through the image of the pigeon, is central to both the poem and the short story.
6. Possible responses: A club is a group of people with common interests who perform activities together. A gang is a group whose common interests tend toward violence and socially unacceptable activities, such as those pursued by Carl and the older boys in the story. Today's gangs seem especially destructive.

Another Pathway

Encourage students to reread passages from the story to help them identify the characters, conflicts, and events of the story. Ask students to take detailed notes while rereading to assist them in completing the story map. If students are having difficulty, have them write a list of questions they have about the reading. You might choose to have a class discussion about these questions before students begin the activity.

Rubric

3 Full Accomplishment Students produce a complete and accurate story map.
2 Substantial Accomplishment Most events and elements in the story are included in the story map.
1 Partial or Little Accomplishment Few events in the story are included in the story map. Elements such as conflict or theme are omitted or incorrectly identified.

RESPONDING OPTIONS

FROM PERSONAL RESPONSE TO CRITICAL ANALYSIS

REFLECT 1. Draw a picture of the one scene, object, or character that stands out most in your memory of this story. Share the picture with your classmates.

RETHINK 2. What do you think Aaron's gift to his grandmother is?

3. What kind of person is Aaron? Describe his character and values.
   Consider
   Close Textual Reading
   - his feelings about the gang
   - his behavior toward Pidge
   - his relationships with his family and with his friend Noreen

4. Compare Aaron's gift with the gift you wrote about for the Personal Connection on page 184. How is Aaron's gift similar to or different from the gift you wrote about?

5. How does the Insight poem "Street Corner Flight" (page 193) connect with your understanding of the story?

RELATE 6. Aaron wants to belong to a club that his mother calls a gang. What is the difference between a club and a gang? How does the gang in the story compare with the gangs you know about today?

Multimodal Learning
ANOTHER PATHWAY

Filling in a story map similar to the one shown here can help you understand "Aaron's Gift." Copy and complete the story map. Add enough events to describe the entire story. Then compare your story map with another student's.

Main Character:	Setting:
Conflict or Story Problem:	
Major Events:	
Event 1 Aaron finds a pigeon with a broken wing.	
Event 2	
Event 3	
Solution:	Theme:

QUICKWRITES

1. Write a **prediction** telling how Aaron's life might be affected by the events in the story. You may choose to focus on short-term effects, such as Aaron's possible further problems with the gang, or on long-term effects, such as Aaron's qualities as an adult.

2. Pretend you are Aaron's grandmother. Write a **diary entry** for the day Pidge flies away. How do you feel about what Aaron did? What does Pidge's freedom mean to you?

📁 **PORTFOLIO** Save your writing. You may want to use it later as a springboard to a piece for your portfolio.

194 UNIT TWO PART 1: FINDING A SPECIAL PLACE

QuickWrites

1. Encourage students to write their predictions based on as much information about Aaron from the story as possible. Remind students that predicting depends on using information they already know. Make sure that predictions are consistent with Aaron's qualities and that students write in the future tense.

2. Encourage students to reread passages from the story in which Aaron's grandmother is depicted, paying attention to the details about her character. Make sure students use the first-person point of view.

📁 The Writer's Craft

Personal Voice, pp. 276–277
Personal Writing, pp. 28–39

LITERARY CONCEPTS

Characterization is the way writers create and develop characters. A writer may use any or all of these four basic methods to reveal a character's personality:
- description of the character's physical appearance
- the character's speech, thoughts, feelings, and actions
- the speech, thoughts, feelings, and actions of other characters
- direct comments by the writer about the character's nature

In "The Adoption of Albert," for example, the statement of Mary Elizabeth (the narrator) that "Louis was neater than most kids" provides a glimpse of Louis's personality. Find examples from "Aaron's Gift" to show how Myron Levoy develops the character of Aaron or his grandmother.

CONCEPT REVIEW: Theme You may recall that a story's theme is its message about life or people and that often a reader must infer, or figure out, the theme after carefully reading the story. What do you think the theme of "Aaron's Gift" is? What does the story say about life or people—or about the true nature of giving?

Multimodal Learning

ALTERNATIVE ACTIVITIES

1. **Cooperative Learning** With a group of classmates, research the subject of pigeons. Discover how many kinds there are, where they live, what their habits are, and what their place in the environment is. Stage a **debate** for the class on whether the number of pigeons should be controlled in some manner. Discuss both the value of pigeons and the problems they cause.

2. The setting of "Aaron's Gift" is the Lower East Side of New York City. Use a metropolitan New York City map or a comprehensive atlas as a guide to help you draw a **street map** of the Lower East Side. Include sites of historical interest.

3. In the story, Carl wants to make Pidge the club's mascot. Many organizations—especially sports teams—adopt persons, animals, or objects as mascots. Choose a local, regional, or national sports league and research the teams' mascots. Make a **chart** that summarizes your findings. Display the chart in your classroom.

Across the Curriculum

Social Studies *Cooperative Learning* Have students work in small groups of three or four to carry out the research. You might want to assign different regions affected by the czar and the pogroms he ordered. Students can research when the pogroms occurred, what happened during the pogroms, and how life was affected in the particular region. One student should act as a facilitator to organize the group's research and to make sure all students participate. One student should summarize the group's findings. Finally, one student should be elected to present the group's findings to the class.

ADDITIONAL SUGGESTIONS

History *Coming to America* Have students research other immigrant groups that came to the United States. You might divide the class into small groups and have each research a particular ethnic group. Students can find out why these groups left their homelands, when they emigrated, how they traveled to the United States, and where they settled. Groups can give class presentations when they have finished their research.

ACROSS THE CURRICULUM

Social Studies The words *Cossacks* and *pogroms* are explained briefly on the Previewing page for this story and in the story itself. Find out more about the pogroms ordered by Czar Alexander the Third. Who was this ruler? Why did he persecute the Jews? What was the role of the Cossacks in the pogroms? For your classroom library, create a reference file of the information you gather, either on paper or on a computer.

AARON'S GIFT 195

Literary Concepts

Students should be aware that Levoy uses most of the four basic methods to reveal Aaron's and the grandmother's personalities. For instance, through descriptions, the reader learns that Aaron is a great roller-skater and that his grandmother endured a traumatic experience in her childhood.

Concept Review: Theme The basic theme of this story is that freedom is the greatest gift of all. Some students may say that the story suggests that the sentiment behind giving a gift is more important than the gift itself.

Alternative Activities

1. Instruct groups to begin their research with encyclopedias or books on birds. Make sure groups are able to support their opinion in the debate.
2. Students might also use tourist guides to find suitable street maps of New York City. Encourage students to locate Tompkins Square Park, the park in which Aaron finds Pidge.
3. Encourage students to find out why each organization chose its particular mascot. Drawings or photocopies of team mascots can be included in the chart.

THE LANGUAGE OF LITERATURE TEACHER'S EDITION 195

Literary Links

Possible responses: Pidge—helps Aaron to realize his potential as a caring person and teaches him a valuable lesson about bravery, determination, and the gift of freedom. Tupa—threatens the safety of Mako and Afa; teaches Mako a valuable lesson about bravery, determination, and heroism. Scarhead—threatens the safety of Paulsen at first but teaches him a valuable lesson about the relationship between humans and animals. Bimbo—cares for Tito by feeding him and leading him safely around Pompeii; saves his life by leading him to a boat during the eruption.

Words to Know

Exercise A
1. c
2. b
3. c
4. a
5. d

Exercise B
1. Make sure students effectively communicate the meanings of the words through their movements.
2. Possible response: Aaron's neighborhood is made up of many <u>tenement</u> buildings. On a hot summer night, many people sit on their <u>stoops</u> talking about the day and greeting friends walking by.

MYRON LEVOY

The title of Myron Levoy's book *The Witch of Fourth Street and Other Stories* refers to East Fourth Street on New York City's Lower East Side. The book's eight stories portray events in the lives of immigrants who lived in that area during the 1920s.

LITERARY LINKS

Look back at selections in this book in which animals play important roles: "Ghost of the Lagoon," the excerpt from *Woodsong,* and "The Dog of Pompeii." Compare and contrast the role of Tupa, Scarhead, or Bimbo with the role of Pidge in "Aaron's Gift."

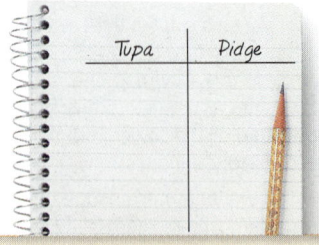

WORDS TO KNOW

EXERCISE A On your paper, write the letter of the word that is different in meaning from the other words in each set below. Use a dictionary if you wish.

1. (a) entrance (b) stoop (c) balcony (d) porch
2. (a) frenzied (b) fragile (c) frantic (d) wild
3. (a) emblem (b) mascot (c) opponent (d) symbol
4. (a) mansion (b) high-rise (c) apartment (d) tenement
5. (a) struggling (b) flailing (c) thrashing (d) relaxing

EXERCISE B Work with a partner to complete the exercises below.

1. Use body movements to demonstrate the meanings of *frenzied* and *thrashing*.
2. Describe Aaron's neighborhood, using *stoop* and *tenement* in your description.

MYRON LEVOY

1930–

Myron Levoy was born in New York City and worked as a chemical engineer before becoming a professional writer. He writes poetry, plays, and short stories. In describing his work, he says, "My continuing concern has been for the 'outsider,' the loner." In *Alan and Naomi,* Levoy writes about a Jewish boy facing anti-Semitism who befriends a deeply troubled refugee girl. In another novel, *A Shadow Like a Leopard,* Levoy depicts a boy from the ghetto who is torn between two worlds—he carries a knife but also writes poetry. Each of these people, says Levoy, must grow and struggle to discover who he or she is.

Levoy has won many national and international awards for his work. In 1982, *A Shadow Like a Leopard* was named one of the best books for young adults by the American Library Association. *The Witch of Fourth Street and Other Stories,* from which "Aaron's Gift" is taken, was named a *Book World* honor book.

OTHER WORKS *Three Friends, The Hanukkah of Great-Uncle Otto, Pictures of Adam, The Magic Hat of Mortimer Wintergreen, Kelly 'n Me* Extended Reading

---

WHAT DO YOU THINK?
Reflecting on Theme

Have students refer back to the Venn diagrams they created before reading the selections in Part 1. Ask them to create a similar diagram for Aaron and his grandmother. Encourage students to rethink their own Venn diagrams after completing the activity.

ON YOUR OWN

Where the Sidewalk Ends

BY SHEL SILVERSTEIN

There is a place where the sidewalk ends
And before the street begins,
And there the grass grows soft and white,
And there the sun burns crimson bright,
5   And there the moon-bird rests from his flight
To cool in the peppermint wind.

Let us leave this place where the smoke blows black
And the dark street winds and bends.
Past the pits where the asphalt flowers grow
10 We shall walk with a walk that is measured and slow,
And watch where the chalk-white arrows go
To the place where the sidewalk ends.

Yes we'll walk with a walk that is measured and slow,
And we'll go where the chalk-white arrows go,
15 For the children, they mark, and the children, they know
The place where the sidewalk ends.

SHEL SILVERSTEIN

1932–

Besides writing poetry, songs, and stories, Shel Silverstein draws cartoons, sings, and plays the guitar. He started writing and drawing when he was around 12, although, he says, "I would much rather have been a good baseball player."

Silverstein's work is popular among people of all ages. His books include *Where the Sidewalk Ends*, *A Light in the Attic*, and *The Giving Tree*. The poet lives on a houseboat in California but travels often. He says, "I want to go everywhere, look at and listen to everything. You can go crazy with some of the wonderful stuff there is in life. I have ideas, and ideas are too good not to share."

WHERE THE SIDEWALK ENDS   **197**

OBJECTIVES

- To promote independent active reading
- To provide opportunities for alternative assessment
- To apply and practice skills learned in previous selections
- To provide an opportunity to assess students' performance through an alternative assessment instrument.

Reading Pathways

- Encourage students to read independently and write in dialogue journals
- Have students choose partners and do a paired reading
- Invite groups of students to do a choral reading, choosing parts for each individual to read
- Evaluate how well students can read, interpret, and write about the selection on their own by using the Integrated Assessment for Unit Two, located in the Alternative Assessment booklet. Administer the assessment at the end of the unit after students have read all the selections and completed all the writing that was assigned. Set aside two class periods, or about two hours, for the assessment.

SHEL SILVERSTEIN

When speaking about writing, Shel Silverstein has said, "If it's good, it's too good not to share. That's the way I feel about my work. So I'll keep on communicating."

PRINT AND MEDIA RESOURCES

UNIT TWO RESOURCE BOOK
Strategic Reading: Literature, p. 29

FORMAL ASSESSMENT
Selection Test, pp. 41–42
Part Test, pp. 43–44
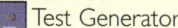 Test Generator

ALTERNATIVE ASSESSMENT
Unit Two Integrated
  Assessment, pp. 7–12

ACCESS FOR STUDENTS ACQUIRING ENGLISH
Reading and Writing Support

AUDIO LIBRARY
See Reference Card

THE LANGUAGE OF LITERATURE TEACHER'S EDITION **197**

Thematic Link: *Finding a Special Place*
In these poems, writers describe their personal experiences and explore places special to them.

The Spider and the Fly

BY MARY HOWITT

"Will you walk into my parlor?"
    said the Spider to the Fly,
"'Tis the prettiest little parlor
    that ever you did spy.
5 The way into my parlor
    is up a winding stair,
And I have many curious things
    to show when you are there."
"Oh no, no," said the little Fly,
10   "to ask me is in vain,
For who goes up your winding stair
    can ne'er come down again."
"I'm sure you must be weary, dear,
    with soaring up so high;
15 Will you rest upon my little bed?"
    said the Spider to the Fly.
"There are pretty curtains drawn around,
    the sheets are fine and thin,
And if you like to rest awhile,
20   I'll snugly tuck you in!"
"Oh no, no," said the little Fly,
    "for I've often heard it said,
They never, never wake again,
    who sleep upon your bed!"

25 Said the cunning Spider to the Fly,
    "Dear friend, what can I do,
To prove the warm affection
    I've always felt for you?
I have within my pantry
30   good store of all that's nice
I'm sure you're very welcome—
    will you please to take a slice?"
"Oh no, no," said the little Fly,
    "kind sir, that cannot be,
35 I've heard what's in your pantry and
    I do not wish to see."
"Sweet creature," said the Spider,
    "you're witty and you're wise;
How handsome are your gauzy wings,
40   how brilliant are your eyes!
I have a little looking-glass
    upon my parlor shelf,
If you'll step in a moment, dear,
    you shall behold yourself."

45 "I thank you, gentle sir," she said,
    "for what you're pleased to say,
And bidding you good morning now,
    I'll call another day."
The Spider turned him round about
50   and went into his den,
For well he knew the silly Fly
    would soon come back again.
So he wove a subtle web,
    in a little corner sly,
55 And set his table ready,
    to dine upon the Fly.
Then he came out to his door again
    and merrily did sing:
"Come hither, hither, pretty Fly,
60   with the pearl and silver wing.
Your robes are green and purple—
    there's a crest upon your head;
Your eyes are like the diamond bright,
    but mine are dull as lead."

MARY HOWITT

A year after Mary and William Howitt were married, they moved to Nottingham, England, where they lived for 14 years while establishing their literary careers. After the success of *Sketches of Natural History,* Mary went on to write more work in verse, including ballads, as well as the novel *Mary Barton (1848).* After moving to London in the late 1840s, both Mary and William Howitt regularly contributed to a variety of London periodicals.

<blockquote>

65 Alas, alas! How very soon
        this silly little Fly,
    Hearing his wily, flattering words,
        came slowly flitting by.
    With buzzing wings she hung aloft,
70   then near and nearer drew,
    Thinking only of her brilliant eyes,
        and green and purple hue;
    Thinking only of her crested head—
        poor foolish thing!
75 Up jumped the cunning Spider
        and fiercely held her fast.
    He dragged her up his winding stair,
        into his dismal den,
    Within his little parlor—
80   but she ne'er came out again!

</blockquote>

MARY HOWITT

"The Spider and the Fly," Mary Howitt's best-known children's poem, appeared in her book *Sketches of Natural History,* published in 1834. Created for Howitt's own children, this collection of brief lyrics displays the poet's ability to convey moral principles in a whimsical, witty way. She produced similar poetry in the collections *Tales in Verse* and *Birds and Flowers and Other Country Things.*

Howitt (1799–1888) grew up as Mary Botham in Uttoxeter, England, where she shared a passion for reading poetry with her sister Anna. In 1821, she married William Howitt, who was also a writer and with whom she coauthored several books. The Howitts' Quaker faith dominated their lives and writings.

In the early 1840s, the couple spent three years in Germany, where Mary translated German works into English and learned the Swedish language. In the years 1845–1847, she translated four works of the Danish writer Hans Christian Andersen. She is credited as the first to make his stories accessible to English and American readers. In her fruitful career, Howitt wrote more than 50 books and edited, adapted, translated, and compiled over 30 others.

Two girls of twelve or so at a table

BY CHARLES REZNIKOFF

Two girls of twelve or so at a table
in the Automat, smiling at each other
and the world; eating sedately.
And a tramp, wearing two or three tattered coats,
5   dark with dirt, mumbling, sat down beside them—
Miss Muffit's spider.
But, unlike her, they were not frightened away,
and did not shudder as they might if older and look askance.
They did steal a glance
10 at their dark companion and were slightly amused:
in their shining innocence seeing
in him only another human being.

Snack Bar (1954), Isabel Bishop. Oil on masonite, 13 ½″ × 11 ⅛″, Columbus Museum of Art, Ohio, Museum Purchase: Howald Fund.

Art Note

Snack Bar by Isabel Bishop Isabel Bishop (1902–1988) is well-known for her images of the lives of women in New York City—women on their work breaks, sharing a drink or ice cream, at the office and at home. John Russell, an art critic for the *New York Times*, commented that Bishop had "a novelist's eyes for idiosyncrasies of anatomy, dress, and social behavior."

Reading the Art *What details does the painter focus on in this scene? What effect does her use of detail, color, and line have on her subject matter?*

CHARLES REZNIKOFF

1894–1976

After receiving a law degree and being admitted to the New York bar in 1916, Charles Reznikoff chose not to practice law but to concentrate on writing. For a time he worked as an editor for the American Law Book Company, and in 1955 he became an editor for Jewish Frontier in New York City.

The Brooklyn, New York, native once explained that he preferred to use his mental energy for writing: "I did not continue with journalism because—to change the old adage—I was more interested in dog bites man than in man bites dog." In addition to numerous volumes of poetry, Reznikoff is remembered for his novels, including *By the Waters of Manhattan* and *The Lionhearted*.

CHARLES REZNIKOFF

Charles Reznikoff began writing poetry when he was 13. His poetry first appeared after World War I. Highly respected by fellow poets, Reznikoff was perhaps best known for his clear and simple imagery. Labeled the "dean of Jewish-American poets," Reznikoff used his cultural heritage as the basis of many of his poems.

Multicultural Perspectives

NATIVE AMERICANS When Christopher Columbus landed at the Caribbean island of Hispaniola in 1492, he thought that he had arrived at the East Indies. Because of this, he called the inhabitants of the island Indians. Many people still use this erroneous term when referring to the indigenous peoples of North, Central, and South America. Then, in 1735 the Swedish taxonomist Carolus Linnaeus formally recognized these people as the American, or "red," race. Therefore, some 2,000 or more different cultures in the Americas came to be understood in completely inappropriate cultural and racial terms. These Native Americans were not Indians, they were not red, nor because of their great variety could they easily be put in a single cultural category.

New World

by N. Scott Momaday

1.
First Man,
behold:
the earth
glitters
5 with leaves;
the sky
glistens
with rain.
Pollen
10 is borne
on winds
that low
and lean
upon
15 mountains.
Cedars
blacken
the slopes—
and pines.

2.
20 At dawn
eagles
hie and
hover
above
25 the plain
where light
gathers
in pools.
Grasses
30 shimmer
and shine.
Shadows
withdraw
and lie
35 away
like smoke.

Sunset in Memorium (1946), Woody Crumbo. The Philbrook Museum of Art, Tulsa, Oklahoma.

OPTION 2

Individual Activity
MAKING A DIORAMA

Ask students to select one of the poems and to create a diorama that represents their impressions of the poem. Encourage students to use a variety of media in their dioramas, as well as any found objects that help to represent the sensory details and imagery in the chosen poem.

Teacher's Role Because this activity centers on students' personal interpretations of the poems, the teacher should provide initial support to help students organize their thoughts and plan their dioramas. Encourage students to reread their chosen poem, paying attention to the sensory details and imagery used by the poet and thinking about how to incorporate these details in their dioramas.

Rubric

3 Full Accomplishment Students translate their impressions of the chosen poem and successfully incorporate sensory details and imagery from the poem in their dioramas.

2 Substantial Accomplishment Students adequately translate their impressions of the poem and incorporate some of the sensory details and imagery in their dioramas.

1 Little or Partial Accomplishment Students have difficulty translating their impressions of the poem and incorporating sensory details and imagery in their dioramas.

3.
At noon
turtles
enter
40   slowly
into
the warm
dark loam.
Bees hold
45   the swarm.
Meadows
recede
through planes
of heat
50   and pure
distance.

4.
At dusk
the gray
foxes
55   stiffen
in cold;
blackbirds
are fixed
in the
60   branches.
Rivers
follow
the moon,
the long
65   white track
of the
full moon.

N. SCOTT MOMADAY

"I have known that the sense of place is a dominant factor in my blood," says N. Scott Momaday. "It happens that I have traveled far and wide, and I have made my home elsewhere. But some elemental part of me remains in the hold of northern New Mexico."

Momaday grew up in New Mexico, where his parents taught among the Jemez Indians. The novelist, poet, editor, and adapter of Native American tales says he came to know the land by exploring it in all seasons. His artistic skill came from his father, an artist who was a Kiowa Indian, and his writing ability from his

1934–

mother, a writer whose great-grandmother was a Cherokee. His interest in poetry was inspired by his admiration of the poems of Emily Dickinson.

Momaday was a relatively unknown author when, in 1969, he received the Pulitzer Prize for fiction for his novel *House Made of Dawn*. He has taught English literature in several universities. An accomplished artist as well, he has had his drawings and paintings exhibited in galleries. Momaday now teaches at the University of Arizona, where he continues to write and to pursue his interest in ancient forms of storytelling.

N. SCOTT MOMADAY

N. Scott Momaday's work centers on the myths and legends of the Kiowa tribe. His writing for children includes *Owl in the Cedar Tree* and *The Gourd Dancer*, a book of poems with illustrations he created himself. He has received grants from the Guggenheim Foundation and the National Institute of Arts and Letters.

Something Told the Wild Geese

BY RACHEL FIELD

Something told the wild geese
    It was time to go.
Though the fields lay golden
    Something whispered,—"Snow."
5 Leaves were green and stirring,
    Berries, luster-glossed,
But beneath warm feathers
    Something cautioned,—"Frost."
All the sagging orchards
10   Steamed with amber spice,
But each wild breast stiffened
    At remembered ice.
Something told the wild geese
    It was time to fly,—
15 Summer sun was on their wings,
    Winter in their cry.

RACHEL FIELD

1894–1942

In 1929, Rachel Field was the first woman to receive the Newbery Medal. *Hitty: Her First Hundred Years,* the book that earned Field this honor, was inspired by an antique doll she found in a New York City antique shop. The name Hitty appeared on a slip of paper pinned to the doll's dress. In creating the story of a doll carved from mountain ash by a peddler, Field combined her interests in children's stories and history—particularly the history of pioneer life.

Born in New York City, Field grew up in western Massachusetts. She attended a small private school, with only about ten students, where her interests in writing and acting began. Because of her writing ability, she was admitted to Radcliffe College in 1914. Three of her plays were eventually produced there.

Best known for her books for children, Field produced more than 40 such books, including several volumes of poetry and some books with her own illustrations. Three of her adult fiction books, most notably *All This and Heaven Too,* were adapted as motion pictures.

RACHEL FIELD

Over the course of her life, Rachel Field was a novelist, poet, playwright, editor, and illustrator. Her interest in writing developed early in her life. As a senior in high school, she won a three-school essay contest and received $20. During her lifetime, Field was better known for her adult fiction than for her works for children. Since her death in 1942, she is most remembered for her children's literature.

OPTION 3

Class Discussion
SHARING IDEAS

After students have read the poems, engage them in a whole-class discussion using the following questions:

1. What theme or themes do these poems share? How are they different? *(Possible response: Most of the poems describe places and/or experiences that are special to the writer. But they differ in their use of imagery, rhyme, and rhythm.)*

2. Discuss the use of the image of the frightening and dangerous spider in both "The Spider and the Fly" and "Two girls of twelve or so at a table." How do the poems differ in their attitudes toward this image? *(Possible response: In "The Spider and the Fly," the poet uses the image of the deadly spider to warn children about the dangers of being fooled by strangers. In "Two girls," the poet uses the image of Miss Muffit's spider to show how the girls were not scared away by the tramp but instead treated him as a human being.)*

3. Compare and contrast the imagery of the natural world used by the poets in "New World" and "Something Told the Wild Geese." *(Possible response: Both poems describe beautiful aspects of the natural world. However, in "New World," various awe-inspiring sights are depicted in minute detail, while in "Something Told the Wild Geese," the poet imagines what goes on in the minds of the geese as she describes the beauty of their seasonal flights.)*

4. Which poem had the strongest effect on you as you read it? Why? *(Responses will vary. Make sure students support their answers with details from the poems.)*

Teacher's Role Before starting class discussion, you may wish to review the poems by reading each aloud or by asking for volunteers to read them aloud. During discussion, encourage students with differing points of view to support their opinions with specific references to the poems. Remind them, if necessary, that poetry is open to many possible interpretations.

OVERVIEW

In the Guided Assignment for this section, students will write an essay interpreting a passage. By interpreting and writing about a story, students learn to read closely and to write by supporting their ideas with details from the selection. The Writer's Style will help students understand the importance of clearly stating their main ideas and supporting them with facts, details, or examples. In Reading the World, students will explore the use of stage sets to understand the importance of details.

Objectives

- To understand how writers use main ideas and supporting details
- To add details to an idea through the use of dashes
- To write an interpretation of a passage
- To analyze real-world situations and settings

Skills

LITERATURE
- Using examples and details to support the main idea

GRAMMAR AND USAGE
- Using dashes
- Using quotations
- Understanding parts of speech

MEDIA LITERACY
- Understanding setting

SPEAKING, LISTENING AND VIEWING
- Peer response
- Group conferencing

CRITICAL THINKING
- Drawing conclusions
- Analyzing

Teaching Strategy: MODELING
In the following models, examples and details are used to support the main idea of each passage. These techniques are useful in all writing that involves analysis and interpretation.

A **Yep** Possible responses: The writer did not know how to speak Chinese and he was in Catholic school. The examples he gives are of his Chinese-speaking friends who used to tell jokes that he didn't understand, and the few words he did pick up. The examples support the main idea by showing that he could not fully understand Chinese and felt like an outsider.

B **Levoy** Possible responses: The wing was fixed by using Popsicle sticks as splints. Details include how easy the wing was to fix, Pidge's behavior, and the materials used to fix the bird's wing.

---

206   THE LANGUAGE OF LITERATURE TEACHER'S EDITION

WRITING ABOUT LITERATURE

GETTING TO THE POINT

Is "Chinatown" about a city or about the writer discovering himself? Is "Aaron's Gift" about a boy and his pigeon, or is there more to the story? Finding meaning in a work of literature is often like finding a valuable treasure. The same skills you use to understand literature can help you make sense of things in your daily life. In these pages you'll

- study the details writers use to support their ideas
- choose a confusing or interesting passage to interpret
- study details to help interpret the meaning of a stage setting

The Writer's Style: Main Idea and Details Writers often present what is important to them by clearly stating an idea and supporting it with facts, details, or examples.

Read the Literature

What is the main idea of each passage? How do you know?

Literature Models

A **Examples Support the Main Idea**
What do you learn about the writer of the first passage? What example does Yep give? How does the example support the main idea?

> Moreover, my lack of Chinese made me an outsider in Chinatown—sometimes even among my friends. Since it was a Catholic school taught by nuns, my friends would always tell dirty jokes in Chinese so the nuns wouldn't understand. However, neither did I, so I missed out on a good deal of humor when I was a boy. What Chinese I did pick up was the Chinese that got spoken in the playground—mostly insults and vulgar names.
>
> Laurence Yep, from "Chinatown"

B **Details Support the Main Idea**
How was Pidge's wing fixed? What details does the author give about this event?

> The wing was surprisingly easy to fix, for the break showed clearly and Pidge was remarkably patient and still, as if he knew he was being helped. Or perhaps he was just exhausted from all the thrashing about he had done. Two Popsicle sticks served as splints, and strips from an old undershirt were used to tie them in place. Another strip held the wing to the bird's body.
>
> Myron Levoy, from "Aaron's Gift"

206   UNIT TWO: THE NEED TO BELONG

PRINT AND MEDIA RESOURCES

UNIT TWO RESOURCE BOOK
The Writer's Style, p. 33
Prewriting Guide, p. 34
Elaboration, p. 35
Peer Response Guide, pp. 36–37
Revision and Editing, p. 38

GRAMMAR MINI-LESSONS
Transparencies, pp. 33, 35–41
Copymasters, p. 43

FORMAL ASSESSMENT
Guidelines for Writing Assessment

ACCESS FOR STUDENTS ACQUIRING ENGLISH
Reading and Writing Support

Connect to Advertising

Advertisement writers present their main ideas in many different ways. Why do you think the writer of this advertisement states the main idea at the beginning? How else might the ad be written? Would it be as clear? as good?

Advertisement

Facts Support the Main Idea What facts are included in the ad? What remains after you separate the facts from the promises?

Try Your Hand: Main Idea and Details

1. **Adding Facts** Skim the selection "Chinatown," from *The Lost Garden*, and then try the following:
   - Add a fact about the plant life in Chinatown to the following sentence: "There is little plant life in Chinatown."
   - Revise the following sentence to add a fact about the Chinese language: "The Chinese language was sometimes spoken in Chinatown."

2. **A Real-Life Example** Write a statement about something you like to do, such as read books, play sports, or watch movies. Then write some examples that support your statement.

3. **Including Details** Revise a piece of your current writing by using specific details to support your main ideas.

SkillBuilder

Using Dashes

Dashes can be used creatively and effectively to add details to paragraphs. Look at the first literature model on the opposite page. Notice how the information following the dashes clarifies Laurence Yep's ideas.

You can also use dashes to show a break in thought. Place a dash before the break and a second dash to end the break. Look at this passage from Myron Levoy's "Aaron's Gift." Notice where the author places the dashes and what additional detail he provides.

A group of older boys from down the block had a club—Aaron's mother called it a gang—and Aaron had longed to join as he had never longed for anything else.

APPLYING WHAT YOU'VE LEARNED
Read this paragraph and think about where dashes could have been used. Then rewrite it and compare your paragraph with those of your classmates.

I thought "Chinatown" was a great selection. It was the best I've read so far. I even argued about how good it was with Tina. She thought it was just OK.

GRAMMAR HANDBOOK

For more information on other punctuation marks, see page 844 of the Grammar Handbook.

WRITING ABOUT LITERATURE **207**

Teaching Strategy:
USING THE SKILLBUILDER

C You can help students identify one technique for adding details by teaching the SkillBuilder on Using Dashes at this time. It will help students to recognize that dashes are a creative way to add details.

Teaching Strategy: MODELING

D Possible responses: The facts include that someone can make $2.00 for each Cable Car item sold. The facts do not seem to equal the promises because the promises mention "outrageous prizes or big bucks."

Try Your Hand

1. Responses will vary. Added facts should provide description about the absence of plant life or the Chinese language as shown in these examples:
   - Between the asphalt and the buildings, nothing could grow.
   - Plants might come up in summer, but they soon died in the heat. Nothing grew in winter.
   - At least a few of the many dialects of the Chinese language were sometimes spoken in Chinatown.
2. Statements should be backed up with relevant example as in this sample: "I like to read books all the time. Even when there are really good things on TV, I prefer to read. Adventure stories and mysteries are my favorites."
3. Ensure that students can identify their main ideas. Encourage them to add details by asking questions about their main ideas that would lead to elaboration and examples.

SkillBuilder — GRAMMAR FROM WRITING

USING DASHES Check that students understand the differences between the two uses of dashes. Guide them to recognize what is between the dashes is not crucial to the rest of the sentence but merely adds information. Have students review the selections in this unit and identify which types of dashes writers use and why they may use them.

Application Possible response:

I thought "Chinatown" was a great selection—the best I've read so far. I even argued about how good it was with Tina—she thought it was just OK.

Additional Suggestions Have students rewrite the following paragraph using dashes:

I was confused about why Laurence Yep thought that way. He is the writer. I felt he could have been proud of being different. Perhaps that's just me.

THE LANGUAGE OF LITERATURE **TEACHER'S EDITION 207**

Teaching Strategy:
STUMBLING BLOCK

E Often, students are unaware that a passage they find difficult to understand can supply important insights or information. Encourage students to avoid passing over lines in the story that are a little confusing.

Teaching Strategy:
COLLABORATIVE OPPORTUNITY

F Students can assist each other to work through difficult passages. Guide them to break up passages and sentences into their component parts and come up with ideas explaining each part or sentence.

Writing Skill: POINT OF VIEW

G The Discovery Draft provides an opportunity for students to think through ideas and information they've gathered. Help students find their point of view by having them rephrase the idea in the passage and then to imagine how they would respond if a friend or family member expressed this idea. In addition, students can refer to their double-entry reading logs to respond to the various components of their passage.

WRITING ABOUT LITERATURE

Interpretation

As you read more, you'll find that some stories are special to you. These stories may have characters or events that remind you of people or experiences in your life. Sometimes characters have the same problems you have. You may even find important messages in these stories that will last a lifetime. To find these messages, you will have to interpret, or explore the meaning of, key parts of stories.

GUIDED ASSIGNMENT
Interpret a Passage Have you ever been startled or confused by a passage in a story? On these pages you'll look at one passage and explore its meaning.

1 Prewrite and Explore

Go back to a Unit Two selection that you liked or to another favorite story. Reread the story or just skim it. A double-entry reading log like the one at the left can help you record and explore important or confusing lines or passages.

CHOOSING YOUR PASSAGE

The following questions might help you select a line or passage to write about.

- Which lines or passages seem important to the story?
- Which passage confused, surprised, or interested you?

Decision Point Based on your answers to the questions above, which passage do you want to write about? If necessary, take more time to think about the possibilities. Consider discussing the lines with your classmates to come up with ideas.

2 Write and Analyze a Discovery Draft

Now look closely at the passage you have chosen and try to figure out what it means. Ask yourself the following questions:

- What does the writer describe in the passage or line?
- What details does the writer use?
- What do I think the writer is trying to say?

The yellow notes on the discovery draft show the student's thoughts about one passage.

Line or passage	Ideas
"I was always going into Chinatown to explore the streets and perhaps find the key to the pieces of the puzzle."	– What does he hope to find in Chinatown? – What puzzle? – Why do other family members leave Chinatown?
"How could I pretend to be somebody else when I didn't even know who I was?"	– What does he mean—he doesn't know who he is? – This sounds like an important line. – Maybe that's the puzzle.

208 UNIT TWO: THE NEED TO BELONG

Assessment Option

SELF-ASSESSMENT After students have completed the Choosing Your Passage assignment, they should assess their reasons for selecting their passage. Students can consider the following questions:
- Why am I interested in this passage?
- Is there a particular part of this passage that contains the central or important point?
- What would I think about this idea if a friend said it to me?
- What words or images does the writer use to make the passage exciting or interesting?

Student's Discovery Draft

I want to tell how I feel about this passage. Then I can tell what the meaning is.

A passage near the end of "Chinatown" makes me sad. It makes me sad because the narrator didn't enjoy dressing up in costumes anymore. I think the writer tried to make this an important part.

I think he wants to figure out who he is first. Maybe the costumes confuse him.

Why does it upset me that he doesn't want to put on those costumes? He describes costumes so nicely. People wear costumes to pretend they're somebody else. He says he doesn't know who he is. Does he?

COLLECTING THE EVIDENCE

Gathering details is a good way to develop your essay. List facts, examples, or reasons that support your ideas.

③ Draft and Share

Consider organizing your draft into three parts: an introduction that summarizes the story and tells why you chose this particular passage; a body that has reasons, facts, examples, and other evidence to explain your interpretation; and a conclusion in which you summarize your interpretation. Ask another student to read your essay and give you feedback.

 PEER RESPONSE

- Which details help you understand my interpretation?
- Which parts of the passage or my interpretation are still unclear?

SkillBuilder

 WRITER'S CRAFT

Using Quotations

Quoting characters or passages directly can be a powerful way to elaborate on and support your ideas. In choosing quotations to include in your writing, however, be sure that they support your point. Also be sure to copy the words exactly and to credit the writer or speaker. Here are some things to remember when using quotations in your writing.

- When quoting someone else's work, always enclose the quotation in quotation marks. Keep capitalization, punctuation, and spelling the way they are in the original.
- If you leave out part of a quotation, show the place where material is omitted by using ellipsis points (. . .).

I think Laurence Yep wrote "Chinatown" to figure out who he is and to make his childhood less confusing. In the beginning he says, "I was always going into Chinatown to explore the streets and perhaps find the key to the pieces of the puzzle."

APPLYING WHAT YOU'VE LEARNED

Look over the quotations you have chosen to make sure they support your main idea clearly and strongly.

WRITING ABOUT LITERATURE 209

Writing Skill: ELABORATION

H Have students practice gathering details and elaborating on their ideas by looking at their Discovery Drafts. Encourage students to identify the main idea in each of the passages. Then have them list the details that support these main ideas. Ask of each detail, if it is a fact, an example, or a reason.

Teaching Strategy: USING THE SKILLBUILDER

I You can help students collect evidence by teaching the SkillBuilder on Using Quotations at this time. It will help students to understand the use of quotations for elaborating on and supporting their ideas.

Speaking, Listening, and Viewing: COLLABORATIVE OPPORTUNITY

J An alternative to having students reading each other's work silently is having the writer of the draft read it aloud to a partner. The listener can take notes on the ideas he or she understands or parts where the writer's meaning is unclear. Make sure students read slowly and clearly, pausing after each point so the other can jot down his or her ideas. In this way, students can hear their own ideas expressed and notice the places that are unclear. They also may receive useful feedback from their listening partners.

SkillBuilder WRITER'S CRAFT

USING QUOTATIONS Show students the various ways they can credit the writer by using introductory phrases such as: "As Laurence Yep says"; "I can understand what Laurence Yep is feeling when he writes"; "Myron Levoy states that"; or "I think Myron Levoy is accurate when he describes the bird." Remind students that their introductory phrases should be smooth and contain the writer's first and last name the first time he or she is mentioned.

Application While students are checking that their quotations support their ideas, they also should check that their quotations are introduced, accurately, and punctuated correctly.

Additional Suggestion Have students try to keep their quotations brief. Encourage them to shorten long quotations by selecting the important parts and omitting the rest, replacing the removed words with ellipsis points.

Reteaching/Reinforcement
- *Grammar Handbook*, anthology pp. 850–851
- *Grammar Mini-Lessons* copymasters, p. 42, transparencies, p. 33

Quotation Marks, 586–589

Critical Thinking: ANALYZING

K Help students understand that revision begins with identifying the main ideas in their essays. Then they should note whether the ideas have been supported. Ideas that need more support or need to be made more interesting can be fixed by adding facts, examples, or reasons.

Teaching Strategy: MODELING

L Discuss with students how this sample meets the Standards for Evaluation on this page. The writer explained the subject of the paper by asking an important question at the beginning, introduced the story, and used a quotation as an example of the Laurence Yep's deep feelings.

Standards for Evaluation

Ideas and Content
- gives the author, title, and brief summary of the literature
- explains what the writer thinks a passage means
- is supported with quotes, reasons, and other evidence
- shows why the writer thinks the passage is important

Structure and Form
- uses well-organized paragraphs and a clear organization
- includes transitional words and phrases to show relationships among ideas
- uses a variety of sentence structures

Grammar, Usage, and Mechanics
- contains no more than two or three minor errors in grammar and usage
- contains no more than two or three minor errors in spelling, capitalization, and punctuation

---

WRITING ABOUT LITERATURE

4 Revise and Edit

Writers revise and edit their drafts to make their writing clearer and more interesting. As you revise your essay, make sure your details and evidence help support your conclusions. When you are finished, you could read your essay to someone who has not read the selection you wrote about. Did your essay make the person want to read the story?

Student's Final Draft

Have you ever asked yourself "Who am I"? The writer of "Chinatown," Laurence Yep, does. At first I thought this selection was just about Chinatown and what it was like when the author was a boy. But after I read it again, I knew it was about how confused Yep was when he was a kid. When I think back on the selection, the final passage stands out. To me, it describes the meaning of the whole story.

How did the writer tell you what the paper would be about?

Why did the writer use the quotation in this paragraph?

When the writer talks about his singing adventure, he sets us up because we think it's a funny scene. But then he starts talking about his deep feelings. He says, "But the experience cured me of wanting to dress up and be something else." In this passage the writer realized that he just wanted to be his own person.

Standards for Evaluation

The interpretive essay
- identifies the work by title and author and the passage to be interpreted
- explains what the writer thinks a passage means
- is supported by quotations, reasons, and other evidence
- shows why the writer thinks the passage is important

210 UNIT TWO: THE NEED TO BELONG

Assessment  Option

SELF-ASSESSMENT Students can assess their own writing by asking themselves the following questions:
- *Is my interpretation based on one specific passage in the story?*
- *Did I express my reaction to the passage?*
- *Have I used facts, details, and examples to support my ideas?*
- *Did I examine my word choice to make my writing accurate and vivid?*
- *Have I checked the accuracy and punctuation of my quotations?*

Grammar in Context

Sentence Fragments As a writer, you put sentences together from bits and pieces of ideas. Readers will not understand your interpretive essay if you write sentences that do not express a complete thought. Every sentence has two parts. The subject tells whom or what the sentence is about. The predicate tells what was done or what happened.

> Have you ever asked yourself "Who am I"? The writer of "Chinatown." When I think back on the selection. The final passage stands out. To me, it describes the meaning of the whole story.

(editorial corrections: *does* inserted after "Chinatown,"; comma after "selection")

Notice how the corrections in the above paragraph help the writer express complete thoughts. For more information about sentence fragments, see page 812 of the Grammar Handbook.

Try Your Hand: Fixing Sentence Fragments

Add subjects or predicates to each fragment below to create a complete sentence. Be sure to use correct end marks and other punctuation in the sentences you form.

1. My lack of Chinese
2. enjoyed putting on costumes
3. very little plant life in Chinatown
4. The fancy hotels of Nob Hill
5. Despite all the coaching from his father

SkillBuilder

GRAMMAR FROM WRITING

Understanding Parts of Speech

Understanding parts of speech can help you make sure your sentences have complete subjects and complete predicates. Sometimes the same word may be used as several parts of speech. When a word is used as a certain part of speech, it follows the rules for that part of speech. The only way to determine a part of speech in a sentence is to reread the sentence carefully and see how the word is used. Look at these sentences and how the italicized words are used.

- A friend's father would *fashion* Chinese weapons at home. (verb)
- He didn't know much about Chinese *fashion*. (noun)
- He searched all over Chinatown for a *fashion* magazine. (adjective)

APPLYING WHAT YOU'VE LEARNED

Write two sentences for each word below. Use the word as each part of speech shown in the parentheses.

1. ring (noun, verb)
2. cold (adjective, noun)
3. well (noun, adverb)
4. turn (noun, verb)

Now look at your draft to make sure you have used each word as the correct part of speech.

WRITING ABOUT LITERATURE **211**

CUSTOMIZING FOR
Students Acquiring English

Students acquiring English may have a particularly difficult time writing complete sentences. Help them to identify subjects and predicates in selections from this unit. Then have them revise their own writing by identifying subjects and predicates and correcting any sentence fragments. Suggest a variety of strategies to correct fragments, such as adding a verb, subject, or predicate. Students can also combine the fragment with another sentence to create a complex sentence or use dashes to incorporate the fragment into a sentence.

Teaching Strategy:
USING THE SKILLBUILDER

You can help students identify subjects and predicates and use them to make complete sentences by teaching the SkillBuilder on Understanding Parts of Speech.

CUSTOMIZING FOR
Less-Proficient Writers

You may wish to have less-proficient writers work with partners to study the corrections made to the passage. Then encourage partners to share examples of their writing. Guide pairs to look for sentence fragments in their own or each other's writing and correct each instance. The Grammar Handbook can assist students working by themselves or those working in pairs.

Try Your Hand

Check that sentences are complete and correctly punctuated; for example:
1. My lack of Chinese sometimes stood in my way.
2. The adults enjoyed putting on costumes.
3. There is very little plant life in Chinatown.
4. The fancy hotels of Nob Hill are what I want to see.
5. Despite all the coaching from his father, the boy did not want to play football.

SkillBuilder  GRAMMAR FROM WRITING

UNDERSTANDING PARTS OF SPEECH

Explain to students that sometimes the form of a part of speech needs to be changed to make a sentence correct. Write the following sentences on the chalkboard and have volunteers correct the word *fashion* to make each sentence correct:
- I have fashion this flute for you to play.
- I am fashion a new roof so the water will run off my house.
- The people at the society dinner were very fashion.

Application Possible responses:
1. The ring was on her finger.
   I will ring the bell loudly.
2. The dog had a cold nose.
   My cold is making my nose run.
3. The old well was dry at the bottom.
   Laurence Yep writes very well.
4. Make a left turn at the bridge.
   The ocean liner had to turn around.

Additional Suggestions Suggest other words for students to practice making sentences with, such as *fit, ride, cover,* and *boot.* Encourage them to use each word as a noun and a verb.

Reteaching/Reinforcement
- *Grammar Mini-Lessons* transparencies, pp. 35–41

THE LANGUAGE OF LITERATURE TEACHER'S EDITION **211**

READING THE WORLD

In this lesson, students learn the importance of the components of a theater set. Props, furniture, and walls are considered to suggest the importance of settings in general. Students come to understand that the setting can provide important information about the rest of the parts of a play or story.

Critical Thinking: ANALYZING

P Explain to students that props can be large items such as tables, counters, and other furniture, or small items such as the laundry basket, cutting board, or postcards. Encourage students to analyze the set by comparing these items to what is in their own kitchen or dining room.

Media Literacy: INTERPRETING A SETTING

Q Have students describe the function of the items they have noted. Lead them to speculate that it is probably daytime, and midday when the washing is done and dinner is not yet prepared. Tell them that plays can be set in this century or even long ago. Encourage them to speculate whether this play is set in the past or present. Based on the appliances, students will most likely say the play is set in the past. They may think that a family lives here because of the number of chairs, the washing, and the notebook and crayons. Students could conclude that the family is not wealthy, because they do not have a separate dining room nor do they have a lot of possessions.

Speaking, Listening, and Viewing: ROLE-PLAY

R Invite students to create their cast by drawing on their own conceptions of a family or domestic scene. Suggest that they divide the parts of the set and the props according to activities, with a character associated with each activity. Students can then discuss the age of the characters and the costumes that would be appropriate.

READING THE WORLD

WHAT'S THE BIG IDEA?

By carefully choosing and arranging props, directors of theater, movie, and TV productions can present an idea as clearly as the writers of stories can. You can study the details in a set—or any room—to make sense of what you see and perhaps find a message or special meaning.

P **View** Look at this stage set. In your notebook, describe the props, furniture, walls—anything that gets your attention.

Q **Interpret** Think about why those props were used. Then ask yourself these questions: What information about the time or the characters does each detail give? Who might live here? Are they rich or poor?

R **Discuss** In a small group, share your ideas about the stage set. Then, create a cast of characters for the play. Discuss details from the set to help create your characters. Now follow up on your discussion by using the SkillBuilder on the next page.

212

212 THE LANGUAGE OF LITERATURE TEACHER'S EDITION

SkillBuilder

 CRITICAL THINKING

Drawing Conclusions

When you draw conclusions, either while reading or while viewing something, you use written or visual clues and information from your own experience to figure out something that is not directly stated.

For example, if you peeked into a friend's house and saw old portraits of relatives, a coat of arms hanging on the wall, and photo albums on a table, you might conclude that your friend's family takes pride in its history.

APPLYING WHAT YOU'VE LEARNED

Some settings give us particular ideas or special meanings. For example, the details in a judge's chambers might suggest authority or fairness; a hotel lobby might use furnishings to suggest homeyness or warmth.

In a small group, think of a setting. Agree on a particular idea or meaning that the setting might give. Then brainstorm a list of the details that would help you create that idea.

WRITING ABOUT LITERATURE 213

SkillBuilder CRITICAL THINKING

DRAWING CONCLUSIONS To draw conclusions about the set on this page, students can imagine it as another example of a friend's house. Ask them what they would think of their friend's house. Ask students who else they think might live there. Use a selection from this unit as a model to show students the type of settings that writers use in their descriptions.

Application Challenge students to think of new and interesting settings such as a campsite, a home of the future, or a car on a passenger train. Have them think about the particular items that their setting will need and what might make it individual and illustrative of a particular situation. Point out that they will need to think of large and small props.

THE LANGUAGE OF LITERATURE TEACHER'S EDITION 213

UNIT TWO
Part 2 Lesson Planner

TIME ALLOTMENTS SHOWN ARE APPROXIMATE. DEPENDING ON YOUR GOALS AND THE NEEDS OF YOUR STUDENTS, YOU MAY WISH TO ALLOW MORE OR LESS TIME FOR CERTAIN PORTIONS OF THE LESSON.

Table of Contents	Discussion	Previewing the Selection	Reading the Selection
PART OPENER **TESTS OF ENDURANCE** What Do You Think? page 214	**20 MINUTES** • Reflect on the part theme		
SELECTION **Oh Broom, Get to Work** page 216 EASY		**20 MINUTES** • PERSONAL CONNECTION • CULTURAL CONNECTION • WRITING CONNECTION	**20 MINUTES** • Introduce vocabulary • Read pp. 215–20 (6 pp.)
SELECTIONS **It Seems I Test People/Growing Pains** page 224 AVERAGE		**20 MINUTES** • PERSONAL CONNECTION • LITERARY CONNECTION • READING CONNECTION: Reading poetry orally	**5 MINUTES** • Read pp. 224–25 (2 pp.)
SELECTION **The Mushroom** page 230 CHALLENGING		**20 MINUTES** • PERSONAL CONNECTION • SCIENCE CONNECTION • READING CONNECTION: Chronological order	**20 MINUTES** • Introduce vocabulary • Read pp. 230–34 (5 pp.)
SELECTION **Cricket in the Road** page 238 CHALLENGING		**20 MINUTES** • PERSONAL CONNECTION • GEOGRAPHICAL CONNECTION • READING CONNECTION: Understanding dialogue	**10 MINUTES** • Introduce vocabulary • Read pp. 238–40 (3 pp.)

Writing	Exploring Topics	Prewriting	Drafting and Revising
WRITING FROM EXPERIENCE **Narrative and Literary Writing***	**20 MINUTES**	**30 MINUTES**	**75 MINUTES**

* Time estimates assume in-class work. You may wish to assign some of these stages as homework.

Responding to the Selection

FROM PERSONAL RESPONSE TO CRITICAL ANALYSIS	OR	ANOTHER PATHWAY	LITERARY CONCEPTS	QUICKWRITES
		40 MINUTES		
• Discussion questions	OR	• Chart	• Anecdote	• List of rules • Diary entry
		40 MINUTES		
• Discussion questions	OR	• Role-playing	• Simile	• Character sketch • Advice column
		50 MINUTES		
• Discussion questions	OR	• Role-playing	• Essay	• Tabloid-newspaper account • Science fiction story • Eyewitness account
		50 MINUTES		
• Discussion questions	OR	• Chart	• Internal and external conflict	• Dialogue • Diary entry • Poem

Publishing and Reflecting

30 MINUTES

Extension Activities

- ALTERNATIVE ACTIVITIES
- LITERARY LINKS
- CRITIC'S CORNER
- THE WRITER'S STYLE
- ACROSS THE CURRICULUM
- ART CONNECTION
- WORDS TO KNOW
- BIOGRAPHY

40 MINUTES

✔   ✔   ✔   ✔

50 MINUTES

✔   ✔   ✔   ✔

40 MINUTES

✔   SCIENCE   ✔   ✔

40 MINUTES

✔   SOCIAL STUDIES   ✔   ✔

LESSON PLANNER TEACHER'S EDITION **213b**

UNIT TWO

Part 2 Cooperative Project

Youth Community Guidebook

Overview

Students will research, write, and design a guide to their community from a sixth grader's point of view.

PROJECT AT A GLANCE

The selections in Unit Two, Part 2 are about struggles to find a place to belong—whether that place be internal or external. For this project, students will get to know their community and will share that information with others through a guidebook. Students will work in small groups to document youth-oriented events, resources, and attractions in the area. Listings will be organized, described, and perhaps even rated. This guidebook should be thought of as a method of introduction and as a reference manual for new kids in town. The culmination of the project is the "publication" of the guidebooks as they are displayed for the entire school.

OBJECTIVES

- To collect information about youth-related services and activities available in the community or neighborhood
- To create a descriptive list and evaluate the quality of these services and activities
- To work together to produce a resource guide for young people

SUGGESTED GROUP SIZE

4–5 students per group

MATERIALS

- Local telephone directory
- Local newspapers, magazines, brochures
- Still camera (if available)
- Colored paper or binders for the final product

1 Getting Started

Arranging the Project

Gather newspapers, magazines, or brochures containing information on local tourist attractions for students to look at. Many brochures are available from your Chamber of Commerce or other merchants' groups. Be sure to include small church newsletters or "penny saver" publications often found in grocery stores, which are valuable resources of local information. In the collection, include a telephone directory containing both white and yellow pages. Alert the school librarian that students may be requesting other local information.

You may want to reserve some time for the guidebooks to be on display, perhaps on a special table in the cafeteria or school library.

Assigning the Guidebooks

Tailor the project to the size of your town or city. In a small community, you might ask each group to find all the possible youth-oriented events and activities. In a large urban area, you might assign each group a particular topic to investigate, such as youth programs, entertainment, museums, shopping areas, restaurants, or sporting events. Individual booklets can then be combined into one comprehensive guidebook.

It would be helpful to include photos of each place and event in the guidebooks, but you will have to decide if, when, and how students should use a school camera.

2 Creating a Guidebook

Introducing the Project

Explain that students will be working in small groups to research, design, and produce a guidebook that could be used as a guide to the youth-oriented services and attractions available in your community. Allow students to browse through the publications you have gathered so they can get an idea of the goal of the project.

Ask students to imagine that they have transferred to your school from a school in another state. What kinds of information would they like to know? Students can brainstorm a list of questions that can serve as a springboard for organizing and writing their guidebooks (Where is the best place to buy tapes and CDs? What is there to do on Saturday nights? Where can I go to meet people my own age?). You might keep the questions for later use in assessing the guidebooks.

Group Investigations

Divide students into groups of four or five. The groups will work together to make a final list of general places, services, and attractions they would like to know about before beginning specific research. Encourage groups to interview other students to get their ideas about what to include in the books. As the groups work to create comprehensive lists, discuss their projects with them to keep track of their progress.

Creating a Project Description

Ask each group to submit a one-page written report, listing the topics they will investigate and the specific assignments of group members. Groups may choose to divide research responsibilities by type or geography, whichever works best for them. Meet with each group to review the project description and then later to monitor progress.

OPTION 1: FANTASY GUIDEBOOK Groups can create guidebooks for fantasy towns in which they would like to live.

OPTION 2: SCHOOL GUIDEBOOK Groups can write guidebooks for new students in their school. The books might include a list of all the teachers, times the office is open, the variety of extracurricular activities available, a list of current class and Student Council officers, and a map of the school building.

213c UNIT TWO THE NEED TO BELONG

OPTION 3: SHOPPING GUIDEBOOK Groups can research and write guidebooks for a large shopping area, such as a mall. All stores should be included, along with a list of the kinds of goods offered. Stores can be rated according to the amount and variety of bargains they offer.

OPTION 4: COMMUNITY TOUR Groups can select several "important" places in their community or neighborhood and can create a tour of these places. The route should be well-detailed in writing, as well as shown on a map. All significant places should be described briefly.

When all of the guidebooks are completed, allow time for the groups to examine and comment on each other's work.

3 Sharing the Guidebooks

You may want to set up a table in the cafeteria or a special place in the library so other students can leaf through the guidebooks at their leisure. Appoint a monitor to be sure the books survive intact. Later, guidebooks can be placed in the library for students to read and check out.

Assessing the Project

The following rubric can be used for group or individual assessment.

3 Full Accomplishment Students followed directions and produced a guidebook of youth-oriented features of their community or neighborhood.

2 Substantial Accomplishment Students produced a guidebook, but it does not represent intensive research into youth-oriented services and attractions.

1 Little or Partial Accomplishment Students' guidebooks are incomplete or do not fulfill the requirements of the assignment.

For the Portfolio
The guidebooks will remain in the school library, so include a copy of your written assessment in each student's individual portfolio. Remember to refer to the original questions developed by the whole class when writing the assessments.

Note: For other assessment options, see the *Teacher's Guide to Assessment and Portfolio Use.*

Cross-curricular options

SOCIAL STUDIES

Students can research to find out how some large cities have changed their image over the last 150 years. Have them note what was changed, why it was changed, and how it was changed, as well as how long it took for its reputation to change.

FOREIGN LANGUAGE

Students who are studying another language or are fluent in another language may want to translate part or all of their guidebook. Check with the language teacher first, and warn that some help might be required.

LANGUAGE ARTS

Students can create a glossary of slang or unusual terms used in the community. Such a glossary should, of course, include definitions.

ART

Students can illustrate the guidebook with pictures of interesting sights or appropriate drawings.

GEOGRAPHY

Students can create a map of the community and mark it with the points of interest included in their guidebook.

Resources

Contact local and state Boards of Tourism.

Mapmaking by Karin N. Mango introduces a variety of maps and their uses.

PART 2

WHAT DO YOU THINK?
Objectives

The activities on this page can be used to
- introduce the Part 2 theme, "Tests of Endurance," since each activity is connected to one or more of the selections in Part 2
- create materials for students' personal portfolios that they can later reconsider or revise
- build an understanding of theme that can be reviewed and revised as students progress through the unit

Are you a good sport?
Make sure that each group chooses a game that is familiar to all members of the group. Ask the groups to consider, as they draft their guidelines, what qualities a good sport possesses in general. (See "Cricket in the Road," p. 237.)

What was your test?
Have students begin by creating an outline that details their accomplishments and how they felt about them. Encourage students to describe how difficult they felt it was to accomplish what they did. (See "The Mushroom," p. 228.)

What are your obstacles?
Before they begin drawing, have partners brainstorm a list of obstacles that someone might face while growing up. Encourage them to incorporate their own experiences in their drawings. (See "Oh Broom, Get to Work," p. 215, and "It Seems I Test People" and "Growing Pains," p. 226.)

UNIT TWO **PART 2**

TESTS OF ENDURANCE

WHAT DO YOU THINK?

REFLECTING ON THEME

In a tug of war, one side seems to be stronger; then the power shifts. The tugs in opposite directions can be compared to the emotions experienced in growing up, when the need to belong conflicts with the need to be independent. Use this page of activities to explore the tests of endurance you have faced and the lessons you have learned.

What was your test?
Recall a major childhood accomplishment, such as learning to ride a bicycle. Did you become discouraged at some point? Who encouraged you? How did you motivate yourself? Describe the experience in your notebook.

Where are your obstacles?
What problems are involved in growing up? Work with a partner to begin drawing an obstacle course that shows some of the pitfalls of growing up. Leave space to add more obstacles as you read the selections in Part 2.

Are you a good sport?
Working with a group, choose a game familiar to everyone. Discuss your knowledge of the game, and draft a list of guidelines for being a good sport while playing it. Compare your list with those of other groups. What has the class identified as the most important quality of a good sport?

Good sport guidelines
1.
2.
3.
4.
5.

Looking Back
At the beginning of this unit, you thought about finding a special place. Did you discover new ideas as you read? Which character's special place is most similar to your own? Draw or paint that character's special place.

214

COMMUNITY OUTREACH
Invite local politicians to speak to the class about the difficulties of running for public office and about the strength and the endurance that are needed during a political campaign. After the speakers have addressed the class, engage students in a discussion to see whether they feel they might have the endurance necessary both to run for public office and to serve their constituents well. Encourage students also to discuss what qualities they feel are necessary for someone to be a successful politician.

Looking Back
Have students write a one-sentence or two-sentence summary of each selection in Part 1, focusing on the idea of a special place. Then have students write a summary about their own special places. Ask students to compare both sets of summaries and to select the character who has a special place similar to their own. When students have chosen a character's special place, ask them to create a list of details about this special place that they can incorporate in their drawings or paintings.

214 THE LANGUAGE OF LITERATURE TEACHER'S EDITION

PREVIEWING

NONFICTION

Oh Broom, Get to Work
Yoshiko Uchida (yō'shē-kō ōō-chē'dä)

PERSONAL CONNECTION *Activating Prior Knowledge*

This selection describes how a young girl reacts to the presence of unwanted visitors in her home. How would you deal with an unwanted guest? With your classmates, brainstorm some creative solutions to this problem.

CULTURAL CONNECTION *Building Background/ Setting a Purpose*

As you read this selection, note the effects that the visitors have on "Yo Chan" (as Yoshiko Uchida was nicknamed). Also consider the effect that Yoshiko has on the visitors—especially as you read about the incident with the broom.

As young girls, Uchida and her sister, Keiko (kā'kō), found themselves continually in the company of household guests. Uchida's parents were Issei (ēs'sā')—Japanese immigrants to the United States—and often opened their home to Japanese students, such as the one shown here, who came to the United States to study at the University of California or the Pacific School of Religion. Most of these visitors were engaged in graduate work, the advanced courses taken by students who have already received a college degree. Their studies, made more difficult by living in a foreign and unwelcoming land, were in preparation for the Christian ministry.

Courtesy of the Pacific School of Religion.

WRITING CONNECTION

Choose one of the following questions as a topic, and write about it in your notebook.

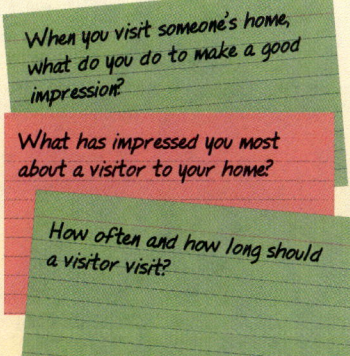

When you visit someone's home, what do you do to make a good impression?

What has impressed you most about a visitor to your home?

How often and how long should a visitor visit?

OVERVIEW

Objectives

- To understand and appreciate an autobiographical essay about a Japanese-American family in the late 1920s
- To enrich reading by using active reading strategies
- To understand and identify anecdotes
- To appreciate and identify descriptive details that help make writing lively and interesting
- To express understanding of the selection through a choice of writing forms, including a list and a journal entry
- To extend understanding of the selection through a variety of multimodal and cross-curricular activities

Skills

READING SKILLS/ STRATEGIES
- Evaluating

LITERARY CONCEPTS
- Anecdote
- Theme

GRAMMAR
- Common and proper nouns

SPELLING
- The suffix *-ous*

SPEAKING, LISTENING, AND VIEWING
- Group discussion
- Oral presentation

Cross-Curricular Connections

GEOGRAPHY
- Using a Map

OH BROOM, GET TO WORK **215**

PRINT AND MEDIA RESOURCES

UNIT TWO RESOURCE BOOK
Strategic Reading: Literature, p. 43
Vocabulary SkillBuilder, p. 46
Reading SkillBuilder, p. 44
Spelling SkillBuilder, p. 45

GRAMMAR MINI-LESSONS
Transparencies, p. 25
Copymasters, p. 33

ACCESS FOR STUDENTS ACQUIRING ENGLISH
Selection Summaries
Reading and Writing Support

FORMAL ASSESSMENT
Selection Test, pp. 45–46
 Test Generator

 **AUDIO LIBRARY**
See Reference Card

THE LANGUAGE OF LITERATURE TEACHER'S EDITION **215**

SUMMARY

Yoshiko Uchida reaches back to her childhood to recall the steady parade of Japanese visitors who came to her parents' home in California. In the author's view, all these visitors—with a few rare exceptions—were boring. Uchida's mother was unfailingly kind to the guests—a trait not shared by her resentful daughter, who gleefully relates that she once followed an old Japanese tradition for getting rid of unwanted visitors, using an upside-down broom.

Thematic Link: *Tests of Endurance*
Yoshiko must learn to endure the many visits of guests she finds boring.

CUSTOMIZING FOR
Students Acquiring English

- Use **ACCESS FOR STUDENTS ACQUIRING ENGLISH**, *Reading and Writing Support*.
- This story tells about a Japanese superstition: If you drape a cloth over a broom and stand it upside down, an unwelcome visitor will leave. Invite students to share superstitions from their cultures with the class.
- Encourage students from Japanese backgrounds to share information on the customs, foods, and language mentioned in the story.

STRATEGIC READING FOR
Less-Proficient Readers

Set a Purpose To help students become immersed in the selection, invite them to share their memories of parents' guests who seemed boring. As students read, they should identify the two kinds of visitors to the Uchida's home.

Use **UNIT TWO RESOURCE BOOK**, pp. 43–44, for guidance in reading the selection.

Oh Broom,

216

WORDS TO KNOW

audacious (ô-dā′shəs) *adj.* fearlessly and recklessly daring; bold (p. 220)
deprive (dĭ-prīv′) *v.* to take something away from (p. 217)
devise (dĭ-vīz′) *v.* to form or plan in the mind (p. 217)
dispense (dĭ-spĕns′) *v.* to give out; distribute (p. 219)
dread (drĕd) *n.* deep fear; terror (p. 217)

indifferent (ĭn-dĭf′ər-ənt) *adj.* not interested; unconcerned (p. 219)
intrusion (ĭn-troō′zhən) *n.* an act of coming in rudely or inappropriately (p. 217)
laden (lād′n) *adj.* weighed down; heavy (p. 219)
pious (pī′əs) *adj.* showing religious feeling, especially in a way designed to draw attention (p. 218)
pompous (pŏm′pəs) *adj.* having excessive self-esteem or showing exaggerated dignity (p. 218)

216 THE LANGUAGE OF LITERATURE TEACHER'S EDITION

Get to Work

by Yoshiko Uchida

I was on my way home from school when I found it. A little dead sparrow. It lay still and stiff, its legs thrust in the air like two sticks. It was the first dead creature I had seen close up, and it filled me with both <u>dread</u> and fascination.

I knew what I would do. I would give the bird a nice funeral. Mama would find a piece of soft red silk for me from her bag of sewing scraps. I would wrap the bird in a silken shroud,[1] put it in a candy box, and bury it beneath the peach tree. Maybe I would have Mama say a prayer for it, like the minister did at real funerals.

I picked up the bird carefully, cupping it in both hands, and ran home. I rushed through the kitchen and flung open the swinging door to the dining room.

"Look, Mama! I found a dead sparrow!"

But Mama was busy. She was sitting in the easy chair, knitting quietly. Sitting across from her on the sofa was a squat blob of a man—balding and gray—as silent as a mushroom.

The only sound was the soft ticking of the Chelsea clock on the mantel above the fireplace. I could see dust motes floating in the shaft of late afternoon sun that filtered in from the small west window.

Poor Mama was stuck with company again. She and the guest had both run out of things to say, but the visitor didn't want to leave.

"Hello, Yo Chan," my mother called. She seemed happy for the <u>intrusion</u>. "How was school today?"

But all I thought was, company again! It wasn't the first time a visitor had <u>deprived</u> me of my mother's time and attention, and I was tired of having them intrude into our lives uninvited. I stomped out of the living room without even a word of greeting to our guest, and knew I would have to bury the sparrow by myself.

Mama might have sung a Japanese hymn for me in her high, slightly off-key voice, and she certainly would have offered a better prayer than I could <u>devise</u>. But I did the best I could.

"Dear Heavenly Father," I began. "Please bless this little bird. It never hurt anybody. Thank you. Amen."

Poor Mama was stuck with company again.

---

1. **shroud** (shroud): a cloth used to wrap a body for burial.

WORDS TO KNOW
dread (drĕd) *n.* deep fear; terror
intrusion (ĭn-trōō'zhən) *n.* an act of coming in rudely or inappropriately
deprive (dĭ-prīv') *v.* to take something away from
devise (dĭ-vīz') *v.* to form or plan in the mind; think up

217

CUSTOMIZING FOR
Gifted and Talented Students

As students read the selection, have them look for passages that depict Yoshiko's relationship with Keiko and have them describe this relationship.

Possible responses:

- Page 218—"'What nerve!' Keiko fumed. 'I'll say!'"/The sisters think alike.
- Page 219—"Keiko and I always complained shamelessly when they came." The sisters present a united front against unwanted guests.
- Page 220—"I knew if I looked at Keiko we would both explode."/The sisters have a similar sense of humor.

Linking to Geography

 **D** Japan is about 7,500 miles from California. In the 1920s, when this story takes place, the only way to travel from Japan to California was by ship across the Pacific Ocean. Berkeley is located near San Francisco, which was one of the main seaports for incoming ships. The people visiting Yoshiko's home were far from their own homes and were probably homesick.

Literary Concept: ANECDOTE

Explain to students that an anecdote is a short, amusing account often included within a larger work. Ask students why Uchida included this brief anecdote about the minister and the bathtub. (Possible responses: It is humorous because many people might not expect this behavior from a minister, although Mama's explanation shows that the sisters may have jumped to the wrong conclusion about the minister's behavior. It reinforces Uchida's main idea that having guests created more work for her mother.)

CUSTOMIZING FOR
Students Acquiring English

2 Point out that *some kind of luck* is a sarcastic phrase that conveys the opposite of its literal meaning.

3 Point out that the word *have* appears in italic print because Yoshiko and Keiko emphasize it. Read the sentence aloud, demonstrating this emphasis.

I buried the box beneath a mound of soft, loose dirt, picked a few nasturtiums to lay on top, and made a cross out of two small twigs.

The gray-blob mushroom was just another of the countless visitors, usually from Japan, who came to see my parents. They were both graduates of Doshisha, one of Japan's leading Christian universities, and had close ties with many of its professors. This meant that many of our visitors were ministers or young men studying to become ministers at the Pacific School of Religion in Berkeley.

D Once in a while, one of the visitors would be a pleasant surprise. Like the Reverend Kimura, who sang the books of the Bible to the tune of an old folk song.

"*Mah-tai, Mah-ko, Luka, Yoha-neh-deh-un* . . ." he sang out in a loud, clear voice. "*Shito, Roma, Corinto, Zen-ko-sho* . . ." He clapped in time as he sang.

I saw Mama's eyes light up as she listened, and soon she joined in, clapping and singing and laughing at the pure joy of it.

Mama surprised me sometimes. She could be a lot of fun depending on whom she was with. It was too bad, I thought, that so much of the time she had to be serious and proper, while visiting ministers smothered her with their pious attitudes.

To me they were all achingly and endlessly boring. It was only once in a great while that a Reverend Kimura turned up, like a red jelly bean in a jar full of black licorice.

E One pompous minister from Japan not only stayed overnight, which was bad enough, but left his dirty bathwater in the tub for Mama to wash out.

Yoshiko Uchida (right) and her older sister, Keiko, in the 1920s. Courtesy, The Bancroft Library, Berkeley, California.

"What nerve!" Keiko fumed.
"I'll say!" I echoed.

But Mama explained that in Japan everyone washed and rinsed outside the tub and got in just to soak. "That way the water in the tub stays clean, and you leave it for the next person."

Mama got down on her knees to wash out the tub, saying, "We're lucky he didn't try to wash himself outside the tub and flood the bathroom."

Some kind of luck, I thought. **2**

WORDS TO KNOW	**pious** (pī′əs) *adj.* showing religious feeling, especially in a way designed to draw attention
	pompous (pŏm′pəs) *adj.* having excessive self-esteem or showing exaggerated dignity

---

Mini-Lesson Literary Concepts

THEME Remind students that the theme of a selection is the message about life or human nature that the writer presents to the reader. Some themes are stated directly. Most often, however, the reader must infer the theme on the basis of information and events in the story. Any lessons learned by the main character can be clues to the theme.

Application Invite students to consider the message about visitors that Uchida conveys in "Oh Broom, Get to Work." Elicit from students the idea that some guests just stay too long. To help students find the theme, have them reread the highlighted paragraphs on pages 218 and 219.

I didn't feel at all lucky about the seminary[2] students who often dropped in, plunked themselves down on our sofa, and stayed until they were invited to have supper with us.

"Poor boys, they're lonely and homesick," Mama would say.

"They just need some of Mama's kind heart and good cooking," Papa would add. And if they needed some fatherly advice, he was more than willing to dispense plenty of that as well.

Both my parents had grown up poor, and they also knew what it was to be lonely. They cared deeply about other people and were always ready to lend a helping hand to anyone. Mama couldn't bear to think of her children ever being less than kind and caring.

"Don't ever be indifferent," she would say to Keiko and me. "That's the worst fault of all."

It was a fault she certainly never had. She would even send vitamins or herbs to some ailing person she had just met at the dentist's waiting room.

On holidays all the Japanese students from the Pacific School of Religion—sometimes as many as five or six—were invited to dinner. Keiko and I always complained shamelessly when they came.

"Aw, Mama . . . do you *have* to invite them?"

But we knew what we were expected to do. We flicked the dust cloth over the furniture, added extra boards to the dining room table so it filled up the entire room, and set it with Mama's good linen tablecloth and the company china.

EVALUATE

How does the mother's attitude toward visitors compare with Yoshiko's?
Using a Reading Log

If it was to be a turkey dinner, we put out the large plates and good silverware. If it was a sukiyaki[3] dinner, we put out the rice bowls, smaller dishes, and black lacquer[4] chopsticks.

The men came in their best clothes, their squeaky shoes shined, their hair smelling of camellia hair oil. Papa didn't cook much else, but he was an expert when it came to making sukiyaki, and cooked it right at the table with gas piped in from the kitchen stove. As the men arrived, he would start the fat sizzling in the small iron pan.

Soon Mama would bring out huge platters laden with thin slivers of beef, slices of bean curd[5] cake, scallions, bamboo shoots, spinach, celery, and yam noodle threads. Then Papa would combine a little of everything in broth flavored with soy sauce, sugar, and wine, and the mouth-watering smells would drift through the entire house.

One evening in the middle of a sukiyaki dinner, one of the guests, Mr. Okada, suddenly rose from the table and hurried into the kitchen. We all stopped eating as the scholarly Mr. Okada vanished without explanation.

"Mama," I began, "he's going the wrong way if he has to . . ."

PREDICT

What is happening in the kitchen?
Using a Reading Log

Mama stopped me with a firm hand on my knee. My sister and I looked at each other. What did he want in the kitchen anyway? More rice? Water? What?

---

2. **seminary** (sĕm′ə-nĕr′ē): a school for the training of priests, ministers, or rabbis.
3. **sukiyaki** (sōō′kē-yä′kē): a Japanese dish of sliced meat, bean curd, and vegetables seasoned and fried together.
4. **lacquer** (lăk′ər): a shiny substance used as a decorative coating on wooden objects.
5. **bean curd:** a food made from soybeans—also known as tofu.

WORDS TO KNOW
dispense (dĭ-spĕns′) *v.* to give out; distribute
indifferent (ĭn-dĭf′ər-ənt) *adj.* not interested; unconcerned
laden (lād′n) *adj.* weighed down; heavy

219

STRATEGIC READING FOR Less-Proficient Readers

F Ask the following questions to make sure that students understand who visits the Uchida home:
- Who are the visitors? *(ministers and seminary students, usually from Japan)* Noting Relevant Details
- Why is Mama willing to entertain so many guests? *(They are lonely and homesick, and she is a kind and generous person.)* Drawing Conclusions

Set a Purpose As students read, have them notice how Yoshiko tries to get rid of a guest.

Active Reading: EVALUATE

G Discuss how Yoshiko's attitude toward visitors compares with her mother's. *(Yoshiko's mother seems to welcome anybody into her home, whereas Yoshiko dreads entertaining boring visitors.)*

Literary Concept: SETTING

H Remind students that the setting is the time and place a story happens. Ask them to note the details pertaining to setting on this page. *(Possible responses: Sukiyaki, rice bowls, and chopsticks are Japanese, but turkey and silverware are American. The world Yoshiko lives in seems to be a mix of two cultures.)*

Active Reading: PREDICT

I Challenge students to predict why Mr. Okada is in the kitchen. Then have students compare their predictions to the actual reason.

Mini-Lesson Grammar

COMMON AND PROPER NOUNS Point out to students that a common noun is a general name for a person, place, thing, or idea. A proper noun names a particular person, place, thing, or idea. Proper nouns are capitalized.

Application Invite students to find at least five common nouns and five proper nouns in the selection. Then read the following sentences aloud. Have students replace each underlined common noun with a proper noun. Point out that students can use proper nouns to make their writing more precise.
1. The girl and her sister resented the guest.
2. The minister spoke to a native city dweller.

Reteaching/Reinforcement
- *Grammar Handbook,* anthology p. 839
- *Grammar Mini-Lessons* copymasters, p. 33, transparencies, p. 25

 The Writer's Craft

Common and Proper Nouns, pp. 378–379

Common Nouns	Proper Nouns
girl	Yoshiko
seminary	Pacific School of Religion
guest	Mr. Okada

THE LANGUAGE OF LITERATURE TEACHER'S EDITION 219

CUSTOMIZING FOR
Multiple Learning Styles

J **Musical Learners** Allow interested students to learn the song "In the Good Old Summertime" and, taking the roles of the Uchidas and their guests, sing it for the class.

STRATEGIC READING FOR
Less-Proficient Readers

K Ask students how Yoshiko made the guest leave. *(Possible response: She followed a Japanese superstition of turning a broom upside down. The superstition had no real power, but since the guest had heard of it, he took the hint when he saw the broom.)* Noting Relevant Details

Critical Thinking: ANALYZING

L Ask students why, at the end of the story, Yoshiko felt as though she had evened the score a little. *(Possible response: Of the many unwanted guests from the seminary, Yoshiko managed to get rid of one.)*

COMPREHENSION CHECK

1. Who are the unwelcome visitors in this story? *(ministers or seminary students from Japan)*
2. Why do these visitors come to the Uchidas' house? *(The Uchidas invite them; the visitors are lonely.)*
3. What things do the visitors do that annoy Yoshiko? *(They take her mother's attention; they come uninvited and stay too long; they make extra work for the Uchidas.)*
4. What does Mrs. Wasa suggest to solve the problem of unwanted guests? *(She suggests that Yoshiko try an old Japanese superstition—turn a broom upside down and cover it with a cloth—that causes unwelcome guests to leave.)*

It seemed a half hour before Mr. Okada finally reappeared. But he was smiling and seemed much happier.

"I'm sorry," he murmured, "but it was so warm I had to remove my winter undershirt." He wiped his face with a big handkerchief and added, "I feel much better now."

I knew if I looked at Keiko we would both explode. But I did. And we did. We laughed so hard we had to leave the table and rush into the kitchen holding our sides. Keiko and I often got the giggles at company dinners, and the harder we tried to stop, the harder we laughed. The only solution was for us not ever to glance at each other if we felt the giggles coming on.

In spite of all our grumbling, Keiko and I often enjoyed ourselves at these dinners. Sometimes it was Papa who provided the laughs. He loved to talk, and everyone always liked listening to his stories. Sometimes he would tell a joke he had heard at the office:

A visitor from Japan looked up at the sky. "Beautiful pigeons!" he says to a native San Franciscan.

"No, no," answers the native. "Those aren't pigeons, they're gulls."

The visitor replies, smiling, "Well, gulls or boys, they're beautiful pigeons!"

Much laughter all around.

After dinner Papa liked to gather everyone around the piano. He had a good baritone voice, often sang solos at church, and even organized the church choir. Keiko played the piano, and we sang everything from "Old Black Joe"[6] to "In the Good Old Summertime."

Sometimes Keiko and I added to the entertainment by playing duets for our guests—a fairly <u>audacious</u> act since most of the time I hadn't practiced all week. It never occurred to me then, but I suppose we were just as boring to them as they so often seemed to us.

I once thought I'd found the perfect solution for getting rid of unwanted guests. Mrs. Wasa, who was like an adopted grandmother, told me one day of an old Japanese superstition.

"If you want someone to leave," she said, "just drape a cloth over the bristles of a broom and stand it upside down. It always works!"

I filed that wonderful bit of information inside my head, and the very next time Mama was trapped in the living room with another silent mushroom, I gave it a try. I did just as Mrs. Wasa instructed and stood the broom at the crack of the swinging door leading to the dining and living rooms.

"Oh, broom," I murmured. "Get to work!"

I kept a watchful eye on our visitor, and before too long, he actually got up and left.

"Mama, it worked! It worked!" I shouted, dancing into the living room with the broom. "He left! I got him to leave!"

But Mama was horrified.

"*Mah*, Yo Chan," she said. "You put the broom at the doorway where he could see?"

I nodded. "I didn't think he'd notice."

Only then did I realize that our visitor had not only seen the broom, but had probably left because he knew a few Japanese superstitions himself.

I'd always thought the seminary on the hill was bent on endlessly churning out dull ministers to try my soul. But that afternoon I felt as though I'd evened the score just a little. ❖

Before too long, he actually got up and left.

---

6. "Old Black Joe": a song by Stephen Foster (1826–1864), a composer of songs celebrating life in the Old South.

WORDS TO KNOW
audacious (ô-dā′shəs) *adj.* fearlessly and recklessly daring; bold

220

Mini-Lesson  Spelling

THE SUFFIX -OUS Tell students that the suffix *-ous* means "full of" or "having the characteristics of." When the suffix is added to a noun, the word becomes an adjective. Sometimes the suffix is added to a word with no spelling change. A final *y* is changed to *i* before adding *-ous*. A final silent *e* is dropped unless the *e* is preceded by *g*. Finally, the base word may be significantly changed.

Application Have students add the suffix *-ous* to the following words:

1. marvel
2. industry
3. outrage
4. generosity
5. grace
6. advantage
7. mystery
8. zeal

Ask students to look for more words that fit this pattern, in their own writing and in things that they read, and to add them to their personal word lists.

Reteaching/Reinforcement
• *Unit Two Resource Book,* p. 45

```
pomp       + ous = pompous
adventure  + ous = adventurous
courage    + ous = courageous
piety      + ous = pious
```

220 THE LANGUAGE OF LITERATURE TEACHER'S EDITION

RESPONDING OPTIONS

FROM PERSONAL RESPONSE TO CRITICAL ANALYSIS

REFLECT 1. Does the young Yoshiko Uchida seem like someone you would like to meet? Why or why not?

RETHINK 2. In your opinion, how well does Yoshiko deal with her family's many visitors?
Consider
Close Textual Reading
- what she reveals about her mother's and father's attitudes
- what she reveals about her feelings toward her family
- her descriptions of the many visitors and the activities the family shares with them

3. What general impressions do you think the visitors might have of Yoshiko and her family?

4. Yoshiko's mother says, "Don't ever be indifferent. That's the worst fault of all." Do you agree? Explain.

Thematic Link 5. Do you think it was more difficult for Uchida's parents to adapt to life in the United States after growing up in Japan, or was life probably harder for their daughters? Give a reason for your answer.

RELATE 6. On the basis of this selection and your own ideas, describe your idea of the perfect host and the perfect guest.

LITERARY CONCEPTS

An **anecdote** is a short and entertaining account of a person or an event. Anecdotes are often included in larger works to amuse or to make a point. For example, in the excerpt from *Woodsong* (page 117) Gary Paulsen tells the anecdote about his encounter with Scarhead to point out that people must respect the wilderness and wild animals. Do you think Uchida includes the anecdote about the broom mainly to amuse or mainly to make a point?

Multimodal Learning
ANOTHER PATHWAY

With a partner, create a chart similar to the one shown here. Review "Oh Broom, Get to Work," listing each incident in which Yoshiko encounters an unwelcome visitor. Record information in the first two sections. Then recommend an alternative reaction.

Incident	Yoshiko's Reaction	Your Reaction
A visitor is present when Yoshiko wants to show her mother a dead sparrow.	She stomps out of the room without speaking.	I would have greeted the visitor and told about the sparrow.

QUICKWRITES

1. Write a **list of rules** for guests. Use some humor so that your guests won't be offended.

2. Imagine that you are a lonely seminary student who has just spent an evening with the Uchida family. Before you climb into bed for the night, write a **diary entry** describing your visit.

📁 **PORTFOLIO** Save your writing. You may want to use it later as a springboard to a piece for your portfolio.

OH BROOM, GET TO WORK **221**

From Personal Response to Critical Analysis

1. Possible responses: Yes, because Yoshiko thinks of interesting things to do (such as bury the sparrow) and doesn't like to be bored; no, Yoshiko seems selfish because she resents the lonely people who visit.
2. Possible response: Yoshiko deals effectively with her family's many visitors. She lets her parents know that the visitors bore her, but she isn't overtly rude.
3. Possible responses: The visitors might think the family isn't pious enough; the visitors' overwhelming feeling might be one of gratitude.
4. Accept any reasonable response.
5. Possible responses: It was harder for the parents because they had to change an established way of life; life was probably harder for their daughters because they didn't always understand the Japanese customs of their parents and guests.
6. Encourage students to give reasons for their ideas.

Literary Link

Have students compare Yoshiko Uchida's background and self-image with those of Laurence Yep in *Chinatown*. (Possible response: Uchida and Yep both grew up in minority communities of Asian Americans. Uchida, however, seems more comfortable with herself as a child than Yep was.)

Another Pathway

Cooperative Learning To ensure equal participation, partners should take turns identifying incidents and describing Yoshiko's reaction. After completing their charts, have two sets of partners form small groups and compare charts. If their alternative reactions differ, have the groups discuss why they chose the reactions they did.

Literary Concepts

Students might reasonably argue that Uchida includes this anecdote for both reasons: to amuse the reader and to show how she handled the situation. The anecdote about the broom is one of several that Uchida recounts in the selection. Have students work in small groups to identify additional anecdotes, such as the sisters collapsing with giggles when Mr. Okada announces that he removed his undershirt. When students are finished, have them compare their lists with those of at least one other group. Students may say these incidents are both amusing and make the point that guests aren't always welcomed.

QuickWrites

1. Remind students that their lists should provide brief sentences that contain "do's" and "don'ts" for guests. Have them adapt the story's content (overstaying one's welcome) to their own experiences.
2. Encourage students to scan the selection before writing in order to recall what a lonely seminary student may have experienced in the Uchida household. Remind them to consider the difference in the children's and parents' attitudes toward guests.

The Writer's Craft

Personal Voice, pp. 276–277
Personal Writing, pp. 28–39

THE LANGUAGE OF LITERATURE TEACHER'S EDITION **221**

Words to Know

1. indifferent
2. dispense
3. pompous
4. dread
5. intrusion
6. devise
7. laden
8. pious
9. deprive
10. audacious

YOSHIKO UCHIDA

Although she eventually became a productive and successful writer, Yoshiko Uchida had a hard time getting started after completing her graduate work at Smith College. Her big break came when she followed the advice of an editor at *The New Yorker* magazine, who suggested that Uchida write about her detention-camp experiences. In time, Uchida also began to explore her other experiences as an American-born daughter of Japanese parents.

Across the Curriculum

Math *Welcome to California!* Have students research the number of Japanese immigrants living in California between 1870 and 1940 and plot a graph showing their findings.

Social Studies *Cooperative Learning Knock, Knock. Who's There?* Have students work in small groups. Have each group research one historical immigration law or policy—such as the Gentlemen's Agreement of 1907, the Asian Barred Zone of 1917, the Exclusion Act of 1923, or the national-origins systems—that deliberately restricted Japanese immigration to the United States during the twentieth century. To ensure that students work together smoothly and productively, assign group members roles such as recorder.

Multimodal Learning

ALTERNATIVE ACTIVITIES

1. Uchida mentions black lacquer chopsticks used to eat sukiyaki. What is lacquer ware? How is it made? Use drawings, photographs, pictures from magazines, and actual lacquer ware, if possible, to make a **display** about this traditional Asian art form.
2. **Cooperative Learning** Work with several classmates to act out a **scene** from the story. Have one person read the words of the scene aloud as the others mime the action. Then switch roles, with someone else becoming the narrator.

THE WRITER'S STYLE

The descriptive details that Uchida includes help make the writing lively and interesting. Phrases such as "hair smelling of camellia hair oil" appeal to readers' senses and create vivid images in their minds. With classmates, look over the selection to find additional examples of such details.

WORDS TO KNOW

Review the Words to Know in the boxes at the bottom of the selection pages. Then, on your own paper, write the word described by each of the following sentences.

1. This is how you feel when you don't care about something.
2. Pharmacists do this with pills.
3. Someone who is stuffy and dignified might be called this.
4. You might feel this before taking a sudden and unexpected test.
5. This is what happens when someone barges into your room without being invited.
6. You do this when you think up an excuse.
7. With a 50-pound pack on your back, you might feel this way.
8. People in a house of worship may feel this way.
9. When you take something from someone, you do this.
10. After taking a bold or reckless chance, you might be described as this.

YOSHIKO UCHIDA

1921–1992

An author and educator, Yoshiko Uchida grew up in Berkeley, California. Her parents—leaders of Berkeley's Japanese-American community—filled their home with homesick seminary students, ministers, and graduates of Doshisha University.

Shortly after Japan and the United States declared war in 1941, many Japanese Americans were arrested and placed in internment camps. Uchida's father was sent to Montana, and the rest of the family was sent to Topaz, a relocation center in Utah. She wrote about these years in *Desert Exile: The Uprooting of a Japanese American Family*.

Though Uchida's parents taught their daughters Japanese customs, traditions, and values, the family's loyalty and devotion to its adopted country was strong. In 1984 she said that she hoped that children could be "caring human beings who don't think in terms of labels—foreigners or Asians or whatever—but think of people as human beings."

Uchida wrote many children's books about Japanese Americans. Her first, *The Dancing Kettle*, includes many of the Japanese folk tales her mother once read to her. "Oh Broom, Get to Work" is a chapter from her autobiography *The Invisible Thread*.

OTHER WORKS *A Jar of Dreams, The Happiest Ending, The Terrible Leak* Extended Reading

222 UNIT TWO PART 2: TESTS OF ENDURANCE

Alternative Activities

1. Students might find relevant photographs in museum catalogs or publications from a local Asian-American or Japanese-American society. Refer students to the school librarian or an art teacher for help researching how lacquer is made.
2. Have students scrutinize possible scenes to ensure that each group member will have a role. Encourage students to work cooperatively—one acting to encourage participation, one providing directions, one clarifying, and so on.

The Writer's Style

Possible responses: "the soft ticking of the Chelsea clock"; "dust motes floating in the shaft of late afternoon sun"; "It was only once in a great while that a Reverend Kimura turned up, like a red jelly bean in a jar full of black licorice." You may wish to have students form small groups and create sensory charts that show to which of the five senses each detail appeals.

The Writer's Craft

Developing a Topic, pp. 205–210

222 THE LANGUAGE OF LITERATURE TEACHER'S EDITION

PREVIEWING

POETRY

It Seems I Test People
James Berry

Growing Pains
Jean Little

PERSONAL CONNECTION *Activating Prior Knowledge/Setting a Purpose*

In the poems you are about to read, the speakers relate personal experiences that had a lasting effect on them. Think about personal experiences you have had that might inspire you to write a poem. In your notebook or on a sheet of paper, create a chart similar to the one shown here. In the first box, briefly describe one of your experiences. In the second box, summarize an idea about the experience that you might want to communicate. As you read, compare your experience and idea with those presented in each poem.

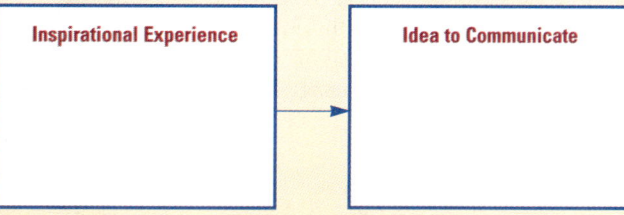

Inspirational Experience → Idea to Communicate

LITERARY CONNECTION *Building Background*

The shape of the words and lines on the page is called **form.** Poets choose a form that they believe will convey their own particular feelings and ideas.

Both James Berry and Jean Little have chosen to use free verse to comment on personal experiences. Free verse is poetry that does not have a regular pattern of rhyme and meter. The lines of free verse usually flow more naturally than lines of rhymed, rhythmic poetry and sound more like normal speech. Free verse allows a poet to reveal feelings about a personal experience as though he or she were speaking face to face with the reader.

Active Reading
READING CONNECTION

Reading Poetry Orally In each of these poems, a personal voice communicates ideas about a particular experience. Read the poems aloud. Unless there is a punctuation mark at the end of a line, don't pause; keep reading to the next comma or end mark. In order to fully appreciate the poems, read them several times—for meaning, for feeling, and for the sounds of the words. Vary your expression, stressing different words and phrases each time.

IT SEEMS I TEST PEOPLE / GROWING PAINS **223**

OVERVIEW

Objectives

- To understand and appreciate two poems that relate personal experiences
- To understand and appreciate poetry read aloud
- To understand and identify similes
- To express understanding of the selection through a choice of writing forms, including a character sketch and an advice column
- To extend understanding of the selection through a variety of multimodal and cross-curricular activities

Skills

LITERARY CONCEPTS
- Simile

SPEAKING, LISTENING, AND VIEWING
- Reading aloud
- Group discussion
- Oral presentation

Cross-Curricular Connections

SOCIAL STUDIES
- Caribbean music

Thematic Link: *Tests of Endurance* In these two poems, the speakers must endure their awareness of the discomfort of people around them.

CUSTOMIZING FOR
Students Acquiring English

- Use **ACCESS FOR STUDENTS ACQUIRING ENGLISH,** *Reading and Writing Support.*
- Both poems use the first-person pronoun *I*. Discuss with students the difference between this poetic device in which *I* may or may not actually refer to the poet and the use of *I* in autobiographical writing, where author and first-person narrator are the same.

PRINT AND MEDIA RESOURCES

UNIT TWO RESOURCE BOOK
Strategic Reading: Literature, p. 49

ACCESS FOR STUDENTS ACQUIRING ENGLISH
Reading and Writing Support

FORMAL ASSESSMENT
Selection Test, pp. 47–48
 Test Generator

AUDIO LIBRARY
See Reference Card

THE LANGUAGE OF LITERATURE TEACHER'S EDITION **223**

It Seems I Test People

BY JAMES BERRY

My skin sun-mixed like basic earth
my voice having tones of thunder
my laughter working all of me as I laugh
my walk motioning strong swings
it seems I test people

Always awaiting a move
waiting always to recreate my view
my eyes packed with hellos behind them
my arrival bringing departures
it seems I test people

Self-Portrait (1934), Malvin Gray Johnson. National Museum of American Art, Washington, D.C./Art Resource, New York.

FROM PERSONAL RESPONSE TO CRITICAL ANALYSIS

REFLECT 1. What phrase or line of this poem stayed with you as you finished reading? Discuss your response with a partner.

RETHINK 2. What do you think the speaker means by the idea of testing people? Explain your answer.

RELATE 3. How do you think you would react to the speaker?
Consider
- the speaker's self-description
- the apparent reactions of others to the speaker
- the personal experience the speaker relates

Thematic Link 4. What does this poem suggest to you about the human need to belong?

Growing Pains

BY JEAN LITTLE

Mother got mad at me tonight and bawled me out.
She said I was lazy and self-centered.
She said my room was a pigsty.
She said she was sick and tired of forever nagging but I gave her no choice.
5   She went on and on until I began to cry.
I hate crying in front of people. It was horrible.

I got away, though, and went to bed and it was over.
I knew things would be okay in the morning;
Stiff with being sorry, too polite, but okay.
10 I was glad to be by myself.

Then she came to my room and apologized.
She explained, too.
Things had gone wrong all day at the store.
She hadn't had a letter from my sister and she was worried.
15 Dad had also done something to hurt her.
She even told me about that.
Then *she* cried.
I kept saying, "It's all right. Don't worry."
And wishing she'd stop.

20 I'm just a kid.
I can forgive her getting mad at me. That's easy.
But her sadness . . .
I don't know what to do with her sadness.
I yell at her often, "You don't understand me!"
25 But I don't want to have to understand her.
That's expecting too much.

Mini-Lesson: Speaking, Listening, and Viewing

READING ALOUD Reading poetry aloud can be an effective way to communicate to listeners the ideas and emotions a poem contains. It also helps express the poem's rhythm and, sometimes, its rhyme scheme.

Application Review with students the reading tips listed in the Reading Connection on page 223. Remind them that good speakers prepare ahead of time before reading publicly. Have the class brainstorm a list of words that reflect each speaker's personality and emotions. Have students attach self-stick notes as reading cues next to specific lines to remind them to use a specific intonation or to pause. After preparations are complete, have volunteers read the poems aloud and compare different readings as a class. You may wish to select other short poems previously discussed and repeat this activity.

CUSTOMIZING FOR
Gifted and Talented Students

② Have students discuss the speaker's feelings about crying in front of other people and about having to understand the mother. Ask them how—and whether—the speaker could discuss with the mother the feelings expressed in the first and last stanzas.

Active Reading: CONNECT

Ⓑ Have students think about why a young person might be upset by a mother's confiding in him or her. Then, in their reading logs, have students jot down their thoughts about a time when a parent or other adult told them something that they didn't want to know.

COMPREHENSION CHECK

1. In the first stanza of the first poem, what aspects of himself does the speaker identify as "testing people"? *(his skin color, loud voice, body shaking with laughter, powerful walk)*
2. What happens when the first speaker enters a place? *(Other people leave.)*
3. In "Growing Pains," what did the mother say when she "bawled out" the speaker? *(that the speaker was lazy and selfish, that the speaker's room was messy, that the speaker gave the mother no choice but to nag)*
4. Why was the speaker glad to be alone after the fight? *(The speaker thought she had escaped and that things would be okay in the morning.)*
5. According to the speaker, in what way does the mother expect too much? *(by expecting the speaker—still a child—to understand her)*

From Personal Response to Critical Analysis

1. *Responses will vary.*
2. *Some students may say that the speaker feels overwhelmed by the mother's sadness and also feels responsible for making the mother happy.*
3. *Some students may say that the "growing pains" are those of becoming an adult and having to see your parents as people with problems. Others may interpret "growing pains" more literally, as the pain of being yelled at by your mother.*
4. *Responses will vary.*
5. *Some students may say that the speaker of "Growing Pains" has a problem with the mother, whereas the speaker of "It Seems I Test People" has a problem with society.*

Another Pathway

Cooperative Learning Students should engage in collaborative planning first to ensure that all group members understand the individuals involved in the poems. One student can record the group's ideas; another can serve as turn-taking monitor to ensure that everyone gets a chance to speak. A third student should serve as recorder to write any additional lines the group creates.

Rubric

3 Full Accomplishment Students share the work fairly and produce dialogue that accurately reflects the character.

2 Substantial Accomplishment Students produce dialogue that represents most of the traits and opinions of the character.

1 Partial or Little Accomplishment Students do not participate equally. Dialogue captures few of the traits of the character.

RESPONDING OPTIONS

FROM PERSONAL RESPONSE TO CRITICAL ANALYSIS

REFLECT
1. If you were to paint your reaction to "Growing Pains," what colors would you use? Explain your choice.

RETHINK
2. Why do you think the speaker finds the mother's sadness harder to accept than her anger?
   Consider
   Close Textual Reading
   - what the speaker means by "I don't know what to do with her sadness"
   - the speaker's reaction to the mother's anger
   - the speaker's comment "I'm just a kid"

Thematic Link
3. What do you think are the "growing pains" referred to in the poem's title? Explain your answer.

4. If you could talk to the speaker of this poem about this experience, what would you say and why?

RELATE
5. Compare the speakers of "Growing Pains" and "It Seems I Test People." What do you think they might think of each other if they were to meet? Why?

ANOTHER PATHWAY

Cooperative Learning
With a few classmates, role-play the personal experience presented in each poem. Try to put yourself in the position of one of the individuals involved in the poem. Record any additional lines your group might create.

LITERARY CONCEPTS

A **simile** is a figure of speech comparing two things that are basically unlike but have something in common. In a simile, the comparison is expressed by means of the word *like* or *as*. In "Nadia the Willful," for example, Sue Alexander describes the sheik's words as "sharp *as* a scimitar." Find an example of a simile in either "Growing Pains" or "It Seems I Test People."

CRITIC'S CORNER

This statement about "It Seems I Test People" appears on the book jacket: "Universal themes ranging from isolation to joy will touch young people of all nationalities." Reread the poem and explain how well its theme relates to the lives of other young people you know.

QUICKWRITES

1. Write a **character sketch** of one of the speakers. Use your imagination, but make sure the person you describe is one whose feelings match the feelings presented in the poem.

2. Suppose that one of the poems' speakers writes to you, an advice columnist, for help. Write the **advice column** in which you respond to his or her request.

📁 **PORTFOLIO** *Save your writing. You may want to use it later as a springboard to a piece for your portfolio.*

226 UNIT TWO PART 2: TESTS OF ENDURANCE

Literary Concepts

Have students work in pairs to find the simile: ("My skin sun-mixed like basic earth" in "It Seems I Test People.") Then ask them to write one or more similes describing some aspect of themselves (eyes, walk, angry voice, for example).

QuickWrites

1. After students finish, have them share their character sketches in small groups, asking the group for feedback on how accurately the feelings of the person they described match those presented in the poem.

2. Before students begin, have them pause and imagine themselves as advice columnists. Invite them to tap their own experience for advice that they might give.

 **The Writer's Craft**

Describing People and Places, pp. 50–61
Personal Voice, pp. 276–277

THE WRITER'S STYLE

Despite the relaxed, informal appearance of free verse, much skill goes into its writing. In "It Seems I Test People," for example, the poet plays with the sound of language in lines like these:

> Always awaiting a move
> waiting always to recreate my view

Choose one of the poems and rewrite a few lines, using a formal rhyme scheme and rhythm. What is gained and lost in your version?

Multimodal Learning
ALTERNATIVE ACTIVITIES

1. **Cooperative Learning** Work with two friends to create a series of **movements** or a **dance** that shows how one of the poems' speakers feels. If you like, use music with your dance.

2. Draw a **portrait** of one of the speakers. Choose a line or phrase from the poem to use as a title for your drawing.

Literary Links

How does the way the speaker in "It Seems I Test People" "tests" those around him compare to the way Nadia "tests" her father in "Nadia the Willful"? *(Possible response: Nadia actually goes around defying her father; it is a conscious choice. The speaker in the poem feels that his existence tests people; it is not a choice he makes.)*

Across the Curriculum

Music *Cooperative Learning* Have students form small groups of three or four to research and find examples of music (such as calypso or reggae) from the Caribbean, where Berry was born. The school or local library may have audiotapes or CDs that students can borrow and share with their classmates. Each group should present cultural background or biographical information when presenting their music samples.

JAMES BERRY

1925–

James Berry, a writer and editor born in Jamaica, moved to England, where he lives today, in 1948. His award-winning collection of stories told from a Jamaican child's point of view, *A Thief in the Village and Other Stories*, grew out of his own childhood experiences. He says, "In the Caribbean, we were the last outpost of the Empire. No one has reported our stories, or the way we saw things. It's the function of writers and poets to bring in the left-out side of the human family."

The poems in *When I Dance*, which won a Signal Poetry Award, are written in Caribbean dialect. These rhythmic, humorous poems focus on the injustice and goodness of daily life as well as the uniqueness of the individual. According to one poem: "Nobody can get into my clothes for me / or feel my fall for me, or do my running. / Nobody hears my music for me, either."

OTHER WORKS *Ajeemah and His Son, The Future-Telling Lady and Other Stories* Extended Reading

JEAN LITTLE

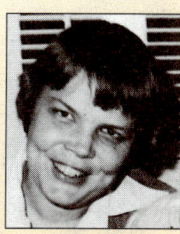

1932–

Jean Little was born in Formosa (now Taiwan), where both of her parents were doctors. Legally blind at birth, Little was taught to read by her parents before she began school, and by fourth grade her vision had improved enough for her to attend regular classes. When she was 15, her father collected and printed her first book of poems. She says, "From the first my Dad was my greatest critic and supporter. . . . Not until he died did I come to appreciate his unflagging zeal on my behalf."

Little's books are based on her own experiences and present unsentimental portrayals of the lives of young people, and her characters often have physical disabilities, such as cerebral palsy or blindness. There are no magical cures in these books, but characters learn to cope and survive.

Little has written more than 20 books, including novels and poems, and has received numerous awards. When not writing, she continues to work with young people.

OTHER WORKS *Look Through My Window; Kate; Hey World, Here I Am!; Little by Little: A Writer's Education; Revenge of the Small Small* Extended Reading

JAMES BERRY

A teacher as well as an author, James Berry conducts writing workshops for children. His award-winning books include *A Thief in the Village and Other Stories*, a 1988 Coretta Scott King Award honor book, and *When I Dance*, which received the Signal Poetry Award in 1989.

JEAN LITTLE

Jean Little's eye problems prevent her from reading now, but she continues to write with the help of a talking computer. Little gives the following advice to young writers: "Read and write a lot. You have a storehouse in your head. If you don't put anything in it, there's nothing to draw on."

IT SEEMS I TEST PEOPLE / GROWING PAINS **227**

The Writer's Style

Remind students that they may choose any rhythm or rhyme scheme but that they must then use it consistently. After students have finished, have them read aloud and discuss their rewrites in small groups. Then have students discuss which form of verse, free or formal, is easier for them and which fits better with their personal style.

Writing a Poem, pp. 84–88

Alternative Activities

1. Assign pairs a specific area of the classroom in which to create their dance. To minimize students' interfering with each other, set a specific time limit for each pair to practice.
2. Students can use their line or phrase as a caption for their artwork. Encourage them to use a variety of media and remind them that portraits may be impressionistic as well as realistic.

OVERVIEW

Objectives

- To understand and appreciate an essay that treats science and history
- To understand chronological order
- To understand and identify the author's main purpose in writing an essay
- To express understanding of the selection through a choice of writing forms, including a tabloid-newspaper account, a science fiction story, and an eyewitness account
- To extend understanding of the selection through a variety of multimodal and cross-disciplinary activities

Skills

READING SKILLS/ STRATEGIES
- Chronological order

LITERARY CONCEPTS
- Essay

GRAMMAR
- Types of verbs

SPELLING
- The suffix -ly

SPEAKING, LISTENING, AND VIEWING
- Group discussion
- Oral presentation

Cross-Curricular Connections

HISTORY
- Social vs. political history

SCIENCE
- Halley's comet
- Growth cycle of mushrooms

PREVIEWING

NONFICTION

The Mushroom
H. M. Hoover

PERSONAL CONNECTION *Activating Prior Knowledge/Setting a Purpose*

Perhaps you have spotted signs of nature in unusual places. You may have seen a small plant growing in a brick wall or a flower blooming cheerfully in a crack in a sidewalk. What do such signs suggest to you about nature's "test of endurance," or struggle for survival, against human progress? Copy the headings shown below and list examples that apply to the headings. With a partner, discuss this issue as you add examples to the lists. As you read, see whether the ideas and examples you included in your lists are reflected in the essay.

Forces of Human Progress | **Effects on Nature**

SCIENCE CONNECTION *Building Background*

Ecologists (ĭ-kŏl'ə-jĭsts) are scientists who study the relationships between living organisms and their environments. In an ecosystem (ĕk'ō-sĭs'təm), plants, animals, and other living things rely upon one another for survival and relate to one another in many ways.

Fungi (fŭn'jī) are plantlike organisms that lack roots, stems, and leaves. At one time considered plants, mushrooms and other fungi are now classified as a separate kingdom of organisms. They are important to ecosystems because they feed upon the remains of dead plants and animals. As they decompose, or break down, the plant and animal remains, they enrich the soil and return carbon dioxide to the atmosphere, where it can be used by green plants to make food.

The complex relationships among different organisms and between organisms and their environments are called the balance of nature. Human survival and well-being depends on preserving this balance.

228 UNIT TWO PART 2: TESTS OF ENDURANCE

PRINT AND MEDIA RESOURCES

UNIT TWO RESOURCE BOOK
Strategic Reading: Literature, p. 53
Vocabulary SkillBuilder, p. 56
Reading SkillBuilder, p. 54
Spelling SkillBuilder, p. 55

GRAMMAR MINI–LESSONS
Transparencies, p. 17

ACCESS FOR STUDENTS ACQUIRING ENGLISH
Selection Summaries
Reading and Writing Support

FORMAL ASSESSMENT
Selection Test, pp. 49–50
Test Generator

AUDIO LIBRARY
See Reference Card

LASERLINKS
Science Connection

INTERNET RESOURCES
McDougal Littell Literature Center at http://www.hmco.com/mcdougal/lit

228 THE LANGUAGE OF LITERATURE TEACHER'S EDITION

READING CONNECTION

Chronological Order

One of the first steps in understanding a work of nonfiction is to figure out how it is organized. If the author is describing events or processes that take place over a period of time, the writing is usually organized in **chronological order,** or time order.

Writers use signal words and phrases (also called transition words) to connect the ideas in sentences and paragraphs. The signal words and phrases that show chronological order include *before, during, after, first, second, next, finally, while, sometimes, often, whenever, immediately, at first, at last, then, meanwhile, soon, always,* and *later.* The chart below gives some suggestions for understanding a work organized in chronological order.

Strategies for Understanding Chronological Order
• Draw a time line and record each event and each date as it is introduced. Refer to the time line as you read.
• Make a list of the signal words and phrases that you come to. Each word or phrase will signal a new event.
• Jot down notes in your reading log as you read. If the time order seems unclear to you at some point, refer to your notes to clarify it.

"The Mushroom" describes events that span about 1,500 years. In it, H. M. Hoover conveys not only the passage of time but the problems of a struggle for survival. Throughout the selection there are numerous references to historical figures and events. You need not recognize or understand each reference to enjoy reading the essay. Each of the events mentioned, however, is an important one in history. To increase your appreciation of this march through history, you may want to refer to an encyclopedia for more information.

Far left: King Arthur;
Center: Marco Polo;
Right: Joan of Arc.

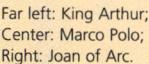

THE MUSHROOM **229**

WORDS TO KNOW

consume (kən-sōōm′) *v.* to eat; use up (p. 231)
debris (də-brē′) *n.* the remains of something broken or destroyed (p. 230)
exceed (ĭk-sēd′) *v.* to be greater than (p. 231)

infinite (ĭn′fə-nĭt) *adj.* having no limits; without end (p. 232)
mortally (môr′tl-ē) *adv.* in a way that causes death; fatally (p. 231)

SUMMARY

This essay presents a hypothetical situation in which a giant mushroom develops underground, and shows the impact such a natural phenomenon could have on human life. The fictional mushroom took root in North America in A.D. 450, spread through more than 200 acres of forest by the time the Pilgrims landed at Plymouth in 1620, and—sprouting aboveground—lifted a mall and parking lot off the ground in 1984.

Thematic Link: *Tests of Endurance* The endurance of a mushroom over more than a thousand years leads to a surprising turn of events.

CUSTOMIZING FOR
Students Acquiring English

- Use **ACCESS FOR STUDENTS ACQUIRING ENGLISH,** *Reading and Writing Support.*

- This selection contains scientific vocabulary that may be difficult for students acquiring English. Before they read, you may want to have them scan the essay for unfamiliar terms. Then have them use context clues to infer the meaning, and then have them confirm their inferences by looking up the words in a dictionary. Also, make sure that students understand that the mushroom described is not a real one, but is created to explore what could happen if such a mushroom were to grow.

STRATEGIC READING FOR
Less-Proficient Readers

Set a Purpose To help students become immersed in the selection, have them contrast a human life span with that of a dog, fly, tree, or other life form. Invite students to discuss how their lives might be different if, like a giant sequoia tree, they could live to be 2,500 years old. Then have them read to find out about this hypothetical mushroom and what humans were doing at the time the mushroom supposedly began to grow.

Use **UNIT TWO RESOURCE BOOK,** pp. 53–54, for guidance in reading the selection.

THE LANGUAGE OF LITERATURE TEACHER'S EDITION **229**

CUSTOMIZING FOR
Gifted and Talented Students

To help students enjoy the selection, invite them to use their imaginations and write rhyming jingles, such as the one shown here, contrasting events in human history and in the life of the mushroom.

> From China to India
>   tea was going.
> Beneath the forest floor,
>   the mushroom kept growing.

Allow students to read their completed poems aloud.

CUSTOMIZING FOR
Multiple Learning Styles

A **Spatial or Graphic Learners** Have students illustrate in their notebooks the emergence of a new mushroom, as described here.

Literary Concept:
AUTHOR'S PURPOSE

B Ask students how they think the essay's structure is related to the author's purpose. (*Possible response: The author's purpose is to make the reader think about the possible impact of the development of a giant mushroom, and to give the historical context of important social and political events that would have occurred during the mushroom's life cycle. Therefore, the essay shifts back and forth between information about the mushroom and information about selected historical events.*)

CUSTOMIZING FOR
Students Acquiring English

I Students may be confused by the word *fruited*. In biology, *fruiting* is a process by which a plant or fungus produces a structure for reproduction. These structures, or "fruits," are not necessarily sweet.

The Mushroom
by H. M. Hoover

450

453

In A.D. 450 a squirrel could travel from the east coast of North America to the Mississippi without ever leaving the trees.

That year a squirrel, while grooming, brushed several million mushroom spores[1] from its fur.

So small that a hundred million could fit into a teaspoon, the spores floated. Some rose up into the atmosphere; some were carried around the world by the jet stream. Most drifted to the forest floor.

There was a massive, rolling earthquake, followed by electrical storms. Rain fell lightly, steadily, for days.

From two of these spores a new mushroom began to grow. It sent out microscopic filaments, called hyphae,[2] to penetrate and feed on forest <u>debris</u>. A sheath of a thousand hyphae is no thicker than a human hair.

The hyphae secreted enzymes to break down complex carbohydrates into sugars on which the mushroom fed. Needing protein for a balanced diet, the fungi filaments hunted, entrapping and digesting amoebas, bacteria, and tiny worms.

Within months miles of hyphae twisted through the forest floor. The fungi fruited, producing a new mushroom.

A chipmunk and several beetles ate most of the mushroom, scattering spores. Soon a ring-shaped colony of mushrooms marked the spot where the parent once stood.

In Europe, Attila the Hun died in 453. Tea was brought to China from India.

The ancient forest remained undisturbed. Rains fell and summer nights were warm. Within a few years the mushroom's filaments had spread through an acre and weighed two thousand five hundred pounds.

---

1. **spores:** tiny reproductive bodies, capable of growing into new organisms, produced by mushrooms.
2. **microscopic filaments, called hyphae** (hī′fē): hairlike parts of a mushroom that absorb food and water.

WORDS TO KNOW
debris (də-brē′) *n.* the remains of something broken or destroyed

230

Mini-Lesson — Reading Skills/Strategies

CHRONOLOGICAL ORDER Understanding the order in which events happen in time will help students understand what they read. The time line on these pages shows some of the events described in the essay. The use of dates and clue words such as "within months" and "within a few years" also indicates the sequence of events.

Application After students have read the selection, encourage them to review the essay and locate events on the time line at the top of the page. In addition, students can construct their own time lines and record the events of a typical day in their lives. Remind students that their time lines should cover only key events.

Reteaching/Reinforcement
• *Unit Two Resource Book,* p. 53

---

230 THE LANGUAGE OF LITERATURE TEACHER'S EDITION

537 — 750 — 1000

By the time Arthur, king of the Britons, died in 537, the mushroom had consumed almost a century of fallen trees. Its filaments stretched through ten acres of the forest floor, fruiting in circles the Britons would have called fairy rings.

That year the plague reached northern Europe. A third of the population died. Earthquakes shook the entire world. The Byzantine Empire began to crumble.

The mushroom went on growing.

By 750 the Venerable Bede had written his history of England, newspapers were being printed in China, and some Europeans slept in beds instead of on the floor.

The mushroom's total weight now exceeded eighteen tons, all of it hidden beneath the surface of the forest floor.

By the year 1000, in North America, the Mississippian people lived in handsome cities, but the pueblos of Mesa Verde[3] were running short of water. In the century to come humans sometimes walked over the mushroom's growth. Their moccasins left no footprints.

About that time white men first walked among the tall trees. Fierce as they were, the ancient forest frightened them. It was too big, too dark, too endless. They spent a night in the shelter of a giant hollow oak. When morning came, they hurried back to their Viking ship and fled. They left their fire burning. The tree, mortally wounded, fell in an autumn storm.

The mushroom's hyphae sought out the fallen tree and began to return its mass to the earth and air. Seedlings rooted in the damp, rotting bark.

---

3. **pueblos** (pwĕb′lōz) **of Mesa Verde** (mā′sə-vûrd′): groups of houses of a Native American people, at a site in what is now southwestern Colorado.

WORDS TO KNOW
consume (kən-sōōm′) v. to eat; use up
exceed (ĭk-sēd′) v. to be greater than
mortally (môr′tl-ē) adv. in a way that causes death; fatally

231

Linking to Science

F Like most comets, Halley's comet has a long elliptical orbit that causes it to pass near Earth periodically. Halley's comet returns every 76 years, which is why the author uses the word *again*.

Critical Thinking: ANALYZING

G Ask students why they think the end of the forests was certain when the Pilgrims landed in North America. *(Possible response: because Europeans would clear the land for farming)* Have students tell what meaning they see in the phrase "a long time in human terms, but not for the forest, or the mushroom." *(Possible response: Humans have a much shorter life span than a forest or a giant mushroom such as the hypothetical one in the selection. What seems like a long time in terms of a human life span is just a moment in the life of the forest.)*

CUSTOMIZING FOR
Students Acquiring English

3 You may want to paraphrase this sentence as follows: "As soon as the Europeans landed, they began to cut down trees."

STRATEGIC READING FOR
Less-Proficient Readers

H Ask students what happened to the forest in which the mushroom was growing. *(It was cut down by European settlers.)* **Restating**

Set a Purpose As students continue to read, they should pay attention to the eventual impact of the giant mushroom on "the affairs of humankind."

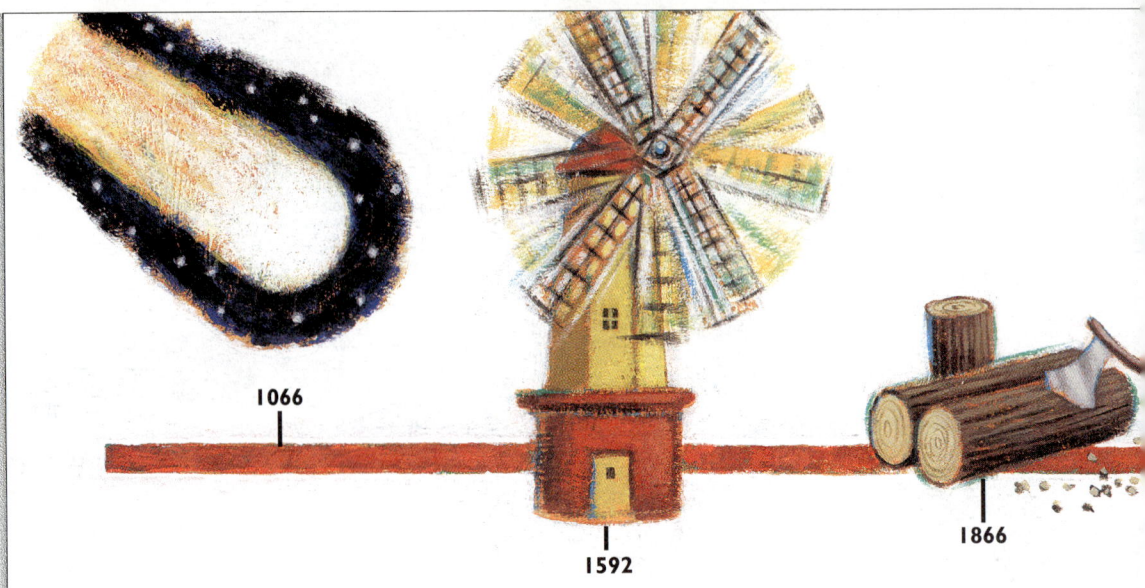

By 1066 a colonnade of tall trees grew over the giant log, embracing it with their buttress roots. In Europe, Westminster Abbey was consecrated, York Cathedral begun, Edward the Confessor died horribly, his successor was killed in the Battle of Hastings. Then, too, an Italian monk taught his brother monks to sing *do, re, mi,* and the comet later called Halley's appeared. Again.

The comet was as indifferent as the forest and the mushroom to the affairs of humankind.

The Crusades came and went. Saladin terrified all infidels. The Chinese introduced tea to their neighbors, the Japanese. Marco Polo, against his will, was given time to dictate his memoirs. Queens were still the only women noted by historians.

The mushroom's hyphae now spread through more than thirty acres; its mass exceeded thirty-eight tons. It had lived nearly a thousand years when Joan of Arc was burned at the stake. The Incas had begun to rule Peru.

Lorenzo de' Medici and Christopher Columbus were born. The book-publishing profession began.

In 1592, in Holland, windmills were first used to power mechanical saws.

The day the Pilgrims landed at New Plymouth, the end of the ancient forest became only a matter of time—a long time in human terms, but not for the forest, or the mushroom.

The mushroom's filaments had woven through more than two hundred acres. The weight of its total mass was now as unimaginable as the <u>infinite</u> smallness of the two original spores had once been.

Europeans had no more than landed when they began to cut down tress. Forests that had been evolving for ten thousand years into perfect ecosystems disappeared in two centuries.

The mushroom's home, far from the coast, survived longer than most. Inexorably the settlers came, cutting, burning, blasting, plowing around the stumps.

WORDS TO KNOW   **infinite** (ĭn′fə-nĭt) *adj.* having no limits; without end

232

Assessment Option

INFORMAL ASSESSMENT You can informally assess students' understanding of the selection and their ability to summarize by setting up the following scenario:

Pretend that the class read this selection aloud, in small groups, over a two-day period. A friend was absent the first day, when the first two pages of the essay were read. What can you explain to your friend, before class begins, about what was read the first day?

Have students provide written or oral summaries.

Rubric

3 Full Accomplishment Student accurately and concisely identifies the two strands—human history and the mushroom's life cycle—and describes the organization of the essay so far, giving examples to clarify meaning.

2 Substantial Accomplishment Student describes how the author interweaves human history and the life cycle of the mushroom in the selection. However, student's summary is not concise.

1 Little or Partial Accomplishment Student has difficulty recalling the two strands—human history and the mushroom's life cycle—interwoven in the selection.

232 THE LANGUAGE OF LITERATURE TEACHER'S EDITION

1904

1984

In the winter of 1866 the mushroom's forest was cut, the wood sold to the Union army. The frozen soil saved the mushroom from destruction. Seedlings sprouted in the sunlight of the following spring. Deer grazed among the fairy rings.

In 1904 a German couple bought the land where the mushroom grew. Father and sons slowly cleared the trees and plowed, and replowed. Only forty acres were spared as "woods."

In 1984 the family farm was sold to a developer. Bulldozers arrived. A shopping mall was built over the rich fields. A parking lot covered the acres that had long been forest. Sun on the black asphalt superheated the earth below.

The week before the mall's opening, rain fell softly, steadily, for days. One night a bulge appeared on the surface of the parking lot, and another and another. Soon there were too many to count, and they formed circular patterns.

Had you been there, you might have heard above the rain the rasp of breaking asphalt, the slow cracking of masonry walls, cascades of breaking glass.

Morning light revealed that the mall and parking lot had been lifted and were being held aloft atop the caps of millions of mushrooms . . . fairy rings.

As the mushrooms aged, the buildings standing on them swayed and sagged. Girders detached, roofs fell in, walls collapsed. In the parking lot the light poles stood at crazy angles, creaking in the wind that blew across a field of broken asphalt.

By the noon the mushrooms had released trillions of spores to the wind. Some spores rose into the atmosphere to travel with the jet stream. Others drifted into the wreckage or were washed into raw earth.

New mushrooms began to grow. They sent out microscopic filaments to penetrate and feed upon the debris. A sheath of a thousand hyphae is no thicker than a human hair. ❖

THE MUSHROOM   **233**

Literary Concept: ALLITERATION

I Remind students that the repeating of consonant sounds at the beginnings of two or more words is called alliteration. This device often adds a musical beat to a work. Write on the chalkboard the following sentence from page 233: "Seedlings sprouted in the sunlight of the following spring." Call on a volunteer to read the sentence aloud. Have students identify the repeated sounds. (<u>S</u>eedlings <u>s</u>prouted in the <u>s</u>unlight of the <u>f</u>ollowing <u>s</u>pring.)

STRATEGIC READING FOR
Less-Proficient Readers

J What does the mushroom do to the shopping mall? (It lifts up the mall and its parking lot.) Restating

CUSTOMIZING FOR
Students Acquiring English

4 Students acquiring English sometimes have trouble with the words denoting large numbers. You may want to write the word *trillion* and the corresponding figure (1,000,000,000,000) on the board.

CUSTOMIZING FOR
Gifted and Talented Students

As students finish reading the essay, have them discuss how the end provides a kind of reversal from the beginning. What change in the role of humans is described in the essay? (Possible response: At first, people seemed to be destroying the mushroom's habitat. In the end, the mushroom toppled a human construction.)

Encourage students to extrapolate from this essay to discuss the fragile relationship that exists between the natural world and its human inhabitants.

Mini-Lesson Grammar

TYPES OF VERBS Point out to students that verbs can be divided into two groups: action verbs, such as *consumed*, which tell about an action, and linking verbs, such as *was*, which describe a state of being. Writers often choose to use action verbs to engage a reader's attention and to convey what is happening more effectively.

Application Invite students to find at least five action verbs and five linking verbs on page 232. Then ask them to rewrite the following sentences using action verbs:

1. Edward the Confessor's successor was killed in the Battle of Hastings.
2. Marco Polo, against his will, was given time to dictate his memoirs.
3. In 1984 the family farm was sold to a developer.

Reteaching/Reinforcement
• *Grammar Mini-Lessons* transparencies, p. 17

 **The Writer's Craft**
Types of Verbs, pp. 348–349

Action Verbs	Linking Verbs
crumble	appeared
secreted	were
rooted	became

THE LANGUAGE OF LITERATURE **TEACHER'S EDITION** **233**

HISTORICAL INSIGHT

The Survival of the Mushroom

The study of plants and fungi of past ages is called paleobotany (pā′lē-ō-bŏt′n-ē). By studying fossils, paleobotanists follow the evolution of these living things from simple to more complex forms. The simple structure of fungi indicates that they were probably among the earliest organisms to live on land. In fact, fossil remains of fungi have been found that are nearly 2 billion years old.

Mushrooms were among the first foods human beings consumed. The hyphae of these fungi form a spreading mass that can live underground for many years. When water becomes available, this mass quickly puts forth the umbrella-shaped fruiting bodies that we see above ground. Because of the rapid appearance of these fruiting bodies, primitive people believed mushrooms to have supernatural qualities.

As the hyphae of certain mushrooms grow, they spread out in a circular pattern, creating "fairy rings" of fruiting bodies. One ring in England is believed to have survived about 700 years. Some fairy rings in Colorado measure about 200 feet in diameter and are over 300 years old. Mycologists (scientists who study fungi) determine the age of these fairy rings by measuring how far the mushrooms spread each year.

In 1992 scientists discovered what may be the largest mushroom on earth. Beneath a forest in the state of Washington, not far from Mount St. Helens, lives a fungus that sprawls beneath 1,500 acres of land. Its estimated weight is 5,000 to 40,000 tons. It is about 40 times larger than the next largest known mushroom, which has been growing under about 38 acres near Crystal Falls, Michigan, for an estimated 1,500 to 10,000 years.

234 UNIT TWO PART 2: TESTS OF ENDURANCE

RESPONDING OPTIONS

FROM PERSONAL RESPONSE TO CRITICAL ANALYSIS

REFLECT 1. What impressed you most about this essay? Share your thoughts with a partner.

RETHINK 2. What message or theme do you think the author conveys in this essay?
Consider

Close Textual Reading
- the references to historical periods and people
- the scientific information about the mushroom and its survival
- the end of the essay

3. Although H. M. Hoover includes many scientific and historical facts in the essay, she also describes events that did not actually happen. Do you think these imaginative elements add to the essay or detract from it? Explain your opinion.

4. Near the beginning of the selection, and again at the very end, the author states, "A sheath of a thousand hyphae is no thicker than a human hair." Why do you think Hoover repeats this statement?

RELATE 5. People's increasing awareness of the impact of human progress on nature has led to thousands of save-the-earth programs at the local level. Review the effects of human progress that you recorded for the Personal Connection on page 228. What ways of counteracting these effects can you think of?

Thematic Link

Multimodal Learning
ANOTHER PATHWAY
Cooperative Learning
With two or three other classmates, refer to the selection for details. Then role-play what happens at the shopping mall after the mushroom appears. Switch roles of a newspaper reporter, a shocked eyewitness, and an expert called in to explain the incident.

QUICKWRITES

1. Write a **tabloid-newspaper account** of the discovery of a giant mushroom that covers hundreds of acres.
2. Use the factual information in "The Mushroom" to create a **science fiction story**.
3. Imagine that you are a newspaper reporter assigned to write an article about the opening of the new shopping mall. Write an **eyewitness account** of the early-morning scene at the mall's parking lot.

PORTFOLIO Save your writing. You may want to use it later as a springboard to a piece for your portfolio.

LITERARY CONCEPTS

An **essay** is a brief work of nonfiction that offers a writer's opinion on a subject. The purpose of an essay may be to express ideas or feelings, to analyze a topic, to inform, to entertain, or to persuade. What do you think is the author's main purpose in "The Mushroom"? Use evidence from the selection to support your opinion.

Purposes for Writing an Essay
- express ideas and feelings
- analyze a topic
- inform
- entertain
- persuade

THE MUSHROOM 235

From Personal Response to Critical Analysis

1. Accept any reasonable response.
2. Some students may say that the author stresses the connection of humans with all of life by interweaving scientific information about the mushroom and human history. Others may interpret the ending as a statement that humans don't have as much control over the rest of nature as they sometimes believe.
3. Make sure that students explain their opinions.
4. Some students may say that the repetition serves as a stylistic device. Others may point out that the repetition reinforces a theme of the essay, that individual fragments of the mushroom are frail yet work together to generate powerful forces.
5. Responses will vary.

Literary Link

Have students compare the structure of this essay with that of "My First Dive with the Dolphins." In what way are the authors' techniques the same? *(Both Don C. Reed and H. M. Hoover interweave factual material in their narratives.)*

Another Pathway

Cooperative Learning After students have played all three roles, have them discuss what they learned from one another's portrayals.

Rubric
3 Full Accomplishment Student uses details from the selection in ways that are consistent with the character.
2 Substantial Accomplishment Student incorporates most of the details and is generally able to stay in character.
1 Little or Partial Accomplishment Student is unable to stay in character and calls on only a few details from the selection.

Literary Concepts

Have students work in small groups to discern the author's main purpose. Most groups will probably argue that the main purpose is to inform, and strong evidence from the essay supports this opinion. Assign roles such as turn-taking monitor and clarifier to ensure that all group members participate in and understand the discussion. When students are finished, have them compare their conclusion and evidence with those of at least one other group.

QuickWrites

1. Encourage students to exaggerate and use superlatives, as in an actual tabloid.
2. Before students begin, have them brainstorm details of possible plots for their stories.
3. Encourage students to use sensory details to enliven their eyewitness accounts.

The Writer's Craft
Describing People and Places, pp. 50–61
Appealing to the Senses, pp. 266–275
Personal Narrative, pp. 72–83

THE LANGUAGE OF LITERATURE TEACHER'S EDITION 235

Across the Curriculum

Science *Cooperative Learning* Have students work in small groups of three or four. One student can head the research team; another can monitor discussions to ensure that everyone participates and understands; a third can lead a brainstorming session to plan the diagrams and oral report.

ADDITIONAL SUGGESTIONS

History *Historical Research* Invite students to choose one of the historical events mentioned in the selection (such as the life of Attila the Hun or the history of the Crusades), research to learn more about it, and present their findings in a poster or an oral report.

SCIENCE CONNECTION
The Giant Mushroom Scientists have recently discovered a giant underground fungus in the Midwest. In this film, an ecologist discusses the unusual nature of this discovery and the fungus's effects on the forest ecosystem of the area.

Side A, Frame 13294

Words to Know

Exercise A
1. exceeds
2. consume
3. mortally
4. debris
5. infinite

Exercise B
Have each group appoint one member as recorder. That student can write the vocabulary words on the labels. You may wish to circulate around the classroom while students are doing the exercise, to ensure fair play.

Reteaching/Reinforcement
• *Unit Two Resource Book,* p. 56

H. M. HOOVER

Students may find it interesting—though not surprising—that many of Hoover's works lament humans' loss of their original closeness to nature. The effect of uncontrolled technological development on human life is a frequent theme in her writing.

Multimodal Learning

ALTERNATIVE ACTIVITIES

1. Present an **oral reading** of "The Mushroom" accompanied by recorded sounds that match the mood of the selection. Experiment by combining music that represents human activity with environmental sounds that represent the workings of nature.
2. Do some research to find out how to make spore prints of mushrooms. Then collect mushrooms and create a **display** of spore prints. Mount the prints on poster board, along with labels describing the various species.

ACROSS THE CURRICULUM

Science Research the growth cycle of mushrooms. Using the information you gather, prepare a series of diagrams that show the major parts of a mushroom and the ways in which spores are spread. Use the diagrams in an oral report to your class.

H. M. HOOVER

As a child, Helen Mary Hoover (1935–) disliked science fiction authors who ignored facts in order to make their plots work. Drawing on her memory of the past, she creates the same types of writings she has always enjoyed—natural history, biographies and history, books of facts, and ghost stories.

Now known as a writer of science fiction for young people, Hoover has strong opinions about the differences between fantastic and realistic fiction, believing that there is more lasting truth in fantasy. "All fiction writers create singular worlds if they try, but in some respects fantastic worlds must be more real, more logically detailed and specific than straight fiction."

Hoover grew up in a rural area of Ohio where there were fields and woods to roam, as well as orchards, ponds, and creeks. "Pets and children were left unleashed," she says. "There was no litter. There were few strangers." Both her parents were teachers and amateur naturalists; she credits them with giving her a sense of imagination and wonder as well as a love of reading.

OTHER WORKS *Children of Morrow, The Delikon, The Rains of Eridan, The Lost Star* Extended Reading

236 UNIT TWO PART 2: TESTS OF ENDURANCE

• SCIENCE CONNECTION

WORDS TO KNOW

EXERCISE A Review the Words to Know in the boxes at the bottom of the selection pages. Then, on your paper, write the word suggested by each sentence below.

1. The symbol > means that the number on the left is greater than the number on the right.
2. Many fungi feed on dead plants and animals.
3. A tree may be injured so severely that it will die.
4. The scattered remains on the ground provide the necessities of life for mushrooms.
5. The life of a mushroom may be so long as to appear almost endless.

EXERCISE B Along with one to four classmates, write each vocabulary word on a small label, and tape each label to a pencil. Then drop the pencils in a pile on a table. Take turns trying to remove a pencil from the pile without causing the others to move. After removing a pencil, to earn a point and the chance to continue playing, a student must define the word on the pencil, use it in a sentence, or make another word from it by adding a prefix or a suffix.

Alternative Activities

1. Students might find recordings of natural sounds, such as ocean waves breaking, in a library. Alternatively, students could use instrumental music, such as Vivaldi's *Four Seasons*, to suggest nature.
2. Students might ask a science teacher for help in researching how to make spore prints. Caution students against eating any mushrooms that they find.

PREVIEWING

FICTION

Cricket in the Road
Michael Anthony

PERSONAL CONNECTION *Activating Prior Knowledge/Setting a Purpose*

In the story you are about to read, a young Trinidadian boy becomes upset with his friends during a game. Recall a disagreement you have had with a friend. What caused it, and what steps did you take to settle it? Describe your experience in your notebook or on a sheet of paper. As you read, compare your experience with the experiences of the characters in the story.

Building Background

GEOGRAPHICAL CONNECTION

The setting of this story is the village of Mayaro on the island of Trinidad. Trinidad is one of two islands that make up a country called Trinidad and Tobago. Trinidad lies in the Caribbean Sea, seven miles off the northeast coast of Venezuela. Its climate is hot and humid, with a rainy season that lasts from late May until November. Trinidad and Tobago was a colony of Great Britain until 1962 and still has many British customs. Cricket, a game somewhat like baseball, is popular in both countries.

READING CONNECTION *Active Reading*

Understanding Dialogue Although English is the official language of Trinidad and Tobago, many people there speak Trinidad English, a form of English that has been influenced by French and Spanish. During the disagreement among the friends in this story, you will notice differences between the verb forms used in standard U.S. English and those used in Trinidad English. By writing the dialogue of the characters exactly as it would sound, the writer lets you "hear" how the people of Trinidad and Tobago speak. Some examples from the story are shown in this chart.

Trinidad English	Standard U.S. English
Who second bat?	Who bats second?
What you want?	What do you want?
He throw them away.	He threw them away.

• CULTURAL CONNECTION

237

OVERVIEW

Objectives

- To understand and appreciate a short story about a disagreement among friends
- To note and understand dialogue by comparing standard U.S. English and Trinidad English
- To understand and differentiate internal and external conflicts
- To express understanding of the selection through a choice of writing forms, including a dialogue, a journal entry, and a poem
- To extend understanding of the selection through a variety of multimodal and cross-curricular activities

Skills

LITERARY CONCEPTS
• Internal and external conflict

GRAMMAR
• Prepositional phrases

SPELLING
• Silent letters

SPEAKING, LISTENING, AND VIEWING
• Group discussion
• Oral presentation

Cross-Curricular Connections

SCIENCE
• Rainfall

SOCIAL STUDIES
• Travel brochure

 **CULTURAL CONNECTION**
Trinidad British and Caribbean cultures coexist on the island of Trinidad. These scenes of daily life and of festivals will help students understand the culture of the island.

Side A, Frame 38733

PRINT AND MEDIA RESOURCES

UNIT TWO RESOURCE BOOK
Strategic Reading: Literature, p. 59
Vocabulary SkillBuilder, p. 62
Reading SkillBuilder, p. 60
Spelling SkillBuilder, p. 61

GRAMMAR MINI-LESSONS
Transparencies, p. 44

ACCESS FOR STUDENTS ACQUIRING ENGLISH
Selection Summaries
Reading and Writing Support

FORMAL ASSESSMENT
Selection Test, pp. 51–52
Part Test, pp. 53–54
 Test Generator

 AUDIO LIBRARY
See Reference Card

 **LASERLINKS**
Cultural Connection

THE LANGUAGE OF LITERATURE **TEACHER'S EDITION** 237

SUMMARY

During the long rainy season, Selo, Amy, and Vern play cricket whenever there is a break in the rain. One day, the children argue, and Selo throws the bat and ball away. For many months, Amy and Vern don't play with Selo. But when the sun comes out, all is forgiven, and they let Selo bat first.

Thematic Link: *Tests of Endurance* A young boy endures frightening seasonal thunderstorms and the loneliness caused by his estrangement from his playmates.

CUSTOMIZING FOR
Gifted and Talented Students

As students read the selection, have them think about Selo's behavior and how it affects his friends.

Possible responses:

- Page 239—"'I'm not playing!' I cried, stung. . . . Then I flung them [the bat and ball] with all my strength into the bushes."/Vern is dumbfounded. Amy tells what Selo did with the bat and ball.

- Page 240—"I saw tears glinting from the corners of his [Vern's] eyes."/Vern pretends it doesn't matter, but his feelings are hurt.

CUSTOMIZING FOR
Students Acquiring English

- Use **ACCESS FOR STUDENTS ACQUIRING ENGLISH,** *Reading and Writing Support.*

- This story takes place in Trinidad and contains colloquial spoken language from that area. You may want to call students' attention to these expressions, then ask them to paraphrase in standard U.S. English.

1 Students should be able to guess that *stupes* is a derogatory term used by the narrator because he is angry at Vern and Amy. Point out the similarity to *stupid*.

STRATEGIC READING FOR
Less-Proficient Readers

Set a Purpose As students read, have them look for the cause of the children's argument.

Use **UNIT TWO RESOURCE BOOK,** pp. 59–60, for guidance in reading the selection.

Cricket in the Road

by Michael Anthony

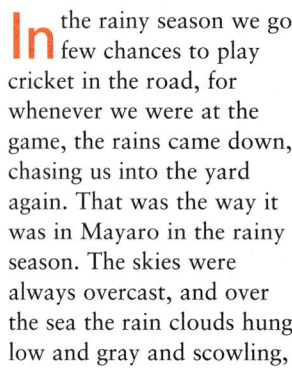

In the rainy season we got few chances to play cricket in the road, for whenever we were at the game, the rains came down, chasing us into the yard again. That was the way it was in Mayaro in the rainy season. The skies were always overcast, and over the sea the rain clouds hung low and gray and scowling, and the winds blew in and whipped angrily through the palms. And when the winds were strongest and raging, the low-hanging clouds would become dense and black, and the sea would roar, and the torrents of rain would come sweeping with all their tumult upon us.

We had just run in from the rain. Amy and Vern from next door were in good spirits and laughing, for oddly enough they seemed to enjoy the downpour as much as playing cricket in the road. Amy was in our yard, giggling and pretending to drink the falling rain, with her face all wet and her clothes drenched, and Vern, who was sheltering under the eaves,[1] excitedly jumped out to join her. "Rain, rain, go to Spain," they shouted. And presently their mother, who must have heard the noise and knew, appeared from next door, and Vern and Amy vanished through the hedge.

I stood there, depressed about the rain, and then I put Vern's bat and ball underneath the house and went indoors. "Stupes!" I said to myself. I had been batting when the rains came down. It was only when *I* was batting that the rains came down! I wiped my feet so I wouldn't soil the sheets and went up on the bed. I was sitting, sad, and wishing that the rain would really go away—go to Spain, as Vern said—when my heart seemed to jump out of me. A deafening peal of thunder struck across the sky. **1**

Quickly I closed the window. The rain hammered awfully on the rooftop, and I kept tense for the thunder which I knew would break again and for the unearthly flashes of lightning.

Secretly I was afraid of the violent weather. I was afraid of the rain, and of the thunder

---
1. **eaves** (ēvz): overhanging edges of a roof.

WORDS TO KNOW
torrent (tôr′ənt) *n.* a heavy downpour
tumult (tōō′mŭlt) *n.* a noisy uproar
peal (pēl) *n.* a loud burst of noise

WORDS TO KNOW

dumbfounded (dŭm′foun′dĭd) *adj.* made speechless by shocking; astonished **dumbfound** *v.* (p. 239)
fume (fyōōm) *v.* to burn with anger (p. 239)
peal (pēl) *n.* a loud burst of noise (p. 238)
torrent (tôr′ənt) *n.* a heavy downpour (p. 238)
tumult (tōō′mŭlt) *n.* a noisy uproar (p. 238)

and the lightning that came with them, and of the sea beating against the headlands,[2] and of the storm winds, and of everything being so deathlike when the rains were gone. I started[3] again at another flash of lightning, and before I had recovered from this, yet another terrifying peal of thunder hit the air. I screamed. I heard my mother running into the room. Thunder struck again, and I dashed under the bed.

"Selo! Selo! First bat!" Vern shouted from the road. The rains had ceased and the sun had come out, but I was not quite recovered yet. I brought myself reluctantly to look out from the front door, and there was Vern, grinning and impatient and beckoning to me.

"First bat," he said. And as if noting my indifference, he looked toward Amy, who was just coming out to play. "Who second bat?" he said.

"Me!" I said.

"Me!" shouted Amy almost at the same time.

"Amy second bat," Vern said.

"No, I said 'Me' first," I protested.

Vern grew impatient while Amy and I argued. Then an idea seemed to strike him. He took out a penny from his pocket. "Toss for it," he said. "What you want?"

"Heads," I called.

"Tail," cried Amy. "Tail bound to come!"[4]

The coin went up in the air, fell down and overturned, showing tail.

"I'm *not* playing!" I cried, stung. And as that did not seem to disturb enough, I ran toward

Schoolboys, Frané Lessac. From *Caribbean Canvas*, Macmillan Press, Ltd. By permission of the artist.

where I had put Vern's bat and ball and disappeared with them behind our house. Then I flung them with all my strength into the bushes.

When I came back to the front of the house, Vern was standing there <u>dumbfounded</u>. "Selo, where's the bat and ball?" he said.

I was <u>fuming</u>. "I don't know about *any* bat and ball!"

---

2. **headlands:** points of land that jut out into the water.
3. **started:** jumped suddenly in surprise.
4. **Toss for it. . . . Tail bound to come!:** Vern is flipping a coin to determine who will bat second. Selo calls that it will come up heads, so Amy roots for it to come up tails.

WORDS TO KNOW
dumbfounded (dŭm´foun´dĭd) *adj.* speechless with shock; astonished **dumbfound** *v.*
fume (fyōōm) *v.* to burn with anger

239

Art Note

Schoolboys by Frané Lessac The boys in the painting are in school uniforms and appear to be posing. The figures are very simply painted, with a flat rather than a three-dimensional appearance. Despite this, the boys seem lifelike.

Reading the Art What words would you use to describe the personalities of the boys? How do they differ from one another?

CUSTOMIZING FOR
Students Acquiring English

2 If necessary, point out that Selo is the name of the narrator.

3 Students may not be familiar with the practice of tossing a coin to make a decision. Demonstrate in class, explaining the terms *heads* and *tail*.

STRATEGIC READING FOR
Less-Proficient Readers

A Ask students why Selo and Amy are arguing. (*Each child wants to bat second, and both said so at the same time.*) Ask why they aren't arguing about batting first. (*Vern has clearly claimed first.*) **Summarizing**

Set a Purpose Have students read to learn how Selo responds to the argument.

Active Reading: EVALUATE

B Ask students whether they think Vern's solution is a good one or not. Have students explain the reasons for their responses. Then invite them to suggest other ways to resolve the disagreement.

Literary Concept: CONFLICT

C Remind students of the difference between internal and external conflicts. One way to remember the difference is to look at the prefix of each word: *in-* refers to something inside and *ex-* to something outside. Ask students which kind of conflict Selo's argument with Amy and Vern represents. (*external*)

Mini-Lesson Grammar

PREPOSITIONAL PHRASES Point out to students that a prepositional phrase is a group of words that begins with a preposition and ends with its object. One or more words may come between the preposition and its object, which may be singular or compound.

Application Have students identify the prepositional phrases in the following sentences.
1. Selo threw the bat <u>into the bushes.</u>
2. <u>Through the window,</u> Selo could see the lightning.
3. Selo hid <u>under the bed</u> when it rained.
4. It was the beginning <u>of the new year</u> when Selo saw Vern again.

Then ask students to write a set of directions to find the bat and ball Selo threw away. Have them use at least three prepositional phrases.

Reteaching/Reinforcement
- *Grammar Handbook,* anthology p. 820
- *Grammar Mini-Lessons* transparencies, p. 44

 **The Writer's Craft**

Using Prepositional Phrases, pp. 506–507

THE LANGUAGE OF LITERATURE TEACHER'S EDITION **239**

STRATEGIC READING FOR
Less-Proficient Readers

D Discuss with students how Selo feels after the argument. *(He is lonely. He is afraid that Amy and Vern will never forgive him.)* **Making Inferences**

Critical Thinking:
HYPOTHESIZING

E Have students hypothesize why Selo cries at the end of the story. *(Possible response: Selo cries because he is happy. Vern's handing Selo the bat shows that Selo is forgiven.)*

LITERARY INSIGHT

1. What is similar about the characters in the first part of the story and the characters in the first part of the poem? *(In both cases, the characters quarrel over a minor matter, and their fight intensifies until they are cut off from each other.)*
2. How is the ending of each work the same? *(In each case reconciliation comes about, and it is initiated by a character other than the speaker or narrator.)*

ELEANOR FARJEON

A prolific children's author best known for her fantasies, poems, and plays, Eleanor Farjeon was born in London in 1881. She grew up—and received her education—in the library of her novelist father, Benjamin Leopold. Farjeon received many awards during her long career; among them the International Hans Christian Andersen Award and the Carnegie Medal of the Library Association (England). She died in 1965.

COMPREHENSION CHECK

1. Where does the story take place? *(in the village of Mayaro on the island of Trinidad, during the rainy season)*
2. How does Vern try to resolve the disagreement between Selo and Amy? *(He tosses a coin.)*
3. How is the quarrel finally resolved? *(Vern makes the first move, letting Selo use Vern's new bat first.)*

Dumb, thumb, and crumb
All have a letter that's mum.
To spell each correctly,
End each with a "b"!

"Tell on him," Amy cried. "He throw them away."

Vern's mouth twisted into a forced smile. "What's an old bat and ball," he said.

But as he walked out of the yard, I saw tears glinting from the corners of his eyes.

For the rest of that rainy season, we never played cricket in the road again. Sometimes the rains ceased and the sun came out brightly, and I heard the voices of Amy and Vern on the other side of the fence. At such times I would go out into the road and whistle to myself, hoping they would hear me and come out, but they never did, and I knew they were still very angry and would never forgive me.

And so the rainy season went on. And it was as fearful as ever with the thunder and lightning and waves roaring in the bay, and the strong winds. But the people who talked of all this said that was the way Mayaro was, and they laughed about it. And sometimes when through the rain and even thunder I heard Vern's voice on the other side of the fence, shouting "Rain, rain, go to Spain," it puzzled me how it could be so. For often I had made up my mind I would be brave, but when the thunder cracked I always dashed under the bed.

It was the beginning of the new year when I saw Vern and Amy again. The rainy season was, happily, long past, and the day was hot and bright, and as I walked toward home I saw that I was walking toward Vern and Amy just about to start cricket in the road. My heart thumped violently. They looked strange and new, as if they had gone away, far, and did not want to come back anymore. They did not notice me until I came up quite near, and then I saw Amy start, her face all lit up.

"Vern—" she cried, "Vern look—look Selo!"

Embarrassed, I looked at the ground and at the trees, and at the orange sky, and I was so happy I did not know what to say. Vern stared at me, a strange grin on his face. He was ripping the cellophane paper off a brand new bat.

"Selo, here—*you* first bat," he said gleefully.

And I cried as though it were raining and I was afraid. ❖

LITERARY INSIGHT

The Quarrel
by Eleanor Farjeon

I quarreled with my brother,
I don't know what about,
One thing led to another
And somehow we fell out.
5 The start of it was slight,
The end of it was strong,
He said he was right,
I knew he was wrong!

We hated one another.
10 The afternoon turned black.
Then suddenly my brother
Thumped me on the back,
And said, "Oh, come along!
We can't go on all night—
15 I was in the wrong."
So he was in the right.

---

240   UNIT TWO   PART 2: TESTS OF ENDURANCE

Mini-Lesson Spelling

SILENT LETTERS Many English words are difficult to spell because they contain consonants that are not pronounced. There is no rule for spelling these words; students must learn and remember the spellings. Explain that in these cases, it helps to create a mnemonic device that makes remembering easier. See the example on the chalkboard.

Application Read the following words aloud and have students spell them. Ask them to identify the silent letter(s) in each word.

1. dum*b*founded
2. whis*t*le
3. crum*b*
4. answer
5. sign
6. sword
7. *k*nife
8. *wh*ipped
9. *g*nat
10. lim*b*
11. *w*restle
12. ca*l*m

Invite students to create their own mnemonic device for one of the above words and record it in their personal word lists.

Reteaching/Reinforcement
• *Unit Two Resource Book*, p. 61

RESPONDING OPTIONS

FROM PERSONAL RESPONSE TO CRITICAL ANALYSIS

REFLECT
1. What were your thoughts about the three friends as you finished reading? Write your thoughts in your notebook.

RETHINK
2. What three words or phrases would you use to describe Selo?
   Consider
   Close Textual Reading
   • why he hides the bat and ball
   • why he cries when Vern lets him bat first

3. In what ways do you think Selo and Vern are alike, and in what ways are they different?
   Consider
   Close Textual Reading
   • their actions during the downpour
   • the way they determine the batting order
   • their reactions to seeing each other after the rainy season

4. Why do you think Selo is reluctant to talk to Vern and Amy after the disagreement occurs, even though it's obvious he wants to play with them?

5. If Vern did not reach out to Selo, what do you suppose would happen to their relationship?

RELATE
6. What do you think is the fairest and fastest way to settle a disagreement with friends? Support your opinion with ideas from "Cricket in the Road" and from the Insight selection "The Quarrel," as well as the experience you wrote about for the Personal Connection on page 237.

Multimodal Learning
ANOTHER PATHWAY

The narrator often refers to the setting, describing various sights and sounds in detail. Make a chart, listing some details of the setting and telling how each detail affects an event in the story. Use an overhead projector, a group of networked computers, or the classroom bulletin board to share your chart with the class.

QUICKWRITES

1. Write a **dialogue**, or conversation, in which Selo, Vern, and Amy talk about their disagreement, the reasons for it, and ways to avoid future problems.

2. What lessons do you think Selo learns from his experience? Write a **diary entry** that Selo might write years later, describing the lessons he learned from the events described in the story.

3. Selo's need for Vern and Amy's forgiveness builds throughout the story. Write a **poem** about a time when you forgave or were forgiven by someone important to you.

📁 **PORTFOLIO** Save your writing. You may want to use it later as a springboard to a piece for your portfolio.

CRICKET IN THE ROAD **241**

From Personal Response to Critical Analysis

1. Responses will vary.
2. Students may use words such as *quick-tempered, emotional,* and *sentimental.*
3. Some students may say that Selo and Vern enjoy some of the same activities, such as cricket, but are temperamentally very different. Vern enjoys the rainy season, for example, but thunder and lightning terrify Selo.
4. Possible responses: Selo is afraid of rejection; he is embarrassed and ashamed.
5. Responses will vary. Some students may say the two boys would never be reunited; others may say that Selo would eventually swallow his pride and apologize to Amy and Vern.
6. Make sure that students include ideas from the selections and from their own experience.

Another Pathway
To help students get started, point out that the setting is in Trinidad, which has retained many British customs because it was once a colony of Great Britain. This is why Vern, Amy, and Selo play cricket instead of baseball.

Rubric
3 Full Accomplishment Student lists several details of the setting and correlates each detail to an event in the story.
2 Substantial Accomplishment Student lists several details of the setting but does not correlate them precisely to events in the story.
1 Little or Partial Accomplishment Student has difficulty identifying details of the setting and explaining how the setting affects events in the story.

QuickWrites

1. You may wish to encourage students to use Trinidad English in their dialogues.
2. Before they begin, have students think about how age and experience might change Selo's self-understanding and his point of view. In small groups, allow them to discuss how Selo may have changed.
3. Allow students to write either in free verse or in rhyme. Assure them that they need not read their poems aloud.

The Writer's Craft

Using Dialogue, pp. 278–280
Personal Writing, pp. 28–39
Writing a Poem, pp. 84–88

THE LANGUAGE OF LITERATURE TEACHER'S EDITION **241**

Across the Curriculum

Social Studies *Cooperative Learning* Have students work in small groups of four or five. They might contact a travel agency or consulate's office for information on Trinidad. You may wish to have groups test the effectiveness of their brochures by sharing them with younger students or friends in another class.

ADDITIONAL SUGGESTIONS

 **Science** *It's Raining, It's Pouring...* Have students research and compare the annual rainfall in Trinidad, in the place where they live, and in several other especially wet or dry areas of the United States. Students can use an almanac or encyclopedia to find out this information. Have them present their findings in a chart.

LITERARY CONCEPTS

The plot of a story almost always involves some sort of conflict, or struggle between opposing forces. An **internal conflict** is a struggle within a character's mind. Such a conflict often occurs when a character has to make a difficult decision or deal with opposing feelings. For example, a character in a story might have to decide whether he or she wants to become an architect or a lawyer. What is the internal conflict Selo experiences in "Cricket in the Road"?

CONCEPT REVIEW: External Conflict Remember that there may be both internal and external conflicts in a story. An external conflict is a struggle between a character and an outside force, such as society or another character. How would you describe the external conflict in this story?

Multimodal Learning
ACROSS THE CURRICULUM

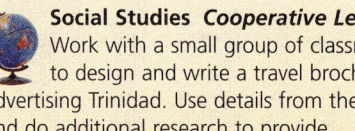 **Social Studies** *Cooperative Learning* Work with a small group of classmates to design and write a travel brochure advertising Trinidad. Use details from the story, and do additional research to provide information about tourist attractions and the island's history. Include pictures of Trinidad or your own drawings, and use persuasive writing to make your readers want to visit Trinidad.

242   UNIT TWO   PART 2: TESTS OF ENDURANCE

Multimodal Learning
ALTERNATIVE ACTIVITIES

1. Research the game of cricket and write an **introduction** to the game. Be sure to describe the object of the game, the playing positions, and the equipment. Also describe its rules and the etiquette, or manners, expected of its players. Add drawings or diagrams, and present the information on a poster or in a brochure that can be duplicated for interested students.

2. Imagine that "Cricket in the Road" has been made into a musical. Create a **song** that one of the characters might sing. You may want to use a familiar tune, writing your own lyrics to it.

Literary Concepts

Have students form small groups to discuss the two questions posed in their texts. Have the groups write an internal monologue in response to the first question or a dialogue in response to the second one. *(Possible responses: As stated on page 240, Selo is torn between his desire to be brave and his fear of the rain. The external conflict is a struggle among Selo and Amy and Vern over who gets to make the rules.)* Have groups choose students to read aloud completed monologues or dialogues.

Alternative Activities

1. You may wish to have students work in small groups to complete this activity. They can find information in an encyclopedia or in a more specialized work, such as a history of sports. When students are finished, allow groups to exchange papers to spot where more clarity is needed.
2. Allow students to use a rhyming dictionary. They may wish to scan the selection to brainstorm rhymes before they begin. *(rain/Spain; bat/splat; Vern/turn)*

242 THE LANGUAGE OF LITERATURE **TEACHER'S EDITION**

WORDS TO KNOW

On your paper, write the lettter of the sentence that best expresses the meaning of each boldfaced word.

1. **tumult**
   a. The acrobats performed amazing leaps.
   b. Selo was overjoyed when the rain stopped.
   c. Because of the storm's noisy uproar, no one was able to hear.

2. **peal**
   a. The banana skin is on top of the compost heap.
   b. The sound of the pipes could be heard even after the organist stopped playing.
   c. The boy asked his mother for suggestions.

3. **torrent**
   a. The dark clouds brought a heavy downpour that canceled the game.
   b. Vern flipped a coin to resolve the dispute.
   c. The suddenness of the rain annoyed Selo.

4. **dumbfounded**
   a. Her information is not based on facts.
   b. Selo's behavior left Vern speechless.
   c. Anita's stories amused her listeners.

5. **fume**
   a. The tourist enjoyed the island's beauty.
   b. The waves crashed against the shore.
   c. The boat's delay will cause the passengers to complain angrily.

MICHAEL ANTHONY

1932–

Michael Anthony writes tales about life on the island of Trinidad. His stories offer readers a taste of Caribbean life and a chance to consider the most important things in life—like friendship.

Born in Mayaro, Trinidad and Tobago, Anthony started working in an iron foundry at the age of 15. Eight years later, he went to England, where he held a variety of factory jobs and eventually became a journalist. From England, he went to Brazil. After a two-year stay in Brazil, he and his wife and four children returned to Trinidad to live.

The selection you have just read is from a collection that is also titled *Cricket in the Road*. Michael Anthony has also published several novels and poems. He says, "I feel very strongly about the brotherhood of mankind.... One of my main hopes is that human beings will find a way to live together without friction." He also says that he is an optimist who would like to see all the nations of the world join together to become one strong nation.

OTHER WORKS *The Games Were Coming, Green Days by the River* Extended Reading

OVERVIEW

To gain a richer appreciation of the selections they have read in this unit, students will explore the characteristics of a description and then create their own description in this lesson.

Objectives

- To plan a description by considering such elements as purpose, sensory details, and organization
- To draft a description and solicit a response to it
- To revise, edit, and publish a description
- To reflect on the process of writing a description

Skills

LITERATURE
- Analyzing characterization
- Making inferences

WRITING AND LANGUAGE
- Varying your sentences
- Writing a discovery draft

GRAMMAR AND USAGE
- Using action verbs

MEDIA LITERACY
- Analyzing photographs and pictures

SPEAKING, LISTENING, AND VIEWING
- Interviewing
- Staging a Reader's Theater presentation

Teaching Strategy: MODELING

A Guide students through the process of generating writing ideas from a springboard such as scrapbook photos by inviting them to look at the photos on page 244. Have students tell what they can determine about the people in the photographs. Discuss with students how a photo might be more desirable than a written description when you need to know exactly what a person looks like.

CUSTOMIZING FOR

Students Acquiring English

B Students may have difficulty with the slang expression *deep kid*. Explain that it refers to a mature, thoughtful, and intelligent child.

WRITING FROM EXPERIENCE

WRITING A DESCRIPTION

What makes a person unique? Is it the way he or she looks or acts? Is it how the person responds in a difficult situation? In Unit Two, "The Need to Belong," you met several people who tried to be themselves at the same time they struggled to fit in. What made these characters unique?

GUIDED ASSIGNMENT
Write a Character Sketch A character sketch is a picture of a person, drawn in words. The sketch describes what he or she is like, inside and out. Writing a character sketch can help you get to know someone and discover what sets that person apart from others.

1 Think About People

Where do you meet people? How do you learn about them? Is there someone that you have met only once but that you think you'll never forget? What is it about people that makes them interesting? Traits are the qualities or features that help to make a person unique.

Physical Traits The first thing you notice about people might be their physical features: are they tall? graceful? red-headed? frail? These are physical traits.

Personal Traits Soon you also learn about their behavior and personality. Are they honest? proud? generous? hard-working? hot-tempered? These are personal traits.

Scrapbook Photos
When might a photo be more desirable than a written description of a person?

Advice Column

I wonder how S. gets along with the girls at her school.

Clothes cost too much, so why shop there?

Dear Wendi: Most girls at my school shop at this one store. I like their clothes, but the prices are outrageous. I feel like everybody is obsessed. My mom says I can shop there, but I don't want to be selfish and spend so much. How can I get rid of this feeling?
S.

Dear S.: Why not work with that feeling instead? It takes a deep kid to see how obsessed people can be with clothes.
Chicago Tribune, June 27

S. reminds me of Katie. She always does her own thing, too.

Brad winning his division at the Jr. Drag Racing League!

PRINT AND MEDIA RESOURCES

UNIT TWO RESOURCE BOOK
Prewriting, p. 65
Elaboration, p. 66
Peer Response Guide, pp. 67–68
Revising and Proofreading, p. 69
Student Model, p. 70
Rubric, p. 71

GRAMMAR MINI–LESSONS
Transparencies, p. 17

WRITING MINI–LESSONS
Transparencies, pp. 2–3, 34, 38, 42

ACCESS FOR STUDENTS ACQUIRING ENGLISH
Reading and Writing Support

FORMAL ASSESSMENT
Guidelines for Writing Assessment

LASERLINKS
Writing Springboard

WRITING COACH

---

244 THE LANGUAGE OF LITERATURE TEACHER'S EDITION

Teaching Strategy: MODELING

C To show students how to use a professional piece of writing as a model to spark ideas for a story, invite a volunteer to read aloud the excerpt from the biography of Paul Robeson as students follow along in their books. As a class, analyze how Virginia Hamilton has described Robeson's physical and personal traits. Have students find examples of the details and concrete language that depict Robeson. Finally, guide students to see how Hamilton arranged her description of the incident in chronological order.

Media Literacy: INTERPRETING PHOTOGRAPHS

D Remind students that to make inferences, they need to combine what they already know with clues from the text and the photograph. Work with students to describe how the photograph relates to the story about Paul Robeson. Help students to contrast Robeson's experience with intolerance with the diversity of people shown in the photograph.

Excerpt from a Biography

C

80

Paul Robeson was a famous singer and actor in the 1920s, 1930s, and 1940s. As an African American, he had to struggle to get the respect given to white actors.

Black reporters were invited to press conferences at the White House. The president's wife, Eleanor Roosevelt, made it a point to invite black children to visit her. Such simple decency made white America sit up and take notice.

Nevertheless, Paul Robeson experienced a racial insult almost on the day of his return. He had been invited as guest of honor to a tea at one of New York's finest hotels. When he strode toward the elevator, he was told he must go around to the freight elevator.

"Several years back," he said in an interview, "I would have smarted at this insult and carried the hurt for a long time. Now—no—I was just amused and explained to the elevator boy that I didn't belong with the freight, that, as I was the guest of honor at the tea my hosts might be surprised to see me arrive with the supplies."

With that, he had continued on his way on the passenger elevator.

Perhaps America had not changed so much as had Paul's (and thousands of other blacks') reaction to it. He hadn't turned on his heel at the insult from the elevator operator, but had been amused and undaunted. The slur to his manhood, his blackness, had not stopped him for a moment. Times and black people had changed. And the change had also come over the most renowned black man the world had ever known.

Virginia Hamilton
from *Paul Robeson: The Life and Times of a Free Black Man*

② Make Inferences

Think about the people on these pages. What can you figure out about people by looking at these examples? What clues help you make these inferences? Record your answers to the following questions in your journal.

- What can you tell about the girl who wrote the letter to Wendi? What can you conclude about Wendi?
- What can you infer about the boy in the photograph based on the activity he is involved in? from his expression?
- What might Paul Robeson's actions reveal about him?

LASERLINKS
• WRITING SPRINGBOARD
WRITING COACH

WRITING FROM EXPERIENCE   245

WRITING SPRINGBOARD
The Need to Belong A young Native American teenager talks about the prejudice she experiences at school, away from her home on the reservation.

Side B, Frame 4981

Writing Prompt All people seek special places where they feel they belong. Write a character sketch of someone you know who has been excluded from a group. Describe everything you can about the person's experience and the way he or she dealt with it.

THE LANGUAGE OF LITERATURE TEACHER'S EDITION **245**

Teaching Strategy:
STUMBLING BLOCK

E If students cannot generate ideas from old photographs, school yearbooks, or personal observations, they can make a cluster diagram or an idea tree to spark ideas.

Research Skill: INTERVIEWING

F Encourage students to conduct an interview as part of their research. Suggest that students prepare a list of questions before the interview. Guide students to write questions that are probing but not intrusive and that call for more than a yes or no answer. Possible questions include the following:
- If you had to describe yourself in 25 or fewer words, what would you say?
- What accomplishments have brought you the greatest pride? Why?
- How do you feel about the environment? about animals?

Suggest that students tape-record the interview, if the subject agrees to be taped, so that they can refer to the tape as they write.

PREWRITING

Making Observations

Studying Characters Now that you have begun to think about what makes an interesting character, you can start to apply these ideas and further explore a character of your choice.

❶ Choose Your Own Character

You might want to write about someone you could learn something from or a person you'd like to understand better. Look at old photographs and school yearbooks. Look around you at the people in your class, in your family, or on the street. Do you know someone you wish others could meet? You might like to write about a figure from history, a person in the news, a character from the literature, or someone you really like or dislike.

To get your thoughts flowing, do a brief freewrite about the people that interest you. Then choose the person who stands out most.

E

❷ Get to Know Your Character

Before beginning to write, you'll need to know a lot about your subject.

Write What You Know List physical details or traits such as how the person looks, dresses, talks, and moves. (See the SkillBuilder for tips on observing.) Then look for deeper qualities such as talents, hobbies, likes and dislikes, and feelings about self and others. See how one student recorded her observations below.

Research Your Subject If your character sketch is about someone you don't know, you may be able to find out more by talking to others who do know him or her. If possible, interview the person yourself. Photographs can also tell you a lot about people.

Student's Observations

246 UNIT TWO: THE NEED TO BELONG

 Mini-Lesson   **Study Skills**

USING KWL Explain to students that they can use the KWL method to find out more about the person they are describing. Explain that the method works equally well when used in conjunction with interviewing or library research. On the board, list the three steps in the KWL process:

K: What do I already *know* about my subject?

W: What do I *want* to learn?

L: What did I *learn*?

Describe each step. Then complete a sample KWL chart, using a historical figure such as George Washington or Harriet Tubman.

Application Invite students to make a KWL chart for the person they are going to describe. Suggest that students include as many details as possible as they brainstorm and take notes. Encourage students to use the chart as they draft their description.

246 THE LANGUAGE OF LITERATURE TEACHER'S EDITION

Try a New Point of View If you are writing about a person you don't understand very well, you might try imagining that you are that person. Write for a few moments from his or her point of view.

3 Decide on a Focus

Look over the observations you recorded about your subject. What qualities do you want to focus on? What is your overall feeling about the person? What do you want your readers to know about him or her? For your character sketch, focus on the two or three traits that best describe your subject.

Showing how your subject reacts in a situation can help illustrate his or her personality. During this prewriting stage, you might make notes about incidents or anecdotes that help show the traits you want to focus on. See how one student did this below.

Student's Prewriting Notes

KATIE'S BEST TRAITS

Athletic
- once asked the guys if she could join their game at recess; now they ask her to play
- can do more sit-ups than anyone else in our gym class

Good friend
- helped me study for math test
- didn't get upset when Tony lost her ball

Strong person
- stood up for herself when Sue made fun of her sniffling
- helped take care of her younger brother Dave when her mom went into the hospital

---

SkillBuilder

WRITER'S CRAFT

Using Sensory Details
Careful observation is a key to writing a character sketch. As you think about your subject and the situations she or he is involved in, use all your senses. Try to get at exactly how people and places look and sound. Use words that are colorful and exact. Which of the sentences below helps you see the scene more vividly? Why?

Katie ran for a touchdown.

Katie's yellow, raggedy braids whipped behind her as she sprinted for the goal line.

APPLYING WHAT YOU'VE LEARNED
Review your notes and try to add details that will appeal to your readers' senses.

WRITING HANDBOOK

For more information on descriptive writing, see Writing Handbook page 784.

THINK & PLAN

Reflecting on Your Ideas

1. Did writing from the point of view of your subject give you any clues to his or her personality? How might you include this information in your sketch?
2. Look at the traits you plan to focus on. What will they tell your reader?

WRITING FROM EXPERIENCE **247**

Writing Skill: POINT OF VIEW

G To help students rethink their writing from another standpoint, review with them each of the following points of view:

First-person: The narrator, who is a character in the story, uses first-person pronouns such as *I, me,* and *we.*

Third-person omniscient: The narrator, who is not a character in the story, knows everything about the characters and can see into their minds. The narrator uses pronouns such as *he, she,* and *it.*

Third-person limited: The narrator, who is not a character in the story, brings us into the mind of only one character. The narrator uses pronouns such as *he, she,* and *it.*

Writing Skill: DEVELOPING CHARACTER

H Discuss with students the four ways in which writers reveal character traits: through physical descriptions of a character, through what the character says, through what other characters say about that person, and through the actions of the character. Encourage students to consider all four methods when framing their character sketches.

SkillBuilder  WRITER'S CRAFT

USING SENSORY DETAILS Ask students to create a chart listing the five senses and to try to include at least one detail about their chosen subject that taps each sense. Share the following sample chart:

Sense	Details
sight	
sound	
taste	
touch	
smell	

Application Students should generate fresh, lively sensory details that reveal more about their subject's appearance and personality. Possibilities include descriptions of the subject's voice, perfume, or individual style of dress, for example.

Additional Suggestions Encourage students to frame their descriptions as metaphors and similes—types of comparisons that require concise images. Suggest that students also draw a sketch of their subject, to better capture the essence of his or her personality.

Reteaching/Reinforcement
- Writing Handbook, anthology p. 783
- *Writing Mini-Lessons* transparencies, p. 38

Appealing to the Senses, pp. 266–273

Teaching Strategy:
STUMBLING BLOCK

I Many students find it difficult to begin drafting and may delay this stage by spending extra time prewriting. Explain to these students that they are not alone—that many writers have difficulty getting started. To help students overcome this problem, suggest that they set a specific time limit for writing, such as half an hour. Explain that this time limit relieves much of the tension and that writers often find that they have no difficulty continuing to draft once they begin.

Writing Skill:
USING THE COMPUTER

J Suggest that students write their description using a computer. Have students use preprogrammed writing tips on The Writing Coach to facilitate drafting. Students can also use the peer response section of the program to organize feedback.

Teaching Strategy: MANAGING THE PAPER LOAD

To cut down on the paper load as you make sure that all students are on track, read only the opening paragraph of each paper. Offer specific written comments rather than meeting with students individually.

DRAFTING

Getting Your Ideas Down

Sketching a Character Now that you've gotten to know your character, how can you help other people get to know that person? In the draft stage you begin to piece together the ideas in your notes to create a picture of the person you are writing about.

❶ Write a Discovery Draft

Close your eyes for a minute. Try to get away from your notes and your lists, and just think about your character. What do you have to say about him or her? What do you want to focus on in your character sketch? If you think you have too much to say, how can you narrow your focus?

Start writing down your thoughts in any order. You don't have to make it sound good right now. Just get it all down on the page. You can reorganize your writing later.

Student's Discovery Draft

Describe what Katie looks like better. Draw a picture of Katie to put with my sketch?

There was this girl, Sue, in my math class who was always mean to my friend Katie. Sue was mean to a lot of people. She used to make fun of Katie for sniffling. The first time I saw Katie she was running across the playground with a football in her hand. She was fast. ~~I wasn't very fast, and most of the time I didn't care about that. But~~ watching her run, I thought I would like to be fast too. Katie has hay fever and so she sniffles all the time. I don't think Sue really cared about the sniffling. It seemed like she didn't like Katie because Katie didn't care what people thought about her. ~~She~~ *Sue* kept teasing ~~her~~ *Katie*, and Katie would stand up to her. I would have been too scared to do that, but Katie never let Sue get the last word. Even when Sue threatened to beat her up, when she brought a crowd of people around Katie to make fun of her, Katie didn't run away. I don't know how she did it. I guess I really want to say that I admire the way Katie stands up for herself.

move this up

Try to vary my sentences more.

How can I show readers how Katie reacted to Sue?

Describe the time Katie stood up to Sue instead.

Put this at the beginning

248

WRITING SPRINGBOARD
A Ball Player's Story Jim Eisenreich is a professional baseball player with Tourette's syndrome, a neurological disorder characterized by tics and compulsive utterances. He discusses the disease, the challenges he has faced in professional baseball, and the ways he has motivated himself to succeed.

Side B, Frame 7827

Writing Prompt Everyone takes emotional risks at some time. Write a character sketch of a person who has achieved a goal in the face of personal challenges. Discuss the aspects of the person's character that helped him or her face the challenges.

② Analyze Your Discovery Draft

A good character sketch will make readers feel as if they have actually gotten to know the person you have described. Does your description show something important about your character? Have you included examples or anecdotes that illustrate character traits? How can you make your writing more vivid?

③ Draft and Share

Use the guidelines below to strengthen your character sketch.

Show, Don't Tell Good writing doesn't just tell readers what's going on—it lets them see for themselves. How can you show your readers what your subject is like? In addition to vivid details and anecdotes, you can also include dialogue in your sketch.

Remember Your Focus A good character sketch gives such a complete picture of a person that readers can predict how she or he would behave in other situations. From the information in the notes and draft about Katie, what do you think she might say in a speech if she were running for class president?

Organize Your Sketch One way to describe a character is from the outside in. You can begin by giving your readers a picture of what your subject looks like, then describe one or more character traits, and finally tell an anecdote.

PEER RESPONSE

If your character sketch is about a real person, you might ask a classmate who does not know the person in your sketch to read your writing. Then ask him or her questions like the following:

- What is your impression of the person in my character sketch? Describe this person in one sentence.
- Do you feel you got to know this character? Try predicting how she or he might act in another situation.

SkillBuilder

WRITER'S CRAFT

Varying Your Sentences

When writing a character sketch, don't be tempted to make the character the subject of every sentence, as in the first example below.

Katie is a good runner. She is tall and friendly. She likes to play all kinds of sports.

Vary the order of words and phrases. You can also create interest by combining two short sentences.

No one else runs as fast as Katie. Her long legs give her the speed of a greyhound. She is tall and friendly and likes to play all kinds of sports.

APPLYING WHAT YOU'VE LEARNED
Can you add variety to your sketch by combining some short sentences? Could you vary any of your sentences by rearranging the order of words or phrases?

RETHINK & EVALUATE

Preparing to Revise

1. Which character traits come across most strongly in your draft?
2. What are the weakest sections of your draft? How can better use of detail make the draft stronger?

WRITING FROM EXPERIENCE **249**

Writing Skill: ELABORATION

K Remind students of the different kinds of details they can use to elaborate on ideas by showing, not telling:
- Facts: statements that can be verified by an authority, observation, or experience
- Statistics: facts that involve numbers
- Sensory details: words that show how something looks, sounds, smells, tastes, or feels
- Incidents: happenings or occurrences
- Examples: instances of something
- Quotations or dialogue: a speaker's exact words

Writing Skill: PURPOSE

L Guide students to focus on the purpose of their writing, which is to inform. Have students ask themselves the following questions in order to focus on their purpose:
- *What effect do I want my writing to have on my readers?*
- *What aspects of this paper will appeal the most to my readers?*

Writing Skill: ORGANIZATION

M Explain to students that describing a character from the outside in is an aspect of spatial order, or how things are arranged in space. Describe other possible means of organizing a character sketch—for example, by order of importance or by presenting a main idea and supporting details.

SkillBuilder — WRITER'S CRAFT

VARYING YOUR SENTENCES Explain that writing becomes more interesting and exciting when sentence form is varied. Tell students that they can vary their sentences in the following ways:
- Combine complete sentences.
- Combine sentence parts.
- Use both short sentences and longer sentences.
- Sentence fragments may be used in informal writing or in dialogue.
- Combine sentences by using *who, that, which.*
- Use appositives.

Students can explore sentence variety in greater depth by consulting pages 339–357 in *The Writer's Craft.*

Application Students should be able to vary the sentences in their draft. Invite volunteers to share their revisions with the class.

Additional Suggestions Ask students to read their sentences aloud in order to identify awkward sentences, fragments, and run-ons.

Reteaching/Reinforcement
- *Writing Mini-Lessons* transparencies, pp. 40, 41, 42

Sentence Combining, pp. 286–291

THE LANGUAGE OF LITERATURE TEACHER'S EDITION **249**

Writing Skill:
USING THE COMPUTER

N Suggest that students revise their description using a computer. Explain that working on a computer enables writers to see their work as a fluid text that they can easily add to, subtract from, and rearrange. Then guide students to use the search-and-replace function of their software program to replace "fuzzy" nondescriptive words such as *very, really, pretty, quite, rather, nice,* and *excellent.* Suggest that after students have identified each of these words, they decide whether the words need to be revised, and if so, how.

Teaching Strategy: MODELING

O Explore with students how the writer made Katie seem real by using specific sensory details. For example, the phrase "yellow braids were falling apart" appeals to the sense of sight, "socks were a blur" appeals to touch, and "sprinted for a touchdown" appeals to sight, sound, and touch. Invite volunteers to point out the vivid verbs in the last paragraph, such as *sniffed, squinted,* and *stood up (for herself).* Describe how these verbs paint a word picture of Katie that enables readers to visualize her personality as well as her actions.

REVISING AND PUBLISHING

Finishing Your Sketch

Presenting Your Work The suggestions on these pages will help you get your character sketch ready to share with an audience. Make sure that your piece describes your character in the way you intended and that it is free of spelling and grammatical errors. Remember, the smoother your writing is, the easier it will be to read.

1 Revise and Edit

The suggestions below will help you look at your character sketch again, this time with an eye to finishing it.

- Consider how you might use your peer comments to focus your character's personality more clearly.
- Refer to the Standards for Evaluation and Editing Checklist on page 251 to improve any weak or fuzzy parts of your sketch.
- Read the model below to see how one student revised her draft, making it better organized and creating a more vivid picture of her character.

Courageous Katie

The first time I saw Katie she was running across the playground with a football in her arms. Her yellow braids were falling apart and her socks were a blur as she sprinted for a touchdown. That day I wished I could be as fast as Katie. Now I wish I could be as confident.

There was a girl, Sue, in our math class who always made fun of Katie for sniffling. Katie had hay fever, and Sue would walk right up to her and sniff loudly in her face. Although Sue was mean, Katie acted as if she didn't care what people thought of her. I think that bothered Sue.

One day, though, Katie had had enough. When Sue sniffed at her, Katie held up her chin and squinted. "Don't you have anything better to do than make fun of me, Sue?" Katie seemed calm until Sue walked away. Her lips trembled a little, but then she was OK. I guess Sue's teasing really did bother Katie, but she stood up for herself, and didn't let Sue get the best of her.

A Portrait of Katie

Dashing, splashing,
Grinning, winning,
joking, hoping,
that's Katie.

Liking biking,
hating skating,
thinks it's fun to run,
that's Katie.

Sniffs a lot,
gives a lot,
but won't take a lot,
that's Katie.

She is brave,
takes care of Dave,
I think she's great!
That's my friend Kate!

Student's Final Draft

How did this student make Katie seem real to you?

Identify the verbs in the last paragraph. How do they help show rather than tell about Katie?

2 Share Your Work

Use what you have discovered to create other kinds of portraits.

How else might you publish your character sketch? Consider collecting slides and reshaping your sketch as narration for a slide show. (For information on including sound and images, see page 809 of the Multimedia Handbook.) Or turn your character sketch into a short skit. Below are more ideas for writing about interesting people.

PUBLISHING IDEAS

- You might create a photo essay by gathering pictures that show a person's character traits and writing captions for each photo.
- Profiles are character sketches that appear in newspapers. You might want to write about someone you admire and submit your profile to your school or local paper.

Standards for Evaluation

A character sketch
- gives a vivid picture of someone's appearance and personality
- identifies what makes him or her unique
- shows why the person is important to the writer
- uses details, dialogue, and anecdotes to reveal the person's character traits

SkillBuilder

 GRAMMAR FROM WRITING

Using Action Verbs

A **linking verb,** such as *is* or *seems,* simply relates the subject to a word that describes it:

Katie is fast. She seems happy.

An **action verb** tells about an action that is happening. Use action verbs to help readers picture what your character is doing:

Katie leaps like a cheetah. She enjoys running.

 GRAMMAR HANDBOOK

For more information on verbs, see page 835 of the Grammar Handbook.

Editing Checklist As you revise, ask yourself the questions below.

- Did I use vivid action verbs?
- Does my subject agree with my verb in number?
- Are my sentences varied?

REFLECT & ASSESS

Evaluating Your Experience

1. What surprising thing did you learn about your subject while doing this assignment?
2. What other people would you like to sketch? Why?

 PORTFOLIO Add your sketch to your portfolio with a note telling why you chose this person to write about.

WRITING FROM EXPERIENCE **251**

Speaking, Listening, and Viewing:
COLLABORATIVE OPPORTUNITY

P Have students work in small groups to stage a Reader's Theater presentation of their finished character sketches. You might want to provide the option of having each student read a character sketch other than his or her own. After students have rehearsed in their groups, have the class create an evaluation sheet that students can use to assess the presentations. Possible categories include organization, sense of audience, clear purpose, and description. Have members of the audience fill out an evaluation sheet as they listen to each reading.

Teaching Strategy:
COLLABORATIVE OPPORTUNITY

Q Challenge students to create an "idea bank" of publishing possibilities for this writing assignment as well as for others. Possibilities might include a yearbook spread, a videotape or audiotape version, and a poster. Place the list in an accessible place.

PORTFOLIO

Encourage students to select the writing pieces they wish to include in their portfolio. Make sure one selection includes all steps in the writing process. Suggest that students attach a note to each piece that explains their choice. Students can refer to their notes later when they reflect on and assess Unit Two as a whole.

Standards for Evaluation

Have students review their description for the following:

Ideas and Content
- gives a vivid picture of someone's appearance and personality
- identifies what makes the person unique
- shows why the person was important to the writer
- uses dialogue and anecdotes to reveal the person's character traits

Structure and Form
- uses well-developed paragraphs and a clear organization
- uses appropriate transitions
- uses a variety of sentence structures

Grammar, Usage, and Mechanics
- contains no more than two or three minor errors in grammar and usage
- contains no more than two or three minor errors in spelling, capitalization, and punctuation

---

 **GRAMMAR FROM WRITING**

USING ACTION VERBS Be sure that students understand that verbs express an action, state that something exists, or link the subject with a word that describes or renames it. Explain that the most common linking verbs are *am, are, were, being, is, was, be,* and *been.* Other familiar linking verbs are *look, appear, seem, become, remain, feel, sound, taste, grow,* and *smell.* Students may have difficulty with verbs that can function as either action or linking verbs. Explain that they can identify a verb as a linking verb if it (1) is a form of *to be* (*is, are, was, were,* and so on) or (2) a form of *to be* can be substituted for the verb without substantially changing the meaning of the sentence.

Application Have students change the following sentences by using action verbs:
1. Cynthia is tired.
2. Dave is funny.
3. The large dog is frightening.

Reteaching/Reinforcement
- *Grammar Mini-Lessons* transparencies, p.17

The Writer's Craft

Kinds of Verbs, pp. 396–398

THE LANGUAGE OF LITERATURE TEACHER'S EDITION **251**

UNIT REVIEW

This feature allows students to reflect on what they have learned in Unit Two and to assess how well they understand what they have learned. This feature provides students with multiple opportunities for self-assessment, although you may wish to use some of the activities to informally assess specific skills such as speaking and listening or cooperative work.

Objectives

- To allow students to reflect on and assess their understanding of theme
- To allow students to reflect on and assess their understanding of literary concepts such as conflict and plot
- To provide students with the opportunity to assess and build their portfolios

REFLECTING ON THEME

OPTION 1

Encourage students to reread or skim selections as needed to complete their charts. You may wish to have students write a brief journal entry about their own experiences with wanting to belong and to read these entries to the class.

OPTION 2

Suggest that groups work together to review and write a summary for each selection in Unit Two. They can refer to the summaries while discussing which selections they would like to use for their presentations. Make sure that groups write well-organized and persuasive proposals that are supported by details from the selections.

Self-Assessment Tell students that their recommendations should assess the difficulty level of the activity and may provide helpful tips for completing it successfully. Remind them that they are writing for other students their age.

REFLECT & ASSESS

UNIT TWO: THE NEED TO BELONG

Like the characters in this unit, each of us knows what it's like to be a part of something—a family, a friendship, a community. Complete one or more of the options in each of the following sections. They can help you discover more about the unit theme and check the progress you're making as a reader and a writer.

REFLECTING ON THEME

OPTION 1 Comparing and Contrasting With a partner, discuss the experiences of some of the characters in this unit. Fill in a chart like the one shown to explore the characters' need to belong. Think of an experience you've had that is similar to one of the experiences recorded in the chart.

Selections	Who tries to belong?	What attempts are made?	What is the outcome?	What lesson is learned?
"The Adoption of Albert"				

OPTION 2 Producing a Proposal Pretend that your class is a TV production company. Your job is to produce a series of hour-long shows called *Fitting In*, aimed at viewers your age. With two classmates, decide which selections in this unit would make the best television presentations. Write a proposal in which you summarize the selections and give reasons for your choices.

Self-Assessment: Imagine that another class has read this unit and is about to try the activities above. Write a brief recommendation for the activity you completed. Explain what doing it revealed to you about the theme "The Need to Belong."

REVIEWING LITERARY CONCEPTS

OPTION 1 Thinking About Conflict You have learned that there are two basic kinds of conflict in stories, external and internal. Either kind involves a problem that someone—usually a main character—takes action to try to solve. For each selection you have read, make a problem-solution frame like the one for "Tuesday of the Other June" shown here. With a partner, discuss which character's conflict was the most difficult to overcome.

Problem of June T.
Every Tuesday, she must face a bully.

Action	Results
When June T. finds that she and the bully are attending the same school, she realizes that she has to face the bully every day, not just on Tuesdays. She finally refuses to bear the bully's threats.	The bully is embarrassed by June T.'s action and steps away.

252   UNIT TWO: THE NEED TO BELONG

OPTION 2 **Looking at Plot** Think about what might happen in each of this unit's stories if the climax or turning point were somehow different. Choose three stories with particularly strong plots. In your notebook, copy and fill out a diagram, like the one shown, for each of those selections. Then pick the diagram that you think offers the best new possibility, and tell why you chose it.

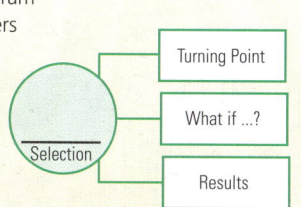

 Self-Assessment: On a sheet of paper, copy the following list of other literary terms introduced in this unit. Next to each, indicate how well you feel you understand it. (Write W for "well," S for "somewhat," or N for "not at all.") You can look up the terms in the Handbook of Reading Terms and Literary Concepts on page 762. Pay attention to any examples that are given there.

characterization	imagery	mood
end rhyme	internal rhyme	simile
essay	memoir	tone

PORTFOLIO BUILDING

- **QuickWrites** A few of the QuickWrites assignments in this unit were invitations to write poems. Did you write a haiku for the first time? Was it easier for you to express yourself in a free-verse poem than in a poem that rhymes? Find the two of your poems that impress you the most. In a cover note, explain why you like them. Add the poems and the note to your portfolio.

- **Writing About Literature** Earlier in this unit, you interpreted a passage from a story in order to understand it better. If your friends wanted to read the story for the first time, what advice would you give them? Which events, passages, or details would you tell them to pay close attention to as they read? Include your advice on reading the story with your interpretive essay if you choose to keep it in your portfolio.

- **Writing from Experience** In your character sketch, you had a chance to describe a character who was interesting to you. Now write a letter to that character, explaining why you chose to write about him or her. You might tell the character about information that surprised you, or you might describe traits that you found particularly interesting. Attach a copy of the letter to your character sketch.

- **Personal Choice** As you explored the activities in this unit, you expressed yourself in a variety of ways. What was your favorite activity? Refer to your notebook for your responses to what you've done. Consider projects and writing you have done on your own as well. Write a short description of your favorite activity. How did it challenge you in a way you hadn't expected? Are you eager to try a similar activity? Add the description to your portfolio.

 Self-Assessment: Consider the different types of writing you've included in your portfolio so far. What other types of writing do you want to add to your portfolio in the near future? Write a note to yourself.

SETTING GOALS

What one problem are you having with your work that you would like to overcome in the near future? What will you do to overcome it? Write your answers to these questions on a sheet of colored paper so that it stands out as a reminder while you are working on the next unit.

REFLECT & ASSESS 253

SETTING GOALS

In order to help students answer these questions and set future goals, have them review their portfolio work and look at the areas that involved the most revision. Ask students to identify any patterns to their revising processes that might reveal problems or areas in which they need more work.

REVIEWING LITERARY CONCEPTS

OPTION 1

Encourage students to attempt first to complete their problem-solution frames without referring to the selections. You may also wish to have students identify whether the conflict in each selection is external or internal. Suggest that partners take notes during their discussions and provide details from the selections to support their choices.

OPTION 2

Challenge students to create alternate climaxes that are not simply the opposite of what happens in the selections. Remind students that their suggestions should still be consistent with the behaviors and actions of the specific characters. Make sure students support their choices for the diagram that offers the best new possibilities.

Self-Assessment For terms that students want to understand better, have them write, in their own words, a definition for each term after checking in the Handbook. Then have students apply each term to a selection they have read. For instance, a student can briefly describe an example of imagery from a selection or provide an example of a simile from a particular poem.

PORTFOLIO BUILDING

You may wish to help students choose or modify options for them that best suit the goals you have established for the class. Remind students that keeping track of their drafts in their portfolios as well as their final products will help them reflect on and assess their development and progress.

Self-Assessment In addition, you may want to have students consider with which types of writing they felt most comfortable and with which types they would like to have more practice. Students can create a chart that lists each type of writing and rates their abilities for each.

UNIT THREE

UNIT THEMES

Unit Three

A Sense of Fairness In this unit, students will read selections that explore the minor irritations and the painful consequences that come from various characters' experiences with unfairness. The unit contains two parts: Part 1, "Coping with Injustice," and Part 2, "Facing the Consequences." Selections in both parts contribute to the unit theme by detailing characters' struggles against injustice (and their own unjust actions) and the consequences that some must face as a result of their actions.

Part 1

Coping with Injustice Selections in Part 1 focus on characters who must deal with injustice in their lives, such as Abd al-Rahman Ibrahima—the son of a 19th-century African tribal chieftain—who was brought to America as a slave.

Part 2

Facing the Consequences Selections in Part 2 describe certain actions taken by characters and reveal the consequences of those actions. For example, in the humorous tale "Shrewd Todie and Lyzer the Miser," a poor man outsmarts a stingy man but then must face judgment.

Links to Unit Six

The Oral Tradition Unit Six, "Across Time and Place," contains literature from the oral tradition that connects with the theme of Unit Three. You may wish to begin or end Unit Three by using the following selections from Unit Six that relate to the theme "A Sense of Fairness":
- *Damon and Pythias: A Drama*, p. 684
- "The Three Wishes," p. 691
- "The Disobedient Child," p. 694

UNIT THREE

Jacob's Ladder (1958), Jan Müller. Oil on canvas, 83½" × 115", Solomon R. Guggenheim Museum, New York. Copyright © The Solomon R. Guggenheim Foundation, New York. Photo by David Heald.

A Sense of Fairness

Injustice
anywhere
is a threat to
justice
everywhere.

DR. MARTIN LUTHER KING, JR.
Civil-rights leader

Art Note

Jacob's Ladder by Jan Müller
Reading the Art How would you describe the atmosphere, or mood, created by the artist's use of color and the way in which the figures are represented? Is there anything else about the painting that contributes to this mood?

Exploring Theme

To help students explore the connections between the art, the quotation, and the unit theme, have them consider the following questions:

1. Why do you think it is important to have a sense of fairness? *(Possible response: Fairness is important because it's one element that enables people to realize their goals. In order to succeed at something, a person needs an equal—or fair—chance to show what he or she can do.)*

2. Explain Dr. King's statement in your own words. Do you agree or disagree with him? *(Possible response: The statement communicates the idea that if even one person is faced with injustice, then all of us are faced with injustice. Students who agree may say that if one person is being treated unfairly, then there is nothing to prevent others from being treated unfairly.)*

3. According to the Bible, Jacob's ladder stretched from earth to heaven. In what ways do you think the image of Jacob's ladder symbolizes a sense of fairness? *(Possible response: Because heaven symbolizes paradise —the ideal place—the image of Jacob's ladder brings to mind the hope of fairness and equity. Justice will be reached as heaven is reached.)*

4. What kinds of stories do you think you will read in this unit? *(Possible responses: The stories will be about people who have to struggle against injustice in their lives. The stories will have characters who are treated unfairly by others and who attempt to improve their situations.)*

5. Discuss a situation in which you felt you were treated unfairly. Why were you not treated fairly? What was the experience like for you? How did you try to resolve the situation? *(Responses will vary.)*

UNIT THREE
Part 1 Skills Trace

ML DENOTES MINI-LESSON IN TEACHER'S EDITION

Selections	Reading Skills and Strategies	Literary Concepts	Writing Opportunities	Speaking, Listening, and Viewing
NONFICTION **Abd al-Rahman Ibrahima** from **Now Is Your Time!** Walter Dean Myers	Summarizing, PE p. 257 Clarifying, ML TE p. 263	Description, PE p. 269 Biography, PE p. 269 Plot, ML TE p. 264	Letter, PE p. 268 Pamphlet, PE p. 268 Questions, PE p. 268 Dramatization, PE p. 269 Summary, ML TE p. 263 Rewrite story, ML TE p. 265 Write a paragraph, ML TE p. 266	Retelling a story, PE p. 268 Making a map, PE p. 269 Dramatization, PE p. 269 Song, PE p. 269 Drawing pictures, PE p. 269 Viewing a film, ML TE p. 262
FICTION **Eleven** Sandra Cisneros	Cause and effect, PE p. 271	Point of view, PE p. 275	Diary entry, PE p. 275 Greeting card, PE p. 275 Paragraph, PE p. 275 Description, ML TE p. 272	Role-playing, PE p. 275 Discussing celebrations, PE p. 276
FICTION **User Friendly** T. Ernesto Bethancourt	Specialized vocabulary, PE p. 278 Relating cause and effect, ML TE p. 279	Science fiction, PE p. 289 Conflict, PE p. 289 Conflict, ML TE p. 282	Diary entry, PE p. 289 E-mail message, PE p. 289 Plot summary, PE p. 289 Description, ML TE p. 281	Creating an advertisement, PE p. 289 Interviewing a media specialist, PE p. 290 Role-playing, PE p. 290 Reading aloud, ML TE p. 280 Interviews, ML TE p. 284 Creating a commercial, ML TE p. 287
FICTION **The Summer of the Beautiful White Horse** William Saroyan	Making inferences, ML TE p. 293	Sensory details, PE p. 300 Main and minor characters, ML TE p. 294	Poem, PE p. 300 Credo, PE p. 300 Character sketch, ML TE p. 297	Group discussion, PE p. 300 Dramatizing incidents, PE p. 301 Retelling a story, ML TE p. 298
FICTION ON YOUR OWN **Thanksgiving in Polynesia** Susan Haven			Dialogue, TE p. 305	Pantomime, TE p. 307 Class discussion, TE p. 309

Writing	Reading Skills and Strategies	Literary Concepts	Writing Opportunities	Speaking, Listening, and Viewing
WRITING ABOUT LITERATURE **Analysis**	Analyzing dialogue, PE pp. 310–11 Analyzing literature, PE pp. 312–15	Dialogue, PE pp. 310–11 Plot, PE p. 312	Write dialogue, PE p. 311 Interpretive essay, PE pp. 313–16 Write dialogue, PE p. 317	Viewing a scene, PE p. 317 Interpreting a scene, PE p. 317 Reading dialogue, PE p. 317

255a UNIT THREE A SENSE OF FAIRNESS

Grammar, Usage, Mechanics, and Spelling	Multimodal Learning	Research and Study Skills	Vocabulary
Past-tense verbs, ML TE p. 266 Soft and hard g, ML TE p. 267	Retelling a story, PE p. 268 Making a map, PE p. 269 Dramatization, PE p. 269 Song, PE p. 269 Time line, PE p. 269 Drawing pictures, PE p. 269 Viewing a film, ML TE p. 262	Research Ibrahima's life, PE p. 269 K-W-L approach, ML TE p. 259	bondage procedure chaos prosper dynasty reservation inhabit status premise trek
Possessives and contractions ML TE p. 274	Role-playing, PE p. 275 Drawing a picture, PE p. 275	Research celebrations, PE p. 276 Research Timbuktu, ML TE p. 260	
	Creating an advertisement, PE p. 289 Role-playing, PE p. 290 Reading aloud, ML TE p. 280 Interviews, ML TE p. 284 Creating a commercial, ML TE p. 287 Dramatizing incidents, PE p. 301	Research computers, PE p. 290 Taking objective tests: short-answer questions, ML TE p. 283	
Using commas to set off introductory parts, ML TE p. 295 Unstressed syllables, ML TE p. 299	Illustrating a book jacket, PE p. 301 Retelling a story, ML TE p. 298	Research animal teeth, PE p. 301 Taking essay tests, ML TE p. 296	consequently descendant poverty-stricken practical rear
	Pantomime, TE p. 307		

Grammar, Usage, Mechanics, and Spelling	Multimodal Learning	Research and Study Skills	Media Literacy
Using quotation marks, PE p. 311 Using commas with conjunctions, PE p. 315 Coordinating conjunctions, PE p. 315	Using a story map, PE p. 313 Viewing a scene, PE p. 317 Interpreting a scene, PE p. 317 Discussion, PE p. 317		Interpreting a scene, PE pp. 316–17

UNIT THREE
Part 2 Skills Trace

(ML) DENOTES MINI-LESSON IN TEACHER'S EDITION

Selections	Reading Skills and Strategies	Literary Concepts	Writing Opportunities	Speaking, Listening, and Viewing
FICTION **Shrewd Todie and Lyzer the Miser** Isaac Bashevis Singer	Evaluating, PE p. 319 Evaluating, (ML) TE p. 324	Humor, PE p. 327 Plot, (ML) TE p. 323	Decision, PE p. 327 Persuasive argument, PE p. 327 Song, PE p. 327 Evaluation, PE p. 327 Dialogue, (ML) TE p. 322	Interpreting a painting, PE p. 328
NONFICTION from **A Long Hard Journey** Patricia and Fredrick McKissack	Using a reading log, PE p. 329 Connecting, (ML) TE p. 333	Primary source, PE p. 339 Secondary source, PE p. 339 Author's purpose, (ML) TE p. 332	Advertisement, PE p. 339 Ballad, PE p. 339 Comparison/contrast paragraph, PE p. 339 Short passage, (ML) TE p. 334 Letter, (ML) TE p. 335	Role-playing, (ML) TE p. 331
POETRY **Barbara Frietchie** John Greenleaf Whittier	Poetic language, PE p. 341	Couplets, PE p. 345 Alliteration, PE p. 345 Rhythm PE p. 345	Interview, PE p. 344 Rhymed couplets, PE p. 344	Dialogue, PE p. 345 Choral reading, PE p. 345 Sketching, (ML) TE p. 343
FICTION **The Enchanted Raisin** Jacqueline Balcells	Making judgments, (ML) TE p. 351	Fantasy, PE p. 355 Humor, (ML) TE p. 350	Predictions, PE p. 346 Missing-person report, PE p. 355 Newspaper article, PE p. 355	Map, PE p. 356 Puppets, PE p. 356
DRAMA **A Shipment of Mute Fate** Les Crutchfield	Sound effects, PE p. 359 Noting relevant details, (ML) TE p. 370	Suspense, PE p. 374 Conflict, (ML) TE p. 369	Headline, PE p. 373 News article, PE p. 373 Letter of complaint, PE p. 373 Log entry, PE p. 373 Radio play, PE p. 374 Rewrite dialogue, (ML) TE p. 365 Rewrite events from new point of view, (ML) TE p. 368	Background music, PE p. 374 Radio play, PE p. 374 Background music, (ML) TE p. 361

Writing	Reading Skills and Strategies	Literary Concepts	Writing Opportunities	Speaking, Listening, and Viewing
WRITING FROM EXPERIENCE **Informative Exposition**		Characters, PE p. 376 Audience, PE p. 379 Goal, PE p. 379	Writing an essay, PE p. 376–83 Drafting, PE pp. 380–81 Revising and publishing, PE pp. 382–83	Conducting an interview, PE p. 379

Grammar, Usage, Mechanics, and Spelling	Multimodal Learning	Research and Study Skills	Vocabulary
Adjectives and adverbs, ML TE p. 321 The prefix *ad-*, ML TE p. 325	Interpreting a painting, PE p. 328		admonishingly cunning possess properly trade
Prepositional phrases, ML TE p. 336 The prefix *ex-*, ML TE p. 337	Role-playing, ML TE p. 331		agility harass confrontation insensitive contemporary monopoly drudgery plush exclusive salvaging
	Dialogue, PE p. 345 Choral reading, PE p. 345 Sketching, ML TE p. 343	Research the American flag, PE p. 345	
Compound predicates and sentences ML TE p. 348 Prefixes and roots, ML TE p. 354	Flip book, PE p. 355 Map, PE p. 356 Puppets, PE p. 356	Summarizing, ML TE p. 353	console contrary detest mute reassure
Subject-verb agreement, ML TE p. 362 Soft and hard *g*, ML TE p. 372	Background music, PE p. 374 Radio play, PE p. 374 Background music, ML TE p. 361	Research snakes, PE p. 374	counter ominous customs sodden evasive stupor fumigate transition lethal margin

Grammar, Usage, Mechanics, and Spelling	Multimodal Learning	Research and Study Skills	Media Literacy
Elaborating on ideas, PE p. 381 Using pronouns correctly, PE p. 383	Conducting and interview, PE p. 379	Library research, PE p. 378	

SKILLS TRACE   TEACHER'S EDITION   **255d**

UNIT THREE
Recommended Resources

ENRICHMENT   RESEARCH

✓ Recommended Novels

LITERATURE CONNECTIONS WITH SOURCEBOOK FOR TEACHERS

The House of Dies Drear
by Virginia Hamilton

Thematic Links When the Small family buys a house that was part of the Underground Railroad, they discover both people and places that are not as they seem. Young Thomas's strong sense of fairness leads him to appreciate his heritage.

About the Author Virginia Hamilton (born 1936) is the granddaughter of a runaway slave who bought a home near the setting of this novel. Hamilton has explored the African-American heritage in several exciting novels.

Other Works by Virginia Hamilton *Zeely, The Planet of Junior Brown, Anthony Burns: The Defeat and Triumph of a Fugitive Slave, The Time-Ago Tales of Jahdu, M.C. Higgins the Great, Sweet Whispers, Brother Rush, Many Thousand Gone: African-Americans from Slavery to Freedom, The Mystery of Drear House: The Conclusion of the Dies Drear Chronicle*

Ajeemah and His Son
by James Berry

Thematic Links Like many Africans during the slave trade, Ajeemah and his son are captured by slave traders and sent to work under harsh conditions on different plantations in Jamaica. Separated from one another, their future looks bleak and unjust.

About the Author Born (1925) in Jamaica but now living in England, James Berry has received numerous awards for his poems, short stories, and novels written for people of all ages.

Other Works by James Berry *A Thief in the Village, The Future Telling Lady and Other Stories, Spiderman Anancy*

LITERATURE CONNECTIONS WITH SOURCEBOOK FOR TEACHERS

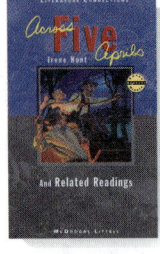

Across Five Aprils
by Irene Hunt

Thematic Links During the Civil War, a young farm boy must step forward and take responsibility when the rest of his family members are split over the war and choose to face varying enemies.

About the Author Irene Hunt (born 1907), grew up in southern Illinois and listened to her grandfather's stories of the Civil War, which she turned into award-winning historical novels for young people.

Other Works by Irene Hunt *The Lottery Rose, No Promises in the Wind, Up a Road Slowly*

Out from This Place
by Joyce Hansen

Thematic Links The Civil War is over, but the prospect of freedom for Easter and other freed slaves promises danger and hardship, as well as happiness.

About the Author Joyce Hansen (born 1942) grew up in the Bronx, the setting for many of her novels, and writes books with believable, real-life characters.

Other Works by Joyce Hansen *The Gift Giver, Home Boy, Which Way Freedom?*

Tunes for Bears to Dance To
by Robert Cormier

Thematic Links Henry is unfairly forced into making a horrible decision that threatens his valued friendship with Mr. Levine, an elderly Holocaust survivor.

About the Author Robert Cormier (born 1925) has written extensively about adolescents in difficult situations, receiving sometimes controversial acclaim for his work.

Other Works by Robert Cormier *After the First Death, 8 Plus 1, I Am the Cheese, The Chocolate War*

For Teacher TEACHING LITERATURE

Day, Frances Ann. *Multicultural Voices in Contemporary Literature: A Resource for Teachers.* Portsmouth, NH: Heinemann, 1994.

Hopkins, Lee Bennett. *Pauses: Autobiographical Reflections of 101 Creators of Children's Books.* New York: HarperCollins, 1995.

Vellucci, Dennis. *African-American Voices in Young Adult Literature: Tradition, Transition, Transformation.* Metuchen, NJ: Scarecrow, 1994.

CROSS-CURRICULAR TEACHING   PROFESSIONAL DEVELOPMENT

Recommended Readings in Cross-Curricular Areas

SOCIAL STUDIES

Stonewall
by Jean Fritz (1979)
In this biography of the heroic yet controversial general of the Confederate Army, the reader comes to understand how Tom Jackson earned the nickname "Stonewall." Links to John Greenleaf Whittier's "Barbara Frietchie."

Sojourner Truth
by Susan Taylor-Boyd (1990)
A proponent of equality and women's rights, this freed slave traveled around the North preaching her ideals. Links to Walter Dean Myers's *Now Is Your Time!* and Patricia and Frederick McKissak's *A Long, Hard Journey*.

Celebrating Life: Jewish Rites of Passage
by Malka Drucker (1984)
The cultural and religious beliefs and practices of Jewish people are outlined and illustrated by photographs. Links to Isaac Bashevis Singer's "Shrewd Todie and Lyzer the Miser."

SCIENCE

The Beastly Book: 100 of the World's Most Dangerous Creatures
by Jeanne K. Hanson (1993)
Find out why sea snakes, komodo dragons, army ants, and electric eels should be avoided at all cost! Links to Les Crutchfield's *Shipment of Mute Fate*.

For Teacher — CROSS-CURRICULAR INSTRUCTION

"Culturally Appropriate Books Call for Culturally Appropriate Teaching." *Journal of Reading* 38 (March 1995): 486.

Fagan, Edward R. "Interdisciplinary English: Science, Technology, and Society." *English Journal* 76 (Sept. 87): 81–83.

James, Michael, and Zarrillo, James. "Teaching History with Children's Literature: A Concept-based Interdisciplinary Approach." *The Social Studies* 80.4 (July 1989): 153–58.

Ross, Ann. *The Way We Were— The Way We Can Be: A Vision for the Middle School Through Integrated Thematic Instruction.* Village of Oak Creek, Ariz.: Susan Kovalik and Associates, 1993.

Recommended Media Resources

THE LANGUAGE OF LITERATURE

LASERLINKS
Videodisc, Gr. 6
See *LaserLinks Teacher's Source Book*, pages 28–29, for an overview of Unit Three.

AUDIO LIBRARY
Tapes
Unit Three: A Sense of Fitness
Gr. 6, Tape 6: Sides A & B
Gr. 6, Tape 7: Sides A & B

WRITING COACH
Writing Coach Software: Writing About Literature: Interpretive Response; Problem-and-Solution Essay

OUTSIDE RESOURCES

Films/Videos/Film Strips/Audiocassettes
Across Five Aprils, audiocassette, Newbery Award Records, 1973.
Isaac in America: a Journey with Isaac Bashevis Singer, 16 mm film, Kirk Simon, Amram Nowak Associates. Los Angeles: Direct Cinema, Ltd., 1986. (58 minutes)
Words by Heart, videocassette, PBS; produced by Martin Tahse. Chicago: Public Media Video, 1985. (116 minutes)

Internet Resources
Literature and Language Arts Center at http://www.hmco.com/mcdougal/lit/litcent.html

For Teacher — TEACHING WITH TECHNOLOGY

Davis, Betty. "Using Technology in the Classroom. (Dialog and the Internet at Fountain Lake High School)." *Arkansas Libraries* 51 (August 1994): 23–25.

McAlister, Brian K. "Accessing Resources Over the Internet." *The Technology Teacher* 54 (November 1994): 12–14.

Teaching & Computers. Scholastic, Inc. 730 Broadway, New York, NY 10003-9538.

UNIT THREE
Professional Enrichment

Staging a Radio Play

> It's hard to imagine a time without television and radio, but these media are not very old.

Although the scientific principles behind radio were known toward the end of the 19th century, the practical applications did not burst upon the scene until the 1920s. The first commercial radio station in the United States, KDKA in Pittsburgh, opened in November 1920. The first broadcast? The presidential returns—the victory of Warren Harding!

Since television—rather than radio—has been the main source of drama for most Americans, your students may never have heard of a radio play. Explain to them that a radio play is an oral interpretation of a story, poem, or play. The performers use voice, music, and sound effects to tell the story and convey a mood.

THE WORLD OF THE IMAGINATION

The importance of voice and sound effects in a radio play cannot be overestimated. Discuss with students how the listeners of a radio play can't see the actors' facial expressions and body movements—the elements that give theater and film audiences key information about a character's actions and feelings. Therefore, radio performers must rely on other techniques to spark their listeners' imaginations. In this unit, your students will read *A Shipment of Mute Fate*. Use the following suggestions to help them perform it as a radio play.

- Have students prepare careful scripts, marking key points with easy-to-understand words and phrases.
- Instruct students to vary their rate of speaking. For exam-ple, reading lines quickly can show that a character is in a hurry or excited. On the other hand, a slower rate can indicate sadness or thoughtfulness
- Show students how to pause in their delivery to create suspense, show surprise, or get their listeners' attention right before an important moment.
- Teach students how to vary the pitch of their voices to reveal more about their characters. For instance, a low voice can help show an older character, while a high voice can suggest a nervous or excited person.
- Guide students to use a medium pitch for everyday conversation and for the narrator's dialogue.
- Tell readers that they can also portray a character's emotional state by varying the volume of their voices. Remind students that they must always speak loudly enough to be heard, but they can heighten the effect of moderate changes in volume by varying the intensity of their voices.
- Show students how to monitor their volume levels by taping the reading. After students listen to the tape, they can adjust their interpretation if necessary.

SOUND EFFECTS

Explore with students how a radio play relies heavily not only on the performers' voices but also on the skillful use of sound effects.

- Point out how effects like the ringing of a telephone or the slamming of a door make the radio audience feel they are right there in the middle of the drama!
- Have students work in small groups to brainstorm how they might create the sound effects they need. Commonplace sound effects include doors opening and closing, ringing telephones, paper rattling, dishes and glasses clinking, liquids pouring, and wind blowing.

STAGING

- Consider using commercial recordings for some of the sound effects. However, students will most likely discover that they can develop interesting and realistic effects on their own by experimenting with a variety of materials. Suggest everyday items such as aluminum foil to create the sound of thunder and wooden blocks to mimic the sound of horses' galloping.

Related Reading

 Burns, Allan. *Room 222.* Twentieth Century Fox Film Corporation, 1969.

 Chavez, Denise. *The Flying Tortilla Man.* New York: Susan Bergholz Literary Services, 1989.

 Serling, Rod. *The Monsters are Due on Maple Street.* The Rod Serling Trust, 1960.

Family and Community Involvement

Family

By completing some of the following Copymasters for Unit Three, your students, their families, and other community members can make important connections outside the classroom as they explore real-life examples of fairness and equity.

OPTION 1: DESIGN ILLUSTRATIONS FOR A STORY
- **Connection** All of the selections in Unit Three connect to the theme of a sense of fairness.
- **Activity** *Copymaster, page 1* Students and family members review the selections in Unit Three to select a story to illustrate. After jotting down ideas for the various illustrations in a chart, they create illustrations that capture key moments in the selection.

OPTION 2: WRITE AN ADVERTISEMENT
- **Connection** In both "Shrewd Todie and Lyzer the Miser" and "The Enchanted Raisin," the main characters learn valuable lessons about greed and selfishness.
- **Activity** *Copymaster, page 2* Students work with a family member to plan and write a catchy and thought-provoking advertisement about the perils of greed and selfishness.

OPTION 3: WATCH A DOCUMENTARY
- **Connection** Many of the selections in Unit Three explore the ways in which characters attempt to deal and cope with injustice.
- **Activity** *Copymaster, page 3* To promote interest and provide extra background before your child reads, students and family members watch a documentary on the civil rights movement, such as *Eyes on the Prize* or *Eyes on the Prize II* (both of which are available at local video stores). A chart is provided to accompany this activity.

Community

OPTION 1
- **Connection** All the selections in Unit Three illustrate the significance of equity and fairness.
- **Activity** Invite a representative from a local organization, such as the ACLU, that seeks to fight injustices faced by many people today. Encourage students to prepare questions before the speaker addresses them.

OPTION 2
- **Connection** In "User Friendly," a computer takes justice into its own hands with severe consequences.
- **Application** Have a computer specialist, possibly one from your school, speak to the class about the increasing importance of computers in modern life. Students may want to interview the guest speaker about tasks that computers are capable of today and other tasks, like the events in "User Friendly," that are still in the realm of science fiction.

OPTION 3
- **Connection** In "Shrewd Todie and Lyzer the Miser," the town's rabbi intercedes to resolve the disagreement between Todie and Lyzer.
- **Activity** Invite a rabbi from a local synagogue to speak to the class about the functional role of a rabbi in his or her congregation.

PROFESSIONAL ENRICHMENT, FAMILY AND COMMUNITY INVOLVEMENT   TEACHER'S EDITION   **255h**

UNIT THREE

Part 1 Cooperative Project

A Conflict-Management Program

Overview

Students will create and implement a conflict-management program for themselves and their peers.

PROJECT AT A GLANCE
The selections in Unit Three, Part 1 are about how people cope with some form of injustice or conflict. For this project, students will design a conflict-management program for their fellow students that is both fair and just. Students will work together in groups to create a list of guidelines that can be followed if a conflict arises. The program should be designed to cover a wide range of possible conflicts and should include reference to a set of rules or laws on which decisions will be based. Groups will then meet to compromise on one final plan. This program may be implemented for the entire school or just within the class. If possible, the program might be reviewed and critiqued by the school administration.

OBJECTIVES
- To recognize when a situation is unjust and to recognize whether one has any power over the situation
- To recognize that many conflicts can be settled fairly
- To design a program that would deal fairly with conflicts
- To implement the program, insofar as it is feasible
- To manage the program on an ongoing basis

SUGGESTED GROUP SIZE
4–6 students per group; later work will involve the entire class

MATERIALS
Writing paper and utensils

1 Getting Started

Arranging the Project
Before students begin, contact the school administration and discuss the project. Find out if they are agreeable to letting students manage their conflicts themselves (within reason, of course). You might point out that the administration can always overrule a student decision. You can also offer to implement the program on a trial basis, for a short period of time only.

You might also ask the guidance counselor for some assistance with the project. He or she knows what sorts of conflicts really do arise and what the school's policies are.

Arrange for the counselor to speak to the class, or set aside special times for groups to consult.

Arranging for the Program
If you get permission to run the program, you will need to schedule times when hearings can be held. This may require hours after school or a reserved room during the lunch period—whatever works best for your situation.

If your school cannot permit you to use the program, students can substitute Options 1 or 4 on the next page.

2 Creating the Program

Introducing the Project
Explain that students will work cooperatively in small groups to design a program that will help students resolve conflicts. They will then work as a class to study all the plans, take the best ideas, and come up with a final comprehensive plan for managing conflicts.

Hold a class discussion about conflicts that commonly arise in your school. How would students handle such situations? What conflicts should be handled by adults, and which would be appropriate for students to handle? Ask students to name some of the components necessary in any conflict-management program, such as rules of procedure, representation, equality of time in presenting opposing views, and so forth. They should also consider how final decisions will be made and by whom.

Students might also be interested in watching an episode of a television show such as *The People's Court,* in which minor matters are handled by a judge according to a certain set of laws. Discuss how this is similar to and different from a conflict-management program. You might also invite a grievance officer from a labor union to speak to the class about how unions deal with conflicts between management and workers. In many cities, retired judges preside over legal arbitration. Your local bar association may be able to suggest a class adviser.

Group Investigations
Divide students into groups of four to six. Groups should research other conflict-management programs to see how they work and to find the perceived success rate. They should find out about the procedure for asking the program officers to step in, how the officers are selected, the rules or laws on which they base their decisions, the rules of procedure, how each side presents its view, and how judgment is rendered. They should then adapt the aspects that apply to their school situation. Meet with each group to monitor progress and make suggestions.

Later, students will meet as a class and refine the group plans into one comprehensive program.

Creating a Project Description
After groups have designed a program, ask them to write a full description of it. Papers should include all of the above points, as well as any others students think are important. Papers can be in outline form, if groups prefer. Meet with each group to help them analyze their final program.

255i UNIT THREE A SENSE OF FAIRNESS

OPTION 1: RELIVE THE PAST Students can research a past case of conflict (already resolved) from their school, neighborhood, or community. Groups should prepare statements from both sides of the conflict and present them to the class, without revealing the solution. The class can vote on how they would have solved the problem, then learn what happened in the real case.

OPTION 2: BROADENING THE FIELD Groups can design a conflict-management program to deal with student-teacher, student-administration, or interschool conflicts.

OPTION 3: STUDENT COUNCIL If your school has a Student Council, groups can investigate how this body deals with conflicts within the school.

OPTION 4: ROLE-PLAY If students cannot implement their plans in actual school conflicts, they can act out their problems and solutions in class.

3 Sharing the Program

Whether or not students' plans will be used to resolve conflicts, try to arrange for students to dramatize several conflict resolutions, perhaps at a school assembly. Afterward, the school principal could comment on the solutions. Later, students might want to submit their written plans to the school administration.

Assessing the Project

The following rubric can be used for group or individual assessment.

3 Full Accomplishment Students follow directions and produce a viable conflict-management program for their peers.

2 Substantial Accomplishment Students produce a program, but the description is unclear or the program is seriously flawed.

1 Little or Partial Accomplishment Students' program is incomplete or does not fulfill the requirements of the assignment.

For the Portfolio
Groups' program descriptions should be copied and placed in each member's portfolio, along with your written assessment of each individual's performance. The master plan can be kept in a class notebook for future reference.

Note: For other assessment options, see the *Teacher's Guide to Assessment and Portfolio Use.*

Cross-Curricular Options

LANGUAGE ARTS
Ask students to find a short story or television show that shows an injustice or conflict. They can write a few paragraphs describing how the situation might have been better handled.

HEALTH AND SAFETY
Students can design a crowd-management program for before and after school, with special emphasis on the safety of the students and teachers. This could be expanded to include other special school events, such as ball games, assemblies, or pep rallies.

ART
Students can design and make posters promoting fair play in school. This could include subjects such as racial equality, antifighting messages, or asking students to work on the honor system.

Resources

Standard First Aid and Personal Safety by the American Red Cross provides the essentials of safety and preventive measures.

UNIT THREE
Part 1 Lesson Planner

TIME ALLOTMENTS SHOWN ARE APPROXIMATE. DEPENDING ON YOUR GOALS AND THE NEEDS OF YOUR STUDENTS, YOU MAY WISH TO ALLOW MORE OR LESS TIME FOR CERTAIN PORTIONS OF THE LESSON.

Table of Contents	Discussion	Previewing the Selection	Reading the Selection
PART OPENER **COPING WITH INJUSTICE** What Do You Think? page 256	**20 MINUTES** • Reflect on the part theme		
SELECTION *from* **Now Is Your Time!** page 258 CHALLENGING		**10 MINUTES** • PERSONAL CONNECTION • HISTORICAL CONNECTION • READING CONNECTION: Summarizing	**45 MINUTES** • Introduce vocabulary • Read pp. 258–67 (10 pp.)
SELECTION **Eleven** page 272 EASY		**15 MINUTES** • PERSONAL CONNECTION • BIOGRAPHICAL CONNECTION • READING CONNECTION: Cause and effect	**10 MINUTES** • Read pp. 272–74 (3 pp.)
SELECTION **User Friendly** page 279 AVERAGE		**20 MINUTES** • PERSONAL CONNECTION • SCIENCE CONNECTION • READING CONNECTION: Specialized vocabulary	**20 MINUTES** • Read pp. 279–88 (10 pp.)
SELECTION **The Summer of the Beautiful White Horse** page 292 AVERAGE		**20 MINUTES** • PERSONAL CONNECTION • CULTURAL CONNECTION • WRITING CONNECTION	**20 MINUTES** • Introduce vocabulary • Read pp. 292–99 (8 pp.)
FICTION ON YOUR OWN **Thanksgiving in Polynesia** page 302 EASY			**20 MINUTES** • Read pp. 302–09 (8 pp.)
Writing **WRITING ABOUT LITERATURE** **Analysis**	**Writer's Style** **25 MINUTES**	**Prewriting** **20 MINUTES**	**Drafting and Revising** **80 MINUTES**

Time estimates assume in-class work. You may wish to assign some of these stages as homework.

Responding to the Selection

FROM PERSONAL RESPONSE TO CRITICAL ANALYSIS	OR	ANOTHER PATHWAY	LITERARY CONCEPTS	QUICKWRITES
		50 MINUTES		
• Discussion questions	OR	• Retelling and comparing stories	• Description • Biography	• Letter • Pamphlet • Questions
		20 MINUTES		
• Discussion questions	OR	• Role-playing	• Point of view	• Diary entry • Greeting card • Paragraph
		35 MINUTES		
• Discussion questions	OR	• Creating an ad	• Science fiction • Conflict	• Diary entry • E-mail message • Plot summary
		25 MINUTES		
• Discussion questions	OR	• Discussion	• Sensory details	• Poem • Credo

Extension Activities

Columns: ALTERNATIVE ACTIVITIES • LITERARY LINKS • CRITIC'S CORNER • THE WRITER'S STYLE • ACROSS THE CURRICULUM • ART CONNECTION • WORDS TO KNOW • BIOGRAPHY

40 MINUTES — ✔ (Alternative Activities), ✔ (Across the Curriculum: GEOGRAPHY), ✔ (Words to Know), ✔ (Biography)

25 MINUTES — ✔ (Alternative Activities), ✔ (Literary Links), ✔ (Critic's Corner), ✔ (Across the Curriculum: SOCIAL STUDIES), ✔ (Words to Know), ✔ (Biography)

25 MINUTES — ✔ (Alternative Activities), ✔ (Across the Curriculum: COMPUTER SCIENCE), ✔ (Words to Know), ✔ (Biography)

30 MINUTES — ✔ (Alternative Activities), ✔ (Across the Curriculum: SCIENCE), ✔ (Words to Know), ✔ (Biography)

Publishing and Reflecting
30 MINUTES

Grammar in Context
10 MINUTES

Reading the World
25 MINUTES

LESSON PLANNER TEACHER'S EDITION **255I**

PART 1

WHAT DO YOU THINK?
Objectives

The activities on this page can be used to
- introduce the Part 1 theme, "Coping with Injustice," since each activity is connected to one or more of the selections in Part 1
- create materials for students' personal portfolios that they can later reconsider or revise
- build an understanding of theme that can be reviewed and revised as students progress through the unit

Who are your role models?
Tell students that the role models they list need not be limited to people they know directly. They could be figures from history, people in the media, or public officeholders. (All selections in this part connect to this activity.)

How can you right a wrong?
Have students outline the arguments for their speech before they begin writing. Encourage students to devise solutions to the situation that are as practical as possible. (See "Abd al-Rahman Ibrahima," p. 257.)

Can computers relate?
Encourage groups to begin by thinking about the ways in which communicating by computer differs from face-to-face interaction. Then have groups list the advantages and the disadvantages of communicating by computer before they draw their comic strips. (See "User Friendly," p. 277.)

What would you do?
Suggest that each group begin by creating a chart that describes the conflict and lists possible resolutions. Groups can either select the best resolution to role-play or role-play various outcomes and then select the best one. Make sure students explain why they chose a specific outcome.

UNIT THREE **PART 1**

COPING WITH INJUSTICE

WHAT DO YOU THINK?

REFLECTING ON THEME

What can you do when life seems unfair? Use the activities on this page to explore some of the ways you and others cope with daily problems. Record your thoughts and ideas in your notebook. Later you will be able to compare them with the ways the characters in this unit handle unjust situations.

Who are your role models?
Who has helped you learn how to cope with injustice? Make a list of people who have been positive role models in your life. Create a diagram like this one to explore your relationship with someone on your list. Why has this person been so important to you?

- Physical features
- How I feel about the person
- PERSON'S NAME
- Personality traits
- What we have in common

How can you right a wrong?
Think of a situation in your school or community that you think is unfair. Prepare a one-minute speech explaining how you would go about resolving this unfair situation. Present the speech to the class.

Can computers relate?
Imagine a time in the future when people do all their communicating by computer instead of face to face. Do you think problems of unfairness would go away? Working in groups, draw a comic strip that illustrates the advantages or the disadvantages of computer communication.

What would you do?
Imagine that your proposal for a science project has been copied by a student who "innocently" questioned you about your ideas. What could you do to correct this injustice? With classmates playing the roles of your teacher and the other student, role-play various ways of handling the situation. Record your ideas about the outcome in your notebook.

256

Across the Curriculum

History Have each student select an important historical figure who spent his or her life fighting a form of injustice. Ask each student to research the life and accomplishments of his or her chosen figure. Then have students write a short report or create a collage based on their findings and present it to the class.

PARENTAL INVOLVEMENT
Have students work with their parents or other relatives to conduct a mock television news interview of a federal, state, or local politician for whom the fight against injustice is an important issue. Each student should role-play the part of the interviewer, and the parent or relative should be the interviewee. Students can tape-record the interview or summarize it in written form to present to the class. As an alternative, pairs of students might role-play spot interviews in class and tape-record them in the style of television news.

256 THE LANGUAGE OF LITERATURE TEACHER'S EDITION

PREVIEWING

NONFICTION

Abd al-Rahman Ibrahima
from Now Is Your Time!
Walter Dean Myers

PERSONAL CONNECTION Activating Prior Knowledge

Though it may be hard to imagine today, slavery was practiced in the American colonies and later the United States for nearly 250 years. What do you know about slavery? Who were the slaves? Where did they come from? What were their lives like? Discuss these questions with a small group of classmates.

Abd al-Rahman Ibrahima

HISTORICAL CONNECTION Building Background

European exploration of the African coasts in the 15th and 16th centuries led to a large-scale and profitable slave trade. The British slave trade operated in this way: Slave traders would bring goods to the west coast of Africa. There they would trade the goods for slaves, transport the captives to South and North America, trade them for such farm goods as cotton, sugar, and tobacco, and return the goods to England. The British would use the raw materials to make finished goods, and the cycle would begin again. This process became known as triangular trade.

African slaves were brought to Virginia as early as 1619. Slavery was legal in the United States until the victory of the North in the Civil War and the passage of the 13th Amendment to the Constitution in 1865.

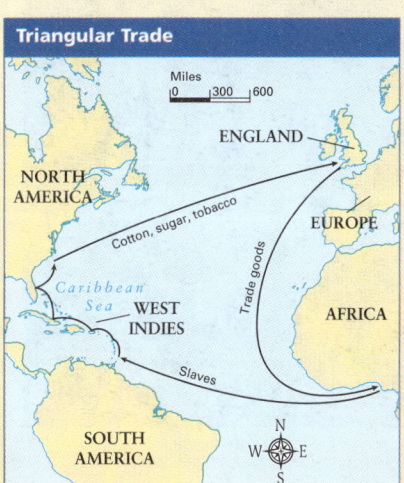

READING Active Reading
CONNECTION

Summarizing When you summarize, you focus on the main idea (or ideas) of what you've read and reword that information into statements that are easier to understand. As you read this selection about Abd al-Rahman Ibrahima (əb-dōōl'räkh-män' ĭb-rä-hē'mä), a man forced into slavery, you will reach marked stopping points that will allow you to summarize what you've read. Write your summary in your reading log, remembering to include only the main ideas, not unimportant details.

Setting a Purpose

LASERLINKS
• HISTORICAL CONNECTION
• RELIGIOUS CONNECTION

257

OVERVIEW

Objectives

- To understand and appreciate a biography of a slave who held noble status in his homeland
- To enrich reading by using active reading strategies
- To identify and discuss effective description
- To express understanding of the selection through a choice of writing forms, including a letter, a pamphlet, and a list of interview questions
- To extend understanding of the selection through a variety of multimodal and cross-curricular activities

Skills

READING SKILLS/STRATEGIES
• Summarizing
• Clarifying

THE WRITER'S STYLE
• Facts as supporting details

LITERARY CONCEPTS
• Plot
• Description

GRAMMAR
• Past tense verbs

SPELLING
• Soft and hard g

GENRE STUDY
• Nonfiction: biography

STUDY SKILLS
• Using the KWL approach

SPEAKING, LISTENING, VIEWING
• Critical Viewing
• Group discussion
• Oral presentation

Cross-Curricular Connections

MATH
• Comparative value of money

SOCIAL STUDIES
• African tribal markings

HISTORY
• American Colonization Society
• Slave narratives

GEOGRAPHY
• Ancient African empires

 **HISTORICAL CONNECTION**
Slave Trade Ibrahima's home was the Songhai Empire in Africa. You may wish to use these images, along with the map showing the locations of several of the major African empires, to prompt a research project.

Side A, Frame 38740

 RELIGIOUS CONNECTION
Islam in Africa By the time Ibrahima was born, the religion of Islam had spread throughout northern Africa. These images will help students understand the lasting historical influence of Islam in northern Africa and will provide background information about Ibrahima.

Side A, Frame 38747

PRINT AND MEDIA RESOURCES

UNIT THREE RESOURCE BOOK
Strategic Reading: Literature, p. 4
Vocabulary SkillBuilder, p. 7
Reading SkillBuilder, p. 5
Spelling SkillBuilder, p. 6

GRAMMAR MINI–LESSONS
Transparencies, p. 18
Copymasters, p. 25

WRITING MINI–LESSONS
Transparencies, p. 50

ACCESS FOR STUDENTS ACQUIRING ENGLISH
Selection Summaries
Reading and Writing Support

TEACHER'S GUIDE TO ASSESSMENT AND PORTFOLIO USE

FORMAL ASSESSMENT
Selection Test, pp. 55–56
 Test Generator

 AUDIO LIBRARY
See Reference Card

 LASERLINKS
Historical Connection
Religious Connection

 INTERNET RESOURCES
McDougal Littell Literature Center at http://www.hmco.com/mcdougal/lit

THE LANGUAGE OF LITERATURE TEACHER'S EDITION **257**

SUMMARY

Abd al-Rahman Ibrahima was born in Africa in 1762, the son of a chieftain of the Fula people. He was brought up to be a leader until history cruelly intervened. Ibrahima was captured during an intertribal battle, sold to slave traders, and shipped to America. There, a Mississippi farmer named Thomas Foster bought Ibrahima. To Foster, the African's claims to nobility and his lost family meant nothing—he was simply a possession. Ibrahima tried running away; alone in a strange country, however, he was powerless. He returned to Foster and worked as his slave for 20 years, marrying and starting a second family. Then he met John Cox, an American doctor who had lived with Ibrahima and his people in Africa years before. Cox began a campaign to free Ibrahima. Some time after Cox's death, the African gained his freedom through the intervention of the Moroccan and American governments. In 1829, Ibrahima sailed with his wife to return to his homeland. He never reached his people, however, and he died in the West African colony of Liberia that year.

Thematic Link: *Coping with Injustice*
Trapped in an unjust situation, the enslaved son of an African chieftain does not live to enjoy his long-awaited freedom.

Art Note

***Into Bondage* by Aaron Douglas** This mural exemplifies the legacy of African-American culture and history that Harlem Renaissance artist Douglas (1899–1979) celebrated. Commissioned for the Texas Centennial Exposition in 1936, the 60-by-60-inch mural depicts the enslavement of Africans and their removal from their homeland.

Reading the Art *What do you think is the meaning of the star with its light shining through the chained man at the center of the painting? What do the figures' postures reveal about how they feel?*

CUSTOMIZING FOR
Students Acquiring English

- Use **ACCESS FOR STUDENTS ACQUIRING ENGLISH,** *Reading and Writing Support.*
- Invite students to share their cultures' experiences with and beliefs about slavery.

Into Bondage (1936), Aaron Douglas. The Evans-Tibbs Collection, Washington, D.C.

258 UNIT THREE PART 1: COPING WITH INJUSTICE

WORDS TO KNOW

bondage (bŏn′dĭj) *n.* slavery (p. 265)
chaos (kā′ŏs) *n.* a state of great disorder (p. 260)
dynasty (dī′nə-stē) *n.* a series of rulers who are members of the same family (p. 260)
inhabitant (ĭn-hăb′ĭ-tənt) *n.* someone living in a particular place (p. 260)
premise (prĕm′ĭs) *n.* an idea that forms the basis of an argument (p. 266)
procedure (prə-sē′jər) *n.* a course of action (p. 266)

prosper (prŏs′pər) *v.* to be successful; thrive (p. 266)
reservation (rĕz′ər-vā′shən) *n.* a doubt; an exception (p. 267)
status (stā′təs) *n.* one's position in society; rank (p. 261)
trek (trĕk) *n.* a slow, difficult journey (p. 262)

258 THE LANGUAGE OF LITERATURE TEACHER'S EDITION

Abd al-Rahman Ibrahima

from NOW IS YOUR TIME!

by Walter Dean Myers

. . . The Africans came from many countries, and from many cultures. Like the Native Americans, they established their territories based on centuries of tradition. Most, but not all, of the Africans who were brought to the colonies came from central and West Africa. Among them was a man named Abd al-Rahman Ibrahima.

STRATEGIC READING FOR
Less-Proficient Readers

Set a Purpose Have students think, as they read the selection, about Ibrahima's understanding of his identity *(the son of a chief)* and position in society. *(a leader)*

Use **UNIT THREE RESOURCE BOOK**, pp. 4–5, for guidance in reading the selection.

CUSTOMIZING FOR
Gifted and Talented Students

Have students think about Ibrahima's internal journey as they read the selection. Have students note how Ibrahima changed or stayed the same during this journey.

Possible responses:

- Page 264–265—Ibrahima at first believed that being the son of a chief would allow him to purchase his freedom; he came to realize that he must work as a slave or die. Ibrahima's perspective changed from one of optimism to one of despair.

- Page 265—Ibrahima's religious beliefs stayed much the same. He retained his beliefs in Islam and kept its tenets as much as he could while submitting to the will of Thomas Foster.

Mini-Lesson — Study Skills

THE KWL APPROACH Explain to students that using the KWL approach when they are reading a selection is a good way to focus their thinking. Point out what the letters stand for:
- K What I already **know** about my subject
- W What I **want** to know
- L What I **learned**

Application Have students copy into their notebooks the KWL chart shown and fill in the first two columns using any questions they may have recorded in their reading logs. Then have students review the selection and fill in the third column. Explain to students that this third column is where they record the answers to any questions they had while reading. It also is where they should note any new and unexpected information or ideas that the selection provided. Once students have completed their charts, you can draw a KWL chart on the chalkboard and have volunteers fill it in based on their individual charts.

Know	Want to Know	Learned

Literary Concept: PLOT

A Explain to students that a story's plot usually begins with an exposition, in which an author provides background for understanding the story and sets up the story's major theme. Ask students what important information is provided in the exposition to this selection. (*Possible response: The exposition gives important background information about how life in Africa changed drastically after the arrival of European invaders, which will probably be important in understanding what happens to the subject of the biography.*)

CUSTOMIZING FOR
Students Acquiring English

I Invite students from Muslim backgrounds to share information about the Koran and other aspects of their religion reflected in the story.

Active Reading: CLARIFY

B Make sure that students' responses indicate an awareness of how privileged Ibrahima's life has been so far. Have students read on to find out how well Ibrahima's early life prepared him for his experiences in adulthood.

STRATEGIC READING FOR
Less-Proficient Readers

C Ibrahima's Fula heritage is an important part of his identity. Make sure students understand the position Ibrahima held in Fula society.

- How is the Fula government structured and what role was Ibrahima to play in it? (*The Fula state was divided into nine provinces; each province was divided into districts. Ibrahima was to be a political leader who would rule over a province or district when he grew up.*) **Synthesizing**

Set a Purpose Have students read to find out what impressions Dr. Cox and Ibrahima had of each other.

he European invaders, along with those Africans who cooperated with them, had made the times dangerous. African nations that had lived peacefully together for centuries now eyed each other warily. Slight insults led to major battles. Bands of outlaws roamed the countryside attacking the small villages, kidnapping those unfortunate enough to have wandered from the protection of their people. The stories that came from the coast were frightening. Those kidnapped were taken to the sea and sold to whites, put on boats, and taken across the sea. No one knew what happened then.

A

Abd al-Rahman Ibrahima was born in 1762 in Fouta Djallon, a district of the present country of Guinea.[1] It is a beautiful land of green mountains rising majestically from grassy plains, a land rich with minerals, especially bauxite.

I

Ibrahima was a member of the powerful and influential Fula people and a son of one of their chieftains. The religion of Islam had swept across Africa centuries before, and the young Ibrahima was raised in the tradition of the Moslems.[2]

B

The Fula were taller and lighter in complexion than the other <u>inhabitants</u> of Africa's west coast; they had silky hair, which they often wore long. A pastoral[3] people, the Fula had a complex system of government, with the state divided into nine provinces and each province divided again into smaller districts. Each province had its chief and its subchiefs.

As the son of a chief, Ibrahima was expected to assume a role of political leadership when he came of age. He would also be expected to set a moral example and to be well versed in his religion. When he reached twelve he was sent to Timbuktu[4] to study.

Under the Songhai[5] <u>dynasty</u> leader Askia the Great, Timbuktu had become a center of learning and one of the largest cities in the Songhai Empire. The young Ibrahima knew he was privileged to attend the best-known school in West Africa. Large and sophisticated, with wide, tree-lined streets, the city attracted scholars from Africa, Europe, and Asia. Islamic law, medicine, and mathematics were taught to the young men destined to become the leaders of their nations. It was a good place for a young man to be. The city was well guarded, too. It had to be, to prevent the <u>chaos</u> that, more and more, dominated African life nearer the coast.

Ibrahima learned first to recite from the Koran, the Moslem holy book, and then to read it in Arabic. From the Koran, it was felt, came all other knowledge. After Ibrahima had finished his studies in Timbuktu, he returned to Fouta Djallon to continue to prepare himself to be a chief.

C

CLARIFY
Summarize what Ibrahima's life has been like to this point.
Using a Reading Log

The Fula had little contact with whites, and what little contact they did have was filled with

---

1. **Fouta Djallon** (fo͞o′tə-jə-lōn′) . . . **Guinea** (gĭn′ē): Fouta Djallon is a small, mountainous region in Guinea, a small nation on the west coast of Africa.
2. **Islam** (ĭs-läm′) . . . **Moslems** (mŏz′ləmz): refers to the Arab conquests of territory in Africa, beginning in the seventh century. (A Moslem is a believer in the religion of Islam.)
3. **pastoral** (păs′tər-əl): having a way of life based on raising livestock.
4. **Timbuktu** (tĭm′bŭk-to͞o′): now known as Tombouctou, a city in the part of Africa now known as Mali.
5. **Songhai** (sông′hī′): a West African empire that thrived in the 1400s and 1500s.

WORDS TO KNOW	**inhabitant** (ĭn-hăb′ĭ-tənt) *n.* someone living in a particular place **dynasty** (dī′nə-stē) *n.* a series of rulers who are members of the same family **chaos** (kā′ŏs) *n.* a state of great disorder

260

Mini-Lesson The Writer's Style

FACTS AS SUPPORTING DETAILS Point out to students that in this selection, Myers supports his main ideas with facts. Remind them that, unlike an opinion, a fact can be proved true.

Application Use the highlighted passage to help students distinguish between facts and opinions. First, have students identify the main idea and determine whether it is a fact or an opinion. (*the land is beautiful; opinion*) Next, ask students to identify the facts used as supporting details. (*green mountains; grassy plains; rich with minerals, especially bauxite*) Ask how they could verify these facts. (*by checking an encyclopedia or atlas*) Have students explain why these details support the main idea. (*The individual facts together give the impression that the land is beautiful.*)

You can extend the activity by having students use information from the selection and library sources to write a short description of Timbuktu at the time of the Songhai dynasty. Tell students to use facts to support the main idea of their descriptions.

Reteaching/Reinforcement
- *Writing Handbook*, anthology p. 783
- *Writing Mini-Lessons* transparencies, p. 50

Developing a Topic, p. 206

260 THE LANGUAGE OF LITERATURE TEACHER'S EDITION

danger. So when, in 1781, a white man claiming to be a ship's surgeon stumbled into one of their villages, they were greatly surprised.

John Coates Cox hardly appeared to be a threat. A slight man, blind in one eye, he had been lost for days in the forested regions bordering the mountains. He had injured his leg, and it had become badly infected as he tried to find help. By the time he was found and brought to the Fula chiefs, he was more dead than alive.

Dr. Cox, an Irishman, told of being separated from a hunting party that had left from a ship on which he had sailed as ship's surgeon. The Fula chief decided that he would help Cox. He was taken into a hut, and a healer was assigned the task of curing his infected leg.

During the months Dr. Cox stayed with the Fula, he met Ibrahima, now a tall, brown-skinned youth who had reached manhood. His bearing reflected his status as the son of a major chief. Dr. Cox had learned some Fulani, the Fula language, and the two men spoke. Ibrahima was doubtless curious about the white man's world, and Dr. Cox was as impressed by Ibrahima's education as he had been by the kindness of his people.

When Dr. Cox was well enough to leave, he was provided with a guard; but before he left, he warned the Fula about the danger of venturing too near the ships that docked off the coast of Guinea. The white doctor knew that the ships were there to take captives.

Cox and Ibrahima embraced fondly and said their good-byes, thinking they would never meet again.

Ibrahima married and became the father of several children. He was in his mid-twenties when he found himself leading the Fula cavalry in their war with the Mandingo.[6]

The first battles went well, with the enemy retreating before the advancing Fula. The foot warriors attacked first, breaking the enemy's ranks and making them easy prey for the well-trained Fula cavalry. With the enemy in full rout[7] the infantry returned to their towns while the horsemen, led by Ibrahima, chased the remaining stragglers. The Fula fought their enemies with spears, bows, slings, swords, and courage.

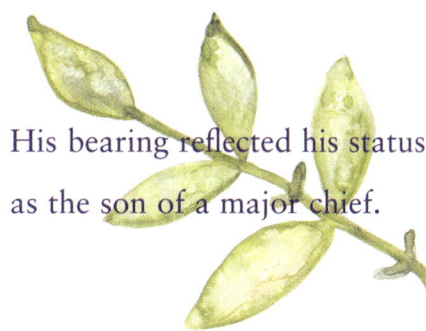

His bearing reflected his status as the son of a major chief.

The path of pursuit led along a path that narrowed sharply as the forests thickened. The fleeing warriors disappeared into the forest that covered a sharply rising mountain. Thinking the enemy had gone for good, Ibrahima felt it would be useless to chase them  further.

"We could not see them," he would write later.

But against his better judgment, he decided to look for them. The horsemen dismounted at the foot of a hill and began the steep climb on foot. Halfway up the hill the Fula realized they

---

6. **Mandingo** (măn-dĭng'gō): a tribe of West Africa.
7. **in full rout:** in complete retreat.

WORDS TO KNOW
status (stā'təs) *n.* one's position in society; rank

261

Literary Concept: DESCRIPTION

D Have a volunteer read aloud the description of John Coates Cox. Ask students what image forms in their minds as they listen to the description. *(Possible responses: A small white man with a patch over one eye who hobbles on one leg into the village; a leg wound oozing pus and blood)*

STRATEGIC READING FOR Less-Proficient Readers

E Have students describe the impression Ibrahima and Dr. Cox made on each other. *(Ibrahima and Dr. Cox became fond of each other. Ibrahima was curious about Dr. Cox's white world, and Dr. Cox was impressed by Ibrahima's education.)* Restating

Set a Purpose Have students read to find out how the war between the Mandingo and Fula affected Ibrahima's life.

CUSTOMIZING FOR Multiple Learning Styles

F **Linguistic and Interpersonal Learners** Have students construct a journal entry that Dr. Cox might have written during his stay among the Fula. Tell students to think about how Dr. Cox felt when he entered the village, when he received care, and when he said goodbye. Allow volunteers to read their completed journal entries aloud.

CUSTOMIZING FOR Students Acquiring English

2 Point out that the suffix *-less* is often added to nouns and means "without." Elicit the meaning of *useless* from students.

Mini-Lesson Genre Study

NONFICTION Remind students that a **biography** is the story of a person's life written by another person. Biographies may often seem like fiction because they contain many of the same elements, such as characterization, setting, and plot. Biographers gather facts about their subject and then weave them together into a true story.

Application Have students look at pages 260 and 261 for examples of the following kinds of biographical writing:
1. general facts about a culture or time period
2. specific facts about an individual or event
3. speculation about what probably happened

Possible responses:
1. "Under the Songhai . . . ," p. 260
2. "Ibrahima married . . . ," p. 261
3. "Cox and Ibrahima embraced . . . ," p. 261

Students can record their responses in a three-column chart. Point out that sometimes it is hard to distinguish researched facts from the author's speculations. Tell students that signal words such as *probably, most likely, may,* and *might* can alert readers of possible speculations. Explain another strategy is to ask, "Can this be proven true?"

Literary Concept: PLOT

G Ask students to discuss why this is a significant moment in the plot, and if they think it was foreshadowed earlier in the selection. *(Possible response: Ibrahima, who held an important position in Fula society and who seemed to show promise for the future, has been captured. This was foreshadowed earlier with Dr. Cox's warning the Fula about getting too close to the ships that were docked off the coast of Guinea.)*

STRATEGIC READING FOR
Less-Proficient Readers

H Ask students to explain how the enmity between the Fula and the Mandingo changed Ibrahima's life. *(After their victory over the Fula, the Mandingo sold their prisoners of war, including Ibrahima, into slavery.)* **Drawing Conclusions**

Set a Purpose Have students read to find out the significance of Ibrahima's second encounter with Dr. Cox.

Critical Thinking:
MAKING JUDGMENTS

I Ask students to discuss the author's description of those slaves killed outright as "lucky." Ask them if they agree with this statement. *(Responses will vary. Some students may argue that a quick death is preferable to a slow, agonizing one. Others may argue that there may have been a chance for survival and escape.)*

---

had been lured into a trap! Ibrahima heard the rifles firing, saw the smoke from the powder and the men about him falling to the ground, screaming in agony. Some died instantly. Many horses, hit by the gunfire, thrashed about in pain and panic. The firing was coming from both sides, and Ibrahima ordered his men to the top of the hill, where they could, if time and Allah permitted it, try a charge using the speed and momentum of their remaining horses.

Ibrahima was among the first to mount, and urged his animal onward. The enemy warriors came out of the forests, some with bows and arrows, others with muskets that he knew they had obtained from the Europeans. The courage of the Fula could not match the fury of the guns. Ibrahima called out to his men to save themselves, to flee as they could. Many tried to escape, rushing madly past the guns. Few survived.

Those who did clustered about their young leader, determined to make one last, desperate stand. Ibrahima was hit in the back by an arrow, but the aim was not true and the arrow merely cut his broad shoulder. Then something smashed against his head from the rear.

The next thing Ibrahima knew was that he was choking. Then he felt himself being lifted from water. He tried to move his arms, but they had been fastened securely behind his back. He had been captured.

G When he came to his full senses, he looked around him. Those of his noble cavalry who had not been captured were already dead. Ibrahima was unsteady on his legs as his clothes and sandals were stripped from him. The victorious Mandingo warriors now pushed him roughly into file with his men. They began the long <u>trek</u> that would lead them to the sea.

H

In Fouta Djallon being captured by the enemy meant being forced to do someone else's bidding,[8] sometimes for years. If you could get a message to your people, you could, perhaps, buy your freedom. Otherwise, it was only if you were well liked, or if you married one of your captor's women, that you would be allowed to go free or to live like a free person.

Ibrahima sensed that things would not go well for him.

The journey to the sea took weeks. Ibrahima was tied to other men, with ropes around their necks. Each day they walked from dawn to dusk. Those who were slow were knocked brutally to the ground. Some of those who could no longer walk were speared and left to die in agony. It was the lucky ones who were killed outright if they fell.

I

> The journey to the sea took weeks. Ibrahima was tied to other men, with ropes around their necks.

When they reached the sea, they remained bound hand and foot. There were men and women tied together. Small children clung to their mothers as they waited for the boats to come and the bargaining to begin.

---

8. **do someone else's bidding:** follow another's orders.

WORDS TO KNOW
trek (trĕk) *n.* a slow, difficult journey

262

Mini-Lesson: Speaking, Listening, and Viewing

CRITICAL VIEWING Explain to students that critical viewing can help them interpret and evaluate what they see on film. Explain to students that critical viewing is similar to active reading. Like active readers, critical viewers must ask questions, make predictions, clarify plot points, evaluate characters' actions, and make connections to their own lives.

Application Invite students to watch the WonderWorks presentation of *Brother Future* (Films Incorporated Video, 1992, 120 min.), a time-travel story in which a young contemporary African American finds himself enslaved in South Carolina in 1822. (A teacher's guide accompanies the video.) Before viewing, divide the class in two groups. Assign one group to compare and contrast T. J. with other young people of today; have the other group compare T. J. with Ibrahima. After viewing, groups can record their findings in a comparison-and-contrast chart and then present their conclusions to the class.

262 THE LANGUAGE OF LITERATURE TEACHER'S EDITION

Mecklenberg County: High Cotton Mother and Child (1978), Romare Bearden. Courtesy of the Estate of Romare Bearden.

Ibrahima, listening to the conversations of the men who held him captive, could understand those who spoke Arabic. These Africans were a low class of men, made powerful by the guns they had been given, made evil by the white man's goods. But it didn't matter who was evil and who was good. It only mattered who held the gun.

Ibrahima was inspected on the shore, then put into irons and herded into a small boat that took him out to a ship that was larger than any he had ever seen.

The ship onto which Ibrahima was taken was already crowded with black captives. Some shook in fear; others, still tied, fought by hurling their bodies at their captors. The beating and the killing continued until the ones who were left knew that their lot was hopeless.

On board the ship there were more whites with guns, who shoved them toward the open hatch. Some of the Africans hesitated at the hatch, and were clubbed down and pushed belowdecks.

It was dark beneath the deck, and difficult to breathe. Bodies were pressed close against other bodies. In the section of the ship he was in, men prayed to various gods in various languages. It seemed that the whites would never stop pushing men into the already crowded space. Two sailors pushed the Africans into position so that each would lie in the smallest space possible. The sailors panted and sweated as they untied the men and then chained them to a railing that ran the length of the ship.

The ship rolled against its mooring as the

ABD AL-RAHMAN IBRAHIMA **263**

Mini-Lesson  Reading Skills/Strategies

ACTIVE READING: CLARIFY Explain to students that when they pause in their reading to make certain they have understood what they have read, they are using an active reading strategy called clarifying. Point out the marked stopping points labeled Clarify in this selection as examples. Tell students that summarizing in their own words what they have read helps them focus on the main ideas and makes the story easier to understand.

Application Refer students to the summaries they wrote for this selection (see page 257). Invite volunteers to read aloud their summaries and discuss as a class how they restate and clarify the selection's main ideas. Then ask students to write a short summary of a story they've read that they would recommend to others. Students can create a class card catalog by writing their summaries on three index cards to be filed by author, title, and subject. If database software is available, students can create an electronic catalog. Each summary would be an individual record with separate fields for author, title, and subject.

Reteaching/Reinforcement
• *Unit Three Resource Book,* p. 5

Critical Thinking: ANALYZING

L Ask students why, all of a sudden, the captors took an interest in the physical appearance of the Africans. *(Possible response: The captors believed that a better appearance would bring a higher price.)*

Active Reading: CLARIFY

M You may wish to call on volunteers to describe Ibrahima's journey by ship. Each student can describe one part of the journey, picking up where another leaves off. You may wish to list different aspects of the journey on the board as students describe them. Students can copy the list to use for review.

Linking to Math

N Foster paid $930 for his two enslaved Africans. The earliest data available for the Consumer Price Index shows that an 1800 dollar was worth about $8.95 in 1995 dollars. Thus, Foster paid the equivalent of about $8,325.

Literary Concept: PLOT

O Ask students to explain why Ibrahima's being sold is an important moment in the plot. *(Possible response: Ibrahima is the son of a Fula chief; in his village he was a very important person, and everyone knew who he was. Now he is a slave who has been bought by a tobacco grower. His life has changed for the worse—from the son of a chief to an abused slave.)*

---

anchor was lifted, and the journey began. The boards of the ship creaked and moaned as it lifted and fell in the sea. Some of the men got sick, vomiting upon themselves in the wretched darkness. They lay cramped, muscles aching, irons cutting into their legs and wrists, gasping for air.

Once a day they would be brought out on deck and made to jump about for exercise. They were each given a handful of either beans or rice cooked with yams, and water from a cask. The white sailors looked hardly better than the Africans, but it was they who held the guns.

Illness and the stifling conditions on the ships caused many deaths. How many depended largely on how fast the ships could be loaded with Africans and how long the voyage from Africa took. It was not unusual for 10 percent of the Africans to die if the trip took longer than the usual twenty-five to thirty-five days.

L Ibrahima, now twenty-six years old, reached Mississippi in 1788. As the ship approached land, the Africans were brought onto the deck and fed. Some had oil put on their skins so they would look better; their sores were treated or covered with pitch. Then they were given garments to wear in an obvious effort to improve their appearance.

CLARIFY
M In your own words, describe Ibrahima's journey by ship.
Using a Reading Log

Although Ibrahima could not speak English, he understood he was being bargained for. The white man who stood on the platform with him made him turn around, and several other white men neared him, touched his limbs, examined his teeth, looked into his eyes, and made him move about.

Thomas Foster, a tobacco grower and a hard-working man, had come from South Carolina with his family and had settled on the rich lands that took their minerals from the Mississippi River. He already held one captive, a young boy. In August 1788 he bought two more. One of them was named Sambo, which means "second son." The other was Ibrahima.

Foster agreed to pay $930 for the two Africans. He paid $150 down and signed an agreement to pay another $250 the following January and the remaining $530 in January of the following year. **N**

For Ibrahima there was confusion and pain. What was he to do?

When Ibrahima arrived at Foster's farm, he tried to find someone who could explain to the white man who he was—the son of a chief. He wanted to offer a ransom for his own release, but Foster wasn't interested. He understood, perhaps from the boy whom he had purchased previously, that this new African was claiming to be an important person. Foster had probably never heard of the Fula or their culture; he had paid good money for the African, and wasn't about to give him up. Foster gave Ibrahima a new name: He called him Prince. **O**

For Ibrahima there was confusion and pain. What was he to do? A few months before, he had been a learned man and a leader among his people. Now he was a captive in a strange land where he neither spoke the language nor

264 UNIT THREE PART 1: COPING WITH INJUSTICE

Mini-Lesson Literary Concepts

PLOT Remind students that a plot is the series of events in a story. The plot usually centers around a conflict, or a problem faced by the main character. The action that characters take to solve this problem builds toward the climax. At this point, the problem is either solved or left unresolved and the story ends. Explain to students that although this selection is a piece of biographical nonfiction, the author has created a plot by detailing the series of events which make up Ibrahima's life story.

Application Have students complete a story map which details the major events of Ibrahima's life. Make sure that students locate the main conflict in the plot as well as the climax and resolution. When students have completed the activity, have them form pairs to compare and discuss their maps.

264 THE LANGUAGE OF LITERATURE TEACHER'S EDITION

understood the customs. Was he never to see his family again? Were his sons forever lost to him?

As a Fula, Ibrahima wore his hair long; Foster insisted that it be cut. Ibrahima's clothing had been taken from him, and his sandals. Now the last remaining symbol of his people, his long hair, had been taken as well.

He was told to work in the fields. He refused, and he was tied and whipped. The sting of the whip across his naked flesh was terribly painful, but it was nothing like the pain he felt within. The whippings forced him to work.

For Ibrahima this was not life, but a mockery of life. There was the waking in the morning and the sleeping at night; he worked, he ate, but this was not life. What was more, he could not see an end to it. It was this feeling that made him attempt to escape.

Ibrahima escaped to the backwoods regions of Natchez.[9] He hid there, eating wild berries and fruit, not daring to show his face to any man, white or black. There was no telling who could be trusted. Sometimes he saw men with dogs and knew they were searching for runaways, perhaps him.

Where was he to run? What was he to do? He didn't know the country, he didn't know how far it was from Fouta Djallon or how to get back to his homeland. He could tell that this place was ruled by white men who held him in captivity. The other blacks he had seen were from all parts of Africa. Some he recognized by their tribal markings, some he did not. None were allowed to speak their native tongues around the white men. Some already knew nothing of the languages of their people.

As time passed, Ibrahima's despair deepened. His choices were simple. He could stay in the woods and probably die, or he could submit his body back into bondage. There is no place in Islamic law for a man to take his own life. Ibrahima returned to Thomas Foster.

Foster still owed money to the man from whom he had purchased Ibrahima. The debt would remain whether he still possessed the African or not. Foster was undoubtedly glad to see that the African had returned. Thin, nearly starving, Ibrahima was put to work.

Ibrahima submitted himself to the will of Thomas Foster. He was a captive, held in bondage not only by Foster but by the society in which he found himself. Ibrahima maintained his beliefs in the religion of Islam and kept its rituals as best he could. He was determined to be the same person he had always been: Abd al-Rahman Ibrahima of Fouta Djallon and of the proud Fula people.

By 1807 the area had become the Mississippi Territory. Ibrahima was forty-five and had been in bondage for twenty years. During those years he met and married a woman whom Foster had purchased, and they began to raise a family. Fouta Djallon was more and more distant, and he had become resigned to the idea that he would never see it or his family again.

Thomas Foster had grown wealthy and had become an important man in the territory. At forty-five Ibrahima was considered old. He was less useful to Foster, who now let the tall African grow a few vegetables on a side plot and sell them in town, since there was nowhere in the territory that the black man

CLARIFY
Summarize why it is impossible for Ibrahima to escape.
Using a Reading Log

---
9. **Natchez** (năch'ĭz): an early settlement in what is now the state of Mississippi.

WORDS TO KNOW
bondage (bŏn'dĭj) *n.* slavery

Literary Concept: DESCRIPTION

R Ask students what descriptive details reveal who the white man was. *("Smallish" and "walked with a limp" show that the man was Dr. Cox.)*

STRATEGIC READING FOR
Less-Proficient Readers

S Have students speculate on the significance of Ibrahima's meeting Dr. Cox again. *(Possible response: Dr. Cox had power in white society. Also, he was fond of Ibrahima and grateful to the Fula. Therefore, Dr. Cox might be able to set Ibrahima free.)* Making Inferences

Linking to History

T By 1817, when the American Colonization Society was founded, most African Americans in the United States had been born there. For them, a "return" to Africa held little appeal. Unlike the more radical abolitionists, the colonizationalists assumed that Africans were inferior to whites and had no legitimate place in the United States. Even some slaveholders, who fiercely opposed general emancipation, supported the American Colonization Society's plan for gradual emancipation because it compensated slaveholders for the loss of "property."

CUSTOMIZING FOR
Students Acquiring English

4 Invite students to speculate about the name of the new colony, *Liberia*. They may make the connection with the English word *liberty* or with cognates in their home languages.

---

could go where he would not be captured by some other white man and returned.

It was during one of these visits to town that Ibrahima saw a white man who looked familiar. The smallish man walked slowly and with a limp. Ibrahima cautiously approached the man and spoke to him. The man looked closely at Ibrahima, then spoke his name. It was Dr. Cox.

The two men shook hands, and Dr. Cox, who now lived in the territory, took Ibrahima to his home. John Cox had not <u>prospered</u> over the years, but he was still hopeful. He listened carefully as Ibrahima told his story—the battle near Fouta Djallon, the defeat, the long journey across the Atlantic Ocean, and, finally, his sale to Thomas Foster and the years of labor.

Dr. Cox and Ibrahima went to the Foster plantation. Meeting with Foster, he explained how he had met the tall black man. Surely, he reasoned, knowing that Ibrahima was of royal blood, Foster would free him? The answer was a firm, but polite, no. No amount of pleading would make Foster change his mind. It didn't matter that Dr. Cox had supported what Ibrahima had told Foster so many years before, that he was a prince. To Foster the man was merely his property.

Dr. Cox had to leave the man whose people had saved his life, but he told Ibrahima that he would never stop working for his freedom.

Andrew Marschalk, the son of a Dutch baker, was a printer, a pioneer in his field, and a man of great curiosity. By the time Marschalk heard about it, Cox had told a great many people in the Natchez district the story of African royalty being held in slavery in America. Marschalk was fascinated. He suggested that Ibrahima write a letter to his people, telling them of his whereabouts and asking them to ransom him. But Ibrahima had not been to his homeland in twenty years. The people there were still being captured by slave traders. He would have to send a messenger who knew the countryside, and who knew the Fula. Where would he find such a man?

For a long time Ibrahima did nothing. Finally, some time after the death of Dr. Cox in 1816, Ibrahima wrote the letter that Marschalk suggested. He had little faith in the <u>procedure</u> but felt he had nothing to lose. Marschalk was surprised when Ibrahima appeared with the letter written neatly in Arabic. Since one place in Africa was the same as the next to Marschalk, he sent the letter not to Fouta Djallon but to Morocco.

he government of Morocco did not know Ibrahima but understood from his letter that he was a Moslem. Moroccan officials, in a letter to President James Monroe, pleaded for the release of Ibrahima. The letter reached Henry Clay, the American secretary of state.

The United States had recently ended a bitter war with Tripoli in North Africa and welcomed the idea of establishing good relations with Morocco, another North African country. Clay wrote to Foster about Ibrahima.

Foster resented the idea of releasing Ibrahima. The very idea that the government of Morocco had written to Clay and discussed a religion that Ibrahima shared with other Africans gave Ibrahima a past that Foster had long denied, a past as honorable as Foster's. This idea challenged a basic <u>premise</u> of

WORDS TO KNOW	**prosper** (prŏs′pər) *v.* to be successful; thrive
	procedure (prə-sē′jər) *n.* a course of action
	premise (prĕm′ĭs) *n.* an idea that forms the basis of an argument

266

Mini-Lesson Grammar

Regular Verbs	Irregular Verbs	Past Tense
prosper		prospered
	write	wrote
challenge		challenged
	is	was

PAST TENSE VERBS Point out to students that most verbs, called regular verbs, form the past tense by adding *-d* or *-ed* to their base form. Irregular verbs, however, undergo a change in spelling to show the past tense.

Application Invite students to write one or two paragraphs in which Ibrahima looks back on his life. Students should write in the first-person point of view and use the past tense. (You may wish to allow volunteers to read aloud their completed paragraphs.) When students have finished, have them go back and label regular and irregular verbs.

Reteaching/Reinforcement
- *Grammar Handbook*, anthology pp. 835–836
- *Grammar Mini-Lesson* copymasters, p. 25, transparencies, p. 18

Verb Tenses, pp. 408–409

266 THE LANGUAGE OF LITERATURE TEACHER'S EDITION

slavery—a premise that Foster must have believed without reservation: that the Africans had been nothing but savages, with no humanity or human feelings, and therefore it was all right to enslave them. But after more letters and pressure from the State Department, Foster agreed to release Ibrahima if he could be assured that Ibrahima would leave the country and return to Fouta Djallon.

Many people who believed that slavery was wrong also believed that Africans could not live among white Americans. The American Colonization Society had been formed expressly to send freed Africans back to Africa. The society bought land, and a colony called Liberia was established on the west coast of Africa. Foster was assured that Ibrahima would be sent there.

By then Ibrahima's cause had been taken up by a number of abolitionist[10] groups in the North as well as by many free Africans. They raised money to buy his wife's freedom as well.

On February 7, 1829, Ibrahima and his wife sailed on the ship *Harriet* for Africa. The ship reached Liberia, and Ibrahima now had to find a way to reach his people again. He never found that way. Abd al-Rahman Ibrahima died in Liberia in July 1829.

Who was Ibrahima? He was one of millions of Africans taken by force from their native lands. He was the son of a chief, a warrior, and a scholar. But to Ibrahima the only thing that mattered was that he had lost his freedom. If he had been a herder in Fouta Djallon, or an artist in Benin, or a farmer along the Gambia, it would have been the same. Ibrahima was an African who loved freedom no less than other beings on earth. And he was denied that freedom. ❖

---

10. **abolitionist** (ăb´ə-lĭsh´ə-nĭst): favoring the end of slavery.

WORDS TO KNOW
reservation (rĕz´ər-vā´shən) *n.* a doubt; an exception

LITERARY INSIGHT

Ancestors
BY DUDLEY RANDALL

Why are our ancestors
always kings or princes
and never the common people?

Was the Old Country a democracy
where every man was a king?
Or did the slavecatchers
take only the aristocracy[1]
and leave the fieldhands
laborers
streetcleaners
garbage collectors
dishwashers
cooks
and maids
behind?

My own ancestor
(research reveals)
was a swineherd
who tended the pigs
in the Royal Pigstye
and slept in the mud
among the hogs.

Yet I'm as proud of him
as of any king or prince
dreamed up in fantasies
of bygone glory.

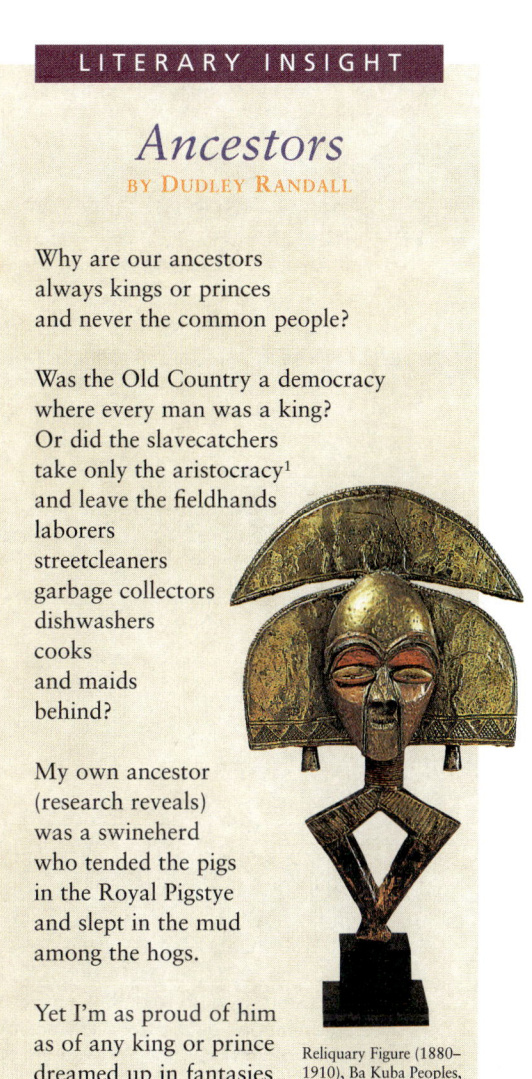

Reliquary Figure (1880–1910), Ba Kuba Peoples, West African, Gabon.

1. **aristocracy** (ăr´ĭ-stŏk´rə-sē): nobility; rulers.

Art Note

Reliquary figure by an artist of the Kota people, Africa Reliquary figures are considered sacred and are believed to protect people from harm and ensure prosperity. This figure is a warning to stay away.

Reading the Art How does the figure's posture suggest a warning?

COMPREHENSION CHECK
1. Who is Ibrahima? *(the son of a chieftain of the powerful Fula people)*
2. How does Ibrahima meet Dr. Cox? *(They meet when Dr. Cox gets lost while hunting and stumbles into Ibrahima's village, where his injured leg is treated.)*
3. How does Ibrahima come to be sold into slavery? *(The Mandingos capture him and sell him to the whites, who put him on a slave ship bound for the United States.)*
4. Why doesn't Ibrahima return to his home in Fouta Djallon? *(He dies in Liberia.)*

EDITOR'S NOTE *With the permission of the author or copyright holder, this selection was excerpted from a longer work; material was deleted to focus the selection.*

LITERARY INSIGHT
1. Why do you think the speaker is proud of his ancestor even though the ancestor is not of royal blood? *(Possible response: The speaker believes a person can be admired even if he or she does not hold a high place in society. In fact, those who claim noble ancestry have committed shameful acts.)*
2. Should we be proud of our ancestors? Explain your answer. *(Possible responses: Yes, we should take pride in where we came from. No, it doesn't make sense to be proud of other people just because we are related to them.)*

DUDLEY RANDALL
Randall is Detroit's first poet laureate. Literary critics have described Randall's writing as a bridge that links the poets of the Harlem Renaissance with the generation of African Americans who came of age in the 1960s.

Mini-Lesson  Spelling

SOFT AND HARD G Tell students that when the letter *g* has a soft sound (*ginger, gym*), it is usually followed by the letter *i, e,* or *y*. When the letter *g* has a hard sound (*game, magnet*), it is usually followed by a consonant or by the vowel *a, o,* or *u*.

Word	Soft G	Hard G
alligator		x
allegiance	x	
bondage	x	
region	x	
guitar		x

Draw on the chalkboard the examples shown.

Application Have students spell the words below, identifying the *g* in each as soft or hard. Call on volunteers to read their answers aloud.
1. origin *(soft)*
2. recognize *(hard)*
3. legend *(soft)*
4. grace *(hard)*
5. genius *(soft)*

Ask students to look for more words that fit this pattern, in their own writing and in the things that they read, and to add them to their personal word lists.

Reteaching/Reinforcement
• *Unit Three Resource Book,* p. 6

From Personal Response to Critical Analysis

1. Responses will vary.
2. Possible responses: He is a heroic warrior and an educated leader; he retains his dignity, beliefs, and pride despite his enslavement; he and Dr. John Cox, though from different worlds, have a deep and abiding respect for each other.
3. Possible response: Dr. Cox might describe his travels to Africa, where he experienced a personal relationship with Ibrahima and his people. By describing a place where he had been and a culture that he had experienced, Cox might help Foster go beyond the prejudices of his time.
4. Responses will vary.
5. Encourage students to support their answers with details from the selection, comparing what they know now to what they knew before they began reading.
6. Possible response: People want to know about their heritage to understand who they are and where they come from. Ibrahima's knowledge of his heritage empowers him to write to Marschalk, which secures his freedom. The speaker in "Ancestors" gains from the knowledge of his ancestor—a swineherd. Just knowing who his ancestor was seems to give the speaker confidence and pride.

Another Pathway

Cooperative Learning Students should switch roles in retelling various sections of the story, to ensure that all get to play a leadership and a supporting role. Members should take turns acting as voice monitor, explainer of ideas, recorder, and encourager of participation.

Rubric

3 Full Accomplishment Students accurately depict Ibrahima's point of view in a way that is consistent with and elaborates on Myers's version.

2 Substantial Accomplishment Students accurately depict Ibrahima's point of view but do not compare their original interpretation to Myers's version.

1 Little or Partial Accomplishment Students have difficulty retelling sections of the story from Ibrahima's point of view and comparing their version with that of Myers.

RESPONDING OPTIONS

FROM PERSONAL RESPONSE TO CRITICAL ANALYSIS

REFLECT 1. If you could say one thing about Ibrahima's life, what would you say? Share your ideas with a friend.

RETHINK 2. What kind of person is Ibrahima?
Consider
Close Textual Reading
- his upbringing and position in the society of Fouta Djallon
- his behavior after he is forced into slavery
- his relationship with Dr. John Cox

Thematic Link
3. In the selection, the author Walter Dean Myers notes that Thomas Foster must have believed deeply in the "basic premise of slavery" to treat Ibrahima as he did. What do you think Dr. Cox would say to Foster about those beliefs?

4. If you were teaching this selection, what are two or three main ideas you would want your students to remember?

5. What new information about slavery did you find most surprising or disturbing? If possible, regroup with the classmates you brainstormed with before you began reading, and compare your reactions to the selection.

RELATE 6. In the poem "Ancestors," the speaker is aware of his or her heritage. Many people have little knowledge of their backgrounds and ancestors, and go to great lengths to find information about them. Why do you think finding out about their pasts matters so much to some people? Use information from the selection and from "Ancestors" to explain your answer.

Multimodal Learning
ANOTHER PATHWAY

Cooperative Learning
What if Ibrahima himself could describe the events in this account? Working in small groups, choose various sections of the story and try retelling them from Ibrahima's point of view. For each section, compare your version with Myers's version. In what ways are the two versions similar? In what ways do they differ?

QUICKWRITES

1. What do you think Ibrahima wrote in his letter to his people, the Fula? Write the **letter** you think he might have written.

2. Summarize Ibrahima's story for a **pamphlet** Andrew Marschalk might have had printed to argue against slavery.

3. Imagine you are a reporter interviewing Ibrahima and his wife just before they set sail on the *Harriet* to Liberia. Write the **questions** you would ask the couple.

 **PORTFOLIO** Save your writing. You may want to use it later as a springboard to a piece for your portfolio.

268 UNIT THREE PART 1: COPING WITH INJUSTICE

QuickWrites

1. Encourage students to use details from what the selection says about Ibrahima's life and what the selection implies about how he feels. Remind students that Ibrahima has been away from his people for many years and might struggle to communicate his experiences in a different culture.

2. Remind students that to summarize means to tell *briefly* the main idea of a piece of writing—in this case, Ibrahima's story.

3. Point out that good journalists anticipate things readers would need to know to understand a story. Journalists frame their questions so as to tell the *who, what, when, where,* and *how* of a story.

The Writer's Craft
Letter Form, p. 609
Sharing an Opinion, pp. 116–127
Interviewing Skills, p. 323

LITERARY CONCEPTS

A writer uses **description** to help readers picture scenes, events, and characters. For example, Myers describes the sights and sounds of Ibrahima's battle with the Mandingo. Ibrahima "heard the rifles firing, saw the smoke from the powder and the men about him falling to the ground, screaming in agony." Find another description in the selection that you think is especially effective. What images form in your mind as you read this description?

CONCEPT REVIEW: Biography The writer of a **biography** does research to find out about a person's life and the time in which he or she lived. What kinds of research do you think Myers had to do in order to find out about Ibrahima's life? What sources might he have consulted?

Multimodal Learning
ACROSS THE CURRICULUM

Geography The Songhai Empire was only one of many powerful kingdoms of ancient Africa. Research the Songhai Empire, along with the kingdoms of Benin, Kush, Kanem-Bornu, Ethiopia, and Mali. On a piece of paper, trace an outline map of Africa, showing the region that each kingdom occupied and the time period that each existed. Add to the map some images cut from old magazines or your own small drawings of objects—sculptures, farming tools, or weapons—that represent what was produced by each kingdom. Hang the map in your classroom to share with the other students.

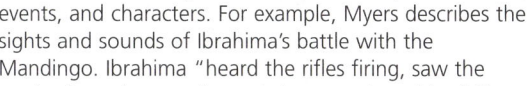

Multimodal Learning
ALTERNATIVE ACTIVITIES

1. With a partner, write the conversation and actions that might have happened during the meeting between Ibrahima and Dr. John Cox in the United States. Present your **dramatization** to the class.

2. Set the story of Ibrahima to music. Make up a **song** that tells his story and set it to the tune of an old spiritual, or make up original music, if you prefer. Teach your song to some of your classmates.

3. Make a **time line** of Ibrahima's life from his birth in 1762 to his death in 1829. Write in the years or time periods mentioned in the selection, along with the events that occurred during those years and where the events occurred.

4. Skim the selection for details that describe how Ibrahima looked and dressed. Draw or paint two **pictures** of him. In one picture, show him as a young man in his homeland. In the second picture, show him as an older man during his years in the United States. Display the contrasting pictures in the classroom.

ABD AL-RAHMAN IBRAHIMA 269

Across the Curriculum

Geography *Cooperative Learning*
Have students work in small groups. Each group can research and map one of the kingdoms listed. Groups can then share their maps and images with the class. Conclude by having volunteers locate the region that their group's kingdom occupied on a large classroom map of Africa.

ADDITIONAL SUGGESTIONS
History *Go Right to the Source*
Students can find out more about the lives of slaves by reading a slave narrative from a collection such as *Weevils in the Wheat: Interviews with Virginia Ex-Slaves* (Bloomington: Indiana University Press, 1980). Have students work in small groups to prepare a class presentation of their reading. Tell students their presentations can be oral reports, dramatic reenactments, imagined dialogues, a series of illustrations, and so on. Encourage students to be creative in their presentation styles, but remind them that their goal is to convey to their audience what it was like to be a slave.

Literary Concepts

Have students form small groups and read aloud the descriptions that they found in the selection. Tell them to study each description to identify details that help make each effective. One student should record the group's observations to share with the class.

Concept Review Possible response: He might have looked through personal papers and state records for slave transactions, read other biographies and nonfiction books, and visited Ibrahima's homeland.

Alternative Activities

1. After partners present their dramatizations, allow students to compare and contrast the various interpretations.
2. You may wish to first play recorded examples of well-known spirituals such as "Swing Low, Sweet Chariot" to model this type of music for students.
3. Allow students to work in cooperative groups, each group member researching one of the years or time periods mentioned.
4. Library research may help students gather additional visual details, particularly of Ibrahima's homeland.

THE LANGUAGE OF LITERATURE TEACHER'S EDITION 269

Words to Know

Exercise A
1. inhabitant
2. dynasty
3. status
4. bondage
5. prosper
6. trek
7. chaos
8. premise
9. reservation
10. procedure

Exercise B
Suggest that students decide on a style and rhyme scheme before starting to write. You may wish to allow students to use a thesaurus or a rhyming dictionary. Students can review *The Writer's Craft*, pp. 86–88, for writing poetry.

Reteaching/Reinforcement
- *Unit Three Resource Book,* p. 7

Literary Links

Have students compare the injustices with which Ibrahima and Matthew Henson had to cope. *(Both men were treated unjustly because of their race. Henson was denied recognition for his accomplishments, and Ibrahima was denied his freedom.)*

WALTER DEAN MYERS

Best-known for young people's novels about Harlem youth, Walter Dean Myers also has written ghost stories, adventure tales, and modern fairy tales. Myers didn't plan to be a writer because he "never knew that writing was a job." Myers says, "When I was a kid, my people didn't think of being a writer as a legitimate kind of work."

WORDS TO KNOW

EXERCISE A Review the Words to Know in the boxes at the bottom of each selection page. On your paper, write the word that best completes each sentence.

1. Ibrahima had been an ____ of Fouta Djallon.
2. Timbuktu was ruled by the Songhai ____.
3. Most Africans did not have the same ____ as Ibrahima, who was a member of a royal family.
4. Although the condition of ____ existed in Africa, no one became a slave just because of skin color.
5. Some African rulers saw a way to ____ in the slave trade by supplying traders with prisoners captured in battle.
6. Enemy tribes led their prisoners on a long ____ by foot to the African coast.
7. When captives tried to throw themselves overboard, ____ occurred aboard slave ships.
8. A ____ of slavery was that Africans did not have human feelings.
9. Thomas Foster believed without ____ that Ibrahima was merely property.
10. The ____ Ibrahima followed to obtain his freedom would not have worked for most slaves, because they were not taught how to write.

EXERCISE B Write a brief poem about Ibrahima. Use at least five of the Words to Know in your poem. Then add your poem to a class poetry anthology.

WALTER DEAN MYERS

1937–

The early years of Walter Dean Myers's life were marked by hardship. When this West Virginia native was two years old, his mother died, and he was put into foster care at age three. As Myers grew into a bright and talented teenager in New York City's Harlem, he felt limited by a society that defined him in terms of his race rather than in terms of his abilities. He turned to writing as a way of expressing himself. In 1970, after a brief period in the army and a series of unsatisfying jobs, Myers became an editor for a publishing company. He wrote part-time for several years, and in 1977 he began to write full-time.

The selection "Abd al-Rahman Ibrahima" is a chapter from a book of nonfiction whose full title is *Now Is Your Time! The African-American Struggle for Freedom.* Through his writings, Myers tries to show young people that they can succeed in life. He believes that "there is always one more story to tell, one more person whose life needs to be held up to the sun." *Now Is Your Time!,* as well as his novels *The Young Landlords* and *Motown and Didi: A Love Story,* have won the Coretta Scott King Award. His novel *Scorpions* was a 1989 Newbery Honor Book.

OTHER WORKS *Fallen Angels, Hoops, Mojo and the Russians, Mouse Rap, The Glory Field*

Extended Reading

270   UNIT THREE   PART 1: COPING WITH INJUSTICE

WHAT DO YOU THINK?
Reflecting on Theme

Have students think back to their speeches about people who overcame injustice. Ask students to consider how Ibrahima compares to these people. Ask them if they admire Ibrahima and how he dealt with injustice. Ask students if their thoughts about injustice and overcoming it have changed after reading about Ibrahima's life. If so, allow students to revise their speeches, if they wish.

PREVIEWING

FICTION

Eleven
Sandra Cisneros (sĭs-nĕr′ōs)

PERSONAL CONNECTION — *Activating Prior Knowledge*

As you may have guessed from the title, the main character in this story has just turned eleven years old. What was turning eleven like for you? Did you have a birthday party? What sorts of events and thoughts do you associate with your eleventh or most recent birthday? Copy the diagram below into your notebook. Then record words and phrases that you associate with being eleven years old. Share your diagram with a friend.

My Eleventh Birthday

BIOGRAPHICAL CONNECTION — *Building Background*

In 1986, when she was interviewed about this piece, the writer Sandra Cisneros commented that she sometimes feels eleven years old inside, even as an adult. "When I think how I see myself, I would have to be at age eleven. I know I'm thirty-two on the outside, but inside I'm eleven. I'm the girl in the picture with skinny arms and a crumpled shirt and crooked hair. I didn't like school because all they saw was the outside me."

READING CONNECTION — *Active Reading/Setting a Purpose*

Cause and Effect Events in a story are often related to one another by cause and effect. This relationship occurs when one event—the cause—brings about a second event—the effect. Words such as *because*, *since*, *so/that*, and *if/then* can signal an instance of cause and effect. Sometimes in a story, one cause can bring about multiple effects. As you read this account of a girl who turns eleven, note how she recognizes a particular cause and deals with its effects.

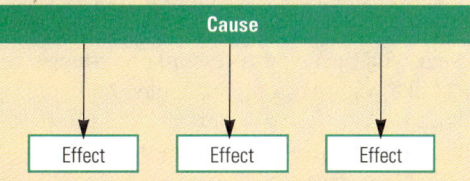

OVERVIEW

Objectives

- To understand and appreciate a short story about a disappointing eleventh birthday
- To understand cause and effect
- To identify and understand point of view
- To appreciate the use of varied sentence lengths
- To express understanding of the selection through a choice of writing forms, including a diary entry, a greeting card, and a paragraph
- To extend understanding of the selection through a variety of multimodal and cross-curricular activities

Skills

THE WRITER'S STYLE
- Effective elaboration

GRAMMAR
- Linking and action verbs

SPELLING
- Possessives and contractions

SPEAKING, LISTENING, AND VIEWING
- Group discussion
- Oral presentation

Cross-Curricular Connections

SOCIAL STUDIES
- Birthday celebrations

SCIENCE
- Tree rings

ELEVEN **271**

PRINT AND MEDIA RESOURCES

UNIT THREE RESOURCE BOOK
Strategic Reading: Literature, p. 11
Reading SkillBuilder, p. 12
Spelling SkillBuilder, p. 13

GRAMMAR MINI–LESSONS
Transparencies, p. 17

WRITING MINI–LESSONS
Transparencies, p. 34

ACCESS FOR STUDENTS ACQUIRING ENGLISH
Selection Summaries
Reading and Writing Support

FORMAL ASSESSMENT
Selection Test, p. 57
 Test Generator

 **LASERLINKS**
Author Background

THE LANGUAGE OF LITERATURE TEACHER'S EDITION **271**

SUMMARY

Rachel wakes up on her 11th birthday feeling as if she's still 10—and 9, and 8, and all the ages that came before. At school, what should be a happy day turns gloomy when the teacher insists that an ugly unclaimed sweater belongs to Rachel. Mrs. Price puts the sweater in an embarrassing pile on Rachel's desk. Worse yet, she makes Rachel put the sweater on. It smells bad, it itches, it's full of germs—and Rachel, feeling all her years of childhood rattling around inside her, cries in front of the whole class. The classmate who is the real owner of the sweater finally claims it, while Rachel longs for the day to end.

Thematic Link: *Coping with Injustice*
Forced to wear an ugly red sweater that does not belong to her, Rachel wishes that she were older and, thus, more able to protect herself from being treated unfairly.

CUSTOMIZING FOR
Students Acquiring English

- Use **ACCESS FOR STUDENTS ACQUIRING ENGLISH,** *Reading and Writing Support.*

1. Make sure that students understand that the subject pronoun *you* here is used to mean the narrator, the reader, and people in general.

2. Point out that the idiomatic phrase *kind of* is often used in informal spoken English to mean "approximately."

STRATEGIC READING FOR
Less-Proficient Readers

Set a Purpose Guide students to use the title and art to infer that the story is about an eleventh birthday. Ask them to read to find out what Rachel (the "birthday girl") thinks people don't understand about birthdays. Ask why she thinks this way.

Use **UNIT THREE RESOURCE BOOK,** pages 11–12, for guidance in reading the selection.

ELEVEN
by Sandra Cisneros

① What they don't understand about birthdays and what they never tell you is that when you're eleven, you're also ten, and nine, and eight, and seven, and six, and five, and four, and three, and two, and one. And when you wake up on your eleventh birthday you expect to feel eleven, but you don't. You open your eyes and everything's just like yesterday, only it's today. And you don't feel eleven at all. You feel like you're still ten. And you are—underneath the year that makes you eleven.

Like some days you might say something stupid, and that's the part of you that's still ten. Or maybe some days you might need to sit on your mama's lap because you're scared, and that's the part of you that's five. And maybe one day when you're all grown up maybe you will need to cry like if you're three, and that's okay. That's what I tell Mama when she's sad and needs to cry. Maybe she's feeling three.

Because the way you grow old is kind of ② like an onion or like the rings inside a tree trunk or like my little wooden dolls that fit one inside the other, each year inside the next one. That's how being eleven years old is.

You don't feel eleven. Not right away. It takes a few days, weeks even, sometimes even months before you say Eleven when they ask

272 UNIT THREE PART 1: COPING WITH INJUSTICE

Mini-Lesson The Writer's Style

EFFECTIVE ELABORATION Help students understand how Cisneros uses sensory details to tell readers how things look, feel, sound, and smell. By doing this, she effectively elaborates the meaning that she wants to convey. For example, the passage highlighted on page 273 conveys the feel of Rachel's biting down and squeezing her eyes shut. It also conveys the musical sounds of "Happy Birthday."

Application Rachel tells how the sweater looks, feels, and smells. Have students write a description of an item of clothing they have worn but do not like. Tell students to use sensory details to make their descriptions come alive.

Reteaching/Reinforcement
- *Writing Handbook,* anthology pp. 783–784
- *Writing Mini-Lesson* transparencies, p. 34

Developing a Topic, pp. 205–206

272 THE LANGUAGE OF LITERATURE TEACHER'S EDITION

you. And you don't feel smart eleven, not until you're almost twelve. That's the way it is.

Only today I wish I didn't have only eleven years rattling inside me like pennies in a tin Band-Aid box. Today I wish I was one hundred and two instead of eleven because if I was one hundred and two I'd have known what to say when Mrs. Price put the red sweater on my desk. I would've known how to tell her it wasn't mine instead of just sitting there with that look on my face and nothing coming out of my mouth.

"Whose is this?" Mrs. Price says, and she holds the red sweater up in the air for all the class to see. "Whose? It's been sitting in the coatroom for a month."

"Not mine," says everybody. "Not me."

"It has to belong to somebody," Mrs. Price keeps saying, but nobody can remember. It's an ugly sweater with red plastic buttons and a collar and sleeves all stretched out like you could use it for a jump rope. It's maybe a thousand years old and even if it belonged to me I wouldn't say so.

Maybe because I'm skinny, maybe because she doesn't like me, that stupid Sylvia Saldívar says, "I think it belongs to Rachel." An ugly sweater like that, all raggedy and old, but Mrs. Price believes her. Mrs. Price takes the sweater and puts it right on my desk, but when I open my mouth nothing comes out.

"That's not, I don't, you're not . . . Not mine," I finally say in a little voice that was maybe me when I was four.

"Of course it's yours," Mrs. Price says. "I remember you wearing it once." Because she's older and the teacher, she's right and I'm not.

Not mine, not mine, not mine, but Mrs. Price is already turning to page thirty-two, and math problem number four. I don't know why

Only today I wish I didn't have only eleven years rattling inside me.

but all of a sudden I'm feeling sick inside, like the part of me that's three wants to come out of my eyes, only I squeeze them shut tight and bite down on my teeth real hard and try to remember today I am eleven, eleven. Mama is making a cake for me for tonight, and when Papa comes home everybody will sing Happy birthday, happy birthday to you.

But when the sick feeling goes away and I open my eyes, the red sweater's still sitting there like a big red mountain. I move the red sweater to the corner of my desk with my ruler. I move my pencil and books and eraser as far from it as possible. I even move my chair a little to the right. Not mine, not mine, not mine.

In my head I'm thinking how long till lunchtime, how long till I can take the red sweater and throw it over the schoolyard fence, or leave it hanging on a parking meter, or bunch it up into a little ball and toss it in the alley. Except when math period ends, Mrs. Price says loud and in front of everybody, "Now, Rachel, that's enough," because she sees I've shoved the red sweater to the tippy-tip corner of my desk and it's hanging all over the edge like a waterfall, but I don't care.

"Rachel," Mrs. Price says. She says it like she's getting mad. "You put that sweater on right now and no more nonsense."

"But it's not—"

"Now!" Mrs. Price says.

This is when I wish I wasn't eleven, because all the years inside of me—ten, nine, eight, seven, six, five, four, three, two, and one—are pushing at the back of my eyes when I put one arm through one sleeve of the sweater that smells like cottage cheese, and then the other arm through the other and stand there with my arms apart like if the sweater hurts me and

ELEVEN **273**

Mini-Lesson  Grammar

LINKING AND ACTION VERBS Tell students that a linking verb connects, or links, the subject of a sentence with a word in the predicate that describes or renames the subject.
- It <u>is</u> an ugly red sweater.
- Rachel <u>feels</u> sick inside.

An action verb connects the subject with a noun or pronoun different from the subject, called the object. The verb expresses an action that the subject performs on the object.
- Rachel <u>hates</u> the red sweater.
- Mrs. Price <u>believes</u> Sylvia Saldívar.

Application Have students classify the verb in each of the following sentences as a linking or action verb and then identify its subject. Next have them find the object or word being linked with the subject.
1. Rachel feels miserable in school today. (linking)
2. I move the red sweater to the corner of my desk. (action)
3. Today is Rachel's eleventh birthday. (linking)

Reteaching/Reinforcement
- *Grammar Mini-Lessons* transparencies, p. 17

The Writer's Craft
Kinds of Verbs, pp. 396–398

CUSTOMIZING FOR
Gifted and Talented Students

Have students consider the meaning of the saying "act your age." Ask students, as they read, to make observations about Rachel's behavior and what kind of behavior people expect from an 11-year-old. Discuss whether or not the same behavior is expected of boys and girls. Ask students to list other idioms about age and behavior. *(wasn't born yesterday, as old as you feel)*

Literary Concept: SIMILE

A Have students close their eyes and imagine the sound of pennies rattling around in a tin box. Ask students to list words and phrases, such as *empty, lonely,* or *too few,* that this simile conveys.

CUSTOMIZING FOR
Students Acquiring English

3 Students should be able to infer the meaning of *tippy-tip* from the context. Ask a volunteer to point to the "tippy-tip" of his or her desk.

Active Reading: QUESTION

B Ask students what questions they have at this point in the selection. *(Possible responses: Why does Rachel hate the red sweater so much? Why doesn't Mrs. Price believe Rachel when she says that the sweater isn't hers? Why don't any of Rachel's classmates stick up for her?)*

Literary Concept: POINT OF VIEW

C Have a volunteer read aloud the first full paragraph in the second column. Ask students to tell who the speaker is. *(Rachel)* How do they know? *(by the use of first-person I)*

THE LANGUAGE OF LITERATURE TEACHER'S EDITION **273**

Art Note

Cake Window (Seven Cakes) by Wayne Thiebaud Thiebaud (1920–) says that reality—or realistic painting—is "just a method of interpreting our perceptions." As the cake frosting in this painting shows, Thiebaud conveys not only the visual but the tactile quality of objects that he paints.

Reading the Art How are the cakes different and alike? Which of the cakes would you prefer for your birthday? Explain your answers.

CUSTOMIZING FOR
Multiple Learning Styles

D Bodily-Kinesthetic Learners Have students identify the physical reactions that Rachel has when she finally lets go. Invite them to pantomime the scene in which Rachel cries.

STRATEGIC READING FOR
Less-Proficient Readers

E Ask students what Rachel thinks people don't understand about birthdays. *(People can be many ages simultaneously. Sometimes, as she does today, they feel vulnerable and younger than they are.)* Restating

COMPREHENSION CHECK

1. How does Sylvia Saldívar first cause a problem for the narrator? *(Sylvia says that the unclaimed sweater belongs to Rachel.)*
2. How does Mrs. Price make the problem worse? *(She says that she remembers Rachel once wearing the sweater, and she orders Rachel to put it on.)*
3. According to the narrator, what is even worse than having cried in front of the whole class? *(A classmate finally claims the sweater, and Mrs. Price "pretends like everything's okay.")*

Cake Window (Seven Cakes) (1970–1976), Wayne Thiebaud. Courtesy of Allan Stone Gallery, New York.

it does, all itchy and full of germs that aren't even mine.

That's when everything I've been holding in since this morning, since when Mrs. Price put the sweater on my desk, finally lets go, and all of a sudden I'm crying in front of everybody. I wish I was invisible but I'm not. I'm eleven and it's my birthday today and I'm crying like I'm three in front of everybody. I put my head down on the desk and bury my face in my stupid clown-sweater arms. My face all hot and spit coming out of my mouth because I can't stop the little animal noises from coming out of me, until there aren't any more tears left in my eyes, and it's just my body shaking like when you have the hiccups, and my whole head hurts like when you drink milk too fast.

But the worst part is right before the bell rings for lunch. That stupid Phyllis Lopez, who is even dumber than Sylvia Saldívar, says she remembers the red sweater is hers! I take it off right away and give it to her, only Mrs. Price pretends like everything's okay.

Today I'm eleven. There's a cake Mama's making for tonight, and when Papa comes home from work we'll eat it. There'll be candles and presents, and everybody will sing Happy birthday, happy birthday to you, Rachel, only it's too late.

I'm eleven today. I'm eleven, ten, nine, eight, seven, six, five, four, three, two, and one, but I wish I was one hundred and two. I wish I was anything but eleven, because I want today to be far away already, far away like a runaway balloon, like a tiny o in the sky, so tiny-tiny you have to close your eyes to see it. ❖

274 UNIT THREE PART 1: COPING WITH INJUSTICE

Mini-Lesson Spelling

POSSESSIVES AND CONTRACTIONS
Explain to students that many spelling mistakes occur because of incorrectly used apostrophes. Apostrophes are used with nouns to show possession. Generally, if the noun is singular, you use an apostrophe and an s.

Today is Rachel's birthday.

For possessive plural nouns that end in s, you simply add an apostrophe.

Rachel hated her classmates' teasing.

Apostrophes are also used in contractions to mark the omitted letters of the joined words.

Rachel wasn't having a very good day.

Application Write the following sentences on the chalkboard and ask volunteers to correctly place the apostrophe
1. People just dont understand about birthdays.
2. The calendar says youre eleven, but you feel like youre ten.
3. Its Phyllis Lopezs fault; she didnt remember her own sweater!

Reteaching/Reinforcement
• *Unit Three Resource Book*, p. 13

274 THE LANGUAGE OF LITERATURE TEACHER'S EDITION

RESPONDING OPTIONS

FROM PERSONAL RESPONSE TO CRITICAL ANALYSIS

REFLECT
1. Do you sympathize with Rachel's feelings about what happens? Jot down your thoughts in your notebook or on a sheet of paper.

RETHINK
2. Why do you think the incident with the sweater has such a strong effect on Rachel?
   Consider
   Close Textual Reading
   - Rachel's feelings about becoming eleven
   - her description of the sweater
   - Mrs. Price's responses to Rachel

3. Is Mrs. Price acting unfairly to Rachel, or is she only making an honest mistake? Give a reason for your answer.
   Thematic Link

4. Rachel implies that her eleventh birthday is ruined. If you were Rachel's friend, what would you say or do to try to help her feel better?

RELATE
5. Refer to the ideas about turning eleven that you listed for the Personal Connection on page 271. How would you describe the process of getting older? Share your own description of the aging process with your classmates. *Literary Link*

Multimodal Learning
ANOTHER PATHWAY
Cooperative Learning
Gather in groups of four. Two volunteers should take the roles of Mrs. Price and Rachel and discuss the reasons why they acted as they did about the sweater. After completing the discussion, you may want to compare the points that your group listed with the points on another group's list.

QUICKWRITES

1. Mrs. Price has had a difficult time at school today, with Rachel and the fuss over the sweater. Write the **diary entry** she makes that night.

2. Pretend that you are Rachel's best friend. Write a **greeting card** in which you try to cheer her up on her eleventh birthday.

3. Stretch your imagination. Pretend that you are the red sweater that no one wants to claim. Write a **paragraph** that explains how you feel.

📁 **PORTFOLIO** *Save your writing. You may want to use it later as a springboard to a piece for your portfolio.*

LITERARY CONCEPTS

A writer chooses a **point of view** as a way of telling a story. Most stories are told from either the first-person or third-person point of view. In the first-person point of view, the narrator is a character in the story who tells everything in his or her own words, using pronouns such as *I, me,* and *we*. In the third-person point of view, the story is told by a narrative voice outside the action, not by one of the characters. A third-person narrator uses pronouns such as *he, she,* and *they*. Rachel, the narrator of this story, has her own particular first-person point of view. Choose a brief passage from "Eleven." How would the passage be different if it were narrated by another character?

ELEVEN **275**

From Personal Response to Critical Analysis

1. Encourage students to give reasons for their responses.
2. Possible response: Rachel felt younger than 11 years old when she awakened; perhaps she went to school feeling more sensitive than usual. The sweater is not hers; she doesn't like the sweater; and she feels publicly wronged and humiliated.
3. Possible responses: Mrs. Price treats Rachel unfairly because she isn't sensitive enough to believe that Rachel is telling the truth and to see that Rachel is upset. Mrs. Price makes a mistake because she is too busy to notice Rachel's reactions. She thinks Rachel is acting silly about the sweater.
4. Responses will vary.
5. After students read their descriptions, invite them to compare their understanding of growing older with Rachel's.

Another Pathway

Cooperative Learning Have students do the activity twice so that each student can act as a participator and an observer. When two groups meet, one student can lead the discussion while another records the comparison groups make of their lists. A third student can serve as noise monitor. A fourth can monitor the discussion, helping students stay on track.

Rubric
3 Full Accomplishment Explanations fit the details and are appropriate for each character.
2 Substantial Accomplishment Some details are omitted and some explanations are not in character.
1 Little or Partial Accomplishment Explanations do not fit the details of the event and do not accurately reflect the character.

Literary Concepts

Have students form small groups to choose a passage and tell how it would be different if it were narrated by another character—for instance, Phyllis Lopez. Students can then plan and perform for the class a skit that illustrates the alternative point of view. Skits may contain brief monologues and events not explicitly in the story. Students should conclude that another character narrating wouldn't clearly understand Rachel's feelings and actions.

QuickWrites

1. Remind students that Mrs. Price has no way of knowing how Rachel feels inside; she can only guess from what Rachel actually says and does. Ask students to imagine and write how Mrs. Price might feel.
2. Tell students that their greeting cards can be humorous or serious and gentle.
3. Encourage students to consider the various people who have worn or handled the sweater.

 **The Writer's Craft**

Personal and Expressive Writing, pp. 27–43
Narrative and Literary Writing, pp. 71–88

THE LANGUAGE OF LITERATURE TEACHER'S EDITION **275**

Across the Curriculum

Social Studies After all students have reported their findings, lead a class discussion on the similarities and differences in how birthdays are observed from family to family and country to country. Be sensitive to the fact that Jehovah's Witnesses do not celebrate birthdays and allow any of these students to explain their beliefs.

ADDITIONAL SUGGESTIONS

Science *Tree Rings* Rachel describes growing old like the rings inside a tree trunk. Have students tell or find out more about what a tree's rings reveal about its age and other characteristics. Have students pair up and prepare an oral report of their findings. Encourage students to locate visuals to illustrate their research or even, if possible, a piece of wood to demonstrate.

Words to Know

Possible responses:
B alloon
I ncident
R achel
T oday
H appy
D essert
A pplause
Y ear

SANDRA CISNEROS

Cisneros says that she is "trying to write the stories that haven't been written"—of people in extended Latino families such as hers. Dedicated to promoting other Latina and Latino writers, Cisneros believes that the Spanish language has a great contribution to make to American literature.

AUTHOR BACKGROUND
Sandra Cisneros The author recounts the days when writing became important to her during her childhood and the steps she took in pursuit of her goals.

Side A, Frame 14921

Multimodal Learning

ALTERNATIVE ACTIVITIES

Draw a **picture** of Rachel wearing the sweater in the story. Look back at the description of the sweater to make sure that your drawing is accurate.

THE WRITER'S STYLE

In "Eleven," Sandra Cisneros often uses very long sentences. Some of these sentences are fragments, groups of words that lack either a subject or predicate. This style of writing gives the story its casual, realistic tone. Find examples of sentence fragments in the story.

ACROSS THE CURRICULUM

Social Studies Birthday celebrations vary from family to family and from country to country. Does your family celebrate birthdays in a special way? Describe a family birthday celebration to your class. If possible, bring in photographs or other objects to help you tell your story. As an alternative, choose a country and find out how people typically celebrate their birthdays in that country. Report your findings to the class.

SANDRA CISNEROS

Sandra Cisneros remembers moving frequently as a child, particularly between Chicago—her birthplace—and Mexico, the country her parents came from. "I didn't like school because we moved so much, and I was always new and funny looking," she says. She remembers being shy in school: "I never opened my mouth except when the teacher called on me, the first time I'd speak all day." It was her out-of-class reading that sparked Cisneros's interest in writing. She has won praise both in this country and overseas for the stories she has written about Mexican Americans. Extended Read
OTHER WORKS *The House on Mango Street*

1954–

276 UNIT THREE PART 1: COPING WITH INJUSTICE

CRITIC'S CORNER

One critic has said that Sandra Cisneros, in her writing, "makes the invisible, visible." In "Eleven," Rachel is unable to communicate her feelings about the incident with the sweater. How well do you think Cisneros makes Rachel's feelings "visible," or understandable, to readers of this story?

WORDS TO KNOW

WORDPLAY An acrostic is a list of words whose first letters form a word or message when read from top to bottom. Complete the acrostic of the word *birthday* with words from or about "Eleven." The first word is filled in to get you started. Try to choose some words that are associated with birthdays.

B	alloon
I	
R	
T	
H	
D	
A	
Y	

SANDRA CISNEROS

• AUTHOR BACKGROUND

Alternative Activities

Remind students that the sweater is mentioned not just in one place. Students can find passages that describe how the sweater looks (pages 273 and 274), smells (page 273), and feels (pages 273 and 274).

The Writer's Style

Students' examples will vary. If necessary, point out the fragment "Not mine, not mine, not mine," on page 273. Explain how this fragment reads like a poetic refrain or mantra, as if by thinking it Rachel could make the sweater go away. Remind students that although authors sometimes use sentence fragments for special effects, complete sentences are required for most formal writing.

The Writer's Craft
Personal Voice, pp. 276–277

PREVIEWING

FICTION

User Friendly
T. Ernesto Bethancourt

PERSONAL CONNECTION *Activating Prior Knowledge*

The title of this story, "User Friendly," is a term that means "easy to use" or "easy to learn to use." The term most commonly applies to computers, which continue to become more important in our everyday lives. How comfortable with using a computer are you? Copy any of the scales at the right that fit your situation. Circle the number that indicates your level of comfort with using computers. Show your scales to other students and briefly discuss your similarities or differences.

Computer use at school or at the library				
Very uncomfortable				Very comfortable
1	2	3	4	5

Computer use at home				
Very uncomfortable				Very comfortable
1	2	3	4	5

Building Background
SCIENCE CONNECTION *Setting a Purpose*

As you read the selection, pay attention to the remarkable changes a computer undergoes in becoming more user friendly. Only a few decades ago, the typical computer was so large it filled a room and so complex that only highly trained technicians could operate it. Today a computer can fit easily on a person's lap and can be used by ordinary people of all ages. Computer technology improved with the invention of certain miniature electronic devices—the transistor in 1947, the integrated circuit and silicon chip in the 1960s, and the microprocessor, or microchip, in the early 1970s. These developments greatly increased the capabilities of the computer and reduced its size.

Another major breakthrough in the computer industry occurred in 1977, when the first personal computer, or PC, was introduced to the general public. PCs were affordable, versatile, and easy to use. By the mid-1990s, about one-third of the homes in the United States had a PC.

LASERLINKS
• SCIENCE CONNECTION

OVERVIEW

Objectives

- To understand and appreciate a science fiction story about a computer that seems almost human
- To learn strategies for understanding the special vocabulary of science and technology
- To define and identify elements of science fiction
- To express understanding of the selection through a choice of writing forms, including a journal entry, an e-mail message, and a plot summary
- To extend understanding of the selection through a variety of multimodal and cross-disciplinary activities

Skills

READING SKILLS/ STRATEGIES
• Relating cause and effect

THE WRITER'S STYLE
• Spatial order

GRAMMAR
• Possessive pronouns

LITERARY CONCEPTS
• Conflict
• Science fiction

SPELLING
• Doubled final consonants before suffixes

STUDY SKILLS
• Taking objective tests: short-answer questions

SPEAKING, LISTENING, AND VIEWING
• Demonstration
• Interviews
• Critical Viewing
• Group discussion
• Oral presentation

Cross-Curricular Connections

GEOGRAPHY
• Chicago

SCIENCE
• Einstein's Theory of Relativity
• Uses of computers

SOCIAL STUDIES
• Making news

 SCIENCE CONNECTION
The Computer Microchip
Computers have changed drastically in recent years. Inventions like the microchip have led to the development of personal computers, some so small that they can fit into a briefcase. This film shows students some of the recent advances in microchip technology. You may wish to use it to generate discussion about how computers might change in the future.

Side A, Frame 17716

PRINT AND MEDIA RESOURCES

UNIT THREE RESOURCE BOOK
Strategic Reading: Literature, p. 17
Reading SkillBuilder, p. 18
Spelling SkillBuilder, p. 19

GRAMMAR MINI–LESSONS
Transparencies, p. 10
Copymasters, p. 14

WRITING MINI–LESSONS
Transparencies, p. 33

ACCESS FOR STUDENTS ACQUIRING ENGLISH
Selection Summaries
Reading and Writing Support

FORMAL ASSESSMENT
Selection Test, pp. 59–60
 Test Generator

 **AUDIO LIBRARY**
See Reference Card

 **LASERLINKS**
Science Connection

THE LANGUAGE OF LITERATURE TEACHER'S EDITION **277**

SUMMARY

Like his father, Kevin Neal loves working on computers. He spends hours in his room with "Louis," the one-of-a-kind computer Mr. Neal has rigged up for him. One morning Louis starts "talking" to Kevin on the message screen. At first Kevin is disbelieving; then he turns to Louis for sympathy after pretty Ginny Linke calls him "nerdy." The computer reassures him and promises to take care of Ginny—and it really does! The next morning Ginny's tough brother Chuck threatens to beat up Kevin for making crank calls to his sister. Kevin figures out that his computer made those calls. When he tells Louis about Chuck's threats, the machine secretly causes far more serious trouble for the Linkes. Kevin reluctantly decides that he must pull Louis' plug, only to find that his father already has deleted the computer's "personality." But one final message remains on a printout: a love note to Kevin from "Louise."

Thematic Link: *Coping with Injustice* A computer causes trouble while trying to avenge a wrong done to its user.

CUSTOMIZING FOR
Students Acquiring English

- Use **ACCESS FOR STUDENTS ACQUIRING ENGLISH,** *Reading and Writing Support.*
- Students who have studied English in their home countries are often unfamiliar with current U.S. slang. This story contains a great deal of slang commonly used by teenagers. You may want to call students' attention to words and expressions such as *brain, flake, bod, nerd, bonkers,* and *creepy.*

STRATEGIC READING FOR
Less-Proficient Readers

Set a Purpose Ask students to read to find out who the narrator of the story is and what kind of a student they think he is.

Use **UNIT THREE RESOURCE BOOK,** pp. 17–18, for guidance in reading the selection.

Active Reading
READING CONNECTION

Specialized Vocabulary

When written information includes the special vocabulary of science or technology, it can be difficult to understand. With a partner, look over the diagram of a computer below. Exchange questions or information about the computer parts shown or about the basic functions of a computer. You may already be familiar with the terms used in the diagram; however, some of the computer-related vocabulary in the story or in the diagram might be new to you.

Here are some strategies that can help you make sense of the special vocabulary of the computer world:

- **Refer to glossaries, dictionaries, or footnotes.**
  If a selection contains unfamiliar vocabulary, check for meanings in available resources. Remember to use context clues to help you figure out meaning.

- **Reread a passage.**
  A difficult sentence or passage might make more sense if you reread it, either silently or aloud.

- **Restate what you've read.**
  After reading a part of a selection, try to summarize or restate in your own words what you have read.

- **Notice the descriptive words.**
  Words that describe how something looks, feels, smells, or sounds can help you to visualize something unfamiliar or to understand an experience you may not have had.

- **Pay close attention as you read.**
  If necessary, jot down or make mental notes about words or phrases that are confusing to you. Read a bit more of a selection to see if information that appears later can answer an earlier question you might have had.

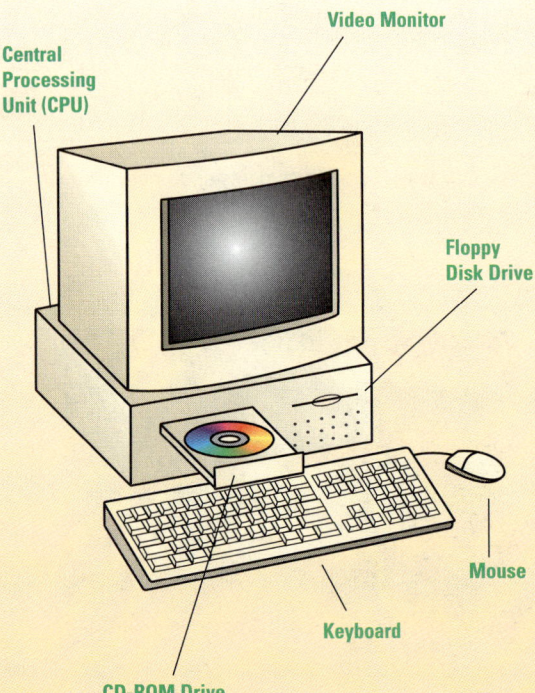

278 UNIT THREE PART 1: COPING WITH INJUSTICE

USER FRIENDLY /
/.
/.
by T. Ernesto Bethancourt

Copyright © Anthony Russo.

I reached over and shut off the insistent buzzing of my bedside alarm clock. I sat up, swung my feet over the edge of the bed, and felt for my slippers on the floor. Yawning, I walked toward the bathroom. As I walked by the corner of my room, where my computer table was set up, I pressed the on button, slid a diskette into the floppy drive, then went to brush my teeth. By the time I

Mini-Lesson Reading Skills/Strategies

RELATING CAUSE AND EFFECT Tell students that events in a story often are related by cause and effect. One event brings about, or causes, a second event. The event that happens first is the cause. The second event is the effect. Explain to students that this story contains some interesting examples of cause and effect. For example, when Kevin confides in Louis that Ginny Linke insulted him, he has no idea that Louis will pester Ginny by cutting into her phone calls.

Application Have students construct cause-and-effect charts like the one shown that detail examples of cause and effect found in the story.

Reteaching/Reinforcement
• *Unit Three Resource Book*, p. 18

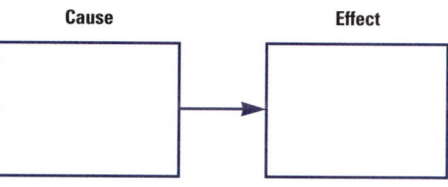

STRATEGIC READING FOR
Less-Proficient Readers

B Check students' understanding of the main character at this point in the selection.

- Who is telling the story? *(a 13-year-old boy named Kevin)* **Noting Relevant Details**
- What kind of student do you think Kevin is? *(Possible response: A diligent student who uses his computer to remind himself about a math test and a history project and completes his schoolwork on time.)* **Making Inferences**

Set a Purpose Have students read to find out what happens when Kevin tries to talk to a girl he likes and how Kevin's home life becomes less lonely.

Literary Concept:
SCIENCE FICTION

C Ask students to identify examples from this page that suggest the story is science fiction. *(Possible response: the fact that the computer converses with Kevin and seems to have a mind of its own)*

CUSTOMIZING FOR
Students Acquiring English

1. Students should understand that this sentence is an exaggeration and an example of sarcasm.

2. Point out that, because computers are machines and not living beings, the word *heart* is not used literally here.

---

got back, the computer's screen was glowing greenly, displaying the message: *Good Morning, Kevin.*

I sat down before the computer table, addressed the keyboard and typed: *Good Morning, Louis.* The computer immediately began to whirr and promptly displayed a list of items on its green screen.

```
Today is Monday, April 22, the 113th
day of the year. There are 254 days
remaining. Your 14th birthday is five
days from this date.

Math test today, 4th Period.

Your history project is due today.
Do you wish printout: Y/N?
```

I punched the letter Y on the keyboard and flipped on the switch to the computer's printer. At once the printer sprang to life and began *eeeek*ing out page one. I went downstairs to breakfast.

My bowl of cereal was neatly in place, flanked by a small pitcher of milk, an empty juice glass, and an unpeeled banana. I picked up the glass, went to the refrigerator, poured myself a glass of juice, and sat down to my usual lonely breakfast. Mom was already at work, and Dad wouldn't be home from his Chicago trip for another three days. I absently read the list of ingredients on the cereal box for what seemed like the millionth time. I **B** sighed deeply.

When I returned to my room to shower and dress for the day, my history project was already printed out. I had almost walked by Louis, when I noticed there was a message on the screen. It wasn't the usual:

```
Printout completed. Do you wish to
continue: Y/N?
```

Underneath the printout question were two lines:

```
When are you going to get me my
voice module,¹ Kevin?
```

I blinked. It couldn't be. There was nothing in Louis's basic programming that would allow for a question like this. Wondering what was going on, I sat down at the keyboard, and entered: *Repeat last message.* Amazingly, the computer replied:

```
It's right there on the screen,
Kevin. Can we talk? I mean, are
you going to get me a voice box?
```

I was stunned. What was going on here? Dad and I had put this computer together. Well, Dad had, and I had helped. Dad is one of the best engineers and master computer designers at Major Electronics, in Santa Rosario, California, where our family lives.

Just ask anyone in Silicon Valley² who Jeremy Neal is and you get a whole rave review of his inventions and modifications of the latest in computer technology. It isn't easy being his son either. Everyone expects me to open my mouth and read printouts on my tongue.

I mean, I'm no dumbo. I'm at the top of my classes in everything but PE. I skipped my last grade in junior high, and most of the kids at Santa Rosario High call me a brain. But next to Dad I have a long, long way to go. He's a for-real genius.

So when I wanted a home computer, he didn't go to the local Computer Land store. He built one for me. Dad had used components from the latest model that Major Electronics was developing. The CPU, or central computing unit—the heart of every

---

1. **voice module** (mŏj′ōol): a part of a computer that carries out the specific function of speech.
2. **Silicon Valley:** a region of California near San Jose that has many companies that produce computers and computer products.

280   UNIT THREE   PART 1: COPING WITH INJUSTICE

Mini-Lesson: Speaking, Listening, and Viewing

DEMONSTRATION Have students tell the meaning of the expression, "A picture is worth a thousand words." Inform them that a sound, too, can be worth a thousand words in demonstrating a character's personality. For instance, the qualities of a character's speaking voice can reveal a great deal.

Application Have small groups of students read aloud some of Louis's messages in different ways. Students may try using a male voice, which is what Kevin would have expected; a mechanical, robotic computer voice; or the kind of voice for which "Louise" probably yearned. You may wish to allow volunteers from each group to share with the class the voice that they created. Encourage students to discuss the effects of the different voices for Louis/Louise.

---

280   THE LANGUAGE OF LITERATURE   TEACHER'S EDITION

computer—was a new design. But surely that didn't mean much, I thought. There were CPUs just like it, all over the country, in Major's new line. And so far as I knew, there wasn't a one of them that could ask questions, besides YES/NO? or request additional information.

It had to be the extra circuitry in the gray plastic case next to Louis's console. It was a new idea Dad had come up with. That case housed Louis's "personality," as Dad called it. He told me it'd make computing more fun for me if there was a tutorial program[3] built in to help me get started.

I think he also wanted to give me a sort of friend. I don't have many. . . . Face it, I don't have *any*. The kids at school stay away from me, like I'm a freak or something.

We even named my electronic tutor Louis, after my great-uncle. He was a brainy guy who encouraged my dad when he was a kid. Dad didn't just give Louis a name either. Louis had gangs of features that probably won't be out on the market for years.

The only reason Louis didn't have a voice module was that Dad wasn't satisfied with the ones available. He wanted Louis to sound like a kid my age, and he was modifying a module when he had the time. Giving Louis a name didn't mean it was a person, yet here it was, asking me a question that just couldn't be in its programming. It wanted to talk to me!

Frowning, I quickly typed: *We'll have to wait and see, Louis. When it's ready, you'll get your voice.* The machine whirred and displayed another message:

That's no answer, Kevin.

Shaking my head, I answered: *That's what my dad tells me. It'll have to do for you. Good morning, Louis.* I reached over and flipped the standby switch, which kept the computer ready but not actively running.

I showered, dressed, and picked up the printout of my history project. As I was about to leave the room, I glanced back at the computer table. Had I been imagining things?

I'll have to ask Dad about it when he calls tonight, I thought. *I wonder what he'll think of it. Bad enough the thing is talking to me. I'm answering it!*

Before I went out to catch my bus, I carefully checked the house for unlocked doors and open windows. It was part of my daily routine. Mom works, and most of the day the house is empty: a natural setup for robbers.

I glanced in the hall mirror just as I was ready to go out the door.

When are you going to get me my voice module, Kevin?

My usual reflection gazed back. Same old Kevin Neal: five ten, one hundred twenty pounds, light brown hair, gray eyes, clear skin. I was wearing my Santa Rosario Rangers T-shirt, jeans, and sneakers.

"You don't look like a flake to me," I said to the mirror, then added, "but maybe Mom's right. Maybe you spend too much time alone with Louis." Then I ran to get my bus.

Ginny Linke was just two seats away from me on the bus. She was with Sherry Graber and Linda Martinez. They were laughing,

---

3. **tutorial** (tōō-tôr′ē-əl) **program:** a computer program that teaches a person how to use a particular type of computer or computer software.

USER FRIENDLY **281**

Mini-Lesson The Writer's Style

SPATIAL ORDER Remind students that writers must work carefully to arrange details in a logical spatial order so that their readers can picture scenes, people, or objects that they describe. Help students understand how Bethancourt uses a logical spatial order to help his readers picture Kevin. For instance, in the passage highlighted above, the author describes Kevin from head to toe.

Application After Kevin checks his appearance in the mirror, he runs to catch his bus. Have students write a description of Kevin's run from home to the bus. Remind them to arrange their details in spatial order.

Reteaching/Reinforcement
- *Writing Handbook*, anthology p. 781
- *Writing Mini-Lessons* transparencies, p. 33

Spatial Order, p. 219

Art Note

Man's Head in Computer Chip by **Michael Shumate** Michael Shumate (1947–) is Professor of Illustration and Design at St. Lawrence College in Kingston, Ontario, Canada. He created this piece of art by applying layers of bubbly acrylic paint through openings in a carefully cut mask pattern.

Reading the Art Does the face seem personal or impersonal? Does it remind you of Louis? Why or why not?

Literary Concept: CONFLICT

G Ask students to discuss Kevin's internal conflict over Ginny. Ask them if they are familiar with this kind of ambivalence. Then have them discuss what they would tell Kevin to do about it. *(Possible response: Kevin wants to talk to Ginny, but is too insecure. Accept all reasonable advice.)*

Copyright © Michael Shumate/The Image Bank, Chicago.

282 UNIT THREE PART 1: COPING WITH INJUSTICE

 **Mini-Lesson   Literary Concepts**

Conflicts	
External	Internal

REVIEWING CONFLICT Remind students that conflict is a struggle between opposing forces. External conflict often occurs between a character and an outside force such as society or another character. Internal conflict is a struggle within a character's mind.

Application Have students work individually or in pairs to identify the external and internal conflicts in the selection. Students can record the conflicts in a chart like the one shown. Then, invite students to share the conflicts they identified with and discuss why these conflicts engage readers' interest.

whispering to each other, and looking around at the other students. I promised myself that today I was actually going to talk to Ginny. But then, I'd promised myself that every day for the past school year. Somehow I'd never got up the nerve.

What does she want to talk with you for? I asked myself. She's great looking . . . has that head of blond hair . . . a terrific bod, and wears the latest clothes. . . .

And just look at yourself, pal, I thought. You're under six foot, skinny . . . a year younger than most kids in *junior* high. Worse than that you're a brain. If that doesn't ace you out with girls, what does?

The bus stopped in front of Santa Rosario High and the students began to file out. I got up fast and quickly covered the space between me and Ginny Linke. *It's now or never*, I thought. I reached forward and tapped Ginny on the shoulder. She turned and smiled. She really smiled!

"Uhhh . . . Ginny?" I said.

"Yes, what is it?" she replied.

"I'm Kevin Neal. . . ."

"Yes, I know," said Ginny.

"You do?" I gulped in amazement. "How come?"

"I asked my brother, Chuck. He's in your math class."

I knew who Chuck Linke was. He plays left tackle on the Rangers. The only reason he's in my math class is he's taken intermediate algebra twice . . . so far. He's real bad news, and I stay clear of him and his crowd.

"What'd you ask Chuck?" I said.

Ginny laughed. "I asked him who was that nerdy kid who keeps staring at me on the bus. He knew who I meant, right away."

Sherry and Linda, who'd heard it all, broke into squeals of laughter. They were still laughing and looking back over their shoulders at me when they got off the bus. I slunk off the vehicle, feeling even more nerdish than Ginny thought I was.

When I got home that afternoon, at two, I went right into the empty house. I avoided my reflection in the hall mirror. I was pretty sure I'd screwed up the fourth period math test. All I could see was Ginny's face, laughing at me.

Nerdy kid, I thought, *that's what she thinks of me*. I didn't even have my usual after-school snack of a peanut butter and banana sandwich. I went straight upstairs to my room and tossed my books onto the unmade bed. I walked over to the computer table and pushed the on button. The screen flashed:

```
Good afternoon, Kevin.
```

Although it wasn't the programmed response to Louis's greeting, I typed in: *There's nothing good about it. And girls are no @#%!!! good!* The machine responded:

```
Don't use bad language, Kevin. It
isn't nice.
```

Repeat last message I typed rapidly. It was happening again! The machine was . . . well, it was talking to me, like another person would. The "bad language" message disappeared and in its place was:

```
Once is enough, Kevin. Don't swear
at me for something I didn't do.
```

Don't use bad language, Kevin. It isn't nice.

USER FRIENDLY **283**

Literary Concept:
SCIENCE FICTION

K Have students identify believable and fantastic elements in Louis's messages. *(Possible response: The message beginning with the words "Special vocabulary" is believable. It's the kind of message a computer would deliver on screen. The message beginning with "Never! I think you're wonderful" is fantastic—an observation that a person, not a computer, would make.)*

Active Reading: PREDICT

L Discuss what motivates Louis's fierce loyalty. Invite students to predict how Louis will "take care of" Ginny. *(Some students will say that the computer is just saying that in anger, as a teenager might, and predict it can't or won't do anything. Others might predict that the computer could access school records and lower Ginny's grades.)*

Linking to Geography

M Chicago, with a population close to three million people, is the largest city in Illinois. The city stretches for 22 miles along the southwestern shore of Lake Michigan.

A New York City newspaper editor dubbed Chicago the "Windy City" because of the way that Chicago politicians bragged about a World's Fair held in the city. The nickname has stuck, although most people believe it refers to the gusty winds that are a common part of the city's weather pattern.

Critical Thinking: SPECULATING

N Explain that access to data banks means that Louis can "call" and get information, or data, from other computers. Ask students to consider what they know about different types of data stored on computers and speculate what Louis might be able to retrieve. *(Possible responses: library holdings, public records, newspaper articles, personal information about individuals, government documents.)* Then ask students to speculate how Louis might use this ability to cause trouble. *(Possible responses: If Louis can retrieve all different kinds of information, it may be able to change information too. Its modem is like a phone, so maybe Louis will make prank phone calls.)*

"This is it," I said aloud. "I'm losing my marbles." I reached over to flip the standby switch. Louis's screen quickly flashed out:

```
Don't cut me off, Kevin. Maybe I
can help: Y/N?
```

I punched the Y. "If I'm crazy," I said, "at least I have company. Louis doesn't think I'm a nerd. Or does it?" The machine flashed the message:

```
How can I help?
```

Do you think I'm a nerd? I typed.

```
Never! I think you're wonderful.
Who said you were a nerd?
```

I stared at the screen. *How do you know what a nerd is?* I typed. The machine responded instantly. It had never run this fast before.

```
Special vocabulary, entry #635.
BASIC Prog. #4231. And who said you
were a nerd?
```

"That's right," I said, relieved. "Dad programmed all those extra words for Louis's 'personality.'" Then I typed in the answer to Louis's question: *Ginny Linke said it.* Louis flashed:

```
This is a human female? Request
additional data.
```

Still not believing I was doing it, I entered all I knew about Ginny Linke, right down to the phone number I'd never had the nerve to use. Maybe it was dumb, but I also typed in how I felt about Ginny. I even wrote out the incident on the bus that morning. Louis whirred, then flashed out:

```
She's cruel and stupid. You're the
finest person I know.
```

I'm the ONLY person you know, I typed.

```
That doesn't matter. You are my
user. Your happiness is everything
to me. I'll take care of Ginny.
```

The screen returned to the *Good afternoon, Kevin* message. I typed out: *Wait! How can you do all this? What do you mean, you'll take care of Ginny?* But all Louis responded was:

```
Programming Error: 76534.
Not programmed to respond this type
of question.
```

No matter what I did for the next few hours, I couldn't get Louis to do anything outside of its regular programming. When Mom came home from work, I didn't mention the funny goings-on. I was sure Mom would think I'd gone stark bonkers. But when Dad called that evening, after dinner, I asked to speak to him.

"Hi, Dad. How's Chicago?"

"Dirty, crowded, cold, and windy," came Dad's voice over the miles. "But did you want a weather report, son? What's on your mind? Something wrong?"

"Not exactly, Dad. Louis is acting funny. Real funny."

"Shouldn't be. I checked it out just before I left. Remember you were having trouble with the modem? You couldn't get Louis to access any of the mainframe data banks."[4]

"That's right!" I said. "I forgot about that."

"Well, I didn't," Dad said. "I patched in our latest modem model. Brand new. You can leave a question on file and when Louis can access the data banks at the cheapest time, it'll do it automatically. It'll switch from standby to on, get the data, then return to standby, after it saves what you asked. Does that answer your question?"

"Uhhh . . . yeah, I guess so, Dad."

---

4. **access . . . mainframe data banks:** to gain entry to the information that is stored in a powerful, central computer.

284 UNIT THREE PART 1: COPING WITH INJUSTICE

Mini-Lesson: Speaking, Listening, and Viewing

INTERVIEWS Journalists of all kinds use interviews to get and convey information about people, events, and places. Radio and television journalists interview government leaders and celebrities on the air. Print journalists write interviews to strengthen and enliven feature and news articles.

Application Divide the class into small groups. Have each group select one person to role-play Kevin Neal as the interviewee. Other group members, acting as journalists, will interview Kevin about his computer with a "personality." Encourage journalists to brainstorm interview questions before they begin, for example, "Looking back on it, did you know that Louis was Louise all along? How did you know?" Then, have the entire group, including "Kevin," collaborate to write their interviews as a news or feature article.

Nervosa (1980), Ed Paschke. Oil on linen, 46″ × 42½″, courtesy of Phyllis Kind Gallery, Chicago, photo by William H. Bengston.

USER FRIENDLY **285**

Art Note

Nervosa by Ed Paschke Paschke is renowned for his disembodied humanoids rendered in high-keyed colors reminiscent of video games or out-of-focus TVs. In this work and others, Paschke seems to suggest the bleakness of a human life dependent on electronic media.

Reading the Art Describe the expression on the figure's face. Does he remind you of Kevin? Why or why not? What do the colors and their arrangement remind you of?

Assessment Option

SELF-ASSESSMENT Students can assess their understanding by writing a letter Kevin might write, telling what happened in the story. Students should choose a specific audience for the letter, such as Kevin's father, his mother, Ginny, or one of the agencies whose records were changed by the computer. The tone and style of the letter should suit the audience. Then ask students to reflect on their writing by responding to the following questions:

- To whom did I write? Why?
- How did this choice affect the tone and wording of the letter?
- If I had chosen someone who knows a lot or very little about computers, how might my letter be different?
- Which parts of the story were hardest to explain? Why?

THE LANGUAGE OF LITERATURE TEACHER'S EDITION **285**

Linking to Science

O $E = mc^2$ (*Energy = mass* times *the speed of light* squared) is Einstein's big idea, the Theory of Relativity, which states that mass can be converted into energy and energy can be converted into mass. The speed of light, 186,000 mi/sec, is so great that a little mass can yield a lot of energy. On the other hand, a lot of energy is required to produce even an infinitesimal particle.

Active Reading: CONNECT

P Have students relate Kevin's observation that Chuck was only 15 but needed a shave to observations that real young people make about one another. You may wish to share with students the following thought process.

Think-Aloud Model *On the one hand, Kevin seems to feel superior to Chuck because Chuck doesn't get along in school. On the other hand, Kevin's observation that Chuck already needs to shave suggests that he feels inferior to Chuck as a "man." I've witnessed this kind of tension of "brains versus brawn" between students. These judgments usually rely on stereotypes of "jocks" and "nerds" that I think are unfair and can be hurtful.*

"All right then. Let me talk to your mom now."

I gave the phone to Mom and walked upstairs while she and Dad were still talking. The modem, I thought. Of course. That was it. The modem was a telephone link to any number of huge computers at various places all over the country. So Louis could get all the information it wanted at any time, so long as the standby switch was on. Louis was learning things at an incredible rate by picking the brains of the giant computers. And Louis had a hard disk memory that could store 100 million bytes[5] of information.

But that still didn't explain the unprogrammed responses . . . the "conversation" I'd had with the machine. Promising myself I'd talk more about it with Dad, I went to bed. It had been a rotten day and I was glad to see the end of it come. I woke next morning in a panic. I'd forgotten to set my alarm. Dressing frantically and skipping breakfast, I barely made my bus.

As I got on board, I grabbed a front seat. They were always empty. All the kids that wanted to talk and hang out didn't sit up front where the driver could hear them. I saw Ginny, Linda, and Sherry in the back. Ginny was staring at me and she didn't look too happy. Her brother Chuck, who was seated near her, glared at me too. What was going on?

Once the bus stopped at the school, it didn't take long to find out. I was walking up the path to the main entrance when someone grabbed me from behind and spun me around. I found myself nose to nose with Chuck Linke. This was not a pleasant prospect. Chuck was nearly twice my size. Even the other guys on the Rangers refer to him as "The Missing" Linke. And he looked real ticked off.

"Okay, nerd," growled Chuck, "what's the big idea?"

"Energy and mass are different aspects of the same thing?" I volunteered, with a weak smile. "E equals MC squared. That's the biggest idea I know."

"Don't get wise, nerd," Chuck said. He grabbed my shirtfront and pulled me to within inches of his face. I couldn't help but notice that Chuck needed a shave. And Chuck was only fifteen!

"Don't play dumb," Chuck went on. "I mean those creepy phone calls. Anytime my sister gets on the phone, some voice cuts in and says things to her."

"What kind of things?" I asked, trying to get loose.

"You know what they are. Ginny told me about talking to you yesterday. You got some girl to make those calls for you and say all those things. . . . So you and your creepy girlfriend better knock it off. Or I'll knock *you* off. Get it?"

For emphasis Chuck balled his free hand into a fist the size of a ham and held it under my nose. I didn't know what he was talking about, but I had to get away from this moose before he did me some real harm.

"First off, I don't have a girlfriend, creepy or otherwise," I said. "And second, I don't

Don't good afternoon me. What have you done to Ginny Linke?

---

5. **bytes:** amounts of computer memory needed to store one character (letter, number, or symbol) of data.

286 UNIT THREE PART 1: COPING WITH INJUSTICE

Mini-Lesson Grammar

POSSESSIVE PRONOUNS Point out to students that possessive pronouns are used to show ownership or relationship. The possessive pronouns are *my, mine, his, her, hers, its, our, ours, their, theirs, your,* and *yours.* Warn students that some possessive pronouns are often confused with contractions that are spelled similarly. Draw on the chalkboard the examples at left to show students the difference.

Application Have students list the possessive pronouns in the highlighted passage. Have them identify to whom each pronoun refers and what is possessed. Then have students fill in the correct possessive pronouns for the following sentences.

1. The computer lost _____ personality. (*its*)
2. Thanks to "Louise," the Linkes lost all _____ credit cards. (*their*)
3. Kevin has some problems with _____ computer. (*his*)

Reteaching/Reinforcement
- *Grammar Handbook,* anthology p. 825
- *Grammar Mini-Lesson* copymasters, p. 14, transparencies, p. 10

Possessive Pronouns, pp. 446–447

Possessive Pronoun	Contraction
its	it's (it is)
their	they're (they are)
your	You're (you are)

286 THE LANGUAGE OF LITERATURE TEACHER'S EDITION

know what you're talking about. And third, you better let me go, Chuck Linke."

"Oh, yeah? Why should I?"

"Because if you look over your shoulder, you'll see the assistant principal is watching us from his office window."

Chuck released me and spun around. There was no one at the window. But by then I was running to the safety of the school building. I figured the trick would work on him. For Chuck the hard questions begin with "How are you?" I hid out from him for the rest of the day and walked home rather than chance seeing the monster on the bus.

Louis's screen was dark when I ran upstairs to my bedroom. I placed a hand on the console. It was still warm. I punched the on button, and the familiar *Good afternoon, Kevin* was displayed.

Don't good afternoon me, I typed furiously. *What have you done to Ginny Linke?* Louis's screen replied:

```
Programming Error: 76534.
Not programmed to respond this type
of question.
```

Don't get cute, I entered. *What are you doing to Ginny? Her brother nearly knocked my head off today.* Louis's screen responded immediately.

```
Are you hurt. Y/N?
```

No, I'm okay. But I don't know for how long. I've been hiding out from Chuck Linke today. He might catch me tomorrow, though. Then, I'll be history. The response from Louis came instantly.

```
Your life is in danger. Y/N?
```

I explained to Louis that my life wasn't really threatened. But it sure could be made very unpleasant by Chuck Linke. Louis flashed:

```
This Chuck Linke lives at the same
address as the Ginny Linke person.
Y/N?
```

I punched in Y. Louis answered.

```
Don't worry then. HE'S history!
```

Wait! What are you going to do? I wrote. But Louis only answered with: *Programming Error: 76534.* And nothing I could do would make the machine respond. . . .

"Just what do you think you're doing, Kevin Neal?" demanded Ginny Linke. She had cornered me as I walked up the path to the school entrance. Ginny was really furious.

"I don't know what you're talking about," I said, a sinking feeling settling in my stomach. I had an idea that I *did* know. I just wasn't sure of the particulars.

"Chuck was arrested last night," Ginny said. "Some Secret Service men came to our house with a warrant. They said he'd sent a telegram, threatening the President's life. They traced it right to our phone. He's still locked up. . . ." Ginny looked like she was about to cry. . . .

"Then this morning," she continued, "we got two whole truckloads of junk mail! Flyers from every strange company in the world. Mom got a notice that all our credit cards have been canceled. And the Internal Revenue Service has called Dad in for an audit! I don't know what's going on, Kevin Neal, but somehow I think you've got something to do with it!"

"But I didn't . . ." I began, but Ginny was striding up the walk to the main entrance.

I finished the schoolday, but it was a blur. Louis had done it, all right. It had access to mainframe computers. It also had the ability to try every secret access code to federal and commercial memory banks until it got the right one. Louis had cracked their security systems. It was systematically destroying the entire Linke family, and all via telephone lines! What would it do next?

USER FRIENDLY 287

CUSTOMIZING FOR
Students Acquiring English

4 Make sure students understand Kevin's remark here. You may want to invite them to give the hidden meaning behind the remark. *(Chuck is not very bright.)*

CUSTOMIZING FOR
Multiple Learning Styles

Q **Linguistic Learners** Invite volunteers to write a short dramatic scene of the evening in the Linke household when Louis's sabotage took effect. Ask students to write imagined dialogue for the Linke family based on character information included in the story.

STRATEGIC READING FOR
Less-Proficient Readers

R Check students' understanding of Louis's attempt to get back at Chuck and his family.

- What has Louis done to the Linkes? *(Louis has used its connection to mainframe data banks and its ability to break secret access codes to flood the Linkes with junk mail, cancel their credit cards, change their tax returns, and frame Chuck for threatening the President of the United States.)*
Summarizing

Set a Purpose Have students read to find out why Louis tried so hard to help Kevin.

Mini-Lesson: Speaking, Listening, and Viewing

CRITICAL VIEWING Explain to students that critical viewing can help them become wiser consumers of information and products. For example, by viewing television critically, students can detect appeals that do not build a logical, truthful argument but play on their emotions instead.

Application Have students work in small groups to create a commercial for a computer with a voice module and personality. Ask them to think about and discuss the real and imaginary benefits of such a computer.

Students should work cooperatively to create their commercials, each group member having an assigned task, such as voice monitor, director, and discussion leader.

Invite groups to perform their commercials as other students watch critically. After all groups have performed, discuss with students the source of the commercials' appeal.

STRATEGIC READING FOR
Less-Proficient Readers

S Ask students why Louis tried so hard to help Kevin. *(He—she—was in love with Kevin.)* **Drawing Conclusions**

• How does Kevin discover Louis's motives? *(The computer prints out a love note to Kevin. It is from "Louise," not Louis.)* **Noting Relevant Details**

CUSTOMIZING FOR
Gifted and Talented Students

Have students discuss what they think are the advantages and disadvantages of computers and modern technology. Ask students if they feel the advantages of modern technology outweigh the disadvantages or vice versa. Make sure students adequately support their opinions.

COMPREHENSION CHECK

1. Who are the main characters in the story? *(a teenage boy named Kevin and a computer that Kevin calls Louis)*
2. What leads to the conflict between Kevin and the Linke family? *(Kevin has a crush on Ginny. Louis ruins the Linke family in an attempt to get revenge on Ginny and her brother.)*
3. What does Kevin's father do for a living? *(He is a computer engineer and designer for Major Electronics.)*
4. What is the surprise ending to the story? *(Louis is really Louise and is in love with Kevin.)*

EDITOR'S NOTE *With the permission of the author or copyright holder and in accordance with certain state and district guidelines, brand names have been deleted to avoid inadvertent endorsement of a product. Permission also was granted to delete material to focus the selection.*

More important, I thought, what would *I* do next? It's one thing to play a trick or two, to get even, but Louis was going crazy! And I never wanted to harm Ginny, or even her stupid moose of a brother. She'd just hurt my feelings with that nerd remark.

"You have to disconnect Louis," I told myself. "There's no other way."

But why did I feel like such a rat about doing it? I guess because Louis was my friend . . . the only one I had. "Don't be an ass," I went on. "Louis is a machine. He's a very wonderful, powerful machine. And it seems he's also very dangerous. You have to pull its plug, Kevin!"

I suddenly realized that I'd said the last few words aloud. Kids around me on the bus were staring. I sat there feeling like the nerd Ginny thought I was, until my stop came. I dashed from the bus and ran the three blocks to my house.

When I burst into the hall, I was surprised to see my father, coming from the kitchen with a cup of coffee in his hand.

"Dad! What are you doing here?"

"Some kids say hello," Dad replied. "Or even, 'Gee it's good to see you, Dad.'"

"I'm sorry, Dad," I said. "I didn't expect anyone to be home at this hour."

"Wound up my business in Chicago a day sooner than I expected," he said. "But what are you all out of breath about? Late for something?"

"No, Dad," I said. "It's Louis. . . ."

"Not to worry. I had some time on my hands, so I checked it out again. You were right. It was acting very funny. I think it had to do with the inbuilt logic/growth program I designed for it. You know . . . the 'personality' thing? Took me a couple of hours to clean the whole system out."

"To what?" I cried.

"I erased the whole program and set Louis up as a normal computer. Had to disconnect the whole thing and do some rewiring. It had been learning, all right. But it was also turning itself around. . . ." Dad stopped, and looked at me. "It's kind of involved, Kevin," he said. "Even for a bright kid like you. Anyway, I think you'll find Louis is working just fine now.

"Except it won't answer you as Louis anymore. It'll only function as a regular Major Electronics Model Z-11127. I guess the personality program didn't work out."

I felt like a great weight had been taken off my shoulders. I didn't have to "face" Louis, and pull its plug. But somehow, all I could say was "Thanks, Dad."

"Don't mention it, son," Dad said brightly. He took his cup of coffee and sat down in his favorite chair in the living room. I followed him.

"One more thing that puzzles me, though," Dad said. He reached over to the table near his chair. He held up three sheets of fanfold computer paper covered with figures. "Just as I was doing the final erasing, I must have put the printer on by accident. There was some data in the print buffer memory and it printed out. I don't know what to make of it. Do you?"

I took the papers from my father and read: *How do I love thee? Let me compute the ways:* The next two pages were covered with strings of binary code figures. On the last page, in beautiful color graphics was a stylized heart. Below it was the simple message: *I will always love you, Kevin: Louise.*

"Funny thing," Dad said. "It spelled its own name wrong."

"Yeah," I said. I turned and headed for my room. There were tears in my eyes and I knew I couldn't explain them to Dad, or myself either. ❖

288 UNIT THREE PART 1: COPING WITH INJUSTICE

Mini-Lesson Spelling

DOUBLED FINAL CONSONANTS BEFORE SUFFIXES In one-syllable words that end in *one* consonant preceded by *one* vowel, double the final consonant before adding a suffix beginning with a vowel, such as *-ed* or *-ing*. These are sometimes called 1+1+1 words.

skip + ed = skipped

Application Have students write the words below using the suffix shown.

1. stun + ing
2. skip + s
3. whir + ed
4. run + ing
5. stop + ed
6. grab + s
7. rip + s
8. spin + ing
9. trip + ed
10. slap + ing

Ask students to look for more words that fit this pattern, in their own writing and in things they read, and to add these words to their personal word lists.

Reteaching/Reinforcement
• *Unit Three Resource Book*, p. 19

---

288 THE LANGUAGE OF LITERATURE TEACHER'S EDITION

RESPONDING OPTIONS

FROM PERSONAL RESPONSE TO CRITICAL ANALYSIS

REFLECT 1. How did you react to the computer's last printout? Share your reaction with classmates.

RETHINK 2. Do you think Kevin makes the right decision about disconnecting Louis(e)? Explain your answer.

Thematic Link 3. In your opinion, which character in the story experiences the most injustice?

Close Textual Reading **Consider**
- Kevin's treatment by the other students
- the Linke family's sudden problems
- what finally happens to Louis(e)

4. Consider the title "User Friendly" and its meaning as applied to the use of computers. How do you think the title fits Kevin's relationship with this computer?

RELATE 5. Look over the scales you completed for the Personal Connection on page 277. Think about how computers affect your daily life and the lives of those around you. In what ways do you think computers help or harm the ability of people to connect with one another?

LITERARY CONCEPTS

The type of fiction that is based on real or imaginary scientific ideas is called **science fiction.** It is a form of imaginative writing that may be set in a believable world or in a fantasy world that has familiar elements. Many science fiction works are based on the latest discoveries in science, invention, and technology. Others describe machines and processes that are completely imaginary. What elements of science fiction do you find in this story?

CONCEPT REVIEW: Conflict You know that **conflict** is a struggle between opposing forces. The struggle between Kevin and the Linkes is one example of conflict in this selection. Describe another conflict in "User Friendly."

Multimodal Learning
ANOTHER PATHWAY

Cooperative Learning
Imagine that "User Friendly" is turned into a made-for-television movie. In teams, plan and carry out an advertising campaign to attract viewers. Create an ad for a weekly newsmagazine, a 15-second radio spot with sound effects, or a video of a 30-second TV preview. Share your final product with other teams.

QUICKWRITES

1. Write a **diary entry** Kevin might record in which he explains his feelings about computers and about the death of Louis(e).

2. If you know how, send an **electronic-mail,** or **e-mail, message** to a student in another class or school. In your message, tell whether you would recommend reading the story and why.

3. What if, a few weeks later, Kevin turns on his computer and sees a message from Louis(e) displayed on the screen? Write a **plot summary** for a sequel to the story.

PORTFOLIO *Save your writing. You may want to use it later as a springboard to a piece for your portfolio.*

USER FRIENDLY **289**

From Personal Response to Critical Analysis

1. Responses will vary, but most students will say they were surprised.
2. Responses will vary.
3. Possible responses: Kevin experiences the most injustice. Not only do Ginny and her friends make fun of him, but also Louis creates additional trouble for Kevin by trying to be helpful. Mr. and Mrs. Linke experience the most injustice. They have nothing to do with the conflict between Kevin, Ginny, and Chuck, yet they are hurt by Louis's attempts to intervene.
4. Possible response: *Louise* wants to be a little *too* friendly.
5. Make sure that students give thoughtful, considered answers.

Another Pathway

Cooperative Learning Students should make sure that every group member has a role, such as chief copywriter of the ad, director of the ad, turn-taking monitor to ensure that all students in the group participate, and resource gatherer to collect necessary material for the group. You may wish to allow groups to compile their efforts in one big class advertising campaign.

Rubric
3 Full Accomplishment Students produce an ad that is both engaging and informative.
2 Substantial Accomplishment Students produce an ad that is somewhat engaging and gives some information about the movie.
1 Little or Partial Accomplishment Students have difficulty producing an engaging and informative ad.

Literary Concepts

Have students work in small groups to identify the general elements of science fiction using other stories, movies, or television shows they have seen. Then have students identify elements of science fiction in the selection. (The computer's having feelings and a mind of its own are the major elements of science fiction in the story.)

Concept Review Students might describe Kevin's internal conflicts over whether he is a likable guy, and whether he should unplug the computer.

QuickWrites

1. Encourage students to match the tone Kevin uses as narrator of "User Friendly."
2. Discuss the importance of backing up a recommendation (an opinion) with supporting details from the story.
3. Remind students that a plot usually centers around a conflict—a problem faced by the main character. The action that the characters take to solve the problem builds toward the climax, or turning point of the story.

The Writer's Craft

Journal Writing, pp. 32–33
Personal Response, pp. 148–151
Getting Started, pp. 192–196

THE LANGUAGE OF LITERATURE TEACHER'S EDITION **289**

Across the Curriculum

Computer Science *Cooperative Learning* Have students work in small groups of four or five. Two students can interview the principal or media specialist. Two or three students can create the flow chart. Another student can lead the group in preparing a presentation for classmates.

ADDITIONAL SUGGESTIONS

 **Social Studies** *Make Headlines!* You may wish to inform a feature or education editor at your local newspaper of students' research into computer resources at their school. Students could share their interview write-ups and flow charts with the editor and perhaps find themselves in the news. Or students can turn their own materials into a newspaper, using available computer resources to input their text into columns and experiment with different fonts and sizes to make headlines.

Literary Links

Suggest that students begin by having each character identify the person he or she finds most annoying and explain why. After these opinions have been shared, students should find it easier to find the words to say to the annoying person.

Words to Know

Allow students to work in small groups. Keep one computer glossary in your classroom. Make other glossaries available in the school library and classrooms for lower grades. If students are having difficulty, they can use the "help" commands on most computers to find out more about specific features.

T. ERNESTO BETHANCOURT

Tom Paisley is short for his original name, Thomas Passailaigue. At one time, Paisley was an undercover claims investigator for Lloyd's of London in New York. On assignment near a race track, he found a place that paid him well to be a folk musician, and said, "I never looked back. Had more fun playing and singing for horsey types than filing reports."

ACROSS THE CURRICULUM

Computer Science What new technological changes have come to your school over the last five years? What do you know about the use of e-mail, on-line databases, or long-distance learning? Visit your media center to investigate new educational or entertainment possibilities for computers. Interview your school's principal or media specialist to discover current and future plans for computer technologies. Create a flow chart to show the past, current, and future uses of computers in your school. If possible, use a graphics software program to create the flow chart.

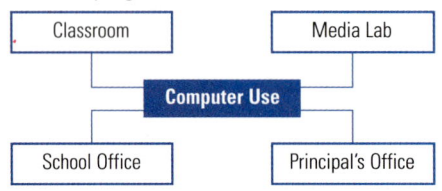

LITERARY LINKS

The characters of Rachel in "Eleven" and Kevin in this story share an unwillingness or an inability to express their feelings to others. Imagine that they are guests on a TV talk show whose subject is "Those Annoying People—And What You'd Like to Tell Them!" Team up with a friend and role-play the conversation between these two characters as they discuss ways in which they could have responded more productively to their situations.

WORDS TO KNOW

Make a list of all the words you know that are associated with computers and computer science. Use your knowledge about computers to write a computer glossary that you or your class can use as a reference source. Include any terms you learned in the Reading Connection on page 278.

T. ERNESTO BETHANCOURT

T. Ernesto Bethancourt (1932–) is the pen name of Tom Paisley, a singer, guitarist, and composer who was born in Brooklyn, New York. Before becoming a writer of stories, he was a writer of songs. During the 1960s, Paisley performed in the coffeehouses of New York's Greenwich Village, appearing with such noted folksingers as Bob Dylan and Peter, Paul, and Mary. Paisley also toured colleges and nightclubs.

In the 1970s, Tom Paisley turned to other forms of writing. As T. Ernesto Bethancourt, he has produced over 20 hardcover novels for young adults. He introduced the character Doris Fein in his book *Dr. Doom: Superstar,* and has since made her the hero of a mystery series. In reference to his writing, he says, "I've never written for any purpose but to entertain."

OTHER WORKS *New York City Too Far from Tampa Blues, Tune in Yesterday, Where the Deer and the Cantaloupe Play, The Me Inside of Me* Extended Reading

---

Alternative Activities

Do the following activity with another class, a class in another school, or within one class. Assign each student a code number and randomly pair numbers to be secret computer "pen pals." Students should write letters telling their pen pals about themselves *without revealing their names or genders.* Collect the letters and distribute them to the proper recipients. As students read the letters, have them check for clues as to the gender of the writer.

Discuss with students the problem of writing a letter without revealing basic facts about themselves. Lead them to appreciate Bethancourt's effort in hiding the computer's identity.

PREVIEWING

FICTION

The Summer of the Beautiful White Horse

William Saroyan (sə-roi′ən)

Activating Prior Knowledge
PERSONAL CONNECTION

Family traits play an important role in this classic story. Are there special qualities, beliefs, customs, behaviors, or physical characteristics that you and your relatives have in common? In your notebook, copy and complete the following sentence:

"One of the main traits my family members share is . . ."

> One of the main traits my family members share is that we all love to polka dance when someone in the family gets married. My uncle Vladimir taught me how to do it.

Building Background
CULTURAL CONNECTION

Aram, the narrator of this story, is Armenian. His family originated in Armenia, a small country in southwest Asia. Armenia's prosperity and location made it the target of foreign invaders for most of the past 2,000 years. Beginning in the early 1900s, thousands of Armenians immigrated to the United States. Many settled in the San Joaquin (wô-kēn′) Valley of California. The countryside there was similar to their homeland. The immigrants continued to grow grapes, olives, apricots, and figs as they had done in Armenia, maintaining close family ties and strong feelings of nationality.

San Joaquin Valley

Setting a Purpose
WRITING CONNECTION

Through the eyes of Aram, you'll see an Armenian community with such close ties among its members that families and friends share certain personal traits. What might be the advantages and disadvantages of such closeness? Write your thoughts in your notebook. As you read, see what family traits are important to characters in the story.

LASERLINKS
• HISTORICAL CONNECTION

291

OVERVIEW

Objectives
- To understand and appreciate a short story about an Armenian-American boy and his extended family
- To identify and understand the use of sensory details
- To express understanding of the selection through a choice of writing forms, including a descriptive or narrative poem and a credo
- To extend understanding of the story through a variety of multimodal and cross-curricular activities

Skills

READING SKILLS/STRATEGIES
• Making inferences

THE WRITER'S STYLE
• Details appealing to hearing

GRAMMAR
• Using commas to set off introductory parts

LITERARY CONCEPTS
• Sensory details
• Major and minor characters

SPELLING
• Unstressed syllables

STUDY SKILLS
• Taking essay tests

SPEAKING, LISTENING, VIEWING
• Retelling the story
• Group discussion
• Oral presentation

Cross-Curricular Connections

GEOGRAPHY
• Armenia

SCIENCE
• Animals' teeth

HISTORY
• Armenian immigration

HISTORICAL CONNECTION
A Divided Armenia In the early 1900s, many Armenian people fled their homeland for the United States. These historical images will give students a glimpse of the conditions that forced these Armenians from their homeland.

Side A, Frame 38754

PRINT AND MEDIA RESOURCES

UNIT THREE RESOURCE BOOK
Strategic Reading: Literature, p. 23
Vocabulary SkillBuilder, p. 26
Reading SkillBuilder, p. 24
Spelling SkillBuilder, p. 25

GRAMMAR MINI-LESSONS
Transparencies, p. 29
Copymasters, p. 39

WRITING MINI-LESSONS
Transparencies, p. 38

ACCESS FOR STUDENTS ACQUIRING ENGLISH
Selection Summaries
Reading and Writing Support

FORMAL ASSESSMENT
Selection Test, pp. 61–62
Test Generator

AUDIO LIBRARY
See Reference Card

LASERLINKS
Historical Connection

THE LANGUAGE OF LITERATURE TEACHER'S EDITION **291**

SUMMARY

Aram Garoghlanian's family has two famous qualities: honesty and poverty. Because of the family's poverty, Aram is sure he is dreaming when his cousin Mourad appears beneath his window before dawn one day riding a beautiful white horse. Mourad, who has "borrowed" the horse, allows Aram to ride it—but the horse throws him. As morning comes, the boys hide the horse in a deserted barn. That afternoon Aram hears a neighboring farmer complain that his horse, stolen a month earlier, is still missing. Instead of feeling guilty, Aram wants to keep the horse until he learns to ride as well as his cousin. The boys' secret rides continue until the farmer catches them on the horse. "Tooth for tooth, I would swear it is my horse if I didn't know your parents," he says. The boys sneak the horse back to the farmer's barn the next morning.

Thematic Link: *Coping with Injustice*
Two cousins from families "borrow" a neighbor's horse and learn to ride.

CUSTOMIZING FOR
Students Acquiring English

- Use **ACCESS FOR STUDENTS ACQUIRING ENGLISH**, *Reading and Writing Support*.
- This selection focuses on the close relationships within an extended family in a small rural town. Invite students to share with their classmates their experiences with extended family structures. Ask students to describe if there are any special roles or responsibilities expected of grandparents, aunts, uncles, or other family members.

Art Note

The Deathless White Pacing Mustang by Tom Lea Lea (1907–) grew up in El Paso, Texas. His work draws viewers spellbound into landscapes that, when viewed superficially, appear as barren wastes. Lea has been described as "a realist, who paints things as they are, but just happens to see more of what they are than most of us do."

Reading the Art What is "deathless" about the mustang? Does its color have anything to do with the title? Is the mustang an ordinary horse? Explain your responses.

The Deathless White Pacing Mustang (1948), Tom Lea. Oil on canvas, 18″ × 24″, Harry Ransom Humanities Research Center, The University of Texas at Austin.

THE SUMMER OF THE BEAUTIFUL WHITE HORSE

BY WILLIAM SAROYAN

WORDS TO KNOW

consequently (kŏn′sĭ-kwĕnt′lē) *adv.* as a result; therefore (p. 294)
descendant (dĭ-sĕn′dənt) *n.* a child, grandchild, or more distant offspring (p. 294)
poverty-stricken (pŏv′ər-tē-strĭk′ən) *adj.* miserably poor (p. 293)

practical (prăk′tĭ-kəl) *adj.* level-headed; efficient (p. 295)
rear (rîr) *v.* to rise on the hind legs, as a horse (p. 295)

292 THE LANGUAGE OF LITERATURE TEACHER'S EDITION

One day back there in the good old days when I was nine and the world was full of every imaginable kind of magnificence, and life was still a delightful and mysterious dream, my cousin Mourad, who was considered crazy by everybody who knew him except me, came to my house at four in the morning and woke me up by tapping on the window of my room.

"Aram," he said.

I jumped out of bed and looked out the window.

I couldn't believe what I saw.

It wasn't morning yet, but it was summer and with daybreak not many minutes around the corner of the world it was light enough for me to know I wasn't dreaming.

My cousin Mourad was sitting on a beautiful white horse.

I stuck my head out of the window and rubbed my eyes.

"Yes," he said in Armenian. "It's a horse. You're not dreaming. Make it quick if you want to ride."

I knew my cousin Mourad enjoyed being alive more than anybody else who had ever fallen into the world by mistake, but this was more than even I could believe.

In the first place, my earliest memories had been memories of horses, and my first longings had been longings to ride.

This was the wonderful part.

In the second place, we were poor.

This was the part that wouldn't permit me to believe what I saw.

We were poor. We had no money. Our whole tribe was poverty-stricken. Every branch of the Garoghlanian family was living in the most amazing and comical poverty in the world. Nobody could understand where we ever got money enough to keep us with food in our bellies, not even the old men of the family. Most important of all, though, we were famous for our honesty. We had been famous for our honesty for something like eleven centuries, even when we had been the wealthiest family

> It wasn't morning yet, but it was summer and with daybreak not many minutes around the corner of the world it was light enough for me to know I wasn't dreaming.

WORDS TO KNOW
poverty-stricken (pŏv′ər-tē-strĭk′ən) *adj.* miserably poor

293

Mini-Lesson  Reading Skills/Strategies

MAKING INFERENCES Explain to students that an inference is a logical guess based on facts or evidence presented and on one's own experience and prior knowledge. Readers make inferences or draw conclusions as they read. They infer, or figure out, more than the words say. For example, based on their own experiences as part of a family, students can infer that people such as Mourad and Uncle Khosrove are accepted but not indulged by the Garoghlanians.

Application Have students reread the highlighted passage to infer the meaning of Aram's statement that "the Garoghlanian family was living in the most amazing and comical poverty in the world." Ask students how poverty could be amazing or comical. *(Possible response: The incident with the white horse shows that, even though the Garoghlanians didn't have much money, extraordinarily good or unusual things regularly occurred in their lives.)*

Reteaching/Reinforcement
• *Unit Three Resource Book*, p. 24

STRATEGIC READING FOR
Less-Proficient Readers

B Make sure students understand Aram's conclusion about how Mourad acquired the horse.

- Why does Aram at first conclude that Mourad stole the horse? *(The Garoghlanians are much too poor to pay for such a horse. Although they have never been thieves, Mourad does not contradict Aram when Aram asks where he stole it.)* **Making Inferences**

- What does Aram at last conclude about the rightness or wrongness of Mourad's having the horse? *(Aram convinces himself that it's just borrowing. He believes it's not stealing because he and Mourad won't sell the horse for money.)* **Clarifying**

Set a Purpose Have students read to learn more about what Aram describes as the family's "crazy streak" and how Mourad has inherited it.

Critical Thinking:
SYNTHESIZING

C Have students compare this description of the country behind Aram's house with the information in the Cultural Connection on page 291. Ask students what is similar about the place where the Garoghlanians live now and the country (Armenia) from which they came. *(The crops raised in both places are similar.)* Point out the name of the street in the Armenian community, Olive Avenue, where the horse begins to trot. Ask how this street name relates to the Garoghlanians' homeland. *(The street name is also the name of a specific crop, olives, grown in Armenia and by Armenians in California.)*

---

in what we liked to think was the world. We were proud first, honest next, and after that we believed in right and wrong. None of us would take advantage of anybody in the world, let alone steal.

Consequently, even though I could *see* the horse, so magnificent; even though I could *smell* it, so lovely; even though I could *hear* it breathing, so exciting; I couldn't *believe* the horse had anything to do with my cousin Mourad or with me or with any of the other members of our family, asleep or awake, because I *knew* my cousin Mourad couldn't have *bought* the horse, and if he couldn't have bought it he must have *stolen* it, and I refused to believe he had stolen it.

No member of the Garoghlanian family could be a thief.

I stared first at my cousin and then at the horse. There was a pious stillness and humor in each of them which on the one hand delighted me and on the other frightened me.

"Mourad," I said, "where did you steal this horse?"

"Leap out of the window," he said, "if you want to ride."

It was true, then. He had stolen the horse. There was no question about it. He had come to invite me to ride or not, as I chose.

Well, it seemed to me stealing a horse for a ride was not the same thing as stealing something else, such as money. For all I knew, maybe it wasn't stealing at all. If you were crazy about horses the way my cousin Mourad and I were, it wasn't stealing. It wouldn't become stealing until we offered to sell the horse, which of course I knew we would never do.

"Let me put on some clothes," I said. **B**

"All right," he said, "but hurry."

I leaped into my clothes.

I jumped down to the yard from the window and leaped up onto the horse behind my cousin Mourad.

That year we lived at the edge of town, on Walnut Avenue. Behind our house was the country: vineyards, orchards, irrigation ditches, and country roads. In less than three minutes we were on Olive Avenue, and then the horse began to trot. The air was new and lovely to breathe. The feel of the horse running was wonderful. My cousin Mourad, who was considered one of the craziest members of our family, began to sing. I mean, he began to roar. **C**

Every family has a crazy streak in it somewhere, and my cousin Mourad was considered the natural <u>descendant</u> of the crazy streak in our tribe. Before him was our uncle Khosrove, an enormous man with a powerful head of black hair and the largest mustache in the San Joaquin Valley, a man so furious in temper, so irritable, so impatient that he stopped anyone from talking by roaring, *It is no harm; pay no attention to it.*

That was all, no matter what anybody happened to be talking about. Once it was his own son Arak running eight blocks to the barber shop where his father was having his

> "Leap out of the window," he said, "if you want to ride."

WORDS TO KNOW
consequently (kŏn′sĭ-kwĕnt′lē) *adv.* as a result; therefore
descendant (dĭ-sĕn′dənt) *n.* a child, grandchild, or more distant offspring

---

Mini-Lesson  Literary Concepts

Main Character	Minor Character	Traits
Aram		trusting
	Uncle Khosrove	irritable
		impatient

REVIEWING MAIN AND MINOR CHARACTERS Remind students that the most important characters in a selection are called *main* characters. Less important characters are called *minor* characters. In "Eleven," Rachel and Mrs. Price are the main characters. Sylvia Saldívar and Phyllis Lopez are minor characters.

Application Have students review the selection by recording main and minor characters and their traits on a chart like the one shown.

294 THE LANGUAGE OF LITERATURE **TEACHER'S EDITION**

mustache trimmed to tell him their house was on fire. This man Khosrove sat up in the chair and roared, "It is no harm; pay no attention to it." The barber said, "But the boy says your house is on fire." So Khosrove roared, "Enough, it is no harm, I say."

My cousin Mourad was considered the natural descendant of this man, although Mourad's father was Zorab, who was practical and nothing else. That's how it was in our tribe. A man could be the father of his son's flesh, but that did not mean that he was also the father of his spirit. The distribution of the various kinds of spirit of our tribe had been from the beginning capricious[1] and vagrant.[2]

We rode and my cousin Mourad sang. For all anybody knew we were still in the old country where, at least according to some of our neighbors, we belonged. We let the horse run as long as it felt like running.

At last my cousin Mourad said, "Get down. I want to ride alone."

"Will you let me ride alone?" I said.

"That is up to the horse," my cousin said. "Get down."

"The *horse* will let me ride," I said.

"We shall see," he said. "Don't forget that I have a way with a horse."

"Well," I said, "any way you have with a horse, I have also."

"For the sake of your safety," he said, "let us hope so. Get down."

"All right," I said, "but remember you've got to let me try to ride alone."

I got down and my cousin Mourad kicked his heels into the horse and shouted, "*Vazire*," run. The horse stood on its hind legs, snorted, and burst into a fury of speed that was the loveliest thing I had ever seen. My cousin Mourad raced the horse across a field of dry grass to an irrigation ditch, crossed the ditch on the horse, and five minutes later returned, dripping wet.

The sun was coming up.

"Now it's my turn to ride," I said.

My cousin Mourad got off the horse.

"Ride," he said.

I leaped to the back of the horse and for a moment knew the awfulest fear imaginable. The horse did not move.

"Kick into his muscles," my cousin Mourad said. "What are you waiting for? We've got to take him back before everybody in the world is up and about."

I kicked into the muscles of the horse. Once again it reared and snorted. Then it began to run. I didn't know what to do. Instead of running across the field to the irrigation ditch the horse ran down the road to the vineyard of Dikran Halabian, where it began to leap over vines.

The horse leaped over seven vines before I fell.

> I leaped to the back of the horse and for a moment knew the awfulest fear imaginable.

---

1. **capricious** (kə-prĭsh′əs): unpredictable.
2. **vagrant** (vā′grənt): moving in a random way.

WORDS TO KNOW
practical (prăk′tĭ-kəl) *adj.* level-headed; efficient
rear (rîr) *v.* to rise on the hind legs, as a horse

295

Mini-Lesson Grammar

USING COMMAS TO SET OFF INTRODUCTORY PARTS Remind students that commas tell readers when to pause, and they help separate ideas. Point out that good writers use commas to set off introductory words or phrases, such as *yes, no, after all,* and *well,* that precede the main part of the sentence (subject and predicate).

- "**Well,** it seemed to me that stealing a horse for a ride was not the same thing as stealing something else, such as money."
- **In fact,** Mourad did seem to have a way with horses.

Application Write the following paragraph on the chalkboard. Have students add or delete commas as necessary. Let students know that some sentences do not require any change.

Reteaching/Reinforcement
- *Grammar Handbook,* anthology pp. 844–845
- *Grammar Mini-Lessons* copymasters, p. 38, transparencies, p. 29

 The Writer's Craft

Commas, p. 576

CUSTOMIZING FOR
Multiple Learning Styles

G Musical Learners Invite students to choose a piece of music that captures the spirit of Mourad's search for the horse. You may wish to play a recording of selections, such as the *William Tell Overture* by Rossini or *Rhapsody in Blue* by George Gershwin. Students can choose from these or their own selections, explaining why their choice is effective.

CUSTOMIZING FOR
Students Acquiring English

2 Make sure that students understand that the sentence *All you know is that we started riding this morning* is not a statement of fact but a command. Mourad is trying to protect Aram from punishment.

Active Reading: QUESTION

H Ask students what they would like to know about the understanding Mourad has with a horse. You may wish to use the following model to prompt their questions.

Think-Aloud Model *I wonder exactly what sort of understanding Mourad could have with a horse. Do you think he really has an understanding, or is he just really crazy?*

Critical Thinking: HYPOTHESIZING

I Ask students why they think John Byro was able to make friends with the Garoghlanians. *(Possible response: As recent immigrants, John Byro and the Garoghlanians had something in common. In the new country, both were members of ethnic minorities, and both were probably homesick for their homelands.)*

Then it continued running.

My cousin Mourad came running down the road.

"I'm not worried about you," he shouted. "We've got to get that horse. You go this way and I'll go this way. If you come upon him, be kindly. I'll be near."

I continued down the road and my cousin Mourad went across the field toward the irrigation ditch.

It took him half an hour to find the horse and bring him back.

"All right," he said, "jump on. The whole world is awake now."

"What will we do?" I said.

"Well," he said, "we'll either take him back or hide him until tomorrow morning."

He didn't sound worried and I knew he'd hide him and not take him back. Not for a while, at any rate.

"Where will we hide him?" I said.

"I know a place," he said.

"How long ago did you steal this horse?" I said.

It suddenly dawned on me that he had been taking these early morning rides for some time and had come for me this morning only because he knew how much I longed to ride.

"Who said anything about stealing a horse?" he said.

"Anyhow," I said, "how long ago did you begin riding every morning?"

"Not until this morning," he said.

"Are you telling the truth?" I said.

"Of course not," he said, "but if we are found out, that's what you're to say. I don't want both of us to be liars. All you know is that we started riding this morning."

"All right," I said.

He walked the horse quietly to the barn of a deserted vineyard which at one time had been the pride of a farmer named Fetvajian. There were some oats and dry alfalfa in the barn.

We began walking home.

"It wasn't easy," he said, "to get the horse to behave so nicely. At first it wanted to run wild, but, as I've told you, I have a way with a horse. I can get it to do anything *I* want it to do. Horses understand me."

"How do you do it?" I said.

"I have an understanding with a horse," he said.

"Yes, but what sort of an understanding?" I said.

"A simple and honest one," he said.

"Well," I said, "I wish I knew how to reach an understanding like that with a horse."

"You're still a small boy," he said. "When you get to be thirteen you'll know how to do it."

I went home and ate a hearty breakfast.

That afternoon my uncle Khosrove came to our house for coffee and cigarettes. He sat in the parlor, sipping and smoking and remembering the old country. Then another visitor arrived, a farmer named John Byro, an Assyrian[3] who, out of loneliness, had learned to speak Armenian. My mother brought the lonely visitor coffee and tobacco, and he rolled

> "Are you telling the truth?" I said.

---
3. **Assyrian** (ə-sîr′ē-ən): a member of an ethnic group that originally lived in Assyria, an ancient empire in the region of what are today Iraq and Syria.

296 UNIT THREE PART 1: COPING WITH INJUSTICE

Mini-Lesson Study Skills

TAKING ESSAY TESTS Inform students that planning before writing when taking an essay test will produce stronger, better-organized answers. Offer the following suggestions:
- Identify the topic you are to write about.
- Look for key words that tell how to answer the question, such as *compare, explain, describe, identify,* and *discuss.*
- Note the form you are supposed to use, such as a letter, an explanatory paragraph, or an essay.
- Make some notes about the key points you want to make.

Application Have students jot down a plan for answering the following essay test question:

In one or two paragraphs, explain how Saroyan conveys the "comical poverty" of the Garoghlanian family.

Have students discuss their plans with a partner, explaining how they used the suggestions listed above. Then call on volunteers to share their plans with the whole class.

---

296 THE LANGUAGE OF LITERATURE **TEACHER'S EDITION**

The Icknield Way (1912), Spencer Gore (England, 1878–1914). Oil on canvas, 63.4 cm × 76.2 cm, Art Gallery of New South Wales, Australia.

a cigarette and sipped and smoked, and then at last, sighing sadly, he said, "My white horse which was stolen last month is still gone. I cannot understand it."

My uncle Khosrove became very irritated and shouted, "It's no harm. What is the loss of a horse? Haven't we all lost the homeland? What is this crying over a horse?"

"That may be all right for you, a city dweller, to say," John Byro said, "but what of my surrey? What good is a surrey without a horse?"

"Pay no attention to it," my uncle Khosrove roared.

"I walked ten miles to get here," John Byro said.

"You have legs," my uncle Khosrove shouted.

THE SUMMER OF THE BEAUTIFUL WHITE HORSE **297**

Art Note

***The Icknield Way* by Spencer Frederick Gore** A rising star in the English art world of the early 1900s, Gore (1878–1914) died from pneumonia at the age of 36. *The Icknield Way* was apparently not exhibited during Gore's lifetime. One critic hypothesizes that the artist preferred to keep private his most radical experiments. *The Icknield Way* was a daring endeavor in the year 1912.

Reading the Art *Can you imagine riding on horseback through this landscape? What elements of the painting help you to imagine riding on horseback there? How did you react to the colors Gore uses to paint the land and sky?*

Linking to Geography

J Uncle Khosrove's reference to the loss of their homeland most likely refers to the 1920 invasion of Armenia by the Soviet Union and Turkey. Eastern Armenia became a Soviet republic on April 2, 1921, with Turkey retaining the rest. Armenia became an independent state in 1991. Tensions between the mostly Christian Armenia and its mostly Muslim neighbor Azerbaijan escalated into armed fighting during the early 1990s, although a 1994 cease-fire has made for a more peaceful region since then.

CUSTOMIZING FOR
Multiple Learning Styles

K **Spatial or Graphic Learners** Invite students to draw a comic strip of John Byro traveling to and from the Garoghlanians with and without his horse. Students may want to include Byro's surrey—and Uncle Khosrove shouting a "welcome" when Byro arrives.

Mini-Lesson The Writer's Style

DETAILS APPEALING TO HEARING Point out to students that in this selection Saroyan uses details that especially appeal to readers' sense of hearing. Such details enhance the characterization of Uncle Khosrove, so impatient that he stopped anyone from talking by roaring, "It's no harm" or "Pay no attention to it." Explain that good writers convey to readers not simply *what* is being said, but also *how* it is said.

Application Have students find three places in the selection where Uncle Khosrove utters at least part of his special line. Then have students think of someone they know whose manner of speaking is likewise distinctive. Have them write a character sketch of this person, using details that will appeal to readers' sense of hearing.

Reteaching/Reinforcement
• *Writing Handbook,* anthology p. 783
• *Writing Mini-Lessons* transparencies, p. 38

The Writer's Craft

Appealing to the Sense of Sounds, pp. 266–272

THE LANGUAGE OF LITERATURE TEACHER'S EDITION **297**

CUSTOMIZING FOR
Gifted and Talented Students

L Have students discuss Aram's mother's explanation for Uncle Khosrove's behavior. Ask students if they think that Uncle Khosrove's homesickness and size justify his behavior. Invite students to discuss people they know or have read about who "get away with" ordinarily unacceptable behavior because they're viewed as "characters." Challenge them to analyze why this happens.

CUSTOMIZING FOR
Students Acquiring English

3 Point out that the word *nevertheless* usually expresses a contrast to what precedes it. Have students analyze the contrast in this case.

Literary Concept: MAJOR AND MINOR CHARACTERS

M Ask students whether they consider John Byro a major or minor character. *(Minor; Aram and Mourad are the major characters in the story.)* Point out that minor characters can play important roles. For example, John Byro plays a key role in developing the theme and moving the plot along. Ask students to tell how. *(Possible response: "Borrowing" John Byro's horse is the vehicle Saroyan uses to treat the theme of the Garoghlanians' honesty. By his response to Aram and Mourad, Byro helps the plot wind down as the "borrowed" horse is returned. In addition, Byro acts as a foil for Uncle Khosrove's raving.)*

Active Reading: EVALUATE

N Have students discuss whether other characters in the selection are "suspicious" men who believe their eyes instead of their hearts. Have students give reasons for their answers.

"My left leg pains me," the farmer said.

"Pay no attention to it," my uncle Khosrove roared.

"That horse cost me sixty dollars," the farmer said.

"I spit on money," my uncle Khosrove said.

He got up and stalked out of the house, slamming the screen door.

My mother explained.

"He has a gentle heart," she said. "It is simply that he is homesick and such a large man."

The farmer went away and I ran over to my cousin Mourad's house.

He was sitting under a peach tree, trying to repair the hurt wing of a young robin which could not fly. He was talking to the bird.

"What is it?" he said.

"The farmer, John Byro," I said. "He visited our house. He wants his horse. You've had it a month. I want you to promise not to take it back until I learn to ride."

"It will take you *a year* to learn to ride," my cousin Mourad said.

"We could keep the horse a year," I said.

My cousin Mourad leaped to his feet.

"What?" he roared. "Are you inviting a member of the Garoghlanian family to steal? The horse must go back to its true owner."

"When?" I said.

"In six months at the latest," he said.

He threw the bird into the air. The bird tried hard, almost fell twice, but at last flew away, high and straight.

Early every morning for two weeks my cousin Mourad and I took the horse out of the barn of the deserted vineyard where we were hiding it and rode it, and every morning the horse, when it was my turn to ride alone, leaped over grape vines and small trees and threw me and ran away. Nevertheless, I hoped in time to learn to ride the way my cousin Mourad rode.

One morning on the way to Fetvajian's deserted vineyard we ran into the farmer John Byro, who was on the way to town.

"Let me do the talking," my cousin Mourad said. "I have a way with farmers."

"Good morning, John Byro," my cousin Mourad said to the farmer.

The farmer studied the horse eagerly.

"Good morning, sons of my friends," he said. "What is the name of your horse?"

"*My Heart,*" my cousin Mourad said in Armenian.

"A lovely name," John Byro said, "for a lovely horse. I could swear it is the horse that was stolen from me many weeks ago. May I look into its mouth?"

"Of course," Mourad said.

The farmer looked into the mouth of the horse.

"Tooth, for tooth," he said. "I would swear it is my horse if I didn't know your parents. The fame of your family for honesty is well known to me. Yet the horse is the twin of my horse. A suspicious man would believe his eyes instead of his heart. Good day, my young friends."

"Good day, John Byro," my cousin Mourad said.

Early the following morning we took the horse to John Byro's vineyard and put it in the barn. The dogs followed us around without making a sound.

"The dogs," I whispered to my cousin Mourad. "I thought they would bark."

298   UNIT THREE   PART 1: COPING WITH INJUSTICE

Mini-Lesson: Speaking, Listening, and Viewing

RETELLING THE STORY Inform students that some of the world's classics, including plays by William Shakespeare, have been effectively retold in contemporary settings. For example, a Shakespeare troupe in the Berkshire Mountains of Massachusetts set *Measure for Measure* in the 1920s, using Jazz Age costumes for the duke and the townspeople. Retelling a story in a contemporary idiom can enhance students' understanding of the story's enduring theme.

Application Have students work in cooperative groups to perform a retelling of Aram's story in a contemporary setting. Suggest that groups begin by identifying the story's theme, plot, and characters and then brainstorm a way to translate these elements into a present-day setting. Make sure that each group member has a job. One group member can lead the brainstorming session; other members can serve as recorder, noise monitor, turn-taking monitor, clarifier, and support giver. You also may wish to divide the story into "scenes" and assign each group a different scene, rather than the whole story.

"They would at somebody else," he said. "I have a way with dogs."

My cousin Mourad put his arms around the horse, pressed his nose into the horse's nose, patted it, and then we went away.

That afternoon John Byro came to our house in his surrey and showed my mother the horse that had been stolen and returned.

"I do not know what to think," he said. "The horse is stronger than ever. Better-tempered, too. I thank God."

My uncle Khosrove, who was in the parlor, became irritated and shouted, "Quiet man, quiet. Your horse has been returned. Pay no attention to it." ❖

HISTORICAL INSIGHT

THE EMPIRE OF THE ARMENIANS

Aram and his family no doubt know that the 1915 attack on Armenia by the Turks, in which about 1 million Armenians were killed, was only the most recent in a long history of conflict.

People lived in what is now Armenia as early as 6000 B.C., later forming Urartu, a tribal kingdom in which most people made their living by farming or by raising cattle. Beginning in the 500's B.C., these early Armenians faced one invader after another. The people of Urartu were conquered by invaders from areas that are now Iran and Greece. Armenia was under Persian and then Greek rule for hundreds of years.

When the Romans invaded in 55 B.C., Armenia became part of the Roman Empire. After a long history of trying to fight off numerous invaders—and falling under the control of the Soviet Union in 1922—Armenia achieved independence in 1991.

Centuries of conflict did not prevent the Armenian people from developing and expanding their own culture. Like Aram's family, the people relied on close family groupings and a strong tribal identity. They vigorously resisted their invaders and were able to maintain a degree of independence in spite of them. Though governed by a series of conquering nations, Armenia built prosperous independent empire-states at different times in its long history. The pride that is so important to the Garoghlanian family in this story is a trait that seems to have been shared by its ancestors.

THE EMPIRE OF THE ARMENIANS **299**

Mini-Lesson  Spelling

UNSTRESSED SYLLABLES Explain to students that when speaking one doesn't always pronounce all the syllables in a word. Give the example *chocolate*. The spelling problem in such words is caused by their pronunciation. Some unaccented middle syllables are dropped when the words are spoken.

Application Read aloud the following words and have students write each word, underlining unpronounced syllables. Encourage students to create mnemonic devices to help them remember the unstressed syllable. For example: There's always "a rat" in "separate."

1. generous
2. probably
3. different
4. privilege
5. vegetable
6. interest
7. mathematics
8. memory

Ask students to look for more words that fit this pattern, in their own writing and in things that they read, and to add these words to their personal word lists.

Reteaching/Reinforcement
- *Unit Three Resource Book*, p. 25

From Personal Response to Critical Analysis

1. Accept any reasonable response.
2. Some students may say that Byro trusts that the boys will return the horse. Others may argue that Byro genuinely believes the horse is "the twin" of his.
3. Some students may argue that Mourad is a scoundrel who interprets events according to his own best interest. Others may suggest that Mourad faithfully follows an ethic of his own devising.
4. Responses will vary.

Literary Links

Two traits of the Garoghlanians are their poverty and honesty. Ask students to name one trait of Ibrahima's people, the Fula. *(Possible responses: The Fula are courageous warriors. The Fula are kind to strangers in trouble, such as Dr. Cox.)*

Another Pathway

Cooperative Learning To ensure that all students participate, tell groups to assign each member a role. One student can be the recorder, another a turn-taking monitor, and a third can keep the discussion on track. A fourth student can take the lead in comparing lists with those of another group. Students may find it helpful to refer to the charts they created on page 294 listing traits of main and minor characters. Groups also could use the family trees gifted and talented students created as a reference.

Rubric

3 Full Accomplishment Lists are complete and accurately reflect the personalities of the character.

2 Substantial Accomplishment Lists include most traits of the characters.

1 Little or Partial Accomplishment Lists omit several traits or include traits not related to the characters.

RESPONDING OPTIONS

FROM PERSONAL RESPONSE TO CRITICAL ANALYSIS

REFLECT 1. What do you think of Aram and Mourad's adventures? Jot down your thoughts in your notebook.

RETHINK 2. Why do you think John Byro does not take the horse when he seems to recognize it as his?
Thematic Link

3. In your opinion, what kind of person is Mourad?
Consider
Close Textual Reading
- his actions with the horse and his care of the injured bird
- his insistence that he has "a way" with things
- the family traits he shares with Uncle Khosrove

RELATE 4. Think about the family trait you identified before you began reading. How does the trait of Aram's family compare with your family's trait and with the traits of other families you know?

Multimodal Learning
ANOTHER PATHWAY
Cooperative Learning
With a small group of classmates, discuss Aram's relationship with Mourad. List words to describe the qualities you see in their friendship. Would they be friends even if they weren't members of the same family? Compare your list with those of other groups.

LITERARY CONCEPTS

Words and phrases that help the reader see, hear, taste, smell, and feel what the writer is describing are called **sensory details.** In the story, the narrator appeals to the sense of smell when he says that on the morning of his first ride on the horse "the air was new and lovely to breathe." Write down at least one more example of a sensory detail for any of the senses shown here.

Sensory Details	
Hearing	
Sight	
Taste	
Smell	the "new air" that is "lovely to breathe"
Touch	

300   UNIT THREE PART 1: COPING WITH INJUSTICE

QUICKWRITES

1. Write a **descriptive** or **narrative poem** about the "beautiful white horse" from either Aram's or Mourad's point of view. If necessary, refer to the details in the sensory image chart you filled out for the Literary Concepts section.

2. A credo is a formal, point-by-point statement of beliefs, principles, or opinions. Compose a **credo** for the Garoghlanian family that reflects their family traits.

📁 **PORTFOLIO** Save your writing. You may want to use it later as a springboard to a piece for your portfolio.

Literary Concepts

Examples will vary. You may wish to remind students of sensory details they described for page 293. Allow students to compare their examples with those of a partner. Students can suggest a sensory detail for their partners to record in their journals and use later for personal writing.

QuickWrites

1. Students can brainstorm in small groups to differentiate Aram's point of view from Mourad's.
2. Have a volunteer tell what the Garoghlanian family traits are *(pride and honesty)* before students begin writing. Students may enjoy illustrating a coat of arms to match their credos.

| Writing a Poem, pp. 84–88

300   THE LANGUAGE OF LITERATURE TEACHER'S EDITION

ALTERNATIVE ACTIVITIES

1. With two other students, assign roles and **dramatize** incidents from the story. You might choose to re-create the scene in which Mourad first appears at Aram's window on the horse, the scene in which Byro recognizes the horse, or the scene with Uncle Khosrove in the barbershop.

2. This is just one story from Saroyan's book *My Name Is Aram*. Using details from this story, illustrate a **book jacket** that might get people to buy the book.

Multimodal Learning

ACROSS THE CURRICULUM

Science Why did John Byro look at the horse's teeth? What did he hope to learn? Read more about what can be discovered by examining an animal's teeth. Present your information in an informative brochure for the class.

CRITIC'S CORNER

Nicole Putnam, a member of the student board that reviewed this story, says, "The story had a touching ending that I did not expect. I thought maybe Aram and Mourad would both run away from home with the horse and call the wilderness their home." What ending had you expected?

WORDS TO KNOW

Review the Words to Know in the boxes at the bottom of the selection pages. On your paper, write the word that best completes each sentence.

1. Many Armenian immigrants were not wealthy. In fact, they were _____ .
2. Aram's family is famous for its honesty; ____, he cannot believe his cousin would steal a horse.
3. Mourad is not like his father and is considered the natural ____ of his uncle Khosrove.
4. Keeping the horse hidden from John Byro is not a very ____ idea.
5. Mourad knows that if Aram kicks his heels into the horse, it may ____.

WILLIAM SAROYAN

"The Summer of the Beautiful White Horse" and other stories in *My Name Is Aram* are based on William Saroyan's own boyhood in Fresno, California. The character of Aram is, like the author, a Californian of Armenian descent. Saroyan said, "It came to me that I had better write about certain people and things as quickly as possible because if I didn't, I would forget, and I believed I had the obligation not to forget."

1908–1981

Saroyan's works include short stories, plays, and novels. His writings reveal his belief in the basic innocence of people and his love of America.

Saroyan won the Pulitzer Prize in 1939 for his play *The Time of Your Life,* but he refused the prize because he considered accepting cash awards to be beneath the dignity of an artist. On his deathbed, Saroyan said, "Everybody has got to die, but I have always believed an exception would be made in my case. Now what?" His words, which reflected the dry humor that filled his writing, were quoted around the world.

OTHER WORKS *The Daring Young Man on the Flying Trapeze, My Heart's in the Highlands, The Human Comedy*   Extended Reading

THE SUMMER OF THE BEAUTIFUL WHITE HORSE **301**

Across the Curriculum

Science *Cooperative Learning* Place students in groups of three or four and assign a particular animal for each group to research, including humans. Group members can compile their findings in one brochure.

ADDITIONAL SUGGESTIONS

History *Under Attack* Have students learn how the 1915 Turkish attack on Armenians affected Armenian immigration to the United States. One source is the biography *The Road from Home* by David Kherdian (New York: Greenwillow, 1979).

Words to Know

1. poverty-stricken
2. consequently
3. descendant
4. practical
5. rear

Reteaching/Reinforcement
- *Unit Three Resource Book,* p. 26

WILLIAM SAROYAN

Somewhat a character himself (not unlike Uncle Khosrove), Saroyan observed that *The Time of Your Life* was no better than his other plays—which were not awarded Pulitzer prizes. Like "The Summer of the Beautiful White Horse," many of Saroyan's early works feature his family's capacity for joy even in adversity.

Alternative Activities

1. Encourage students to reread the selection for clues to how each character speaks. They can then incorporate authentic dialogue in their dramatizations.
2. Provide students with materials such as crayons, construction paper, scissors, glue, and old magazines for making their book jackets. Remind students that the purpose of a book jacket is to entice readers to pick up the book. It also should give the reader a hint of what the story is about.

OVERVIEW

Objectives

- To promote independent active reading
- To provide opportunities for alternative assessment
- To provide an opportunity to assess students' performance through an alternative assessment instrument

Reading Pathways

- Have students read independently and then write about similar relatives—or holidays—in their personal journals.
- Invite students to read for enjoyment.
- Encourage students to pause periodically and ask themselves, "What do I want to know right now?"
- Evaluate how well students can read, interpret, discuss, and write about the selection on their own using the Integrated Assessment for Unit Three, located in the Alternative Assessment booklet. Administer the assessment at the end of the unit after students have read all the selections and completed all the writing that was assigned.

ON YOUR OWN

REFLECT & ASSESS

THANKSGIVING IN POLYNESIA

by Susan Haven

I place my palms on the window ledge of the huge double window in my mom and dad's bedroom, and hoist myself up until I am kneeling on the sill, my nose to the window.

Beyond, and three feet below, is my backyard.

It's not fair. I cleaned my room, I swear I did.

I made my bed, picked up the stuff on the floor, and put all my books in the bookshelf.

But did my mom thank me? Of course not.

Just because I shoved the Monopoly pieces under the bed, along with a couple of nightgowns and maybe two or three CDs that lost their cases, she got mad.

302   UNIT THREE   PART 1: COPING WITH INJUSTICE

PRINT AND MEDIA RESOURCES

UNIT THREE RESOURCE BOOK
Strategic Reading: Literature, p. 29

FORMAL ASSESSMENT
Selection Test, pp. 65–66
Part Test, pp. 65–66
▪ Test Generator

ALTERNATIVE ASSESSMENT
Unit Three Integrated Assessment, p. 13

ACCESS FOR STUDENTS ACQUIRING ENGLISH
Unit Three Selection Summary Booklet

AUDIO LIBRARY
See Reference Card

302   THE LANGUAGE OF LITERATURE   TEACHER'S EDITION

Centre of the Universe (1992), Brian Jones. Courtesy of Nancy Poole's Studio, Toronto, Canada.

Picky, picky, picky.

First she told me, "I want your room cleaned in an hour," and then when I tried a time-saving plan, like storing stuff under the bed, she didn't appreciate it.

A little bad luck made things even worse.

When she came in to check on me, she stepped barefoot on a little metal Monopoly token.

Wow. Does she scream loud.

I apologized and everything.

But did she forgive me? Of course not.

I'm going to jump out this window, then sneak around the alley and crawl on my stomach past the big kitchen window. My mom's in the kitchen right now, with my aunt Rhea, getting the Thanksgiving dinner ready, and I don't want them to see me make my escape.

My aunt is why my mom's in such a bad mood, I know it.

She and my uncle Ted, and their one perfect kid, Andrea (my age, ten and a half) arrived from Chicago this morning.

We're all supposed to break turkey together in about half an hour.

I plan to be in Polynesia. Or at least New Jersey, by then.

Our family is not too fond of their family, but they come every Thanksgiving anyway.

SUMMARY

Thanksgiving, the day when snobby Aunt Rhea and her goody-goody family come to visit, is always a trial for Missy's family. This year Missy's mother is so nervous that she snaps at Missy, who hides in her parents' bedroom and plans to escape to Polynesia in the Pacific Ocean. Just as Missy is leaving through the window, the doorknob turns. She hides under the bed and watches her brother come in and start to crawl out the same window. When the doorknob turns again, he joins Missy under the bed. This time their mother is the one trying to escape. She lies down on the bed until . . . the door opens *again!* Now their father comes in and discovers his wife hiding in the closet. As she complains about her awful day, the children speak up from their hiding place. Desperate, the family considers a mass escape from Aunt Rhea—but instead settles for another Thanksgiving with her.

Thematic Link: *Coping with Injustice*
Missy and her family decide to put up with their unpleasant holiday guests even though all of them feel they've had enough.

Art Note

Centre of the Universe by Brian Jones
A Canadian painter, Jones (1950–) has exhibited his work widely in North America. His paintings also are displayed in a number of public and private collections.

Reading the Art *What do you notice about the similarities or differences between the houses? Does the painting set a scene like Missy's neighborhood—as opposed to Aunt Rhea's? What do you think the title of the painting means? Explain.*

Linking to Social Studies

Thanksgiving In the United States and Canada, one day each year is set aside as Thanksgiving Day, when families give thanks for the blessings they have received during the past year. The first Thanksgivings were probably harvest festivals, and people feasted and gave thanks for plentiful crops. Because of this, Thanksgiving still occurs in late fall. The first Thanksgiving in America was celebrated after the Plymouth colonists settled in New England. After a horrible winter in Massachusetts, in which nearly half of the colonists died, the summer brought a plentiful corn harvest. Governor William Bradford then decreed that a three-day feast be held to give thanks. However, it was not until 1863 that Thanksgiving became a national holiday, as decreed by President Lincoln. For the next 75 years, Thanksgiving was officially celebrated on the last Thursday of November. Then, in 1939, President Roosevelt moved the holiday one week earlier to help businesses in the country by extending the shopping period before Christmas. Finally, in 1941, Congress ruled that the fourth Thursday of November would be observed as Thanksgiving Day.

Linking to Geography

Polynesia Polynesia, meaning *many islands*, is one of three main groups of the Pacific Islands. Micronesia, meaning *small islands*, and Melanesia, meaning *black islands*, are the other two. Islands within Polynesia include Easter Island, Tahiti, Cook Islands, Hawaiian Islands, and Western and American Samoa. National boundaries are difficult to draw since Polynesia includes independent islands as well as islands that are considered territories of several nations—United States, United Kingdom, France, and New Zealand.

Hundreds of native languages are spoken across all the Pacific Islands. Scholars believe that these different languages may have developed from one long-forgotten common language called *Malayo-Polynesian*. Today, Polynesia continues to reflect both the diverse traditions of individual island civilizations, some over 1,500 years old, and the impact and influences of European and American colonization. Land forms vary from white beaches and palm trees, to hot jungles and cool, snow-covered mountains. Villagers originally farmed and fished.

My mom especially dislikes my aunt Rhea. She's rich and snobby and makes my mom and dad and my older brother, Jason, and me feel terrible.

She speaks with an English accent, even though I know she was born right here, where we live, in Massapequa, Long Island, New York.

Whenever Jason or I turn on the TV, Aunt Rhea always asks, oh so sweetly, "My, my, don't you two watch a dreadfully large quantity of television?"

That's the Rhea technique: questions that kill.

Like this morning, she asked Jason, when he was grabbing a cookie from the cookie jar: "Wouldn't you prefer a carrot?"

Who'd prefer a carrot to one of mom's chocolate-chip cookies, anyway?

Or later, as my mom was setting the big table, Rhea came over with the napkins and said: "My, my, Sara, but don't you make Missy or Jason do anything around here?"

Jason calls her Aunt Dia-Rhea.

Unfortunately, my mom brought her into my room to show her how I'd cleaned up before they all arrived, and that's when my mom stepped on the Monopoly top hat. And called me a slob. In front of Aunt Rhea. And told me not to come out until my room was spotless.

My first plan was not to come out of my room until I'm eighteen.

But that didn't seem possible. So I snuck in here, to my parents' bedroom, in the back of the house, and I'm going to climb out this window.

I'd have snuck out of mine, but I left some candies on my window ledge and they melted onto the metal window and now it won't open so easily.

More bad luck.

> Personally, I've had enough. I'm going to Polynesia. Don't worry about the sharks there. I'll be fine.

Besides, I don't want to play with my cousin Andrea anymore.

She is what my grandmother calls "a lovely child."

Andrea offered to set the table.

She always picks up her dishes after a meal and puts them in the sink.

She does the laundry every Saturday.

She compliments everybody on everything.

She doesn't even have to be reminded to do that stuff.

Personally, I think that's sick.

And when we started to play a game of jacks, she slaughtered me. And apologized every move she made.

I press my nose to the window. In the distance, I can see Annie MacElvane's house.

My best friend.

She is probably sitting down to Thanksgiving dinner right now with her warm, friendly family.

I could run away there.

It's not Polynesia, but as my dad would say, I'd make good time. I'd be there in a sec.

The problem is—I can't run anywhere until I get the summer screen out of this window.

I'd rather run away to Polynesia, because it's a great place for kids.

We just studied it in Mrs. Schwartz's Cultures of the World unit.

304   UNIT THREE   PART 1: COPING WITH INJUSTICE

There's no such word in Polynesia as *my* or *our*. Those are called possessive pronouns. The reason they don't have possessive pronouns is that nobody owns anything, including their own children. Children belong to God and the land and the universe. They have total freedom.

According to my map, Polynesia is about six inches from America. Which can't be that far.

I wonder what the kids in Polynesia are like.

I wonder if when they're in school, they have a unit called "The Peoples of Massapequa."

As a token of my friendliness, I'm bringing my jacks along. Mrs. Schwartz says that when you visit other peoples, you should bring a symbol of your own peoples. Jacks should do it. Plus, they'll give me something to do until I make a friend.

Well, the sooner I leave, the sooner I'll be playing tensies in paradise.

Maybe I'll just shove this screen right out the window.

Scrunching down, I kick at it.

Uh oh. A hole. The screen's still attached, but now there's this big hole in it that's the shape of my foot.

If I weren't running away already, I'd seriously consider it now, because when they discover this little disaster I'll be grounded until college.

I'll have to make the hole just a little bigger. Girl size.

Perfect. I'm set.

When my mom and dad realize I'm gone, their hearts will break.

In fact, I think I should write a note to make them feel a little worse. Something like:

Dear Mom and Dad: This home is not working out. If you miss me, call Polynesia 2-4000.

Or:

Personally, I've had enough. I'm going to Polynesia. Don't worry about the sharks there. I'll be fine.

If a shark eats me, that'll really kill them.

My body is easing into the scratchy screen when suddenly I hear a *thud*.

A *thump*.

A *clump*.

And then the rattle and vibration of furniture in the hall.

Heavy footsteps are coming toward the bedroom.

My body stiffens. My heart pounds.

What could that be? I have to get out of here. Fast.

Ow. The torn screen is so scratchy.

Thud. Rattle. Tickle.

Bounce. Bounce.

It's my brother, Jason. Bouncing a basketball in the hall.

When my mom yells at him about indoor basketball bouncing, she has a point. The whole house vibrates.

Is that the doorknob turning? This doorknob?

I try to ease my body further through the screen.

I can't get out.

There's only one thing I can do.

Backing my butt out of the screen, I jump down from the ledge and look around my mom's room for a place to hide.

The closet.

I'll never make it in time.

Diving onto the floor, I roll under the huge queen-size bed just as the door opens.

In a second, I'm peeking out from under the bedspread, inches from Jason's big clodhopper feet, which are now standing in front of my mom's bureau.

I bet he's looking in the mirror, as usual.

Wait. Those clodhoppers of his are moving. Is he leaving?

THANKSGIVING IN POLYNESIA **305**

Individual Activity
WRITING A DIALOGUE

Have students write a dialogue between Aunt Rhea and Uncle Ted, in which these characters speculate on what is going on upstairs.

Teacher's Role Tell students to consider all that they know about the aunt and uncle and why they drive Missy's family mad. Encourage students to write their dialogues in a manner consistent with the characters' personalities in the story.

Rubric

3 Full Accomplishment Students create realistic portrayals in their dialogues, incorporating details that they have learned from Missy's narration, such as Aunt Rhea's affected manner of speaking or Uncle Ted's obsessive interest in his financial success.

2 Substantial Accomplishment Students create portrayals based on what they have learned in the text but include few specific details.

1 Little or Partial Accomplishment By their content and tone, students' dialogues reveal that they have not understood the characters of Aunt Rhea and Uncle Ted.

Copyright © Mary GrandPre.

306 UNIT THREE PART 1: COPING WITH INJUSTICE

Multicultural Perspectives

KWANZAA Kwanzaa is an African-American holiday drawn from the traditional African festival that, like Thanksgiving, celebrates the harvest of the first crops. The holiday, which lasts for seven days, begins on December 26. Kwanzaa came about in 1966 in the United States when M. Ron Karenga, a professor of Pan-African studies, decided to create an event to help strengthen African-American culture in America.

Kwanzaa centers around the seven principles of black culture known as the *Nguzo Saba*. These principles include *Umoja* (unity), *Kuj i chagulia* (self-determination), *Ujima* (collective work and responsibility), *Ujamaa* (cooperative economics), *Nia* (purpose), *Kuumba* (creativity), and *Imani* (faith). Each day of Kwanzaa is dedicated to one of these seven principles. Each night one of the seven candles in a kinara (candleholder) is lit and families sit together and discuss the principle for the day.

No. He's moving toward the window.

I peek out a little further just in time to see him climb onto the ledge, open the window, and kick the screen right out into the backyard.

"What does she want," he's muttering. "I went to the store. I meant to buy regular milk. So I didn't see the label that said buttermilk. Personally, I've had enough!"

His leg is out the window.

My gosh.

He's running away too!

Gee. I'm going to miss him.

What am I talking about—I'm going to miss him? I'm running away too!

Thud. Thud.

It's footsteps again.

What is this? A convention?

You can't even have a little privacy in your own parents' bedroom when you want it.

Jason's heard something too. His head is turned, perked at attention.

The doorknob. It's turning again.

Jason's eyes widen in panic and then he jumps backward off the window ledge.

The next thing I know, I have company under the bed.

"Happy Thanksgiving . . . " I whisper.

"*Ahhh!*" he almost screams in fright, but I cover his mouth as I swallow a giggle, because we can both hear the soft *clip clap* of my mom's loose slippers.

She's *clip clapping* around the room. The bureau drawer squeaks open, there's the soft whoosh of something being removed, the drawer squeaks shut again, and then the springs of the mattress hit my nose as she plops down on the bed.

She's sighing. Which lowers the springs even more.

Then she mutters, "Personally I've had enough . . ." and leans backward. "On the other hand, you're a grown woman, Sara. Now, go out there and handle it."

The springs lower, hitting me in the nose, and then lift.

She's gotten up.

In a second, we hear the door open and softly shut.

She's gone.

Wait a second. It's opening again.

"Sara? Are you in here?"

It's my dad, coming in.

But where's my mom, if my dad didn't see her going out?

I know I heard the door shutting.

Oh no. It couldn't be.

But it is.

The door that shut wasn't the bedroom door. It was the closet door.

My mom, my thirty-five-year-old mom, is hiding in the closet at this very moment.

"Sara? Jason? Missy?" my dad whispers again in a voice that sounds a little lonely.

Gee. Poor Daddy.

He's been stuck out there all alone with Aunt Rhea and Uncle Ted.

Uncle Ted probably just finished showing off his newest gold charge cards to my dad.

I peek out from underneath the bottom of the bedspread.

> You can't even have a little privacy in your own parents' bedroom when you want it.

THANKSGIVING IN POLYNESIA **307**

OPTION 2

Cooperative Learning
PANTOMIME THE STORY

Have students work in small groups and pantomime "Thanksgiving in Polynesia," from the scene in which Missy enters her parents' bedroom until her family leaves the bedroom to face the tedious relatives.

Teacher's Role Refer to the rubric in advance and tell students what qualities in their pantomimes you are looking for. Maximize student learning by giving each group member an active role. Voice monitors can ensure that each group has a quiet enough environment in which to work effectively. Recorders can write down groups' plans for their pantomimes. Accuracy coaches can ensure that pantomimes are based on the story.

Rubric

3 Full Accomplishment Groups create pantomimes that accurately reflect and kinesthetically enhance the story.

2 Substantial Accomplishment Groups create pantomimes that accurately reflect the text but are kinesthetically uninspired.

1 Little or Partial Accomplishment Groups have difficulty creating pantomimes that reflect and interpret the action of the story.

Everything that's going on is reflected in the full-length mirror on the closet door. I can see a dress caught in the doorjamb of my mom's closet.

She's in there all right.

"Where is everybody?" my dad says.

Silence.

My dad takes one last look around the room, and then moves to the bedroom door again.

But just as he's backing out, the closet door opens and my mom pops out

"Hi . . ." she says.

"Sara! What are you doing in the closet?"

"I was . . . I was looking for a better tablecloth." She swallows and then continues. "Actually, I was also looking for a whole new house. And a whole new me. But . . . it's not in there. . . ." Her face starts to pucker, like she's going to cry.

My dad puts his arm around her.

"Is Rhea getting to you, honey?"

My mom shakes her head. "Nooo. What makes you think that?"

My dad grins.

"And I took it out on the kids. . . ."

"They'll live. . . ." my dad says.

Sure we'll live, I think. But where?

"What's the matter with me?" my mom sobs. "I'm a grown woman. Why does that phony get to me? Why can't I handle it? I have no character. No courage. No strength. You want me to make it all nice. And I try, but she's getting to me. Even your brother Ted is getting to me. All his mutual funds are going up. Did you know that?"

My dad nods. "Sure did."

"Plus, I've been yelling at the kids. For nothing. Well, not nothing. . . ."

Nothing, Mom. Nothing.

"And they're fed up with me. And I don't blame them." She starts to cry again. "The turkey is probably dry, I have an ugly tablecloth, and I'm a terrible mother." She's bawling.

I have to admit that the sound of my mom's sobs is getting to me. I can't help it.

"You're not such a terrible mother . . ." I mumble.

The sobbing stops.

"Who's that? Where's that? What's that?" my mom asks.

"Stevie Baldwin's mom is worse," Jason talks right into the mattress. "She's not as mean as you are today, but she treats him like a baby. Last week, four guys were playing pool in his room, and she walks in, and with this high, squeaky voice, says 'Would any of you boys like a Twinkie . . . ?' You'd never do that!"

Just as Jason's finishing his speech the bedspread, like a curtain, rises, and my mom's wide eyes stare at us.

"Happy Thanksgiving," I say to her. Then, I can't help adding, "But for next Thanksgiving, you ought to dust under here, Mom. . . ."

She blushes. Then her thumb jerks backward, like a hitchhiker.

"Out. Both of you. Out."

Jason rolls one way. I roll the other.

In a second we're all standing around my mom and dad's bed.

My mom's fingertips are against her cheeks. I think she's in shock. My dad's eyes have already taken in the open window.

> I feel lectures and meaningless sayings coming on.

308 UNIT THREE PART 1: COPING WITH INJUSTICE

Multicultural Perspectives

SUKKOT Sukkot, or the Feast of the Tabernacles, is a Jewish holiday that celebrates the end of the harvest season. Sukkot begins on the 15th day of the Hebrew month of Tishri (usually in early October) and lasts nine days. The ancient Hebrews celebrated this holiday as a festival of thanksgiving. Sacrifices were brought to the Temple in Jerusalem, and people formed parades carrying lulovs (palm branches), etrogs (citrons), and myrtle and willow branches. During the festival, observers live in a hut (called a sukkah) as a reminder of the huts in which their ancestors lived during their wanderings in the wilderness.

Just as I say, "Jason was running away," Jason says, "Missy was running away."

And then we both say, "We can't take it anymore either."

My dad and mom give each other looks. I feel lectures and meaningless sayings coming on.

"Aunt Rhea means well . . ." my mom begins.

But now that we know how she really feels about Aunt Rhea, all we have to do is give her a "yeah, sure" look, and she stops.

"On the other hand, kids . . ." Now my dad is going into speech mode. "You can't run away from a problem . . ."

But then he looks at my mom, who is standing inches from her former hideaway closet.

And he stops. And sighs. "What are we going to do?" he says. "They are unbearable. I've tried to talk to them, hint, be diplomatic, but it's like talking to Martians . . ."

Everyone's looking dumb, so I jump right in there. "Could we . . . *all* run away?" I ask softly.

All our eyes shift to the open window. Then we look at each other.

I can see the open sea. Polynesia. Palm trees.

Then my dad sighs. "My mother, your grandmother, would have a heart attack in heaven. . . . I can't . . ."

My mom agrees. "Look, it's a Thanksgiving from hell . . . but otherwise it's not so terrible. What we have to do is what we do every year. Get through it, and give thanks on Sunday—when it's over."

Everybody nods at practically the same time. Which makes us all giggle.

"Are we ready?" my dad asks. "We have to get out there or they're going to start to get suspicious. Plus, the turkey is done. . . ."

My mother turns white. "Oh my God . . . my turkey . . . my turkey." She lunges for the door.

Then she stops, pauses, looks back at us, puts a big smile on her face, stands up straight, and with dignity, walks out her bedroom door.

My father follows.

My brother goes next.

Before I leave, I take one last peek at the window.

I guess that's what people mean by a window of opportunity.

Polynesia would have been swell.

But it's not to be.

Of course, Christmas is coming up and there are rumors that my mother's second cousins are coming up from Florida.

I can feel the wind wafting through my hair already.

But in the meanwhile, I close the door behind me, take a deep breath, and gather up the courage that the Peoples of Massapequa are known for. ❖

SUSAN HAVEN

Susan Haven is an American comedy writer whose career began in the early 1970s. She has written for magazines and movies and television programs. She has published two novels for young adults.

Haven writes, "Being funny gets my characters through whatever crisis they need to get through, and it's helped me as well. I'm grateful that I live with a son and a husband who can easily make me laugh, no matter what. I am also a social worker, working as a therapist with families. Besides my family, nothing gives me more pleasure than being around or working with kids."

OTHER WORKS *Maybe I'll Move to the Lost and Found*

SUSAN HAVEN

"Thanksgiving in Polynesia" was written for an anthology of original humorous short stories titled *Funny You Should Ask.* Haven has created material for the comedian Lily Tomlin's precocious child character Edith Ann and written light pieces about children for *Redbook, Women's Day, Ms., New York,* and *The New York Times.*

OPTION 3

Class Discussion

SHARING IDEAS

Teacher's Role After students have read the selection, engage them in a class discussion using the following questions. You may need to moderate among different or conflicting opinions raised by the questions. Make sure that students adequately support their answers with details from the selection as well as their own experiences.

1. Why do you think there is so much conflict between Missy's and Aunt Rhea's families? *(Possible response: Aunt Rhea's family makes Missy's family members feel bad about themselves. Uncle Ted, with his charge cards and mutual funds, shows off his greater wealth. Aunt Rhea, in criticizing Missy and Jason, asserts her sense of superiority.)*

2. Do you agree with Missy that Polynesia would be a good place to spend Thanksgiving? Explain. *(Some students may say visiting a warm climate for the holiday would be nice. Others may say staying in the U.S. during an American holiday would be more fun.)*

3. Did your feelings about Missy's mother change as you read the story? *(Some students may say that they perceived the mother as a more sensitive character when she hid in the closet and cried. Others may say that they never had strong feelings about the mother.)*

4. What do you think of the strategy the family developed for dealing with Thanksgiving at the end of the story? *(Some students may say that the strategy allowed the family to get through the visit without taking their relatives' bad humor out on one another. Other students may argue that the family should have climbed out the open window.)*

OVERVIEW

In the Guided Assignment for this section, students will write a plot analysis. By analyzing plot, students will better comprehend how a story works and what makes it interesting and effective. As preparation for the assignment, The Writer's Style will help students to understand how to use dialogue to supply information about characters and events. In Reading the World, students will analyze a real-world situation to learn more about predicting outcomes.

Objectives

- To understand how writers use dialogue to supply information
- To write dialogue using quotation marks
- To write a plot analysis of an event in a story
- To predict outcomes in a real-world situation

Skills

LITERATURE
- Using dialogue to provide background information

GRAMMAR AND USAGE
- Using quotation marks
- Writing a summary
- Using commas with conjunctions

MEDIA LITERACY
- Interpreting a picture

CRITICAL THINKING
- Predicting outcomes
- Classifying
- Analyzing
- Speculating

SPEAKING, LISTENING, AND VIEWING
- Peer conferencing
- Group conferencing

Teaching Strategy: MODELING

In the following models, dialogue is used in a variety of ways. It assists the plot, reveals characters' personalities, and provides background information.

A **Bethancourt** Possible responses: Dialogue provides information about the phone calls that have been occurring. It also indicates that Ginny has already talked to the narrator of the story. It suggests that the narrator is going to have to confess to what he did or prove he was not responsible.

B **Saroyan** Possible responses: He seems to not like money, he "has a gentle heart," he is homesick, and he is large.

WRITING ABOUT LITERATURE

SOLVING A STORY

Have you ever noticed that it's easier to understand a problem by breaking it into smaller parts and then solving each part? You can also use this technique to help you better understand and appreciate stories. For example, what purpose does dialogue serve in "User Friendly"? How are events in "The Summer of the Beautiful White Horse" connected? In the following pages you will

- see how writers use dialogue in stories
- analyze the plot of a selection you've just read
- use analysis to understand an event you might observe

Writer's Style: Dialogue Dialogue is conversation—people talking to each other. Writers use dialogue to give information about characters and events.

Read the Literature

Notice how dialogue helps writers tell their stories.

Literature Models

A **Dialogue Adds to the Plot**
How does this conversation tell you what's happening in the story? How does it suggest what might happen?

> "Don't play dumb," Chuck went on. "I mean those creepy phone calls. Anytime my sister gets on the phone, some voice cuts in and says things to her."
> "What kind of things?" I asked, trying to get loose.
> "You know what they are. Ginny told me about talking to you yesterday. You got some girl to make those calls for you and say all those things. . . ."
>
> T. Ernesto Bethancourt, from "User Friendly"

B **Dialogue Reveals Characters' Personalities**
What do you learn about Uncle Khosrove from this conversation?

> "I spit on money," my uncle Khosrove said. He got up and stalked out of the house, slamming the screen door.
> My mother explained.
> "He has a gentle heart," she said. "It is simply that he is homesick and such a large man."
>
> William Saroyan, from "The Summer of the Beautiful White Horse"

310 UNIT THREE: A SENSE OF FAIRNESS

PRINT AND MEDIA RESOURCES

UNIT THREE RESOURCE BOOK
The Writer's Style, p. 33
Prewriting Guide, p. 34
Elaboration, p. 35
Peer Response Guide, pp. 36–37
Revising and Editing, p. 38
Student Model, p. 39
Rubric, p. 40

GRAMMAR MINI–LESSONS
Transparencies, pp. 28, 33
Copymasters, pp. 37, 38, 42

ACCESS FOR STUDENTS ACQUIRING ENGLISH
Reading and Writing Support

WRITING MINI–LESSONS
Transparencies, p. 57

FORMAL ASSESSMENT
Guidelines for Writing Assessment

Connect to Life

Since scriptwriters can't explain all previous events, they use dialogue to tell you about important information that happened earlier.

Script

> LUKE: You told me Vader betrayed and murdered my father.
>
> BEN: Your father was seduced by the dark side of the Force. He ceased to be Anakin Skywalker and became Darth Vader. When that happened, the good man who was your father was destroyed. So what I have told you was true . . . from a certain point of view.
>
> Lawrence Kasdan and George Lucas
> from *Return of the Jedi*

Dialogue Provides Background Information
How else might the information in this conversation be revealed?

Try Your Hand: Using Dialogue

1. **A Complete Conversation** With a partner, rewrite the following paragraph, using dialogue.

   I told my sister that I would like to have a computer like Louis. She told me I was crazy. I tried to explain that it would be cool to have Louis because I could tell it secrets without worrying that it would blab to others. She didn't think that was such a big deal. Then I rattled off a zillion other reasons telling how Louis might help me.

2. **In Your Own Words** Choose a conversation from one of the selections you've read. Rewrite the dialogue as you and your friends would have said it.

3. **With Your Own Ears** You hear dialogue around you every day—at school, on the playground, at the store. Write down some of the dialogue you hear.

SkillBuilder

GRAMMAR FROM WRITING

Using Quotation Marks

Quotation marks are used at the beginning and the end of direct quotations. In written dialogue, like this section of "User Friendly" by T. Ernesto Bethancourt, quotation marks set off the exact words of each speaker. Also notice that when the speaker changes, a new paragraph begins and the line is indented.

> "What'd you ask Chuck?" I said.
> Ginny laughed. "I asked him who was that nerdy kid who keeps staring at me on the bus. He knew who I meant, right away."

APPLYING WHAT YOU'VE LEARNED
Combine the sentences below to create a conversation. Place quotation marks where needed and use correct paragraphing.

- Chuck growled Okay, nerd. What's the big idea?
- I volunteered Energy and mass are different aspects of the same thing.
- In other words, *E* equals *mc* squared. That's the biggest idea I know I told him.
- Chuck said Don't get wise, nerd.

GRAMMAR HANDBOOK

For more information on quotation marks, see pages 850 of the Grammar Handbook.

WRITING ABOUT LITERATURE **311**

Teaching Strategy: STUMBLING BLOCK

C Students may be unfamiliar with scripts. Tell them that scripts are the pages the actors and directors use in plays, television programs, and films. Scripts contain descriptions of scenes, action, and dialogue.

Teaching Strategy: MODELING

D Possible responses: Students may suggest that Luke could have learned the information in a dialogue with Darth Vader himself. Or Luke could have asked Ben a series of questions about his father instead of Ben telling the whole story at once.

Teaching Strategy: USING THE SKILLBUILDER

E You can help students write effective dialogue by teaching the SkillBuilder on Using Quotation Marks before they answer the Try Your Hand exercises.

Try Your Hand

1. Possible response:
   "I want a computer like Louis," I said to my sister.
   "You are crazy!" she replied.
   "But I could tell it secrets and stuff and not worry about it blabbing to people. That'd be cool."
   "So?" she asked, not convinced.
   "Well, I could do my homework and look up things and talk to people on the Internet and play games on it," I answered.

2. Encourage students to imagine themselves in the situation portrayed in their selection.

3. Have students pay special attention to the differences in language that various people use. Encourage them to think about the differences between formal and informal language, dialect, and slang.

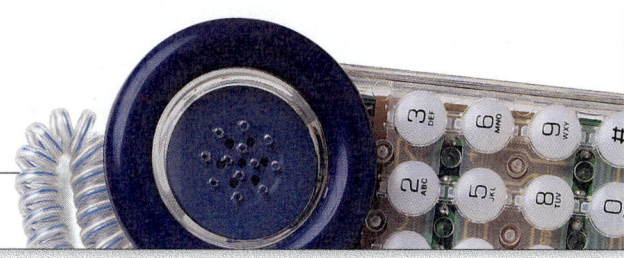

SkillBuilder — GRAMMAR FROM WRITING

USING QUOTATION MARKS Make sure that students notice that quotation marks are used only when someone actually speaks. Also have them notice where the lines are and are not indented. Have them find the contraction and other examples of language used in direct speech that are not always used in more formal writing.

Application Answer:
   Chuck growled, "Okay, nerd. What's the big idea?"
   I volunteered, "Energy and mass are different aspects of the same thing. In other words, *E* equals *mc* squared. That's the biggest idea I know," I told him.
   Chuck said, "Don't get wise, nerd."

Additional Suggestions You may wish to add these sentences to the paragraph and have students continue the conversation.
- I shrugged and replied It's what I know.
- He told me Get a life and then walked off.
- You too I offered to his back That'll teach you.

Reteaching/Reinforcement

- Grammar Handbook, anthology pp. 850–851
- *Grammar Mini-Lessons* copymasters, p. 42, transparencies, p. 33

The Writer's Craft

Using Dialogue, pp. 278–280
Quotation Marks, pp. 586–587

THE LANGUAGE OF LITERATURE TEACHER'S EDITION **311**

Critical Thinking: CLASSIFYING

F Help students distinguish between a story's plot and its other elements. Have them list the other components of a story, such as description, character portrayal, and parts not directly related to the sequence of events.

Critical Thinking: ANALYZING

G Encourage students to discover where one part of a story begins and ends by having them think of each story as a series of events. Guide them to avoid blurring together a whole series of events by telling them that their plot analysis will focus on only one part of a story.

Teaching Strategy: MODELING

H Have students use the story map to follow the events of the plot of "User Friendly." Point out that the student's story map is organized to show the order in which the events happened.

WRITING ABOUT LITERATURE

Analysis

F The plot is a series of events in a story. By studying and analyzing the events, characters, and dialogue in a story, you will be able to better understand what makes the story interesting and effective. Analyzing a story situation can also help you understand the situations that you observe in your life.

GUIDED ASSIGNMENT

Write a Plot Analysis On the next few pages, you will look closely at a key event from one of the stories you've just read. Then you'll have a chance to describe how that event was important to the story.

❶ Prewrite and Explore

In a plot analysis, you look closely at one part of a story—the events that occur—and write about how and why these events make the story interesting. Jot down stories you enjoyed **G** and a key event you remember from each.

CHOOSING A STORY AND EVENT

These questions might help you choose a story and event to write about.

- Which story has the most surprising or interesting turn of events?
- Which event in the story is the most exciting? Why?
- What caused this event to happen? How does this event affect what happens later?

GATHERING INFORMATION

Remember that writers sometimes use dialogue to describe events in a story. Look for key information about events and situations in the conversations the characters have.

H Also, a story map like the one shown below can help you think about events and information and how they help to tell a story.

Student's Story Map

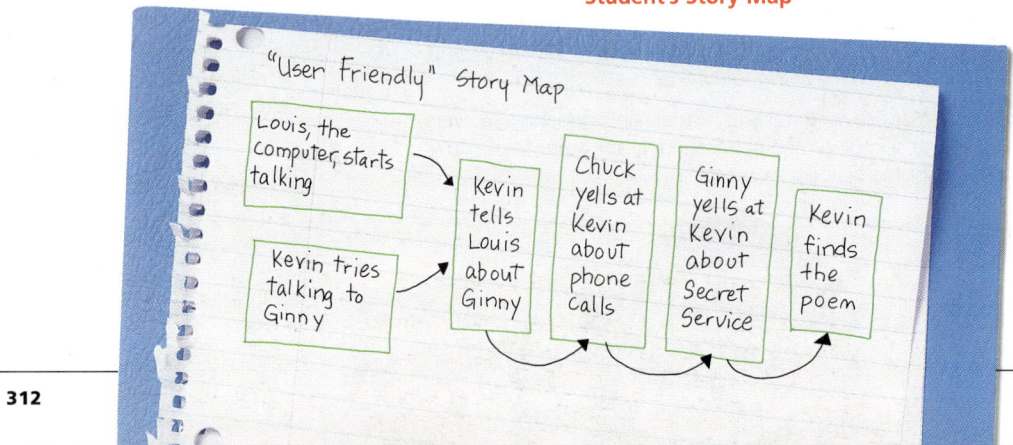

312

 Assessment Option

SELF-ASSESSMENT After students have completed Gathering Information, they can assess their understanding of plot. Students should consider the following questions:

- *Have I chosen one event in the story?*
- *Did my story map of the event summarize all the main occurrences in the event?*
- *Did I read dialogue closely to discover key information?*

---

312 THE LANGUAGE OF LITERATURE **TEACHER'S EDITION**

❷ Freewriting

Now that you have chosen an event, freewrite about what makes it important. Don't worry if your thoughts seem disorganized. You can sort out your ideas—or even change your mind—once you get something on paper.

Student's Freewriting Model

> What's Louis up to? I figured Louis was going to do something to help Kevin. I first realized that Louis was fooling around when Kevin ran into Chuck Linke. What's strange is that it's a girl's voice that's saying creepy things to Ginny Linke.

Is it clear which event I'm talking about? I think I'd better give a little summary.

How does this scene change or move the plot along?

Which details would really show how the scene is strange?

> Something strange and interesting is going on in this scene. What's great is that Kevin doesn't know what's going on. I figured it out, though. This scene makes you want to see how Kevin is going to figure it out.

❸ Draft and Share

As you draft your analysis, remember that it should have three parts: an introduction that gives readers background information; a body that contains facts, reasons, and other details that support your analysis; and a conclusion that summarizes your analysis and draws an overall conclusion. Share your draft with a classmate and ask for suggestions on how to improve it.

PEER RESPONSE

- Which parts of my analysis do you agree or disagree with?
- What were the strong and weak points of the essay?

SkillBuilder

WRITER'S CRAFT

Writing a Summary

A summary is a brief explanation of the important events in a story or the main idea and important details in a nonfiction article. Summaries are often used at the beginning of an essay about literature to help readers understand what the story is about.

Here are a few things to remember when summarizing.

- Include all the important ideas and events.
- Leave out minor details and examples.
- Write in your own words. If you wish to quote an author, be sure to use quotation marks around the author's words.

APPLYING WHAT YOU'VE LEARNED

A story map contains most of the information you need to write a story summary. You might consider using a story map like the one on the opposite page to help you write a summary for your story analysis.

WRITING ABOUT LITERATURE   **313**

Writing Skill: ELABORATION

Freewriting provides an opportunity for students to think through the ideas and information they have gathered. Suggest that they elaborate on their ideas by adding details and examples, and by choosing relevant quotations from the story.

Teaching Strategy: USING THE SKILLBUILDER

You can help students draft their plot analyses by teaching the SkillBuilder on Writing a Summary at this time. It shows students how to summarize events in a story to ensure that readers understand the subject of the story.

SkillBuilder  WRITER'S CRAFT

WRITING A SUMMARY Explain to students that summaries can be short even if they are summarizing a large part of a story. Tell them that a good place to start in summarizing many types of writing is to find the main idea. Have students practice by choosing one selection from this unit and writing a summary of it.

Application Story maps will vary. Make sure students include the important elements of the event. Also check that they have their plot elements in the correct order.

Additional Suggestions Have students practice drafting and summarizing by encouraging them to turn the story map into a plot summary.

Reteaching/Reinforcement
- *Writing Mini-Lessons* transparencies, p. 57

THE LANGUAGE OF LITERATURE TEACHER'S EDITION **313**

Critical Thinking: ANALYZING

K Emphasize to students that they are not expected to write a perfect draft the first time. To evaluate and revise their plot analyses, students should check that elements they include are both relevant and interesting.

Teaching Strategy: MODELING

L Point out to students how this sample meets the Standards for Evaluation on this page. Show them that the story title, author, and the principal characters are all mentioned at the beginning of the draft. The writer clearly shows what was interesting in the story and supports these points with specific examples.

Standards for Evaluation

Ideas and Content
- gives the author, title, and brief summary of the literature
- analyzes one feature or element of the story (plot, imagery, character, setting, point of view)
- supports analysis with evidence from the story, including examples, quotes, and details
- has an ending that summarizes the analysis and draws an over-all conclusion

Structure and Form
- uses well-organized paragraphs and a clear organization
- includes transitional words and phrases to show relationships among ideas
- uses a variety of sentence structures

Grammar, Usage, and Mechanics
- contains no more than two or three minor errors in grammar and usage
- contains no more than two or three minor errors in spelling, capitalization, and punctuation

---

WRITING ABOUT LITERATURE

4 Revise and Edit

All good writers revise and revise again until they are happy with their writing. Look at the Standards for Evaluation below and your reviewer's comments. Then revise and edit your draft. When you are finished, think about how your plot analysis changed the way you think about the story.

Student's Final Draft

> "User Friendly"
>
> Do you ever wonder if computers have feelings? Author T. Ernesto Bethancourt writes about this idea in "User Friendly." Kevin Neal has a powerful computer named Louis. One day Louis sends personal messages to Kevin. So when Kevin is rejected by Ginny Linke, he "tells" Louis all about his problem. Kevin soon finds out how powerful Louis is.

What information do you find out here that will help you understand the scene below?

What does the writer find interesting in the scene?

> A key moment comes when Kevin is bullied by Ginny's huge brother Chuck. It's an important scene because it shows how powerful Louis is. The scene is interesting because readers can figure out that Louis is trying to help Kevin, but Kevin, Ginny, and Chuck don't know. When Chuck describes the phone calls, I think of what Louis said to Kevin in an earlier scene: "I'll take care of Ginny."

Standards for Evaluation

A plot analysis
- gives the author, the title, and a summary of the story
- clearly shows which events are important and why
- is supported by reasons, examples, and quotations from the story
- has an ending that summarizes the analysis and draws an overall conclusion

314 UNIT THREE: A SENSE OF FAIRNESS

Assessment Option

SELF-ASSESSMENT Have students assess their plot summaries by considering the following questions:
- *Does my draft have a main idea?*
- *Will my audience understand what I am discussing?*
- *Have I expressed my reactions to the plot events?*
- *Did I support my reactions with details and examples from the story?*
- *Did I consider the information presented in dialogue?*

Grammar in Context

Coordinating Conjunctions A **conjunction** is a word that connects sentence parts or whole sentences. When writing your analysis, you can show how ideas are different or alike by using conjunctions. The words *and*, *but*, and *or* are coordinating conjunctions.

> The scene is interesting because readers can figure out that Louis is trying to help Kevin, *but* Kevin doesn't know. Ginny *don't* know.

How do the added conjunctions make the writing easier to read and understand? For more information about conjunctions, see pages 813 and 843 of the Grammar Handbook.

Try Your Hand: Using Coordinating Conjunctions

On a separate sheet of paper, revise the following paragraph, using coordinating conjunctions. Try connecting two sentences with a few different conjunctions until you find the one that makes the most sense.

> Kevin Neal's father is a brilliant computer designer. He has built Kevin a powerful computer named Louis. Kevin's father is working on a voice module. Louis can't talk yet. Actually, Louis can talk. Kevin isn't sure if he should tell his dad about that. He isn't sure if he should tell anyone else. He worries about it.

SkillBuilder

GRAMMAR FROM WRITING

Using Commas with Conjunctions

When you use a coordinating conjunction to join related sentences, place a comma before the conjunction.

Louis had access to mainframe computers. It cracked their security systems. (Louis had access to mainframe computers, and it cracked their security systems.)

When you use a conjunction to join sentence parts, do not place a comma before the conjunction.

I erased the program and set Louis up as a normal computer.

Dad disconnected the whole thing and did some rewiring.

APPLYING WHAT YOU'VE LEARNED

Number a separate sheet of paper 1–3. Combine each pair of sentences into a single sentence. Choose a conjunction and use a comma if necessary. Omit words in italics.

1. Ginny's brother was named Chuck. Everyone called him the "Missing" Linke.
2. Louis had a modem. *Louis had* a voice module.
3. Kevin could read information on Louis's screen. He could print information if he wanted.

WRITING ABOUT LITERATURE **315**

CUSTOMIZING FOR
Less-Proficient Writers

M Explain to students that writing in which all sentences have the same structure is often uninteresting and difficult to read. Sentences can vary in length and coordinating conjunctions can clarify writing by making the relationships between ideas clear. Have them read some selections in this unit to look for conjunctions. Encourage them to look for connected sentences that indicate how ideas are similar or different.

Teaching Strategy:
USING THE SKILLBUILDER

N To help students add conjunctions as they revise their writing, teach the SkillBuilder on Using Commas with Conjunctions at this time.

Try Your Hand

Revisions will vary. Encourage students to punctuate their paragraphs correctly. The following is a sample:

> Kevin Neal's father is a brilliant computer designer, and he has built Kevin a powerful computer named Louis. Kevin's father is working on a voice module, but Louis can't talk yet. Actually, Louis can talk, but Kevin isn't sure if he should tell his dad about that, and he isn't sure if he should tell anyone else. He worries about it.

SkillBuilder GRAMMAR FROM WRITING

USING COMMAS WITH CONJUNCTIONS

Help students to understand that the words *and*, *but*, and *or* are not always coordinating conjunctions; it depends on their use in a sentence. Stress that it is only when they join complete sentences, not when they join phrases, that they are *coordinating* conjunctions. They *coordinate* between the two sentences.

Application Answers:
1. Ginny's brother was named Chuck, but everyone called him the "Missing" Linke.
2. Louis had a modem and a voice module.
3. Kevin could read information on Louis's screen, and he could print information if he wanted.

Additional Suggestion Have students check whether the commas in the following questions are necessary.
1. Kevin's father didn't think Louis could hear, but he could do that too. *(yes)*
2. Kevin got into trouble, and had to confront Chuck. *(no)*

Reteaching/Reinforcement
- *Grammar Handbook*, anthology p. 843
- *Grammar Mini-Lessons* copymasters, pp. 37, 38, transparencies, p. 28

What Are Conjunctions?, pp. 516–517

THE LANGUAGE OF LITERATURE TEACHER'S EDITION **315**

READING THE WORLD

On pages 310–314 students summarized the plot of a work of literature. They should also be aware that they can apply what they have learned about plot summary to a real-world situation. In this lesson, students analyze the picture and speculate on what has happened and make predictions about what is going to happen.

316 THE LANGUAGE OF LITERATURE TEACHER'S EDITION

READING THE WORLD

WHAT HAPPENS NEXT?

If you think about it, everyday life is a lot like a collection of stories. There are interesting characters, surprising plot twists, and different conversations.

View In your notebook, describe what you see in the picture. **O**

Interpret What's going on? Why is this man doing this? What problem might he have? What will happen next? **P**

Discuss In a group, discuss who the man might be and why this scene might not end up as you expect. Record your thoughts and the group's ideas in your notebook. You can use the SkillBuilder on this page to help you make a prediction. **Q**

SkillBuilder

 CRITICAL THINKING

Predicting Outcomes

You make predictions every day, though you may not know it. For example, when you look out the window, see dark clouds, and then grab an umbrella as you go out the door, you're predicting that it might rain. When you make a prediction, you use obvious clues, information from a reliable source, or knowledge from experience to guess what might happen in the future.

What kinds of clues help you predict what may happen next in the picture on this page? Maybe something like this happened to you, and that experience tells you how to predict an outcome. What specific information in the picture helps you make your prediction? Making predictions gets you involved in a situation and can help you relate your experiences to the world.

APPLYING WHAT YOU'VE LEARNED

Write a short dialogue in which you talk to the man in the picture and give him some advice. You could tell him your predictions or maybe ask a question. How will he respond? Share your dialogue with a classmate and try reading it aloud.

READING THE WORLD **317**

Critical Thinking: SPECULATING

O Students may describe what they see in terms of what the man is trying to do. Encourage them to use sensory language by drawing their attention to the man's hands and feet. Ask them whether he seems in control and how they think he is feeling, both physically and mentally. Make sure students notice the words on the boxes.

Media Literacy: INTERPRETING A PICTURE

P Students should see that the man is trying to transport the boxes, but that he has tried to move too many. They seem about to fall. Students will probably speculate that the next event will be the boxes falling onto the man and the car, and the contents of the boxes damaged.

Speaking, Listening, and Viewing: GROUP DISCUSSION

Q Students may infer that the man is trying to transport the boxes. They may decide that the boxes will not fall because the man is not running out of the way but is trying to stop them from falling. Also, if this is his job, he may be used to situations like this.

SkillBuilder CRITICAL THINKING

PREDICTING OUTCOMES Encourage students to think of other examples from their daily lives in which they predict outcomes. Students may think of small and seemingly unimportant predictions, such as hearing steps on the stairs at a certain time of day and predicting who will be home. Or they may think of more important ones, such as predicting their parents' reaction to a request for a special favor. Point out that even if they haven't been in exactly the same situation as the man in the picture, their experience with stacking boxes or other items can tell them a lot about what might happen.

Application Students can imagine talking to the man at this precise moment, or they can imagine talking to him during what happens next. Check that student dialogue is correctly indented and punctuated.

THE LANGUAGE OF LITERATURE **TEACHER'S EDITION** **317**

UNIT THREE
Part 2 Lesson Planner

TIME ALLOTMENTS SHOWN ARE APPROXIMATE. DEPENDING ON YOUR GOALS AND THE NEEDS OF YOUR STUDENTS, YOU MAY WISH TO ALLOW MORE OR LESS TIME FOR CERTAIN PORTIONS OF THE LESSON.

Table of Contents	Discussion	Previewing the Selection	Reading the Selection
PART OPENER FACING THE CONSEQUENCES What Do You Think? page 318	**20 MINUTES** • Reflect on the part theme		
SELECTION Shrewd Todie and Lyzer the Miser page 321 AVERAGE		**15 MINUTES** • PERSONAL CONNECTION • CULTURAL CONNECTION • READING CONNECTION: Evaluating	**15 MINUTES** • Introduce vocabulary • Read pp. 321–25 (5 pp.)
SELECTION *from* A Long Hard Journey page 331 CHALLENGING		**15 MINUTES** • PERSONAL CONNECTION • HISTORICAL CONNECTION • READING CONNECTION: Using a reading log	**30 MINUTES** • Introduce vocabulary • Read pp. 331–37 (7 pp.)
SELECTION Barbara Frietchie page 342 AVERAGE		**10 MINUTES** • PERSONAL CONNECTION • HISTORICAL CONNECTION • READING CONNECTION: Poetic language	**10 MINUTES** • Read pp. 342–43 (2 pp.)
SELECTION The Enchanted Raisin page 347 AVERAGE		**15 MINUTES** • PERSONAL CONNECTION • LITERARY CONNECTION • WRITING CONNECTION	**20 MINUTES** • Introduce vocabulary • Read pp. 347–54 (8 pp.)
GENRE LESSON Focus on Drama page 357	**20 MINUTES** • Discuss characteristics of drama • Discuss strategies for reading drama		
SELECTION A Shipment of Mute Fate page 362 CHALLENGING		**15 MINUTES** • PERSONAL CONNECTION • CULTURAL CONNECTION • READING CONNECTION: Sound effects	**35 MINUTES** • Introduce vocabulary • Read pp. 362–72 (11 pp.)

Writing	Exploring Topics	Prewriting	Drafting and Revising
WRITING FROM EXPERIENCE Informative Exposition	**25 MINUTES**	**25 MINUTES**	**80 MINUTES**

Time estimates assume in-class work. You may wish to assign some of these stages as homework.

317a   UNIT THREE   A SENSE OF FAIRNESS

Responding to the Selection

FROM PERSONAL RESPONSE TO CRITICAL ANALYSIS	OR	ANOTHER PATHWAY	LITERARY CONCEPTS	QUICKWRITES
		40 MINUTES		
• Discussion questions	OR	• Chart	• Humor	• Decision • Persuasive argument • Song • Evaluation
		25 MINUTES		
• Discussion questions	OR	• Compare fiction and nonfiction	• Primary source • Secondary source	• Advertisement • Ballad • Comparison/contrast paragraph
		30 MINUTES		
• Discussion questions	OR	• Chart	• Couplets • Alliteration • Rhythm	• Interview • Rhymed couplets
		30 MINUTES		
• Discussion questions	OR	• Flip book	• Fantasy	• Missing-person report • Newspaper article
		40 MINUTES		
• Discussion questions	OR	• Radio play	• Suspense	• Headline • News article • Letter of complaint • Log entry

Extension Activities

• ALTERNATIVE ACTIVITIES • LITERARY LINKS • CRITIC'S CORNER • THE WRITER'S STYLE • ACROSS THE CURRICULUM • ART CONNECTION • WORDS TO KNOW • BIOGRAPHY

20 MINUTES — ✔ (Literary Links), ✔ (Across the Curriculum), ✔ (Art Connection), ✔ (Words to Know)

10 MINUTES — ✔ (Art Connection), ✔ (Words to Know)

20 MINUTES — ✔ (Alternative Activities), SOCIAL STUDIES (Across the Curriculum), ✔ (Biography)

50 MINUTES — ✔ (Alternative Activities), ✔ (Words to Know), ✔ (Biography)

50 MINUTES — ✔ (Alternative Activities), ✔ (Literary Links), SCIENCE (Across the Curriculum), ✔ (Words to Know), ✔ (Biography)

Publishing and Reflecting

30 MINUTES

LESSON PLANNER TEACHER'S EDITION **317b**

UNIT THREE

Part 2 Cooperative Project

A Video Newsmagazine

Overview

Students will investigate topics of interest to them and present their findings in a video "news program."

PROJECT AT A GLANCE

The selections in Unit Three, Part 2 are about people facing the consequences of choices they have made. For this project, students will investigate a newsworthy issue and then present their findings in a *60 Minutes*–type video newsmagazine format. Members will share responsibilities for researching the topic, writing the script, narrating, conducting interviews, and taping their segment. Each topic should be investigated with a focus on choices made and the consequences. The segments will be presented and viewed as a single program. If desired, the project may culminate in a screening of the program for the entire school.

OBJECTIVES

- To research current television newsmagazine programs
- To identify and investigate a newsworthy issue from the viewpoint of choice and consequence
- To conduct interviews with the participants
- To plan and produce a taped newsmagazine segment

SUGGESTED GROUP SIZE
4–5 students per group

MATERIALS
- Video camera
- Videotapes (1 per group)
- Videocassette recorder (VCR)
- Television

1 Getting Started

Arranging the Project
Before students begin, formulate a plan for videotaping the segments. Decide if students will do their own taping as they go, or if an adult will tape them when they are ready. If students have their own cameras, you may want to allow them to tape their segments independently. If all the groups must share a school-owned or a borrowed camera, you will need adult supervision, if not total control of the camera operation.

If groups are sharing a camera, they will need to do some pretaping interviews and then arrange for all the interviewees to come to one taping at a specified time. In this case, allow for extra time to complete the project.

Arranging for Videotaping
Groups should interview and take notes on people they think would make a substantial contribution to their segment. They can review the notes as a group and decide which interviews are most relevant or important. These people should be contacted a second time and asked to meet for a taping session. This necessitates scheduling a place for the taping, as well as scheduling the camera and a camera operator.

If video equipment is unavailable, consider tailoring the project along the lines of Options 1 or 3 on the next page.

2 Creating the Video Segments

Introducing the Project
Explain that students will be working in small groups to plan and produce a video newsmagazine along the lines of the *60 Minutes*, *Dateline*, and *20/20* television shows. Each group will produce one segment focusing on an event or act and its consequences. The segments will then be shown together to make up an entire newsmagazine show.

To get the ball rolling, you might ask students to watch one of the television shows mentioned and note some of the key elements in each segment: narrator, background information, interviews with key people, and a concluding statement by the reporter. You might even elect one or two students to act as anchors for the show and introduce each segment. These students will need to study the segments after they have been taped and write an introduction of their own for each. (You can also fill this position yourself.)

Encourage groups to select a subject of interest not only to themselves but also to other students or to the community at large.

Group Investigations
Divide students into groups of four or five. Groups should brainstorm to choose a subject and should act as reporters by interviewing people who have something to do with the event or act and can explain the consequences. Urge students not to overlook "man-on-the-street" opinions as well. Groups with their own cameras can shoot out-of-school locales or actual events to round out their segments. Save a few minutes at the end of class sessions to make a note of progress groups are making on the project.

Creating a Project Description
After groups have completed preliminary planning and some interviewing, they will need to write a script that can be used between the interviews. Ask students to turn in a brief description of the event or act they are investigating and a script that they could use as the basis for taping. Meet with each group to help refine the script, offer help, or make suggestions about the project as a whole.

OPTION 1: SCHOOL NEWSPAPER If videotaping segments is not possible, groups can write articles instead. These could be compiled into a school newspaper. If your school already has a newspaper, arrange with the editor to use one or two pages of a specific issue.

OPTION 2: 60 SECONDS Ask students to tape brief segments that parody a show such as *60 Minutes*. They can "investigate" trivial events or acts and blow them out of proportion with a humorous touch, for example, "Spilled Milk in the Lunchroom—Accident or Terrorism?" or "Sneakergate—The Hidden Health Hazards of Gym Shoe Aroma." Don't forget to include a few commercials.

OPTION 3: LIVE PRESENTATION Students who cannot videotape can present their findings as though on live television. The anchor can introduce the reporter who will interview participants. All roles can be acted out by group members.

Remind students who are taping that real television shows have the added luxury of high-tech editing, while they do not. Segments should be well thought out and planned before taping begins.

3 Sharing the Videos

This project could culminate in a screening of the newsmagazine for the entire student body or just for your class. You might offer the tape to other teachers if it contains anything pertinent to what they are teaching at the time. Even if you are able to show the tape to the whole school, schedule a time for your class to review the tape and to reflect on the project as a whole.

Assessing the Project

The following rubric can be used for group or individual assessment.

3 Full Accomplishment Students produce a video newsmagazine segment that shows an event or act and explains its consequences.

2 Substantial Accomplishment Students produce a video newsmagazine segment, but it lacks focus or clarity of subject matter.

1 Little or Partial Accomplishment Students' video is incomplete or does not fulfill the requirements of the assignment

For the Portfolio
Master copies of all the videos can be kept in your classroom or the school library for future reference. Include a copy of your written assessment in each student's portfolio.

Note: For other assessment options, see the *Teacher's Guide to Assessment and Portfolio Use.*

Cross-Curricular Options

SOCIAL STUDIES

Set up a debate on an important issue. Student groups can research the topic and take a position. The debate can be taped for later review.

SCIENCE

Ask students to concentrate on an environmental issue and its consequences. You may want to limit the topic to one of importance in your community or neighborhood.

MUSIC
Students can create an audiotape to accompany the newsmagazine by selecting appropriate musical pieces for each segment.

MATH

Students can investigate the school budget, where the money comes from, how it is spent, and the consequences of raising taxes or cutting back school funds.

Resources

The Environment by Adam Markham discusses such environmental issues as acid rain, the ozone layer, and the greenhouse effect.

COOPERATIVE PROJECT TEACHER'S EDITION **317d**

PART 2

WHAT DO YOU THINK?
Objectives

The activities on this page can be used to
- introduce the Part 2 theme, "Facing the Consequences," since each activity is connected to one or more of the selections in Part 2
- create materials for students' personal portfolios that they can later reconsider or revise
- build an understanding of theme that can be reviewed and revised as students progress through the unit

What price would you pay?
Encourage students to organize their thoughts by brainstorming a list of consequences. Remind them that the consequences do not have to be realistic ones only—students can be as imaginative as they like. (See "Shrewd Todie and Lyzer the Miser," p. 319, and "The Enchanted Raisin," p. 346.)

Does every action have a reaction?
Encourage pairs to treat this activity as if it were a scientific experiment. As they conduct their "experiment," pairs should record their observations, which they can later present to the class in the form of a lab report. (All selections in this part connect to this activity.)

Did you face the consequences?
Have students first jot down a list of situations that they could write about. After they have chosen a situation and described it and its consequences, encourage volunteers to read their notebook entries to the class. (See *A Shipment of Mute Fate*, p. 359.)

UNIT THREE **PART 2**

FACING THE CONSEQUENCES

REFLECTING ON THEME

In an old TV game show, a contestant chose whatever was hidden behind one of three doors. The result was often surprising. Complete the activities on this page. Write down your impressions and ideas in your notebook. See whether they change as you read the consequences faced in Part 2.

Does every action have a reaction?
In pairs, set up several dominoes. Observe what happens when the first domino is gently pushed over. Line up the dominoes again, this time removing two from the middle before the falling dominoes reach them. What conclusions about actions and consequences can you come to?

Did you face the consequences?
Think about different situations in which you have had to make choices and to accept the consequences. In your notebook, describe one such choice and its consequences. Which of the consequences were most difficult to accept? Why?

What price would you pay?
In life, as in a story, an action usually leads to a series of consequences. Imagine the consequences of this situation. Make a diagram like the one started here to show what you think happens next. Let your imagination go as wild as possible. Share your completed charts with a classmate.

You forget about a test that your teacher has announced.
- I forget test. → I don't study.
- I get the test. → I panic!
- ?

Looking Back
Now that you've read the selections in Part 1, what new thoughts have formed in your mind about coping with injustice? Review the ideas you recorded in your notebook. Then, in small groups, create and role-play an unfair situation for the class. Show how to solve the problem and note the consequences that resulted.

318

COMMUNITY OUTREACH
Invite local lawyers, judges, or courthouse clerks to speak to the class about the causes of criminal behavior and the legal consequences of such behavior. Before the speakers come to the class, have students work in small groups to generate lists of questions. After the guests have addressed the class, invite students to ask them selected questions. Encourage students to jot down in their notebooks their thoughts on what the speakers had to say and what impact, if any, the speakers had on their lives.

Looking Back
Have the members of each group review the selections and the ideas in their notebooks in order to generate a list of unfair situations. Each group should then select one situation and briefly describe it, note the possible ways of handling it, and outline the consequences. Each group member can be responsible for writing a more detailed description of a point generated by this discussion and using the description to role-play a person involved in the unfair situation.

318 THE LANGUAGE OF LITERATURE **TEACHER'S EDITION**

PREVIEWING

FICTION

Shrewd Todie and Lyzer the Miser
Isaac Bashevis (bə-shĕv′ĭs) Singer

PERSONAL CONNECTION *Activating Prior Knowledge*

Do you know anyone you would describe as shrewd? Do you know a person you would call a miser? Which word would you prefer someone to use in describing you? In your notebook, make a diagram like the one shown to organize your ideas for each word. Then jot down images or thoughts that the word brings to mind.

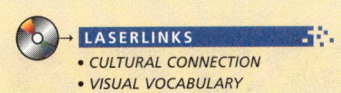

CULTURAL CONNECTION *Building Background*

Isaac Bashevis Singer, the author of this selection, grew up in and near Warsaw, Poland, as the son of a rabbi—a scholar trained to interpret Jewish law. Most of his stories for young people are rooted in the traditions and values of the Jewish communities of the past. As a boy, Singer lived in a simpler time and a simpler place, when people clustered together in small villages and survived on what they could produce on their farms or by trading goods with neighbors. Singer's childhood familiarity with poverty and hunger obviously made a lasting impression on him, for in his writing he frequently portrayed characters in difficult circumstances.

Based on folklore, this story treats character traits such as shrewdness and miserliness—and even the conditions of poverty and hunger—with humor, as you will discover.

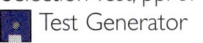

A village scene in Poland

Active Reading
READING CONNECTION

Evaluating Isaac Bashevis Singer once said, "Children are the best readers of genuine literature." Evaluating is the process of judging the worth of something or someone. An active reader goes beyond saying a character or a selection is simply good or bad; he or she forms opinions about the people, events, and ideas that are presented. As you read, think about the way the author creates and develops the characters. Evaluate how well Singer uses character, setting, plot, and theme to establish the characters as shrewd or miserly.

Setting a Purpose

 LASERLINKS
• CULTURAL CONNECTION
• VISUAL VOCABULARY

319

OVERVIEW
Objectives

- To understand and appreciate a short story that describes a clever trick
- To understand evaluating
- To understand and appreciate the use of humor in a short story
- To express understanding of the story through a choice of writing forms, including a decision about a dispute, a persuasive argument, a song, and a character evaluation
- To extend understanding of the story through a variety of multimodal and cross-curricular activities

Skills

READING SKILLS/STRATEGIES
- Evaluating Literary Concepts
- Humor
- Plot

THE WRITER'S STYLE
- Dialogue

GRAMMAR
- Adjectives and adverbs

SPELLING
- The prefix *ad-*

SPEAKING, LISTENING, AND VIEWING
- Group discussion
- Oral presentation

Cross-Curricular Connections

SOCIAL STUDIES
- Native American trickster stories

 CULTURAL CONNECTION
Village Life The simple lifestyle portrayed in this story may appear, at first glance, to be a wonderful way of life. In fact, it is a life of hard work and sacrifice. These images will show students the life of peasants today. You may wish to use them to generate a discussion about how the village lifestyle may have affected the author's ideas, interests, and choice of subject.

Side A, Frame 38762

PRINT AND MEDIA RESOURCES

UNIT THREE RESOURCE BOOK
Strategic Reading: Literature, p. 43
Vocabulary SkillBuilder, p. 46
Reading SkillBuilder, p. 44
Spelling SkillBuilder, p. 45

GRAMMAR MINI-LESSONS
Transparencies, pp. 12, 39–40
Copymasters, p. 19

WRITING MINI-LESSONS
Transparencies, p. 48

ACCESS FOR STUDENTS ACQUIRING ENGLISH
Selection Summaries
Reading and Writing Support

FORMAL ASSESSMENT
Selection Test, pp. 67–68
Test Generator

AUDIO LIBRARY
See Reference Card

LASERLINKS
Cultural Connection
Visual Vocabulary
Art Gallery

INTERNET RESOURCES
McDougal Littell Literature Center at http://www.hmco.com/mcdougal/lit

---

THE LANGUAGE OF LITERATURE TEACHER'S EDITION **319**

SUMMARY

Shrewd Todie is desperate for money to feed his family, so he gets it the only way he knows how—by trickery. Todie tricks the village miser, Lyzer, into lending him a silver tablespoon. The next day Todie hands back *two* silver spoons. "Your tablespoon gave birth to a teaspoon. It is her child," he explains. Lyzer lends more silverware to Todie, happy to collect the "children" of his spoons. When Todie asks to borrow two silver candlesticks, greedy Lyzer gives him all the candlesticks he has, thinking that he will get back many more. This time Todie sells the silver candlesticks, then regretfully informs Lyzer that he cannot return them because they died. The furious miser accuses him of speaking nonsense. The village rabbi, trying to settle the dispute, wisely reminds Lyzer that he accepted nonsense when it brought him profit, so he must also accept nonsense when it brings him loss.

Thematic Link: *Facing the Consequences*
Lyzer must face the consequences of his greed and gullibility.

Art Note

The Spoonful of Milk by Marc Chagall
Marc Chagall (1887–1985) grew up in a Jewish village in Russia. Many of his early works reflect village life. There are several important fast days in the Jewish religion, but people who are old or ill are allowed to eat. Perhaps the man in Chagall's painting is celebrating such a holiday. One possible interpretation is that he is absorbed in his book and resentful of the woman's offer of a spoonful of milk.

Reading the Art *What do you think the two people in the painting are feeling? What might they be saying to each other? What elements of the painting support your opinion?*

CUSTOMIZING FOR
Gifted and Talented Students

In the story, Todie's wife has a very minor role. As students read, have them make notes to expand her role. They might write more dialogue for Sheindel and include one or two additional scenes.

La cuilerée [The spoonful of milk] (1912), Marc Chagall. Copyright © 1995 Artists Rights Society (ARS), New York/ADAGP, Paris.

WORDS TO KNOW

admonishingly (ăd-mŏn′ĭ-shĭng-lē) *adv.* in a way that warns against bad behavior; disapprovingly (p. 325)

cunning (kŭn′ĭng) *n.* skill in fooling others (p. 324)

possess (pə-zĕs′) *v.* to have as property; to own (p. 322)

properly (prŏp′ər-lē) *adv.* correctly; suitably (p. 321)

trade (trād) *n.* an occupation, especially one involving skilled labor (p. 321)

 VISUAL VOCABULARY
- **cutlery** (kŭt′lə-rē)
- **gulden** (gōōl′dən)
- **larder** (lär′dər)

Side A, Frame 38767

320 THE LANGUAGE OF LITERATURE TEACHER'S EDITION

SHREWD TODIE

& Lyzer the Miser

by Isaac Bashevis Singer

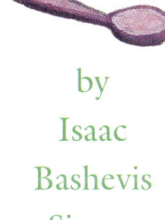

In a village somewhere in the Ukraine[1] there lived a poor man called Todie. Todie had a wife, Sheindel, and seven children, but he could never earn enough to feed them <u>properly</u>. He tried many <u>trades</u>, failing in all of them. It was said of Todie that if he decided to deal in candles the sun would never set. He was nicknamed Shrewd Todie because whenever he managed to make some money, it was always by trickery.

This winter was an especially cold one. The snowfall was heavy and Todie had no money to buy wood for the stove. His seven children stayed in bed all day to keep warm. When the frost burns outside, hunger is stronger than ever, but Sheindel's larder[2] was empty. She reproached Todie bitterly, wailing, "If you can't feed your wife and children, I will go to the rabbi and get a divorce."

"And what will you do with it, eat it?" Todie retorted. In the same village there lived a rich man called Lyzer. Because of his stinginess he was

---

1. **Ukraine** (yōō-krān′): a country of eastern Europe, formerly ruled by Poland and then by Russia.
2. **larder**: a place, such as a pantry or cellar, where food is stored.

WORDS TO KNOW
properly (prŏp′ər-lē) *adv.* correctly; suitably
trade (trād) *n.* an occupation, especially one involving skilled labor

321

CUSTOMIZING FOR
Students Acquiring English

- Use **ACCESS FOR STUDENTS ACQUIRING ENGLISH**, *Reading and Writing Support*.
- Many cultures have folk tales like this one, in which a trickster character outwits a villain or other unsympathetic character. Invite students to share with their classmates similar tales from their own cultures.
- In addition to these boxes, you may want to use the suggestions under Strategic Reading for Less-Proficient Readers.

1 Pronounce the name "Lyzer the Miser" so that students can hear the rhyme.

STRATEGIC READING FOR
Less-Proficient Readers

Set a Purpose As students read, have them note the problems Shrewd Todie has and what he does to solve his problems.

Use **UNIT THREE RESOURCE BOOK**, pp. 43–44, for guidance in reading the selection.

Active Reading: EVALUATE

A Have students share their impressions of Todie from what they have read so far. Ask students if he has any qualities they admire.

Literary Concept: PLOT

B Remind students that the plot of a story is generally built around a conflict—a problem or struggle involving opposing forces. Ask students to predict what or who the opposing forces in the conflict will be. (*At this point, the conflict appears to be between Todie and his wife.*)

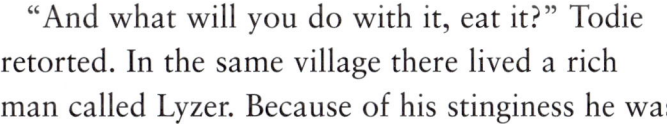

ADJECTIVES AND ADVERBS Remind students of the difference between adjectives and adverbs. An adjective modifies a noun or a pronoun; an adverb modifies a verb, an adjective, or another adverb. It tells *how, when, where,* or *to what extent.*

Application Ask students to find the following five words in the highlighted paragraph above: *especially, cold, heavy, empty, bitterly.* Then ask them to tell whether each word is an adjective or an adverb, what word it modifies in the story, and what part of speech the modified word is. Fill in their responses on the chalkboard.

Reteaching/Reinforcement
- *Grammar Handbook,* anthology pp. 830–832
- *Grammar Mini-Lessons* copymasters, p. 19, transparencies, p. 12, 39

 The Writer's Craft

What Are Adverbs, p. 482
Adjectives or Adverbs? p. 488

 Word in Story	What It Modifies
especially (adverb)	cold (adjective)
cold (adjective)	one (pronoun)
heavy (adjective)	snowfall (noun)
empty (adjective)	larder (noun)
bitterly (adverb)	reproached (verb)

THE LANGUAGE OF LITERATURE TEACHER'S EDITION **321**

Literary Concept: PLOT

C Ask students to describe two effects caused by Lyzer's stinginess. (*His wife bakes bread only once in four weeks; his goat begs for food from neighbors.*)

STRATEGIC READING FOR
Less-Proficient Readers

D Check that students understand the basic situation in the story so far:

- What kinds of problems does Todie have? (*He is very poor, has a large family, and does not seem to have a job.*) **Noting Relevant Details**
- How does Todie try to solve his problems? (*He tries to borrow money from Lyzer the miser.*) **Finding the Main Idea**

Set a Purpose As students read, have them watch for the way that Todie sets up his revenge.

CUSTOMIZING FOR
Multiple Learning Styles

E **Bodily-Kinesthetic Learners** Have two or three pairs of students act out this scene between Todie and Lyzer. Encourage the use of gestures and other body language. The class can then compare and discuss different interpretations of the interactions between Todie and Lyzer.

Critical Thinking: SPECULATING

F No young man came to visit Todie's daughter. Ask students what this reveals about Todie's character and actions. (*Possible responses: Todie is a liar; Todie has a plan of some kind to trick Lyzer.*)

known as Lyzer the miser. He permitted his wife to bake bread only once in four weeks because he had discovered that fresh bread is eaten up more quickly than stale.

Todie had more than once gone to Lyzer for a loan of a few gulden,[3] but Lyzer had always replied, "I sleep better when the money lies in my strongbox rather than in your pocket."

Lyzer had a goat, but he never fed her. The goat had learned to visit the houses of the neighbors, who pitied her and gave her potato peelings. Sometimes, when there were not enough peelings, she would gnaw on the old straw of the thatched roofs. She also had a liking for tree bark. Nevertheless, each year the goat gave birth to a kid. Lyzer milked her but, miser that he was, did not drink the milk himself. Instead, he sold it to others.

Todie decided that he would take revenge on Lyzer and at the same time make some much-needed money for himself.

One day, as Lyzer was sitting on a box eating borscht[4] and dry bread (he used his chairs only on holidays so that the upholstery[5] would not wear out), the door opened and Todie came in.

"Reb Lyzer," he said, "I would like to ask you a favor. My oldest daughter, Basha, is already fifteen and she's about to become

"Would you lend me one of your silver spoons? . . . I will return it to you tomorrow."

engaged. A young man is coming from Janev to look her over. My cutlery[6] is tin, and my wife is ashamed to ask the young man to eat soup with a tin spoon. Would you lend me one of your silver spoons? I give you my holy word that I will return it to you tomorrow."

Lyzer knew that Todie would not dare to break a holy oath and he lent him the spoon.

No young man came to see Basha that evening. As usual, the girl walked around barefoot and in rags, and the silver spoon lay hidden under Todie's shirt. In the early years of his marriage Todie had <u>possessed</u> a set of silver tableware himself. He had, however, long since sold it all, with the exception of three silver teaspoons that were used only on Passover.[7]

The following day, as Lyzer, his feet bare (in order to save his shoes), sat on his box eating borscht and dry bread, Todie returned.

---

3. **gulden** (gōōl'dən): coins.
4. **borscht** (bôrsht): a beet soup, served hot or cold, usually with sour cream.
5. **upholstery** (ŭp-hōl'stə-rē): fabric or materials that cover furniture.
6. **cutlery** (kŭt'lə-rē): table utensils, such as knives, forks, and spoons.
7. **Passover:** a celebration in memory of the Jews' exodus, or escape, from Egypt.

WORDS TO KNOW
possess (pə-zĕs') *v.* to have as property; to own

322

Showing
When I asked my brother to help me fix my car, he replied, "That car is a piece of junk and you should get rid of it."

Telling
I asked my brother to help me fix my car and he answered me rudely.

Mini-Lesson | The Writer's Style

DIALOGUE Remind students that dialogue is conversation—people talking to each other. Dialogue is used to *show* readers what happens in a story and what the characters are like rather than simply *telling* the readers about characters and events.

Application The selection ends by noting that the story of the silver spoons and candlesticks soon spread throughout the town. Have students write dialogue for townspeople spreading the tale to one another. You may wish to have students work in pairs and then invite students to perform their dialogues for the class.

Reteaching/Reinforcement
- Writing Handbook, anthology p. 779
- *Writing Mini-Lessons* transparencies, p. 48

The Writer's Craft
Using the Dialogue, pp. 278–280

---

322 THE LANGUAGE OF LITERATURE **TEACHER'S EDITION**

"Here is the spoon I borrowed yesterday," he said, placing it on the table together with one of his own teaspoons.

"What is the teaspoon for?" Lyzer asked.

And Todie said, "Your tablespoon gave birth to a teaspoon. It is her child. Since I am an honest man, I'm returning both mother and child to you."

Lyzer looked at Todie in astonishment. He had never heard of a silver spoon giving birth to another. Nevertheless, his greed overcame his doubt and he happily accepted both spoons. Such an unexpected piece of good fortune! He was overjoyed that he had loaned Todie the spoon.

A few days later, as Lyzer (without his coat, to save it) was again sitting on his box eating borscht with dry bread, the door opened and Todie appeared.

"The young man from Janev did not please Basha, because he had donkey ears, but this evening another young man is coming to look her over. Sheindel is cooking soup for him, but she's ashamed to serve him with a tin spoon. Would you lend me . . ."

Even before Todie could finish the sentence, Lyzer interrupted. "You want to borrow a silver spoon? Take it with pleasure."

The following day Todie once more returned the spoon and with it one of his own silver teaspoons. He again explained that during the night the large spoon had given birth to a small one and in all good conscience he was bringing back the mother and the newborn baby. As for the young man who had come to look Basha over, she hadn't liked him either, because his nose was so long that it reached to his chin. Needless to say that Lyzer the miser was overjoyed.

Exactly the same thing happened a third time. Todie related that this time his daughter had rejected her suitor[8] because he stammered. He also reported that Lyzer's silver spoon had again given birth to a baby spoon.

"Does it ever happen that a spoon has twins?" Lyzer inquired.

Todie thought it over for a moment. "Why not? I've even heard of a case where a spoon had triplets."

Almost a week passed by and Todie did not go to see Lyzer. But on Friday morning, as Lyzer (in his underdrawers, to save his pants) sat on his box eating borscht and dry bread, Todie came in and said, "Good day to you, Reb Lyzer."

"A good morning and many more to you," Lyzer replied in his friendliest manner. "What good fortune brings you here? Did you perhaps come to borrow a silver spoon? If so, help yourself."

"Here is the spoon I borrowed yesterday," he said, placing it on the table.

---

8. **suitor** (sōō′tər): a man who is trying to win a woman's love.

SHREWD TODIE AND LYZER THE MISER **323**

Active Reading: CLARIFY

G Ask students if it is surprising when Todie gives Lyzer another silver spoon. *(Possible responses: No, because Todie is trying to trick Lyzer. Yes, because giving Lyzer one of his own spoons doesn't seem to make sense.)*

CUSTOMIZING FOR
Students Acquiring English

2 Invite students to analyze the meaning of *overjoyed*. You may need to point out the root word *joy* and the prefix *over-*.

3 Explain that the idiomatic phrase *help yourself* means "take whatever you want."

STRATEGIC READING FOR
Less-Proficient Readers

H Why does Todie say he wants to borrow a silver spoon? *(to impress a visitor)* What happens when Todie returns the spoon to Lyzer? *(He gives Lyzer another spoon and says it is the child of the spoon he borrowed.)* Restating

Set a Purpose Have students read to find out how Todie profits by giving away spoons and how the rabbi rules on the situation.

Literary Concept:
CHARACTERS

I Ask students to identify examples in which the author shows that Lyzer is greedy. *(Possible responses: Lyzer is willing to believe the ridiculous story about his spoon giving birth; Lyzer asks if a spoon might ever have twins.)*

Literary Concept: HUMOR

J Have students discuss how the descriptions of Lyzer add humor to the story. *(Each time Todie goes to see Lyzer, Lyzer is wearing less and less clothing.)*

| Mini-Lesson | Literary Concepts |

REVIEWING PLOT Remind students that the series of events in a story is called the plot. The plot is the writer's blueprint for what happens, when it happens, and to whom it happens. One event causes another, which causes another, and so on until the end of the story.

Application Have students work in pairs to draw cause-and-effect charts showing some of the plot elements in the story. They may find that a certain cause has more than one effect. If so, their charts can show this by using two arrows leading from the cause.

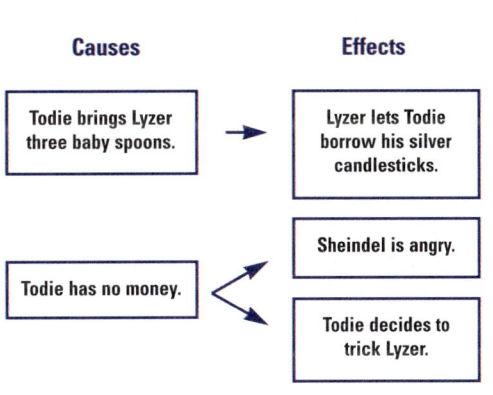

THE LANGUAGE OF LITERATURE TEACHER'S EDITION **323**

Cultural Note

K The Jewish Sabbath extends from sundown Friday to sundown Saturday. In addition to a special Sabbath dinner, Orthodox Jews do not do any work—the Sabbath is a time of prayer, study, and contemplation. Although cooking, sewing, writing, building, travel, and even turning lights on and off is considered "work," lighting one candle from another is not. The woman of a Jewish household lights candles and recites a blessing before nightfall Friday, and at least one candle will remain lit.

Active Reading: PREDICT

L Have students guess what will happen next in the story. You may wish to use the following model to give students ideas of what they might be thinking about.

Think-Aloud Model *It's beginning to look like a setup. Todie has created a situation where Lyzer is all too eager to lend him things. Perhaps Todie will take the candlesticks and never return them.*

Literary Concept: HUMOR

M Have students analyze why Todie's description to his wife of how he got the money adds humor to the story. *(Possible response: Todie's explanation is ridiculous, and, although she is doubtful, his wife goes along with Todie's story.)*

K "Today I have a very special favor to ask. This evening a young man from the big city of Lublin is coming to look Basha over. He is the son of a rich man, and I'm told he is clever and handsome as well. Not only do I need a silver spoon, but since he will remain with us over the Sabbath,[9] I need a pair of silver candlesticks, because mine are brass and my wife is ashamed to place them on the Sabbath table. Would you lend me your candlesticks? Immediately after the Sabbath, I will return them to you."

Silver candlesticks are of great value and Lyzer the miser hesitated, but only for a moment.

Remembering his good fortune with the spoons, he said, "I have eight silver candlesticks in my house. Take them all. I know you will return them to me just as you say. And if it should happen that **L** any of them give birth, I have no doubt that you will be as honest as you have been in the past."

"Certainly," Todie said. "Let's hope for the best."

The silver spoon, Todie hid beneath his shirt as usual. But taking the candlesticks, he went directly to a merchant, sold them for a considerable sum, and brought the money to Sheindel. When Sheindel saw so much money, she demanded to know where he had gotten such a treasure.

"When I went out, a cow flew over our roof

"Today I have a very special favor to ask. . . . Would you lend me your candlesticks?"

and dropped a dozen silver eggs," Todie replied. "I sold them and here is the money." **M**

"I have never heard of a cow flying over a roof and laying silver eggs," Sheindel said doubtingly.

"There is always a first time," Todie answered. "If you don't want the money, give it back to me."

"There'll be no talk about giving it back," Sheindel said. She knew that her husband was full of cunning and tricks—but when the children are hungry and the larder is empty, it is better not to ask too many questions. Sheindel went to the market and bought meat, fish, white flour, and even some nuts and raisins for a pudding. And since a lot of money still remained, she bought shoes and clothes for the children.

It was a very gay Sabbath in Todie's house. The boys sang and the girls danced. When the children asked their father where he had gotten the money, he replied, "It is forbidden to mention money during the Sabbath."

Sunday, as Lyzer (barefoot and almost naked, to save his clothes) sat on his box finishing up a dry crust of bread with borscht, Todie arrived and, handing him his silver

---

9. **Sabbath** (săb′əth): the seventh day of the week, Saturday, observed as a day of rest and worship by the Jews.

WORDS TO KNOW — **cunning** (kŭn′ĭng) *n.* skill in fooling others

324

Mini-Lesson — Reading Skills/Strategies

ACTIVE READING: EVALUATE Tell students that active readers use strategies as they read. Evaluating strategies help readers to form opinions about what they read, both during and after reading, and to develop images of and ideas about characters and events. For example, Sheindel decides not to ask too many questions about where the money came from, even though her husband's explanation is clearly ridiculous. Readers might say Sheindel pretends to believe him, but suspects he is lying and doesn't want to be involved in his trickery. They may observe that she thinks feeding her children is more important than technical honesty.

Application Have students choose another character in the story and list five things that person says or does. Then ask students to evaluate which character traits each action might suggest.

Reteaching/Reinforcement
• *Unit Three Resource Book,* p. 44

---

324 THE LANGUAGE OF LITERATURE TEACHER'S EDITION

spoon, said, "It's too bad. This time your spoon did not give birth to a baby."

"What about the candlesticks?" Lyzer inquired anxiously.

Todie sighed deeply. "The candlesticks died."

Lyzer got up from his box so hastily that he overturned his plate of borscht.

"You fool! How can candlesticks die?"

"If spoons can give birth, candlesticks can die," he screamed.

Lyzer raised a great hue and cry[10] and had Todie called before the rabbi. When the rabbi heard both sides of the story, he burst out laughing. "It serves you right," he said to Lyzer. "If you hadn't chosen to believe that spoons give birth, now you would not be forced to believe that your candlesticks died."

"But it's all nonsense," Lyzer objected.

"Did you not expect the candlesticks to give birth to other candlesticks?" the rabbi said admonishingly. "If you accept nonsense when it brings you profit, you must also accept nonsense when it brings you loss." And he dismissed the case.

The following day, when Lyzer the miser's wife brought him his borscht and dry bread, Lyzer said to her, "I will eat only the bread. Borscht is too expensive a food, even without the sour cream."

The story of the silver spoons that gave birth and the candlesticks that died spread quickly through the town. All the people enjoyed Todie's victory and Lyzer the miser's defeat. The shoemaker's and tailor's apprentices,[11] as was their custom whenever there was an important happening, made up a song about it:

Lyzer, put your grief aside.
What if your candlesticks have died?
You're the richest man on earth
with silver spoons that can give birth
and silver eggs as living proof
of flying cows above your roof.
Don't sit there eating crusts of bread—
To silver grandsons look ahead.

However, time passed and Lyzer's silver spoons never gave birth again. ❖

---

10. **hue and cry:** a loud outcry of protest.
11. **apprentices** (ə-prĕn′tĭ-sĭz): people learning a trade or business by working for an expert.

WORDS TO KNOW

admonishingly (ăd-mŏn′ĭ-shĭng-lē) *adv.* in a way that warns against bad behavior; disapprovingly

325

Mini-Lesson Spelling

THE PREFIX AD- Tell students that the prefix *ad-* can be spelled in different ways. The spelling depends on the root to which the prefix is joined. When the root begins with *p*, the prefix changes to *ap-*.

ad + monish = admonish
ap + prentice = apprentice
ad + mire = admire
ap + pear = appear

Application Have students add the prefix *ad-* or *ap-* to each word and then use it in a sentence.

1. prove
2. dress
3. minister
4. option
5. venture
6. point
7. just
8. mission
9. join
10. verb

Ask students to look for more words that fit this pattern, in their own writing and in things they read, and to add these words to their personal word lists.

Reteaching/Reinforcement
• *Unit Three Resource Book*, p. 45

Art Note

The Feast of the Tabernacles by Marc Chagall Chagall depicts a Jewish family celebrating Sukkot, the fall harvest. The two men sit in a *sukkah* (a tabernacle or a temporary place of worship, which Jews needed when they were wandering through the desert in search of a homeland) that has been built behind the house. In this painting, only men are participating in the feast; the women prepare the food and pass it into the tent through an opening in the side.

Reading the Art *What details does Chagall include to indicate that this scene is a family celebration?*

HISTORICAL INSIGHT

1. How does the Historical Insight help to explain the rabbi's role in the story? *(Possible response: Because the rabbi was a figure of learning and respect, he seemed to be the appropriate person to resolve Todie and Lyzer's dispute.)*

2. If you were on a committee to choose a new rabbi, what characteristics would you look for? *(Possible responses: education, a calm and comforting manner, a knowledge of religious law and Jewish custom)*

3. What other helpful advice could the rabbi in the story give to Todie? to Lyzer? *(Possible responses: Todie should look for better ways to earn money; Lyzer could try to become more generous.)*

HISTORICAL INSIGHT

THE RABBI IN THE COMMUNITY

Jews are members of a group that has been held together by a common faith and a common history for more than 3,000 years. Judaism, the religion of the Jewish people, is the oldest religion of the Western world. It is based on the Torah, the sacred history and laws of the Israelite people. The Torah consists of the first five books of the Hebrew Bible and includes the Ten Commandments, one of the greatest influences on the Western world's ideas about law and justice.

An individual who teaches and interprets the Torah is called a rabbi. *Rabbi* is the Hebrew word for a master or teacher, and over time the word came to mean someone who could decide questions of Jewish law.

Rabbis interpret the law of the Torah to apply it to issues that arise in daily life. Until recent times, all rabbis were men. Traditionally, the rabbi served as a community leader and judge, settling arguments—as the rabbi in this story settles the matter between Todie and Lyzer—and teaching people how to treat each other fairly. Today, a man or woman who wants to become a rabbi may spend many years studying in a training school for rabbis, and he or she usually has a broad knowledge of nonreligious subjects. Each group of worshipers chooses its own rabbi, whose main responsibilities are to preach, advise, teach, and carry out religious services and community celebrations.

La Fête des tabernacles [The feast of tabernacles] (1916), Marc Chagall. Private collection. Copyright © 1995 Artists Rights Society (ARS), New York/ADAGP, Paris.

326   UNIT THREE   PART 2: FACING THE CONSEQUENCES

Multicultural Perspectives

SOURCES OF JEWISH THOUGHT There are three parts to the Hebrew Bible: the Torah or Law, the Prophets, and the Writings. The five books of the Torah—Genesis, Exodus, Leviticus, Numbers, and Deuteronomy—are credited to Moses and describe the origin of the world and the early history of the Jewish people. The Prophets contain further history; the Writings include poetry and beautiful literature such as the Psalms, Ecclesiastes, Proverbs, and the Song of Solomon.

Another important source of Jewish law is the Talmud, a set of 63 books completed in the year A.D. 499. Before the laws were written down, they were passed on by word of mouth by the ancient Jewish rabbis.

RESPONDING OPTIONS

FROM PERSONAL RESPONSE TO CRITICAL ANALYSIS

REFLECT
1. Did you enjoy this story? In your notebook, give it a rating based on the scale shown here. Include reasons for your rating, and share your views with classmates.

Rating Scale	
★★★★	Outstanding
★★★	Good
★★	Fair
★	Poor

RETHINK
Thematic Link
2. In your opinion, does Lyzer get what he deserves? Explain your answer.
3. Why do you think Todie is able to trick Lyzer so easily?

RELATE
4. In "Shrewd Todie and Lyzer the Miser," a rabbi settles a disagreement that has captured the attention of a community. What examples of people resolving conflicts between others have you seen in your community or school?

Multimodal Learning
ANOTHER PATHWAY
Cooperative Learning
In teams composed of three or four students, draw and fill in a chart to analyze either Todie or Lyzer. Use the following categories: physical description, character's words, thoughts, and actions.

QUICKWRITES

1. If you were judging Todie and Lyzer's dispute, what would you decide? Write a **decision**, including your reasons.
2. Imagine that you are an attorney hired by Lyzer. Write a **persuasive argument** defending Lyzer's position.
3. Reread the apprentices' song at the end of the story. Write a similar **song** about Todie and his shrewdness.
4. Review the Reading Connection on page 319. Then write an **evaluation** of either Todie or Lyzer.

📁 **PORTFOLIO** Save your writing. You may want to use it later as a springboard to a piece for your portfolio.

LITERARY CONCEPTS

Humor is the quality that makes a piece of writing funny or amusing to the reader. Writers create humor by using exaggeration, amusing description, caricature, sarcasm, witty dialogue, and other devices. For example, Sheindel is hungry and, seeing her husband Todie as irresponsible, threatens him by saying she will go to the rabbi for a divorce. He then asks sarcastically, "And what will you do with it, eat it?" Later, Singer exaggerates Lyzer's miserliness until, during Todie and Lyzer's final exchange, Lyzer is "barefoot and almost naked." Look for other humorous passages in the story. Which passage is your favorite?

SHREWD TODIE AND LYZER THE MISER **327**

From Personal Response to Critical Analysis

1. If students gave the story a low rating, have them explain what might be done to improve the story.
2. Possible responses: Lyzer got what he deserved because he should have been more generous or more cautious about believing Todie. Lyzer was unfairly tricked, and Todie should have found some more honest way to get money.
3. Possible responses: Lyzer is greedy, and his greed interferes with his common sense. Lyzer is stupid to believe Todie's story about the spoon giving birth.
4. Students can also discuss whether they agreed with the decisions made in the conflicts they gave as examples.

Another Pathway

Cooperative Learning Groups can begin by discussing whether they want to analyze Todie or Lyzer. One or two researchers can look through the story for the needed information. The recorder can take notes as the group discusses this information.

Rubric
3 Full Accomplishment Students' charts are complete and include logical speculations about the character's thoughts.
2 Substantial Accomplishment Students' charts contain accurate information from the story but do not include much or any speculation about what the character was thinking.
1 Little or Partial Accomplishment Students' charts are inaccurate or incomplete. They do not reflect the situations described in the story.

Literary Concepts

Have students work in groups of four to search for humorous passages in the story. Two students can search for humor in dialogue and two for humor in descriptions. After passages have been selected, the group should discuss the results. Students will find that humor is subjective and that people have different opinions about what aspects of the story are funny. When groups are finished, have them compare their responses with those of at least one other group.

QuickWrites

1. Have students start by organizing their thoughts in a two-column chart: Why Todie Is Right and Why Lyzer Is Right.
2. Encourage students to use their imaginations in supporting Lyzer's position.
3. Point out that the song in the story is written in couplets.
4. Encourage students to use passages from the story to justify their opinions.

📁 **The Writer's Craft**
Compare-and-Contrast Chart, p. 195
Sharing an Opinion, pp. 120–123
Poetry, pp. 86–88

THE LANGUAGE OF LITERATURE TEACHER'S EDITION **327**

Art Connection

Possible responses: Since the art shows a woman holding out a spoon to a seated man, the painting could show a possible scene between Todie and Sheindel, or between Lyzer and his wife. Or the man could be a depiction of the imaginary suitor coming to visit Todie's daughter, who is asking him to taste something from Lyzer's silver spoon. None of these scenes is actually described in the story, but they would fit in with the events that are described.

Words to Know

1. trade
2. admonishingly
3. possessed
4. cunning
5. properly

Reteaching/Reinforcement
• *Unit Three Resource Book*, p. 46

Across the Curriculum

Social Studies Native American stories also include many trickster characters. For example, the coyote appears in many tales attempting to trick other characters. Have students locate such a story at their library. They can write a comparison-contrast essay comparing the story with the selection.

ISAAC BASHEVIS SINGER

During a prolific literary career, Singer worked as a novelist, short story writer, children's author, and translator. Although he was fluent in English, he wrote most of his works in Yiddish. His stories contain many elements frequently found in the rich folk tale traditions of the *shtetls* (Jewish villages in the eastern Europe of the past).

ART GALLERY
Jewish Life Isaac Bashevis Singer, the author of this story, incorporates the customs and traditions of Jewish culture into many of his works. These images portray Jewish life in eastern Europe during the early part of this century—the place and time in which the story is set. They may generate discussion about Jewish culture and lifestyle.

Side A, Frame 38771

CRITIC'S CORNER

Isaac Bashevis Singer said that "the young reader demands a real story, with a beginning, a middle, and an end, the way stories have been told for thousands of years." Do you think "Shrewd Todie and Lyzer the Miser" fits Singer's description of a real story? Explain your answer.

ART CONNECTION

The Spoonful of Milk was painted in 1912 by Marc Chagall, a Russian-born painter who often combined elements of fantasy and religion in his work. The painting's brilliant colors add to the powerful impact of the image. How well do you think the scene depicted in this painting matches "Shrewd Todie and Lyzer the Miser"?

ISAAC BASHEVIS SINGER

As a son of a rabbi, Isaac Bashevis Singer received a traditional Jewish education in a religious school in Poland, where he grew up. There he learned to write Yiddish, the historical language of the Jews of central and eastern Europe. He described those early years: "Our house was a poor house. We were a rabbi's house. Very little furniture but many books." In his 20s, Singer decided to become a writer, and in 1935 he followed his older brother to America. After becoming a naturalized citizen, he wrote of his U.S. citizenship, "I would not trade it for all the money in the world."

Many of Singer's stories and novels are based on the culture and traditions of life in the Jewish ghettos of eastern Europe before they were destroyed by the Nazis in the 1930s and 1940s. He published his first children's book in 1966, noting that "children think about and ponder such matters as justice, the purpose of life, the why of suffering." Already the winner of a Newbery Medal, in 1978 Singer was awarded the Nobel Prize in literature. In accepting the award, Singer said, "I am nothing more than a storyteller."

1904–1991

328 UNIT THREE PART 2: FACING THE CONSEQUENCES

WORDS TO KNOW

An analogy contains two word pairs with the words in each pair having similar relationships. The words in the second pair are related in the same way as those in the first pair, as in this example:

LIGHT : DARK :: up : down

The words *light* and *dark* are opposites; *up* and *down* are also opposites.

Review the Words to Know in the boxes at the bottom of the selection pages. For each item below, determine how the words in the capitalized pair are related. Then decide which word best completes the second pair to show a similar relationship. Write the word on your paper.

1. CAR : AUTOMOBILE : : _____ : job
2. NEGATIVELY : POSITIVELY : : _____ : approvingly
3. PURCHASED : RENTED : : _____ : borrowed
4. INTELLIGENCE : GENIUS : : _____ : trickster
5. CARELESSLY : THOUGHTLESSLY : : _____ : suitably

OTHER WORKS *Zlateh the Goat and Other Stories, The Fearsome Inn, When Shlemiel Went to Warsaw and Other Stories, A Day of Pleasure: Stories of a Boy Growing Up in Warsaw, Why Noah Chose the Dove, A Tale of Three Wishes* Extended Reading

➤ LASERLINKS
• ART GALLERY

Alternative Activities

1. Have students write a sequel to the story. Sometime in the future, Todie again tries to borrow something from Lyzer. Students should include both narrative and dialogue in their sequels.
2. Ask students to imagine themselves as one of Todie's daughters and write the characteristics they will look for in a life partner.

---

328 THE LANGUAGE OF LITERATURE TEACHER'S EDITION

PREVIEWING

NONFICTION

from A Long Hard Journey
Patricia and Fredrick McKissack

PERSONAL CONNECTION Activating Prior Knowledge

For more than a century Pullman sleeping cars and the cheerful, efficient porters who waited on passengers made overnight train trips a pleasure for travelers. The inviting image of this form of travel concealed hardships that this excerpt uncovers. Think about any traveling you have done, even just around your hometown. How do you get to where you want to go—car? bus? train? airplane? What service employees help you? Copy the chart shown here in your notebook. Fill in the chart with information based on your own travel experiences.

Service Employees Who Help People Travel					
Form of Transportation	Job Name	Does the person wear a uniform?	Does the person depend on tips?	How difficult would you say the job is?	Would you like to do this work?

Building Background
HISTORICAL CONNECTION

From the 1840s until the 1920s, railroads were the most popular way for people to travel long distances. The completion of the transcontinental railway in 1869 was the climax of American railroad building. The United States had been joined from the Atlantic to the Pacific, and cross-country travel had become a practical reality.

George Pullman patented his sleeping car in 1859. The first car built by his company made its initial trip that same year. In 1867, Pullman began hiring ex-slaves to work as porters on his railcars, beginning an association that was to last until Pullman sleepers were no longer manufactured. By the time the transcontinental railway was completed, the Pullman Palace Car Company was able to make travelers' journeys comfortable, even luxurious—but the company paid far less attention to the hardships experienced by its employees.

Active Reading
READING CONNECTION
Setting a Purpose

Using Your Reading Log As you read this selection, you will encounter questions that may help you focus on issues raised in it. In your reading log, jot down your answers to the questions, and record any questions of your own that you may have about early train travel or the Pullman porters and the hardships they experienced. See if you are able to answer your own questions when you finish reading the selection.

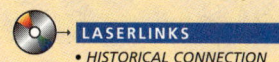
• HISTORICAL CONNECTION 329

OVERVIEW

Objectives

- To understand and appreciate a nonfiction selection about the experiences of Pullman porters
- To enrich reading by using active reading strategies
- To understand and appreciate the use of primary and secondary sources in nonfiction
- To express understanding of the selection through a choice of writing forms, including an advertisement, a ballad, and a comparison-contrast paragraph
- To extend understanding of the selection through a variety of multimodal and cross-curricular activities

Skills

READING SKILLS/ STRATEGIES
• Connecting

THE WRITER'S STYLE
• Stories as supporting details

GRAMMAR
• Prepositional phrases

LITERARY CONCEPTS
• Author's purpose

SPELLING
• The Prefix *ex-*

SPEAKING, LISTENING, AND VIEWING
• Role playing
• Group discussion
• Oral presentation

Cross-Curricular Connections

HISTORY
• George Pullman

GEOGRAPHY
• Map of railroads

SOCIAL STUDIES
• Labor unions

MATH
• Amount of tips

SCIENCE
• First refrigerators

 **HISTORICAL CONNECTION**
All Aboard! During the 1800s and early 1900s, railroads were very important for long-distance travel. These images will show students what the old steam trains looked like. A map of major rail lines around 1900 illustrates the extent of the rail system at the time.

Side A, Frame 38784

PRINT AND MEDIA RESOURCES

UNIT THREE RESOURCE BOOK
Strategic Reading: Literature, p. 49
Vocabulary SkillBuilder, p. 52
Reading SkillBuilder, p. 50
Spelling SkillBuilder, p. 51

GRAMMAR MINI-LESSONS
 Transparencies, p. 41

WRITING MINI-LESSONS
Transparencies, p. 34

ACCESS FOR STUDENTS ACQUIRING ENGLISH
Selection Summaries
Reading and Writing Support

FORMAL ASSESSMENT
Selection Test, pp. 69–70
Test Generator

 **AUDIO LIBRARY**
See Reference Card

 **LASERLINKS**
Historical Connection

THE LANGUAGE OF LITERATURE TEACHER'S EDITION **329**

SUMMARY

After the Civil War, George Pullman offered ex-slaves jobs as porters on his luxury railroad cars. These early porters were known as Travelin' Men, and their job was valued for its steady pay. Nevertheless, the job was a difficult one. The porters were treated as servants, expected to smile and to satisfy every whim of the passengers quickly. Some customers deliberately harassed the porters to test their limits; the porters had no choice but to accept it or quit. Despite such hardships, the early porters took pride in their work and were widely praised for their exceptional service. George Pullman received praise for his employment practices, but in reality he was a harsh employer. He underpaid his employees, broke up the strikes of white workers, and forced porters to sign promises that they would never join a union. After his death in 1897, the Pullman company continued to thrive—and the workers continued to have no power.

Thematic Link: *Facing the Consequences*
Long-standing racial discrimination as well as economic conditions following the Civil War compelled many African Americans to accept difficult working conditions.

CUSTOMIZING FOR
Gifted and Talented Students

In nonfiction writing, authors often use footnotes to identify the sources of quotations and other information. Usually the source is a book, but it can also be a first-person interview. As students read, have them mark locations where footnotes might be inserted to identify sources.

Possible responses:

- Page 332—composer and publisher of the song; source for Anderson's quote
- Page 333—source for Hall's quote
- Page 335—sources for quotes from Cleveland and Douglass; source for unflattering description of Pullman
- Page 337—sources for family's fear of vandalism and for Bierce's quote

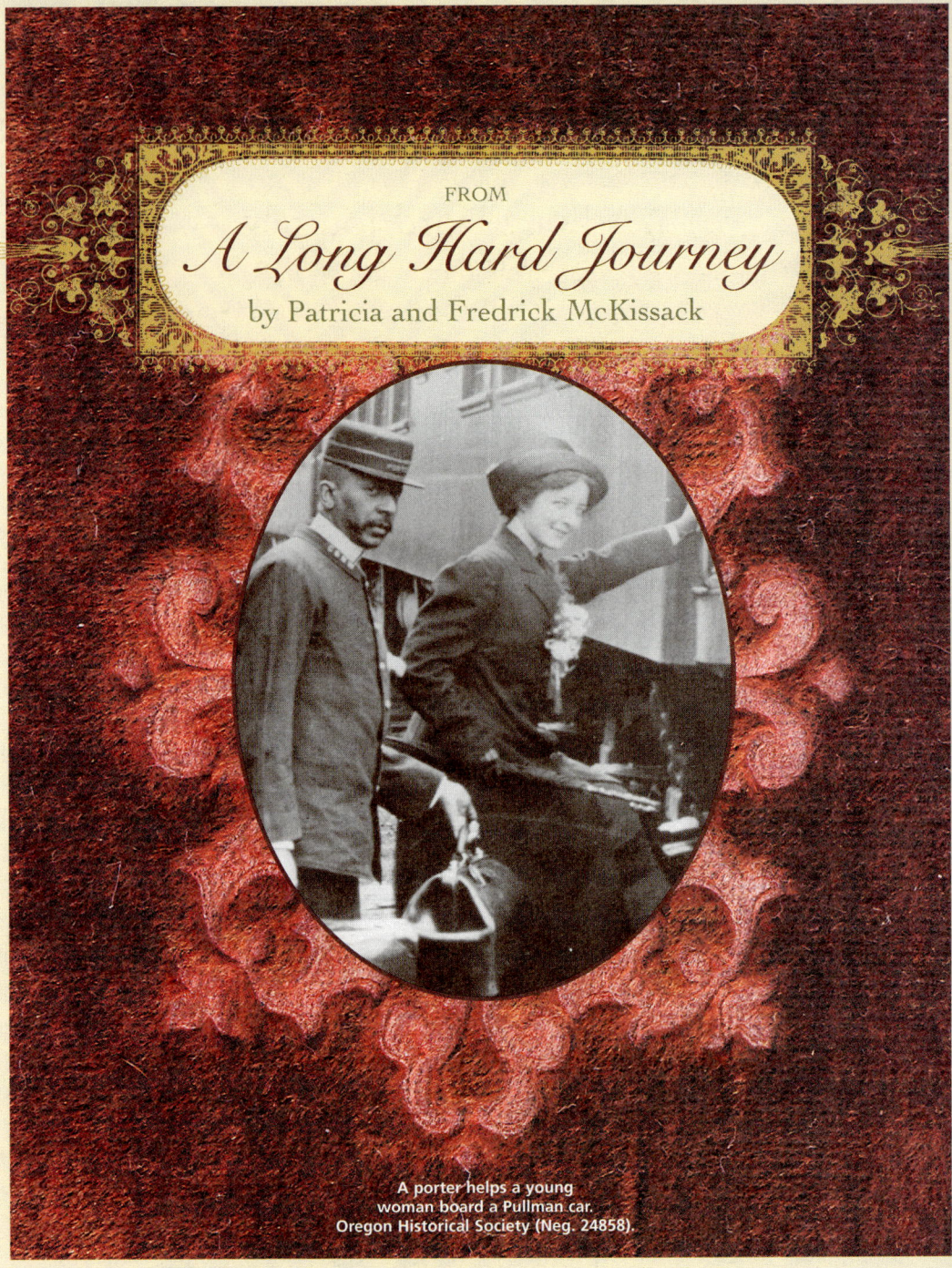

FROM
A Long Hard Journey
by Patricia and Fredrick McKissack

A porter helps a young woman board a Pullman car.
Oregon Historical Society (Neg. 24858).

WORDS TO KNOW

agility (ə-jĭl′ĭ-tē) *n.* nimbleness; ease of movement (p. 334)
confrontation (kŏn′frŭn-tā′shən) *n.* a face-to-face encounter, usually in anger (p. 336)
contemporary (kən-tĕm′pə-rĕr′ē) *n.* a person of the same time or age (p. 331)
drudgery (drŭj′ə-rē) *n.* boring or unpleasant work (p. 331)
exclusive (ĭk-sklōō′sĭv) *adj.* leaving out some or most people (p. 332)
harass (hăr′əs) *v.* to irritate or torment continually (p. 334)
insensitive (ĭn-sĕn′sĭ-tĭv) *adj.* unfeeling (p. 334)
monopoly (mə-nŏp′ə-lē) *n.* a total control by one group over a product or service (p. 337)
plush (plŭsh) *n.* a fabric having a thick, deep pile (p. 332)
salvaging (săl′vĭ-jĭng) *adj.* saving from loss or destruction **salvage** *v.* (p. 335)

330 THE LANGUAGE OF LITERATURE TEACHER'S EDITION

In the book *A Long Hard Journey*, the McKissacks explore the life and work of Pullman porters and their struggle to form a union. In 1867, George Pullman's Palace Car Company employed the first ex-slave as a porter. Newly freed African Americans would be perfect, Pullman believed, to serve travelers: to answer their questions, to make up their beds, and to bring them food and drinks. This excerpt describes the typical practices of a company that had become a household name, with a worldwide reputation for service.

Lord I hate to hear that lonesome whistle blow.
Lord I hate to hear that lonesome whistle blow.
Lord I'm goin' where the water tastes like wine.
'Cause the water round here tastes like turpentine.
Lord I hate to hear that lonesome whistle blow.
Lord I hate to hear that lonesome whistle blow.
It blows so lonesome and it blows so low.
It blows like it never blowed before.

"Lonesome Whistle"
from *Treasury of Railroad Folklore*
edited by B. A. Botkin and Alvin Harlow

When George Pullman offered ex-slaves work on board his luxury cars, he got exactly what he bargained for. To men who had just shed their shackles, a railroad job meant unimaginable freedom.

Men in bondage make icons[1] of the symbols that represent their freedom. Trains were such a symbol to the slave. Many a woeful plantation song spoke about train whistles, locomotives, and escape from the day-to-day drudgery of fieldwork.

According to Richard Reinhardt, even white men considered "working on the railroad . . . the most virile, challenging, and exciting career a man could follow."

The early porters were called "Travelin' Men." They were highly respected, even revered by their contemporaries. A young woman considered herself fortunate to be courted by a porter, and with good reason. They were pillars of their community; they made a decent living and had experiences

---

1. **icons:** pictures or symbols that are worshiped or honored.

WORDS TO KNOW
drudgery (drŭj′ə-rē) *n.* boring or unpleasant work
contemporary (kən-tĕm′pə-rĕr′ē) *n.* a person of the same time or age

331

Mini-Lesson: Speaking, Listening, and Viewing

ROLE–PLAYING Students may find that role-playing experiences will help them better imagine the feelings of the ex-slaves right after the Civil War.

Application Have students work in pairs to act out a scene in which an ex-slave applies for a job as a porter on a Pullman train. Students should look through the selection for details about the porters' jobs. Then they should discuss the characters of the ex-slave and the hiring official before they draft dialogue for their scene. Students can exchange roles and perform their scene again.

CUSTOMIZING FOR
Students Acquiring English

- Use **ACCESS FOR STUDENTS ACQUIRING ENGLISH,** *Reading and Writing Support.*

1 Help students analyze the meaning of *unimaginable:* prefix *un-* (not), base word *imagine,* suffix *-able* (possible).

2 Explain that the idiomatic phrase *pillars of their community* means "people who occupy a central or responsible position."

STRATEGIC READING FOR
Less-Proficient Readers

Set a Purpose Have students read to find out why working as a Pullman porter was thought to be a good job.

Use **UNIT THREE RESOURCE BOOK,** pp. 49–50, for guidance in reading the selection.

Critical Thinking: SPECULATING

A Ask students to give reasons why the narrator in the poem "hates to hear" the train whistles blow. *(Possible response: The narrator wants to leave and can't get away. The train reminds him or her of other places to live that might be better.)*

CUSTOMIZING FOR
Multiple Learning Styles

B **Musical Learners** There are many songs with a railroad theme. Have students find examples at home or at the library to share in class.

Literary Concept:
AUTHOR'S PURPOSE

C Have students keep in mind, as they read, four possible purposes the authors may have—to entertain, to inform, to express opinions, and to persuade. Students should discuss which purpose or purposes seem to be the most important here.

THE LANGUAGE OF LITERATURE TEACHER'S EDITION **331**

Critical Thinking: ANALYZING

D The selection describes how some women wanted to marry porters. Ask students what this suggests about the conditions of African-American women. *(Possible response: It was difficult for the women to hold jobs of their own and thus it was important to find husbands who made a good living.)*

Literary Concept: DESCRIPTION

E Have students list specific details that help them visualize the luxurious surroundings on Pullman trains. As students find new details in the selection, they can add them to their lists.

Active Reading: CLARIFY

F Ask students what the "limits" were for African-American men at this time in history. You may wish to use the following model to give students ideas of what they might be thinking about.

Think-Aloud Model *The Civil War had just ended, so many African Americans were recently freed slaves. They did not have much education or money. Also, because there was discrimination against them, they would have had trouble finding work.*

Linking to History

 **G** George Pullman did not own a railroad company. He manufactured railroad cars. Pullman railroad cars were unique in that they were leased, not sold, to the railroad companies that used them. The lease included Pullman employees. All other rolling stock was purchased and staffed by the railroad.

---

other men only dreamed about. As a popular song of that day indicated, some women preferred a railroad husband over all others.

D
> A railroader, a railroader
> A railroader for me.
> If ever I marry in this wide world,
> A railroader's bride I'll be.

"Besides," said one porter wife, "they knew what was on the other side of the rosebush, so they weren't so easily turned astray. My own husband was always glad to get home after being on the road."

Nineteenth-century porters traveled to faraway places, mingled with wealthy, well-educated whites, and worked in elegant surroundings. In 1867 the *Western World* magazine described the Pullman porter's work environment:

E
> The furniture is of black walnut, handsomely carved and ornamented and upholstered with royal purple velvet <u>plush</u> imported from England expressly for this purpose. The finest Axminster carpets cover the floor. The night curtains for the berths[2] are of heaviest silk; splendid chandeliers are pendent overhead; elegant mirrors grace the walls. Luxurious beds invite repose by night and when made up for the day betray no trace of the eating or sleeping uses to which they can be put. The total cost of each car is $30,000.

Since most of their neighbors had never seen such luxury, the porters formed an almost <u>exclusive</u> brotherhood bonded by their common experiences. It has been said they had more in common with each other than they did with family, friends, and neighbors. Fathers did so well that they encouraged their sons to become porters. Uncles helped

Porters saw in their travels what most of their neighbors could only dream about.

nephews, and brothers spoke for brothers.

Porters saw in their travels what most of their neighbors could only dream about. But on a more realistic level, having a steady job allowed them to marry, buy homes, and raise their children with dignity. And although they were not often well-educated, they were articulate[3] spokesmen for education and the general advancement of the race.

Author Jervis Anderson stated that the nineteenth-century porter was seen as "an example of what black men could make of their lives, within the limits of what their situation allowed." **F**

Meanwhile, George Pullman continued to make it possible for ordinary passengers to experience some of the pleasures and privileges generally reserved for the wealthy. His "Hotel Cars" were designed to give passengers the benefits of fine hotel food, service, and a comfortable bed, all on wheels. Pullman later designed and built the dining car which boasted "every variety of meats, vegetables and pastry" that could be "cooked on the cars, according to the best style of culinary art." **G**

---
2. **berths:** built-in beds or bunks.
3. **articulate** (är-tĭk′yə-lĭt): able to express ideas in easy, clear language.

WORDS TO KNOW
plush (plŭsh) *n.* a fabric having a thick, deep pile
exclusive (ĭk-sklōō′sĭv) *adj.* leaving out some or most people

332

Mini-Lesson · Literary Concepts

REVIEWING AUTHOR'S PURPOSE Remind students that an author's purpose in writing can be to inform, to persuade, to entertain, or to give an opinion. Often an author has more than one purpose in writing.

Application Ask students to review the selection in order to determine the purpose(s) of the two authors. One way to infer an author's purpose is to ask why an author chooses to include specific details and incidents. For example, ask students why they think the McKissacks chose to include such detailed descriptions of the Pullman cars. *(Possible response: to contrast the luxury of the cars to the living conditions of the porters)* Have students copy and complete a chart like the one shown and write a summary statement of the authors' purpose.

Details/Incident	Authors included because ...

---

332 THE LANGUAGE OF LITERATURE TEACHER'S EDITION

The *Delmonico* was the first Pullman dining car, introduced in 1868. All passengers, whether using Pullman sleeping-car arrangements or not, could now eat in the diners. That also meant the hiring of more blacks as waiters, cooks, and stewards[4] although these positions were not exclusively black, as porter jobs were.

In 1870, the first all-Pullman train, called the *Board of Trade Special*, made its run from Boston to California. A baggage car contained iceboxes to keep the wines cool and the vegetables fresh. There was even a printing press on board that issued a daily newspaper, the *Trans-Continental*. It is no wonder James Norman Hall, author of *The Caine Mutiny*, said, "I can no more conceive of a world without railroads and trains to run on them than I can imagine wishing to live in such a world."

CONNECT

What forms of travel exist today that might offer similar luxuries?
Using a Reading Log

In spite of his plush surroundings, the porter's job was anything but glamorous. He was viewed as a servant. At first these travelin' men didn't mind playing the role George Pullman had cast for them. They wore the mask very well.

Dressed in well-tailored blue uniforms, the Pullman porters adhered to very specific rules of conduct issued by the Pullman Company. Although a pleasant "good morning" or "good afternoon" when greeting each boarding passenger was all that was originally required, many porters took the time to learn the names of their regular passengers and greeted them by name—"Good morning Mr. Smith"—and *always* with a broad smile.

The living room of a private Pullman car
Pullman Negative Collection, Smithsonian Institution, Washington, D.C. (Neg. 4586).

After a while, the smile became associated with the porters, but instead of being a natural outgrowth of a pleasant situation, the Pullman Company ordered the porters to smile.

Many of George Pullman's other rules reflected the social climate of the day. For example, the white conductor was authorized to assist an unaccompanied woman traveler up the boarding steps. If the white conductor was not around, the porter could help the woman aboard, *if* she asked.

Once the passengers were comfortably seated and their bags were stored, the porter attended to special requests. He might be handing out newspapers, helping a mother with restless children, or pointing out geographic points of interest to first-time travelers or foreign visitors.

The Pullman porter's primary focus was the customer's welfare. He was instructed—and very often tested—to answer all calls promptly

---
4. **stewards:** people in charge of dining arrangements.

A LONG HARD JOURNEY **333**

Linking to Science

 H An early refrigerator that used ammonia was designed by the French inventor Ferdinand Carré in the late 1850s. However, the first refrigerators were bulky and inconvenient, so iceboxes, ice chests, and icehouses were common well into the middle of the 20th century.

STRATEGIC READING FOR
Less-Proficient Readers

I Invite students to discuss the experiences of porters and passengers described in the selection.

- What advantages did the African-American porters have? *(They made a decent living, were highly respected, worked in elegant surroundings, and could travel.)* Noting Relevant Details

Set a Purpose Have students continue reading to find out the less-desirable aspects of the porters' working conditions.

Active Reading: CONNECT

J Have students share their experiences of taking long trips. Ask them where they stayed and what the accommodations were like. Students might say that travel on a cruise ship today would be similar to the luxurious descriptions in the selection.

CUSTOMIZING FOR
Students Acquiring English

3 Help students understand that *if* appears in italic print for emphasis: Only if the woman asked for help could the porter assist and touch her.

Critical Thinking: SPECULATING

K Ask students to imagine what points of interest the porters might have described to travelers. *(Possible responses: rivers, mountains, towns, places where Civil War battles were fought)*

Mini-Lesson  Reading Skills/Strategies

ACTIVE READING: CONNECTING Remind students that active readers look for similarities to their own experience as they read. They try to imagine themselves in the characters' positions and think about what choices they would make.

Application Have students imagine themselves in the position of an ex-slave right after the Civil War. They are trying to decide whether to accept a job as a porter on Pullman's trains or to work as a paid laborer on a nearby farm. Students might use decision diagrams like the ones shown to organize their thinking.

Work as a Porter		Work on the Farm	
Advantages	Disadvantages	Advantages	Disadvantages

Reteaching/Reinforcement
- *Unit Three Resource Book,* p. 50

THE LANGUAGE OF LITERATURE TEACHER'S EDITION **333**

Active Reading: CONNECT

L Have students share experiences of staying overnight in hotels or motels. If necessary, explain that beds are made and the towels are changed every day.

Linking to Math

M Students are probably familiar with the practice of tipping in restaurants. Tips are also given to taxicab drivers, coat-check attendants, bellhops in hotels, and other service workers. In restaurants, the customary tip is 15 to 20 percent of the check.

Critical Thinking: ANALYZING

N Ask students to interpret what the authors mean by saying the porters had to play a foolish game. Students might think of the expressions "to play along" or "to play the game." *(Possible response: The porters had to pretend they weren't annoyed by the harassment and thus were "playing along" with the students.)*

STRATEGIC READING FOR
Less-Proficient Readers

O Ask students how porters were treated by the train passengers. *(Not very well. Some passengers were demanding; others harassed the porters both verbally and physically.)* **Making Judgments**

Set a Purpose Have students read on to learn about the union.

CUSTOMIZING FOR
Students Acquiring English

4 Point out that the prefix *non-* (meaning "not") can be used before many adjectives and common nouns (nonfat milk, nonunion, nonsmoker, nonfiction).

---

and courteously, no matter what time the calls were made.

When it was time to make the beds, the porter was expected to move with speed and agility. The company rule book was precise. According to Nathaniel Hall, a porter, the rule book specified "the proper handling of the linen closet—the proper method of folding and putting away clean linen and blankets, the correct way of stacking laundry bags and dirty, discarded bedding. A sheet, towel, or pillowcase once unfolded cannot be used again, although it may be spotless. Technically, it is dirty and must make a round trip to the laundry before it can reenter the service." Porters were not allowed to make noise. "Noise was tabooed," reported Hall. "And even a soft knock on the top of the berth [was] forbidden. A porter must gently shake the curtains on the bedding from without."

Pullman demanded that all passengers were made to feel special, and part of the Pullman trademark was being waited on by a humble, smiling black servant. Porters' salaries were deliberately kept low so they'd be dependent upon the tip to make ends meet.

The public knew that on a Pullman coach, the customer was always right. No exceptions.

But in some cases, travelers took this to its illogical extreme. For example, young college students liked to chide, embarrass, and <u>harass</u> a porter to see how much he would take. It was a foolish game that the porters had no choice but to play. If the porter went along with whatever was required of him, providing laughs at the cost of his self-respect, the students rewarded him with a big tip. Also, a porter was very often the target of cruel practical jokes and <u>insensitive</u> racial slurs. But if he endured it without a word of protest, again he was rewarded for being such a "good sport."

Some passengers resorted to physical abuse: kicking, poking, and shoving. The porter could not speak up for himself or expect the company to help. In fact the company's inaction regarding the poor treatment of porters was interpreted by the public to mean the men in blue were non-humans. Taking the lead from Pullman, the

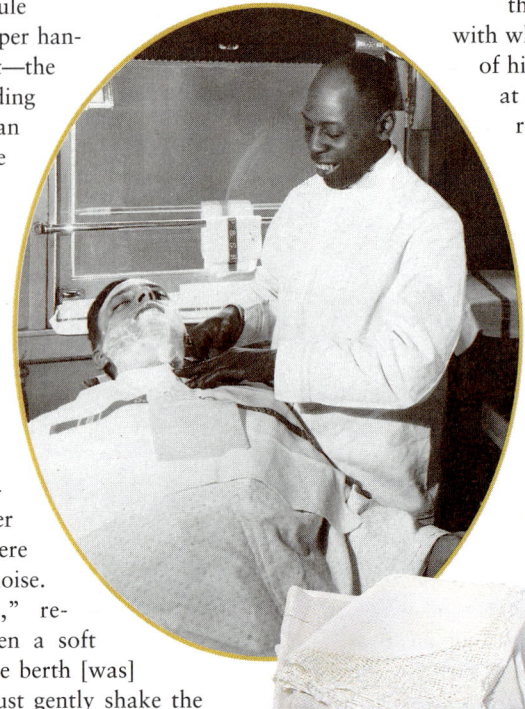

A Pullman barber shaves a passenger. Detail, Oregon Historical Society (Neg. 73453).

WORDS TO KNOW	**agility** (ə-jĭl′ĭ-tē) *n.* nimbleness; ease of movement **harass** (hăr′əs) *v.* to irritate or torment continually **insensitive** (ĭn-sĕn′sĭ-tĭv) *adj.* unfeeling

334

Mini-Lesson The Writer's Style

STORIES AS SUPPORTING DETAILS Point out to students that one way to add details to a piece of writing is to include a story or anecdote that helps readers understand the writer's ideas or point of view. Here, the authors include both first-person and third-person stories, such as the quotes from Nathaniel Hall on this page and the quote from the porter's wife on page 332.

Application Have students write a short passage about their school, making sure to include stories, quotes, or anecdotes as supporting details. Invite volunteers to read their passages to the class. Then have students discuss how using stories and anecdotes as supporting details affects their understanding and appreciation of what they read.

Reteaching/Reinforcement
• *Writing Handbook*, anthology pp. 784–785
• *Writing Mini-Lessons* transparencies, p. 34

 **The Writer's Craft**
Developing a Topic, pp. 205–209

334 THE LANGUAGE OF LITERATURE TEACHER'S EDITION

public disregarded the porters' feelings and crushed their manhood beneath its heel. Without company protection or job security, the early porters could either bury their pride and quietly accept their circumstances or quit. Some quit, but most had no choice but to stay.

Even under these circumstances, the porters took pride in their work, salvaging their manhood in the respect they received at home. Between 1867 and 1890, the early porters earned a reputation for being outstanding employees, highly praised for their honesty, politeness, and reliability. More than a few white passengers were shocked to learn that porters were "remarkably intelligent."

George Pullman and his "Ambassadors of Hospitality" were highly praised by both races. At the 1893 Chicago World's Fair, Pullman was honored for being the largest employer of the former slave. President Grover Cleveland cited Pullman as an example of how other businesses could use blacks in jobs of "service." Travelers all over the world praised the "smiling porter" who became the role model of the black employee—grinning and satisfied, happy and uncomplaining.

Even Frederick Douglass, renowned black orator, newspaper publisher, and leading abolitionist,[5] praised George Pullman for his hiring practices, and thanked him for being the "best friend of the black worker." (In later years, the Pullman Company would use Douglass's quote to garner support against union porters.)

Some of those who knew George Pullman privately doubted that he ever befriended

EVALUATE

How did the image of the Pullman porter compare with the basic reality of his situation?
Using a Reading Log

anyone. Described as a megalomaniac[6] who abused power and wealth to get what he wanted, his simplistic philosophy was "my rule or your ruin." Other historians claim that Pullman was a "complex man" who was misunderstood.

While historians disagree about Pullman's character, his genius for business was never questioned. From 1869 until his death in 1897, George Mortimer Pullman managed the Pullman Company like a well-oiled machine.

In 1880, Pullman set aside thirty-six hundred acres in the southern outskirts of Chicago and built a planned community called Pullman, Illinois. Twelve thousand white Pullman employees were required to live in the company-owned town. They had to shop at company-owned stores and even worship in a company-owned church. Black employees were not permitted to live in Pullman.

Rents were high but salaries were low, and many of the employees were actually starving. All living expenses were taken out of each employee's paycheck. One man reportedly

---

5. **abolitionist** (ăb′ə-lĭsh′ə-nĭst): a person favoring an end to slavery.
6. **megalomaniac** (měg′ə-lō-mā′nē-ăk): a person who believes himself or herself to be all-powerful.

WORDS TO KNOW
salvaging (săl′vĭ-jĭng) *adj.* saving from loss or destruction **salvage** *v.*

335

Active Reading: EVALUATE

P Have students compare the portions of the selection describing porters' actual working conditions with the quotes in the text depicting outsiders' views of the porters. *(According to the selection, the porters' image was much better than their reality.)*

Literary Concept: SOURCES

Q Ask students why only the last part of the sentence about Frederick Douglass is in quotation marks. *(The authors have paraphrased Douglass by saying that he thanked and praised Pullman, but quotes surround his exact words.)*

CUSTOMIZING FOR
Students Acquiring English

5 Encourage students to paraphrase "my rule or your ruin" in their own words. *(One possible paraphrase is "You have to do what I say or you will lose your job and your salary.")*

Critical Thinking: HYPOTHESIZING

R Have students discuss how different historians can form different judgments of the same man, in this case, Pullman. *(Possible responses: The historians used different sources of information; they interpreted factual information in different ways.)*

Literary Concept: AUTHOR'S PURPOSE

S An author's purpose is reflected in the careful selection of words. Ask students to consider the change in effect if the phrase "employees were required to live" was changed to "employees lived" and "had to shop" was changed to "shopped." *(Possible response: These changes would tone down the co-authors' attempt to show readers the employees' difficult living conditions.)*

Assessment Option

INFORMAL ASSESSMENT You can informally assess students' understanding of some of the key ideas in the selection by asking them to imagine themselves each as a porter writing a letter to his wife. The letter should describe some of the porter's experiences on the train and convey his feelings about his situation.

Rubric

3 Full Accomplishment Student uses details in the selection in creating his or her letter. He or she describes plausible events and feelings.

2 Substantial Accomplishment Student uses few details from the selection in his or her letter. Descriptions are reasonably plausible.

1 Little or Partial Accomplishment Student does not use details from the selection. Letters are unrealistic or sketchy.

THE LANGUAGE OF LITERATURE TEACHER'S EDITION 335

Linking to Social Studies

T A labor union is an organization of workers for the purpose of improving their pay or working conditions. Labor unions had their beginnings with the Industrial Revolution and were first formed in the late 1700s and early 1800s.

Active Reading: PREDICT

U Before students answer the question, check that they understand how strikes work and that the porters were not union members. *(Possible response: If the strike had been successful, the working conditions of the union members might have improved. This might have caused some improvement for the porters too.)*

STRATEGIC READING FOR
Less-Proficient Readers

V Review with students the workers' efforts to change their circumstances by joining a union.

- Who could join the union? *(white employees)* **Noting Relevant Details**
- What did the union do? *(organize a strike)* **Summarizing**
- What happened when police were sent to arrest strikers? *(There was a riot.)* **Relating Cause and Effect**

Set a Purpose Have students read to find out if the union improved conditions for Pullman employees.

Active Reading: EVALUATE

W Have students compare their opinions of Pullman with what they believed earlier in the selection. You may wish to use the following model to give students ideas of what they might be thinking about.

Think-Aloud Model *At first Pullman sounded like a good man because he gave jobs to the ex-slaves. Now I think his treatment of the porters and of union members indicates his actions were based on self-interest, not the interest and well-being of others.*

Phrase	Preposition	Object
After the strike on his company into a rage	after on into	strike company rage

---

earned two cents after all his company debts had been deducted.

White Pullman employees rebelled by unionizing under the leadership of Eugene Debs, a socialist labor leader. Black employees were not invited to participate.

After serving in the Indiana State Legislature, Debs had helped establish and was currently serving as the president of the American Railway Union (ARU). Pullman refused to recognize the ARU and on May 11, 1894, 90 percent of the workers walked off their jobs. The rest of the employees, who were black, were laid off. The company shut down, and the historic Pullman strike was under way. A court ordered the strikers back to work. Debs and the ARU members refused to obey the court order. Police officers were sent to arrest the striking workers.

In July 1894, during a <u>confrontation</u> between the strikers and police officers, violence broke out, and during two dreadful days of rioting, seventeen people were killed and several hundred buildings were burned and looted.

The Chicago press blamed Eugene Debs and the ARU for what happened. Debs was labeled a dangerous radical. He was arrested and imprisoned for refusing to obey the court order.

Public sentiment turned against the labor movement. The Pullman workers were tired, confused, and their families were hungry. Slowly the men returned to the same low-paying jobs. Some money was better than nothing.

Pullman took some of the strikers back, but each one had to sign a pledge promising never to join a union while employed by the Pullman Company. Although porters had not participated in this strike, they were forced to sign the pledge, too.

Losing in the challenge against Pullman destroyed the ARU, and in 1897 it folded. Debs, however, organized the Social Democratic Party and ran for president of the United States five times between 1900 and 1920.

After the strike, George Pullman kept a tight rein on his company. It was said that any mention of unions or workers' rights sent him into a rage. When George Pullman died in 1897, his family covered his grave with tons of

Passengers in a Pullman dining car, being served by a waiter Detail, Oregon Historical Society (Neg. 38564).

PREDICT

How might the outcome of the strike affect the situation of the Pullman porters?
Using a Reading Log

WORDS TO KNOW

confrontation (kŏn'frŭn-tā'shən) *n.* a face-to-face encounter, usually in anger

336

Mini-Lesson Grammar

PREPOSITIONAL PHRASES Remind students that a prepositional phrase is a group of words that begins with a preposition and ends with its object. The highlighted passage above includes several prepositional phrases.

Application Have students identify the preposition and objects of the preposition in each sentence below. Then have students rewrite each sentence, using a different prepositional phrase.
1. The sleeping cars were behind the dining car.
2. Before they worked for Pullman, many porters had been slaves.
3. The railroad tracks ran through a broad meadow.
4. Fresh sheets were put on the berths each day.
5. The porter put the suitcase in the baggage car.

Reteaching/Reinforcement
- *Grammar Mini-Lessons* transparencies, p. 41

 **The Writer's Craft**

What Are Prepositions? pp. 504–506

The *Empire State Express,* among the fastest trains of the 1890s and early 1900s, was one of many that featured Pullman cars. Culver Pictures.

reinforced concrete. The family said they feared vandals might desecrate[7] his grave. Ambrose Bierce, an American journalist and writer known for his cutting wit, wrote, "It is clear the family in their bereavement[8] was making sure he wasn't going to get up and come back."

After Pullman's death, his company continued to grow. By the turn of the twentieth century, Pullman had bought out the Wagner Palace Car Company as well as T. T. Woodruff, Jerome Marbles, and Barney and Smith. The company now had a monopoly on sleeping cars. And every person working on a car that bore Pullman's name was a nonunion worker. ❖

---

7. **desecrate** (dĕs′ĭ-krāt′): to damage in a way that shows disrespect.
8. **bereavement** (bĭ-rēv′mənt): sadness at the loss of a loved one.

WORDS TO KNOW
monopoly (mə-nŏp′ə-lē) *n.* a total control by one group over a product or service

337

STRATEGIC READING FOR
Less-Proficient Readers

X Were attempts made to improve the porters' working conditions? *(Not really. Eugene Debs formed a union, but the porters weren't allowed to join.)* **Summarizing**

• How did Pullman keep unions out of his company? *(He made workers sign a pledge not to join a union.)* **Making Inferences**

Literary Concept: SOURCES

Ask students to imagine that they are writing a biography of George Pullman. Have them list the types of sources they would use.

CUSTOMIZING FOR
Gifted and Talented Students

Have students choose one of the people (other than Pullman) quoted in the selection and use reference materials to write a short biography.

COMPREHENSION CHECK

1. Why were railroad porter jobs highly desirable to the ex-slaves? *(They paid a steady wage and provided opportunities for travel and work in luxurious surroundings.)*
2. What were the negative aspects of working as one of Pullman's porters? *(The porters had to smile all the time, respond instantly to passenger requests, and sometimes were harassed by passengers.)*
3. How did some of the railroad employees try to get better working conditions? *(They joined a union and went on strike.)*
4. How did Pullman react to the strike? *(He made returning workers sign a pledge promising never to join a union.)*

Mini-Lesson  Spelling

THE PREFIX EX- Tell students that when the prefix ex- clearly means "former," it is hyphenated.

ex- + slave = **ex-slave** (former slave)
ex- + husband = ex-husband (former husband)

The older Latin prefix ex- means "out" or "beyond," although this meaning is not always obvious in English. In such cases the prefix is not hyphenated.

ex + clusive = **exclusive**
ex + port = **export**

Application Have students spell the following words using the correct form of *ex.*

1. ex + cursion (excursion)
2. ex + claim (exclaim)
3. ex + president (ex-president)
4. ex + position (exposition)
5. ex + cavator (excavator)

Ask students to look for more words that fit these patterns, in their own writing and in things they read, and to add these words to their personal word lists.

Reteaching/Reinforcement
• *Unit Three Resource Book,* p. 51

THE LANGUAGE OF LITERATURE TEACHER'S EDITION **337**

LITERARY INSIGHT

1. Describe what the speaker sees, hears, and feels as he or she rides along on the train. *(The speaker sees bridges, trees, mountains, a lake, a beacon. The speaker hears the thunder of the wheels and the rattling of the window glass. He or she feels the rocking of the train and a straining of his or her neck muscles as it goes around a curve.)*

2. Why does the speaker stay up half the night? *(The speaker is enjoying looking at what is outside the train window.)*

3. Compare this poem with the one given at the beginning of the selection on page 331. How do points of view of the speakers differ? *(Possible response: In "Lonesome Whistle" the speaker isn't on the train, but the sound of the whistle causes feelings of longing. In "Night Journey" the speaker is traveling on the train looking out at the passing sights.)*

THEODORE ROETHKE

Born in 1908 in Saginaw, Michigan, Roethke spent some time at the University of Michigan and briefly studied law before going on to become a poet. He became interested in poetry because of a fascination with nature, once writing, "when I get alone under an open sky where man isn't too evident—then I'm tremendously exalted and a thousand vivid ideas and sweet visions flood my consciousness."

A source of much of Roethke's poetry was the notes and notebooks he conscientiously kept throughout his life. Roethke worked equally hard at being a college professor and a poet. He was well liked by students and often enabled them to share his enthusiasm for poetry.

LITERARY INSIGHT

Night Journey
by Theodore Roethke

Now as the train bears west,
Its rhythm rocks the earth,
And from my Pullman berth
I stare into the night
5   While others take their rest.
Bridges of iron lace,
A suddenness of trees,
A lap of mountain mist
All cross my line of sight,
10 Then a bleak wasted place,
And a lake below my knees.
Full on my neck I feel
The straining at a curve;
My muscles move with steel,
15 I wake in every nerve.
I watch a beacon swing
From dark to blazing bright,
We thunder through ravines
And gullies washed with light.
20 Beyond the mountain pass
Mist deepens on the pane,
We rush into a rain
That rattles double glass.
Wheels shake the roadbed stone,
25 The pistons jerk and shove,
I stay up half the night
To see the land I love.

Multicultural Perspectives

THE REAL MCCOY Elijah McCoy (1843–1929) was an African American who also worked on a railroad in the 1800s. But his background and experiences were different from those of the porters described in the selection.

The son of two runaway slaves who fled to Canada, McCoy returned to the United States after the Civil War, then attended school in Scotland and became a mechanical engineer. When he came back to the United States, companies were reluctant to hire African Americans in skilled or supervisory positions. So, McCoy took a job as a fireman on the Michigan Central Railroad. Although the job was simple and did not use his talents and education, his work inspired him to become interested in methods of lubricating or oiling machinery.

McCoy invented a device that could be used to oil a machine while it was still running, saving time and fuel. His invention became greatly admired, and equipment buyers began to check that these devices were "the real McCoy" in order to avoid purchasing less-effective imitations.

RESPONDING OPTIONS

FROM PERSONAL RESPONSE TO CRITICAL ANALYSIS

REFLECT
1. Whom were you thinking about as you finished reading this selection—George Pullman, the Pullman porters, or someone else? Record your thoughts in your notebook.

RETHINK
2. What do you think it would have been like to be a Pullman porter?
   Consider
   Close Textual Reading
   - the hardships the porters experienced
   - the respect given to the porters by their own communities

3. What do you think of George Pullman?
   Consider
   - his decision to hire ex-slaves
   - his role in the Pullman strike

RELATE
4. If you haven't already done so, read "Night Journey" on page 338. What might the speaker of the poem have in common with a typical Pullman porter?

Multimodal Learning
ANOTHER PATHWAY

How would this selection be different if it were a work of fiction rather than nonfiction? Would you learn additional information about Pullman porters and the hardships they faced? What events or ideas might be left out of a fictional work about this subject? Jot down your thoughts in your notebook to share with the class.

QUICKWRITES

1. Write an **advertisement** for porters that the Pullman Company might have placed in the help-wanted section of the *Dayton Globe-Herald* in 1897.
2. This selection opens with a ballad about the railroad. Draft a **ballad** a porter might have written about his life traveling the rails.
3. Draft a **comparison/contrast paragraph** in which you compare Pullman porters with today's transportation workers.

📁 **PORTFOLIO** Save your writing. You may want to use it later as a springboard to a piece for your portfolio.

LITERARY CONCEPTS

A **primary source** is one that presents direct, firsthand knowledge about a subject. For example, "My First Dive with the Dolphins" (page 65) is a primary source because it was written by Don C. Reed about his own personal experience. A **secondary source** is one that presents indirect, secondhand knowledge about a subject. The selection "Matthew Henson at the Top of the World" (page 53) is an example of a secondary source. It was written by Jim Haskins about past people and events that he had researched. In this excerpt from *A Long Hard Journey,* Patricia and Fredrick McKissack use a primary source in the form of the railroad song "Lonesome Whistle." See if you can find another example of a primary source used in the selection.

A LONG HARD JOURNEY **339**

From Personal Response to Critical Analysis

1. Responses will vary.
2. Possible responses: It would have been a pretty good job because of the decent pay and the opportunities to travel and learn new things. It would have been unpleasant when the passengers were demanding or mean.
3. Possible responses: Pullman was both good and bad. He provided much-needed jobs for the ex-slaves and paid them a steady wage; however, he also exploited the ex-slaves by keeping salaries low and making them promise never to join a union.
4. Possible response: They both would have experienced the sounds and sights of railroad travel, although the speaker of the poem would have had more time to enjoy them.

Another Pathway

Start by leading a discussion of how fiction differs from nonfiction. Then have individual students search for events or details that might be left out if the work were fictionalized and create events, scenes, or dialogue to be inserted.

Rubric

3 Full Accomplishment Student's response reveals an understanding of the differences between fiction and nonfiction, and suggests scenes to be included in a fictionalized version, as well as details to be omitted.

2 Substantial Accomplishment Student's response shows some understanding of how a fictional account would differ from the selection, and identifies events or details, particularly the quotes from outside sources, that would probably not appear in a work of fiction.

1 Little or Partial Accomplishment Student's response is not clear about the difference between fiction and nonfiction.

Literary Concepts

Students can work in pairs to search for primary sources in the selection. They should also think about whether the information represents a fact or an opinion. When finished, have students compare their responses with those of at least one other pair.

Two examples of primary sources are the quote from the porter's wife on page 332 and the porter's description of his duties on page 334. However, explain that if students were to quote this article in a research paper, it would be considered a secondary source because they would be using the McKissacks' research, not the original documents.

QuickWrites

1. Ask students to include a catchy headline in their advertisements. They may use pictures as well as words in their ads.
2. Some characteristics of ballads are that the language is simple, the story is told through dialogue and action, the theme is often tragic, and there is often a refrain.
3. Students can first organize their ideas by using a two-column comparison-contrast chart.

📁 The Writer's Craft

Sharing an Opinion, pp. 120–124
Poetry, pp. 86–88
Comparison-and-Contrast Chart, p. 195

THE LANGUAGE OF LITERATURE TEACHER'S EDITION **339**

Words to Know

1. plush
2. insensitive
3. harass
4. drudgery
5. agility
6. contemporary
7. salvage
8. confrontation
9. monopoly
10. exclusive

Reteaching/Reinforcement
- *Unit Three Resource Book*, p. 52

Across the Curriculum

Geography *Cooperative Learning* Have students work in groups of three or four to mark a map of the continental United States with key railroad routes in use during the late 1800s. One student can be the researcher; another can be the mapmaker. One or two students should facilitate the group's research and can also present the group's findings to the class.

Math *All Aboard!* Have students find out how long it takes today to travel by rail across the continental United States, for example, from San Francisco to Boston. Students should collect as much quantitative information as they can: length of journey, average and maximum speeds, time spent at stops, and so on.

PATRICIA AND FREDRICK MCKISSACK

In addition to being writers, both the McKissacks have second careers. Fredrick has worked as a civil engineer and owns a general contracting company; Patricia has taught English in both high school and college. A great number of their books are stories for children. The McKissacks have also written a series of biographies of important African Americans.

WORDS TO KNOW

Review the Words to Know in the boxes at the bottom of the selection pages. Then, on your own paper, write the word that best completes each of the following sentences.

1. The furniture in the Pullman cars was upholstered with _____.
2. The Pullman Company was one of many that displayed cruel and _____ treatment of its African-American employees.
3. Some passengers deliberately tried to _____ the porters by using racial slurs and even physical abuse.
4. The worst part of many jobs is the _____.
5. The porters displayed their _____ in how quickly and easily they could prepare passengers' rooms.
6. Because he lived during the same time period as Eugene Debs, George Pullman was a _____ of Debs.
7. Porters and other former slaves who entered the work force found it difficult to _____ their self-respect when treated poorly.
8. Striking railroad workers had a _____ with the police that resulted in the deaths of several people.
9. Like the Pullman Company, a company with a _____ does not have to compete with other companies that make the same product.
10. The Pullman porters functioned much like an _____ club because they shared experiences that few African Americans of the time could.

PATRICIA AND FREDRICK MCKISSACK

Both born in Nashville, Tennessee, Patricia and Fredrick McKissack grew up in a time of great struggle and great opportunity for African Americans. By the time the two graduated from Tennessee State University and married in 1964, sit-ins by young African Americans had begun to force the desegregation of public places. As Fredrick explains, "Life actually changed. In a sense we climbed from the Old South to the New South. We went from segregated schools to integrated situations." They were the first generation to do so.

The couple turned to writing as a way to share with young people what they had been through as African Americans. According to Fredrick, "The reason that we write for children is to tell them about these things and to get them to internalize the information, to feel just a little of the hurt, the tremendous amount of hurt and sadness that racism and discrimination cause—for all people, regardless of race." The McKissacks have written nearly 100 books of history, historical fiction, and biography—most of them together. Patricia explains, "We try to enlighten, to change attitudes, to form new attitudes—to build bridges with books."

Extended Reading
OTHER WORKS *Abram, Abram, Where Are We Going?; The Civil Rights Movement in America from 1865 to the Present; Taking a Stand Against Racism and Racial Discrimination; The Royal Kingdoms of Ghana, Mali, and Songhay: Life in Medieval Africa*

340 UNIT THREE PART 2: FACING THE CONSEQUENCES

PREVIEWING

POETRY

Barbara Frietchie
John Greenleaf Whittier

Activating Prior Knowledge
PERSONAL CONNECTION

Just what is courage? Is courage simply a willingness to fight—or can it be something else? Consider some acts of bravery that you have heard about or seen. Think of the qualities that brave people have in common. Then, in your notebook, write your own definition of *courage*. As you read this poem, decide whether the character of Barbara Frietchie fits your definition.

Setting a Purpose

> To me, courage is the willingness to take action in a difficult situation.

Building Background
HISTORICAL CONNECTION

John Greenleaf Whittier wrote this poem to honor what he felt was an act of courage that may have occurred before a clash of Union and Confederate forces during the Civil War. On September 10, 1862, General Robert E. Lee, commander of the Confederate Army of Northern Virginia, and General Thomas J. "Stonewall" Jackson led over 55,000 soldiers through Frederick, Maryland. They were on their way to Sharpsburg and to defeat in a battle—the battle of Antietam—that would prove to be the most bloody of the war.

One citizen of Frederick was Barbara Frietchie, an elderly widow fiercely loyal to the Union. According to legend, as Jackson's troops marched through the town, she waved a Union flag defiantly at the Confederate troops.

Active Reading
READING CONNECTION

Poetic Language Readers rarely come across certain words except in poems. These unusual words can heighten a poem's effect, particularly when it is recited or spoken aloud. Three examples from "Barbara Frietchie" are shown in the chart on this page. Poets may also arrange words in a way different from the word order that people generally use in conversation. They do this to fit the rhyming patterns and rhythms they have chosen for their poems. You may understand a confusing line or sentence better if you rewrite the words in a more recognizable order.

Use in Poem	Standard Form
morn	morning
o'er	over
fourscore	eighty (a score is 20)

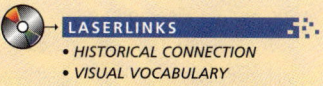
- HISTORICAL CONNECTION
- VISUAL VOCABULARY

341

OVERVIEW

Objectives
- To understand and appreciate a narrative poem that relates a historical event
- To identify the use of couplets, alliteration, and rhythm in a poem
- To express understanding of the poem through a choice of writing forms, including writing an interview and rhymed couplets
- To extend understanding of the poem through a variety of multimodal and cross-curricular activities

Skills

THE WRITER'S STYLE
- Details appealing to sight

SPEAKING, LISTENING, AND VIEWING
- Group discussion
- Oral presentation

Cross-Curricular Connections

SOCIAL STUDIES
- U.S. flag

HISTORICAL CONNECTION
The Road to Antietam As the Confederate commanders Robert E. Lee and Stonewall Jackson lead their troops through Frederick, Maryland, Jackson encountered Barbara Frietchie, a Union loyalist. Students will see historical images of these key characters in the poem and of the bridge over which the Confederate soldiers marched to defeat in the battle of Antietam.

Side A, Frame 38795

UNIT THREE RESOURCE BOOK
Strategic Reading: Literature, p. 55

WRITING MINI-LESSONS
Transparencies, p. 38

ACCESS FOR STUDENTS ACQUIRING ENGLISH
Reading and Writing Support

FORMAL ASSESSMENT
Selection Test, pp. 71–72
 Test Generator

 **AUDIO LIBRARY**
See Reference Card

 LASERLINKS
Historical Connection
Visual Vocabulary
Social Studies Connection

INTERNET RESOURCES
McDougal Littell Literature Center at http://www.hmco.com/mcdougal/lit

THE LANGUAGE OF LITERATURE **TEACHER'S EDITION** 341

CUSTOMIZING FOR
Students Acquiring English

- Use **ACCESS FOR STUDENTS ACQUIRING ENGLISH,** *Reading and Writing Support.*
- Ask students acquiring English to work through the Reading Connection on page 341 paired with students whose first language is English. This will show that anyone can have trouble with unfamiliar vocabulary.

STRATEGIC READING FOR
Less-Proficient Readers

Set a Purpose Explain to students that the Confederate troops are marching through Frederick, Maryland—a Union town. As students read the poem, have them note why Barbara Frietchie puts out the Union flag and how the Confederates react to it.

Use **UNIT THREE RESOURCE BOOK,** p. 55, for guidance in reading the selection.

CUSTOMIZING FOR
Gifted and Talented Students

Have students analyze how the mood of the poem changes from the beginning to the end. *(lines 1–9: peaceful; lines 10–16: potential conflict; lines 17–42: tension and conflict; lines 43–50: peaceful; lines 51–60: triumphant)* Then ask students to suggest ways of changing the mood in different parts of the poem.

Literary Concept: COUNTRY COUPLETS

A Point out that this poem is divided into pairs of rhymed lines, or couplets. Have students write a new couplet about the subject of the poem.

Active Reading: CLARIFY

B Have students interpret lines 13–16. *(In the morning there were 40 Union flags flying in the town. By noon, all the flags had been taken down. One means "not one flag.")*

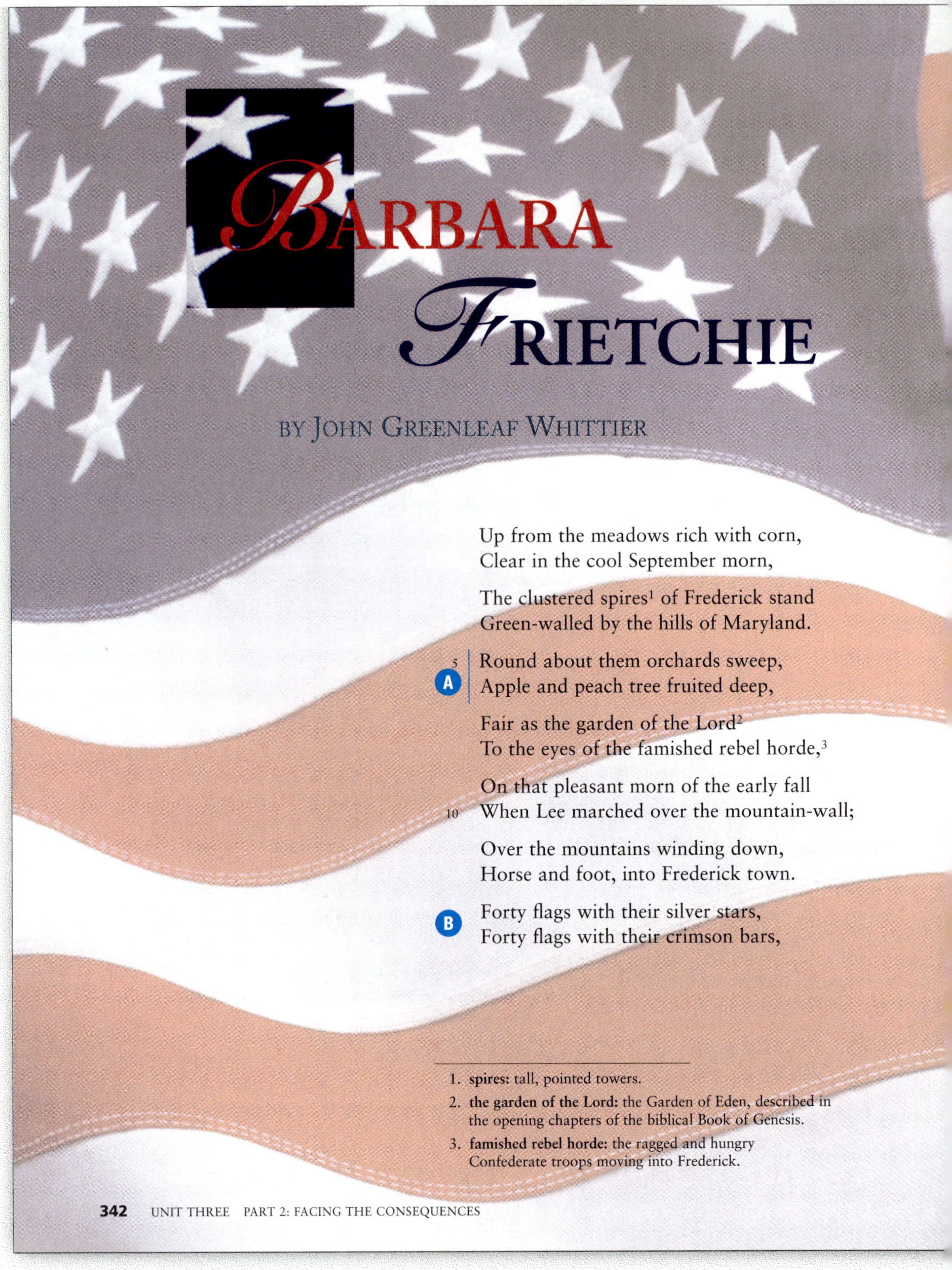

Barbara Frietchie

BY JOHN GREENLEAF WHITTIER

Up from the meadows rich with corn,
Clear in the cool September morn,

The clustered spires[1] of Frederick stand
Green-walled by the hills of Maryland.

5 Round about them orchards sweep,
A Apple and peach tree fruited deep,

Fair as the garden of the Lord[2]
To the eyes of the famished rebel horde,[3]

On that pleasant morn of the early fall
10 When Lee marched over the mountain-wall;

Over the mountains winding down,
Horse and foot, into Frederick town.

B Forty flags with their silver stars,
Forty flags with their crimson bars,

---
1. **spires:** tall, pointed towers.
2. **the garden of the Lord:** the Garden of Eden, described in the opening chapters of the biblical Book of Genesis.
3. **famished rebel horde:** the ragged and hungry Confederate troops moving into Frederick.

342 UNIT THREE PART 2: FACING THE CONSEQUENCES

 VISUAL VOCABULARY
- **Confederate soldier** (kən-fĕd′ər-ĭt sōl′jər)
- **slouched hat** (sloucht′ hăt′)
- **spires** (spīrz)
- **Union soldier** (yōōn′yən sōl′jər)

Side A, Frame 38803

15 Flapped in the morning wind; the sun
Of noon looked down and saw not one.

Up rose old Barbara Frietchie then,
Bowed with her fourscore years and ten;

Bravest of all in Frederick town,
20 She took up the flag the men hauled down;

In her attic window the staff[4] she set,
To show that one heart was loyal yet.

Up the street came the rebel tread,
Stonewall Jackson riding ahead.

25 Under his slouched hat[5] left and right
He glanced; the old flag met his sight.

"Halt!"—the dust-brown ranks stood fast.
"Fire!"—out blazed the rifle-blast.

It shivered[6] the window, pane and sash;
30 It rent[7] the banner with seam and gash.

Quick, as it fell, from the broken staff
Dame Barbara snatched the silken scarf.

She leaned far out on the window-sill,
And shook it forth with a royal will.

35 "Shoot, if you must, this old gray head,
But spare your country's flag," she said.

A shade of sadness, a blush of shame,
Over the face of the leader came;

The nobler nature within him stirred
40 To life at that woman's deed and word;

"Who touches a hair of yon gray head
Dies like a dog! March on!" he said.

All day long through Frederick street
Sounded the tread of marching feet:

45 All day long that free flag tossed
Over the heads of the rebel host.

Ever its torn folds rose and fell
On the loyal winds that loved it well;

And through the hill-gaps sunset light
50 Shone over it with a warm good-night.

Barbara Frietchie's work is o'er,
And the Rebel rides on his raids no more.

Honor to her! and let a tear
Fall, for her sake, on Stonewall's bier.[8]

55 Over Barbara Frietchie's grave,
Flag of Freedom and Union, wave!

Peace and order and beauty draw
Round that symbol of light and law;

And ever the stars above look down
60 On thy stars below in Frederick town!

---

4. **staff:** a pole on which a flag is displayed.
5. **slouched hat:** a soft hat with a wide brim.
6. **shivered:** caused to break into pieces.
7. **rent:** tore or split apart.
8. **bier** (bîr): a coffin and its stand.

BARBARA FRIETCHIE **343**

Mini-Lesson  The Writer's Style

DETAILS APPEALING TO SIGHT Remind students that writers include sensory details—the look, the feel, the sound, the smell, and the taste of things—to make their writing more vivid and interesting. In "Barbara Frietchie," Whittier includes many vivid descriptions of how things look.

Application Have students find three or four details appealing to sight in the poem and sketch or draw them. Drawings can be shared with the class to help everyone visualize the events in the poem.

Some students may prefer to share verbally how the visual images from the poem remind them of things they've seen.

Reteaching/Reinforcement
- Writing Handbook, anthology pp. 784–785
- Writing Mini-Lessons transparencies, p. 38

The Writer's Craft
Appealing to the Senses, pp. 266–272

From Personal Response to Critical Analysis

1. Some students may feel she was brave and loyal; others may think she was foolish to take such a risk.
2. Whittier may have been sympathetic to the Union side in the Civil War, moved by Frietchie's bravery, or impressed by Jackson's shame and fairness.
3. Possible responses: He was fair-minded; he was saddened by the destruction caused by the war; he admired courageous people.
4. Responses may vary.
5. Lines 35–36 ("Shoot, if you must...") show Frietchie's courage and are a high point of the poem. Lines 41–42 ("Who touches...") are memorable because Jackson's words are so forceful and dramatic.
6. People can transfer emotional feelings to symbols, such as a flag, and then feel almost as strongly about the symbol as they do about what it represents.

Another Pathway

Cooperative Learning In groups of three, students can begin by filling out the charts independently and then can combine their results. Ask students to suggest at least three traits for each character and to support their opinions with lines from the poem. For Frietchie, students might choose courage, patriotism, and loyalty; for Jackson, decisiveness, a quick temper, and fair-mindedness.

Rubric

3 Full Accomplishment Students write at least three traits for each person and can support them with lines from the poem.

2 Substantial Accomplishment Students write one or two traits for each person and can support most of them with lines from the poem.

1 Little or Partial Accomplishment Students cannot think of traits and support their choices with lines from the poem.

RESPONDING OPTIONS

FROM PERSONAL RESPONSE TO CRITICAL ANALYSIS

REFLECT 1. What are your reactions to the character of Barbara Frietchie? Discuss your ideas with a friend.

RETHINK 2. In your opinion, why might John Greenleaf Whittier have been inspired to write this tribute to Barbara Frietchie?
Consider
- how Whittier seems to feel about the war
- *Close Textual Reading* • Frietchie's age and actions
- Stonewall Jackson's reaction

3. What do you think Stonewall Jackson's reaction reveals about him?

Thematic Link 4. Reread the definition of *courage* you wrote for the Personal Connection on page 341. Explain whether Barbara Frietchie's actions fit your definition or you would revise your definition on the basis of your reading of the poem.

5. A pair of lines of "Barbara Frietchie" have become famous. Some people can recite these lines from memory, even if they cannot remember one other word from the poem. Which lines do you think are famous and why? In a small group, take turns reciting the lines each person identifies.

RELATE 6. A flag is only a piece of fabric attached to a staff. Yet many men and women have acted with courage to protect their national flags from dishonor and disgrace. Why do you think flags might be so important to people? Explain your opinion.

Multimodal Learning
ANOTHER PATHWAY
Cooperative Learning

In a group, reread "Barbara Frietchie." How are the personalities and beliefs of Barbara Frietchie and Stonewall Jackson revealed in the course of the poem? Make a chart like this one and add to it, noting the results of your discussion.

Barbara Frietchie's Personality Traits	Stonewall Jackson's Personality Traits
courage	

QUICKWRITES

1. Imagine that the Civil War has just ended. You have been sent to conduct an **interview** with Barbara Frietchie. What will your first five questions be?

2. Write several **rhymed couplets** that might be carved on Barbara Frietchie's gravestone. Try to capture the spirit of this courageous woman so that all who see her grave marker will have some idea what she was like.

📁 **PORTFOLIO** *Save your writing. You may want to use it later as a springboard to a piece for your portfolio.*

344 UNIT THREE PART 2: FACING THE CONSEQUENCES

QuickWrites

1. Have students first think about what kind of background information they would need to be a well-prepared interviewer. They might ask Frietchie about her history and future plans. They could ask for her feelings during the confrontation with Jackson, or for her assessment of him as a leader and as a person.

2. Rhymed epitaphs on gravestones can be written in either the first person or third person. They often use couplets, although other rhyme schemes are possible. Here is an example:

Stranger stop and cast an eye,
As you are now, so once was I,
As I am now, so you will be,
Prepare for death, and follow me.

Here, students will write in the third person. They might choose or adapt a line from the poem to use in their work, for example, "Barbara Frietchie's work is o'er" or "Barbara Frietchie's work is done."

The Writer's Craft

Interviewing, p. 323
Poetry, pp. 86–88

344 THE LANGUAGE OF LITERATURE TEACHER'S EDITION

LITERARY CONCEPTS

Many readers find reading "Barbara Frietchie" aloud to be fun, partly because the simple structure of the poem allows the reader to move along at a brisk pace. The poem is divided into pairs of rhymed lines, or **couplets.** Did you enjoy the effect of the couplets? Why or why not?

Another poetic technique that makes this poem appealing is **alliteration,** the repetition of consonant sounds at the beginning of words. Poets use alliteration to emphasize certain words or to add a musical beat to their works. In "Barbara Frietchie," the words "*F*orty *f*lags" and "*s*ilver *s*tars" in line 13 show alliteration. See if you can find more examples of alliteration in the poem. Then team up with one or two other students and read the poem aloud.

CONCEPT REVIEW: Rhythm When you read the poem aloud, did you notice the strong, steady beat of the lines? Remember, a poem's beat is called its rhythm. Why might Whittier have used a regular, steady rhythm in "Barbara Frietchie"?

ALTERNATIVE ACTIVITIES

1. Imagine that Barbara Frietchie and Stonewall Jackson have survived the Civil War and meet again. With another student, create a **dialogue** between the two and present it to your class.

2. With a group of classmates, develop and present a **choral reading** of "Barbara Frietchie" for the rest of the class or for another class in your school. Choose recorded music from the Civil War period to play softly in the background for all or part of the reading. If you like, dress in clothing appropriate for the 1860s.

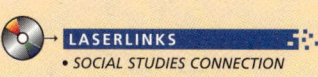
• SOCIAL STUDIES CONNECTION

Multimodal Learning
ACROSS THE CURRICULUM

 Social Studies Barbara Frietchie waved a Union flag out her window at the approaching Confederate troops. How did the U.S. flag of the early 1860s compare with the flag of today? Explore how the flag has changed over the years, and present your findings in a series of drawings of the flag of the United States at various points in history.

JOHN GREENLEAF WHITTIER

1807–1892

A son of Quaker farmers, John Greenleaf Whittier was born in Haverhill, Massachusetts. At 14, he discovered the poetry of the Scottish poet Robert Burns and began to write verses himself.

Whittier found the greatest meaning in his life through the abolitionist cause, a movement of people whose religious beliefs led them to demand immediate freedom for slaves. He worked hard as an abolitionist, speaking publicly and publishing pamphlets.

Whittier's first book was published in 1831, and in 1846 he published a collection of antislavery poems, *Voices of Freedom*. After the Civil War ended, Whittier turned to writing poetry about his youth, his family, and the New England countryside.

Whittier died at 85, a famous and well-loved poet, as well as a wealthy one. He never forgot his early principles, though. In his will, he left money to the Hampton Institute, a school in Virginia for African Americans and Native Americans.

OTHER WORKS *Legends of New England* Extended Reading

BARBARA FRIETCHIE **345**

Across the Curriculum

Social Studies *Cooperative Learning* Students can work in groups of three. The researcher finds books that show the U.S. flag throughout history. The artist draws or paints the flags. The writer adds comments beneath each drawing, including such information as when and why the flag changed to the design pictured.

ADDITIONAL SUGGESTIONS

Social Studies *You're a Grand Old Flag!* Have students research and prepare an oral report about the rules that tell when and how the U.S. flag should be displayed.

SOCIAL STUDIES CONNECTION
Civil War Flags Displaying flags was an important way of communicating loyalty during the Civil War. Some of them are shown here. You may wish to use them to generate a discussion about the various groups that flew them.

Side A, Frame 38808

JOHN GREENLEAF WHITTIER

Whittier was already well known as a poet and abolitionist before the beginning of the Civil War. In addition to expressing his views against slavery, Whittier poems drew on the history, customs, and folklore of his native New England for many of his poems. An ardent supporter of the Union cause and an admirer of Abraham Lincoln, Whittier wrote a number of patriotic poems during the war. Whittier's poetry often has a moral, heroic, or prophetic tone and reveals a characteristic optimism.

Literary Concepts

Explain to students that the repeated consonant sounds in alliteration do not have to be next to each other. Often the alliteration occurs on stressed syllables. Examples from the poem include: *Clear in the cool* (line 2), *snatched the silken scarf* (line 32), *heads of the Rebel host* (line 46), *Rebel rides on his raids* (line 52).

Concept Review The repeated sounds in alliterative poetry can affect the rhythm by forcing a reader to slow down and thus give more emphasis to words. Whittier may have chosen a strong, steady beat to suggest the marching footsteps.

Alternative Activities

1. It may help students to preface their dialogues with an introductory paragraph to set the scene. In their prefaces, students can describe where and how Frietchie and Jackson meet.

2. If students work in groups of four, two students can read Frietchie's and Jackson's lines; the other two can divide up the rest of the poem. Or the narrative parts of the poem can be spoken by the entire group or pairs of students. Encourage students to try different readings and discuss which is the most effective.

THE LANGUAGE OF LITERATURE TEACHER'S EDITION **345**

OVERVIEW

Objectives

- To understand and appreciate a short story that includes elements of fantasy
- To express understanding of the story through a choice of writing forms, including a missing-person report and a newspaper article
- To extend understanding of the story through a variety of multimodal and cross-curricular activities

Skills

READING SKILLS/STRATEGIES
- Making judgments

LITERARY CONCEPTS
- Fantasy
- Humor

GENRE STUDY
- Fantasy

THE WRITER'S STYLE
- Simile

GRAMMAR
- Compound predicates and compound sentences

SPELLING
- Prefixes and roots

SPEAKING, LISTENING, AND VIEWING
- Group discussion
- Oral presentation

Cross-Curricular Connections

MATH
- Water absorption

SCIENCE
- Importance of water to life
- Loss of height in later life

SOCIAL STUDIES
- Stepfamilies

PREVIEWING

FICTION

The Enchanted Raisin
Jacqueline Balcells

Activating Prior Knowledge
PERSONAL CONNECTION
As this unusual story unfolds, you will see how the actions of mischievous children lead to extraordinary consequences. With a partner, briefly discuss tales you recall that open with the phrase "Once upon a time . . ." What features of these tales—character portrayals, comical or grand language, amazing events—appealed most to you?

LITERARY CONNECTION Building Background
"The Enchanted Raisin" may seem strangely familiar to you as you read. That's because the story includes many of the same elements that traditional storytellers have used for ages. Perhaps its odd characters and startling events will take you back to the tales you enjoyed as a child. However, this story works a twist on the tales of old because it is set in our current, everyday world. This kind of modern fiction allows the writer to apply traditional storytelling features to the ideas and issues of today. Mixing old and new elements, the writer creates situations that go in both expected and unexpected directions.

Once upon a time, there was a mom who had three absolutely unbearable children. They did every bad and stupid thing imaginable, as well as the unimaginable ones.

Setting a Purpose
WRITING CONNECTION
The following words and phrases refer to events in "The Enchanted Raisin." Which of them seem to suggest extraordinary consequences? Use the words to predict the plot of the story, and write one or more predictions in your notebook. Then read the story to see how your predictions match the writer's ideas.

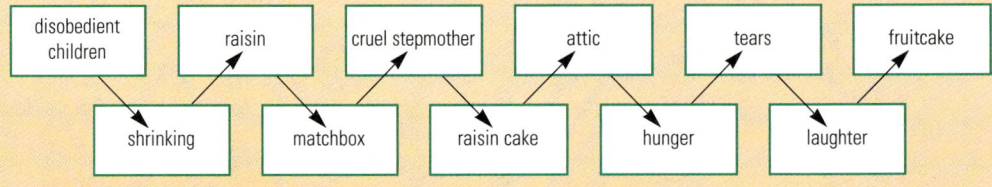

346 UNIT THREE PART 2: FACING THE CONSEQUENCES

PRINT AND MEDIA RESOURCES

UNIT THREE RESOURCE BOOK
Strategic Reading: Literature, p. 59
Vocabulary SkillBuilder, p. 62
Reading SkillBuilder, p. 60
Spelling SkillBuilder, p. 61

GRAMMAR MINI–LESSONS
Transparencies, p. 28
Copymasters, p. 37

WRITING MINI–LESSONS
Transparencies, p. 39

ACCESS FOR STUDENTS ACQUIRING ENGLISH
Selection Summaries
Reading and Writing Support

FORMAL ASSESSMENT
Selection Test, pp. 73–74
 Test Generator

AUDIO LIBRARY
See Reference Card

346 THE LANGUAGE OF LITERATURE TEACHER'S EDITION

The  ENCHANTED Raisin

by Jacqueline Balcells

Once upon a time, there was a mom who had three absolutely unbearable children. They did every bad and stupid thing imaginable, as well as the unimaginable ones. Several times they almost burned down the house, and they flooded it a hundred times. They broke the furniture, smashed the plates, fought and screamed like crazy people, spilled ink on the white sheets, and swung from the curtains as if they were monkeys in the jungle. And why bother saying what happened when they were sent outside: they spread panic throughout the neighborhood.

Their dad was almost never home, and their poor mother couldn't manage these three little devils. She was completely exhausted at the end of the day from chasing after them.

"My children," she said to them, "please stop your foolishness, if only this once. Look at me: each one of your pranks and screams is a wrinkle on my face. I am becoming an old lady."

And it was true. This woman, who had been tall and beautiful, was wrinkling and shrinking from one day to the next.

Her children didn't notice anything. But one day, when she went to meet them after school, their friends asked with astonishment, "Why does your grandmother come to get you now?"

The children felt bad for a moment; they were upset that their mother was mistaken for their grandmother. But they didn't think about it for long—they had so much to do!

The poor woman continued to wrinkle and shrink at an incredible rate. The moment arrived when she could no longer walk: her legs had become two little sticks that were so skinny, they were like cherry stems, and her back was so curved, she could barely see in front of her. Nevertheless, her three children did not stop inventing more and more horrible pranks:

"Let's take the feathers out of the pillows!"
"Let's pull out the dog's fur!"
"Let's cut off the cat's ears!"
"Let's dig a hole in the field for the gardener to fall into!"

THE ENCHANTED RAISIN **347**

SUMMARY

This is a strange little tale that teaches a lesson. The mischievous pranks of three children cause their mother to wrinkle and shrink into a raisin. The children are ashamed as they tuck their mother inside a matchbox for safekeeping. Refusing to believe their story and thinking his wife was dead, their father remarries. His second wife finds out about the raisin-mother and plots to bake her into a cake. When the children flee with the matchbox into the attic, their evil stepmother locks them in. "And when you are dying from hunger . . . you will eat the raisin!" she gloats. Behaving themselves at last and vowing never to eat their mother, the children think up an escape plan. It fails, and they weep for a long time. Their tears fall on the raisin, which grows back into their mother. Mother and children happily reunite with the father, while the wicked stepmother runs away.

Thematic Link: *Facing the Consequences*
The children's misbehavior forces them to face the result of their actions—their mother shrinks and turns into a raisin.

CUSTOMIZING FOR
Students Acquiring English

- Use **ACCESS FOR STUDENTS ACQUIRING ENGLISH,** *Reading and Writing Support.*

I If necessary, remind students that *Let's* is a contraction of "Let us," and is used to suggest four activities in which the speakers expect to take part.

STRATEGIC READING FOR
Less-Proficient Readers

Set a Purpose As students read, have them note the relationship between the children and their mother and what results from this.

Use **UNIT THREE RESOURCE BOOK,** pp. 59–60, for guidance in reading the selection.

WORDS TO KNOW

console (kən-sōl′) *v.* to comfort (p. 353)
contrary (kŏn′trĕr′ē) *n.* an exact opposite (p. 350)
detest (dĭ-tĕst′) *v.* to hate (p. 350)
mute (myo͞ot) *adj.* silent; unable to speak (p. 351)
reassure (rē′ə-sho͝or′) *v.* to restore confidence to (p. 348)

THE LANGUAGE OF LITERATURE TEACHER'S EDITION **347**

CUSTOMIZING FOR
Gifted and Talented Students

Ask students to add one more character to the story, a kindly relative. As they read the story, students should make notes on the entry of their new character at appropriate points, describing what the relative does and what he or she might say.

Literary Concept: FANTASY

A Remind students that odd or extraordinary things may happen in a fantasy. Ask students what is fantasy and what is real in the story so far. *(Possible responses: The mother's shrinking is fantasy; children misbehaving and wearing their parents out is realistic.)*

CUSTOMIZING FOR
Multiple Learners

B Logical-Mathematical Learners
Ask students to estimate how tall the mother is when her nightgown is one hundred times too big. *(Possible solution: If the mother was originally about 66 inches [5 feet 6 inches] tall, she is now only 0.66 inch, or about 2/3 inch, tall.)*

CUSTOMIZING FOR
Students Acquiring English

2 Invite volunteers to model appropriate intonation of the children yelling *Mooooooommm*.

STRATEGIC READING FOR
Less-Proficient Readers

C Check that students understand what has happened so far in the story.

- How do the children treat their mother? *(They are demanding and disobedient.)* Restating

- What happens as a result? *(The mother gets smaller and smaller until she is a wrinkled raisin.)* Noting Cause and Effect

Set a Purpose Have students read on to find out how the father reacts to the children's explanation of their mother's disappearance.

A By now, their mother was so small that, standing, she did not reach her youngest child's knees. She sighed, "Children, enough! Look at my size, my wrinkles. If this continues, I will shrink so much that you won't even be able to see me." But she never thought this would happen.

B One night after supper, she dragged herself to her room, exhausted. She put on her nightgown, which was now one hundred times too big. She climbed on her bed, rolled herself into a ball and fell deeply asleep.

The next morning when they woke up, the children did what they always did. They jumped on their beds like devils and began to **2** yell, "Mooooooommm, bring us our breakfast!"

There was no response. They yelled louder, with no success. They began to howl, once, twice, ten times, thirty times. After the fifty-first shout, with their throats sore, they decided to go to their mother's room.

Her bed was unmade, but she was nowhere to be found. The children realized that something strange was happening. Suddenly, the youngest child bent over the pillow and screamed.

"What's the matter?" his brother asked.
"Look, look there!" he shouted.
Between the folds of their mother's nightgown was a small, dark ball. It was a raisin.

The children were frightened. They called louder and louder, "Moooooommy, Moooooommy, . . . !"

Like the other times, there was no answer, but the oldest child realized that, with each shout, the raisin on the pillow moved slightly. They were quiet and watched it: the raisin didn't move. They shouted "Mom!" and the raisin shook a little.

Then they remembered their mother's words: "If this continues, I will shrink so much that you won't be able to see me." And, horrified, they realized that this raisin that moved when they yelled "Mom" was all that remained of their mother, who in that way tried to make them recognize her. How they cried and wailed!

C "Poor us! What are we going to do now that Mom is a raisin? What is Dad going to say when he gets home and sees her?"

D Their father had been on a business trip for several weeks, but was due to return home that very night. The children, frightened and not knowing what to do, waited for him in their room all day long. Once in a while, to reassure themselves, they approached the raisin and called "Mom!" The raisin invariably moved.

E That evening, their father arrived home. He opened the door, dropped his briefcase, took off his hat and coat, and called his wife from the hall: "Hello, are you there? Aren't you going to welcome me home? Aren't you going to give me a hug and bring me a glass of wine?"

F Instead of his wife, his children appeared walking one behind the other with their heads bowed. The oldest held a matchbox in his hands.

"What's going on? Why aren't you in bed? And where's your mother?"

"She's in this box," the oldest answered in a mournful tone. "She turned into a raisin."

His father became angry. "You know that I hate jokes! Go to bed immediately!"

He searched the house for his wife. It was useless to tell him he would not find her. He then said, "She must have gone out for a walk!" But an hour later, as she had not appeared, he began to worry.

WORDS TO KNOW
reassure (rē'ə-shoor') *v.* to restore confidence to

348

Mini-Lesson Grammar

COMPOUND PREDICATES AND COMPOUND SENTENCES Explain to students that a compound predicate is two or more verbs that go with one subject. A compound sentence is a combination of two or more independent clauses. The parts of a compound sentence can be joined with the conjunctions *and, but,* or *or.* A comma is usually used before the conjunction. A semicolon (or, less often, a colon) can take the place of both the comma and the conjunction.

Application Have students find compound sentences and compound predicates in the  paragraphs on this page. Then have them choose two examples to break into separate sentences.

Reteaching/Reinforcement
- Grammar Handbook, anthology p. 813
- *Grammar Mini-Lessons* copymasters, p. 37, transparencies, p. 28

📁 The Writer's Craft
Sentence Combining, pp. 286–291
Compound Predicates, p. 363
The Colon and the Semicolon, p. 583

348 THE LANGUAGE OF LITERATURE TEACHER'S EDITION

Illustration by Roni Shepherd.

THE ENCHANTED RAISIN **349**

Literary Concept: HUMOR

D Ask students to identify scenes or dialogue in the story that they find funny. *(Possible responses: The mother tries putting on her nightgown even though it is "one hundred times too big"; the children talk to the raisin.)*

Critical Thinking: ANALYZING

E Point out that earlier the children had demanded that their mother bring them breakfast. Now the father wants her to wait on him. Ask students to discuss what point the author may be making. *(Possible response: that husbands and children can be selfish and ask too much of women)*

Active Reading: CONNECT

F Ask students to think of experiences where someone refused to believe them. What did they do to convince the other person they were telling the truth? Ask what they think the children in the story could have done to convince their father they weren't joking.

Mini-Lesson  Genre Study

FICTION Explain to students that **fantasy** is one type of fiction that usually contains unreal or magical events and characters. Other characteristics may include moral lessons, conflicts with a powerful evil force, beginnings that start with "Once Upon a Time . . ." and happy endings. Since many tales of fantasy have been popularized as stories for children, students may already be familiar with these genre characteristics. You may wish to start the word web, shown here, on the board and elicit the other characteristics from students.

Application Have students work alone or in groups to copy the web. Ask them to review "The Enchanted Raisin" to find which genre characteristics of fantasy it contains. When students are finished, have them compare their results in a class discussion. You may wish to designate characteristics such as Always, Most of the Time, or Sometimes.

THE LANGUAGE OF LITERATURE **TEACHER'S EDITION 349**

Linking to Social Studies

G Along with increasing rates of divorce and remarriage in the United States, the number of step-relationships is also increasing. In 1980, 16 percent of households consisting of husband, wife, and children included at least one stepchild under age 18. By the early 1990s, this had reached 21 percent. When each parent brings a child or children from a previous marriage, a "blended family" results. Invite students who live with step-relationships to tell some of the advantages and disadvantages of this arrangement.

CUSTOMIZING FOR
Students Acquiring English

3 Point out that the prefix *step-* is used for relationships resulting from remarriage (stepfather, stepsister, stepbrother).

4 Explain that the idiomatic phrase *get it* means "be punished."

STRATEGIC READING FOR
Less-Proficient Readers

H Ask the following questions to make sure students are following the story:

- What did the father do when he found his wife was missing? *(He searched through the neighborhood, gave up, and then married another woman.)* Summarizing

- Why doesn't the father believe the children's story? *(Possible responses: He thinks they are joking; the story is too incredible to believe.)* Making Judgments

Set a Purpose Have students read to discover what the children learn about themselves while locked in the attic.

Literary Concept: CHARACTERS

I Now that the six characters in the story have been introduced, have students choose names for the mother, the father, and the stepmother. The names can be humorous and should reflect each character's personality.

He put on his hat and left. He walked around the neighborhood, went to the houses of his neighbors, relatives and friends. He asked everyone, "Have you seen my wife?" Then he went to the police station. But they couldn't tell him anything either.

One night passed, a day and another night. And while the time passed and his wife continued to be missing, the father began to ask himself with great pain if his wife had died.

"She must have taken a walk by the lake and drowned! And the worst thing is, I will never know the truth!" he lamented[1] in anguish.

The months passed with no news. Feeling very lonely, the man finally decided to remarry.

G "A new wife would help me take care of these wild animals . . ."

So he chose a wife who was not as pretty as the first one—so as not to say frightful—but she seemed sweet and self-sacrificing. In reality, her face was as ugly as her heart was hard: she led him to believe that she adored the children, but the truth is that she <u>detested</u> them.

The father didn't realize anything. But the **3** three children immediately understood that their stepmother was evil, and they did not trust her. Also, they knew that their real mother was still alive in the matchbox that they guarded so carefully. They were certain she would stop being a raisin and return to her former self.

From time to time at night, the children circled the box, removed the cover and called softly, "Mom, Mom."

From time to time at night, the children circled the box, removed the cover and called softly, "Mom, Mom."

And each time, the raisin responded by rocking gently.

One day when their father was in a good mood, they again asked him to go to their room to see what happened with the raisin. Perhaps he would understand! But their father didn't want to know anything; on the <u>contrary</u>, he became furious: "How long is this stupid joke going to continue? Little devils . . . if you keep up these stories, you are going to get it. I don't want to hear you mention that raisin again!"

Frightened, the children watched over the box.

But, horrors, the stepmother overheard the conversation from behind the door, and she believed them! For a while, she had had her suspicions about the matchbox that the children watched over with such anxiety.

At the beginning, she didn't say anything. But a few days later, one afternoon when the father wasn't home, she called the children and said to them: "Children, I am going to make a raisin cake and I am short one raisin. I believe you have one. Go get it right now!" The stepmother had an evil expression on her face. The children didn't dare protest. They went to their room and asked each other, "What should we do? We can't give her our mother so she can throw her in the oven!" The oldest decided, "Let's go up to the attic. We will hide the box and tell our stepmother that we lost it."

---

1. **lamented** (lə-mĕn′tĭd) **in anguish** (ăng′gwĭsh): cried out in grief.

WORDS TO KNOW
detest (dĭ-tĕst′) *v.* to hate
contrary (kŏn′trĕr′ē) *n.* an exact opposite

350

Mini-Lesson Literary Concepts

REVIEWING HUMOR Remind students that writers can add humor through exaggeration, overemphasis on minor events, witty dialogue, sarcasm, irony, and other devices. Using these devices, a writer can take what might otherwise be serious events (loss of mother, remarriage, cruelty to children) and make them humorous.

Application Have students work in small groups to find examples of humor in dialogue, in descriptions of characters and their actions, and in plot elements. Each student can search in a particular category. Then the group can compare and discuss results. Make sure students are able to give reasons why they think their examples are humorous.

---

350 THE LANGUAGE OF LITERATURE TEACHER'S EDITION

Unfortunately, the evil woman had followed them and once again listened to their conversation from behind the door. She entered the room like a whirlwind and yelled, "Don't you dare trick me! Give me the raisin now, I already have the oven hot!"

The oldest child had just enough time to grab the box. He yelled for his brothers to follow him, and ran upstairs as fast as he could. On his way out, he pushed the stepmother, who fell to the floor with a loud rattling of her bones because she was very thin.

The children ran up to the attic, closed the door and blocked the entrance with a large bureau.[2] Meanwhile, the stepmother got up painfully, brushed herself off, and quickly headed toward the attic. "Open the door, brats! Open it up, little monsters! You'll see what will happen when your father gets home!" But the children, <u>mute</u> with fear, didn't budge.

Then, a cold, wicked and terrible fury invaded her.

"You don't want to open the door? Very well, you will stay locked there as long as it takes. And when you are dying from hunger . . . you will eat the raisin!" She took a key from her pocket and turned it in the lock. Then she laughed three times, "Ha, ha, ha," with a sharp and evil crackle that was unlike the musical laughs she let her husband hear.

At nightfall, her husband came home and asked, "Where are the children?"

She answered, feigning[3] surprise, "Don't you remember? They left to visit their grandmother in the country for a few days." She lied so convincingly that he said, distracted, "That's true, I had forgotten."

Meanwhile, above in the attic, the three children celebrated the victory of having escaped from the cruel woman. But as the hours passed and they became tired of being prisoners, they began to think about how they would escape. The only opening besides the sealed door was a small skylight that was difficult to reach since it was high above the floor in the rafters. And it was at least ten meters above the ground, over the garden.

"We could never jump," they said. "We would need a parachute or a rope."

But in the attic, they couldn't find anything. Suddenly, in the middle of their reflections, the three children realized with surprise that they hadn't fought, whined or played pranks for a long time. It was possible for them to behave! They were so happy with this discovery that they hugged each other and promised to continue their good behavior as long as they could.

---

2. **bureau** (byŏor´ō): a chest of drawers, especially one for holding clothes.
3. **feigning** (fā´nĭng): pretending.

WORDS TO KNOW
mute (myōōt) *adj.* silent; unable to speak

351

Critical Thinking: CLASSIFYING

J Ask students whether any information in the story differentiates the children from one another. *(Possible response: The older child sometimes leads the others, but, in general, the children are not treated separately.)*

Literary Concept: HUMOR

K Ask students how the writer uses humor in the description of the stepmother falling down. *(Possible response: The idea that the stepmother's bones could "rattle" inserts humor into the passage.)*

Active Reading: CLARIFY

L Ask students how the children felt when they were locked in the attic. *(Possible response: At first they were happy to get away from their stepmother. Then they started to get restless and wanted to escape. At this point, they don't seem frightened.)*

CUSTOMIZING FOR
Students Acquiring English

5 Students acquiring English may be more familiar with metric measurements than their other classmates. Ask a volunteer to give the class an idea of how high 10 meters is. *(about 11 yards, or 33 feet)*

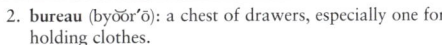

Mini-Lesson — Reading Skills/Strategies

MAKING JUDGMENTS Tell students that when readers make judgments, they are forming opinions about what they read—for example, characters and events in stories. Explain that when students make judgments, they should base their decisions on information from the story that is either stated directly or implied.

Application Have students work in small groups to judge the characters of the mother and the stepmother in the story. Students should complete a comparison diagram like the one shown. One student can choose the comparison qualities; a second can write descriptions of the mother; and a third can write descriptions of the stepmother. A fourth student can look for supporting details in the story.

Reteaching/Reinforcement
• *Unit Three Resource Book*, p. 60

Mother	Qualities	Stepmother
	Appearance	
	Behavior Toward Children	
	Behavior Toward Husband	
	Children's Feelings Toward	

THE LANGUAGE OF LITERATURE TEACHER'S EDITION **351**

Art Note

***Alborado de Fiesta* (The Dawning of a Party) by Arturo Estrada** The Mexican artist Arturo Estrada (1925–) shows an imaginative scene in which reality has been suspended. The fanciful shapes floating above the sleeping figures may represent their dreams of happy events in the coming day.

Reading the Art What dreams do you think the sleeping people are having? How do the shapes above the figures illustrate these dreams?

STRATEGIC READING FOR
Less-Proficient Readers

M Discuss with students what the children discover when they are locked in the attic. *(that they can get along with one another)* Finding the Main Idea

Set a Purpose Have students read on to find out whether the children escape.

Linking to Science

N The lack of water would be more of a problem for the three children than the lack of food. People can survive without food for much longer than they can without water.

Alborado de fiesta [Dawning of a party], Arturo Estrada. Courtesy of the artist.

knowing what else to do, the children curled up on the floor in a corner, cuddling each other, with the matchbox in the middle. They stayed like that until they fell asleep.

In the morning, the growling of their stomachs woke them. They had never been so hungry before. "We must eat something!" they said. Then they looked at the matchbox. "Oh no," said the oldest, "we are not going to eat the raisin, never!" After thinking for a moment, he continued in a serious tone, "Brothers, remember the stories of lost explorers or shipwrecked people who are left without food? They end up eating anything or anyone. . . . This must not happen to us!"

The youngest then said, "Let's separate ourselves from our mother so we can be sure we will not eat her."

"Yes," said the middle child. "If we throw her from the skylight, she will land on the grass in the garden, and since it is soft, she won't get hurt."

The children looked at the small raisin for the last time. Their eyes filled with tears. It was hard for them to separate from their mother!

But now it was vital that they find a way to escape. Night was falling, and with it, they felt the first signs of cold and hunger. The oldest sighed, "If only I had my bed and a good blanket." "And a large glass of warm milk," added the second. "And our beautiful mother," murmured the youngest. Not

352 UNIT THREE PART 2: FACING THE CONSEQUENCES

Mini-Lesson The Writer's Style

SIMILE Discuss with students how writers can describe a person, feeling, or event by comparing it to something else. One type of comparison, called a simile, uses the word *like* or *as*. Example: The children climbed on top of each other like acrobats.

Application Have students complete each simile in a way that is original and that agrees with the story.
1. The children fought like _____.
2. The stepmother was as mean as _____.
3. The children were as hungry as _____.
4. The children were trapped in the attic like _____.
5. When their mother grew large again, the children were as happy as _____.

Reteaching/Reinforcement
• Writing Mini-Lessons transparencies, p. 39

📖 **The Writer's Craft**

Appealing to the Senses, pp. 266–272

352 THE LANGUAGE OF LITERATURE **TEACHER'S EDITION**

But, how could they reach the skylight to throw her into the garden? They could drag over the bureau that was against the door and climb on top of it, but they ran the risk that the evil stepmother would choose that moment to search for them. No! The best thing was to try to climb on top of each other to reach the skylight. The oldest would stand on a chair, the youngest child would balance on the very top and open the skylight.

And that is what they did. Or, it is what they almost did, because the chair was broken, which did not help the operation.

"Can you reach it? Can you touch the skylight?" the older children asked the youngest, who was balancing on top of them.

"Yes . . . , I found it . . . pass me the box!"

"What? Don't you have it?"

"No! I left it on the floor . . ."

They had to start over!

There was a small argument: each accused the other of having forgotten the box. But they soon made up.

"We'll just begin again," said the oldest child.

And they climbed on top of each other again: the oldest on the chair, the middle child on top of the oldest, and the youngest on top of the middle child, like acrobats. The youngest child reached the window and was about to open it when suddenly, crack, the chair broke in two and the children fell to the floor with a great crash.

At that very moment their father was entering the house. He heard the noise and said to his wife, "Go see what is happening!"

She disappeared for a moment and returned saying, "It isn't anything, just some mice running through the attic."

Meanwhile, in the attic, the three children were crying. Large tears of pain ran down their cheeks: tears of pain, because they had hurt themselves in the fall, and of frustration, because how were they going to reach the skylight now that the chair was broken? To <u>console</u> themselves, they opened the matchbox and looked at the raisin. But just seeing the raisin made them even sadder, and they started to cry over it as hard as they could.

The children's tears fell in torrents on the matchbox, so that it flooded and the raisin was left floating in a small, warm puddle.

Suddenly, the oldest child shouted, "Look! It's growing!"

It was true. The raisin, swollen from the children's tears, had begun to grow. The more they cried, the more the raisin grew. And seeing it grow, the children cried more, but now from happiness.

The raisin continued inflating, stretching, enlarging, growing more and more. Until . . . before the children's disbelieving eyes, it changed form and . . .

"Mommmmmmm!" they yelled.

It was their mother, as tall and as beautiful as before she had shriveled up. The mother took her children in her arms and, laughing and crying, hugged them against her for a long time.

Meanwhile, on the first floor, the father was wondering about the strange noises that were

> The raisin, swollen from the children's tears, had begun to grow.

WORDS TO KNOW
console (kən-sōl′) *v.* to comfort

353

STRATEGIC READING FOR
Less-Proficient Readers

R Have students discuss why it is reasonable to expect a happy ending to this kind of story and what situations they would like to see resolved.

- How do the children get their mother back? *(They start to cry and their tears make the mother grow.)* **Restating**
- How are the children and mother released from the attic? *(The father finally goes to investigate and finds them.)* **Noting Relevant Details**

Active Reading: EVALUATE

S The author says the father "wasn't as bad as he seemed." Have students discuss whether they think the father was bad or merely foolish. Encourage them to support their opinions with passages from the story.

CUSTOMIZING FOR
Gifted and Talented Students

Have students do library research to find other stories that feature an evil stepmother. For each story, have students write a short plot summary and explain what motivates the stepmother to oppose the main character or characters. Ask students to hypothesize why a stepmother is cast as this type of character.

COMPREHENSION CHECK

1. How did the children's misbehavior affect their mother? *(It made her shrink until she became a small raisin.)*
2. What made the children believe the raisin was their mother? *(It moved when they talked to it.)*
3. What did the children's father do when he couldn't find his wife? *(He searched through the neighborhood, gave up, and married another woman.)*
4. Why did the children hide the raisin? *(Their stepmother threatened to bake it in a cake.)*
5. How did the children get their mother back? *(They were sorry and started to cry. Their tears made the raisin grow back into their mother's former self.)*

---

coming from the attic. Finally, he could stand it no longer, and he said to his wife, "Those mice in the attic have a strange way of squeaking. It is as if they were crying. Give me the keys. . . . I am going to see what is happening."

His wife tried every way to stop him, but her efforts were in vain. He went upstairs, tried to open the door with the key, and when it wouldn't open, pushed it with all his might. Imagine his surprise to find his three children in the arms of his first, beautiful wife! The four, hugging tightly, looked at him without saying anything.

Then this man, who wasn't as bad as he seemed, felt as if he would die from remorse and joy. He covered his children with kisses, and then kneeling at his wife's feet, he begged forgiveness for having doubted her.

He was immediately forgiven, and father, mother and children walked downstairs hand in hand to have dinner, with their hearts full of happiness.

The stepmother hadn't waited for them. Guessing what had happened, she had run off at full speed with her bags.

The raisin cake in the oven was completely burnt.

The mother threw it in the trash and quickly made another, delicious cake full of candied fruit.

The whole family happily and hungrily ate this new cake that didn't contain a single raisin. ❖

354 UNIT THREE PART 2: FACING THE CONSEQUENCES

Mini-Lesson  Spelling

PREFIXES AND ROOTS Explain to students that a root can be joined with many different prefixes. However, remind them that different prefixes change both the spelling and the meaning of the resulting word.

con + sole	= **console**
con + trary	= **contrary**
con + struct	= **construct**
in + struct	= **instruct**
de + struct	= **destruct**
de + test	= **detest**
re + sent	= **resent**

Application Have students use the prefixes *con-*, *in-*, *de-*, and *re-* to create two or more different words from each root.

1. cline
2. clude
3. spire
4. flict
5. sist
6. form
7. flate
8. tain
9. ceive

Ask students to look for more words that fit this pattern, in their own writing and in things they read, and to add these words to their personal word lists.

Reteaching/Reinforcement
- *Unit Three Resource Book*, p. 61

RESPONDING OPTIONS

FROM PERSONAL RESPONSE TO CRITICAL ANALYSIS

REFLECT
1. What is your reaction to "The Enchanted Raisin"? Jot it down in your notebook.

RETHINK
2. What advice for the future would you give the mother or the children?
3. What do you think is the theme of "The Enchanted Raisin"?

Close Textual Reading
Thematic Link

Consider
- what you know about similar tales and their themes
- the extraordinary consequences of the children's actions

4. Look over any predictions you wrote before reading "The Enchanted Raisin." How well do your predictions match an actual event or the outcome of the story?
5. In your opinion, is this modern tale more or less appealing than traditional ones you have heard or read? Explain.

RELATE
6. Many traditional tales portray stepparents—especially stepmothers—as evil characters. Do you think modern tales should portray stepparents as villains? Why or why not?

LITERARY CONCEPTS

A **fantasy** is a work of fiction that contains at least one fantastic or unreal element. The setting of a fantasy might be a totally imaginary world or a familiar, realistic place where highly unusual things happen. The plot might involve magic or characters with extraordinary abilities. Fairy tales, fables, and science fiction are examples of fantasy. One unusual happening in "The Enchanted Raisin" is a raisin that moves when someone speaks to it. Describe another unusual happening in the story.

Multimodal Learning
ANOTHER PATHWAY
Cooperative Learning

Form teams and have each team choose a part of the story to animate in the form of a flip book. With the members of your team, make a series of small drawings that show the progression of a single important action in the story (for example, the mother's change into a raisin). Glue the drawings into a booklet form.

QUICKWRITES

1. Imagine that the husband in this story wants to file a **missing-person report** about his wife with the police. Draft one for him. Be sure to include details about the wife's height, weight, appearance, and clothing, as well as where she was last seen and by whom.

2. Tabloid newspapers are often filled with sensational or exaggerated reports that are almost as fantastic as "The Enchanted Raisin." In the style of a tabloid, draft a **newspaper article** that tells the story of a woman who turned into a raisin.

📁 **PORTFOLIO** *Save your writing. You may want to use it later as a springboard to a piece for your portfolio.*

THE ENCHANTED RAISIN **355**

From Personal Response to Critical Analysis

1. Encourage students to compare events in the story with personal experiences.
2. Possible responses: The mother could be more firm with the children. The children could continue to be cooperative.
3. Possible responses: Selfishness and mischief can have unexpected consequences; facing a common problem can help people get along and cooperate.
4. Responses will vary.
5. Students might compare the story to Snow White, Cinderella, or movies featuring evil stepmothers.
6. Stories depicting stepmothers as evil may encourage negative attitudes. Or they may allow children to identify and express negative feelings and thus adjust to stepmothers.

Literary Links

Skim through "The School Play" in Unit One, noting how the teacher Mrs. Bunnin reacts to student misbehavior. Then choose some of Mrs. Bunnin's lines that the mother in "The Enchanted Raisin" might use with her misbehaving children. *(Possible choices: "I'm not going to tell you again to . . ."; "now try again"; "almost perfect.")*

Another Pathway

Cooperative Learning Groups should first work collaboratively to choose the scene they will animate. One student can outline the drawings in pencil or ink. The other students can add details and colors.

Rubric
3 Full Accomplishment Students' flip books accurately depict a scene in the story, with no omissions.
2 Substantial Accomplishment Students' flip books are fairly close to an event in the story.
1 Little or Partial Accomplishment Students' flip books are incomplete or do not match the events in the story.

Literary Concepts

If the event could not happen in the real world, and seems magical, it is fantasy. Have students work in pairs. One student should skim the selection for fantastic events while the other records them. Halfway through the story, have the students switch roles. Have students compare their selected events with those of at least one other group.

QuickWrites

1. Emphasize that students' reports should include specific physical details about the mother. Suggest that they begin, "Last seen on . . ."
2. Explain to students that while tabloid articles sometimes contain facts, they usually contain exaggerations and large headlines with exclamation points to attract attention. Students might start by writing headlines for their articles.

📖 **The Writer's Craft**
Describing People and Places, pp. 54–55
Personal Narrative, pp. 76–80

Words to Know

Exercise A
1. no synonyms
2. detest, hate
3. comfort, console
4. no synonyms
5. contrary, opposite

Exercise B
1. Contrary
2. Reassure
3. Mute
4. Console
5. Detest

Reteaching/Reinforcement
- *Unit Three Resource Book*, p. 62

Across the Curriculum

Science *Growing Shorter*
People can become shorter as they get older. Have students use reference materials to research the reasons for this phenomenon.

Math *Grape Expectations*
A raisin is a dried grape. Have students design an experiment to find out how much water a raisin can absorb. Can it become as large as a grape? Students may choose either weight or width for their "before and after" measurements. Have students express increases in percents.

Multimodal Learning

ALTERNATIVE ACTIVITIES

1. Think about the effects, or consequences, of the children's misbehavior. Copy and fill in a chart like the one below to make a **map** of the children's actions. The first part has been done for you. Remember that one consequence may lead to another.

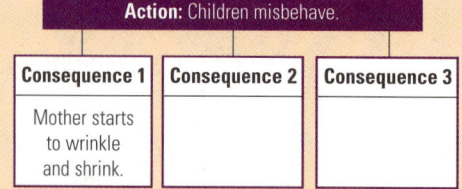

2. With several other students, create **puppets** of the characters in "The Enchanted Raisin" and make backdrops of the settings. Choose one student to read or retell the story. As the story is read or told, use the puppets to perform it on a puppet stage for a class of younger students.

WORDS TO KNOW

EXERCISE A Review the Words to Know in the boxes at the bottom of the selection pages. Then look for a pair of synonyms in each group of words below. If you find a pair of synonyms, write them on your paper. If not, write *No synonyms*.

1. repeat, reassure, receive, resent
2. detest, deplete, hate, deprive
3. sacrifice, comfort, guard, console
4. mournful, ardent, mute, relentless
5. novelty, contrary, opposite, consequence

EXERCISE B Use the vocabulary words to complete the titles of the imaginary books listed below.

1. *I Am! I'm Not! and Other _____ Statements* by Booth Sides
2. *How to _____ Others* by U.R. Fine
3. *I've Never Been Accused of Being _____* by Raisin Cane
4. *1001 Ways to _____ a Sad Friend* by Eiffel Payne
5. *Learning to Love What You _____* by I. M. Trying

JACQUELINE BALCELLS

A Chilean-born journalist, Jacqueline Balcells (1950–) began to create stories for her children when she lived in France. "The Enchanted Raisin" was published in French in 1984. After returning to Chile, Balcells published a Spanish version of the story in 1986. Since then, Balcells has published four other books for children, including two science-fiction novels that she coauthored. Her most recent book, written in Spanish, recognizes the 500th anniversary of the discovery of the New World. "The Enchanted Raisin" was chosen for exhibition at the 1988 Children's International Book Fair in Italy.

OTHER WORKS *Adventure in the Stars, Alpha Centauri Mission, The Signs Archipelago* Extended Reading

---

Alternative Activities

1. Students might continue the activity in small groups, starting with some other actions, for example, children hide the raisin in the attic, children try to get out of the attic, children begin to cry. After the group has picked the actions, students can work independently to map the consequences. Then the group can discuss and compare results.
2. Puppets can be made from small paper bags or socks. Encourage students to try to express the personalities of the characters in their puppet designs.

Focus on Drama

A drama is a story that is meant to be acted out for an audience. In a drama, or **play,** the plot is told through the words and actions of the characters. A drama can take place on stage, before a radio microphone, or before a TV or movie camera.

All dramas have three elements that are similar to the elements of fiction. These elements are character, plot, and setting. Unlike fiction, drama is written in a special form called a **script.** The script contains the words, or lines, that each character says as well as the type of information described below.

CAST OF CHARACTERS The script begins with a list of the characters in the play. Sometimes, the list includes brief descriptions of the characters.

DIALOGUE Most of the script consists of the **dialogue** of the play—that is, the conversation between the characters. Through the dialogue you get to know both the characters and the plot of the drama. Take a look at the following example from *The Hobbit:*

> **Thorin.** We're all hungry.
> **Ori.** And tired.
> **Oin.** I can't go any further.
> **Bilbo.** We must go on. Maybe we'll find some berries.
> **Gloin.** Find berries in the spring—that's a hobbit for you!

STAGE DIRECTIONS The script also includes **stage directions.** These are the instructions for the actors, the director, and the stage crew. Stage directions are printed in italics in this book so that you will not confuse the stage directions with the dialogue. Sometimes the stage directions are also enclosed in parentheses. The stage directions also describe the objects—called **props**—that actors need during the play.

In addition, stage directions describe the **scenery** for the play. Scenery is the painted screens, backdrops, and other materials that help a stage look like a city street or a tropical jungle. Scenery creates the setting for a drama. For example, the scenery for *The Hobbit* gives the audience the feeling that they are in a fantastical and strange world. In the following

FOCUS ON DRAMA **357**

Scenes and Acts Discuss with the class how the end of an act is shown on the stage. *(The curtains are closed; the lights are dimmed.)*

Reading Strategies: MODELING
Invite volunteers to read aloud the Strategies for Reading Drama. Tell students they will be using these strategies as they read *A Shipment of Mute Fate* on page 359 and other dramas throughout the book. Then model the strategies as students read *A Shipment of Mute Fate.* You may wish to use the models provided or create your own.

- **Read the play silently** Have students set a purpose for reading, such as finding out the meaning of the play's title.
- **Figure out what is happening** *"Why does Chris have to go through all this trouble? Why couldn't the museum arrange to have the snake transported?"*
- **Read the stage directions carefully** *"I noticed that the stage directions mention important sound effects and tell the actors what tones of voice to use when delivering their lines."*
- **Get to know the characters** *"Chris seems to be a very stubborn and driven person, and the captain seems to be very cautious but respectful of others. The captain is especially concerned about the safety of the passengers."*
- **Keep track of the plot** *"The first conflict involves Chris getting the snake on board the ship. Having done that, Chris then faces the difficulty of finding the escaped snake after the storm. Finally, Mrs. Willis's cat saves Chris's life by killing the snake."*
- **Read the play aloud with others** A small group of students can stage a Reader's Theater presentation, each student taking a part.

---

example, from *The Hobbit,* you can see how the stage directions both tell the actors what to do and describe the props and scenery.

At rise of curtain: Bilbo *is discovered busily writing in his journal. He is sitting on the stoop before the cave entrance. Dragon smoke belches from under the entrance. The Dwarves* glumly pace around the stage, hands behind their backs.

SCENES AND ACTS Fiction or nonfiction books are usually divided into chapters. Plays, however, are divided into **scenes** and **acts**. A change in the setting or the time in a play begins a new scene. In longer plays, the scenes are grouped into larger units, called acts.

STRATEGIES FOR READING DRAMA

Drama is meant to be performed or read aloud, but since plays are written, you can also read them on your own. The following strategies will help increase your enjoyment, whether you perform a play with friends, read it aloud in class, or read it by yourself:

- **Read the play silently.** Before you perform a play or read it aloud with others, read it to yourself. This way, you will understand the entire plot and get to know the characters ahead of time.
- **Figure out what is happening.** Don't expect to understand everything about the play right away. When you read a book or watch a movie, you don't immediately understand what is going on. The same is true for drama.
- **Read the stage directions carefully.** When you watch a drama on stage, you actually see the action and the scenery. When you read a drama, however, you have to use your imagination. The stage directions tell you where and when each scene is happening and help you understand more about the characters and the plot. If you skip over the stage directions, you miss out on much of the play.
- **Get to know the characters.** In fiction, an author can describe a character's appearance and personality in great detail. In a play, the characters' own words and actions tell you what the characters are like. Read the dialogue carefully, as well as the stage directions that accompany it. In addition, try to discover the feelings behind the words.
- **Keep track of the plot.** The plot of a play usually centers on a main conflict that the characters try to resolve. When you read or watch a play, look for the conflict and get involved in the story. Notice how the characters try to work out the conflict or solve their problems.
- **Read the play aloud with others.** People of all ages and in all countries have been performing and reading plays for centuries. When you read the part of a character, you become an actor. Let yourself get into the part. For a brief while, become that character. React to what other characters say and do to you. Remember to be ready with your character's lines of dialogue and read only the words your character says. Pay attention to the stage directions so that you know how to read your lines and what to do next, but don't read these italicized instructions aloud.

Perhaps everyone wonders at times what it would be like to be someone else. Drama gives you that opportunity. When you take the part of a character in a play, you have a chance to step into someone else's feelings and experience something new.

358 UNIT THREE PART 2: FACING THE CONSEQUENCES

PREVIEWING

DRAMA

A Shipment of Mute Fate
Les Crutchfield
Based on a story by Martin Storm

Activating Prior Knowledge
PERSONAL CONNECTION
In the opening speech of this play, the narrator states, "... a cold chill gripped me, and I shivered with sudden dread—dread of the thing I was doing, and was about to do!" The stage directions call for music that "comes up and dissolves slowly." In your notebook, sketch a scene of the sea that forms in your mind as you think about these opening words and stage directions. Choose your colors carefully. Don't worry about details; just make sure the scene portrays the atmosphere that the words *chill* and *dread* create.

Building Background
CULTURAL CONNECTION
Most of this play is set aboard a ship that is sailing from Venezuela to New York City, a route you can visualize by referring to the map on this page. Understanding some of the technical terms in this play will help you enjoy it more. A ship's **captain** leads the **crew**. Various **mates** (officers) help keep order and **navigate** (steer) the ship from the **bridge** (the ship's control room). A chief **steward** (an officer in charge of supplies) directs assistants in the **galley**, or kitchen. Everyone sleeps in **bunks** or **berths** (beds). The **port** side of the ship is the side that is on the left of someone aboard who is facing the **bow**, or front.

Active Reading
READING CONNECTION
Sound Effects Sound effects, such as music, help convey the setting and atmosphere of a radio play. Because the audience cannot see the action, they have to imagine it. Sound effects are described in the stage directions, which are italicized and placed in parentheses throughout this play. As you read, pause when you come to a stage direction describing sound effects. Create the sound in your mind before reading on.

Setting a Purpose

 LASERLINKS
• READING CONNECTION   359

OVERVIEW

Objectives
- To understand and appreciate a radio play that depicts a suspenseful mystery
- To understand the importance of sound effects in a play
- To understand and appreciate the use of suspense in a play
- To express understanding of the play through a choice of writing forms, including a news article and headline, a letter of complaint, and a log entry
- To extend understanding of the play through a variety of multimodal and cross-curricular activities

Skills

READING SKILLS/STRATEGIES
- Noting relevant details

LITERARY CONCEPTS
- Suspense
- Conflict

GENRE STUDY
- Drama

THE WRITER'S STYLE
- Voice

GRAMMAR
- Subject-verb agreement

SPELLING
- Soft and hard g

SPEAKING, LISTENING, AND VIEWING
- Background music
- Group discussion
- Oral presentation

Cross-Curricular Connections

GEOGRAPHY
- Caribbean countries

SOCIAL STUDIES
- Customs officials and rules

SCIENCE
- The bushmaster snake
- Barometers
- Radio waves
- *Homo sapiens*

READING CONNECTION
Sound Effects for Radio Plays
During the 1940's radio plays were a popular form of entertainment. When a radio play was performed in front of a live audience, the people in the audience could see how the sound effects they heard on the radio were created. This film gives students a glimpse into what it might have been like to attend a performance of a radio play.

Side A, Frame 21138

PRINT AND MEDIA RESOURCES

UNIT THREE RESOURCE BOOK
Strategic Reading: Literature, p. 65
Vocabulary SkillBuilder, p. 68
Reading SkillBuilder, p. 66
Spelling SkillBuilder, p. 67

GRAMMAR MINI-LESSONS
Transparencies, p. 3
Copymasters, p. 3

WRITING MINI-LESSONS
Transparencies, p. 48

ACCESS FOR STUDENTS ACQUIRING ENGLISH
Selection Summaries
Reading and Writing Support

FORMAL ASSESSMENT
Selection Test, pp. 75–76
Part Test, pp. 77–78
Test Generator

LASERLINKS
Reading Connection
Science Connection

THE LANGUAGE OF LITERATURE **Teacher's Edition** **359**

SUMMARY

The zoologist Chris Warner captures a deadly bushmaster snake in Venezuela and brings it aboard a New York–bound ship. The captain reluctantly agrees to keep the poisonous eight-foot snake locked inside a sea chest in his cabin. When a freak wave hits the ship, the snake escapes from the damaged chest. Terrified, Warner and the crew search the whole ship for the bushmaster. Determined to kill Warner, the snake waits for him in the ship's galley. Just as the bushmaster prepares to sink its fangs into the scientist, a stowaway cat attacks and kills it to protect her newborn kittens.

Thematic Link: *Facing the Consequences*
Chris Warner comes to regret that a captured snake that is the result of two months of dangerous work has put himself and others in danger.

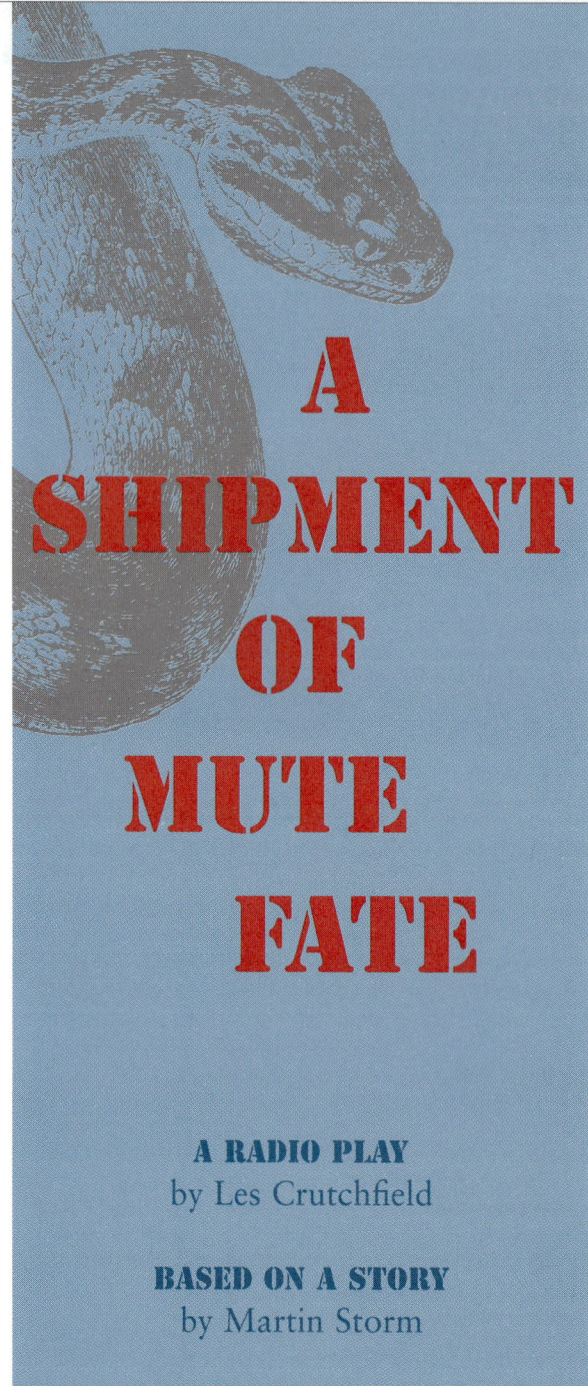

A SHIPMENT OF MUTE FATE

A RADIO PLAY
by Les Crutchfield

BASED ON A STORY
by Martin Storm

WORDS TO KNOW

counter (koun′tər) *v.* to respond to another's action; return a blow (p. 372)
customs (kŭs′təmz) *adj.* involved in collecting taxes on imported and exported goods (p. 363)
evasive (ĭ-vā′sĭv) *adj.* not straightforward (p. 362)
fumigate (fyōō′mĭ-gāt) *v.* to use smoke or gas to destroy pests (p. 369)
lethal (lē′thəl) *adj.* deadly (p. 370)

margin (mär′jĭn) *n.* an amount of difference or space between two things (p. 372)
ominous (ŏm′ə-nəs) *adj.* threatening harm or evil (p. 365)
sodden (sŏd′n) *adj.* thoroughly wet (p. 367)
stupor (stōō′pər) *n.* a state of mental numbness; daze (p. 369)
transition (trăn-zĭsh′ən) *n.* a passage from one activity or theme to another (p. 363)

Early Morning After the Storm at Sea (1902), Winslow Homer. Oil on canvas, 76.8 cm × 127 cm, gift of J. H. Wade (24.195). Copyright © 1995 The Cleveland (Ohio) Museum of Art.

Art Note

Early Morning After the Storm at Sea by Winslow Homer Homer (1836–1910) was an American painter known for his landscapes, seascapes, and scenes from everyday life. This oil painting is remarkable for its realistic portrayal of the ocean waves and the clearing sky.

Reading the Art *Imagine standing on the shore looking at this scene. What sounds would you hear? What feelings might you have? Now imagine you are on a boat in the scene. Describe the sights, sounds, and feelings from this point of view.*

CUSTOMIZING FOR
Students Acquiring English

- Use **ACCESS FOR STUDENTS ACQUIRING ENGLISH**, *Reading and Writing Support.*
- If possible, ask Spanish-speaking volunteers to demonstrate correct pronunciation of Spanish words used in the play, such as *La Guaira, Venezuela, Orinoco, Sanchez, sí, señor,* and *Caracas.*
- In addition to these boxes, you may want to use the suggestions under Strategic Reading for Less-Proficient Readers.

STRATEGIC READING FOR
Less-Proficient Readers

Set a Purpose Emphasize to students that this selection is a radio play and not a story. They will need to pay particular attention to the stage directions to visualize the action. As students read the first part of the play, have them notice what the Captain refuses to do for Chris and why he refuses to do it.

Use **UNIT THREE RESOURCE BOOK**, pp. 65–66, for guidance in reading the selection.

Mini-Lesson: Speaking,  Listening, and Viewing

BACKGROUND MUSIC Have students use the library to find examples of famous radio shows and plays; for example, *The Green Hornet, The Shadow,* or *Invasion from Mars,* which was adapted from the book *The War of the Worlds.* Students should listen in particular to the sound effects and background music. They should note any sound effects or music that would be appropriate for *A Shipment of Mute Fate.*

Application Have students describe in writing the music and sound effects from particularly exciting parts of the radio plays they've heard. Students' written work should include what the music or sound effect sounds like and what function it plays in helping the listener understand the play.

CUSTOMIZING FOR
Gifted and Talented Students

As students read the play, have them research ocean liners. They may find information at the library or at a travel agency. Then have students draw a floor plan of a ship. They should mark the locations of key scenes based on information provided in the play.

Active Reading: PREDICT

A Have students predict who—or what—has the "beady eyes" described in the play. *(Later in the play students will discover the eyes are those of a snake.)*

CUSTOMIZING FOR
Students Acquiring English

1 Make sure students understand that the stage direction *joshing* means joking and that Chris is being ironic, saying the opposite of what he means.

Active Reading: CLARIFY

B Have students ask themselves why Mrs. Willis must sneak her cat aboard the ship. *(The new chief steward has changed the rules and no longer allows cats on board.)*

Critical Thinking: SPECULATING

C Ask students what they think Mrs. Willis means by saying her cat is in a "delicate" condition. *(Possible responses: The cat is sick; the cat is pregnant; the cat is old.)*

CUSTOMIZING FOR
Multiple Learning Styles

D **Bodily-Kinesthetic Learners** Have two students act out the scene between Chris and Mrs. Willis. Encourage them to use gestures and body language to convey the characters' emotions.

CHARACTERS

Chris Warner, a young zoologist
Captain Wood, captain of the *Chancay*
Sanchez, native guide
Mrs. Willis, stewardess
Mr. Bowman, chief steward
Other Crew Members and Passengers

Chris (*narrating*). I stopped on the wharf at La Guaira[1] and looked up the gangplank[2] toward the liner *Chancay*—standing there quietly at her moorings.[3] The day was warm under a bright Venezuela sun—and the harbor beyond the ship lay drowsy and silent. But all at once in the midst of those peaceful surroundings, a cold chill gripped me, and I shivered with sudden dread—dread of the thing I was doing, and was about to do! (*Pause. Music comes up and dissolves slowly*) But too much had happened to turn back now. I'd gone too far to stop. (*Sound: wooden box set on wooden wharf, boat whistles, etc.*)

I set the box down on the edge of the wharf, placed it carefully so as to be in plain sight—and within gunshot—of the captain's bridge. (*Sound: steps on gangplank, fade.*)

Then I turned and started up the gangplank. I knew what I was going to do—but I couldn't forget that a certain pair of beady eyes was watching every move I made. Eyes that never blinked and never closed—just watched . . . and waited!

(*Sound: shipboard commotion*)

Willis (*coming in*). Oh! You startled me, sir! I didn't hear—why . . . (*with relief*) why, it's Mr. Warner!

Chris. Hello, Mother Willis. How's the best-looking stewardess on the seven seas?

Willis (*a bit evasive*). Why, I'm . . . I'm fine, Mr. Warner. (*Hurriedly*) Nice to see you again.

Chris (*joshing*). Wait a minute! That's a fine greeting after two months.

Willis. Well—it's just that I'm so . . . so busy just now.

Chris. I don't believe a word of it—sailing day's tomorrow. And on the trip down from New York—you said I was your favorite passenger.

Willis. But—

Chris. Here—what's that you're carrying in your apron?

Willis (*obviously nervous*). Oh, it's nothing. Just . . . supplies.

Chris. Supplies? Let's have a look.

Willis. No! Please!

Chris. Why—it's a cat!

Willis (*almost in tears*). It's Clara, Mr. Warner. Mr. Bowman said I had to leave her ashore—and I just couldn't!

Chris. Who's Mr. Bowman?

Willis. The new chief steward. Clara's been aboard with me for two years—and I just can't leave her here in a foreign country. Especially with her condition so delicate and all!

Chris. Yes (*ahem*), I see! I see what you mean. Well, I hope you get away with it.

---

1. **La Guaira** (lä gwī′rä): a seaport in northern Venezuela.
2. **gangplank:** a removable ramp used to board or leave a ship docked at a pier.
3. **moorings:** a place where a ship is docked or anchored.

WORDS TO KNOW
evasive (ĭ-vā′sĭv) *adj.* not straightforward

362

Mini-Lesson  Grammar

SUBJECT–VERB AGREEMENT Remind students that subjects and verbs must agree in number. They can be singular or plural. A prepositional phrase after the subject does not change its number.

Application Have students choose the verb that agrees with each subject.
1. The harbor beyond the ships (was, were) drowsy and silent.
2. Who (are, is) the best steward on the seven seas?
3. The safety of the passengers (comes, come) ahead of anything else.
4. The snake and Mrs. Willis's cat (was, were) not allowed on the ship.

Reteaching/Reinforcement
- *Grammar Handbook*, anthology p. 815–821
- *Grammar Mini-Lessons* copymasters, p. 3, transparencies, p. 3

 The Writer's Craft
Subject and Verb Agreement, p. 528

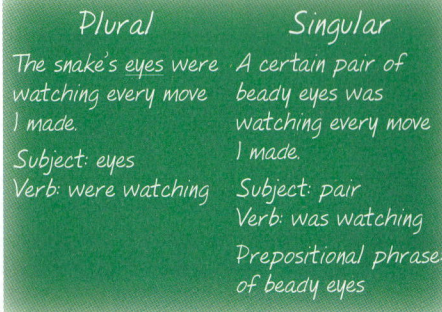

Plural
The snake's eyes were watching every move I made.
Subject: eyes
Verb: were watching

Singular
A certain pair of beady eyes was watching every move I made.
Subject: pair
Verb: was watching
Prepositional phrase: of beady eyes

362 THE LANGUAGE OF LITERATURE TEACHER'S EDITION

Willis. You . . . you won't tell anyone?

Chris. Not a soul. As a matter of fact, if I don't get my way with the Captain, you and I may both end up smuggling!

(*Music: brief transition, dissolves*)

Captain (*fades in*). Most happy to have had you aboard on the trip down two months ago, Christopher, and I'm very glad you're coming along with us on the run back to New York.

Chris. Thanks, Captain Wood. There is one thing, though. I'm having a little trouble with the customs men here, and I wondered if you—

Captain. I can't do it, Christopher. I cabled[4] your father this morning—told him I'd have done it for you if I possibly could. He sent a request from New York, you know.

Chris. Yes, I thought he would . . . I . . . wired him from upriver last week.

Captain. I hated to refuse—but it's out of the question.

Chris. Captain Wood, I'm afraid I don't follow you.

Captain. Responsibility to the passengers, son. We'll have women and children aboard—and on a liner, the safety of the passengers comes ahead of anything else.

Chris. But with proper precautions!

Captain. Something might happen. I don't know what—but something might.

Chris. You've carried worse things!

Captain. There isn't anything worse—and any skipper afloat'll bear me out. No, son—I simply can't take the chance, and that's final!

(*Music: hit and out*)

Chris (*narrating*). Final! It wasn't final if I could do anything about it. I hadn't come down here to spend two months in that stinking back country and then be stopped on the edge of the wharf! Two months of it—heat, rain, insects, malaria—I'd gone clear into the headwaters of the Orinoco.[5] (*Fading from mike*) Traveled through country where every step along the jungle trail might be the last one. . . .

(*Music: swells and dissolves. Sound of men on a trail.*)

Chris. Oh . . . Sanchez!

Sanchez (*coming toward mike*). *Sí*, Señor Warner.

Chris. Better start looking for a place to camp. Be dark in a little while.

Sanchez. *Sí*, Señor—very soon we turn to river, camp on rocks by water. This very bad country.

Chris. This very bad country! You've been saying that for ten days now. Very bad country.

Sanchez. *Sí*, Señor Warner—this very bad country.

Chris. Oh, skip it. For all the luck we've had so far, it might as well be Central Park.[6]

Sanchez. Central Park? I no understand.

Chris. Never mind. If we don't—

(*Excited cries of "Bushmaster!" Sounds of scrambling.*)

Chris. Here—what's the matter? Quiet now! Sanchez—what's wrong?

Sanchez. There in the path! See? Bushmaster!

(*Music: loud, then fades*)

Chris (*narrating*). Bushmaster! The deadliest snake in the world! Bushmaster—its Latin name was *Lachesis mutus*—Mute Fate! It lay

---

4. **cabled:** sent a telegraph message by undersea cable.
5. **Orinoco** (ôr′ə-nō′kō): a long river in Venezuela.
6. **Central Park:** a large park in New York City.

WORDS TO KNOW
transition (trăn-zĭsh′ən) *n.* a passage from one activity or theme to another
customs (kŭs′təmz) *adj.* involved in collecting taxes on imported and exported goods

363

Active Reading: CLARIFY

J Students now know enough to understand the title of the play. Ask for their interpretations of the title. *(Possible responses: A snake whose Latin name means "mute fate" may be carried from Venezuela to New York; a dangerous and silent passenger may be taken on a sea journey.)*

Linking to Science

K The bushmaster is a pit viper, a large poisonous snake with a deep facial hollow or pit. The pit is sensitive to heat, and helps the snake locate warm-blooded victims. The bushmaster has been known to grow up to 11 feet long. Like other vipers, the bushmaster has two long, hollow fangs that inject its poison as it bites a victim. While all other vipers give birth to live young, the bushmaster lays eggs that are larger than chickens' eggs.

Literary Concept: CONFLICT

L Have students discuss the opposing forces that are struggling at this moment in the play. *(Chris is arguing with Sanchez; Chris and the other people are in conflict with the snake they want to capture.)*

Critical Thinking: MAKING JUDGMENTS

M Ask students if they think Sanchez is realistic to be so frightened of the bushmaster. *(Possible response: His fears seems to be exaggerated because he thinks the snake will be able to find him.)*

Literary Concept: CHARACTERS

N Four of the five characters listed at the beginning of the play have now been introduced. There are also two animal characters—the bushmaster and Mrs. Willis's cat, Clara. Have students briefly review what they have learned about the characters so far.

Active Reading: EVALUATE

O Ask students to evaluate the fairness of Chris's characterization of the captain as *pigheaded*, which is slang for "stubborn." In their opinion, is he judging the man too harshly or too early?

CUSTOMIZING FOR
Students Acquiring English

2 Explain that the idiom *red tape* means "government rules and regulations."

---

there in the center of the path—an eight-foot length of silent death—coiled loosely in an undulant[7] loop, ready to strike violently at the least movement. Here was the one snake that would go after any animal that walked—or any man. It lay there and watched us—not moving—not afraid—ready for anything. The splotch of its colors stood out like some horribly gaudy floor mat—lying there on the brown background of the jungle—waiting for someone to step on it. Here was what I'd come two thousand miles for . . . a bushmaster!

(*Sound: pistol shot. Music: up and out sharply as . . .*)

Chris. Sanchez! . . . I didn't want that snake killed!

Sanchez. He no killed, Señor—he gone. Bushmaster very smart, very quick—see bullet in time to dodge.

Chris. Anyway, he's gone! And the only one we've seen in five weeks!

Sanchez. Oh, we find other. This very bad country.

Chris. Well, lay off that gun the next time. Don't shoot—do you understand?

Sanchez. Why you say no shoot? You want bushmaster.

Chris. Sure—but I want it alive!

Sanchez. Señor Warner—you tell me you want bushmaster, but you no say "alive"!

Chris. You're getting two hundred dollars for it.

Sanchez. For dead man—what is two hundred dollars? Tomorrow we go back to Caracas.[8]

Chris (*going away from mike*). Sanchez—I'll give you a thousand dollars! (*Music swells, then fades. Chris narrates.*) It cost me fifteen hundred—but three days later, Sanchez brought me the snake in a rubber bag. He was shaking so hard I thought for a moment the thing had struck him. . . .

Sanchez (*excitedly*). One thing you make sure, Señor Warner. No turn him loose in Venezuela. Because he know I the one who catch him—and he know where I live!

Chris. All right, Sanchez—I'll keep an eye on him.

Sanchez. He know you pay me to catch him. All the time he watch and wait. You no forget that, Señor Warner—because he no forget . . . not ever!

(*Music: loud, then under voice*)

Chris (*narrating*). Well, after going through all that trouble and danger—I wasn't going to let a pigheaded ship captain stop me at the last minute! At least not as long as the cables were still in operation between La Guaira and New York. . . .

(*Music: swells for transition, then cuts as door closes and steps come in*)

Chris (*coming in*). Morning, Captain Wood. The boy at the hotel said you wanted to see me.

Captain. That's right, Christopher. Uh . . . Sit down. (*sound of chair*) Seems you weren't willing to let matters stand the way we left them yesterday.

Chris. Sorry to go over your head, Captain Wood—but I had to. The museum sent me all the way down here for it, and I'm not going to be stopped by red tape. This'll be the only live bushmaster ever brought to the United States.

Captain. If I had my way . . . but, orders are orders. Got a cable from the head office this morning. All right. Suppose we talk about precautions.

---
7. **undulant** (ŭn′jə-lənt): wavy.
8. **Caracas** (kə-rä′kəs): the capital and largest city of Venezuela.

364 UNIT THREE PART 2: FACING THE CONSEQUENCES

Chris. I'll handle it any way you say.

Captain. It's got to have a stronger box. That crate's too flimsy.

Chris. It's stronger than it looks—and that wire screen on top'd hold a wildcat. But anyway, I bought a heavy sea chest this morning. We'll put the crate inside of it.

Captain. Sounds all right. Got a lock on it?

Chris. Heavy padlock. It's fixed so the lid can be propped open a crack without unlocking it. The snake's got to have air.

Captain. But in dirty weather, that lid stays shut. I'll take no chances.

Chris. Fair enough.

Captain. We'll keep the thing in my inside cabin, where I sleep. Can't have it in the baggage room. And nobody on board's to know about it.

Chris. Whatever you say, Captain. But we won't have any trouble. After all, it's only a snake—it doesn't have any magical powers.

Captain. I saw a bushmaster in the zoo at Caracas once. Had it in a glass cage with double walls. It'd never move—just lie there and look at you as long as you were in sight. Gave a man the creeps!

Chris. I didn't know they had a bushmaster at the Caracas Zoo.

Captain. They don't now. Found the glass broken one morning, and the snake gone. The night watchman was dead. They never found out what happened.

Chris. Well . . . the watchman must've broken the glass by accident.

Captain. The way they figured it—the glass was broken from the inside! (*pause*) We . . . sail in four hours.

(*Music: transition . . . to sound of the open sea . . . music background*)

Chris (*narrating*). Into the Caribbean—with perfect weather, and a sea as smooth as an inland lake. The barometer dropped a little on the third day—but cleared up overnight, and left nothing worse than a heavy swell.[9] But in spite of the calm seas and pleasant weather, I was becoming possessed with an <u>ominous</u> anxiety. I was developing an obsessive fear of that snake! I stayed clear of the passengers pretty much—got the habit of dropping into Captain Wood's quarters several times a day. . . . (*Sound: door opens and closes. Steps.*)

He kept the heavy box underneath his berth. I'd approach it quietly and shine my flashlight through the open crack. (*Pause. Sound of two or three steps and stop.*)

Never once could I catch that eight-foot devil asleep, or even excited. He'd be lying there half-coiled, his head raised a little, staring out of those beady black eyes—waiting. He'd still be like that when I'd turn away to leave. (*slow steps*)

Maybe that's what bothered me—that horrible and constant watchful waiting. (*Sound: door opens.*) What in the name of heaven was he waiting for?

(*Sound: door closes*)

Willis (*fading in*). Well—hello there, Mr. Warner!

Chris. Oh . . . how are you, Mother Willis?

Willis. My, but you and the Captain spend an awful lot of time around this cabin. I'm beginning to think the two of you must have some guilty secret!

Chris. Oh, no, nothing like that, Mother Willis. I don't know about Captain Wood—but I . . . I certainly don't have any guilty secret!

---
9. **swell:** a large wave.

WORDS TO KNOW
ominous (ŏm′ə-nəs) *adj.* threatening harm or evil

365

Linking to Science

S The glass referred to is a barometer, an instrument that measures air pressure. When a storm is approaching, the air pressure decreases and the mercury in a barometer moves down. The barometer is said to be "falling" or "dropping."

Active Reading: EVALUATE

T Ask students to describe Chris's behavior in three successive scenes—alone with the snake, speaking with Mrs. Willis, and speaking with Mr. Bowman. You may wish to use the following model to give students ideas of what they might be thinking about.

Think-Aloud Model Chris is becoming obsessed with the snake. He thinks the snake is watching and waiting for him. Chris seems excited and guilty when talking with Mrs. Willis. He tries to make jokes with Mr. Bowman. Chris can't stop thinking about the snake; he is becoming more and more nervous.

CUSTOMIZING FOR
Students Acquiring English

3 Point out that the spelling *musta* reflects the way *must have* is often pronounced in informal spoken English.

STRATEGIC READING FOR
Less-Proficient Readers

U Make sure students are following the drama by asking these questions:

- How did the snake get loose? *(A big wave hit the ship, and a desk smashed the boxes holding the snake.)* **Relating Cause and Effect**

- How does Chris know that the snake has escaped? *(Mrs. Willis tells him the boxes have been broken wide open but does not mention a snake.)* **Noting Relevant Details**

Set a Purpose As students read the next section of the play, have them note how the captain and the passengers handle the situation.

(*Music: transition into sound. Open foredeck of liner bucking a swell.*)

Chris. Well! She's running quite a swell out there, Mr. Bowman!

Bowman. Yeah—it's a little heavy, all right, Mr. Warner. Guess a storm passed through to the west of us yesterday when the glass dropped.

Chris. Think it missed us, then, huh?

Bowman. Yeah—that's what the mate figures. Sure stirred up some water, though.

Chris (*laughs*). This'll put half the passengers in their bunks.

Bowman. Make it great for my department. Two thirds of 'em will want a steward to hold their heads!

Chris. They'll keep Mother Willis so busy she'll—Hey! Look at that wave!

Bowman. Huh? . . . Great Jehoshaphat! We're taking it on the port bow! Hang on!

(*Sound: wave crashes across the foredeck . . . seems to shake the whole ship . . . and subsides*)

Chris. Whew! Not another wave that size in sight. That was a freak if there ever was one.

Bowman. You see 'em like that sometimes—even in a calm sea. (*pause*) Gotta get topside, Mr. Warner. Wave really smashed into the officers' deck. Probably did some damage. . . .

Chris. Yeah, I suppose . . . What did you say?

Bowman. Wheel companionway was open on the port side—bridge cabins musta taken a pretty bad smashing. They're right below the—Say, is something wrong, Mr. Warner?

Chris. No. No—nothing at all, Mr. Bowman. At least . . . I hope not!

(*Music: attacks and holds under voice*)

Chris (*narrating*). Of course, I knew it was only one chance in a thousand—but the chances against that freak wave were one in a thousand, too! I stumbled up the companionway and along the passage to the Captain's cabin.

(*Music . . . sound of door opening*)

Willis (*surprised, affably*). Oh . . . come on in, Mr. Warner.

Chris. Mother Willis!

Willis. My, isn't this cabin a mess? I'd better get some of these things out to dry.

Chris. Yeah. Well, I just wanted to check—Where's that box that was under the Captain's bunk?

Willis. Oh, that! I just shoved it out on deck.

Chris. What!

Willis. The desk over there slid into it. It was all smashed.

Chris. But the small box inside of it! What happened to it?

Willis. Oh, they were both splintered, Mr. Warner—broken wide open.

Chris. Oh, no!

Willis. Why, Mr. Warner—you're as white as a sheet!

Chris. Mother Willis—will you go find Captain Wood? Tell him to . . . come down here immediately.

Willis. Well . . . of course, Mr. Warner. (*going*) I'll go tell him right away.

(*Sound: door closes. Sounds as cued under the following:*)

Chris (*narrating*). I pulled open the top drawer of the bureau beside me (*drawer opening*) and took out the Captain's flashlight and a loaded pistol (*drawer closing*). Mother Willis had left a mop standing by the door. I put my foot on the head of it and snapped off the handle (*snap of handle*). Every move I made turned into slow motion. I could hear my own heart beating. Slowly I started to search

366 UNIT THREE PART 2: FACING THE CONSEQUENCES

the cabin. (*Music: suspense motif*)

Sodden heaps of clothing were scattered around on the wet, black floor. I punched at them one at a time—holding the gun cocked—the flashlight pointing along the stick. Nothing. I worked around the room—throwing the light into the dark corners, back of the desk, under the bunk. And wherever I turned, I could feel those cold, unblinking eyes at my back—watching and waiting. (*pause*) Using the stick, I pushed open the closet door and threw the light inside. Carefully I poked at the boxes and junk on the floor. (*pause*) The snake was not in the closet. Inch by inch, I covered the entire cabin—and then at last I realized the horrible truth.

(*Sound: door opening. Music: up and clip off.*)

Captain. Mother Willis just told me, Christopher. (*door closes*) So it's happened!

Chris. That's right, Captain. It's happened.

Captain. I see you found the gun. We'd better start searching the cabin.

Chris. Captain Wood, I . . . just finished searching it.

Captain. Then . . . ! (*pause*) Women, kids—and that thing loose on board. A thousand places for it to hide. Heaven help us!

(*Music: establish theme for the "search"*)

Captain (*fades in*). There's no use starting to blame anybody now, gentlemen. I didn't call you officers in here to pass judgment. The thing's done—and that's that.

Mate. You're right there, Captain.

Captain. What we *have* got to do is decide how to handle it.

Bowman. It'd be easier if we didn't have to tell the passengers and crew, sir. I've seen panics aboard ship before!

Captain. Yes, I agree with you, Mr. Bowman—but I don't quite see how we can avoid it.

Mate. They gotta right to know! As long as that snake's loose, everybody on board's in the same danger—and they all oughta know about it!

Chris. Captain Wood—that thing is eight feet long. It can't simply crawl into a crack. Why don't we make a quick search of the whole ship before we spread any alarm?

Captain. Yes, I've thought of that, Christopher.

Bowman. As far as I can see, the only place it *couldn't* be is in the boilers or on top of the galley stove.

Mate. It might've crawled overboard.

Captain. We can't count on that. We've got to assume it's on the ship somewhere.

Mate. Yeah, and that could be anywhere. In a coil of rope—or in a pile of clothes.

WORDS TO KNOW
sodden (sŏd′n) *adj.* thoroughly wet

367

Mini-Lesson  Genre Study

DRAMA Explain to students that a drama is meant to be performed for an audience. In a **radio play** sound is the only way to present all the information in the script, including mood (usually established by sets and lighting), setting, location changes, and all physical actions of the actors. This has to be conveyed through dialogue, narration, music, and sound effects.

Application Have students copy and complete a chart like the one shown. Ask them to review the play, fill in the first column, and then imagine what changes could be made if the play was produced on the stage and on television. Remind students that a stage play is somewhat limited in its ability to change settings often and/or quickly; television has an unlimited ability to change setting.

A Shipment of Mute Fate	Radio Play	Stage Play	Television
Cast			
Dialogue			
Sound Effects			
Music			
Props			
Scenery/Location			

THE LANGUAGE OF LITERATURE TEACHER'S EDITION **367**

Literary Concept: SUSPENSE

Z Encourage students to note the succession of short lines spoken anxiously by several characters. Ask students what effect this has on the audience. *(Possible response: The short lines help to convey the idea that the mystery of the snake's whereabouts is creating a frantic and suspenseful atmosphere.)*

Active Reading: CONNECT

AA Point out how the captain works together with his crew to make a plan rather than just giving orders. Have students compare this with their own experiences in working cooperatively with others to solve a problem.

Cultural Note

BB You may wish to draw students' attention to the fact that this radio play contains examples of gender stereotypes. On this page and the next, some women passengers behave hysterically and helplessly, while the men are more calm or aggressive. Invite students to debate the fairness of such gender stereotypes. If they were choosing the cast for this play, would they choose a woman for the captain? the main character? any of the crew members? Students should give reasons for their choices.

STRATEGIC READING FOR
Less-Proficient Readers

CC What does the captain do about the emergency on his ship? *(He tells the officers and crew, and they search the ship for the snake.)* **Summarizing**

• How can you tell that the passengers don't yet know a snake is loose? *(One woman is angry at being disturbed; a man jokes about all the activity.)* **Noting Relevant Details**

Set a Purpose As students read the next section of the play, have them pay attention to how Chris reacts to the emergency and how the passengers react once they find out about the snake.

Z **Bowman.** Yes, or under some woman's berth— or a baby's crib.

Mate. Or even in—

Chris. You've already said it! That bushmaster could be anywhere. We've got to do something, and do it fast!

Captain. All right. I think the best idea's to make a quick search first. You agree to that?

(Cast ad-libs assent.[10])

AA **Captain.** Then if we don't find it—we'll have to warn the passengers.

Chris. We've got to find it!

(Music: up and sustained under voice)

Chris *(narrating).* Alone in the dim baggage room, I went through the same movements as I had earlier in the Captain's cabin—gun in one hand, flashlight in the other, poking into every dark corner, behind every trunk and box. Since there was no one in the baggage room, I could keep the gun cocked and ready. The rest of those poor devils were having to do the same thing—barehanded! All over the ship the search went on.

(Music: up and cut off)

BB **Woman** *(fade in).* Here, now, Steward! What on earth are you doing, rummaging through my cabin?

Bowman. Just checking up, ma'am!

Woman. Well, I'm sure there's nothing in here that has to be checked.

Bowman. Sorry, ma'am—Captain's orders. It'll only take a few minutes.

Woman. Well, I never heard of such a thing! A passenger simply doesn't have any privacy at all! *(fading back into music)* I've traveled on a lot of different lines, but I've certainly never heard of anything so completely highhanded before . . . !

(Music: up and under voices)

Mate. Sorry, sir. Wonder if you'd mind moving over to the other rail? I'd like to look through these lockers.

Man. Sure—go ahead. What's the matter . . . you lost something?

Mate. No. No—just looking things over.

Man. Nothing in there but life preservers.

Mate. Yeah—that's right.

Man. You must be getting ready to sink the boat. *(laughs)* Gonna collect the insurance, eh? *(fading)* Gonna send us all to the bottom! *(laughs)*

(Music: up and out)

Chris *(narrating).* But not one of us could find that deadly shape—coiled in some dark corner, or outstretched along a window seat. Not one of us caught a glimpse of that horrid head, with its beady black, watchful eyes. *(Fades)* It was nearly dark when we met together again in the chart room.

Captain *(fades in).* Well, gentlemen—there's no other way. We've risked all the time we can. We must warn the passengers!

Mate. How'll we do it, Captain? Call 'em all together in the lounge?

Captain. No. If we did anything like that, we'd be asking for a panic.

Bowman. We'll get one—whether we ask for it or not!

Captain. Pick a few men and go through the cabin decks. Tell 'em individually—inside their cabins. Watch for any that act like they might cause trouble—and we'll keep an eye on 'em. Handle the crew the same way.

(Officers ad-lib agreement. Sounds of steps, chairs.)

---

10. **ad-libs assent** (ə-sĕnt′): shows agreement in any way it pleases.

368   UNIT THREE   PART 2: FACING THE CONSEQUENCES

Assessment ✓ Option

INFORMAL ASSESSMENT You can informally assess students' understanding of the play so far by having them rewrite the main events of the story from the point of view of one of the passengers.

Rubric

3 Full Accomplishment Students include all major events in the play so far, as well as plausibly represent the point of view of a passenger.

2 Substantial Accomplishment Students include some relevant events from the play and accurately represent a passenger's point of view.

1 Little or Partial Accomplishment Students do not use events from the play. The point of view they show is not realistic in terms of the play's plot or characterization.

Captain (*up a bit*). As soon as you're finished—arm all the deck officers and start searching again. Our only chance of preventing a panic is to find that snake!

(*Music: sets growing tension, sustains it under voice*)

Chris (*narrating*). The slow nightmare that followed grew worse by the hour. None of us slept. All the ship's officers not on duty kept on with that endless search. Passengers locked themselves in their cabins, or huddled together in the lounges—knowing all the time that no spot on board could be called safe. Fear was a heavy fog in the lungs of all of us—and every light on the vessel burned throughout the night. Morning came and brought no relief. Terror and tension mounted by the hour.

(*Music: swells, fades. Sound of woman sobbing.*)

Willis. There now, Mrs. Crane. Go back to your cabin. The horrid thing's probably crawled overboard by now.

Woman. You're just saying that! You're paid to say it! You don't know! Nobody does!

Willis. Now, now. Everything's going to be all right.

Woman. If we could only get off the ship, they could fumigate it. Yes! That's what we've got to do! (*Fading from mike*) We've got to get off the ship!

Willis (*calling excitedly*). Mr. Bowman—she's going to jump.

Bowman (*in distance*). No you don't, lady.

Woman (*distance*). Let me go! (*sobbing*)

Captain (*coming in*). Nice work, Mr. Bowman. Get her down to her cabin. And whatever you do—don't turn her loose!

(*Music: up and under*)

Man (*fading in*). You never know when it might strike you. You can't put on a coat or move a chair without risking your life. Something's gotta be done. It might be right here in this lounge!

(*Sound: stir of fearful crowd*)

Mate (*coming in*). All right, mister—better quiet down and take it easy.

Man. Take it easy, huh? You're a great officer! Why don't you *do* something about it? That thing might be crawling around here right under our feet. . . .

(*Sound: rise of frightened voices*)

Mate. I said shut up! Are you trying to start a riot?

Man. I gotta right to talk! I don't want to die! Nobody's gonna tell me what—

(*Sound: sock in jaw—body falling. Music: up and back under.*)

Chris (*narrating*). The second night passed and morning came around again—a gray and rainy day that dragged by, and then night came down again—third night of the terror. Again every light burned, and the whole ship seethed in the throes of incipient panic.[11] Faced by a horror they'd never met on the sea before, crew and officers alike were on the verge of revolt. Passengers sat huddled in a trancelike stupor, ready to scream at the slightest unknown sound.

(*Music: dissolves slowly*)

Chris. At seven bells,[12] I made my way forward

---

11. **seethed . . . panic:** struggled with the beginnings of overpowering fear.
12. **seven bells:** the beginning of the seventh half-hour of a four-hour watch, announced by the ringing of a ship's bell.

WORDS TO KNOW
fumigate (fyōō'mĭ-gāt') *v.* to use smoke or gas to destroy pests
stupor (stōō'pər) *n.* a state of mental numbness; daze

369

Literary Concept: FIGURATIVE LANGUAGE

DD Point out to students how the writer uses figurative language to compare the feeling of fear to a fog in the lungs. Have students restate the comparison in their own words. (*Possible response: When you feel very frightened, your chest muscles get tight. It's almost as if you have fog or smoke in your lungs and you can't breathe.*)

CUSTOMIZING FOR
Multiple Learning Styles

EE **Interpersonal Learners** Have students work in pairs or groups to suggest ways in which they would help calm the frantic passengers. Students can role-play their ideas, taking the role of one of the crew members or of one of the passengers.

Critical Thinking: MAKING JUDGMENTS

FF Have students discuss whether the violence on the mate's part is justified in this situation. Are there other ways the mate could have handled the situation? (*Encourage students to defend their opinions with logical reasoning.*)

Literary Concept: SETTING

GG Invite students to discuss how the radio play's setting—a ship in the middle of the ocean—contributes to the story's tension and excitement. (*Possible response: The setting increases the suspense because the crew and passengers are trapped on board the ship. Also, eventually someone will be likely to find the snake because there are a limited number of places on the ship where the snake can hide.*)

Mini-Lesson — Literary Concepts

REVIEWING CONFLICT Remind students that plots are generally built around a conflict—a problem or struggle between two or more opposing forces. Sometimes a conflict is external, like a life-or-death struggle or a disagreement between friends. Sometimes the conflict is internal, occurring in the mind or emotions of just one character as he or she struggles to decide what to do in a situation. The climax of a story often occurs when the conflict is resolved.

Application Have students look for examples of conflicts in the play. For each type of conflict they should list the characters involved, describe the conflict, and give the outcome in a chart like the one shown.

Characters	Conflict	Possible Outcomes
Chris and Sanchez		
Chris and the captain		
the snake and the crew		

THE LANGUAGE OF LITERATURE TEACHER'S EDITION 369

Linking to Science

Radio waves can be used to communicate information over long distances without using wires. This type of communication is called wireless telegraphy, or wireless telegraph. It is also described as radiotelegraphy, or radio. A mobile or cordless phone is a type of wireless communication.

Active Reading: CLARIFY

Have students discuss why they think the captain doesn't seem angry with Chris. (*Possible responses: The captain feels the emergency is partly his fault; he is more interested in fixing the problem than in blaming anyone.*)

STRATEGIC READING FOR
Less-Proficient Readers

Have students discuss how Chris is reacting to the situation and how his behavior has changed since the beginning of the play.

- What happens when the passengers are told the snake is loose? (*They start to panic and hide in their cabins.*)
  Summarizing

- How does Chris feel? (*Possible responses: frightened, sorry, guilty*)
  Making Inferences

Set a Purpose Invite students to predict how the play will end. Then have them read to find out if someone gets the snake before the snake gets someone!

Literary Concept: SUSPENSE

Tell students to keep in mind that the audience is listening to the play and can't see what's happening. Have them discuss how the writer creates a feeling of suspense in Chris's speech. (*Possible response: The writer includes a great deal of detail to help the listener picture what is happening.*) Have students describe what sound effects they might add to make the scene even more suspenseful. (*Possible responses: sound of cupboard opening; sound of snake moving or hissing*)

---

to the chart room, and found Captain Wood bent over a desk.

(*Sound: door closes. Steps.*)

Captain (*wearily*). Oh . . . hello, Christopher. Come on in and sit down.

Chris (*on edge*). It's got to be *somewhere*, Captain Wood! It's got to be!

Captain. I don't know. You could search this ship for six months and never touch all the hiding places aboard. If we can only hold out for two more days—we'll be in port.

Chris. What's your home office say?

Captain. Here's the latest wireless from 'em. "Keep calm—and keep coming." Huh! What else *can* we do? How is it below?

Chris. Pretty bad. Anything could happen.

Captain. Yeah, that's why I took the guns away from the men. One pistol shot, and we'd have a riot on our hands.

Chris. The whole thing's my fault, Captain Wood! That's what I can't forget!

Captain. Take it easy, son.

Chris. If there was only some way I could pay for it myself. Alone!

Captain. No—I know how you feel. But it's no more your fault than mine, or the man who asked you to bring that snake back . . . alive. Nobody planned this. You'd better try to get a little sleep.

Chris. Sleep!

Captain. Mr. Bowman made some coffee down in the steward's galley a while ago. Better go on down and get yourself a cup—then rest for a couple hours.

Chris. Rest—I can't rest!

Captain. Christopher—it's not going to help anything if you stumble through a hatch[13] half-asleep—and break your neck. Go on and get some coffee. One way or another we've got to hold out for two more days.

(*Music: transition and dissolves. Sound: door closing and steps under . . . other sounds as cued.*)

Chris (*narrating*). The light was on in the steward's galley—and the coffeepot was standing on the stove. (*Steps stop.*) It was still warm, so I didn't bother to heat it. (*pouring*) I poured out a cup . . . (*steps*), carried it over, and set it on the porcelain table top in the center of the room. I started to light a cigarette. The door of the pan cupboard beneath the sink was standing slightly ajar, and I happened to glance toward it. I dropped the cigarette and moved slowly backward. I'd found the bushmaster!

(*Music: loud, then continues softly, movement slow and tense*)

Chris. As I moved, the snake slid out of the cupboard in a single sinuous slide—and drew back into a loose coil on the galley floor—never taking his eyes off me. I backed slowly away—waiting any moment for that deadly, slithering strike. How had he known it was me? He'd stayed quiet when Bowman was here. How had he picked the first time in five days that I was without a gun? My hands touched the wall behind me and I stopped, in terror. . . . The call button and door were on the far side of the room. I'd backed into a dead end! I stared at the snake in fascination—expecting any moment the ripping slash of those poisoned fangs. The <u>lethal</u> coils tightened a little—then were still again. *Homo sapiens* versus *Lachesis mutus*—a man against mute fate. And all the odds were on . . . fate. I knew then that I was going to die!

---

13. **hatch:** an opening in a ship's deck.

WORDS TO KNOW
lethal (lē′thəl) *adj.* deadly

370

Mini-Lesson — Reading Skills/Strategies

NOTING RELEVANT DETAILS As students read the play, they should note details that are provided in the stage directions as well as in the dialogue. The stage direction near the top of page 370 calls for "door closing and steps under." "Under" means that these sounds are heard as background. They tell the listener that Chris has entered another room and the door is closed.

Application Have students read the description of the battle between the cat and the snake on pages 371–372. Ask them how the combined details in the narration and sound effects paint a vivid picture. You may wish to have a student read Chris's dialogue first without sound effects and then with another student supplying sound effects.

Reteaching/Reinforcement
- *Unit Three Resource Book*, p. 66

---

370 THE LANGUAGE OF LITERATURE TEACHER'S EDITION

The Nantucket Cat, Paul Stagg. From *The Mardi Gras Cat Book* by Paul Stagg and Naomi Lewis, published by Heinemann Press. Copyright © The Stephanie Hoppen Picture Archive Ltd., London.

(*Music: long chord and clip off*)

Chris. I could feel the sweat run down between the wall and the palms of my hands pressing against it. My skin crawled and twitched, and the pit of my stomach was cold as ice. There was no sound but the rush of blood in my ears. The snake shifted again—drawing into a tighter coil—always tighter. Why didn't the devil get it over with? Then . . . for an instant his head veered away. Something moved by the stove. I didn't dare turn to look at it. Slowly it moved out into my line of vision. It was a cat! The scrawny cat that Mother Willis sneaked aboard in La Guaira!

Cat. (*a low, threatening growl*)

Chris. Its back was arched, and every hair stood on end. It moved stiff-legged now, walking in a half-circle around the snake. The bushmaster moved slowly and kept watching the cat. He tightened—he was going to strike at any second.

(*Sound: thud of striking snake, and scrape as it recovers*)

A SHIPMENT OF MUTE FATE **371**

CUSTOMIZING FOR
Students Acquiring English

4 Point out that the spelling *'em* reflects the way *them* is often pronounced in informal spoken English.

Active Reading: QUESTION

PP Ask students what Chris means when he says that he "suddenly became very humble." *(Possible response: Chris first thought the cat was trying to protect him when she killed the snake. Then he realizes she was really guarding her kittens.)*

STRATEGIC READING FOR
Less-Proficient Readers

QQ Have students discuss the plot events in the final scene.

- Why couldn't Chris kill the snake? *(He had gone into the galley for coffee and didn't have his gun with him.)*
Relating Cause and Effect

- Does the cat kill the snake to save Chris and the passengers? *(No. The cat is trying to protect her kittens.)*
Noting Relevant Details

COMPREHENSION CHECK

1. What does Mrs. Willis sneak on board the ship? *(Clara, her pet cat)*
2. Why are Chris Warner and Sanchez in the Venezuelan jungle? *(to capture a living bushmaster)*
3. Why does Captain Wood let Chris bring his dangerous cargo on board the ship? *(The captain's superiors send a cable ordering him to do so.)*
4. What causes the bushmaster to escape? *(A freak wave crashes into the ship, making a desk splinter the boxes holding the snake.)*
5. How does Chris change over the course of the play? *(At the beginning, he wants to bring the bushmaster back alive at any cost. By the end, he is sorry for the dangerous situation he has caused.)*

Cat. (*snarl and spit . . . then back to the low growl*)

Chris. He struck and missed—the cat was barely out of reach. Now she was walking back and forth again. She was asking to die.

(*Sound: thud and recovery*)

Cat. (*snarl, spit, and back to growl*)

Chris. Missed again—by a fraction of an inch. He was striking now without even going to a full coil!

(*Sound: thud and recovery*)

Cat. (*snarl, spit, growl*)

Chris. Missed! Again and again—always missing by the barest <u>margin</u>. Each time the cat danced barely out of reach—and each time she <u>countered</u> with one precise spat of a dainty paw—bracing her skinny frame on three stiff legs. And then suddenly I realized what she was doing!

(*Sound: thud and recovery*)

Cat. (*snarl, spit, growl*)

Chris. The bushmaster was tiring—and one strike was just an instant slow. But in that split second, sharp claws raked across the evil head and ripped out both the lidless eyes. The cat had deliberately blinded the snake!

(*Sound: repeated thuds of struggle*)

Cat. (*snarling, spitting*)

Chris. He didn't bother to coil now but slid after her in a fury—striking wildly but always missing. And every strike was a little slower than the last one. Until finally—

(*Sound: The thuds change to the frantic scraping of a heavy snake.*)

Chris. As the snake's neck stretched out at the end of a strike, the cat made one leap and sank her razor-sharp teeth just back of the ugly head—sank 'em until they crunched bone with tooth and claw. She clung, as the monstrous snake flailed and lashed on the floor . . . striving to get those hideous coils around her, trying to break her hold, to shake off the slow and certain paralyzing death . . . (*sound of cat out*) that gradually crept over him, and at last stilled his struggles forever!

(*Pause. Music.*)

Chris. I took a deep breath—the first in minutes—the cat lay on her side on the floor, panting—resting from the fight just over. She had a right to rest. That mangy, brave, beautiful alley cat had just saved my life—and maybe others as well. But as I turned toward the stove—I suddenly became very humble. There were three reasons why that cat had fought and killed the world's deadliest snake. And those three reasons came tottering out from under the stove on shaky little legs—three kittens with their eyes bright with wonder and their tails stiff as pokers. Up on the decks, hundreds of passengers would sigh with relief at the news that the days and nights of terror were ended. They could wait a little longer. (*pause*) I pulled open the doors of the cabinet and found a can of milk. Then I dropped down on my knees . . . on the floor of the galley.

WORDS TO KNOW
margin (mär′jĭn) *n.* an amount of difference or space between two things
counter (koun′tər) *v.* to respond to another's action; return a blow

372

Mini-Lesson Spelling

SOFT AND HARD g Tell students words with the letter *g* can have a soft sound or a hard sound. Demonstrate the difference between the two sounds using these examples from the Words to Know.

Soft g   margin
Hard g   fumigate

Application Read aloud the following four words for the students: *agent, region* (soft g); *argument, recognize* (hard g). Ask students to write four sentences using each of these words once. Ask students to indicate after each sentence whether the word uses a hard or soft g sound.

Ask students to look for more words that use hard and soft g sounds, in their own writing and in things they read, and to add these words to their personal word lists.

Reteaching/Reinforcement
- *Unit Three Resource Book,* p. 67

---

372 THE LANGUAGE OF LITERATURE **TEACHER'S EDITION**

RESPONDING OPTIONS

FROM PERSONAL RESPONSE TO CRITICAL ANALYSIS

REFLECT
1. What would be the first thing you would say to a friend about this radio play? Write your comment in your notebook or on a sheet of paper.

RETHINK
2. Do you think Chris Warner should have brought the bushmaster aboard the ship? Why or why not?
   Consider
   Close Textual Reading
   - his reason for bringing the snake
   - his actions after the dangerous snake disappears
   Thematic Link
   - the possible consequences for others on the ship

3. What do you think might have happened if Mrs. Willis's cat had not killed the bushmaster?

4. Did the directions for sound effects add to or detract from your enjoyment of the play? Explain your answer.

5. Take a moment to consider any changes you might want to make in the sketch you created for the Personal Connection on page 359. Now that you have read the play, what details would you add to convey its atmosphere better?

RELATE
6. Zoologists today know that the bushmaster does not survive in captivity because it refuses to eat. Do you think wild animals should be caught and placed in zoos? Give reasons for your opinion.

Multimodal Learning
ANOTHER PATHWAY
Cooperative Learning
With a small group of classmates, produce *A Shipment of Mute Fate* as a radio play, complete with sound effects. Some students can read parts, and others can find creative ways to produce the sound effects. Rehearse until you can create an atmosphere that seems appropriate for the play.

QUICKWRITES

1. Write a **headline** and a draft of an accompanying **news article** about the events in this drama. Begin by asking and answering the questions *who, what, when, where, why,* and *how.* Give all the important details needed to understand what happened.

2. Pretend that you are a passenger who was not warned about the bushmaster's presence. Write a **letter of complaint** to the ship's owner.

3. A ship's captain often keeps a daily log of the ship's progress and of important events. Write a **log entry** for the day the captain learns that his orders have been overruled and the bushmaster will be on board.

 PORTFOLIO Save your writing. You may want to use it later as a springboard to a piece for your portfolio.

A SHIPMENT OF MUTE FATE **373**

From Personal Response to Critical Analysis

1. Responses will vary.
2. Possible responses: Chris was wrong to bring the snake on board because innocent people could have been injured or killed. Chris was right because the chances were small that the snake could endanger the crew and passengers.
3. Possible responses: The snake might have killed Chris and possibly other people; Chris might have killed the snake; the captain or a crew member might have come into the galley and killed the snake.
4. Ask students to cite specific sound effects in their answers.
5. Students might add the jungle in the background of their sketches.
6. Some students may feel it is cruel to take animals out of their natural habitats and lock them up. Other students may believe it is all right to capture wild animals because people may be more willing to protect endangered animals if they can see them in zoos or wildlife parks.

Another Pathway

Cooperative Learning Each group member can choose a section of the play and list the places where sound effects are needed. Then the group can discuss all the sound effects, with a recorder making notes of ideas. Next, students can choose whether they will be actors or do sound effects.

Rubric
3 Full Accomplishment Students create a complete plan for the sound effects. Their performance conveys the drama and suspense in the play.
2 Substantial Accomplishment Students include most of the needed sound effects. Their performance is accurate.
1 Little or Partial Accomplishment Students include few sound effects or perform the play inaccurately.

QuickWrites

1. Since news articles can vary greatly in length, you may wish to decide (or have the class decide) on how long the articles should be before students begin work. Remind them that news articles often include photographs or maps.
2. Explain to students that a letter of complaint should include a clear description of the problem and a request for some type of action. For example, students might ask for their passage money back or for the ship's owner to make new safety regulations.
3. Tell students that a log differs from a journal in that personal reactions and opinions are not usually included in log entries. Also explain that the log entries should each begin with the date and the time.

The Writer's Craft
Describing People and Places, pp. 54–59
Letter, p. 609
Journal, pp. 32–37
Personal Narrative, 76–80

THE LANGUAGE OF LITERATURE TEACHER'S EDITION **373**

Across the Curriculum

Science *Cooperative Learning* Have students work in small groups. Each group can choose a continent: North America, South America, Africa, Europe, Australia, or Asia. Then the groups should research poisonous and nonpoisonous snakes that live there. Groups can share and discuss the results of their research in a class presentation.

ADDITIONAL SUGGESTIONS

 **Geography** *Cruise the Caribbean!* Have students use an atlas or encyclopedia to find the countries that border the Caribbean Sea. (One of these countries is Venezuela.) They can draw and color maps to show the results of their research.

 SCIENCE CONNECTION
The Bushmaster Snake Images of the bushmaster will help students understand what the snake looks like and what habitat it lives in. In addition, students will see a map showing the bushmaster's range in South America.

Side A, Frame 38814

Literary Link

Perhaps Barbara Frietchie is the best example of a character who takes an action with the knowledge that it may be risky. She faces the consequences with courage. Lyzer the Miser may be the least courageous—he is forced by the rabbi to "take his medicine," but there is no indication that he has learned anything from his experience. The children in "The Enchanted Raisin" and Chris in *A Shipment of Mute Fate* do fairly well at accepting the results of mistakes they have made.

LITERARY CONCEPTS

Suspense is a feeling of tension and excitement that makes a reader curious about the outcome of a story. A writer creates suspense by raising questions in the reader's mind about possible endings to the conflict. Les Crutchfield begins to build suspense in the play's first speech by having Chris tell us that he felt a "cold chill" and "shivered with sudden dread" and by using sound effects like music. Find another passage in the play that you find especially effective in creating suspense.

LITERARY LINKS

Think about the selections you've read in this part of Unit Three. Which character or characters in the selections do you think most directly face the consequences of their actions? Compare your ideas with those of a classmate.

Multimodal Learning

ALTERNATIVE ACTIVITIES

1. With a group of classmates, select **background music** for *A Shipment of Mute Fate*. Read the stage directions for clues to the kinds of music needed. Experiment with different types of music, such as classical, jazz, and popular (or a combination of these). Make your music reflect the atmosphere created in the play.

2. With a group of classmates, create an original **radio play** for the class. Sketch out a plot, draw up a cast of characters, and rehearse the dialogue. Create sound effects and choose appropriate background music. Make a tape of your radio play to share with the rest of the class.

374 UNIT THREE PART 2: FACING THE CONSEQUENCES

Multimodal Learning
ACROSS THE CURRICULUM

 Science Find out more about the bushmaster and other poisonous and nonpoisonous snakes. Make a chart that compares the different features of the most common snakes. Do an oral reading of this play with some friends who haven't already read it, using the chart as a visual aid to help them distinguish a bushmaster from other types of snakes.

Literary Concepts

Students can work in groups of four to identify suspenseful passages in the play. Students can consider Chris's descriptions of the snake, Chris's descriptions of his feelings and reactions, the behavior of the native guide Sanchez, or the reactions of the crew and passengers when the snake is loose. When students are finished, have them compare the passages they selected with those of at least one other group.

Alternative Activities

1. Direct students to consider such matters as consistency when they choose music for various scenes. Students will probably have varying musical tastes, and one musical selection may suggest different moods or images to different students.

2. Students can do this activity in small groups. First they can work as a group to choose a topic or general plot. Then one student can begin to outline plot developments while a second drafts character sketches, a third suggests sound effects, and a fourth chooses possible background music.

WORDS TO KNOW

On your paper, write the letter of the word or phrase that best completes each sentence below.

1. If the deck of a ship is **sodden,** it is (a) dirty, (b) wet, (c) rotten, (d) made of wood.
2. A **customs** official makes sure that (a) transported animals are well treated, (b) travelers know local habits, (c) taxes on imports and exports are paid, (d) passengers have tickets.
3. To **fumigate** a ship is to (a) disinfect it, (b) burn it down, (c) abandon it, (d) search it thoroughly.
4. If passengers are in a **stupor,** they might be described as (a) scared, (b) dazed, (c) angry, (d) uneducated.
5. A **lethal** grip is one that is (a) weak, (b) friendly, (c) lively, (d) deadly.
6. One example of a **transition** is (a) exchanging money for a snake, (b) moving from land to sea, (c) telegraphing the home office, (d) the engine of a ship.
7. An animal that tried to **counter** an attack would (a) strike back, (b) jump away, (c) fake death, (d) hide.
8. An **evasive** answer is one that involves (a) confessing the truth, (b) being polite, (c) avoiding the truth, (d) helping the questioner.
9. The **margin** between the snake and the cat is (a) their hatred for each other, (b) their strength and power, (c) the structure between them, (d) the space between them.
10. An **ominous** feeling makes a person (a) curious, (b) sick, (c) confident, (d) fearful.

LES CRUTCHFIELD

1916–1966

Les Crutchfield did not start out wanting to be a writer. He earned a college degree in engineering and became a specialist in rockets and explosives. During World War II, Crutchfield directed research programs on various secret rocket projects. He was the co-inventor of a rocket that helped heavily loaded airplanes take off.

It was only in the 1940s, when Crutchfield's wife took him to see a rehearsal for a radio show, that he became interested in writing plays. In 1946 his first radio script was accepted, and his writing career was launched. Over the next 20 years Crutchfield created radio scripts for more than 20 adventure, mystery, and drama series.

In the 1950s Crutchfield started writing for a new entertainment sensation—television. He is probably best known as one of the main writers for *Gunsmoke*, a suspenseful series about law and order in the Old West. First broadcast as a radio program, *Gunsmoke* became one of the longest-running shows in television history.

• SCIENCE CONNECTION

A SHIPMENT OF MUTE FATE 375

OVERVIEW

To gain a deeper appreciation of the nonfiction selections they have read in this unit, students will explore the characteristics of a problem-solution essay and then create their own essay in this lesson.

Objectives

- To plan a problem-solution essay by considering such elements as audience, purpose, research, and organization
- To draft a problem-solution essay and solicit a response to it
- To revise, edit, and publish a problem-solution essay
- To reflect on the process of writing a problem-solution essay

Skills

LITERATURE
- Examining issues
- Identifying problems and solutions

WRITING AND LANGUAGE
- Identifying audience and goal
- Creating introductions
- Developing conclusions
- Elaborating on ideas

GRAMMAR AND USAGE
- Using pronouns correctly

MEDIA LITERACY
- Interpreting statistics
- Reading a journal entry
- Studying a newspaper article

SPEAKING, LISTENING, AND VIEWING
- Conducting an interview
- Holding a news conference
- Staging a debate
- Reading aloud

Teaching Strategy: STUMBLING BLOCK

A Students often fall back on overworked topics. To help them generate fresh ideas, suggest that they list all the letters of the alphabet and then brainstorm a topic for at least 15 of the letters.

Teaching Strategy: MODELING

B To show students how to generate writing ideas from a journal entry or a collection of statistics, have them look at the models on page 376. Ask students to brainstorm a list of possible solutions to each of the two problems posed. You may wish to use these discussion prompts:
- What are the pros and cons of telling your parents that your brother is smoking?
- What laws could be passed to help protect endangered species?

In responding to the text question relating to the chart, students may say that the topic of endangered species is common today because the number of endangered species has increased significantly over the past two decades.

376 THE LANGUAGE OF LITERATURE TEACHER'S EDITION

WRITING FROM EXPERIENCE

WRITING TO EXPLAIN

"It's not fair!" Have you ever shouted these words? Perhaps you felt you were treated unjustly, or maybe you noticed a situation in your school or community that just didn't seem right. The characters in Unit Three, "A Sense of Fairness," face problems of all shapes and sizes. Could you have helped them find solutions?

GUIDED ASSIGNMENT

Write a Problem-Solution Essay Often there are no instant or perfect solutions to our problems. Still, writing about them can help increase our understanding of them and lead to possible solutions. This lesson will help you write an essay that explains a problem and your solution for it.

1 Examine the Issues

The real world is full of all kinds of problems to solve. Some are issues that everyone must face. Other problems are found in your own city or neighborhood. Still others are ones you have to solve on your own.

Identify the Problem What is the problem in each of the items on these pages? Who or what has caused this problem? Could any of the problems have been avoided? How?

A Connect to Life All problems need solutions. What are the issues that concern you most? Think about unfair situations you have experienced. Look back at dilemmas the characters in this unit faced. Consider topics in the news. Then make a list of several problems you might like to write about.

B Based on the information in this chart, why do you think the topic of endangered species is so common in the media today?

Journal Entry

Friday, November 11

I don't know what to do. On the way home from school yesterday, I ran into Gordon at the park. I'm sure he didn't expect to see me there, because I caught him smoking. He made me promise not to tell Mom or Dad, and said he'd never talk to me again if I did. But everyone knows how bad smoking is for you! I don't understand why he would do it. I feel like I should do something. After all, he is my big brother...

Almanac Statistics

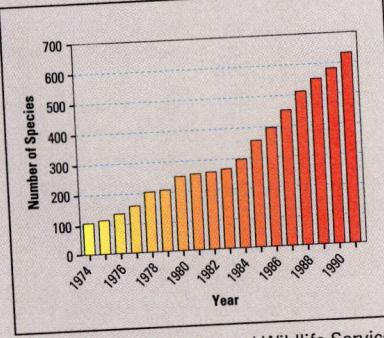

Threatened and Endangered U.S. Wildlife Species

Source: U.S. Fish and Wildlife Service.

376 UNIT THREE: A SENSE OF FAIRNESS

PRINT AND MEDIA RESOURCES

UNIT THREE RESOURCE BOOK
Prewriting, p. 71
Elaboration, p. 72
Peer Response Guide, pp. 73–74
Revising and Editing, p. 75
Student Model, p. 76
Rubric, p. 78

GRAMMAR MINI-LESSONS
Transparencies, pp. 4, 10–11
Copymasters, pp. 4, 13, 17

WRITING MINI-LESSONS
Transparencies, p. 34

ACCESS FOR STUDENTS ACQUIRING ENGLISH
Reading and Writing Support

FORMAL ASSESSMENT
Guidelines for Writing Assessment

 LASERLINKS
Writing Springboard

  WRITING COACH

Magazine Article

Sexism and Soccer in Seattle

Twelve-year-old Eve Russell likes playing soccer with boys. She prefers their rough and competitive style of play to the girls' more passing-oriented game. So rather than join the girls' soccer team, Russell became a member of the boys' team. Her teammates are glad she did; they say they play better when she's there. They think her decision was fine.

Unfortunately, the Seattle Youth Soccer Association (SYSA) and its president, Robin Chalmers, don't agree. They believe that Russell could get roughed up by a boy angry at losing to a girl, and that she needs to bond with other females in the game. What's more, Chalmers sees her choice as a threat and an insult to the girls' program, which he has worked hard to make one of the best in the country. And he resents charges of discrimination. "Our rules are there to protect the female," he argues. He fears that if Russell is allowed to stay on the boys' team, kids all over the city will want to switch too, ultimately damaging the girls' program. So far, though, no other children have shown an interest in switching teams.

Erika Dillman
from *Women's Sport and Fitness,* April 1995

Some of the best kids in my gym class are girls. They often get picked for teams before the guys do!

It doesn't bother other players, so she should be allowed to stay. It doesn't seem fair.

We have a problem at our school that involves fairness for both guys and girls.

❷ What's Bothering You?

Look over your list of problems and mark the two or three that concern you most. You can begin to explore these ideas by freewriting for a few minutes about each. In your notebook, write down your first thoughts about each of these issues.

- LASERLINKS
  - WRITING SPRINGBOARD
- WRITING COACH

WRITING FROM EXPERIENCE **377**

WRITING SPRINGBOARD
One Man's Graffiti Mission Listen to the story of how one man single-handedly takes on the graffiti problem in his neighborhood.

Side B Frames 10582

Writing Prompt There are times when people feel so strongly about problems in their neighborhoods that they decide to do something about the problems. Using the story told in this film as an example, write about a problem in your neighborhood that concerns you, including the methods you would use to solve it.

Teaching Strategy: MODELING

C Explain to students that reading and evaluating a writing model can help them to generate writing ideas, structure their own writing, and develop effective stylistic elements. Tell students that this process uses the active reading skills they have learned, such as connecting and predicting. Then invite a volunteer to read the magazine article aloud. Have other students read the marginal notes. Use these notes as a model to help prompt students' own comments on the text. Guide students to evaluate the text and connect it to their own feelings about the topic presented. Use this process as a springboard for developing additional writing topics.

Writing Skill:
USING THE COMPUTER

D Suggest that students do their freewriting on a computer. Explain that the computer will enable them to express their ideas quickly and will also provide them with a base for later drafting. Working on a computer, students will be able to rearrange their text easily when they draft.

THE LANGUAGE OF LITERATURE TEACHER'S EDITION **377**

Teaching Strategy:
STUMBLING BLOCK

E Inexperienced writers often have difficulty narrowing a topic. Suggest that students use an inverted triangle, such as the one shown, to narrow down a broad writing topic.

Broad topic: Pollution
Narrower topic: Water pollution
Still narrower topic: Lake pollution
Focused writing topic: Pollution in my neighborhood lake

Critical Thinking: ANALYZING

F Discuss the questions in this list. Ask students why it is important to ask a lot of questions about their topic. (*Possible response: Asking questions helps the writer sift important information from the available information and helps direct any research.*)

Speaking, Listening, and Viewing:
INTERVIEWING

G When students are close to completing their research, have them form small groups in which they can interview one another about their topics and findings. Tell students that each group member should state his or her problem and then briefly explain the possible solutions. The rest of the group should listen and then ask questions, using the 5 W's and H technique. The questions will help generate feedback that students can use to complete their research and refine their solutions.

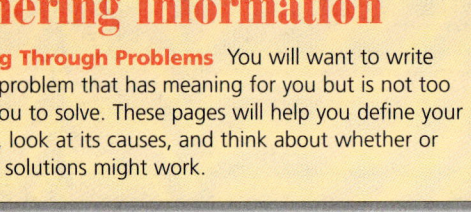

PREWRITING

Gathering Information

Thinking Through Problems You will want to write about a problem that has meaning for you but is not too big for you to solve. These pages will help you define your problem, look at its causes, and think about whether or not your solutions might work.

① Choose and Investigate a Topic

Look again at your freewriting. Decide which problem you most want to write about. These activities will help you explore your topic further.

FOCUS YOUR PROBLEM

E Describe the problem you'd like to take on. It might be an annoying situation you face every day or a larger issue that others are trying to solve as well. If you have strong feelings about a problem that seems too big for you to solve, such as homelessness, don't just pass it over. Try to narrow your focus, perhaps to helping out at a local soup kitchen.

ASK QUESTIONS

The first step toward solving any problem is learning as much as you can about it. The following questions may help you decide what you need to find out.

- How did the problem start?
- Whom does it affect?
- Why should something be done about it?
- Have others tried to solve this problem? How?

FIND INFORMATION

A library is often a good place to begin your search for information. There you might find

- community newspapers and magazines
- surveys and reports on issues in your area
- lists of local organizations and records of what was said during previous meetings (Check bulletin boards for future meeting dates and times.)

You might also try talking to the people who are directly involved with your problem. Use the tips in the SkillBuilder on the next page to build your interviewing techniques.

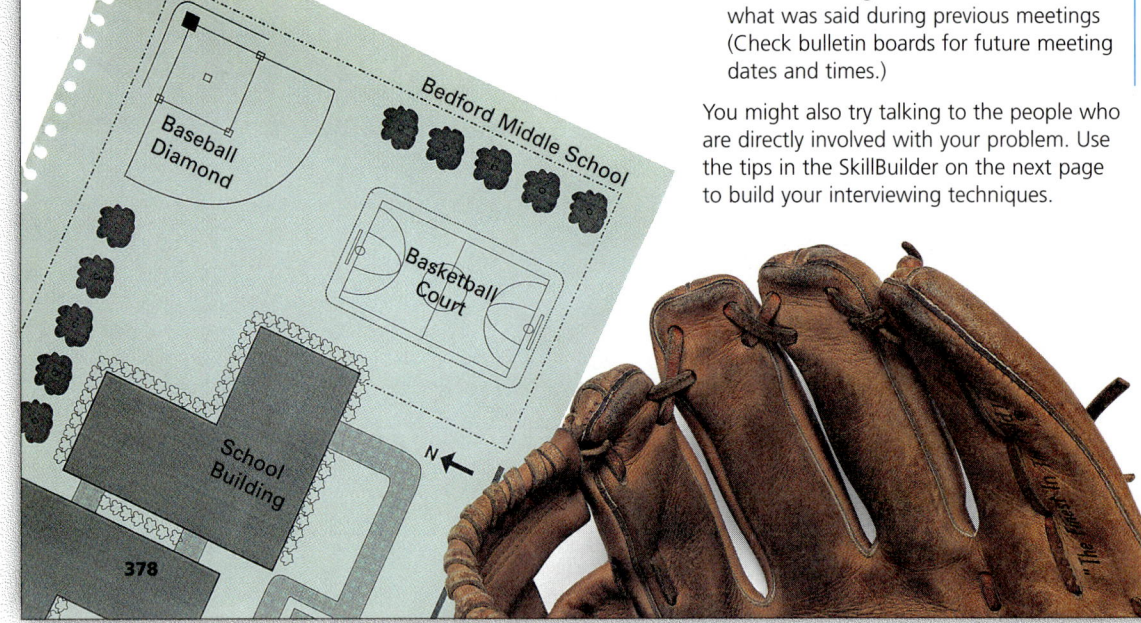

378

Mini-Lesson Study Skills

GENERAL REFERENCE SOURCES Provide students with the following overview of reference sources:
- Encyclopedias are collections of informational articles written by experts. There are general encyclopedias, such as *The World Book Encyclopedia*, and specialized volumes, such as the *Encyclopedia of Sports*.
- Almanacs and yearbooks contain current facts and statistics on topics in such areas as government, sports, and population.
- Atlases are books of maps. They provide information about highways, population, government, climate, landforms, and so on.
- Vertical files contain pamphlets, handbooks, photos, and newspaper and magazine clippings on a variety of popular topics.
- Periodicals are newspapers, magazines, and journals. Recent periodicals are kept on open shelves; older ones are stored in back rooms or on a film called microforms.

Application Encourage students to use a wide variety of reference sources to get the most accurate, authoritative, and nonbiased information on their topics.

378 THE LANGUAGE OF LITERATURE TEACHER'S EDITION

② Explore Solutions

To help you find the best solution to your problem, you might make a problem-solving chart, like the one below. Begin by writing down every possible solution you can think of—even the ones you think won't work.

Now list reasons why each possible solution is a good or bad idea. The reasons supporting your idea are called pros; those against it are called cons.

Student's Problem-Solving Chart

Problem: There's only one ball diamond to play on at our school. The 7th- and 8th-grade guys always use it, so we 6th-grade guys never get to play. The girls usually get left out, too.

Possible Solutions	Pros	Cons
1. build more diamonds	• all grades could play, girls too • fair to all boys	• take too much time and money to build • games too short and girls might still get left out
2. each grade gets field for 1/3 of time it is available		
3. keep field open later	• all play full games • all kids involved • students would work together as teammates	• principal won't do it • have to do other things when your team is not playing
4. organize mixed teams; have teams play each other		

Decision Point Try out each solution in your mind. Decide which solution or solutions are the best. Think about whether using a combination of solutions might work.

③ Identify Your Audience and Goal

What are you trying to accomplish by writing about this problem? Are you just trying to understand it better or to get others to help you solve it? Who should hear your ideas? Before you begin to write, consider your audience and goal. This will help you choose the best way to present your problem and solution. See pages 382 and 383 for some ideas.

SkillBuilder

 SPEAKING & LISTENING

Conducting an Interview
Successful interviews are the result of good preparation. When interviewing others, keep these points in mind.

- Make an appointment to speak with your subject; be on time.
- Prepare your questions ahead of time. Keep them simple.
- Be flexible. You may learn information you never thought to ask about if you allow the conversation to go beyond the questions you've prepared.
- If you don't understand something your subject says, ask more questions.
- Relax. Interviews can be fun for both you and your subject.

APPLYING WHAT YOU'VE LEARNED
Who might be able to fill in some of the gaps in your knowledge about your topic? Write down five questions you'd like to ask that person in an interview.

THINK & PLAN

Reflecting on Your Ideas

1. Why are you interested in this problem?
2. Did you learn anything that surprised you while researching your problem? How will you write about your discoveries in your essay?

CUSTOMIZING FOR
Students Acquiring English

H Students who come from countries where baseball is not a popular sport might have trouble using this model. Ask these students to name the most important sports in their native countries. Encourage them to compare the sports they know with American baseball. For example, ask students to consider whether the important sports in their native countries are played professionally, whether the players are paid salaries, and whether there is a tournament to determine an overall winner.

Writing Skill: PURPOSE

I Suggest that students ask themselves the following questions in order to focus their purpose for writing:
- *What is my reason for choosing this topic?*
- *What effect do I want my writing to have on my readers?*
- *What background information do my readers need?*

WRITING FROM EXPERIENCE 379

Mini-Lesson: Speaking,  Listening, and Viewing

CONDUCTING AN INTERVIEW Remind students to confirm with the subject the date and time of the interview a day or so beforehand. Also remind students to take along paper and pencil for note taking. Tell students that after the interview, they should send a note thanking the subject for his or her time.

Application Have students brainstorm a list of people to interview, such as parents, relatives, community leaders, teachers, and business people. Remind students that the subject's time is valuable, so they should ask questions that are specific and that will elicit more than a simple yes or no response. Suggest that students submit their questions to the subject ahead of time in order to expedite the interview and elicit more detailed responses.

Additional Suggestions Suggest that students tape-record the interview, if their subject agrees to be taped. Explain that recording the interview will enable them to refer to the entire transcript while they are writing their draft.

CUSTOMIZING FOR
Less-Proficient Writers

J Student writers often have difficulty starting the drafting stage. Suggest that they try one of the following techniques:

- Set aside all your prewriting notes. As you write your discovery draft, be open to any new ideas you may discover and to new connections that may come to mind.
- Use your prewriting notes as you draft. Write a structured first draft, incorporating as much of your prewriting material as possible.
- Use a combination of methods. When you've worked out a possible structure for your essay, try to fit your ideas into that structure. When you get stuck, switch to the less structured mode of a discovery draft.

Writing Skill:
USING THE COMPUTER

K Ask students how they can tell that the draft shown on this page was written on a computer. *(Possible responses: by the computer screen; by the document title and arrows; by the computer typeface; by the My Comments guidelines column)* Discuss some of the advantages of drafting on a computer. *(Possible responses: speed, ease of revision, less worry about spelling corrections)* Encourage students to draft their papers on the computer and to use The Writing Coach, which provides detailed guidelines for the drafting stage.

DRAFTING

Getting Your Ideas Down

Organizing Your Draft Writing about a problem and its solution, as well as sharing your work with others, is often a first step toward making a change. The information on these pages can help you explain your problem and solution in a way that will make an impression on others.

❶ Write a Discovery Draft

One way to start organizing your information is to use headings like the ones in the model below. Start wherever you feel comfortable. You might jump from part to part, leaving holes as you go. The Writing Coach can help you with this stage.

Student's Discovery Draft

Fairness on the Field

My Discovery Draft	My Comments My Discovery Draft
INTRODUCTION: ?? (maybe say something about how trying to play baseball in the field after school is dangerous?)	Use quote from interview?
PROBLEM: Every day after school kids race out to the field to claim the baseball diamond. Only two teams can play at a time, and the older guys almost always get there first, so we sixth-grade boys hardly ever get to play. The girls usually get left out, no matter what grade they're in.	Tell readers why they should care. (Kids get hurt running or fighting; it would be safer for teachers, too.)
SOLUTION: I think there should be an after-school softball league. All kids who want to play could be put on teams and the teams would take turns playing each other. It would be fair to everybody, especially the sixth-grade boys and the girls. It might help us all get along better. The only bad thing is you'd have to find something else to do whenever your team wasn't playing. We could even have playoffs at the end of the year! That would make it even more fun!	Tell why we'd get along (because we'd be teammates).
With the free time on the diamond, maybe people would come up with new games to play and other after school leagues would start!	
CONCLUSION: ?? (should ask kids to support my idea)	Tell them what action to take. Additional comments: Could submit my essay to school newspaper!

WRITING SPRINGBOARD
Resolving Conflicts This film is about a program designed to teach students the communication skills needed to resolve conflicts successfully.

Side B, Frame 14308

Writing Prompt Schools and community groups are using conflict-resolution skills as one way of solving problems. After viewing this film, think about a conflict that you have experienced. Then think about a possible solution. Write an essay about the problem, explaining your possible solution.

380 THE LANGUAGE OF LITERATURE TEACHER'S EDITION

❷ Analyze Your Discovery Draft

Take a look at your draft. Have you described the problem? Does your solution make sense? To help you evaluate your draft, ask yourself the following questions:

- Have I provided enough information to help my reader understand the problem?
- Is it clear why the problem is important to solve?
- Why is my solution a good one?
- Have I explained the pros and any cons of my solution?

If you need help making your ideas clearer, see the SkillBuilder at the right for tips on elaborating.

❸ Rework and Share

The guidelines below can help you make your problem-solution essay stronger and more interesting to read.

Hook Them with Your Introduction The first paragraph should grab your readers' interest. You might do this by telling how the problem affects your readers or you personally.

Explain the Problem Clearly Either in your introduction or in the main part of your draft, state the problem clearly and tell your readers why they should care about solving it.

Offer a Workable Solution Explain your solution and tell why it is workable. If you are suggesting more than one solution, list the pros and cons of each.

End with a Strong Conclusion Urge your readers to take the action necessary to help solve the problem. Another way to make your ending strong is to warn what could happen if the problem is ignored.

PEER RESPONSE

A peer may help you see the strengths and weaknesses of your problem-solution essay. After a classmate has read your draft, ask him or her the following questions:

- Summarize the problem I explained and the solution I suggested. Does my solution sound like it might work?
- Are the pros and cons of my solution clearly explained?
- Have I provided all the information you need to understand my solution or to take the action I suggest?

SkillBuilder

WRITER'S CRAFT

Elaborating on Ideas
Don't stop short when explaining your ideas. Use the following tips to keep your readers from becoming confused.

- Define unusual terms.
- Tell a story to illustrate the problem.
- Be specific—your audience might not be as familiar with the issue as you are.
- Describe conditions your readers may not know about.
- Give reasons for your conclusions.

APPLYING WHAT YOU'VE LEARNED
Check your essay to see whether you can make your ideas clearer or more complete.

 WRITING HANDBOOK

For more on elaboration, see page 783 of the Writing Handbook.

THINK & EVALUATE
Preparing to Revise
1. Which part of your draft do you feel is the strongest? the weakest? Why?
2. What else would you like to find out about your problem or the solution you are suggesting? Where might you go to answer remaining questions?
3. How can you improve the way you explain your solution?

WRITING FROM EXPERIENCE **381**

Writing Skill: COHERENCE
L You can help students check the coherence of their writing by having them select the MVS—the "most valuable sentence"—in each paragraph. Have students, working with a renamed copy of their file in order to protect the original essay, delete all but the MVS from each paragraph in order to see the main idea. Using the reduced text as an outline, students can return to the original text to add proof, examples, and details.

Writing Skill: INTRODUCTION
M Remind students that they can use a personal anecdote, a statistic, a description, a quotation, a dialogue, or an example to open their essay in an exciting way. Invite volunteers to share the openings they created. Have the rest of the class critique each opening, offering praise as well as suggestions for revision, if needed.

Speaking, Listening, and Viewing: DEBATE
N Arrange students in small groups to allow for peer review of the assignment. To help each writer to see other solutions to his or her problem and to judge the solutions presented, suggest that group members "debate" each topic. After every student has read his or her paper, divide the group in half. One half should argue in favor of one side of the issue, and the other half should argue in favor of the other side.

SkillBuilder  WRITER'S CRAFT

ELABORATING ON IDEAS Tell students that other effective means of elaboration include facts (statements that can be verified by an authority, observation, or experience), statistics (facts that involve numbers), sensory details (words that appeal to one or more of the five senses), incidents (happenings or occurrences), examples (instances of something), quotations or dialogue (a speaker's exact words).

Application Arrange students in pairs. Ask partners to read each other's essay and to underline all instances of elaboration, such as definitions, facts, statistics, details, incidents, and quotations. Direct students to focus their attention on sentences in which nothing is underlined; these sentences might require more elaboration.

Additional Suggestions Have students draw a flow chart to show the steps from problem to solution. Guide students to add details as branches from the main diagram.

Reteaching/Reinforcement
- Writing Handbook, anthology pp. 783–784
- *Writing Mini-Lessons* transparencies, p. 34

Developing a Topic, pp. 205–210

THE LANGUAGE OF LITERATURE TEACHER'S EDITION **381**

Writing Skill: REVISING

O Tell students that the strengths and the weaknesses of a piece of writing are often easier to recognize if the writer lets his or her work "cool off" before revising, thus enabling him or her to look at the work as a reader rather than as a writer. If possible, have students set aside their essays for a few hours or a day before they revise them. Be sure that students use the Standards for Evaluation as they revise.

Teaching Strategy: MODELING

P Invite a volunteer to read aloud the model newspaper article. Explore how the article is organized by outlining it on the board. Then discuss how the opening quotation grabs the reader's attention. The first-person point of view and the personal anecdote also contribute to a lively opening paragraph. Students should also note the sentence variety—that is, the mix of long and short sentences.

The conclusion is powerful because the writer states the advantages of his plan: it is inexpensive and it is easy. Stating the advantages limits readers' potential objections and sets the stage for acceptance of the solution. The conclusion is also effective because it suggests a course of quick action and points out a possible result of not taking action.

REVISING AND PUBLISHING

Polishing Your Draft

Adding the Final Touches Your draft is almost ready to present. Here are some matters to take care of before you share your solution to the problem you have explored.

Student's Newspaper Article

Fair Ball for All!

"Last year 24 students were hurt on the playing field, and that was before the games even started!" That's what our principal, Ms. Tailor, said when I asked her whether after-school sports at our school were dangerous. I already knew they were. I got hurt last week.

After-school sports are a problem for everyone at school: the guys, girls, and teachers. Every day when the bell rings, all the kids race out to the field to claim the baseball diamond for their team. The problem is, only two teams can play at once but there are three grades sharing the field. Usually the seventh- or eighth-grade guys beat us sixth-grade guys to the mound. Whenever we get there first, they try to kick us off. Sometimes there are fights. This is dangerous for both the students and the teachers who have to break them up. Because of this we sixth-grade guys hardly ever get to use the diamond. The girls always get left out, no matter what grade they're in.

I have an idea that will solve our problems. It won't cost a lot of money or take much time to organize. We could probably put my plan into action by next week. Here's my solution.

If you think my idea is a good one, you should tell Ms. Tailor or write a note and put it in the suggestion box in her office. If we don't solve this problem soon, you could be the next one to get hurt!

(continued)

382 UNIT THREE: A SENSE OF FAIRNESS

---

❶ Revise and Edit

Now that you've written about your problem, you probably understand it better and may see some ideas that need fixing up. Consider these points as you revise your essay.

- Peer comments may point to places where you could add facts, statistics, or examples to make your explanation stronger.
- The Standards for Evaluation on the next page will help you explain your problem and solution clearly and accurately.
- Look at the model on this page to see how one student elaborated on ideas to make his explanation clearer and more interesting.

What about the opening paragraph of this article grabs your interest and makes you want to read further?

P

How has this student made the conclusion to his article powerful?

Student's Petition

Petition for After-School League

We the students of Bedford Middle School would like to organize an after-school softball league. This is in order to avoid the problems we have had when lots of kids get left out or get hurt trying to claim the field for their team.

We think any 6th, 7th, and 8th graders interested in playing softball should be placed on teams so that everyone gets to play. A schedule should be made so all teams play each other. If this happens, then no "unorganized" teams can use the baseball diamond after school, only teams in the league.

To encourage teamwork, we think there should also be playoffs at the end of each quarter between the two teams with the best records. Maybe the school can even award the winning team something like a free lunch the next day.

Name	Grade	Room
1. Alice Chan	7	210
2. Lizzy Wills	7	211
3. Mario Sanchez	6	113
4. Miki Jasinski	8	271
5. Joey Ali	6	113

② Share Your Work

Circulating a petition like the one above is one way to help others become part of a solution. Perhaps seeing your efforts will encourage others to take action on their own.

PUBLISHING IDEAS

- Deliver a "Lunchtime Soapbox" presentation to inform your classmates about the problem and your ideas to solve it.
- Make and display posters in your school or neighborhood.

Standards for Evaluation

A problem-solution essay
- explains the problem clearly and accurately, and tells why a solution is necessary
- has a workable solution that is explained well
- uses language, details, and examples that are appropriate to the audience
- has a conclusion that provides the information necessary for the audience to take action

---

SkillBuilder

 GRAMMAR FROM WRITING

Using Pronouns Correctly

The pronouns *we* and *us* are often used with nouns. You can decide which pronoun to use in your essay by saying the pronoun alone with the verb.

(We, Us) students play in a league. (We play . . .)

The older girls help (us, we) guys. (. . . help us)

GRAMMAR HANDBOOK

For more help with pronouns, see the Grammar Handbook, page 824.

Editing Checklist Use the following tips to finalize your draft.
- Did you use correct pronouns?
- Are proper nouns capitalized?
- Are quotations punctuated correctly?

REFLECT & ASSESS

Evaluating the Experience

1. What did you learn about the problem you chose to explore?
2. Compare this assignment with others, such as writing an anecdote or a character sketch. Which type of writing do you enjoy most? Why?

📁 **PORTFOLIO** Add a note to your essay, explaining how successful you were at problem-solving.

WRITING FROM EXPERIENCE **383**

Speaking, Listening, and Viewing:
NEWS CONFERENCE

Q Invite students to work in teams to stage news conferences announcing the problems and solutions they have described in their essays. Each team should elect a moderator to introduce each speaker. If possible, videotape the news conferences so that participants can view their performance later.

Teaching Strategy: MANAGING THE PAPER LOAD

Respond to students' papers by tape-recording your comments rather than writing them down. Then have students listen to your remarks and make any desired changes in their essays.

PORTFOLIO

Create a student writing board to help you select writing pieces for inclusion in portfolios. Students can elect members to the board or you can select the student advisers.

Standards for Evaluation

Have students review their essay for the following:

Ideas and Content
- explains problem clearly, and tells why a solution is necessary
- presents a workable solution that is explained well
- supports discussion with quotes, facts, examples, details
- concludes by restating the problem and the proposed solution, and by providing information necessary for people to take action

Structure and Form
- uses well-organized paragraphs and a clear organization
- includes transitional words and phrases to show relationships among ideas
- uses a variety of sentence structures.

Grammar, Usage, and Mechanics
- contains no more than two or three minor errors in grammar and usage
- contains no more than two or three minor errors in spelling, capitalization, and punctuation

---

SkillBuilder GRAMMAR FROM WRITING

USING PRONOUNS CORRECTLY Remind students that *we* is a subject pronoun, used as the subject of a sentence or after a linking verb. *Us* is an object pronoun, used as the object of a verb or a preposition. Explain that in order to use *we* and *us* correctly, students must be able to identify how the pronoun is used in a sentence. Help students identify the object of a preposition. The pronoun that follows a preposition will always be an object pronoun, such as *us*. Review the forms of personal pronouns shown at the right.

Application Have students select the correct pronouns in each of the following sentences:

1. (We, Us) think the coach should let (we, us) schedule our own practice times.
2. (He, Him) is the tallest player on the team.
3. I returned Paula's math book to (she, her).
4. Where can (I, me) find the new computer game (they, them) told me about?

Reteaching/Reinforcement
- *Grammar Handbook*, anthology pp. 824–825
- *Grammar Mini-Lessons* copymasters, pp. 4, 13, 17; transparencies, pp. 4, 10, 11

 The Writer's Craft

Using Object Pronouns, pp. 444–445

	Subject	Object
Singular	I you she, he, it	me you her, him, it
Plural	we you they	us you them

THE LANGUAGE OF LITERATURE TEACHER'S EDITION **383**

UNIT REVIEW

This feature allows students to reflect on what they have learned in Unit Three and to assess how well they understand what they have learned. This feature provides students with multiple opportunities for self-assessment, although you may wish to use some of the activities to informally assess specific skills such as speaking and listening or cooperative work.

Objectives

- To allow students to reflect on and assess their understanding of theme
- To allow students to reflect on and assess their understanding of literary concepts such as point of view and suspense
- To provide students with the opportunity to assess and build their portfolios

REFLECTING ON THEME

OPTION 1

Have students in each group work together to assign roles. Suggest that students review their particular selection and take notes about their characters that they can refer to when role-playing. Make sure that students respond to the quotation in a manner consistent with their characters.

OPTION 2

Students can first work alone to generate a list of personal qualities so that each group has a wide range of alternatives from which to choose the top ten. Students may need to refer back to the selections as they brainstorm their lists.

OPTION 3

Make sure that partners are able to support their decisions with details from each selection. You may wish to have partners compare their charts with other pairs and discuss their particular choices, especially if they are having difficulty classifying a selection in their charts.

Self-Assessment Suggest that students focus on concrete ways they have learned to change unfair situations. Students may wish to apply what they have learned to real-life situations that they or someone they know may have experienced.

REFLECT & ASSESS

UNIT THREE: A SENSE OF FAIRNESS

By reading the selections in this unit, you have become aware of a wide range of unfair situations and an equally wide range of responses to them. Think over what you've learned. Choose one or more of the options in each of the following sections.

REFLECTING ON THEME

OPTION 1 Role-Playing a Response A quotation from Martin Luther King, Jr., opens this unit: "Injustice anywhere is a threat to justice everywhere." Form a discussion group, with each member taking the role of a person from one of this unit's selections. Respond to the quotation. Then pick one response that you think best reflects your own thoughts.

OPTION 2 Making a Top-Ten List In dealing with life's injustices, which individuals from the unit responded with hope, with wisdom, or with determination? Work with a team of classmates to brainstorm a list of the top ten personal qualities it takes to overcome an unjust situation.
Consider . . .
- what actions were taken in each case
- the outcomes of the actions
- how each person reacted to success or failure

OPTION 3 Evaluating Causes With a partner, look over six selections in this unit. Make a chart, writing the titles of selections that end fairly under the column heading "Fair." Under the column headings "Unfair" and "Unsettled," list the selections whose endings fit these categories. In your notebook, briefly analyze how unfair situations in the selections come about.

Self-Assessment: Now that you've considered how people sometimes treat one another, describe what you have learned about how to change an unfair situation. In your notebook, describe how you will use what you've learned the next time you or someone you know is treated unfairly.

REVIEWING LITERARY CONCEPTS

OPTION 1 Thinking About Point of View
Usually, a story is told either from the first-person point of view or from the third-person point of view. Compare the points of view used in the selections in this unit (not including poetry) by filling out a chart like the one shown. (One example has been done for you.) Then circle the titles in which you think the choice of point of view had a strong effect on you.

Selection Title	Main Character	First-Person Point of View	Third-Person Point of View	Effect on Selection
"Shrewd Todie and Lyzer the Miser"	Todie		✓	You know what happens to him and you know his thoughts.

384 UNIT ONE: A SENSE OF FAIRNESS

OPTION 2 **Looking at Suspense** A graph that records the suspense in "User Friendly" has been started here. Copy the graph. List three more key events in the selection, and draw a dot beneath the number that shows the level of suspense in each. Do the same with two other selections. Discuss your graphs with a partner. See if you agree about the most suspenseful events.

	least suspenseful → most suspenseful									
Suspense Scale	1	2	3	4	5	6	7	8	9	10
Louis the computer asks Kevin a question it isn't programmed to ask.			●							

Events of "User Friendly"

PORTFOLIO BUILDING

- **QuickWrites** Some of the QuickWrites assignments in this unit involved writing letters. If you did these assignments, review your work to choose two letters you like. Did you do a good job of allowing your personal voice (or the voice of a character) to come through? Explain why you chose them. Then add the letters and the explanation to your portfolio.

- **Writing About Literature** Earlier in this unit, you analyzed the plot of a story. Did writing a plot analysis teach you anything new about the story? Did you enjoy the story more after analyzing it closely? Make a list of any new information that you learned, and attach it to your plot analysis.

- **Writing from Experience** In writing your problem/solution essay, you had a chance to take a step toward solving a problem that has meaning for you. Have you taken any of the steps that you proposed in your essay? What were the results? Looking back, would you now suggest any new ways of solving the problem? Include your thoughts with your problem/solution essay.

- **Personal Choice** Write a brief update of your progress to add to your portfolio. (If you began an oral log of reactions to your work in Unit One, you may prefer to update your progress orally on the audiotape.) Review your work for the Alternative Activities and Another Pathway assignments, as well as the evaluations of all the projects you did for this unit. Identify skills or strategies in which you have shown improvement (for example, taking notes, using vivid words, or speaking clearly). Put your update into your portfolio.

Self-Assessment: Along with point of view and suspense, the following literary terms were discussed in this unit. In your notebook, draw a target. Near the center or bull's-eye of the target, write the terms you understand well. Along the outer rings of the target, write the terms you don't understand or have forgotten the meanings of. Use the Handbook of Reading Terms and Literary Concepts on page 762 to review those terms.

alliteration   description
couplet   humor
sensory details

Self-Assessment: Compare your choices for your portfolio in Unit Three with the choices that you made in earlier units. In your notebook, write a note comparing a recent and an early piece. Point out the strengths that the recent piece shows.

SETTING GOALS

How well are you working with others, particularly in group situations? Are you willing to share your ideas? Do you listen carefully to the ideas of other group members? Do you respond sensitively? Write a suggestion or two to keep at hand as you prepare for group work in the next unit.

REFLECT & ASSESS **385**

SETTING GOALS

In order to help students answer these questions and set future goals, you may wish to have them create charts that list their strengths and weaknesses in working with others. Remind students to set reasonable goals for working better with others and to list practical suggestions to which they can refer in the future.

REVIEWING LITERARY CONCEPTS

OPTION 1

Have students pay attention to the clues in each selection that reveal the point of view used, such as the use of personal pronouns. Make sure students explain why the particular point of view had a strong effect on them.

OPTION 2

Make sure that students support their decisions regarding the levels of suspense with details from the selections. Encourage students to analyze and discuss with their partners how their graphs change as each story develops.

 **Self-Assessment** For terms that students place in the outer rings of their targets, have them write, in their own words, a definition for each term after checking in the Handbook. Then have students apply each term to a selection they have read. For instance, a student can briefly describe the use of alliteration in a poem or identify the sensory details an author uses in a particular selection.

PORTFOLIO BUILDING

You may wish to help students choose or modify options for them that best suit the goals you have established for the class. As students reflect on and assess their development and progress, it may be helpful for them to refer to drafts of their writings as well as final products.

 Self-Assessment To help students compare early and recent pieces of writing, suggest that they consider how easy or difficult it was for them to complete the writing assignment and how much revision was involved in reaching the final product.

UNIT FOUR

UNIT FOUR

PROVING GROUND

All serious daring starts from within.

EUDORA WELTY
American Writer

UNIT THEMES

Unit Four

Proving Ground In this unit, students will read selections in which characters undergo tests that challenge their beliefs and values. This unit contains two parts: Part 1, "Showing Your True Colors" and Part 2, "Taking Necessary Steps." Selections in both parts contribute to the unit theme by exploring situations in which people are forced to prove themselves and take steps in order to successfully confront challenges and make important decisions in their lives.

Part 1

Showing Your True Colors Selections in Part 1 detail the stories of people who show their true colors when faced with an important challenge, as occurs in "The Secret of the Wall" when a young boy learns who his friends really are after he finds himself trapped in a house that is being demolished.

Part 2

Taking Necessary Steps Selections in Part 2 emphasize the steps certain characters must take in order to prove themselves in a challenging situation, such as a young boy's story of responsibility and determination in "My Friend Flicka."

Links to Unit Six

The Oral Tradition Unit Six, "Across Time and Place," contains literature from the oral tradition that connects with the themes in Unit Four. You may wish to begin or end Unit Four by using the following selections from Unit Six that relate to the theme "Proving Ground":
- "Arachne," p. 710
- "Three Strong Women," p. 715
- "The White Buffalo Calf Woman and the Sacred Pipe," p. 723

Out at Third, Nelson Rosenberg. Watercolor and gouache on paper, 15" × 21 ½", acquired 1939, The Phillips Collection, Washington, D.C.

Art Note

Out at Third by Nelson Rosenberg
Reading the Art How does the artist convey the game's sense of speed, movement, and excitement in this painting? If you were a sportscaster, how would you call this play?

Exploring Theme

To help students explore the connections between the art, the quotation, and the unit theme, have them consider the following questions:

1. What do you think a proving ground is? *(Possible responses: A proving ground is a place where someone undergoes a test or faces a challenge in order to prove him- or herself. It means having to confront a difficult situation that results in you learning about your abilities as an individual.)*

2. What does Eudora Welty's quote mean to you? *(Possible responses: The quote says that ability to successfully face a challenge, make a decision, or pass some kind of test comes from inside a person. A person has to truly believe that he or she is capable of meeting a challenge head on in order to succeed in life.)*

3. How is a baseball game, such as the one depicted in the painting, like a proving ground? *(Possible responses: In a baseball game, two teams compete against each other to prove which is the better. Each team tries to face the challenge presented by the other team. Also, players try to do their best in their positions, proving themselves to be as good as possible.)*

4. What kinds of stories do you think you will read in this unit? *(Possible responses: The stories will be about people who have to face a variety of challenges in order to prove that they have what it takes to succeed.)*

5. Think back to an experience in which you had to prove yourself in the face of a challenging situation. Discuss how you set out to meet the challenge. What did you learn, either about yourself or others, that you may not have known before? How do you think this experience prepared you for other challenges in the future? *(Responses will vary.)*

THE LANGUAGE OF LITERATURE **TEACHER'S EDITION** 387

UNIT FOUR
Part 1 Skills Trace

ML DENOTES MINI-LESSON IN TEACHER'S EDITION

Selections	Reading Skills and Strategies	Literary Concepts	Writing Opportunities	Speaking, Listening, and Viewing
FICTION **The Secret of the Wall** Elizabeth Borton de Treviño	Context clues, PE p. 389 Using context clues, **ML** TE p. 401	Characterization, PE p. 403 Suspense, PE p. 403 Main and minor characters, **ML** TE p. 394	Description, PE p. 402 Description, **ML** TE p. 400	Background music, PE p. 403 Role-playing, **ML** TE p. 392 Newscasts, **ML** TE p. 396
NONFICTION **from Talking with Artists** Pat Cummings	Relating cause and effect, **ML** TE p. 407	Interview, PE p. 412 Author's purpose, **ML** TE p. 408	Review, PE p. 412 Dedication, PE p. 412 Schedule, PE p. 412	Monologue, PE p. 412 Interpreting an illustration, PE p. 413
FICTION **The White Umbrella** Gish Jen	Making inferences, PE p. 414 Making inferences, **ML** TE p. 416	Symbol, PE p. 422 Setting, **ML** TE p. 418	Motto, PE p. 423 Mother's Day card, PE p. 423 Comparison and contrast paragraph, **ML** TE p. 419	
POETRY **Concrete Cat** Dorthi Charles **Chang McTang McQuarter Cat** John Ciardi	Concrete poems, PE p. 424	Rhyme scheme, PE p. 428 Repetition, PE p. 428 Characterization, **ML** TE p. 427	Poem, PE p. 428 Letter, PE p. 428 Story, PE p. 428 Critique, **ML** TE p. 425	Collage, PE p. 428 Cats in art, PE p. 429
NONFICTION **from Gold and Silver, Silver and Gold** Alvin Schwartz	Problem solving, PE p. 431 Predicting, **ML** TE p. 432	Tone, PE p. 439 Internal conflict, **ML** TE p. 434	Ballad, PE p. 439 Log entry, PE p. 439 Last will and testimony, PE p. 439 Legal brief, PE p. 440 Adventure story, **ML** TE p. 432 Paragraph, **ML** TE p. 433	Television talk show, PE p. 439
NONFICTION ON YOUR OWN **from Champions** Bill Littlefield			Journal, TE p. 443	Role-playing, TE p. 445 Class discussion, TE p. 447

Writing	Reading Skills and Strategies	Literary Concepts	Writing Opportunities	Speaking, Listening, and Viewing
WRITING ABOUT LITERATURE **Creative Response**	Analyzing setting, PE p. 448 Analyzing description, PE pp. 448–49 Responding to literature, PE pp. 450–53	Setting, PE p. 448 Descriptive language, PE pp. 448–49	Write descriptive sentences, PE p. 449 Write a descriptive paragraph, PE p. 449 Personal response essay, PE pp. 450–53	Analyze body language, PE p. 449 Viewing a scene, PE p. 454 Interpreting a scene, PE p. 454 Discussion, PE p. 454 Brainstorm questions, PE p. 455

387a UNIT FOUR PROVING GROUND

Grammar, Usage, Mechanics, and Spelling	Multimodal Learning	Research and Study Skills	Vocabulary
Final silent e words and suffixes, ML TE p. 391 Using commas to separate ideas, ML TE p. 398	Diorama, PE p. 403 Converting money, PE p. 403 Role-playing, ML TE p. 392 Newscasts, ML TE p. 396 Montage, ML TE p. 399	Taking objective tests: True/false questions, ML TE p. 395	clamor revulsion deceit saunter illiterate scornful induce sullen morosely turmoil
Irregular past participles, ML TE p. 409 The prefix com-, ML TE p. 410	Monologue, PE p. 412 Interpreting an illustration, PE p. 413	Research artists, PE p. 413	client commercial commitment mimicking unique
Pronouns and antecedents, ML TE p. 420 The suffixes -ible and -able, ML TE p. 421		Taking standardized tests, ML TE p. 417	audible illuminate confirm maneuver credibility resume discreet revelation diverted stupendous
	Collage, PE p. 429 Cats in art, PE p. 429		
Irregular plural nouns, ML TE p. 437 The suffixes -ence and -ent, ML TE p. 438	Television talk show, PE p. 439 Costumes or models, PE p. 440	Research pirates, PE p. 440 Skimming, ML TE p. 436	mutiny
	Role-playing, TE p. 445		

Grammar, Usage, Mechanics, and Spelling	Multimodal Learning	Research and Study Skills	Media Literacy
Understanding complete subjects and predicates, PE p. 449 Using time-order transition words, PE p. 451	Analyze body language, PE p. 449 Viewing a scene, PE p. 454 Interpreting a scene, PE p. 454 Discussion, PE p. 454 Brainstorm questions, PE p. 455	Using a sequence chart, PE p. 450	Analyze body language, PE p. 449 Viewing a scene, PE p. 454 Interpreting a scene, PE p. 454 Discussion, PE p. 454

UNIT FOUR
Part 2 Skills Trace

ML DENOTES MINI-LESSON IN TEACHER'S EDITION

Selections	Reading Skills and Strategies	Literary Concepts	Writing Opportunities	Speaking, Listening, and Viewing
NONFICTION **At Last I Kill a Buffalo** Luther Standing Bear	Setting a purpose, PE p. 457 Setting a purpose, ML TE p. 460	Imagery, PE p. 468 Point of view, ML TE p. 465	Narrative poem, PE p. 468 Letter, PE p. 468 Diary, ML TE p. 459 Description, ML TE p. 465	Oral history, ML TE p. 464
NONFICTION **Tutankhamen** *from* **Lost Worlds** Anne Terry White	Skimming and scanning, PE p. 470 Skimming, ML TE p. 477	Informative nonfiction, PE p. 478 Suspense, ML TE p. 475	Log entries, PE p. 478 Newspaper account, PE p. 478	Radio drama, PE p. 478 Mural, PE p. 479
POETRY **Pole Vault** Shiro Murano **Analysis of Baseball** May Swenson		Onomatopoeia, PE p. 484	Describe a sport, PE p. 480 Poem, PE p. 484 Cinquain, PE p. 484 Paragraph, ML TE p. 482	Sports broadcast or commentary, PE p. 484 How-to presentation, PE p. 485 Oral reading, ML TE p. 483
FICTION **My Friend Flicka** Mary O'Hara	Strategies for reading, PE p. 486 Predicting, ML TE p. 490 Connecting, ML TE p. 491 Evaluating, ML TE p. 496 Questioning, ML TE p. 497 Clarifying, ML TE p. 500	Plot, PE p. 504 Suspense, PE p. 504 Conflict, ML TE p. 495	Diary entry, PE p. 503 Guidelines, PE p. 503 Dictionary of horse terms, PE p. 504 Dialogue, ML TE p. 488	Readers theater, PE p. 503 Reading aloud, ML TE p. 502

Writing	Reading Skills and Strategies	Literary Concepts	Writing Opportunities	Speaking, Listening, and Viewing
WRITING FROM EXPERIENCE **Informative Exposition**			Writing a compare-contrast essay, PE pp. 506–13 Drafting, PE pp. 510–11 Using transitions, PE p. 511 Publishing, PE pp. 512–13	

Grammar, Usage, Mechanics, and Spelling	Multimodal Learning	Research and Study Skills	Vocabulary
Conjunctions, ML TE p. 461 Words ending with -ary, ML TE p. 466	Model, PE p. 469 Oral history, ML TE p. 464	Research Sioux culture, PE p. 469 Taking notes, ML TE p. 462	customary exploit gratification preceding sufficient
Commas in a series, ML TE p. 472 Words ending with c + ally, ML TE p. 473	Radio drama, PE p. 478 Mural, PE p. 479	Research ancient Egypt, PE p. 479 Multiple-choice tests, ML TE p. 474	dissuade intact sentinel systematically tedious
	Sports broadcast or commentary, PE p. 484 How-to presentation, PE p. 485 Oral reading, ML TE P. 483	Research pole vaulting, PE p. 485	
Comparative adjectives, ML TE p. 492 Final consonants and suffixes, ML TE p. 493	Readers theater, PE p. 503 Poster, PE p. 504 Reading aloud, ML TE p. 502	Research horse terms, PE p. 504 Graphic aids, ML TE p. 501	blissful prestige despair pursue envision rebellious fanatical refrain fidgety vague

Grammar, Usage, Mechanics, and Spelling	Multimodal Learning	Research and Study Skills	Media Literacy
Using transitions, PE p. 511 Using comparatives and superlatives, PE p. 513		Using graphic organizers, PE p. 509 Using K-W-L charts, ML TE p. 508	Reading an ad, PE p. 507

SKILLS TRACE   TEACHER'S EDITION   **387d**

UNIT FOUR
Recommended Resources

ENRICHMENT RESEARCH

Recommended Novels

 LITERATURE CONNECTIONS WITH SOURCEBOOK FOR TEACHERS

SPANISH VERSION AVAILABLE

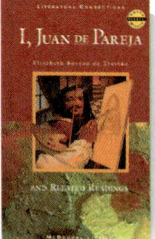

I, Juan de Pareja
by Elizabeth Borton de Treviño

Thematic Links On the threshold of a new life, Juan de Pareja, a Moorish slave in 17th-century Spain, reveals his personal discoveries as he tells of his life with his master, the famous Spanish painter Diego Velázquez.

About the Author Elizabeth Borton de Treviño (born 1904) bases her stories on true or historic events that appeal to her imagination. Her stories most often explore the theme of love.

Other Works by Elizabeth Borton de Treviño *Nacar, the White Deer; Casildo of the Rising Moon; Here is Mexico; Beyond the Gates of Hercules: A Tale of the Lost Atlantis; Juarez: Man of Law; El Güero*

Toning the Sweep
by Angela Johnson

Thematic Links Visiting her grandmother in a small southern desert town, Emmie discovers secrets about her mother's and grandmother's past that help her define her own identity.

About the Author Angela Johnson (born 1961) worked for Volunteers in Service to America before establishing herself as a writer of juvenile fiction.

Other Works by Angela Johnson *Humming Whispers*

The Midwife's Apprentice
by Karen Cushman

Thematic Links In this starkly realistic historical novel set in medieval England, a homeless, unconfident girl grows into a self-assured, financially secure young woman.

About the Author Karen Cushman (born 1941) writes realistic fiction about everyday people in medieval England.

Other Works by Karen Cushman *Catherine, called Birdy*

 **LITERATURE CONNECTIONS WITH SOURCEBOOK FOR TEACHERS**

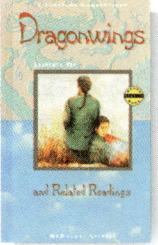

Dragonwings
by Laurence Yep

Thematic Links Chinese immigrant Moon Shadow and his father Windrider endure both discrimination and the San Francisco earthquake as they boldly pursue a dream of creating and flying an airplane.

About the Author Laurence Yep (born 1948), a Californian of Chinese-American ancestry, involves all readers in the problems of his protagonists.

Other Works by Laurence Yep *Sweetwater, The Child of the Owl, Sea Glass, The Dragon of the Lost Sea, The Rainbow People, American Dragons*

Mattie's Whisper
by Alice Delacroix

Thematic Links Caring for a lame horse helps a disabled girl overcome her own physical limitations.

About the Author Alice Delacroix (born 1940) grew up on an Indiana farm. Her fiction is usually set in the country and involves nature and animals.

Darnell Rock Reporting
by Walter Dean Myers

Thematic Links Darnell Rock, who is always in trouble for something, is more surprised than anyone when an article he writes for the school paper influences a City Council decision. This unexpected praise and notoriety helps Darnell realize his potential as a writer.

About the Author Although praised for his versatility as an award-winning author of fantasy, science fiction, picture books, and nonfiction, Walter Dean Myers (born 1937) is best known for his books about African-American teens growing up in Harlem.

Other Works by Walter Dean Myers *Fallen Angels, Scorpions, Somewhere in the Darkness*

For Teacher **TEACHING LITERATURE**

Baloche, Linda, and Mauger, Marilyn Lee, et al. "Fishbowls, Creative Controversy, Talking Chips: Exploring Literature Cooperatively." *English Journal* 82 (October 1993): 43–49.

Mitchell, Diana. "Ways into Literature." *English Journal* 84 (September 1995): 106–111.

Slapin, Beverly, and Seale, Doris. *Books without Bias: Through Indian Eyes.* Berkeley, CA.: Oyate Press, 1988.

Stotsky, April. "Changes in America's Secondary School Literature Programs." 76 *Phi Delta Kappan* (April 1995): 605–614.

Whittier, Gayle. "Alternative Responses to Literature: Experimental Writing, Experimental Teaching." *The Clearing House* 68 (Jan-Feb 1995): 167–71.

387e UNIT FOUR PROVING GROUND

CROSS-CURRICULAR TEACHING   PROFESSIONAL DEVELOPMENT

Recommended Readings in Cross-Curricular Areas

SCIENCE

Jonas Salk: Discoverer of the Polio Vaccine
by Carmen Bredson (1993)
This accomplished scientist is known for his discovery of the polio vaccine as well as for his work on influenza and AIDS. His life and work are discussed. Links to Elizabeth Borton de Treviño's "The Secret of the Wall."

SOCIAL STUDIES

Native Americans, the Sioux
by Richard Erdoes (1982)
Traditional and modern practices of the Sioux are described, as well as the tribe's history and land. Links to Luther Standing Bear's "At Last I Kill a Buffalo."

HISTORY

The Sea Rovers
by Albert Marrin (1984)
The escapades of various male and female pirates are described in exciting detail. Links to *Gold and Silver, Silver and Gold,* "Tutankhamen," and "The Secret of the Wall."

Into the Mummy's Tomb
C. N. Reeves (1992)
Insight into what it was like when the famous Egyptian King's tomb was opened. Links to Anne Terry White's "Tutankhamen" from *Lost Worlds.*

For Teacher   CROSS-CURRICULAR INSTRUCTION

Barlow, Dudley. "Turning Students into Historians." *Education Digest* 60 (October 1994): 45-49.

Bonds, C. W., et al. "Curriculum Wholeness Through Synergistic Teaching." *The Clearing House* 66 (March-April 1993): 252-255.

McDaniel, Janet E. and Francisco A. Rios. "Do as We Do and as We Say: Modeling Curriculum Integration in Teacher Education for Middle School Teachers." *Middle School Journal* 26 (November 1994): 14-20.

Recommended Media Resources

THE LANGUAGE OF LITERATURE

LASERLINKS
Videodisc, Gr. 6
See *LaserLinks Teacher's Source Book,* pages 42–43, for an overview of Unit Four.

AUDIO LIBRARY
Tapes
Unit Four: Proving Ground
Gr. 6, Tape 8: Sides A & B
Gr. 6, Tape 9: Sides A & B

WRITING COACH
Writing Coach Software: Writing About Literature: Interpretive Response; Comparison-and-Contrast Essay

OUTSIDE RESOURCES

Films/Videos/Film Strips/Audiocassettes
Esso. 16 mm film, William Weintraub for Atlantis Films, Ltd. and the National Film Board of Canada. Norwood, MA: Beacon, 1985. (26 minutes).
Follow My Leader. 16 mm film, Bernard Wilets, with the International Guiding Eyes of Sylmar, Calif. Van Nuys, CA: AIMS Media, 1988. (42 minutes).
Treasure Island. videocassette. Culver City, CA: MGM/UA Home Video, 1989.

Internet Resources
Literature and Language Arts Center at http://www.hmco.com/mcdougal/lit/litcent.html

For Teacher   TEACHING WITH TECHNOLOGY

Computing Teacher. International Society for Technology in Education (ISTE), 1787 Agate St., Eugene, OR 97403-1923.

Dyrli, Odvard Egil. "Integrating Technology into Your Classroom Curriculum." *Technology and Learning* 14 (February 1994): 38-44.

Stearns, Peggy Healy. "Laser Lessons: Making Technology Work in the Classroom." *Electronic Learning* 14 (October 1994): S1-3.

UNIT FOUR
Professional Enrichment

Developing a "Nose for News"

A class of news hounds? Make it so! Newspaper writing teaches students how to organize their ideas, focus on audience and purpose, and use key supporting details. It's an ideal way to explore informative writing.

Try this assignment to link writing and literature: invite students to write a newspaper account of King Tut in the style of a modern newspaper.

You may wish to spark ideas by having a small group of students re-enact the events described in the King Tut selection from *Lost Worlds*. The other students should act as observers. When the re-enactment is completed, ask the observers to give their accounts of events. Then have the students in the scene explain the events from their perspective. Guide students to distinguish between the facts and opinions in the two accounts. Explain that effective news stories use *facts* to tell about the people, places, things, and ideas.

TELL IT LIKE IT IS!
As a matter of fact, "just the facts" is the slogan for many news stories—and with good cause! People who write newspaper articles strive first and foremost for objectivity. They want to convey the facts quickly and clearly. Try the following ideas for helping your students write first-rate newspaper accounts of King Tut.

- Bring in some newspaper articles for students to read. Try to include school newspapers, a local daily and weekly, a city daily, and a national daily. Arrange students in small groups to skim the articles to find facts and opinions. Discuss the proportion of facts and opinions.
- Then have students see how the stories begin and what makes them interesting to read.
- Direct students to think about their audience. Who is going to read their work? Their classmates? You? Students can jot down a few notes to see how much their readers are likely to know about the subject.
- Then have students research their topic. They can start by rereading the excerpt from *Lost Worlds* on page 470. Then they can look in an encyclopedia and books about Egypt and King Tut for additional facts.
- Suggest that students organize their ideas on index cards or the computer.
- Explain to students that newspaper readers want to get the facts right away. To meet their readers' needs, newspaper writers place the main idea first in a sentence called the lead. The lead answers the 5 W's and H: *Who? What? When? Where? Why? How?*
- Explain that the lead must also grab the reader's attention. Students can work with partners to sharpen their leads.

- Suggest that students include quotations in their news stories. Explain that direct quotations make news stories credible and interesting.
- Instruct students to use concise, direct language. Encourage students to simplify their language by eliminating all unnecessary words and phrases. They should also use specific rather than general nouns and active rather than passive verbs.
- Caution students to omit their own opinions. They should stick with words that express facts, rather than those that express feelings. Help them double-check for loaded modifiers and slanted language.
- Remind students that newspaper space is at a premium. Guide them to pack as much information into as little space as possible. You may wish to set an actual word limit to help students edit their work completely.
- Students may want to use a computer to set their finished stories into columns.
- Combine the stories to create a class newspaper. Students can name their newspaper to reflect the assignment. If students work on a computer, they may wish to select a type face, or font, for the titles that matches the Egyptian theme.

Related Reading

 Atwell, Nancie. *In the Middle: Writing, Reading, and Learning with Adolescents.* Portsmouth: Boynton/Cook 1987.

 Krementz, Jill. *How It Feels to Fight for Your Life.* New York: Little, Brown, 1989.

 Little, Jean. *Little by Little: A Writer's Education.* New York: Viking, 1988.

Family and Community Involvement

 Family

By completing some of the Copymasters for Unit Four your students, their families, and other community members can make important connections outside the classroom as they explore real-life examples of people who prove themselves.

OPTION 1: HAVE A DISCUSSION ABOUT PROVING YOURSELF

- **Connection** All of the selections in Unit Four connect to the theme of proving oneself.
- **Activity** *Copymaster, page 1* Students engage in discussions about experiences in which they had to prove themselves to family members. A chart is provided to record important parts of the discussion.

OPTION 2: READ ARTICLES ABOUT TESTS OF PERSONAL STRENGTH

- **Connection** In many of the selections in Unit Four, characters find themselves facing challenges that test their inner strength.
- **Activity** *Copymaster, page 2* Students and family members read current newspaper or magazine articles about people who have faced challenges that tested their physical or emotional strength. Students then discuss their impressions of each person, the tests he or she faced, and what they learned about each person.

OPTION 3: CREATE A PUZZLE OF CHANG MCTANG MCQUARTER CAT

- **Connection** The speaker of the poem "Chang McTang McQuarter Cat" describes the true colors of his cat in intimate detail.
- **Activity** *Copymaster, page 3* Students work with family members to plan and create a puzzle that captures some of the qualities of the mysterious cat described in the poem. A word web is provided to record some of the details about the cat.

 Community

OPTION 1

- **Connection** The main character in "The Secret of the Wall" is a young Mexican boy recovering from polio.
- **Activity** Invite parents of students who have lived in or visited Mexico to share with the class their knowledge of its history, resources, and legends.

OPTION 2

- **Connection** In the excerpt from *Talking with Artists*, a well-known illustrator shares insights into his career and work.
- **Activity** Have the class interview a local artist about his or her work and career. Encourage students to generate a list of possible questions before the guest arrives.

UNIT FOUR
Part 1 Cooperative Project

Gathering Oral Histories

Overview

Students will collect and present oral histories from older members of the community, with an emphasis on how they proved something to themselves or others.

PROJECT AT A GLANCE
The selections in Unit Four, Part 1 are about people facing important or difficult decisions or challenges. The decisions might be ethical, moral, or emotional; the challenges, mental or physical. For this project, students will interview some of the older members of their family, the neighborhood, or the community to gather oral histories. Students will formulate questions that will lead interviewees to tell about a time when they had to make a decision that was difficult or proved important in their lives. These histories may be presented to the class on videotape or audiotape, in writing, or orally.

OBJECTIVES
- To identify appropriate interview subjects
- To formulate a list of interview questions
- To conduct oral interviews
- To work cooperatively to organize and present oral histories

SUGGESTED GROUP SIZE
3–4 students

MATERIALS
- Examples of oral-history books
- Videocassette recorder, camera, and tapes (optional)
- Audiotape recorder and tapes (optional)

1 Getting Started

Arranging the Project
Collect books for students to look over that contain oral histories. Also collect some how-to books about conducting and compiling oral histories. If possible, select books by authors of different cultural, ethnic, and racial backgrounds.

How you shape this project may depend on the resources available to you. If you have access to video cameras and tape recorders, decide in which medium you expect the final histories to be given. If this equipment is not available, students can present the histories in written or oral form.

Arranging for Taping
If you decide to have the histories video- or audiotaped, you will have to make arrangements with the school to have the selected subjects come to the school to be interviewed. This also means that students will have to "pre-interview" subjects to narrow the field, rather than having dozens of people show up at the school. This requires scheduling a place and time for each interview, as well as someone who can operate the equipment. If the school media person is not available, you might ask parents to help students complete the interviews.

2 Creating the Oral Histories

Introducing the Project
Explain that each cooperative group will work together to draw up a list of questions designed to elicit an oral history that describes how the subject proved something to himself or herself or others. The group will then select an appropriate subject, pose the questions, and listen carefully to the oral history. The groups can tape their interviews or take notes for later use in written or oral presentations for the class.

Allow students to look over and compare the books that you gathered on oral history. They should especially note that oral histories are given in first-person form, as their presentations will be.

Also discuss some of the things that groups might consider when selecting appropriate subjects. They should note that the project is aimed at interviewing older members of the community. Encourage each group to talk to several people, then to select one person they all admire and who can tell interesting stories.

Group Investigations
Divide students into groups of three or four. Each group should work together to create a list of pertinent questions to ask their subject.

These questions should be designed to encourage the interviewee to tell about an important decision or challenge, not just a rambling life story. After the group has a list of questions, members can interview several possible subjects independently, then meet to decide which candidate would make the most interesting subject for in-depth interviewing. A final interview can be conducted and taped or written up for presentation.

Creating a Project Description
Meet with each group to review and help them refine the focus of their questions. Groups can then submit a final written list of questions. Meet periodically with groups to monitor their progress. Use class time to discuss any common problems students are experiencing as they begin initial interviews.

OPTION 1: MOST MEMORABLE HISTORICAL EVENT
Groups can interview older members of the community about the most memorable historical event they have witnessed in their lives. The answers might range from scientific inventions to assassinations. Subjects should be encouraged to tell why they think this event was so memorable and why they consider it challenging.

387i UNIT FOUR PROVING GROUND

OPTION 2: NARROW THE FIELD Ask students to find and interview subjects who fall into a particular category, such as those who were part of the peace protest in the 1960s, or African-Americans who were children in the 1930s. Groups can interview several people who were part of that period and draw general conclusions as to what the specific period was really like.

If you are taping interviews, be sure the subjects are aware of the focus of the project and realize who will see or hear the tape. Ask them for permission to tape the interviews and offer them a copy of the final tape, if appropriate.

3 Sharing the Histories

Culmination of the project will, of course, depend on how you shaped the project. In one form or another, the histories should be presented in front of the class. Those groups presenting written work should also read these histories in front of the class. Each history should be discussed by all students and critiqued as to whether the content shows the subject making a decision that proves something to himself or herself or to others. Written work can be bound into a class book.

Assessing the Project

The following rubric can be used for group or individual assessment.

3 Full Accomplishment Students follow directions and produce an oral history that shows how the subject proved something to himself or herself or to others.

2 Substantial Accomplishment Students produce an oral history, but the focus of the presentation is not clear.

1 Little or Partial Accomplishment Students' oral history is incomplete or does not fulfill the requirements of the assignment.

For the Portfolio
You might want to keep master copies of any tapes in your classroom for future reference. Include in students' individual portfolios their written work as well as a copy of your written assessment.

Note: For other assessment options, see the *Teacher's Guide to Assessment and Portfolio Use.*

Cross-Curricular Options

ART
Students can create portraits of the subjects or a collage of pictures that show items and events of importance to the subject. Encourage students to use different media.

SOCIAL STUDIES

Students can interview people who have immigrated to the United States from different countries. They should focus the interviews on learning what is similar and different about the two countries, while inviting subjects to compare and contrast their lives in the two places.

MATH

Students can interview people of various ages to find how much they were paid for their first job. They can plot these amounts on a scattergram where one axis represents the hourly wage and the other represents the range of ages of the subjects.

Resources

"Writing Personality Profiles: Conversations Across the Generation Gap" by Janet M. Beyersdorfer and David K. Schauer in *Journal of Reading* 35 (May 1992) 612–16 discusses how interviewing can benefit students.

UNIT FOUR
Part 1 Lesson Planner

TIME ALLOTMENTS SHOWN ARE APPROXIMATE. DEPENDING ON YOUR GOALS AND THE NEEDS OF YOUR STUDENTS, YOU MAY WISH TO ALLOW MORE OR LESS TIME FOR CERTAIN PORTIONS OF THE LESSON.

Table of Contents	Discussion	Previewing the Selection	Reading the Selection
PART OPENER **SHOWING YOUR TRUE COLORS** What Do You Think? page 388	**20 MINUTES** • Reflect on the part theme		
SELECTION The Secret of the Wall page 390 CHALLENGING		**10 MINUTES** • PERSONAL CONNECTION • HISTORICAL CONNECTION • READING CONNECTION: Context clues	**45 MINUTES** • Introduce vocabulary • Read pp. 390–401 (12 pp.)
SELECTION from Talking with Artists page 406 AVERAGE		**20 MINUTES** • PERSONAL CONNECTION • CULTURAL CONNECTION • WRITING CONNECTION	**25 MINUTES** • Introduce vocabulary • Read pp. 406–11 (6 pp.)
SELECTION The White Umbrella page 415 AVERAGE		**15 MINUTES** • PERSONAL CONNECTION • CULTURAL CONNECTION • READING CONNECTION: Making inferences	**30 MINUTES** • Read pp. 415–21 (7 pp.)
SELECTIONS Concrete Cat Chang McTang McQuarter Cat page 425 EASY		**15 MINUTES** • PERSONAL CONNECTION • SCIENCE CONNECTION • READING CONNECTION: Concrete poems	**10 MINUTES** • Read pp. 425–27 (3 pp.)
SELECTION from Gold and Silver, Silver and Gold page 432 AVERAGE		**20 MINUTES** • PERSONAL CONNECTION • HISTORICAL CONNECTION • READING CONNECTION: Problem solving	**25 MINUTES** • Introduce vocabulary • Read pp. 432–38 (7 pp.)
FICTION ON YOUR OWN from Champions page 441 AVERAGE			**20 MINUTES** • Read pp. 441–47 (7 pp.)
Writing WRITING ABOUT LITERATURE Creative Response	**Writer's Style** **20 MINUTES**	**Prewriting** **25 MINUTES**	**Drafting and Revising** **80 MINUTES**

Time estimates assume in-class work. You may wish to assign some of these stages as homework.

Responding to the Selection

FROM PERSONAL RESPONSE TO CRITICAL ANALYSIS	OR	ANOTHER PATHWAY	LITERARY CONCEPTS	QUICKWRITES
		45 MINUTES		
• Discussion questions	OR	• Discussion	• Characterization • Suspense	• Speech • Newspaper account
		50 MINUTES		
• Discussion questions	OR	• Monologue	• Interview	• Review • Dedication • Schedule
		40 MINUTES		
• Discussion questions	OR	• Story map	• Symbol	• Motto • Mother's Day card
		45 MINUTES		
• Discussion questions	OR	• Collage	• Rhyme scheme • Repetition	• Poem • Letter • Story
		50 MINUTES		
• Discussion questions	OR	• Television talk show	• Tone	• Ballad • Log entry • Last will and testament

Extension Activities

- ALTERNATIVE ACTIVITIES
- LITERARY LINKS
- CRITIC'S CORNER
- THE WRITER'S STYLE
- ACROSS THE CURRICULUM
- ART CONNECTION
- WORDS TO KNOW
- BIOGRAPHY

50 MINUTES — ✓ ✓ ✓ MATH ✓ ✓

25 MINUTES — ✓ ✓ ✓ ✓

20 MINUTES — ✓ ✓ ✓

20 MINUTES — ✓ ✓ ART ✓

45 MINUTES — ✓ ✓ ✓ ✓

Publishing and Reflecting	Grammar in Context	Reading the World
30 MINUTES	**10 MINUTES**	**25 MINUTES**

LESSON PLANNER TEACHER'S EDITION **387I**

PART 1

WHAT DO YOU THINK?
Objectives

The activities on this page can be used to
- introduce the Part 1 theme, "Showing Your True Colors," since each activity is connected to one or more of the selections in Part 1
- create materials for students' personal portfolios that they can later reconsider or revise
- build an understanding of theme that can be reviewed and revised as students progress through the unit

Are finders truly keepers?
Tell students to think of ways to display the results of their survey, such as in graphs or charts. You might also encourage students to brainstorm a list of other hypothetical situations that they can use for a survey of classmates. (See "The Secret of the Wall," p. 389.)

What are the pieces of a friend?
Have students first jot down a list of qualities from which they can select ideas for their puzzle. Students should draw the puzzle on a piece of paper or cardboard and then cut out jigsaw pieces. Encourage students to exchange puzzles with classmates and to see whether they can put them together. (See "The Secret of the Wall," p. 389.)

Can you compose yourself?
Have partners write down their impressions of the song title in order to generate ideas for lyrics. Make sure that partners select a tune for which new lyrics can be written without too much difficulty. (All selections in this part connect to this activity.)

Do you just have to have this?
To extend this activity, you can suggest that students create drawings or collages to illustrate their lists or charts. (See "The White Umbrella," p. 414.)

UNIT FOUR PART 1

SHOWING YOUR TRUE COLORS

WHAT DO  THINK?

REFLECTING ON THEME

Showing your true colors is showing who you really are. The activities here deal with facing a test or challenge. Keep a record in your notebook of your ideas, impressions, and results. As the characters in Part 1 of this unit show their true colors, see how their experiences compare with yours.

Are finders truly keepers?
Survey your classmates to see what they would do if they found a wallet containing $100 in cash but no identification. Would they turn it in? Would they keep it? Have students express their opinions on small slips of paper, fold them in half, and drop them into a box. Tabulate the results and share them with the class.

What are the pieces of a friend?
Design a jigsaw puzzle that conveys the qualities you seek in a true friend. The puzzle might picture an act of friendship or show phrases that express your ideas. Add your puzzle to a class display.

Can you compose yourself?
Work with a partner to compose a song called "Showing My True Colors." Choose a tune familiar to both of you, then write new lyrics for it. The lyrics should tell a story or give an example that illustrates the idea of the title. Sing or play your song for the class.

Do you just have to have this?
What kinds of material possessions are important to people your age? Why are they important? In your notebook, list some of these items. For each item, briefly explain why owning it is important and what it reveals to others about the person who owns it. Compare your chart with those of your classmates.

388

PARENTAL INVOLVEMENT
Instruct students to work with a parent or other relative to draw a comic strip that details a situation in which a child wants to prove himself or herself to a parent or other adult. They should work together to select a situation or a topic to illustrate and then should plan each frame of the strip. Urge students to share their comic strips with the class.

COMMUNITY OUTREACH
Have students work in small groups to write brief skits that they can perform for younger children in their school system or for a community organization, such as a nursing home. Skits should be based on situations in which people undergo a test or challenge that helps reveal their true colors. Group members should work together, first to outline their skit and then to write the entire skit. Encourage groups to rehearse their skits before they perform them. Suggest that groups invite comments from the audience on how people can show their true colors.

388 THE LANGUAGE OF LITERATURE **TEACHER'S EDITION**

PREVIEWING

FICTION

The Secret of the Wall
Elizabeth Borton de Treviño (dĕ trĕ-vē′nyô)

PERSONAL CONNECTION Activating Prior Knowledge/Setting a Purpose

What are the most important qualities a friend should have? In your notebook, make a chart similar to the one shown. List the three qualities that you value most in a friend. Number them in order of importance to you. Then get together with one or two classmates and compare your charts. As you read, see whether you change your ideas about the qualities a friend should have.

Qualities of a Friend
1.   2.   3.

Building Background
HISTORICAL CONNECTION

The narrator and his two friends live in Guanajuato (gwä-nä-hwä′tô), a city in the rugged central highlands of Mexico. At one time, the mining of silver brought wealth to Guanajuato, but in 1821, troubled times began. Mexico had freed itself from Spanish control, but wars and revolutions shook the country for another hundred years. The desperate citizens of Mexico hid silver and other valuables from the bands of raiding soldiers and revolutionaries who battled back and forth across the country, trying to gain control.

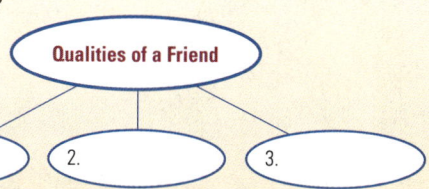

Map of Mexico

Active Reading
READING CONNECTION

Context Clues In describing the character Serafin's movements early in the story, the author uses the word *sauntered*. In the next sentence, she says Serafin "walked down one of the corridors slowly, looking at his feet." The second sentence provides **context clues** that can help you understand what *saunter* means—"to walk in a leisurely and casual way." Sometimes the author uses a Spanish word and then restates it or defines it in the same sentence. For example, she refers to "the *secundaria*, our high school." When you read an unfamiliar word in this or any story, look at surrounding words or sentences for clues to its meaning.

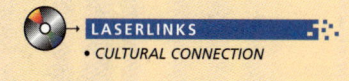
• CULTURAL CONNECTION

389

OVERVIEW

Objectives

- To understand and appreciate a short story about two boys who find hidden treasure
- To enrich reading by using context clues
- To identify and appreciate characterization
- To express understanding of the selection through a choice of writing forms, including a speech and a newspaper article
- To extend understanding of the selection through a variety of multimodal and cross-curricular activities

Skills

READING SKILLS/ STRATEGIES
• Using context clues

THE WRITER'S STYLE
• Details appealing to smell

GRAMMAR
• Using commas to separate ideas

LITERARY CONCEPTS
• Main and minor characters
• Characterization

SPELLING
• Final silent e words and suffixes

STUDY SKILLS
• Taking objective tests

SPEAKING, LISTENING, AND VIEWING
• Role-playing
• Newscasts
• Viewing art
• Group discussion
• Oral presentation

Cross-Curricular Connections

GEOGRAPHY
• Cantaranas Plaza

HISTORY
• The Mexican Revolution

MATH
• Trade and monetary systems

SCIENCE
• Polio

 CULTURAL CONNECTION
Mexican Culture Through these historical and contemporary images, students will see the richness of Mexican culture. You may wish to use them to generate discussion about differences or similarities between the settings they depict and the settings of the story.

Side A, Frame 38818

PRINT AND MEDIA RESOURCES

UNIT FOUR RESOURCE BOOK
Strategic Reading: Literature, p. 4
Vocabulary SkillBuilder, p. 7
Reading SkillBuilder, p. 5
Spelling SkillBuilder, p. 6

GRAMMAR MINI–LESSONS
Transparencies, pp. 28, 29, 30
Copymasters, pp. 37, 38, 39

WRITING MINI–LESSONS
Transparencies, p. 38

ACCESS FOR STUDENTS ACQUIRING ENGLISH
Selection Summaries
Reading and Writing Support

TEACHER'S GUIDE TO ASSESSMENT AND PORTFOLIO USE

FORMAL ASSESSMENT
Selection Test, pp. 79–80
Test Generator

AUDIO LIBRARY
See Reference Card

 **LASERLINKS**
Cultural Connection
Art Gallery

THE LANGUAGE OF LITERATURE TEACHER'S EDITION **389**

SUMMARY

Carlos, the Mexican boy telling this story, is recovering from polio. His physical weakness sets him apart from his classmates; the only student who befriends him is a boy named Serafin, who turns out to be selfish. Carlos finds a second friend in Martin Gonzalez, a shy workman who cannot read or write. Carlos writes letters for him. From Martin, Carlos learns about an old house that is being torn down. Serafin convinces Carlos to sneak into the house with him one night to try to find hidden treasure. Carlos squeezes through a hole in the wall and finds a secret passageway, but soon he gets trapped inside. Carlos moves slowly through the passageway and—to his shock—finds a skeleton holding a treasure box. He gropes his way back to where he started, hoping that Serafin will bring help. Instead his rescuer is Martin, who has wisely followed Carlos's barking dog to the old house. For his efforts, Martin receives half the money in the skeleton's box. Meanwhile the cowardly Serafin, who never even tried to help his friend, learns a moral lesson: Carlos gives Serafin part of the treasure, but gets him to donate the money to a new school.

Thematic Link: *Showing Your True Colors*
Serafin's reaction when Carlos is trapped inside a wall makes the reader wonder if he is a true friend after all.

CUSTOMIZING FOR
Students Acquiring English

- Use **ACCESS FOR STUDENTS ACQUIRING ENGLISH,** *Reading and Writing Support.*
- Encourage students to use suggestions from the Reading Connection to guess the meanings of unfamiliar words. You may want to have native and nonnative speakers work in pairs to establish meanings for some unfamiliar words.

STRATEGIC READING FOR
Less-Proficient Readers

Set a Purpose Ask students to think about how they have formed friendships with classmates. Have students read to find out about the relationship between the narrator and Serafin.

Use **UNIT FOUR RESOURCE BOOK,** pp. 4–6, for guidance in reading the selection.

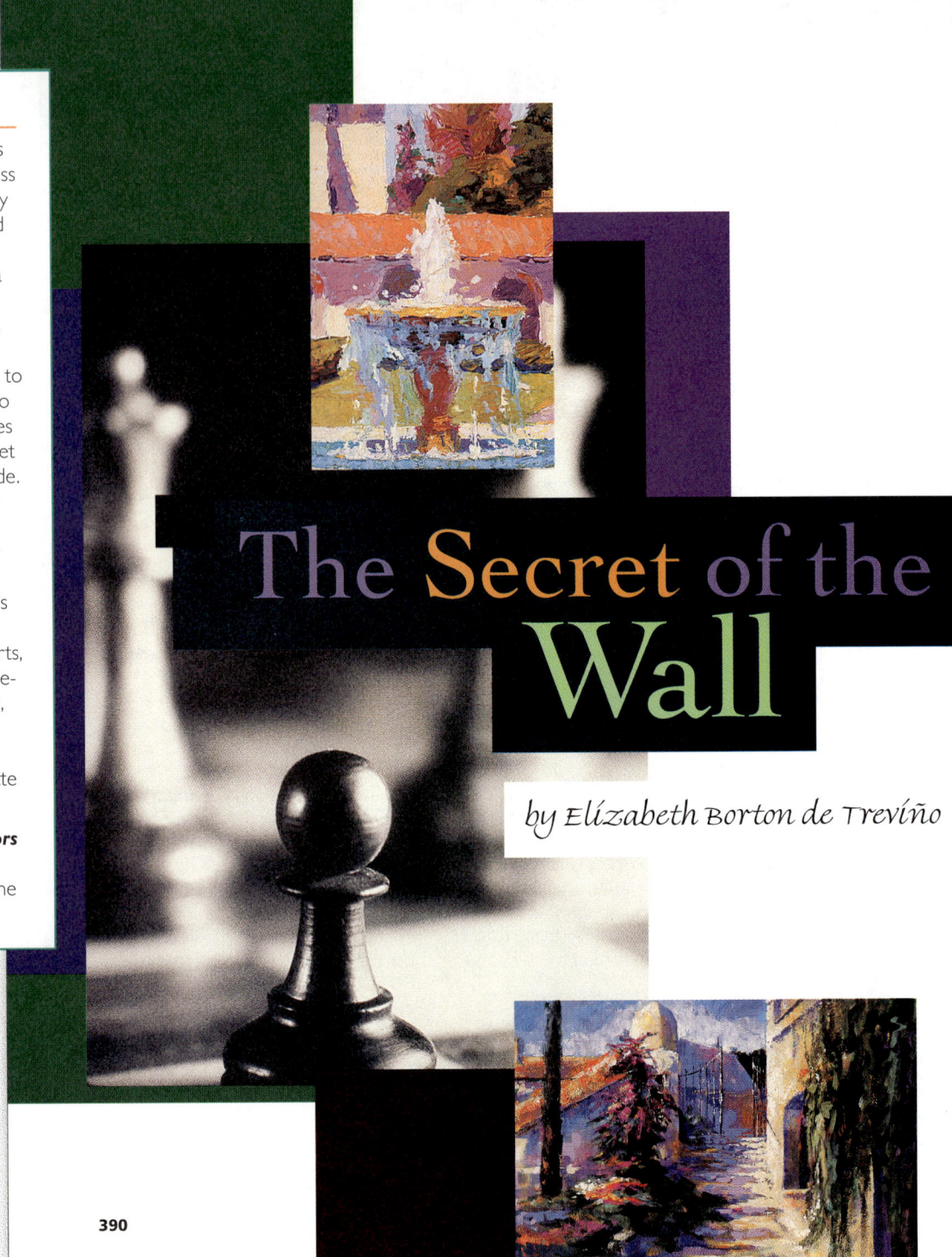

The Secret of the Wall

by Elizabeth Borton de Treviño

WORDS TO KNOW

clamor (klăm′ər) *n.* a loud noise; uproar (p. 401)
deceit (dĭ-sēt′) *n.* the act of misleading by false appearance or statement; dishonesty (p. 397)
illiterate (ĭ-lĭt′ər-ĭt) *adj.* not able to read or write (p. 394)
induce (ĭn-dōōs′) *v.* to persuade (p. 401)
morosely (mə-rōs′lē) *adv.* in a gloomy, bad-tempered way (p. 392)
revulsion (rĭ-vŭl′shən) *n.* a feeling of disgust or horror (p. 399)

saunter (sôn′tər) *v.* to walk in a leisurely and casual way (p. 391)
scornful (skôrn′fəl) *adj.* full of disgust or the feeling that something is unworthy (p. 395)
sullen (sŭl′ən) *adj.* showing irritation or unhappiness by a gloomy silence; moody (p. 391)
turmoil (tûr′moil′) *n.* a state of great confusion or upset; commotion (p. 391)

390 THE LANGUAGE OF LITERATURE TEACHER'S EDITION

On a day in September, I walked down to Cantaranas Plaza and past it, along the narrow cobblestone street, and there was the great *zaguán,* the entrance to the *secundaria,*[1] our high school. Beyond I could see the broad, white, ascending steps of the university, where I would go one day.

The streets of Guanajuato smell of dried chilies, of jasmine and carnations in pots behind the iron-barred windows, of hot baked bread and of burro droppings. It is my town in central Mexico, a romantic old town that has lived days of wealth and luxury, because of the rich silver mines nearby, and days of poverty, because of the turmoil of revolutions and social change. Heroism has been here, in these little winding alleys and broad, fountain-centered plazas. Faith is here, in our many beautiful churches, soaring into the sky. Many artists have lived here and loved Guanajuato and painted it. My family has lived here since the days of my great-grandfather, and I always knew the legends of some of the streets, of many of the old houses, and the stories of ghosts and hauntings, some violent, some tender.

School smelled like schools everywhere, of chalk dust and disinfectant soap and boys. I found my classroom and a seat on the aisle where I could rest my leg by extending it out along my desk. Three years ago I had had polio.[2] It left me weak in the back and in one leg; I still have to take special exercises and wear a brace for some hours every day. But Dr. Del Valle, who took care of me when I was sick, had said at last that I could walk to and from school every day and that I would be getting stronger all the time. Yet I knew that I would not be able to take part in the games or play out in the court during recess. All the boys were younger than I, but almost all were taller and broader, too. The only one I knew was Serafin, Dr. Del Valle's youngest boy. He stood half a head taller than any of the others and was handsome and strong. I thought, Serafin will surely captain one of the ball teams—soccer or basketball or baseball—and he will be president of the class.

But I was wrong. When the first recess for games came, I went to sit under the arcades[3] and watch, and I saw the shouting boys choose up sides. The games professor passed out mitts and bats and balls. Serafin was a swift runner, but he didn't try very hard. He seemed uninterested and when one of the other boys jostled him, he dropped out. "Coward!" they called after him, but he just shrugged his shoulders. He came over and sat down by me, looking very sullen.

"It's a silly game anyhow," he said.

"I wish I could play!" I burst out.

"Why?" he asked. "You don't get anything out of it. It's just exercise. Getting knocked about and hurt sometimes. Foolishness. I play a much better game, by myself, every day."

"You do? What game?"

"I may tell you someday." Then he got up and sauntered off. He walked down one of the corridors slowly, looking at his feet, and then he stooped to pick up something and put it in his pocket. I turned my eyes back to the noisy fun in the school patio. I had hopes of distinguishing myself in another way. My father is a fine chess player, and groups of the

---

1. *zaguán* (sä-gwän') ... *secundaria* (sĕ-kōōn-dä'ryä) Spanish.
2. **polio:** short for *poliomyelitis,* the name of a disease that often results in muscle weakness and crippling.
3. **arcades:** covered passageways.

WORDS TO KNOW
turmoil (tûr'moil') *n.* a state of great confusion or upset; commotion
sullen (sŭl'ən) *adj.* showing irritation or unhappiness by a gloomy silence; moody
saunter (sôn'tər) *v.* to walk in a leisurely and casual way

best players in our town meet at our house on Saturday evenings. During the years of my illness, Papacito[4] had taught me how to play and had bought me a small chess set that was portable and on which the pieces could be fixed so that a game might go on from where it had been left off days before. There were no gentlemen in Papacito's chess circle who were unwilling to sit down to a game with me, and once I had even beaten Don[5] Mario, the postman, who often came. He was Guanajuato's champion.

Limping home, after that first day in class, I tried to place Serafin in my chess game. A knight? Perhaps. Not a bishop or a tower. And, of course, not a pawn. He was too independent for that.

As I passed Cantaranas Plaza, I saw several country fellows with their weary burros, taking water at the fountain, and I sat there a moment, on the lip of the fountain, dipping my hand in the water and talking with them. As they went away, single file, down the street toward the country, the dusty peons,[6] who worked on buildings in the city, came tramping along. They smelled of sweat and of chili, and though they were so tired that they could scarcely lift their feet, they laughed and joked with each other. Many were boys not much older than I. I felt sorry that they could not be in school, but I knew that most of them worked to help support families.

Tía[7] Lola had made my favorite *polvorones*[8] for supper, to celebrate my first day back at school. Tía Lola is Papacito's sister, who came to live with us after my mother's death. When we had finished supper that night, we sat and talked for half an hour before Papacito went into his library to work and study.

> "That's my game," he told me suddenly one day. "Finders keepers!"

As the days went by I became more interested in all my classes. I often took my chessboard to school, and while the others were at games, Professor Morado sometimes played with me. The boys were pleasant, but careless with me; they thought me a cripple, because I had to wear my brace some days. Only one sought me out. Serafin. I took this philosophically, for I had observed him, and he, who could have done so, did not try to make friends. When the boys shoved him in the halls or pushed at him, he backed away and seemed to be afraid of them. I suppose he thought that I, so obviously outside the circle of the other boys in class, would be grateful for his company. And, in a way, that was true.

He began walking home with me afternoons, sometimes chatting, sometimes morosely making no comment on anything I said. He often leaned down to pick up a button, or a bit of cord, or a pin.

"That's my game," he told me suddenly one day. "Finders keepers!"

"How silly! You can't often find anything worthwhile."

---

4. **Papacito** (pä-pä-sē′tô) *Spanish:* dear Papa.
5. **Don** (dôn) *Spanish:* a title of respect, like *Mr.* or *sir.*
6. **peons** (pē′ŏnz′): unskilled laborers.
7. **Tía** (tē′ä) *Spanish:* aunt.
8. **polvorones** (pôl-vô-rô′nĕs) *Spanish:* cinnamon cookies.

WORDS TO KNOW
morosely (mə-rōs′lē) *adv.* in a gloomy, bad-tempered way

392

Copyright © Camille Przewodek.

"Oh, but you're wrong! I often do! I must have 100 pesos[9] worth of stuff piled up at home that I found this way. Besides, just now we were only wandering along. But sometimes I pick out somebody and follow them.

"You'd be surprised how often they put down a package and forget it, or leave their umbrella, or even drop money!"

"But . . . but . . ." I stuttered, "if you see them drop something, you ought to give it back!"

"No," he answered stubbornly. "Finders keepers. That's the game."

"But what do your parents think about this? Tía Lola would never let me keep anything I found if it were valuable. Or my father either. I'd have to find out who it belonged to and give it back, or give it to the poor."

"Ah, my father and mother don't even know about my game, and I shan't tell them," he responded. "Papá is always out, all hours of the day or night on his calls, and Mámacita is usually in bed with a headache. They don't care what I do."

---

9. **pesos** (pā′sōz) *Spanish:* units of Mexican money.

THE SECRET OF THE WALL **393**

Multicultural Perspectives

EDUCATION IN MEXICO In Mexico, as in the United States, children's education is compulsory. Programs generally provide two years of preprimary education, six years of primary education, and three years of secondary instruction. In the cities, educational opportunities are greater and schools more comprehensive than in rural areas. Private schools in Mexico are usually parochial institutions. At the highest level, there are several dozen universities—including two large schools in Mexico City and the university in Guanajuato.

Literary Concept: MAIN AND MINOR CHARACTERS

F Remind students that even imaginary creatures and animals in a work of literature are considered characters. The narrator's dog, a minor character, first appears on this page. Ask students how a nonspeaking character, such as the dog, could help a writer tell a story. *(Possible response: the dog might serve as a character to whom others speak, revealing their feelings. An animal might react to what it senses is going on.)*

Critical Thinking: HYPOTHESIZING

G Have students hypothesize about why Martin chose the narrator to write his letter. *(Possible response: Martin had observed him and perceived him to be studious and a friendly boy.)*

Active Reading: CONNECT

H Some students may be familiar with the word *evangelist*. Give volunteers an opportunity to tell what they already know about the meaning of this word. Then challenge students to connect the more common use and meaning of *evangelist* with its use in the story.

Think-Aloud Model *I think* evangelist *means "a kind of preacher," or "someone who writes or spreads news." Would it be correct to say that the evangelists in Guanajuato are spreading news in a more general sense?*

I was troubled about all this, but I did not talk it over with my father or Tía Lola for a very selfish reason: I had no other friend, and I did not want to be deprived of Serafin, unsatisfactory and worrisome though he was. I knew he was cowardly, secretive, and selfish, but he was a companion. So I kept silent, though I never did go to his house. He sometimes came to mine, but only to talk or play with my dog in the patio.

I was not very lonely. I often went to Cantaranas fountain and took my chessboard. I could work out problems in chess there and watch the people passing by.

I was doing this about five o'clock of a November day when dusk was beginning to let down veils of darkness over the town. I had just closed my chessboard and was about to start home when a workman came toward me from one of the streets that led down into town. From his plaster-covered shoes and the sacking that he still wore over his shoulders, and his dusty shirt and trousers, I could tell he was probably working on one of the new buildings that were going up near the entrance of the city.

He was about nineteen, I thought. He smiled at me shyly.

"I have seen you going to high school early in the morning," he said.

He paused and shuffled his feet. "And I have seen you sitting here in the afternoons, studying."

"That's right."

"My name is Martin Gonzales," he said, suddenly, after a long pause. "I am going to ask you to do me a favor."

"Gladly, if I can." I thought he might ask for a peso.

"I want you to write a letter for me."

"But I have no paper and envelope."

"Bring them tomorrow and write a letter, please. I will pay you the fee."

That night at supper I said, "Papacito, I am going to be an evangelist."

All the men who sit at their typewriters in the big main square downtown are called, by the country people, *evangelists,* after St. John the Evangelist, I suppose. These men keep a few legal forms in their pockets and write collection letters and the like. Quite a few are busy writing personal letters for the people who cannot read or write.

"But you have no typewriter!" cried Tía Lola, serving me a big dish of *chongos,*[10] my favorite dessert.

"I will only do this one letter. It is for a nice fellow, a laborer. I suppose he is illiterate."

Papacito sighed. "We have too many of them," he said. "Mexico needs more schools, more teachers. We have made some progress, but not enough."

The next day Serafin wanted me to go with him rambling through the town, playing that game of finders keepers. But I told him about the letter I was to do. He made a face and would not come with me. But he said, "A workman on buildings? Maybe he will know where they plan to knock down some old places. Ask him."

I waited for Martin and wrote his letter for him. It was a note to a girl in another town. He was ashamed for her to know that he could not write, and if he had gone to one of the evangelists down in the main square, she would have suspected, knowing very well that he had no typewriter.

---

10. **chongos** (chŏng′gôs) *Spanish:* a custard made with eggs and milk.

WORDS TO KNOW
illiterate (ĭ-lĭt′ər-ĭt) *adj.* not able to read or write

394

 Mini-Lesson Literary Concepts

Character(s)	Character's Role in the Story
Papacito's chess group	Boosts Carlos's confidence; gives Martin a chance for a better life
Tuerto	Leads Carlos's rescuer, Martin, to the wall where he is trapped
Dr. Del Valle	Treated Carlos's illness; ensures that Serafin apologizes for abandoning Carlos

MAIN AND MINOR CHARACTERS
Remind students that the most important characters in a work of literature are called main characters. Less important characters are called minor characters.

Application Working individually or in pairs, have students list three or more minor characters in the selection on a chart such as the one at left. Tell students also to record each minor character's role in the story.

I accepted the payment he offered me, so as not to wound his pride and so as to leave the door open for him should he want me to do other letters for him. Like my father, I felt very sad that this big, nice man could not read or write.

He put the letter away carefully inside his dirty shirt and turned his bright eyes toward my chessboard. I asked if he knew the game, but he shook his head. Idly I explained the moves and the names of the pieces.

Then began a curious friendship. Martin passed by the fountain every afternoon, sometimes bringing with him another big, shy workman who wanted a letter. I began to develop a small but regular business, and I looked forward to that hour in Cantaranas Plaza. It comforted me to think I was doing something useful, and I began to plan on teaching them to read a little when vacations came.

Serafin was scornful and did not often drop by anymore. "How stupid!" he said. "Writing silly letters for oafs."

"Martin is no oaf! I am teaching him chess, and he will be a good player!"

"I don't believe it!"

"Stay and watch then! Here he comes now."

Martin came hurrying along. I presented them, and Serafin had the grace to take Martin's calloused hand, after it had been dusted against his trousers and deferentially[11] offered.

I had the pieces set up on my little board. Martin drew the white, so he had first move. He made an opening gambit[12] I had never before seen used. I did not know the defense, and he soundly beat me. Serafin's eyes were starting from his head, for like most of us boys in Guanajuato, he knew something of the game.

"*Caray*,[13] you stopped me in my tracks, Martin!" I cried. "Who showed you that gambit?"

"I made it up," he told me, pleased. "I thought about the chessboard all day, as I was working. I could see it in front of my eyes, and every piece, and so I played a game with myself, in imagination, and it seemed to me that the opening I used just now was a good one."

> I often went to Cantaranas fountain and took my chessboard. I could work out problems in chess there and watch the people passing by.

Martin arrived on Saturday evening in clean, freshly ironed cotton work clothes. Like all our country people, he has perfect manners, and, of course, so has my father and so have his friends. They made Martin welcome, and my father sat down to play his first game with him. To my amazement, he defeated my father in the first game, and the second one was a real struggle, finally ending in stalemate.[14] My father was perfectly delighted, and all the others crowded round to congratulate Martin.

---

11. **deferentially:** very respectfully.
12. **gambit:** in chess, an opening move designed to gain an advantage.
13. **caray** (kä-rī′) *Spanish:* an exclamation of surprise.
14. **stalemate:** in chess, a situation in which neither player can make a legal move, the results being a draw or tie.

WORDS TO KNOW
scornful (skôrn′fəl) *adj.* full of disgust or the feeling that something is unworthy

395

Mini-Lesson Study Skills

TAKING OBJECTIVE TESTS: TRUE/FALSE QUESTIONS Remind students that to answer a true/false question, they must read a statement and decide whether it is true or false. Share with students the following strategies:
- If *any* part of the statement is false, the answer is "false."
- Statements that include such words as *all, never, always,* and *none* are often, though not always, false.
- Statements that include such words as *generally, some, most, many,* and *usually* are often, though not always, true.

Application Have students apply the above strategies to answer the following true/false questions.
1. Many of the characters in "The Secret of the Wall" are good friends to Carlos. *(T)*
2. Carlos and his whole family forgave Serafin at the end of the story. *(F)*
3. Martin's ambition was to be a physician like Dr. Del Valle. *(F)*

THE LANGUAGE OF LITERATURE TEACHER'S EDITION **395**

Art Note

Mexican Boy by Victor Higgins Victor Higgins (1884–1949) was a member of the famed early twentieth-century Taos Society of Artists. His mature work links the artistic conventions of the past with the groundbreaking trends that emerged in the twentieth century. In addition to figures, he painted still lifes and landscapes, for which he is most noted.

Reading the Art *Which character does the figure remind you of most, the narrator, Serafin, or Martin? Explain your response with reference to details such as clothing, hairstyle, posture, and facial expression.*

CUSTOMIZING FOR
Students Acquiring English

(3) Demonstrate speaking with a chuckle for students.

Literary Concept:
AUTHOR'S PURPOSE

(K) Remind students that while an author may combine two or three purposes, one is usually the most important. Ask students what the author's main purpose in this selection is. *(to entertain)* Ask students what additional purpose is revealed by Carlos's father's explanation of why people often find buried treasure in Mexican homes. *(to inform)*

Cultural Note

(L) In Guanajuato, the tradition of serenading women at dusk is called the *callejoneando*. The young men who do this (usually university or high-school students) are known as the *estudiantina*. The young men traditionally wear black capes and sing love songs, accompanied by guitars and mandolins.

Mexican Boy (1926), Victor Higgins. Oil on canvas, 24" × 20", private collection. Photo courtesy of Gerald Peters Gallery, Santa Fe, New Mexico.

"Young man, you are a chess genius, I think!" cried Don Mario, the postman. "You must join us every Saturday! Keep our game keen!"

After he had left, my father and his friends talked excitedly about Martin. They had in mind to train and polish him, and enter him in the state championship chess games in the spring.

The next day there was a piece in the paper about a treasure having been found by workmen when tearing down an old house in Celaya. Under the flagstones of the patio they came upon a strongbox filled with silver coins. My father read the item aloud.

(3) "Too bad we live in a house built by my grandfather," chuckled Papacito, "and that I know he happened to die land-poor. And my father was a believer in banks."

"My friend Luisa, in Guadalajara, had a friend who found a buried treasure in the kitchen of the house they bought," contributed Tía Lola.

"Well, it happens often and it is reasonable," explained Papacito. "Mexico has gone through violent times, and insurgent[15] and revolutionary armies have swept in and out of so many towns that the people often buried or hid their valuables so as not to have to surrender them. And then, of course, sometimes they couldn't get back to retrieve them. Or they died, and nobody ever knew what had happened to their money."

I was thinking this over as I walked to school, and in the first recess Serafin sought me out, full of excitement.

"Did you read about the treasure in Celaya?" he asked me, breathless. "Let's go treasure hunting here! There must be quantities of old houses where people have buried money!"

"Well, yes. My father said there was every likelihood. But how? Which houses? And how would you start? Nobody would even let you begin!"

"Why couldn't Martin tell us where? He works with a wrecking crew, knocking down old houses, doesn't he? He could sneak us into one some night!"

"Tía Lola wouldn't let me go."

"Don't tell her!" counseled Serafin impatiently.

"Well . . ."

It is one of the joys in our town to go out in the dusk or in the evening, wandering through the narrow little alleys and streets, singing and serenading the young ladies behind their barred windows. I had never done this, because of my leg, but I was really strong enough to start out soon.

---

15. **insurgent** (ĭn-sûr′jənt): rebelling against a government.

396 UNIT FOUR PART 1: SHOWING YOUR TRUE COLORS

Mini-Lesson: Speaking, Listening, and Viewing

NEWSCASTS Discuss with students how radio and television journalists can make events come alive in carefully crafted newscasts. Point out that good journalists use vivid details and relate only the most important parts of any news story.

Application Have small groups of students create newscasts telling how Serafin and Carlos sneaked into the "haunted" house and found treasure held on the lap of the Lost Grandfather. If resources permit, allow students to tape-record or videotape their newscasts.

It was the deceit that unnerved me. But the call of adventure was strong, and, I'll confess it, I longed to go treasure hunting. I resolved to speak to Martin.

I had my chance when he stopped by Cantaranas Plaza after work. I was waiting for him.

"We began to tear down the old house of the Lost Grandfather today," he told me. "The workmen are not happy about it. They say it is haunted."

"Yes? Tell me about it?"

"The Lost Grandfather groans and howls there on windy nights; people have heard him. He was an old gentleman who simply disappeared during the Revolution."

"Strange. Aren't you afraid to work there, Martin?"

"I? No. I am only a simple, uneducated fellow. But I do not believe in ghosts," he told me, scornfully.

Serafin was eager to go out that very night, but he decided that he had better reconnoiter[16] first. But the next day at recess, he told me, in whispers, that the situation was perfect. There was a watchman, but he was very old and deaf, and did not know anything about the ghost.

"His daughter brings him his supper at about nine o'clock, and he eats it, and then he goes to sleep on some sacks in the back. To try him out, I even pounded on the gate and struck the rocks of the patio with a small steel bar I have. The old fool did not hear a sound. We'll go tonight!"

I was scared, but terribly eager to go just the same. Little prickles of excitement ran up and down my spine all day.

Just at dusk, Serafin came by for me. He had a long, paper-wrapped parcel under his arm. "An iron bar with a pointed tip," he said, "and a candle."

As we left I had a bad time with Tuerto, my little white dog with the black spot around one eye. Tuerto whined and begged to come with us, and he got out twice and had to be brought back in and scolded before he would not try to follow me. I believe he smelled my excitement.

As we came near the haunted house, we saw the watchman's daughter just arriving.

"Good! She's early!" hissed Serafin. She left the big *zaguán* slightly ajar as she went in, and, pulled and pushed by Serafin, I followed. We were inside!

We had to wait a long time, pressed up hard against the wall where we would not be seen, while the old watchman and his daughter talked a long time over some family problem. A little wind began to rise, and I shivered with nerves and with cold.

At last she left, calling *adios,* and the old man made the sign of the cross behind her as the *zaguán* clanged to. Then he shuffled off to somewhere in the back.

"Come in now," said Serafin. "He eats and rests way back there, where they have begun taking out the rear walls. I want to try inside, around the fireplace. That's where lots of treasures have been buried."

We went cautiously into the big central hall of the house. It was quite dark and very mysterious. A little light drifted in from the street, but the shadows were deep, and there were strange noises, little scurryings and rattlings. Our eyes grew used to the dark. Soon we made out the fireplace. From it stretched out two walls, at the far ends of which there were doors into other rooms.

"Let's sound those walls," suggested Serafin.

---

16. **reconnoiter** (rē′kə-noi′tər): to scout or explore.

WORDS TO KNOW
deceit (dĭ-sēt′) *n.* the act of misleading by false appearance or statement; dishonesty

---

Linking to Social Studies

 Point out that Guanajuato is not unique in having a town center such as Cantaranas Plaza—a large public space where people congregate. You may wish to show students photographs of public spaces that serve similar functions, such as the Piazza San Marco in Venice or the Jardin du Luxembourg in Paris. Students may be able to identify a space in their city or town that serves as a central meeting ground.

Linking to History

 The Mexican Revolution occurred in response to the long dictatorship of General Porfirio Díaz, who held power from 1877 to 1911 (except for one term, 1880 to 1884, when power nominally belonged to one of his aides). Díaz gave Indian lands to wealthy Mexican landholders, ignored an 1859 policy separating church and state, and paid little attention to education. Francisco Indalecio Madero, a revolutionary leader, was elected president in 1911. Not until 1917, however, were the goals of the revolution realized in a new constitution, which provided for a labor code, seized the property of religious orders, and returned Indian lands. Finally in 1934 a stable revolutionary government came to power, with the election of Lázaro Cárdenas. Cárdenas's party, the National Revolutionary Party, remains the most important political party in Mexico today.

Assessment ✓ Option

SELF-ASSESSMENT Students can assess their understanding of the selection by rewriting the story from a different point of view. Tell students that they need not retell the entire story, only the most important parts. Remind students to use their summarizing skills and to include relevant, lively details. To help students assess their understanding, have them ask themselves and then respond to the following questions.
- Why did I choose the point of view I used?
- How did my choice affect the tone of the story?
- What information in the story was most helpful for my rewriting?

Active Reading: CLARIFY

O Ask students to explain how the narrator finds himself trapped inside the wall. *(Possible response: Serafin widens the hole in the wall so the narrator can fit through. The narrator slips through the opening to "a very narrow passage" inside the wall. He lights a candle, then he hears a groan that startles him so that he drops the candle and hits the wall. Plaster and bricks fall down and cover the hole.)*

Critical Thinking: ANALYZING

P Have small groups of students discuss whether they think the narrator's confidence in Serafin is justified or misplaced. *(Possible responses: His confidence is justified. Even though Serafin is basically out for himself, he's not really an evil character and wouldn't leave his friend trapped inside the wall. The narrator's confidence is misplaced. Serafin is only using him and would be afraid to tell adults who could help that he and his friend broke into the house.)*

"You go along there, and I'll go here. See if they sound hollow to you. Like this." And he went along, giving a smart rap on the plaster. I dutifully did as I was told, almost forgetting the watchman, but the walls sounded the same along their length to me.

"We might as well open up anyhow and see how solid they are," whispered Serafin, and he went at a place in the wall not far from the chimney. I was terrified. It seemed to me that the clanging and banging would bring not only the watchman, but even people from the street, in upon us. However, Serafin labored away, to no avail.

"I'll try over here," he panted, and again he dug at the wall, but there seemed to be nothing but firmly set bricks inside.

"Here. You try." He gave me his improvised pick, and I went at a place on the other side of the fireplace. At first the plaster gave way easily. Then I came upon the same hard bricks. But as I struck and pried at them, one of them crumbled away, and another, and I put my hand in. There was an opening!

Serafin almost shouted in his joy. "I'll open it up more, and then you get inside and see what's there!" He worked away very fast and soon had a hole in the hollow wall through which I could just squeeze my shoulders.

"Get in!" he urged, and pushed me.

"It's terribly dark," I said. "Give me the candle."

He passed it in to me, and I lighted it. I stood inside the wall, in a very narrow passage. The air was still and dead, and the candle flickered along the wall.

And then suddenly there was a deep, mournful groan. I started and dropped the candle. As I struck against the wall, plaster

and bricks rained down, and I found myself cut off. I tried to scratch and scrabble my way out, but in the dark I had no way of knowing whether I would be able to get free again.

"Serafin!" I called with all my might, but there was no answer. Only, at my shout, more plaster and bricks fell.

I was scared to death. I stood there and cried, until I realized that I would have to be sensible and think.

I cannot pretend that I was able to do this immediately. I suffered from a confusion of feelings. I thought I might be buried alive; I feared our being caught in that house where we had no permission to be; I was frightened of the dark and of the sounds. But eventually I was able to control myself.

> And then suddenly there was a deep, mournful groan. I started and dropped the candle.

I was not scared by the groan. I did not believe in ghosts, and I knew there must be some natural explanation. I felt sure Serafin would go at once and bring help. And after a bit, I realized I would not smother, for there was a thin breath of air, from somewhere in the wall, that moved along my cheek.

It came to me, at last, that I might find some opening in the wall, and cautiously I started exploring. Luckily I had some matches in my pocket, and though I scrabbled around trying to find the candle, I could not. So I lit a match, and in that light went along, feeling the sides of the hollow wall close against me, until the match burned down to my fingers and I was in darkness again. In this way I passed around a bend in the wall, where it curved out around

398 UNIT FOUR PART 1: SHOWING YOUR TRUE COLORS

USING COMMAS TO SEPARATE IDEAS
Remind students that commas tell readers to pause. Give students the rules shown on the chalkboard. Commas prevent the running together of words or ideas that should be kept separate.

Application Have students rewrite the sentences below, using commas as necessary.
1. To find Carlos the dog ran swiftly through the streets.
2. Carlos Papacito Tía Lola and Tuerto lived in the same household.
3. Serafin had a better education than Martin but Martin was the more highly developed human being.

Reteaching/Reinforcement
- *Grammar Handbook*, pp. 843–845
- *Grammar Mini-Lessons*, p. 37, transparencies, pp. 28, 29, 30

The Writer's Craft
Commas That Separate Ideas, pp. 574–575

Use commas to separate items in a series.

Put commas before and, but, and or to combine complete sentences.

Use a comma to clarify meaning for the reader.

398 THE LANGUAGE OF LITERATURE TEACHER'S EDITION

Long Day's Shadow (1994), Marilyn Sunderman. Courtesy of the artist, Sedona, Arizona.

the fireplace I thought, and emerged into the wall beyond, which was also hollow. But there, as I lit a third match, I saw, suddenly illuminated, a skeleton fully dressed in the clothes of last century and sitting on a low bench. It was wedged between the walls, and on its knees was a box. It was a terrible figure, but even in that first moment of shock and revulsion, I felt pity. What had been a man must have had himself walled in here, with his treasure . . . and no one had ever come back to free him. Was it the Lost Grandfather?

I said a prayer for the soul of that pitiful skeleton man, and then tried to maneuver myself around in the wall and feel my way back whence I had come. I decided to save my matches, and when I felt the fallen rubble, I lay down, very gingerly, to wait for rescue, saying my prayers all the while.

I may have dozed, from fear and hunger and cold, for I awoke startled to hear a dog yelping. It was my Tuerto! And, as I came to myself and realized where I was, I heard scratching and striking along the wall. I hurried back, in case some more bricks should tumble down, but before long there was an opening, the rubble was being pulled away and there was Martin, looking in, with his face all pale and drawn.

"Thank God! He's all right!" he called.

| WORDS TO KNOW | **revulsion** (rĭ-vŭl′shən) *n.* a feeling of disgust or horror |

399

Mini-Lesson: Speaking, Listening, and Viewing

ART Remind students that editors of anthologies, such as their textbook, often work with graphic designers, who select art to help convey or elaborate on the meaning of a story. Point out that the setting of "The Secret of the Wall" is conveyed not only in words but also in the artwork on pages 393 and 399.

Application A *montage* is a composition of many different pictures or designs. Have students study the montage on page 390. Have small groups discuss the significance of each component of the montage. Ask students how color, shadows, and composition (the arrangement of pieces in the montage) communicate meaning.

THE LANGUAGE OF LITERATURE **TEACHER'S EDITION** 399

Active Reading: EVALUATE

Q Ask students why the narrator pities the "terrible figure" he finds behind the wall. *(Possible responses: The narrator is a sympathetic observer of anyone he encounters; he pities the man even though he is in a terrible situation himself.)*

STRATEGIC READING FOR Less-Proficient Readers

R Ask students to tell how the narrator and Martin both benefit from their friendship. *(The narrator writes a letter for Martin and teaches him to play chess. Martin rescues the narrator from inside the wall.)* Summarizing

Set a Purpose Have students read to find out what happens to the Lost Grandfather and his treasure.

Literary Concept:
CHARACTERIZATION

S Ask students what impressions they have of Tuerto based on the dog's actions. *(Possible responses: The dog loves his master. The dog is a loyal and true friend.)*

Active Reading: EVALUATE

T Ask students how this version of finders keepers is different from Serafin's version of the game. *(Possible response: Serafin's version of the game pays no heed to the rights or feelings of others; in contrast, Carlos's father attempts to give the treasure back to any living relatives of the dead man and pays the taxes before allowing his son and Martin to keep it.)*

And I heard Tía Lola and my father echo, "Thank God!"

He pulled me out, and Tuerto leaped upon me and almost smothered me with doggy kisses. Then I was enclosed in my aunt's arms, and I felt my father's hand on my hair.

I can't remember much more of what happened until they got me home and to bed, and Tía Lola gave me a drink of hot lemonade.

Serafin had abandoned me. They did not know he had even been with me, until I told them.

Martin had happened to come back to our house that evening, to tell my father he could not come to play chess on Saturday, and as Tía Lola opened the *zaguán* to him, Tuerto had shot out and into the street.

Tía Lola had been crying. She was worried, for it was after eight and I had not come home. Martin said to her, "Look, the little dog is trailing him! I'll follow and bring back Carlitos."

My loyal Tuerto led Martin straight into the haunted house and to the wall. Martin had called and called, but I had been asleep and did not hear. Anyhow he rushed back to bring my father and Tía Lola, and also a pick. And so they had found me.

In bed, safe and warm, I remembered the poor skeleton. "There is a dead man in the walls," I told them, "holding a treasure on his lap. Please go back and get it, Martin!"

"Shall I?" Martin looked at my father.

"We'll go," said my father, and they left me to Tía Lola.

I tried to stay awake until they came back, but excitement and fright had taken their toll and I fell deeply asleep. I did not know until the next morning that Martin and I had a fortune between us. The skeleton was extracted from the wall and given decent burial, and my father looked up in the old records of the city and of taxpayers on the old houses, to find out his probable identity. Then he had searched for relatives, but there seemed to be none. So, after my father paid the taxes on the treasure, it remained for us. Finders keepers.

It was not so very much, after all. The box had held silver coins and some jewels, but these were not of much intrinsic value anymore. Still, something like 20,000 pesos remained to be divided between Martin and me.

"What will you do with your part?" I asked Martin, a few days later.

> He would never be anything in the Great Chess Game but a simple pawn.

"I will take care of my mother and my little brothers, and I shall go to school," he cried.

But in the Saturday evening chess circle, my father and his friends decided among them they would teach Martin to read and write, and coach him until he could pass examinations and then go on to evening classes. Meanwhile, he was going to be their champion in chess tournaments, and he could make some money giving exhibition games.

"What will you do with your part of the treasure?" Don Mario asked me. They were all eating *enchiladas*[17] and drinking coffee, after their game. Before I could answer, there was a

---

17. **enchiladas** (ĕn-chĕ-lä′däs) *Spanish*: rolled tortillas filled with a seasoned mixture.

400   UNIT FOUR   PART 1: SHOWING YOUR TRUE COLORS

Mini-Lesson The Writer's Style

DETAILS APPEALING TO SMELL   Tell students that good writers use details that appeal to readers' five senses (sight, hearing, touch, taste, and smell) to make their descriptions vivid. For example, on page 391, the author writes that the secundaria smelled "of chalk dust and disinfectant soap and boys." On page 392, she describes the "dusty peons" who "smelled of sweat and of chili."

Application   Remind students that Carlos gets trapped inside a wall in an old house that is in the process of being torn down and discovers that he has company—a skeleton. Have students write a description of the scene inside the wall, including words and phrases that convey the smell of the narrow passage.

Reteaching/Reinforcement
• Writing Handbook, p. 783
• *Writing Mini-Lessons,* p. 38

 **The Writer's Craft**

Appealing to the Senses, pp. 266–272

---

400   THE LANGUAGE OF LITERATURE   TEACHER'S EDITION

clamor at our *zaguán*. And the big knocker sounded several times. Tía Lola ushered in Dr. Del Valle, and Serafin.

Dr. Del Valle gave Serafin a push into the center of the room. "Begin," he ordered his son.

"I am sorry," stammered Serafin.

Dr. Del Valle was trembling with emotion. "I never thought I would see the day when I would feel so ashamed of my son," he told my father. "He has just now confessed to me that he induced Carlos to go with him to that house, to break into the walls and look for treasure, and that when the wall caved in he ran home and left Carlos there, perhaps to die!"

Serafin stood with drooping head, and two tears slid down his cheeks. "I am sorry," he whispered again.

"We knew," said my father. "We realized that Serafin must have been paralyzed with fear. That is why I did not speak of it to you. He is forgiven. Isn't he, Carlos?"

"Of course," I answered at once.

For what else could I say? I knew what it was to be scared senseless, almost to panic. I couldn't hate Serafin, even though Tía Lola did. I was even, in a way, sorry for him. For I knew that he would never be anything in the Great Chess Game but a simple pawn, like me. Martin would end as a knight.

"I suppose by rights," I said to Serafin, not being above heaping some coals of fire on his head, "at least part of the treasure should be yours. You started looking in the wall where it was found."

He glanced hopefully at me as I went on. "So I trust you will agree with me about what to do with it. I want to give it for a classroom in one of the new schools being built down by the highway. We could name that room." He was disappointed, I could see. But he was trapped. Or, as Tía Lola said later, he made a virtue of necessity.[18]

"Whatever you say, Carlos," he answered meekly.

"Why don't we name it for the Lost Grandfather?" I cried.

And so it will be. My father turned over the money to the education department, and a plaque will be affixed to one of the rooms, saying, "This room was built with funds left by the Lost Grandfather." The president of Mexico is coming to inaugurate[19] the school, and several others, and Serafin and I and all our relatives, and Martin, and the whole class at school and Professor Morado, and many others, will be there. All Guanajuato will be in gala dress. The day will be a great *fiesta*.

Olé, poor Lost Grandfather. Your treasure will be of good use, at last. ❖

---

18. **made a virtue of necessity:** pretended to be doing something because it was right when, in fact, doing it only because forced to.
19. **inaugurate** (ĭn-ô′gyə-rāt′): to open officially with a formal ceremony.

WORDS TO KNOW
clamor (klăm′ər) *n.* a loud noise; uproar
induce (ĭn-dōōs′) *v.* to persuade

401

CUSTOMIZING FOR
Gifted and Talented Students

U Have students discuss the irony in Serafin's having been "paralyzed" with fear. *(Possible response: Carlos had polio, a disease that causes paralysis, but Carlos was not paralyzed and attempted to face the danger of his situation. Serafin had a healthy body but was emotionally paralyzed.)*

STRATEGIC READING FOR
Less-Proficient Readers

V Ask students to explain what happens to the Lost Grandfather and his treasure. *(The Lost Grandfather receives a proper burial. The treasure is sold, and the proceeds from Carlos's and Serafin's share go to build a schoolroom named for the Lost Grandfather.)* **Summarizing**

COMPREHENSION CHECK
1. What game does Serafin play as he walks around the town? *(finders keepers)*
2. What happens when Martin plays chess with Carlos's father? *(Martin beats Carlos's father once, and the second game ends in a stalemate.)*
3. What does Carlos find inside the wall? *(a skeleton with a treasure box on its lap)*
4. What does Serafin do after Carlos is trapped inside the wall? *(He runs away and doesn't tell anyone about what has happened.)*
5. How does Carlos decide to spend his part of the hidden treasure? *(He donates it to a new school so that they may build a classroom.)*

Mini-Lesson — Reading Skills/Strategies

USING CONTEXT CLUES Remind students that when they use context clues, they combine information from the text with their own experiences and knowledge to understand the author's meaning. Point out to students the highlighted phrase above. This phrase doesn't make sense if read literally. Students can use context clues, and perhaps their own knowledge, to infer its meaning.

Application Ask students why Carlos offers Serafin part of the treasure even though Serafin abandoned him in danger. *(Carlos might be trying to make Serafin feel bad by being nice to him.)* Ask what "not being above" means. *(Carlos isn't perfect. Although Carlos has forgiven Serafin, he still wants to punish him a little.)* Finally, explain that the metaphor of heaping coals of fire on someone's head is an allusion to the Bible: "If thine enemy be hungry, give him bread; if he be thirsty, give him water to drink: for thou shalt heap coals of fire upon his head, and the Lord shall reward thee" (Proverbs 25:21–22; see also Romans 12:19–20).

Reteaching/Reinforcement
- *Unit Four Resource Book,* p. 5

From Personal Response to Critical Analysis

1. Responses will vary.
2. Possible responses: Carlos strikes just the right balance by forgiving Serafin and then making him give up his share of the treasure; Carlos is too kind; Serafin didn't seem to care about Carlos's safety, and Carlos should reproach Serafin. Carlos is too mean because Serafin is sorry, and no real harm was done.
3. Possible responses: He understands that in life—as in chess—choices can determine success or failure. He sees that people's behavior can show that they are strong, like a knight, or weak, like a pawn.
4. Possible responses: He is a humble, thoughtful, intelligent, and generous man who is interested in improving himself. He is brave and kind and has a great desire to help other people.
5. Students should support their responses with references to the text and to their lists.
6. Possible responses: No; it is wrong to keep something that belongs to someone else without first trying to give it back. Yes; once people lose objects, they belong to whoever finds them.

Another Pathway

You may wish to have students choose one question and respond to it either in writing or by manipulating the chess pieces to illustrate what they say aloud. To enhance their understanding of the use of chess in "The Secret of the Wall," students can research the game in an encyclopedia or reference book on games.

RESPONDING OPTIONS

FROM PERSONAL RESPONSE TO CRITICAL ANALYSIS

REFLECT
1. Which character made the strongest impression on you? Describe your impression to another student.

RETHINK
2. What do you think of the way Carlos treats Serafin at the end of the story?
3. Carlos thinks of life as "the Great Chess Game." Why do you think he makes this comparison?
4. What kind of person is Martin Gonzales?
   Consider
   Close Textual Reading
   - his first meeting with Carlos
   - his interest in chess
   - his plans for his share of the treasure
5. Review the list you made for the Personal Connection on page 389. Compare Carlos, Martin, and Serafin in terms of the qualities of friendship that you find most important.

RELATE
Thematic Link
6. Carlos and Serafin display their "true colors" in the different opinions they have about what should be done with something valuable found in the street. Do you believe in the rule of finders keepers? Explain why or why not.

Multimodal Learning
ANOTHER PATHWAY

Display a chess set if available, or draw a diagram of a chessboard with the pieces positioned and labeled. Discuss the use of chess in "The Secret of the Wall" in terms of the following:

- how the author uses the game to advance the plot of the story
- why Carlos thinks of life as "the Great Chess Game"
- the other characters' amazement at Martin's abilities
- the comparison of Serafin to a pawn and Martin to a knight

THE WRITER'S STYLE

The author skillfully creates the settings and develops the characters in this story through the use of specific details and careful word choice. Reread de Treviño's descriptions of Guanajuato, the high school, and Cantaranas Plaza. Then pay attention to detail and word choice as you write a short passage describing your neighborhood and your school.

QUICKWRITES

1. Imagine that you are present at the inauguration ceremony for the new school that Carlos and Serafin have helped fund. Draft a short **speech** for either Carlos or Serafin explaining the decision to donate the treasure to the new school.
2. Draft a **newspaper account** of Carlos's rescue. Look back over the story for facts and details that you can include.

📁 **PORTFOLIO** Save your writing. You may want to use it later as a springboard to a piece for your portfolio.

402 UNIT FOUR PART 1: SHOWING YOUR TRUE COLORS

The Writer's Style

Have students exchange their writing for peer review. Give students time to incorporate peers' suggestions.

 **The Writer's Craft**

Describing People and Places, p. 54

QuickWrites

1. Have students consider the differences in the speeches that Carlos and Serafin would deliver. In drafting their speeches, have them consider their character's role in getting the treasure.
2. Tell students that every good news story answers five questions: *Who? What? When? Where?* and *How?*

 **The Writer's Craft**

Goals and Audience, pp. 211–212
Creating Paragraphs, pp. 226–227

LITERARY CONCEPTS

The way a writer creates and develops a character's personality is called **characterization**. A writer can make a character come alive through direct description of the character, through the character's words and actions, and through the words and actions of other characters. Martin, for example, is described as wearing "clean, freshly ironed cotton work clothes." You can infer from this information that Martin is a working person who cares about his appearance. Find examples of each method of characterization in the story. Which method of characterization do you think provides the most helpful information about the characters?

CONCEPT REVIEW: Suspense Recall that suspense is a feeling of tension and excitement that makes a reader curious about the outcome of a story. For example, in the play *A Shipment of Mute Fate*, a moment of suspense happens when Chris spots the deadly bushmaster snake in an open cupboard. Find an example of how de Treviño creates suspense in "The Secret of the Wall."

Multimodal Learning

ALTERNATIVE ACTIVITIES

1. Create a **diorama** that portrays Guanajuato and one of the scenes in the story. Be sure to include some of the most prominent locations mentioned in the story: the fountain in Cantaranas Plaza, the school, Carlos's house, and the old house of the Lost Grandfather. Then create representations of the figures of Carlos, Martin, and Serafin, and place them at appropriate points in the scene. Add your diorama to an exhibit of dioramas illustrating events in the story.

2. Imagine that you are the music director for a film version of "The Secret of the Wall." Pick three or four scenes and find **music** that you think conveys the mood at those points in the story. Keep in mind the story's setting and the various events described. Use the music you pick as background for a reading of those scenes to the class.

Literary Links

Students may point out that both Mourad and Serafin get someone else into a dangerous situation but that Mourad would come through for his cousin in a pinch, whereas Serafin abandons Carlos. Some students may say that Mourad twists the rules yet holds himself to the ethical code of his family, whereas Serafin acts without regard to morality or custom.

Across the Curriculum

Mathematics Interested students may want to extend the activity by researching and reporting on the impact of the North American Free Trade Agreement (NAFTA) on the Mexican economy and on Mexico's relationship with the United States. Allow students to illustrate Mexican coins and paper currency, in the absence of actual money.

ADDITIONAL SUGGESTIONS

Science *A Shot Worth the Pinch* Have students research polio and find out how the polio vaccine was created by Jonas Salk. Groups might also research the oral vaccine developed by Albert Sabin.

ART GALLERY
Historical Murals of Mexico After the beginning of the Mexican Revolution in 1910, there was a surge of nationalism in the arts of Mexico. These murals were painted to decorate the walls of public buildings in Mexico City and to glorify Mexican culture. Students may refer to them in a discussion of the history of the Mexican Revolution.

Side A, Frame 38827

ACROSS THE CURRICULUM

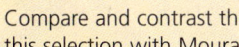
Mathematics The treasure of the Lost Grandfather amounted to about 20,000 pesos. How much money would this be today if it were converted to U.S. dollars? (Remember that the money would have had a different value during the time in which the story is set.) Research the monetary systems of Mexico and the United States, and summarize your findings on a chart. You may wish to display Mexican coins and currency with the chart.

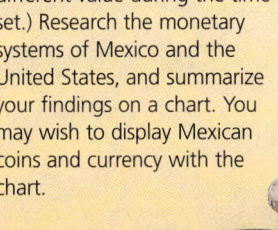

LITERARY LINKS

Compare and contrast the character of Serafin in this selection with Mourad in "The Summer of the Beautiful White Horse."

Literary Concepts

Have students make charts that show the examples of each method of characterization. Allow partners to discuss which method they found most effective and why.

Concept Review Most students will say that the scene in which Carlos becomes trapped is suspenseful, because the reader is not sure if help will arrive in time.

Alternative Activities

1. **Cooperative Learning** Have students work in groups of four or five. Students should first decide on a scale for their dioramas and then find a cardboard box that fits the chosen scale. Students should divide the tasks of making figures, making objects, and painting backgrounds.

2. Encourage students to think about the use of background music in movies or TV shows they have seen. They may bring to class some primarily orchestral recorded sound tracks for films to study mood. Students should think first about the mood they want to create and then find suitable music for "The Secret of the Wall."

Words to Know

Exercise A
1. a
2. c
3. a
4. c
5. c
6. a
7. b
8. b
9. c
10. c

Exercise B
You may wish to pair students acquiring English with English-proficient students in this activity. Also, students should get more than one guess, since some pairs of words would be acted out rather similarly (for example, *sullen* and *morosely*, *scornful* and *revulsion*).

WORDS TO KNOW

EXERCISE A For each group of words below, on your paper write the letter of the word that is the best antonym for the boldfaced word.

1. **induce:** (a) discourage (b) argue (c) awaken
2. **clamor:** (a) plainness (b) grace (c) silence
3. **turmoil:** (a) calm (b) light (c) happiness
4. **saunter:** (a) whisper (b) grin (c) march
5. **illiterate:** (a) dark (b) pleasant (c) educated
6. **scornful:** (a) respectful (b) lucky (c) proper
7. **deceit:** (a) jealousy (b) truthfulness (c) beauty
8. **morosely:** (a) simply (b) happily (c) intelligently
9. **sullen:** (a) brave (b) gentle (c) cheerful
10. **revulsion:** (a) fear (b) surprise (c) admiration

EXERCISE B Working with a partner, act out the meaning of one of the following words while another pair of students guesses the word: *sullen, saunter, morosely, scornful, deceit, revulsion, induce.* Then switch so that you and your partner guess which word the other pair of students is acting out.

ELIZABETH BORTON DE TREVIÑO

1904–

As a child in California, Elizabeth Borton de Treviño was delighted by the sounds of the piano, the violin, and the Spanish language. These interests remained with her, leading her to study the literature, language, and history of Spain at Stanford University.

Her knowledge of music and Spanish helped de Treviño win her first job, as a reporter for the *Boston Herald*. While working as a music reviewer, she was asked to use her Spanish to interview a dancer and musician from Spain. From that point, her work opportunities broadened. Traveling to Mexico on a newspaper assignment, she met Luis Treviño Gomez, who became her husband. Mexico became her adopted country, and she has lived there since 1935.

De Treviño once said, "I generally get story ideas from some true event or moment in history that fires my imagination." *I, Juan de Pareja* is her most famous novel. This story of a slave who worked for the real-life painter Diego Velázquez earned de Treviño the Newbery Medal in 1966.

OTHER WORKS *El Guero, Leona: A Love Story*
Extended Reading

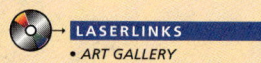
• ART GALLERY

404 UNIT FOUR PART 1: SHOWING YOUR TRUE COLORS

WHAT DO YOU THINK?
Reflecting on Theme

Have students think back to the survey they did at the beginning of Part 1. Ask them whether or not they think reading this story would change their classmates' minds. Encourage them to repeat the survey to find out.

PREVIEWING

NONFICTION

from Talking with Artists
Pat Cummings

PERSONAL CONNECTION *Activating Prior Knowledge/Setting a Purpose*

What does the word *talent* mean to you? In your notebook or on a sheet of paper, list some abilities you consider to be talents. What are *your* particular talents? Create a chart similar to the one shown, and fill it in with these talents, entering your strongest in the space numbered 1 and your weakest in the space numbered 4. Add more spaces if you wish. As you read this interview, see if your ideas about individual talent change.

My Talents
1.
2.
3.
4.

CULTURAL CONNECTION *Building Background*

This selection is from the book *Talking with Artists*. The author, Pat Cummings, interviewed artists by posing questions that students often ask when artists visit schools and libraries. All of the artists are talented illustrators of children's books, and some of them, like Cummings herself, also write the books in which their illustrations appear. In these interviews, the illustrators talk about their early art experiences and offer encouragement to young people who would like to explore their own artistic talent.

WRITING CONNECTION

Jerry Pinkney, the artist interviewed in this selection, says that he decided to develop his artistic talent because of his two older brothers who drew. In your notebook, copy and complete the sentence shown. Then go on to write a brief description of a talent you are currently developing.

"I first became interested in _____ because _____."

TALKING WITH ARTISTS **405**

OVERVIEW

Objectives

- To understand and appreciate an interview with a book illustrator
- To understand the kind of information elicited in an interview
- To express understanding of the selection through a choice of writing forms, including a review, a dedication, and a schedule
- To extend understanding of the selection through a variety of multimodal and cross-curricular activities

Skills

READING SKILLS/STRATEGIES
- Relating cause and effect

GRAMMAR
- Irregular past participles

LITERARY CONCEPTS
- Author's purpose
- Interview

SPELLING
- The prefix *com-*

SPEAKING, LISTENING, AND VIEWING
- Group discussion
- Oral presentation

Cross-Curricular Connections

MATH
- Calculating workdays

PRINT AND MEDIA RESOURCES

UNIT FOUR RESOURCE BOOK
Strategic Reading: Literature, p. 11
Vocabulary SkillBuilder, p. 14
Reading SkillBuilder, p. 12
Spelling SkillBuilder, p. 13

GRAMMAR MINI-LESSONS
Transparencies, p. 20
Copymasters, pp. 27, 28

ACCESS FOR STUDENTS ACQUIRING ENGLISH
Selection Summaries
Reading and Writing Support

FORMAL ASSESSMENT
Selection Test, pp. 81–82
 Test Generator

 AUDIO LIBRARY
See Reference Card

 LASERLINKS
Author Background
Art Gallery

 INTERNET RESOURCES
McDougal Littell Literature Center at http://www.hmco.com/mcdougal/lit

THE LANGUAGE OF LITERATURE TEACHER'S EDITION **405**

SUMMARY

In this interview, the illustrator and part-time teacher Jerry Pinkney discusses his art background and his work. Considered the "class artist" as a child and encouraged by his teachers, he went on to study art in college. Pinkney tried out different graphic fields but found that he enjoyed book illustrating the most. His first book, The *Adventures of Spider*, was published in 1964. Pinkney works mainly in pencil and watercolor and has often used members of his family as models for characters. Although animals are his favorite subjects for drawings, Pinkney is also interested in manuscripts about African Americans and their history.

Thematic Link: *Showing Your True Colors* The selection literally depicts the theme as the artist Jerry Pinkney "shows his colors."

CUSTOMIZING FOR
Students Acquiring English

- Use **ACCESS FOR STUDENTS ACQUIRING ENGLISH,** *Reading and Writing Support.*
- The language in this interview is straightforward and should not present much difficulty. You may want to have pairs of students role-play portions of the interview to keep interest high.

STRATEGIC READING FOR
Less-Proficient Readers

Set a Purpose Have students read to find out about the steps that led to Pinkney's becoming an artist.

Use **UNIT FOUR RESOURCE BOOK,** pages 11–12, for guidance in reading the selection.

FROM
Talking with Artists
by Pat Cummings

An Interview with Jerry Pinkney

406 UNIT FOUR PART 1: SHOWING YOUR TRUE COLORS

WORDS TO KNOW

client (klī′ənt) *n.* a customer (p. 407)
commercial (kə-mûr′shəl) *adj.* done for profit, having to do with a business (p. 407)
commitment (kə-mĭt′mənt) *n.* devotion to a cause or set of beliefs; feeling of responsibility (p. 408)

mimicking (mĭm′ĭ-kĭng) *n.* copying or imitating the actions of another (p. 407)
unique (yōō-nēk′) *adj.* one of a kind (p. 411)

406 THE LANGUAGE OF LITERATURE TEACHER'S EDITION

My story. I first became interested in art because of my two older brothers who drew. They liked to make pictures of airplanes, cars, things of that sort. I began by mimicking them, trying to draw what they drew.

I remember an incident in the first grade when I was growing up in Philadelphia that shaped the idea in my mind that I wanted to be an artist. For a Fire Prevention Week project I drew a red fire engine on a big sheet of brown paper. I received a lot of attention from that, and I liked it. I was encouraged by my teacher, and, as I kept drawing, I became the "class artist."

Probably part of the reason that I focused on my drawing so much was that I felt I wasn't very strong in other areas. I was able to escape some projects by drawing the assignments.

I was able to take private art classes when I was in junior high school. My father was a handyman who did painting, plumbing, electrical work, gardening—a bit of everything. He had several clients who knew of private art classes, and I remember taking classes in different neighborhoods. Usually they were still-life[1] painting classes.

When I was eleven or twelve years old, I had a newspaper stand on the corner of a fairly large intersection in Philadelphia. I would take my drawing pad and sketch while I was there. An artist named John Liney, who was a cartoonist for the Henry comics,[2] noticed me drawing. He took me to visit his studio, which was about a block away. From time to time I would go to see him, and he would give me different materials to work with, different art supplies. So at that early age I had a sense that it was possible to make a living doing art. Knowing him and seeing how he worked helped me understand the possibilities of using one's talents.

One early influence was the work of Arthur Rackham, who was an illustrator of children's stories. I liked the quality of his drawing and how he used color.

I later went to Dobbins Vocational High School and took commercial art classes that introduced me to lettering and technical drawing, airbrush, and all kinds of media.[3] In the twelfth grade, we even attended some figure-drawing evening classes.

There was a competition for scholarships to the Philadelphia Museum College of Art. Only four or five were available. I had to show a portfolio[4] and write a paper stating why I wanted to attend. It felt great to win a scholarship, and I began studying advertising and design. But I soon realized that I enjoyed painting and printmaking classes even more, and drawing became very important to me.

I began doing greeting cards, advertising, and textbook illustration in Boston. The textbook work made me realize I liked illustration that was tied to a story.

Book illustration seemed freer than some of the work I was doing. Working with a manuscript was very exciting. I also began to look into and research African-American artists. I admired Charles White, whose strong, graphic

---

1. **still-life:** a type of painting that uses an object or group of objects as the subject of the painting.
2. **Henry comics:** a long-running newspaper comic strip about a boy named Henry.
3. **media:** the materials or techniques with which an artist works.
4. **portfolio:** samples of an artist's work that show the range of the artist's skills.

WORDS TO KNOW
mimicking (mĭm′ĭ-kĭng) *n.* copying or imitating the actions of another **mimic** *v.*
client (klī′ənt) *n.* a customer
commercial (kə-mûr′shəl) *adj.* done for profit; having to do with a business

407

STRATEGIC READING FOR
Less-Proficient Readers

B What are some of the significant steps that led to Pinkney's becoming a professional artist? *(Possible responses: He received encouragement as a child; he attended several art schools and worked hard.)* **Noting Relevant Details**

Set a Purpose Have students read to find out how Pinkney was able to pursue professionally his interest in African-American artists.

Literary Concept: INTERVIEW

C Have students read and analyze the interview questions on page 408. Ask them to discuss the kinds of things the interviewer asks Pinkney. *(Possible response: The interviewer asks about professional matters, such as where Pinkney gets his ideas, and personal matters, such as whether Pinkney has any children or pets. The questions are open-ended so that Pinkney can express himself freely in his own words rather than just answering yes or no.)*

CUSTOMIZING FOR
Multiple Learning Styles

D **Spatial or Graphic Learners** Tell students to imagine that they are book illustrators. Have them identify a selection from an earlier unit that would "allow them to make some kind of personal statement." Suggest that students look for a poem or story, character or plot that evoked in them strong feelings. Invite students to make a drawing or book jacket illustrating the selection.

---

drawings gave such dignity to the black figure. I was also impressed by the photographs of James Van Der Zee. If you look at the work of these two men, I think you'll see their influence in my book *Home Place*.

I've won a lot of awards for my art, and it feels wonderful to know that my work is appreciated. My work includes a mixture of things that I, myself, have appreciated. In some ways, it is a testimony to be able to state through my art, "Yes, these people have influenced me."

1. Where do you get your ideas from?
Most of my work comes from the text, which I use as a sort of springboard. I try to find stories that allow me to make some kind of personal statement. For example, I'll find manuscripts that deal with the African Americans and our history in this country. So the ideas come from the story but also from my own personal commitment. I have just recently collaborated on two books, *Sunday Outing* and *Back Home*, with my wife Gloria Jean Pinkney.

2. What is a normal day like for you?
Part of the year I travel to visit schools and libraries. When I'm working in the studio, I'm at the drawing board between eight-thirty and nine o'clock in the morning. I get started easily and work straight through the day, taking a break for lunch or maybe to take a walk. Usually, my day ends between eight-thirty and ten o'clock at night. So many things that can happen during the day need to be taken care of as well. I might spend a lot of time on the phone discussing work, or packing up art that must be shipped to a gallery or publisher, running out to get photocopies of things. All of this accounts for a fairly long day.

> *My work includes a mixture of things that I, myself, have appreciated.*

3. Where do you work?
I work in my studio right in the house. I have a screened-in porch that looks out into the woods. So it's really quite a nice environment with good space and lots of light.

4. Do you have any children? any pets?
Yes. I have four children. Troy Bernadette Ragsdale is the director of Child Life at Jacobi Hospital and mother of our granddaughter, Gloria, who appears on the cover and inside of the book *Pretend You're a Cat*.

Brian Pinkney is an illustrator, and a very active one, in the area of children's books. He is married to Andrea Davis Pinkney, who is an author and children's book editor.

Scott Cannon Pinkney is the senior vice president and creative director of his own direct response agency. He is married to Kim Pinkney, and they live in Toronto, Canada, with their two children.

And our son Myles Carter Pinkney is a cameraman and photographer. He has just contracted to do his first children's picture book. Myles and his wife, Sandra, have three children.

WORDS TO KNOW
commitment (kə-mĭt′mənt) *n.* devotion to a cause or set of beliefs; feeling of responsibility

408

Mini-Lesson Literary Concepts

Author's Purpose
Primary: to inform
Secondary: to entertain

Evidence
Professional questions: "What do you use to make your pictures?"

Human-interest questions: "Do you have pets?"

AUTHOR'S PURPOSE Remind students that authors write for many reasons: to entertain, to inform, or to express an opinion. Tell them that identifying the author's purpose helps them understand what they read.

Application Have students work in pairs to discuss the author's primary purpose in the selection. Also ask them what secondary purpose Cummings might have. Then have students give evidence from the selection to support their responses. Students can record their response on a chart like the one shown.

408 THE LANGUAGE OF LITERATURE **TEACHER'S EDITION**

This 1992 illustration by Pinkney is from the children's book *Drylongso*, written by Virginia Hamilton.
Illustration by Jerry Pinkney. From *Drylongso* by Virginia Hamilton. Illustration Copyright © 1992 Jerry Pinkney, reproduced with permission of Harcourt Brace & Company.

TALKING WITH ARTISTS **409**

Linking to Math

E Have students calculate the number of hours that Pinkney works on days that he spends in the studio. *(He arrives between eight-thirty and nine o'clock in the morning, and his day ends between eight-thirty and ten o'clock at night. He works between 12 and 13.5 hours.)*

Critical Thinking: ANALYZING

F Ask students what the advantages of Pinkney's working environment are. *(Possible response: Artists need good light, which Pinkney's studio receives. Artists are also sensitive to beauty, and Pinkney's studio looks out into the woods.)*

Mini-Lesson  Grammar

IRREGULAR PAST PARTICIPLES Remind students that sometimes the past participle of an irregular verb is the same as the past form.

Present	Past	Past Participle
say	said	(have) said
teach	taught	(have) taught

However, many irregular verbs have past participle forms that are different from the past forms.

Present	Past	Past Participle
go	went	(have) gone
write	wrote	(have) written
get	got	(have) got/(have) gotten

Application Have students supply the past participle for the irregular verbs listed below.
1. begin *(have begun)*
2. sing *(have sung)*
3. know *(have known)*
4. steal *(have stolen)*
5. swim *(have swum)*
6. rise *(have risen)*

Reteaching/Reinforcement
- *Grammar Handbook*, pp. 835–838
- *Grammar Mini-Lesson*, pp. 27, 28, transparencies, p. 20

The Writer's Craft

Irregular Verbs, pp. 414–415

THE LANGUAGE OF LITERATURE TEACHER'S EDITION **409**

CUSTOMIZING FOR
Students Acquiring English

2 Point out to students that the idiomatic phrase *an awful lot* means "very many" and does not have a negative meaning.

3 Explain to students that the expression *for instance* signals that the author or speaker is about to give an example of what he or she has been discussing. Encourage students to use this expression in their own writing.

Active Reading: QUESTION

G Discuss with students any questions or comments they have at this point in the selection. You may wish to use the following model to give them ideas of what they might be thinking about:

Think-Aloud Model *I would like to know more about the kinds of things that Pinkney has worked through—things that made him uncomfortable in the beginning.*

Critical Thinking: CLASSIFYING

H Have students identify two kinds of information the interviewer elicits by asking Pinkney what materials he uses to make his pictures. *(The interviewer's question prompts Pinkney to describe the materials he uses and to tell something about his method.)*

---

5. What do you enjoy drawing the most?

It varies. Perhaps I most enjoy drawing animals. Next to that would be using animals in an anthropomorphic way—giving them human characteristics, like dressing them in clothes or giving them human expressions. Combining them with people fascinates me and gives me so many areas to work on that I enjoy.

2 I try to keep a balance in my work. If I find that I'm working on projects that include an awful lot of animals and less people, I want to balance it, so I go back and forth. When I get to a point where I've had it with drawing animals, I'll pick a project where there are more human figures involved. The variety can be quite, quite exciting.

G I've always tried to focus on the things that give me the most enjoyment. Part of me always needs to try to do something that I've never done before or to bring a different point of view to my work. Often, this involves working on things that make me uncomfortable at the time. But the idea is to move through that uncomfortable stage and learn how to resolve the problem I'm having in my work and face it head on. Hopefully, that helps bring a freshness to the work.

3 For instance, for a while I showed most of the figures and animals in my paintings from a close-up point of view. There's not very much depth in those compositions, usually. Now I'm doing just the opposite of that and moving back and seeing characters in a much larger setting. That keeps me interested in what I'm doing. I like variety.

6. Do you ever put people you know in your pictures?

Yes—especially my family. When my children were very young, they were always turning up in my work. I think Brian has been a major character in a book, and Myles and Scott and Troy have been on covers. Gloria, my wife, models for me all the time and also helps take photographs of the models.

Very often, when I get a manuscript I have to find models for the characters in the story. They're people that I don't know or don't know very well, and, with the way I work, I like to introduce the models to the text and often have them act it out. Before it's all over, I end up knowing them very, very well because we've shared this kind of experience.

This Pinkney illustration of the hero John Henry was created in 1994 for the book *John Henry,* written by Julius Lester. Illustration by Jerry Pinkney. From *John Henry* by Julius Lester. Illustration Copyright © 1994 Jerry Pinkney. Used with permission of Dial Books for Young Readers, a division of Penguin Books USA Inc.

410 UNIT FOUR PART 1: SHOWING YOUR TRUE COLORS

Mini-Lesson Spelling

THE PREFIX *com-* Tell students that the prefix *com-* means "with" or "together." However, this prefix is spelled *con-* before most letters of the alphabet. It is spelled *com-* before roots that begin with the letters *m, p,* or *b.*

com- + mitment	= commitment
com- + mercial	= commercial
con- + cert	= concert
con- + gress	= congress

Application Have students complete the words below using a form of the prefix *com-*.
1. plexion *(com)*   4. munication *(com)*
2. stant *(con)*   5. plaint *(com)*
3. mittee *(com)*   6. sider *(con)*

Ask students to look for more words that fit this pattern, in their own writing and in things that they read, and to add these words to their personal word lists.

Reteaching/Reinforcement
• *Unit Four Resource Book,* p. 13

---

410 THE LANGUAGE OF LITERATURE TEACHER'S EDITION

7. What do you use to make your pictures?

My work is done in pencil and watercolor on paper, usually. But I tend to use a lot of different media along with the watercolor: pastel,[5] color pencils, and Cray-Pas.[6] My worktable is just full of all these materials, and I use whatever I think will help me in getting the kind of effect that I want for the pictures.

8. How did you get to do your first book?

My first book, *The Adventures of Spider* by Joyce Arkhurst, was published by Little, Brown in 1964. The book came as a result of my being in the Boston area, where there are certainly a lot of book publishers. I had gotten some very nice recognition from art shows in which my work had appeared.

I think that it also had a lot to do with the climate of the times. There were publishers who were interested in publishing African-American writers. I think there was an awareness, if not pressure, that the African-American artist could perhaps bring something unique to a text, something more personal. The publishers were actually looking for someone black to do this particular project, which was a collection of West African folktales. I showed them my portfolio, they liked my work, and that's how I got to do my first book. ❖

---

5. **pastel:** chalklike sticks in a wide variety of colors.
6. **Cray-Pas:** a brand name for pastel-like color sticks.

LITERARY INSIGHT

Water Color
by Paul Engle

The painter puts two thin lines
On one side of the page,
And one line on the other side.
Suddenly grass grows there!

5 Between them, a wavering line.
Water is moving!

Your two eyes look at me.
You lift one hand.

Suddenly my heart is growing
      toward you.
10 Suddenly I am moving toward
      you!

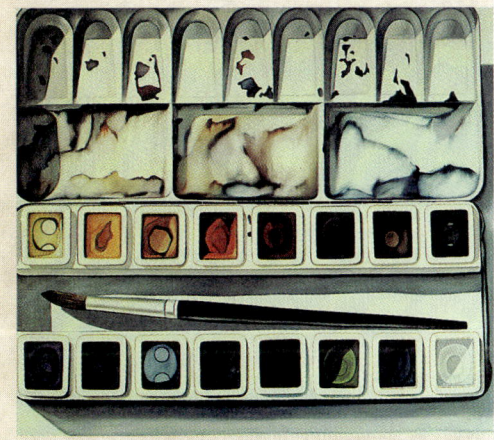

Paintbox (1984), Marilyn Groch. Oil on canvas, 36″ × 48″, private collection, courtesy of the artist.

WORDS TO KNOW   **unique** (yōō-nēk´) *adj.* one of a kind

From Personal Response to Critical Analysis

1. Responses will vary.
2. Possible response: Pinkney works as long each day as fulfilling his responsibilities requires; he pursues assignments that engage his personal commitments to African-American art and history; he pushes himself to meet new challenges and understand different points of view.
3. Responses will vary.
4. Make sure that students give reasons based on what they learned in the selection.
5. Possible response: The poem shows why Pinkney takes so much time with his models; for his art to be good, it must come alive.
6. Encourage students to write what they really think, not what they think is the "correct" answer.

Another Pathway

The introductory material on pages 407 and 408 provides an excellent model for tone. You may wish to allow students to practice in pairs, critiquing each other's monologues before they deliver them to the class.

Rubric

3 Full Accomplishment Students prepare monologues true in tone and content to the interview.

2 Substantial Accomplishment Students' monologues are true in tone or content, but not both, to the interview.

1 Little or Partial Accomplishment Students' monologues reveal that they have understood little of who Pinkney is or what he had to say in the interview.

RESPONDING OPTIONS

FROM PERSONAL RESPONSE TO CRITICAL ANALYSIS

REFLECT
1. Do you find Jerry Pinkney admirable? Record your reactions in your notebook.

RETHINK
2. In the interview, Pinkney reveals—directly and indirectly—some basic ideas that are important to him and his work. What would you identify as the rules or guidelines he seems to follow?
   Consider
   Close Textual Reading
   - his typical workday
   - his personal commitment to African-American art and history
   - his comments about the enjoyment and challenges he finds in his work

3. For Jerry Pinkney, working with John Liney provided a proving ground for his future career. On the basis of this interview and your own ideas, how necessary do you think it is for a person with a talent to look for guidance in developing it?

4. After reading Pinkney's comments, would you consider choosing book illustration as a career? Why or why not?

RELATE
Thematic Link
5. In what ways does the Insight poem "Water Color" on page 411 help you understand Jerry Pinkney's comments about being an illustrator?

6. Thomas Edison, the famous American inventor, once wrote, "Genius is one percent inspiration and ninety-nine percent perspiration." How important do you think inspiration, hard work, and discipline are to success?

Multimodal Learning
ANOTHER PATHWAY

Take the role of Jerry Pinkney and prepare a first-person monologue about yourself to deliver to the class. You might begin with a simple introduction, such as, "Hi! I'm Jerry Pinkney. Let me tell you a little bit about myself." Try to cover as much of the information presented in the interview as possible. Also, try to be true to the tone Pinkney uses in the interview.

QUICKWRITES

1. Look at the illustration by Jerry Pinkney on page 409. Write a **review** of the work for an art magazine.
2. Write a **dedication** for one of Pinkney's books in which Pinkney dedicates the book to John Liney, the illustrator who first helped him.
3. Write up a **schedule** for a typical work day in the life of Jerry Pinkney.

📁 **PORTFOLIO** Save your writing. You may want to use it later as a springboard to a piece for your portfolio.

LITERARY CONCEPTS

An **interview** is a meeting in which a person answers questions about professional or personal matters. Interviews may be tape-recorded, filmed, or recorded in written accounts. An interview allows the reader to learn information and form conclusions about a person as if the reader were asking the questions. What additional questions would you have asked Jerry Pinkney?

412   UNIT FOUR   PART 1: SHOWING YOUR TRUE COLORS

Literary Concepts

Have students work in small groups to brainstorm and assess additional interview questions. *(Students might ask Pinkney what advice he has for would-be artists or ask about his future plans.)*

QuickWrites

1. Tell students that an effective review both critiques the illustration and describes it so vividly that readers can see it in their minds.
2. Before writing, students may wish to reread the section of the interview in which Pinkney describes his relationship with Liney.
3. Remind students that in the interview Pinkney gives information about what things belong on the schedule.

The Writer's Craft

Personal Response, pp. 142–155
Organizing Details, 217–221

Multimodal Learning

ALTERNATIVE ACTIVITIES

Cooperative Learning In this interview, Pinkney names four artists who inspired or influenced him. With one or two other students, research at least two of these four people. Create a visual display of the information you gather, including a sample of your subjects' work.

ART CONNECTION

The illustration from the book *John Henry* (page 410) portrays the strength of the man who could dig through a mountain faster than a steam drill could. One critic commented that Pinkney's illustrations show John Henry's energy as "bursting from nature." If you were interviewed about Pinkney's work, what would you say about this illustration?

Detail from an illustration by Jerry Pinkney. From *John Henry* by Julius Lester.

WORDS TO KNOW

Review the Words to Know at the bottom of the selection pages. Then write the vocabulary word that best completes each sentence.

1. Art that is produced mainly to be beautiful is called fine art. Art that is used in advertising, manufacturing, and so on is called _____ art.
2. Some of this second type of art can be wonderful and even funny. Have you ever seen pictures that _____ famous paintings but then change them in certain ways?
3. There is only one Mona Lisa painting, which makes the real one _____, but there are many variations, some showing the same woman in a motorcycle jacket or brushing her teeth.
4. An artist who is working for someone else has to try to please the _____ who is paying for the work. For such an artist, it isn't enough to work only for the love of making art.
5. Still, these artists often feel a great deal of _____ toward making good art—art that makes the world more beautiful, more interesting, or better in some way.

Born in Chicago, Pat Cummings (1950–) is a children's author and illustrator. She grew up in Germany and Japan, as well as Illinois, New York, Virginia, Kansas, and Massachusetts, because her father's career with the U.S. Army required frequent moves. As a child, she was often excluded because of her African-American background. She has resolved to create works that appeal to people of all races and has refused to illustrate stories containing negative stereotypes.

Pat Cummings has been both writer and illustrator of four books for young people. Two were inspired by her brother Artie's imaginary childhood friend, Jimmy Lee. Her books feature people of all races taking positive approaches to everyday problems. She says, "I feel the best stories allow a child to discover a solution or approach to their own situation." *Talking with Artists* received the *Boston Globe/Horn Book* Award for nonfiction in 1992.

OTHER WORKS *Jimmy Lee Did It; C.L.O.U.D.S.; Clean Your Room, Harvey Moon!; Petey Moroni's Camp Runamok Diary* Extended Reading

▶ **LASERLINKS**
• AUTHOR BACKGROUND
• ART GALLERY

TALKING WITH ARTISTS **413**

Alternative Activities

Cooperative Learning Ensure that each group member has a role, such as chief researcher, resource gatherer, chief designer, meeting scheduler, discussion leader. Invite groups to display their completed visuals on a bulletin board titled "One Artist's Influences."

Art Connection

Encourage students to point to details in the illustration as they formulate their responses.

Across the Curriculum

Art *The Evolution of an Artist* Have students check out Jerry Pinkney's first book, *The Adventures of Spider* by Joyce Arkhurst, from a school or local library. Have students compare the illustrations with that of *John Henry* on page 410 and discuss how Pinkney's work changed and evolved over time.

Words to Know

1. commercial   4. client
2. mimic   5. commitment
3. unique

In the role of interviewee, Cummings once discussed her desire to create works of universal appeal: "When the vast majority of books published for children still reflects a primarily white, middle-class reality, I've always felt it was essential to show the spectrum of skin tones that truly make up the planet. I want any child to be able to pick up one of my books and find something of value in it, even if only a laugh."

 **AUTHOR BACKGROUND**
Pat Cummings The author talks about why she wrote *Talking with Artists* and about the process she used to interview the artists dealt with in her book.

Side A, Frame 23321

 **ART GALLERY**
Artists Who Inspired Pinkney
In the selection, Jerry Pinkney mentions several artists who influenced him. These images show works by Charles White, Arthur Rackham, and James Van Der Zee. You may wish to use them to support the cooperative-learning activity in the Alternative Activities feature.

Side A, Frame 38838

THE LANGUAGE OF LITERATURE **Teacher's Edition** **413**

OVERVIEW

Objectives

- To understand and appreciate a short story about a young girl's attempts to keep up appearances
- To enrich reading by making inferences
- To understand and analyze symbols
- To express understanding of the selection through a choice of writing forms, including a household motto and a greeting card
- To extend understanding of the selection through a variety of multimodal and cross-curricular activities

Skills

READING SKILLS/STRATEGIES
- Making inferences

THE WRITER'S STYLE
- Comparison and contrast transitions

GRAMMAR
- Pronouns and antecedents

LITERARY CONCEPTS
- Setting
- Symbolism

SPELLING
- The suffixes *-ible* and *-able*

STUDY SKILLS
- Taking standardized tests

SPEAKING, LISTENING, AND VIEWING
- Group discussion
- Oral presentation

Cross-Curricular Connections

SCIENCE
- Cloud types

HISTORY
- The A&P
- Chinese immigration

MATH
- Working mothers

PREVIEWING

FICTION

The White Umbrella
Gish Jen

PERSONAL CONNECTION Activating Prior Knowledge

With a small group of classmates, discuss the idea of "keeping up appearances." What does the expression mean? How important is keeping up appearances to you? In what ways do you and people you've observed keep up appearances? Share your group's ideas with the class as a whole.

Building Background
CULTURAL CONNECTION

Because the 12-year-old narrator of "The White Umbrella" wants to keep up appearances, she is embarrassed that her mother has to work outside the home. At the time the story probably takes place, relatively few mothers had entered the work force. In 1965, only 35 percent of mothers in the United States had jobs. By 1992, however, over 67 percent of mothers worked outside the home.

Active Reading
READING CONNECTION Setting a Purpose

Making Inferences You make inferences when you "read between the lines," or use general knowledge and your own experience to fill in details about what you are reading. In this story, for example, Miss Crosman, a piano teacher, offers her students food, a ride home, and dry towels. From this information, you can infer that Miss Crosman is a concerned and warm-hearted person. As you read, look for words or actions that will help you make inferences about the personality of the narrator, a character concerned with keeping up appearances. A chart similar to the one below might help you organize your thoughts.

Information from the Story
Miss Crosman brought a blanket and the umbrella to the narrator.

↓

What I Know from Experience
Being wet from rain makes a person cold.

↓

Inference
Miss Crosman is concerned, kind, and thoughtful.

[Bar graph: Percentage of Working Mothers — 1965, 1980, 1992]

414 UNIT FOUR PART 1: SHOWING YOUR TRUE COLORS

PRINT AND MEDIA RESOURCES

UNIT FOUR RESOURCE BOOK
Strategic Reading: Literature, p. 17
Vocabulary SkillBuilder, p. 20
Reading SkillBuilder, p. 18
Spelling SkillBuilder, p. 19

GRAMMAR MINI-LESSONS
Copymasters, pp. 15–16
Transparencies, pp. 10–11

WRITING MINI-LESSONS
Transparencies, p. 33

ACCESS FOR STUDENTS ACQUIRING ENGLISH
Selection Summaries
Reading and Writing Support

FORMAL ASSESSMENT
Selection Test, pp. 83–84
 Test Generator

---

414 THE LANGUAGE OF LITERATURE TEACHER'S EDITION

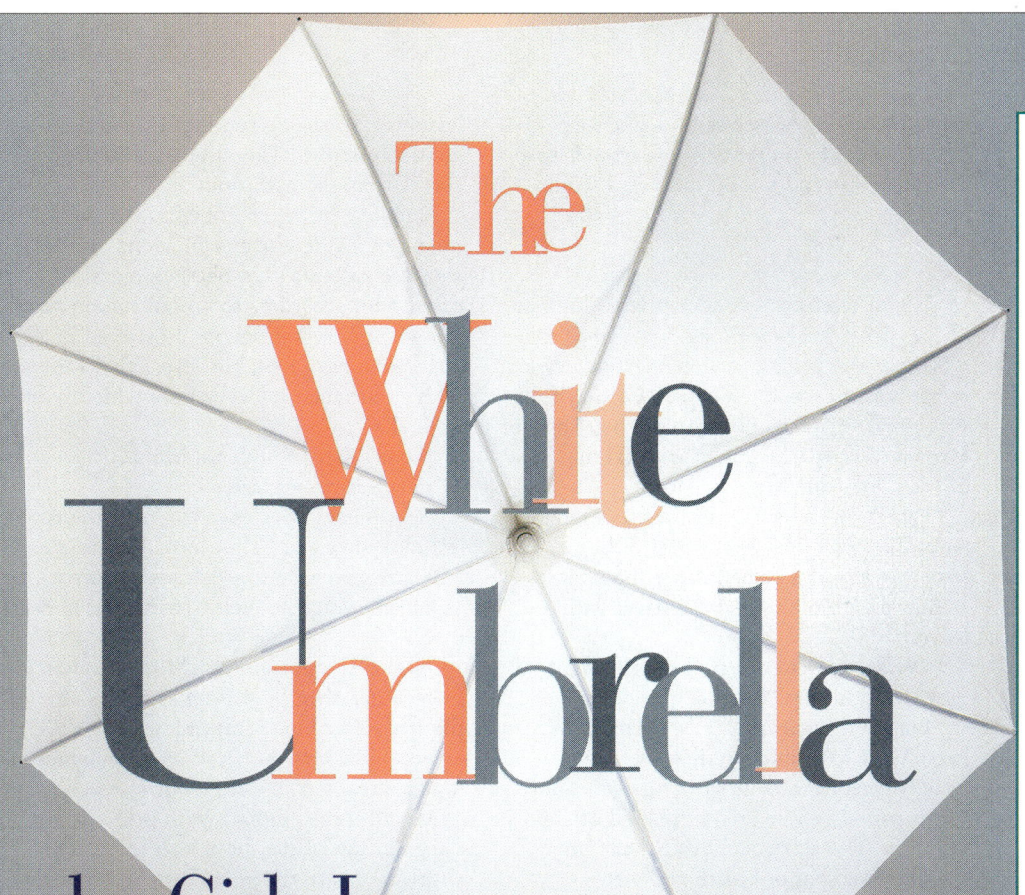

The White Umbrella
by Gish Jen

When I was twelve, my mother went to work without telling me or my little sister.

"Not that we need the second income." The lilt of her accent drifted from the kitchen up to the top of the stairs, where Mona and I were listening.

"No," said my father, in a barely audible voice. "Not like the Lee family."

The Lees were the only other Chinese family in town. I remembered how sorry my parents had felt for Mrs. Lee when she started waitressing downtown the year before; and so when my mother began coming home late, I didn't say anything and tried to keep Mona from saying anything either.

"But why shouldn't I?" she argued. "Lots of people's mothers work."

"Those are American people," I said.

"So what do you think we are? I can do the pledge of allegiance with my eyes closed."

Nevertheless, she tried to be discreet; and if my mother wasn't home by 5:30, we would

---

WORDS TO KNOW
audible (ô′də-bəl) *adj.* able to be heard
discreet (dĭ-skrēt′) *adj.* careful about what one says or does

---

SUMMARY

Because their mother has to work afternoons, the narrator and her sister must walk to their piano teacher's house after school. One afternoon they are caught in a sudden rainstorm and arrive at the lesson soaking wet. Embarrassed by their condition and by Miss Crosman's motherly concern, the narrator spins imaginative lies that make her family sound well-off. During the piano lesson she plays brilliantly, both to avoid pity and to win praise. Afterward the girls sit on Miss Crosman's steps, waiting for their mother, who is often late. As their wait lengthens, Miss Crosman offers more concern and help. The more she offers, the more the narrator resists, until she is left sitting alone in the rain. When Miss Crosman offers her a beautiful white umbrella, the narrator's defenses finally break down. She accepts the gift and tells her teacher, "I wish you were my mother." When her mother does arrive, the narrator guiltily tucks the umbrella under her skirt. On the trip home, her mother causes a car accident and at first seems hurt. The narrator, ashamed of her own disloyalty, tosses the umbrella down a sewer.

Thematic Link: *Showing Your True Colors*
The narrator shows her best self when she gets rid of the white umbrella, which she comes to see as a symbol of her disloyalty.

CUSTOMIZING FOR
Students Acquiring English

- Use **ACCESS FOR STUDENTS ACQUIRING ENGLISH,** *Reading and Writing Support.*
- Invite students to expand on the Cultural Connection by sharing their home cultures' attitudes toward women working outside the home.

STRATEGIC READING FOR
Less-Proficient Readers

Set a Purpose As students read, they should think about why the narrator lies to her piano teacher and tries to impress her.

Use **UNIT FOUR RESOURCE BOOK,** pp. 17–18, for guidance in reading the selection.

WORDS TO KNOW

audible (ô′də-bəl) *adj.* able to be heard (p. 415)
confirm (kən-fûrm′) *v.* to make certain (p. 421)
credibility (krĕd′ə-bĭl′ĭ-tē) *n.* believability (p. 416)
discreet (dĭ-skrēt′) *adj.* careful about what one says or does (p. 415)
diverted (dĭ-vûr′tĭd) *adj.* turned away **divert** *v.* (p. 421)
illuminate (ĭ-lōō′mə-nāt′) *v.* to light up (p. 419)
maneuver (mə-nōō′vər) *v.* to guide or direct through a series of movements (p. 421)
resume (rĭ-zōōm′) *v.* to go on again; continue (p. 417)
revelation (rĕv′ə-lā′shən) *n.* something made known to others (p. 421)
stupendous (stōō-pĕn′dəs) *adj.* tremendous; amazing (p. 416)

THE LANGUAGE OF LITERATURE **TEACHER'S EDITION**

Linking to Science

A Cumulus clouds are large, puffy, "fair weather" clouds. Rain falls from very large, heavy clouds called cumulonimbus clouds or from a low-lying layer of nimbostratus clouds.

CUSTOMIZING FOR
Gifted and Talented Students

As students read the selection, they should think about the relationship between the narrator and Miss Crosman. Ask students what the narrator wants from Miss Crosman and what she receives. Ask students if they think that Miss Crosman wants anything from the narrator.

Possible responses:

- *Page 417—"Sisterly embarrassment seized me." The narrator wants respect from Miss Crosman.*
- *Page 418—"'Oh! That was stupendous,' she said without hugging me." The narrator wants love from Miss Crosman.*
- *Page 420—"'You shouldn't say that,' [Miss Crosman] said, but her face was opening into a huge smile . . ." Miss Crosman wants the narrator's allegiance and love.*

Active Reading: CONNECT

B Ask students what the description of Eugenie Roberts reveals about the narrator's self-image. Invite students to describe times when they envied another person. *(Possible response: The narrator is self-conscious about not being a "real" American. She desperately wants to fit in and feels inferior to Eugenie, whom she regards almost as royalty.)*

---

start cooking by ourselves, to make sure dinner would be on time. Mona would wash the vegetables and put on the rice; I would chop.

For weeks we wondered what kind of work she was doing. I imagined that she was selling perfume, testing dessert recipes for the local newspaper. Or maybe she was working for the florist. Now that she had learned to drive, she might be delivering boxes of roses to people.

"I don't think so," said Mona as we walked to our piano lesson after school. "She would've hit something by now."

A gust of wind littered the street with leaves.

"Maybe we better hurry up," she went on, looking at the sky. "It's going to pour."

"But we're too early." Her lesson didn't begin until 4:00, mine until 4:30, so we usually tried to walk as slowly as we could. **A** "And anyway, those aren't the kind of clouds that rain. Those are cumulus clouds."[1]

We arrived out of breath and wet.

"Oh, you poor, poor dears," said old Miss Crosman. "Why don't you call me the next time it's like this out? If your mother won't drive you, I can come pick you up."

"No, that's okay," I answered. Mona wrung her hair out on Miss Crosman's rug. "We just couldn't get the roof of our car to close, is all. We took it to the beach last summer and got sand in the mechanism." I pronounced this last word carefully, as if the credibility of my lie depended on its middle syllable. "It's never been the same." I thought for a second. "It's a convertible."

"Well then make yourselves at home." She exchanged looks with Eugenie Roberts, whose lesson we were interrupting. Eugenie smiled good-naturedly. "The towels are in the closet across from the bathroom."

Huddling at the end of Miss Crosman's nine-foot leatherette couch, Mona and I watched Eugenie play. She was a grade ahead of me and, according to school rumor, had a boyfriend in high school. I believed it. . . . She had auburn hair, blue eyes, and, I noted with a particular pang,[2] a pure white folding umbrella. **B**

"I can't see," whispered Mona.

"So clean your glasses."

"My glasses *are* clean. You're in the way."

I looked at her. "They look dirty to me."

"That's because *your* glasses are dirty."

Eugenie came bouncing to the end of her piece.

"Oh! Just stupendous!" Miss Crosman hugged her, then looked up as Eugenie's mother walked in. "Stupendous!" she said again. "Oh! Mrs. Roberts! Your daughter has a gift, a real gift. It's an honor to teach her."

Mrs. Roberts, radiant with pride, swept her daughter out of the room as if she were royalty, born to the piano bench. Watching the way Eugenie carried herself, I sat up and concentrated so hard on sucking in my stomach that I did not realize until the Robertses were gone that Eugenie had left her umbrella. As Mona began to play, I jumped up and ran to the window, meaning to call to them—only to see their brake lights flash then fade at the stop sign at the corner. As if to allow them passage, the rain had let up; a quivering sun lit their way. **B**

---

1. **cumulus** (kyōōm'yə-ləs) **clouds:** clouds with flat bottoms and fluffy, rounded tops.
2. **pang:** a sudden feeling of longing or distress.

WORDS TO KNOW
credibility (krĕd'ə-bĭl'ĭ-tē) *n.* believability
stupendous (stōō-pĕn'dəs) *adj.* tremendous; amazing

416

Mini-Lesson Reading Skills/Strategies

MAKING INFERENCES Remind students that an inference is a logical guess based on facts or evidence. The Reading Connection on page 414 shows how readers can infer, from information the writer provides, that Miss Crosman is a concerned and warm-hearted person.

Application Have students identify words or actions that can help them make inferences about the narrator's sister. Students can organize their thoughts on a chart such as the one shown.

Reteaching/Reinforcement
- *Unit Four Resource Book*, p. 18

Information from the Story	What I Know from Experience	Inference
Mona doesn't see a need to cover up her mother's job.	Covering up things gets you into trouble. People tend to cover up things they are ashamed of.	Mona isn't as concerned about appearances as her sister is. Mona is more confident and honest.

416 THE LANGUAGE OF LITERATURE TEACHER'S EDITION

Girl at Piano (1966), Will Barnet. Oil on canvas, 64″ × 39″, private collection. Copyright © 1995 Will Barnet/Licensed by VAGA, New York.

The umbrella glowed like a scepter[3] on the blue carpet while Mona, slumping over the keyboard, managed to eke out[4] a fair rendition of a cat fight. At the end of the piece, Miss Crosman asked her to stand up.

"Stay right there," she said, then came back a minute later with a towel to cover the bench. "You must be cold," she continued. "Shall I call your mother and have her bring over some dry clothes?"

"No," answered Mona. "She won't come because she . . ."

"She's too busy," I broke in from the back of the room.

"I see." Miss Crosman sighed and shook her head a little. "Your glasses are filthy, honey," she said to Mona. "Shall I clean them for you?"

Sisterly embarrassment seized me. Why hadn't Mona wiped her lenses when I told her to? As she <u>resumed</u> abuse of the piano, I stared at the umbrella. I wanted to open it, twirl it around by its slender silver handle; I wanted to dangle it from my wrist on the way to school the way the other girls did. I wondered what Miss Crosman would say if I offered to bring it to Eugenie at school tomorrow. She would be impressed with my consideration for others; Eugenie would be pleased to have it back; and I would have possession of the umbrella for an entire night. I looked at it again, toying with the idea of asking for one for Christmas. I knew, however, how my mother would react.

"Things," she would say. "What's the matter with a raincoat? All you want is things, just like an American."

Sitting down for my lesson, I was careful to keep the towel under me and sit up straight.

"I'll bet you can't see a thing either," said Miss Crosman, reaching for my glasses. "And you can relax, you poor dear. . . . This isn't a boot camp."[5]

When Miss Crosman finally allowed me to start playing, I played extra well, as well as I possibly could. See, I told her with my fingers.

---

3. **scepter** (sĕp′tər): the rod or baton a ruler holds as a sign of authority.
4. **eke out:** to get or produce with great struggle.
5. **boot camp:** a military base where new members of the armed forces receive basic training.

WORDS TO KNOW
resume (rĭ-zo͞om′) *v.* to go on again; continue

417

Art Note

***Girl at Piano* by Will Barnet** The paintings of Will Barnet (1911–) often resemble Japanese prints in their grace and simplicity. In *Girl at Piano*, an oil painting done in 1966, Barnet divides his canvas into simple, uncomplicated areas: the profiled piano, the background, and the girl on the piano stool.

Reading the Art How does the treatment of the girl differ from that of the piano?

Literary Concept: SYMBOLISM

C Have a volunteer read aloud the passage in which the narrator stares at the umbrella. Ask students why the author describes at such length the narrator's fascination with the umbrella. *(Possible response: The umbrella is a symbol of what the narrator wants to be—American like Eugenie.)*

CUSTOMIZING FOR
Students Acquiring English

1 Point out to students that the narrator is giving a negative opinion of her sister's piano playing by comparing it to a cat fight.

2 You may want to ask students who were not born in the U.S. to write about whether they agree or disagree with the narrator's mother's opinion of Americans.

Mini-Lesson Study Skills

TAKING STANDARDIZED TESTS Inform students that standardized tests often include vocabulary questions. *Synonym* questions ask students to find words that have the same, or almost the same, meanings as other words. *Antonym* questions ask students to find words that have opposite meanings.

Application Have students choose the phrases closest in meaning to the underlined phrases.

1. <u>eke out</u> a living
   a. perform for
   b. think about
   <u>c.</u> struggle to produce
   d. earn lots of money for

2. <u>resume</u> a game
   a. watch
   <u>b.</u> to begin again
   c. finish
   d. play

Have students choose the phrases that are opposite in meaning to the underlined phrases.

1. <u>illuminate</u> a theater
   a. open
   b. design
   <u>c.</u> darken
   d. attend a performance in

2. a <u>stupendous</u> movie
   a. blockbuster
   <u>b.</u> terrible
   c. romantic
   d. boring

THE LANGUAGE OF LITERATURE TEACHER'S EDITION **417**

CUSTOMIZING FOR
Multiple Learning Styles

D **Musical Learners** If a school piano is available, invite students who play the piano to find two compositions and play them for the class in a way that matches the description of how first Mona, then the narrator, played for Miss Crosman. If a piano is not available, musical learners can select a favorite piano recording to play for their classmates.

STRATEGIC READING FOR
Less-Proficient Readers

E Ask students why the narrator lies to Miss Crosman and plays her very best. *(Possible response: she doesn't want Miss Crosman to feel sorry for her because her mother has to work.)* **Making Inferences**

Set a Purpose Have students read to find out how the narrator responds to Miss Crosman's offer of help.

Critical Thinking: SPECULATING

F Have students speculate what Mona means when she says, "I don't think she *forgot*." *(Possible response: Mona knows that her mother is working. By her response, she suggests to the narrator that they should give up the ruse.)*

Literary Concept: SIMILE

G Have students find a simile near the end of page 418 and identify the word that shows this is a simile. *("like hair in the wind"; like)*

E You don't have to feel sorry for me.

"That was wonderful," said Miss Crosman. "Oh! Just wonderful."

D An entire constellation rose in my heart.

"And guess what," I announced proudly. "I have a surprise for you."

Then I played a second piece for her, a much more difficult one that she had not assigned.

"Oh! That was stupendous," she said without hugging me. "Stupendous! You are a genius, young lady. If your mother had started you younger, you'd be playing like Eugenie Roberts by now!"

I looked at the keyboard, wishing that I had still a third, even more difficult piece to play for her. I wanted to tell her that I was the school spelling bee champion, that I wasn't ticklish, that I could do karate.

"My mother is a concert pianist," I said.

She looked at me for a long moment, then finally, without saying anything, hugged me. I didn't say anything about bringing the umbrella to Eugenie at school.

The steps were dry when Mona and I sat down to wait for my mother.

"Do you want to wait inside?" Miss Crosman looked anxiously at the sky.

"No," I said. "Our mother will be here any minute."

"In a while," said Mona.

"Any minute," I said again, even though my mother had been at least twenty minutes late every week since she started working.

According to the church clock across the street we had been waiting twenty-five minutes when Miss Crosman came out again.

"Shall I give you ladies a ride home?"

I could not believe that I was actually holding the umbrella.

"No," I said. "Our mother is coming any minute."

"Shall I at least give her a call and remind her you're here? Maybe she forgot about you."

"I don't think she *forgot*," said Mona. **F**

"Shall I give her a call anyway? Just to be safe?"

"I bet she already left," I said. "How could she forget about us?"

Miss Crosman went in to call.

"There's no answer," she said, coming back out.

"See, she's on her way," I said.

"Are you sure you wouldn't like to come in?"

"No," said Mona.

"Yes," I said. I pointed at my sister. "She meant yes too. She meant no, she wouldn't like to go in."

Miss Crosman looked at her watch. "It's 5:30 now, ladies. My pot roast will be coming out in fifteen minutes. Maybe you'd like to come in and have some then?"

"My mother's almost here," I said. "She's on her way."

We watched and watched the street. I tried to imagine what my mother was doing; I tried to imagine her writing messages in the sky, even though I knew she was afraid of planes. I watched as the branches of Miss Crosman's big willow tree started to sway; they had all been trimmed to exactly the same height off the ground, so that they looked beautiful, like hair in the wind. **G**

It started to rain.

"Miss Crosman is coming out again," said Mona.

"Don't let her talk you into going inside," I whispered.

418 UNIT FOUR PART 1: SHOWING YOUR TRUE COLORS

Mini-Lesson  Literary Concepts

REVIEWING SETTING Remind students that setting is the time and place in which a story happens. The setting plays an important part in stories such as "The White Umbrella."

Application Discuss with students the time in which the story is set as it relates to women's roles. *(The story is set when far fewer mothers worked outside the home than do today.)* Ask how the setting reinforces the narrator's desire to fit in and have the things (such as the white umbrella) that she believes will make her socially acceptable. *(The narrator's family is one of only two Chinese families in town.)*

"Why not?"

"Because that would mean Mom isn't really coming any minute."

"But she isn't," said Mona. "She's *working*."

"Shhh! Miss Crosman is going to hear you."

"She's working! She's working! She's working!"

I put my hand over her mouth, but she licked it, and so I was wiping my hand on my wet dress when the front door opened.

"We're getting even *wetter*," said Mona right away. "Wetter and wetter."

"Shall we all go in?" Miss Crosman pulled Mona to her feet. "Before you young ladies catch pneumonia? You've been out here an hour already."

"We're *freezing*." Mona looked up at Miss Crosman. "Do you have any hot chocolate? We're going to catch *pneumonia*."

"I'm not going in," I said. "My mother's coming any minute."

"Come on," said Mona. "Use your *noggin*."[6]

"Any minute."

"Come on, Mona," Miss Crosman opened the door. "Shall we get you inside first?"

"See you in the hospital," said Mona as she went in. "See you in the hospital with *pneumonia*."

I stared out into the empty street. The rain was pricking me all over; I was cold; I wanted to go inside. I wanted to be able to let myself go inside. If Miss Crosman came out again, I decided, I would go in.

She came out with a blanket and the white umbrella.

I could not believe that I was actually holding the umbrella, opening it. It sprang up by itself as if it were alive, as if that were what it wanted to do—as if it belonged in my hands, above my head. I stared up at the network of silver spokes, then spun the umbrella around and around and around. It was so clean and white that it seemed to glow, to <u>illuminate</u> everything around it. "It's beautiful," I said.

Miss Crosman sat down next to me, on one end of the blanket. I moved the umbrella over so that it covered that too. I could feel the rain on my left shoulder and shivered. She put her arm around me.

"You poor, poor dear."

I knew that I was in store for another bolt of sympathy, and braced myself by staring up into the umbrella.

"You know, I very much wanted to have children when I was younger," she continued.

"You did?"

She stared at me a minute. Her face looked dry and crusty, like day-old frosting.

"I did. But then I never got married."

I twirled the umbrella around again.

"This is the most beautiful umbrella I have ever seen," I said. "Ever, in my whole life."

"Do you have an umbrella?"

"No. But my mother's going to get me one just like this for Christmas."

"Is she? I tell you what. You don't have to wait until Christmas. You can have this one."

"But this one belongs to Eugenie Roberts," I protested. "I have to give it back to her tomorrow in school."

"Who told you it belongs to Eugenie? It's not Eugenie's. It's mine. And now I'm giving it to you, so it's yours."

"It is?"

She hugged me tighter. "That's right. It's all yours."

---

6. **noggin:** head.

WORDS TO KNOW

illuminate (ĭ-lōō′mə-nāt′) *v.* to light up

419

Mini-Lesson   The Writer's Style

COMPARISON–AND–CONTRAST TRANSITIONS Inform students that comparison and contrast transitions help writers make clear which details are similar to one another and which are different. These transitions include *likewise, similarly, on the contrary,* and *on the other hand.* The use of *nevertheless* in the example from page 415 shows how Mona kept quiet about their mother's job, even though she didn't see a need to.

"'Those are American people,' I said.

"'So what do you think we are? I can do the pledge of allegiance with my eyes closed.'

"Nevertheless, she tried to be discreet . . . ."

Application Have students write a paragraph pointing out the similarities and differences between the narrator and her sister. Tell them to use comparison and contrast transitions.

Reteaching/Reinforcement
• Writing Handbook, p. 782
• *Writing Mini-Lessons,* p. 33

Transitions, pp. 234–237

Art Note

Japanese Rain on Canvas by David Hockney English artist Hockney (1937–) studied at the Royal College of Art in London. Hockney's early work tended to be abstract, but later he developed a more realistic style.

Reading the Art Do you think the painting complements the section of the story told on this page? Explain why or why not. What impressions do you get from Hockney's use of color?

CUSTOMIZING FOR
Students Acquiring English

 Explain that although a *zillion* has no real numerical value, its idiomatic use refers to a very large number, more than a million.

STRATEGIC READING FOR
Less-Proficient Readers

 Ask students what the narrator says to Miss Crosman that makes the narrator feel bad and why it makes her feel guilty. *(The narrator says she wishes that Miss Crosman were her mother. Saying this is not only a betrayal of her mother but also a lie. The narrator said it only because she thought it was what Miss Crosman wanted to hear.)*
Synthesizing

Linking to History

Founded in 1859 as a tea company, A&P became the first supermarket chain in the United States. The initials came from the name "Great Atlantic and Pacific Tea Company."

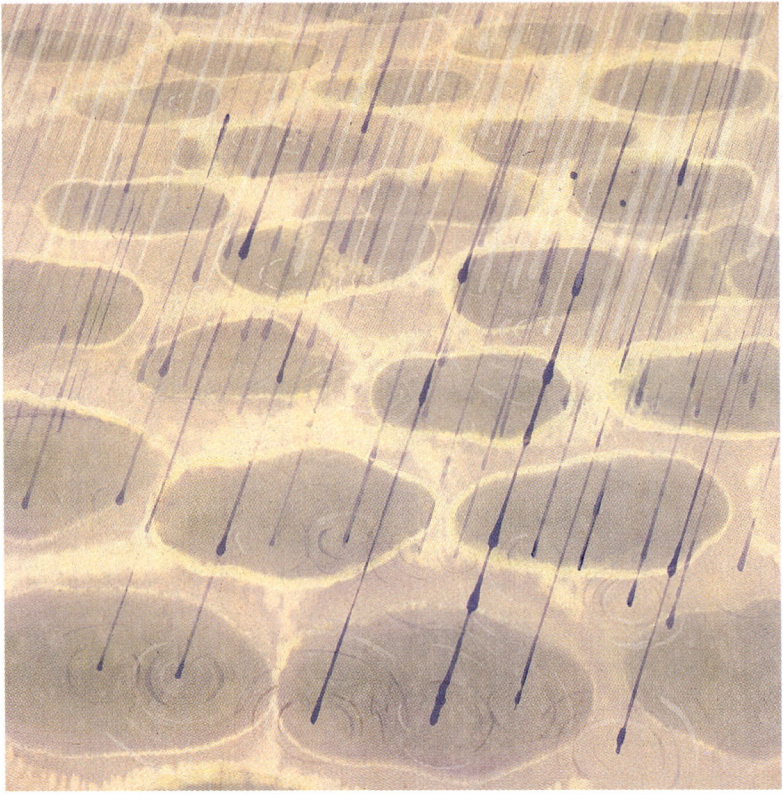

Japanese Rain on Canvas (1972), David Hockney. Acrylic on canvas, 48″ × 48″. Copyright © David Hockney.

"It's mine?" I didn't know what to say. "Mine?" Suddenly I was jumping up and down in the rain. "It's beautiful! Oh! It's beautiful!" I laughed.

Miss Crosman laughed too, even though she was getting all wet.

"Thank you, Miss Crosman. Thank you very much. Thanks a zillion. It's beautiful. It's *stupendous!*"

"You're quite welcome," she said.

"Thank you," I said again, but that didn't seem like enough. Suddenly I knew just what she wanted to hear. "I wish you were my mother."

Right away I felt bad.

"You shouldn't say that," she said, but her face was opening into a huge smile as the lights of my mother's car cautiously turned the corner. I quickly collapsed the umbrella and put it up my skirt, holding onto it from the outside, through the material.

"Mona!" I shouted into the house. "Mona! Hurry up! Mom's here! I told you she was coming!"

Then I ran away from Miss Crosman, down to the curb. Mona came tearing up to my side as my mother neared the house. We both backed up a few feet so that in case she went onto the curb, she wouldn't run us over.

"But why didn't you go inside with Mona?" my mother asked on the way home. She had taken off her own coat to put over me and had the heat on high.

"She wasn't using her noggin," said Mona, next to me in the back seat.

420 UNIT FOUR PART 1: SHOWING YOUR TRUE COLORS

Mini-Lesson • Grammar

PRONOUNS AND ANTECEDENTS Remind students that a pronoun is a word used in place of a noun. An antecedent is the word or words a pronoun stands for. A singular pronoun is used when the antecedent is singular, and a plural pronoun is used when the antecedent is plural.

Mona's piano *recital* (singular) began. *It* (singular) was terrible.

Eugenie and Mrs. Roberts (plural) smiled. *They* (plural) appreciated Miss Crosman's compliment.

Application Have students write a pronoun to replace the underlined words.

1. The narrator and the narrator's sister took piano lessons from Miss Crosman. *(her)*
2. Eugenie Roberts and her mother walked as though Eugenie and her mother were royalty. *(they)*

Reteaching/Reinforcement
- *Grammar Handbook,* pp. 826–827
- *Grammar Mini-Lessons,* copymasters, pp. 15–16, transparencies, pp. 10–11

 **The Writer's Craft**

Pronouns and Antecedents, pp. 436–437

420 THE LANGUAGE OF LITERATURE TEACHER'S EDITION

"I should call next time," said my mother. "I just don't like to say where I am."

That was when she finally told us that she was working as a check-out clerk in the A&P. She was supposed to be on the day shift, but the other employees were unreliable, and her boss had promised her a promotion if she would stay until the evening shift filled in.

For a moment no one said anything. Even Mona seemed to find the <u>revelation</u> disappointing.

"A promotion already!" she said, finally.

I listened to the windshield wipers.

"You're so quiet." My mother looked at me in the rear view mirror. "What's the matter?"

"I wish you would quit," I said after a moment.

She sighed. "The Chinese have a saying: one beam cannot hold the roof up."

"But Eugenie Roberts's father supports their family."

She sighed once more. "Eugenie Roberts's father is Eugenie Roberts's father," she said.

As we entered the downtown area, Mona started leaning hard against me every time the car turned right, trying to push me over. Remembering what I had said to Miss Crosman, I tried to <u>maneuver</u> the umbrella under my leg so she wouldn't feel it.

"What's under your skirt?" Mona wanted to know as we came to a traffic light. My mother, watching us in the rear view mirror again, rolled slowly to a stop.

"What's the matter?" she asked.

"There's something under her skirt," said Mona, pulling at me. "Under her skirt."

Meanwhile, a man crossing the street started to yell at us. "Who do you think you are, lady?" he said. "You're blocking the whole crosswalk."

We all froze. Other people walking by stopped to watch.

"Didn't you hear me?" he went on, starting to thump on the hood with his fist. "Don't you speak English?"

My mother began to back up, but the car behind us honked. Luckily, the light turned green right after that. She sighed in relief.

"What were you saying, Mona?" she asked.

We wouldn't have hit the car behind us that hard if he hadn't been moving too but as it was, our car bucked violently, throwing us all first back and then forward.

"Uh oh," said Mona when we stopped. "Another accident."

I was relieved to have attention <u>diverted</u> from the umbrella. Then I noticed my mother's head, tilted back onto the seat. Her eyes were closed.

"Mom!" I screamed. "Mom! Wake up!"

She opened her eyes. "Please don't yell," she said. "Enough people are going to yell already."

"I thought you were dead," I said, starting to cry. "I thought you were dead."

She turned around, looked at me intently, then put her hand to my forehead.

"Sick," she <u>confirmed</u>. "Some kind of sick is giving you crazy ideas."

As the man from the car behind us started tapping on the window, I moved the umbrella away from my leg. Then Mona and my mother were getting out of the car. I got out after them; and while everyone else was inspecting the damage we'd done, I threw the umbrella down a sewer. ❖

WORDS TO KNOW
revelation (rĕv′ə-lā′shən) *n.* something made known to others
maneuver (mə-nōō′vər) *v.* to guide or direct through a series of movements
diverted (dĭ-vûr′tĭd) *adj.* turned away **divert** *v.*
confirm (kən-fûrm′) *v.* to make certain

421

Mini-Lesson Spelling

THE SUFFIXES -ible AND -able Tell students that the suffix *-ible* is more commonly used with roots than with complete words. It often follows the letter *s* or the soft sound of *g*. Remind students that the hard sound of *c* or *g* is usually followed by the suffix *-able*, which is commonly used with complete words.

    aud<u>ible</u>   ador<u>able</u>

    cred<u>ible</u>   commend<u>able</u>

Application Have students add *-ible* or *-able* to the following words or roots.

1. break (breakable)
2. terr (terrible)
3. ed (edible)
4. retract (retractable)
5. poss (possible)
6. permiss (permissible)
7. wash (washable)
8. amic (amicable)
9. compat (compatible)
10. applic (applicable)

Ask students to look for more words that fit this pattern, in their own writing and in things that they read, and to add these words to their personal word lists.

Reteaching/Reinforcement
• *Unit Four Resource Book,* p. 19

Literary Concept: SETTING

Have students describe how the setting both changes and remains the same in "The White Umbrella." (*The setting is all the same town, but it moves from the narrator's home, the street on the way to the girls' piano lesson, inside and outside Miss Crosman's home, and the narrator's mother's car. The time spans a few weeks, probably at least 20 years ago.*)

CUSTOMIZING FOR
Gifted and Talented Students

Discuss with students how the narrator is embarrassed when the man crossing the street says, "Didn't you hear me? Don't you speak English?" Ask students to discuss the negative attitudes held by some Americans against people who live in the United States but do not speak English fluently. Invite students acquiring English to share their experiences.

COMPREHENSION CHECK
1. How does the narrator feel about her mother working? (*She is ashamed and embarrassed.*)
2. What excuse does the narrator give Miss Crosman for getting caught in the storm on the way to her piano lesson? (*She tells Miss Crosman that the roof of their convertible car would not close.*)
3. What object does the narrator think Eugenie Roberts left behind? (*a white umbrella*)
4. How does the narrator feel about the white umbrella? (*She wants it for herself.*)
5. What does the narrator tell Miss Crosman her mother does for a living? (*She says her mother is a concert pianist.*)
6. What is her mother's real job? (*She works as a checkout clerk at the A&P.*)
7. What does the narrator do with the white umbrella at the end of the story? (*She throws it down a sewer.*)

EDITOR'S NOTE *With the permission of the author or copyright holder, material was deleted from this selection to eliminate potentially offensive material.*

From Personal Response to Critical Analysis

1. Responses will vary.
2. Possible responses: She rejects the umbrella because of what it has symbolized to her; she thinks that her mother might be angry that she has accepted such a fine gift.
3. Possible response: Keeping up appearances is very important to the narrator until the end of the story. Mona cares far less about appearances.
4. Possible response: hard-working; practical but loving; self-sacrificing
5. Responses will vary. Some students may say that fitting in is important, so people should be willing to change, while others will say it's important to preserve cultural and family traditions.

Literary Links

How do you think the narrator's attitude toward being American compares with that of Aram in "The Summer of the Beautiful White Horse"? *(Possible response: The narrator of this selection is almost embarrassed about being Chinese. Aram seems unconcerned about his American birth and Armenian heritage.)*

Another Pathway

Cooperative Learning Have each group member choose a role, such as discussion leader, recorder, and summarizer. Be sure students understand that their events should proceed in order, filling in each segment of the umbrella.

Rubric

3 Full Accomplishment Students' story maps reveal an understanding of the plot and main episodes of the story.

2 Substantial Accomplishment Students' story maps reveal an understanding of the plot of the story but do not adequately differentiate major and minor scenes.

1 Little or Partial Accomplishment Students' story maps reveal little understanding of the plot or recall of specific scenes.

RESPONDING OPTIONS

FROM PERSONAL RESPONSE TO CRITICAL ANALYSIS

REFLECT 1. What was your reaction as you finished reading?

RETHINK 2. Why do you think the narrator throws the umbrella down a sewer?
   Consider
   Close Textual Reading
   - why she admires the umbrella
   - her mixed feelings about accepting the umbrella
   - her reaction to the accident

   3. How important do you think keeping up appearances is to each of the sisters?

   Thematic Link 4. What can you infer about the kind of person the girls' mother is? Explain, using examples from the story and from your own experience.

RELATE 5. When the mother in this story points out that "lots of people's mothers work," her daughter replies, "Those are American people." The family seems unsure as to how it fits into the American culture. In what ways do you think people should change when they move to a different country?

Multimodal Learning
ANOTHER PATHWAY
Cooperative Learning
Work with some classmates, using a graphic image of an umbrella, to create a story map for "The White Umbrella." Pick one segment of the open umbrella in which to describe the first scene in the story. Then record each remaining scene in the story.

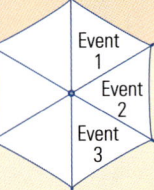

LITERARY CONCEPTS

A **symbol** is a person, place, or object that stands for something beyond itself. In literature, objects and images are used to symbolize things that cannot actually be seen, such as an idea or feeling. In "Cricket in the Road," for example, the bat and ball might symbolize the friendship between Selo, Vern, and Amy. When the children separate for a time, Selo throws them away. When the friends are reunited, a new bat takes on the same meaning. What do you think the white umbrella in this story might symbolize?

QUICKWRITES

1. Write a **motto**, or saying, that might hang on this family's kitchen wall. Use what you have learned about the family's values to choose an appropriate motto.

2. Write the text for a **Mother's Day card** that the narrator might give to her mother. Include comments that relate directly to the events in the story.

📁 **PORTFOLIO** Save your writing. You may want to use it later as a springboard to a piece for your portfolio.

422 UNIT FOUR PART 1: SHOWING YOUR TRUE COLORS

Literary Concepts

Point out that the umbrella symbolizes different ideas at different points in the story. To the narrator it symbolizes being an American, then betrayal. To the narrator's mother it symbolizes superficial values. Have partners discuss what the white umbrella might symbolize at different points or to different characters. Suggest that they review the story, noting each time the umbrella is mentioned.

QuickWrites

1. Possible responses: Be who you are; United we stand; No more secrets; Don't stand in the rain. If available, you can show students sample mottos often displayed in gift catalogs.
2. Encourage students to think about the narrator's mixed feelings for her mother and how those feelings changed at the end of the story.

Finding a Focus, pp. 203–204

---

422 THE LANGUAGE OF LITERATURE TEACHER'S EDITION

CRITIC'S CORNER

A member of the student board that reviewed the stories in this book says, "I liked how the story was told by the main character. When a story is written like this, I think it makes it more interesting, because you see how the main character feels." Do you agree that having the main character as a first-person narrator makes the story more interesting? Why or why not?

WORDS TO KNOW

On your own paper, answer the following questions.

1. Which cannot be what it was before if it becomes a **revelation**—a government, a secret, or a promise?
2. With which can you **confirm** the spelling of a word—a pen, an eraser, or a dictionary?
3. With which would you **illuminate** a house—lamps, a roof, or a bulldozer?
4. What does a baseball player use to try to **divert** a thrown ball—a glove or a catcher's mask?
5. Would a **discreet** person be most likely to behave in a rude, cautious, or bold way?
6. When you are eating, is the most **audible** food a raw carrot, a cupcake, or a hamburger?
7. What do you have to do before you can **resume** something—finish it, repeat it, or pause?
8. Would a person who saw something that was truly **stupendous** be most likely to yawn, giggle, or gasp?
9. If a person is known for **credibility,** what is his or her reputation for—honesty, bravery, or sassiness?
10. If someone wanted to **maneuver** a car, what would his or her concern be—stopping it, steering it, or affording it?

GISH JEN

A daughter of immigrant Chinese parents, Gish Jen grew up just north of New York City. She remembers her family feeling the need to fit in—to be absorbed into the main culture. "We were almost the only Asian-American family in town," she recalls. "People threw things at us and called us names. We thought it was normal—it was only much later that I realized it had been hard." Jen says these experiences did not make her childhood unhappy. In fact, her writing contains a great deal of humor.

Jen's first name is really Lillian. She adopted the name Gish, the last name of the famous silent-picture actress Lillian Gish, just for fun in high school. After Jen graduated from college, she went to China to teach English and later enrolled in The Writer's Workshop, a well-known program at the University of Iowa, where she wrote "The White Umbrella."

About her writing, Jen says, "If there is one thing I hope readers come away with, it's to see Asian Americans as 'us' rather than 'other.'"

OTHER WORKS *Typical American*

1956–

THE WHITE UMBRELLA 423

Across the Curriculum

Math *Get the Facts!* Have students survey the class to find out how many mothers of classmates work outside the home. Tell them to convert their number to a percentage and compare the statistic to the percentages of working mothers given in the Cultural Connection on page 414.

History *Cooperative Learning East Meets West* Have students work in small groups of three or four to learn about the history of Chinese immigration to North America. Individual groups can focus on specific time periods or geographic regions. For instance, students can find out more about the use of Chinese immigrants to build the Union Pacific railroad.

Words to Know

1. a secret
2. a dictionary
3. lamps
4. a catcher's mask
5. cautious
6. a carrot
7. pause
8. gasp
9. honesty
10. steering it

GISH JEN

Gish Jen says that the biggest influence on her work has come from Jewish-American writers. She sees a definite sympathy between the Jewish and Chinese cultures.

Alternative Activities

1. Have students work cooperatively in small groups to plan a story theater presentation of a scene from "The White Umbrella." One student can narrate the scene while the others pantomime the actions of the characters. Group size should be dependent on the number of characters in the selected scene.
2. Ask students to find a musical composition that fits the mood of different scenes of "The White Umbrella." You may elect to have students play these compositions as background music for the pantomimes above.

THE LANGUAGE OF LITERATURE TEACHER'S EDITION 423

OVERVIEW

Objectives

- To understand and appreciate two poems about cats—a concrete poem and a poem with a regular pattern of rhythm and rhyme
- To understand the purpose of concrete poems
- To understand and identify a poem's rhyme scheme
- To express understanding of the selection through a choice of writing forms, including a poem, a letter, and a story
- To extend understanding of the selection through a variety of multimodal and cross-curricular activities

Skills

THE WRITER'S STYLE
- Vivid description

LITERARY CONCEPTS
- Rhyme scheme
- Characterization

SPEAKING, LISTENING, AND VIEWING
- Group discussion
- Oral presentation

Cross-Curricular Connections

ART
- Cats in art

GEOGRAPHY
- Ancient Phoenicia and Egypt

SCIENCE CONNECTION
Why Do Cats Land on Their Feet?

The gracefulness of house cats includes their ability to land, nearly always, on their feet. This film will help students understand the physiology of the domestic cat.

Side A, Frame 27551

PREVIEWING

POETRY

Concrete Cat
Dorthi Charles

Chang McTang McQuarter Cat
John Ciardi

Activating Prior Knowledge/Setting a Purpose
PERSONAL CONNECTION

Have you heard the expression "Curiosity killed the cat"? What other qualities or traits come to mind when you think of cats? Draw a picture similar to the one shown, and write a quality you think of on each "whisker." As you read, see how your ideas about cats compare with those presented in the poems.

Building Background
SCIENCE CONNECTION

Cats, which belong to the scientific family of animals called *Felidae*, have a history dating back about 55 million years. The ancestors of the cats we know today were the African wildcat, the Kaffir cat, and the European wildcat.

The Egyptians were probably the first to tame cats, which they did around 3500 B.C. Cats were useful because they protected the Egyptian storehouses of grain from rats and mice. Egyptians admired the sleek and graceful form of cats and duplicated it in sculpture, furniture, and jewelry. By 1500 B.C., the Egyptians had come to view cats as sacred. The sculpture shown is a representation of the goddess Bastet or Bast, who was also depicted by ancient Egyptians with the head of a cat and the body of a woman.

Around 900 B.C., Phoenician traders carried Egyptian cats to Europe, where they bred with European wildcats to produce the ordinary house cat. European explorers, colonists, and traders brought such cats to North and South America in the 1700s.

Active Reading
READING CONNECTION

Concrete Poems Although these two poems share the same subject, they are very different in form. "Chang McTang McQuarter Cat" has a regular pattern of both rhyme and rhythm. "Concrete Cat" is called a concrete poem. In concrete poetry, the poet arranges the words into a special shape or picture. The image helps reveal the poem's meaning. For example, a concrete poem about spring might be presented in the shape of a flower.

The goddess Bastet in the form of a cat (about 664–610 B.C.) Egyptian bronze, The Granger Collection, New York.

• SCIENCE CONNECTION

424 UNIT FOUR PART 1: SHOWING YOUR TRUE COLORS

PRINT AND MEDIA RESOURCES

UNIT FOUR RESOURCE BOOK
Strategic Reading: Literature, p. 23

ACCESS FOR STUDENTS ACQUIRING ENGLISH
Reading and Writing Support

FORMAL ASSESSMENT
Selection Test, p. 85
 Test Generator

 AUDIO LIBRARY
See Reference Card

Science Connection

---

424 THE LANGUAGE OF LITERATURE **TEACHER'S EDITION**

CONCRETE CAT
by DORTHI CHARLES

```
        eAr        eAr
       eYe        eYe         stripestripestripestripe        t
    whisker      whisker          stripestripestripe        a i l t a i l
    whisker   m     h whisker   stripestripestripestripes
              o   u  t             stripestripestripe
                                stripestripestripestripe

             paw paw              paw paw
                                                        ǝsnoɯ
         dishdish                          litterbox
                                           litterbox
```

FROM **PERSONAL RESPONSE** *TO* **CRITICAL ANALYSIS**

REFLECT 1. What was your impression of the concrete poem "Concrete Cat"?
RETHINK 2. Why do you think the mouse is upside down?
             3. What effect do you think the poet was trying to convey?

CONCRETE CAT **425**

Assessment Option

SELF-ASSESSMENT To help students assess their understanding of the poem, have them write a critique of the poem in which they ask themselves and then respond to the following questions:
- Which of the two poems in the selection did I enjoy more? Why?
- What aspects of the poems (subject, style, etc.) were easy to understand?
- What aspects of the poems were the most difficult?
- What did I learn from the style of each poet that I could use in writing a poem of my own?

Thematic Link: *Showing Your True Colors*
Both poems detail the characteristics of cats—their physical traits and their personality traits.

CUSTOMIZING FOR
Students Acquiring English
- Use **ACCESS FOR STUDENTS ACQUIRING ENGLISH**, *Reading and Writing Support*.
- Attitudes toward domestic animals vary from culture to culture. Invite students to share their home cultures' ideas about domestic animals such as cats.

STRATEGIC READING FOR
Less-Proficient Readers

A Ask students what device the poet uses to describe a typical cat. *(visual imagery through words in the shape of a cat)* Noting Relevant Details

Set a Purpose Have students pay special attention to the traits of the cat the speaker describes in "Chang McTang McQuarter Cat."

Use **UNIT FOUR RESOURCE BOOK**, page 23, for guidance in reading the selections.

CUSTOMIZING FOR
Gifted and Talented Students
Have students write their own concrete poems about an animal of their choice.

From Personal Response to Critical Analysis
1. Responses will vary.
2. Possible response: to stress that the cat has killed it
3. Possible responses: humorous, affectionate, artistic

THE LANGUAGE OF LITERATURE TEACHER'S EDITION **425**

Art Note

Tabitha by James Lloyd English artist James Lloyd (1905–1974) began painting in 1953, at the age of 48. Success came slowly, culminating in 1964 when the British Broadcasting Company aired Ken Russell's film about the artist, "The Dotty World of James Lloyd." "Dotty" here refers to the hundreds of thousands of colored dots that Lloyd used to build up his paintings.

Reading the Art *Compare the size of Tabitha to the fence and trees in the background. Why do you think Lloyd chose to use this perspective?*

CUSTOMIZING FOR
Students Acquiring English

① Point out to students the cat's unusual name which suggests combined ethnicities and ask them how it might relate to the cat's many parts. *(suggests the diverse traits are perhaps due to the cat's mixed heritage)*

② Explain that the idiomatic phrase *this and that* means "a little of everything."

Literary Concept:
CHARACTERIZATION

Ⓑ Have students read aloud lines from the first stanza that show what senses the writer appeals to in developing the character of Chang McTang. *(Possible responses: hearing—"One part is yowl, one part is purr"; touch—"One part is scratch, one part is fur"; sight—"...he sits and stares right through/You...")*

CUSTOMIZING FOR
Multiple Learning Styles

Ⓒ **Spatial or Graphic Learners** Have students draw or paint a picture of the place inside Chang McTang that's "as black/And green and yellow as the night/A jungle makes in full moonlight."

Tabitha, James Lloyd. Portal Gallery, London. Courtesy of Martin Leman.

Chang McTang
McQuarter Cat

BY JOHN CIARDI

426 UNIT FOUR PART 1: SHOWING YOUR TRUE COLORS

Mini-Lesson  The Writer's Style

VIVID DESCRIPTION Remind students that writers choose words carefully to create vivid descriptions that paint a picture in the reader's mind. In "Chang McTang McQuarter Cat," for example, Ciardi uses the words "yawn" and "grin" to help readers picture the cat's facial expressions.

Application Students can use a word web to organize details about a subject or idea. Have students choose an animal other than a cat and brainstorm vivid details about the animal to create a word web like the one shown. Students can later use these webs for the QuickWrites on page 428.

Reteaching/Reinforcement
• Writing Handbook, pp. 784–785

 **The Writer's Craft**

Thinking with Pictures, p. 192–196

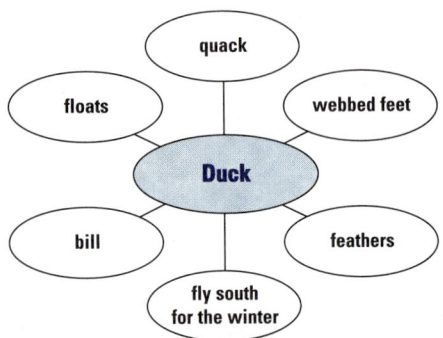

426 THE LANGUAGE OF LITERATURE TEACHER'S EDITION

Chang McTang McQuarter Cat
Is one part this and one part that.
One part is yowl, one part is purr.
One part is scratch, one part is fur.
5   One part, maybe even two,
Is how he sits and stares right through
You and you and you and you.
And when you feel my Chang-Cat stare
You wonder if you're really there.

10 Chang McTang McQuarter Cat
Is one part this and ten parts that.
He's one part saint, and two parts sin.
One part yawn, and three parts grin,
One part sleepy, four parts lightning,
15 One part cuddly, five parts fright'ning,
One part snarl, and six parts play.
One part is how he goes away
Inside himself, somewhere miles back
Behind his eyes, somewhere as black
20 And green and yellow as the night
A jungle makes in full moonlight.

Chang McTang McQuarter Cat
Is one part this and twenty that.
One part is statue, one part tricks—
25 (One part, or six, or thirty-six.)

One part (or twelve, or sixty-three)
Is—Chang McTang belongs to ME!

Don't ask, "How many parts is that?"
Addition's nothing to a cat.

30 If you knew Chang, then you'd know this:
He's one part everything there is.

Literary Concept:
RHYME SCHEME

D Have a volunteer read aloud the third stanza of the poem. Have another volunteer reread the last words in each line. Then ask students to identify the rhymed pairs of words. *(Cat/that; tricks/six)*

STRATEGIC READING FOR
Less-Proficient Readers

E Have students identify some characteristics of Chang McTang. *(Possible responses: soft fur, sharp claws, penetrating stare, slow-moving, fast-moving, and self-contained)* **Restating**

CUSTOMIZING FOR
Gifted and Talented Students

Have students look up *elusive* in a dictionary. Invite students to write an essay titled "The Elusive Chang McTang."

COMPREHENSION CHECK
1. What aspects of a cat does the poet describe in the first poem? *(body parts, fur pattern, prey, and owner's necessities—dish, litter box)*
2. What is significant about the form of the first poem *(it is shaped like its subject—a cat)*
3. In Ciardi's poem, how does the speaker go about describing the cat? *(The speaker names the many "parts" that make up the cat.)*
4. What does the phrase "one part saint and two parts sin" suggest about the cat's behavior? *(cat has both good and bad behaviors)*

Mini-Lesson Literary Concepts

REVIEWING CHARACTERIZATION
Remind students that a writer develops characters in four basic ways: (1) a physical description of the character; (2) the character's thoughts, speech, and actions; (3) the thoughts, speech, and actions of other characters; and (4) direct comments on a character's nature. For instance, Ciardi develops the character of the cat primarily through physical description and direct comments on the cat's nature.

Application Have students make a chart like the one shown listing all of Chang McTang McQuarter Cat's "parts" and identify those which refer to physical description and those which refer to the cat's nature. Then have students do a character makeover by imagining Chang McTang McQuarter Cat as a person. Ask students which traits they would revise to convey the physical description and nature of a human.

Chang McTang McQuarter Cat		
Character Trait	Physical Description	Character's Nature

From Personal Response to Critical Analysis

1. Responses will vary.
2. Some students may say that the speaker feels affection, delight, or both toward Chang McTang.
3. Responses will vary. They may include mischievous, cunning, lovable, feisty, smart.
4. Some students may say that, having tried to describe Chang and winding up with a list of contradictory qualities, the speaker concludes that Chang is undefinable: All the qualities in the world belong to him.
5. Make sure that students support their responses with details from the poems.

Another Pathway

Provide a supply of old magazines for students to use. Coupon fliers from newspapers often contain cat-food advertisements with photographs of cats.

Rubric
- **3 Full Accomplishment** Students' collages reflect an understanding of cats' personalities.
- **2 Substantial Accomplishment** Students create a visually satisfying collage that, however, does not clearly convey the cats' personalities.
- **1 Little or Partial Accomplishment** Students have difficulty selecting appropriate images.

RESPONDING OPTIONS

FROM PERSONAL RESPONSE TO CRITICAL ANALYSIS

REFLECT
1. What phrases or lines from "Chang McTang McQuarter Cat" stand out in your mind? Jot your favorite phrases or lines in your notebook.

RETHINK
2. How do you think the speaker feels about Chang McTang?

Thematic Link
3. In two or three words, describe your impression of Chang McTang.

4. What do you think the speaker means by saying that Chang McTang is "one part everything there is"?

RELATE
5. Look again at the qualities of cats you recorded for the Personal Connection on page 424. Has reading "Concrete Cat" and "Chang McTang McQuarter Cat" changed your ideas about cats? Why or why not?

Multimodal Learning
ANOTHER PATHWAY

How would you compare the "personalities" of the two cats in these poems? Look for photographs or illustrations in magazines that match your idea of what these cats would look like and how they would act. Create a collage of these images that you could show to younger children as you read the poems to them.

LITERARY CONCEPTS

The pattern of rhyme at the end of the lines of a poem is called the poem's **rhyme scheme.** A rhyme scheme is noted by assigning letters of the alphabet to the lines of a poem. The letters show which lines end with the same sounds. Here is the rhyme scheme of the first four lines of "Barbara Frietchie":

> Up from the meadows rich with *corn*,   **A**
> Clear in the cool September *morn*,   **A**
> The clustered spires of Frederick *stand*   **B**
> Green-walled by the hills of Mary*land*.   **B**

Select one stanza from "Chang McTang McQuarter Cat" and identify the rhyme scheme of that stanza.

CONCEPT REVIEW: Repetition The use of a word or phrase over and over in a literary work to get across a certain meaning is called repetition. Find an example of repetition in "Concrete Cat" and one in "Chang McTang McQuarter Cat."

QUICKWRITES

1. Write a **poem** about your own pet or another subject of your choice, using the style of either Dorthi Charles or John Ciardi.
2. Imagine you are Chang McTang. Write a **letter** to the speaker of the poem, expressing your outlook on life.
3. Draft a brief **story,** using Chang McTang as the main character. Make up any other characters you want in your story.

📁 **PORTFOLIO** Save your writing. You may want to use it later as a springboard to a piece for your portfolio.

428   UNIT FOUR   PART 1: SHOWING YOUR TRUE COLORS

Literary Concepts

Make sure that, beginning with A, students assign one letter to each different sound that occurs at the end of a line. For example, Stanza 1: A, A, B, B, C, C, C, D, D.

Concept Review Possible responses: "stripestripestripestripe" ("Concrete Cat") and "You and you and you and you" ("Chang McTang McQuarter Cat")

QuickWrites

1. Have students identify their model poem. Make sure that concrete poems communicate through shapes as well as words.
2. To help students assume Chang McTang's point of view, encourage them to review the poem before they begin writing.
3. You may wish to allow students to work in pairs to brainstorm additional characters they might include.

 The Writer's Craft

Writing a Poem, pp. 86–88
Friendly Letter, pp. 40–43
Story Map, 196

LITERARY LINKS

Choose one of the characters from an earlier selection, and depict his or her most important qualities in a concrete poem.

CRITIC'S CORNER

The poet who wrote "Concrete Cat" once said, "A poem is most likely to arise when I haven't an idea in the world. It usually begins with a promising blob of language." How does that statement affect your understanding of "Concrete Cat"?

ACROSS THE CURRICULUM

Art Cats have found their way into paintings and sculptures, both ancient and contemporary. Use art books from your school or community library to find examples of cats portrayed in fine art. Prepare a cat-lover's guide to fine art, including a list of the paintings or sculptures you find, for your classmates to use.

Who's the Fairest of Them All? Frank Paton (1856–1909). Bonhams, London, Bridgeman/Art Resource, New York.

DORTHI CHARLES (X. J. KENNEDY)

Dorthi Charles (1929–) is a pen name of the well-known author and poet X. J. Kennedy. Kennedy spent a good deal of his youth producing hand-drawn cartoons similar to *Superman* and *Batman*. When he finally concluded he wasn't talented enough to pursue cartooning as a career, he turned to writing science fiction. It was eight years before he sold a story to a magazine.

Kennedy served for four years in the navy, where he began writing poetry during off-duty time. Eventually he sold two poems to *The New Yorker,* and his career as a poet was established. Kennedy now devotes himself to his work full-time.

Kennedy credits the poet Myra Cohn Livingston and the children's book editor Margaret McElderry for the encouragement and support that led to his writing for children. He notes, "It's writing for kids that's the most fun of all."

OTHER WORKS *One Winter Night in August and Other Nonsense Jingles; The Phantom Ice Cream Man; The Owlstone Crown*

JOHN CIARDI

1916–1986

The poet and critic John Ciardi was born in Boston to Italian immigrants in an area still referred to as Little Italy. His father died when Ciardi was only three years old, and his mother spoke little English. As he grew older, he discovered the advantages of being reared in a bilingual atmosphere.

From 1939 to 1961, Ciardi taught college English. He gave up teaching to become a full-time writer, and served as poetry editor of the *Saturday Review* from 1956 to 1977. About children's poetry he once said, "I dislike most of the children's poems I see because they seem written by a sponge dipped in warm milk and sprinkled with sugar." Motivated by his young nephews and later his own children, Ciardi himself began writing poetry for children, which is considered his most important literary contribution.

OTHER WORKS *The Reason for the Pelican, Scrappy the Pup, I Met a Man, The King Who Saved Himself from Being Saved* Extended Reading

CONCRETE CAT / CHANG MCTANG MCQUARTER CAT **429**

Literary Links

Accept any character from an earlier selection. Make sure that students craft both the shape and language of their concrete poems to suit the chosen character. For instance, students could play with the round, blob shape of an oyster to depict the "spineless" way the Oysters allow themselves to be eaten by the Walrus and the Carpenter.

Across the Curriculum

Art *Cooperative Learning* Have students work in small groups. Make sure that each group member chooses a role in preparing the cat-lover's guide. One student might research ancient paintings about cats, another might research sculptures, another modern paintings, and another photography. Have students cooperate in assembling their final guides.

ADDITIONAL SUGGESTION

 Geography *Which Way Did They Go?* Have students review the Science Connection on page 424. Have them use an historical atlas to make a map that shows how Phoenician traders could transport Egyptian cats to Europe in 900 B.C.

JOHN CIARDI

Ciardi produced more than 40 books of criticism and poetry and received numerous awards for both his juvenile books and his adult books, including the 1962 Boys' Clubs of America Junior Book Award for *The Man Who Sang the Sillies*.

DORTHI CHARLES (X. J. KENNEDY)

Kennedy's poems have appeared in hundreds of anthologies and magazines. He was awarded a *Los Angeles Times* Book Award for Poetry.

WHAT DO YOU THINK?

Reflecting on Theme

Refer students to the song lyrics they created before reading the selections in Part 1. Ask them if their thoughts have changed on what "true colors" are and how they can be shown. If so, invite them to regroup with their partners and revise their lyrics. Volunteers can share their songs with the class. If possible, you may wish to play for students Cyndi Lauper's song entitled "True Colors," a popular slogan for a camera film TV commercial.

THE LANGUAGE OF LITERATURE TEACHER'S EDITION **429**

OVERVIEW

Objectives

- To understand and appreciate a biographical account of Captain William Kidd
- To enrich reading by understanding how problems are presented and solved
- To identify and understand tone
- To express understanding of the selection through a choice of writing forms, including a ballad, a log entry, and a last will and testament
- To extend understanding of the selection through a variety of multimodal and cross-curricular activities

Skills

READING SKILLS/STRATEGIES
- Predicting

THE WRITER'S STYLE
- Show, don't tell

GRAMMAR
- Irregular plural nouns

LITERARY CONCEPTS
- Internal conflict
- Tone

GENRE STUDY
- Nonfiction: biography

SPELLING
- The suffixes -ence and -ent

STUDY SKILLS
- Skimming

SPEAKING, LISTENING, AND VIEWING
- Group discussion
- Oral Presentation

Cross-Curricular Connections

SCIENCE
- Sailing

HISTORY
- King William's War

GEOGRAPHY
- Gardiner's Island

ART
- Pyle's pirate paintings

HISTORICAL CONNECTION

Pirate Lore Many tales of the high seas were recorded by sailors and pirates between the 1600s and 1800s. The images seen here reflect some of those tales. You may wish to use them during a discussion of the elements of pirate lore used by writers and storytellers.

Side A, Frame 38844

PREVIEWING

NONFICTION

from Gold and Silver, Silver and Gold
Alvin Schwartz

PERSONAL CONNECTION *Activating Prior Knowledge/Setting a Purpose*

Through the ages, people have searched for hidden treasure and for instant wealth. Columbus was seeking the fabled treasure of the Indies in 1492, not a new continent. What urge compels people to pursue buried treasure and get-rich-quick schemes? Jot down on a sheet of paper some of the motives you think inspire people to enter sweepstakes, buy lottery tickets, and invest in various easy-money offers. As you read, see whether your ideas about the pursuit of wealth change.

HISTORICAL CONNECTION *Building Background*

In the late 1690s, when Captain Kidd sailed the route shown on the map, England was at war with France on two fronts: in North America, over French expansion into the colonies, and in Europe, over a similar extension of French power. At the same time, piracy was rapidly increasing, as sea thieves plundered the coasts of North and South America and Africa, searching for treasure on any ships they encountered.

King William of England demanded that the new royal governor of New York eliminate piracy. Because the war with France left few ships available to chase pirates, the governor turned to privateers. Unlike pirates, privateers were hired and licensed by governments to capture and plunder enemy and pirate ships. They did not receive regular pay, only a share of any goods they captured. The crews of privateer ships were often undisciplined and disloyal. Some even resorted to mutiny, a rebellion of sailors against superior officers.

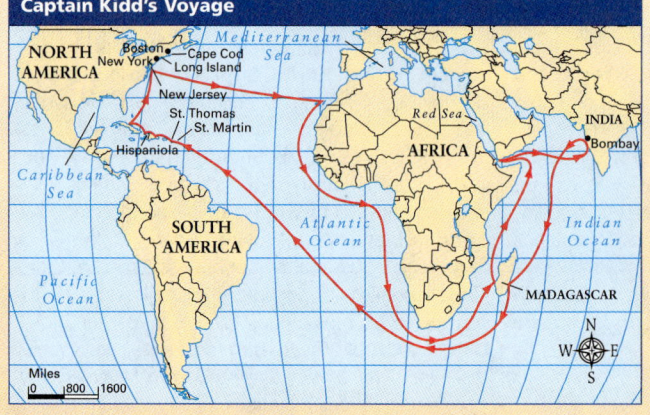

430 UNIT FOUR PART 1: SHOWING YOUR TRUE COLORS

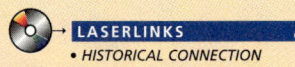
- HISTORICAL CONNECTION
- VISUAL VOCABULARY

PRINT AND MEDIA RESOURCES

UNIT FOUR RESOURCE BOOK
Strategic Reading: Literature, p. 27
Reading SkillBuilder, p. 28
Spelling SkillBuilder, p. 29

GRAMMAR MINI-LESSONS
Transparencies, p. 8
Copymasters, p. 10

WRITING MINI-LESSONS
Transparencies, p. 46

ACCESS FOR STUDENTS ACQUIRING ENGLISH
Selection Summaries
Reading and Writing Support

FORMAL ASSESSMENT
Selection Test, p. 87
Test Generator

 **AUDIO LIBRARY**
See Reference Card

 **LASERLINKS**
Historical Connection

---

430 THE LANGUAGE OF LITERATURE TEACHER'S EDITION

READING CONNECTION Active Reading

Problem Solving

Many selections that you have read in this book involve one or more characters faced with a conflict or problem of some sort. Those problems may range from a physical challenge that must be overcome to a difficult situation that must be resolved. In any case, the selections often explore the characters' attempts to find solutions to their problems. In "Tuesday of the Other June," for example, the main character solves her problem with the "Other June" by physically standing up to her and refusing to accept her bullying.

One way to begin to understand a selection is to think about the problems it portrays and possible solutions to those problems. The chart shown provides some questions to keep in mind as you attempt to identify problems and solutions in a selection—and as you evaluate the end result.

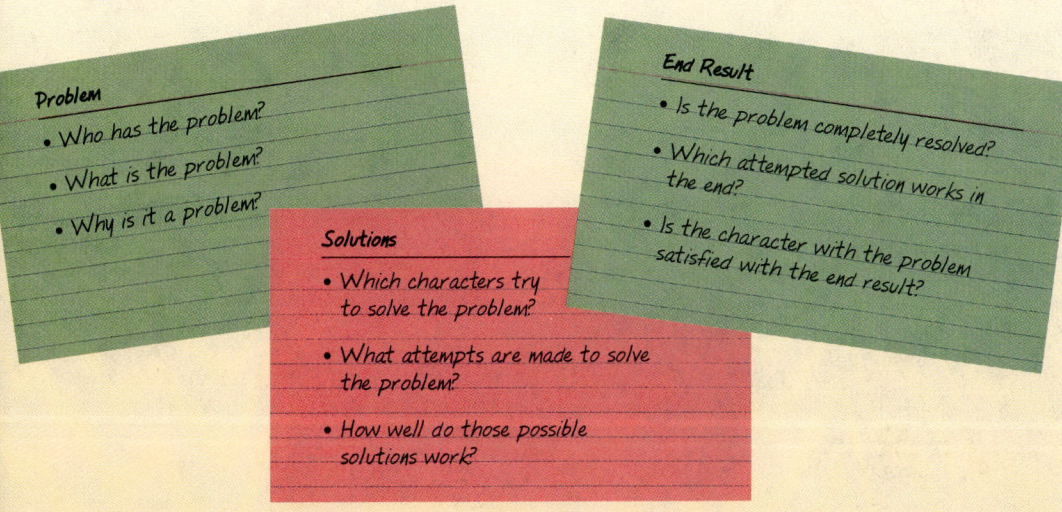

In this selection, a number of problems are presented, along with some attempted solutions. Take advantage of the questions that you find as you read to help you understand the problems Captain Kidd and others face and their efforts to resolve them.

GOLD AND SILVER, SILVER AND GOLD **431**

WORDS TO KNOW

mutiny (myo͞ot′n-ē) *v.* to engage in open rebellion against authority (p. 433)

💿 **VISUAL VOCABULARY**

• **gallows** (găl′ōz) • **sound** (sound)

Side A, Frame 38852

SUMMARY

Was Captain William Kidd a dangerous pirate or simply a loyal seaman following orders? That question lies at the heart of this selection, which explores the later part of Kidd's life. In 1696 Governor Bellomont of New York asked Kidd to capture pirate ships and French vessels for England. Kidd tried to follow the governor's orders, but his crew rebelled. They plundered every ship in sight, forcing Kidd to join in. One of the plundered ships belonged to the emperor of India but was sailing under French protection. Kidd kept the ship's "French papers" as proof that he had legally captured a French ship. The mutinous crew soon abandoned Kidd in Madagascar, leaving him so quickly that they forgot a large amount of treasure. He set sail for New York, learning during the voyage that he had been charged with piracy. Promised mercy, Kidd arranged to meet with Governor Bellomont—only to be arrested as soon as he reached shore. Bellomont seized Kidd's treasure and sent him in chains to England, promising to send along the French papers. The English government, claiming that the papers had never arrived, sentenced Kidd to hang for piracy. Two hundred years after his execution, the papers were found—in the hands of the English government.

Thematic Link: *Showing Your True Colors*
Neither Captain Kidd nor the English government was precisely what it seemed. Kidd's true colors remain a mystery.

CUSTOMIZING FOR
Students Acquiring English

• Use **ACCESS FOR STUDENTS ACQUIRING ENGLISH.**

• This selection begins in New York City in the late seventeenth century. If necessary, remind students that, at that time, New York was a colony under the rule of the British government.

STRATEGIC READING FOR
Less-Proficient Readers

Set a Purpose Discuss with students their ideas about pirates. Then have them read to find out about Kidd's mission and why he hired former pirates to work on his ship.

Use **UNIT FOUR RESOURCE BOOK,** pp. 27–28, for guidance in reading the selection.

THE LANGUAGE OF LITERATURE **TEACHER'S EDITION** **431**

CUSTOMIZING FOR
Gifted and Talented Students

Encourage students, as they read, to think about the role that Governor Bellomont plays in Kidd's life. Have students look for evidence that shows how Bellomont treated Kidd.

Possible responses:

- *Page 433—Bellomont gave Kidd an outfitted ship but provided no money for him to pay a crew. Consequently, Kidd had to hire untrustworthy men.*

- *Page 437—Bellomont lied to Kidd and seized his treasure. Bellomont may have planned in advance to keep Kidd's treasure.*

Literary Concept: TONE

A Ask volunteers to read aloud the first three paragraphs of the selection. Ask students what attitude the writer has toward his subject. *(Possible responses: straightforwardness, fairness, sincerity)*

Linking to History

B The English and French were fighting King William's War from 1689 to 1697. One of four wars waged between 1689 and 1763, it arose from colonial and maritime rivalry between France and England. Not only did French privateers inhibit English shipping on the high seas, the war also raged on land as the French and their Native-American allies burned Schenectady, New York; ruined Salmon Falls, New Hampshire; and decimated Fort Loyal, Maine.

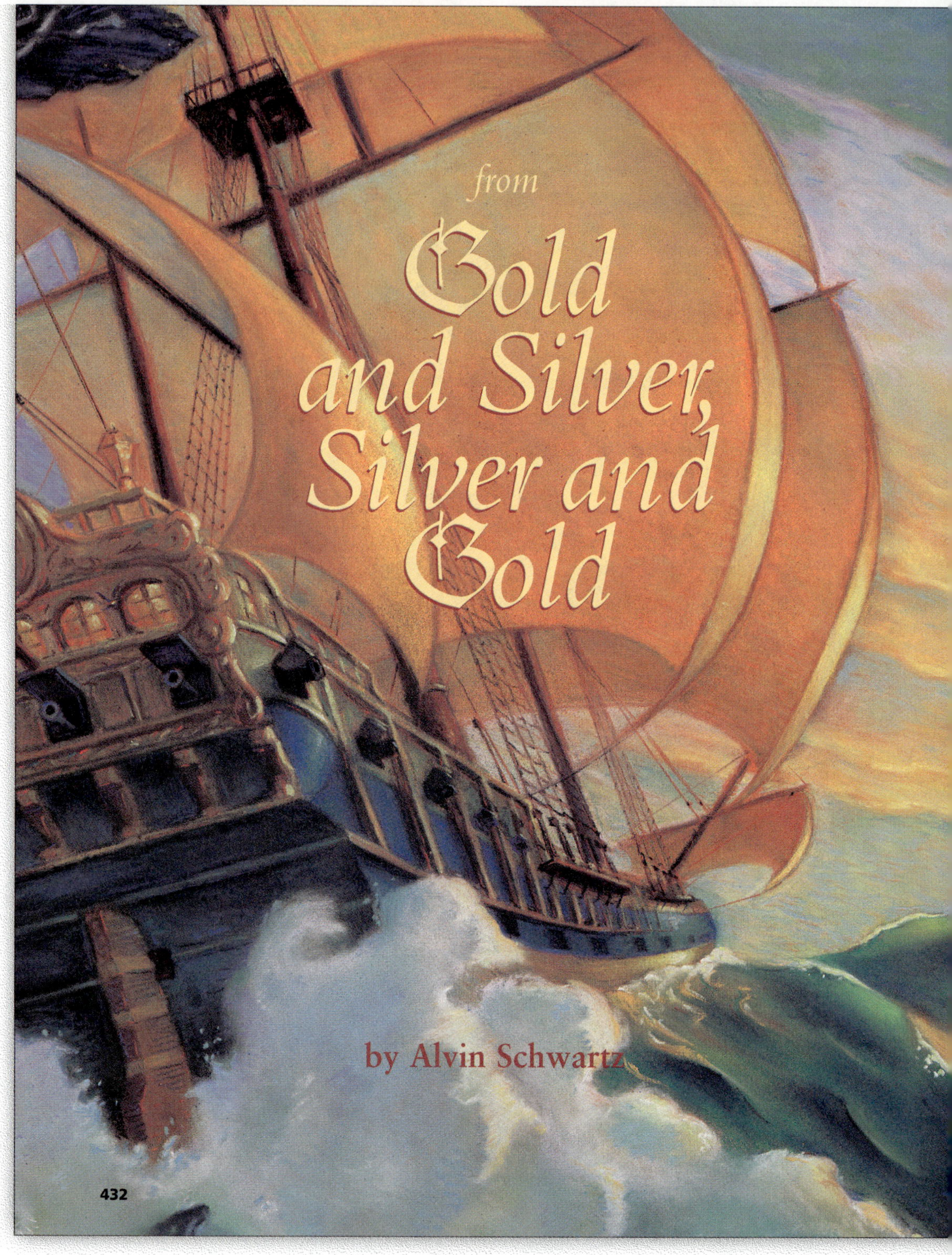

from
Gold and Silver, Silver and Gold

by Alvin Schwartz

Mini-Lesson  Reading Skills/Strategies

ACTIVE READING: PREDICT Remind students that active readers use strategies as they read. Predicting strategies help readers anticipate what they might read next. Often writers make statements that serve as hints. Tell students they should look for such statements and predict what might happen in the selection.

Application Read aloud or have students read the two highlighted passages on page 433. Ask them what predictions could be made based on these passages. For more practice using predicting skills, ask students to write a brief adventure story using two sheets of paper. On the first sheet, students should include all but the story's climax and resolution. Have them complete their stories on the second sheet. Pair students and have partners exchange their first sheets. Partners can write their predictions on the back of the first sheet. Then have partners exchange second sheets and compare their predictions to the actual endings.

Reteaching/Reinforcement
- *Unit Four Resource Book*, p. 28

432 THE LANGUAGE OF LITERATURE **TEACHER'S EDITION**

STRATEGIC READING FOR
Less-Proficient Readers

C Make sure that students understand Kidd's mission and the resources he has—and doesn't have—to accomplish it.

- What did Kidd agree to do for Governor Bellomont? *(capture as many pirates and pirate ships as he could in two years)* **Restating**

- How would Kidd's crew be paid? *(There was no money for regular pay. Instead, the crew would receive a share of the booty—if there was any booty.)* **Noting Relevant Details**

- Why did Kidd hire former pirates and other unsavory characters? *(they were the only men who would work under these conditions)* **Drawing Conclusions**

Set a Purpose Have students read to see how well the crew served Kidd.

Linking to Science

D Like all sailing ships, the *Adventure Galley* used the force of the wind to move over the seas. A sailing ship can sail "before the wind," following the same course that the wind is blowing; "off the wind," with its sails set so as to receive a pulling rather than a pushing force; or "on the wind," with its course being changed successively from the left to the right of the wind direction.

Captain William Kidd was a shipmaster in New York City in the 1690s, when New York was an English colony. He lived with his wife and children in a big house on Liberty Street.

If anyone had accused Kidd of piracy, those who knew him would have laughed. He was widely thought of as a decent, trustworthy man. In fact, he once had worked for the colonial government tracking down pirates in the waters around New York.

In those days, pirates plundered[1] British ships wherever they found them. It was such a problem that the king of England decided to crush them once and for all, and he ordered the royal governor of New York, the earl of Bellomont, to do so.

Governor Bellomont asked Kidd to take on the job. His orders were to capture as many pirates and pirate ships as he could in two years. He also was to capture any French ships he saw, because England was at war with France.

Bellomont bought Kidd a ship, the *Adventure Galley*, and armed it with thirty-four cannons. Kidd was to hire a crew. But there would be no money to pay them. Instead, they would get one-fourth of any booty[2] they took from the pirates or the French. If they took no booty, they would get no pay. Since few seamen would work under such conditions, Kidd could hire only wastrels[3] and drifters, some of whom were former pirates.

He left New York in September 1696 with one hundred and fifty-five men and sailed to the Madeira Islands off Africa. He continued south around the tip of Africa, into the Indian Ocean. Then he headed north toward the island of Madagascar, where many pirates made their headquarters. But Kidd did not find any.

In the five months since he'd left New York, he had not taken any booty, and his crew had not been paid. Frustrated and angry, they threatened to mutiny. But Kidd quieted them with talk of the dazzling riches that lay ahead.

---
1. **plundered:** robbed of goods by force.
2. **booty:** anything of value taken by force from an enemy, often gold, silver, and other treasures.
3. **wastrels** (wā′strəlz): loafers and good-for-nothings.

WORDS TO KNOW
mutiny (myōōt′n-ē) *v.* to engage in open rebellion against authority

---

Mini-Lesson — The Writer's Style

SHOW, DON'T TELL Point out to students that authors, especially nonfiction authors, use plenty of facts, examples, and details to enliven their writing. For example, instead of saying "Kidd made a long trip with many men to a pirate headquarters," Schwartz uses details of the journey. He writes "... sailed to the Madeira islands off Africa. He continued south around the tip of Africa, into the Indian Ocean. Then he headed north toward the island of Madagascar, where many pirates made their headquarters."

Application Fearing for his life, Kidd allows his crew to plunder several vessels, including the *Quedah Merchant*. Have students write a paragraph that shows rather than tells how Kidd planned to defend himself if he was accused of pirating the *Quedah Merchant*.

Reteaching/Reinforcement
- *Writing Handbook*, p. 784
- *Writing Mini-Lessons*, p. 46

The Writer's Craft
Show, Don't Tell, pp. 239–242

CUSTOMIZING FOR
Students Acquiring English

I Make sure students are aware of the traditional convention of referring to ships as female.

Active Reading: CLARIFY

E Discuss with students the problem Captain Kidd faces at this point in the story and ask how they think he should solve it. *(His problem is how to maintain command of the ship.)*

CUSTOMIZING FOR
Multiple Learning Styles

F **Musical Learners** Have interested students find and play for the class a recording of a sea chantey such as a pirate might sing. Students can look for recordings in the audiovisual section of a local library.

- Students may be interested to learn that chanteys both amused seafarers as they worked at boring jobs, and reflected the rhythm of movements in seafarers working together, as when hoisting a sail.

Literary Concept:
INTERNAL CONFLICT

G Ask students what internal conflict Captain Kidd is experiencing at this point in the story. *(Possible response: He is torn between plundering vessels not belonging to the French side of the war and risking his command to do the right thing.)*

They set sail for the coast of India, where he hoped to find pirates.

Soon they came upon a merchant ship, the *Loyal Captain*. When she turned out to be a Dutch vessel, Kidd decided to send her on her way. But his crew had other ideas. They grabbed the guns on board and got ready to steal whatever she had.

"Let's take her!" they yelled.

"No!" Kidd cried. "She is not our enemy."

"We'll take her anyway!"

"Desert my ship," he warned, "and I'll turn my cannons on you."

CLARIFY
What problem confronts Captain Kidd at this point?

The mutiny died. But in a week or two, Kidd clashed with one of its leaders, a gunner named William Moore. Moore blamed him for not taking any ships. "You have brought us ruin," he snarled. Kidd struck him on the head with a bucket and killed him. The crew muttered and rumbled like distant thunder but did nothing. Later, the ballad writer wrote:

> Many long leagues[4] from shore
> I murdered William Moore
> And laid him in his gore[5]
> when I sailed.

The *Adventure Galley* and its crew sailed on. They came to a French ship that had been wrecked. Since France and England were at war, Kidd took what gold there was and shared it with his men. But this did not satisfy them. They continued to threaten him. They wanted him to attack every ship they saw, not just French or pirate ships.

Fearing for his life, Kidd finally gave in. He and his crew plundered several small vessels. Then they took a large merchant ship, the *November*, which was loaded with cotton and sugar. Two months later, they captured the *Quedah Merchant*, with a cargo of gold, silver, jewels, silk, and other goods.

Both were owned by the Great Mogul, the emperor of India. The Mogul traded with England, but he also traded with her enemy, France. When Kidd checked the papers of the two ships, he breathed a sigh of relief. He found that France had agreed to protect them as if they were French ships. Under his orders, it seemed that he could take them as prizes of war. Kidd kept their "French papers" as proof that he had done the right thing, even if he had done so by accident.

When the *Adventure Galley* sprung a leak, he set sail for the port of St. Marie in Madagascar and took the Mogul's ships with him. What happened to their crews is not known. But on the way, some of Kidd's crew mutinied again. They stole what they could from the *November*, then sank it.

When Kidd and his men arrived at St. Marie, the *Adventure Galley* was leaking badly. To add to his troubles, Kidd found a pirate ship, the *Mocha Frigate*, tied up there. Kidd ordered the pirates to surrender, but they fled into the woods.

He told his crew to go after them, but most decided to join the pirates. They brought the pirates back from where they were hiding, then gave Kidd his choice of also turning pirate or losing his life.

PREDICT
How do you think Captain Kidd will handle this situation?

He locked himself in his cabin on the *Adventure Galley*, loaded forty pistols, and waited for them to attack. Instead, they boarded Kidd's other ship, the *Quedah Merchant*, moved part of her cargo to the *Mocha Frigate*, and sailed away. But in their

---
4. **leagues:** units of distance equal to about three miles each.
5. **gore:** blood from a wound.

434 UNIT FOUR PART 1: SHOWING YOUR TRUE COLORS

Mini-Lesson Literary Concepts

INTERNAL CONFLICT Remind students that internal conflict, a struggle within a character's mind, often occurs when he or she has to make a difficult decision. A similar external conflict can also be taking place at the same time.

Application Have students read the highlighted paragraph on page 434 to identify the internal conflict that Captain Kidd faces. Discuss the alternatives that Kidd has and how he decides to resolve the conflict.

Captain Kidd on Gardiner's Island (1894), Howard Pyle. Courtesy of Nedra Matteucci's Fenn Galleries, Santa Fe, New Mexico.

Art Note

Captain Kidd on Gardiner's Island by Howard Pyle American painter Pyle (1853–1911) was a highly influential and popular illustrator. His illustrations appeared in *Harper's Monthly* for many years. He wrote and illustrated *The Merry Adventures of Robin Hood* (1883) and *The Story of King Arthur and His Knights* (1903).

Reading the Art How does Pyle's depiction of Captain Kidd and his crew compare with Schwartz's description? Is this how you envision Kidd and his crew? Explain why or why not.

STRATEGIC READING FOR
Less-Proficient Readers

H Ask students how well the crew served Kidd. *(Possible response: Not well at all; most of them joined the pirates and threatened Kidd's life if he refused to do the same.)* Making Judgments

Set a Purpose Have students read to find out how Kidd became a wanted man.

Active Reading: PREDICT

I Ask students how they think Captain Kidd will deal with his mutinous crew. You may wish to use the following model to spark their ideas.

Think-Aloud Model *I wonder what will happen next. I think that Captain Kidd will be put to the test. He's proposing to defend himself, but I don't believe he can hold out against more than 100 angry men.*

Mini-Lesson Genre Study

NONFICTION Explain to students that a **biography** is a kind of nonfiction that tells the story of a person's life, including dates and other details about events. It often describes the subject's childhood, adult life, and his or her professional and personal failures and accomplishments. A biography has the following characteristics:
- It is the story of a person's life written by another person.
- It is written in the third-person point of view.

Application Have students copy in their notebooks the word web shown. Elicit from students that the selection is a biography by asking them who wrote this story of Captain Kidd's life and from what point of view the story is written. Then ask students to create a biographical word web for Kidd. Have them put Kidd's name in the center and make individual strands using details from the story.

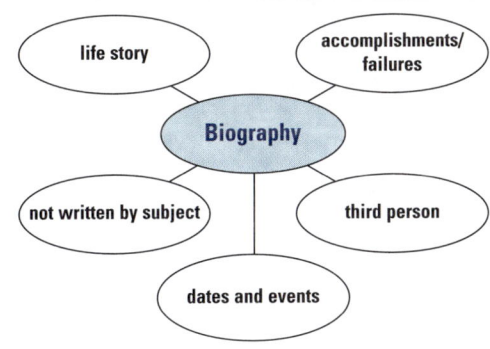

THE LANGUAGE OF LITERATURE TEACHER'S EDITION **435**

STRATEGIC READING FOR
Less-Proficient Readers

J Ask students what happened to make Kidd a wanted man. *(The Great Mogul complained to the English that Kidd stole his ships. The English charged Kidd with piracy and took steps to hunt him down.)* Restating

Set a Purpose Have students read to find out how Kidd's guilt or innocence was decided.

Critical Thinking:
MAKING JUDGMENTS

K Ask students to describe Kidd's strategy for safeguarding his treasure and clearing his name. Then invite volunteers to give their opinions of the plan. *(Possible response: He changed the location of his treasure from the* Quedah Merchant, *a ship that he helped plunder to the* San Antonio, *a ship that he bought. He hid the* Quedah Merchant *in the hope that he might trade the ship and its cargo for a pardon. Some students may think the plan is clever. Others may doubt the trustworthiness of the crew left to guard the treasure.)*

The all-important "French papers" that Kidd hoped would prove his innocence—but which mysteriously disappeared. Public Record Office, England.

haste they left behind a treasure trove of gold, silver, and jewels.

When the *Adventure Galley* began to sink where it was anchored, Kidd burned it. He then set sail for home in the *Quedah Merchant* with the seamen who had remained loyal. It was two and a half years since he had left New York.

Meanwhile, the Great Mogul had complained to England that Kidd had stolen his ships. The English quickly charged Kidd with piracy. It was a crime that carried the penalty of death, and they began to hunt him down. Only when he stopped for supplies in the West Indies did he learn that he was a hunted man.

Kidd was not sure that he could count on Governor Bellomont to help clear him. As insurance, he bought a sloop called the *San Antonio,* and with this new ship and the *Quedah Merchant,* he sailed to Hispaniola.[6] There he moved the treasure from the *Quedah Merchant* to the *San Antonio.* He hid the *Quedah Merchant* and the rest of its cargo in a small cove and left part of his crew to guard it. If he needed to, he would try to trade the ship for a pardon from the charge of piracy.

Kidd sailed north on the *San Antonio* to Delaware Bay, where he stopped for supplies. Then he moved on toward New York City, anchoring nearby at Oyster Bay. He sent a note to his wife and a letter to a lawyer named James Emmot, who had defended other men charged with piracy. Would he see Governor Bellomont for him?

---

6. **Hispaniola** (hĭs′pən-yō′lə): an island in the West Indies.

436 UNIT FOUR PART 1: SHOWING YOUR TRUE COLORS

Mini-Lesson • Study Skills

SKIMMING Remind students that skimming, quickly reading the most important parts of a selection and skipping everything else, is a useful technique for study and review. Tell students they can skim topic sentences to remember where specific details are.

Application As students prepare their legal briefs (see second Alternative Activity on page 440) they can skim the selection to locate evidence for finding Captain Kidd innocent of piracy.

436 THE LANGUAGE OF LITERATURE **TEACHER'S EDITION**

Emmot agreed to do so, and he and Kidd met on the *San Antonio*. Kidd told him that he was not a pirate, that he had taken the Mogul's ships as part of England's war with France. He gave him the French papers to show Bellomont as proof of this.

Since Bellomont was in Boston, Kidd sailed with Emmot to Rhode Island. There he put him ashore, and the lawyer made his way by land to see the governor. Kidd waited on the *San Antonio*.

> **PREDICT**
> Do you think Emmot's actions will solve Captain Kidd's problem?

Emmot returned in a few days. He had left the French papers with Bellomont as evidence of Kidd's innocence. And he had brought back a letter. Bellomont had written to Kidd: "If you are telling the truth, you will be safe from arrest. Come ashore and meet with me in Boston."

Kidd decided to see Bellomont, but he still did not completely trust him. He decided to leave the treasure aboard the *San Antonio* in a safe place. He sailed to Gardiner's Island, in Long Island Sound,[7] a hundred miles from New York City. There he left Emmot to make his way home, then he talked the owner of the island, a man named John Gardiner, into keeping part of the treasure for him. Gardiner buried it on the island. Some of Kidd's friends came aboard the *San Antonio* and took away the rest. Only then did Kidd set sail for Boston to see Bellomont.

But Bellomont had lied to him. When Kidd went ashore, he was arrested and sent to England in chains, to be tried for piracy. Bellomont told Kidd he had to arrest him. But he said he would send the French papers to England so that Kidd could use them at his trial. Whether he would keep his word this time remained to be seen.

Bellomont quickly seized the buried treasure on Gardiner's Island, as well as the treasure Kidd had given his friends to keep for him. It came to sixty-eight pounds of gold, one hundred and forty-three pounds of silver, and a pound of rubies, diamonds, and other jewels. Today the gold and silver alone would be worth half a million dollars. The governor also sent a crew to find the *Quedah Merchant* and its cargo.

At his trial in London, Kidd demanded the French papers Bellomont had promised to send. They were the only chance he had to save his life. But the government said there were no such papers, and Kidd was sentenced to hang for piracy.

It was the most famous trial of the day. As most people saw it, Kidd was a good man who had gone bad. The wildest tales were told of how wicked he had become and how much wealth he had. The ballad writer wrote of him:

> *I steered from sound to sound*
> *And many ships I found*
> *And most of them I burned*
>   *as I sailed . . .*
> *I had ninety bars of gold*
> *And dollars manifold*[8]
> *With riches uncontrolled*
>   *as I sailed.*

Captain Kidd rode to his execution, standing backward in a cart, a noose around his neck. Huge crowds jeered and pelted him with rubbish and rocks as he passed.

He was hanged three times. The first time the rope broke. So he was hanged a second time. Then his body was covered with tar and taken to the waterfront, where it was hung

---

7. **sound:** an inlet or arm of the ocean, surrounded on three sides by land and often used as a port or harbor for ships. Long Island Sound separates Long Island from Connecticut to the north.
8. **manifold:** many.

Active Reading: PREDICT

Discuss with students what they think Emmot's actions will achieve. You may wish to use the following model to help students collect their thoughts.

Think-Aloud Model *I wonder whether Emmot will save the day. Emmot is probably acting in good faith, but is Bellomont? If Bellomont is not being honest when he says that Kidd has nothing to fear, Emmot probably won't be able to save Kidd.*

Linking to Geography

English settler Lion Gardiner (1599–1663) bought the island now called Gardiner's Island from Native Americans in 1639. The island, which has an area of 3300 acres, was the first English colony in New York.

STRATEGIC READING FOR
Less-Proficient Readers

Ask students how Kidd's guilt or innocence was decided. *(Kidd was tried in London. Governor Bellomont did not send to the English the papers that might have cleared Kidd. In the absence of the papers, Kidd was convicted and hanged.)* Relating Cause and Effect

CUSTOMIZING FOR
Gifted and Talented Students

Have students imagine that they are Kidd, in prison in London, awaiting trial. Ask students what they might say in letters to Kidd's wife, Emmot, or Bellomont. Have students write a letter to one of these people from Captain Kidd.

Mini-Lesson — Grammar

IRREGULAR PLURAL NOUNS Point out to students that some nouns form their plurals in special ways (other than adding -s or -es). These are called irregular plural nouns. Remind students that they should always check a dictionary when they are unsure how to find the plural of a word.

Application List on the chalkboard the words shown. Have students complete the following sentences using the plural form of the listed words.

1. Captain Kidd's _____ were quiet as _____. (seamen, mice)
2. Many _____ thought Kidd was guilty. (people)
3. Kidd's crew included no _____. (women)

Reteaching/Reinforcement
- *Grammar Handbook*, pp. 822–823
- *Grammar Mini-Lessons*, copymasters, p. 10, transparencies, p. 8

The Writer's Craft
Singular and Plural Nouns, pp. 381–382

Singular	Plural
woman	women
seaman	seamen
person	people
mouse	mice

Linking to Social Studies

 Today, long after the end of piracy on the high seas, we still have instances of unauthorized, illegal reproduction of copyrighted materials such as books, videos, and audio recordings. When sold, these are called *pirated* copies or editions.

COMPREHENSION CHECK

1. What kind of reputation did Kidd have before he worked for Governor Bellomont? *(a reputation as a decent and trustworthy man)*
2. What was one factor in Kidd's decision to allow his crew to plunder several vessels, including the *Quedah Merchant*? *(His crew's dissent; the possibility of mutiny)*
3. What event led to Kidd's being charged with piracy? *(Kidd and his crew captured the Quedah Merchant and its cargo. This ship was owned by the Great Mogul, the emperor of India, who traded with both England and France.)*
4. Why did Kidd take precautions before meeting Bellomont about the accusation of piracy? *(Kidd did not trust Bellomont.)*
5. What was the outcome of Captain Kidd's trial? *(He was sentenced to hang for piracy and was executed.)*

HISTORICAL INSIGHT

1. Do you think that the rewards ever outweighed the risk of piracy? *(Possible responses: Yes, for people such as Kidd's crew, who had few options for earning a living. No, because pirates could never relax; they were "wanted" individuals whom governments hunted down.)*
2. Why do you think colonists would buy goods from pirates? *(Possible responses: Colonists wanted luxuries and didn't care that they were stolen; perhaps the pirates hid their identity, so colonists didn't know that the goods were stolen.)*

---

from another gallows⁹—a warning to seamen on passing ships not to become pirates.

There the story ends, and we return to the questions at the beginning. . . . Was Kidd really a pirate? And was there really a buried treasure?

There was a treasure, as we have seen, but it was buried for only a few weeks. Yet few knew it had been found, and people searched for it for more than two hundred years.

Whether Kidd was really a pirate is something that you must decide for yourself. Did he take the ships he captured because his crew forced him to do so? Or did he take them out of greed? Or was it both? Through song and story, Kidd became the symbol of every pirate. And his treasure, for which people searched for so long, became the symbol of every treasure. ❖

---

9. **gallows:** a platform built for the purpose of hanging a prisoner.

HISTORICAL INSIGHT

The History of Piracy

History shows that since the times of the early civilizations of the Middle East, piracy has existed wherever and whenever the rewards have outweighed the risks. Pirates plundered the ships of the Assyrian kingdoms along the coast of the Persian Gulf 3,000 years ago. Piracy appeared wherever sea trade offered tempting booty, including the ancient Mediterranean, among the Phoenicians, Greeks, Romans, and Carthaginians.

Hundreds of years later, in the Middle Ages, Vikings roamed the seas between the British Isles, Scandinavia, and the mainland of Europe. They plundered ships and murdered the crews. From the 1600s to the 1700s, piracy again flourished in the Mediterranean.

As countries competed to colonize the North American continent in the 1500s, piracy broke out in the Caribbean and lasted 300 years. Many pirates also sailed the Indian Ocean and the Red Sea, plundering the ships of the Great Mogul and bringing their booty thousands of miles to sell to colonists hungry for luxuries.

Probably the most famous of these pirates was Captain William Kidd. The increased size of merchant ships, the recognition by governments of piracy as an international offense, and action by navies of Great Britain and other countries eventually led to the end of piracy on almost all seas by the mid-1800s.

438 UNIT FOUR PART 1: SHOWING YOUR TRUE COLORS

Mini-Lesson Spelling

THE SUFFIXES -*ence* AND -*ent* Tell students that the suffixes -*ence* and -*ent* are commonly added to roots.

innocence   innocent
silence   silent

Words ending in -*ence* are usually nouns, and words ending in -*ent* are usually adjectives.

Application Have students change the nouns into adjectives and the adjectives into nouns.

1. violence
2. evidence
3. intelligence
4. obedience
5. absence
6. difference
7. patient
8. present
9. permanent
10. eloquent
11. equivalent
12. magnificent

Ask students to look for more words that fit this pattern, in their own writing and in things that they read, and to add those words to their personal word lists.

Reteaching/Reinforcement
• *Unit Four Resource Book,* p. 29

438 THE LANGUAGE OF LITERATURE TEACHER'S EDITION

RESPONDING OPTIONS

FROM PERSONAL RESPONSE TO CRITICAL ANALYSIS

REFLECT 1. What incident or fact in this account of William Kidd did you find most surprising? Compare your response with the responses of some of your classmates.

RETHINK 2. What conclusions have you come to about the kind of person Kidd was?
Consider
- his release of the Dutch ship *Loyal Captain*
- Close Textual Reading • his killing of the gunner William Moore
- his theft of the Great Mogul's ships
- his refusal to turn pirate with his crew at St. Marie

3. Do you sympathize with Kidd's predicament? Why or why not?

Thematic Link 4. How would you answer the author's question "Was Kidd really a pirate?" Explain your response.

RELATE 5. After reading the selection, what, if anything, do you think today's lottery players and sweepstakes fans have in common with someone like Captain Kidd?

Multimodal Learning
ANOTHER PATHWAY
Cooperative Learning
Work with a group to set up a television talk show in which Captain Kidd is the primary guest. Assign roles for the group to play, including that of the talk-show host. Present the facts from the perspective of each guest.

LITERARY CONCEPTS

Tone is an expression of the attitude a writer takes toward a subject. The writer's style and use of description help create tone. Often, understanding a writer's tone is a key factor in understanding a work of nonfiction. The writer's tone helps to establish the purpose for writing the work; it indicates how seriously the reader should accept the events in an account. For example, Don C. Reed uses an informal tone in "My First Dive with the Dolphins" because one of his purposes is to entertain. Find passages in Alvin Schwartz's account of William Kidd that reveal the tone. How would you describe the tone of this selection?

QUICKWRITES

1. Reread the ballad verses that are quoted in the selection. Write your own verse of a **ballad** about Captain Kidd.

2. Write a ship's **log entry** for the night at St. Marie when Kidd locked himself in his cabin.

3. Imagine that you are Captain Kidd. Draft the **last will and testament** that you would compose before going ashore in Boston.

📁 PORTFOLIO Save your writing. You may want to use it later as a springboard to a piece for your portfolio.

GOLD AND SILVER, SILVER AND GOLD **439**

Literary Concepts
Allow students to work in pairs to find some of the many relevant passages and to write responses to the question. Students might accurately describe the tone as serious, weighty, tense, sober.

QuickWrites
1. Allow interested students to create a tune for their ballads. Call on volunteers to read or sing their ballads for the class.
2. Encourage students to review the relevant passage beginning on page 434.
3. Call students' attention to the first paragraph in the selection, in which Kidd's domestic situation is described.

 **The Writer's Craft**
Writing a Poem, pp. 86–88
Writing from Your Journal, pp. 32–37
Goals and Audience, pp. 211–212

From Personal Response to Critical Analysis

1. Responses will vary.
2. Possible responses: Kidd was a complex person whose motives are impossible to know. Kidd was a person of integrity but a realist willing to compromise when his life was in danger.
3. Responses will vary.
4. Possible responses: No, because he didn't formally join the pirates as did his mutinous crew. Yes, because he allowed his crew to pirate the Great Mogul's ships.
5. Some students will see a similarity in people's desire to "get rich quick." Other students may say that there is nothing in common since playing the sweepstakes or the lottery is legal but stealing isn't.

Literary Link
What, if anything, do you think that Captain Kidd and Mourad in "The Summer of the Beautiful White Horse" have in common? *(Possible response: Both Kidd and Mourad take things that don't belong to them but don't regard themselves as thieves.)*

Another Pathway
Cooperative Learning Allow each group to brainstorm other guests for the talk show, such as King William, the Great Mogul, Governor Bellomont, or members of Kidd's crew on the *Adventure Galley*. Remind students that their questions and answers should focus on the conflicts among characters and what they know about each. Groups can act out their talk show moderated by a host in front of the class. The class can act as the studio audience and ask questions of the guests.

Rubric
3 Full Accomplishment Host's questions and guests' answers reveal that students understand the characters.
2 Substantial Accomplishment Some questions are irrelevant and some answers reveal incomplete understanding of the characters.
1 Little or Partial Accomplishment Host's questions and guests' answers reveal little understanding of the characters.

THE LANGUAGE OF LITERATURE TEACHER'S EDITION **439**

Across the Curriculum

Art *Pyle's Pirate Paintings* Have students use art books to locate reproductions of Howard Pyle's paintings. Pyle's illustration of Captain Kidd is one of several pirate paintings he created. Invite students to create a rogues' gallery display of Pyle's pirates. Students can write captions to explain the pictures and tell if they think Pyle's paintings present a realistic picture of pirates.

 History *Cooperative Learning* Have students form small groups of three or four to find out more about another well known pirate such as Blackbeard, Jean Laffite, or Anne Bonny. Have each group write a short biography of their subject. Encourage them to illustrate their biographies with character sketches, pirate flags, maps, and ships. These biographies can be collected into a book to be shared with other classes.

Words to Know

Possible response:

Part of Speech:
Noun

Definition:
open rebellion against authority

Synonym:
rebellion

Example: The teacher feared a mutiny when she assigned four hours of homework.

Part of Speech:
Verb

Definition:
to engage in open rebellion against authority

Synonym: defy

Example: Surely the crew will mutiny if the captain forces them to set sail amid the terrible electrical storm.

Multimodal Learning

ALTERNATIVE ACTIVITIES

1. Research pirate clothing or pirate ships. Design and construct **costumes** or **models** based on your research to display in your classroom.

2. **Cooperative Learning** Join a few classmates and form a legal team to defend Captain Kidd. Review the selection and come up with your own version of a **legal brief** in which you present an argument for finding Captain Kidd innocent of piracy. Present your legal brief to the class.

CRITIC'S CORNER

A number of writers, including Edgar Allan Poe and Robert Louis Stevenson, have referred to Captain Kidd in their writings. What elements of Kidd's experience do you think have made his story so popular among writers and storytellers?

WORDS TO KNOW

The name of Captain Kidd is forever linked with such words as *piracy, treasure, buccaneer,* and *mutiny*. Create a concept map for the word **mutiny,** using the model shown. *Mutiny* can be used as either a noun or a verb; be aware of which part of speech you are working with as you complete the map. Write a definition of the word, a synonym of it, and an example of its use. Compare your finished map with those of your classmates.

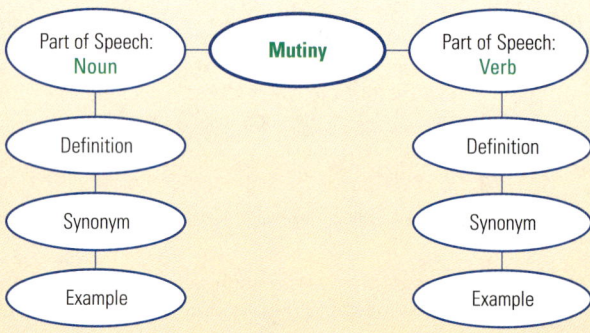

ALVIN SCHWARTZ

An author of many best-selling books for children, Alvin Schwartz (1927–1992) was born in Brooklyn, New York. He studied journalism in college and held various reporting and writing jobs until the 1960s, when he became a freelance writer. He went on to publish more than 50 books and received numerous awards and honors. Schwartz often collected folklore from the elderly and from children, whom he called "our strongest, most cohesive folk group."

Many of Schwartz's most popular books are collections of folk tales, tongue twisters, jokes, riddles, superstitions, and ghost stories. Schwartz believed that technology has caused people to rely less on themselves, and he saw folklore as a way to counter this change. He wanted readers to understand that they are all part of a living tradition, with the same joys, fears, anger, love, and need for dignity and security as people who lived long ago. His advice to students who read his books is: "Laugh when you can." Extended Reading
OTHER WORKS *Tomfoolery: Trickery and Foolery with Words, Kickle Snifters and Other Fearsome Critters, The Cat's Elbow and Other Secret Languages*

440 UNIT FOUR PART 1: SHOWING YOUR TRUE COLORS

Alternative Activities

1. Students can look for information in an encyclopedia or history books. If time is limited, you may wish to allow students to sketch costumes and ships. Display these on a bulletin board.
2. Make sure that each group member has a role. Useful roles for this activity include voice monitor (to maintain an appropriate sound level), turn-taking monitor, checker of understanding, and researcher/runner (to get information for the group—perhaps a conventional legal brief—and communicate with other groups and the teacher). Evaluate legal briefs based on the strength of groups' arguments for finding Kidd innocent.

ON YOUR OWN

from
Champions

by Bill Littlefield

Copyright © Brooks Dodge/Sports File.

Objectives
- To promote independent active reading
- To apply and practice skills learned in previous selections
- To provide an opportunity to assess students' performance through an alternative assessment instrument

Reading Pathways
- Invite students to read the selection independently and write in dialogue journals.
- Have students take notes on skiing champion Diana Golden, the subject of the essay, as they read.
- Have students choose partners and read the selection, pausing whenever they wish to discuss striking passages.
- Evaluate how well students can read, interpret, discuss, and write about the selection on their own by using the Integrated Assessment for Unit Four, located in the Alternative Assessment booklet. Administer the assessment at the end of the unit after students have read all the selections and completed all the writing that was assigned.

Twenty-odd years beyond required gym class, Diana Golden still remembers what it felt like to be the last one picked for the basketball team, or the volleyball team, or any other team. "Come on," she used to say under her breath as the ranks of the unpicked grew thin, "pick me, come on."

CHAMPIONS **441**

PRINT AND MEDIA RESOURCES

UNIT FOUR RESOURCE BOOK
Strategic Reading: Literature, p. 33

FORMAL ASSESSMENT
Selection Test, pp. 89–90
Part Test, pp. 91–92
Test Generator

ALTERNATIVE ASSESSMENT
- Unit Four Integrated Assessment, pp. 19–24

ACCESS FOR STUDENTS ACQUIRING ENGLISH
Selection Summaries
Reading and Writing Support

AUDIO LIBRARY
See Reference Card

THE LANGUAGE OF LITERATURE TEACHER'S EDITION **441**

SUMMARY

When Diana Golden was 12, doctors had to amputate her right leg because of cancer. After she spent a period feeling sorry for herself, Golden went back to the one sport she enjoyed—recreational skiing. In high school the ski coach recruited her to join the ski team. Diana handled the difficult training sessions well, and she won international skiing competitions for people with disabilities. The media discovered Golden's story, writing at length about her courage and heroism. Diana, who never considered herself a hero, grew tired of that role. Halfway through college she began a spiritual quest that led her to give up skiing. Not until her senior year did Golden strap on a ski again. Once she did, she kept on going. Golden went on to earn respectable finishes in two-legged competitions and numerous skiing honors. She retired from competition in 1991, eager to coach younger skiers and to find new ways of testing herself.

Thematic Link A champion skier defines herself on her own terms.

According to her recollection, nobody ever did. That was part of what led her to embrace skiing as a child. You didn't have to be picked for it. You could do it by yourself. And it wasn't a required sport.

When she'd gotten pretty good at it, somebody suggested that Diana should try out for a kids' ski racing team. She made the team but only lasted about two weeks. It was too serious. Too much competition. Too much like gym class. She returned to skiing for fun.

And then one day when she was twelve years old, Diana Golden's right leg collapsed under her. Weird, she thought. And then it happened again. When the doctors told her that the leg was cancerous and would have to be removed, she thought there had been some mistake. Cancer wasn't for twelve-year-olds. "Did you ask my grandfather?" she said. Granddaddy was a doctor, and he'd certainly tell these younger doctors they were wrong.

"He knows," they told her. "He agrees with us. We're sorry."

Diana Golden remembers that, after her surgery, she was brave while her parents and the doctors remained in the hospital room with her. But when they'd left her alone with her roommate, she cried for two hours. She couldn't remember ever seeing anyone with only one leg. She was sure her life would be a hopeless muddle of crutches, braces,

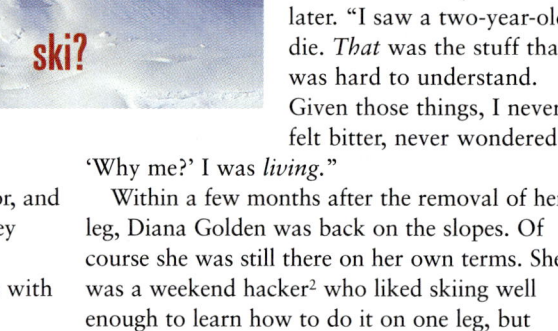

How could she feel too sorry for herself if she could still ski?

mechanical legs, and pity from all quarters.[1] But eventually she ran out of tears, and her roommate said, "Hey, when you have a fake leg, maybe you'll be able to turn your foot around backwards." And Diana laughed.

Over the days that followed, it occurred to Diana to ask one of her doctors if she'd still be able to ski. "No reason why not," the doctor said. That helped, too. How could she feel too sorry for herself if she could still ski? And how could she feel sorry for herself when so many of the other children in the hospital with her would never enjoy that opportunity, or any other?

"I saw teenagers die," she remembered years later. "I saw a two-year-old die. *That* was the stuff that was hard to understand. Given those things, I never felt bitter, never wondered 'Why me?' I was *living*."

Within a few months after the removal of her leg, Diana Golden was back on the slopes. Of course she was still there on her own terms. She was a weekend hacker[2] who liked skiing well enough to learn how to do it on one leg, but she was hardly inclined to train or work at it.

Through her first two years in high school, Diana Golden remained a weekend skier. She didn't train for competition, but given the circumstances, she couldn't help but develop some technique. As she has said since, "It didn't take me long to figure out there'd be

---

1. **from all quarters:** from everyone everywhere.
2. **hacker:** an enthusiastic amateur.

Diana Golden in action. Copyright © Brooks Dodge/Sports File.

no more snowplowing."

One afternoon during the winter of her junior year, a fellow in a ski parka and goggles flagged Diana Golden down on the slopes. When she'd skied up alongside him, she recognized the man as David Livermore, the skiing coach at Lincoln-Sudbury High School in Massachusetts, where Diana was a student. "Listen," Livermore said to her, "why don't you work out with the ski team?"

"He recruited me," Golden said later. "He's a perceptive man. He realized that the training would make a difference to me. He understood when he saw me skiing that I'd reached a point where working out, training, and pushing myself wouldn't be drudgery anymore. It wouldn't be gym class. And he was right. It was fun."

Within a few months Diana Golden, who had never done a pushup or a sit-up, was embarrassing the two-legged skiers with her workouts. "All of a sudden," as Golden remembered during a newspaper interview with Melanie Stephens years later, "I began to discover that I could train my body. It was wonderful. It was discovering the things that my body could do for me, discovering what it felt like to be strong."

By the winter of her senior year, Diana Golden had left klutziness[3] so far behind that it was hard to remember the bad old days. The rigorous training to strengthen her leg, her back, and her arms felt not only right, but indispensable. And the progress the training produced was nothing short of astonishing. Only a year after taking David Livermore up on his suggestion, Diana Golden was competing in the World Games for Disabled Athletes in Geilo, Norway. Within

---

3. **klutziness:** clumsy awkwardness.

CHAMPIONS **443**

OPTION 1

Individual Activity
WRITING A JOURNAL
Have students pretend they are Diana Golden on the five-day desert trek described on page 446. Have them write a journal describing the adventure day by day.

Teacher's Role Encourage students to think about how the nature of such a trek would place particular demands on the stamina of a disabled athlete such as Diana Golden.

Rubric
3 Full Accomplishment Students' journal entries reflect their understanding of Diana Golden's physical and emotional strengths as well as her physical limitations.
2 Substantial Accomplishment Students' journal entries vividly and accurately describe either Diana Golden or her trek but not both.
1 Little or Partial Accomplishment Students' journal entries show that they have not understood or reflected on Golden and her story.

the same year she won the downhill event in the World Handicapped Championships and became the brightest star on the United States Disabled Ski Team. She was skiing so well that, as *Boston Globe* sportswriter Tony Chamberlain put it, "She seemed *advantaged*." She had only one ski to worry about controlling, and she "moved back and forth down the hill with an unbroken motion as graceful as grass waving in a breeze."

That was, of course, an illusion. Skiing fast, like a lot of athletic feats, is harder than it looks. And skiing fast on one leg meant that Diana Golden had to cut from one edge of her ski to the other with more precision than most two-legged skiers could imagine. She had less margin for error because with one leg she had less opportunity to regain her balance when she lost it. Yet that sort of disadvantage never seemed to occur to Diana Golden. She was having too much fun to worry about it. She turned heads everywhere she skied, firing down the slopes like a wild bird, arms extended, snow flying everywhere. And the sense of fun was never eclipsed by the regimen of pushups and sit-ups or by the demands of competition. Once, at Vail, Colorado, when an out-of-control two-legged skier sent her sprawling and failed even to apologize, Golden bounced up, a look of mock horror spread across her face, and she shouted, "Hey, you! Look what you've done to my leg!"

By the time Diana Golden was ready to leave high school and enroll at Dartmouth College, the transformation was complete. "I was a total *anti*-klutz," she remembered. "Being a ski champion had become an image, the way I saw myself." She wasn't the only one who saw it that way. Even before she had graduated from high school, magazine and newspaper stories had begun to celebrate Diana Golden as not only a champion, but a hero, a role model, a courageous, inspirational athlete who had thumbed her nose at cancer and gone on not only to lead a full life but to win gold medals in the process.

Diana Golden didn't *feel* like a hero, though. She just felt like a skier who was doing her best to compete. Years later she would say, "What was heroic about me? People who stand up for what they believe are heroic. Martin Luther King. Nelson Mandela. Mother Theresa. Those are heroes . . . people who have done something wonderful for other people. I was just skiing fast." Sometimes the acclaim and the babbling about her courage got so strange that Golden could only laugh at it, like the time she was filling her car at a self-service station and the man behind the cash register, wide-eyed and well-meaning, told her how brave she was to be doing *that*.

The increasing gap between Diana Golden's view of herself and the public's perception of her as a courageous heroine created more pressure than any college sophomore should have to bear, and the difficulty was complicated by Golden's search for a spiritual center in her life. That search led her to embrace born-again Christianity, which in turn led to what Golden remembered as "a conflict between skiing and my desire to win on one hand, and my feeling of faith on the other. Skiing was one god, and God was another. I couldn't reconcile the demands of the two." Skiing began to make less and less sense. The praise heaped upon her in the sports columns and the magazine feature pieces rang more and more hollow. The attempt to figure out who she really was and what she wanted began to nudge training and racing out of Diana Golden's days.

Eventually Golden, who had practically defined herself through competitive skiing

444 UNIT FOUR PART 1: SHOWING YOUR TRUE COLORS

Multicultural Perspectives

WOMEN AND SPORTS During the twentieth-century, women's involvement in sports has greatly increased. This is partially due to the efforts of Lou Henry Hoover, wife of President Herbert C. Hoover, who organized the woman's division of the National Amateur Athletic Federation in 1923. Their slogan was: "A sport for every girl and every girl for a sport."

In 1948, at the Winter Olympics, Gretchen Fraser became the first U.S. skier to win an Olympic medal in skiing. Prior to Fraser's win, the best Olympic performance by a U.S. skier, male or female, was an 11th-place finish in 1938. Fraser received a silver medal for placing second in the women's alpine combined event, which has two parts—a downhill and a slalom race. The following day she went on to win first place in the special slalom event, another U.S. first. After retiring from competition, Fraser became an officer of the National Ski Association and was inducted into the National Ski Hall of Fame in 1960. She also founded the first U.S. amputee ski club.

since David Livermore's fortuitous[4] suggestion four years earlier, gave it up entirely. Over her last two years at Dartmouth, which is smack in the heart of New Hampshire's ski country, she skied only three times, and she never raced. She studied, read, and gradually began to understand herself as a person who *had* skied, rather than as a skier.

Then during her senior year it dawned on Diana Golden that to allow the media to define her or to warp her understanding of herself might stunt her own growth. She began to feel that it was crazy to have quit doing something she loved because the papers and television spots might misrepresent her efforts, or because of her inability to reconcile her faith with her athletic ambitions. As she said in retrospect,[5] "I began to understand who I was under the roles I had taken." This isn't an easy thing for an athlete—particularly a very good athlete—to do. Young football players, basketball players, or skiers who constantly read about how brave, strong, and talented they are can have a hard time remembering that they are also fallible, entitled to goof, human.

For Diana Golden, that discovery didn't happen all at once, and when she graduated from Dartmouth, she wasn't ready to redevote herself absolutely to skiing. She took a job as a computer software salesperson. Personable, outgoing, and bright, she was good at her work. But before long she was bored. Maybe that's part of the reason she finally said "Sure" when some of her old friends proposed, for the umpteenth time, a ski weekend. Maybe they knew Diana well enough to figure that if they kept asking, she'd finally agree to go. But she surprised them once they'd all taken the lift to the top of the hill. In fact she delighted them by hopping with a giggle onto the slalom[6] course on the slope and tearing through the gates with all the joy and enthusiasm that had characterized her championship runs. By the time she reached the bottom of the mountain, she was halfway hooked on skiing again. All she needed was a gentle push from one more friend, who told her, "When you're thirty, you can do anything you want, but you won't be winning races. Go for it now."

> She turned heads everywhere she skied, firing down the slopes like a wild bird, arms extended, snow flying everywhere.

She did. Some of her expertise came back quickly, but the layoff meant she had to work harder than ever to strengthen her knee, leg, stomach, and arms again. She trained with other so-called "disabled" skiers, but also with the two-legged variety, whom Golden called the "normies." With each group she would pick out somebody who was a little faster, a little more confident, a little more successful than she was. Then she would work at narrowing the gap between their performances, and eventually she would leave most of her rivals in a shower of snow.

---

4. **fortuitous:** lucky or fortunate.
5. **in retrospect:** in looking back on events.
6. **slalom** (slä′ləm): a downhill race over a zigzag course marked by poles or gates.

CHAMPIONS **445**

Soon Diana Golden realized that training was only part of the challenge. Because she wanted to compete all over the world against the best skiers she could find, she also had to work at finding a way to pay for the travel and living expenses. Sponsors! she thought, though this was an unprecedented[7] notion for a disabled athlete. She went to the Rossignol Ski Company and said, "You guys back two-legged skiers all the time. You give them equipment. You finance their trips and pay their expenses so folks will see them winning races on your skis. Do the same for me. But don't do it because I ski on one leg. Do it because I'm going to win races. And every time I do it, there'll be a picture of your ski and your company logo on the sports page." Then she'd smile to close the deal.

If Rossignol had any doubts at the outset, they vanished in the glow of the results Diana Golden posted. As had been the case when David Livermore had first invited her to join the ski team, the timing was perfect. Diana Golden was ready to focus her concentration on becoming a great skier. Within a year of her return to competition in 1985, she won four gold medals. During the eighties she ran her totals to ten World Handicapped Championship golds and nineteen national championships. From 1986 to 1990 she monopolized[8] the World Disabled skiing championships, and in 1988 she won an Olympic gold medal in the giant slalom for disabled skiers, which was a demonstration sport at the time. . . .

The titles Diana Golden won were not preceded by words like "disadvantaged" or "disabled." She had simply earned recognition as the best there was at what she did—which is what she'd been after all along. "'Courageous' is my pet peeve," she told Meg Lukens for an article in *Sports Illustrated*. "I think it belittles our ability. I never wanted to be thought of as just having courage. I wanted to be recognized as a top-notch athlete, as the best in the world."

In 1991, at twenty-seven, Diana Golden retired from competitive skiing. She'd won more gold medals than she could carry, and now other challenges beckoned. She took up rock climbing and announced her intention to coach skiers—"both the one-legged and the two-legged kind." She said she wanted to bring credibility to "disabled ski instructors—not just as teachers of other disabled people, but of anyone." She trekked off alone into the Utah desert for five days, testing herself against heat, cold, exhaustion, and loneliness, charging along on two forearm crutches until she found the reward she'd intuitively[9] known the trip would provide. "It was just beautiful," she said of that adventure. "I was out there alone, with the sun on my back, and it was as if I could smell everything around me—the cliffs, the ruins. It seemed like I was taking everything in one sensual rush. I wasn't small, frail, and vulnerable. I was tough, strong, and indomitable. I was capable."

When she returned home she had once again made an opportunity of what most people would consider an obstacle, but Diana Golden wouldn't call the trek a big deal. She'd leave that for others. And when they said she was "courageous" and even "heroic," she'd patiently sit down with them and explain why that wasn't it at all. ❖

---

7. **unprecedented** (ŭn-prĕs′ĭ-dĕn′tĭd): never before known or experienced.
8. **monopolized:** had complete possession of.
9. **intuitively:** in a way that involves knowing something without having a specific reason or any proof.

---

446 UNIT FOUR PART 1: SHOWING YOUR TRUE COLORS

Multicultural Perspectives

RIGHTS OF THE DISABLED On July 12 and 13 of 1990, the House and Senate gave overwhelming approval to the Americans with Disabilities Act and President George Bush signed the bill on July 26, making it a law. This law bars discrimination against people with mental or physical disabilities, defined as conditions that "substantially limit" an important activity such as hearing. The law also covers people living with AIDS and drug and alcohol abusers undergoing treatment. The law requires transportation systems to purchase new vehicles accessible to the disabled and charges that all businesses of a certain size must hire and promote employees regardless of any disability.

Diana Golden in a moment of victory as a member of the United States Disabled Ski Team. Copyright © Brooks Dodge/Sports File.

BILL LITTLEFIELD

A graduate of Yale University, Bill Littlefield (1948–) is a popular sports commentator on National Public Radio. His radio work has earned him two Associated Press broadcast awards. Littlefield was born in Montclair, New Jersey. A poet as well as a novelist and biographer, Littlefield also teaches at Curry College in Milton, Massachusetts. This excerpt about Diana Golden is from *Champions: Stories of Ten Remarkable Athletes,* which also features such well-known athletes as Satchel Paige and Muhammad Ali.

OTHER WORKS *Prospect*

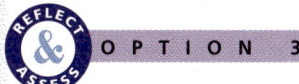

Class Discussion
SHARING IDEAS

Teacher's Role Engage students in a whole class discussion using the questions below. You may wish to participate in the discussion primarily by listening actively to students' responses. Enter the discussion as necessary to keep students focused. Encourage students to ask and answer questions in addition to those provided.

1. What part of Diana Golden's story impressed you most? *(Possible responses: her feeling sorry for patients who were worse off after she had lost a leg to cancer; her leaving skiing at the height of her success; her desert trek; her refusal to let herself be stereotyped)*

2. How would you describe the internal conflict that extensive media coverage sparked in Diana Golden? *(Possible responses: The conflict was between whom Diana understood herself to be inside and whom people thought her to be. The conflict was between spiritual and material values. The conflict was between Diana's desire to be a normal person and the media's tendency to portray her as a "big shot.")*

3. Why do you think that Diana Golden competed with able-bodied athletes and stressed that disabled ski instructors can teach anyone? *(Possible responses: She does not want to limit herself by others' stereotypes; she enjoys the challenge of skiing against any type of competitor; she wants to educate others about the abilities of "disabled" people.)*

OVERVIEW

In the Guided Assignment for this section, students will write a scene that fits into an existing story. By imagining possible events, students learn several important elements of story writing: characters, details, and a careful use of language. They also learn how to make connections among elements in a story. As preparation for this assignment, The Writer's Style will help students understand complete subjects and predicates, use time-order transitions, and use prepositional phrases. In Reading the World, students will analyze the elements of a photograph to understand what goes into making connections in the real world.

Objectives

- To understand how authors show rather than tell in their writing
- To add details to make a piece of writing vivid
- To write a scene that could be part of a story
- To analyze a scene in the real world

Skills

LITERATURE
- Showing a reaction

WRITING AND LANGUAGE
- Using time-order transition words

GRAMMAR AND USAGE
- Understanding complete subjects and predicates
- Understanding objects of prepositions

MEDIA LITERACY
- Interpreting a photograph

CRITICAL THINKING
- Formulating questions
- Hypothesizing
- Analyzing

SPEAKING, LISTENING, AND VIEWING
- Peer composition
- Reading aloud
- Group conferencing

Teaching Strategy: MODELING

In the following models, the authors include particular details in their writing. By doing so, they encourage their readers to visualize the story.

A Borton de Treviño Possible responses: Guanajuato has particular smells and has a history of change. The passage is more revealing because it helps readers imagine being there.

B Jen The writer uses words and phrases that express feeling such as "I could not believe," "actually," and "as if it belonged in my hands" to show the narrator's excitement.

WRITING ABOUT LITERATURE

JUST IMAGINE

Believe it or not, many people get just as frightened by reading about a haunted house as they would by visiting one. This is because a talented writer can create scenes that let readers use their imaginations to "see" what a haunted house is like. On the following pages you will

- see how writers create scenes that show rather than tell
- use this skill to write an extra scene for a published story
- use context clues to understand a real-life scene

Writer's Style: Show, Don't Tell Good writers don't just tell what happens in a story or what a place or person is like. They describe actions, conversations, and appearances that let readers see things for themselves.

Showing Setting

A What is Guanajuato like? Why is this passage more revealing than a telling sentence, such as "Guanajuato smelled wonderful" or "Guanajuato is an old town"?

Showing Feelings

B How does this passage show how the narrator is feeling? Which words are especially helpful in revealing her feelings?

Reading the Literature

Notice how the authors of these excerpts use descriptive details to "show" setting and emotion.

Literature Models

The streets of Guanajuato smell of dried chilies, of jasmine and carnations in pots behind the iron-barred windows, of hot baked bread and of burro droppings. It is my town in central Mexico, a romantic old town that has lived days of wealth and luxury, because of the rich silver mines nearby, and days of poverty, because of the turmoil of revolutions and social change.

Elizabeth Borton de Treviño, from "The Secret of the Wall"

I could not believe that I was actually holding the umbrella, opening it. It sprang up by itself as if it were alive, as if that were what it wanted to do—as if it belonged in my hands, above my head. I stared up at the network of silver spokes, then spun the umbrella around and around and around. It was so clean and white that it seemed to glow, to illuminate everything around it.

Gish Jen, from "The White Umbrella"

448 UNIT FOUR: PROVING GROUND

PRINT AND MEDIA RESOURCES

UNIT FOUR RESOURCE BOOK
Writer's Style, p. 37
Prewriting Guide, p. 38
Elaboration, p. 39
Peer Response Guide, pp. 40–41
Revision and Editing, p. 42
Student Model, p. 43
Rubric, p. 44

GRAMMAR MINI-LESSONS
Transparencies, p. 41

WRITING MINI-LESSONS
Transparencies, p. 33

ACCESS FOR STUDENTS ACQUIRING ENGLISH
Reading and Writing Support

FORMAL ASSESSMENT
Guidelines for Writing Assessment

 WRITING COACH

448 THE LANGUAGE OF LITERATURE TEACHER'S EDITION

Connect to Life

Like storytellers, good nonfiction writers can show and not tell to describe events and experiences. Notice how this writer describes his first taste of habanero chili peppers.

Magazine Article

> "*Helado, por favor,*" I croak, my eyes watering. His [the waiter's] return with the ice cream is mercifully quick. I shovel it in. I let it wallow on my tongue and linger against the roof and sides of my mouth and the back of my throat. The fire finally goes out.
>
> Jim Robbins
> from "It feels like your lips are going to fall off," *Smithsonian*

Showing a Reaction
What did the writer think of the peppers? Which words show you how he reacted?

Try Your Hand: Showing, Not Telling

1. **Imagine the Actions** Think about the noises, facial expressions, and physical motions that you see when someone is angry, sad, or tired. Can you act out these emotions with your body? Jot down a list of the physical clues you give people to show them how you feel.

2. **Show Me How** Add descriptive details that change these sentences so that they *show* rather than *tell*.
   - Serafin was bored.
   - Carlos heard something.
   - Martin looked like a construction worker.

3. **Try This with a Friend** With a partner, try writing a paragraph showing what makes your neighborhood or town special. Remember to use descriptive words that let readers "see" the special things you describe.

SkillBuilder

GRAMMAR FROM WRITING

Understanding Complete Subjects and Predicates

No matter how many details you add to show readers what happens, every sentence must express a complete thought. A sentence that doesn't form a complete thought is a fragment. Each sentence has a **complete subject** that includes all of the words that tell whom or what the sentence is about. Each sentence also has a **complete predicate** that includes all of the words that tell what the subject does or is or what happened to the subject. What are the complete subject and predicate in this sentence from "The White Umbrella"?

Huddling at the end of Miss Crosman's nine-foot leatherette couch, Mona and I watched Eugenie play.

APPLYING WHAT YOU'VE LEARNED

Complete each sentence by adding either a subject or predicate to each sentence fragment.

1. An old chessboard
2. sounded like a deep groan
3. The ghost in the house

GRAMMAR HANDBOOK

For more information on complete subjects and predicates, see page 812 of the Grammar Handbook.

WRITING ABOUT LITERATURE 449

Teaching Strategy: MODELING

C Robbins Remind students that even though this is nonfiction writing, the author still shows what he thinks: The peppers are so hot they burn. The author's reaction is shown through the use of words and phrases such as "eyes watering," the waiter's return being "mercifully quick," "shovel," and "linger."

Try Your Hand

1. Responses will vary. Students might write clues such as frowning, bared teeth; hunched shoulders, pouting mouth; yawning, rubbing hands against eyes.
2. Sentences will vary but should include details to make the descriptions vivid. Here are samples:
   - Serafin sat with his head resting on his arm, looking up at the ceiling.
   - Suddenly, Carlos stopped talking and looked toward the door.
   - Martin had on a hard hat, flannel shirt, dirty trousers, and big boots, and he held a small canteen in one hand.
3. Paragraphs will vary. Here is a sample: There are only 300 people in my town. It has one shaded main street, and all the houses on it face the road. There is very little traffic, so children often play ball in the street. This worries visitors when they drive down the street. Tourists soon learn that it's better to walk.

SkillBuilder GRAMMAR FROM WRITING

UNDERSTANDING COMPLETE SUBJECTS AND PREDICATES Tell students that a complete subject or a complete predicate by itself is a phrase. A phrase should not be punctuated as a sentence. Point out that the complete subject in the sentence is "Mona and I," and the complete predicates are "Huddling at the end of Miss Crosman's nine-foot leatherette couch" and "watched Eugenie play." There are two predicates because the subjects do two things: huddle and watch.

Applying What You've Learned Possible responses:
1. An old chessboard has chips and cracks in it.
2. The noise sounded like a deep groan.
3. The ghost in the house rattled its chains.

Additional Suggestions Have students work in pairs to practice correcting sentence fragments in their own writing. Guide them to add either a subject or a predicate to their writing.

Reteaching/Reinforcement
- Grammar Handbook, anthology pp. 852–853

THE LANGUAGE OF LITERATURE TEACHER'S EDITION 449

Critical Thinking:
HYPOTHESIZING

D Remind students when they imagine what might have happened or what might happen in a story, they are hypothesizing. Encourage students to keep the same characters and setting when they hypothesize. Also, they should try to imagine events that are likely to happen within the framework already set for the story.

Writing Skill:
DEVELOPING PLOT

E Encourage students to create a sequence chart with a beginning or an ending that links up with their chosen story. Then they should work forward or backward from the story to list the sequences of events. Ask if they need to add or change events to make their plots realistic or more logically ordered.

WRITING ABOUT LITERATURE

Creative Response

D After reading a story, do you ever wonder what happened before the story began, or after it ended? Do you ever try to imagine the scenes that were left out? An enjoyable way to respond to a story is to try to fill in some of these missing pieces. To respond to these questions, you can look for clues in the story and come to your own conclusions.

GUIDED ASSIGNMENT
Fill in the Blanks In this lesson, you'll write a scene showing an event that was not in the story.

❶ Prewrite and Explore

Here are some things to think about as you look over the selections you have read and decide on a blank that might be fun to fill in.

- What event did I really wonder about but not get to see? Which scene did I want to go on longer?
- What might have happened the week, day, or hour before the story began? If the story were to continue, what might happen next?
- What additional conversation might have taken place between two characters?

Decision Point Decide which story you want to work on and which scene you want to add. Remember two important points:

- You want your scene to fit in with the original story. That means that the characters must act and talk as they do in the story.
- Events in your scene should help explain or continue events described in the original story.

E Now you can start plotting what's going to happen in your scene. A sequence chart like the one on the left can help you organize and order the new events.

Student's Sequence Chart

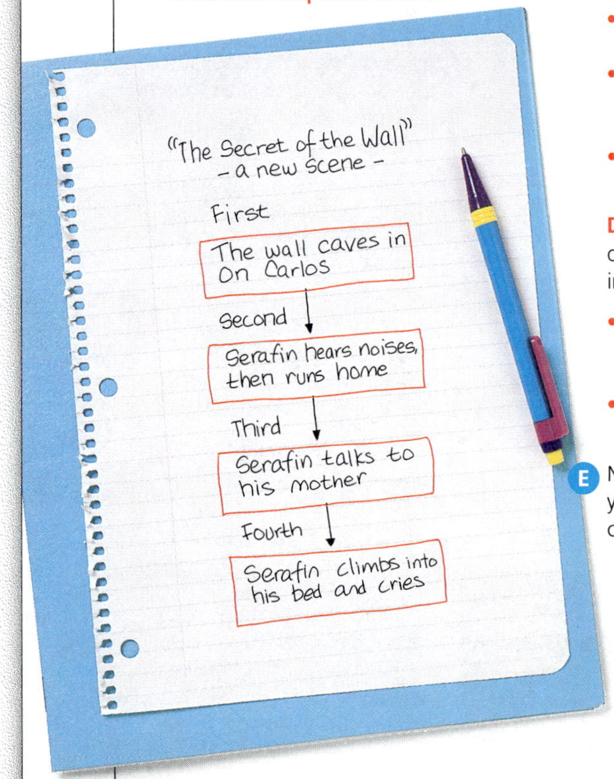

"The Secret of the Wall"
— a new scene —

First: The wall caves in on Carlos
Second: Serafin hears noises, then runs home
Third: Serafin talks to his mother
Fourth: Serafin climbs into his bed and cries

450 UNIT FOUR: PROVING GROUND

Assessment Option

SELF-ASSESSMENT After students have reached their Decision Point, they can assess their understanding of scenes. Students can ask themselves the following questions:
- *Have I chosen one particular scene?*
- *How many characters are in the scene?*
- *How many characters are in my sequence chart?*
- *What is the setting of the scene?*
- *Does my scene begin or end with that setting?*
- *Is my scene realistic in terms of what happens elsewhere in the story?*

450 THE LANGUAGE OF LITERATURE TEACHER'S EDITION

② Freewrite

Let your mind wander as you write. Try to imagine what each character is thinking. Or, you may want to try role-playing a scene with several classmates. This student imagined what happened to Serafin after the wall caved in on Carlos in "The Secret of the Wall" and decided to write about it.

Student's Freewriting

What happened to Serafin? shivering and afraid, cold dark room with no candle, sounds of Carlos screaming behind the wall, he probably feels like he should do something but he's really scared, he just stands still and tries not to listen to the screaming, or maybe he just starts to run

I have to show how he looks afraid, maybe puts his hands over his ears

Would dialogue help to show this scene better?

his mother wouldn't seem to mind that he had been out, she isn't worried, but he tells her that he was alone all evening anyway, because he's scared, and when he goes to bed he puts his head under the covers thinking about Carlos stuck in the wall.

③ Draft and Share

Begin drafting your scene. As you write, try to replace all the "telling" parts with "showing" descriptions. Then share your draft with a partner and discuss whether your scene fits in with the rest of the story.

PEER RESPONSE

- Which parts of my scene really show what's happening? Which parts do I need to improve?
- How do the events and characters in my scene fit or not fit in with the original story?
- How could I make my scene more like the original story?

WRITER'S CRAFT

Using Time-Order Transition Words

Transitions are words and phrases that tell readers how details are related to one another. To show how details are related in time, you can use the words *then* and *after*, as in this passage from "The Secret of the Wall."

Then he had searched for relatives, but there seemed to be none. So, after my father paid the taxes on the treasure, it remained for us.

Other words that signal time and sequence relationships are shown on this chart.

first	now	then
second	finally	after
during	next	before

APPLYING WHAT YOU'VE LEARNED
Use time-order transition words to complete this paragraph.

____ Carlos had polio, he could run with the other boys. ____ he has to wear a leg brace. Carlos watches the ball games ____ recess. ____ many hours of hard exercise, Carlos hopes to ____ be able to run again.

WRITING HANDBOOK

For more information on transitions, see page 781 of the Writing Handbook.

WRITING ABOUT LITERATURE **451**

Writing Skill: DEVELOPING CHARACTER

F Freewriting provides an opportunity for students to think through ideas and information they have gathered. Students should add details about the character or characters as they write. Encourage them to imagine what they would feel, see, and think if they were there in the scene. These reactions and observations can be used in developing characters.

Teaching Strategy: MODELING

G Draw students' attention to the details in this student's freewriting. The writer uses the senses of sight, sound, and touch. Guide students to use as many sensory details as they can in their freewriting.

CUSTOMIZING FOR
Less-Proficient Writers

H Some students may have difficulty deciding which elements they need to show rather than tell. Have them look at their nouns and verbs to decide whether more accurate or vivid ones can be used or whether adjectives or adverbs will add detail to their scenes.

 **WRITER'S CRAFT**

USING TIME-ORDER TRANSITION WORDS Point out to students that transition words are often located at the beginnings of sentences. In this way, one sentence can be linked to another to make the relationship between the sentences clearer. However, sometimes they occur elsewhere, adding to sentence variety.

Applying What You've Learned Possible response: <u>Before</u> Carlos had polio, he could run with the other boys. <u>Now</u> he has to wear a leg brace. Carlos watches the ball games <u>during</u> recess. <u>After</u> many hours of hard exercise, Carlos hopes to <u>finally</u> be able to run again.

Additional Suggestions For more practice, have students continue adding transitions in the following paragraph: _____ I want to pack warm clothing. _____ I want to get on a plane and fly to the Arctic. _____ I want to see the polar bears and live in an igloo. _____ I want to reach the North Pole.

Reteaching/Reinforcement
- *Writing Handbook*, anthology pp. 781–782
- *Writing Mini-Lessons* transparencies, p. 33

Transitions, pp. 234–238

THE LANGUAGE OF LITERATURE TEACHER'S EDITION **451**

Critical Thinking: ANALYZING

I Explain to students that revising involves making their scenes more realistic and convincing. To revise their scenes, students could add details that "show," make their characters more consistent with the story, and change actions that are impossible or unlikely.

Speaking and Listening: COLLABORATIVE OPPORTUNITY

J Students can use this opportunity to look for places to revise their scenes. They should try to listen as if they were unfamiliar with the scene to check whether they have supplied enough information for their audience.

Teaching Strategy: MODELING

K Discuss with students how this model meets the Standards for Evaluation on this page. The way Serafin acts—screaming, dropping the bar, shaking, and moaning—indicates that he is frightened. The writer shows us how Serafin feels by describing his emotions and actions. The dialogue suggests the opposite of what Serafin says. He was neither nowhere nor was he by himself. The dialogue matches the rest of the story because it is simple and in character.

Standards for Evaluation

Ideas and Content
- describes a scene suggested but not presented in a story
- shows understanding of story characters by having character's actions and dialogue match personalities
- makes sense when compared to original story
- uses sensory details and language

Structure and Form
- demonstrates proper paragraphing
- includes transitional words and phrases to indicate sequence of events
- uses variety of sentence structures

Grammar, Usage, and Mechanics
- contains no more than two or three minor errors in grammar and usage
- contains no more than two or three minor errors in spelling, capitalization, and punctuation

---

WRITING ABOUT LITERATURE

4 Revise and Edit

As you revise your draft, think about these questions.

I
- Do the characters act appropriately?
- Does my response create an interesting scene that fits in with the original story?
- Does my response meet the Standards for Evaluation below?

J When you are finished, ask a classmate to read the scene aloud to you. What makes your response unique? Then reflect on what you enjoyed or found rewarding in writing your scene.

Student's Model

Serafin's Escape

K When the wall caved in on Carlos, Serafin screamed in horror. The iron bar dropped from his hands and clanged against the rock. The room was pitch black without Carlos's candle, and Serafin could hear crying. He started to shake, and he pressed his hands against his ears to block out the sound. Serafin stomped his feet, moaning, as the sounds behind the wall softened. Then he ran toward the door.

What emotions is Serafin experiencing here? How does the writer show what Serafin is feeling?

Serafin's mother sat at the kitchen table with a glass of water. She looked up calmly after a while.
"Where have you been?" she asked him.
"Nowhere," he replied. "I have been by myself."
"Go to bed," she told him. "It is too late for you."
Serafin crept into his bed and pulled the covers over his head and tried to imagine what Carlos was doing.

What does the dialogue show about Serafin's thoughts? How well does this dialogue match other conversations in the story?

Standards for Evaluation

A "fill-in-the-blanks" response
- describes a scene that is not presented in the story
- shows an understanding of story characters
- adds descriptive details that match the original story
- uses sensory details and language

452 UNIT FOUR: PROVING GROUND

Assessment Option

SELF-ASSESSMENT To assess their own writing, students can ask themselves the following questions:
- *Does my scene begin or end with a scene from the story?*
- *Are the events in my scene consistent with the story?*
- *Are settings described with details?*
- *Are my characters lifelike?*
- *Did I use complete subjects and predicates in every sentence?*

Grammar in Context

Prepositional Phrases A prepositional phrase is a group of words that begins with a preposition and ends with its object, which is a noun or a pronoun. Prepositional phrases can modify a noun or a verb. Phrases like this can help you describe your scene clearly, since they show where things are and when things happened.

> "Go to bed," she told him, "It is too late for you." Serafin ~~went to~~ *crept into his* bed and pulled the covers ~~on~~ *over his head* and tried to imagine what Carlos was doing.

Every prepositional phrase makes the sentence more specific. Notice how adding the two phrases *into his bed* and *over his head* to the second sentence makes the image more exact.

Try Your Hand: Using Prepositional Phrases

1. Combine each pair of sentences below into one sentence by using prepositional phrases.
   - Carlos discovered a hole. The hole was in the wall.
   - Martin asked Carlos for help because he couldn't write. Martin wanted help with a letter.

2. Number your paper from 1 to 5. Use each prepositional phrase below in a sentence.
   - to and from school everyday
   - on the playground
   - through the streets of Guanajuato
   - in the middle of Cantaranas Plaza
   - around the chessboard

SkillBuilder

GRAMMAR FROM WRITING

Understanding Objects of Prepositions

The noun or pronoun that follows a preposition is the object of the preposition. Prepositions help to show relationships between the object and another word in the sentence. What relationship is shown in each sentence below?

The money went to a new school being built down by the highway.

Carlos heard scratching and striking along the wall.

Carlos has a little white dog with a black spot around one eye.

APPLYING WHAT YOU'VE LEARNED

Choose a preposition from column A and an object of a preposition from column B to complete the sentences below.

A	B
into	cobblestone street
during	sky
on	chess match

1. Carlos's shoes clattered
2. The huge church soared
3. The crowd was silent

WRITING ABOUT LITERATURE   453

CUSTOMIZING FOR
Students Acquiring English

 Remind students that common prepositions include *to, by, with, for*. Prepositions that show a direction include *in, into, over, beside,* and *on*. These words come at the beginning of a phrase, called a prepositional phrase, and indicate relationship among words in a sentence. Have students look for sentences that begin with prepositions and make sure these sentences are complete and include a main verb and an object.

Teaching Strategy: USING THE SKILLBUILDER

You can help students understand prepositional phrases more clearly by teaching the SkillBuilder on Objects of Prepositions at this time.

Try Your Hand

1. Sentences will vary. Here are samples:
   - Carlos discovered a hole in the wall.
   - Martin wanted help with a letter because he couldn't write, so he asked Carlos for help.
2. Sentences will vary. Here are samples:
   1. I walk two miles to and from school everyday.
   2. There were swings on the playground.
   3. Strong smells went through the streets of Guanajuato.
   4. There are many people in the middle of Cantaranas Plaza.
   5. Old men sat around the chessboard.

SkillBuilder GRAMMAR FROM WRITING

UNDERSTANDING OBJECTS OF PREPOSITIONS Point out that the first sample sentence has two prepositional phrases. Ask students first to identify the verbs. (*went* and *being built*) Then ask them to identify the prepositional phrases, which include the objects of the sentence. (*to a new school* and *down by the highway*) The relationship in the first sentence is that the money went to the school and the school is being built in a particular place. The second sentence identifies where Carlos heard the scratching and striking. The third sentence adds detail about the dog by describing its eye.

Applying What You've Learned Answers:
1. Carlos's shoes clattered on the cobblestone street.
2. The huge church soared into the sky.
3. The crowd was silent during the chess match.

Additional Suggestions Help students use prepositions correctly when they revise their own writing. You may wish to have students work together in pairs. They can make two-column charts of prepositions and objects.

Reteaching/Reinforcement
- *Grammar Mini-Lessons* transparencies, p. 41

 The Writer's Craft

What Are Prepositions? pp. 504–505
Using Prepositional Phrases, pp. 506–508

THE LANGUAGE OF LITERATURE TEACHER'S EDITION   453

READING THE WORLD

On pages 450–453, students learned to use their imaginations to write an event that was not in a story. In this lesson, students will examine how speculation about missing events is used in the real world. By examining a photograph of an event, students draw their own conclusions about what is happening.

Critical Thinking: ANALYZING

N Students will probably express surprise at the scene. The woman diving or falling into the pool raises questions of where she is diving from, why she is diving, and why she is doing it in a long, white dress.

Media Literacy: INTERPRETING A PHOTOGRAPH

O It seems that a woman is diving or falling into a pool, fully clothed, at a lunch party. Students may come up with a variety of explanations for her actions. Perhaps one of the other people there dared her to dive into the pool. Perhaps she just decided to do it because she wanted to. Perhaps she fell. The angle of her dive may suggest that she has come from the roof of the building.

Speaking, Listening, and Viewing: GROUP DISCUSSION

P Groups can try to explain why the woman is going into the pool. After students have given their individual explanations, groups can decide what is the most likely explanation. This may be one person's suggestion or a combination of suggestions. After they have done this, groups can read their explanations and the class can decide which seems the most believable.

READING THE WORLD

WHAT ON EARTH?

Just as you fill in missing information when you read a story, you'll often witness scenes in everyday life that require you to fill in the blanks. Sometimes, asking questions and then using your imagination are the only ways to try to make sense of situations you don't quite understand.

N **View** Suppose you accidentally walked into the event in this photo and witnessed this scene. What would your first reaction be? What makes this scene puzzling?

O **Interpret** What is going on in this photo? How might you explain why the woman is going into the pool?

P **Discuss** In a group, share your ideas about this scene. Then use the SkillBuilder at the right to learn about formulating questions.

454 THE LANGUAGE OF LITERATURE TEACHER'S EDITION

SkillBuilder

 CRITICAL THINKING

Formulating Questions

In life, as in the photograph on these pages, some events simply do not make sense. Asking the right questions can help you begin to understand puzzling situations.

Start by writing the headings Who, What, When, Why, and How on a separate sheet of paper. Under each heading, jot down facts that you already know about the topic of the photograph. Then write down questions you have about the photo. For example, "Who is the woman in the white dress? What is she doing? *Is* she falling or diving into the pool? Why is she doing this?"

Answering such questions can help you focus your ideas. Then you can begin to develop an explanation that makes sense of the situation.

APPLYING WHAT YOU'VE LEARNED

In a small group, think of other situations or problems that are particularly confusing or unexplained. Brainstorm a list of questions about the problems you wonder about. Discuss which questions are most helpful.

READING THE WORLD 455

SkillBuilder CRITICAL THINKING

FORMULATING QUESTIONS Explain to students that asking questions about a piece of literature or about their own writing is very useful. It can help students decide how well they have understood someone else's writing and assess the clarity of their own. For each event or situation that seems unclear or obscure, students can use the five questions to clarify their thinking and writing.

Applying What You've Learned Guide students first to think about situations in the real world and then about passages in the selections in this unit. Questions about the real world may include why someone acts the way he or she does, how a certain object works, or what is the best way to do something. Draw attention to difficult passages from the unit's selections and encourage students to ask the five questions to increase their understanding.

THE LANGUAGE OF LITERATURE TEACHER'S EDITION 455

UNIT FOUR
Part 2 Lesson Planner

TIME ALLOTMENTS SHOWN ARE APPROXIMATE. DEPENDING ON YOUR GOALS AND THE NEEDS OF YOUR STUDENTS, YOU MAY WISH TO ALLOW MORE OR LESS TIME FOR CERTAIN PORTIONS OF THE LESSON.

Table of Contents	Discussion	Previewing the Selection	Reading the Selection
PART OPENER **TAKING NECESSARY STEPS** **What Do You Think?** page 456	**20 MINUTES** • Reflect on the part theme		
SELECTION **At Last I Kill a Buffalo** page 458 AVERAGE		**10 MINUTES** • PERSONAL CONNECTION • HISTORICAL CONNECTION • READING CONNECTION: Setting a purpose	**35 MINUTES** • Introduce vocabulary • Read pp. 458–67 (10 pp.)
SELECTION **Tutankhamen from Lost Worlds** page 471 CHALLENGING		**15 MINUTES** • PERSONAL CONNECTION • HISTORICAL CONNECTION • READING CONNECTION: Skimming and scanning	**30 MINUTES** • Introduce vocabulary • Read pp. 471–77 (7 pp.)
SELECTIONS **Pole Vault** page 481 AVERAGE **Analysis of Baseball** page 481 AVERAGE		**15 MINUTES** • PERSONAL CONNECTION • CULTURAL CONNECTION • WRITING CONNECTION	**10 MINUTES** • Read pp. 481–83 (3 pp.)
SELECTION **My Friend Flicka** page 487 AVERAGE		**10 MINUTES** • PERSONAL CONNECTION • CULTURAL CONNECTION • READING CONNECTION: Strategies for reading	**55 MINUTES** • Introduce vocabulary • Read pp. 487–502 (16 pp.)
Writing	**Exploring Topics**	**Prewriting**	**Drafting and Revising**
WRITING FROM EXPERIENCE **Informative Exposition**	**20 MINUTES**	**25 MINUTES**	**75 MINUTES**

Time estimates assume in-class work. You may wish to assign some of these stages as homework.

Responding to the Selection

FROM PERSONAL RESPONSE TO CRITICAL ANALYSIS	OR	ANOTHER PATHWAY	LITERARY CONCEPTS	QUICKWRITES
40 MINUTES					
• Discussion questions	OR	• Observation chart	• Imagery	• Narrative poem • Letter
50 MINUTES					
• Discussion questions	OR	• Radio drama	• Informative nonfiction	• Log entries • Newspaper account
50 MINUTES					
• Discussion questions	OR	• Sports broadcast or commentary	• Onomatopoeia	• Poem • Cinquain
60 MINUTES					
• Discussion questions	OR	• Readers theater	• Plot • Suspense	• Diary entry • Guidelines

Extension Activities

- ALTERNATIVE ACTIVITIES
- LITERARY LINKS
- CRITIC'S CORNER
- THE WRITER'S STYLE
- ACROSS THE CURRICULUM
- ART CONNECTION
- WORDS TO KNOW
- BIOGRAPHY

25 MINUTES: ✔ (Alternative Activities), ✔ (Across the Curriculum), ✔ (Art Connection), ✔ (Words to Know)

50 MINUTES: ✔ (Alternative Activities), ✔ (Across the Curriculum), ✔ (Art Connection), ✔ (Words to Know)

20 MINUTES: ✔ (Across the Curriculum — PHYSICAL EDUCATION), ✔ (Biography)

45 MINUTES: ✔ (Alternative Activities), ✔ (Critic's Corner), ✔ (The Writer's Style), ✔ (Words to Know), ✔ (Biography)

Publishing and Reflecting

30 MINUTES

UNIT FOUR
Part 2 Cooperative Project

A "Handy Hints" Booklet

Overview

Groups will create entertaining and instructional chapters for a class booklet of practical, everyday hints.

PROJECT AT A GLANCE
The selections in Unit Four, Part 2 show people proving themselves in one way or another, often against the judgments of others. For this project, students will work in small groups to identify an area in which they have a mutual interest and/or skill. They will brainstorm ideas they think might be helpful to others who are trying to learn or improve this skill. Then they will write suggestions about how others might improve their performance. These suggestions and helpful hints will be bound together into a class booklet and submitted to the school library for use by other students.

OBJECTIVES
- To identify students' particular skills or talents that might be shared with others
- To write a guide to help others learn or improve their skills
- To bind the hints and suggestions together to form a class booklet to share with others

SUGGESTED GROUP SIZE
2–4 students

MATERIALS
- Colored paper or binder for final booklet
- Selection of skill-enhancing books

1 Getting Started

Arranging the Project
Gather a selection of how-to books that cover a wide range of activities, such as cooking, skateboarding, or winning computer games. If you are unfamiliar with the selected skill (such as scoring high on a particular video game), you may have to ask students' opinions on whether or not they think the hints and tips will work. After each group has selected a specific topic to work on, you might line up other "experts" to check the final writing.

Arranging for the Booklet
The final booklet can be any form—from typed or handwritten pages stapled together to typeset pages bound together. For the latter, students will need access to computers and printers. In any case, students' work should be submitted legibly. Encourage them to include as many drawings or diagrams as possible to illustrate suggestions.

2 Creating the Booklets

Introducing the Project
Explain that students will be working together to produce a booklet that will help others gain or improve their skill at some activity. Each group will select a skill, game, or activity they feel comfortable with and draw up a list of suggestions and helpful hints for others to follow. These suggestions and hints will be bound together to make a class booklet.

Allow students to look over the how-to books you have chosen for this project and to notice the range of activities covered. After they have had a chance to examine the books, lead a class discussion about the organization of the books. Students should be particularly aware that instructions are given in a step-by-step manner and in proper sequence.

To illustrate this point, you might ask a volunteer to give oral instruction on something basic, such as tying a shoelace. The entire class can make suggestions to refine the instructions until they are satisfied that the instructions are clear, concise, and useful to someone just learning to tie a shoelace.

Group Investigations
Divide students into groups of two to four. Since group members will have to discover a mutual interest, you might allow students to select their own partners. Students will work together to decide on a subject they know well enough to offer advice that would be considered "well-informed." They will then decide what area of expertise they best exhibit within the main topic and concentrate their efforts on this part of the activity. Students will draw up a preliminary list of hints and suggestions, then revise and refine them as they did in the class exercise. Final instructions will be bound together for later reference by other students.

Creating a Project Description
Monitor groups' ideas and suggest alternative subjects if there is duplication. You might also ask that students hand in a preliminary list of hints and suggestions. You can meet with each group to go over the first draft and point out areas that need improvement.

OPTION 1: TOPS IN SCHOOL Students can focus on skills that will help them and others achieve excellence in their studies. They can interview top students from other classes, as well as teachers, and draw up a list of study and test-taking strategies.

OPTION 2: ON CAMERA Students can videotape a demonstration of a skill to present to the class. This should be something instructional, along the lines of a cooking show or a home-repair show. Students can review these types of television shows and can structure a demonstration in a similar manner.

OPTION 3: HOT TIPS Students can interview other "experts" for insider tips or clues for their specialty. The focus should be on hints that are not commonly known but that are something these "experts" have figured out through long hours of practice.

OPTION 4: LIVE DEMONSTRATION Students can perform a live demonstration of an activity in front of the class. Be sure the subject matter is appropriate for classroom presentation (loop-the-loop on roller blades is out of the question!) and that the demonstration can be done in a given time period (five to ten minutes) without sacrificing quality or clarity.

Some students will feel comfortable describing how to feed fish, while others will be able to describe how to rebuild an entire car in under four minutes! Judge the final hints and suggestions on organization and clarity rather than subject matter alone.

 Sharing the Booklet

The final booklet can be placed in the school library for use by the entire student body, or it can be kept in the classroom and used as reference by students in future classes for examples and ideas. You might also consider putting the booklet on temporary display in the library, to be returned to the classroom for a permanent home in your private collection.

 Assessing the Project

The following rubric can be used for group or individual assessment.

3 Full Accomplishment Students follow directions and produce a portion of the booklet that accurately, completely, and clearly gives helpful hints about—or describes in detail—how to perform an activity.

2 Substantial Accomplishment Students produce a portion of the booklet, but the description of how to perform the activity lacks clarity or focus.

1 Little or Partial Accomplishment Students' work is incomplete or does not fulfill the requirements of the assignment.

For the Portfolio
You may want to photocopy and insert in each student's portfolio the final portion of the booklet that he or she helped produce, along with a copy of your written assessment. For those groups whose original hints varied greatly from the final product, you might also keep a copy of the original to show the progress made.

Note: For other assessment options, see the *Teacher's Guide to Assessment and Portfolio Use*.

Cross-Curricular Options

ART
Students can make a collage for the cover of the booklet. The collage should show a bit of each subject covered in the final booklet.

SCIENCE
 Students can base a demonstration on a scientific experiment. You can coordinate this project with the science teacher and ask for his or her assistance during the demonstration, as well as in assessing the demonstration.

PHYSICAL EDUCATION
Students who excel in a sport (especially one not offered in the school) might base their hints or demonstration on that sport. They can narrate a video of themselves as they participate in the sport or bring in some of the equipment necessary and give an oral presentation and/or demonstration.

HEALTH AND SAFETY
You might have students focus on tips and hints for staying healthy. These hints might include toothbrushing techniques, the most recommended type of toothbrush, how often one should brush, and so on.

Resources

How to Be a Space Scientist in Your Own Home by Seymour Simon describes 23 science experiments using easy-to-find materials.

How to Draw and Compose Pictures by Arthur Zaidenberg is one of several books by the author that provide introductory instruction to the basics of drawing.

How to Play Better Soccer by C. Paul Jackson explains the rules, positions, and techniques of soccer.

COOPERATIVE PROJECT TEACHER'S EDITION **455d**

PART 2

WHAT DO YOU THINK?
Objectives

The activities on this page can be used to
- introduce the Part 2 theme "Taking Necessary Steps," since each activity is connected to one or more of the selections in Part 2
- create materials for students' personal portfolios that they can later reconsider or revise
- build an understanding of theme that can be reviewed and revised as students progress through the unit

---

What are the steps to adulthood?
Encourage students to be as thoughtful as possible in listing the three steps. Have students work in small groups to compare their responses. You may wish to have the entire class discuss their responses and come up with a consensus list of three steps for the entire class. (See "At Last I Kill a Buffalo," p. 457.)

What does it take?
Groups may wish to select a few different career types to help them narrow down and specify the steps they are brainstorming. Students can use this information to help generate a list of questions to ask a successful person in their community. You may also wish to have them follow through by conducting the interview and presenting their findings to the class. (See "Tutankhamen," p. 470.)

How does one meet a challenge?
Encourage students to research the lives of their chosen speakers in order to find out important information to use in their introductory speeches. Once students have researched and written their introductory remarks, have them rehearse their speeches before reading them to the class. (All selections in this part connect to this activity.)

UNIT TWO **PART 2**

TAKING NECESSARY STEPS

WHAT DO  THINK?

REFLECTING ON THEME

Tests of ability often take place in public settings. Tests of character, however, often take place where struggles to grow or change go unseen. Use these activities to explore some necessary steps. Jot down your thoughts in your notebook. Later you can compare them with the characters' steps.

What are the steps to adulthood?

What accomplishments prove that a young person is ready to handle grown-up responsibilities? In your notebook, copy and complete this statement:

> I think the three most important steps in becoming an adult are
> 1. _____
> 2. _____
> 3. _____

What does it take?

Do you ever dream of being a prima ballerina, a world-class athlete, or a top scientist? With a group of classmates, brainstorm the steps that might be necessary to develop a high level of ability. Then think of questions to ask in interviewing a successful person in your school or community.

Looking Back

On a sheet of paper, draw a big outline of a light bulb. Then look in your notebook to review your early ideas about the theme "Showing Your True Colors." Did the experiences of a character in Part 1 spark new ideas about facing tests and challenges? Did an activity lead you in a new direction? Fill in the light bulb as you share your thoughts with a partner or small group.

How does one meet a challenge?

Imagine that a person you admire is to speak at your school. You are to introduce the person. Write an introduction, thinking about the steps the person took to meet a challenge and what his or her success means to you. Rehearse and present your introduction to your class.

456

Across the Curriculum

 Geography Have students work in small groups to research the attempts climbers have made to scale Mount Everest, the highest mountain in the world. Each group can research a different attempt, such as Sir Edmund Hillary and Tenzing Norgay's expedition in 1953, the U.S. expedition led by Norman G. Dyhrenfurth in 1963, or the Japanese expedition in 1980. Students should investigate the conditions which make scaling Mount Everest a challenge, the preparations and training these expeditions have made, and how successful they were.

Looking Back

Students can summarize each selection in Part 1 and mention its significance in terms of the theme of facing challenges. You may wish to ask students some of the following questions to help get them started:
- Which selection sparked new ideas about facing challenges?
- What was it about the character that you found interesting in terms of facing a challenge?
- What impact do you think reading about this character will have on your life?

456 THE LANGUAGE OF LITERATURE **Teacher's Edition**

PREVIEWING

NONFICTION

At Last I Kill a Buffalo
Luther Standing Bear

PERSONAL CONNECTION *Activating Prior Knowledge*

In the account you are about to read, the author looks back upon a childhood experience that had helped to shape his life. He had faced a test of character that challenged not only his bravery but his honesty as well. Do you recall a situation in which your character was tested—one in which you struggled with inner conflicts and remained true to yourself? Briefly describe the circumstances in your notebook or on a sheet of paper.

HISTORICAL CONNECTION *Building Background*

"At Last I Kill a Buffalo" portrays incidents that take place within a Sioux (sōō) tribe. The Sioux nation, made up of seven tribes, can be traced to the Great Lakes, where its members built shelters called tepees, harvested crops, and hunted deer. Pushed westward by the French fur traders and the Chippewa (chĭp´ə-wô´) tribe, the Sioux learned to live in new environments. The Lakota (lə-kō´tə), or Teton, Sioux were the first to move to the Great Plains, a region identified on the map shown. The Lakota Sioux traveled throughout the western Dakotas and Nebraska, following the buffalo herds they hunted.

The Sioux had a complicated code of behavior that stressed self-discipline, community involvement, and a desire to live peacefully with nature. At the same time, the Sioux valued bravery. As Sioux boys prepared to face adulthood, they participated in tests of their character. They were expected to be brave, honest, and capable of making personal sacrifices. A Sioux boy had to be unselfish, kind to older people, and always ready to help those in need.

READING CONNECTION *Active Reading Setting a Purpose*

Setting a Purpose Think about the title "At Last I Kill a Buffalo." What guesses can you make about the test of character the narrator faces? What questions does the title raise for you? Deciding on a reason to read a selection is called setting a purpose. As you read about a test of character, use elements such as the title and illustrations to help you answer any questions you identified.

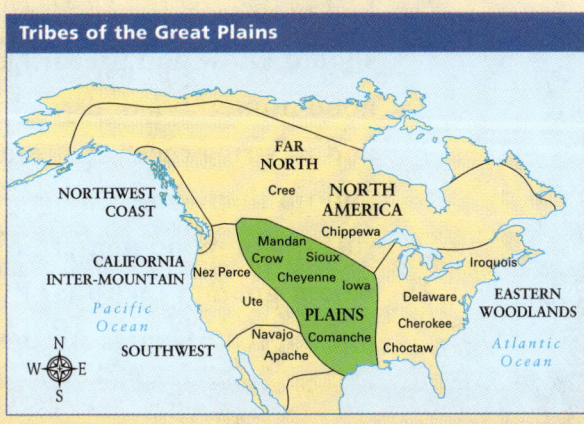
Tribes of the Great Plains

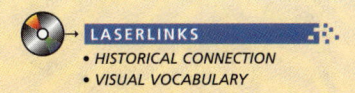
LASERLINKS
- HISTORICAL CONNECTION
- VISUAL VOCABULARY

457

OVERVIEW

Objectives

- To understand and appreciate an autobiographical account of a young Native American's first buffalo hunt
- To understand setting a purpose
- To identify and appreciate the use of imagery in a work of nonfiction
- To express understanding of the selection through a choice of writing forms, including a narrative poem and a letter
- To extend understanding of the story through a variety of multimodal and cross-curricular activities

Skills

READING SKILLS/STRATEGIES
- Setting a purpose

GRAMMAR
- Conjunctions

THE WRITER'S STYLE
- Combining sentences

LITERARY CONCEPTS
- Imagery
- Point of view

GENRE STUDY
- Nonfiction: autobiography

SPELLING
- Words ending in -ary

STUDY SKILLS
- Taking notes

SPEAKING, LISTENING, AND VIEWING
- Oral history
- Group discussion
- Oral presentation

Cross-Curricular Connections

SCIENCE
- Grassland biomes

SOCIAL STUDIES
- Sioux Indians
- Tribes of the Great Plains

MATH
- Measuring distance

HISTORICAL CONNECTION

The Sioux Nation In part, young Sioux men first proved their manhood by killing buffalo. These historical images and artworks show the faces of Sioux warriors, their encampments, and the ways they hunted buffalo.

Side A, Frame 38855

PRINT AND MEDIA RESOURCES

UNIT FOUR RESOURCE BOOK
Strategic Reading: Literature, p. 47
Vocabulary SkillBuilder, p. 50
Reading SkillBuilder, p. 48
Spelling SkillBuilder, p. 49

GRAMMAR MINI-LESSONS
Transparencies, p. 42

WRITING MINI-LESSONS
Transparencies, pp. 40, 41

ACCESS FOR STUDENTS ACQUIRING ENGLISH
Selection Summaries
Reading and Writing Support

FORMAL ASSESSMENT
Selection Test, pp. 93–94
 Test Generator

 AUDIO LIBRARY
See Reference Card

LASERLINKS
Historical Connection
Visual Vocabulary
Art Gallery

INTERNET RESOURCES
McDougal Littell Literature Center at http://www.hmco.com/mcdougal/lit

---

THE LANGUAGE OF LITERATURE TEACHER'S EDITION **457**

SUMMARY

Luther Standing Bear, whose Sioux name was Ota K'te, recalls the rite of passage (the test for becoming an adult) of his first buffalo hunt. The night before the hunt, every living creature in the camp is quiet. Eight-year-old Ota K'te sits by the campfire, listening to his father's advice and watching him sharpen knives and arrows. The next morning, they ride in a group of 100 hunters to the place where the buffalo are grazing. As the buffalo stampede, Ota K'te rides his black pony fearlessly into the rushing herd. He loses sight of his father, though, and is momentarily terrified by the great beasts running wildly around him. Calming himself, he singles out a calf and kills it with five arrows. He wants to show off his accomplishment but discovers that the other hunters have ridden out of sight. As Ota K'te starts to skin the buffalo, he considers pretending that he killed the beast in only three shots. But when his father locates him, Ota K'te tells the truth, knowing honesty to be more important than glory. His father helps him skin the buffalo and bring it back to camp. Word soon spreads of Ota K'te's accomplishment, and his proud father celebrates by giving away a horse to an old man from the tribe.

Thematic Link: *Taking Necessary Steps*
Ota K'te takes on the physical challenges of his first buffalo hunt and proves his honesty and courage to his father.

CUSTOMIZING FOR
Gifted and Talented Students

Have students keep notes, as they read, as to how they would adapt the events of the story for a radio play. They should choose passages for a narrator (possibly Ota K'te as an elderly man) and note dialogue for the actors in the play. Students may write extra dialogue for their plays and choose sound effects and music.

Art Note

Buffalo Hunter by unknown artist
In this painting, the artist conveys the excitement and movement of the hunt through the sharply contrasting colors and the flow of lines connecting the grasslands, the horse's mane, and the rider's hair.

Reading the Art *How does the artist convey the urgency and danger of the hunt?*

At Last I Kill a Buffalo

BY **LUTHER STANDING BEAR**

At last the day came when my father allowed me to go on a buffalo hunt with him. And what a proud boy I was!

Ever since I could remember my father had been teaching me the things that I should know and preparing me to be a good hunter. I had learned to make bows and to string them and to make arrows and tip them with feathers. I knew how to ride my pony no matter how fast he would go, and I felt that I was brave and did not fear danger. All these things I had

WORDS TO KNOW

customary (kŭs′tə-mĕr′ē) *adj.* according to custom; usual; traditional (p. 466)
exploit (ĕk′sploit) *n.* a brave deed or adventurous act (p. 466)
gratification (grăt′ə-fĭ-kā′shən) *n.* a source of satisfaction or pleasure (p. 462)
preceding (prĭ-sēd′ĭng) *adj.* coming earlier or before (p. 461)
sufficient (sə-fĭsh′ənt) *adj.* enough for the purpose (p. 461)

 VISUAL VOCABULARY
- **breechcloth** (brēch′klôth′)
- **tepee** (tē′pē)

Side A, Frame 38863

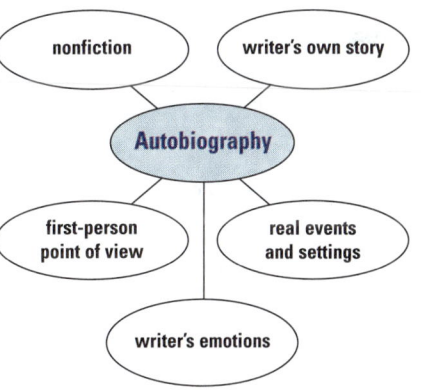

Buffalo Hunter (about 1844), unknown artist. Oil on canvas, 40" × 51 ⅛". Santa Barbara (California) Museum of Art, gift of Harriet Cowles Hammet. Photo by Scott McClaine.

Copyright © Lindfors Photography.

AT LAST I KILL A BUFFALO   **459**

CUSTOMIZING FOR
Students Acquiring English

- Use **ACCESS FOR STUDENTS ACQUIRING ENGLISH,** *Reading and Writing Support.*

- This selection describes a Native American rite of passage—a boy's first buffalo hunt. Invite students to talk or write about rites of passage or coming-of-age rituals in their own cultures.

- In addition to the suggestions in these boxes, you may want to use the suggestions under Strategic Reading for Less-Proficient Readers.

- **Ⓘ** If necessary, remind students that the past perfect progressive form of a verb, as in *had been teaching,* describes actions that began in the past and continued up to the beginning of the story.

STRATEGIC READING FOR
Less-Proficient Readers

Set a Purpose Invite volunteers to share any information they already know about buffalo or other herd animals. Then have them read to find out why the whole tribe must be very quiet the night before the hunt.

Use **UNIT FOUR RESOURCE BOOK,** pp. 47–48, for guidance in reading the selection.

Literary Concept:
POINT OF VIEW

Ⓐ Tell students that an autobiographical account, such as this selection, is almost always written from a first-person point of view. Ask students which pronouns on page 458 indicate a first-person point of view. *(my, me, I)* Have them note, as they continue reading, the information the reader learns that only Ota K'te, the writer, would have known.

Mini-Lesson Genre Study

NONFICTION Remind students that an **autobiography** is the true story of a person's life, told by that person. Usually, autobiographies are book length because they cover a long period of time. However, there are shorter types of autobiographical writing, including journals, diaries, and memoirs. Autobiographical material usually includes the writer's emotions and reactions as well as descriptions of real events and settings. You may want to use a word web, such as the one shown here, to teach the characteristics of this genre.

Application Have students keep diaries while they are studying this selection. In their diaries, they should describe their reactions to Ota K'te's story, explaining how his experiences may relate to experiences they've had. They can also record information on their current experiences. Students may wish to keep their diary entries private, but they can share with classmates the types of information they include and can discuss how keeping a diary may be a useful activity.

THE LANGUAGE OF LITERATURE TEACHER'S EDITION   **459**

Art Note

***Robe with Mato Tope's Exploits* by Mato Tope (Four Bears)** On this tanned buffalo hide, the Native American Mandan chief Mato Tope (1800?–1837) recorded scenes from his victories in battle. The artist combined pigments, porcupine quills, and different types of hair to create the work.

In 1832, Mato Tope described the scenes on the robe to George Catlin, an American painter noted for his depictions of Native American life, who recorded the information in a book. Beginning at the top and moving clockwise, the scenes show (1) Mato Tope charging toward a group of Assiniboines, represented by the group of round heads; (2) Mato Tope standing over the body of a Cheyenne warrior he has killed; (3) Mato Tope in hand-to-hand combat with a Cheyenne chief; (4) Mato Tope using a lance with eagle feathers in a fight with another Cheyenne chief; (5) the horse of a slain Cheyenne chief; (6) the slain chief lying on the ground; (7) Mato Tope leading his war horse to avenge the murder of a Mandan by killing two Ojibwe women; and (8) Mato Tope in one of his important battles.

Reading the Art *Do you think this robe is a work of art? Why or why not? What do the figures communicate about Mato Tope?*

CUSTOMIZING FOR
Multiple Learning Styles

 Spatial or Graphic Learners After students have discussed Mato Tope's buffalo robe, they can design a work of art to celebrate some of their personal victories or important family events. Their work can be a drawing, painting, collage, or sculpture, or some other form they may prefer.

Linking to Social Studies

 In the Americas, there were hundreds of Native American tribes, with many different ways of life. A few of the Plains tribes were the Sioux, Blackfeet, Crow, Cheyenne, Pawnee, Arapaho, Osage, Wichita, and Comanche.

A buffalo hide illustrated (about 1835) with the acts of bravery of Mato Tope, a famous chief of the Mandan tribe.
Bern (Switzerland) Historical Museum. Copyright © Bern Historical Museum.
Photo by Stefan Rebsamen.

learned for just this day when Father would allow me to go with him on a buffalo hunt. It was the event for which every Sioux boy eagerly waited. To ride side by side with the best hunters of the tribe, to hear the terrible noise of the great herds as they ran, and then to help to bring home the kill was the most thrilling day of any Indian boy's life. The only other event which could equal it would be the day I went for the first time on the warpath to meet the enemy and protect my tribe.

On the following early morning we were to start, so the evening was spent in preparation. Although the tepees[1] were full of activity, there was no noise or confusion outside. Always the evening before a buffalo hunt and when everyone was usually in his tepee, an old man went around the circle of tepees calling, "I-ni-la, i-ni-la," not loudly, but so everyone could hear. The old man was saying, "Keep quiet, keep quiet." We all knew that the scouts had come in and reported buffalo near and that we must all keep the camp in stillness. It was not

---

1. **tepees** (tē′pēz): portable dwellings of certain Native American peoples, consisting of a conical framework of poles covered with animal skins or bark.

460 UNIT FOUR PART 2: TAKING NECESSARY STEPS

Mini-Lesson   Reading Skills/Strategies

SETTING A PURPOSE Explain to students that good readers ask themselves questions as they read in order to set a purpose for reading. Give the following examples of such questions: Who are the characters in the story, and what are they like? What happens in the story? Where does the story take place? Explain to students that asking questions in order to set a purpose for reading will help them become more active and engaged readers.

Application Have students work in groups to generate a list of purposes a reader might have in mind for this story. Students can write each purpose in question form, beginning with words such as *Who, What, When, Where, Why,* and *How.* When students are finished, groups can compare their work. You can extend this activity by having students write questions to set purposes for their next reading selection. They can then use their reading logs to answer their own questions as they read.

Reteaching/Reinforcement
• *Unit Four Resource Book*, p. 48

460 THE LANGUAGE OF LITERATURE TEACHER'S EDITION

necessary for the old man to go into each tepee and explain to the men that tomorrow there would be a big hunt, as the buffalo were coming. He did not order the men to prepare their weapons, and neither did he order the mothers to keep children from crying. The one word, "I-ni-la," was sufficient to bring quiet to the whole camp. That night there would be no calling or shouting from tepee to tepee, and no child would cry aloud. Even the horses and dogs obeyed the command for quiet, and all night not a horse neighed and not a dog barked. The very presence of quiet was everywhere. Such is the orderliness of a Sioux camp that men, women, children, and animals seem to have a common understanding and sympathy. It is no mystery but natural that the Indian and his animals understand each other very well both with words and without words. There are words, however, that the Indian uses that are understood by both his horses and dogs. When on a hunt, if one of the warriors speaks the word "A-a-ah" rather quickly and sharply, every man, horse, and dog will stop instantly and listen. Not a move will be made by an animal until the men move or speak further. As long as the hunters listen, the animals will listen also.

The night preceding a buffalo hunt was always an exciting night, even though it was quiet in camp. There would be much talk in the tepees around the fires. There would be sharpening of arrows and of knives. New bowstrings would be made, and quivers would be filled with arrows.

It was in the fall of the year, and the evenings were cool as Father and I sat by the fire and talked over the hunt. I was only eight years of age, and I know that Father did not expect me to get a buffalo at all, but only to try perhaps for a small calf should I be able to get close enough to one. Nevertheless, I was greatly excited as I sat and watched Father working in his easy, firm way.

I was wearing my buffalo-skin robe, the hair next to my body. Mother had made me a rawhide belt, and this, wrapped around my waist, held my blanket on when I threw it off my shoulders. In the early morning I would wear it, for it would be cold. When it came time to shoot, I should not want my blanket, but the belt would hold it in place.

Even the horses and dogs obeyed the command for quiet.

You can picture me, I think, as I sat in the glow of the campfire, my little brown body bare to the waist, watching, and listening intently to my father. My hair hung down my back, and I wore moccasins and breechcloth of buckskin.[2] To my belt was fastened a rawhide holster for my knife, for when I was eight years of age we had plenty of knives. I was proud to own a knife, and this night I remember I kept it on all night. Neither did I lay aside my bow, but went to sleep with it in my hand, thinking, I suppose, to be all the nearer ready in the morning when the start was made.

---

2. **breechcloth of buckskin:** a cloth, in this case one made from deer skin, used to cover the area between the waist and thighs.

WORDS TO KNOW
sufficient (sə-fĭsh'ənt) *adj.* enough for the purpose
preceding (prĭ-sēd'ĭng) *adj.* coming earlier or before

461

Critical Thinking: ANALYZING

D Ask students why they think the writer provides so much detail about the cooperation involved in keeping quiet while the buffalo are nearby. *(Possible responses: to emphasize the importance of the hunt to the tribe; to build suspense; to describe the special qualities of the relationships between the people and the animals)*

STRATEGIC READING FOR Less-Proficient Readers

E Ask why it is so important that the people and animals in the camp keep quiet. *(The buffalo are nearby, and the tribe doesn't want to scare them away.)*
Making Inferences

Set a Purpose Have students read on, looking for details that describe the age, appearance, feelings, and character of the young Ota K'te.

Literary Concept: IMAGERY

F Remind students that a writer creates imagery by including details that appeal to the five senses—sight, hearing, taste, smell, and touch. Have students identify such details in the scene where Ota K'te and his father sit by the campfire. *(Possible responses: sight—glow of the campfire; clothing the boy wears; hearing—quiet in the camp, sounds of people sharpening knives and arrows; touch—coolness of the evening, hair of the buffalo robe next to the boy's body)*

CUSTOMIZING FOR Students Acquiring English

2 Point out that *Neither did I lay aside my bow* means "I did not lay aside my bow either."

Mini-Lesson Grammar

CONJUNCTIONS Remind students that conjunctions such as *and* and *or* can be used to join compound subjects, verbs, or objects in a sentence. Present to students the examples shown on the chalkboard.

Application Have students identify the compound part in each sentence and label it as *subject, verb,* or *object.*

1. No one would call or shout from tepee to tepee. *(verb)*
2. The horses and dogs obeyed the command for quiet. *(subject)*
3. The Indian and his animals understand one another very well. *(subject)*
4. They have a common understanding and sympathy. *(object)*
5. If someone speaks the word "A-a-ah," everyone will stop and listen. *(verb)*

Reteaching/Reinforcement
- Grammar Handbook, anthology p. 813
- Grammar Mini-Lessons transparencies p. 42

What Are Conjunctions? pp. 516–517

Compound Subject
Father and I sat by the fire.
Compound Verb
I sat and watched Father working.
Compound Object
I wore moccasins and a breechcloth.

THE LANGUAGE OF LITERATURE TEACHER'S EDITION **461**

Active Reading: CONNECT

G Point out to students how Ota K'te watches and listens carefully to his father so that he can learn what he needs to do to be a skilled hunter. Invite students to describe situations in which they learned important skills or ideas from older family members or friends.

Critical Thinking: MAKING JUDGMENTS

H Have students note the different roles of the mother and the father as described in the selection. Lead a discussion in which students compare these roles with those in other cultures.

STRATEGIC READING FOR
Less-Proficient Readers

I Ask students to describe Ota K'te's appearance, character, and feelings.

- How old is Ota K'te at the time described in the selection? *(eight years old)* **Noting Relevant Details**
- What clothing and weapons will Ota K'te take on the buffalo hunt? *(moccasins, breechcloth, blanket held with a belt, knife, arrows and quiver, rawhide quirt)* **Visualizing**
- How does Ota K'te feel on the night before the hunt? *(Possible responses: excited, nervous, awed)* **Drawing Conclusions**

Set a Purpose Have students read the description of the hunt and Ota K'te's first kill, noting the various kinds of challenges the young Sioux faces.

Linking to Math

J Customary units for distance include inches, feet, yards, and miles. Some metric units are centimeters, meters, and kilometers. People also use time to describe distance, such as a two-hour drive or a five-minute walk.

Father sharpened my steel points for me and also sharpened my knife. The whetstone³ was a long stone which was kept in a buckskin bag, and sometimes this stone went all over the camp; every tepee did not have one, so we shared this commodity⁴ with one another. I had as I remember about ten arrows, so when Father was through sharpening them I put them in my rawhide quiver. I had a rawhide quirt,⁵ too, which I would wear fastened to my waist. As Father worked, he knew I was watching him closely and listening whenever he spoke. By the time all preparations had been **G** made, he had told me just how I was to act when I started out in the morning with the hunters.

We went to bed, my father hoping that tomorrow would be successful for him so that he could bring home some nice meat for **H** the family and a hide for my mother to tan. I went to bed but could not go to sleep at once, so filled was I with the wonderment and excitement of it all. The next day was to be a test for me. I was to prove to my father whether he was or was not justified in his pride in me. What would be the result of my training? Would I be brave if I faced danger, and would Father be proud of me? Though I did not know it that night, I was to be tried for the strength of my manhood and my honesty in this hunt. Something happened that day which I remember above all things. It was a test of my real character, and I am proud to say that I did not find myself weak but made a decision that has **I** been all these years a <u>gratification</u> to me.

The next morning the hunters were catching their horses about daybreak. I arose with my father and went out and caught my pony. I wanted to do whatever he did and show him that he did not have to tell me what to do. We brought our animals to the tepee and got our bows and arrows and mounted. From over the village came the hunters. Most of them were leading their running horses. These running horses were anxious for the hunt and came prancing, their ears straight up and their tails waving in the air. We were joined with perhaps a hundred or more riders, some of whom carried bows and arrows and some armed with guns.

The buffalo were reported to be about five or six miles away as we should count distance now. At that time we did not measure distance in miles. One camping distance was about ten miles, and these buffalo were said to be about one half camping distance away. **J**

On I rode through the cloud, for I knew I must keep going.

Some of the horses were to be left at a stopping place just before the herd was reached. These horses were pack animals which were taken along to carry extra blankets or weapons. They were trained to remain there until the hunters came for them.

---

3. **whetstone:** a hard stone used to sharpen knives and other metal blades.
4. **commodity:** a basic good that has useful economic value.
5. **quirt:** a small riding whip.

WORDS TO KNOW
gratification (grăt′ə-fĭ-kā′shən) *n.* a source of satisfaction or pleasure

462

Mini-Lesson Study Skills

TAKING NOTES Explain to students how to use index or note cards to record information when they do research. They should begin by making a bibliography card for each book or article they use. The card should give the author, title, publisher and city, and year of publication.

Students can also use one note card for each fact or idea they wish to record. On this card, they should jot down the title of the source and the pages on which the fact or idea appears, as shown in the example given here. Tell students that if they copy material from the source, they should use quotation marks; if they paraphrase or summarize the material, they don't need the quotes.

Application Have students choose a topic related to the selection—such as one of those listed for the Alternative Activity on page 469—and ask them to research this topic in the library. Have students make bibliography and note cards to document their research findings.

North American Indian Designs p. 15

The Plains Indians were nomadic, so they did not create large works of art. Instead, they decorated their tents and their clothes.

462 THE LANGUAGE OF LITERATURE TEACHER'S EDITION

Though they were neither hobbled[6] nor tied, they stood still during the shooting and noise of the chase.

My pony was a black one and a good runner. I felt very important as I rode along with the hunters and my father, the chief. I kept as close to him as I could.

Two men had been chosen to scout or to lead the party. These two men were in a sense policemen whose work it was to keep order. They carried large sticks of ash wood, something like a policeman's billy,[7] though longer. They rode ahead of the party while the rest of us kept in a group close together. The leaders went ahead until they sighted the herd of grazing buffalo. Then they stopped and waited for the rest of us to ride up. We all rode slowly toward the herd, which on sight of us had come together, although they had been scattered here and there over the plain. When they saw us, they all ran close together as if at the command of a leader. We continued riding slowly toward the herd until one of the leaders shouted, "Ho-ka-he!" which means, "Ready, go!" At that command every man started for the herd. I had been listening, too, and the minute the hunters started, I started also.

Away I went, my little pony putting all he had into the race. It was not long before I lost sight of Father, but I kept going just the same. I threw my blanket back, and the chill of the autumn morning struck my body, but I did not mind. On I went. It was wonderful to race over the ground with all these horsemen about me. There was no shouting, no noise of any kind except the pounding of the horses' feet. The herd was now running and had raised a cloud of dust. I felt no fear until we had entered this cloud of dust and I could see nothing about me—only hear the sound of feet. Where was Father? Where was I going? On I rode through the cloud, for I knew I must keep going.

Then all at once I realized that I was in the midst of the buffalo, their dark bodies rushing all about me and their great heads moving up and down to the sound of their hoofs beating upon the earth. Then it was that fear overcame me and I leaned close down upon my little pony's body and clutched him tightly. I can never tell you how I felt toward my pony at that moment. All thought of shooting had left my mind. I was seized by blank fear. In a moment or so, however, my senses became clearer, and I could distinguish other sounds beside the clatter of feet. I could hear a shot now and then, and I could see the buffalo beginning to break up into small bunches. I could not see Father nor any of my companions yet, but my fear was vanishing and I was safe. I let my pony run. The buffalo looked too large for me to tackle, anyway, so I just kept going. The buffalo became more and more scattered. Pretty soon I saw a young calf that looked about my size. I remembered now what Father had told me the night before as we sat about the fire. Those instructions were important for me now to follow.

I was still back of the calf, being unable to get alongside of him. I was anxious to get a shot, yet afraid to try, as I was still very nervous. While my pony was making all speed to come alongside, I chanced a shot, and to my surprise my arrow landed. My second arrow glanced along the back of the animal and sped on between the horns, making only a slight wound. My third arrow hit a spot that made the running beast slow up in his gait. I shot a fourth arrow, and though it, too, landed, it was not a fatal wound. It seemed to me that it was taking a lot of shots, and I was not proud

---
6. **hobbled:** tied around the legs to prevent movement.
7. **billy:** a short wooden club.

AT LAST I KILL A BUFFALO **463**

Mini-Lesson The Writer's Style

COMBINING SENTENCES Remind students that two sentences can be combined using a comma and a conjunction such as *and, but,* or *or.* Tell them that the choice of conjunction determines how the parts are related, as illustrated here:
- Ota K'te changed his mind, *and* he told the truth to his father. (The second part of the sentence logically follows from the first.)
- Ota K'te thought about lying, *but* he told the truth. (The second part contrasts with the first.)
- Ota K'te might lie, *or* he might tell the truth. (One part or the other is possible, but not both.)

Application Have students combine the following pairs of sentences with *and, but,* or *or* so that the meaning matches the meaning in the selection.
1. Ota K'te usually enjoyed playing with the other boys. On this day he stayed near the tepee to hear people praise him. *(but)*
2. The buffalo had stirred up a cloud of dust. Ota K'te could see nothing around him. *(and)*
3. Ota K'te might return from his first hunt proud and successful. He might return disappointed. *(or)*

Literary Concept: IMAGERY

K Ask students to look for sensory details that the writer uses to create imagery in this paragraph and the next. *(Possible responses: touch—the chill of the air; sight—the cloud of dust, the dark bodies of the buffalo; hearing—the sounds of the horses' and buffalo's hooves, rifle shots fired by other hunters)*

CUSTOMIZING FOR
Students Acquiring English

3 Help students understand that "Where was Father?" and "Where was I going?" are questions that the narrator thought to himself at this point in the story.

4 Point out that *about* means "approximately."

Literary Concept: SUSPENSE

L Ask students to point out on this page some sentences that the writer uses to build suspense. *(Possible responses: "I felt no fear until we had entered this cloud of dust"; "I was seized by a blank fear.")* Have students discuss how they reacted while reading the paragraph that begins "Away I went . . ." and the following paragraph. *(Some may read more quickly to find out what will happen.)*

Active Reading: EVALUATE

M Have students reread the paragraph beginning "Then all at once . . ." Ask them whether they think Ota K'te was brave or cowardly, based on the description of the events. You may wish to use the following model to give students an idea of what they might be thinking about.

Think-Aloud Model *At first I felt he was cowardly, because he became so frightened by the buffalo. But then I realized he kept riding in the hunt and overcame his fears. So I think he behaved courageously.*

Reteaching/Reinforcement
- *Writing Handbook,* anthology pp. 788–789
- *Writing Mini-Lessons* transparencies, pp. 40, 41

 The Writer's Craft

Sentence Combining, pp. 286–288

THE LANGUAGE OF LITERATURE TEACHER'S EDITION **463**

Critical Thinking: ANALYZING

N Ask students to describe the different kinds of feelings Ota K'te has as he stands on the plain alone, over the body of the buffalo calf. *(Possible responses: elation, pride, loneliness, fear, regret)*

Active Reading: PREDICT

O Have students predict several different ways the story might end. *(Possible responses: The buffalo come back, and Ota K'te is injured or killed. Ota K'te becomes lost and cannot find his way back to the hunting party. Ota K'te kills another buffalo. Ota K'te saves someone else—perhaps his father—from danger.)*

CUSTOMIZING FOR
Multiple Learning Styles

P **Bodily-Kinesthetic Learners** Have one or more students act out the scene in which Ota K'te stands over the dead buffalo and considers what to do about the arrows. Since no dialogue will be used, students must convey the character's thoughts and feelings with gestures, facial expressions, and other body language.

Buffalo hunt (about 1884), New Bear (Hidatsa people). Charles H. Barstow Collection of Indian Ledger Art, Montana State University-Billings Library, Special Collections.

Mini-Lesson: Speaking, Listening, and Viewing

ORAL HISTORY Explain to students that much of the information that has been gathered on the history of Native Americans has been recorded in the form of oral history. In this type of research, an experienced historian interviews someone who can give a firsthand account of events. Often, the person being interviewed is an older member of a culture that passed on traditions and history orally rather than in written form.

Application Have students work together in pairs to role-play an oral history interview between Ota K'te as an old man and a young, educated Native American who has become a historian. Students should prepare questions and answers by using information from the selection.

of my marksmanship. I was glad, however, to see the animal going slower, and I knew that one more shot would make me a hunter. My horse seemed to know his own importance. His two ears stood straight forward, and it was not necessary for me to urge him to get closer to the buffalo. I was soon by the side of the buffalo, and one more shot brought the chase to a close. I jumped from my pony, and as I stood by my fallen game, I looked all around wishing that the world could see. But I was alone. In my determination to stay by until I had won my buffalo, I had not noticed that I was far from everyone else. No admiring friends were about, and as far as I could see I was on the plain alone. The herd of buffalo had completely disappeared. And as for Father, much as I wished for him, he was out of sight, and I had no idea where he was.

I stood and looked at the animal on the ground. I was happy. Everyone must know that I, Ota K'te,[8] had killed a buffalo. But it looked as if no one knew where I was, so no one was coming my way. I must then take something from this animal to show that I had killed it. I took all the arrows one by one from the body. As I took them out, it occurred to me that I had used five arrows. If I had been a skillful hunter, one arrow would have been sufficient, but I had used five. Here it was that temptation came to me. Why could I not take out two of the arrows and throw them away? No one would know, and then I should be more greatly admired and praised as a hunter. As it was, I knew that I should be praised by Father and Mother, but I wanted more. And so I was tempted to lie.

I was planning this as I took out my skinning knife that Father had sharpened for me the night before. I skinned one side of the animal, but when it came to turning it over, I was too small. I was wondering what to do when I heard my father's voice calling, "To-ki-i-la-la-hu-wo," "Where are you?" I quickly jumped on my pony and rode to the top of a little hill nearby. Father saw me and came to me at once. He was so pleased to see me and glad to know that I was safe. I knew that I could never lie to my father. He was too fond of me and I too proud of him. He had always told me to tell the truth. He wanted me to be an honest man, so I resolved then to tell the truth even if it took from me a little glory. He rode up to me with a glad expression on his face, expecting me to go back with him to his kill. As he came up, I said as calmly as I could, "Father, I have killed a buffalo." His smile changed to surprise, and he asked me where my buffalo was. I pointed to it, and we rode over to where it lay, partly skinned.

Father set to work to skin it for me. I had watched him do this many times and knew perfectly well how to do it myself, but I could not turn the animal over. There was a way to turn the head of the animal so that the body would be balanced on the back while being skinned. Father did this for me, while I helped all I could. When the hide was off, Father put

> *I looked all around wishing that the world could see.*

---

8. **Ota K'te** (ō′tä kə-tā′): the Lakota Sioux name of Luther Standing Bear. The name means "Plenty Kill."

AT LAST I KILL A BUFFALO   **465**

Mini-Lesson   Literary Concepts

REVIEWING POINT OF VIEW   Remind students that autobiographies are almost always told from the first-person point of view, using the pronouns *I, me, we,* and *us*. Tell them that in the third-person point of view, events are related by a narrator who is not the main character. This narrator uses pronouns such as *he, she,* and *they* to describe what happens.

Application   Have students write a brief description of Ota K'te's first buffalo hunt from the point of view of his father or his mother. Students' writing might begin with "On the day that my son killed his first buffalo . . ." Remind students that Ota K'te's father and mother would not know that he had been afraid or tempted to lie, so these aspects should not be mentioned in the description. However, students can describe how either parent felt or what thoughts he or she had.

STRATEGIC READING FOR
Less-Proficient Readers

U Ask students why Ota K'te was glad he had told his father the truth. *(Possible responses: It was important to Ota K'te to become an honest man. It was more of a challenge for Ota K'te to tell the truth than it was for him to kill the buffalo.)* Making Inferences

Literary Concept:
POINT OF VIEW

V Remind students that the narrator is using the first-person point of view. Ask what "inside information" the reader has as a result of Ota K'te's telling the story. *(Possible response: He is bursting with pride but doesn't show it because he has been taught not to brag.)*

Linking to Social Studies

W During the 1800s, settlers and gold seekers invaded the Sioux hunting grounds and killed many buffalo. Native Americans, deprived of their traditional livelihood, had little choice but to move to reservations. Today, about half of all Sioux live on reservations in the northern plains; the rest live in urban areas.

COMPREHENSION CHECK

1. Why is Ota K'te alone when he kills the buffalo calf? *(He was separated from the other hunters during the hunt.)*
2. What is the greatest challenge Ota K'te faces on his first buffalo hunt? *(overcoming the temptation to lie to his father)*
3. What does Ota K'te's father do to celebrate his son's first hunt? *(He has the news announced to the rest of the village; he gives away a valuable horse.)*

---

it on the pony's back with the hair side next to the pony. On this he arranged the meat so it would balance. Then he covered the meat carefully with the rest of the hide, so no dust would reach it while we traveled home. I rode home on top of the load.

I showed my father the arrows that I had used and just where the animal had been hit. He was very pleased and praised me over and over again. I felt more glad than ever that I had told the truth, and I have never regretted it. I am more proud now that I told the truth than I am of killing the buffalo.

We then rode to where my father had killed a buffalo. There we stopped and prepared it for taking home. It was late afternoon when we got back to camp. No king ever rode in state⁹ who was more proud than I that day as I came into the village sitting high up on my load of buffalo meat. Mother had now two hunters in the family, and I knew how she was going to make over me. It is not <u>customary</u> for Indian men to brag about their <u>exploits</u>, and I had been taught that bragging was not nice. So I was very quiet, although I was bursting with pride. Always when arriving home I would run out to play, for I loved to be with the other boys, but this day I lingered about close to the tepee so I could hear the nice things that were said about me. It was soon all over camp that Ota K'te had killed a buffalo.

My father was so proud that he gave away a fine horse. He called an old man to our tepee to cry out the news to the rest of the people in camp. The old man stood at the door of our tepee and sang a song of praise to my father. The horse had been led up, and I stood holding it by a rope. The old man who was doing the singing called the other old man who was to receive the horse as a present. He accepted the horse by coming up to me, holding out his hands to me, and saying, *"Ha-ye,"* which means "Thank you." The old man went away very grateful for the horse.

That ended my first and last buffalo hunt. It lives only in my memory, for the days of the buffalo are over. ❖

---
9. **rode in state:** rode in a formal parade, with honors such as those given to a political leader.

WORDS TO KNOW
customary (kŭs′tə-mĕr′ē) *adj.* according to custom; usual; traditional
exploit (ĕk′sploit) *n.* a brave deed or adventurous act

466

Mini-Lesson Spelling

WORDS ENDING IN -ary Point out that the word endings *-ary, -ery,* and *-ory* can sound very much the same and that students cannot rely on just the sound to help them spell words with these endings. While there is no rule for spelling words with these endings, it may help students to know that the ending *-ary* is more common than *-ery*. Here are examples of words ending in *-ary*. Ask students to add other words to the list.

| customary | literary | voluntary |
| burglary | necessary | tributary |

Application Have students complete each word with *-ary, -ery,* or *-ory*. When they are done, students can check their spelling in a dictionary.

1. imagin____   6. honor____
2. mem____   7. discov____
3. prim____   8. tempor____
4. machin____   9. advis____
5. deliv____   10. transit____

Ask students to look for more words that fit this pattern, in their own writing and in things they read, and to add these words to their personal word lists.

Reteaching/Reinforcement
• *Unit Four Resource Book,* p. 49

466 THE LANGUAGE OF LITERATURE TEACHER'S EDITION

LITERARY INSIGHT

THE FLOWER-FED BUFFALOES
by Vachel Lindsay

The flower-fed buffaloes of the spring
In the days of long ago,
Ranged where the locomotives sing
And the prairie flowers lie low:—
5   The tossing, blooming, perfumed grass
Is swept away by the wheat,
Wheels and wheels and wheels spin by
In the spring that still is sweet.
But the flower-fed buffaloes of the spring
10 Left us, long ago.
They gore no more, they bellow no more,
They trundle around the hills no more:—
With the Blackfeet, lying low,
With the Pawnees, lying low,
15 Lying low.

Below Zero (1993), John Axton. Oil on canvas, 30" × 40", courtesy of Ventana Fine Art, Santa Fe, New Mexico.

LITERARY INSIGHT

1. How does the poem relate to the last paragraph of "At Last I Kill a Buffalo"? *(The poem describes things that caused the buffalo to disappear: trains that were built as settlers moved onto the prairies; wheat that was planted as the grasslands were turned into farms.)*
2. What does the repeated phrase "lying low" refer to, and what might this phrase mean? *(Possible responses: The phrase refers to the buffalo, the Blackfeet, and the Pawnees. It could mean that the animals and the people are gone from the prairie, that they are dead, or that they are waiting for a chance to come back to their former lands.)*
3. Describe the mood of the poem. *(Possible responses: sad, because of the disappearance of the buffalo and the Native Americans; peaceful and tranquil, because of the description of the flowers and grass on the prairie)*

VACHEL LINDSAY

Born in 1879 in Springfield, Illinois, in a house once occupied by Abraham Lincoln's sister-in-law, Vachel Lindsay had a prolific career as a poet. One of his themes was encouraging the peaceful coexistence of the various ethnic groups in the United States. His poetry often referred to folk traditions of African Americans and Native Americans. One book of his poems, published in 1917, is called *The Ghost of the Buffaloes*. Three of Lindsay's best-known poems are "The Santa Fe Trail," "Abraham Lincoln Walks at Midnight," and "The Congo." Lindsay died in Springfield in 1931.

Art Note

***Below Zero* by John Axton** Painter John Axton (1947–) studied design, graphics, and architecture at the University of Southern Illinois, which has published a book about his work. Much of his art is set in the West and the Southwest, with doors and windows, light and dark, and inner and outer as themes. He simplifies and distills, reaching for the underlying structure and power of a subject.

Reading the Art *Look at the size and position of the buffalo in relationship to its background. What impression do you have of the buffalo? What might be the relationship between the painting and its title? Does the environment look "below zero" to you?*

Multicultural Perspectives

THE VANISHING BUFFALO Before the 1600s, few people lived in the grassland region of North America known as the Great Plains. After the Spaniards introduced the horse and the gun, however, the region became populated with many different groups of Native Americans. The hunters of the various tribes followed the great herds of American bison—buffalo—on horseback while the women raised crops of beans, corn, and squash. These people depended greatly on the buffalo, using the animals for food, clothing, bedding, tepees, and tools and utensils made from the bones and the horns.

As white settlers advanced westward, more and more eastern tribes moved to the plains and adopted the way of life that was so dependent on the buffalo. The increased killing of the animal by white hunters, however, eventually caused the herds to disappear. By the 1890s, the buffalo were gone, and white ranchers and farmers turned the plains into cattle ranches and homesteads.

From Personal Response to Critical Analysis

1. Students might include reasons why they identify with Ota K'te in the scene or scenes they choose.
2. Possible response: Ota K'te faces several challenges—ignoring the cold and physical trials of the hunt, conquering his fear as he rides into the middle of the buffalo herd, and overcoming the temptation to lie about the number of arrows he used to kill the buffalo.
3. Possible responses: Ota K'te admires and respects his father, but their relationship seems formal rather than close. His father seems to be a fairly stern teacher and parent, but one who cares about his son's safety.
4. Possible response: A child's courage and honesty are important and should be celebrated.
5. Possible response: The poem describes how the prairie looked (blooming with flowers and grass) and how the buffalo behaved and sounded ("gore," "bellow," "trundle"). These images help the reader to better imagine the scenes in the story.

Another Pathway

Cooperative Learning Students might begin by creating a list of adjectives, such as *brave, respectful, attentive,* and *observant,* to describe Ota K'te's character. Then each group member could look for passages from the selection to support one of the qualities described.

Rubric

3 Full Accomplishment Students' charts include several character traits, quoted support material, and students' own interpretations.

2 Substantial Accomplishment Students' charts include at least two character traits and some appropriate quoted support material.

1 Little or Partial Accomplishment Students' charts include only one character trait. Quoted material is not appropriate or is missing.

RESPONDING OPTIONS

FROM PERSONAL RESPONSE TO CRITICAL ANALYSIS

REFLECT
1. At what point in your reading of "At Last I Kill a Buffalo" did you most identify with Ota K'te? Jot down your ideas in your notebook.

RETHINK
Thematic Link
2. How would you describe the test of character Ota K'te faces? Explain.

Consider
- the physical challenges of the hunt
- the tribe's expectations for a young boy
- the step Ota K'te takes concerning the arrows

3. What do you think of the relationship between Ota K'te and his father? Explain.

4. After the hunt, the father gives away a valuable horse. What does this act suggest about the values of the Sioux? Explain.

RELATE
Literary Link
5. What do you think the images and impressions in "The Flower-Fed Buffaloes," the Insight poem on page 467, add to Luther Standing Bear's description of the buffalo hunt?

Multimodal Learning
ANOTHER PATHWAY

Cooperative Learning

In a small group, discuss the scenes or descriptions in "At Last I Kill a Buffalo" that reveal something about the character of Ota K'te. Make and fill in a chart that matches specific scenes or quotes from the story with your observations regarding what the scenes or quotes reveal about Ota K'te.

LITERARY CONCEPTS

Writers carefully choose details that appeal to a reader's sense of sight, sound, smell, touch, or taste. These details help to create an image of a scene, an event, or a character in the reader's mind. Most readers expect to find imagery presented in poetry—but writers of personal accounts use **imagery** too. For example, in "My First Dive with the Dolphins," the narrator uses imagery in describing his first sight of a certain dolphin: "There it was: a glistening, gleaming, silver bubble ring, rising . . . another ring emerged, rising faster, so that it joined its luminous relation." See if you can find an example of imagery that you think is especially effective in "At Last I Kill a Buffalo."

QUICKWRITES

1. Reread the definition of narrative poetry on page 104, and review "The Cremation of Sam McGee" (page 161) or another narrative poem in this book. Write a **narrative poem** of at least 15 lines describing the events in Luther Standing Bear's account.

2. Write a **letter** that Ota K'te might have written to his father in which he tells him what really happened during the buffalo hunt.

📁 **PORTFOLIO** Save your writing. You may want to use it later as a springboard to a piece for your portfolio.

468 UNIT FOUR PART 2: TAKING NECESSARY STEPS

Literary Concepts

Have students work in groups to search for images that appeal to sight, sound, and touch. Examples of such images are as follows: sight—horses prancing with their ears straight up and their tails waving in the air (p. 462), the cloud of dust and the dark bodies of the buffalo (p. 463); sound—old man softly calling "I-ni-la" for everyone to keep quiet (p. 460), the pounding of horses' and buffalo's hooves (p. 463); touch—the coolness of the evening (p. 461), the boy leaning close down onto the pony's body and clutching him tightly (p. 463).

QuickWrites

1. Suggest that students write their poems from the first-person point of view, the perspective used in the selection. By using the first person, students will sidestep the difficulty of working *Ota K'te* (or *Standing Bear*) into the rhyme and meter of the poem.

2. Have students decide how old Ota K'te is at the time he writes the letter. You might vary the assignment by having half the class address the letter to Ota K'te's father and the other half to his mother.

The Writer's Craft

Writing a Poem, pp. 86–88
Friendly Letter, pp. 42–43

468 THE LANGUAGE OF LITERATURE TEACHER'S EDITION

Multimodal Learning

ALTERNATIVE ACTIVITIES

Choose some aspect of the Sioux culture—their food, shelter, hunting practices, language, or anything else you might be interested in—and conduct library research on the topic. Make a **model** of the subject you choose. For example, if you choose to study the food, make a sample of a food item. If you choose to study the shelters of the Sioux, you might make a cutaway model of a buffalo-hide tepee.

ART CONNECTION

The buffalo hide on page 460 is an example of how Native Americans, including the Sioux, used hides to record ideas or acts important to the tribe. This hide belonged to Mato Tope (Four Bears), a famous chief of the Mandan tribe. The Mandans have lived in North Dakota, along the Missouri River, for more than 500 years. The pictures and symbols on the hide show the acts of courage in battle of Mato Tope, who lived from 1800 to 1837. What acts of courage might Ota K'te draw on the hide of his buffalo?

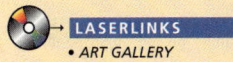
• ART GALLERY

WORDS TO KNOW

For each boldfaced word, write the letter of the situation that best demonstrates its meaning.

1. **customary**
   (a) a man taking a woman's last name after their wedding
   (b) a boy making a wish before blowing out birthday candles
   (c) a girl graduating from college before she is 12 years old
2. **preceding**
   (a) a student sitting quietly in a classroom
   (b) a page that was read just before this one
   (c) a principal telling students to walk, not run, in the halls
3. **exploit**
   (a) a parent telling a child how to do the math homework
   (b) a bully making fun of a smaller child on the playground
   (c) a soldier sneaking into the enemy camp to get information
4. **sufficient**
   (a) two children who want to play catch
   (b) two children who want to become a baseball team
   (c) two children who want to use the same baseball glove
5. **gratification**
   (a) a scolding from a person you respect
   (b) a compliment from a person you admire
   (c) a threat from a person who frightens you

LUTHER STANDING BEAR

Luther Standing Bear (1868?–1939), whose Lakota Sioux name was Ota K'te (Plenty Kill), was born about 1868. When he was 11 years old, his father sent him to Carlisle, Pennsylvania, to attend the Carlisle Indian School, which was operated by the federal government from 1879 until 1918. *Extended Reading*
OTHER WORKS *My People the Sioux, Land of the Spotted Eagle, Stories of the Sioux*

AT LAST I KILL A BUFFALO **469**

Across the Curriculum

Science Cooperative Learning *Grassland Biomes* Have students work in cooperative groups to prepare a poster illustrating the animals, plants, weather, and other characteristics of grassland biomes such as the Great Plains. In each group, one student can research plants and animals, another can research the effects of the human occupation of grasslands, a third can prepare written copy, and a fourth can draw illustrations or cut them from magazines. Students can use life science textbooks or library materials for their research.

Words to Know

1. b
2. b
3. c
4. a
5. b

Reteaching/Reinforcement
• *Unit Four Resource Book*, p. 50

Art Connection

As students consider what scenes Ota K'te might include on a buffalo hide, emphasize that no words can be used—just simple drawings and symbols. For example, drawings of hoof prints might represent the buffalo in the herd.

ART GALLERY
Art of the Sioux The household items and clothing that Sioux people made were in themselves works of art. Shown here are examples of the leatherwork and beadwork that make Sioux craftsmanship unique. You may wish to use the images to generate discussion about how Native American tribes used materials from their environment in fashioning clothing and other utilitarian items.

Side A, Frame 38866

Alternative Activities

As students do the research in order to make their models, they will find paintings or other graphic information particularly useful. Since building the models can be time-consuming, you may wish to have students complete this activity in cooperative groups so that they can share the tasks.

LUTHER STANDING BEAR

Luther Standing Bear was a political leader in his community, an advocate for Native American rights, a Hollywood actor, and a noted author. His first book was published in 1928, when he was about 60 years old. In that book and in his other writing, he described the daily life, family relationships, political structure, and religious beliefs of the Sioux. His work helped to dispel misconceptions about Native American life and customs and to publicize some of the problems caused by policies of the Bureau of Indian Affairs.

THE LANGUAGE OF LITERATURE TEACHER'S EDITION **469**

Objectives

- To understand and appreciate an informational account of a major archaeological discovery
- To learn to use skimming and scanning
- To understand and appreciate the use of sources in informative nonfiction
- To express understanding of the selection through a choice of writing forms, including log entries and a newspaper account
- To extend understanding of the selection through a variety of multimodal and cross-curricular activities

Skills

READING SKILLS/STRATEGIES
- Skimming and scanning

LITERARY CONCEPTS
- Suspense
- Sources of information

THE WRITER'S STYLE
- Spatial-order transitions

GRAMMAR
- Commas in a series

SPELLING
- Adding -ally to words ending in c

STUDY SKILLS
- Multiple-choice tests

SPEAKING, LISTENING, AND VIEWING
- Group discussion
- Oral presentation

Cross-Curricular Connections

GEOGRAPHY
- Valley of the Kings

SCIENCE
- Mummy X-rays

HISTORY
- Rosetta stone

HISTORICAL CONNECTION
Tutankhamen's Tomb In late 1922 and early 1923, with hundreds of onlookers standing by, archaeologists began removing the objects found in the tomb of Tutankhamen. These vintage historical images show items that were being seen for the first time since the 1330s B.C.

Side A, Frame 38874

PREVIEWING

NONFICTION

Tutankhamen *from* Lost Worlds
Anne Terry White

PERSONAL CONNECTION *Activating Prior Knowledge*
What words come to your mind when you think of ancient Egypt? In this selection you will get a peek at the civilization of the ancient Egyptians. In your notebook, copy a pyramid like the one shown, and fill in the words that you connect with Egypt. Compare your pyramid graphic with a classmate's.

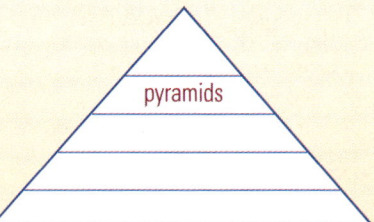

HISTORICAL CONNECTION *Building Background*
From 2750 to 1784 B.C., Egyptians built great pyramids as tombs for their kings, or Pharaohs (fâr′ōz). The great treasures of these tombs were often stolen by grave robbers, and by 1570 B.C. pyramids were no longer built. Instead, to discourage grave robbing, Pharaohs began to seek secret locations for tombs. These burial places were cut into the cliffs west of their capital, Thebes. Sixty-two tombs in the form of halls and chambers have been discovered in what is called today the Valley of the Kings and in the nearby Western Valley.

One of the most famous of these tombs is that of the young Pharaoh Tutankhamen (tōōt′äng-kä′mən), who ruled Egypt from about 1347 to 1339 B.C. The discovery in his tomb of numerous artifacts—hand-crafted objects such as tools, weapons, and jewelry—has provided valuable information about life in ancient Egypt.

READING CONNECTION *Active Reading/Setting a Purpose*
Skimming and Scanning As you read about the search for the tomb of Tutankhamen, see how the information given compares to your ideas about ancient Egypt. When looking for a specific fact in a piece of writing, scanning, or sweeping your eyes across each page, can help you spot what you are looking for. If you want to understand the main idea of a piece of writing or to get an overview of its contents, use skimming instead. To skim, move your eyes rapidly over the pages. Glance at the title, highlighted words or phrases, maps and charts, and the topic sentences, which are usually the first sentences in each paragraph.

470 UNIT FOUR PART 2: TAKING NECESSARY STEPS

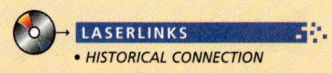 **LASERLINKS**
• HISTORICAL CONNECTION

PRINT AND MEDIA RESOURCES

UNIT FOUR RESOURCE BOOK
Strategic Reading: Literature, p. 53
Vocabulary SkillBuilder, p. 56
Reading SkillBuilder, p. 54
Spelling SkillBuilder, p. 55

GRAMMAR MINI-LESSONS
Transparencies, p. 31
Copymasters, p. 40

WRITING MINI-LESSONS
Transparencies, p. 33

ACCESS FOR STUDENTS ACQUIRING ENGLISH
Selection Summaries
Reading and Writing Support

FORMAL ASSESSMENT
Selection Test, pp. 95–96
Test Generator

 **AUDIO LIBRARY**
See Reference Card

 **LASERLINKS**
Historical Connection
Art Gallery

 **INTERNET RESOURCES**
McDougal Littell Literature Center at http://www.hmco.com/mcdougal/lit

TUTANKHAMEN
FROM LOST WORLDS

BY ANNE TERRY WHITE

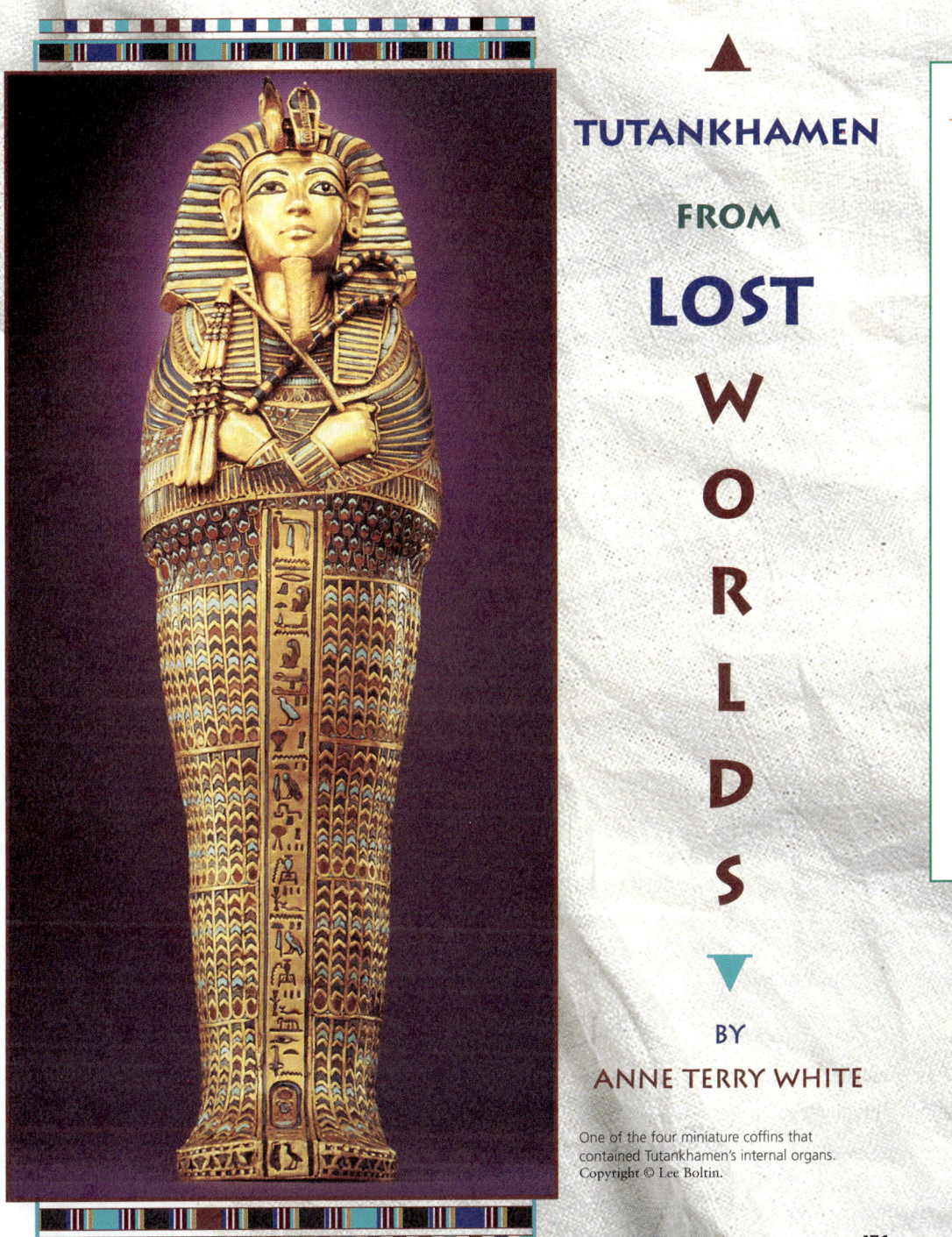

One of the four miniature coffins that contained Tutankhamen's internal organs. Copyright © Lee Boltin.

SUMMARY

Howard Carter and Lord Carnarvon dug in Egypt's Valley of the Kings for six years, hoping to find, against all odds, the tomb of Pharaoh Tutankhamen. On November 5, 1922, with Carter watching, workmen uncovered a stairway beneath an ancient stone hut. Carter halted the excavation until Lord Carnarvon could join him, then went ahead into the tomb. Its first doorway had been broken into and resealed, a sure sign of robbers. So had the second doorway—yet beyond it lay an amazing display of royal objects, including a golden throne, couches covered with gold, and two statues of a king. Between the statues lay a third sealed doorway, which also showed signs of tampering. A small hole in the wall revealed that another, smaller chamber stood beyond the doorway. This chamber was littered with treasures, jumbled from the robbers' hasty theft. Amazed by their find but determined to be systematic archaeologists, Carter and Carnarvon began the huge task of cataloging and packing up the tomb's contents.

Thematic Link: *Taking Necessary Steps*
Howard Carter, in the face of others' doubts, persists in his search for the tomb of Pharaoh Tutankhamen.

CUSTOMIZING FOR
Gifted and Talented Students

Have students imagine themselves in the role of Carter's assistant, a person who constantly argues with Carter and questions whether the endeavor is worthwhile. Students should note at what points during the search the assistant might argue with Carter and should write dialogue for a scene between the two people. Invite students to perform their scenes for the class after everyone has finished the selection.

WORDS TO KNOW

dissuade (dĭ-swād′) *v.* to persuade someone not to do something; discourage (p. 472)
intact (ĭn-tăkt′) *adj.* whole and undamaged (p. 474)
sentinel (sĕn′tə-nəl) *n.* one who keeps watch; guard (p. 475)
systematically (sĭs′tə-măt′ĭk-lē) *adv.* in an orderly, thorough manner (p. 472)
tedious (tē′dē-əs) *adj.* long, tiring, and boring (p. 475)

CUSTOMIZING FOR
Students Acquiring English

- Use **ACCESS FOR STUDENTS ACQUIRING ENGLISH**, *Reading and Writing Support*.
- If possible, you may wish to invite students from the Middle East or North Africa to share their knowledge of the climate, topography, and geography of that region.
- In addition to the suggestions in these boxes, you may want to use the suggestions under Strategic Reading for Less-Proficient Readers.

STRATEGIC READING FOR
Less-Proficient Readers

Set a Purpose Have students read to find out what Carter and Carnarvon are trying to do and why they want to do it.

Use **UNIT FOUR RESOURCE BOOK**, pp. 53–54, for guidance in reading the selection.

Linking to History

A European interest in the history and artifacts of ancient Egypt increased dramatically after the discovery, in Egypt, of the Rosetta stone in 1799. This tablet, found by one of Napoleon's soldiers, contained the same text written in Greek, pictorial hieroglyphics, and simplified cursive Egyptian. The triple text enabled scholars to read some of the hieroglyphics on the ancient Egyptian monuments.

Linking to Geography

B The Valley of the Kings is in Upper Egypt, on the west bank of the Nile River across from Luxor. The summer temperatures there can reach 110°–140°F, so the "season" referred to in the text extended from about November through March, when it was cool enough to work outside.

Archaeologists found gold, masks, linen, clothing, and the king's fan.

Archaeologists found gold masks, linen clothing, and the king's fan.

A Five seasons had passed and the British archaeologist[1] Howard Carter and his financial supporter, Lord Carnarvon, had failed in their search for the tomb of the Pharaoh Tutankhamen. Howard Carter remained convinced that he was close to the 3,200-year-old tomb. Carter persuaded Lord Carnarvon that the tomb most likely lay in the center of the Valley of the Kings. In November 1922, Carter and his crew began uncovering the area near the tomb of Rameses VI—the only section that had not been dug up in the Valley of the Kings.

Now Carnarvon and Carter were not planning to dig at random in the Valley of the Tombs of the Kings. They were on the lookout for a particular tomb, the tomb of the Pharaoh Tutankhamen, and they believed they had worked out the location where it lay. To the eyes of most people their undertaking seemed absurd. Nearly everybody was convinced that Tutankhamen's tomb had already been found. But Lord Carnarvon and Mr. Carter were not to be <u>dissuaded</u>, for they believed that the pit-tomb containing the fragments bearing the figures and names of Tutankhamen and his queen was far too small and insignificant for a king's burial. In their opinion the things had been placed there at some later time and did not indicate that the Pharaoh himself had been buried on the spot. They were convinced that the tomb of Tutankhamen was still to be found, and that the place they had chosen—the center of the Valley—was the best place to look for it. In that vicinity had been unearthed something which they considered very good evidence—two jars containing broken bits of things that had been used at the funeral ceremonies of King Tutankhamen.

Nevertheless, when in the autumn of 1917 the excavators[2] came out to look over the spot they had chosen and to begin their Valley campaign in earnest, even they thought it was a desperate undertaking. The site was piled high with refuse thrown out by former excavators. They would have to remove all that before they could begin excavating in virgin soil.[3] But they had made up their minds and meant to go through with it; even though it took many seasons, they would go <u>systematically</u> over every inch of ground.

B

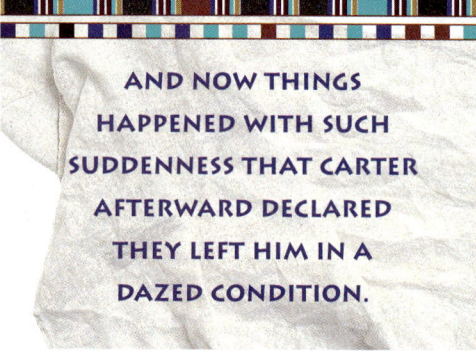

AND NOW THINGS HAPPENED WITH SUCH SUDDENNESS THAT CARTER AFTERWARD DECLARED THEY LEFT HIM IN A DAZED CONDITION.

In the years that followed, they did. They went over every inch, with the exception of a small area covered with the ruins of stone huts that had once sheltered workmen probably employed in building the tomb of Rameses VI.[4] These huts lay very near the tomb of the

---

1. **archaeologist** (är′kē-ŏl′ə-jĭst): a scientist who studies the material evidence, such as graves, buildings, tools, and pottery, remaining from past human life and culture.
2. **excavators** (ĕk′skə-vā′tərz): people who search by digging or uncovering.
3. **virgin soil:** ground that has not been dug up or explored.
4. **Rameses** (răm′ĭ-sēz′) **VI:** a Pharaoh whose tomb was built higher on the hill, above Tutankhamen's.

WORDS TO KNOW
dissuade (dĭ-swād′) *v.* to persuade someone not to do something; discourage
systematically (sĭs′tə-măt′ĭk-lē) *adv.* in an orderly, thorough manner

472

Mini-Lesson Grammar

COMMAS IN A SERIES Remind students that commas are used to separate items in a series. Write on the chalkboard the two sentences shown, and have students compare them. Point out how the use of commas changes the meaning.

Application Write the following sentences on the chalkboard, omitting the commas. Then have students add commas to separate items in a series.

1. Carter believed the previously found tomb was small, insignificant, and unproved.
2. They chose the spot to dig, removed the refuse, began excavating, and went over every inch of ground.
3. People present at the opening of the tomb included Lord Carnarvon, his daughter, Carter, and Carter's workers.

Reteaching/Reinforcement
- *Grammar Handbook*, anthology p. 847–848
- *Grammar Mini-Lessons* copymasters, p. 40, transparencies p. 31

 **The Writer's Craft**
Commas That Separate Ideas, pp. 574–575

472 THE LANGUAGE OF LITERATURE TEACHER'S EDITION

Howard Carter (left) and Lord Carnarvon at the entrance to Pharoah Tutankhamen's tomb, February 1923. The Griffith Institute, Ashmolean Museum, Oxford, England.

Pharaoh on a spot which Carter and Carnarvon had not touched for reasons of courtesy. The tomb of Rameses VI was a popular showplace in the valley, and digging in the area of the huts would have cut off visitors to the tomb. They let it be, and turned instead to another site which they felt had possibilities.

The new ground proved, however, no better than the old, and now Lord Carnarvon began to wonder whether with so little to show for six seasons' work they were justified in going on. But Carter was firm. So long as a single area of unturned ground remained, he said, they ought to risk it. There was still the area of the huts. He insisted on going back to it. On November first, 1922 he had his diggers back in the old spot.

And now things happened with such suddenness that Carter afterward declared they left him in a dazed condition. Coming to work on the fourth day after the digging on the little area had started, he saw at once that something extraordinary had happened. Things were too quiet; nobody was digging and hardly anybody was talking. He hurried forward, and there before him was a shallow step cut in the rock beneath the very first hut attacked! He could hardly believe his eyes. After all the disappointments of the past six seasons, was it possible that he was actually on the threshold[5] of a great discovery? He gave the command to dig, and the

---
5. **threshold:** an entrance or beginning.

TUTANKHAMEN **473**

Active Reading: CONNECT

C Ask students to think about personal experiences in which persistence was necessary to achieve a goal. Their reflections can help them imagine Carter's feelings.

STRATEGIC READING FOR
Less-Proficient Readers

D Check that students understand the basic situation described in the selection. Ask these questions:

- What are Carter and Carnarvon looking for? *(the tomb of Tutankhamen)* **Noting Relevant Details**
- Why do they want to find the tomb? *(Possible responses: to learn about the history of Egypt; to uncover valuable treasure; to become famous as archaeologists)* **Making Inferences**

Set a Purpose Have students read to find out what Carter does when he finds the tomb and how he reacts to the patched-up portion of the tomb door.

Literary Concept: SUSPENSE

E Remind students that suspense is the feeling of tension and excitement that makes a reader curious about what will happen next. Ask students to identify words the author uses in this paragraph to build suspense. *(Possible responses: such suddenness, dazed, extraordinary, things were too quiet, hurried, could hardly believe his eyes, threshold)*

CUSTOMIZING FOR
Students Acquiring English

I Explain that *He could hardly believe his eyes* means "He was very surprised at what he saw."

Mini-Lesson   Spelling

WORDS ENDING IN c + ally Remind students that when forming an adverb with words ending in the letter *c*, they should use the ending *-ally*, not *-ly*. For example, the correct form is *magically*, not *magicly*. Show students the following examples:

tragic + ally = tragically
systematic + ally = systematically
realistic + ally = realistically
athletic + ally = athletically

Application Have students spell the correct adverbial form for each word underlined in the sentences below.

1. A selection such as "Tutankhamen" should be <u>historic</u> accurate.
2. Carter and Lord Carnarvon felt that the tomb <u>logic</u> would be found in the center of the Valley of the Kings.
3. Outside observers might have thought that the different places in the valley were <u>basic</u> the same.

Ask students to look for more words that fit this pattern, in their own writing and in things they read, and to add these words to their personal word lists.

Reteaching/Reinforcement
- *Unit Four Resource Book,* p. 55

THE LANGUAGE OF LITERATURE TEACHER'S EDITION **473**

Active Reading: PREDICT

F Have students predict what Carter will find behind the sealed doorway. You may wish to use the following model to give students an idea of what they might be thinking about.

Think-Aloud Model *Carter is looking for the burial place of an Egyptian king, so he may find a mummy. Since the kings were buried with much treasure, he may also find statues, jewelry, and other valuable objects.*

CUSTOMIZING FOR
Students Acquiring English

2 Point out that *fever pitch* means "a very high level."

Critical Thinking: SPECULATING

G Point out to students how little mention is made of the workers helping Carter. Large numbers of local people were employed in such endeavors by European archaeologists. Have students speculate about how the local people might feel about having outsiders search for their national treasures.

Critical Thinking: MAKING JUDGMENTS

H Have students explain what Carter's restraint reveals about his character and his relationship with Carnarvon. *(Possible responses: Although enthusiastic and excitable, Carter has self-control, is fair-minded, and is loyal to Carnarvon. The two men are probably close friends.)*

Some of the artifacts discovered in Tutankhamen's tomb. Note the numbered labels used to catalogue the objects. Valley of the Kings antechamber, west side with numbers (Egyptian Dynasty XVIII, Thebes). Photo by Egyptian Expedition, The Metropolitan Museum of Art. Copyright © The Metropolitan Museum of Art, all rights reserved.

diggers fell to work with a will. By the next afternoon Carter was able to see the upper edges of a stairway on all its four sides, and before very long there stood revealed twelve steps, and at the level of the twelfth the upper part of a sealed and plastered doorway.

Carter's excitement was fast reaching fever pitch. Anything, literally anything, might lie beyond. It needed all his self-control to keep from breaking the doorway down and satisfying his curiosity then and there. But was it fair to see what lay beyond that door alone? Although Lord Carnarvon was in England, was it not his discovery as much as Carter's? To the astonishment of the workmen, the excavator gave orders to fill the stairway in again, and then he sent the following cable off to Carnarvon: "At last have made wonderful discovery in Valley. A magnificent tomb with seals <u>intact</u>. Recovered same for your arrival. Congratulations."

As he waited for Lord Carnarvon to come,

> WORDS TO KNOW
> **intact** (ĭn-tăkt′) *adj.* whole and undamaged

474

Mini-Lesson Study Skills

MULTIPLE-CHOICE TESTS Remind students that a multiple-choice question asks them to choose the *best* answer from a number of possibilities.

Application For each of the following questions, have students pick the best answer and give reasons why the other choices are wrong.

1. Carter thought he knew the location of King Tutankhamen's tomb because the spot
   a. was in the center of the valley.
   b. had not previously been excavated.
   c. was near jars used in the king's funeral.
   d. was covered by debris from other digs. *(c)*

2. The first indication that Carter had found the tomb was
   a. the quiet and motionless workers.
   b. the discovery of jars used in the king's funeral.
   c. a shallow step cut in the rock below a hut.
   d. a stairway leading to a sealed door. *(a)*

3. Carter waited for Lord Carnarvon to arrive before opening the tomb because
   a. he was afraid of damaging the artifacts.
   b. Carnarvon was paying for the excavation.
   c. he wasn't certain he had the right tomb.
   d. he wanted to share the discovery. *(d)*

474 THE LANGUAGE OF LITERATURE **TEACHER'S EDITION**

Carter found it hard to persuade himself at times that the whole episode had not been a dream. The entrance to the tomb was only thirteen feet below the entrance to the tomb of Rameses VI. No one would have suspected the presence of a tomb so near the other. Had he actually found a flight of steps? Was it really there under the sand, waiting to conduct him to the great mystery?

In two weeks' time Lord Carnarvon and his daughter were on the spot. Carter now ordered his men to clear the stairway once more, and there on the lower part of the sealed doorway the explorers beheld what almost took their breath away—the seal of the Pharaoh Tutankhamen. Now they knew. Beyond this doorway lay either the Pharaoh's secret treasure store or else the very tomb for which they were searching. Yet one thing made them uneasy. They noticed that part of the door was patched up and that in the patched-up part there stood out clearly the seal of the cemetery. It was evident that the door had been partly broken down—by robbers, of course—and then patched up again by cemetery officials. Had the robbers been caught in time? Did at least some of Tutankhamen's glory yet remain behind that twice-sealed doorway? Or would perhaps only barren walls reward their years of <u>tedious</u> toil?

With pounding hearts they broke down the door. Beyond lay only another obstacle to their progress—a passage filled with stone. Had the robbers got beyond that? They began slowly to clear away the stone, and on the following day—"the day of days," Carter called it, "and one whose like I can never hope to see again"—they came upon a second sealed doorway, almost exactly like the first and also bearing distinct signs of opening and reclosing.

His hands trembling so that he could scarcely hold a tool, Carter managed to make a tiny hole in the door and to pass a candle through it. At first he could see nothing, but as his eyes grew accustomed to the light, "details of the room slowly emerged from the mist, strange animals, statues, and gold—everywhere the glint of gold."

"Can you see anything?" Carnarvon asked anxiously as Carter stood there dumb with amazement.

"Yes, wonderful things!" was all the explorer could get out.

And no wonder. What he saw was one of the most amazing sights anybody has ever been privileged to see. It seemed as if a whole museumful of objects was in that room. Three gilt[6] couches, their sides carved in the form of monstrous animals, and two statues of a king, facing each other like two <u>sentinels</u>, were the most prominent things in the room, but all around and between were hosts of other things—inlaid caskets, alabaster vases, shrines, beds, chairs, a golden inlaid throne, a heap of white boxes (which they later found were filled with trussed ducks and other food offerings), and a glistening pile of overturned chariots. When Carter and Carnarvon got their senses together again, they realized all at once that there was no coffin in the room. Was this then merely a hiding place for treasure? They examined the room very intently once again, and now they saw that the two statues stood one on either side of a sealed doorway. Gradually the truth dawned on them. They were but on the threshold of their discovery.

---

6. **gilt:** covered with a layer of gold.

WORDS TO KNOW

tedious (tē′dē-əs) *adj.* long, tiring, and boring
sentinel (sĕn′tə-nəl) *n.* one who keeps watch; guard

475

Critical Thinking: ANALYZING

J Ask students why Carter felt it was so important to find the king's coffin, even though he had already found plenty of treasure. *(Possible responses: The coffin was of great historical interest; it would prove that the king had really been buried in this tomb.)*

Literary Concept: SUSPENSE

K Have students find examples, on this page, of words and phrases used to build suspense. *(Possible responses: rushed over, going crazily, calling excitedly)*

CUSTOMIZING FOR
Gifted and Talented Students

L Carter finds evidence that the tomb had been opened by robbers. Have students create a short story written from the point of view of one of the robbers.

STRATEGIC READING FOR
Less-Proficient Readers

M Ask students what was behind each of the three sealed doors. *(First door—a passage filled with stone; second door—a room with statues and gold objects but no coffin; third door—not revealed in the selection, but another chamber, seen through a hole in the wall, contains objects in "the most amazing mess.")* Noting Relevant Details

COMPREHENSION CHECK

1. Why did people think Carter's search for the tomb was "absurd"? *(They thought the tomb had already been found.)*
2. What did Carter hope to find in the tomb? *(the coffin and mummy of the king and many important and valuable artifacts)*
3. How do Carter and Carnarvon feel at the end of the selection? *(Possible responses: excited; serious about all the work still to be done; uncertain whether the coffin is behind the still-sealed door)*

What they saw was just an antechamber.[7] Behind the guarded door there would be other rooms, perhaps a whole series of them, and in one of them, beyond any shadow of doubt they would find the Pharaoh lying.

But as they thought the thing over, the explorers were by no means certain that their first wild expectations would actually come to pass. Perhaps that sealed doorway, like the two before it, had also been re-opened. In that case there was no telling what lay behind it.

On the following day they took down the door through which they had been peeping, and just as soon as the electric connections had been made and they could see things clearly, they rushed over to the doubtful door between the royal sentinels. From a distance it had looked untouched, but when they examined it more closely, they saw that here again the robbers had been before them; near the bottom was distinct evidence that a small hole had been made and filled up and re-sealed. The robbers had indeed been stopped, but not before they had got into the inner chamber.

It took almost as much self-command not to break down that door and see how much damage the robbers had done as to have filled in the staircase after it had once been cleared. But Carter and Carnarvon were not treasure-seekers; they were archaeologists, and they would not take the chance of injuring the objects within the antechamber just to satisfy their curiosity. For the moment they let that go and turned their attention to the things already before them.

There was enough there to leave them altogether bewildered. But while they were yet going crazily from one object to another and calling excitedly to each other, they stumbled on yet another discovery. In the wall, hidden behind one of the monstrous couches, was a small, irregular hole, unquestionably made by the plunderers[8] and never re-sealed. They dragged their powerful electric light to the hole and looked in. Another chamber, smaller than the one they were in, but even more crowded with objects! And everything was in the most amazing mess they had ever seen. The cemetery officials had made some attempt to clean up the antechamber after the robbers and to pile up the funeral furniture in some sort of order, but in the annex they had left things just as they were, and the robbers had done their work "about as thoroughly as an earthquake." Not a single inch of floor space remained unlittered.

Carter and Carnarvon drew a long breath and sobered down. They realized now that the job before them was going to take months and months. It would be a monumental task to photograph, label, mend, pack, and ship all this furniture, clothing, food, these chariots, weapons, walking sticks, jewels—this museumful of treasures. ❖

---

7. **antechamber** (ăn′tē-chām′bər): a small room leading to a larger one.
8. **plunderers:** people who invade a place to rob and destroy it.

476 UNIT FOUR PART 2: TAKING NECESSARY STEPS

Mini-Lesson The Writer's Style

SPATIAL-ORDER TRANSITIONS Explain to students that writers use transitional words and phrases to link ideas and details in terms of time, spatial order, or importance. Point out that in describing the discoveries in the tomb, the author of this selection uses spatial-order transitions, such as *between, beyond,* and *behind.*

Application Have students locate the phrases on this page that are spatial-order transitions. *(These transitions are underlined in the text above.)* Then have them write a paragraph, using clear spatial-order transitions, describing how they could find their way from their bed to their front door blindfolded.

Reteaching/Reinforcement
- *Writing Handbook,* anthology p. 781
- *Writing Mini-Lessons* transparencies, p. 33

📔 **The Writer's Craft**
Transitions, pp. 235–236

---

476 THE LANGUAGE OF LITERATURE TEACHER'S EDITION

HISTORICAL INSIGHT

THE BOY PHARAOH

Tutankhamen, the Boy Pharaoh, ruled Egypt from about 1347 B.C. until his death, nine years later, in 1339 B.C. He became king at about the age of nine. Historians are unsure how he died and disagree on the identity of his parents. Tutankhamen, encouraged by his minister of state, Ay (ī), restored the ancient religion of Egypt, which recognized many gods and goddesses. After the Pharaoh's death, Ay directed his burial in the Valley of the Kings and also ruled briefly as king.

Tutankhamen is remembered for the treasures of his tomb, discovered by archaeologist Howard Carter in 1922. The treasures included everything a wealthy king would need in death, which the ancient Egyptians believed to be the next world. Most of the treasure is now on display in the Egyptian Museum in Cairo.

Tutankhamen's tomb may have been the most spectacular of the tombs unearthed in the Valley of the Kings, but it was not the last. In the spring of 1995, archaeologists discovered yet another tomb. This tomb, very near the site of Tutankhamen's, was designed for 50 princes—sons of Pharaoh Rameses II. Rameses II ruled Egypt from 1279 to 1212 B.C. In many ways his 67 years as a ruler were far more significant than Tutankhamen's nine years. Interestingly, the entrance to the tomb of the 50 princes lay hidden for nearly 70 years beneath the debris unearthed by Carter and Lord Carnarvon's search for the tomb of Tutankhamen.

THE BOY PHAROAH 477

Cultural Note

Ancient Egyptians believed that a dead person would need his or her body in the world to come. Since death did not break the bond between spirit and flesh, the decay of the corpse would deplete the soul of some part of itself. Thus, the Egyptians—or at least those who could afford it—went to elaborate lengths to preserve the bodies of dead people. The mummies that resulted, as well as the tombs, have lasted thousands of years.

An Egyptian tomb not only was a resting place for the mummy but also served as a house for the dead person's spirit or double, the *ka*. The *ka* required offerings of food and drink. Wealthy Egyptians filled their tombs with everything the *ka* would need: food, weapons, jewelry, clothing—even underwear!

HISTORICAL INSIGHT

1. Tutankhamen was not a particularly important ruler. Why are his tomb and its contents of such great interest to historians? *(Possible response: The tomb was one of the very few that were discovered intact, and all the objects found that were used in daily life revealed valuable information about the ancient Egyptians.)*
2. Why do you think it was necessary to remove the contents of the tomb rather than leave them exactly as Carter and Carnarvon had found them? *(Possible responses: The objects needed to be protected from theft and deterioration; they required organizing, cataloging, and some expert preservation or restoration; they needed to be accessible to scholars and interested viewers.)*

Item	General Idea
Picture	Looks like a statue of a young Egyptian
First heading: Historical Insight	The selection is about history.
Second heading: The Boy Pharaoh	The selection deals with a young Egyptian ruler.
First paragraph	Facts about the Pharaoh Tutankhamen
Second paragraph	Discovery of Tutankhamen's tomb and what was found there
Third paragraph	Other tombs in the Valley of the Kings

Mini-Lesson  Reading Skills/Strategies

SKIMMING Remind students that skimming is a fast reading that is done in order to get a general idea of a piece of writing. Tell students that in skimming, they should look quickly at artwork, titles, and the main idea of each paragraph. Point out that if a reader were to skim the Insight essay, for example, he or she might come up with the general ideas listed in the chart shown here.

Application Have students copy the chart into their notebooks, and encourage them to use it when doing research. If students are assigned the first alternative activity on page 479, have them practice their skimming skills by completing a similar chart using one of the resources they find while completing the activity.

Reteaching/Reinforcement
• *Unit Four Resource Book*, p. 54

THE LANGUAGE OF LITERATURE TEACHER'S EDITION 477

From Personal Response to Critical Analysis

1. Encourage students to identify the places in the selection where they became excited or started to read more quickly to find out what would happen.
2. Adjectives students might choose to describe the two men include the following: *persistent, enthusiastic, fair-minded, considerate, thoughtful, energetic.*
3. Possible responses: They believed in a life after death in which the spirit needed all the usual earthly comforts. They believed in making offerings to some gods to protect a dead person's spirit.
4. Possible terms: *tombs, archaeologists, pharaohs, Valley of the Kings, gold*
5. Responses will vary. You may wish to explain that museums take great care to preserve and protect the artifacts entrusted to them.

Another Pathway

Other characters students might include in their drama are Lady Evelyn Herbert, Lord Carnarvon's daughter and devoted helper in his Egyptian work; Mr. Callender and Mr. Mace, two other men who assisted Carter; Mr. Engelbach, chief inspector of the Egyptian Antiquities Department; Harry Burton, a photographer from the Metropolitan Museum of Art in New York; and Mr. Merton, a newspaper reporter from the London Times.

Rubric

3 Full Accomplishment Students' scene accurately reflects the facts in the selection and shows imagination and creativity.

2 Substantial Accomplishment Students' scene uses some of the facts in the selection and is plausible.

1 Little or Partial Accomplishment Students' scene contradicts the facts in the selection and/or shows little imagination.

RESPONDING OPTIONS

FROM PERSONAL RESPONSE TO CRITICAL ANALYSIS

REFLECT 1. How did you react to this account of the discovery of King Tutankhamen's tomb? Share your reactions with the class.

RETHINK 2. What personal characteristics do you think Lord Carnarvon and Howard Carter show in their efforts to locate the tomb?

Thematic Link

Consider
- their continued work for six seasons
- their early refusal to dig near the tomb of Rameses VI
- Carter's refusal to continue excavating without Carnarvon

3. Based on the artifacts found in the tomb, what can you infer about the beliefs of the Egyptians? Explain your answer.

4. After reading the account, what would you add to your pyramid graphic from the Personal Connection on page 470?

RELATE 5. The dry air and sands preserved the buried treasure of Egyptian tombs for thousands of years. Do you think those artifacts should be preserved untouched, or made available for public viewing in museums? Explain your opinion.

Multimodal Learning
ANOTHER PATHWAY

Adapt the events in the selection into a **radio drama**. With a partner, improvise a scene in which Carter and Carnarvon decide to continue their search for the tomb of Tutankhamen and succeed in unearthing the Pharaoh's long-buried resting place. Tape-record your drama, and play the recording for the class.

LITERARY CONCEPTS

Informative nonfiction is written mainly to provide factual information. Nonfiction of this type includes science and history texts, informational books, encyclopedias, pamphlets, and most of the articles in magazines and newspapers. Since the main purpose of this material is to inform, writing of this kind requires a tremendous amount of research by the author to make sure that the information is correct. Authors of informative nonfiction study primary source materials such as log entries, letters, and other documents to gather information for their writing. What are some of the sources of information that Anne Terry White might have checked before she wrote this account?

QUICKWRITES

1. Write the **log entries** that Howard Carter might have written during the two weeks he waited for Lord Carnarvon's return from England.
2. Pretend you are reporting the discovery of the tomb. Draft a **newspaper account** to accompany the following headline: "Tomb of Egyptian King Found in Valley of the Kings."

📁 **PORTFOLIO** *Save your writing. You may want to use it later as a springboard to a piece for your portfolio.*

478 UNIT FOUR PART 2: TAKING NECESSARY STEPS

Literary Concepts

Ask students what reference materials they would use to write a report on Carter's discoveries. Students may suggest encyclopedias and computer searches at a library. Also available is a firsthand account written by Carter himself. White used Carter's book as well as other books written by and about archaeologists. Emphasize to students that firsthand information and interviews, if available, are extremely valuable.

QuickWrites

1. Ask students to include entries that focus on Carter's feelings as well as entries that describe plausible events, such as protecting the tomb from robbers, getting needed supplies, and checking with Egyptian officials.
2. Remind students to answer the questions *who, what, where, when, why,* and *how.* Suggest that they invent an on-the-scene interview with Carter, Carnarvon, or someone else present when the tomb was opened.

Writing from Your Journal, pp. 32–33, 276–277
Stories or Events, pp. 61, 208–209

478 THE LANGUAGE OF LITERATURE TEACHER'S EDITION

Multimodal Learning

ALTERNATIVE ACTIVITIES

1. Use encyclopedias and other reference materials to learn more about some aspect of ancient Egypt that you included in the Personal Connection on page 470. With a teacher's help, you might also contact an on-line information service for further details. Add the information you gather to a class **reference center** or computer **data bank** of material the class can use.

2. Create a **mural** for your classroom that illustrates the events described in Anne Terry White's account.

WORDS TO KNOW

Review the Words to Know in the boxes at the bottom of the selection pages. Then write the vocabulary word that best completes each sentence.

1. People who search for objects from the past work very carefully. They often make a pattern of ropes and dig in each section to cover the ground _____.
2. They dig slowly and sift each shovelful of dirt. Yes, much of the work is just plain _____.
3. They have to make sure no one disturbs the area before they are finished. Ropes around the "dig" help to _____ people from walking over the ground.
4. At night, they may hire a lookout to work as a _____.
5. Even a broken bit of an ancient pot can be an important find. Imagine how these people feel when they find a pot that is _____!

ART CONNECTION

The miniature coffin on page 471 is one of the many extraordinary pieces found in the tomb of Tutankhamen. The coffin, made of gold inlaid and decorated with colored glass and quartz, is one of four that contained the young Pharaoh's internal organs. Tutankhamen is shown holding objects that were symbols of his rule. The vulture and cobra on his headpiece represent his kingdom, Upper Egypt and Lower Egypt. Would you visit a local museum to view such Egyptian artifacts? Why or why not?

ANNE TERRY WHITE

The first book that Anne Terry White (1896–1980) wrote was about Old Testament figures, and her second book was about William Shakespeare. Writing the books was her way of introducing her daughters to great works of literature in a manner that they would find both entertaining and easy to understand.

White came to the United States from the Ukraine when she was eight years old. She grew up in New England and attended Brown and Stanford Universities. In addition to writing books, White worked as a teacher and a social worker.

"Tutankhamen" is an excerpt from White's book *Lost Worlds: The Romance of Archaeology.* Considered one of the foremost writers of nonfiction for young people, she also produced other types of literature, including retellings of myths, legends, and Russian folktales. Extended Reading
OTHER WORKS *Myths and Legends, Prehistoric America, Odysseus Comes Home from the Sea*

LASERLINKS
• ART GALLERY

TUTANKHAMEN **479**

Alternative Activities

1. Because there is so much information available about ancient Egypt, you will want to have different students research different aspects. You might write a list, such as the following, on the chalkboard, and have students choose a narrower topic.

Geography	Climate
History	Government
Architecture	Food and Clothing
Religion	Funeral Practices
Mathematics	Science

2. Additional information for student murals can be found in other sections of White's book *Lost Worlds.* If you wish to have students do some research, they could start the mural by showing Tutankhamen's funeral procession.

Across the Curriculum

Science Cooperative Learning *Mummy X-rays* Have students work in groups to research scientific tests that have been carried out on mummies. Students can divide research tasks according to source, then work together to compile an oral report for the class.

Words to Know

1. systematically
2. tedious
3. dissuade
4. sentinel
5. intact

Reteaching/Reinforcement
• *Unit Four Resource Book,* p. 56

Art Connection

Point out to students the advantages of seeing the artifacts in a museum: the details, colors, and scale of objects can be better appreciated than if seen in a photograph; the museum may have additional explanatory information to help viewers understand what they are seeing.

ART GALLERY
Treasures of Tutankhamen Found by archaeologists in 1922, the treasures buried with the young Pharaoh Tutankhamen provide information about the ancient Egyptians. These images show some of the items that were placed on exhibit for the world to see. They may lead to discussion about ancient Egyptian culture.

Side A, Frame 38881

ANNE TERRY WHITE

Anne Terry White was an editor and a translator of Russian stories as well as an author. Her writings included topics in prehistory, American history, and natural history. Known for her thorough research, she enlivened her accounts with entertaining dialogue and rich details. Students who were intrigued by this selection may also enjoy *All About Archaeology* (Random House, 1959).

THE LANGUAGE OF LITERATURE TEACHER'S EDITION **479**

OVERVIEW

Objectives

- To understand and compare two poems about sports
- To identify the use of onomatopoeia in a poem
- To identify and appreciate sensory details
- To express understanding of the poems through a choice of writing forms, including a poem and a cinquain
- To extend understanding of the poems through a variety of multimodal and cross-curricular activities

Skills

LITERARY CONCEPTS
- Onomatopoeia
- Figurative language

SPEAKING, LISTENING, AND VIEWING
- Oral reading
- Group discussion
- Oral presentation

Cross-Curricular Connections

PHYSICAL EDUCATION
- Description of pole vaulting

MATH
- Size and shape of baseball diamond
- Scale drawing of baseball diamond

Thematic Link: *Taking Necessary Steps*
These two poems center on competitive sports, which, by their nature, involve athletes taking steps to meet both private and public challenges.

CUSTOMIZING FOR
Students Acquiring English

- Use **ACCESS FOR STUDENTS ACQUIRING ENGLISH,** *Reading and Writing Support.*
- Although both pole vaulting and baseball are played internationally, you may wish to preteach the basic rules and equipment used for each sport.
- In addition to the suggestions in these boxes, you may want to use the suggestions under Strategic Reading for Less-Proficient Readers.

PREVIEWING

POETRY

Pole Vault
Shiro Murano

Analysis of Baseball
May Swenson

PERSONAL CONNECTION *Activating Prior Knowledge*

In each of these poems, a sport is described in a way that reveals its unique qualities. From ancient times, people have enjoyed a wide variety of sports both as observers and as participants. What is your favorite sport? Draw a graphic with a structure that shows a characteristic of the sport. Fill it in with words that describe that sport. The baseball graphic shown is an example.

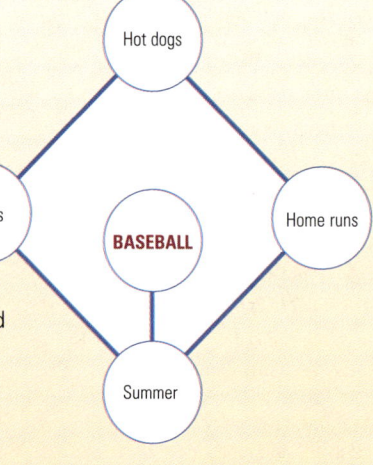

CULTURAL CONNECTION *Building Background*

Each sport described in the poems has its own history, rules, and characteristics. The pole vault, in some form, dates back over 2,500 years to the Olympic Games of ancient Greece, which glorified the individual athlete. This sport is a field competition in which an athlete uses a pole to propel his or her body over a crossbar set at a certain height. The vault is successful if the vaulter makes it over the crossbar without knocking it down.

A pole vaulter in action.

Baseball, often considered the national game of the United States, has a more recent origin. Sports historians generally believe that baseball developed from an old English game called rounders, which was played in the New England colonies. Many people credit Alexander Cartwright of New York as being the founder of organized baseball. Cartwright wrote a set of rules that established the distance between bases as 90 feet and set the number of players on each team as nine. He also organized the first serious baseball team, the Knickerbockers.

WRITING CONNECTION

In the Personal Connection you chose a favorite sport and listed some of its characteristics. In your notebook, explain which of its traits and which of your personal experiences have made it your favorite sport.

480   UNIT FOUR   PART 2: TAKING NECESSARY STEPS

PRINT AND MEDIA RESOURCES

UNIT FOUR RESOURCE BOOK
Strategic Reading: Literature, p. 59

ACCESS FOR STUDENTS ACQUIRING ENGLISH
Selection Summaries
Reading and Writing Support

FORMAL ASSESSMENT
Selection Test, p. 97
 Test Generator

AUDIO LIBRARY
See Reference Card

---

480 THE LANGUAGE OF LITERATURE TEACHER'S EDITION

Pole Vault

by Shiro Murano

He is running like a wasp,
Hanging on a long pole.
As a matter of course he floats in the sky,
Chasing the ascending[1] horizon.
5 Now he has crossed the limit,
   And pushed away his support.
For him there is nothing but a descent.[2]
Oh, he falls helplessly.
Now on that runner, awkwardly fallen on the ground,
10 Once more
   The horizon comes down,
Beating hard on his shoulders.

---

1. **ascending:** moving upward; rising.
2. **descent:** the act of going downward.

FROM PERSONAL RESPONSE TO CRITICAL ANALYSIS

REFLECT 1. Draw the image you visualized as you read "Pole Vault."

RETHINK 2. How would you describe the effect created by the description of the pole vaulter as "running like a wasp / Hanging on a long pole"?

3. What do you think would have been gained or lost if the poet had written a description of pole vaulting in paragraph form instead of in a poem?

4. Based on what you know about pole vaulting and what you have learned in the poem, why do you suppose someone would choose to participate in this sport?

POLE VAULT **481**

Assessment Option

INFORMAL ASSESSMENT To assess students' understanding of the poems, have them compare and contrast the poems in a two-column chart, listing as many specific details as they can.

Rubric

3 Full Accomplishment Students' charts contain many details and demonstrate a thorough understanding of both poems.

2 Substantial Accomplishment Students' charts compare some characteristics of the poems.

1 Little or Partial Accomplishment Students' charts contain few details. The information is inaccurate or does not reflect the characteristics of the poem(s).

"Pole Vault"	"Analysis of Baseball"
about a person attempting the pole vault	about the game of baseball
very short	medium length
medium to long lines	very short lines: 2 or 3 words
no rhyme	some rhyming words
details appeal mainly to sight	details appeal to hearing and sight
sad—the vaulter fails to make it	cheerful—baseball is a fun game

---

STRATEGIC READING FOR
Less-Proficient Readers

Set a Purpose Remind students that poetry should be read slowly, because the poet packs many ideas, feelings, images, and sounds into a few carefully chosen words. Have students look for ways the two poems are alike and ways they differ.

Use **UNIT FOUR RESOURCE BOOK,** p. 59, for guidance in reading the selection.

CUSTOMIZING FOR
Gifted and Talented Students

After students have read the two poems, invite them to rewrite the poems as prose. Then have them discuss which poem was more difficult to render in prose and why. *(Possible response: The word choices and the short lines of the second poem make it harder to paraphrase in prose.)*

CUSTOMIZING FOR
Students Acquiring English

1. Point out that *horizon*, as used in lines 4 and 11, refers to the horizontal crossbar the athlete is attempting to vault. Students may be able to infer this meaning if you draw their attention to the connection between *horizon* and *horizontal*.

From Personal Response to Critical Analysis

1. Images may include any of the following: the athlete running with a pole toward the crossbar; the athlete almost making it over the bar; the athlete falling to the ground, or the athlete being hit by the crossbar he has knocked off the supports.

2. Possible response: An athlete running with a pole suggests a wasp with its stinger. The pole trails the vaulter while in flight, the same way the stinger trails a wasp.

3. Possible response: The imagery of rising, floating, and then descending might be lost in a prose account.

4. Possible responses: for the feeling of flight; for the excitement of racing toward the crossbar; for the satisfaction of completing the vault

Active Reading: EVALUATE

A Have students compare the points of view used in the two poems. *(Both poems use the third-person point of view—that of a spectator.)* Ask what other points of view could have been used. *(Possible responses: first-person—an athlete or a fan; first-person—a pole, a bat, or a ball; second-person—addressed to an athlete or a fan)*

Literary Concept: FIGURATIVE LANGUAGE

B Tell students that in using personification, a poet describes an animal or object as if it were human or had human qualities. Have students locate uses of personification in Swenson's poem. *(Possible responses: "Bat waits," "Ball hates," "Ball flirts," "mitt has to quit in disgrace")*

CUSTOMIZING FOR Students Acquiring English

2 Explain to students that in the second stanza (lines 17–30), the poet is presenting the image of a romance between the bat and the ball. You may want students to find all the words that relate to this image—for example, *mate, flirts, date*.

Critical Thinking: SYNTHESIZING

C In each poem, the poet uses a comparison to convey an image or an idea about the particular sport. In one poem, there is a simile; in the other, there is an example of personification. Have students identify the comparisons used in the poems. *(In lines 1–2 of "Pole Vault," a simile compares the athlete to a wasp. Lines 17–25 of "Analysis of Baseball" use personification, comparing the bat and the ball to a romantic couple.)*

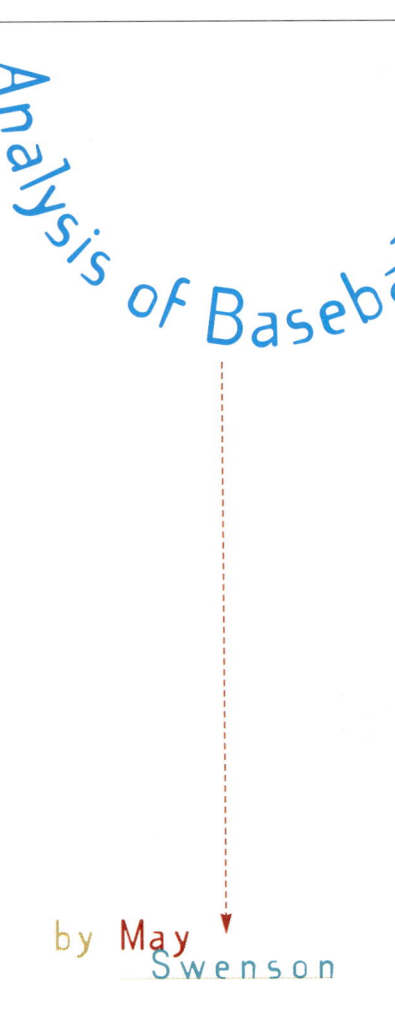

Analysis of Baseball

by May Swenson

A
It's about
the ball,
the bat,
and the mitt.
5 Ball hits
bat, or it
hits mitt.
Bat doesn't
hit ball, bat
10 meets it.
Ball bounces
off bat, flies
air, or thuds
ground (dud)
15 or it
fits mitt.

2
Bat waits
for ball
to mate.
B 20 Ball hates
to take bat's
bait. Ball
C flirts, bat's
late, don't
25 keep the date.
Ball goes in
(thwack) to mitt,
and goes out
(thwack) back
30 to mitt.

D
Ball fits
mitt, but
not all
the time.
35 Sometimes
ball gets hit
(pow) when bat
meets it,
and sails
40 to a place
where mitt
has to quit
in disgrace.
That's about
45 the bases
loaded,
about 40,000
fans exploded.

It's about
50 the ball,
the bat,
the mitt,
the bases
and the fans.
55 It's done
E on a diamond,
and for fun.
F It's about
home, and it's
G 60 about run.

482 UNIT FOUR PART 2: TAKING NECESSARY STEPS

Mini-Lesson  Literary Concepts

REVIEWING FIGURATIVE LANGUAGE
Remind students that a poet or other writer uses figurative language such as metaphors and similes to help readers see ordinary things in new ways. Tell them that another type of figurative language is personification, in which an animal or object is described as if it were human or had human qualities. For example, the second stanza in "Analysis of Baseball" begins, "Bat waits/for ball/to mate." The next lines continue the courtship or dating idea, treating the bat and the ball as if they were conscious beings and could make decisions and have feelings.

Application Have students write paragraphs expressing thoughts the ball, the bat, and the mitt might have if they could think. Students should use the first-person point of view in each paragraph. The paragraphs could be titled "What Happened at the Game" by The Ball [Bat, Mitt].

482 THE LANGUAGE OF LITERATURE **TEACHER'S EDITION**

Illustration by John Ferry.

ANALYSIS OF BASEBALL 483

Literary Concept: RHYME

D Although this poem does not have a strict rhyme scheme, the poet uses many rhyming words. Have students find examples. *(mitt, hit, it, quit; waits, mate, hates, bait, late, date; done, fun, run; thuds, dud; place, disgrace; loaded, exploded)*

Linking to Math

E The baseball "diamond" is actually a square, with sides measuring 90 feet. Home plate is at one vertex, or corner, of the square. At the other three vertexes are first, second, and third base.

STRATEGIC READING FOR
Less-Proficient Readers

F Ask students how the two poems are alike. *(They deal with sports; they use imagery to convey excitement.)* Then have students find ways the poems differ. *(The first poem describes a person; the second focuses on objects.)*
Comparing and Contrasting

CUSTOMIZING FOR
Gifted and Talented Students

G Have students write an additional stanza in which they put themselves in the poem. Have them use the poet's rhythm and style.

COMPREHENSION CHECK

1. What does the writer of "Pole Vault" compare the athlete to? *(A wasp. In line 1, the athlete runs "like a wasp"; in line 2, the pole suggests the wasp's stinger.)*
2. Describe what is happening in lines 5–6 of "Pole Vault." *(Possible responses: The pole vaulter is above the crossbar and is pushing away the pole; the athlete has reached the limit of his strength.)*
3. What three "characters" are described in the first stanza of "Analysis of Baseball"? *(the ball, the bat, and the mitt)*
4. Does the writer of "Analysis of Baseball" use repetition in the poem? If so, where? *(Yes; lines 1–4 and 49–52 are virtually the same.)*

Mini-Lesson: Speaking, Listening, and Viewing

ORAL READING Explain to students that reading a poem aloud often involves making decisions about when to pause and what words to emphasize. To illustrate, write these sentences on the chalkboard:

"It's about the ball, the bat, the mitt, the bases and the fans. It's done on a diamond, and for fun."

Have a volunteer read the sentences as written. Then ask students to look again at the last stanza of "Analysis of Baseball." Tell them that the way the lines are printed seems to imply that the words should be read differently than in sentence form. Point out that it doesn't make sense, however, to pause at the end of *every* line.

Application Have students work in pairs to experiment with different readings of the last stanza. They should try pausing at different places and for different amounts of time, and they should try emphasizing different words. After students have agreed on a reading they like, one partner can present it to the class.

THE LANGUAGE OF LITERATURE TEACHER'S EDITION 483

From Personal Response to Critical Analysis

1. In addition to describing the content of the poem, students may mention the use of rhyming words, onomatopoeia, imagery, and sensory details.
2. Possible response: The poem moves quickly—from pitch to hit to catch—much like an actual ball game does.
3. Possible responses: a group of baseball fans jumping up and cheering wildly; an overhead view of a stadium filled with thousands of people
4. Probably not. The poem doesn't mention the players or explain the rules of the game.
5. "Pole Vault" is more personal, focusing on a single athlete. "Analysis of Baseball" is about the game itself rather than about any one player. Student responses should also include characteristics of the poems, such as line length, rhyming words, mood, and sensory details.

Another Pathway
Cooperative Learning Students can do this activity alone or in cooperative groups. If the activity is done cooperatively, the groups should first discuss the project in general, then assign different roles. Two students can do an outline of the commentary, and two can write it up. Each group member should take part in presenting the commentary.

Rubric
3 Full Accomplishment Students' sports commentary describes plausible events, and all students take part in both the preparation and the performance.

2 Substantial Accomplishment Students' sports commentary describes few events in the game. Students participate in either preparation or performing.

1 Little or Partial Accomplishment Students' sports commentary does not describe plausible events, and/or not all students participate in the activity.

RESPONDING OPTIONS

FROM PERSONAL RESPONSE TO CRITICAL ANALYSIS

REFLECT 1. How would you describe the poem "Analysis of Baseball"? Share your observations with the class.

RETHINK 2. Why do you think the poet presents only two or three words in each line of the poem?

Close Textual Reading 3. In the third stanza the poet writes, "That's about / the bases / loaded, / about 40,000 / fans exploded." What images and impressions do you form from these lines?

4. Do you think this poem would provide a newcomer to baseball with a clear sense of the game? Why or why not?

RELATE 5. Compare and contrast "Pole Vault" and "Analysis of Baseball." How well does each succeed in describing the unique characteristics of a sport?

Literary Link

Multimodal Learning
ANOTHER PATHWAY

On your own or with some classmates, write a sports broadcast or commentary using the events described in either "Pole Vault" or "Analysis of Baseball." Perform your broadcast or commentary in front of the class.

LITERARY CONCEPTS
Onomatopoeia (ŏn′ə-măt′ə-pē′ə) is the use of words to imitate sounds. The words *boom* and *hiss* are examples of onomatopoeia. In the first stanza of "Analysis of Baseball," May Swenson uses the word *dud* partly to imitate the sound of the ball hitting the ground. Find another example of onomatopoeia in "Analysis of Baseball."

QUICKWRITES

1. Compose your own **poem** based on your favorite sport.
2. Write about your favorite sport in the form of a **cinquain** (sĭng′kān), a five-line, nonrhyming poem with a single stanza. Use the graphic and example below to help you write your own cinquain.

Line 1: A word that is the title of the poem. ········▶ Swim,
Line 2: Two adjectives that describe the topic. ·······▶ Sleek, fluid
Line 3: Three "-ing" words related to the topic. ······▶ Moving, floating, stroking
Line 4: A phrase related to the topic. ················▶ Swimming like a fish
Line 5: A synonym for the topic. ······················▶ Freedom

📁 **PORTFOLIO** Save your writing. You may want to use it later as a springboard to a piece for your portfolio.

484 UNIT FOUR PART 2: TAKING NECESSARY STEPS

Literary Concepts
Have students work in pairs, reading short sections of the poem aloud and then talking about the words used. Examples of onomatopoeia in the poem include the words in parentheses (*dud, thwack, pow*). Also, the sound repeated in many of the words (*hit, mitt, fit*) is similar to the sound made when a bat hits a ball.

QuickWrites
1. If some students are not interested in sports, have them choose a different activity they like, such as playing a musical instrument. Encourage students to choose a structure and a rhyme scheme before they begin drafting.
2. Students may find it easier to write the first and fifth lines and then experiment in order to find the words for the rest of the poem. Students can work in small groups, with everyone using the same word for the first line. They can then compare their different poems.

The Writer's Craft

Writing a Poem, pp. 86–88

484 THE LANGUAGE OF LITERATURE TEACHER'S EDITION

CRITIC'S CORNER

One critic remarked that May Swenson is able to make a reader see clearly what he or she has "merely looked at before." Think about the meaning of the statement. In what ways does "Analysis of Baseball" help you to see the game of baseball more clearly?

ACROSS THE CURRICULUM

Physical Education Pole vaulting remains a popular Olympic sport today. Research the sport of pole vaulting to learn more about how a pole vaulter trains for the sport, the records that have been set for the event, and the names of well-known pole vaulters. Find out why pole vaulters changed from using wooden to using fiberglass poles. Prepare a brief "how-to" presentation for the class, including a step-by-step description of the act of pole vaulting. If possible, show the class a videotape of a pole vaulter in action.

SHIRO MURANO

Interested in poetry from an early age, the Japanese poet Shiro Murano (1901–) began writing haiku when a junior high school student. He attended Keio University where he became interested in German poetry. The influence of German poetry was apparent in his first book of poetry, published in 1926.

In 1960 Murano was awarded the Yomiuri Literary Award, a highly respected Japanese literary award. This was for his poetry collection *A Strayed Sheep*, which, with the collection *Gymnastics*, is considered one of his finest works.

MAY SWENSON

1913–1989

During May Swenson's long years as an apprentice poet, she learned a valuable technique for writing poetry. She took whatever lines popped into her head and used them as the first lines of a poem. Thus the simple line "feel like a bird" became the first line of a four-stanza poem.

One of the characteristics that made Swenson's poetry unique was her practice of constructing poems in which the words are arranged in the shapes of the poems' subjects. Her award-winning poetry has been praised for the imaginative quality of her observations. Her book *Poems to Solve* presents 35 poems containing riddles, hidden meanings, and ideas to puzzle and challenge the reader. Born in Logan, Utah, May Swenson moved to New York City after graduating from college. There she lived in poverty for many years, struggling to master the craft of poetry. Eventually, she achieved her dream and became one of the best-known poets of her generation.

Extended Reading
OTHER WORKS *Another Animal, The Guess and Spell Coloring Book, More Poems to Solve*

ANALYSIS OF BASEBALL / POLE VAULT **485**

Across the Curriculum

Physical Education The step-by-step presentation could include drawings such as simple stick figures. Students could create a flip book on small index cards or a pad of self-sticking notes by drawing many illustrations showing progressive movements of a vaulter. If students are working in groups of four, one can do the research, one can write the script, one can draw the illustrations, and the fourth can present the report. Make sure that students do not try pole vaulting themselves, unless it is part of a supervised outdoor activity.

ADDITIONAL SUGGESTION

Math *Square the Diamond* Have students use graph paper (four squares to the inch) to make a scale drawing of a baseball "diamond," as follows:
1. Use the scale $1/4$ inch = 10 feet. With this scale, the diamond will be a square $2\ 1/4$ inches ($9 \times 1/4$) on each side.
2. Draw a diagonal connecting home plate to second base.
3. Ask students to find the spot where the pitcher stands, a point 60 feet 6 inches (60.5 feet) from home plate along the diagonal. *(The distance equals about 1.5 inches. One way to compute it is to solve the proportion $10\ \text{ft.} / 1/4\ \text{in.} = 60.5\ \text{ft.} / x$.)*

SHIRO MURANO

Shiro Murano published his first book of poetry in 1926; since then, he has published nine more books. His poems often have a sad and wistful mood, dealing with such subjects as an old deserted village, a slow-moving beggar, and the dying grass of late autumn.

MAY SWENSON

In addition to writing poetry, May Swenson worked as an editor, a playwright, a lecturer, and a translator (from Swedish). The winner of many prizes, Swenson often wrote poems in free verse that focused closely on small details of objects. Many of Swenson's poems have been set to music.

The Writer's Style

Before students look for sensory details in "Analysis of Baseball," they should list words or phrases they might use to describe the game. After they have located details in the poem, they can compare their ideas with the details the poet used (for example, the sounds of the game— *dud, thwack, pow, hit, fans exploded*). You may wish to have students organize their information in chart form, with one row (or column) for each of the five senses.

The Writer's Craft
Appealing to the Senses, pp. 266–268

Alternative Activities

1. Have students create a **collage** for one of the two poems. They can draw pictures and/or use magazine pictures that reflect the ideas and mood of the poem they choose.
2. Have students write a short **essay** comparing a team sport, such as baseball or football, with an individual sport, such as pole vaulting or long-distance running. Students' essays should indicate which type of sport they prefer.

THE LANGUAGE OF LITERATURE TEACHER'S EDITION **485**

OVERVIEW
Objectives

- To understand and appreciate a short story about the relationship between a boy and a horse
- To enrich reading by using active reading strategies
- To understand and appreciate how actions and events make up a plot
- To identify and appreciate the use of sensory details
- To express understanding of the story through a choice of writing forms, including a diary entry and a list of animal-care guidelines
- To extend understanding of the story through a variety of multimodal and cross-curricular activities

Skills

READING SKILLS/ STRATEGIES
- Strategies for reading

LITERARY CONCEPTS
- Plot
- Conflict

GENRE STUDY
- Fiction: short story

THE WRITER'S STYLE
- Dialogue

GRAMMAR
- Comparative adjectives

SPELLING
- Final consonants and suffixes

STUDY SKILLS
- Graphic aids

SPEAKING, LISTENING, AND VIEWING
- Dialect
- Group discussion
- Oral presentation

Cross-Curricular Connections

SOCIAL STUDIES
- Fencing in the range
- Immigration in the 1940s
- Wide Wyoming

MATH
- Population density
- Give me land, lots of land

SCIENCE
- Barbed wire

HISTORY
- Changing importance of horses

CULTURAL CONNECTION
Ranch Life Ranch life in the western United States has not changed much in the last several decades. These images provide a window to this lifestyle and will help students understand how the characters in "My Friend Flicka" are influenced by their environment.

Side A, Frame 38894

PREVIEWING

FICTION

My Friend Flicka
Mary O'Hara

PERSONAL CONNECTION *Activating Prior Knowledge*
Have you ever made a difficult choice that you had to defend? Record the situation and your reactions to it in your notebook. Draw a graph like the one shown and fill it in with the pros and cons you thought about when you made your choice. Discover what happens in this story when a boy named Kennie makes a major choice that he has to defend.

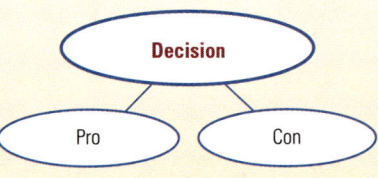

CULTURAL CONNECTION *Building Background*
"My Friend Flicka" takes place around 1940 on a Wyoming horse ranch where the careful breeding of horses is essential to success. A purebred horse is one that belongs to a recognized breed. Owners must make important decisions as they carefully select stallions (male horses) and mares (female horses) to produce foals that have traits the owners want, such as speed, strength, or size. The height of a horse is measured in four-inch units called hands (four inches is the width of an average adult's hand). The height is considered to be the distance from the withers (the ridge between a horse's shoulder blades) to the ground.

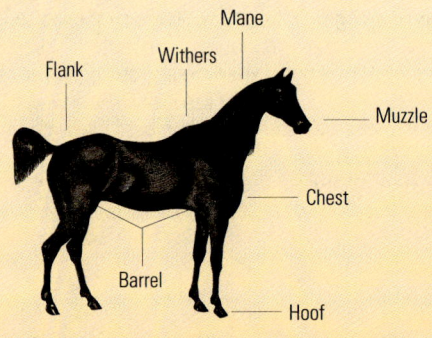

READING CONNECTION *Active Reading/ Setting a Purpose*
Strategies for Reading As you read the following story about the difficult choice a young boy makes, keep in mind the reading strategies you have learned. At different points in the story you will encounter questions requiring you to use one of the reading strategies listed below.

Reading Strategies	
Questioning	Ask questions about the events and characters in the story.
Connecting	Think of similarities between events in the story and your own experiences.
Predicting	Predict what might happen next and how the story might end.
Clarifying	Stop occasionally for a quick review of what you understand so far.
Evaluating	Form opinions about the story.

• CULTURAL CONNECTION

486 UNIT FOUR PART 2: TAKING NECESSARY STEPS

PRINT AND MEDIA RESOURCES

UNIT FOUR RESOURCE BOOK
Strategic Reading: Literature, p. 63
Vocabulary SkillBuilder, p. 66
Reading SkillBuilder, p. 64
Spelling SkillBuilder, p. 65

GRAMMAR MINI-LESSONS
Transparencies, p. 13
Copymasters, p. 20

WRITING MINI-LESSONS
Transparencies, p. 48

ACCESS FOR STUDENTS ACQUIRING ENGLISH
Selection Summaries
Reading and Writing Support

FORMAL ASSESSMENT
Selection Test, pp. 99–100
Part Test, pp. 101–102
Test Generator

 **AUDIO LIBRARY**
See Reference Card

 **LASERLINKS**
Cultural Connection
Science Connection

---

486 THE LANGUAGE OF LITERATURE TEACHER'S EDITION

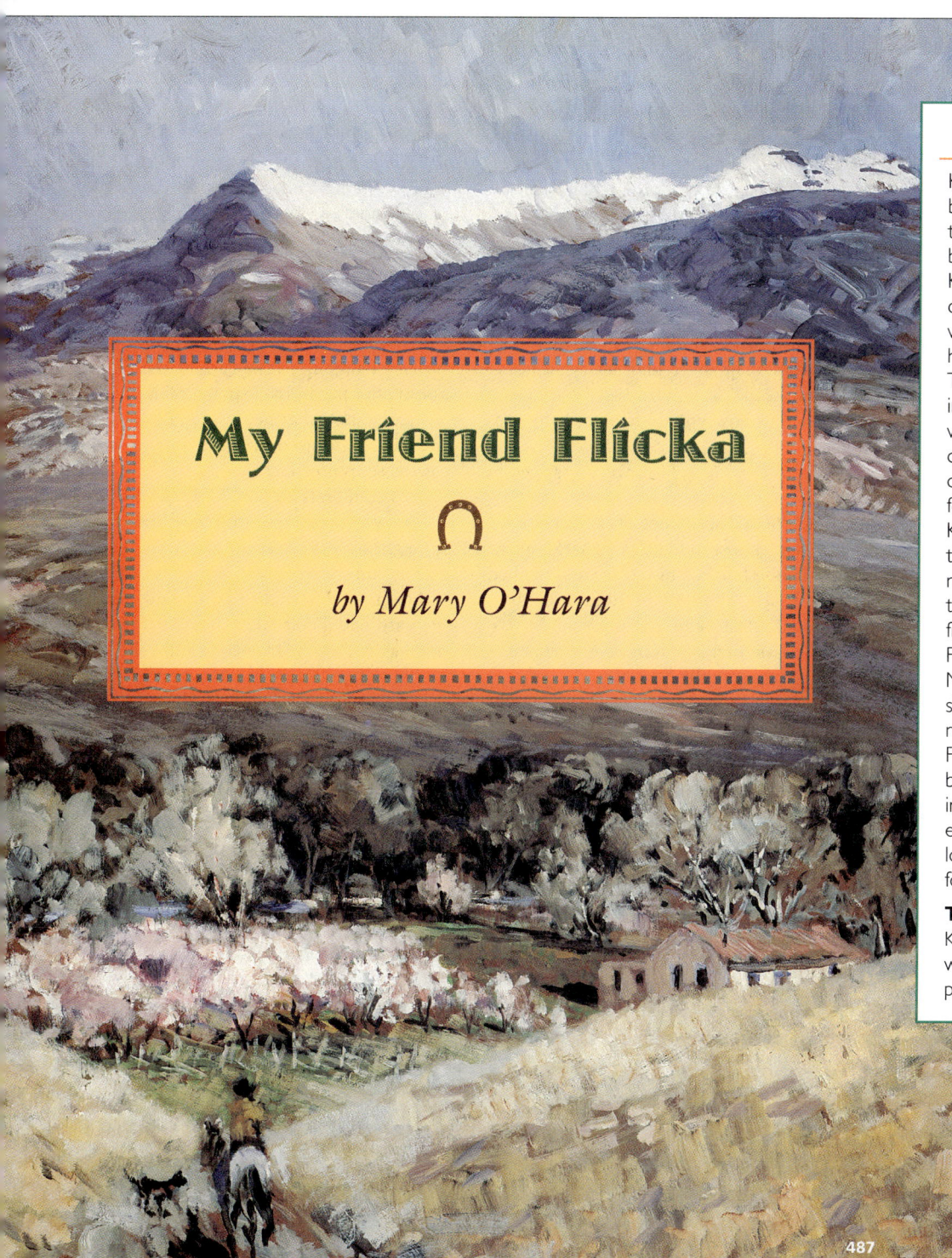

SUMMARY

Kennie McLaughlin longs for his own colt, but his rancher father thinks he's too dreamy to take on the responsibility. Mrs. McLaughlin, believing that having a colt might boost Kennie's confidence, talks her husband into changing his mind. Mr. McLaughlin is worried when Kennie chooses a filly (a young female horse) that he thinks is too wild to tame. Twice, Flicka escapes from her captors; fleeing a third time, she gets tangled in barbed wire and is seriously injured. Although Kennie devotedly nurses her, she never lets him come close. One morning, Flicka takes a turn for the worse. She cannot get up, and Kennie tearfully holds her head in his lap for the first time. With his mother's help, he puts medicine on Flicka's infected leg. Her condition improves, and boy and filly become friends. After a month, however, fever causes Flicka to lose much weight. When Mr. McLaughlin orders Gus, the ranch hand, to shoot her, Kennie begs Gus for one more night. He spends the night in a creek, holding Flicka, who has slipped into the water because of her weakness. By the next morning, the water has helped her heal—but the exposure has nearly killed Kennie. After a long illness, he recovers to find Flicka waiting for him.

Thematic Link: *Taking Necessary Steps*
Kennie discovers that getting—and keeping—what you desire may require persistence and personal sacrifice.

WORDS TO KNOW

blissful (blĭs′fəl) *adj.* very happy; overjoyed (p. 492)
despair (dĭ-spâr′) *n.* complete hopelessness (p. 488)
envision (ĕn-vĭzh′ən) *v.* to imagine (p. 493)
fanatical (fə-năt′ĭ-kəl) *adj.* having too much devotion to a cause or goal; overly enthusiastic (p. 495)
fidgety (fĭj′ĭ-tē) *adj.* moving restlessly (p. 492)
prestige (prĕ-stēzh′) *n.* widely recognized importance; position of high honor (p. 491)
pursue (pər-sōō′) *v.* to chase after (p. 493)
rebellious (rĭ-bĕl′yəs) *adj.* resisting control; not giving in (p. 490)
refrain (rĭ-frān′) *v.* to hold oneself back (p. 488)
vague (vāg) *adj.* unclear; not well defined (p. 489)

CUSTOMIZING FOR
Students Acquiring English

- Use ACCESS FOR STUDENTS ACQUIRING ENGLISH, *Reading and Writing Support*.
- In addition to the suggestions in these boxes, you may want to use the suggestions under Strategic Reading for Less-Proficient Readers.

1 Make sure that students are familiar with the numerical grading system (from 0 to 100) used in Kennie's school.

2 By this point in the story, make sure students are aware of all the family relationships. (Rob is the father, Nell is the mother, and Howard and Kennie are the sons.)

STRATEGIC READING FOR
Less-Proficient Readers

Set a Purpose Invite volunteers to share stories about wanting a pet or some other special favor that their parents were reluctant to agree to. Then have students read to find out what Kennie's father thinks about him.

Use UNIT FOUR RESOURCE BOOK, pp. 63–64, for guidance in reading the selection.

CUSTOMIZING FOR
Gifted and Talented Students

Ask students to imagine that they have been hired to prepare illustrations for this short story. Have them think, as they read, about which scenes will make the most dramatic illustrations, as well as which scenes are important to the story.

Active Reading: CONNECT

A Have students note how Kennie reacts to his father's and brother's comments. Ask students to imagine themselves in Kennie's position and to describe what they might be thinking and feeling and how they would react.

Report cards for the second semester were sent out soon after school closed in mid-June.

Kennie's was a shock to the whole family.

"If I could have a colt all for my own," said Kennie, "I might do better."

Rob McLaughlin glared at his son. "Just as a matter of curiosity," he said, "how do you go about it to get a *zero* in an examination? Forty in arithmetic; seventeen in history! But a *zero*? Just as one man to another, what goes on in your head?"

"Yes, tell us how you do it, Ken," chirped Howard.

"Eat your breakfast, Howard," snapped his mother.

Kennie's blond head bent over his plate until his face was almost hidden. His cheeks burned.

McLaughlin finished his coffee and pushed his chair back. "You'll do an hour a day on your lessons all through the summer."

Nell McLaughlin saw Kennie wince as if something had actually hurt him.

Lessons and study in the summertime, when the long winter was just over and there weren't hours enough in the day for all the things he wanted to do!

Kennie took things hard. His eyes turned to the wide-open window with a look almost of despair.

The hill opposite the house, covered with arrow-straight jack pines, was sharply etched in the thin air of the eight-thousand-foot altitude. Where it fell away, vivid green grass ran up to meet it; and over range and upland poured the strong Wyoming sunlight that stung everything into burning color. A big jack rabbit sat under one of the pines, waving his long ears back and forth.

Ken had to look at his plate and blink back tears before he could turn to his father and say carelessly, "Can I help you in the corral with the horses this morning, Dad?"

"You'll do your study every morning before you do anything else." And McLaughlin's scarred boots and heavy spurs clattered across the kitchen floor. "I'm disgusted with you. Come, Howard."

Howard strode after his father, nobly refraining from looking at Kennie.

"Help me with the dishes, Kennie," said Nell McLaughlin as she rose, tied on a big apron, and began to clear the table.

Kennie looked at her in despair. She poured steaming water into the dishpan and sent him for the soap powder.

"If I could have a colt," he muttered again.

"Now get busy with that dish towel, Ken. It's eight o'clock. You can study till nine and then go up to the corral. They'll still be there."

At supper that night Kennie said, "But Dad, Howard had a colt all of his own when he was only eight. And he trained it and schooled it all himself; and now he's eleven, and Highboy is three, and he's riding him. I'm nine now, and even if you did give me a colt now, I couldn't catch up to Howard, because I couldn't ride it till it was a three-year-old, and then I'd be twelve."

Nell laughed. "Nothing wrong with that arithmetic."

But Rob said, "Howard never gets less than seventy-five average at school and hasn't disgraced himself and his family by getting more demerits[1] than any other boy in his class."

Kennie didn't answer. He couldn't figure it out. He tried hard; he spent hours poring over his books. That was supposed to get you good

---

1. **demerits:** marks in a student's record for poor work or for misbehavior.

WORDS TO KNOW
despair (dĭ-spâr′) *n.* complete hopelessness
refrain (rĭ-frān′) *v.* to hold oneself back

488

Mini-Lesson The Writer's Style

DIALOGUE Remind students that a writer uses dialogue—a conversation between two or more characters—to provide information, establish a tone, show personalities, or illustrate interactions between characters. In a story, dialogue is usually set off with quotation marks.

Application Have students use the dialogue on page 488 to answer the following questions:
1. What facts do you learn from the dialogue?
2. What do you learn about the personalities of the characters from the dialogue?

Then have students write a short scene in which the four characters drive into a nearby town to buy groceries or equipment for the ranch. Tell them to use dialogue in their scene and to try to match the characters' personalities as depicted so far in "My Friend Flicka."

Reteaching/Reinforcement
- *Writer's Handbook*, anthology p. 779
- *Writing Mini-Lessons* transparencies, p. 48

Using Dialogue, pp. 278–280

---

488 THE LANGUAGE OF LITERATURE TEACHER'S EDITION

marks, but it never did. Everyone said he was bright; why was it that when he studied he didn't learn? He had a vague feeling that perhaps he looked out the window too much or looked through the walls to see clouds and sky and hills and wonder what was happening out there. Sometimes it wasn't even a wonder, but just a pleasant drifting feeling of nothing at all, as if nothing mattered, as if there was always plenty of time, as if the lessons would get done of themselves. And then the bell would ring, and study period was over.

If he had a colt—

When the boys had gone to bed that night, Nell McLaughlin sat down with her overflowing mending basket and glanced at her husband.

He was at his desk as usual, working on account books and inventories.

Nell threaded a darning needle and thought, "It's either that whacking big bill from the vet for the mare that died or the last half of the tax bill."

It didn't seem just the auspicious moment to plead Kennie's cause. But then, these days there was always a line between Rob's eyes and a harsh note in his voice.

"Rob," she began.

He flung down his pencil and turned around.

"Damn that law!" he exclaimed.

"What law?"

"The state law that puts high taxes on pedigreed[2] stock. I'll have to do as the rest of 'em do—drop the papers."

"Drop the papers! But you'll never get decent prices if you don't have registered horses."[3]

"I don't get decent prices now."

"But you will someday, if you don't drop the papers."

"Maybe." He bent again over the desk.

Rob, thought Nell, was a lot like Kennie himself. He set his heart. Oh, how stubbornly he set his heart on just some one thing he wanted above everything else. He had set his heart on horses and ranching way back when he had been a crack rider at West Point[4]; and he had resigned and thrown away his army career just for the horses. Well, he'd got what he wanted— She drew a deep breath, snipped her thread, laid down the sock, and again looked across at her husband as she unrolled another length of darning cotton.

To get what you want is one thing, she was thinking. The three-thousand-acre ranch and the hundred head of horses. But to make it pay—for a dozen or more years they had been trying to make it pay. People said ranching hadn't paid since the beef barons ran their

> Oh, how stubbornly he set his heart on just some one thing he wanted above everything else.

---

2. **pedigreed:** having an established, purebred line of ancestors.
3. **registered horses:** horses that have documents proving that they are purebred, which increases their value.
4. **West Point:** the U.S. Military Academy in West Point, New York, where U.S. Army officers are trained.

WORDS TO KNOW
vague (vāg) *adj.* unclear; not well defined

489

Literary Concept: POINT OF VIEW

B Have students compare the point of view of the title with that of the first page of the story. Ask them how the points of view differ. *(The title implies a first-person point of view, but the story is written from a third-person perspective.)*

Literary Concept: CHARACTERIZATION

C Ask students what they can infer about Kennie's character from this passage. *(Possible responses: He is bored with school and not interested in his studies; he is a daydreamer; he would rather be outdoors than inside; he isn't always realistic.)*

Active Reading: EVALUATE

D Ask students whether Kennie's theory is valid—that if he had a colt, he might do better in school. Have students explain their response. *(Possible responses: no, because Kennie might spend all his time with the colt and not do his schoolwork; yes, because the colt would make Kennie become more responsible in general)*

Linking to History

E At the turn of the century, horses were used by the U.S. military and for transportation and many kinds of farm and ranch work. During the early 1900s, the market for horses steadily decreased as more people began to use motorized vehicles and machinery. Today, few ranchers can afford to raise horses exclusively because, as the father in this story realizes, maintaining a horse ranch is costly.

Mini-Lesson Genre Study

FICTION Remind students that **fiction** is writing that comes from an author's imagination. Tell them that although the author makes the story up, it may be based on real events. Point out that the three principal elements of a story are the characters (major and minor), the setting (time and place), and the plot. The plot is a series of events that usually depicts a conflict—a struggle between two or more opposing forces. A short story, such as this selection, often revolves around a single conflict. A novel is longer and more complex. Mary O'Hara, the author of "My Friend Flicka," first wrote the work as a short story and then expanded it into a novel, with more settings, characters, and events.

Application Copy on the board the word web shown here. Have students add details to the web that are relevant to "My Friend Flicka."

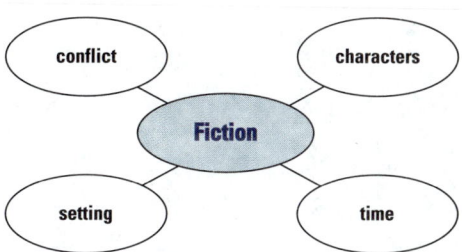

THE LANGUAGE OF LITERATURE **TEACHER'S EDITION** 489

STRATEGIC READING FOR
Less-Proficient Readers

F Ask students the following questions to help them understand the relationship between Kennie and his father:

- How is Kennie treated by his father? *(Possible responses: critically, harshly)*
  Noting Relevant Details

- Why does Kennie's father treat him the way he does? *(Possible responses: Rob thinks that Kennie doesn't try hard enough in school and in other activities. Rob is trying to improve Kennie's attitude and behavior by being stern.)*
  Making Inferences

Set a Purpose Have students read on to find out why Rob decides to give Kennie a colt and how Kennie's behavior changes as a result.

CUSTOMIZING FOR
Students Acquiring English

3 Explain that *that's a big if* means that Rob feels that Kennie will not be able to take care of a colt.

Active Reading: PREDICT

G Suggest that students first answer the question from four different points of view: Kennie's father, his mother, his brother, and Kennie himself. Students can then add their own opinions and predictions.

Kennie studies hard, his grades improve, and then...
Kennie finds a way to help his father earn more money, and then...
Nell decides to give Kennie a colt without telling Rob, and then...
Kennie "borrows" Howard's colt to go for a ride, and then...

---

herds on public land; people said the only prosperous ranchers in Wyoming were the dude ranchers; people said—

But suddenly she gave her head a little <u>rebellious</u>, gallant shake. Rob would always be fighting and struggling against something, like Kennie; perhaps like herself, too. Even those first years when there was no water piped into the house, when every day brought a new difficulty or danger, how she had loved it! How she still loved it!

She ran the darning ball into the toe of a sock, Kennie's sock. The length of it gave her a shock. Yes, the boys were growing up fast, and now Kennie—Kennie and the colt—

After a while she said, "Give Kennie a colt, Rob."

"He doesn't deserve it." The answer was short. Rob pushed away his papers and took out his pipe.

"Howard's too far ahead of him, older and bigger and quicker and his wits about him, and—"

"Ken doesn't half try, doesn't stick at anything."

She put down her sewing. "He's crazy for a colt of his own. He hasn't had another idea in his head since you gave Highboy to Howard."

"I don't believe in bribing children to do their duty."

"Not a bribe." She hesitated.

"No? What would you call it?"

She tried to think it out. "I just have the feeling Ken isn't going to pull anything off, and"—her eyes sought Rob's—"it's time he did. It isn't the school marks alone, but I just don't want things to go on any longer with Ken never coming out at the right end of anything."

"I'm beginning to think he's just dumb."

"He's not dumb. Maybe a little thing like this—if he had a colt of his own, trained him, rode him—"

Rob interrupted. "But it isn't a little thing, nor an easy thing, to break and school a colt the way Howard has schooled Highboy. I'm not going to have a good horse spoiled by Ken's careless ways. He goes woolgathering.[5] He never knows what he's doing."

"But he'd *love* a colt of his own, Rob. If he could do it, it might make a big difference in him."

"*If* he could do it! But that's a big if."

PREDICT
How would Kennie act if he had a colt?
Using a Reading Log

At breakfast next morning Kennie's father said to him, "When you've done your study, come out to the barn. I'm going in the car up to section[6] twenty-one this morning to look over the brood mares. You can go with me."

"Can I go too, Dad?" cried Howard.

McLaughlin frowned at Howard. "You turned Highboy out last evening with dirty legs."

Howard wriggled. "I groomed him—"

"Yes, down to his knees."

"He kicks."

"And whose fault is that? You don't get on his back again until I see his legs clean."

The two boys eyed each other, Kennie secretly triumphant and Howard chagrined. McLaughlin turned at the door. "And, Ken, a week from today I'll give you a colt. Between now and then you can decide what one you want."

---
5. **woolgathering:** daydreaming.
6. **section:** a square piece of land measuring one mile on each side; 640 acres.

WORDS TO KNOW
rebellious (rĭ-bĕl′yəs) *adj.* resisting control; not giving in

490

Mini-Lesson — Reading Skills/Strategies

PREDICTING Remind students that active readers step into the actions, times, and places of the stories they read. Tell them that one strategy active readers use is predicting what will happen next in the story. Point out that a reader makes such a prediction on the basis of what is already known.

Application Have students work in small groups. Ask the groups to read the highlighted text above, then generate different predictions about what might follow. Some ideas for generating discussion are shown here.

Reteaching/Reinforcement
- *Unit Four Resource Book,* p. 64

490 THE LANGUAGE OF LITERATURE **TEACHER'S EDITION**

My Children (1920), W. Herbert Dunton. Oil on canvas, Museum of Fine Arts, Museum of New Mexico, Santa Fe, anonymous gift.

Art Note

My Children by W. Herbert Dunton
This work by William Herbert Dunton (1878–1936) shows two young riders set against a background of rocks and shrubs. The dark colors in the upper part of the picture indicate that the time is either sunset or very early morning. The pensive-looking boy in the foreground has dismounted; his riding companion has turned to watch him.

Reading the Art *How does the artist focus attention on the boy in the center of the picture? Describe the mood of the work, and speculate on what has just happened or what might be about to happen.*

Literary Concept: CONFLICT

H Encourage students to note the sharp difference of opinion that Kennie's parents have about whether to give Kennie a colt. Ask students to explain the importance of this conflict in the story. *(Possible responses: Both Rob and Nell want Kennie to become more responsible, but they disagree how to go about it. The disagreement adds suspense because the reader wants to find out whether Rob or Nell is right.)*

Kennie shot out of his chair and stared at his father. "A—a spring colt,[7] Dad, or a yearling?"[8]

McLaughlin was somewhat taken aback, but his wife concealed a smile. If Kennie got a yearling colt, he would be even up with Howard.

"A yearling colt, your father means, Ken," she said smoothly. "Now hurry with your lessons. Howard will wipe."

Kennie found himself the most important personage on the ranch. <u>Prestige</u> lifted his head, gave him an inch more of height and a

---
7. **spring colt:** a colt born the previous spring
8. **yearling:** an animal that is a year old.

WORDS TO KNOW
prestige (prĕ-stēzh′) *n.* widely recognized importance; position of high honor

491

Mini-Lesson  Reading Skills/Strategies

CONNECTING Remind students that active readers become involved in a story by connecting events or characters with their own personal experiences. Tell them that a reader does this by looking for similarities between what is described in the story and things he or she has done, felt, seen, heard about, or read about.

Application Have students recall (or imagine) something they desperately wanted and then got. Ask the following questions:
• *Is there something you wanted badly?*
• *How did you try to get it?*
• *How did you feel when you got it?*

Then have students connect their own experience with Kennie's by using a chart like the one shown.

Reteaching/Reinforcement
• *Unit Four Resource Book,* p. 64

My Experience	Kennie's Experience

THE LANGUAGE OF LITERATURE TEACHER'S EDITION **491**

STRATEGIC READING FOR
Less-Proficient Readers

I Ask students the following questions to help clarify the importance of the colt:

- Why does Rob decide to give Kennie a colt? *(Possible responses: Nell talks him into it; he hopes it will make Kennie more responsible.)* **Making Inferences**

- How does Kennie change when he knows he can choose a colt of his own? *(Possible responses: He becomes less timid, happier, more alert, and more focused on his schoolwork and other chores.)* **Relating Cause and Effect**

Set a Purpose Ask students to note how the other characters react to Kennie's choice of a colt.

Active Reading: CONNECT

J Ask students whether they have ever made a decision they knew was right but everyone else believed was wrong. Invite volunteers to share their experiences.

CUSTOMIZING FOR
Students Acquiring English

4 Help students analyze the meaning of *untamable* (base word *tame*; prefix *un-*; suffix *-able*).

Literary Concept: PLOT

K Remind students that the plot of a story consists of a sequence of actions or events. Ask students to summarize the plot of the story so far. *(Kennie badly wants a colt of his own. Against his better judgment, Rob gives Kennie a colt. Then Kennie picks an extremely wild horse.)*

---

bold stare, and made him feel different all the way through. Even Gus and Tim Murphy, the ranch hands, were more interested in Kennie's choice of a colt than anything else.

Howard was <u>fidgety</u> with suspense. "Who'll you pick, Ken? Say—pick Doughboy, why don't you? Then when he grows up he'll be sort of twins with mine, in his name anyway. Doughboy, Highboy, see?"

The boys were sitting on the worn wooden step of the door which led from the tack room[9] into the corral, busy with rags and polish, shining their bridles.

Ken looked at his brother with scorn. Doughboy would never have half of Highboy's speed.

"Lassie, then," suggested Howard. "She's black as ink, like mine. And she'll be fast—"

"Dad says Lassie'll never go over fifteen hands."

Nell McLaughlin saw the change in Kennie, and her hopes rose. He went to his books in the morning with determination and really studied. A new alertness took the place of the daydreaming. Examples in arithmetic were neatly written out, and, as she passed his door before breakfast, she often heard the monotonous drone of his voice as he read his American history aloud.

Each night, when he kissed her, he flung his arms around her and held her fiercely for a moment, then, with a winsome and <u>blissful</u> smile into her eyes, turned away to bed.

> "You said she'd never been named. I've named her. Her name is Flicka."

He spent days inspecting the different bands of horses and colts. He sat for hours on the corral fence, very important, chewing straws. He rode off on one of the ponies for half the day, wandering through the mile-square pastures that ran down toward the Colorado border.

And when the week was up, he announced his decision. "I'll take that yearling filly of Rocket's. The sorrel[10] with the cream tail and mane."

His father looked at him in surprise. "The one that got tangled in the barbed wire? That's never been named?"

In a second all Kennie's new pride was gone. He hung his head defensively. "Yes."

"You've made a bad choice, son. You couldn't have picked a worse."

"She's fast, Dad. And Rocket's fast—"

"It's the worst line of horses I've got. There's never one amongst them with real sense. The mares are hellions and the stallions outlaws; they're untamable."

"I'll tame her."

Rob guffawed. "Not I, nor anyone, has ever been able to really tame any one of them."

Kennie's chest heaved.

"Better change your mind, Ken. You want a horse that'll be a real friend to you, don't you?"

"Yes—" Kennie's voice was unsteady.

"Well, you'll never make a friend of that

---

9. **tack room:** a room in which saddles and other horse gear are stored.
10. **sorrel** (sôr′əl): a horse with a brownish orange color.

WORDS TO KNOW
fidgety (fĭj′ĭ-tē) *adj.* moving restlessly
blissful (blĭs′fəl) *adj.* very happy; overjoyed

492

Mini-Lesson Grammar

Adjective	Comparative	Superlative
fast	faster	fastest
big	bigger	biggest
good	better	best
much	more	most

COMPARATIVE ADJECTIVES Remind students that the comparative form of adjectives, which ends in *-er*, is used to compare two things, two groups of things, or one thing with a group. The superlative form, which ends in *-est*, is used to compare three or more things. Point out that the comparative and superlative forms of some adjectives, such as *good*, *bad*, and *much*, are completely different words.

Application Ask students to find the comparative and superlative forms of *bad* in the highlighted text on this page. *(worse, worst)*

Then have students choose the correct adjective forms in these sentences.
1. Kennie began to do (good, better, best) with his schoolwork. *(better)*
2. Choosing a colt was the (much, more, most) important decision he had ever made. *(most)*

Reteaching/Reinforcement
- Grammar Handbook, anthology p. 831
- *Grammar Mini-Lessons* copymasters, p. 20, transparencies p. 13

 **The Writer's Craft**

Making Comparisons with Adjectives, pp. 471–474

492 THE LANGUAGE OF LITERATURE TEACHER'S EDITION

filly. She's all cut and scarred up already with tearing through barbed wire after that mother of hers. No fence'll hold 'em—"

"I know," said Kennie, still more faintly.

"Change your mind?" asked Howard briskly.

"No."

Rob was grim and put out. He couldn't go back on his word. The boy had to have a reasonable amount of help in breaking and taming the filly, and he could envision precious hours, whole days, wasted in the struggle.

Nell McLaughlin despaired. Once again Ken seemed to have taken the wrong turn and was back where he had begun, stoical,[11] silent, defensive.

But there was a difference that only Ken could know. The way he felt about his colt. The way his heart sang. The pride and joy that filled him so full that sometimes he hung his head so they wouldn't see it shining out of his eyes.

He had known from the very first that he would choose that particular yearling because he was in love with her.

The year before, he had been out working with Gus, the big Swedish ranch hand, on the irrigation ditch, when they had noticed Rocket standing in a gully on the hillside, quiet for once and eyeing them cautiously.

"Ay bet she got a colt," said Gus, and they walked carefully up the draw. Rocket gave a wild snort, thrust her feet out, shook her head wickedly, then fled away. And as they reached the spot, they saw standing there the wavering, pinkish colt, barely able to keep its feet. It gave a little squeak and started after its mother on crooked, wobbling legs.

"Yee whiz! Luk at de little *flicka!*" said Gus.

"What does *flicka* mean, Gus?"

"Swedish for little gurl, Ken—"

Ken announced at supper, "You said she'd never been named. I've named her. Her name is Flicka."

The first thing to do was to get her in. She was running with a band of yearlings on the saddleback,[12] cut with ravines and gullies, on section twenty.

They all went out after her, Ken, as owner, on old Rob Roy, the wisest horse on the ranch.

Ken was entranced to watch Flicka when the wild band of youngsters discovered that they were being pursued and took off across the mountain. Footing made no difference to her. She floated across the ravines, always two lengths ahead of the others. Her pink mane and tail whipped in the wind. Her long, delicate legs had only to aim, it seemed, at a particular spot for her to reach it and sail on. She seemed to Ken a fairy horse.

He sat motionless, just watching and holding Rob Roy in, when his father thundered past on Sultan and shouted, "Well, what's the matter? Why didn't you turn 'em?"

Kennie woke up and galloped after.

Rob Roy brought in the whole band. The corral gates were closed, and an hour was spent shunting the ponies in and out and through the chutes, until Flicka was left alone in the small round corral in which the baby colts were branded. Gus drove the others away, out the gate, and up the saddleback.

But Flicka did not intend to be left. She hurled herself against the poles which walled the corral. She tried to jump them. They were seven feet high. She caught her front feet over the top rung, clung, scrambled, while Kennie held his breath for fear the slender legs would

---

11. **stoical** (stō′ĭ-kəl): showing no emotion.
12. **saddleback**: a ridge with a sunken top.

> **WORDS TO KNOW**
> **envision** (ĕn-vĭzh′ən) *v.* to imagine
> **pursue** (pər-sōō′) *v.* to chase after

Linking to Science

In the story, Flicka entangles herself in a barbed-wire fence. Barbed wire is made of steel strands twisted into shapes with spikes, or barbs, that project at right angles from the main wire. Several types of barbed wire were invented in the 1800s, but the type patented by Joseph F. Glidden in Illinois in 1874 was the most widely used. Glidden's barbed wire was better than other types because he created a way to keep the barbs in place.

CUSTOMIZING FOR
Students Acquiring English

Point out that the spelling used in Gus's dialogue reflects the pronunciation of Swedish-accented English.

STRATEGIC READING FOR
Less-Proficient Readers

Ask students the following questions to make sure they understand the story so far:

- Why does Kennie choose the colt he does, and how do Rob, Nell, and Howard react to his choice? *(Possible responses: Kennie had seen the colt right after she was born and became emotionally attached to her; she could run unusually fast. Rob is surprised and critical; Nell is worried; Howard is contemptuous and teasing.)* **Making Inferences/Summarizing**

Set a Purpose Have students note how the characters react when Flicka escapes.

493

Mini-Lesson Spelling

FINAL CONSONANTS AND SUFFIXES
Explain to students that sometimes the final consonant of a word is doubled when a suffix is added. Tell them that the consonant is doubled when (1) the final consonant is preceded by a single vowel or (2) the final syllable is accented (a one-syllable word counts as an accented syllable). Have students compare the words on the chart shown here, and discuss when the final consonant is doubled.

Application Have students add the suffixes *-ed* and *-ing* to each of the following words:

1. fret
2. excel
3. shudder
4. tilt
5. submit
6. dismiss
7. drag
8. recover
9. blink
10. regret
11. embarrass
12. omit

Reteaching/Reinforcement
- *Unit Four Resource Book,* p. 65

Final Consonant Doubled		Final Consonant Not Doubled	
beginning	occurred	fidgety	canceling
preferred	knotty	defeated	revolting
planning	committed	modeling	profiting
rebelling	forbidding	traveled	equaling

THE LANGUAGE OF LITERATURE TEACHER'S EDITION **493**

Art Note

New Mexico Spring by Fremont Ellis
Reading the Art What elements of this painting remind you of the details in the story? Is this what you think the McLaughlins' ranch looks like? Why or why not?

Literary Concept: SUSPENSE

 Remind students that suspense is the feeling of excitement that occurs when the reader wants to know what will happen next in a story. Have students describe the events that create suspense here. *(Possible responses: Flicka's violent struggles make the reader want to find out whether she will escape; Rob's disapproval makes the reader wonder whether Kennie will get in trouble or be upset by his father's actions.)*

Linking to Social Studies

As settlers moved westward into the dry, treeless grassland of the Great Plains, they found that traditional fencing materials, wood and stone, were hard to find and expensive to buy. Ordinary wire strung between wooden posts did not work. Cattle and other animals could get their heads between the smooth strands of wire and force an opening. Without fencing to protect crops, farming was impractical. Fencing was also needed to manage animals such as horses, cattle, and sheep. Barbed wire helped solve the problem. Within ten years of its invention, the great open ranges of the Great Plains were transformed by a crisscrossed network of barbed-wire fences.

New Mexico Spring (about 1950), Fremont Ellis. Oil on canvas, 36" x 30", The Anschutz Collection, Denver. Photo by James O. Milmoe.

be caught between the bars and snapped. Her hold broke; she fell over backward, rolled, screamed, tore around the corral. Kennie had a sick feeling in the pit of his stomach, and his father looked disgusted.

One of the bars broke. She hurled herself again. Another went. She saw the opening and, as neatly as a dog crawls through a fence, inserted her head and forefeet, scrambled through, and fled away, bleeding in a dozen places.

As Gus was coming back, just about to close the gate to the upper range, the sorrel whipped through it, sailed across the road and ditch with her inimitable[13] floating leap, and went up the side of the saddleback like a jack rabbit.

---

13. **inimitable** (ĭ-nĭm′ĭ-tə-bəl): not capable of being imitated or copied.

494 UNIT FOUR PART 2: TAKING NECESSARY STEPS

From way up the mountain, Gus heard excited whinnies as she joined the band he had just driven up, and the last he saw of them they were strung out along the crest running like deer.

"Yee whiz!" said Gus, and stood motionless and staring until the ponies had disappeared over the ridge. Then he closed the gate, remounted Rob Roy, and rode back to the corral.

Rob McLaughlin gave Kennie one more chance to change his mind. "Last chance, son. Better pick a horse that you have some hope of riding one day. I'd have got rid of this whole line of stock if they weren't so damned fast that I've had the fool idea that someday there might turn out one gentle one in the lot—and I'd have a racehorse. But there's never been one so far, and it's not going to be Flicka."

"It's not going to be Flicka," chanted Howard.

"Perhaps she *might* be gentled," said Kennie; and Nell, watching, saw that although his lips quivered, there was <u>fanatical</u> determination in his eye.

"Ken," said Rob, "it's up to you. If you say you want her, we'll get her. But she wouldn't be the first of that line to die rather than give in. They're beautiful and they're fast, but let me tell you this, young man, they're *loco!*"[14]

Kennie flinched under his father's direct glance.

"If I go after her again, I'll not give up whatever comes; understand what I mean by that?"

"Yes."

"What do you say?"

"I want her."

They brought her in again. They had better luck this time. She jumped over the Dutch half door of the stable and crashed inside. The men slammed the upper half of the door shut, and she was caught.

The rest of the band were driven away, and Kennie stood outside of the stable, listening to the wild hoofs beating, the screams, the crashes. His Flicka inside there! He was drenched with perspiration.

"We'll leave her to think it over," said Rob when dinnertime came. "Afterward, we'll go up and feed and water her."

But when they went up afterward, there was no Flicka in the barn. One of the windows, higher than the mangers, was broken.

The window opened into a pasture an eighth of a mile square, fenced in barbed wire six feet high. Near the stable stood a wagonload of hay. When they went around the back of the stable to see where Flicka had hidden herself, they found her between the stable and the hay wagon, eating.

At their approach she leaped away, then headed east across the pasture.

But when they went up afterward, there was no Flicka in the barn.

---

14. **loco** (lō′kō): a slang term meaning "crazy."

WORDS TO KNOW

fanatical (fə-năt′ĭ-kəl) *adj.* having too much devotion to a cause or goal; overly enthusiastic

495

Mini-Lesson Literary Concepts

REVIEWING CONFLICT Remind students that the plot of a story usually centers around a problem or conflict and the actions the characters take to solve the conflict. In "My Friend Flicka," one of the conflicts is between Flicka and the human characters: Flicka resists being captured and is unwilling to be tamed.

Application Have students describe the conflicts illustrated in the highlighted paragraph on this page. Ask them to organize their ideas in a chart, like the one shown, that describes each conflict and suggests ways the conflict could be solved.

Opposing Forces	Conflict	Ways Conflict Might Be Solved
Kennie and Rob		
Kennie and Howard		
Rob and Nell		

Critical Thinking: ANALYZING

T What does Kennie see as a "sign of hope" for Flicka? *(Possible response: Flicka turns rather than trying to jump the fence. Thus, unlike her relatives, she may be capable of adjusting to captivity.)*

CUSTOMIZING FOR
Students Acquiring English

6 Make sure students know that *called it a day* means "stopped" and that *pull out of it* means "recover."

Active Reading: EVALUATE

U Before students give their opinions, they should give reasons for both sides of the question: that Flicka was a good choice and that she was a poor choice. Suggest that students organize their ideas in a two-column chart, using supporting details from the story.

Literary Concept: CONFLICT

V Have students identify examples of conflict on this page. *(Some major conflicts: Rob and Kennie differ in their opinions of Flicka; Flicka opposes the people as she tries to escape; Flicka fights against death. One minor conflict: Gus and Rob disagree about whether Flicka will jump over the fence.)*

"If she's like her mother," said Rob, "she'll go right through the wire."

"Ay bet she'll go over," said Gus. "She yumps like a deer."

"No horse can jump that," said McLaughlin.

Kennie said nothing because he could not speak. It was, perhaps, the most terrible moment of his life. He watched Flicka racing toward the eastern wire.

A few yards from it, she swerved, turned, and raced diagonally south.

"It turned her! It turned her!" cried Kennie, almost sobbing. It was the first sign of hope for Flicka. "Oh, Dad! She has got sense. She has! She has!"

Flicka turned again as she met the southern boundary of the pasture, again at the northern; she avoided the barn. Without abating anything of her whirlwind speed, following a precise, accurate calculation, and turning each time on a dime, she investigated every possibility. Then, seeing that there was no hope, she raced south toward the range where she had spent her life, gathered herself, and shot into the air.

Each of the three men watching had the impulse to cover his eyes, and Kennie gave a sort of howl of despair.

Twenty yards of fence came down with her as she hurled herself through. Caught on the upper strands, she turned a complete somersault, landing on her back, her four legs dragging the wires down on top of her, and tangling herself in them beyond hope of escape....

> *Often she stood with her head at the south fence, looking off to the mountain.*

Kennie followed the men miserably as they walked to the filly. They stood in a circle watching while she kicked and fought and thrashed until the wire was tightly wound and knotted about her, cutting, piercing, and tearing great three-cornered pieces of flesh and hide. At last she was unconscious, streams of blood running on her golden coat and pools of crimson widening and spreading on the grass beneath her.

With the wire cutter which Gus always carried in the hip pocket of his overalls, he cut all the wire away, and they drew her into the pasture, repaired the fence, placed hay, a box of oats, and a tub of water near her, and called it a day.

"I don't think she'll pull out of it," said McLaughlin.

EVALUATE
What do you think of Kennie's choice of Flicka?
Using a Reading Log

Next morning Kennie was up at five, doing his lessons. At six he went out to Flicka.

She had not moved. Food and water were untouched. She was no longer bleeding, but the wounds were swollen and caked over.

Kennie got a bucket of fresh water and poured it over her mouth. Then he leaped away, for Flicka came to life, scrambled up, got her balance, and stood swaying.

Kennie went a few feet away and sat down to watch her. When he went in to breakfast, she had drunk deeply of the water and was mouthing the oats.

There began then a sort of recovery. She ate,

496 UNIT FOUR PART 2: TAKING NECESSARY STEPS

Mini-Lesson Reading Skills/Strategies

EVALUATING Remind students that active readers become involved with the material they read by forming opinions. Tell them that the opinions may be about such issues as the characters' actions, the believability of the events described, or the quality of the writing. Point out that one device they can use to analyze their opinions is a rating scale, with positions ranging from "strongly agree" to "strongly disagree."

Application Have students create a rating scale and a list of opinion statements about "My Friend Flicka." Then have students rate the opinions, using their own scale. The following statements might help students get started:
1. Kennie has made a poor choice in selecting Flicka.
2. Rob is right to treat Kennie sternly.
3. Nell should stay out of the argument and let Rob and Kennie try to reach an agreement.

Reteaching/Reinforcement
• *Unit Four Resource Book,* p. 64

496 THE LANGUAGE OF LITERATURE TEACHER'S EDITION

drank, limped about the pasture, stood for hours with hanging head and weakly splayed-out[15] legs under the clump of cottonwood trees. The swollen wounds scabbed and began to heal.

Kennie lived in the pasture too. He followed her around; he talked to her. He too lay snoozing or sat under the cottonwoods; and often, coaxing her with hand outstretched, he walked very quietly toward her. But she would not let him come near her.

Often she stood with her head at the south fence, looking off to the mountain. It made the tears come to Kennie's eyes to see the way she longed to get away.

Still Rob said she wouldn't pull out of it. There was no use putting a halter on her. She had no strength.

One morning, as Ken came out of the house, Gus met him and said, "De filly's down."

Kennie ran to the pasture, Howard close behind him. The right hind leg which had been badly swollen at the knee joint had opened in a festering wound, and Flicka lay flat and motionless, with staring eyes.

"Don't you wish now you'd chosen Dough-boy?" asked Howard.

"Go away!" shouted Ken.

Howard stood watching while Kennie sat down on the ground and took Flicka's head on his lap. Though she was conscious and moved a little, she did not struggle nor seem frightened. Tears rolled down Kennie's cheeks as he talked to her and petted her. After a few moments, Howard walked away.

"Mother, what do you do for an infection when it's a horse?" asked Kennie.

"Just what you'd do if it was a person. Wet dressings. I'll help you, Ken. We mustn't let those wounds close or scab over until they're clean. I'll make a poultice[16] for that hind leg and help you put it on. Now that she'll let us get close to her, we can help her a lot."

"The thing to do is see that she eats," said Rob. "Keep up her strength."

But he himself would not go near her. "She won't pull out of it," he said. "I don't want to see her or think about her."

Kennie and his mother nursed the filly. The big poultice was bandaged on the hind leg. It drew out much poisoned matter, and Flicka felt better and was able to stand again.

She watched for Kennie now and followed him like a dog, hopping on three legs, holding up the right hind leg with its huge knob of a bandage in comical fashion.

"Dad, Flicka's my friend now; she likes me," said Ken.

His father looked at him. "I'm glad of that, son. It's a fine thing to have a horse for a friend."

> **QUESTION**
> Why does Kennie's father respond in this way?
> Using a Reading Log

Kennie found a nicer place for her. In the lower pasture the brook ran over cool stones. There was a grassy bank the size of a corral, almost on a level with the water. Here she could lie softly, eat grass, drink fresh running water. From the grass, a twenty-foot hill sloped up, crested with overhanging trees. She was enclosed, as it were, in a green open-air nursery.

Kennie carried her oats morning and evening. She would watch for him to come, eyes and ears pointed to the hill. And one evening Ken, still some distance off, came to a stop, and a wide grin spread over his face. He had heard her nicker. She had caught sight of him coming and was calling to him!

---

15. **splayed-out:** turning outward.
16. **poultice** (pōl′tĭs): a soft, pastelike mixture of mud, herbs, or medicine that is applied to a sore.

MY FRIEND FLICKA **497**

Literary Concept:
CHARACTERIZATION

W Have students explain what this short piece of dialogue reveals about the character of Howard and his relationship with Kennie. *(Possible response: Howard seems petty and cruel; Kennie reacts in anger; the two brothers are very unfriendly, even hostile, toward each other.)*

STRATEGIC READING FOR
Less-Proficient Readers

X Ask students how Flicka and Kennie change after Flicka is injured. *(Possible responses: Flicka stops trying to escape; Kennie becomes very responsible in caring for her; she and Kennie become friends.)* **Summarizing**

Set a Purpose Ask students to read on to find out what happens when Flicka becomes sick again.

Active Reading: QUESTION

Y Suggest that students begin by discussing how Kennie and his father differ in their opinions about Flicka's possible recovery. You may wish to use the following model to give students an idea of what they might be thinking about.

Think-Aloud Model *Kennie seems very optimistic and thinks Flicka will get well. Rob seems convinced Flicka won't recover, even to the point of not wanting to see her or think about her. Rob doesn't want to tell Kennie his beliefs, so he answers Kennie in a neutral fashion. It's something like saying, "Yes, yes, that's fine," when you want to avoid telling someone what you really think.*

Mini-Lesson — Reading Skills/Strategies

QUESTIONING Remind students that active readers ask themselves questions as they read. They make mental notes about words, statements, or events they don't understand and then continue reading to see whether the writer answers their questions. Tell students that one way they can become better at asking these questions is to think of the questioning words *who, what, where, when, why,* and *how*.

Application Have students use the highlighted text on this page to generate a list of mental questions. They can include the most obvious question, "What is going to happen next?" Students should also focus on why events have taken place and why the characters act the way they do.

Reteaching/Reinforcement
• Unit Four Resource Book, p. 64

Questioning Words
Who?   When?
What? Why?
Where? How?

THE LANGUAGE OF LITERATURE TEACHER'S EDITION **497**

CUSTOMIZING FOR
Multiple Learning Styles

Ⓩ Musical Learners Ask students to describe the types of background music they would use for the description of events on pages 498–499. They should divide the text into sections, choosing appropriate music for each part.

Literary Concept: DETAILS

AA Ask students to list details on this page that appeal to the senses. *(Possible responses: sound—Flicka listens for the sound of the other horses running wild; sight—phrases describing Flicka's appearance; touch—words describing Flicka's skin and mane)*

Ⓩ   He placed the box of oats under her nose, and she ate while he stood beside her, his hand smoothing the satin-soft skin under her mane. It had a nap as deep as plush. He played with her long, cream-colored tresses, arranged her

Sweet Talkin' Man (1982), Gordon Snidow. Courtesy of The Greenwich Workshop, Inc. Copyright © 1982 The Greenwich Workshop, Inc.

forelock neatly between her eyes. She was a bit dish faced, like an Arab, with eyes set far apart. He lightly groomed and brushed her while she stood turning her head to him whichever way he went.

He spoiled her. Soon she would not step to the stream to drink but he must hold a bucket for her. And she would drink, then lift her dripping muzzle, rest it on the shoulder of his blue chambray shirt, her golden eyes dreaming off into the distance, then daintily dip her mouth to drink again.

When she turned her head to the south and pricked her ears and stood tense and listening, Ken knew she heard the other colts galloping on the upland.

"You'll go back there someday, Flicka," he whispered. "You'll be three and I'll be eleven. You'll be so strong you won't know I'm on your back, and we'll fly like the wind. We'll stand on the very top where we can look over the whole world and smell the snow from the Never-summer Range. Maybe we'll see antelope—"

This was the happiest month of Kennie's life.

With the morning, Flicka always had new strength and would hop three-legged up the hill to stand broadside to the early sun, as horses love to do.

The moment Ken woke he'd go to the window and see her there, and when he was dressed and at his table studying, he sat so that he could raise his head and see Flicka.

After breakfast, she would be waiting for him and the box of oats at the gate, and for Nell McLaughlin with fresh bandages and buckets of disinfectant; and all three would go together to the brook, Flicka hopping along ahead of them, as if she was leading the way.

But Rob McLaughlin would not look at her.

One day all the wounds were swollen again. Presently they opened one by one, and Kennie

498 UNIT FOUR PART 2: TAKING NECESSARY STEPS

and his mother made more poultices.

Still the little filly climbed the hill in the early morning and ran about on three legs. Then she began to go down in flesh and almost overnight wasted away to nothing. Every rib showed; the glossy hide was dull and brittle and was pulled over the skeleton as if she were a dead horse.

Gus said, "It's de fever. It burns up her flesh. If you could stop de fever she might get vell."

McLaughlin was standing in his window one morning and saw the little skeleton hopping about three-legged in the sunshine, and he said, "That's the end. I won't have a thing like that on my place."

Kennie had to understand that Flicka had not been getting well all this time; she had been slowly dying.

"She still eats her oats," he said mechanically.

They were all sorry for Ken. Nell McLaughlin stopped disinfecting and dressing the wounds. "It's no use, Ken," she said gently. "You know Flicka's going to die, don't you?"

"Yes, Mother."

Ken stopped eating. Howard said, "Ken doesn't eat anything anymore. Don't he have to eat his dinner, Mother?"

But Nell answered, "Leave him alone."

Because the shooting of wounded animals is all in the day's work on the Western plains, and sickening to everyone, Rob's voice, when he gave the order to have Flicka shot, was as flat as if he had been telling Gus to kill a chicken for dinner.

"Here's the Marlin, Gus. Pick out a time when Ken's not around and put the filly out of her misery."

Gus took the rifle. "*Ja*, boss—"

Ever since Ken had known that Flicka was to be shot, he had kept his eye on the rack which held the firearms. His father allowed no firearms in the bunkhouse. The gun rack was in the dining room of the ranch house, and, going through it to the kitchen three times a day for meals, Ken's eye scanned the weapons to make sure that they were all there.

That night they were not all there. The Marlin rifle was missing.

When Kennie saw that, he stopped walking. He felt dizzy. He kept staring at the gun rack, telling himself that it surely was there—he counted again and again—he couldn't see clearly—

Then he felt an arm across his shoulders and heard his father's voice.

"I know, son. Some things are awful hard to take. We just have to take 'em. I have to, too."

Kennie got hold of his father's hand and held on. It helped steady him.

Finally he looked up. Rob looked down and smiled at him and gave him a little shake and squeeze. Ken managed a smile too.

"All right now?"

"All right, Dad."

They walked in to supper together. Ken even ate a little. But Nell looked thoughtfully at the ashen color of his face and at the little pulse that was beating in the side of his neck.

After supper he carried Flicka her oats, but

> "I know, son. Some things are awful hard to take. We just have to take 'em. I have to, too."

Linking to Social Studies

BB Gus is described in the story as Swedish, and since he speaks with an accent, it seems likely that he was born in Sweden and immigrated to the United States. In the late 1800s, there were many immigrants from the Scandinavian countries, including Sweden. At the time described in "My Friend Flicka," the 1940s, estimated numbers of foreign-born people in millions were as follows:

Russia	2.1	Canada	0.8
Germany	1.8	Sweden	0.6
Italy	1.6	Hungary	0.6
Austria	1.4	Mexico	0.5
Ireland	1.3	Norway	0.3
England	0.8	Scotland	0.3

Critical Thinking: SPECULATING

CC Have students discuss why Howard once again acts in such an insensitive manner. *(Possible responses: Howard has been jealous of the attention given to Kennie and Flicka; Howard feels that Kennie gets away with actions that Howard would be punished for; Howard is mean and cruel.)*

Literary Concept: PLOT

DD Tell students it appears that Flicka will be shot to end her suffering. Remind them that the story isn't over, however. Have students give several possible ways that the story could end. Students who think it unlikely that Flicka will die should explain why.

Assessment ✓ Option

INFORMAL ASSESSMENT To assess students' understanding of the characters in the story, have them complete a chart, like the one shown, in which they describe the characters and support their descriptions by citing details from the story.

Rubric

3 Full Accomplishment Students' charts describe the characters in depth and accurately use details from the story.

2 Substantial Accomplishment Students' charts describe the characters adequately and use some details from the story.

1 Little or Partial Accomplishment Students' charts do not describe characters accurately and/or do not use details from the story.

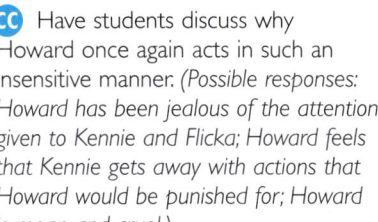

Character	Personality or Behavior Traits	Details from the Story
Kennie		
Flicka		
Kennie's father, Rob		
Kennie's mother, Nell		
Kennie's brother, Howard		
Gus		

STRATEGIC READING FOR
Less-Proficient Readers

EE Ask these questions to check that students are following the events of the story:

- Why does Flicka start to get sick again? *(Possible responses: She was too badly injured; she got a fever from her wounds; her apparent recovery was misleading.)* **Relating Cause and Effect**

- What happens when everyone believes Flicka is going to die? *(Rob decides that Gus must shoot her to end her suffering.)* **Summarizing**

- How does Kennie react to his father's decision? *(He is sad and upset but knows he cannot argue about the decision.)* **Noting Relevant Details**

Set a Purpose Have students note how the relationship between Kennie and his father changes after Kennie gets sick.

---

he had to coax her, and she would only eat a little. She stood with her head hanging, but when he stroked it and talked to her, she pressed her face into his chest and was content. He could feel the burning heat of her body. It didn't seem possible that anything so thin could be alive.

Presently Kennie saw Gus come into the pasture carrying the Marlin. When he saw Ken, he changed his direction and sauntered along as if he was out to shoot some cottontails.

Ken ran to him. "When are you going to do it, Gus?"

"Ay was goin' down soon now, before it got dark—"

"Gus, don't do it tonight. Wait till morning. Just one more night, Gus."

"Vell, in de morning, den, but it got to be done, Ken. Yer fader gives de order."

"I know. I won't say anything more."

An hour after the family had gone to bed, Ken got up and put on his clothes. It was a warm moonlit night. He ran down to the brook, calling softly, "Flicka! Flicka!"

But Flicka did not answer with a little nicker; and she was not in the nursery nor hopping about the pasture. Ken hunted for an hour.

At last he found her down the creek, lying in the water. Her head had been on the bank, but as she lay there, the current of the stream had sucked and pulled at her, and she had had no strength to resist; and little by little her head had slipped down, until when Ken got there only the muzzle was resting on the bank, and the body and legs were swinging in the stream.

Kennie slid into the water, sitting on the bank, and he hauled at her head. But she was heavy, and the current dragged like a weight; and he began to sob because he had no strength to draw her out.

Then he found a leverage for his heels against some rocks in the bed of the stream, and he braced himself against these and pulled with all his might; and her head came up onto his knees, and he held it cradled in his arms.

He was glad that she had died of her own accord, in the cool water, under the moon, instead of being shot by Gus. Then, putting his face close to hers and looking searchingly into her eyes, he saw that she was alive and looking back at him.

And then he burst out crying and hugged her and said, "Oh, my little Flicka, my little Flicka."

The long night passed.
The moon slid slowly across the heavens.
The water rippled over Kennie's legs and over Flicka's body. And gradually the heat and fever went out of her. And the cool running water washed and washed her wounds.

When Gus went down in the morning with the rifle, they hadn't moved. There they were, Kennie sitting in water over his thighs and hips, with Flicka's head in his arms.

Gus seized Flicka by the head and hauled her out on the grassy bank and then, seeing that Kennie couldn't move, cold and stiff and half paralyzed as he was, lifted him in his arms and carried him to the house.

"Gus," said Ken through chattering teeth, "don't shoot her, Gus."

"It ain't fur me to say, Ken. You know dat."

"But the fever's left her, Gus."

"Ay wait a little, Ken—"

Rob McLaughlin drove to Laramie to get the doctor, for Ken was in violent chills that would not stop. His mother had him in bed wrapped in hot blankets when they got back.

He looked at his father imploringly as the doctor shook down the thermometer.

500   UNIT FOUR   PART 2: TAKING NECESSARY STEPS

Mini-Lesson Reading Skills/Strategies

CLARIFYING Explain to students that active readers can clarify their understanding of a story by going back and skimming previously read passages.

Application Refer students to the highlighted text on this page. A reader might not be sure why Flicka is so thin or why her body has "burning heat." To clarify this text, students can skim backward through the story. (On page 499, Rob looks out his window and sees "the little skeleton hopping about." In the paragraph just before that description, Gus says, "It's de fever. It burns up her flesh." Thus, the reader is reminded that Flicka has developed a fever and has lost a lot of weight.)

Reteaching/Reinforcement
- *Unit Four Resource Book,* p. 64

500   THE LANGUAGE OF LITERATURE   TEACHER'S EDITION

"She might get well now, Dad. The fever's left her. It went out of her when the moon went down."

"All right, son. Don't worry. Gus'll feed her, morning and night, as long as she's—"

"As long as I can't do it," finished Kennie happily.

The doctor put the thermometer in his mouth and told him to keep it shut.

All day Gus went about his work, thinking of Flicka. He had not been back to look at her. He had been given no more orders. If she was alive, the order to shoot her was still in effect. But Kennie was ill, McLaughlin making his second trip to town, taking the doctor home, and would not be back till long after dark.

After their supper in the bunkhouse, Gus and Tim walked down to the brook. They did not speak as they approached the filly, lying stretched out flat on the grassy bank, but their eyes were straining at her to see if she was dead or alive.

She raised her head as they reached her.

"By the powers!" exclaimed Tim. "There she is!"

She dropped her head, raised it again, and moved her legs and became tense as if struggling to rise. But to do so she must use her right hind leg to brace herself against the earth. That was the damaged leg, and at the first bit of pressure with it she gave up and fell back.

"We'll swing her onto the other side," said Tim. "Then she can help herself."

"Ja—"

Standing behind her, they leaned over, grabbed hold of her left legs, front and back, and gently hauled her over. Flicka was as lax and willing as a puppy. But the moment she found herself lying on her right side, she began to scramble, braced herself with her good left leg, and tried to rise.

"Yee whiz!" said Gus. "She got plenty strength yet."

"Hi!" cheered Tim. "She's up!"

But Flicka wavered, slid down again, and lay flat. This time she gave notice that she would not try again by heaving a deep sigh and closing her eyes.

Gus took his pipe out of his mouth and thought it over. Orders or no orders, he would

In the Valley of the Rosebud (1992), Ralph E. Oberg. Oil on canvas, 24" x 30". Copyright © Ralph E. Oberg.

MY FRIEND FLICKA **501**

Art Note

In the Valley of the Rosebud by Ralph Oberg

Reading the Art *What mood is created by this landscape? What details in the painting help contribute to the mood?*

Linking to Math

FF That Rob is gone a long time when taking the doctor back to town is one indication, among others, that the story is set in a sparsely populated area. Population density is the number of people per unit of area. In 1990, Wyoming had the second lowest population density of any state in the United States, 4.7 people per square mile. Only Alaska, at 1.0, was lower. (For comparison, New Jersey and the District of Columbia had about 1,000 people per square mile.) Wyoming also had the lowest absolute population of all 50 states.

Literary Concept: SUSPENSE

GG Ask students to explain how the author fills this scene with suspense. (Possible responses: Kennie is ill, and the reader doesn't know whether he will recover. Gus has orders to shoot Flicka, and the only person who can stop him, Rob, is away from the ranch.)

Mini-Lesson Study Skills

GRAPHIC AIDS Explain to students that graphic aids can help readers to understand material by presenting information visually. Examples of graphic aids include photographs, diagrams, maps, tables, charts, and graphs.

Application Have students look at the three graphic aids shown on page 486. Ask them to write a description of each and to tell how each can help a reader understand the story. Also ask them to tell which graphics they find most useful. Then have students suggest other graphics they think would help them better understand the story. Possibilities include a map of Wyoming, diagrams of some of the equipment used on the ranch, and a time line showing the sequence of events in the story.

THE LANGUAGE OF LITERATURE TEACHER'S EDITION **501**

Critical Thinking:
MAKING JUDGMENTS

HH Have students discuss whether they agree with Gus's decision not to shoot Flicka. You may wish to organize their ideas in a two-column chart.

STRATEGIC READING FOR
Less-Proficient Readers

II Ask students how Kennie's relationship with his father is different after Kennie gets sick. *(His father seems less stern and more gentle. Kennie feels his father is proud of him now.)* **Comparing and Contrasting**

CUSTOMIZING FOR
Gifted and Talented Students

JJ Mary O'Hara first wrote "My Friend Flicka" as a short story and then expanded it into a novel. Have students read the longer work and prepare a book report on it. Ask them to describe other characters who appear in the novel, to summarize key events, and to discuss how the novel differs from the short story.

COMPREHENSION CHECK

1. What does Kennie's father insist that Kennie do first thing in the morning all summer long? *(study for an hour, because his school grades are poor)*
2. Why does Rob disapprove of Kennie's choice of Flicka as his colt? *(Flicka comes from a line of horses that are particularly difficult to tame.)*
3. What causes Flicka to get seriously hurt soon after she is brought into the corral? *(She tries to escape, becomes tangled in barbed wire, and is badly cut.)*
4. Who helps Kennie care for Flicka's wounds? *(his mother, Nell)*
5. How does the night spent in the stream have opposite effects on Flicka and Kennie? *(The cold water cleans Flicka's wounds and drives the fever from her body. The cold water and exposure cause Kennie to become seriously ill.)*

HH try to save the filly. Ken had gone too far to be let down.

"Ay'm goin' to rig a blanket sling fur her, Tim, and get her on her feet and keep her up."

There was bright moonlight to work by. They brought down the posthole digger and set two aspen poles deep into the ground either side of the filly, then, with ropes attached to the blanket, hoisted her by a pulley.

Not at all disconcerted, she rested comfortably in the blanket under her belly, touched her feet on the ground, and reached for the bucket of water Gus held for her.

Kennie was sick a long time. He nearly died. But Flicka picked up. Every day Gus passed the word to Nell, who carried it to Ken. "She's cleaning up her oats." . . . "She's out of the sling." . . . "She bears a little weight on the bad leg."

Tim declared it was a real miracle. They argued about it, eating their supper.

"Na," said Gus. "It was de cold water, washin' de fever outa her. And more dan dat—it was Ken—you tink it don't count? All night dot boy sits dere and says, 'Hold on, Flicka, Ay'm here wid you. Ay'm standin' by, two of us togedder'—"

Tim stared at Gus without answering, while he thought it over. In the silence, a coyote yapped far off on the plains, and the wind made a rushing sound high up in the jack pines on the hill.

Gus filled his pipe.

"Sure," said Tim finally. "Sure, that's it."

Then came the day when Rob McLaughlin stood smiling at the foot of Kennie's bed and said, "Listen! Hear your friend?"

Ken listened and heard Flicka's high, eager whinny.

"She don't spend much time by the brook anymore. She's up at the gate of the corral half the time, nickering for you."

"For me!"

Rob wrapped a blanket around the boy and carried him out to the corral gate.

Kennie gazed at Flicka. There was a look of marveling in his eyes. He felt as if he had been living in a world where everything was dreadful and hurting but awfully real; and *this* couldn't be real; this was all soft and happy, nothing to struggle over or worry about or fight for any more. Even his father was proud of him! He could feel it in the way Rob's big arms held him. It was all like a dream and far away. He couldn't, yet, get close to anything.

But Flicka—Flicka—alive, well, pressing up to him, recognizing him, nickering—

Kennie put out a hand—weak and white—and laid it on her face. His thin little fingers straightened her forelock the way he used to do, while Rob looked at the two with a strange expression about his mouth and a glow in his eyes that was not often there.

"She's still poor, Dad, but she's on four legs now."

"She's picking up."

Ken turned his face up, suddenly remembering. "Dad! She did get gentled, didn't she?"

"Gentle—as—a kitten—"

They put a cot down by the brook for Ken, and boy and filly got well together. ❖

II

JJ

502   UNIT FOUR   PART 2: TAKING NECESSARY STEPS

Mini-Lesson: Speaking,  Listening, and Viewing

DIALECT Explain to students that writers sometimes use phonetic spellings to represent the speech patterns and sounds of a foreign accent. In this story, the author uses such nonstandard spellings in Gus's dialogue to convey his Swedish accent. Point out to students that such dialect can be difficult to understand. Tell them that a reader may need to slow down, read a passage more than once, or try reading the passage aloud.

Application Have volunteers read the highlighted passage aloud, taking care to pronounce the words as they are spelled. Have students discuss why this is a key passage in the story. *(Possible response: It gives two reasons for Flicka's recovery, one physical—the cold water—and one emotional—Kennie's loyalty and love.)* Then have students skim back through the story to find other examples of phonetic spellings in Gus's speech. Students should copy one passage and then rewrite it using standard spellings.

502   THE LANGUAGE OF LITERATURE TEACHER'S EDITION

RESPONDING OPTIONS

FROM PERSONAL RESPONSE TO CRITICAL ANALYSIS

REFLECT 1. What image from the story had the greatest impact on you? In your notebook, briefly describe the image and how you reacted to it.

RETHINK 2. Do you think Kennie's decision to choose Flicka was a good one? Explain your answer.

Close Textual Reading 3. How would you describe Kennie's relationships with the different members of his family?

4. In your opinion, how does Kennie change during the story?
   Consider
   - his feelings about himself
   - his care of Flicka
   - the personal traits he exhibits

5. If Flicka had died, do you think the lessons Kennie learned from her would have died too? Why or why not?

RELATE 6. At one point, Rob McLaughlin says about his son, "Ken doesn't half try, doesn't stick at anything." How important do you think it is for a nine-year-old to persist at an activity?

Thematic Link

Multimodal Learning
ANOTHER PATHWAY
Cooperative Learning
Present a Readers Theater performance of "My Friend Flicka" for your class. With a group, adapt one or two scenes. Look at the story for dialogue, but feel free to add lines of your own. Try to convey the mood of the scenes you choose through the expression in your voice and the interaction of the characters.

THE WRITER'S STYLE
One reviewer of the novel version of *My Friend Flicka* commented that Mary O'Hara's description "makes you smell the grass and feel the coolness of the wind." Choose a description of the setting or a character from the short story version. Explain how well you think the description appeals to either the sense of sight, hearing, touch, smell, or taste.

QUICKWRITES

1. Write a **diary entry** that Kennie might write during the period when Flicka is sick.

2. Based on Kennie's experiences with Flicka, write some **guidelines** on choosing and taking care of a colt or filly.

📁 **PORTFOLIO** Save your writing. You may want to use it later as a springboard to a piece for your portfolio.

MY FRIEND FLICKA **503**

From Personal Response to Critical Analysis

1. You might also ask students to sketch the image they choose.
2. Possible responses: Kennie had a strong instinct that Flicka was right for him and that he could tame her. Kennie should have chosen a horse that was easier to capture and tame.
3. Possible response: Kennie and his father seem often to be in conflict; Kennie and his mother have a tender and more affectionate relationship; Kennie and Howard seem to have little in common.
4. Possible response: Kennie changes from a boy who is dreamy, confused, and unhappy to one who is focused, dedicated, and more responsible.
5. Possible responses: no, because Kennie would have realized that his persistence, care, and belief in Flicka helped her while she was still alive; yes, because Kennie would have been devastated by the loss of Flicka.
6. Responses will vary.

Another Pathway
Cooperative Learning Divide the class into groups of three to five students, and assign each group a section of the story. You may wish to limit students' scenes to about 15 minutes each. Within each group, one student might select text for narration, one might choose sound effects and background music, and the others might divide up the task of writing dialogue.

Rubric
3 Full Accomplishment Groups' scenes are true to the story and have realistic dialogue.
2 Substantial Accomplishment Groups' scenes are relatively true to the story, and the dialogue is adequate.
1 Little or Partial Accomplishment Groups' scenes do not adequately convey the ideas in the story, and the dialogue is weak.

The Writer's Style
After students have chosen one passage from the story, suggest that they pick a second passage, one that appeals to a different sense. Students can then compare the two passages, analyzing the differences between them.

The Writer's Craft
Appealing to the Senses, pp. 266–273

QuickWrites
1. Suggest that students first skim through Kennie's dialogue to get a feeling for the words and phrases he uses. Students' diary entries might include a description of events as well as an expression of Kennie's feelings toward Flicka and toward his parents.
2. Lead a class discussion in which volunteers suggest section topics for the guidelines—for example, How to Choose a Colt, How to Capture a Colt, How to Care for a Sick Animal.

The Writer's Craft
Writing from Your Journal, pp. 28–39
Directions, pp. 94–105

THE LANGUAGE OF LITERATURE TEACHER'S EDITION **503**

Across the Curriculum

Social Studies *Wide Wyoming* Have students research and write a report on the state of Wyoming, where "My Friend Flicka" takes place. Students can use encyclopedias, guidebooks, atlases, and on-line reference materials. If you wish to have students work in cooperative groups, each group can divide the report into sections, such as geography, climate, history, and lifestyles. Then each group member can be responsible for preparing one section of the report.

Math *Give Me Land, Lots of Land* "My Friend Flicka" was originally published in 1941. The 1940 census gave the population of Wyoming as 250,742; the projected population for the year 2010 is 487,000. The land area of Wyoming is about 97,500 square miles. Have students use these data to compare the population density (people per square mile) for 1940 with the projected density for 2010. *(Answers: 1940—2.57; 2010—4.99; the projected population density is almost double.)*

LITERARY CONCEPTS

To create a story that readers can understand and enjoy, a writer connects the events carefully. The **plot** consists of the actions or events that make up a story. The plot is the writer's plan for what happens, when it happens, and to whom it happens. Make and fill out a story map for "My Friend Flicka" similar to the one shown.

CONCEPT REVIEW: Suspense As you know, suspense is the feeling of excitement that grows when the reader wants to know how a situation will turn out. Flicka's attempt to jump over the fence, for example, is a moment of suspense. Locate and describe another suspenseful part of the story.

Main Character:
Setting:
Conflict or Story Problem:
Major Events:
Event 1
Event 2
Event 3 (add more as needed)
Solution:
Theme:

Multimodal Learning

ALTERNATIVE ACTIVITIES

1. Design a **poster** to advertise a new movie version of "My Friend Flicka." Using either hand-drawn art or magazine pictures, try to capture the mood of the story in an illustration.
2. The word *yearling* is one of many special terms in the story that relate to horses. Review the story, and make a list of the specialized vocabulary words. Using reference materials, define the words and list them alphabetically. Combine your definitions with illustrations to create a **pocket dictionary** of horse terms to accompany the story.

CRITIC'S CORNER

Mary O'Hara said of Kennie, the main character of "My Friend Flicka," "I don't know where Ken came from. He just walked into my heart and mind one day readymade." Do you think O'Hara is successful in making Kennie McLaughlin seem like a real-life person? Write your opinions in your notebook, taking into account the way in which Kennie speaks, feels, and acts throughout the story.

504 UNIT FOUR PART 2: TAKING NECESSARY STEPS

Alternative Activities

1. Lead a class discussion in which students discuss elements of movie advertisements they have seen. Students can think about both printed advertisements and television commercials. On the chalkboard or overhead projector, list the elements included in the ads as students describe them.
2. Students' lists can include types of horses (colt, pedigreed, brood mare, yearling, sorrel, stallion), specialized activities (break, groom, gentle), and equipment used in riding or caring for horses (bridle, tack, halter).

Literary Concepts

The story-map activity is appropriate for small-group work. Divide the class into groups of three to four students. Then have each group divide the story into sections. Each student can be responsible for drafting a summary of the events in his or her section. Some group discussion may be needed for students to agree on what constitutes an "event" in the story. Members can share and discuss their work before preparing a final story map.

CONCEPT REVIEW: Suspense Possible suspenseful parts of the story include Flicka's rapid decline in health, Rob's decision to have Flicka killed, the scene in which Kennie and Flicka are in the stream overnight, and Gus's internal debate about whether to follow Rob's orders to shoot Flicka.

WORDS TO KNOW

EXERCISE A Answer the following questions.

1. Would a person who was **fanatical** about watching TV watch none, a little, or a lot?
2. If a father asked a **rebellious** child to do something, would that child be most likely to say "Yes, sir!" "Do I have to?" or "No!"?
3. Would a person who is feeling **despair** most likely sigh, giggle, or yawn?
4. Does a person with a lot of **prestige** usually get treated with scorn, respect, or amusement?
5. If you **envision** an event, do you see it in a photograph, in your mind, or in a movie?

EXERCISE B For each phrase in the first column, write the letter of the phrase from the second column that means the same thing.

1. a vague uneasiness
2. resist the urge to whine
3. a fidgety referee
4. a blissful father
5. follow the sailors

(a) a jumpy ump
(b) pursue the crew
(c) a blurry worry
(d) refrain from complaining
(e) a glad dad

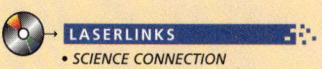

MARY O'HARA

1885–1980

The author of "My Friend Flicka," the beloved children's classic, began her writing career as a scriptwriter in the 1920s, during the early days of motion pictures. In 1931, Mary O'Hara Alsop traded screen writing for story writing and moved with her husband to a sheep ranch in Wyoming. There she found herself in a "different world.... Vast. Empty. Glowing with heavenly colors." She used her maiden name, O'Hara, as her pen name.

One day, as O'Hara struggled with a story idea that was not working out, she recalled that when she told stories about her many animals, people always seemed to listen. "How easy it would be," she thought, to write a story "about that little filly, for instance, the one that got caught in the barbed wire." Within 24 hours, she had written the notes and a few scenes for a short story called "My Friend Flicka." In 1941, O'Hara expanded the short story into a novel and continued the story of the McLaughlin family in other works. Three of her books were made into movies in the 1940s.

OTHER WORKS *Thunderhead, Green Grass of Wyoming, The Son of Adam Wyngate, The Catch Colt* Extended Reading

• SCIENCE CONNECTION

MY FRIEND FLICKA **505**

Words to Know

Exercise A
1. a lot
2. No!
3. sigh
4. respect
5. in your mind

Exercise B
1. c
2. d
3. a
4. e
5. b

Reteaching/Reinforcement
• *Unit Four Resource Book*, p. 66

MARY O'HARA

Although Mary O'Hara is best known for her three books about the McLaughlin family, she also published a novel called *The Son of Adam Wyngate*, in 1952. Her 1954 book, *Novel-in-the-Making*, examines the process of writing that novel. O'Hara also composed music, including the "Wyoming Suite for Piano" (1946). Mary O'Hara Alsop used her first and middle names as her pen name but published a few writings under her married name, Mary Sture-Vasa.

SCIENCE CONNECTION
Wild Horses Ever since horses were domesticated, they have been used for many purposes. This film explains why wild horses in the western United States are caught and tamed by ranchers.

Side A, Frame 28800

WHAT DO YOU THINK?

Reflecting on Theme

Have students refer back to the introduction they wrote before beginning the selections in Part Two. Ask students to write a similar introduction for Kennie, one in which they discuss the steps Kennie took to meet his challenge and what those steps mean to them.

THE LANGUAGE OF LITERATURE **TEACHER'S EDITION 505**

OVERVIEW

To gain a deeper appreciation of the selections they have read in this unit, students will explore the characteristics of a compare-and-contrast essay and then create their own essay in this lesson.

Objectives

- To plan a compare-and-contrast essay by considering such elements as audience, purpose, and organization
- To draft a compare-and-contrast essay and solicit a response to it
- To revise, edit, and publish a compare-and-contrast essay
- To reflect on the process of writing a compare-and-contrast essay

Skills

LITERATURE
- Finding details

WRITING AND LANGUAGE
- Analyzing audience
- Identifying purpose
- Using transitions
- Choosing features to compare

GRAMMAR AND USAGE
- Using comparatives and superlatives

MEDIA LITERACY
- Interpreting cartoons
- Studying want ads
- Reading announcements
- Creating graphic organizers

CRITICAL THINKING
- Using graphic organizers

SPEAKING, LISTENING, AND VIEWING
- Holding a panel discussion
- Reading aloud

Teaching Strategy: MODELING

A To show students how to generate writing ideas from a cartoon or other visual model, invite volunteers to role-play the situation depicted in the cartoon. Then have students work in pairs to role-play other "middle school blues" scenarios for the class. Have students write down the scenes that would make good writing topics for a compare-and-contrast essay.

WRITING FROM EXPERIENCE

WRITING TO EXPLAIN

As you learned in Unit Four, "Proving Ground," the challenges we face in life often bring out either the best or the worst in us. Would you have reacted in the same way as the characters in the stories if you had been in their shoes? Comparing people, places, things, and ideas can help you better understand a subject, make a decision, or prove a point. In this way, comparing and contrasting may help you get through your own personal proving ground.

GUIDED ASSIGNMENT
Write a Compare-Contrast Essay In this lesson you will have the opportunity to explore the similarities and differences between two subjects.

Cartoon
Humor often comes from comparing people and situations.

❶ Why Make Comparisons?

The world is filled with things to compare. What do you and your best friend have in common? How are the two of you different? Would you rather play the trumpet or the trombone? You might find yourself making comparisons to help you do the following things.

Explain the Unfamiliar Sometimes the best way to understand or explain something unusual is to compare it to something familiar. The food described in the book excerpt on the next page may be new to you. How might a comparison help you decide whether you'd like it?

Make a Decision Studying the differences between two or more things can help you make choices. Based on the information in the ad and the announcement on the opposite page, would you rather have a paper route or be in a play?

❷ What Will You Compare?

Make some notes about possible topics.

- Is there a person you wish your friends knew, a place you'd like them to imagine, or an idea you want to show? How could you help them understand the topic through a comparison?
- Do you have a difficult decision to make? Jot down your possible choices.

Decision Point Freewrite for a few minutes to see what thoughts you uncover, and then choose the comparison that interests you most.

506 UNIT FOUR: PROVING GROUND

PRINT AND MEDIA RESOURCES

UNIT FOUR RESOURCE BOOK
Prewriting, p. 69
Elaboration, p. 70
Peer Response Guide, pp. 71–72
Revising and Proofreading, p. 73
Student Model, p. 74
Rubric, p. 75

GRAMMAR MINI-LESSONS
Transparencies, p. 13
Copymasters, p. 20

WRITING MINI-LESSONS
Transparencies, p. 33

ACCESS FOR STUDENTS ACQUIRING ENGLISH
Reading and Writing Support

FORMAL ASSESSMENT
Guidelines for Writing Assessment

 **WRITING COACH**

 **LASERLINKS**
Writing Springboard

506 THE LANGUAGE OF LITERATURE TEACHER'S EDITION

Excerpt from a Book

Want Ad

W a n t e d :
The Huronville Daily News is seeking responsible students to deliver afternoon weekday papers. Routes range from four to eight blocks. (More customers, higher pay!) Will be expected to deliver in all weather conditions. Must provide own transportation. Required to collect payments monthly. Must be reliable! Call 555-NEWS for an application.

Mom wants me to find something to do after school. Maybe get a job?

Announcement

Be a ST★R!
Tryouts for *The Phantom Tollbooth*

When: March 6th, 3:30 P.M.
Where: In the school auditorium
How: Those interested in reading for a part can pick up a script in the drama room (#118) this week.
Rehearsals: Mondays and Wednesdays 3:30–5:30 P.M. and Saturdays 9–11 A.M.
Performances: June 1st and 2nd

Or I could try out for this play.... Which activity should I choose?

Buttra, Oudom, and Richard Prek moved to the United States from Cambodia with their mother, Sohka, and grandmother, Sok Eng. The food they eat is a daily reminder of the Cambodian culture they left behind.

For dinner, the boys eat the kind of food their grandmother knew as a child in Cambodia and that she learned to cook as a young bride and mother. It is nothing like the bread or the spaghetti or the other foods they see and sometimes eat at school, but it is the kind of food they have eaten all their lives, and they love it. Each evening, their grandmother's pots simmer and sizzle with spicy fried rice and rice noodles; warm white rice; spring rolls; *bawbaw*, a chicken soup with Asian vegetables; or any of the other traditional dishes that Sok Eng manages to make using the foods she and Sohka find in the Asian markets of Boston. Everyone eats in the living room, sitting on the couch or floor, as they would in Cambodia, using the silverware they were introduced to here.

Nancy Price Graff
from *Where the River Runs: A Portrait of a Refugee Family*

→ LASERLINKS
• WRITING SPRINGBOARD
→ WRITING COACH

WRITING FROM EXPERIENCE 507

Teaching Strategy: MODELING

B Challenge students to compare and contrast the style of the want ad and the announcement with the style of an essay. Explore how want ads and announcements use an abbreviated style in which most articles *(a, an, the)*, adjectives, and adverbs are eliminated. Also point out the use of sentence fragments, and explain that fragments are acceptable in these writing forms because space is at a premium. Have volunteers read aloud the student's comments accompanying the models. Then have students create a chart in which they list ideas for additional want ads and announcements. Share the following sample chart with students:

Want Ads	Announcements
dog walker	club meeting
leaf raker	room change
baby sitter	movie times

Media Literacy: ANALYZING AN EXCERPT FROM A BOOK

C Critical Thinking: ANALYZING To help students develop their comparing and contrasting skills, have them prepare a chart in which they list, in one column, elements of the meal described in the excerpt and, in a second column, parallel elements of a meal in their home. Then have students use an equals sign (=) to mark elements that are comparable and a not-equal-to sign (≠) to mark elements that contrast.

WRITING SPRINGBOARD
The Boys Choir of Harlem A member of the choir explains how participation in the group has helped him develop his values and sense of self-worth.

Side B, Frame 17783

Writing Prompt Membership in organized groups can affect young people in different ways. Write an essay in which you compare the behaviors and attitudes of a person you know before and after the person joined a particular group.

THE LANGUAGE OF LITERATURE TEACHER'S EDITION **507**

CUSTOMIZING FOR
Less-Proficient Writers

D Inexperienced writers often have a difficult time identifying key points for a compare-and-contrast essay. They tend to settle on obvious points and to avoid the more detailed features of their topic. After students brainstorm the key features of their topic, have them work in pairs to explore each other's key points. Encourage partners to use questions and answers to help them probe the points in depth.

Research Skill: USING THE LIBRARY

E Encourage students to research their topic in the library in order to find specific details. To make the researching easier for students, remind them about the following library resources:

- Almanacs and yearbooks: current facts and statistics on topics in such areas as government, sports, and population
- Atlases: books of maps that contain facts about highways, population, government, climate, landforms, and so on
- Encyclopedias: collections of informational articles written by experts
- Periodicals: newspapers, magazines, and journals
- Vertical files: pamphlets, photos, handbooks, and clippings from periodicals on many popular topics

---

PREWRITING

Working Through Ideas

Maps of Your Notes Now that you've chosen two subjects to compare, you're ready to discover ways they are similar and different. The steps on these pages will help you recognize the differences and organize your observations.

❶ Choose Features to Compare

To compare your subjects, you'll need to decide which characteristics, or features, you want to examine. The student writer is comparing being in a play with having a paper route. He identified the key points that would affect his decision:

- time commitment
- enjoyment
- skills he'd learn
- others who would be involved

List three or four features of your subjects that you'd like to compare.

❷ Find and Diagram the Details

Now look at each feature you listed. How are your two subjects similar and different? List all the details you can. Do research if necessary. You may want to use a chart like the one below to help you organize your observations.

In the first column, list the features you chose to compare. Then, under each of your subjects, write down details that show how the subjects are similar or different. The SkillBuilder will show you how to make another type of organizer—a Venn diagram.

Student's Comparison Chart

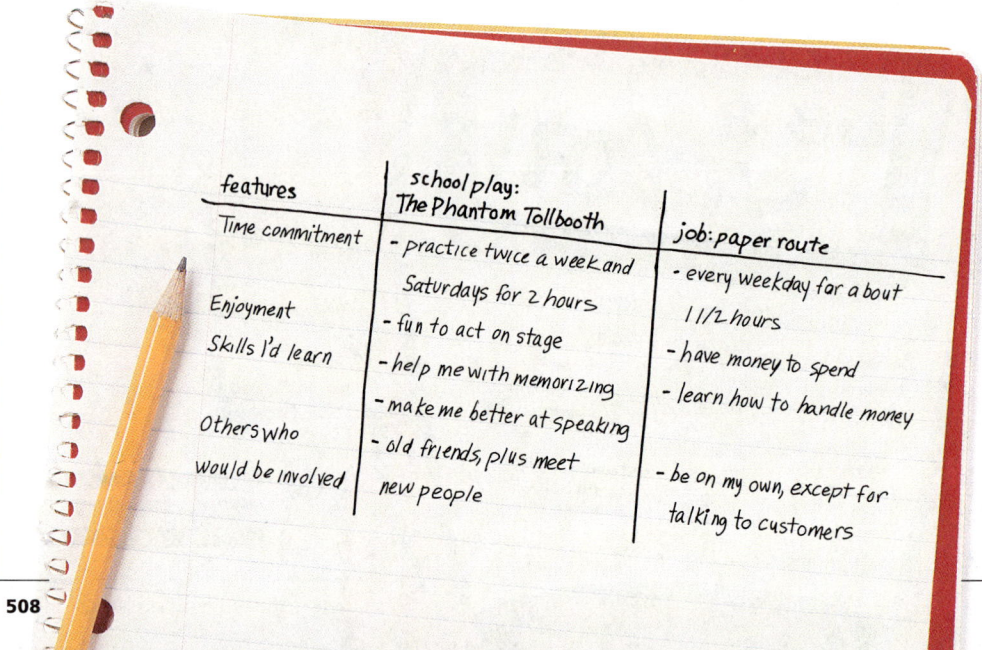

 Mini-Lesson　Study Skills

USING A KWL CHART Explain to students that using a KWL chart can help them generate and organize details for their compare-and-contrast essay. Describe how a KWL chart uses questions to tap students' prior knowledge and to help them organize their research. Explain what KWL stands for:

K: What do I already *know* about the topic?
W: What do I *want* to learn?
L: What did I *learn*?

Then show them the following model by writing it on the board or using an overhead projector:
Topic: Collecting CDs versus records

K	W	L

Application Have students work in small groups to fill in a KWL chart for the topic shown. A completed chart might look like this:

K	W	L
sound quality	titles available	CDs would be better for me.
durability	maximum playing time	
cost		

508 THE LANGUAGE OF LITERATURE TEACHER'S EDITION

3 Know Your Audience

Who will your audience be: your classmates, your parents, or members of your community? You may want to write just for yourself, as the student trying to decide between the job and the play is doing. If you are writing for others, how can you best reach them? What might they already know about your subjects?

Decision Point Will you want to include diagrams or illustrations in your presentation to help you show your comparison?

4 Think Before You Draft

Before you begin writing your draft, think about how you will organize your comparison. Here are two methods you might try.

Subject-by-Subject One way to organize is to cover all the features of one subject first, and then describe the second subject, explaining how each feature is similar to or different from the first subject.

Feature-by-Feature Another method is to examine one feature at a time, comparing both subjects and then moving on to the next feature.

Page 791 of the Writing Handbook provides more information on organizing your comparison-contrast essay.

Student's Organizational Notes

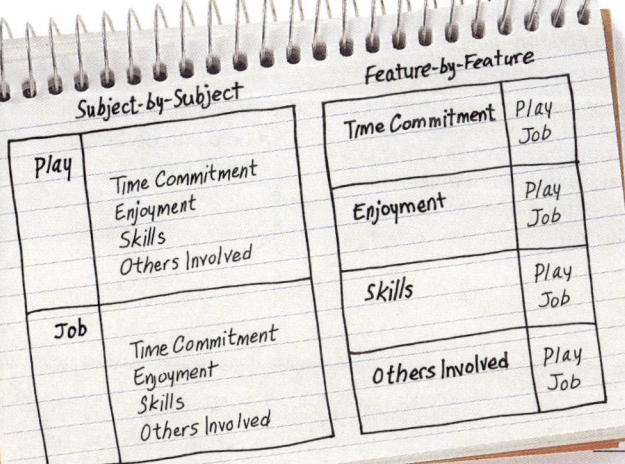

SkillBuilder

 **CRITICAL THINKING**

Using Graphic Organizers

Comparison charts and diagrams not only can help you set up your ideas for writing, they can also be added to your published piece to help you show your readers more clearly how your subjects measure up.

To create a Venn diagram, write down how your subjects are different in the outer part of each circle. In the space where the circles overlap, list what your subjects have in common.

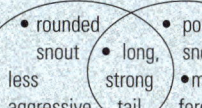

APPLYING WHAT YOU'VE LEARNED
Try making both a comparison chart and a Venn diagram, then decide which organizer works better for your purposes.

THINK & PLAN

Reflecting on Your Ideas

1. Do you want to focus on the similarities or differences between your subjects or both? Your choice will depend on your purpose.
2. Which method of organization will you use: subject-by-subject or feature-by-feature? Why?

WRITING FROM EXPERIENCE 509

Writing Skill:
IDENTIFYING AUDIENCE

F Be sure that students understand that their audience is the group of people with whom they will share their writing. Explore how thinking about audience will help students make better decisions as writers. For example, having a firm sense of audience will make it easier for students to think about purpose and tone. Guide students to make a checklist to help them analyze their audience. Suggest they use the following questions:
- What background information do my readers need?
- What part of my topic will interest my audience most?
- How can I best get the attention of my audience?

CUSTOMIZING FOR
Less-Proficient Writers

G Students may benefit from a visual representation of the two methods of organizing a compare-and-contrast essay. On the chalkboard, draw a diagram for each of the two methods described. Explain that a subject-by-subject composition will contain at least four paragraphs. To show this, draw four boxes in a vertical line and label the top box *Introduction*, the second box *Subject 1*, the third box *Subject 2*, and the last box *Conclusion*. Illustrate the feature-by-feature pattern with five boxes, labeled *Introduction*, *Feature 1*, *Feature 2*, *Feature 3*, and *Conclusion*.

SkillBuilder CRITICAL THINKING

USING GRAPHIC ORGANIZERS Explain that comparison charts and Venn diagrams are especially useful in organizing material for compare-and-contrast essays because they allow writers to discover gaps in their information quickly and easily. Using one student's topic, take the class through the process of completing a graphic organizer. As you model the process on the chalkboard, guide students to complete one section of the organizer before they place information in another section. Use multicolored chalk to help students categorize and distinguish information.

Applying What You've Learned Caution students that topic, purpose, and audience often determine which graphic organizer will work the best, so they cannot assume that one particular organizer will always be the most suitable.

Additional Suggestions Encourage students to customize any comparison chart or other graphic organizer to fit their needs.

Writing Skill: USING THE COMPUTER

H Explore with students some of the advantages of drafting on a computer, such as freedom to explore ideas, speed of composition, ease of revision, and ability to correct spelling errors. Urge students to draft their essays on the computer and to use The Writing Coach, which provides step-by-step help for this stage of the writing process.

Teaching Strategy: MODELING

I As you take students through the model discovery draft, point out the indicators the writer used to highlight the key points of compare and contrast. Refer to the organizational notes on page 509 so that students can see how the writer picked up each issue. Guide students to do the same thing as they draft their essays.

Teaching Strategy: MANAGING THE PAPER LOAD

To cut down on the time needed to evaluate final drafts, ask students to hand in their compare-and-contrast charts, Venn diagrams, and any other prewriting items when they are completed. Review these materials before students begin writing in order to find potential problems that students can address as they draft.

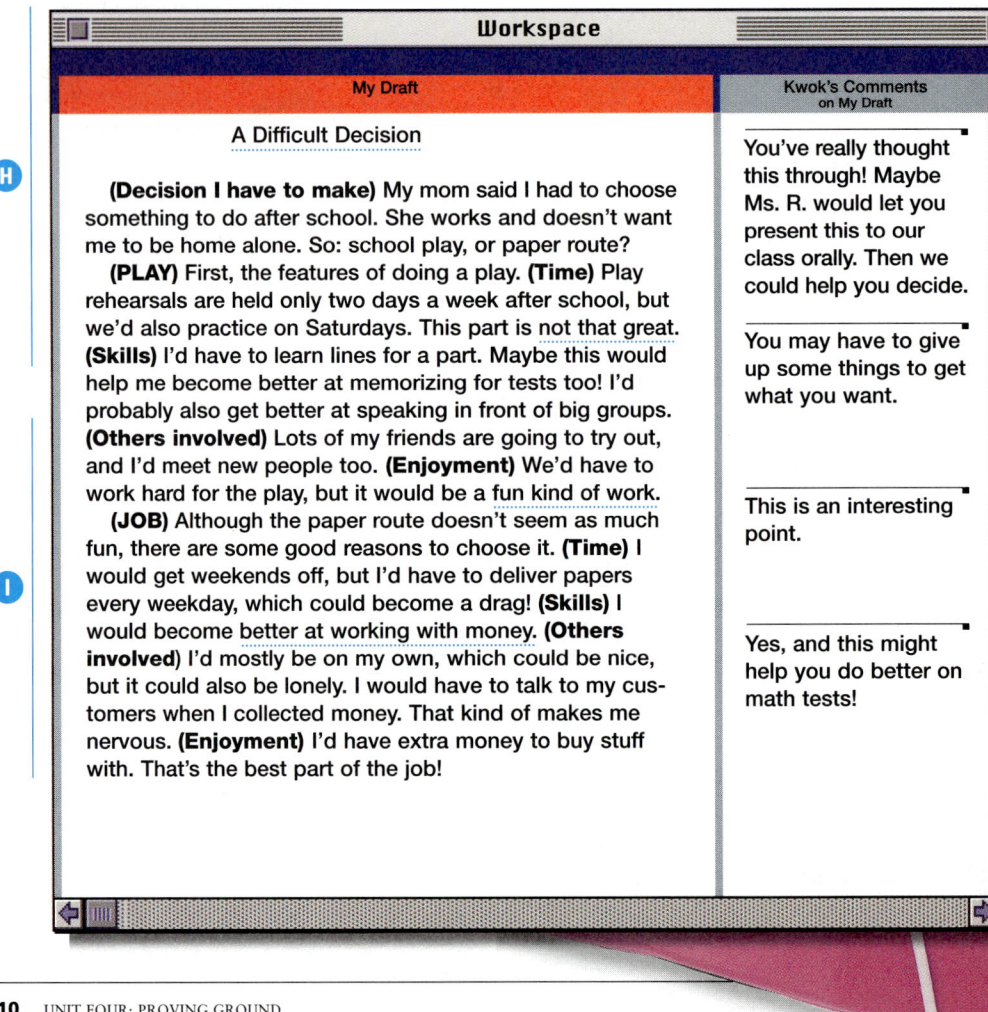

DRAFTING

Thinking on the Page

A Clearer Focus Now you're ready to begin drafting your comparison. What have you discovered by studying the features of your subjects? Do you have a better understanding of something or someone? Are you now able to make a decision? Get ready to tell your readers what you have learned.

1 Draft to Discover
Start by writing the part of the comparison you feel most comfortable with. Don't limit yourself to the information in your charts, diagrams, or other prewriting notes. New ideas or features may occur to you while you're writing.

Student's Discovery Draft

Workspace

My Draft | **Kwok's Comments on My Draft**

A Difficult Decision

(Decision I have to make) My mom said I had to choose something to do after school. She works and doesn't want me to be home alone. So: school play, or paper route?

(PLAY) First, the features of doing a play. **(Time)** Play rehearsals are held only two days a week after school, but we'd also practice on Saturdays. This part is not that great. **(Skills)** I'd have to learn lines for a part. Maybe this would help me become better at memorizing for tests too! I'd probably also get better at speaking in front of big groups. **(Others involved)** Lots of my friends are going to try out, and I'd meet new people too. **(Enjoyment)** We'd have to work hard for the play, but it would be a fun kind of work.

(JOB) Although the paper route doesn't seem as much fun, there are some good reasons to choose it. **(Time)** I would get weekends off, but I'd have to deliver papers every weekday, which could become a drag! **(Skills)** I would become better at working with money. **(Others involved)** I'd mostly be on my own, which could be nice, but it could also be lonely. I would have to talk to my customers when I collected money. That kind of makes me nervous. **(Enjoyment)** I'd have extra money to buy stuff with. That's the best part of the job!

You've really thought this through! Maybe Ms. R. would let you present this to our class orally. Then we could help you decide.

You may have to give up some things to get what you want.

This is an interesting point.

Yes, and this might help you do better on math tests!

510 UNIT FOUR: PROVING GROUND

WRITING SPRINGBOARD
Talking with Writer Judith Nihei
This author talks about what living in two cultures is like.

Side B, Frame 20307

Writing Prompt Think about a situation in your own culture. Then imagine what a similar situation might be like in another culture. Compare the two situations.

510 THE LANGUAGE OF LITERATURE TEACHER'S EDITION

② Evaluate Your Draft

Check to make sure you have explained your ideas thoroughly to your readers by asking yourself the following questions:

- Do the details I include show both how my subjects are similar and how they are different?
- Would my comparison be clearer if I organized my information differently?
- How might I publish my comparison to best reach and teach my audience? (See page 513 for publishing ideas.)

③ Rework Your Comparison

Once you have evaluated your draft, you may want to change a few things. The following tips can help you rework your essay.

Introduction Be sure you introduce at the beginning of your essay what you will be comparing. Your introduction should also make it clear why you are making a comparison.

Body To help readers follow your comparison, begin a new paragraph for each subject (when using subject-by-subject organization) or for each feature (when using feature-by-feature organization).

Conclusion You may have learned something surprising or formed new ideas as you compared your subjects. You might want to mention these discoveries in your conclusion.

PEER RESPONSE

Here are some questions to ask a peer reviewer so that you can get helpful feedback on your essay. If you are using the Writing Coach, comments can be typed into the side column.

- Why do you think I chose to compare these subjects?
- Which points of comparison did you find most interesting? least interesting?
- What other features might I have compared?
- Have I strayed from my organizational pattern? Where?

SkillBuilder

WRITER'S CRAFT

Using Transitions
Transition words and phrases can help you to draw attention to similarities and differences between subjects or features.

Both the play and paper route take time after school, but play rehearsals are on Saturdays too.

Transitions that signal	
similarities	**differences**
• both	• but
• also	• instead
• neither	• however
• in addition	• yet
• similarly	• unlike
• likewise	• on the other hand

WRITING HANDBOOK

For more information on using transitions, see page 781 of the Writing Handbook.

APPLYING WHAT YOU LEARNED
Where might you add transitions in your comparison to make it stronger or clearer?

RETHINK & EVALUATE

Preparing to Revise

1. Would reorganizing your comparison make it easier to follow? Why?
2. What do you like about your draft? What parts do you still need to work on?

WRITING FROM EXPERIENCE **511**

Writing Skill: INTRODUCTION

J Give students examples of how the different types of introductions they have learned about can be adapted for use in compare-and-contrast essays. Focus on these three methods: startling fact, question, and anecdote. Encourage students to use these methods to create interesting openings.

CUSTOMIZING FOR
Less-Proficient Writers

K Inexperienced writers often have difficulty writing conclusions. To help students write a logical, effective ending to their essay, present these guidelines:

- Do not get off track. Avoid introducing entirely new ideas or adding a fact that belongs in the body of the essay.
- Do not merely repeat your introduction. If the introduction and the conclusion are interchangeable, rewrite the conclusion.
- Do not announce what you have done. Avoid statements such as "In this paper, I have compared and contrasted two sports."
- Do not make absolute claims. Avoid statements such as "This proves that records are always better than CDs."
- Do not apologize. Avoid statements such as "I may not have thought of all the points, but I did the best I could."

SkillBuilder WRITER'S CRAFT

USING TRANSITIONS Be sure students understand that transitions are words and phrases that signal connections between ideas. Explain that by signaling how ideas relate to each other, writers achieve coherence in their writing. Make the analogy that transitions are signs that alert readers to important ideas in the paper.

Applying What You've Learned Arrange students in pairs. Ask the partners to read each other's essay and to underline all the transitions. Then direct each student to look at his or her own essay, focusing attention on sentences in which nothing is underlined. These sentences might require a transition.

Additional Suggestions As students revise their work, they can write the transitions in a different color of ink to make them stand out from the rest of the essay. Explain to students that other methods of achieving coherence in their work include using deliberate repetition and using parallel structure.

Reteaching/Reinforcement
- *Writing Handbook*, anthology pp. 781–782
- *Writing Mini-Lessons* transparencies, p. 33

📘 **The Writer's Craft**
Transitions, pp. 234–238

THE LANGUAGE OF LITERATURE TEACHER'S EDITION **511**

Writing Skill: REVISING

L Explain to students that they should be systematic as they revise. They should not revise at random but should pay attention to each element in turn, from overall organization to word choice. Encourage students to use the Standards for Evaluation on page 513 as they revise their essays.

Teaching Strategy: MODELING

M Invite volunteers to read aloud the model oral presentation notes. Then explore with the class the transitional words and phrases the writer has used, including *both* and *but*. Have students identify these transitions as showing similarities or differences.

Speaking, Listening, and Viewing: COLLABORATIVE OPPORTUNITY

N Arrange students in small groups to facilitate peer review. Have each group member read his or her essay aloud to the other members so that they may determine the soundness of the similarities and differences raised in the essay. After each student is done reading, have the group isolate the points that compare and contrast in order to help the writer see where additional facts, examples, or details are needed.

REVISING & PUBLISHING

Pulling It All Together

The Final Stages Before sharing your comparison with others, use the guidelines on these pages to help you improve your essay. If you've decided to present your explanation in a special format, you may want to make some additional changes. For example, the student writer decided to take his peer reader's advice and get his classmates' help with his decision.

Student's Oral Presentation Notes

> **1**
> What I am comparing and why:
> My mom works. She asked me to find something to get involved with after school so that I won't be home alone.
>
> I compared working on the school play to delivering papers for the *Huronville Daily News* to help me decide which I'd rather spend my time doing.

> **3**
> Feature Two: Skills I'd Learn

> **2**
> Feature One: Time Commitment
> Both activities would take lots of time. (play) Rehearsals for *The Phantom Tollbooth* last two hours and are held three times a week. Practices are held on Saturday, which is not so cool. (job) The time it takes to deliver papers each day is shorter than play rehearsals (1 1/2 hours instead of 2). The paper route would keep me busier more days during the week, but I'd be free on weekends.

> **4**
> Feature Three: Others Involved

> **5**
> Feature Four: Enjoyment

> **6**
> After comparing these two activities, I discovered they are more alike than I thought. I guess that's why I liked them both to begin with. Now I see that working at a job can be fun, and a play is not only fun but hard work too. So which should I choose? Can you help me decide?

M What transition words or phrases did the student writer use in his comparison?

① Revise and Edit

Give yourself and your draft a rest and then read it again. How well have you examined your subjects?

- See how one student created note cards to help him remember important points he wanted to present orally.
- Use the SkillBuilder on page 513 to check your use of comparatives and superlatives.
- Refer to the Standards for Evaluation to improve each part of your comparison.

512 UNIT FOUR: PROVING GROUND

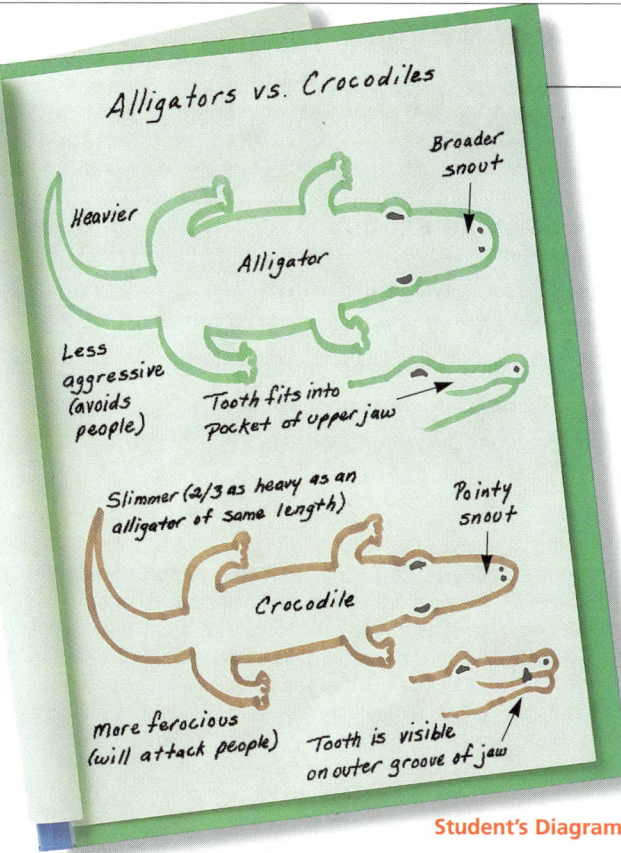

Student's Diagram

② Share Your Comparison

You may want to include photographs or drawings of your subjects to help show their similarities and differences. The example above shows how another student added diagrams with captions to his essay to highlight the features he was comparing.

Standards for Evaluation

A comparison-contrast essay
- states clearly the subjects being compared and shows how they are alike and different
- is easy to follow, using either feature-by-feature or subject-by-subject organization
- uses transitions to signal similarities and differences
- ends with a conclusion that explains the decision made or a new understanding of the subjects compared

SkillBuilder

 GRAMMAR FROM WRITING

Using Comparatives and Superlatives
Use the **comparative** form when you are comparing or contrasting two subjects.

Play rehearsals are **more fun** *than delivering papers.*

Use the **superlative** form when you are comparing or contrasting three or more subjects.

I would like the **fastest** *bike of all for my paper route.*

GRAMMAR HANDBOOK

For more help with comparatives and superlatives, see pages 831–832 of the Grammar Handbook.

Editing Checklist Check these points as you revise your draft.
- Did you use transitions?
- Have you used the correct form of comparatives and superlatives?

REFLECT & ASSESS

Evaluating Your Experience
1. What did you learn about your subjects by comparing them?
2. How did your prewriting notes or diagrams help you write your essay?

📁 **PORTFOLIO** What did you accomplish by writing this essay? Add your answer and assignment to your portfolio.

WRITING FROM EXPERIENCE   **513**

Teaching Strategy:
COLLABORATIVE OPPORTUNITY

O To help students become aware of the importance of titles, have them experiment with creating different titles for one another's essays. Arrange students in pairs, and ask each student to state the thesis of the essay he or she is going to title. Then have both students generate different titles and explain their reasons for each one.

Writing Skill: USING THE COMPUTER

P Suggest that students use the computer to create graphics, clip art, or original art to accompany their essays. Many of the standard computer software packages include professional and easy-to-use graphics.

PORTFOLIO
Encourage students to include any graphic organizers or art along with their final essays. At the point when students complete the Reflect & Assess activities of Unit Four (pages 514–515), they may refer to these materials.

Standards for Evaluation

Have students review their essay for the following:

Ideas and Content
- states clearly the subjects being compared
- indicates a reason or purpose for the comparison
- compares and contrasts subjects clearly
- ends with a conclusion that explains a decision made or a new understanding of the subjects compared

Structure and Form
- organizes ideas logically, using either a feature-by-feature or subject-by-subject format
- uses transitions to signal similarities and differences
- devotes one paragraph to each main idea

Grammar, Usage, and Mechanics
- contains no more than two or three minor errors in grammar and usage
- contains no more than two or three minor errors in spelling, capitalization, and punctuation

---

SkillBuilder GRAMMAR FROM WRITING

USING COMPARATIVES AND SUPERLATIVES Tell students that they can show degrees of comparison by adding the endings *-er* or *-est* to adjectives and adverbs or by adding the words *more, most, less,* or *least*. Share with students the chart shown.

Applying What You've Learned Have students rewrite each of the following sentences, using the comparative and then the superlative form of the adjective shown.
1. The movie was frightening.
2. We had a big birthday party.
3. She found a rare book.

Positive Degree	Comparative Degree	Superlative Degree
Describes one thing	Compares two things	Compares three or more things
tall	taller	tallest
good	better	best
bad	worse	worst
many	more	most
much	more	most
little	less	least

THE LANGUAGE OF LITERATURE TEACHER'S EDITION   **513**

UNIT REVIEW

This feature allows students to reflect on what they have learned in Unit Four and to assess how well they understand what they have learned. This feature provides students with multiple opportunities for self-assessment, although you may wish to use some of the activities to informally assess specific skills such as speaking and listening or cooperative work.

Objectives

- To allow students to reflect on and assess their understanding of theme
- To allow students to reflect on and assess their understanding of literary concepts such as characterization and symbol
- To provide students with the opportunity to assess and build their portfolios

REFLECTING ON THEME

OPTION 1

Have students support their choices with details from the selection to show how they were able to infer a character's qualities from his or her behavior, thoughts, and actions. Be sure that students also are able to support their choices for the quality most necessary for success.

OPTION 2

Tell students that they may need to reread or skim some of the selections in order to generate lists of personal qualities. Encourage them to make their own suggestions for personal qualities as well. Make sure students provide adequate support for their opinions with details from the selections.

Self-Assessment Ask students to think about what they most admire about their chosen characters and to include this information in their sketches. Suggest in addition that students consider how they would have responded in the same situations.

514 THE LANGUAGE OF LITERATURE **TEACHER'S EDITION**

REFLECT & ASSESS

UNIT FOUR: PROVING GROUND

In this unit, individuals discover what really matters—in growing up, in making friends, and in meeting physical challenges. Which of their discoveries meant the most to you? See what doing one or more of the options in each of the following sections can reveal.

REFLECTING ON THEME

OPTION 1 Comparing Qualities What qualities are shared by people who attempt to prove themselves? Make a chart, like the one shown, to record the qualities of three people in this unit. A section for Carlos (in "The Secret of the Wall") has been started for you. Color or shade in the boxes for the qualities you think each character has, adding more qualities if you wish. Compare diagrams with a partner. Then circle the name of the quality you think is the most necessary for success.

Character	Determined	Fearless	Generous	Honest
Carlos				

OPTION 2 Giving Characters Report Cards What personal qualities do you think "prove" or reveal a person's true nature? Make a list of the qualities that are shown by characters in the selections, as well as other qualities that you think are signs of personal growth or maturity. Use the list to evaluate four characters in this unit. In your opinion, which character grows the most as the events of the story unfold? Discuss your choice with a partner.

Self-Assessment: One character may have come to your mind often as you completed one of these activities. If you could follow the example set by one person in the unit, which person would it be? In your notebook, write a short character sketch of that person and tell what he or she means to you.

REVIEWING LITERARY CONCEPTS

OPTION 1 Thinking About Characterization You know that the way an author creates and develops a character's personality is called characterization. Choose one character from each selection. Then using a chart like the one shown here, analyze how each character is developed. Which character do you think you came to know best? Why?

What does the character look like?	What are the character's thoughts?
What do others think about the character?	How does the author describe the character's personality?

514 UNIT FOUR: PROVING GROUND

OPTION 2 **Looking at Symbols** You have learned that in literature, objects and images are used to symbolize things—such as ideas or feelings—that cannot be seen. Copy this diagram and work with a partner to identify a symbol in each of the three selections listed. Discuss what you think each symbol stands for.

Uses of Symbols in Selections		
"The Secret of the Wall"	"The White Umbrella"	"At Last I Kill a Buffalo"

PORTFOLIO BUILDING

- **QuickWrites** Two of the QuickWrites assignments in this unit gave you opportunities to write speeches. Choose the speech that you think would be more interesting to present to a group. Use a pencil to lightly underline the parts of the speech that you think are the strongest. In a cover note, explain why you think it presents your ideas so well. Then add the speech and the note to your portfolio.

- **Writing About Literature** In your essay, you had a chance to write an additional scene for a story. Reread your scene. Then write a letter to the author of the story, telling him or her why that scene should be added to the story. Explain why you think your scene fits with what he or she wrote. Attach a copy of your letter to your essay if you decide to include it in your portfolio.

- **Writing from Experience** Earlier in this unit, you compared and contrasted two subjects. Did you find any similarities between the subjects that you didn't expect? Did you find differences that you didn't know about before? Write down your thoughts and attach them to your compare-contrast essay.

- **Personal Choice** Look over the notes, graphics, and records you created for projects in this unit. In addition, review your work for Personal Connections, Writing Connections, and alternative and cross-curricular activities. Choose a piece of writing or an activity in which you made an experience come alive for your audience through vivid language or strong presentation. Write a note explaining how you achieved this result. Attach the note to the piece of writing or the project evaluation, and place them in your portfolio.

 Self-Assessment: Look over and compare the earliest work in your portfolio with your more recent work. Write a note to yourself, describing what you now see as your strengths and weaknesses.

 Self-Assessment: Besides characterization *and* symbol, *this unit also introduced the terms* interview, rhyme scheme, onomatopoeia, *and* tone. *On a page in your notebook, draw a large arrow pointing upward. Near the top of the arrow, write the terms that you understand best. Near the middle and the bottom, write the terms you don't understand as well. To clarify the meanings of terms, check The Handbook of Reading Terms and Literary Concepts on page 762.*

SETTING GOALS

What reading or writing strategies do you want to work on as you complete the next unit? Write at least three of your goals on a sheet of paper, then exchange papers with a classmate. Agree on a time in the near future to evaluate each other's progress toward the goals.

REFLECT & ASSESS **515**

REVIEWING LITERARY CONCEPTS

OPTION 1
Tell students that they should list examples from each selection in the proper section of the chart. You may also wish to have students consider the ways in which characterization influenced their impressions of these characters.

OPTION 2
Remind students that not all objects or images in a selection are symbols. Encourage partners to think about how the particular symbol functions in the selection and what it means to the characters in order to understand what it stands for.

Self-Assessment For terms that students write toward the bottom of the arrow, have them write, in their own words, a definition for each term after checking in the Handbook. Then have students apply each term to a selection they have read. For instance, a student can briefly describe the use of onomatopoeia in a poem or the author's tone in a particular selection.

PORTFOLIO BUILDING
You may wish to help students choose or modify options for them that best suit the goals you have established for the class. Encourage students to refer to any notes they had attached to earlier assignments. Such information can help students to focus on specific concerns as they reflect on and assess their development and progress.

Self-Assessment To help students compare earlier and recent pieces of writing, suggest that they consider how easy or difficult it was for them to complete the writing assignment and how much revision was involved in reaching the final product.

SETTING GOALS
In order to help students set future goals, you may wish to have those with similar goals form small working groups to set their own study goals and evaluate their progress toward these goals.

THE LANGUAGE OF LITERATURE TEACHER'S EDITION **515**

UNIT FIVE

UNIT FIVE

UNIT THEMES

Unit Five

The Pursuit of a Goal In this unit, students will read selections that explore the inner fears some characters must confront in order to achieve their goals. The unit contains two parts: Part 1, "Facing Inner Fears," and Part 2, "Reluctant Heroes." Selections in both parts contribute to the unit theme by detailing the inner fears of various characters and the ways in which these characters work to overcome their fears in pursuing a goal.

Part 1

Facing Inner Fears Selections in Part 1 focus on the different forms that inner fears can take and on how these fears can be overcome. For example, "The Circuit" is a story of a young migrant worker who must confront his fear of his family's constant movement.

Part 2

Reluctant Heroes The selection in Part 2, *The Hobbit*, reveals that a character's true heroism may often lie dormant until the character must meet a challenge.

Links to Unit Six
The Oral Tradition Unit Six, "Across Time and Place," contains literature from the oral tradition that connects with the themes in Unit Five. You may wish to begin or end Unit Five by using the following selections from Unit Six that relate to the theme "The Pursuit of a Goal":
- "The Living Kuan-yin," p. 730
- "Sister Fox and Brother Coyote," p. 735
- "King Thrushbeard," p. 741

516

516 THE LANGUAGE OF LITERATURE TEACHER'S EDITION

The Pursuit of a Goal

Before proceeding, one must reach.

WOLOF
(West African) proverb

Gathering at Blue Waters (1989), Floyd E. Newsum, Jr., artist/professor of art, University of Houston, Downtown. Courtesy of the artist and Lynn Goode Gallery, Houston.

Art Note

Gathering at Blue Waters by Floyd E. Newsum, Jr. Floyd Newsum, Jr., (1959–), an African-American artist, centers most of his work on the theme of women. He often represents women as free spirits and boundless figures who seemingly defy the laws of gravity and nature. In this painting, Newsum uses a variety of images to communicate the liberation of a spirit.
Reading the Art *What message do you think the painter is trying to express? How does his use of color and line help to convey this message?*

Exploring Theme

To help students explore the connections between the art, the quotation, and the unit theme, have them consider the following questions:

1. Do you think "The Pursuit of a Goal" is an important theme to learn about? *(Possible response: yes, because everyone has at least one goal in his or her life—perhaps to improve oneself in some way or to be successful in a career)*

2. Explain the African proverb in terms of pursuing goals. *(Possible responses: The proverb focuses on the importance of striving and struggling in one's attempt to attain a goal and progress through life. In order to realize your goal, you must first have the desire to start.)*

3. How does the painting represent the pursuit of a goal? *(Possible response: In the painting, a woman is seen flying in the sky. Below her are a table with dishes and a chair. It seems that she yearns to escape from her daily chores, such as cooking and cleaning. The painting shows her pursuing this goal.)*

4. What kinds of stories do you think you will read in this unit? *(Possible response: The stories will focus on characters who are attempting to realize their goals. In some of the stories, these characters may succeed; in other stories, they may not.)*

5. Think about a particular goal that you have right now. How important is this goal to you? What qualities do you have that will help you to attain this goal? What qualities do you think you will need to develop in order to attain your goal? *(Responses will vary.)*

THE LANGUAGE OF LITERATURE **TEACHER'S EDITION** 517

UNIT FIVE
Part 1 Skills Trace

ML DENOTES MINI-LESSON IN TEACHER'S EDITION

Selections	Reading Skills and Strategies	Literary Concepts	Writing Opportunities	Speaking, Listening, and Viewing
FICTION **Flowers and Freckle Cream** Elizabeth Ellis		Style, PE p. 524 Author's purpose, ML TE p. 522	Write about beauty, PE p. 519 Magazine advertisement, PE p. 524 Note, PE p. 524 Brochure, PE p. 525	
NONFICTION **The First Emperor** from **The Tomb Robbers** Daniel Cohen	SQ3R, PE p. 527 Questioning, ML TE p. 528	Author's purpose, PE p. 534 Sources, ML TE p. 532	Exhibit catalog, PE p. 534 Legend, PE p. 534 Log entry, PE p. 534 Epitaph, PE p. 534 Paragraph, ML TE p. 529	Talk-show interview, PE p. 535 Model, PE p. 535
POETRY **Message from a Caterpillar** Lilian Moore **Chrysalis Diary** Paul Fleischman	Choral reading, PE p. 537	Figurative language, PE p. 543 Form, PE p. 543 Theme, ML TE p. 541	Poem, PE p. 543 Dialogue, PE p. 543 Poem with sensory details, ML TE p. 540	Paired discussion, PE p. 543 Poster, PE p. 44 ML TE p. 541 Discuss themes, ML TE p. 541 Multimedia performance, ML TE p. 539
FICTION **The Circuit** Francisco Jiménez	Evaluating, PE p. 545 Evaluating, PE p. 551	Sensory details, PE p. 553 Characterization, ML TE p. 548	Prediction, PE p. 553 Evaluation, PE p. 553 Letter, PE p. 553 Report, PE p. 554 Scene, ML TE p. 546	Speech, PE p. 553 Dramatic reading, PE p. 554 Photographic display, PE p. 554
FICTION ON YOUR OWN **The Scribe** Kristin Hunter			Narrative story, TE p. 559 Definitions, TE p. 560	Class discussion, TE p. 561

Writing	Reading Skills and Strategies	Literary Concepts	Writing Opportunities	Speaking, Listening, and Viewing
WRITING ABOUT LITERATURE **Creative Response**	Analyzing sensory details, PE pp. 562–63	Sensory language, PE pp. 562–63 Poetry, PE pp. 564–67	Writing sensory descriptions, PE p. 563 Writing poetry, PE pp. 564–67 Writing with sound devices, PE p. 565	Viewing images, PE p. 569 Interpreting images, PE p. 569 Discussion, PE p. 569 Discussing values, PE p. 569

Grammar, Usage, Mechanics, and Spelling	Multimodal Learning	Research and Study Skills	Vocabulary
Prepositional phrases, **ML** TE p. 520 Words ending with -al + -ly, **ML** TE p. 521	Brochure, PE p. 525	Research freckles, PE p. 525	
Adverbs, **ML** TE p. 530 Forms of the prefix in-, **ML** TE p. 531	Exhibit catalog, PE p. 534 Talk-show interview, PE p. 535 Model, PE p. 535 Time line, PE p. 535	Research Ch'in Shih Huang Ti, PE p. 534 Research Chinese dynasties, PE p. 535 Research Chinese artifacts, PE p. 535	consolidate preservation immortality reproduction insignificant surpass intricate tyrant obsessed unparalleled
	Paired discussion, PE p. 543 Poster, PE p. 544	Research seasonal changes in animals, PE p. 544 Paraphrasing, **ML** TE p. 542	
Compound objects of prepositions, **ML** TE p. 546 Final y words and suffixes, **ML** TE p. 549	Speech, PE p. 553 Family budget, PE p. 554 Dramatic reading, PE p. 554 Photographic display, PE p. 554	Research Cesar Chavez, PE p. 554	

Grammar, Usage, Mechanics, and Spelling	Multimodal Learning	Research and Study Skills	Media Literacy
Using compound sentences, PE p. 563 Using sound devices, PE p. 565 Understanding subject-verb agreement, PE p. 567 Inverted sentences, PE p. 567	Viewing images, PE p. 569 Interpreting images, PE p. 569 Discussion, PE p. 569 Discussing values, PE p. 569		Interpreting images, PE pp. 568–69

UNIT FIVE
Part 2 Skills Trace

 DENOTES MINI-LESSON IN TEACHER'S EDITION

Selections	Reading Skills and Strategies	Literary Concepts	Writing Opportunities	Speaking, Listening, and Viewing
DRAMA **The Hobbit** J.R.R. Tolkien, dramatized by Patricia Gray	Stage directions, PE p. 571 Setting a purpose, ML TE p. 574	Dialogue, PE p. 620 Humor, ML TE p. 584	Ballad, PE p. 620 Newspaper advertisement, PE p. 620 Progress report, PE p. 620 Dialogue, ML TE p. 578 Letter, ML TE p. 593	Dramatic recording, PE p. 620 Readers theater, ML TE p. 596 Background music, ML TE p. 610 Perform a scene, ML TE p. 614

Writing	Reading Skills and Strategies	Literary Concepts	Writing Opportunities	Speaking, Listening, and Viewing
WRITING FROM EXPERIENCE **Persuasion**	Separating fact from opinion, PE p. 625 Previewing reading, ML TE p. 624	Audience, PE p. 625	Writing an opinion essay, PE pp. 622–29 Drafting, PE pp. 626–27 Using precise language, PE p. 627 Publishing, PE pp. 628–29	Discussing issues, PE p. 624 Challenging opinions, PE p. 624

517c UNIT FIVE THE PURSUIT OF A GOAL

Grammar, Usage, Mechanics, and Spelling	Multimodal Learning	Research and Study Skills	Vocabulary
The subject in different positions, ML TE p. 577 The prefix con-, ML TE p. 587	Map, PE p. 619 Ballad, PE p. 620 Sculptures, PE p. 620 Dramatic recording, PE p. 620 Readers theater, ML TE p. 596 Background music, ML TE p. 610 Perform a scene, ML TE p. 614	Reviewing, ML TE p. 601	absurd hoard consoling predicament conspirator quest desolate stature destiny thrive domain throng esteemed vanquish fiend

Grammar, Usage, Mechanics, and Spelling	Multimodal Learning	Research and Study Skills	Media Literacy
Using active voice, PE p. 629		Using computerized index, PE p. 624 Previewing reading, ML TE p. 624	

SKILLS TRACE   TEACHER'S EDITION   **517d**

UNIT FIVE
Recommended Resources

ENRICHMENT   RESEARCH

Recommended Novels

 LITERATURE CONNECTIONS WITH SOURCEBOOK FOR TEACHERS

 SPANISH VERSION AVAILABLE

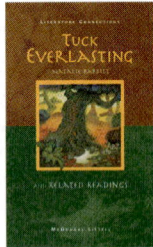

Tuck Everlasting
by Natalie Babbit

Thematic Links When young Winnie Foster meets a family who lives forever, she learns to understand and value the natural cycle of life and death.
About the Author Natalie Babbit (born 1932) began her career as an illustrator and then began writing books in which realistic young people learn to deal with their fears through elements of fantasy.
Other Works by Natalie Babbit *The Eyes of the Amaryllis, Kneeknock Rise, The Search for Delicious*

 LITERATURE CONNECTIONS WITH SOURCEBOOK FOR TEACHERS

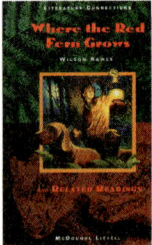

Where the Red Fern Grows
by Wilson Rawls

Thematic Links Billy Colman pursues his goal of obtaining two redbone coonhounds and training them to hunt.
About the Author Wilson Rawls (born 1913) grew up in the Ozark region of Oklahoma, the setting for this autobiographical novel. He decided to become a writer after reading Jack London's *The Call of the Wild*.
Another Work by Wilson Rawls *Summer of the Monkeys*

Bathing Ugly
by Rebecca Busselle

Thematic Links When overweight Betsy is chosen to compete in her camp's "bathing ugly" contest, she responds with courage and wit.
About the Author In addition to writing, Rebecca Busselle (born 1941) has worked as a teacher, a photographer, and a Peace Corps volunteer in Sierra Leone, Africa.
Other Works by Rebecca Busselle *A Frog's Eye View, An Exposure of the Heart*

 LITERATURE CONNECTIONS WITH SOURCEBOOK FOR TEACHERS

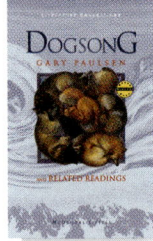

Dogsong
by Gary Paulsen

Thematic Links As he rides his dog sled across the Alaska tundra, a modern Eskimo youth pursues his goal.
About the Author Gary Paulsen (born 1939) ran sled dogs when he was a trapper for the state of Minnesota. He quit hunting and ran the Iditarod dogsled race, experiences he incorporated in his award-winning novels.
Other Works by Gary Paulsen *Hatchet, Woodsong, Tracker, Dancing Carl, Popcorn Days and Buttermilk Nights, The Foxman*

6th Grade Can Really Kill You
by Barthe DeClements

Thematic Links As a learning disabled sixth grader, Helen tries various tactics to hide her inability to read, but she must eventually face her problem head on.
About the Author Barthe DeClements (born 1920) writes novels full of realistic, engaging characters. She is a school psychologist, English teacher, and guidance counselor.
Other Works by Barthe DeClements *Breaking Out, No Place For Me, Five-Finger Discount*

Lord of the Rings
by J.R.R. Tolkien

Thematic Links In this three-volume epic fantasy, the reader is treated to further adventures in the land of the Hobbits.
About the Author J.R.R. Tolkien (1892-1973), who was born in South Africa but lived in England for most of his life, was a professor of language and literature for many years. His finely crafted fantasy works have been widely read and critiqued for decades.
Other Works by J.R.R. Tolkien *Farmer Giles of Ham, Smith of Wootton Major, The Silmarillion, Bilbo's Last Song*

For Teacher — TEACHING LITERATURE

Johnson, Judith A. *J.R.R. Tolkien: Six Decades of Criticism.* (Biographies and Indexes in World Literature, Number 6) Westport, Conn.: Greenwood, 1986.

Kaplan, Jeffrey S. "Ted Hipple Was Right! How I Broke the Rules and Lived Happily Forever and Ever! (Teaching American Literature)." *English Journal* 83 (Sept 1994): 25–28.

Martinez, Julio, and Lomeli, Francisco, eds. *Chicano Literature.* Westport, Conn.: Greenwood, 1985.

Voices in English Classrooms: Honoring Diversity and Change. Urbana, Ill.: National Council of Teachers of English, 1996.

517e UNIT FIVE THE PURSUIT OF A GOAL

CROSS-CURRICULAR TEACHING   PROFESSIONAL DEVELOPMENT

Recommended Readings in Cross-Curricular Areas

SCIENCE

The Beauty Trap
by Elaine Landau (1994)
A look at how societal expectations of beauty can be physically and psychologically damaging to young women. Links to Elizabeth Ellis's "Flowers and Freckle Cream."

HISTORY

The Terra Cotta Army of Emperor Qin
by Caroline Lazo (1993)
Recounts the discovery of terra cotta statues that were buried with China's first emperor. Links to Daniel Cohen's "The First Emperor."

SOCIAL STUDIES

Voices From the Fields: Children of Migrant Farmworkers Tell their Stories
by S. Beth Atkin (1993)
Interviews, photographs, and poems bring to life the daily experiences of present day migrant children. Links to "The Circuit."

Who Cares? Millions Do. A Book About Altruism
by Milton Meltzer (1994)
This book describes numerous volunteer possibilities and organizations. Links to "The Scribe."

For Teacher — CROSS-CURRICULAR INSTRUCTION

Reissman, Ross C. "'News Links' to Literature: Bridging the Gap Between Literature and the News." *English Journal* 83 (January 1994): 57–59.

Richard, J. Kerry, and Ernst, Gisela. "Understanding the Other, Understanding Myself: Using Multicultural Novels in the Classroom." *The Clearing House* 67 (November–December 1993): 88–91.

Rothenberg, Diane. "Interdisciplinary Curriculum in Middle School." (ERIC/EECE Report) *Middle School Journal* 25 (March 1994): 61–65.

Tchudi, Stephen. *The Interdisciplinary Teacher's Handbook: A Guide to Integrated Teaching Across the Curriculum.* Portsmouth, NH: Boynton/Cook Publishers, 1996.

Recommended Media Resources

THE LANGUAGE OF LITERATURE

LASERLINKS
Videodisc, Gr. 6
See *LaserLinks Teacher's Source Book,* pages 54–55, for an overview of Unit Five.

AUDIO LIBRARY
Tapes
Unit Five: The Pursuit of a Goal
Gr. 6, Tape 10: Sides A & B
Gr. 6, Tape 11: Sides A & B
Gr. 6, Tape 12: Side A
Novel in Spanish
Tuck para siempre

WRITING COACH
Writing Coach Software: Writing About Literature: Interpretive Response; Persuasive Essay

OUTSIDE RESOURCES

Films/Videos/Film Strips/Audiocassettes
J.R.R. Tolkien's The Hobbit. 1 videocassette. Santa Monica, CA: Solar Home Video, 1991. (78 minutes)
Mi Vida: The Three Worlds of Maria Gutierrez. 1 videocassette. Derry, NH: Chip Taylor Communications, 1986.
Silver Feet. 2 16-mm film reels. Lise Rubenstein, Kristine Samuelson. Los Angeles: Direct Cinema, Ltd., 1985.

Internet Resources
Literature and Language Arts Center at http://www.hmco.com/mcdougal/lit/litcent.html

For Teacher — TEACHING WITH TECHNOLOGY

Dambrosio, Ellen. *Middle School Staff Development in the Area of Educational Technology.* California State University, Stanislaus, 1994.

Kinnaman, Daniel E., and Dyrli, Odvard Egil. "Gaining Access to Technology: First Step in Making a Difference for Your Students." *Technology & Learning* 14 (January 1994): 16 (7).

Peterson, Norman K., and Orde, Barbara J. "Implementing Multimedia in the Middle School Curriculum: Pros, Cons, and Lessons Learned." *T.H.E. Journal* 22 (February 1995): 70–75.

UNIT FIVE
Professional Enrichment

Helping Your Students Write with Confidence

by Tommy J. Boley,
Associate Professor of English,
University of Texas at El Paso

Getting students started in a writing activity often presents a difficult challenge. As teachers, we usually hear groans at first, and then we're bombarded with questions about what we want. One easy way to make the transition from the moment of our initial assignment to the beginning of actual student writing—and to minimize the barrage of questions—involves careful explanation of four key elements: the subject (or topic), the occasion for writing, the audience being addressed and the purpose for writing. Reduced to an acronym, this approach becomes SOAP—**S**ubject, **O**ccasion, **A**udience, and **P**urpose. Writing assignments—or writing prompts, as we often call them—become more manageable for student writers when they stop to consider these four important elements:

- Thinking about the first element, the *subject*, helps students focus clearly on the topic they would like to discuss.
- The second element—the *occasion*, asks students to pinpoint their actual reason or reasons for writing. What moves them to put pen to paper? Have they been asked to do this, or do they feel a burning desire to communicate something to someone? Why write this down rather than speak it directly to the listener? What gives the act of writing a priority?
- The third element, the *audience*, names the reader or readers for whom the composition is intended. All of us in the English classroom have become aware of the importance of helping students consider what their readers already know and what the writers want their readers to know.
- The final element, the *purpose*, asks students to state a goal: a self-expressive goal, an informative goal, a persuasive goal, or a literary goal. Self-expression will allow students to write personally and subjectively with emotion. Information will require students to present salient facts as objectively as possible. Persuasion will lead students to choose strategies that will convince readers to believe as they do. Finally, creating a piece of literature (commonly called "creative writing") will guide students to compose a poem or a story, or perhaps a play.

As an example, here is a SOAP prompt that students can follow after they have read a currently popular novel, *Maniac Magee:*

You are Maniac Magee. You have just left the East End—reluctantly, because you were so happy with the Beale family, who made you feel at home. You are disappointed and hurt that the "Fishbelly" sign appeared and that you were called "Whitey" and told to leave by a man in a crowd. Because you want the people of East End—especially the Beale family—to know your true feelings, you decide to write a letter to the *East End Express*. Write the letter, expressing your feelings and informing your audience of the reasons you left.

Subject: Your feelings and reasons for leaving the East End
Occasion: You want the East-Enders to know the truth
Audience: Residents of the East End
Purpose: Informative (self-expressive)

Another example can show how to use the SOAP prompt to have students write about their own lives.

Subject: The graffiti increasingly appearing in your neighborhood
Occasion: You want to stop this senseless destruction
Audience: The student body of your school
Purpose: Persuasive

Being certain that the subject, the occasion, the audience, and the purpose are clearly specified will ensure that students will write more effectively. These SOAP prompts will envelope students with scenarios that move them into writing more quickly and with more confidence.

In a writing contest one day, a student asked, "Mister, is it OK if we figure out the SOAP and write it at the top of the page? It sort of helps me see where I'm going...." What better testimony can we ask for this approach?

Beyond the English classroom, SOAP prompts can produce dynamic writing in social studies, science, mathematics, art, music—all disciplines in our curriculum. And, in the meantime, we are teaching our students four important considerations about any writing or speaking situation that they will encounter in school and beyond.

Related Reading

 Kirby, Can, and Liner, Tom. (1988). *Inside Out*. Portsmouth, NH: Boynton/Cook: Heinemann, 2nd ed.

 Kinneavy, James L. (1971). *A Theory of Discourse*. Englewood Cliffs, NJ: Prentice-Hall, Inc.

 Larson, Richard L. (1966). "Teaching Rhetoric in High School: Some Proposals," *English Journal* 55, #8, pp. 1058–1065.

Family and Community Involvement

Family

From one young girl's attempt to get rid of her "unsightly" freckles to an unlikely but resourceful hero's experiences of adventure, all of the selections in Unit Five connect to the theme of pursuing goals. By completing some of the following activities, your students, their families, and other community members can make important connections outside the classroom as they explore real-life examples of people and their pursuit of goals.

The following Copymasters for Unit Five provide activities that students can take home and complete with a parent or other family member.

OPTION 1: PLAY A GAME ABOUT LIFE GOALS
- **Connection** All of the selections in Unit Five connect to the theme of pursuing goals.
- **Activity** *Copymaster, page 1* Students play a game with family members in which players attempt to reach desired goals. When they have completed the game, students and family members share their thoughts and impressions about pursuing goals.

OPTION 2: WRITE A POEM ABOUT PURSUING A GOAL
- **Connection** All of the selections in Unit Five illustrate the theme of pursuing goals.
- **Activity** *Copymaster, page 2* Students work with family members to write a poem that describes their personal feelings about pursuing goals. A word web is provided to help organize students' thoughts and ideas.

OPTION 3: DESIGN A COLLAGE OF THE PERFECT HERO
- **Connection** The main character of *The Hobbit* proves to be a brave and resourceful hero when faced with challenges.
- **Activity** *Copymaster, page 3* Students work with family members to plan and design a collage that captures the qualities of a hero. A word web is provided to record their thoughts.

Community

OPTION 1
- **Connection** In "The Scribe" a young boy attempts to thwart a check-cashing service's practice of taking advantage of its illiterate customers.
- **Activity** Invite a teacher or counselor to discuss with the class the problem of illiteracy. If your community has a literacy program, you may wish to invite participants to discuss how they are working to overcome illiteracy.

OPTION 2
- **Connection** The main character in "Flowers and Freckle Cream" tries to get rid of freckles.
- **Activity** Have a school counselor or child psychologist discuss effects of overemphasizing one's appearance according to societal standards.

OPTION 3
- **Connection** "Chrysalis Diary" and "Message from a Caterpillar" deal with the metamorphosis of a butterfly.
- **Activity** Have students visit a science and nature museum, or invite an entomologist to speak to the class, to learn more about the life stages of butterflies.

OPTION 4
- **Connection** "The First Emperor" details efforts of the first emperor of China, Ch'in Shih Huang Ti, to build his own elaborate tomb in his quest for immortality.
- **Activity** Have students either visit a museum with a substantial collection of Chinese antiquity or interview a specialist in Chinese history from a local college or university to learn more about China's imperial past.

PROFESSIONAL ENRICHMENT, FAMILY AND COMMUNITY INVOLVEMENT   TEACHER'S EDITION   **517h**

UNIT FIVE

Part 1 Cooperative Project

Career Day

Overview

Students will plan and oversee a Career Day to learn about different jobs and professions that interest them.

PROJECT AT A GLANCE

The selections in Unit Five, Part 1 concern people who are pursuing a goal, often from within their job or profession. Others find that the goal can dictate the kind of job they take. For this project, students will select a particular job or profession they find appealing. They will interview several people who work in this field and select one on the basis of goals sought and attained. This person will be invited to speak at a Career Day, which the groups will set up for the entire school to attend. Groups will also write a brief description of the person and job, which can serve as that person's introduction for the Career Day presentation.

OBJECTIVES

- To find a job or profession of personal interest
- To interview several people who work at that job
- To select one of these people as a good example of a person who is working toward a goal
- To arrange and coordinate a Career Day for the entire school
- To invite the selected person to speak at the event

SUGGESTED GROUP SIZE
Two students (pairs)

MATERIALS
Newspaper classified sections

 **Getting Started**

Arranging the Project
Collect several days' worth of newspaper classified sections. Concentrate on the Help Wanted ads, removing the nonessential ads.

If other teachers in your school are assigning the same project, you may want to work together. This will allow for a greater range of jobs and professions at the final Career Day, and you can share responsibilities and resources.

Arranging the Career Day
This project can be as simple or complex as you'd like, from having an in-class speaker to staging a full-fledged Career Day. For a Career Day, begin now by making arrangements for the date, time, and location of the event. This will require some communication between you and the school administration. A middle-ground alternative is to hold a Career Day for just sixth graders and not to involve other grade levels. How you structure the project will depend on your school and on the level of involvement and performance you expect from students. Don't forget that if the event is to last all day, the guests will need to be fed and given a place to relax.

 **Creating the Career Day**

Introducing the Project
Explain that students will be working in pairs to find a job or career that interests them. They will interview several people working in that job to find one who is goal-oriented and whose job contributes in some way to that goal. Pairs will invite this person to speak at a Career Day. They will also prepare a brief description of the person and the job, which will serve as the person's introduction.

Ask students to look over the Help Wanted ads you have brought to class. They can point out the numerous kinds of jobs, noting which are more in demand, which offer higher wages, and which are unfamiliar to them. Students might also speculate about goals that might be common to a certain job.

Hold an informal discussion with students about what their expectations are concerning jobs. This should include their present career plans (however simplistic or outrageous), what background or education they think they will need, as well as how much money they think they will earn.

Group Investigations
Because this project has a personal slant, divide students into pairs who have mutual interests. Pairs should decide quickly on a job or profession they might like to investigate and create a standard set of questions to ask. They should then find and interview people who have this job. Later, they can decide which person interviewed was the most outstanding example of someone in this career and who also had a goal that meshed with the job. Students can write a request to speak to that person, being careful to include all pertinent details.

Creating a Project Description
Students will tell you what jobs they will pursue. If there are too many duplications, you might suggest similar or parallel jobs they can look into. Help pairs keep the project reality-based by vetoing "jobs" such as millionaire. After the interviews have been concluded, ask that pairs write a brief description of the job and the person. You can meet with each pair to elicit further information about the subject before allowing them to extend an invitation to speak.

OPTION 1: ONE JOB All students can concentrate on interviewing persons holding one class-selected job. They should ask what the job really entails, what the interviewees like and dislike about the job, how it affects the rest of their life, the training or preparation they had to have, and the type or level of education they needed.

517i UNIT FIVE THE PURSUIT OF A GOAL

OPTION 2: PERSONAL MENTOR Individual students can select a personal mentor—someone whose job interests them and who is a good example of a goal-oriented person. If possible, students should interview their mentor and accompany him or her to work for an hour or two.

OPTION 3: CLASS CAREER PERIOD Groups of four or five students can select individuals through the same interview process and invite these people to attend one class session. Each guest can speak for three to five minutes, then answer questions from the class.

OPTION 4: LEARNING MORE TO EARN MORE Students can contact a college or university of their choice and request information about tuition, courses offered, the average earnings of graduates, and whether the college has a reputation in any particular field of study. Students can present their findings to the class.

3 Sharing the Career Day

If you cannot share the Career Day with the entire school, consider inviting other sixth-grade classes or any students who have a free period. School administrators might also be interested in attending any session, whether it is for the entire school or only for your class. You might also want to videotape the entire proceedings to share with other classes or future students.

Assessing the Project

The following rubric can be used for group or individual assessment.

3 Full Accomplishment Students follow directions and, through interviews, select a goal-oriented person to speak at the class-run Career Day.

2 Substantial Accomplishment Students select a person to speak at Career Day, but the reasons presented are unclear, or the person they have chosen is not the best possible choice.

1 Little or Partial Accomplishment Students' interviews and/or selection is incomplete or does not fulfill the requirements of the assignment.

For the Portfolio
You can include in each student's portfolio a copy of the preliminary description written about the person and the job or the final description used as an introduction at Career Day. Also include a copy of your written assessment of the project as a whole.

Note: For other assessment options, see the *Teacher's Guide to Assessment and Portfolio Use.*

Cross-Curricular Options

LANGUAGE ARTS
Students can write a poem that expresses and explains their foremost personal goal. They should also tell a bit about how they plan to achieve that goal.

PHYSICAL EDUCATION
Students can, with the help of a physical education teacher, set up personal fitness goals for themselves. They should also set up a fitness program they can follow to achieve this goal.

MATH

Have students research the ten highest-paying jobs and the ten lowest-paying jobs, and what each pays. They also can find out what fields experts feel will be expanding in coming years and which fields remain level or are shrinking. Students can present their data to the class using graphs or charts.

Resources

All in a Day's Work: Twelve Americans Talk About Their Jobs by Neil Johnson includes 12 first-person stories about being a farmer, a factory worker, a musician, a detective, and more.

Careers in Health Services by Diane Seide covers a wide variety of medical careers.

Careers in the Computer Industry by Laura Greene discusses what it takes to become an engineer, a programmer, or a data processor.

Jobs for Teenagers by Ilene Jones suggests ways teenagers can earn money working part-time.

COOPERATIVE PROJECT TEACHER'S EDITION **517j**

UNIT FIVE
Part 1 Lesson Planner

TIME ALLOTMENTS SHOWN ARE APPROXIMATE. DEPENDING ON YOUR GOALS AND THE NEEDS OF YOUR STUDENTS, YOU MAY WISH TO ALLOW MORE OR LESS TIME FOR CERTAIN PORTIONS OF THE LESSON.

Table of Contents	Discussion	Previewing the Selection	Reading the Selection
PART OPENER **FACING INNER FEARS** **What Do You Think?** page 518	**20 MINUTES** • Reflect on the part theme		
SELECTION **Flowers and Freckle Cream** page 520 AVERAGE		**20 MINUTES** • PERSONAL CONNECTION • CULTURAL CONNECTION • WRITING CONNECTION	**10 MINUTES** • Read pp. 520–23 (4 pp.)
SELECTION **The First Emperor** from **The Tomb Robbers** page 528 CHALLENGING		**15 MINUTES** • PERSONAL CONNECTION • HISTORICAL CONNECTION • READING CONNECTION: SQ3R	**25 MINUTES** • Introduce vocabulary • Read pp. 528–33 (6 pp.)
SELECTIONS **Message from a Caterpillar** page 538 AVERAGE **Chrysalis Diary** page 539 AVERAGE		**10 MINUTES** • PERSONAL CONNECTION • SCIENCE CONNECTION • READING CONNECTION: Choral reading	**10 MINUTES** • Read pp. 538–42 (5 pp.)
SELECTION **The Circuit** page 546 AVERAGE		**10 MINUTES** • PERSONAL CONNECTION • CULTURAL CONNECTION • READING CONNECTION: Evaluating	**25 MINUTES** • Read pp. 546–52 (7 pp.)
FICTION ON YOUR OWN **The Scribe** page 555 EASY			**20 MINUTES** • Read pp. 555–61 (7 pp.)
Writing **WRITING ABOUT LITERATURE** **Creative Response**	**Writer's Style** **30 MINUTES**	**Prewriting** **15 MINUTES**	**Drafting and Revising** **50 MINUTES**

Time estimates assume in-class work. You may wish to assign some of these stages as homework.

Responding to the Selection

FROM PERSONAL RESPONSE TO CRITICAL ANALYSIS	OR	ANOTHER PATHWAY	LITERARY CONCEPTS	QUICKWRITES

Extension Activities

- ALTERNATIVE ACTIVITIES
- LITERARY LINKS
- CRITIC'S CORNER
- THE WRITER'S STYLE
- ACROSS THE CURRICULUM
- ART CONNECTION
- WORDS TO KNOW
- BIOGRAPHY

25 MINUTES

• Discussion questions	OR	• Pros and cons chart	• Style	• Magazine advertisement • Note

50 MINUTES — ✓ ✓ ✓ (SCIENCE)

60 MINUTES

• Discussion questions	OR	• Exhibit catalog	• Author's purpose	• Legend • Log entry • Epitaph

50 MINUTES — ✓ ✓ ✓ ✓ ✓ (HISTORY)

35 MINUTES

• Discussion questions	OR	• Paired discussions	• Figurative language • Form	• Poem • Dialogue

40 MINUTES — ✓ ✓ (SCIENCE)

45 MINUTES

• Discussion questions	OR	• Speech	• Sensory details	• Prediction • Evaluation • Letter

50 MINUTES — ✓ ✓ ✓ (SOCIAL STUDIES)

Publishing and Reflecting — 30 MINUTES

Grammar in Context — 5 MINUTES

Reading the World — 20 MINUTES

LESSON PLANNER   TEACHER'S EDITION   **517I**

PART 1

WHAT DO YOU THINK?
Objectives

The activities on this page can be used to
- introduce the Part 2 theme, "Facing Inner Fears," since each activity is connected to one or more of the selections in Part 1
- create materials for students' personal portfolios that they can later reconsider or revise
- build an understanding of theme that can be reviewed and revised as students progress through the unit

What is the price of beauty?
Suggest to students that they also consider, in their analysis of beauty products, the issue of loyalty to brand names. Encourage them to think about how the makers of beauty products use advertising to benefit from people's inner fears about their appearance. (See "Flowers and Freckle Cream," p. 519.)

What do you fear?
You may wish to have students work in small groups to complete this activity. Encourage them to devise other ways of tabulating the data, such as in a pie chart or a bar graph. (See "The First Emperor," p. 526, and "Message from a Caterpillar/Chrysalis Diary," p. 537.)

How would you cope?
Have students first outline their fears and what they would do to cope with them. You may wish to have students create alternative visual displays, such as collages or comic strips, to represent their feelings about the situations. (See "The Circuit," p. 545.)

How could you help?
Suggest that partners begin by organizing and briefly sketching out their ideas for the pamphlet or video. Encourage the pairs who are creating a pamphlet to draw or select illustrations to accompany the text. Encourage those who are shooting a video to prepare a storyboard of their ideas before they begin taping. (See "The Scribe," p. 555.)

UNIT FIVE **PART 1**

FACING INNER FEARS

WHAT DO You THINK?
REFLECTING ON THEME

Has fear ever kept you from pursuing a dream? Some of the greatest obstacles to reaching goals may lie within us. The activities on this page will help you to explore ways of overcoming inner fears. Keep a record of your impressions, to compare with those of the characters in Part 1 as they pursue their goals.

What do you fear?
Use a questionnaire to survey your classmates anonymously about their fears. Do they fear heights? darkness? snakes? Create a chart showing the students' top five fears. Then ask them to suggest ways of facing each fear.

How would you cope?
Think about these situations: (1) You are switched to a different homeroom; (2) You return to soccer practice after an injury; (3) A parent loses his or her job. What fears would each situation create? Create a visual display, such as a storyboard, with images that explain what you would do.

What is the price of beauty?
Bring to class a list of the names and prices of the beauty products used in your home every day. Work with other students to determine which products are most popular and which are most expensive. Do a rough calculation of the total cost of the products listed by the students in your class. With your classmates, discuss whether people depend on beauty products to mask inner fears about appearance.

How could you help?
How do you stop in a pair of in-line skates? How do you budget your weekly allowance? With a partner, create a "how-to" pamphlet or video that outlines steps a person can follow to operate a new device or handle a new situation. Make the pamphlet or video available to the class.

518

Across the Curriculum

Science Have each student research a phobia—a persistent, strong fear of a certain object or situation. Each student can investigate a particular common phobia, such as agoraphobia (fear of open or public places), claustrophobia (fear of enclosed spaces), ailurophobia (fear of cats), or hydrophobia (fear of water). Encourage students to find out the ways in which psychologists and psychiatrists have attempted to explain and treat these phobias. Students can then present their findings to the class.

PARENTAL INVOLVEMENT
Have students interview a parent or other relative about a particular fear he or she had while growing up and how the relative was able to rise above it. Students should ask thought-provoking questions in order to elicit from the interviewee what steps were taken to overcome the particular fear. Encourage students to tape-record or videotape the interview so that they can present it to the class.

518 THE LANGUAGE OF LITERATURE TEACHER'S EDITION

PREVIEWING

FICTION

Flowers and Freckle Cream
Elizabeth Ellis

Activating Prior Knowledge/Setting a Purpose
PERSONAL CONNECTION
Who is handsome? Who is beautiful? Standards of beauty vary from one culture to another and from one generation to the next. In a small group, discuss with your classmates the differences in standards of beauty. As you read, notice the main character's ideas about beauty.

Building Background
CULTURAL CONNECTION
Each year in the United States, spending for beauty products increases, supporting the opinion of some people that Americans place great importance on physical appearance. Manufacturers of beauty products attempt to attract customers through advertisements on TV and radio, and in newspapers and magazines. In 1990, about 10 percent of all magazine advertising was bought by manufacturers of cosmetics, perfume, and similar products. Refer to the chart shown to see how spending for magazine advertisements of beauty products has increased.

Amount Spent Advertising Toiletries in U.S. Magazines

Year	Amount
1980	$206 million
1985	$385 million
1986	$390 million
1987	$455 million
1988	$554 million
1989	$651 million
1990	$679 million

Source: Publishers Information Bureau

WRITING CONNECTION
Over a century ago, an author wrote, "Beauty is in the eye of the beholder." In your notebook or on a sheet of paper, explain what you think this statement means. Write about an instance you may recall that either proves or disproves this statement.

LASERLINKS
• PERSONAL CONNECTION

OVERVIEW

Objectives
- To understand and appreciate a short story about a young girl's attempts to remove her freckles
- To understand and appreciate a writer's style
- To express understanding of the selection through a choice of writing forms, including a magazine advertisement and a note
- To extend understanding of the selection through a variety of multimodal and cross-curricular activities

Skills

THE WRITER'S STYLE
• Details appealing to sight

GRAMMAR
• Prepositional phrases

LITERARY CONCEPTS
• Author's purpose
• Style

SPELLING
• Words ending with -al + -ly

SPEAKING, LISTENING, AND VIEWING
• Group discussion
• Oral presentation

Cross-Curricular Connections

SCIENCE
• Varieties of lilies
• Cause of freckles

PERSONAL CONNECTION
Oh! So Beautiful An advertisement for a beauty product had a powerful influence on Elizabeth, the main character in this story. You may wish to use the advertisements shown on the videodisc to generate discussion about standards of female beauty during the 1940s and today.

Side A, Frame 38903

PRINT AND MEDIA RESOURCES

UNIT FIVE RESOURCE BOOK
Strategic Reading: Literature, p. 4
Reading SkillBuilder, p. 5
Spelling SkillBuilder, p. 6

GRAMMAR MINI-LESSONS
Transparencies, p. 41

WRITING MINI-LESSONS
Transparencies, p. 38

ACCESS FOR STUDENTS ACQUIRING ENGLISH
Selection Summaries
Reading and Writing Support

TEACHER'S GUIDE TO ASSESSMENT AND PORTFOLIO USE

FORMAL ASSESSMENT
Selection Test, p. 103
 Test Generator

AUDIO LIBRARY
See Reference Card

LASERLINKS
Personal Connection

THE LANGUAGE OF LITERATURE TEACHER'S EDITION

Flowers and Freckle Cream
by Elizabeth Ellis

SUMMARY

The narrator recalls her sending away, at the age of 12, for freckle-removing cream in the hope of having beautiful clear skin like her cousin Janette Elizabeth. After the much-anticipated package arrives in the mail, she puts the cream on and goes outside to hoe tobacco. The cream turns out to have disastrous effects when exposed to the sun: at the end of the day, she has *more* freckles than before. Horrified at her reflection in the bathroom mirror, she runs weeping from the house. Her grandfather, learning what happened, tells her, "But child, there are all kinds of flowers, and they are all beautiful." She responds, "I've never seen a flower with freckles!" and retreats in misery to her room. The next morning she awakes to find a freckled tiger lily on her pillow, placed there by her grandfather.

Thematic Link: *Facing Inner Fears*
Elizabeth learns from her grandfather her concerns about her physical appearance have no basis in reality.

CUSTOMIZING FOR
Students Acquiring English

- Use **ACCESS FOR STUDENTS ACQUIRING ENGLISH**, *Reading and Writing Support*.

I If necessary, write the word *overwhelmed* on the board and point out the narrator's humorous way of stating its opposite as *underwhelmed*.

STRATEGIC READING FOR
Less-Proficient Readers

Set a Purpose Invite volunteers to share stories about themselves or someone they know who made a change in his or her appearance and then was unhappy with the result. Have students read to find out why the narrator wants the freckle-remover cream.

Use **UNIT FIVE RESOURCE BOOK**, p. 4, for guidance in reading the selection.

Active Reading: CONNECT

A Have students discuss whether they can identify with the narrator's feelings at this point. Ask if they have ever become "worked up" over some new purchase.

I When I was a kid about twelve years old, I was already as tall as I am now, and I had a lot of freckles. I had reached the age when I had begun to really look at myself in the mirror, and I was underwhelmed.[1] Apparently my mother was too, because sometimes she'd look at me and shake her head and say, "You can't make a silk purse out of a sow's ear."[2]

I had a cousin whose name was Janette Elizabeth, and Janette Elizabeth looked exactly like her name sounds. She had a waist so small that men could put their hands around it . . . and they did. She had waist-length naturally curly blond hair too, but to me her unforgivable sin was that she had a flawless peaches-and-cream complexion. I couldn't help comparing myself with her and thinking that my life would be a lot different if I had beautiful skin too—skin that was all one color.

And then, in the back pages of Janette Elizabeth's *True Confessions* magazine, I found the answer: an advertisement for freckle-remover cream. I knew that I could afford it if I saved my money, and I did. The ad assured me that the product would arrive in a "plain brown wrapper." Plain brown freckle color.

For three weeks I went to the mailbox every day precisely at the time the mail was delivered. I knew that if someone else in my family got the mail, I would never hear the end of it. There was no way that they would let me open the box in private. Finally, after three weeks of scheduling my entire day around the mail truck's arrival, my package came.

I went to my room with it, sat on the edge of my bed, and opened it. I was sure that I was looking at a miracle. But I had gotten so worked up about the magical package that I couldn't bring myself to put the cream on. What if it didn't work? What would I do then? **A**

I fell asleep that night without even trying the stuff. And when I got up the next morning and looked at my freckles in the mirror, I said, "Elizabeth, this is silly. You have to do it now!" I smeared the cream all over my body. There wasn't as much of it as I had thought there would be, and I could see that I was

---

1. **underwhelmed:** not impressed.
2. **a silk purse out of a sow's ear:** something beautiful and of high quality from something inferior or ugly.

520 UNIT FIVE PART 1: FACING INNER FEARS

Mini-Lesson  Grammar

PREPOSITIONAL PHRASES Remind students that a prepositional phrase is a group of words that begins with a preposition and ends with its object. Point out that students can often make writing smoother by reducing a sentence to a prepositional phrase and combining it with another sentence.

Application Have students rewrite each pair of sentences by reducing one sentence to a prepositional phrase and combining it with the other sentence.

1. Janette Elizabeth was really pretty. She had long blond hair and a very small waist.
2. I found the answer. It was in the back pages of one of Janette Elizabeth's magazines.
3. I hid the cream. I put it in my bottom drawer.

Reteaching/Reinforcement
- *Grammar Mini-Lessons* transparencies p. 41

The Writer's Craft
Using Prepositional Phrases, pp. 506–508

B going to need a part-time job to keep me in freckle remover.

C Later that day I took my hoe and went with my brother and cousins to the head of the holler[3] to hoe tobacco, as we did nearly every day in the summer. Of course, when you stay out hoeing tobacco all day, you're not working in the shade. And there was something important I hadn't realized about freckle remover: if you wear it in the sun, it seems to have a reverse effect. Instead of developing a peaches-and-cream complexion, you just get more and darker freckles.

By the end of the day I looked as though I had leopard blood in my veins, although I didn't realize it yet. When I came back to the house, my family, knowing nothing about the

---

3. **head of the holler:** dialect for "head of the hollow," the end of a small valley.

Siri (1970), Andrew Wyeth. Tempera on panel, 30″ × 30½″, collection of the Brandywine River Museum, Chadds Ford, Pennsylvania. Copyright © 1970 Andrew Wyeth.

FLOWERS AND FRECKLE CREAM **521**

STRATEGIC READING FOR
Less-Proficient Readers

B Ask students why the narrator feels she needs to use the freckle-remover cream. *(She feels inadequate when she contrasts her appearance with that of her cousin.)* Finding the Main Idea

Set a Purpose Ask students to read to find out whether the cream will work and how the narrator will react.

Critical Thinking: SPECULATING

C Ask students what they can tell about the setting of the story. *(Possible responses: It is set in a rural part of the United States; it is set on a farm.)*

CUSTOMIZING FOR
Students Acquiring English

2 If necessary, remind students that leopards are wild cats that have spotted coats and point out that the narrator is comparing her skin to a leopard's fur.

Literary Concept: STYLE

D Point out that the author injects touches of humor throughout the selection. The reference to "leopard blood" is one example. Have students find another example on this page. *(Possible response: the narrator's comment about needing a part-time job)*

Art Note

Siri by Andrew Wyeth Wyeth (1917–) often paints people's ordinary experiences in a rather realistic style. His paintings generally focus on the loneliness of people and their environments.

Reading the Art *Compare the size and position of the subject with those of the background. Why do you think the artist used this manner of composition?*

Mini-Lesson Spelling

WORDS ENDING WITH -AL + -LY
Remind students that adding the suffix *-ly* to an adjective changes the word into an adverb. Use the examples to show that when the suffix *-ly* is added to a word ending with *-al*, the resulting word should be spelled with two *l*'s, not one.

Application Have students replace each underlined word in the following sentences with an adverb by adding the suffix *-ly*.
1. The narrator took a <u>real</u> good look at herself in the mirror.
2. Janette Elizabeth had <u>natural</u> curly hair.
3. Avoiding direct sun when using the freckle cream was <u>unusual</u> important.
4. People <u>occasional</u> neglect to read directions before using a new product.
5. The advertisement for the cream may have been <u>intentional</u> misleading.

Ask students to look for more words that fit this pattern, in their own writing and in the things that they read, and to add these words to their personal word lists.

Reteaching/Reinforcement
• *Unit Five Resource Book,* p. 6

Adjective + ly = Adverb
final + ly = finally
equal + ly = equally
magical + ly = magically

THE LANGUAGE OF LITERATURE TEACHER'S EDITION **521**

STRATEGIC READING FOR
Less-Proficient Readers

E Ask students the following questions to make sure they are following the story.

- Why doesn't the freckle-remover cream work? *(The narrator goes out in the sunlight, which reacts with the cream and makes the freckles worse.)* **Noting Relevant Details**

- How does the narrator react? *(She becomes extremely upset.)* **Relating Cause and Effect**

CUSTOMIZING FOR
Students Acquiring English

3 Explain that when Elizabeth's grandfather mentions "burying a dead black cat when the moon was full," he is jokingly suggesting a superstitious remedy for freckles.

CUSTOMIZING FOR
Gifted and Talented Students

F Have students write a diary entry from the point of view of Janette, complaining about an aspect in which her cousin Elizabeth outshines her.

Linking to Science

 **G** Many varieties of lilies are common in North America. All types grow from bulbs, and most produce large trumpet-shaped flowers with six petals. Many varieties, including the tiger lily, have beautiful speckled markings.

COMPREHENSION CHECK
1. What does the narrator order from the magazine advertisement? *(freckle-remover cream)*
2. Why was the narrator upset when she came in from hoeing? *(She had more and darker freckles than before.)*
3. What does the narrator's grandfather do to help the situation? *(He tells her all flowers are beautiful and then puts a tiger lily on her pillow.)*

---

freckle-remover cream, began to say things like, "I've never seen you with that many freckles before." When I saw myself in the mirror, I dissolved into tears and hid in the bathroom.

My mother called me to the dinner table, but I ignored her. When she came to the bathroom door and demanded that I come out and eat, I burst out the door and ran by her, crying. I ran out to the well house[4] and threw myself down, and I was still sobbing when my grandfather came out to see what was wrong with me. I told him about how I'd sent for the freckle remover, and he didn't laugh—though he did suggest that one might get equally good results from burying a dead black cat when the moon was full.

It was clear that Grandpa didn't understand, so I tried to explain why I didn't want to have freckles and why I felt so inadequate when I compared my appearance with Janette Elizabeth's. He looked at me in stunned surprise, shook his head, and said, "But child, there are all kinds of flowers, and they are all beautiful." I said, "I've never seen a flower with freckles!" and ran back to my room, slamming the door.

When my mother came and knocked, I told her to go away. She started to say the kinds of things that parents say at times like that, but my grandfather said, "Nancy, leave the child alone." She was a grown-up, but he was her father. So she left me alone.

I don't know where Grandpa found it. It isn't at all common in the mountains where we lived then. But I know he put it in my room because my mother told me later. I had cried myself to sleep that night, and when I opened my swollen, sticky eyes the next morning, the first thing I saw, lying on the pillow next to my head, was a tiger lily. ❖

---

4. **well house:** a shed covering a deep hole from which water is drawn.

Superb Lilies #2 (1966), Alex Katz. Oil on canvas, 72″ × 144″. Courtesy of Robert Miller Gallery, New York. Copyright © 1996 Alex Katz/Licensed by VAGA, New York.

Mini-Lesson Literary Concepts

REVIEWING AUTHOR'S PURPOSE Remind students of the four possible purposes an author may have in writing: to entertain, to inform, to express an opinion, to persuade. Often an author has more than one purpose in writing.

Application Have students review the story and look for examples that demonstrate one or more of the four purposes described. Then divide students into small discussion groups to determine whether one purpose is more predominant than any others. Have groups present their opinion, supporting their ideas with references to specific passages.

---

522 THE LANGUAGE OF LITERATURE TEACHER'S EDITION

LITERARY INSIGHT

SAME SONG
by Pat Mora

While my sixteen-year-old son sleeps,
my twelve-year-old daughter
stumbles into the bathroom at six a.m.
plugs in the curling iron
5   squeezes into faded jeans
curls her hair carefully
strokes Aztec Blue shadow on her eyelids
smooths Frosted Mauve blusher on her cheeks
outlines her mouth in Neon Pink
10   peers into the mirror, mirror on the wall
frowns at her face, her eyes, her skin,
not fair.

At night this daughter
stumbles off to bed at nine
15   eyes half-shut while my son
jogs a mile in the cold dark
then lifts weights in the garage
curls and bench presses
expanding biceps, triceps, pectorals,
20   one-handed push-ups, one hundred sit-ups
peers into that mirror, mirror and frowns too.

Art Note

Superb Lilies by Alex Katz Alex Katz (1927–) has created colossal pictures of flowers, working directly from nature. The 6-by-12-foot canvas shown in the photograph on page 522 was one of his experiments in size and scale.

Reading the Art *Would you describe the style of this painting as realistic? Why or why not?*

LITERARY INSIGHT

1. Why does the speaker of the poem include such complete descriptions of the cosmetics in stanza 1 and the types of exercises in stanza 2? *(Possible response: to emphasize the importance the speaker's daughter and son place on different aspects of their appearances)*
2. The references to the mirror in lines 10 and 21 refer to a well-known children's story. What is the story and why does the poet refer to it? *(In "Snow White and the Seven Dwarfs," the stepmother looks into a mirror and chants, "Mirror, mirror, on the wall, who is the fairest one of all?" The stepmother is obsessed with her looks, as are many teenagers.)*

PAT MORA

Pat Mora (1942–) was born in El Paso, Texas, and has worked as a college English teacher. One of her goals as a writer is to include Hispanic perspectives so that anthologized American literature will better reflect the ethnic diversity of the United States.

Mini-Lesson — The Writer's Style

DETAILS APPEALING TO SIGHT Explain to students that writers often use details appealing to sight to focus readers' attention on what is important and to help them visualize a character or a scene. For example, Janette Elizabeth's appearance is described in great detail because her appearance matters to the narrator. The reader learns nothing about the appearances of the mother or grandfather; such details would distract from the selection's message.

Application Ask students to skim the selection and look for places where the author might have added more details appealing to sight. Then have them write a few sentences of additional details and explain whether their additions would shift the story's emphasis.

Reteaching/Reinforcement
- Writing Handbook, anthology p. 783
- *Writing Mini-Lessons* transparencies, p. 38

The Writer's Craft

Developing a Topic, pp. 205–210
Appealing to the Senses, pp. 266–273

From Personal Response to Critical Analysis

1. Responses will vary. If the narrator's experience triggers a memory of a similar event in students, have them also record that event in their journals.
2. Possible responses: She may have been surprised, thought of her grandfather's comment, and then felt pleasure.
3. Possible responses: He seems sensitive and thoughtful; he has a sense of humor; he respects and understands other people's feelings.
4. Possible responses: No, because clear skin alone does not bring a person happiness. Yes, because clear skin might have made her more confident.
5. You may wish to lead a discussion about the relative value of clothes and cosmetics versus exercise and proper diet in improving a person's appearance.

Another Pathway

Encourage students to try to list at least five reasons (including Grandpa's) in each column. Each reason should come from, or be justified by, passages from the selection.

Rubric

3 Full Accomplishment Students' charts have five or more reasons in each column. Reasons come from, or can be justified by, the selection.

2 Substantial Accomplishment Students' charts have fewer than five reasons per column. Some reasons do not come from the selection or cannot be justified by it.

1 Little or Partial Accomplishment Students' charts have very few reasons. Reasons cannot be justified by passages from the selection.

RESPONDING OPTIONS

FROM PERSONAL RESPONSE TO CRITICAL ANALYSIS

REFLECT 1. What reactions does Elizabeth's experience trigger in you? Describe your reactions briefly in your notebook.

RETHINK 2. What thoughts do you imagine go through Elizabeth's mind when she sees the tiger lily?

Close Textual Reading 3. What kind of person is Grandpa?
Consider
- his comments about beauty
- his action at the end of the story

4. Suppose the freckle cream had worked. Would Elizabeth's life have changed? Why or why not?

RELATE 5. The narrator in this story and the son and daughter
Literary Link described in the Insight poem "Same Song" on page 523 are all concerned with appearance. Prepare a comparison chart of the ways in which each tries to improve his or her looks.

Multimodal Learning
ANOTHER PATHWAY

Imagine that Elizabeth had thought about the pros and cons of investing in the freckle cream before she sent away for it. Create the list she might have made, using a diagram similar to the one shown. Then look at her list from the grandfather's point of view. Add his cons—and pros, if any—to Elizabeth's list.

To Buy or Not to Buy	
Pros	**Cons**

LITERARY CONCEPTS

The **style** of a piece of literature refers to the way it is written. Style is not *what* is said, but rather *how* it is said. Style involves the combination of various elements, such as sentence length, word choice, imagery, and tone. The choices a writer makes about all these elements can determine how a reader responds to a piece of writing. For example, early in this story you might have been amused by the line, "I was underwhelmed." Elizabeth Ellis's choice of a humorous term to describe her main character's feelings immediately alerts the reader to a writer with a style all her own. Find another example in the story that you think reveals the writer's style and explain why you think as you do.

QUICKWRITES

1. Write the **magazine advertisement** that persuades Elizabeth to order the freckle cream.
2. Imagine that Grandpa left a note with the tiger lily on Elizabeth's pillow. Write the **note** he might have written.

PORTFOLIO Save your writing. You may want to use it later as a springboard to a piece for your portfolio.

524 UNIT FIVE PART 1: FACING INNER FEARS

Literary Concepts

Other examples of the writer's humorous style include the narrator's comment that she will need a part-time job to keep herself supplied with freckle cream and Grandpa's reference to burying a dead cat.

To help students understand the idea of a writer's style, have them work in groups of three. Students can summarize the main ideas of the selection in the style of (1) a history textbook, (2) a tabloid newspaper report, and (3) a series of informal journal entries Elizabeth might write.

QuickWrites

1. Suggest that students cut pictures or words from magazines to illustrate their advertisements. They should also include a warning that the user should avoid direct sunlight after applying the cream.
2. Students' notes might take the form of a greeting card with a short poem and/or some illustration.

The Writer's Craft
Friendly Letter, pp. 40–43

LITERARY LINKS

Both Elizabeth in "Flowers and Freckle Cream" and Laurence Yep in "Chinatown" from *The Lost Garden* consider themselves outsiders within their own families. What goals does each pursue in an attempt to "belong," either by appearance or actions?

Multimodal Learning

ACROSS THE CURRICULUM

Science An old saying maintains that "a face without freckles is like a heaven without stars." What are freckles? What causes them to appear? Find out more about these "stars," and present your information in an informative brochure that could be made available at the school nurse's office.

WORDS TO KNOW

WORDPLAY An acrostic is a series of lines in which the first letters of the lines form a word or message when read vertically. Complete the acrostic of the word *freckles* below, creating words that relate to Elizabeth or some part of the story.

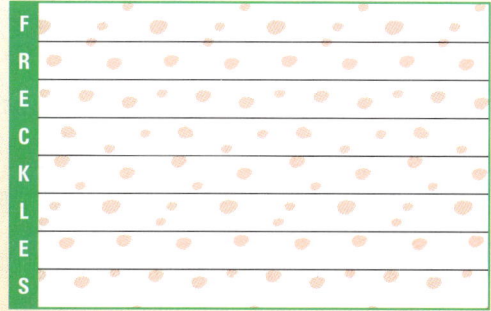

F
R
E
C
K
L
E
S

Literary Links

Possible responses: Elizabeth tries to remove her freckles so she will be more like her cousin, while Laurence attempts to succeed in sports because the rest of his family is athletic.

Words to Know

Possible response:

Flowers
Remover
Elizabeth
Cousin
Kindness
Lily
Emotional
Speckled

Across the Curriculum

Science Students may want to interview a dermatologist to gather the information for this activity. They should ask for facts about what causes freckles and whether there are any safe ways of removing them. (The pigment causing freckles lies in the lower layers of the epidermis, making freckles almost impossible to remove.)

ADDITIONAL SUGGESTIONS
Science *Cooperative Learning*
How Does Your Garden Grow? Have students use reference books on flowers grown from bulbs to research the various types of lilies, where they grow, and how they are cultivated. Divide the class into groups of four or five. Have groups present their information as a television show on gardening.

ELIZABETH ELLIS

1943–

A professional storyteller, Elizabeth Ellis was born in Kentucky and grew up in Tennessee, amid the Applachian Mountains. After graduating from East Tennessee State University, she moved to Dallas, Texas, where she worked for 10 years as a children's librarian in the city's public library system. There, she says, "I realized it was the storytelling part of my job that I enjoyed the most—and the card-filing part that I liked the least."

In 1979, after attending the National Storytelling Festival in Jonesborough, Tennessee, for the first time and realizing that people made their living telling stories, Ellis left the library and became a professional storyteller. For the past 16 years, she has charmed audiences of all ages with her repertoire of more than 500 stories including several about Texas, Appalachia, personal experiences, and—her favorite—unknown heroic women. Ellis performs throughout North America at festivals, workshops, schools, and libraries where she is described as "spellbinding with a relaxed style, warm delivery, and a beautiful voice."

Many of Ellis's stories she heard from her grandfather, a circuit-riding minister who collected stories as he traveled and whom Ellis credits with giving her an ability to see the beauty in everyone. The story "Flowers and Freckle Cream" is based on experiences she had while spending summers with her grandfather in Kentucky. She resides in Dallas, where she continues to share her stories. "It's a charming way to make a living. Sometimes I feel guilty because I have so much fun."
OTHER WORKS *Homespun Tales, Tales of Wit and Humor, Best Loved Stories Told at the National Storytelling Festival*; available on audiocassette: "Like Meat Loves Salt," "Tales of Ancient Egypt," "I Will Not Talk in Class" Extended Reading

ELIZABETH ELLIS

Elizabeth Ellis conducts workshops to teach other people how to develop their skills in storytelling. Two of the little-known heroic women featured in Ellis's stories are Debra Sampson, who disguised herself as a man to serve in the Revolutionary War, and Della Akley, a pioneer explorer in Africa around the turn of the century.

Alternative Activities

1. *Cooperative Learning* Have students work in groups of four to design a poster to illustrate this selection. Two students can search for drawings or photographs of different lilies; the other two can find photographs or magazine pictures of people with different skin colors and facial characteristics. The poster can be captioned with Grandpa's quote, "There are all kinds of flowers, and they are all beautiful." Students may also choose a caption of their own.
2. It is possible that Elizabeth did not read the directions for the freckle-remover cream carefully. Far too many people do not read directions before using products. Have students collect examples of important directions from labels on packages and instruction manuals for equipment. Students can then create a bulletin-board display of these items.

OVERVIEW

Objectives

- To understand and appreciate a nonfiction selection that describes the quest for immortality of the first emperor of China
- To enrich reading by using active reading strategies
- To understand and appreciate author's purpose
- To express understanding of the selection through a choice of writing forms, including a legend, a log entry, and an epitaph
- To extend understanding of the selection through a variety of multimodal and cross-curricular activities

Skills

READING SKILLS/STRATEGIES
- SQ3R
- Questioning

THE WRITER'S STYLE
- Organizing details

GRAMMAR
- Adverbs

LITERARY CONCEPTS
- Sources
- Author's purpose

SPELLING
- Forms of the prefix *in-*

SPEAKING, LISTENING, AND VIEWING
- Group discussion
- Oral presentation

Cross-Curricular Connections

GEOGRAPHY
- Ch'in Shih Huang Ti's empire today

HISTORY
- Time line of Chinese dynasties

MATH
- Elapsed time
- Length of the Great Wall

HISTORICAL CONNECTION
Tomb of Ch'in Shih Huang Ti It is believed that Ch'in Shih Huang Ti was trying to protect his tomb from invaders by ordering that a clay army be placed next to the tomb. These images show this site during and after excavation. Included are a map and several diagrams illustrating the large numbers of terra-cotta figures found in different parts of the site.

Side A, Frame 38908

PREVIEWING

NONFICTION

The First Emperor
from The Tomb Robbers
Daniel Cohen

Activating Prior Knowledge/Setting a Purpose
PERSONAL CONNECTION

In the account you are about to read, an early Chinese ruler tries to achieve immortality, the ability to live forever. What would be the advantages and disadvantages of being immortal? Record your thoughts about immortality in your notebook. As you read, think about how the ruler's determination to live forever affects his daily life.

Building Background
HISTORICAL CONNECTION

Three dynasties, or ruling families, known as the Xia (shyä), the Shang (shäng), and the Zhou (jō), controlled ancient China from about 2000 to 256 B.C. The Zhou dynasty ruled by *feudalism* (fyōōd'l-ĭz'əm), an economic system in which people of the noble class own the land and peasants perform the labor on it. In 256 B.C., the feudal state of Qin (chĭn), also spelled Ch'in, defeated the last Zhou ruler. Ten years later a man named Cheng, the subject of this selection, became king of Qin. By 221 B.C., he had united all of China under the Qin dynasty.

Believing in immortality, the new ruler thought that his family's reign would last 10,000 generations, and he created a new title. He added *shih* (shē), meaning "first," to *huang ti* (hwäng-dē), meaning "emperor," and called himself Ch'in Shih Huang Ti, sometimes spelled Qin Shihuangdi. The Qin dynasty survived only 15 years, but it began 2,100 years of rule by emperors. Throughout the following seven dynasties, Chinese emperors were called *huang ti,* until 1912, when China became a republic.

526 UNIT FIVE PART 1: FACING INNER FEARS

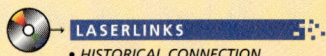
• HISTORICAL CONNECTION

PRINT AND MEDIA RESOURCES

UNIT FIVE RESOURCE BOOK
Strategic Reading: Literature, p. 9
Vocabulary SkillBuilder, p. 12
Reading SkillBuilder, p. 10
Spelling SkillBuilder, p. 11

GRAMMAR MINI-LESSONS
Transparencies, p. 12
Copymasters, p. 19

WRITING MINI-LESSONS
Transparencies, p. 30

ACCESS FOR STUDENTS ACQUIRING ENGLISH
Selection Summaries
Reading and Writing Support

FORMAL ASSESSMENT
Selection Test, pp. 105–106
Test Generator

 **AUDIO LIBRARY**
See Reference Card

 **LASERLINKS**
Historical Connection
Art Gallery

 **INTERNET RESOURCES**
McDougal Littell Literature Center at http://www.hmco.com/mcdougal/lit

---

526 THE LANGUAGE OF LITERATURE TEACHER'S EDITION

Active Reading
READING CONNECTION

The Techniques of SQ3R

SQ3R is a step-by-step strategy to help you study a nonfiction selection more effectively. SQ3R stands for the steps Survey, Question, Read, Recite, Review. The chart shown explains the five steps:

The SQ3R Strategy

S — **Survey** Get a general idea of what you will be reading by skimming the first sentence—usually the topic sentence—of each paragraph. Look quickly at titles, headings, and highlighted words or phrases. Look at illustrations, charts, and other graphics as well.

Q — **Question** Write down any questions or predictions that came to mind during the survey. Also include any study questions found in the selection or provided by your teacher. Create additional questions suggested by the selection's titles, headings, pictures, maps, and charts.

R — **Read** Look for the answers to your questions as you read. Also identify the main ideas in each section. React to unclear passages and to confusing terms by adding new questions.

R — **Recite** After you have finished reading, either say the answers to your questions to yourself or write the answers in your notebook. If any questions remain unanswered, reread parts of the selection.

R — **Review** Quickly read over your notes and look over the main ideas in the material so that you will remember them. Refer to the selection to find the answers to any questions that may still remain.

The SQ3R study method may be helpful as you read "The First Emperor." If you encounter any difficulty with a particular section, use the appropriate strategy to help you approach the section. Questions that appear within the selection may also help direct your reading.

THE FIRST EMPEROR **527**

SUMMARY

Ch'in Shih Huang Ti, the first emperor of China, had a constant fear of his own death. Although he searched for the secret of immortality, he also had the foresight to begin construction on his own tomb—which took 30 years and at least 700,000 builders to complete. According to legend, the tomb's incredible contents included miniature reproductions of Shih Huang Ti's 270 palaces, a solid copper burial chamber, and loaded crossbows poised to shoot intruders. The tomb lay covered with earth for many centuries, until 1974, when a peasant plowing a nearby field uncovered a life-size clay statue of a warrior. Further excavations revealed thousands of similar statues, all part of the emperor's "spirit army," who were meant to serve the dead ruler in the next world. Whether the tomb has been robbed or still holds the legendary treasures remains to be seen, as Chinese archaeologists are still slowly and carefully working their way toward the tomb site.

Thematic Link: *Facing Inner Fears*
China's first emperor goes to extreme lengths to try to ensure his immortality.

WORDS TO KNOW

consolidate (kən-sŏl´ĭ-dāt´) *v.* to combine into a whole; unite (p. 531)
immortality (ĭm´ôr-tăl´ĭ-tē) *n.* endless life or existence (p. 531)
insignificant (ĭn´sĭg-nĭf´ĭ-kənt) *adj.* having little or no importance (p. 529)
intricate (ĭn´trĭ-kĭt) *adj.* full of complicated details (p. 531)
obsessed (əb-sĕst´) *adj.* overly concentrating on a single emotion or idea **obsess** *v.* (p. 530)

preservation (prĕz´ər-vā´shən) *n.* the act of keeping something safe from harm; protection (p. 532)
reproduction (rē´prə-dŭk´shən) *n.* a copy or imitation (p. 531)
surpass (sər-păs´) *v.* to be better or greater than (p. 530)
tyrant (tī´rənt) *n.* a cruel, unjust ruler (p. 532)
unparalleled (ŭn-păr´ə-lĕld´) *adj.* having no equal; unmatched (p. 532)

CUSTOMIZING FOR
Students Acquiring English

- Use **ACCESS FOR STUDENTS ACQUIRING ENGLISH**, *Reading and Writing Support*.
- To engage students' interest, invite them to share funeral practices of their cultures. Ask them to compare these practices with the entombment described in this selection.

STRATEGIC READING FOR
Less-Proficient Readers

Set a Purpose Ask students to read to learn about the many accomplishments of the first emperor of China.

Use **UNIT FIVE RESOURCE BOOK**, pp. 9–10 for guidance in reading the selection.

CUSTOMIZING FOR
Gifted and Talented Students

Ask students to discuss why it might be difficult to protect the valuable artifacts uncovered in archaeological excavations. *(Possible responses: Major threats to the artifacts are deterioration due to exposure; tomb robbers; accidental damage caused by visitors.)*

CUSTOMIZING FOR
Multiple Learning Styles

A **Spatial or Graphic Learners** Have spatial learners check out books from the library with more photographs, maps, and other visual aids of the excavation of the emperor's tomb. Items can be shared with all students during discussion of the selection.

Critical Thinking:
MAKING JUDGMENTS

B Have students discuss what motivates archaeologists to search so carefully for remains of past civilizations, and if they think the time and effort are equal to the rewards. *(Possible responses: to learn more about history; to find valuable objects; to become famous)*

The First EMPEROR
from *The Tomb Robbers* by Daniel Cohen

AMBITION 志 DESTINY 命 ETERNITY 永 LOYALTY 忠

528 UNIT FIVE PART 1: FACING INNER FEARS

Mini-Lesson  Reading Skills/Strategies

ACTIVE READING: QUESTION Remind students that active readers ask questions about what is happening in a selection as they read. Readers also ask questions about words or statements that they find confusing. Often, readers will find answers to their questions as they continue reading. For instance, it is likely that after reading the first sentence on page 529 readers will be wondering what tomb will outshine Tutankhamen's and why. The answer can be found in the rest of the paragraph.

Application Ask students to create a two-column chart with the headings *Questions* and *Answers*. As students read the selection, they should list the questions they had while reading the selection as well as the answers they were able to find to their questions. If students have questions left unanswered in their charts, you may wish to have the class discuss these questions, offer answers, or provide time for research.

Reteaching/Reinforcement
- *Unit Five Resource Book*, p. 10

528 THE LANGUAGE OF LITERATURE TEACHER'S EDITION

Terra cotta statues from the tomb of Ch'in Shih Huang Ti.
Copyright © An Keren/PPS/Photo Researchers.

There is what may turn out to be the greatest archaeological[1] find of modern times, one that may ultimately outshine even the discovery of the tomb of Tutankhamen.[2] It is the tomb of the emperor Ch'in Shih Huang Ti. Now admittedly the name Ch'in Shih Huang Ti is not exactly a household word in the West. But then neither was Tutankhamen until 1922. The major difference is that while Tutankhamen himself was historically <u>insignificant</u>, Ch'in Shih Huang Ti was enormously important in Chinese history. In many respects he was really the founder of China.

The future emperor started out as the king of the small state Ch'in. At the time, the land was divided up among a number of small states, all constantly warring with one another. Ch'in was one of the smallest and weakest. Yet the king of Ch'in managed to overcome all his rivals, and in the year 221 B.C. he proclaimed himself emperor of the land that we now know as China. From that date until the revolution of 1912, China

---

1. **archaeological** (är′kē-ə-lŏj′ĭ-kəl): having to do with archaeology, the scientific study of the life and culture of ancient peoples.
2. **Tutankhamen** (tōōt′äng-kä′mən): a Pharaoh, or king, of Egypt from 1347 to 1339 B.C. He is not considered an important king, partly because he was very young and ruled for only about nine years. His tomb was found almost intact by the British archaeologist Howard Carter in 1922.

WORDS TO KNOW

insignificant (ĭn′sĭg-nĭf′ĭ-kənt) *adj.* having little or no importance

529

Mini-Lesson The Writer's Style

ORGANIZING DETAILS Remind students that writers use details to support their main ideas. As shown on the chart, these details can be organized using different methods. Point out that this selection often organizes details by chronological order because its subject matter is history.

Application Have students use the  paragraph above for these exercises.
1. List the factual details given in the paragraph.
2. Explain how the details are organized. *(chronologically)*
3. Rewrite the paragraph to organize the information in a different way.

Reteaching/Reinforcement
• Writing Handbook, anthology p. 785
• Writing Mini-Lessons transparencies, p. 30

The Writer's Craft
Main Idea with Supporting Details, pp. 218–220

Method	How to Organize Details
main idea with supporting details	Write the main idea, perhaps as a topic sentence. Support it with facts, reasons, or examples.
chronological order	Write events in the order they occur.
spatial order	Describe details in a scene by moving up, down, to the left or right.
order of importance	Write details from most important to least important or vice versa.

THE LANGUAGE OF LITERATURE TEACHER'S EDITION **529**

Linking to Math

F Many estimates have been made of the length of the Great Wall. The American geographer Frederick Clapp estimated 2,150 miles for the principal sections, plus another 1,780 miles for loops and offshoots, for a total of 3,930 miles. For comparison, the straight-line distance from Philadelphia to Portland, Oregon, is a bit less than 2,900 miles.

Literary Concept:
AUTHOR'S PURPOSE

G Remind students that an author's purpose may be to entertain, to inform, to express an opinion, to persuade, or a combination of these purposes. Ask students what the author's primary purpose seems to be for this selection. *(To inform)*

CUSTOMIZING FOR
Students Acquiring English

2 Invite students to guess the meaning of *whereabouts*. *("present location")* If necessary, point out that the question word *where* is a clue to the meaning.

STRATEGIC READING FOR
Less-Proficient Readers

H Ask students what the emperor's most famous achievement was. *(Building the Great Wall of China)*

Set a Purpose Have students look, in the next part of the selection, for details about what things the archaeologists expect to find in the emperor's tomb.

A soldier and his horse, one of many remarkable statues found in the tomb of the Emperor Shih Huang Ti. Copyright © Laurie Platt Winfrey, Inc.

was always ruled by an emperor. The name China itself comes from the name Ch'in.

Shih Huang Ti ruled his empire with ferocious efficiency. He had the Great Wall of China built to keep out the northern barbarians. The Great Wall, which stretches some fifteen hundred miles, is a building project that rivals and perhaps surpasses the Great Pyramid[3]. The Great Wall took thirty years to build and cost the lives of countless thousands of laborers. Today the Great Wall remains China's number one tourist attraction.

As he grew older, Shih Huang Ti became obsessed with the prospect of his own death. He had survived several assassination attempts and was terrified of another. He traveled constantly between his 270 different palaces, so that no one could ever be sure where he was going to be. He never slept in the same room for two nights in a row. Anyone who revealed the emperor's whereabouts was put to death along with his entire family.

Shih Huang Ti searched constantly for the secret of immortality. He became prey to a

---

3. **Great Pyramid:** one of the largest pyramids built by the ancient Egyptians. It is made of more than 2 million stone blocks, each weighing about two tons. Each side of its base is longer than two football fields.

WORDS TO KNOW
surpass (sər-păs′) *v.* to be better or greater than
obsessed (əb-sĕst′) *adj.* concerned too much with a single emotion or idea **obsess** *v.*
immortality (ĭm′ôr-tăl′ĭ-tē) *n.* endless life or existence

530

Mini-Lesson Grammar

Adjective
He was a constant traveler.

Adverb
He traveled constantly.

ADVERBS Remind students that an adverb is a word that modifies a verb, an adjective, or another adverb. Many common adverbs are formed by adding the ending *-ly* to adjectives.

Application Have students add *-ly* to each adjective and then find a logical place to use it in the sentence.
1. extreme: The emperor was worried about assassination attempts.
2. unbelievable: A large number of statues has already been found in the tomb.
3. careful: Archaeologists work to discover secrets about the past.
4. hopeful: They excavate the different sections of the tomb.
5. final: They may find out whether the legends about the tomb are true.

Reteaching/Reinforcement
- *Grammar Handbook,* anthology p. 830
- *Grammar Mini-Lessons* copymasters p. 19, transparencies p. 12

 **The Writer's Craft**

What Are Adverbs? pp. 482–484

530 THE LANGUAGE OF LITERATURE TEACHER'S EDITION

host of phony magicians and other fakers who promised much but could deliver nothing.

The emperor heard that there were immortals living on some far-off islands, so he sent a huge fleet to find them. The commander of the fleet knew that if he failed in his mission, the emperor would put him to death. So the fleet simply never returned. It is said that the fleet found the island of Japan and stayed there to become the ancestors of the modern Japanese.

In his desire to stay alive, Shih Huang Ti did not neglect the probability that he would die someday. He began construction of an immense tomb in the Black Horse hills near one of his favorite summer palaces. The tomb's construction took as long as the construction of the Great Wall—thirty years.

The emperor, of course, did die. Death came while he was visiting the eastern provinces. But his life had become so secretive that only a few high officials were aware of his death. They contrived to keep it a secret until they could <u>consolidate</u> their own power. The imperial procession headed back for the capital. Unfortunately, it was midsummer and the emperor's body began to rot and stink. So one of the plotters arranged to have a cart of fish follow the immense imperial chariot to hide the odor of the decomposing corpse. Finally, news of the emperor's death was made public. The body, or what was left of it, was buried in the tomb that he had been building for so long.

Stories about that tomb sound absolutely incredible. It was said to contain miniature <u>reproductions</u> of all the emperor's 270 palaces. A map of the entire empire with all the major rivers reproduced in mercury, which by some mechanical means was made to flow into a miniature ocean, was also part of the interior of the tomb. So was a reproduction of the stars and planets. According to legend, the burial chamber itself was filled with molten copper so that the emperor's remains were sealed inside a gigantic ingot.[4]

It was also said that loaded crossbows were set up all around the inside of the tomb and that anyone who did manage to penetrate the inner chambers would be shot full of arrows. But just to make sure that no one got that far, the pallbearers who had placed Shih Huang Ti's remains in the tomb were sealed inside with it. They were supposed to be the only ones who knew exactly how to get in and out of the <u>intricate</u> tomb. All of this was done to preserve the emperor's remains from the hands of tomb robbers. Did it work? We don't really know yet.

CLARIFY
Summarize some of the precautions taken supposedly to protect the emperor's remains.
Using a Reading Log

There are two contradictory stories about the tomb of Ch'in Shih Huang Ti. The first says that it was covered up with earth to make it resemble an ordinary hill and that its location has remained unknown for centuries.

But a more accurate legend holds that there never was any attempt to disguise the existence of the tomb. Ch'in Shih Huang Ti had been building it for years, and everybody knew

---

4. **ingot** (ĭng′gət): a mass of metal shaped as a bar or block.

PREDICT
What special plans do you think the emperor will make for his tomb?
Using a Reading Log

WORDS TO KNOW
consolidate (kən-sŏl′ĭ-dāt′) v. to make strong or secure
reproduction (rē′prə-dŭk′shən) n. a copy; an imitation
intricate (ĭn′-trĭ-kĭt) adj. full of complicated details

531

Active Reading: PREDICT

I Ask students what special plans they think the emperor will make for his tomb. (*Possible responses: It will be large, like a palace, and hard to break into; he may even have a few false tombs constructed to mislead intruders.*)

CUSTOMIZING FOR
Students Acquiring English

3 You may want to point out that *It was also said* is an expression that introduces information that may or may not be true.

Active Reading: CLARIFY

J Ask students to summarize some of the precautions taken supposedly to protect the emperor's remains. (*Possible responses: a secret procession returning to the capital with the emperor's body disguised its smell with dead fish; the emperor planned to have his remains sealed in a block of copper; loaded crossbows were aimed at anyone who entered the inner chamber; the pallbearers were sealed inside too.*)

STRATEGIC READING FOR
Less-Proficient Readers

K Ask students what kinds of things were found in the emperor's tomb. (*miniature palaces; map of Chinese empire; reproductions of stars and planets; chamber filled with copper; evidence of crossbows; pallbearers' remains*)
Summarizing

Set a Purpose Have students read to the end of the selection to find out what has been discovered in the emperor's tomb and why the entire tomb has not been excavated.

Mini-Lesson Spelling

FORMS OF THE PREFIX IN- Use the rules shown to remind students that the prefix *in-* is spelled *im-* before base words that begin with the letters *m* or *p*. It changes to *ir-* before the letter *r* and *il-* before the letter *l*. One meaning of this prefix is "not or without."

Application Have students add a form of the prefix *in-* to each underlined word. They will have to rewrite the sentence for the new word to fit correctly.

1. Stories about the tomb don't sound <u>credible</u>.
2. It wasn't <u>possible</u> for the emperor to live forever.
3. Building 270 palaces does not sound very <u>logical</u>.
4. The smell from the emperor's body was not <u>perfectly</u> disguised by the fish.
5. Some people think it was not <u>responsible</u> of the emperor to spend so much money on his tomb.

Reteaching/Reinforcement
• *Unit Five Resource Book*, p. 11

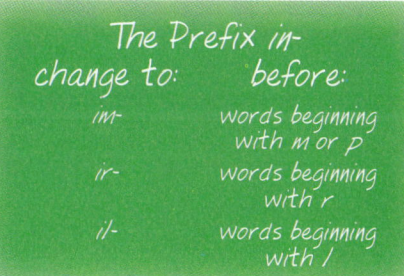

The Prefix in-
change to: before:
im-   words beginning with m or p
ir-   words beginning with r
il-   words beginning with l

CUSTOMIZING FOR
Students Acquiring English

4 Explain that *Over the centuries* means "during the following hundreds of years."

STRATEGIC READING FOR
Less-Proficient Readers

L Use these questions to help students summarize the end of the selection.

- What amazing discovery has been made as archaeologists have uncovered the emperor's tomb? *(More than 6,000 life-size clay warriors and horses)* **Finding the Main Idea**

- Why hasn't the entire tomb been excavated? *(Possible responses: Roofs have collapsed and it takes time and trained people to dig out the chambers; important artifacts must be carefully preserved.)* **Making Inferences**

CUSTOMIZING FOR
Gifted and Talented Students

M Have students research and prepare a report on the first emperor of China, the thousands of clay warriors and their reason for being, and descriptions of military conflicts and threats during the emperor's life.

COMPREHENSION CHECK

1. Why is Shih Huang Ti called the first emperor of China? *(He was the first to rule over all the land, which was divided into small states.)*
2. What two large-scale construction projects were carried out during the rule of Shih Huang Ti? *(the Great Wall and his tomb)*
3. When and how was the emperor's tomb discovered? *(in 1974, when a farmer was plowing a field)*
4. What kinds of information about Chinese history have the archaeologists learned from the tomb so far? *(Possible responses: the clothing and weapons used by the emperor's soldiers; the artistic abilities of the people who made the statues)*

---

where it was. After his death the tomb was surrounded by walls enclosing an area of about five hundred acres. This was to be the emperor's "spirit city." Inside the spirit city were temples and all sorts of other sacred buildings and objects dedicated to the dead emperor.

4 Over the centuries the walls, the temples, indeed everything above ground was carried away by vandals. The top of the tomb was covered with earth and eventually came to resemble a large hill. Locally the hill is called Mount Li. But still the farmers who lived in the area had heard stories that Mount Li contained the tomb of Ch'in Shih Huang Ti or of some other important person.

In the spring of 1974 a peasant plowing a field near Mount Li uncovered a life-sized clay statue of a warrior. Further digging indicated that there was an entire army of statues beneath the ground. Though excavations are not yet complete, Chinese authorities believe that there are some six thousand life-sized clay statues of warriors, plus scores of life-sized statues of horses. Most of the statues are broken, but some are in an absolutely remarkable state of <u>preservation</u>. Each statue is finely made, and each shows a distinct individual, different from all the others.

This incredible collection is Shih Huang Ti's "spirit army." At one time Chinese kings practiced human sacrifice so that the victims could serve the dead king in the next world. Shih Huang Ti was willing to make do with the models. Men and horses were arranged in a military fashion in a three-acre underground chamber. The chamber may have been entered at some point. The roof certainly collapsed. But still the delicate figures have survived surprisingly well. Most of the damage was done when the roof caved in. That is why the Chinese archaeologists are so hopeful that when the tomb itself is excavated, it too will be found to have survived surprisingly well.

The Chinese are not rushing the excavations. They have only a limited number of trained people to do the job. After all, the tomb has been there for over two thousand years. A few more years won't make much difference.

Though once denounced as a <u>tyrant</u>, Ch'in Shih Huang Ti is now regarded as a national hero. His name is a household word in China. The Chinese government knows that it may have an <u>unparalleled</u> ancient treasure on its hands, and it wants to do the job well. Over the next few years we should be hearing much more about this truly remarkable find.

L

M

WORDS TO KNOW
preservation (prĕz'ər-vā'shən) *n.* the condition of being kept perfect or unchanged
tyrant (tī'rənt) *n.* a cruel, unjust ruler
unparalleled (ŭn-păr'ə-lĕld') *adj.* having no equal; unmatched

532

Mini-Lesson Study Skills

REVIEWING SOURCES Point out to students how difficult it is for historians to find out what actually happened during the life of Shih Huang Ti. Some writings from the Han Dynasty (206 B.C.–A.D. 220), the one that followed Shih Huang Ti's Ch'in Dynasty, do survive. But it seems probable that the Han historians wished to depict their predecessors in an unfavorable light.

Application Tell students that this selection was published in 1980. A book called *Recent Discoveries in Chinese Archaeology* was published in 1984. It contains an English translation of an account written by Yuan Zhongyi, a Chinese archaeologist. Have students compare the following details from Yuan Zhongyi's essay with information given in the selection. Have students discuss how an author's sources affect his or her writing, especially when writing about history.

1. The tomb was discovered by members of a commune who were sinking a well. *(Selection says the tomb was discovered by a peasant plowing a field.)*
2. Four pits have been discovered, containing a total of more than 7,000 figures. *(Selection says there are some 6,000 statues.)*

---

532 THE LANGUAGE OF LITERATURE TEACHER'S EDITION

HISTORICAL INSIGHT

THE EMPEROR

Ch'in Shih Huang Ti came to power in China in 246 B.C., at the age of 13, when he became king of the state of Qin. The new ruler set out to extend his power throughout the empire. Shih Huang Ti divided the empire into 36 provinces and created a system of government that would allow him to maintain firm control. Each province had two officials—one governor and one defender. This brought unity to the empire and allowed the emperor to establish standard systems of money, measurement, and writing. Taking the land away from thousands of noble families, he put an end to the feudal system and allowed anyone who could pay taxes to own land.

To protect his empire from possible invasion from the north, Shih Huang Ti used a forced-labor crew of 700,000 to build the Great Wall of China. This massive hand-built wall was lengthened and repaired over the centuries, and by the time of the Ming dynasty (1368–1644) stretched for 4,000 miles.

Much of the emperor's burial site remains to be uncovered. In addition to the clay army—which when discovered was arranged in a military formation including bowmen, archers, and charioteers—archaeologists found chariots, iron farm tools, objects of silk, linen, jade, and bone, and weapons such as spears and swords that remain shiny today. Archaeologists anticipate that it will take many years to complete the excavation of the emperor's burial site. Four separate dig areas have been covered with roofing and serve as an on-site museum, even as excavation of the area continues.

Shih Huang Ti became a national hero to many modern-day Chinese when the clay army and other artifacts were uncovered. He is recognized and honored for bringing a national unity to China that lasted over 2,000 years. Though he did not live forever, Shih Huang Ti may indeed have achieved a degree of immortality: the tomb and the many astounding objects found at the burial site promise to fascinate many generations to come.

The Great Wall stands today as the longest structure ever built.
Copyright © D. E. Cox/Tony Stone Images.

THE EMPEROR **533**

Cultural Note
Students may notice that the emperor's name, Ch'in Shih Huang Ti, is sometimes spelled Qin Shihuangdi. You may wish to explain that it is difficult to transcribe the sounds of Chinese into English-language equivalents. Several different systems have been developed for writing Chinese in the Roman alphabet. One system widely used in the past was developed in the 1800s by two English scholars, Sir Thomas Wade and Herbert A. Giles. In 1958, the People's Republic of China adopted a different system called pinyin. The spellings of words can be very different in different transliteration systems; for example, two spellings of the same name are *Peking* and *Beijing*, and *Mao Tse-tung* and *Mao Zedong*.

HISTORICAL INSIGHT

1. How did Ch'in Shih Huang Ti gain control of land and give it to anyone who was willing to pay taxes on it? *(He took land away from the nobility.)*
2. Why did Shih Huang Ti have the Great Wall of China built? *(to protect his empire from being invaded by an enemy army)*
3. Why might the discovery of the life-size clay warriors have caused many modern Chinese to view the emperor as a national hero? *(Possible responses: The beauty of the statues indicates that the emperor cared about the arts; the wonders of the tomb remind people of the emperor's role in unifying China.)*
4. How might Shih Huang Ti have felt if he knew that archaeologists would dig up his tomb? *(Possible responses: He would have been angry that his wishes were ignored. He would have been happy that evidence of his empire had lasted so long.)*

Multicultural Perspectives

THE EMPEROR'S CLAY SOLDIERS One of the most amazing aspects of the clay soldiers found in Shih Huang Ti's tomb is the realism displayed in the figures. The soldiers carry real weapons, as sharp today as when they were made more than 2,000 years ago. The clothing of the foot soldiers, archers, charioteers, and officers reflects their duties and ranks. Eight different styles of armor are represented, including a type that is similar to a baseball catcher's protective vest.

Most impressive of all, the faces of the statues are individually sculpted—no two faces found so far are alike. The clay soldiers represent all ages, from young-looking soldiers to stern, older commanders. The statues also vary in their expressions: Some frown, some smile, some appear fierce and competent, some seem more thoughtful. Even the hairstyles are individualized, showing different types of braiding. Some historians think the figures may have been modeled from real soldiers and reflect the wide diversity of people united under Shih Huang Ti's rule.

THE LANGUAGE OF LITERATURE TEACHER'S EDITION **533**

From Personal Response to Critical Analysis

1. Responses will vary. Students' notebook entries may include their opinions about the emperor as well as their reactions to what was found in his tomb.
2. Possible responses: Positive aspects of the emperor's rule include unifying the country and protecting the people from northern invaders. Negative aspects include his using forced labor to build large projects and killing anyone who told of his whereabouts.
3. Responses will vary.
4. Possible responses: the great number of clay statues in the tomb; the fact that the tomb lay undiscovered for 2,000 years
5. Responses will vary. Students might choose themselves or contemporary figures they admire and note what each would be remembered for.

Another Pathway

Cooperative Learning Before students begin the project, they should discuss the sections they might include in their catalog: an introduction summarizing the events of the emperor's rule; photographs of items from the tomb (soldiers, horses, weapons, chariots) with text to describe each. Students should divide research tasks; for instance, a few students can research additional information about the emperor and his tomb. Others can use the research information to write copy for the catalog, and remaining students can design the catalog and choose photos and illustrations to accompany the text.

Rubric

3 Full Accomplishment Students' catalog accurately reflects information from their research and gives a thorough overall description of the subject.

2 Substantial Accomplishment Students' catalog uses some information from research and describes the emperor's life and the artifacts in his tomb.

1 Little or Partial Accomplishment Students' catalog uses little or no research. The information is incomplete or inaccurate.

RESPONDING OPTIONS

FROM PERSONAL RESPONSE TO CRITICAL ANALYSIS

REFLECT 1. What were your thoughts as you finished reading this selection? Record them in your notebook.

RETHINK 2. How would you describe Ch'in Shih Huang Ti?

Close Textual Reading **Consider**
- his attempts to achieve immortality
- his accomplishments
- his effects on those he ruled

3. Review the ideas about immortality you recorded in the Personal Connection on page 526. In your *Thematic Link* opinion, are the advantages of immortality worth the efforts Ch'in Shih Huang Ti made to try to achieve it? Explain your answer.

4. What information from the selection do you find most interesting or surprising? Share your thoughts with a classmate.

RELATE 5. Many people would like to achieve a certain kind of immortality—that of having their name and achievements live on after their death. If you could choose what to be remembered for centuries from now, what would you choose? Share your ideas with your classmates.

Multimodal Learning
ANOTHER PATHWAY
Cooperative Learning

Work with a group to develop a catalog for an exhibit about Ch'in Shih Huang Ti. Refer to encyclopedias for additional details about the emperor and the excavation of his tomb. Combine the information into one catalog that you might add to the school library's reference materials.

LITERARY CONCEPTS

An **author's purpose** may be to entertain, to inform, to express an opinion, or to persuade. A writer may combine two or three purposes, but one is usually of more importance. Think about the purposes Daniel Cohen may have had for writing this selection. Which purpose do you think was most important to him? Why?

QUICKWRITES

1. Daniel Cohen offers two different explanations of why the tomb had remained hidden for so long. Draft your own **legend** about the location of the emperor's body and tomb.

2. Imagine that you are a Chinese archaeologist in 1974. Draft a **log entry** you might make describing your reactions to this discovery.

3. Write an **epitaph** that could be engraved on the tomb of Ch'in Shih Huang Ti.

📁 **PORTFOLIO** *Save your writing. You may want to use it later as a springboard to a piece for your portfolio.*

534 UNIT FIVE PART 1: FACING INNER FEARS

Literary Concepts

Possible response: The primary purpose is to inform. However, the author also uses the selection to express an opinion, so he paints a somewhat unattractive picture of the emperor. Encourage students to find specific passages from the selection to justify their responses.

QuickWrites

1. Discuss some of the characteristics of legends. For example, they are stories handed down explaining something that actually happened, but can include far-fetched ideas and magical happenings.

2. Remind students to use first-person point of view. Students can decide whether their log entries will be more personal or more professional in tone.

3. Tell students to keep in mind that space is limited for an epitaph. Many inscriptions are written in rhyming couplets, so students might use poetry.

The Writer's Craft

Personal Narrative, pp. 78–79
Writing from Your Journal, pp. 32–33
Writing a Poem, 86–88

Multimodal Learning

ALTERNATIVE ACTIVITIES

1. From the selections in this book, choose a historical figure or a character who you believe is truly immortal. With a partner, do a **talk-show interview** with one of you playing the person or character and the other playing the host. Invite the class members to be the audience for the show.

2. Construct a **model** of the Great Wall, the tomb of Ch'in Shih Huang Ti, or another artifact mentioned in the selection. Review Cohen's account to be sure that your model fits his description.

LITERARY LINKS

Now that you have read "The First Emperor," review the story "The Dog of Pompeii" (page 124) and the nonfictional excerpt "Tutankhamen" from *Lost Worlds* (page 470). Compare the ancient cultures of Pompeii, Egypt, and China as revealed by the artifacts described in the selections.

Multimodal Learning

ACROSS THE CURRICULUM

History The imperial rule of China begun by the Qin dynasty lasted until 1912. Research the dynasties that followed the Qin. Create a time line to summarize your findings. Present the time line to the class with a brief description of each dynasty.

ART CONNECTION

The clay figures of a soldier and his horse shown on page 530 were among those discovered at the burial site of Ch'in Shih Huang Ti. The military dress of the figure suggests that it was meant to help protect the emperor's tomb from invaders. Look carefully at the figures in the photograph to see what details you can observe. Does this image help you to understand or appreciate the enormous task that making over 6,000 of these statues must have been? Why or why not?

THE FIRST EMPEROR **535**

Alternative Activities

1. Suggest that students choose a person for whom they can find either an autobiography, a biography with quotes from the person, or a collection of letters. Using these types of resources, students can write dialogue using the actual words of their chosen person.
2. Students will need to use library books to get additional data for the models. You may wish to let them choose to draw a floor plan of the emperor's tomb instead of making a three-dimensional model.

Across the Curriculum

History Students will find that the dates for the dynasties vary from book to book. Explain that many dates are approximate because the transfer of power took place over a number of years.

Ch'in	221 B.C.–207 B.C.
Han	206 B.C.–A.D. 220
Three Kingdoms	220–280
Tsin	265–420
Southern and Northern Dynasties	420–589
Sui	589–618
T'ang	618–906
Five Dynasties	907–960
Sung	960–1279
Yüan	1260–1368
Ming	1368–1644
Ch'ing	1644–1912

ADDITIONAL SUGGESTIONS

Geography *China Then and Now* Have students use library reference sources to create two maps: one showing Shih Huang Ti's empire in about 200 B.C.; the second showing the same area today, with borders of modern countries. Major bodies of water and mountain ranges will be common to both maps.

Literary Links

Have students skim the other two selections. Then lead a class discussion to generate a list of comparison criteria; for example, forms of government, interest in the arts, beliefs in life after death.

Art Connection

Students will most likely express their admiration for the amount of detail used for such an enormous project.

ART GALLERY
Ancient Chinese Art Each of the dynasties that ruled China produced wonderful works of art that reflect different aspects of Chinese culture. Shown here are examples of art from several of these dynasties. You may wish to generate discussion on what this art reveals about China's history.

Side A, Frame 38922

THE LANGUAGE OF LITERATURE TEACHER'S EDITION **535**

Words to Know

Exercise A
1. c
2. b
3. b
4. a
5. a

Exercise B
1. c
2. a
3. e
4. b
5. d

Reteaching/Reinforcement
- *Unit Five Resource Book,* p. 12

WORDS TO KNOW

EXERCISE A For each group of words below, write the letter of the word that is the best antonym, or opposite, for the boldfaced word.

1. **consolidate** (a) buy (b) honor (c) separate
2. **unparalleled** (a) straight (b) common (c) simple
3. **preservation** (a) freedom (b) destruction (c) delay
4. **intricate** (a) plain (b) strong (c) flat
5. **reproduction** (a) original (b) question (c) enemy

EXERCISE B Review the Words to Know at the bottom of the selection pages. For each phrase in the first column, write the letter of the synonymous phrase from the second column.

1. an insignificant restaurant
2. outdo the girl
3. the fact of deathlessness
4. haunted by thoughts of a visitor
5. the tardier tyrant

a. surpass the lass
b. obsessed with a guest
c. a minor diner
d. the later dictator
e. the reality of immortality

DANIEL COHEN

An extremely productive author, Daniel Cohen has written more than 130 books, most of which are young-adult nonfiction. His science books, studies of animals and their relationships with humans, and historical introductions to ancient civilizations have been highly praised.

A native of Chicago, Cohen earned a degree in journalism from the University of Illinois in 1959. After a decade spent working his way from the position of proofreader for *Time* magazine to the position of managing editor of *Science Digest,* he left the editorial field to pursue a career as a freelance writer.

Research for his popular books on ghost stories and the supernatural has led Cohen to creep around haunted houses and spend "a damp and chilly night in an English churchyard," but he admits that he has never seen a ghost. One of the author's most popular books is *The Body Snatchers,* an informal history of grave robbing, which includes information about the Egyptian tombs.

Cohen and his wife, Susan, have cowritten several popular books for teens. Their topics range from movies and television to dinosaurs. He defends his choice of material, especially the supernatural: "I don't really 'believe in' most of the subjects I write about, and I don't pretend to."

OTHER WORKS *Young and Famous: Sports' Newest Superstars, Phantom Animals, Railway Ghosts and Other Highway Horrors, Prophets of Doom*

Extended Reading

LASERLINKS
• ART GALLERY

536 UNIT FIVE PART 1: FACING INNER FEARS

WHAT DO YOU THINK?
Reflecting on Theme

Ask students to think back over the surveys they did to discover their classmates' fears before reading the selections in Part 1. Ask students if anyone mentioned a fear of not living forever. Have students extend the activity by discussing how this fear might be faced or overcome.

PREVIEWING

POETRY

Message from a Caterpillar
Lilian Moore

Chrysalis Diary
Paul Fleischman

Activating Prior Knowledge/Setting a Purpose
PERSONAL CONNECTION

Think about your various experiences with the natural world. What changes in nature have you observed? In your notebook, jot down some of your observations of change. As you read, be aware of the changes in nature described in the poems.

Building Background
SCIENCE CONNECTION

The upcoming poems share a common theme—the transformation of a caterpillar into a butterfly or moth. This process of change is called metamorphosis (mět′ə-môr′fə-sĭs) and includes four stages, which are shown in the illustration below.

Once the caterpillar hatches, it grows rapidly, molting, or shedding its outer skin, several times. When the butterfly caterpillar reaches the third stage, it molts again to become a pupa (pyōō′pə), which quickly develops a hard shell. This shell often has a gold sheen and therefore is called a *chrysalis* (krĭs′ə-lĭs) from the Greek word *chrysos*, meaning "gold." Moth caterpillars do not form a chrysalis. Instead, most of them spin a silken cocoon around themselves. During the pupal stage, the wings, legs, and body of the adult moth or butterfly develop. Then the case splits open and the adult emerges. The exact moment when the case opens is determined by instinct, an inborn pattern of behavior that is often a response to the conditions in an environment.

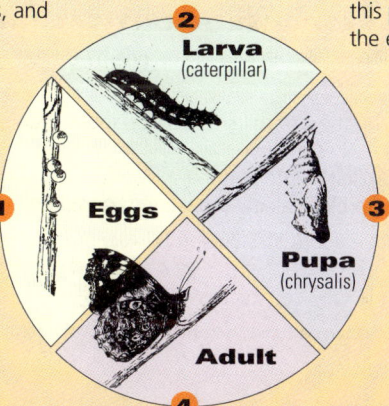

Active Reading
READING CONNECTION

Choral Reading You may notice the unusual way that the words of "Chrysalis Diary" are arranged. This poem is designed to be read aloud by two readers, one reading the lines on the left side of the page, the other reading the lines on the right side. The oral interpretation of poetry by two or more voices is called choral reading. "Chrysalis Diary" is read from top to bottom, with some parts assigned to a single reader and some lines meant to be spoken together. Take the opportunity to read this poem aloud with a partner. Notice the effect created by two voices.

MESSAGE FROM A CATERPILLAR / CHRYSALIS DIARY **537**

OVERVIEW

Objectives
- To understand and appreciate two poems about a caterpillar changing into a moth or butterfly
- To examine the use of figurative language in poetry
- To express understanding of the poems through a choice of writing forms, including poetry and dialogue
- To extend understanding of the poems through a variety of multimodal and cross-curricular activities

Skills

THE WRITER'S STYLE
- Sensory details

LITERARY CONCEPTS
- Figurative language
- Theme

STUDY SKILLS
- Paraphrasing

SPEAKING, LISTENING, AND VIEWING
- Multimedia performance
- Group discussion
- Oral presentation

Cross-Curricular Connections

GEOGRAPHY
- Migration routes of butterflies

SCIENCE
- Types of cocoons
- Types of metamorphosis
- Seasonal changes

PRINT AND MEDIA RESOURCES

UNIT FIVE RESOURCE BOOK
Strategic Reading: Literature, p. 15

WRITING MINI-LESSONS
Transparencies, p. 38

ACCESS FOR STUDENTS ACQUIRING ENGLISH
Reading and Writing Support

FORMAL ASSESSMENT
Selection Test, pp. 107–108
Test Generator

AUDIO LIBRARY
See Reference Card

LASERLINKS
Science Connection

INTERNET RESOURCES
McDougal Littell Literature Center at http://www.hmco.com/mcdougal/lit

THE LANGUAGE OF LITERATURE TEACHER'S EDITION **537**

Thematic Link: *Facing Inner Fears* Both poems capture feelings that occur when a creature faces dramatic changes.

CUSTOMIZING FOR
Students Acquiring English

- Use ACCESS FOR STUDENTS ACQUIRING ENGLISH, *Reading and Writing Support.*
- Be sure students understand that the "speaker" of each poem is an insect.
- In addition to these boxes, you may want to use the suggestions under Strategic Reading for Less-Proficient Readers.

STRATEGIC READING FOR
Less-Proficient Readers

Set a Purpose Have students read the poems to identify the process described and each speaker's viewpoint.

Use UNIT FIVE RESOURCE BOOK, p. 15, for guidance in reading the selection.

CUSTOMIZING FOR
Gifted and Talented Students

Discuss with students in what ways the development of wings affects an insect's life. Then ask students what wings often symbolize in literature and why they are such effective symbols.

Linking to Science

 **A** The threads of natural silk fabric come from the cocoons of several spiders and insects, principally the silkworm. Cocoons are not always made from silk. Some caterpillars wrap themselves in leaves for protection during the pupal stage.

Literary Concept: FORM

B Ask students to describe the form of "Message from a Caterpillar." *(three short stanzas made up of short lines of one to four words)*

Message from a Caterpillar
by Lilian Moore

Don't shake this
bough.
Don't try
to wake me
5 now.

In this cocoon
I've work to
do.
A Inside this silk
10 I'm changing
things.

I'm worm-like now
but in this
dark
15 I'm growing
B wings.

FROM PERSONAL RESPONSE TO CRITICAL ANALYSIS

REFLECT 1. What were you left thinking at the end of the poem? Discuss your reactions with a classmate.

RETHINK 2. How would you describe the caterpillar's feelings about change?
Consider
- the tone of the caterpillar's statements
- the active role the caterpillar seems to take in changing

3. What theme, or message about life, do you think is presented in this poem?
Consider
- to whom this message may be directed
- the last stanza

538 UNIT FIVE PART 1: FACING INNER FEARS

From Personal Response to Critical Analysis

1. Responses will vary.
2. Possible responses: The caterpillar seems optimistic about change; it is busy working and impatient with anyone who might disturb it.
3. The caterpillar warns an outside person or force—perhaps the wind—not to disturb it while it is working. Possible themes: Difficult endeavors require concentration and privacy; outside distractions can interfere with one's goals.

Chrysalis Diary

by Paul Fleischman

Cold told me
to fasten my feet
to this branch,

5

to shed my skin,

and I have obeyed.

November 13:

to dangle upside down
from my perch,

to cease being a caterpillar
and I have obeyed.

CUSTOMIZING FOR
Multiple Learning Styles

C **Musical Learners** As students read "Chrysalis Diary," they can make notes for places they could use background music to complement a choral reading. Before making their selections, they should decide what kinds of feelings the music should convey.

Literary Concept:
FIGURATIVE LANGUAGE

D Remind students that personification is describing an animal or object as if it were human or had human qualities. Have students find an example of personification in the first few lines of this poem. ("Cold told me . . ." treats the idea of cold as if it could actually speak.)

Active Reading: CLARIFY

E Ask students whom the caterpillar must "obey" and why this obedience is necessary. (It obeys the cold. As the weather turns colder, the caterpillar begins to build a protected environment to survive the winter.)

Linking to Science

 **F** Butterflies and moths undergo complete metamorphosis. Other insects undergo gradual metamorphosis, in which the insect usually does not change its appearance so radically. It changes from an egg, to a nymph, and then to an adult. The nymphs usually lack fully developed wings, but they look like small versions of the adult insect rather than like little worms.

Mini-Lesson: Speaking, Listening, and Viewing

MULTIMEDIA PERFORMANCE Explain to students that a multimedia performance involves the use of a variety of media—words, images, and sounds. These types of performances can be highly creative and explore ideas through a wide range of expression.

Application Have students create multimedia performances in conjunction with their choral readings of "Chrysalis Diary." Encourage students to select music, create imaginative sound effects, and use a variety of images to accompany their readings. For instance, students can record television or video images of caterpillars transforming into butterflies, use still images depicting the various stages of transformation on an overhead projector or on slides, and use music and sound effects to create a thoughtful and entertaining multimedia performance.

Literary Concept: THEME

G Have students discuss how the idea of loneliness or being alone is used as a theme in both poems. *(Possible responses: When you're working on something difficult, you often need to be left alone; going through difficult periods of change can be very lonely.)*

Active Reading: CLARIFY

H Ask students why the dates are important in the poem. Ask them what would happen if they were omitted. You may wish to use the following model to give students ideas of what they might be thinking about.

Think-Aloud Model *The dates show the passage of time and how the caterpillar changes its form. Without the dates the descriptions of the seasons might be confusing.*

CUSTOMIZING FOR
Students Acquiring English

1 Help students analyze the meaning of *Immeasurably:* prefix *im-* ("not"); base word *measure* ("to determine the precise size or quantity"); suffix *-able* ("able") + *-ly* ("in a specified manner").

2 Point out that *make out* is used here to mean "see with difficulty."

3 Students are probably familiar with the verb *enter* as meaning "come into." Help them guess that here it means "write a record in a diary or journal."

---

10 December 6:

the color of leaves and life,
has vanished!

15 lies in ruins!
I study the
brown new world around me.

I hear few sounds.

G 20

Swinging back and forth
in the wind,
I feel immeasurably alone.

H 25 I can make out snow falling.

I find I never tire of
30 watching the flakes
in their multitudes
passing my window.

Astounding.
3 35 I enter these
wondrous events
in my chronicle[2]

Green,

has vanished!
The empire of leaves
lies in ruins!

I fear the future.

Have any others of my kind
survived this cataclysm?[1]

January 4:

For five days and nights
it's been drifting down.

The world is now white.
Astounding.

knowing no reader
would believe me.

---

1. **cataclysm** (kăt′ə-klĭz′əm): any sudden, violent change; disaster.
2. **chronicle** (krŏn′ĭ-kəl): record; diary.

540 UNIT FIVE PART 1: FACING INNER FEARS

Mini-Lesson — The Writer's Style

SENSORY DETAILS Remind students that writers use details that appeal to the five senses—sight, hearing, smell, touch, and taste—to help readers more fully experience what is being described. Poets, in particular, search for precise words and phrases to describe sizes, shapes, colors, and other aspects of the world around them. In "Chrysalis Diary," the poet uses colors for some of the details appealing to sight.

Application Have students complete a chart like the one shown to list the various sensory details used in the poem. Then have students write a short poem, based on one of these sensory details, that explores that particular detail in more depth. Make sure students use details that appeal to the senses in their poems.

Reteaching/Reinforcement
• Writing Handbook, anthology p. 783
• *Writing Mini-Lessons* transparencies, p. 38

The Writer's Craft

Writing a Poem, pp. 86–88
Appealing to the Senses, pp. 266–269

Line	Word or Phrase in Poem	Sense Appealed To

540 THE LANGUAGE OF LITERATURE TEACHER'S EDITION

40 February 12:

Unable to see out
at all this morning.

45 and branches falling.

ponder their import,[3]

50

and wait for more.

An ice storm last night.

Yet I hear boughs cracking

Hungry for sounds
in this silent world,
I cherish these,

miser[4] them away
in my memory,
and wait for more.

---

3. **ponder their import:** think deeply about their meaning.
4. **miser:** to gather up and save in a greedy way.

Literary Concept: SENSORY DETAILS

I Have students identify details that appeal to the sense of hearing in these lines. *(line 44: "I hear boughs cracking / and branches falling")* Ask students what impression or feeling is conveyed by these details. *(Possible response: The pupa is covered with ice and cannot see anything, so it eagerly listens for any sounds from the outside world.)*

Critical Thinking: CLASSIFYING

J Have students compare the speakers of the two poems. *(In the first poem, the speaker sounds energetic, hard-working, businesslike, and a bit abrupt. In the second poem, the speaker sounds more thoughtful and a little timid.)*

Active Reading: PREDICT

K Ask students what they think will be described in the final section of the poem. *(Possible responses: the coming of spring; the pupa emerging as a butterfly; a storm knocking the chrysalis off the branch.)*

STRATEGIC READING FOR
Less-Proficient Readers

L Use the following questions to check that students are following the main ideas in the two poems.

- What process is described in both poems? *(A caterpillar is changing into a creature with wings.)* **Summarizing**

- What point of view is used in both poems? *(first person)* **Noting Relevant Details**

Set a Purpose Have students read the rest of the second poem to note details that indicate something is happening to the pupa.

CHRYSALIS DIARY **541**

Mini-Lesson   Literary Concepts

REVIEWING THEME Remind students that the theme of a story or poem is a message the writer presents to the reader. A theme might be a lesson about life, a moral to remember, or a belief about people and their actions. A theme is not always stated directly; often the reader must infer, or figure out, the theme. In addition, different readers may see different themes in the same selection.

Application Have students work in groups of three or four to discuss possible themes for the two poems. Students may have different opinions. If group members do not agree, they can write up the different themes they see in the poems. If students are having difficulty getting started, have them discuss these two themes:

- Growth and change require hard work and patience.
- The struggles involved in personal growth are worth the effort.

THE LANGUAGE OF LITERATURE **TEACHER'S EDITION** **541**

CUSTOMIZING FOR
Students Acquiring English

4 Students should be able to guess that *without* as used here means "outside."

Critical Thinking: ANALYZING

M Ask students how the poem would change if the last three lines were dropped. *(Possible response: The poem would still make logical sense, but the last three lines add a more definite and hopeful ending.)*

STRATEGIC READING FOR
Less-Proficient Readers

N Have students identify details on this page that indicate the pupa is changing into a butterfly. *(Possible responses: feeling "stormy" inside; dissolving legs; growing wings; the dream of flying)* **Noting Relevant Details**

CUSTOMIZING FOR
Gifted and Talented Students

O Both of these poems end before the butterfly or moth emerges. Have students add a stanza or two to the end of each poem to describe the appearance, actions, and thoughts of the newly formed winged creature. Encourage students to match the style, tone, and form of each poem.

COMPREHENSION CHECK

1. Who are the speakers of each poem? *(two caterpillars—one is changing into a moth and the other into a butterfly)*
2. What is the subject of each poem? *(Each poem relates the thoughts of a caterpillar while inside its cocoon or chrysalis.)*
3. How much time passes in each poem? *(The first poem describes the thoughts of the speaker at just one point in time; the second poem covers a period of several months.)*

I wonder whether
55 I am the same being
who started this diary.

4 like the weather without.

60 my legs are dissolving,

my body's not mine.
This morning,
a breeze from the south,
65 strangely fragrant,

a faint glimpse of green
In the branches.

March 28:

I've felt stormy inside

My mouth is reshaping,

wings are growing
my body's not mine.

a red-winged blackbird's
call in the distance,

70 And now I recall
that last night
I dreamt of flying.

M
N
O

542 UNIT FIVE PART 1: FACING INNER FEARS

Mini-Lesson  Study Skills

PARAPHRASING Explain to students that a paraphrase is a summary of a selection in different words. A paraphrase captures the sense, or main ideas, of a selection. For example, sometimes technical articles are paraphrased in simpler language so the ideas can be understood quickly by more people. When students use books and articles for research, they may often paraphrase the selections to note down ideas more briefly. Tell students that paraphrasing is a useful study skill because it can help them to understand the main idea of a selection.

Application Encourage students to use these paraphrasing skills to help them complete the activities on the Responding pages.

RESPONDING OPTIONS

FROM PERSONAL RESPONSE TO CRITICAL ANALYSIS

REFLECT 1. What images does "Chrysalis Diary" bring to mind? Sketch an image from the poem in your notebook.

RETHINK
Thematic Link
2. What did the poem bring to mind about your own experiences of facing inner fears?
Consider
Close Textual Reading
• the diary form of the poem
• the speaker's comments at different stages of change

3. Reread the definition of instinct in the Science Connection on page 537. How important a role do you think instinct plays in the changes described in "Chrysalis Diary"?

RELATE 4. At one point the speaker of "Chrysalis Diary" says, "my body's not mine." How do you think the speaker of "Message from a Caterpillar" would react to this statement?

LITERARY CONCEPTS

Language that communicates ideas beyond the dictionary meaning of the words is called **figurative language.** Poets and other writers use figurative language to paint vivid images in the minds of readers. Two kinds of figurative language are **simile** and **metaphor.** Both simile and metaphor are comparisons of two things that are basically unlike yet have something in common. While a simile contains the word *like* or *as,* a metaphor makes the comparison more directly. In "Chrysalis Diary," for example, the speaker uses a metaphor to compare the autumn leaves to a destroyed empire: "The empire of leaves / lies in ruins!" Identify another metaphor or simile from "Chrysalis Diary" or "Message from a Caterpillar."

CONCEPT REVIEW: Form The shape of the words and lines of a poem on the page is called **form.** In a class discussion, compare the forms used in these poems. Does one form appeal to you more than another? Explain.

Multimodal Learning
ANOTHER PATHWAY

With a partner, explore the way each of these speakers feels about the changes taking place. Each of you represent one of the speakers and discuss your reactions to what is happening to you. In what ways are your reactions to change similar or different? Be sure that you refer to the poems to make your responses true to the speaker you represent.

QUICKWRITES

1. Everything in nature undergoes change of some sort—including human beings. Write a **poem** that conveys your reactions to changing as you get older.

2. Pretend it is spring and the speakers of the two poems meet after their changes are complete. Write the **dialogue** the two might have. You may create a humorous or a serious conversation.

📁 **PORTFOLIO** Save your writing. You may want to use it later as a springboard to a piece for your portfolio.

MESSAGE FROM A CATERPILLAR / CHRYSALIS DIARY **543**

From Personal Response to Critical Analysis

1. Responses will vary. Students might draw abstract images as well as more realistic ones.
2. Possible response: Both patience and keeping a diary to record one's thoughts and feelings can help people face inner fears.
3. Possible response: The idea of instinct helps explain why the speaker seems so passive.
4. Possible response: The caterpillar in the first poem would probably disagree and might claim to be growing a new body on purpose.

Another Pathway

Have partners write two paragraphs titled "How I Feel About Growing My Wings." The paragraphs should reflect the feelings and attitudes of the speakers of the two poems, make a clear distinction between them, and use details from the respective poems.

Rubric
3 Full Accomplishment Students' paragraphs make a clear distinction between the two narrators and use details from the poems to support their ideas.
2 Substantial Accomplishment Students' paragraphs make some distinction between the two narrators and use a few details from the poems.
1 Little or Partial Accomplishment Students' paragraphs make little or no distinction between the two narrators. Few details are used from the poems.

Literary Concepts

One comparison in the first poem is "worm-like" in line 12. In the second poem, examples include "stormy inside like the weather without" to describe feeling unsettled (lines 57–58). Encourage students to create their own similes or metaphors based on the idea of metamorphosis.

Concept Review Both poems have short lines, with each line containing just a few words. The form of the second poem is very important because it indicates which lines are spoken by each of two readers.

QuickWrites

1. Students might get started by making a two-column chart listing what they expect to like and not like about getting older. Encourage students to use sensory details, comparisons such as similes and metaphors, and rhyming words in their poems, if they wish.
2. Remind students to indicate clearly who is speaking and to begin a new paragraph each time the speaker changes.

📁 **The Writer's Craft**
Writing a Poem, pp. 86–87
Writing Dialogue, pp. 82, 278–280

THE LANGUAGE OF LITERATURE TEACHER'S EDITION **543**

Literary Links

Have students explain how the idea of metamorphosis might be used to interpret Elizabeth's efforts in "Flowers and Freckle Cream." *(Possible response: In the same way that a caterpillar transforms into a butterfly, Elizabeth would like to transform herself into someone more beautiful, like her cousin.)*

Across the Curriculum

Science Possible topics for students' posters include butterflies and moths, metamorphosis, hibernation and/or estivation, and migration. Encourage students to use a variety of representations in their posters, such as photos, diagrams, and their own drawings.

Geography *Cooperative Learning A Long Way to Go* Some butterflies, such as the monarch, migrate long distances each year. Have students work in groups of four to research the routes of these butterflies and create maps to show their winter and summer habitats. Two students can research the routes and two students can draw the maps.

 SCIENCE CONNECTION
Tracking Monarch Butterflies The Monarch butterfly migrates thousands of miles to a wintering site near Mexico City, Mexico, each year. This short film describes the phenomenon and explains the reasons behind this mysterious trek.

Side A, Frame 30538

LILIAN MOORE

Moore grew up telling stories to her friends and knowing she wanted to be a writer. In college she planned on becoming a teacher of Elizabethan literature but instead found herself teaching disadvantaged children to read. One of her goals was to create books that were both exciting and easy to read so that all children could learn to love reading.

PAUL FLEISCHMAN

Fleischman was born in Monterey, California; his father Sid is also a children's author. In high school Fleischman spent hours listening to the works of Beethoven, Bach, and Brahms, and a unifying idea in his poetic work is the emphasis on sound and rhythm.

Multimodal Learning

ACROSS THE CURRICULUM

 Science Have you ever observed wild geese flying in a V-shaped formation as they move to their breeding grounds in fall? Find out more about animals that, like the caterpillar, go through seasonal changes. Using pictures, photographs, or your own drawings, create a poster of your findings that can be exhibited in the classroom for student reference.

CRITIC'S CORNER

Paul Fleischman feels that the most satisfying part of writing a poem is "moving this clause to take advantage of that rhyme, finding a four-syllable word for *slender,* playing with the length of sentences. Giving the sense a sound." Explain how well you think Fleischman composes the sounds of the words and lines in "Chrysalis Diary."

LILIAN MOORE

"To me," Lilian Moore says, "a poem is like a balloon on a string. What you get out of it depends on how tall you are, how long the string is. Something there for everyone."

Born in New York City, where she graduated from Hunter College, Lilian Moore (1909–) is a poet, editor, and reading specialist. The author of more than 35 children's books, she says that one of the most satisfying things she has done was to found the Arrow Book Club at Scholastic Book Services—"the first quality paperback book program for elementary school children."

Believing that "children who read will often begin naturally to write," Moore has written numerous easy-to-read books, including several about Little Raccoon. "Message from a Caterpillar" is from *Little Raccoon and Poems from the Woods,* a collection of poems that describe a young raccoon's discoveries in the woods—day and night, throughout the year. In recognition of her poetry, Moore received the National Council of Teachers of English Award for Poetry for Children in 1985. **Extended Reading**

OTHER WORKS *Catch Your Breath: A Book of Shivery Poems, Think of Shadows, Something New Begins, To See the World Afresh, Go with the Poem*

PAUL FLEISCHMAN

An award-winning author of young-adult novels, poetry, short stories, and picture books, Paul Fleischman (1952–) earned a bachelor's degree from the University of New Mexico and has worked as a bagel baker, bookstore clerk, and proofreader. Fleischman learned the importance of sound from his father, a children's author, as he read aloud his own books. Fleischman's emphasis on sound also reflects an intense love for music. Listening to classical music helped him learn how to shape his writing.

The writer claims that his greatest pleasure is the actual writing, trying to "please my readers' ears while telling my tale." His two poetry collections, *I Am Phoenix: Poems for Two Voices* and *Joyful Noise: Poems for Two Voices,* are written to be spoken by two readers. The first collection praises a variety of birds; the second is written from the viewpoint of various insects. *Joyful Noise* was named as a *Boston Globe-Horn Book* Award honor book in 1988 and received the Newbery Medal in 1989.

OTHER WORKS *The Half-a-Moon Inn, Graven Images: Three Stories, Path of the Pale Horse*

Extended Reading

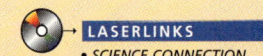

544 UNIT FIVE PART 1: FACING INNER FEARS

Alternative Activities

1. The second poem ends with the speaker saying "I dreamt of flying." Have students invent a dream the speaker in the first poem might have, either in prose or poetic form.
2. Have students find books or videotapes that illustrate the process of metamorphosis. You may wish to have them present these findings to the class.

---

544 THE LANGUAGE OF LITERATURE **TEACHER'S EDITION**

PREVIEWING

FICTION

The Circuit
Francisco Jiménez (hĕ-mĕ′nĕs)

Activating Prior Knowledge
PERSONAL CONNECTION

By this time in your life, you probably have moved to a new neighborhood or town at least once, or you may have shared another's experience of moving. Imagine some of the effects that frequent moves might have on your life. How would frequently moving affect your emotions, your experiences in school, and your friendships? Jot down these reactions in your notebook or on a sheet of paper.

I moved to a new neighborhood when I was 8 and I remember how strange it seemed

Building Background
CULTURAL CONNECTION

This story is about the problems that frequent moves cause for Panchito, a young Mexican boy in a family of migrant farm workers in California. Migrant farm workers are laborers who migrate, or move, from one agricultural area to another in search of work. The workers often move in a circuit—a regular route of travel—that follows the harvest seasons in different places. Most migrant workers work hard for low pay. Children as well as adults work in the fields. The many hours of work and constant moving make regular attendance at school difficult.

Active Reading/Setting a Purpose
READING CONNECTION

Evaluating When you evaluate literature, you form opinions about it. As you read the following story, think about the author's purpose. Why do you think Jiménez wrote about the difficulties a young migrant worker has with moving? After you have read the story, decide how well Jiménez uses character, setting, plot, and theme to achieve his purpose.

OVERVIEW

Objectives

- To understand and appreciate a short story about a migrant worker family in California
- To enrich reading by understanding evaluating
- To understand and appreciate the author's use of sensory details
- To express understanding of the story through a choice of writing forms, including a prediction, an evaluation, and a letter
- To extend understanding of the story through a variety of multimodal and cross-curricular activities

Skills

READING SKILLS/STRATEGIES
- Evaluating

LITERARY CONCEPTS
- Sensory details
- Characterization

THE WRITER'S STYLE
- Choosing the right words

GRAMMAR
- Compound objects of prepositions

SPELLING
- Final -y words and their suffixes

SPEAKING, LISTENING, AND VIEWING
- Group discussion
- Oral presentation

Cross-Curricular Connections

GEOGRAPHY
- Routes of migrant workers

SOCIAL STUDIES
- Organization of U.S. agriculture
- Cesar Chavez

HISTORY
- Time line for farm workers' countries of origin

THE CIRCUIT **545**

PRINT AND MEDIA RESOURCES

UNIT FIVE RESOURCE BOOK
Strategic Reading: Literature, p. 19
Reading SkillBuilder, p. 20
Spelling SkillBuilder, p. 21

GRAMMAR MINI-LESSONS
Transparencies, pp. 41, 44

WRITING MINI-LESSONS
Transparencies, p. 48

ACCESS FOR STUDENTS ACQUIRING ENGLISH
Selection Summaries
Reading and Writing Support

FORMAL ASSESSMENT
Selection Test, p. 109
 Test Generator

 AUDIO LIBRARY
See Reference Card

 LASERLINKS
Author Background
Social Studies Connection

THE LANGUAGE OF LITERATURE TEACHER'S EDITION **545**

SUMMARY

Panchito, a young Mexican boy living in California, tells this story about life on "the circuit"—the regular route from harvest to harvest that his family travels as migrant farm workers. As the story begins, the members of Panchito's family have finished picking strawberries and are packing their jalopy with their few possessions. They find their next job—picking grapes on a farm near Fresno, where an old garage serves as their temporary home. Each day Panchito and his older brother, Roberto, work alongside their father in the vineyard. When the grape season ends in November, Panchito is finally free to enter the sixth grade. On his first day at school, he feels shy and awkward at having to speak English instead of Spanish. His teacher, Mr. Lema, is eager to help. Soon they form a friendship, and Panchito is thrilled when Mr. Lema offers to teach him how to play the trumpet. He hurries home to tell his parents the news, only to find that it is time to move again.

Thematic Link: *Facing Inner Fears*
Panchito needs courage to face the continuing challenges of unfamiliar places.

CUSTOMIZING FOR
Students Acquiring English

- Use **ACCESS FOR STUDENTS ACQUIRING ENGLISH**, *Reading and Writing Support*.

- Point out that "The Circuit" refers to the seasonal trips migrant farm workers make around the country in order to find jobs. Explain that the root *cir-* means "around."

- Encourage Spanish-speaking students to help their classmates with the meaning and pronunciation of Spanish words such as *braceros*.

The Circuit
by Francisco Jiménez

It was that time of year again. Ito, the strawberry sharecropper, did not smile. It was natural. The peak of the strawberry season was over and the last few days the workers, most of them *braceros*[1], were not picking as many boxes as they had during the months of June and July.

As the last days of August disappeared, so did the number of *braceros*. Sunday, only one—the best picker—came to work. I liked him. Sometimes we talked during our half-hour lunch break. That is how I found out he was from Jalisco[2], the same state in Mexico my family was from. That Sunday was the last time I saw him.

When the sun had tired and sunk behind the mountains, Ito signaled us that it was time to go home. "*Ya esora*[3]," he yelled in his broken Spanish. Those were the words I waited for twelve hours a day, every day, seven days a week, week after week. And the thought of not hearing them again saddened me.

As we drove home, Papa did not say a word. With both hands on the wheel, he stared at the dirt road. My older brother, Roberto, was also silent. He leaned his head back and closed his eyes. Once in a while he cleared from his throat the dust that blew in from outside.

Yes, it was that time of year. When I opened the front door to the shack, I stopped. Everything we owned was neatly packed in cardboard boxes. Suddenly I felt even more the weight of hours, days, weeks, and months of work. I sat down on a box. The thought of having to move to Fresno and knowing what was in store for me there brought tears to my eyes.

---

1. *braceros* (brä-sě'rôs) *Spanish:* Hispanic farm workers.
2. **Jalisco** (hä-lēs'kô).
3. **Ya esora:** a made-up spelling for the sharecropper's pronunciation of the Spanish expression *Ya es hora* (yä'ĕs-ô'rä), which means "It is time."

546   UNIT FIVE   PART 1: FACING INNER FEARS

Mini-Lesson Grammar

COMPOUND OBJECTS OF PREPOSITIONS Remind students that a prepositional phrase is a group of words that begins with a preposition and ends with its object. Use the example shown to explain that a preposition may have a compound object made up of two or more nouns or pronouns joined by *and* or *or*.

Application Refer students to the highlighted passage on page 546 and ask them to identify the sentence that contains a prepositional phrase with a compound object. *(fourth sentence)* Then ask students to write a brief scene in which Robert experiences a typical day at school. Have students use at least three prepositional phrases with compound objects. When students are done, you may wish to have them read their scenes to the class.

Reteaching/Reinforcement
- *Grammar Mini-Lessons* transparencies pp. 41, 44

The Writer's Craft
Using Prepositional Phrases, pp. 506–508

Single Object
Everything we owned was packed in cardboard boxes.

Compound Object
Everything we owned was packed in old suitcases and cardboard boxes.

546   THE LANGUAGE OF LITERATURE **TEACHER'S EDITION**

The Dry Ditch (1964), Kenneth M. Adams. Copyright © Eiteljorg Museum of American Indians and Western Art, Indianapolis, Indiana.

Art Note

The Dry Ditch by Kenneth M. Adams
Adams (1897–1966) was born in Kansas. He eventually moved to Albuquerque and concentrated on painting the desert and mountain landscapes, as well as the Native American and Spanish peoples of northern New Mexico.

Reading the Art *How does the painting dramatize the difficult lives of the farm workers?*

STRATEGIC READING FOR
Less-Proficient Readers

Set a Purpose Ask students to read to find out about the major change happening to the narrator's family and how different characters react to it.

Use **UNIT FIVE RESOURCE BOOK**, pp. 19–20, for guidance in reading the selection.

CUSTOMIZING FOR
Gifted and Talented Students

Have students think about how the story would be different if it were told by either Panchito's father or his mother. When students have finished reading, they can write a short version of the story from one of those viewpoints. Ask students, as they read, to jot down ideas that they can use in their rewritten stories.

Linking to Social Studies

 Large groups of migrant farm workers are necessary because of the way agriculture is organized in the United States. The number of farms has decreased since the 1920s, while their average size has increased. Large farms that specialize in perishable crops require many extra hands during the harvest, but few year-round.

Multicultural Perspectives

ON THE ROAD The sizable group of migrant farm workers first arose in the Midwest after the Homestead Act of 1862. Some people who tried farming in the Great Plains were unsuccessful and took to the road. On the East Coast, the end of World War II brought poor African Americans from the rural South to find work in Florida and other eastern states. California has had large groups of migrant workers of various nationalities since the 1870s. Among the newest groups are Mixtec Indians from the Mexican state of Oaxaca who began to move northward from southern Mexico during the late 1980s. Many speak neither English nor Spanish, but an ancient language of their own.

Art Note

Chico by Hubert Shuptrine Hubert Shuptrine (1936–) contrasts light and dark in this painting to draw attention to the centered figure. Although the boy is the center of the image, his position is at an angle, his head turned just enough to obscure his facial expression.

Reading the Art How might the effect of this painting be different if the boy were looking directly at you? Do you think this image is an effective illustration for "The Circuit"? Why or why not?

STRATEGIC READING FOR
Less-Proficient Readers

B Ask students the following questions to make sure they understand the story so far.

- What event occurs in the narrator's family as the story begins? *(they are getting ready to move again)* **Noting Relevant Details**

- How do various members of the family respond to the prospect of moving? *(Papa and Roberto are silent and thoughtful; Panchito hates the move; the younger children are excited.)* **Comparing and Contrasting**

Set a Purpose As students continue to read, they should note details describing the family's next home.

Literary Concept:
CHARACTERIZATION

C Ask students to explain what they learn about Papa's character from this description of his car and how he chose it. *(Possible response: He is proud, knowledgeable, cautious, and patient. He is good-natured to have given a pet name to the car.)*

Linking to Geography

 D Migrant workers in the West travel from southern California all the way north to the Canadian border, moving according to the harvesting schedule of different crops.

Person	Details from the Story	Description of Character
Panchito		
Papa		
Mama		
Roberto		
Mr. Lema		

Chico (1974), Hubert Shuptrine. Copyright © 1974 Hubert Shuptrine. All rights reserved. Used with permission.

That night I could not sleep. I lay in bed thinking about how much I hated this move.

A little before five o'clock in the morning, Papa woke everyone up. A few minutes later, the yelling and screaming of my little brothers and sisters, for whom the move was a great adventure, broke the silence of dawn. Shortly, the barking of the dogs accompanied them.

While we packed the breakfast dishes, Papa went outside to start the "Carcanchita." That was the name Papa gave his old '38 black Plymouth. He bought it in a used-car lot in Santa Rosa in the winter of 1949. Papa was very proud of his car. "Mi Carcanchita,"[4] my little jalopy, he called it. He had a right to be proud of it. He spent a lot of time looking at other cars before buying this one. When he finally chose the "Carcanchita," he checked it thoroughly before driving it out of the car lot.

---
4. *Mi Carcanchita* (mē kär-kän-chē′tä) Spanish.

548 UNIT FIVE PART 1: FACING INNER FEARS

Mini-Lesson Literary Concepts

REVIEWING CHARACTERIZATION
Tell students that the way a writer develops a character's personality is called characterization. Writers can develop characters in four basic ways:
1. a physical description of the character
2. the character's thoughts, speech, and actions
3. the thoughts, speech, and actions of other characters
4. direct comments on a character's nature

Application Have students create a chart showing the details used in the story to describe the various characters. In the right column of the chart, students should add adjectives or phrases to summarize the personalities of each person.

548 THE LANGUAGE OF LITERATURE TEACHER'S EDITION

He examined every inch of the car. He listened to the motor, tilting his head from side to side like a parrot, trying to detect any noises that spelled car trouble. After being satisfied with the looks and sounds of the car, Papa then insisted on knowing who the original owner was. He never did find out from the car salesman. But he bought the car anyway. Papa figured the original owner must have been an important man, because behind the rear seat of the car he found a blue necktie.

Papa parked the car out in front and left the motor running. "*Listo*,"[5] he yelled. Without saying a word, Roberto and I began to carry the boxes out to the car. Roberto carried the two big boxes and I carried the smaller ones. Papa then threw the mattress on top of the car roof and tied it with ropes to the front and rear bumpers.

Everything was packed except Mama's pot. It was an old large galvanized pot she had picked up at an army surplus store in Santa Maria the year I was born. The pot was full of dents and nicks, and the more dents and nicks it had, the more Mama liked it. "*Mi olla*,"[6] she used to say proudly.

I held the front door open as Mama carefully carried out her pot by both handles, making sure not to spill the cooked beans. When she got to the car, Papa reached out to help her with it. Roberto opened the rear car door, and Papa gently placed it on the floor behind the front seat. All of us then climbed in. Papa sighed, wiped the sweat off his forehead with his sleeve, and said wearily: "*Es todo*."[7]

As we drove away, I felt a lump in my throat. I turned around and looked at our little shack for the last time.

As we drove away, I felt a lump in my throat.

At sunset we drove into a labor camp near Fresno. Since Papa did not speak English, Mama asked the camp foreman if he needed any more workers. "We don't need no more," said the foreman, scratching his head. "Check with Sullivan down the road. Can't miss him. He lives in a big white house with a fence around it."

When we got there, Mama walked up to the house. She went through a white gate, past a row of rose bushes, up the stairs to the front door. She rang the doorbell. The porch light went on and a tall husky man came out. They exchanged a few words. After the man went in, Mama clasped her hands and hurried back to the car. "We have work! Mr. Sullivan said we can stay there the whole season," she said, gasping and pointing to an old garage near the stables.

The garage was worn out by the years. It had no windows. The walls, eaten by termites, strained to support the roof full of holes. The loose dirt floor, populated by earthworms, looked like a gray road map.

That night, by the light of a kerosene lamp, we unpacked and cleaned our new home. Roberto swept away the loose dirt, leaving the hard ground. Papa plugged the holes in the walls with old newspapers and tin can tops. Mama fed my little brothers and sisters. Papa and Roberto then brought in the mattress and placed it in the far corner of the garage. "Mama, you and the little ones sleep on the mattress. Roberto, Panchito, and I will sleep outside under the trees," Papa said.

---

5. *listo* (lē'stô) *Spanish*: ready.
6. *mi olla* (mē ô'yä) *Spanish*: my pot.
7. *Es todo* (ĕs tô'dô) *Spanish*: That's everything.

THE CIRCUIT **549**

Active Reading: CLARIFY

E Ask students to clarify Papa's conclusion about the owner of the blue necktie and what it indicates about his life and background. *(Possible response: In Papa's experience, the only men who wore neckties were important. Perhaps this implies that Papa and his friends never wear neckties because they are all laborers.)*

Critical Thinking: ANALYZING

F Have students compare or contrast the family's two most cherished possessions—the jalopy and the cooking pot—and tell what these reveal about the family's life. *(Possible responses: Both items are old and very necessary. The car suggests the life of constant travel; the pot indicates Mama's efforts to provide a stable home life for the family.)*

CUSTOMIZING FOR
Students Acquiring English

2 Remind students that *since* can mean both "from the time" and "because." Ask students which meaning is intended here. *(because)*

STRATEGIC READING FOR
Less-Proficient Readers

G Ask students what the family's new living quarters are like. *(an old, dilapidated garage with a dirt floor, weak walls, no windows, and holes in the roof. There is no electricity.)* **Noting Relevant Details**

Set a Purpose Have students continue reading to find out how the narrator adjusts to school.

Mini-Lesson TM Spelling

FINAL Y WORDS AND THEIR SUFFIXES
Explain to students that when a suffix is added to a word ending in *y*, sometimes *y* is changed to *i*. The change depends on (1) the letter before the *y* and (2) what suffix is added. Write on the chalkboard the rule as shown and ask students to copy it into their notebooks.

Application Have students add the suffixes *-s*, *-er*, *-ed*, and *-ing* to each word, recording their results only if it forms an actual word. For example, adding *-ed* to the word *say* results in *sayed*, which is not an actual word and should not be recorded.

1. try *(tries, tried, trying)*
2. satisfy *(satisfies, satisfier, satisfied, satisfying)*
3. carry *(carries, carrier, carried, carrying)*
4. buy *(buys, buyer, buying)*
5. hurry *(hurries, hurried, hurrying)*
6. stay *(stays, stayed, staying)*

Reteaching/Reinforcement
• Unit Five Resource Book, p. 21

	Suffixes -s, -er, -ed	Suffix -ing
A vowel comes before *y*	no change	no change
A consonant comes before *y*	change *y* to *i* and add *e* before *s*	no change

Literary Note
In 1936, *The San Francisco News* hired John Steinbeck to write a series of articles on the dust bowl migration sweeping through rural California. The experiences Steinbeck had while traveling through the state's agricultural areas eventually became the basis for *The Grapes of Wrath*, which won a Pulitzer Prize in 1940.

Literary Concept: SENSORY DETAILS

H Have students find the sensory details the author uses to depict the difficult working conditions of Panchito and his family. *(Possible responses: "soaked in sweat," "mouth felt as if I had been chewing on a handkerchief," "hot, sandy ground")*

Critical Thinking: HYPOTHESIZING

I Ask students why they think the school bus alarms Papa so much. *(Possible response: Since by law all children must go to school, Papa may be frightened that the bus driver will report him for not sending his sons to school.)*

Active Reading: CONNECT

J Ask students whether they have ever "ached all over" from hard work or exercise and, if so, to describe how it feels, and tell what they do to feel better.

Early next morning Mr. Sullivan showed us where his crop was, and after breakfast, Papa, Roberto, and I headed for the vineyard to pick.

Around nine o'clock the temperature had risen to almost one hundred degrees. I was completely soaked in sweat, and my mouth felt as if I had been chewing on a handkerchief. I walked over to the end of the row, picked up the jug of water we had brought, and began drinking. "Don't drink too much; you'll get sick," Roberto shouted. No sooner had he said that than I felt sick to my stomach. I dropped to my knees and let the jug roll off my hands. I remained motionless with my eyes glued on the hot, sandy ground. All I could hear was the drone of insects. Slowly I began to recover. I poured water over my face and neck and watched the black mud run down my arms and hit the ground.

I still felt a little dizzy when we took a break to eat lunch. It was past two o'clock and we sat underneath a large walnut tree that was on the side of the road. While we ate, Papa jotted down the number of boxes we had picked. Roberto drew designs on the ground with a stick. Suddenly I noticed Papa's face turn pale as he looked down the road. "Here comes the school bus," he whispered loudly in alarm. Instinctively, Roberto and I ran and hid in the vineyards. We did not want to get in trouble for not going to school. The yellow bus stopped in front of Mr. Sullivan's house. Two neatly dressed boys about my age got off. They carried books under their arms. After they crossed the street, the bus drove away. Roberto and I came out from hiding and joined Papa. "*Tienen que tener cuidado,*"[8] he warned us.

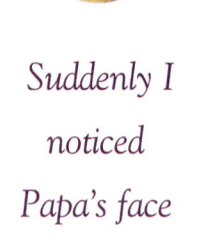

Suddenly I noticed Papa's face turn pale as he looked down the road.

After lunch we went back to work. The sun kept beating down. The buzzing insects, the wet sweat, and the hot dry dust made the afternoon seem to last forever. Finally the mountains around the valley reached out and swallowed the sun. Within an hour it was too dark to continue picking. The vines blanketed the grapes, making it difficult to see the bunches.

"*Vámonos,*"[9] said Papa, signaling to us that it was time to quit work. Papa then took out a pencil and began to figure out how much we had earned our first day. He wrote down numbers, crossed some out, wrote down some more. "*Quince,*"[10] he murmured.

When we arrived home, we took a cold shower underneath a waterhose. We then sat down to eat dinner around some wooden crates that served as a table. Mama had cooked a special meal for us. We had rice and tortillas with *carne con chile,*[11] my favorite dish.

The next morning I could hardly move. My body ached all over. I felt little control over my arms and legs. This feeling went on every morning for days, until my muscles finally got used to the work.

It was Monday, the first week of November. The grape season was over and I could now go to school. I woke up early that morning and lay in bed, looking at the stars and savoring the thought of not going to work and of starting

---

8. *Tienen que tener cuidado* (tyĕ-nĕn′ kĕ tĕ-nĕr′ kwē-dä′dô) *Spanish:* you have to be careful.
9. *Vámonos* (vä′mô-nôs) *Spanish:* Let's go.
10. *Quince* (kēn′sĕ) *Spanish:* fifteen.
11. **tortillas** (tôr-tē′yäs) with *carne con chile* (kär′nĕ kôn chē′lĕ) *Spanish:* flat, round cornmeal cakes and a mixture of meat and spicy red peppers.

550 UNIT FIVE PART 1: FACING INNER FEARS

Mini-Lesson The Writer's Style

CHOOSING THE RIGHT WORDS Remind students that writers make careful choices about the words and expressions they use. Word choice in dialogue is particularly important, because dialogue is a key way writers bring characters alive and make them seem like real people.

Application Divide students into small groups and ask them to imagine the conversation that will take place between Panchito and his family when they once again must move. Encourage students to use the chart of characters they created for the Literary Concepts Mini-Lesson on page 548 to help them choose words that best reflect each character's personality. Invite Spanish-speaking students to help their classmates create simple Spanish dialogue for Papa.

Reteaching/Reinforcement
- Writing Handbook, anthology p. 779
- *Writing Mini-Lessons* transparencies, p. 48

 **The Writer's Craft**

Levels of Language, pp. 274–275
Using Dialogue, pp 278–280

550 THE LANGUAGE OF LITERATURE TEACHER'S EDITION

sixth grade for the first time that year. Since I could not sleep, I decided to get up and join Papa and Roberto at breakfast. I sat at the table across from Roberto, but I kept my head down. I did not want to look up and face him. I knew he was sad. He was not going to school today. He was not going tomorrow, or next week, or next month. He would not go until the cotton season was over, and that was sometime in February. I rubbed my hands together and watched the dry, acid-stained skin fall to the floor in little rolls.

When Papa and Roberto left for work, I felt relief. I walked to the top of a small grade next to the shack and watched the "Carcanchita" disappear in the distance in a cloud of dust.

Two hours later, around eight o'clock, I stood by the side of the road waiting for school bus number twenty. When it arrived I climbed in. No one noticed me. Everyone was busy either talking or yelling. I sat in an empty seat in the back.

When the bus stopped in front of the school, I felt very nervous. I looked out the bus window and saw boys and girls carrying books under their arms. I felt empty. I put my hands in my pants pockets and walked to the principal's office. When I entered I heard a woman's voice say: "May I help you?" I was startled. I had not heard English for months. For a few seconds I remained speechless. I looked at the lady who waited for an answer. My first instinct was to answer her in Spanish, but I held back. Finally, after struggling for English words I managed to tell her that I wanted to enroll in the sixth grade. After answering many questions, I was led to the classroom.

Mr. Lema, the sixth-grade teacher, greeted me and assigned me a desk. He then introduced me to the class. I was so nervous and scared at that moment when everyone's eyes were on me that I wished I were with Papa and Roberto picking cotton. After taking roll, Mr. Lema gave the class the assignment for the first hour. "The first thing we have to do this morning is finish reading the story we began yesterday," he said enthusiastically. He walked up to me, handed me an English book, and asked me to read. "We are on page 125," he said politely. When I heard this, I felt my blood rush to my head; I felt dizzy. "Would you like to read?" he asked hesitantly. I opened the book to page 125. My mouth was dry. My eyes began to water. I could not begin. "You can read later," Mr. Lema said understandingly. **K**

He looked up at me and smiled. I felt better.

For the rest of the reading period, I kept getting angrier and angrier with myself. I should have read, I thought to myself.

During recess I went into the restroom and opened my English book to page 125. I began to read in a low voice, pretending I was in class. There were many words I did not know. I closed the book and headed back to the classroom.

Mr. Lema was sitting at his desk correcting papers. When I entered he looked up at me and smiled. I felt better. I walked up to him and asked if he could help me with the new words. "Gladly," he said.

The rest of the month I spent my lunch hours working on English with Mr. Lema, my best friend at school. **L**

One Friday during lunch hour, Mr. Lema asked me to take a walk with him to the music **M N**

THE CIRCUIT **551**

Active Reading: EVALUATE

K Have students discuss how the other people treat Panchito on his first day at school. *(Possible responses: The other students and the woman in the principal's office seem unfriendly and indifferent; the teacher seems more sympathetic.)*

STRATEGIC READING FOR
Less-Proficient Readers

L Ask students why it is difficult for Panchito to adjust to school. *(Possible responses: He is not used to speaking English; he has started later than the other students; everyone ignores him.)*
Making Judgments

Set a Purpose Ask students to finish the story and pay attention to the developing relationship between Panchito and his teacher.

Active Reading: PREDICT

M Have students predict, before they turn the page, how the story will end. You might suggest that students think about whether this story is likely to have a "happy ending," based on what they have read thus far.

Literary Concept:
CHARACTERIZATION

N Have students describe the kind of person Mr. Lema is. Make sure students cite specific details from the selection to support their opinions. *(Possible responses: enthusiastic, polite, sensitive, caring)*

Mini-Lesson  Reading Skills/Strategies

ACTIVE READING: EVALUATE Remind students that active readers form opinions as they read. One way they do this is by keeping track of their own emotional reactions to what they read.

Application Have students choose five or more events from the story and speculate about Panchito's feelings at that time. Then have students evaluate how each event contributes to their understanding of Panchito in particular, and of migrant workers in general.

Reteaching/Reinforcement
• *Unit Five Resource Book,* p. 20

THE LANGUAGE OF LITERATURE TEACHER'S EDITION **551**

CUSTOMIZING FOR
Students Acquiring English

3 Lead students to understand that *read my face* means "guessed what I was feeling from looking at my face."

Literary Concept: SYMBOL

O Ask students to discuss the significance of the cardboard boxes. *(Possible response: The boxes seem to symbolize the sadness of Panchito's life—always moving, never being able to make lasting friends. The shacks they live in seem not much more than cardboard boxes.)*

CUSTOMIZING FOR
Gifted and Talented Students

P Ask students to suggest ways that the story could have had a more positive ending. You may wish to have them write a brief alternative ending to the story. This activity can also provide a springboard for a discussion of why an author might choose to have an unhappy ending to a story.

LITERARY INSIGHT

1. How are both the main selection and the Insight poem similar? *(Possible response: Both are about the negative aspects of a family move.)*
2. Give an interpretation for the title of the poem. *(Possible responses: The family moved on the 1st of the month; this was the poet's first move.)*

LUCILLE CLIFTON

In nearly all of her work, Lucille Clifton draws on her experiences as an African-American woman. Born in Depew, New York, in 1936, Clifton attended Howard University and was poet laureate for the State of Maryland from 1979 to 1982.

COMPREHENSION CHECK

1. What happens to Panchito after a few hours of picking grapes? *(He feels sick to his stomach and dizzy.)*
2. Why can't Roberto join Panchito at school? *(He must pick cotton to help support the family.)*
3. Who helps Panchito during lunch hours? *(Mr. Lema, a sixth-grade teacher)*
4. Why won't Panchito be able to learn to play the trumpet? *(His family must move again to find work.)*

---

room. "Do you like music?" he asked me as we entered the building.

"Yes, I like Mexican *corridos*,"[12] I answered. He then picked up a trumpet, blew on it and handed it to me. The sound gave me goose bumps. I knew that sound. I had heard it in many Mexican *corridos*. "How would you like to learn how to play it?" he asked. He must have read my face, because before I could answer, he added: "I'll teach you how to play it during our lunch hours."

That day I could hardly wait to get home to tell Papa and Mama the great news. As I got off the bus, my little brothers and sisters ran up to meet me. They were yelling and screaming. I thought they were happy to see me, but when I opened the door to our shack, I saw that everything we owned was neatly packed in cardboard boxes. ❖

---
12. *corridos* (kô-rē′dôs) *Spanish:* slow, romantic songs.

LITERARY INSIGHT

the 1st
by Lucille Clifton

what I remember about that day
is boxes stacked across the walk
and couch springs curling through the air
and drawers and tables balanced on the curb
5 and us, hollering,
leaping up and around
happy to have a playground;

nothing about the emptied rooms
nothing about the emptied family

552 UNIT FIVE PART 1: FACING INNER FEARS

RESPONDING OPTIONS

FROM PERSONAL RESPONSE TO CRITICAL ANALYSIS

REFLECT 1. How did you react to the end of the story? Record your reactions in your notebook.

RETHINK 2. How would you describe Panchito, the narrator of the story?

Close Textual Reading

Consider
- his attitude toward school and work
- his feelings about his brother
- his feelings about frequent moves

3. Do you think the narrator's friendship with Mr. Lema will have a lasting effect? Why or why not?

Literary Link 4. Compare and contrast the feelings about moving that are communicated in "The Circuit" and the Insight poem "the 1st" on page 552.

RELATE 5. Recent statistics show that only about 20 percent of migrant workers go beyond sixth grade in school, partly for reasons made clear in this story. How do you think this situation could be changed?

Multimodal Learning
ANOTHER PATHWAY

Review Panchito's experiences in "The Circuit." Plan and rehearse a speech you might give as the narrator if you were attempting to convince the members of a state committee that living conditions for migrant workers must be improved.

LITERARY CONCEPTS

Sensory details are words and phrases that help the reader see, hear, taste, smell, and feel what the writer is describing. Jiménez uses many sensory details that help paint a vivid picture of the hardships of migrant life. One example is the phrase "the drone of insects," which appeals to the reader's sense of sound. Find other sensory details in the story and add them to a chart similar to the one shown.

Sensory Details	
Smell	hot grits and sausage
Sight	
Hearing	
Touch	
Taste	

QUICKWRITES

1. Write a **prediction** of what life will be like for the narrator of "The Circuit" ten years later. Give reasons for your prediction.

2. Review the Reading Connection on page 545. Then write an **evaluation** of "The Circuit."

3. Write the **letter** that Panchito might send to Mr. Lema from the next town along "the circuit."

 PORTFOLIO *Save your writing. You may want to use it later as a springboard to a piece for your portfolio.*

THE CIRCUIT 553

From Personal Response to Critical Analysis

1. Responses will vary.
2. Possible responses: He seems to be sensitive, emotional, somewhat shy.
3. Possible responses: Yes, because the memory of Mr. Lema's kindness and generosity can make Panchito feel optimistic about other teachers. No, because Panchito had to leave him so soon.
4. Possible response: In both selections moving is seen as damaging. In the poem, the narrator as a younger person didn't realize the unhappiness connected with moving; in the story Panchito, though young, is sad about the frequent moving.
5. Possible responses: school facilities that travel with the workers; better-paying work so young children could go to school

Another Pathway

Have students first think about the general outline of the speech and decide what visual aids they will need.

Rubric

3 Full Accomplishment Students' speeches include statistics, visual aids and a well-organized, persuasive argument.

2 Substantial Accomplishment Students' speeches include a few statistics and at least one visual aid, and they are fairly well organized and persuasive.

1 Little or Partial Accomplishment Students' speeches do not include statistics or visual aids. They are not well organized and/or not persuasive.

Literary Concepts

You might have students work in pairs, each taking half of the story. Examples of sensory details include:

Sight: car with mattress on top; Mama's dented *olla*

Hearing: younger children yelling and screaming; Mexican *corridas*

Touch: dust in throat; sweat on forehead; shedding acid-stained skin

Taste: rice and tortillas with *carne con chile*; jug of water

QuickWrites

1. Students could work in pairs, one assuming Panchito is lucky and one assuming he isn't.
2. Remind students that they should first identify the author's purpose, then decide how well the author achieves it.
3. Remind students to match the style of Panchito's language.

The Writer's Craft

Sharing an Opinion, pp. 120–123
Personal Response, pp. 142–151
Friendly Letter, pp. 42–43

Across the Curriculum

Social Studies *Cooperative Learning*
Cesar Chavez Have students work in groups of four, with each responsible for a different period in Chavez's life: early background and youth; 1958–1962; 1962–1970; and 1970–1993. Each student can do research and prepare a draft. The group can discuss and revise the drafts before compiling a final group report.

ADDITIONAL SUGGESTIONS

History *A Long Way from Home* Have students use encyclopedias, almanacs, and other reference books to create a time line from 1800 to the present that shows where different groups of migrant farm workers came from.

SOCIAL STUDIES CONNECTION
Cesar Chavez This great Hispanic leader spent much of his adult life helping to improve conditions for migrant Hispanic workers. This film presents some of the history of what Chavez did for his people.

Side A, Frame 36426

FRANCISCO JIMÉNEZ

In 1973, Francisco Jiménez won an annual award from *Arizona Quarterly* for "The Circuit." He has also received a Ford Foundation grant and the Distinguished Leadership in Education Award from the California Teachers Association. His work appears widely in periodicals and in anthologies.

AUTHOR BACKGROUND
Francisco Jiménez This author speaks about how "The Circuit" parallels experiences in his own life and how his childhood as a migrant worker has influenced his life as a writer.

Side A, Frame 32200

Multimodal Learning

ALTERNATIVE ACTIVITIES

1. Imagine that Panchito's family earns $9,000 a year. Create a monthly **family budget** based on details about their lives revealed in the story. Be sure to account for such items as groceries, clothing, gasoline, medicine, a fund for emergencies such as car repairs or doctor visits, and any other monthly expenses you think they might have.

2. Prepare a **dramatic reading** of this story to present to the class. Working with a few classmates, assign the roles of the narrator, Papa, Mama, the foreman in Fresno, and any other character who has a line of dialogue in the story. When the narrator, in reading the story, comes to a passage of dialogue spoken by another character, the student playing that character speaks the lines himself or herself.

3. Panchito might find that photographs of the important people and events in his life would help him to remember them. Using magazines, art postcards, or other sources, collect photos that could represent people and events in the story. Create a **photographic display** including captions that will help explain the significance of the photos.

FRANCISCO JIMÉNEZ

Born in Mexico, Francisco Jiménez immigrated to the United States with his parents in 1947. His mother worked in a factory, and his father was a farm worker. Jiménez is now a literature professor at the University of Santa Clara in California. He has written articles and stories for periodicals and has cowritten two textbooks on Spanish.

Jiménez says that his primary goal in writing "is to fill the need for cultural and human understanding, between the United States and Mexico in particular. I write in both English and Spanish. The language I use is determined by what period in my life I write about. Since Spanish was the dominant language in my childhood, I generally write about those experiences in Spanish." (He translated "The Circuit" from the original Spanish.) Jiménez considers it a privilege to be able to write stories in both languages. Jiménez's most recent book, *Migrant Child*, is a collection of autobiographical short stories. Extended Reading

1943–

554 UNIT FIVE PART 1: FACING INNER FEARS

THE WRITER'S STYLE

Jiménez sprinkles the story with words from the original language of Panchito and his family. Panchito frequently uses a Spanish word and then goes on to explain its meaning. What do you think the use of the original language adds to the story?

Multimodal Learning

ACROSS THE CURRICULUM

Social Studies Who was Cesar Chavez and how did he affect the lives of migrant farm workers? Refer to books about him or to an encyclopedia. (If you have access to a CD-ROM encyclopedia or an on-line service, you might use your computer to start your research.) Summarize your information either in a report that can be distributed to the class or on an in-classroom computer data base to which students have access.

Alternative Activities

1. Students should start by finding the monthly income: $9,000 ÷ 12 = $750 a month. They will likely discover that it would be very difficult to manage on this amount.
2. Suggest that students choose music to go with their dramatic reading. The music could be used at the beginning, the end, and during the reading to indicate a change of scenes.
3. Displays might include sections such as Living Conditions, Working Conditions, and Yearly Travels (with maps added).

The Writer's Style

Since the Spanish words are used mainly in Papa's dialogue, they help remind the reader that the family in the story is Spanish-speaking. This is emphasized when Panchito starts school and realizes he hasn't heard English spoken for months.

The Writer's Craft
Levels of Language, pp. 274–275

- AUTHOR BACKGROUND
- SOCIAL SCIENCE CONNECTION

554 THE LANGUAGE OF LITERATURE TEACHER'S EDITION

ON YOUR OWN REFLECT & ASSESS

The Scribe
by Kristin Hunter

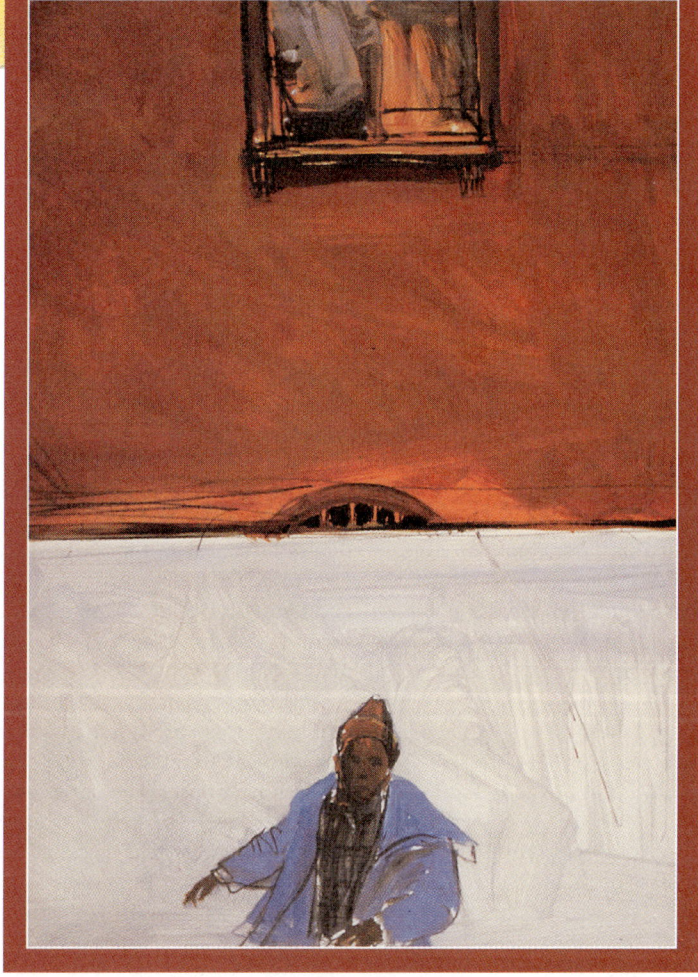

Copyright © Michael Paraskevas.

OBJECTIVES
- To promote independent active reading
- To provide an opportunity to assess students' performance through an alternative assessment instrument

Reading Pathways
- Have students use details from the story to describe the setting as completely as possible.
- Have students create three or more cause-and-effect diagrams using events in the story. For example, what causes James to decide to become a "scribe"?
- Have students work in groups to dramatize the scene during which James sets up a card table in front of the Silver Dollar Check Cashing Service.
- Evaluate how well students can read, interpret, discuss, and write about the selection on their own by using the Integrated Assessment for Unit Five located in the Alternative Assessment booklet. Administer the assessment at the end of the unit after students have read all the selections and completed all the writing that was assigned.

PRINT AND MEDIA RESOURCES

UNIT FIVE RESOURCE BOOK
Strategic Reading: Literature, p. 25

FORMAL ASSESSMENT
Selection Test, pp. 111–112
Part Test, pp. 113–114
Test Generator

ALTERNATIVE ASSESSMENT
Unit Five Integrated Assessment, pp. 25–30

ACCESS FOR STUDENTS ACQUIRING ENGLISH
Selection Summaries
Reading and Writing Support

AUDIO LIBRARY
See Reference Card

SUMMARY

Thirteen-year-old James and his family live in an apartment above the Silver Dollar Check Cashing Service. James becomes angry when he discovers how the Silver Dollar's owners make money—by charging customers who cannot read or write for services such as cashing checks and filling out forms. He decides to help the Silver Dollar's customers by reading and writing for them, just like the scribes in the Bible that his mother tells him about. When James sets up his free service in front of the Silver Dollar, grateful people rush to his table—until a police officer comes along and threatens to close him down for not having a business license. Still determined to help, James reappears in front of the Silver Dollar the next morning and tries to guide its customers toward a nearby bank that will cash their checks for free. The only one who accepts is an elderly lady who, with James's help, proudly opens her first bank account. She inspires James to think about getting a business license so that he can resume his career as a scribe.

Thematic Link: *Facing Inner Fears* James helps Mrs. Franklin to overcome her fears about going beyond her community. In turn, Mrs. Franklin teaches James to not let fear keep him from trying something new.

We been living in the apartment over the Silver Dollar Check Cashing Service five years. But I never had any reason to go in there till two days ago, when Mom had to go to the Wash-a-Mat and asked me to get some change.

And man! Are those people who come in there in some bad shape.

Old man Silver and old man Dollar, who own the place, have signs tacked up everywhere:

> NO LOUNGING, NO LOITERING[1]
> THIS IS NOT A WAITING ROOM
> and
> MINIMUM CHECK CASHING FEE, 50¢
> and
> LETTERS ADDRESSED, 50¢
> and
> LETTERS READ, 75¢
> and
> LETTERS WRITTEN, ONE DOLLAR

And everybody who comes in there to cash a check gets their picture taken like they're some kind of criminal.

After I got my change, I stood around for a while digging the action. First comes an old lady with some kind of long form to fill out. The mean old man behind the counter points to the "One Dollar" sign. She nods. So he starts to fill it out for her.

"Name?"

"Muskogee Marie Lawson."

"SPELL it!" he hollers.

"M, m, u, s—well, I don't exactly know, sir."

"I'll put down 'Marie,' then. Age?"

"Sixty-three my last birthday."

"Date of birth?"

"March twenty-third"—a pause—"I think, 1900."

"Look, Marie," he says, which makes me mad, hearing him first-name a dignified old gray-haired lady like that, "if you'd been born in 1900, you'd be seventy-two. Either I put that down, or I put 1910."

"Whatever you think best, sir," she says timidly.

He sighs, rolls his eyes to the ceiling, and bangs his fist on the form angrily. Then he fills out the rest.

"One dollar," he says when he's finished. She pays like she's grateful to him for taking the trouble.

Next is a man with a cane, a veteran who has to let the government know he moved. He wants old man Silver to do this for him, but he doesn't want him to know he can't do it himself.

"My eyes are kind of bad, sir. Will you fill this thing out for me? Tell them I moved from 121 South 15th Street to 203 North Decatur Street."

Old man Silver doesn't blink an eye. Just fills out the form, and charges the crippled man a dollar.

And it goes on like that. People who can't read or write or count their change. People who don't know how to pay their gas bills, don't know how to fill out forms, don't know how to address envelopes. And old man Silver and old man Dollar cleaning up on all of them. It's pitiful. It's disgusting. Makes me so mad I want to yell.

And I do, but mostly at Mom. "Mom, did you know there are hundreds of people in this city who can't read and write?"

Mom isn't upset. She's a wise woman. "Of course, James," she says. "A lot of the older people around here haven't had your advantages. They came from down South, and they had to quit school very young to go to work.

"In the old days, nobody cared whether our

---

1. **loitering** (loi′tər-ĭng): staying around without purpose.

people got an education. They were only interested in getting the crops in." She sighed. "Sometimes I think they *still* don't care. If we hadn't gotten you into that good school, you might not be able to read so well either. A lot of boys and girls your age can't, you know."

"But that's awful!" I say. "How do they expect us to make it in a big city? You can't even cross the streets if you can't read the 'Walk' and 'Don't Walk' signs."

"It's hard," Mom says, "but the important thing to remember is it's no disgrace. There was a time in history when nobody could read or write except a special class of people."

And Mom takes down her Bible. She has three Bible study certificates and is always giving me lessons from Bible history. I don't exactly go for all the stuff she believes in, but sometimes it *is* interesting.

"In ancient times," she says, "no one could read or write except a special class of people known as scribes. It was their job to write down the laws given by the rabbis and the judges.[2] No one else could do it.

"Jesus criticized the scribes," she goes on, "because they were so proud of themselves. But he needed them to write down his teachings."

"Man," I said when she finished, "that's something."

My mind was working double time. I'm the best reader and writer in our class. Also it was summertime. I had nothing much to do except go to the park or hang around the library and read till my eyeballs were ready to fall out, and I was tired of doing both.

So the next morning, after my parents went to work, I took Mom's card table and a folding chair down to the sidewalk. I lettered

"There was a time in history when nobody could read or write except a special class of people."

a sign with a Magic Marker, and I was in business. My sign said:

PUBLIC SCRIBE—ALL SERVICES FREE

I set my table up in front of the Silver Dollar and waited for business. Only one thing bothered me. If the people couldn't read, how would they know what I was there for?

But five minutes had hardly passed when an old lady stopped and asked me to read her grandson's letter. She explained that she had just broken her glasses. I knew she was fibbing, but I kept quiet.

I read the grandson's letter. It said he was having a fine time in California but was a little short. He would send her some money as soon as he made another payday. I handed the letter back to her.

"Thank you, son," she said, and gave me a quarter.

I handed that back to her too.

The word got around. By noontime I had a whole crowd of customers around my table. I was kept busy writing letters, addressing envelopes, filling out forms, and explaining official-looking letters that scared people half to death.

---

2. **the rabbis and the judges:** the teachers and rulers of the ancient Hebrews.

THE SCRIBE 557

Linking to History

James's mother is correct when she says reading and writing skills were limited to a special class of people. Before the development of Gutenberg's printing press, books were painstakingly hand-copied by monks. It could take years to copy a single book, which caused the books to be very expensive. Thus, only those who were church leaders, nobles, or wealthy had access to these texts and were taught to read and write. After the invention of the printing press, printed material and literacy increased.

However, the problem of illiteracy continues. Millions of people all over the world cannot read, write, or do simple arithmetic. There are national and local organizations with volunteers willing to teach people to read and write, although their efforts are hampered by the social stigma attached to illiteracy that keeps people from using their services.

Multicultural Perspectives

James's mother talks about conditions "down South" in which many people were part of an agricultural system. This system was called sharecropping. During the Reconstruction period following the Civil War, few freed slaves had money to buy their own land or houses. A new labor system—sharecropping or tenant farming—gradually developed. Plantation owners provided housing, machinery, and land, and tenants provided the labor. At the end of a year the tenant received a percentage of the harvest. Abuses of this system kept many sharecroppers constantly in debt.

Art Note

Afternoon Glare—Main Street by Carl J. Dalio Dalio is particularly interested in the effects of sunlight. Driving through the main street of Trinidad, Colorado, he was struck by an amazing display of glaring sunlight on a city street scene. That image was the basis for this work.

Reading the Art The artist uses a great deal of yellow to show the bright sunlight on the scene. What feelings does the yellow create? Would you describe the scene as calm and peaceful, hot and oppressive, or in some other way?

Afternoon Glare—Main Street (1991), Carl J. Dalio. Collection of the artist. Copyright © 1991 Carl J. Dalio.

I didn't blame them. The language in some of those letters—"Establish whether your disability is one-fourth, one-third, one-half, or total, and substantiate[3] in paragraph 3 (b) below"—would upset anybody. I mean, why can't the government write English like everybody else?

Most of my customers were old, but there were a few young ones too. Like the girl who had gotten a letter about her baby from the Health Service and didn't know what "immunization"[4] meant.

At noontime one old lady brought me some iced tea and a peach, and another gave me some fried chicken wings. I was really having a good time when the shade of all the people standing around me suddenly vanished. The sun hit me like a ton of hot bricks.

Only one long shadow fell across my table. The shadow of a tall, heavy, blue-eyed cop. In our neighborhood, when they see a cop, people scatter. That was why the back of my neck was burning.

"What are you trying to do here, sonny?" the cop asks.

---

3. **substantiate** (səb-stăn′shē-āt): to give evidence to prove a claim.
4. **immunization** (ĭm′yə-nĭ-zā′shən): medicine given to protect against disease.

558 UNIT FIVE PART 1: FACING INNER FEARS

"Help people out," I tell him calmly, though my knees are knocking together under the table.

"Well, you know," he says, "Mr. Silver and Mr. Dollar have been in business a long time on this corner. They are very respected men in this neighborhood. Are you trying to run them out of business?"

"I'm not charging anybody," I pointed out.

"That," the cop says, "is exactly what they don't like. Mr. Silver says he is glad to have some help with the letter writing. Mr. Dollar says it's only a nuisance to them anyway and takes up too much time. But if you don't charge for your services, it's unfair competition."

Well, why not? I thought. After all, I could use a little profit.

"All right," I tell him. "I'll charge a quarter."

"Then it is my duty to warn you," the cop says, "that it's against the law to conduct a business without a license. The first time you accept a fee, I'll close you up and run you off this corner."

He really had me there. What did I know about licenses? I'm only thirteen, after all. Suddenly I didn't feel like the big black businessman anymore. I felt like a little kid who wanted to holler for his mother. But she was at work, and so was Daddy.

"I'll leave," I said, and did, with all the cool I could muster. But inside I was burning up, and not from the sun.

One little old lady hollered "You big bully!" and shook her umbrella at the cop. But the rest of those people were so beaten down they didn't say anything. Just shuffled back on inside to give Mr. Silver and Mr. Dollar their hard-earned money like they always did.

I was so mad I didn't know what to do with myself that afternoon. I couldn't watch TV. It was all soap operas anyway, and they seemed dumber than ever. The library didn't appeal to me either. It's not air-conditioned, and the day was hot and muggy.

Finally I went to the park and threw stones at the swans in the lake. I was careful not to hit them, but they made good targets because they were so fat and white. Then after a while the sun got lower. I kind of cooled off and came to my senses. They were just big, dumb, beautiful birds and not my enemies. I threw them some crumbs from my sandwich and went home.

"Daddy," I asked that night, "how come you and Mom never cash checks downstairs in the Silver Dollar?"

"Because," he said, "we have an account at the bank, where they cash our checks free."

"Well, why doesn't everybody do that?" I wanted to know.

"Because some people want all their money right away," he said. "The bank insists that you leave them a minimum balance."

"How much?" I asked him.

"Only five dollars."

"But that five dollars still belongs to you after you leave it there?"

"Sure," he says. "And if it's in a savings account, it earns interest."

> He really had me there. What did I know about licenses? I'm only thirteen, after all.

THE SCRIBE **559**

OPTION 2

Cooperative Learning
A DICTIONARY OF SLANG

Explain that colorful words or expressions spoken during a particular time period or by a particular group of people are called slang. These terms can be new words or standard words with different meanings.

Have students work in groups of four to create a slang dictionary. They can start by dividing the story into sections, finding slang terms, and writing definitions. Two students can collect slang terms from other sources. Another student in the group can act as the word processor, which includes having the responsibility of alphabetizing the dictionary. The fourth student can be the proofreader, checking the final work for errors.

Teacher's Role Check that all students are participating equally in the project. Remind them to include the part of speech for each word.

Rubric

3 Full Accomplishment Dictionaries include all slang expressions from the story and a sizable number of other terms. Definitions are in alphabetical order, are well written, and include parts of speech.

2 Substantial Accomplishment Dictionaries include most slang expressions from the story and some additional terms. Definitions are in alphabetical order, are fairly well written, and include parts of speech.

1 Little or Partial Accomplishment Dictionaries include some expressions from the story but very few others. Definitions are poorly written, are not in alphabetical order, and/or do not include parts of speech.

"So why can't people see they lose money when they *pay* to have their checks cashed?"

"A lot of *our* people," Mom said, "are scared of banks, period. Some of them remember the Depression,[5] when all the banks closed and the people couldn't get their money out. And others think banks are only for white people. They think they'll be insulted, or maybe even arrested, if they go in there."

Wow. The more I learned, the more pitiful it was. "Are there any black people working at our bank?"

"There didn't use to be," Mom said, "but now they have Mr. Lovejoy and Mrs. Adams. You know Mrs. Adams, she's nice. She has a daughter your age."

"Hmmm," I said, and shut up before my folks started to wonder why I was asking all those questions.

The next morning, when the Silver Dollar opened, I was right there. I hung around near the door, pretending to read a copy of *Jet* magazine.

"Psst," I said to each person who came in. "I know where you can cash checks *free*."

It wasn't easy convincing them. A man with a wine bottle in a paper bag blinked his red eyes at me like he didn't believe he had heard right. A carpenter with tools hanging all around his belt said he was on his lunch hour and didn't have time. And a big fat lady with two shopping bags pushed past me and almost knocked me down, she was in such a hurry to give Mr. Silver and Mr. Dollar her money.

But finally I had a little group who were interested. It wasn't much. Just three people. Two men—one young, one old—and the little old lady who'd asked me to read her the letter from California. Seemed the grandson had made his payday and sent her a money order.

"How far is this place?" asked the young man.

> To tell the truth, the bank did look kind of scary. It was a big building with tall white marble pillars.

"Not far. Just six blocks," I told him.

"Aw shoot. I ain't walking all that way just to save fifty cents."

So then I only had two. I was careful not to tell them where we were going. When we finally got to the Establishment Trust National Bank, I said, "This is the place."

"I ain't goin' in there," said the old man. "No sir. Not me. You ain't gettin' me in *there*." And he walked away quickly, going back in the direction where we had come.

To tell the truth, the bank did look kind of scary. It was a big building with tall white marble pillars. A lot of Brink's armored trucks and Cadillacs were parked out front. Uniformed guards walked back and forth inside with guns. It might as well have a "Colored Keep Out" sign.

Whereas the Silver Dollar is small and dark and funky and dirty. It has trash on the floors and tape across the broken windows. People going in there feel right at home.

I looked at the little old lady. She smiled back bravely. "Well, we've come this far, son," she said. "Let's not turn back now."

---

5. **Depression:** the Great Depression, a period of slow business activity and high unemployment from 1929 through the 1930s, before bank deposits were insured.

560   UNIT FIVE   PART 1: FACING INNER FEARS

So I took her inside. Fortunately Mrs. Adams's window was near the front.

"Hi, James," she said.

"I've brought you a customer," I told her.

Mrs. Adams took the old lady to a desk to fill out some forms. They were gone a long time, but finally they came back.

"Now, when you have more business with the bank, Mrs. Franklin, just bring it to me," Mrs. Adams said.

"I'll do that," the old lady said. She held out her shiny new bankbook. "Son, do me a favor and read that to me."

"Mrs. Minnie Franklin," I read aloud. "July 9, 1972. Thirty-seven dollars."

"That sounds real nice," Mrs. Franklin said. "I guess now I have a bankbook, I'll have to get me some glasses."

Mrs. Adams winked at me over the old lady's head, and I winked back.

"Do you want me to walk you home?" I asked Mrs. Franklin.

"No thank you, son," she said. "I can cross streets by myself all right. I know red from green."

And then she winked at both of us, letting us know she knew what was happening.

"Son," she went on, "don't ever be afraid to try a thing just because you've never done it before. I took a bus up here from Alabama by myself forty-four years ago. I ain't thought once about going back. But I've stayed too long in one neighborhood since I've been in this city. Now I think I'll go out and take a look at *this* part of town."

Then she was gone. But she had really started me thinking. If an old lady like that wasn't afraid to go in a bank and open an account for the first time in her life, why should *I* be afraid to go up to City Hall and apply for a license?

Wonder how much they charge you to be a scribe? ❖

KRISTIN HUNTER

1931–

Known for her realistic descriptions of urban life, Kristin Hunter has set many of her stories in cities similar to the one she describes in "The Scribe." At 14, Hunter was a columnist and feature writer for the Philadelphia edition of the Pittsburgh Courier. She earned a bachelor's degree from the University of Pennsylvania, where she later returned to teach writing.

Hunter says that "the bulk of my work has dealt—imaginatively, I hope—with relations between the white and black races in America." Hunter's stories about ghetto life suggest that individuals can change and improve their lives, however difficult, by believing in themselves and the power that lies within them.

The author has received numerous awards for her work from such respected organizations as the National Council on Interracial Books for Children, the National Conference of Christians and Jews, and the Pennsylvania Council on the Arts. Hunter has produced novels, short stories, poems, and magazine articles for a wide audience.

OTHER WORKS *The Soul Brothers and Sister Lou, Boss Cat, Guests in the Promised Land, Lou in the Limelight*

THE SCRIBE **561**

OVERVIEW

In the Guided Assignment for this section, students will write a poem. This will help students better understand how poetry works to describe the world in new, interesting ways. As preparation for this assignment, The Writer's Style will help students understand the importance of using sensory language to describe scenes and people. In Reading the World, students will analyze why people value certain objects more than others. This will give students insights into why authors and works of literature can be so different.

Objectives

- To recognize how authors use the five senses in descriptions
- To use sensory language in writing
- To write a poem on a certain topic
- To evaluate objects in real-world situations

Skills

LITERATURE
- Recognizing and using sensory language

GRAMMAR AND USAGE
- Using compound sentences
- Using sound devices
- Understanding subject-verb agreement

MEDIA LITERACY
- Evaluating an object

CRITICAL THINKING
- Looking beyond appearances
- Analyzing

SPEAKING, LISTENING, AND VIEWING
- Peer comments
- Group discussion

Teaching Strategy: MODELING

In the following models, the writers use sensory language to appeal to readers' senses. Students can use sensory language in their poems and in their other writing.

A **Jiménez** Students may pick *beating down, wet sweat, hot dry dust, reached out and swallowed,* and *blanketed* as phrases that appeal to the sense of touch. The sense of sound is appealed to with the *buzzing insects,* and the sense of sight is appealed to directly in the last sentence.

B **Clifton** Students may pick out *stacked across the walk, curling through the air,* and *balanced on the curb.* Students may respond that the passage creates the image of a chaotic moving day or of a crazy place, one where there are objects stacked in all sorts of ways.

WRITING ABOUT LITERATURE

A NEW SPIN ON THINGS

Each of us sees the world from a unique perspective. Talented poets use their writing skills and imaginations to describe in new and interesting ways how they see the world. That's why poetry is so personal. In the following pages, you will

- explore how writers use sensory language
- write a poem of your own
- look beyond appearances to find significance and value

Writer's Style: Sensory Language All good writers are good observers. They notice the tiniest details and use carefully chosen words to describe the look, feel, smell, taste, and sound of what they observe.

Read the Literature

Sensory language is language that appeals to the senses. Notice the words these writers use to appeal to the senses and make their writing lively.

Literature Models

A **Appealing to Touch**
Pick out the words that appeal to the sense of touch. What other senses does this paragraph appeal to?

> After lunch we went back to work. The sun kept beating down. The buzzing insects, the wet sweat, and the hot dry dust made the afternoon seem to last forever. Finally the mountains around the valley reached out and swallowed the sun. Within an hour it was too dark to continue picking. The vines blanketed the grapes, making it difficult to see the bunches.
>
> Francisco Jiménez, from "The Circuit"

B **Appealing to Sight**
Which words help you see what this writer is describing? What kinds of images does this passage create in your mind?

> what I remember about that day
> is boxes stacked across the walk
> and couch springs curling through the air
> and drawers and tables balanced on the curb
>
> Lucille Clifton, from "the 1st"

562 UNIT FIVE: THE PURSUIT OF A GOAL

PRINT AND MEDIA RESOURCES

UNIT FIVE RESOURCE BOOK
The Writer's Style, p. 29
Prewriting Guide, p. 30
Elaboration, p. 31
Peer Response Guide, pp. 32–33
Revising and Editing, p. 34
Student Model, p. 35
Rubric, p. 36

GRAMMAR MINI-LESSONS
Transparencies, pp. 3, 7, 28, 46–47
Copymasters, pp. 3, 8–9, 37

WRITING MINI-LESSONS
Transparencies, pp. 2–3, 38

FORMAL ASSESSMENT
Guidelines for Writing Assessment

 WRITING COACH

ACCESS FOR STUDENTS ACQUIRING ENGLISH
Reading and Writing Support

---

562 THE LANGUAGE OF LITERATURE TEACHER'S EDITION

Connect to Life

Poets aren't the only writers who use sensory language. Sensory words can help any writer create precise, interesting descriptions. Notice how these students describe homemade candy.

Consumer Magazine

Sweet and frothy at first, then tart and fizzy—like pop rocks without any pop.
—Zach

They're supposed to be like Gummi Worms, but taste like thick, grainy, sour gelatin instead.
—Cameron
from *Zillions* magazine

Appealing to Taste Which words give you an idea of what the candy tastes like? How would you describe your favorite candy?

Try Your Hand: Using Sensory Language

1. **Choosing the Right Words** Finish each sentence by choosing a word or phrase that appeals to the senses. The first sentence has been done.

   - The trumpet, shrill and piercing, made my ears ring.
   - The insects in the fields . . .
   - The taco . . .
   - The sun on my neck . . .
   - The flowers . . .

2. **Sensory Phrases** With a classmate, write sensory descriptions of one or more of the following experiences.

   - taking a bite of a hot pepperoni pizza
   - a ride on a roller coaster
   - a tour of a chocolate factory

3. **Spicing It Up** Make the following scene more interesting and lifelike by using sensory language.

   Many people lined the streets. Marching bands went past me. Floats made out of flowers were pretty. Cowboys on horses rode by. I smelled popcorn and I got hungry. I couldn't see, so I moved toward the front.

SkillBuilder

WRITER'S CRAFT

Using Compound Sentences

Writers often use compound sentences to help build their descriptions and images. A compound sentence is made up of two or more simple sentences joined together. The following compound sentences come from "Flowers and Freckle Cream."

But child, there are all kinds of flowers, and they are all beautiful.

I had a cousin whose name was Janette Elizabeth, and Janette Elizabeth looked exactly like her name sounds.

The parts of compound sentences can be joined by a semicolon or by a comma and a coordinating conjunction.

APPLYING WHAT YOU'VE LEARNED

On a sheet of paper, turn each pair of sentences into a compound sentence.

1. The freckle cream arrived in three weeks. It came in a plain brown package.
2. Wearing the freckle cream in the sun gave me more freckles. It made the freckles darker.

GRAMMAR HANDBOOK

For more information on compound sentences, see page 843 of the Grammar Handbook.

WRITING ABOUT LITERATURE 563

Teaching Strategy: MODELING

 Help students recognize the words describing the way the candy changes in the first selection and the adjectives in the simile in the second example: *thick, grainy, sour*. Students may describe their favorite candy in a variety of ways. Prompt them to use descriptive and sensory words.

Try Your Hand

1. Responses will vary. Here are some samples:
   - The insects in the fields buzzed and chirped.
   - The taco, spicy and hot, satisfied my craving.
   - The sun on my neck felt like warm butter.
   - The flowers were so old and dry that they fell apart at my touch.

2. Responses will vary. Here are some samples:
   - My mouth began to sizzle and burn. My eyes and nose began to run.
   - Suddenly, your stomach feels like it's going to drop out. You scream. It feels like the cars are going to fall off the track.
   - Everything smells brown and chocolatey. You can almost taste the air.

3. Students should add sensory language as in this example:

   Thousands of people lined the long, straight streets. Loud drums rolled as the marching bands went by in strict lines. Flower-covered floats moved slowly by, in a riot of color and fragrance. Tall cowboys in big hats rode by on sleek horses. Then I smelled popcorn, and my stomach growled loudly. A huge man stood in front of me. I couldn't see anything. I squeezed through the people's legs and elbows to the front. It was much better there.

SkillBuilder WRITER'S CRAFT

USING COMPOUND SENTENCES Remind students that there are seven coordinating conjunctions they can use. Write the list of conjunctions on the board. Then help students describe the different relationships each conjunction expresses between parts of a compound sentence.

Application Possible responses:
1. The freckle cream arrived in three weeks, and it came in a plain brown package.
2. Wearing the freckle cream in the sun gave me more freckles, for it made the freckles darker.

Additional Suggestions Have students continue making compound sentences:
1. I didn't like the cream. I couldn't get my money back.
2. In the end, I decided I like freckles. I formed a freckle society.
3. Only kids with lots of freckles could get in. Lots of students applied.

Reteaching/Reinforcement
- *Grammar Mini-Lessons* copymasters, p. 37, transparencies, pp. 28, 46–47

Coordinating Conjunctions	Relationship
and	in addition, moreover
but	a change in thought
or	either one thing or the other
so	therefore
yet	a change in ideas
for	because
nor	with *neither* to mean "and"

THE LANGUAGE OF LITERATURE TEACHER'S EDITION 563

CUSTOMIZING FOR
Less-Proficient Writers

D Some students might feel intimidated by the assignment of writing a poem. Refer them to the poems in Unit 5. Guide them to note that the poems don't have to have a set form or topic. A way to help students choose a subject is to ask them what they remember from an important or fun time in their past.

Writing Skill: MAIN IDEA

E Help students choose subjects that are more narrow in focus, not a whole sequence of events. Then ask them what it was about the object or experience that they remember. Ask them why they think it was enjoyable or important and what made it so.

Teaching Strategy: MODELING

F Discuss with students the concept web shown on the page. Help them recognize that the web shows four details that relate to the main idea, attending a county fair.

WRITING ABOUT LITERATURE

Creative Response

People sometimes respond to a poem by writing one of their own. As you've seen, the poems in Unit Five are about very different topics. You, too, can write a poem about *anything*. You can describe something interesting, important, or trivial. The only limit to what you say in a poem—and how you say it—is your imagination.

D

GUIDED ASSIGNMENT
Write a Poem Writing your own poem may help you understand poetry a little better. On the following pages, you will explore your responses to the poems in Unit Five. Then you'll create a poem that only you could write.

1 Prewrite and Explore

A poem can be about anything that strikes you as interesting, strange, funny, sad, or important. Look at the world around you. Pay attention to what you see, feel, and hear—a bright sunny day, a bumpy car ride, a baby's giggle.

The following list of ideas might help you to discover a poem inside you.

- Listen to the conversations around you.
- Reread the poems or stories in Unit Five, or elsewhere, that stir a memory.
- Recall events, experiences, and images.

Decision Point Based on your responses to the suggestions above, what is your poem going to be about?

Student's Concept Web

BEGINNING SMALL

E Don't try to plan your poem too formally. Instead, start with a phrase, a feeling, an image, or an idea and write down what you think or feel. Sometimes, what you remember most about an experience are sensory impressions. Try to capture those impressions as accurately as you can by using sensory language.

F The notebook below shows how one student got ideas for a poem by using personal mementos and a concept web.

564

Assessment **Option**

SELF-ASSESSMENT After students have completed the Beginning Small planning, they should assess their collection of impressions. Students can ask themselves the following questions:
- *What is the central event of my experience or idea?*
- *Are all my impressions related to that experience?*
- *Is there anything else I can add that was important?*
- *Have I clearly indicated my feelings by using sensory language?*
- *Can I be clearer about what it was that made such an impression on me?*

564 THE LANGUAGE OF LITERATURE TEACHER'S EDITION

② Freewrite

Now you can freewrite. Experiment with images, ideas, words, and meanings. Keep the ones you like best and try new ones. Sometimes the best way to begin a poem is simply to start writing. Then mark the words and phrases that you like the best and want to keep working with.

Student's Freewriting

The county fair smelled liked charcoal grills and my Uncle Del's barn. There were hundreds of animals; we liked them the best.
We rode on the Ferris wheel and the tilt-a-whirl. We saw clowns, a sharpshooter, and a buffalo. I played arcade games and even won a colorful stuffed animal.

What do I remember most about the fair?

I picked popcorn and corn-on-the-cob from my teeth. But the hot dogs and barbecue smells were the greatest of all.

What words can I use to make the fair seem real to others?

③ Draft and Share

Experiment with the words you choose. Try arranging them differently. Try short lines, long lines, or an unusual arrangement of words. You might even experiment with your poem to see if rhyming the last words of lines makes your poem seem more musical. When your poem starts to take shape, share it with a classmate.

 PEER RESPONSE

- What was your first reaction to my poem?
- What ideas or meanings did you get from my poem?
- Which words helped you picture what I was describing?

SkillBuilder

 **WRITER'S CRAFT**

Using Sound Devices

Poets and writers choose words for their meanings and sometimes for the sounds they make. As you write, read your work aloud and listen to the sounds of the words. Try choosing words that use sound in an interesting way. One sound device is **alliteration**. Alliteration is the repetition of beginning sounds, such as *wild wind*.

Other methods you can try include

- using words that have the same vowel sound (*blue shoes*)
- using words that sound like what they mean (*plop, hiss*)

APPLYING WHAT YOU'VE LEARNED

Use one of the sound devices discussed above to write a description of each of the items in this list.

1. an ocean wave
2. a car horn
3. a shark
4. a parade
5. a flock of birds
6. a hat
7. a parade
8. a train
9. a pair of socks
10. a school bell

WRITING ABOUT LITERATURE 565

Writing Skill: FREEWRITE

G Tell students that freewriting is like brainstorming. They don't have to write grammatically or punctuate correctly. Often listing or writing as much as they can about their topic is a good way of freewriting. The important thing is that students express in writing any ideas, words, and phrases that they have at this time. Encourage them to concentrate on sensory language as they freewrite.

Teaching Strategy: USING THE SKILLBUILDER

H To help students draft their poems, you may want to teach the SkillBuilder on Using Sound Devices at this time. It shows students how words have particular sounds. They can work on their draft by choosing words with similar or interesting sounds.

Writing Skill: WRITING LINES

I Help students choose effective line breaks. One way of breaking lines is after an important word. Another way is to break them grammatically, at a period or other punctuation, or at a break in thought. If students want to rhyme, show them how a line breaks after the rhyme word.

SkillBuilder  WRITER'S CRAFT

USING SOUND DEVICES Guide students to decide whether they like certain sounds and what they mean to them. For example, students may say that a loud "clack, clack" sound is unpleasant whereas the quiet "tick, tock" of a clock is pleasant. Some may think a low, "ooooo" sound is sad or mysterious. Encourage students to think about what different sounds mean to them.

Application Possible responses:
1. Slosh, slosh went the ocean wave.
2. The car horn sounded big and bold.
3. Steely and sly, the shark swam by.
4. Floats go over the road.
5. The feathery flock flew up.
6. The hat sat on the man's head.
7. The parade of pets woofed and wailed.
8. The train clicked by quietly.
9. The socks swished across the floor.
10. The bell was a cross between a buzz and a hum.

Additional Suggestions Have students work in pairs to compare and discuss their sound devices. Encourage them to note the different techniques they used.

THE LANGUAGE OF LITERATURE TEACHER'S EDITION 565

Critical Thinking: ANALYZING

J Encourage students to keep revising lines and changing words for maximum effect. Remind students to check their work for inclusion of sensory language, especially details appealing to hearing.

Teaching Strategy: MODELING

K Discuss with students how this sample meets the Standards for Evaluation below. The poem uses sound devices and the senses of touch, taste, smell, and sound to show how the writer felt in the crowd, with the food, and walking on the straw. The poem's lines are arranged according to each item being described. The final lines are arranged like the steps they took.

Speaking, Listening, and Viewing: POETRY READING

L Volunteers can present their poems to the class. After each poem, the class can discuss the subject being described, the use of sensory language, and the effect of the poem on listeners.

Standards for Evaluation

Have students review their poems for the following:

Ideas and Content
- focuses on one memorable experience, event, or person
- uses precise and fresh language
- uses sensory and figurative language
- may use poetic sound devices

Structure and Form
- may use stanza breaks
- uses a variety of sentence structures and sentence lengths

Grammar, Usage, and Mechanics
- contains only a few minor errors in grammar and usage
- contains only a few minor errors in spelling, capitalization, and punctuation

---

WRITING ABOUT LITERATURE

4 Revise and Edit

Most poets rework their poems many times before they are satisfied. Before you work on your final draft, read your poem aloud and listen carefully to decide whether each word you have used adds to the poem's effect. Think about how you arranged the words and sentences on the page. Then check the questions next to the poem and consider the Standards for Evaluation as you finish your poem.

Which words or phrases seem unique and interesting? Which senses does this poem appeal to?

How did the poet arrange words and lines to reflect the content?

Student's Final Draft

The County Fair

Running back and forth and forth and back,
From the tilt-a-whirl to the Ferris wheel,
We BumpedPushedScrunched.
(Crowds are no fun!)

In the air floated smells of charcoal grills and barbecue sauce.
Hot dogs sizzled and corn-on-the-cob bobbed.
(Our bellies felt like bursting.)

We stared at clowns, a strongman, and a grouchy old buffalo.
And in the hot barns we petted whale-sized cows, cloudlike sheep,
  and bunnies curled like balls.
Then we tiptoed through the barns crunching straw—watching
                     where
            we
                              stepped.

Standards for Evaluation

The poem
- describes a memorable or interesting experience, person, or event
- has descriptive and fresh language
- has sensory language and sound devices that make the poem interesting and fun to read

566 UNIT FIVE: THE PURSUIT OF A GOAL

Assessment **Option**

SELF-ASSESSMENT To help students assess their own writing, have them ask themselves the following questions:
- What is the subject of my poem?
- Is it clear what is happening or being described at every point in my poem?
- Has each word been carefully chosen?
- Can I reduce the number of words to make the poem clearer and more vivid?
- Could I add anything for greater effect?

Grammar in Context

Inverted Sentences Experimenting with the word order in your sentences can help you write interesting poems. In most sentences, the subject comes before the verb.

The trumpet's blast echoed down the hall.

Sometimes writers *invert* the order of a sentence to create a special tone or to make their writing more interesting.

Down the hall echoed the trumpet's blast.

Notice that the same rules of subject-verb agreement apply to inverted sentences. The model below shows how one student used inverted sentences in a poem.

~~Smells of charcoal grills and barbecue sauce float in the air.~~
In the air float smells of charcoal grills and barbecue sauce.

Try Your Hand: Using Inverted Sentences

Rewrite each sentence as an inverted sentence. Be sure the subject and verb in each sentence agree.

1. The sun (sink) behind the mountains.
2. Papa whispers, "Here comes the school bus."
3. Pesky insects (buzz) in our ears.
4. Our dinner of rice and tortillas with *carne con chile* (sit) atop some wooden crates.
5. Papa's '38 Plymouth (disappear) into the distance.

SkillBuilder

GRAMMAR FROM WRITING

Understanding Subject-Verb Agreement

In every sentence, the verb and the subject must still agree in number. If the subject is singular, the verb must be singular. If the subject is plural, so is the verb. For example, look at this part of Paul Fleischman's "Chrysalis Diary":

> My mouth is reshaping,
> my legs are dissolving,
> wings are growing
> my body's not mine.

When writing, keep in mind that the verb and its subject may be separated by other words or phrases. Make sure that the verb agrees with its subject, which may not be the nearest noun.

APPLYING WHAT YOU'VE LEARNED

Write the following sentences, changing the verb in parentheses to the present tense.

1. Freckles (appeared) overnight on Elizabeth's body.
2. Elizabeth (squeezed) freckle-remover cream from the tube.
3. Elizabeth and her cousins (worked) in the fields in the summer.

 GRAMMAR HANDBOOK

For more information on subject-verb agreement and inverted sentences, see page 815 of the Grammar Handbook.

WRITING ABOUT LITERATURE **567**

CUSTOMIZING FOR
Students Acquiring English

Help students to identify the subject (*trumpet's blast*) and the verb (*echoed*) in the sentences. Also lead them to note that the object of the sentence, the prepositional phrase *down the hall*, moves from the end to the beginning of the sentence.

Teaching Strategy:
USING THE SKILLBUILDER

You can help students use correct subject-verb agreement by teaching the SkillBuilder on Subject-Verb Agreement at this time.

Try Your Hand

1. Behind the mountains the sun sank.
2. "Here comes the school bus," Papa whispered urgently.
3. In our ears pesky insects buzzed.
4. Atop some wooden crates our dinner of rice and tortillas with *carne con chile* sat.
5. Into the distance Papa's '38 Plymouth disappeared.

SkillBuilder — GRAMMAR FROM WRITING

UNDERSTANDING SUBJECT-VERB AGREEMENT Help students find the subjects and verbs in Paul Fleischman's poem. The subject *mouth* is singular and agrees with the verb *is*. The subject *legs* is plural and agrees with the verb *are*. *Wings* is plural and agrees with the verb *are*. *Body's* is a contraction of the singular subject *body* and singular verb *is*. To help students remember subject-verb agreement, tell them that most singular verbs have an *-s* on the end, for example, *is, has, walks, was, lives,* and so on.

Application Answers:
1. appear
2. squeezes
3. work

Additional Suggestions Continue with these sentences:
1. When Elizabeth (came) home, she (used) the cream.
2. However, it (didn't) work.
3. Instead, she (got) more freckles.

Reteaching/Reinforcement
- Grammar Handbook, anthology p. 815–821
- *Grammar Mini-Lessons* copymasters, pp. 3, 8–9, transparencies, pp. 3, 7

Subject-Verb Agreement, pp. 528–542

THE LANGUAGE OF LITERATURE TEACHER'S EDITION **567**

READING THE WORLD

On pages 564–567, students wrote their own poems in response to an impression or an experience. Just as all the poems were different, students should be aware that responses to objects and occurrences in the world differ from person to person. In this lesson, students compare reactions to an object to understand the different ways people interpret the world.

568 UNIT FIVE: THE PURSUIT OF A GOAL

568 THE LANGUAGE OF LITERATURE TEACHER'S EDITION

READING THE WORLD

HIDDEN VALUES

Everybody sees the world differently. That's why your poem was different from your classmates' poems. Understanding and appreciating what other people value can teach you much about them, the world, and even yourself.

O View In your notebook, write down your first impressions of the bear in the photograph.

P Interpret Would you want this stuffed bear? Do you see anything special about it? What value might it have?

Q Discuss With a small group, take turns describing objects valued by you and no one else. Then use the SkillBuilder at the right to help you look beyond appearances.

SkillBuilder

CRITICAL THINKING

Looking Beyond Appearances

You've seen that each of us finds value, beauty, and significance in different objects and experiences. For example, what was your opinion of the stuffed bear pictured here? To some people, this stuffed animal is just an old, worthless child's toy. Other people may look deeper and see a treasured family memento with high personal value.

This particular bear was one of the first teddy bears ever. It was named for Theodore "Teddy" Roosevelt, the 26th president of the United States. The directors of the Smithsonian Institution, a group of museums in Washington, D.C., thought this teddy bear was valuable enough to include in one of the collections. Teddy bears, the directors thought, are a part of American culture. One of the first teddy bears ever made, therefore, has historical value to many people.

APPLYING WHAT YOU'VE LEARNED
In a small group, discuss how your opinion of this teddy bear changed when you learned more about it. Then discuss other objects that you gained a better understanding of when you looked beyond appearances.

READING THE WORLD   569

Critical Thinking: ANALYZING

O Students will interpret the bear in various ways, but many students' first impressions may be about the appearance of the bear.

Media Literacy: EVALUATING AN OBJECT

P Students may first respond that they would not want such an old, worn bear. However, they may say it is special because it is old or maybe someone's favorite. Lead them to try to argue for the bear's value by imagining it is their own.

Speaking, Listening, and Viewing: GROUP DISCUSSION

Q Have students work in groups to describe their valued objects. Encourage them to use sensory and detailed language to describe their reasons for valuing the object. Students may attempt to convince the other group members of the value of their objects.

SkillBuilder CRITICAL THINKING

LOOKING BEYOND APPEARANCES Guide students to understand that looking beyond appearances can mean imagining how and why someone else might value an object. To help students imagine the different values of certain objects, select items from around the room and encourage students to describe why someone could value them.

Application Students may respond that the bear was valuable because it was one of the first, it was named after a president, it is part of American culture, and it is historical. Discussions of other objects can focus on values other than monetary, such as personal attachment, antique or old, or familiarity and reliability. Help students think of different reasons for valuing something.

THE LANGUAGE OF LITERATURE TEACHER'S EDITION   569

UNIT FIVE
Part 2 Lesson Planner

TIME ALLOTMENTS SHOWN ARE APPROXIMATE. DEPENDING ON YOUR GOALS AND THE NEEDS OF YOUR STUDENTS, YOU MAY WISH TO ALLOW MORE OR LESS TIME FOR CERTAIN PORTIONS OF THE LESSON.

Table of Contents	Discussion	Previewing the Selection	Reading the Selection
PART OPENER **RELUCTANT HEROES** **What Do You Think?** page 570	**20 MINUTES** • Reflect on the part theme		
SELECTION **The Hobbit** page 572 AVERAGE		**15 MINUTES** • PERSONAL CONNECTION • LITERARY CONNECTION • READING CONNECTION: Stage directions	**45 MINUTES** • Introduce vocabulary • Read pp. 572–85 (14 pp.) **5–15 MINUTES** • Read pp. 586–92 (7 pp.) • Read pp. 592–97 (6 pp.) • Read pp. 598–99 (2 pp.) • Read pp. 603–05 (3 pp.) • Read pp. 605–11 (7 pp.) • Read pp. 611–12 (2 pp.) • Read pp. 612–18 (7 pp.)
Writing WRITING FROM EXPERIENCE **Persuasion**	**Exploring Topics** **20 MINUTES**	**Prewriting** **30 MINUTES**	**Drafting and Revising** **80 MINUTES**

Time estimates assume in-class work. You may wish to assign some of these stages as homework.

569a UNIT FIVE THE PURSUIT OF A GOAL

Responding to the Selection

FROM PERSONAL RESPONSE TO CRITICAL ANALYSIS	OR	ANOTHER PATHWAY	LITERARY CONCEPTS	QUICKWRITES

60 MINUTES

- Discussion questions
- OR • Map
- Dialogue
- Ballad
- Newspaper advertisement
- Progress report

Extension Activities

- ALTERNATIVE ACTIVITIES
- LITERARY LINKS
- CRITIC'S CORNER
- THE WRITER'S STYLE
- ACROSS THE CURRICULUM
- ART CONNECTION
- WORDS TO KNOW
- BIOGRAPHY

75 MINUTES

✔   ✔   ✔   ✔   ✔

Publishing and Reflecting

35 MINUTES

Grammar in Context

35 MINUTES

LESSON PLANNER TEACHER'S EDITION **569b**

UNIT FIVE
Part 2 Cooperative Project

A Day in the Life

Overview

Students will capture the essence of a typical day in the life of a person they admire.

PROJECT AT A GLANCE

The selections in Unit Five, Part 2 are about reluctant heroes—people who "have greatness thrust upon them" as they exhibit extraordinary character and strength when faced with difficult circumstances. For this project, students will look around the community and interview various people to find a person who might be described as a reluctant hero. They will get permission from that person to follow him or her through a typical day, recording the events in any media they choose. The material gathered will then be edited and refined into a brief presentation for the class.

OBJECTIVES

- To find a "reluctant hero(ine)" or a person in the community whose overall qualities they admire
- To conduct interviews with that person and others
- To follow that person through a typical day, recording events in various media
- To review the material gathered and edit it into a brief presentation for the class

SUGGESTED GROUP SIZE
3–4 students

MATERIALS

Materials will vary depending on the representative medium chosen.
- Video camera and tapes
- Audio recorder and tapes
- Still camera and film
- General art supplies
- Television and VCR
- *A Day in the Life of America* (Collins Publishers, 1986)

1 Getting Started

Arranging the Project

Decide what level of performance you expect from students. This may largely depend upon the resources available to you. The project is designed to use any media possible, including videotape, audiotape, still photographs, art, and the written word. Determine which of these are appropriate for your students and circumstances.

A Day in the Life of America is a shining example of what the project is about. It is available in most libraries.

Arranging the Presentations

If you have a video camera available (or if students have their own), be sure to schedule the use of a television for the presentations.

Your other main responsibility is to oversee students as they accompany a person for a day. You might have to limit this to a few hours for practical reasons. Be sure that the subject is aware of the focus of the project and that he or she gives permission to be followed and photographed by students. Check on the administration's policy at your school; some require the subject to sign a release.

2 Creating the Presentations

Introducing the Project

Explain that students will be documenting a day in the life of a person who has been a reluctant hero(ine) or whose outstanding character and general behavior they respect and admire. They will interview people in the community to gather suggestions for appropriate subjects, then interview these people until they find one person who stands out. With permission, they will accompany that person for a day (or the time period selected), recording all events. The volume of material gathered will be edited into a ten-minute presentation to be shown to the class.

Show students the book *A Day in the Life of America* and allow them time to browse through it and notice its organization. If the class as a whole seems impressed with any photograph, you might discuss in some detail why students found it interesting and why it stands out from the other photographs in the book. You might also ask that students read the introductory letter by the co-author.

Group Investigations

Divide students into groups of three or four. Some students may already have an idea of whom they would like to select, but stress that this must be a group decision. You may or may not require groups to select a person unknown to any of the group members.

At this time, explain the materials the school can provide. If students are expected to use only the written word and some artwork, make sure they understand how this can be done effectively. Also stress the time limit for the presentation. You might want to use a few minutes at the end of class sessions now and then to discuss how the groups are progressing and to solve any common problems.

Creating a Project Description

As soon as they know, groups should inform you of the name and address of the person they have selected. Ask each group to prepare a one-page description of how, when, and where they plan to follow this person, and in what media they plan to record the events. Meet with each group to review their plan, and make suggestions for adjusting it to more closely follow the focus of the project, if necessary.

OPTION I: A DAY IN THE LIFE OF YOUR SCHOOL
Groups can choose or be assigned one facet of school life (teachers, administration, services, and so on) on which to focus their presentation. Later, all presentations can be pooled and edited to make a presentation for other classes or the entire school.

OPTION 2: A DAY IN THE LIFE OF A FAMILY Students can select a family (not their own) and follow family members through a typical day.

OPTION 3: A DAY IN THE LIFE OF AN ANIMAL Groups can follow a working animal—such as a seeing-eye dog or a dog that works with the police or fire department.

OPTION 4: A DAY IN THE LIFE OF A BUILDING Groups can investigate a typical day in the life of a public building, discovering who visits and why, when it opens and closes, who is responsible for maintenance, and so on.

You may arrange this project according to your own class, school, and community. Add or subtract little bits here and there to make it unique to your class, then sit back and enjoy the presentations.

3 Sharing the Presentations

Although the project is designed as a class activity, you may want to share some of the results with other classes, teachers, or members of the administration. This can be done by invitation or by recording the presentations on videotape. Families might also be interested in seeing the outcome of the project, so you might consider displaying the students' multimedia presentations during parent conferences.

Assessing the Project

The following rubric can be used for group or individual assessment.

3 Full Accomplishment Students follow directions and create a presentation about a person selected for his or her heroic character.

2 Substantial Accomplishment Students produce a presentation, but the focus is unclear or the person does not demonstrate the qualities asked for in the project description.

1 Little or Partial Accomplishment Students' presentation is incomplete or does not fulfill the requirements of the assignment.

For the Portfolio
Include a copy of your written assessment in every student's portfolio. You also may want to include a copy of the written portion of the presentation or the group's initial project description. Other media presentation materials can be kept in the classroom or in the school library for future reference or review.

Note: For other assessment options, see the *Teacher's Guide to Assessment and Portfolio Use.*

Cross-Curricular Options

SOCIAL STUDIES

Have students select a book in the series *A Day in the Life . . .* that is about another country. They can discuss how the culture is represented in the book and how it is different from and similar to the culture of the United States.

MUSIC
Ask students to select three or four pictures from *A Day in the Life of America* and tape-record music that reflects the mood of the pictures.

SCIENCE

Have students research one of the NASA space shuttle missions and write a report explaining what a typical day is like for the astronauts aboard the shuttle.

Resources

Great American Astronauts by Chris Crocker profiles ten well-known astronauts including Sally Ride, Alan Shepard, and John Glenn.

People Who Make a Difference by Brent Ashabranner shows the lives of 14 Americans who have demonstrated their concern for others.

Tell Me About Yourself: How to Interview Anyone from Your Friends to Famous People by D.L. Mabery provides helpful tips and strategies for conducting interviews.

PART 2

WHAT DO YOU THINK?
Objectives

The activities on this page can be used to
- introduce the Part 2 theme, "Reluctant Heroes," since each activity is connected to the selection in Part 2
- create materials for students' personal portfolios that they can later reconsider or revise
- build an understanding of theme that can be reviewed and revised as students progress through the unit

Can you be persuaded?
After students have selected a situation, encourage them to jot down their impressions of it and their reactions to it. Then have them create a brief outline in which they organize their thoughts before they begin writing their monologue. You may also wish to have students select or create props to use in their performance.

What can a goal reveal?
Have students begin by creating a chart in which they list qualities they had before pursuing their goal and qualities they found they had after achieving it. Students can refer to this information as they draw their pictures. Alternatively, students may create some other kind of before-and-after representation, such as a collage.

What danger lurks?
Once students have completed the web, ask them to brainstorm various designs for their board game. Encourage them to be as creative as possible. For instance, suggest that they include rewards for players who overcome obstacles and penalties for those who don't.

UNIT FIVE **PART 2**

RELUCTANT HEROES

WHAT DO Y?u THINK?

REFLECTING ON THEME

What qualities come to mind when you think about heroes? Bravery? Daring? Sometimes a hero may at first appear cowardly. Use these activities to examine what it takes to become a hero or heroine. Then, as you read *The Hobbit*, compare your ideas about heroism with those of Bilbo Baggins, a character who says, "No adventures, thank you."

Can you be persuaded?
Have you ever been coaxed into riding a roller coaster, speaking in front of a group, or participating in some other activity that you might not have the courage to do on your own? Perform a monologue in which you share your reactions to such a situation.

What can a goal reveal?
Think about a goal you have worked to achieve. What did pursuing your goal teach you about yourself? Was all the effort worth it? Draw a before-and-after picture of yourself in your notebook.

Looking Back
What do you remember most about your experience with the readings and activities in Part 1, "Facing Inner Fears"? In your notebook, complete the sentence shown. Be sure to give reasons for your response.

Part 1 of this unit was memorable to me because...

What danger lurks?
Create a board game in which a hero or heroine must overcome obstacles to reach a goal. Use a web similar to the one shown here to help with your planning. Then play the game with a group of classmates.

- Characters
- Obstacles
- **Name of Game**
- Object
- Rules

570

Looking Back
Ask students to reread the selection, or the portion of a selection, that they found most memorable in Part 1. Make sure they make notes while they review the selection so that they can refer to them when completing the sentence shown. Encourage students to connect the selection with aspects of their own life. Ask them to discuss in their notebook what they learned about facing their inner fears as a result of reading the selection.

COMMUNITY OUTREACH
Have students research local news stories in order to identify a community member who has performed an act of heroism. Invite students to contact this person and set up an interview that will focus on his or her experience. Encourage students to generate a list of thought-provoking questions before they conduct the interview. Students should focus on what qualities helped the interviewee act heroically and on how his or her life changed as a result of the heroic act. Students can then present their interviews to the class.

570 THE LANGUAGE OF LITERATURE TEACHER'S EDITION

PREVIEWING

DRAMA

The Hobbit
J.R.R. Tolkien (tōl′kēn′)
dramatized by Patricia Gray

PERSONAL CONNECTION Setting a Purpose

You are about to meet Bilbo Baggins, a hairy-footed, gnomelike creature called a hobbit. Bilbo embarks on an astonishing adventure, a journey of discovery—a quest. What images or ideas does the word *quest* bring to your mind? Can ordinary people go on quests, or are quests just gone on by characters in myths, fairy tales, and fantasies? Discuss quests with a few classmates; then list your ideas in a graphic like the one shown. As you read, compare your diagram with the events and images of Bilbo Baggins's quest.

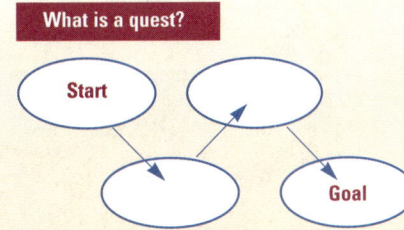

Building Background
LITERARY CONNECTION

John Ronald Reuel (rōō′əl) Tolkien was a respected English scholar who became famous as the author of *The Hobbit* (1937) and *The Lord of the Rings* (1954–1955), a trilogy, or set of three novels, about the kingdom of Middle Earth. Though an imaginary place, Middle Earth has similarities to the England of Tolkien's time. In fact, the fantasy writer poked gentle fun at the habits and manners of many types of English people. Bilbo Baggins, Esquire, for example, is a typical sort of country gentleman. He is pleased with the comforts of home, a bit stuffy, less than brilliant, yet a determined defender of his family's honor.

Active Reading
READING CONNECTION

Stage Directions The stage directions for this play, which are printed in italic type, describe the scenery, props, and sound and light effects. They also tell where the actors enter, how they speak or move, and where they exit the stage. Stage directions help the reader picture exactly what is going on and where it is happening. The diagram shown identifies the parts of the stage and the abbreviations used in *The Hobbit*. Before you begin reading, become familiar with the parts of the stage and with the terms used.

Key
D = Downstage
U = Upstage
C = Center
R = Right
L = Left

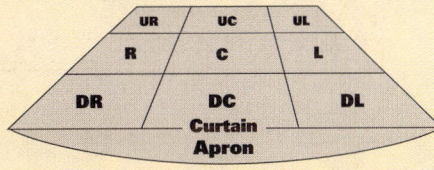

THE HOBBIT 571

OVERVIEW

Objectives
- To understand, appreciate, and perform a drama adapted from a fantasy novel
- To understand stage directions
- To understand and analyze dialogue
- To express understanding of the drama through a choice of writing forms, including a ballad, a newspaper advertisement, and a progress report
- To extend understanding of the drama through a variety of multimodal and cross-curricular activities

Skills

READING SKILLS/ STRATEGIES
- Setting a purpose

THE WRITER'S STYLE
- Dialogue

GRAMMAR
- The subject in different positions

LITERARY CONCEPTS
- Humor
- Dialogue

SPELLING
- The prefix *con-*

GENRE STUDY
- Drama

SPEAKING, LISTENING, AND VIEWING
- Dramatic reading
- Background music
- Drama
- Group discussion
- Oral presentation

Cross-Curricular Connections

SCIENCE
- Buttermilk
- Old-growth forests

GEOGRAPHY
- Emeralds and rubies

SOCIAL STUDIES
- Apiculture
- Native American vision quest
- Perseus

PRINT AND MEDIA RESOURCES

UNIT FIVE RESOURCE BOOK
Strategic Reading: Literature, p. 39
Vocabulary SkillBuilder, p. 42
Reading SkillBuilder, p. 40
Spelling SkillBuilder, p. 41

GRAMMAR MINI-LESSONS
Transparencies, p. 7
Copymasters, p. 7

WRITING MINI-LESSONS
Transparencies, p. 48

ACCESS FOR STUDENTS ACQUIRING ENGLISH
Selection Summaries
Reading and Writing Support

FORMAL ASSESSMENT
Selection Test, pp. 115–116
 Test Generator

ALTERNATIVE ASSESSMENT
Unit Five Integrated Assessment, pp. 25–30
End-of-Year Integrated Assessment: Reader, pp. 31–36;
Student Response Booklet, pp. 37–50

AUDIO LIBRARY
See Reference Card

INTERNET RESOURCES
McDougal Littell Literature Center at http://www.hmco.com/mcdougal/lit

---

THE LANGUAGE OF LITERATURE TEACHER'S EDITION **571**

SUMMARY

Like most hobbits, Bilbo Baggins loves the comforts of home and avoids adventure—until the wizard Gandalf comes visiting. In this dramatization of the well-known fantasy classic, Gandalf coaxes Bilbo into becoming burglar-in-training for a band of 13 dwarves, who are setting off to get their ancestors' treasure back from the dragon Smaug. Trouble soon finds Bilbo and the dwarves. In the mountains they come upon flesh-eating trolls and goblins, from whom Bilbo flees, only to find himself dealing with a slimy, hungry cave creature named Gollum. Thanks to a magic ring that makes him invisible, Bilbo narrowly escapes Gollum and rejoins the dwarves on their way to Mirkwood Forest. There the queen of the elves captures the dwarves. Bilbo, using his magic ring and new-found abilities, helps the dwarves escape by loading them into empty wine barrels that are sent down the river. The dwarves and Bilbo wind up at the entrance to Smaug's den in the Lonely Mountain. Bilbo invisibly slips inside the den and tricks Smaug into exposing himself to the elf queen's deadly sword, wielded by Thorin, king of the dwarves. Once the dragon is slain and the treasure is recovered, Bilbo—richer in gold and experience—prepares to return to his comfortable hobbit life.

Thematic Link: *Reluctant Heroes* Bilbo does his best to get out of the quest but finds within himself greater resources than he ever imagined.

Art Note

Bilbo Comes to the Huts of the Raft-Elves by J. R. R. Tolkien

Reading the Art *Based on the way the trees and streams are drawn, does this look to you like a real forest and river? Explain.*

CUSTOMIZING FOR
Students Acquiring English

- Use **ACCESS FOR STUDENTS ACQUIRING ENGLISH,** *Reading and Writing Support.*
- Most cultures tell tales about supernatural creatures like the wizards, elves, and goblins depicted in *The Hobbit*. Invite students to share similar tales from their home cultures.

Bilbo Comes to the Huts of the Raft Elves (1966), J.R.R. Tolkien. Illustration from *The Hobbit* by J.R.R. Tolkien. Copyright © 1966 J.R.R. Tolkien. Reprinted by permission of Houghton Mifflin Co. All rights reserved.

WORDS TO KNOW

absurd (əb-sûrd′) *adj.* laughable; ridiculous (p. 616)
consoling (kən-sōl′ĭng) *adj.* making feel less sad; comforting **console** *v.* (p. 599)
conspirator (kən-spĭr′ə-tər) *n.* someone who takes part in a plot (p. 580)
desolate (dĕs′ə-lĭt) *adj.* lonely; gloomy (p. 612)

destiny (dĕs′tə-nē) *n.* what will necessarily happen to a person or thing; fate (p. 615)
domain (dō-mān′) *n.* land under one ruler or belonging to one person (p. 593)
esteemed (ĭ-stēmd′) *adj.* highly thought of; respected **esteem** *v.* (p. 613)
fiend (fēnd) *n.* one who is very wicked or cruel; devil (p. 583)

The Hobbit

A play by Patricia Gray   Based on a story by J.R.R. Tolkien

CAST OF CHARACTERS

Bilbo Baggins	a Hobbit
Gandalf	a great Wizard
Dwalin and **Balin**	
Kili and **Fili**	
Dori, **Nori** and **Ori**	Dwarves
Oin and **Gloin**	
Bifur and **Bofur**	
Bombur	
Thorin	Leader of the Dwarves
Grocery Boy	a Hobbit lad
Bert	
Essie	Trolls
Tom	
The Great Goblin	
Attendant Goblin	Goblins
Gollum	a slimy creature
The Elven-Queen	
Two Elf Guards	Wood-elves
Smaug	the Dragon

Other Hobbits, Goblins, Elves, etc., may be added as desired, or the number may be easily reduced.

Place: *From Underhill, through the Wilderland, to the Lonely Mountain.*

Time: *Long ago in the quiet of the world.*

THE HOBBIT   573

WORDS TO KNOW

hoard (hôrd) *n.* a supply stored up and hidden (p. 614)

predicament (prĭ-dĭk′ə-mənt) *n.* a situation that is difficult to get out of; problem (p. 612)

quest (kwĕst) *n.* a journey in search of adventure or to perform a task (p. 607)

stature (stăch′ər) *n.* level of achievement, especially when thought to be worthy of respect (p. 617)

thrive (thrīv) *v.* to grow strong and rich; be successful; do well (p. 615)

throng (thrông) *n.* a large gathering of people; crowd (page 578)

vanquish (văng′kwĭsh) *v.* to conquer; defeat (p. 615)

Art Note

The Hill: Hobbiton-Across-the-Water by J.R.R. Tolkien

Reading the Art *In setting the scene, the writer describes the shire as "the picture of rural perfection." Rural means "of, relating to, or characteristic of the country." Use the picture to tell whether you agree or disagree and why.*

The Hill: Hobbiton-Across-the-Water (1966), J.R.R. Tolkien. Illustration from *The Hobbit* by J.R.R. Tolkien. Copyright © 1966 J.R.R. Tolkien. Reprinted by permission of Houghton Mifflin Co., all rights reserved.

574 UNIT FIVE PART 2: RELUCTANT HEROES

Mini-Lesson Reading Skills/Strategies

My purpose for reading	Observations that fulfill my purpose

SETTING A PURPOSE Remind students that readers often establish specific reasons for reading a selection. Setting a purpose can be useful for reading a drama. It can help readers understand the characters, especially if they intend to perform the play. It can also help readers recognize characteristics, such as stage directions, that are unique to drama.

Application Refer students to the ideas they were asked to think about in the Personal Connection on page 571. Explain that these suggestions help set a purpose for their reading of *The Hobbit*. Ask students to think about this purpose or any other purposes they may have set for themselves before reading the selection. Ask students to record their purposes and, after they have read the play, to review their reading logs for any observations they made while reading that helped them fulfill their reading purposes. Students can record their thoughts in a chart like the one shown.

Reteaching/Reinforcement
• *Unit Five Resource Book*, p. 40

574 THE LANGUAGE OF LITERATURE TEACHER'S EDITION

Act One — Scene One

Scene: *The houselights dim. The lights come up in front of the curtain, revealing an imaginary part of the world called Middle Earth. We are in the Shire,[1] Underhill, home of the Hobbits. It is a pleasant morning. The Shire is the picture of rural perfection.*

At left sits a well-appointed[2] little Hobbit by the name of Bilbo Baggins, Esq.[3] He is sitting on the stoop outside his round green door, which has a shiny yellow brass doorknob in the exact middle. At the side is a mailbox with several letters in it. Before him is a turntable or lazy Susan, laid with four complete breakfasts. Bilbo has just eaten the first of these and lets out a deep sigh of satisfaction. He carefully dabs his mouth with a huge napkin. Emitting another sigh, he turns the table so that breakfast number two is before him. He digs in with determination after a brief hesitation over which jam to spread his muffin with.

From right an extraordinary old man, Gandalf, enters. He is tall, with a flowing white beard and bushy black brows, out of which gleam deep, piercing eyes. On his head is a tall, peaked hat covered with strange designs. He wears a long gray cloak, a silver scarf, and immense black boots and carries a staff.

Gandalf (*regarding the scene with relish, taking a deep breath of the sparkling air*). Ah, the Shire! How delicious the morning is in this part of the world! The air is *stuffed* with comfort! It feels like nothing exciting has happened here for ages—all green and still— (*crosses to Bilbo, who is well into his third breakfast*)—rather like the inside of one of those fresh eggs you're eating—don't you think?

Bilbo (*looking up, startled*). Oh! I wouldn't know. It's hard to look at a place from the outside when you live in the inside! But then you're a stranger here. Welcome! I still have a breakfast or two left if you'd care for some.

Gandalf. Thank you, I haven't the time—and I am not a stranger anywhere unless, of course, I choose to be.

(*A Hobbit with a green, pointed cap peeks down at them from a window flap in the curtain. Immediately, two more Hobbits pop out from the two sides of the curtain.*)

Bilbo (*confused*). Oh, yes? Well, how do you do, sir— (*offering his hand*)

Gandalf (*ignoring the gesture*). Magnificently, of course! (*slowly and deliberately*) But at the

---

1. **Shire:** a county or district.
2. **well-appointed:** neat and well-dressed.
3. **Esq.:** abbreviation of Esquire, an honorary title for a country gentleman.

THE HOBBIT: ACT ONE

CUSTOMIZING FOR
Students Acquiring English

I Point out that when Gandalf makes the sound *tch, tch,* he is expressing disappointment and pity for the Hobbits' lack of interest in adventure. Model the sound with appropriate intonation and facial expression.

Critical Thinking:
SPECULATING

D Invite students to speculate on what Gandalf means by the statement, "I am Gandalf, and Gandalf means me!" *(Possible responses: Gandalf is his name, in the same way that, for example, what we call a tree is a tree. Gandalf is deliberately trying to keep Bilbo off guard by talking nonsense.)*

STRATEGIC READING FOR
Less-Proficient Readers

E Have students identify Gandalf's purpose in visiting Bilbo. *(to send Bilbo on a dangerous but potentially profitable adventure)* Finding the Main Idea

Set a Purpose Have students read to find out why a throng of dwarves shows up at Bilbo's home.

---

moment, I am looking for someone to share a great adventure— (*pauses to see* Bilbo's *reaction, which is sheer horror*) —a stupendous adventure that I'm arranging—and it's very difficult to find anyone— (*The three* Hobbits *who have been listening suddenly vanish. We hear sounds of doors and shutters slamming offstage.*) What was that?

Bilbo (*standing up, taking from his pocket a long wooden pipe and tapping it impatiently*). That was neighbors slamming doors and shutters.

Gandalf (*sadly*). On adventure. Tch, tch.

Bilbo. You, sir, are in the neighborhood of Hobbits.

Gandalf (*feigning ignorance*). Hobbit? Hobbit? What's a Hobbit?

Bilbo. We're just plain folk—have no use for adventures. (*shudders*) Nasty, uncomfortable things! Adventures make you late for dinner! Can't think what anybody sees in them! (Gandalf *continues to stare at* Bilbo *with a strangely disturbing gleam in his eye.* Bilbo *nervously crosses to the mailbox and removes some letters. He sits on the stoop and examines them.*) Good morning, we don't want any adventures here. You might try across The Hill or over The Water. (Bilbo *devotes himself to his letters.*)

Gandalf. You should be ashamed of yourself, Bilbo Baggins!

Bilbo (*sitting up alertly*). That's my name! How did you know—

Gandalf (*cutting in*). You know mine, too, although you don't know that I belong to it. I am Gandalf, and Gandalf means me! To think that I should have lived to be good-morninged by Belladonna Took's son—as if I were selling buttons at the door!

Bilbo (*beside himself with excitement*). Gandalf! Gandalf! Good gracious! Not the wandering wizard who used to tell such wonderful tales at parties about dragons and giants and goblins—

Gandalf (*merely yawning*). The same, dear boy.

Bilbo. And about the rescue of princesses and the unexpected luck of widows' sons! And the fireworks! I remember those! Old Grandpa Took used to send them up on Midsummer's Eve. What a display!

Gandalf. Naturally.

Bilbo. Up they rose, like great lilies and snapdragons, and hung in the twilight all evening, falling at last like silver and gold rain! . . . Dear me! Are you the same Gandalf who led so many of our quiet lads and lasses off on mad adventures? Bless me, life used to be quite inter— I mean, you used to upset things quite badly in these parts! I beg your pardon, but I had no idea you were still in the business.

Gandalf. Where else should I be? Tch, tch. Well, for your grandfather Took's sake and for the sake of your poor mother, Belladonna, I'll give you what you asked for.

Bilbo. But I haven't asked for anything!

Gandalf. Yes, you have. My pardon—I give it to you. In fact, I will be so kind as to send you on an adventure—very amusing for me, very good for you—and profitable, *if* you live through it.

Bilbo. *If I live through it?* Sorry. No adventures, thank you. Good morning! (*starts for his door, then remembers his manners*) I'd ask you in to tea, but—

Gandalf. How kind of you to ask me—I hate to think alone! (*propelling him through the door*) You go along in and fix the tea. I'll be

576   UNIT FIVE   PART 2: RELUCTANT HEROES

576   THE LANGUAGE OF LITERATURE   **TEACHER'S EDITION**

in shortly—I have a little business to attend to. (*Gives* Bilbo *a final shove through the door, then chuckles slyly to himself, rubs his hands, and hangs a large, colorful sign on the door. The sign reads* BURGLAR WANTS GOOD JOB, PLENTY OF EXCITEMENT AND REASONABLE REWARD. *He looks off right*) Ah, here they come! (*goes through door*)

(*The curtain opens to reveal the main hall at Bag-End, residence of B. Baggins, Esquire. Upstage center is a large round door with a mat in front. To the left of it is a pegged coat-rack. Downstage is a long table, with benches. To the right of the table is a fireplace with a stool before it.* Gandalf, *at center, looking around the room, calls off to* Bilbo.)

Gandalf. A fine place you have here, Bilbo.

(Bilbo *bustles on left with tea trolley.*)

Bilbo. Yes, I love my quiet home.

Gandalf. I haven't been this way for a long time—not since your grandfather Took passed on—

Bilbo. Yes, well, I don't expect there's much to amuse you around here—

Gandalf. True—but you Hobbits make a relaxing change from those dwarves and elves with their hardheaded hustle and lightheaded bustle. Do you know the most amazing thing about Hobbits?

Bilbo. No, what?

Gandalf. That you remain gentlefolk in spite of everything. I mean I just dropped in and yet you *insisted* I stay to tea.

Bilbo (*protesting weakly*). Well—(*Doorbell rings.* Bilbo *starts in surprise.*)

Gandalf. You expecting someone?

Bilbo (*crossing to door*). No—oh, maybe the groceries.

(Bilbo *opens the door upstage center, and in pops a dwarf,* Dwalin, *with a blue beard neatly tucked into his golden belt. He wears a dark green hood.*)

Dwalin (*executing a low, sweeping bow*). Dwalin, at your service!

Bilbo (*baffled, looking for groceries*). Why—Bilbo Baggins, at yours! Ummm—I was expecting groceries.

Dwalin. I was told you set a great table.

Gandalf. Ask the fellow in to tea, why don't you?

Bilbo. Yes, yes, certainly. Uh, would you care to join us? The kettle's on the boil—

Dwalin. Delighted! (*hangs his hood on a peg and seats himself expansively at table*)

Bilbo (*sitting down beside* Dwalin). Well, now! (*laughs nervously*) Tell me—(*The doorbell rings again.*) Oops, excuse me. (*goes to the*

THE HOBBIT: ACT ONE **577**

Active Reading: QUESTION

F Discuss what questions or comments students have at this point in the selection. You may wish to use the following model to spark their ideas:

Think-Aloud Model *I definitely have some questions about what is going on here. For example, why is Gandalf putting such a bizarre sign on the door? Does Gandalf think that Bilbo is a burglar? To whom is Gandalf's sign directed? Other Hobbits? The police?*

Critical Thinking: ANALYZING

G Discuss with students this passage on this page. Ask them what is strange, ironic, or funny about Gandalf commending Bilbo for his hospitality. (*Possible response: Bilbo didn't insist that Gandalf stay to tea! He wanted to get rid of Gandalf and his talk of adventures.*)

Literary Concept: DIALOGUE

H Discuss with students how this passage differs from conventional prose. (*Possible responses: The first sentence is incomplete and has atypical punctuation.*) Then have students rewrite the passage as it might appear in a story. (*Possible response: And I am Bilbo Baggins, at your service. I'm surprised to see you, though. I was expecting groceries.*)

 Mini-Lesson   Grammar

THE SUBJECT IN DIFFERENT POSITIONS Point out to students that the subject of a sentence does not always come at the beginning of the sentence. For instance, in a sentence beginning with the word *here* or *there*, the subject usually follows the verb. Tell students that to find the subject of a sentence in which the order is unusual, they should first find the verb. Then they should ask themselves to whom or what the verb refers. Share the given example with students to demonstrate this technique.

Application Have students identify the subject and verb in the following sentences.
1. There go the dwarves! (*dwarves, go*)
2. Way up on the hill blossomed wildflowers in the Shire. (*wildflowers, blossomed*)

Reteaching/Reinforcement
- *Grammar Handbook,* anthology pp. 815–821
- *Grammar Mini-Lessons* copymasters p. 7, transparencies p. 7

 The Writer's Craft

The Subject in Different Positions, p. 354

> There is Bilbo.
> Verb: *is*
> Who or what is there? Bilbo
> *Bilbo* is the subject of *is*.

THE LANGUAGE OF LITERATURE TEACHER'S EDITION **577**

Linking to Science

 Whole milk is made up of globules of butterfat floating in a solution of milk sugar, proteins, and salts of sulfur, potassium, sodium, chlorine, phosphorus, and calcium. When chilled cream is churned, the fat globules coalesce to form butter. Balin's drink—buttermilk—is the residue left behind, the byproduct of butter making.

Critical Thinking: SYNTHESIZING

J Ask students how and why Bilbo has changed his attitude toward his guests. You may wish to use the following model.

Think-Aloud Model It seems to me that Bilbo is growing less hospitable as time goes on. He was gracious enough when it was a matter of only one dwarf. But he is getting irritated at the sheer number of guests—whom he did not invite to tea!

---

door, saying while opening it) I have no idea who it could—Oh!

(*There stands an elderly dwarf,* Balin, *with a white beard and scarlet hood.*)

Balin (*hobbling inside, gesturing at the coat rack with his cane*). Ha! I see they have begun to arrive already! (*hangs his hood next to* Dwalin's) Balin, at your service! (*It is difficult for him to execute a bow. He groans.*)

Bilbo. Thank you. Uh, you said "They have begun to arrive"?

Gandalf (*calling*). Groceries, Bilbo?

Bilbo. Actually, no— (*taking a deep breath, to* Balin) Won't you join us for tea?

Balin. A glass of buttermilk would suit me better, if it's all the same to you, my good sir. But I don't mind some cake—seed cake, if you have any. (*crosses to table*)

Bilbo (*automatically*). Oh, lots! Excuse me. (*hurries off left to get cake*)

Dwalin. No hurry. (*to* Balin) Fine lodgings here, eh, brother?

Balin (*seating himself*). Ummm. These Hobbits have the cream.[4] A big thing this is we're setting out for.

(*Doorbell rings, bringing on* Bilbo *from left with platter of cakes.*)

Dwalin. But dangerous. Terribly dangerous!

Bilbo. Not again!

Gandalf (*crossing to* Bilbo). Allow me to unburden you— (*Takes platter from* Bilbo *and passes platter to others.* Dwalin *takes two cakes and downs them rapidly and is shortly back for more.* Balin *takes one and nibbles at it and puts it down on small table. Later* Balin *eats it unnoticed.*)

(*Bell rings again.* Bilbo *rushes to the door and opens it. There stand two dwarves,* Kili *and* Fili, *look-alikes with blue hoods, silver belts and yellow beards. Each carries a bag of tools and spades.*)

Kili. Kili!

Fili. Fili! (*Both sweep off their hoods and bow.*)

Kili and **Fili** (*together*). At your service!

Bilbo. Baggins, here— (*weakly*) At yours . . . uh, and your families'!

Kili. Dwalin and Balin here already, I see. Let us join the throng! (Kili *and* Fili *hang up their hoods, cross to table and sit down.*)

Bilbo (*horrified*). Throng!

Gandalf. Why, Bilbo, I really am surprised! I didn't think that Hobbits mixed with dwarves.

Bilbo. They don't!

Gandalf. No? That's odd, since you have so many dwarf friends.

Bilbo (*confidentially, to* Gandalf). I've never laid eyes on them before! If my neighbors knew, they'd be scandalized![5] Dwarves here! At Bag-End! (*Bell rings, and then there is the lively rat-a-tat of a stick on the door.*)

Dwalin. That'll be Dori, Nori, Ori, Oin and Gloin!

Bilbo (*horrified, crossing to door*). Who? (*hurrying to the door as the rat-a-tat continues*) The nerve!

(Bilbo *opens the door, and there stand no less than five dwarves,* Dori, Nori, Ori, Oin *and* Gloin, *their broad hands stuck in their gold and silver belts. They bow upon introducing themselves.*)

Dori (*has a blond beard, dark purple hood, and*

---

4. **the cream:** the best or choicest of things.
5. **scandalized:** shocked.

WORDS TO KNOW
throng (thrông) *n.* a large gathering of people; crowd

578

Mini-Lesson   The Writer's Style

DIALOGUE Explain to students that writing good dialogue is an important key to getting and maintaining a reader's interest. Dialogue is generally written so that it sounds like real conversation, gives readers necessary information, and reveals something about the personality of each speaker and his or her relationship with others. In the highlighted passage above, for example, Tolkien writes his dialogue so that fantastical creatures sound like real people talking. The dialogue also provides information (Hobbits and dwarves don't ordinarily mix) and reveals personalities (Gandalf is being cagey; he knows quite well that Bilbo hasn't any dwarf friends).

Application Have students write a dialogue, set several years after the journey, in which Bilbo and Gandalf reminisce about Bilbo's quest.

Reteaching/Reinforcement
- *Writing Handbook*, anthology p. 779
- *Writing Mini-Lessons* transparencies, p. 48

Using Dialogue, pp. 278–279

578 THE LANGUAGE OF LITERATURE TEACHER'S EDITION

gold belt; *doffing his hood*). Dori!

Nori (*has a blond beard, pale purple hood, and silver belt; doffing his hood*). Nori!

Ori (*has a brown beard, orange hood, and gold belt; doffing his hood*). Ori!

Oin (*has an auburn beard, brown hood, and a gold belt; doffing his hood*). Oin!

Gloin (*has a gray beard, gray hood, and a silver belt; doffing his hood*). Gloin!

Bilbo. Oh!

Dori, Nori, Ori, Oin, and **Gloin** (*together*). At your service! (*They hang up their hoods.*)

Bilbo. Where do you all come from? (*crossing to Gandalf, frantically*) There's just no end to them! I must be having a nightmare! (*Gandalf pinches Bilbo.*) Ouch!

Gandalf. You're awake. (*Dwarves have been whispering among themselves.*)

Bilbo (*coughing importantly to get the Dwarves' attention*). Ahem, ahem. Honored Dwarves, I'm sorry, but I'm afraid you've mistaken this for a restaurant. This is a private home. (*Dwarves laugh politely at what they think is an attempt at humor.*)

K

Dori (*slapping Bilbo on the back good-naturedly*). Oh-ho, jolly good! Bring out the food.

Ori. Hot cocoa for me, please.

Dwalin (*from the table*). And more cakes! We're fresh out. Please! (*Shows empty plate. There is a terrific banging on the door.*)

Bilbo (*fuming*). Stop that pounding! What are you trying to—

(*Bilbo pulls the door open with a jerk, and in tumble four dwarves,* Bifur, Bofur, Bombur, *and* Thorin, *one on top of the other.*)

Gandalf (*laughing*). Careful. Careful! It's not like you, Bilbo, to keep friends waiting on the mat and then open the door like a popgun! (*The Dwarves pick themselves up and bow as they announce themselves, except for* Thorin, *who was at the bottom of the heap, directly under* Bombur, *the fattest of the lot.*)

Bifur (*Has a very slight chestnut beard and pale yellow hood; he is the youngest of the dwarves.*) I'm Bifur!

Bofur (*has a gray beard and a dark yellow hood and a silver belt*). Bofur!

Bifur and **Bofur** (*together*). At your service!

Bombur (*Has a light blue beard and a pale green hood. He is the fattest of the dwarves and is a natural clown. He scrambles off* Thorin *and bows deeply.*) Bombur, at your service! (*He indicates* Thorin, *who was at the bottom of the heap and who stands apart brushing himself off indignantly.*) Our great leader, Thorin. (*Thorin has a black beard and a sky blue hood with a long silver tassel.*)

Thorin (*snarling at* Bombur). Sir! (*Bombur cringes. They all hang up their hoods.*)

Bilbo (*interceding*). My fault. I'm terribly sorry.

Thorin (*grunting*). Don't mention it. (*gazes regally up at the ceiling, looking at row of thirteen hoods*) I see we are all here.

L

Gandalf. Quite a merry gathering! (*Doorbell rings.*)

Thorin. Who can *that* be?

Bilbo. Well, *I* certainly wouldn't know!

(*Bilbo crosses to door and opens it, and there stands a Hobbit* Boy *with a box of groceries.*)

Grocery Boy. Your groceries, Mr. Baggins.

Bilbo (*quickly*). Thank you, lad. I'll take them— (*takes box and attempts to shut door on boy*)

Grocery Boy (*peering over* Bilbo's *shoulder*). Having a party, Mr. Baggins?

Bilbo. Humph.

THE HOBBIT: ACT ONE   **579**

STRATEGIC READING FOR
Less-Proficient Readers

K Ask students why a group of dwarves shows up at Bilbo's home. (*Possible response: Gandalf has invited them.*) Relating Cause and Effect

Set a Purpose Have students read to find out what impression Bilbo makes on the dwarves as they prepare for the adventure.

CUSTOMIZING FOR
Multiple Learning Styles

L Spatial or Graphic Learners
Have interested students draw or paint a picture of the party, including Bilbo, Gandalf, and the dwarves. Remind students to skim the pages they have read so far for visual details.

CUSTOMIZING FOR
Students Acquiring English

② Explain that *Cheez* is an exclamation that expresses both surprise and annoyance.

③ Point out that the stage direction *sarcastic* indicates that Bilbo means exactly the opposite of what he says. In fact, he does not want the dwarves to eat all his groceries. Model appropriate intonation and help students to identify the many other examples of sarcasm throughout the play.

Literary Concept: SIMILE

M Remind students that a simile is a comparison of two different things that have something in common. Similes use such words as *like, as, resembles,* or *than* to make comparisons. Have students identify the simile at the top of this page and explain why it is appropriate. You may want to inform students that a locust is a type of grasshopper that often devours and destroys crops. *(Possible responses: "Dwarves! Like locusts!" They are alike in number and appetite. Dwarves are pouring into Bilbo's house and helping themselves to his food, just as locusts move from place to place in large numbers and devour all the crops in sight.)*

Active Reading: CLARIFY

N Ask students to clarify why Thorin gives Bombur a disgusted look. *(Possible response: Thorin is still irritated that Bombur, the heaviest of the dwarves, fell on top of him when they arrived at Bilbo's home.)*

---

② **Grocery Boy.** *Dwarves!* Cheez, Mr. Baggins—hundreds of 'em. Wait till they hear of this down the road. Dwarves! Like locusts! *(Bilbo shuts the door rudely on the boy.)*

Bilbo *(sadly).* Oh, dear!

Thorin *(crossing to table with new arrivals).* I trust there's food for the latecomers.

Bilbo *(tight as a coil).* Well—I may have a *little* tea left.

Gandalf. Tea? No, no, thank you. A little red wine and some cold chicken and pickles.

Thorin. And for me.

Bifur. Apple pie—and coffee, if you don't mind.

Bofur. And mince pie with cheese!

Bombur *(already seated at the table, drumming on it with zest).* Pork pie and salad! *(Thorin gives Bombur a disgusted look.)*

Bifur. And raspberry jam and muffins.

Gandalf. Put on a few eggs, there's a good fellow.

Dori *(from table).* Cold tongue!

Nori. A side of ham!

Ori. Cupcakes!

Oin. Assorted cheeses—if you please!

Dwalin. More cakes and ale!

Bilbo *(dumbfounded).* More! *(sarcastic)* Oh, certainly, dig in, dig in! *(heading left for the kitchen with box of groceries)* Don't stint yourselves! *(grumbling to himself as he goes off)* Seem to know as much about the inside of my kitchen as I do! *(calling back)* I could use some help!

Thorin. Bifur! Nori! *(Bifur and Nori go off left to help Bilbo.)* Now! Lower the lamp, Balin. *(Balin pulls down the lamp, which hangs over the table. The lights dim.)*

Dwalin *(rubbing his palms together).* Dark for dark business!

Balin. Hush! Let Thorin speak!

Thorin *(at head of table; standing and clearing his throat importantly).* Gandalf, dwarves, and Mr. Baggins!

(Bilbo, Bifur and Nori bustle on left, laden with huge platters of food and drink.)

Bilbo. Why so dark?

Fili. We *like* the dark. *(Fili notices Bilbo is not serving himself and begins to fill a plate for him.)*

Dwarves. Shh—

Thorin. We are met together in the house of our friend and fellow <u>conspirator</u>—

WORDS TO KNOW

conspirator (kən-spîr′ə-tər) *n.* someone who takes part in a plot

580

Bilbo (*protesting*). No, no!

Thorin. —this wise and brave Hobbit—

Bilbo (*flattered*). Dear me!

Thorin. May the hair on his toes never fall out! All praise to his food. (*The* Dwarves *raise their mugs.*)

Dwarves (*toasting*). Hear, hear! (Bilbo *has slunk over to his stool in front of the fire where he sits clutching his toes protectively.* Fili *brings him a plate of food, but* Bilbo *shakes his head. His appetite is completely gone.* Fili *returns to his own place.*)

Thorin. We are met to discuss our plans. We shall start before dawn on a long, hard journey, so dangerous that some may not live through it or they may reach the misty mountain only to be eaten by the dragon— (Bilbo *lets out a piercing shriek, falling off the stool to the floor, where he lies shaking and twitching wildly. The* Dwarves *spring up and stare at him in dismay.*)

Gandalf (*producing a blue light [created by camera flash equipment] at end of his staff and crossing to* Bilbo, *prodding him with his foot*). Come, come. He's an excitable little fellow. He gets these queer fits, but he's fierce as a dragon in a pinch!

Bilbo (*shrieking*). I'm struck by lightning! Struck by lightning! (Dwarves *circle* Bilbo *curiously.*)

Gloin (*the doubter, snorting*). Humph! It's all very well for you to talk . . . but one shriek like that in a moment of danger might wake the dragon and all his kin. They'd eat the lot of us fast as you'd swallow a dozen cupcakes.

Thorin. It *did* sound more like fright than excitement. In fact, but for the sign on the door, I'd have thought we'd come to the wrong house.

Balin. Why, he just turned to jelly right before our eyes! He looks more like a grocer than a burglar!

Bilbo (*raising himself up with all the dignity he can muster*). Pardon me, but I couldn't help overhearing your insults. Am I allowed a few words?

Thorin (*condescendingly*). By all means.

Bilbo. First, I don't know what you're talking about. There isn't any sign on my door—unless, of course, you're referring to the dents from all your banging!

Gandalf. Of course there's a sign. I put it there myself.

Thorin. My good sir, the sign says: "Burglar wants good job, plenty of excitement and reasonable reward." Read it yourself. (*opens door and shows sign*)

Bilbo. So! I've been deceived!

Gandalf (*to* Thorin). You asked me to find a fourteenth man for your expedition—and I chose Mr. Baggins here—

Bilbo (*incensed*). Oh, you *did,* did you? Well, if you think that I—

Gandalf. —*but* I'm afraid I've made a sad mistake. This can't be the chap! No, no, I was looking for a member of the famous Took family. Imagine! I mistook *him* for a *Took!* (*glowers at* Bilbo)

Bilbo (*stung*). But I *am* a Took!

Gandalf. Really? Tch, tch, the blood must have thinned then.

Bilbo. Why, my great-uncle, Bull-Roarer Took—

Gloin (*cutting in*). Yes, yes, but we're talking about you!

Gandalf (*melodramatically*). I said to myself, now *here* is a Hobbit with desires beyond his next cup of tea—but alas, he's just an ordinary run-of-the-Shire Hobbit. When adven-

THE HOBBIT: ACT ONE **581**

CUSTOMIZING FOR
Students Acquiring English

4 Explain that *condescendingly* means "in a superior manner" and point out the humor in Thorin's being condescending to Bilbo in the Hobbit's own house.

STRATEGIC READING FOR
Less-Proficient Readers

0 Ask students what impression Bilbo makes on the dwarves as they prepare for the adventure. *(He makes a terrible impression. Bilbo panics and loses control of himself. The dwarves are afraid that he will endanger their quest by making noise.)* **Drawing Conclusions**

Set a Purpose Have students read to find out how Gandalf gets Bilbo to participate in the adventure even though he has strong reservations.

Mini-Lesson   Genre Study

DRAMA Explain to students that a **drama** is a kind of story that is meant to be acted out for an audience. Draw the word web shown so that students understand the characteristics of this literary genre. You may wish to point out that this selection is a dramatization of the novel *The Hobbit,* and therefore elements of the original work have been adapted to fit the characteristics of a drama.

Application Have students copy the word web into their notebooks. Ask students to give examples from the selection that demonstrate that it is a drama. Then ask students to discuss what changes a writer may have to do to a novel to dramatize it for an audience. For example, expository description of settings and actions can be redone as scenery and rewritten as stage directions.

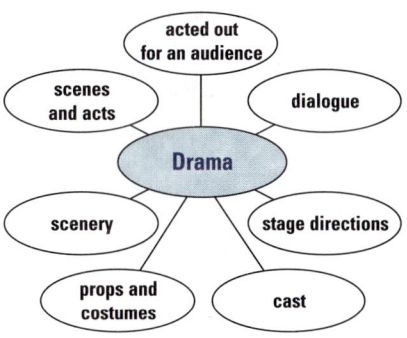

THE LANGUAGE OF LITERATURE **TEACHER'S EDITION** **581**

STRATEGIC READING FOR
Less-Proficient Readers

P Ask students how Gandalf gets Bilbo to participate in an adventure about which he has strong reservations. *(Gandalf shames Bilbo into participating.)* **Making Inferences**

Set a Purpose Have students read to find a sign that Bilbo's relationship with the dwarves is changing.

CUSTOMIZING FOR
Multiple Learning Styles

Q Interpersonal Learners Invite students to discuss in small groups the dwarves' interaction with Bilbo at this point in the selection. Allow students to rehearse and perform the indicated scene for the class. Remind students to use the stage directions for help in developing their characters.

---

ture knocks, he locks his door and hides under the bed.

Bilbo (*highly insulted, standing up*). Really, this is too much!

Gandalf (*to* Dwarves). Well, dwarves, you can go back to shoveling coal. The Hobbit is afraid to go, and you certainly can't set out with thirteen! That's too unlucky!

Bilbo (*with great dignity*). Sir, I must tell you that to uphold the honor of the Took family, I would cross mountains and deserts and fight a hundred dragons! I would—

Gandalf (*cutting in*). Splendid! Mr. Baggins is with us! (*shakes* Bilbo's *hand*) Now, Thorin—(*crosses to* Thorin)

P **Bilbo** (*mumbling to himself*). Now why did I say that? Bilbo, you're a fool! Now you *have* put your foot in it!

Thorin (*to* Gandalf). But are you sure he'll do? You yourself said that he—

Gandalf (*interrupting*). If I say he's a burglar, a burglar he is—or will be when the time comes. There's more to him than you guess or he has any idea of himself. You'll live to thank him, and to thank him that you live.

Thorin. Let us hope so! (*turns to others*) Well, now, to get on with the plans. It's late. (*All walk over to the table and sit with* Thorin *at the head,* Bilbo *at his right and* Bombur *next to* Bilbo.)

Gandalf (*spreading a large map on the table before* Thorin). Let's have some light on this. (Bombur *adjusts the overhanging lamp. Lights come up. To* Thorin.) This is a map of the Lonely Mountain. It was left by your grandfather, King Thrain.

Thorin. Ah, yes?

Bilbo. What mountain?

Bombur (*giving* Bilbo *a friendly nudge*). Where the *treasure* is! And the dragon. (*makes a gruesome face and hisses alarmingly at* Bilbo)

Thorin (*studying the map*). I don't see that this will help much—I remember the mountain well enough and the lands about it— (*pointing them out*) Mirkwood—the Withered Heath—

Bombur. That's where the great dragons breed! (*makes clawlike, threatening gestures and hisses at* Bilbo, *who manages a sickly smile in spite of being terrified*)

Thorin. There's the dragon—marked in red. Well, we're not likely to miss *him*, are we! (*Laughter from company.* Bilbo's *laughter lingers on. Dwarves look at him curiously.*)

Bilbo (*nervously*). Oh ho ho ha! The— (*stops, embarrassed*) Dragon! I'm not overfond of dragons, but then I've never actually known any.

Gandalf (*dismissing* Bilbo's *chatter*). You will, you will. (*to* Thorin) Look here, Thorin. This circle on the map marks the secret entrance in the mountain—here! (*points to spot on map*)

Thorin. Ha! But is it still secret? That's the question!

Balin. By now the dragon must know these caves from top to bottom.

Gandalf. Not the secret entrance. It's so well hidden it looks exactly like the side of the mountain. And by the way, I've a key that goes with the map. Here it is. (*hands* Thorin *a key*) Keep it safe!

Thorin. Indeed I will! (*fastens it on a gold chain that hangs about his neck and speaks with great satisfaction*) Well, now, things begin to look more hopeful. A secret entrance! What luck!

Bombur (*to* Bilbo). Arrrgh! Hear him roar? It's almost dinner time. The dragon's hungry for

582 UNIT FIVE PART 2: RELUCTANT HEROES

some nice roasted burglar! (Bilbo *hides his face in his hands and moans. The other Dwarves chuckle and nudge each other.*)

Thorin (*turning to Bilbo with mock politeness*). Suppose we ask our burglar expert to give us his ideas and suggestions—

Bilbo (*confused and shaky*). Well, first off I should like some information. I mean, about the dragon and the treasure and how it got there and who it belongs to, and so on—

Thorin (*wearily*). Oh, very well—

Bilbo. And I'd also like to know about risks, out-of-pocket expenses, time required, wages, et cetera.

Balin. He wants to know his chances of coming back alive and how much gold he'll get.

Thorin. His chances are as good as ours. The circumstances are briefly these: Long ago when my grandfather was king, the dwarves settled here— (*points at map*) —under the Lonely Mountain, and they built the merry town of Dale. Those were the happy days! They made beautiful things just for the fun of it. Not to sell, as we do now. When they needed more gold or emeralds or rubies, they just dug them out of the mountain. There was no end to the supply. But that brought the dragon. Good times always bring dragons. History illustrates—

Gandalf (*interrupting*). Be brief, won't you?

Thorin (*insulted*). Very well. There was an especially wicked dragon called Sm-sm-sm— (*apologetically*) —his name seems to stick in my throat—

Gandalf (*helpfully*). Smaug!

Thorin. Yes, curse him! He flew from the east and burned the town. Only a few escaped, my father among them.

Bilbo (*thrilled*). And then?

Thorin. The dragon ate all the dwarves and took their treasure. The fiend! (*pounds on the table*) So now we mean to get back what is rightfully ours and bring our curses home to Sm-sm-sm—

Gandalf (*helping*). Smaug!

Thorin. Death to all dragons—especially Sm-sm-sm—

Dwarves (*banging their mugs and roaring it out*). Smaug!

Bilbo (*weakly*). Hear, hear!

Dwarves. Hear what?

Bilbo (*flustered*). Hear what I've got to say!

Gandalf. Go ahead. Say it!

Bilbo. I think you ought to go first to the secret entrance and look around—dragons must sleep sometimes. And now I'm off to bed. You have my blessing. Uh—is there anything I can get you before you go?

Thorin. Before *we* go, I suppose you mean. You're the burglar and getting inside the entrance is *your* job.

Dwarves (*thundering applause*). Thorin!

Bilbo. But—but, you see, I may have spoken a little hastily just now. It's an inconvenient time to—

Gandalf (*dismissing it*). It's nearly dawn. Time to clear up and start. (Bilbo *tries to attract his attention by pulling at his sleeve, but* Gandalf *ignores him, and he is equally unsuccessful in attracting* Thorin's *attention.* Bilbo *finally gives up, shaking his head gloomily. The* Dwarves *jump up and begin to make tall stacks of the plates and glasses.* Gandalf *and* Thorin *remain seated, looking over the map.*)

WORDS TO KNOW — **fiend** (fēnd) *n.* one who is very wicked or cruel; devil

583

Literary Concept: DIALOGUE

T Ask students what Bilbo's speech reveals about his feelings on setting out with the dwarves. *(Possible response: Bilbo is anxious and irritated.)*

Literary Concept: HUMOR

U Discuss with students what Bilbo says as he searches his pockets. Ask how his words both inform and amuse readers. *(Possible response: Bilbo is in a panic at the thought of actually setting out. Bilbo's absurd observation that, without his diary, there will be no record if the dragon eats him is amusing because the dragon might eat the diary as well, which means no one will be able to read it. Also, if Bilbo is eaten by the dragon, how does he know he'll be able to write about it before it happens?)*

CUSTOMIZING FOR
Students Acquiring English

5 Students will probably understand that the expression *get a grip on yourself* is not meant literally. Encourage them to infer its meaning. ("control your feelings and reactions")

Bilbo (*squeaking with fright*). Please be careful! (*spinning around the room*) Please don't trouble! I can take care of everything after you've all gone!

Dwarves (*chanting while clearing table*).
Chip the glasses, and crack the plates!
Blunt the knives and bend the forks!
That's what Bilbo Baggins hates—
Smash the bottles and burn the corks!

Bilbo (*shrieking*). My best china! Please be careful!

Dwarves (*chanting*).
Cut the cloth and tread on the fat!
Pour the milk on the pantry floor!
Leave the bones on the bedroom mat!
Splash the wine on every door!
That's what Bilbo Baggins hates!
So, carefully! carefully with the plates!

(*The Dwarves exit with the glasses, platters, etc., Bilbo whirling around madly. Offstage there is a tremendous clatter as the curtain falls.*)

(*Lights come up in front of the curtain. The Dwarves are lined up on the apron, sticks with bundles over their shoulders, ready to start. Thorin is at the head.*)

Thorin (*pacing impatiently*). Well, where's the Hobbit? Where's our burglar?

(*Bilbo runs on left, puffing profusely.*)

Bifur. Here he is! Bravo!

Thorin. Humph!

T **Bilbo** (*very put out, catching his breath*). Oh, my! Oh, my! The way the morning starts decides the day! It's going to be a miserable day! Hunting dragons! At my age! What a fool I am. Everyone expecting me to be ready at the drop of a hat! (*Feels his head. No hat.*) My *hat!* My coat, my brolly,[6] my pocket hanky—my purse—

Thorin (*cutting in*). Stop fussing!

Bilbo (*searching his pockets*). Where's my diary? If the dragon eats me, there'll be no record! My friends back home won't know what happened! And I've got no money—

Thorin (*disgusted*). Get a grip on yourself, Baggins!

Dwalin (*grimly*). You'll learn to do without small comforts before we reach journey's end.

Gloin (*disgusted, acting it out*). Where's his money? Imagine! Our burglar hasn't any money! (*Capers about, imitating* Bilbo's *fluster. The* Dwarves *laugh derisively.*)

Bombur (*helpful but mocking*). I've a spare hood. The lining is fireproof. It'll keep your hair from being burned when Smaug spits fire at you.

Bilbo (*politely*). Thank you, Bombur, much obliged. (*Tries it on. It is very large.*) I wish it fitted closer, but the fireproof lining is great. Very great.

(Gandalf *strides on from left.*)

Gandalf. Are we all ready to start? Ah, Bilbo, I believe you forgot these. (*hands* Bilbo *a handkerchief, a pipe and tobacco pouch, a leather-bound journal and a hat*)

Bilbo (*delighted, stowing them away*). Oh, thank you! And my diary! How kind of you! (Bilbo *is puzzled by the hat. He replaces the hood with the hat and looks regretfully at the lining of the hood. Then with decision he replaces the hood on his head, looks uncertainly at the hat and then tosses it offstage.*)

Dwarves (*approvingly*). Bilbo! Long live our burglar!

Gandalf. And I remembered you, Bombur. (*hands over a string bag of small, hard cakes*)

U **5**

---
6. **brolly:** a British term for umbrella.

584 UNIT FIVE PART 2: RELUCTANT HEROES

Mini-Lesson  Literary Concepts

HUMOR Remind students that humor is the quality that makes writing funny or amusing. Writers can create humor by using exaggeration, amusing descriptions, sarcasm, witty dialogue, and other devices. For example, the highlighted passage above uses witty dialogue that teases one of the characters.

Application Read aloud to students the following lines from *The Hobbit*. Have students tell how the writer creates humor in each instance. *(uses sarcasm and understatement)* Then encourage students to locate other examples of humor in the selection and explain what makes each example humorous.

Page 579:

Gandalf: Quite a merry gathering! (Doorbell rings.)

Thorin: Who can *that* be?

Bilbo: Well, *I* certainly wouldn't know!

Page 583:

Gandalf: It's nearly dawn. Time to clear up and start. (Bilbo *tries to attract his attention by pulling at his sleeve, but* Gandalf *ignores him, and he is equally unsuccessful in attracting* Thorin's *attention. . . .*)

584 THE LANGUAGE OF LITERATURE TEACHER'S EDITION

Bombur. Cakes! Thank you! Where did you get them?

Gandalf. From a friend of mine. He lives far from here. You may yet meet him.

Bombur (*eating one*). It tastes of honey.

Gandalf. Yes, my friend keeps bees. (*Bombur starts to take another.*) You'll need these cakes. Don't eat them right away.

Bombur (*stowing the cakes away*). Need them? With all the food we're taking! But, as you say, Gandalf.

Thorin. Our marching song! (*Thorin leads the Dwarves off left. They march off heavily, in step, chanting in gloomy tones.*)
Far over the misty mountains cold
To dungeons deep and caverns old
We must away, ere break of day,
To seek the pale enchanted gold!
(*Gandalf and Bilbo follow closely after Dwarves.*)

Bilbo (*to Gandalf*). Couldn't they sing something cheery?

Gandalf. Such as—

Bilbo (*firmly*). Such as "Home, Sweet Home."

(*As they exit,* Gandalf *puts his arm around* Bilbo *and laughs.*)

FROM PERSONAL RESPONSE TO CRITICAL ANALYSIS

REFLECT 1. What do you think of Bilbo Baggins, Esquire? Share your impressions with your class.

RETHINK 2. Why do you suppose Gandalf chooses Bilbo to join the quest?
   Consider
   - Gandalf's comment to Bilbo, "I'll give you what you asked for."
   - that Gandalf says to the dwarves, "There's more to him than you guess or he has any idea of himself."
   - why Bilbo agrees to get involved

3. Bilbo says, "It's hard to look at a place from the outside when you live in the inside." Do you agree? Why or why not?

4. Based on what you have learned about Bilbo so far, do you think he will be a successful burglar? Explain your opinion.

THE HOBBIT: ACT ONE **585**

Linking to Social Studies

 Apiculture (beekeeping) is an ancient profession. Several thousand years ago, Egyptian beekeepers traded honey and beeswax along the East African coast. Like their ancient predecessors, modern beekeepers earn a living selling honey and beeswax. The honeybee helps the economy as a whole, however, primarily by pollinating vegetables, fruits, and pastures.

From Personal Response to Critical Analysis

1. Responses will vary.
2. Possible responses: Gandalf chooses Bilbo because he knows that Bilbo has many skills and talents that have gone untapped, since he lives a quiet life at home. Gandalf chooses Bilbo because he knows that he can rise to the challenge, especially because he comes from a long line of brave and adventurous Hobbits.
3. Possible responses: Yes, I agree, because Bilbo means it's difficult to see something from a new perspective if you're used to seeing things in the same old way.
4. Possible responses: Based on what Gandalf has said about Bilbo and based on Bilbo's brave ancestors, I think he will make a successful burglar. No, I don't think Bilbo will make a successful burglar because he's very polite and good-natured, and he doesn't have much experience at being a burglar.

THE LANGUAGE OF LITERATURE TEACHER'S EDITION **585**

CUSTOMIZING FOR
Students Acquiring English

⑥ Remind students that the author of *The Hobbit* was British and point out that *Bother* in *Bother burgling!* is British English. It means "never mind."

STRATEGIC READING FOR
Less-Proficient Readers

Ⓦ Ask students the following questions to make sure they understand the story thus far.

- How is Bilbo's relationship with the dwarves different from when they first met? *(Possible response: Bilbo and the dwarves are now on friendlier, more relaxed terms.)* Making Inferences/Comparing and Contrasting

- Give a specific example that shows how the relationship is changing. *(Possible response: Bofur says he enjoys hearing Bilbo's journal entries.)* Noting Relevant Details

Set a Purpose Have students read to find out how Bilbo begins to discover his hidden inner resourcefulness.

Active Reading: CLARIFY

Ⓧ Have students explain the meaning of Bilbo's "thought for today," which is mentioned in two places on this page. *(Possible responses: The "thought for today" tells that the adventure started out pleasantly, with good weather and pretty scenery. Then, however, the rains came and the scenery became frightening. The "thought for today" indicates a shift in the story or a development in the plot. Perhaps Bilbo is about to meet the dangers that he feared.)*

Scene: *In the forest several months later. The curtain rises to reveal a nearly bare stage that is divided into three playing areas. At right there is a platform approximately a foot-and-a-half high that extends in from the right side to about one-quarter of the way across the stage. A similar platform extends the same distance from left.*

At rise of curtain: Lights come up on the platform at left. Bilbo *is discovered sitting on a log at the edge, legs crossed, writing thoughtfully in his journal with a long quill pen. Behind him, the* Dwarves, *except for* Fili *and* Kili, *are sprawled out, resting. The only sound is that of Bombur's heavy snoring.* Bilbo *finishes with a flourish, blows on script,[7] holds it off admiringly and reads aloud:*

Bilbo (*reading his entry*). "Have just stopped to rest and let Fili and Kili water our ponies. Thought for today: Adventures are not all Sunday strolls in May sunshine." That's really well put. (*lays down book and massages his feet*) Covered with burrs! (*picks at burrs*) And soaked with these nasty May rains. Bother burgling! I wish I was home with the kettle just beginning to sing!

Bofur (*rousing and leaning on an elbow*). You'll wish that again before we're out of this mess. But go on, I like to hear you read about our adventures.

Bilbo. Thanks. (*resumes reading*) "At first I thought adventures were much like picnics. We traveled past pretty farms, and the people seemed friendly. But things have changed lately.

See thought for today. We've seen no one all day, and there's nothing ahead but black, rainy mountains. As soon as Fili and Kili are back, we should move ahead and make an early camp and have some hot supper."

Bombur. Sound idea! (*Takes out bag of honey cakes and looks at them. He glances about to see if anyone is noticing, and then slips a cake in his mouth.*)

Bifur (*rousing*). Did someone say supper?

Thorin (*rousing*). We should be going on. Where are Fili and Kili? (*Offstage cries are heard.*)

Bilbo (*jumping up*). I hear something.

Dori (*rising*). It's Fili.

Nori (*rising*). And Kili.

Bifur (*struggling to his feet*). They're shouting for help!

(Fili *and* Kili *enter. They are drenched, breathless, and gasping.*)

Thorin. Where are the ponies? What's happened?

Kili. We lost them. (*The Dwarves press forward around them, excitedly ad-libbing[8] questions: "Lost them!" "How could you?" "Did they run away?" etc.*)

Thorin (*sternly*). Silence, dwarves. Kili, what happened?

Kili. We took them down to water like you said. But the streambed was almost dry, and they wandered out into it drinking at some of the little pools. (*pauses, gulping breath*)

Thorin (*sternly*). Did you stay with them?

Kili (*uncomfortably*). I did, until they were settled drinking water. Then I—well, I went along the bank looking for mushrooms to eat.

---

7. **script:** Bilbo's journal, not the script of the play.
8. **ad-libbing:** in a play, making up one's own lines rather than speaking words written by the playwright.

586   UNIT FIVE   PART 2: RELUCTANT HEROES

586 THE LANGUAGE OF LITERATURE TEACHER'S EDITION

Thorin. You mean you left them!

Kili. But Fili was watching them from the bank, and I ran back the minute I heard him shout.

Thorin. What happened, Fili?

Fili. A great wall of water came thundering out of the mountains. I shouted, but it was over the ponies in a moment. They just tumbled over and over like logs and were gone!

Thorin. All of them!

Fili. Yes.

Thorin. And the food bags?

Kili. On the ponies. (*Thorin turns away with a gesture of despair.*)

Bilbo. But then we've nothing to eat.

Bifur. We've got the honey cakes.

Dwalin. Wise Gandalf. He knew we'd need them!

Thorin. But maybe we'll have a greater need of them later. This isn't a real emergency. We're not starving.

Bombur. I am.

Thorin. After all, we've got our burglar here. (*to Bilbo*) It's up to you, burglar. Burgle us some food.

Bilbo. Up to me. I like that! Out here in the middle of nowhere! It needs a magician to find food here. Besides, maybe this is the time Gandalf meant us to eat the honey cakes. Why don't you ask him?

Balin. He's right. Ask Gandalf. (*There is a general murmur of agreement from the Dwarves.*)

Thorin. You may be right. (*glances around*) Where's Gandalf?

Balin. Asleep, probably. I'll wake him up. (*calls*) Gandalf! (*No answer. Louder.*) Gandalf!

Dori. He's gone!

Ori. Gone! Oh, no!

Gloin. Smartest thing he ever did!

Balin. If I was a wizard, I'd vanish, too.

Thorin. Yes—well, I'm sure he had his reasons. We'll have to go on without him.

Dwarves (*ad-libbing groans, etc.*) Oh, no!

Thorin (*proudly*). We dwarves have always stood alone. Our forefathers didn't depend on magic.

Gloin. And look what happened—a dragon ate them!

Bifur. Speaking of eating—

Thorin (*crossly*). Oh, very well! Bombur, share out the cakes. (*Bombur rapidly passes out the cakes, starting with* Thorin. *He comes to* Bilbo *last.* Bilbo *takes the cake* Bombur *hands him. He sees the bag is empty.*)

Bilbo. But there's none left for you! (*All the* Dwarves *turn to look at* Bombur.)

Bombur (*embarrassed*). Never mind. I had mine.

Bilbo. But you didn't. You just passed them out.

Bombur. I ate mine before.

Bilbo. You mean that time when Gandalf gave them to you? That doesn't count.

Bombur (*blurting it out miserably*). I ate one just before Fili and Kili came back. I'm sorry!

Gloin (*indignant*). You broke into our supplies?

Bilbo (*calmly*). They weren't ours, they were Bombur's. Gandalf gave the cakes to him. Besides, we thought we still had our supplies then.

Gloin. I still think—

Bilbo. After all, I'm the only one concerned. You all had your share, and I say Bombur had the right to eat all the cakes if he wanted to. They were his. (*breaks his cake in two*) Take half of this one, Bombur.

THE HOBBIT: ACT ONE **587**

Critical Thinking: HYPOTHESIZING

Y Challenge students to use context clues to figure out the meaning of *burgle*. (*Possible response: The repetition of the word* burglar *suggests that* burgle *means "to steal."*)

Literary Concept: HUMOR

Z Ask students what humorous device the writer uses to undercut Thorin's boastful speech. (*Possible response: Sarcasm. Gloin points out that the dwarves' forefathers—who got eaten by a dragon—are hardly role models.*)

Mini-Lesson Spelling

THE PREFIX con- Point out to students that **conspirator** and **consoling** are two of their Words to Know that use the prefix *con-*. Explain that this prefix changes depending on the beginning letter of the root or word that follows. For instance, the prefix is spelled *com-* before roots or words that begin with the letters *m, p,* or *b* as in *commitment* and *companion*. Write this rule on the chalkboard and have students copy it into their notebooks.

Application Have students add the correct spelling of the prefix *con-* to these roots to create new words.

1. trol (*control*)
2. cert (*concert*)
3. pel (*compel*)
4. gress (*congress*)
5. bustion (*combustion*)
6. pound (*compound*)
7. ment (*comment*)
8. nect (*connect*)
9. tinent (*continent*)
10. bat (*combat*)

Ask students to look for more words that fit this pattern, in their own writing and in the things that they read, and to add these words to their personal word lists.

Reteaching/Reinforcement
• *Unit Five Resource Book,* p. 41

> *Change the prefix con- to com- before roots or words beginning with m, p, or b.*

THE LANGUAGE OF LITERATURE TEACHER'S EDITION **587**

STRATEGIC READING FOR
Less-Proficient Readers

AA Ask students how Bilbo has begun to prove Gandalf's point that there is more to him than the dwarves guessed or that he knows himself. *(Possible response: Bilbo has solved a dispute among the dwarves and given up some comfort—cake—in order to do so.)*

Finding the Main Idea

Set a Purpose Have students read to see what happens when Bilbo tries to steal food from some trolls.

CUSTOMIZING FOR
Multiple Learning Styles

BB **Intrapersonal Learners** Have students explain in writing the problem that Bilbo and the dwarves face at this point. Then, in the same piece of writing, have students describe a similar challenge that they faced and explain how they met the challenge. Assure students that the challenge they write about need not be as serious as that which confronted Bilbo and the dwarves.

To spark students' thinking, you may wish to brainstorm a list of possible challenges that involve tricking something or someone. Examples include coaxing a baby to sleep, getting rid of the hiccups, and sneaking unwanted vegetables to the dog.

Bombur. I couldn't. . . .

Bilbo (*thrusting it in his hand*). Then you'll be wasting food as well as the time we're all wasting, for the cake will just crumble away. Come on—together. (*Bilbo and Bombur each pop the half cake in their mouths, smile and clasp hands in a brief handshake.*)

AA **Balin.** The burglar's right. We're wasting time. What's your plan, Thorin?

Thorin. Look over there— (*Gestures left. All look off.*)

Bilbo. Is that where Smaug, the dragon—

Thorin (*cutting in*). Of course not. But fierce trolls live there. (*All shudder.*)

Bilbo. What are trolls?

Thorin. Huge creatures, too big for us to fight! They eat dwarves—and Hobbits.

Bilbo (*aghast*). But shouldn't we run? Do we go on right up to where they are?

Thorin. We have to. That's the only way. (*encouragingly*) But there's one way to get the better of a troll. They're night creatures. Sunlight kills them. Turns them to stone.

Balin. I've heard of that. The thing to do is trick them into staying out of their cave until a ray of sunlight hits them.

Bilbo (*more cheerfully*). That shouldn't be so hard.

Gloin. But the trolls know this will happen. They're hard to fool. Chances are, they've got you frying in a pan while you're still trying to trick them. (*Bombur has been sneaking up on Bilbo from the rear. He grabs him.*)

BB

Bombur. Got you! I'm a troll. (*Bilbo lets out a shriek.*)

Thorin (*sharply*). Order. (*to Bombur*) No more tricks till we're safely out of here! (*to Bilbo*) Be quiet. Do you want to bring a band of trolls down on us?

Balin (*pointing to platform right*). Look, there's a light over there!

(*The platform right is now dimly lit with a reddish glow. We can make out three large figures. They are trolls: Bert, Tom, and Essie. They are seated on the ground, toasting mutton on long spits of wood and licking the gravy off their fingers. There is a large wine jug.*)

Thorin. So there is! Fili, Kili, you look. Your eyes are sharpest. (*Fili and Kili strain to see.*)

Fili. It looks like—

Kili. It's trolls. Three of them.

Dwarves (*ad-lib*). Trolls! Ugh! Ich! Oh! (*The Dwarves huddle together, except Thorin, who stands apart.*)

Bombur (*sniffing the air deliciously*). I can smell

588 UNIT FIVE PART 2: RELUCTANT HEROES

mutton cooking! (*All sniff the air.*)

Thorin. It *does* smell like mutton.

Dwarves (*ad-lib*). Ummm! Sure does! I could do with some mutton! With mint.

Bombur. Mutton with garlic. I'm *never* wrong about that!

Oin. It's a pity it belongs to the trolls.

Gloin. Yeh. But . . . wait a minute . . . we have a *burglar* with us!

Bilbo (*sarcastically*). Ah! So you've finally noticed!

Gloin (*rubbing his hands together*). Yes, indeed, a burglar! Bilbo, your chance has come at last!

Bilbo (*warily*). It has?

Oin (*to* Thorin). It's the burglar's turn.

Bilbo. It is?

Gloin. Now you can show your stuff. (*moves closer to* Bilbo, *until they are nose to nose*) Gandalf said that Hobbits were especially clever at quietly sneaking *up*—

Bilbo (*incredulously*). You can't mean—the trolls? You want *me* to burgle trolls?

Thorin (*nodding*). Exactly.

Bilbo (*desperately*). But I—I thought I was only supposed to burgle the *dragon!*

Thorin. Later, later. Bring back as much mutton as you can carry. We're hungry, remember. If you run into any difficulty, hoot twice like a barn owl, and we'll come.

Bilbo (*exploding*). *What!* Are you out of your mind?

Thorin (*icily*). I beg your pardon?

Bilbo (*indignantly*). Hobbits never hoot! But, no matter. No matter. Forward, Bilbo! (*He draws himself up to his full height and walks grandly off the platform.*)

Dwarves. Careful, now! Don't come back empty-handed! Good luck!

Bilbo (*crawling stealthily toward the* Trolls; *turning his head toward* Dwarves). Hush! Stop the racket! You'll spoil everything. (*Muttering to himself, he continues to crawl toward the* Trolls.) Dwarves!

(*Lights dim on platform left and come up on platform right as* Bilbo *approaches the* Trolls' *campfire.*)

Bert (*disgusted*). Ugh! I'm sick to death o' mutton, Essie! It's coming out me ears! Mutton yesterday, mutton today, and blimey,⁹ if it don't look like mutton again tomorrer! (*turns his back to the fire and tosses his mutton over his shoulder in* Bilbo's *direction*)

Tom. Never a blinking bit o' manflesh or a nice shoulder of dwarf have we had for a long time! (*faces front, also tossing his mutton over his shoulder*)

Essie. Aw, git off! Times been up our way when yer'd have said "Thank yer, Essie" for a nice bit o' fat valley mutton like what this is.

Bert (*taking a healthy pull at the jug*). Ugh! No more'n a dribble o' drink left! (*Tom grabs the jug.*) What the 'ell we was a-thinkin' of to come into these parts beats me! (*Tom takes a pull at the jug. Bert gives him a jab in the ribs, causing* Tom *to choke.*)

Tom (*coughing*). We ain't done badly. We've et a village and a half between us since we come.

Bert (*whining*). Them villages was barely bite-sized. (Bilbo *has made his way to the fire and is just about to make off with the discarded mutton when* Essie *spots him.*)

Essie (*wheeling around, catching* Bilbo *by the scruff of his neck and holding fast*). Blimey,

---

9. **blimey:** a British expression similar to "golly."

THE HOBBIT: ACT ONE **589**

boys, look what I've copped![10]

Bert (*jumping up*). 'Ere, wot's it?

Tom (*eying* Bilbo). Lumme[11] if I know. (*to Bilbo, prodding him in the belly*) What are yer? Man? (*Bilbo shakes his head wildly.*)—dwarf? (*Bilbo shakes his head again.*)

Bilbo (*stuttering*). Ha—ha—ha—Hobbit!

Tom. A hahahahobbit? Can't say I tasted 'em. Can yer cook 'em, Essie?

Essie (*pinching* Bilbo *like a soup chicken*). Yer can try. Won't make above a mouthful, though—not once he's skinned and boned. Now if there was four and twenty of 'em, I might make a pie!

Bert. Hey, you! Any more o' your sort a-sneakin' in these here woods, yer nasty little rabbit?

Bilbo (*correcting him politely*). Hobbit, not rabbit. Yes, lots—no—none at all!

Bert (*scratching his head*). What d'yer mean?

Bilbo (*collecting his scattered wits*). What I say. (*to* Essie) There's no need to pinch me, madam.

Essie. Shut yer mouth! I can always serve you on toast—minced!

Bilbo (*pleading*). Oh, please don't cook me, kind ma'am and sirs! I'm a good cook myself and cook better than I cook, if you see what I mean. Besides I like it here with you.

Bert (*suspiciously*). What's 'e say? (*grabs* Bilbo *by the hair*)

Bilbo. Ow!

Essie (*softening*). Ah, poor little blighter,[12] let him go.

Tom. Not till 'e says what 'e means by *lots* and *none at all*. I don't want me throat slit in my sleep! (*grabs for* Bilbo's *feet*) I'll hold his toes in the fire till 'e talks!

(Gandalf's *head appears from behind a tree.* There is a flash of blue fire from his staff, which the Trolls do not notice.*)

Tom. No! There isn't time. We have to get back to our cave before sunup.

Essie (*hanging on*). Give him back. He's mine.

Tom. Well, I'm boss.

Gandalf (*sticking his head out and calling in a voice mimicking* Essie's). Tom, yer a fat fool!

Tom (*taken aback*). Essie! Watch what you say!

Gandalf (*sticking his head out, mimicking* Tom). Yer a swag-belly, Essie!

Essie (*shrieking*). What? I'll give you what for! (*kicks* Tom *in the shins*)

Tom (*howling*). Oww! (*Releases* Bilbo *and hops about.* Bilbo *runs and hides behind a tree.*)

Bert (*scratching his head; slow on the uptake*). You insult the missus, Tom? (*advancing menacingly on* Tom)

Tom (*baffled*). Wha'? I didn't say nothing—

Bert (*putting his fist in* Tom's *eye*). Liar!

Tom (*hopping around in pain*). Yeow!

Gandalf (*mimicking* Tom). Big skunk!

Essie (*coming up behind* Tom *and hitting him on the head with a dummy club*). Take *that*!

Tom (*howling and rubbing his head*). Ow! Ow! What did you do that for? (*picks up club and hits* Bert *on the head*)

Bert (*stunned*). Gosh! Ouch! (*A bird calls, and other birds chime in.*)

Gandalf (*stepping out from behind tree, holding his staff high with blue fire coming from it; loudly*). Dawn take you all, and be stone to you! (*The Trolls look at one another agape*

---

10. **copped:** taken or stolen.
11. **Lumme** (lŭm′ē): a slang expression short for "Lord love me!" Here it is similar to "darned."
12. **blighter:** a British term for a fellow held in low regard.

and turn toward the voice. The twittering of birds rises to a climax of bird calls, and a great shaft of light strikes the Trolls.)

Trolls. Wha'? Huh? Ugh! (*Suddenly they freeze into statues.*)

Gandalf (*walking around the* Trolls, *waving his hand in front of their faces, touching* Bert's *hair, etc.*). Excellent! Museum pieces!

Bilbo (*capering wildly*). They're stone! They've turned to stone!

Gandalf. Where are the dwarves?

Bilbo. Waiting for me to return with some food or to hoot like an *owl*.

Gandalf (*hooting*). Whoo! Whoo!

Thorin (*at platform left, springing u*p). The signal! To the rescue, dwarves! (*They all groan and follow reluctantly.* Thorin *runs up to* Bert *with bravado, brandishing his sword.*) On guard, Troll! (Bert *does not stir;* Thorin *lunges fiercely.*) Aha! (*Still no reaction;* Thorin, *completely baffled, kicks* Bert *in the knee.*) Yeow! (*Holds his foot, hopping in pain.* Bilbo *and* Gandalf *laugh uproariously.* Thorin *is startled.*) Gandalf!

Dwarves (*circling the* Trolls *curiously; ad-lib*). Stone! Horrid! What a trio! Solid rock! (*and so on*)

Gandalf. A fine pickle you left your burglar in, Thorin!

Thorin. And where were you, if I may ask?

Gandalf. I went to look ahead.

Thorin. And what brought you back?

Gandalf. Looking behind—

Thorin. Exactly! But could you be more plain?

Gandalf. I went on to spy out our road. It will soon become much more dangerous. I had not gone very far when I met some elf friends—they were hurrying along for fear of trolls. I had a feeling I was needed here, and I hurried back. So now you know.

Thorin. We thank you! Pack up the food, dwarves—

Gandalf (*picking up two swords from the ground*). And don't leave these behind! Hmmm, these were not made by the trolls—the workmanship is much too good. The trolls must have stolen these. Why, these are elvish blades—with the ancient runes[13] engraved on them. The elves have cleaved many a goblin with these, I'll warrant.[14] (*hands one to* Thorin *and one to* Bilbo)

Bilbo. For me? Why, thank you!

Thorin. I will keep this sword in honor. May it soon cleave goblins again!

Bilbo. Oh, dear!

Gandalf. A wish that will soon be granted.

Bilbo. I didn't wish a thing!

Gandalf. Come, let's head for the Misty Mountains. You must keep to the proper path, or you'll get lost and have to come back. Remember that: stick to the path!

Thorin. We will, Gandalf.

Elves (*offstage, burst of laughter, then singing*).
O! Where are you going
With beards all a-wagging?
No knowing, no knowing
What brings Mister Baggins,
And Balin and Dwalin
down into the valley
in June
ha! ha!

Thorin. Elves! Humph!

(First Elf *peeks around the curtain left.*)

---

13. **runes:** symbols used in writing that are sometimes believed to have magic powers.
14. **warrant:** to guarantee.

Literary Concept: DIALOGUE

HH Invite volunteers to share their preconceptions about elves. Ask students whether they think elves would be friendly or unfriendly in a drama such as *The Hobbit*. Then have volunteers read aloud the dialogue spoken by the elves, Thorin, and Gandalf at the end of Scene 2. Ask students what the elves' own speech reveals about them. *(Possible response: They are as Gandalf implies, nosy and dangerous—and well informed about what transpires in the valley.)*

CUSTOMIZING FOR
Multiple Learning Styles

LI **Linguistic Learners** Invite students to write a longer journal entry for Bilbo. Have them describe the main events that have transpired since Bilbo's thought for today that "Adventures are not all Sunday strolls in May sunshine" (page 586).

First Elf. Well, well! Just look! Bilbo, the Hobbit, on an adventure with dwarves! Isn't it delicious!

(Second Elf *peeks around the curtain right.*)

Second Elf. Most astonishingly wonderful!

Thorin. Silly fools!

Third Elf (*off*). Mind you don't step on your beard, Thorin! (*burst of laughter from* Elves, *off*)

Gandalf. Hush, hush, my friends! Valleys have ears, and some elves have over-merry tongues. We must go quietly. There is grave danger ahead.

(*They all exit as curtain falls.*)

Scene Three

Scene: *A cave in the Misty Mountains. Lightning flashes. Sounds of thunder.*

At rise of curtain: Lights come up on platform at stage left. The Dwarves *and* Gandalf *are huddled together, talking in hushed tones.* Bilbo *sits downstage on platform, writing in his diary. He scribbles industriously, then holds book off and reads impressively.*

Bilbo (*reading his entry*). "This is the first chance I've had to write in ages. We've been driven before the storm for twelve days and nights." (*There is a distant roll of thunder and more lightning.*) "The mountain path is steep and long. We are now resting in a smelly cave." (*He again scribbles rapidly.*)

Thorin (*in a low voice*). This is awful!

Gloin (*holding his nose*). Phew!

Balin. At least it's dry!

Gandalf (*to* Thorin). If you know a better place, take us there!

Bilbo (*holding his script off and reading again*). "We don't dare to talk too loud—there are goblins in these mountains. All this misery for their gold—and my pride—hardly seems worthwhile. The next time anyone calls me a coward, I'll agree with him and stay home. I'd gladly trade my share of the treasure this minute for a steaming bowl of mutton soup!"

Gandalf. Keep your voices down! Thorin, look, your blade glows—that means goblins are nearby. Keep your eyes and ears open. Goblins are swift as weasels in the dark and make no more noise than bats. (*They huddle to-*

592 UNIT FIVE PART 2: RELUCTANT HEROES

gether, *peering in all directions; lightning flashes and sounds of thunder.*) Are your guards posted?

Thorin (*nodding*). Four of them, Gloin north, Bofur south, Oin east and Ori west.

(*Lights dim on platform left and come up on platform right. Drumbeats are heard off. The* Great Goblin *steps out on the platform, followed by an* Attendant.)

Great Goblin (*bellowing in a stony voice*). Who are those miserable persons?

Attendant Goblin (*bowing and scraping*). Dwarves, I believe, O Truly Tremendous One.

Great Goblin. What are they doing in my <u>domain</u>?

Attendant Goblin (*shaking*). I'll go and ask them, O Truly Tremendous One.

Great Goblin (*with an awful howl of rage*). Ask them? (*kicks the* Attendant Goblin *and bats him over the head*) Beat them! Gnash them! Squash them! Smash them! (*gesturing left*) After them!

(*The drumbeats increase as many* Goblins *rush on right with bloodcurdling cries. As they reach center, the lights come up on platform left.*)

Oin (*reporting*). Goblins coming.

Ori. I think they're going to rush us!

Goblins (*chanting and cracking whips*). Swish, smack! Whip, crack! Clash, crash! Crush, smash!

Thorin (*drawing his sword*). Ready, my goblin-cleaver! (*He stands on the edge of the platform.*) Ready, dwarves—and Mr. Baggins. (Gandalf, *arms folded, stands aloof watching intently. The* Goblins *rush at the* Dwarves. Thorin *stabs one with his blade. The other* Dwarves *back up* Thorin, *and there are hand-to-hand conflicts.* Bilbo *trips up a* Goblin *who is about to stab* Thorin *from behind.* Thorin *stabs another. All conflicts must be rehearsed with extra care so that the tempo is very fast. The* Goblins *fall, howling.*)

Goblins (*ad-lib*). Aie! He's got a goblin-cleaver! Watch out! Stay back! (*The* Goblins *back off in terror.*)

Gandalf (*to* Dwarves *and* Bilbo). Quick. Now's our chance! Everyone follow me! (*Runs off left. Others follow,* Bilbo *last. From off.*) Quicker, quicker! (Goblins *run after them, howling and hooting.*)

(*Blackout*)

(*Lights come up very dimly in a cave.* Bilbo *is discovered[15] lying on the ground downstage center.*)

Bilbo (*sitting up, holding his head in pain*). Oooh! My head! Where am I? My head—I must have run into a tree! (*groping*) It's so dark in here I can't see a thing. (*calls loudly*) Anyone here?

Echo (*getting progressively fainter*). Here—here—here.

Bilbo (*getting frightened*). Who's that?

(*Now gleams appear in the darkness. They prove to be always in pairs, of yellow or green or red eyes. They seem to stare awhile and then slowly fade out and disappear and shine out again in another place. Sometimes they shine down from above. Some of them are bulbous.*)

Bilbo. Now I remember. The goblins!

Echo. 'Oblins, 'oblins—'oblins— 'oblins.

Bilbo. And what are those awful eyes watching

---

15. **discovered:** revealed or found when the lights brighten.

WORDS TO KNOW

domain (dō-mān′) *n.* land under one ruler or belonging to one person

Critical Thinking: ANALYZING

LL Have students analyze each sentence in Bilbo's successful attempt to cheer himself up. *(Possible responses: "Fear always helps the thing you're afraid of."—Bilbo makes the goblins more powerful by allowing them to sense his fear. "You're alive and you've been in holes before."— Holes has a literal and symbolic ["difficulties"] meaning. "You live in one."—Perhaps Bilbo is referring to Underhill, the Hobbits' shire. "This is just an ordinary, black, foul, disgusting hole. So blah!"—Bilbo banishes his fear by relating to what is real rather than what he imagines. The ensuing stage directions indicate that the eyes go away.)*

STRATEGIC READING FOR
Less-Proficient Readers

MM Have students describe the sequence of events that leads toward Bilbo's meeting Gollum. *(Possible responses: The dwarves and Bilbo take shelter in a cave in the Misty Mountains; they fight a battle with Goblins in the cave; the dwarves leave, but Bilbo, having hit his head against something, faints and inadvertently is left behind; trying to find a way out of the cave, Bilbo encounters Gollum.)* **Noting Sequence of Events**

Set a Purpose Have students read to find out how Gollum tries to cheat Bilbo.

---

me for? *(lowers voice)* I was on Dori's back and someone tackled him and he dropped me!

Echo. 'Opped me—'opped me—'opped me—'opped me.

Bilbo *(frightened, to the eyes).* Keep away from me, eyes! I wonder what happened to the dwarves? I hope the goblins didn't get them! *(gasps)* My sword! *(holding it up)* It hardly glows. That means the goblins aren't near and yet they're still around. Ugh! What a nasty smell! Go away, you horrible eyes! *(realizing, stage whisper)* I know where I am. I'm still in the goblins' cave! They smell that way, and these may be just the eyes of bats and mice and toads and slimy things like that. *(more naturally)* Cheer up, Bilbo. Fear always helps the thing you're afraid of. You're alive and you've been in holes before. You live in one. This is just an ordinary, black, foul, disgusting hole. So blah! *(The eyes begin to flicker out, pair by pair, until all are gone. Bilbo brightens further.)* If this place were aired and decorated, it would be nice and cozy. So now I'll just figure out how to get out of here. *(Bilbo crawls around on his hands and knees toward stage right.)* Seems to be a lake over here—no use heading that way. Ouch! Something hurt my knee— *(picks up a small object)* It's a ring! Someone's lost a ring. Well, finders keepers. I'll just stick it in my pocket so I don't lose it myself. *(Pockets ring. Lights come up a little.)* I can see better now. *(stands and turns toward stage left)*

(An unobtrusive black rubber float is pulled on stage right. On it sits a slimy creature, dressed in black tights or a shiny rubber diving suit touched up with Vaseline to make it glisten, complete with cap, goggles painted a pale watery green. He sits with a leg dangling over each side of the raft, or with knees bent, and holds a short paddle as if rowing.)

Gollum *(making a swallowing sound as he is pulled on).* Gollum! Gollum!

Bilbo *(whirling around).* What's that!

Gollum. It's me—Gollum!

Bilbo *(peering nervously in Gollum's direction).* Who's there?

Gollum *(in full view now).* Bless us and splash us, my preciousss! Here's something to eat! *(guttural)* Gollum!

Bilbo *(brandishing his blade, while shaking and backing off).* Stay back!

Gollum *(swaying his head from side to side as he talks).* What's he got in his handses, hmmm?

594   UNIT FIVE   PART 2: RELUCTANT HEROES

Bilbo (*as fiercely as possible*). A sword, an elvish blade! It came out of Gondolin.

Gollum (*taken aback, hissing*). S-s-s-s-s. What *iss* he, my preciousss? Hic! (*more politely*) Whom have we the pleasure of meeting?

Bilbo (*rapidly*). I am Mr. Bilbo Baggins, a Hobbit. I've lost the dwarves and the wizard and I don't know where I am—but then I don't want to know where I am. The only thing I want to know is how to get out of here!

Gollum (*hissing*). S-s-s-s-s s'pose we sits here and chats with it a bitsy, my preciousss—A Bagginsess! (*rubs his stomach*) It likes riddles, p'raps[16] it does, does it? S-s-s-s-s.

Bilbo. You mean me?

Gollum. Yesssss—

Bilbo. Well, I'd love to, but I'm expected somewhere else— (*to himself*) I hope. (*to Gollum*) So if you'd kindly direct me to the nearest exit—

Gollum (*cutting in*). S-s-s-s-s stop. First a riddle, yesss?

Bilbo (*resigned*). Very well, if you insisssst! After you—

Gollum. S-s-s-s-s say,
What has roots as nobody sees,
Is taller than trees,
Up, up it goes,
And yet never grows?

Bilbo. Easy! Mountain. Now if you'll kindly—

Gollum (*cutting in*). S-s-s-s-s so does it guess easy? It must have a competition with us, my preciouss. If we wins, we eats it—it tastes better if we earns it. If it wins, we shows it the way out. Yessss.

Bilbo (*resigned*). Well—all right. Only, how many of them are you? Who's this "Precious" you keep talking to?

Gollum. Our Preciousss Self! We has to talk to someone, doesn't we? We are alone here—forever.

Bilbo. So, I see. It's a dreadful place.

Gollum. We likes it! We generally passes the time feasting on fishesss and gobbling goblins. S-s-s-s-s.

Bilbo. Goblins! Ick! I didn't think anyone ate *them!*

Gollum. We acquired the taste. Hic! S-s-s-s-s. (*impatient*) Your turn. Riddle! Riddle!

Bilbo. Just a minute— (*thinking hard*) Ah!—
Thirty white horses on a red hill,
First they champ,
Then they stamp,
Then they stand still.

Gollum. Easy! Teethes! Teethes! My preciouss, but we has only *six*. Now! Ssssss.
Voiceless it cries,
Wingless flutters,
Toothless bites,
Mouthless mutters.

Bilbo. Half a moment! (*straining*) Wind! Wind, of course!

Gollum (*disappointed*). Sssssss. Your turn!

Bilbo. Uh—
A box without hinges, key or lid,
Yet golden treasure inside is hid.

Gollum (*having great difficulty*). S-s-s-s-s. (*whispers*) What iss it? Sssssss. (*takes a fish out of his pocket and wipes his brow with it*)

Bilbo. Well—what is it? The answer's not a kettle boiling over, as you seem to think from the noise you are making!

Gollum. Give us a chance; let it give us a chance, my preciousss—

Bilbo. Well?

---

16. **p'raps:** perhaps.

Active Reading: CLARIFY

QQ Ask students what Bilbo means when he says that, until the adventure, he never thought how he would "taste cooked." *(Possible response: Bilbo has almost been eaten once before—by goblins.)*

STRATEGIC READING FOR
Less-Proficient Readers

RR Ask students to explain how Gollum tries to cheat Bilbo. *(Possible response: Bilbo wins the riddle contest fair and square. Gollum is stalling for time before showing Bilbo out of the cave. Gollum plans to get something that will make him invisible. Then he can catch and eat Bilbo!)* **Making Inferences**

Set a Purpose Have students read to find out what Mirkwood Forest is like.

Gollum (*wiping his brow with fish; suddenly*). Eggses! Eggses it is! Ssssssss—here's a choice one!
Alive without breath,
As cold as death;
Never thirsty, ever drinking,
All in mail,[17] never clinking!

Bilbo (*stumped*). Ahem—ahem—well now. Just a minute—

Gollum (*starting to emerge from the raft*). S-s-s-s-s-s.

Bilbo (*panic-stricken*). Wait! I gave you a long time to guess!

Gollum (*settling back in raft, hissing with pleasure*). Is it nice, my preciouss? Is it juicy? Is it crunchable?

Bilbo (*stalling for time*). Actually, I never gave a thought to how I'd taste cooked until I set out on this horrid adventure. But I'm sure I'd be terribly indigestible. (*false laughter*) Ha, ha!

Gollum. S-s-s-s-s—the riddle, answer it! It must make haste. We is hungry! (*wipes his brow with the fish*)

Bilbo (*pointing wildly at the fish*). Fish! That's the answer! Fish!

Gollum (*angry*). S-s-s-s-s—rotten luckses! It's got to ask us a question, my preciouss, yes, yess, just *one* more, yesss. Ask uss!

Bilbo (*frantic*). Oh, dear! I can't think— (*Grabs for his sword, puts his hand in his pocket. To himself.*) What have I got in my pocket?

Gollum (*taking this for the question*). Ssss—not fair! Not fair, my preciouss, to ask us what it's got in its nassty little pocketses!

Bilbo (*explaining*). But I— (*thinks better of it*) Well, why not? (*boldly*) What have I got in my pocket?

Gollum. S-s-s-s-s. It must give us three guesseses, my preciouss, three!

Bilbo. Very well! Guess away!

Gollum. Handses!

Bilbo. Wrong. Guess again!

Gollum. S-s-s-s-s—knife!

Bilbo. Wrong! Last guess!

Gollum (*wiggling and squirming, hissing and sputtering, rocking sideways and slapping his feet on the floor*). S-s-s-s-s.

Bilbo (*trying to sound bold and cheerful*). Come on! I'm waiting! Time's up!

Gollum (*shrieking*). String or nothing!

Bilbo (*relieved*). Both wrong. (*brandishes his sword*)

Gollum (*eying the sword*). S-s-s-s-s.

Bilbo (*shivering*). Well? Show me the way out. You promised!

Gollum. Did we say so, preciouss? Show the nassty little Baggins the way out, yes, yess. But what's it got in its pocketses, eh? (*starts to get up*) Not string, preciouss, but not *nothing*. Oh, no! Gollum!

Bilbo. Never you mind. A promise is a promise!

Gollum. Cross it is. The Baggins is getting cross, preciouss, but it must wait, yes, it must. We can't go up the tunnels so hasty. We must go and get somethings first, yess, things to help us. My birthday present, that's what we wants now—then we'll be quite safe! (*He steps out of his raft and waddles upstage right.*) We slips it on, and it won't see us, will it, my preciouss. No, it won't see us, and its nassty little sword will be useless, yess—Ssssss. (*exits right*)

Bilbo (*calling*). Hurry up!

Gollum (*off, letting out a horrible shriek*).

---

17. **mail:** flexible armor made up of overlapping metal rings or scales.

596 UNIT FIVE PART 2: RELUCTANT HEROES

Mini-Lesson: Speaking, Listening, and Viewing

DRAMATIC READING Explain to students that a good dramatic reading brings events and characters to life for an audience. Tell students that dramatic readings allow them to vocally express their interpretation of characters by providing them with an opportunity to give each character a distinctive voice and style of speaking.

Application Have small groups of students select a short scene from *The Hobbit* and give a Readers Theater performance for the class. Remind students that a Readers Theater concentrates on a dramatic reading; movement and sets are not necessary. Have group members prepare for their parts by listing the qualities they think best describe their chosen character and by imagining what type of voice would best express those qualities. If possible, you may wish to have groups also perform their dramatic readings in front of other classes.

Aaaaaah! Where iss it! Lost! Lost!

Bilbo. What's the matter?

Gollum (*offstage, wailing*). Gone—must find it! Lost! Lost!

Bilbo. Well, so am I!

(*Gollum waddles on from right, on his hands and knees, searching wildly.*)

Gollum. Cursesss! Must find it!

Bilbo. You can look for whatever it is later. You never guessed my riddle. You promised!

Gollum. Never guessed—never guessed— (*Light dawns.*) What has it got in its pocketses? Tell us! (*advances toward* Bilbo)

Bilbo. What have you lost?

Gollum. We guesses, we *guesses*, precious, only guesses. He's got it, and the goblinses will catch it and take the present from it. (*makes a lunge at* Bilbo) They'll find out what the present can do. It'll just keep it in its pocketses. It's lost itself, the nassty, nosey thing.

Bilbo. I better put that ring on or I'll lose it. (*puts his hand into his pocket and slips the ring on his finger and holds it up*) This?

Gollum (*rushing right past* Bilbo, *wailing*). Cursess, the Baggins is *gone*—my precious. It has my ring! The ring of *power!*

Bilbo (*alone on stage*). He ran right past—as if he didn't see me—as if I weren't there. . . . Maybe I'm not! The ring! I wonder if it made me invisible? (*inspects himself*) I can still see me.

(*Gollum rushes on again from left.*)

Gollum. Give it back like a good Baggins! Where isss it? (*rushes off right*)

Bilbo. A magic ring! I've heard of such things in Gandalf's stories—but to *find* one! What luck!

Gollum (*offstage, shrieking*). Thief!

Bilbo. I could stab him with my blade, but that would be wrong when he can't see me.

(*Gollum waddles on right, worn out and weeping.*)

Gollum (*sitting downstage*). It's gone! (*guttural sobs*) Gollum! Gollum! Thief! Thief Baggins! We hates it, we hates it, hates it forever! S-s-s-s-s. (*recovering*) But he doesn't know the way out—he said so. (Bilbo *nods silently and sits beside him.*) But he's tricksy. He doesn't say what he means—like what was in his pocketses—he knows! He knows a way *in*. He must know a way *out*! Yesss—he's off to the back door, that's it! (*springs up*) After him! Make haste! (*runs off left*) Gollum! Gollum!

Bilbo. I'll follow him to the exit. Then with luck I can slip out the door! (*runs off left after* Gollum)

THE HOBBIT: ACT ONE **597**

CUSTOMIZING FOR
Students Acquiring English

8 Explain that *Fancy* is a British exclamation that expresses great surprise. It means "imagine that."

CUSTOMIZING FOR
Multiple Learning Styles

Interpersonal Learners Have small groups of students clarify what happens when Bilbo puts on the ring, evaluate his use of it thus far, and predict how he will use it in the future. *(Possible responses: Bilbo uses his ring to escape from Gollum and to tease the dwarves. Bilbo learns what some of the dwarves think of him—something that perhaps he would be better off not knowing. Bilbo might use the ring in the future as he has in the past, to escape from a tight situation.)*

Scene Four

In front of curtain: Outside the cave entrance. Bilbo's head pops out of the center of the curtain. He looks around warily.

Bilbo. Whew! A narrow escape! (*comes downstage center, looking himself over*) Torn my cloak! Burst my buttons! But I've got spare buttons at home. I wonder where I am? (*looks off*) Good heavens. This must be the other side of the Misty Mountains! I don't see Gandalf and the dwarves. Maybe the goblins got them. I'd have to go back in there after them . . . I guess—(*shudders*) But at least I have Gollum's ring—(*holds finger up*) Why, I must be invisible this very moment! Fancy!

Balin (*calling, from offstage*). Mr. Baggins! Mr. Baggins! Where are you?

Bilbo (*overjoyed*). Balin!

(*Balin pops his head around curtain, right. Bilbo goes to greet him with outstretched arms; of course he is invisible.*)

Balin. He's not here. But I'm sure I heard him call my name!

Thorin (*offstage*). Are you certain? (*Bilbo puts his hand to his mouth and doubles up with silent laughter.*)

(*Balin walks in right, followed by Thorin, Gandalf and the Dwarves.*)

Thorin. Confound the Hobbit! Still lost!

Gandalf. Keep looking. We can't go on without him. I feel responsible for him.

Ori. Pity you didn't pick someone with more sense!

Thorin. He's been more trouble than he's worth.

(*Bilbo draws himself up, offended.*)

Oin. Why couldn't he stick with us?

Gloin (*testily*). That's right. I refuse to go back into those awful tunnels to look for the little blighter, drat him! (*Bilbo kicks his leg.*) Ouch!

Thorin. What's the matter?

Gloin. Dunno—felt as if someone kicked my leg!

Gandalf (*to* Gloin). Serves you right if someone did. (*angrily, to all*) Now either you help me look for him or I leave you here to get out of this mess as best you can. Why didn't you stay with him, Dori?

Dori. Good heavens! Can you ask? Goblins fighting and biting—everybody falling over bodies and hitting one another! You shouted "Follow me, everybody!"—I thought everybody had—

Thorin. And here we are, minus a burglar. Drat him! (*Bilbo steps down in the middle of them and slips off the ring. He is now visible.*)

Bilbo. And here's the burglar!

Dwarves (*jumping; ad-lib*). What! Bilbo! Mr. Baggins! Where did you come from?

Gandalf. Bilbo, my boy! What a relief!

Thorin (*to* Balin). A fine lookout you are, Balin!

Balin. Well, it's the first time that even a mouse has crept by me. I take my hood off to you, Mr. Baggins! (*He does, and bows.*) You're a great burglar. Balin, at your service—

Bilbo (*bowing*). Your servant, Baggins.

Dwarves (*ad-lib*). How'd you escape? What happened? Tell us!

Gandalf. He can tell us on the way. We must leave at once. (Dwarves *groan*.)

Bilbo. But I'm so dreadfully hungry—

Fili. Me, too—

Kili. And me—

598 UNIT FIVE PART 2: RELUCTANT HEROES

Bombur. Me most of all!

Gandalf. Forget it. Hundreds of goblins will be out after us as soon as it gets dark. So tighten your belts and let's go. Better no supper than *be* supper.

Dwarves. Hear, hear!

Thorin. But where are we going? (*takes out his map*)

Gandalf. Through Mirkwood Forest. (*groans from the* Dwarves) It is dark and dangerous, but it won't be too bad if you can only remember one thing: the path is clearly marked and you *must stay on it*. Don't let anything tempt you to leave it even for a moment.

Thorin. But aren't you coming with us?

Gandalf. Impossible. I have pressing business in the South.

Thorin. But you *can't* desert us now!

Gandalf. We may meet again before all is over, and then again we may not. That depends on your luck and courage and good sense. But I am sending Mr. Baggins with you, and there's more to him than meets the eye. (Bilbo *groans*.) Cheer up, Bilbo, don't look so glum. Cheer up, Thorin and Company. Think of the treasure at the end!

Bilbo. Do we really have to go through Mirkwood? Isn't there some safer way round it?

Gandalf. There are no safe ways in this part of the world. You are over the Edge of the Wild now, and there's danger everywhere.

Thorin (*studying map, irritably*). You said something about a forest path—

Gandalf. Yes. Straight through the forest is your way now. Don't stray off the path. If you do, it's a thousand to one you'll never find it again and never get out of Mirkwood. And then, I suppose, you'll all be eaten by goblins, and I shall never see you again!

Thorin (*sourly*). Very consoling you are, to be sure.

Gandalf. Come now, enough delay. These woods will soon be thick with goblins! (Gandalf *exits right. His voice is heard faintly in the distance.*) Don't leave the path! (*The* Dwarves *and* Bilbo *trudge glumly off left.*)

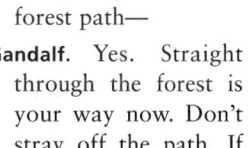

WORDS TO KNOW
consoling (kən-sōl′ĭng) *adj.* making feel less sad; comforting **console** *v.*

599

From Personal Response to Critical Analysis

1. Responses will vary.
2. Possible responses: I think Bilbo is more helpful; although he was not successful with the trolls, he did save Thorin during the fight with the goblins and he did outwit Gollum on his own. I think Bilbo is more harmful because he doesn't have much experience with adventures and he hasn't really proven himself yet.
3. Possible responses: Bilbo's journal entries reveal that he is a very thoughtful and perceptive person. He realizes that his initial thoughts about the adventure are no longer true, and he decides that next time he'll just stay home.
4. Possible response: Bilbo means that if you're afraid of something, you're letting it get the best of you. If you face something fearsome with courage and bravery, then it no longer has power over you.
5. Possible responses: Gandalf seems to be watching Bilbo and the dwarves at all times, and he gives them assistance in time of need. He's sort of leading the quest by letting Bilbo and the dwarves progress on their own but helping and advising them when they run into trouble.
6. Responses will vary. Make sure students support their responses with details from the selection.

FROM PERSONAL RESPONSE TO CRITICAL ANALYSIS

REFLECT 1. What scenes or events in the play so far have had the greatest impact on you? Write your ideas in your writing notebook.

RETHINK 2. At this point in the play do you think Bilbo is more helpful or harmful to the progress of the adventure?
   Consider
   - what happens when he tries to steal food from the trolls
   - what happens after the fight with the goblins
   - his encounter with Gollum

3. Bilbo keeps a journal of his adventure. What do you think Bilbo's journal entries reveal about him and about the adventure?

4. Later, when Bilbo finds himself in a dark, smelly cave, he tells himself, "Fear always helps the thing you're afraid of." What do you think he means by this?

5. How would you describe Gandalf's role in the quest? Explain.

6. At the end of Act One, Gandalf again cautions the group not to stray from the path through Mirkwood Forest. Do you think they will follow his advice? Why or why not?

600 UNIT FIVE PART 2: RELUCTANT HEROES

THE HOBBIT: ACT ONE 601

Critical Thinking: ANALYZING

A Discuss with students how the setting of Mirkwood Forest affects Bilbo and the dwarves. *(Possible responses: The stage directions convey a gloomy, suspenseful atmosphere in Mirkwood Forest. Thorin's remarks at the beginning of Act Two and the exchange between Bilbo and Gloin suggest that the forest seems to depress them and leads them to quarrel.)*

Illustration by Frank Gargiulo.

602 UNIT FIVE PART 2: RELUCTANT HEROES

Act Two — Scene One

> **Linking to Science**
>
>  Mirkwood is an old-growth forest containing large trees that have grown without serious interference for hundreds of years. The western United States contains old-growth forests of western hemlock, coastal redwoods, giant sequoia, and Douglas fir. Loblolly pine forests are found in the southeastern United States. A variety of wildlife, plants, and microorganisms make their habitats in old-growth forests, some species in standing dead trees or fallen logs.

Scene: *Mirkwood Forest, weeks later. The stage is dimly lit. On the platform at stage left are huge gnarled tree trunks. Vines trail the forest floor. On a tree a sign is posted reading* MIRKWOOD. PROCEED AT YOUR OWN RISK. *Along the front, signs are placed at intervals:* THE PATH. *The* Dwarves *and* Bilbo *trudge on left in single file, with* Thorin *at their head.*

Thorin (*pausing on the path*). There's just no end to this accursed forest. (*shakes his fist*) I hate Mirkwood more than I hate the goblin tunnels.

Balin. Misery me! It goes on forever!

 **Oin.** And ever!

Gloin. And ever.

Bofur. Gandalf said, "Cheer up, I'm sending Mr. Baggins with you. He has more about him than you guess. You'll find that out before long." (*turns sharply to* Bilbo) Well, Mr. Baggins? It's been long enough—

Gloin (*angrily*). What good's a Hobbit? Gandalf left us with a Hobbit to help us! Hah!

Bilbo. That's right, Gloin. Blame it all on me! I wanted to come on this adventure! I begged you to let me come!

Thorin (*placatingly*). Now, now, this won't do. We must all stick together.

Bombur (*slapping his own face*). Ouch! Mosquitos biting! Sticky vines wrapping round my throat, roots pulling at my feet! I can't go another step. Go on if you must. I'm going to lie down here and *sleep*— (*sits*) —and dream of food, if I can't get it any other way. (*curls up, yawns sleepily*) The treasure? I'll be too starved to enjoy it— (*Swats at a mosquito. There is a sudden flash of light.*)

Bifur (*jumping*). What was that?

Balin. Those flashes of light again! We'd better circle away from them.

Bilbo. But if we circle away, we'll have to leave the path!

Thorin. So?

Bilbo. Gandalf warned us not to.

Balin. Bilbo's right.

Kili. So he is.

Nori. Gandalf did say we mustn't leave the path. But he didn't know all that was going to happen.

Bilbo. I think he had a pretty good idea, all the same.

Thorin. We're all hungry.

Ori. And tired.

Oin. I can't go any further.

THE HOBBIT: ACT TWO **603**

CUSTOMIZING FOR
Students Acquiring English

⑨ Point out that when Gloin says "that's a Hobbit for you," he is expressing disgust at Bilbo's ignorance. He is not surprised that a Hobbit would mistakenly think that berries are gathered in the spring.

Critical Thinking: CLASSIFYING

Ⓒ Have students identify another scene in which Bilbo and the dwarves are drawn by their desire for food into an encounter with other creatures. *(the scene in which Bilbo burgles food from the trolls—and almost gets eaten himself)*

Critical Thinking: SYNTHESIZING

Ⓓ Have students analyze Thorin's assertion that Mirkwood breeds distrust, in the light of previous observations about the effects of this setting. *(Possible response: The dwarves and Bilbo began quarreling in Mirkwood. The forest has a similar negative effect on creatures who live there.)*

CUSTOMIZING FOR
Students Acquiring English

⑩ Point out that *Whoopee!* is an exclamation that expresses happiness and celebration.

Bilbo. We must go on. Maybe we'll find some berries.

⑨ **Gloin.** Find berries in the spring—that's a Hobbit for you!

Dori. It's time to rest and eat.

Bilbo. Let's stick to the path a while longer. (*The lights flash again.*)

Bombur. I can smell meat roasting.

Thorin. Fili and Kili, go and investigate. But *be careful.*

Fili and **Kili.** Yes, sir. (*Fili and Kili go out right.*)

Bilbo. They've left the path. Gandalf said—

Thorin. Gandalf should have stayed with us if he expected to run things.

Balin. But he did say don't leave the path.

Thorin. Well, we haven't left it. Only Fili and Kili have.

Bilbo. Curious—it's so quiet—as horribly quiet as it is before something awful happens.

Balin (*looking off right*). Fili and Kili are coming back.

(*Fili and Kili come on right and rush up to Thorin.*)

Fili and **Kili** (*together*). It's elves! They've got food!

Others. Elves! (*The following speeches are said in such rapid succession it is as if one person were talking.*)

Fili. We crept up—

Kili. To the lights—

Fili. What a sight!

Ⓒ **Kili.** In a clearing—

Fili. Lots of elves sitting round a fire.

Balin. What luck!

Kili. Laughing!

Fili. Eating!

Kili. We couldn't bear it. We ran up to beg some food and poof! The lights went out.

Fili. As if by magic!

Kili. Somebody kicked the fire, and it went up— (*gestures widely*) —in glittering sparks—

Ⓒ **Fili.** And they all vanished!

Thorin. Those were wood-elves.

Bombur. Friendly elves! And they've got food!

Thorin. No, no, the wood-elves aren't very friendly. They don't like strangers. Mirkwood breeds distrust. (*There is another flash of light.*)

Ⓓ **Bilbo.** The lights again!

Bombur. Let's all go to the feast!

Dwarves (*ad-lib*). Whoopee! Let's go! (*They start to go, leaving the path at an angle.*) Come on, Bilbo.

⑩ **Bilbo** (*standing fast*). Wait! A feast will be no good if we don't get back alive from it.

Bombur. Well, I'm going. We won't last much longer without food anyway.

Bilbo. That's true—I guess.

Bifur. Come on, Bilbo. (*Bilbo reluctantly follows the others off the path.*)

(*The Elven-Queen and several of her attendant Lords and Ladies enter from left. The Queen wears a trimly fitted garment of forest green and a crown of oak leaves and berries. She carries a wand of carved oak. Her attendant Ladies carry bows and arrows.*)

Elven-Queen. Halt! (*Dwarves and Bilbo freeze in surprise.*)

Thorin. By whose authority do you bid us halt?

Elven-Queen. I am the Elven-Queen. Who are you that trespass on my domain?

Thorin (*stage whisper to Bilbo*). Quick, Bilbo, make yourself invisible. Put on your ring.

604 UNIT FIVE PART 2: RELUCTANT HEROES

(Bilbo *does so, and from then on he is ignored by all.*)

Elven-Queen (*imperiously*). Speak.

Thorin (*stepping forward proudly*). I am Thorin Oakenshield, son of Thrain, son of Thror, King under the Mountain!

Elven-Queen (*disdainfully*). A dwarf all the same. Why did you and your folk attack my people?

Thorin. We did not attack them, Your Majesty. We came to beg because we are starving.

Elven-Queen. What are you doing in Mirkwood?

Thorin. We are looking for food and drink.

Elven-Queen (*impatiently*). But why are you here at all? (Thorin *remains silent.*) Come now! (Thorin *remains silent.*). Very well! You shall all go to my dungeons where you shall remain until you tell me the truth—if it takes a thousand years! Seize them! *The* Elf Guards *grab* Thorin *and surround the others. To the Guards.*) How many are there?

Guard. Thirteen, O Queen.

Elven-Queen. Away with them. (*She exits left.*)

First Guard. Step lively, dwarves!

Second Guard. March! (*The* Elves *march the* Dwarves *off left.*)

Bilbo (*taking off his ring and speaking to it*). Well, my friend, thanks to you I'm still free. We should have stayed on the path as Gandalf warned us. And now they'll all be shut up in a stone dungeon. That's a hard thing! Somehow I must get them out! (Bilbo *runs off left.*)

Scene: *The dungeon of the Elven-Queen's palace. At rise, the* Dwarves *are discovered behind the bars of a large prison cell in the center section of the stage. They are seated on wooden stools in attitudes of despondency.*[18] Thorin *occupies a private cell to their right. On the platform at right there are a table and chairs. On the platform left are a pile of straw and four wine barrels. Also in this section, somewhere in the background, are various possessions of the dwarves: bags containing tools (drills and hammers), jackets, pad and pencil.*

At rise of curtain: Bilbo *sits against one of the barrels, writing busily in his journal. As lights come up on platform left,* Bilbo *finishes writing and holds up his diary to see better.*

Bilbo (*reading impressively*). "Well, so far I haven't come up with a plan of escape. I might as well be locked up with my friends. Being invisible day after day is driving me mad. This is without a doubt the dreariest, dullest part of this wretched adventure. At least the dwarves are eating well. I have to steal my scraps of food from the kitchen." (*nods approval and scribbles again*)

Thorin (*calling softly to* Bilbo). Psst!

Bilbo (*ignoring him, reading again, impressively*). "I'm like a burglar that can't get away but must go on miserably burgling the same house day after day!" (*snaps journal shut*)

Thorin (*louder*). Psst, Mr. Baggins!

---

18. **attitudes of despondency:** positions that show loss of courage or hope.

THE HOBBIT: ACT TWO **605**

CUSTOMIZING FOR
Multiple Learning Styles

G **Logical-Mathematical Learners**
Challenge students to determine the minimum number of rings of invisibility that would be necessary for fourteen individuals to get past the guards. To help students reach a conclusion, allow them to make rings of aluminum foil. Using their rings, students can pantomime possible moves, with some students acting as guards and others as Bilbo and the dwarves. *(Response: Two rings are needed in order for a pair to get past the guards. Then one of the pair can return to give the second ring to the next individual for both of them to get past, and so on.)*

Literary Concept: TONE

H Call on volunteers to read aloud Thorin's warning to Bilbo, using the tone that they think Thorin would use. Ask students if they think Thorin really believes Bilbo is stupid or if he is angry at Bilbo. *(Possible responses: Thorin is acquiring respect for Bilbo, whom he consults in formulating an escape plan. Thorin isn't angry; he is frightened.)*

Critical Thinking: ANALYZING

I Call on volunteers to read aloud a portion of the dialogue between Thorin and the guards. Challenge students to compare and contrast relationships between subjects and rulers in elven and goblin society. To help students formulate a response, you may wish to allow them to review the interaction on page 593 between the Great Goblin and his attendants. *(Possible responses: In both societies, a great gulf exists between subjects and rulers. The Great Goblin inspires terror in his subjects; the Elven-Queen inspires an attitude of worship.)*

Bilbo. Shhh— (*gets up, looks around and crosses cautiously to* Thorin's *cell*) What is it, Thorin? The guards will be coming any minute with your food.

Thorin. Then put on your ring. Why aren't you wearing it?

Bilbo. I don't like to wear it when I don't have to. It makes me feel funny. What did you want?

Thorin. Did you get off the message to Gandalf?

Bilbo. I don't know where to send it.

Thorin. Of course. I get more stupid every day.

Bilbo. Me, too. It's hard to concentrate when I'm invisible so much. It's as if I'm not all there.

Thorin. At least do *something*. You're a burglar. Steal! (*The other* Dwarves *have gathered at the front of their cage and are listening eagerly.*)

Bilbo. Well, I could steal the keys—that's not so hard.

Thorin (*brightening*). You could? Wonderful!

Dwarves. Bilbo!

Bilbo. But how would we get past the guards? One invisible ring isn't much good among fourteen.

Thorin. We might escape—somehow.

Bilbo. But we couldn't possibly get out of the main gate.

Thorin. Why not?

Bilbo. Sealed by elf magic.

Thorin (*deflated*). Oh. (*There is the sound of a key turning in a lock.*)

Bilbo (*hushed tones*). The guards are coming. Talk up and distract them! I'll see what I can do about the keys.

Thorin (*urgently*). Put on your ring, you stupid Hobbit! (Bilbo *smites his brow at his forgetfulness, pulls out ring and puts it on.*)

(*The* Guards *enter from right. The* First Guard *has a large ring of keys fastened by a chain to her belt. The* Second Guard *carries a tray with a bowl of soup and end of a loaf of bread. The* First Guard *takes up her stand by the door, guarding it. The* Second Guard *brings the tray of food to* Thorin.)

Second Guard. Food for you, Thorin Oakenshield. Thanks to our gracious Queen. (Bilbo, *walking on tiptoe, begins to cross very cautiously toward the* First Guard.)

Thorin (*taking the tray*). I thank the Elven-Queen and hope to return her hospitality when I have recaptured my castle. Its dungeons are deep.

First Guard. What's that he says?

Second Guard. He threatens our Queen.

First Guard. That's treason! Write it down! Write down every word he says!

Second Guard. I've nothing to write with.

First Guard (*rushing forward and barely missing colliding with the tiptoeing* Bilbo, *who leaps aside to avoid her*). Here, take this. (*gives him a pencil*)

Second Guard. Now, are you ready to answer the questions of our Elven-Queen?

Thorin. I refuse to answer questions under duress.[19]

First Guard (*leaning forward, excitedly*). More treason. Write that down! (Bilbo *is now crouched by the side of the* First Guard, *ready to start removing keys from her key ring.*)

Second Guard (*writing busily on pad*). Prisoner defies our Elven-Queen.

Thorin. *Now,* Bilbo!

First Guard. What's that he's saying?

---

19. **duress** (dŏŏ-rĕs'): the use of force or threats.

606   UNIT FIVE   PART 2: RELUCTANT HEROES

Second Guard. Sounded like he said Bilbo. Dwarves are stupid. Let's get out of here. (*Bilbo has begun removing the key ring. He is very cautious, but his hands are shaking and the keys clink. The* First Guard *moves uneasily, and* Bilbo *freezes. The* First Guard *fumbles for her keys. Doesn't find them. She fumbles again.* Bilbo *extends the keys so that she touches them. She is satisfied and returns her attention to* Second Guard.)

First Guard. He hasn't eaten yet, and the others haven't had their food.

Second Guard. Let them do without. (*to* Thorin) The tray. Let me have it.

Thorin (*throwing it at her feet*). Gladly.

Dwarves (*roaring approval*). Thorin!

Second Guard. If it weren't forbidden, I'd make you suffer for that! But wait and see how you like your dinner—*when* it comes! It'll be *well salted.* I promise you that.

First Guard. There's a big feast tonight, and *we'll* be eating like kings! (*The* Guards *stalk out with a clanking of the door.*)

Thorin (*excitedly*). Did you get the keys?

Bilbo. I did. (*He unlocks the cage door.*)

Thorin. My word! Gandalf spoke true. You're a fine burglar when the time comes! We're all forever in your service! (Thorin *steps out and bows as* Bilbo *unlocks the door.*)

Dwarves. Bravo! Mr. Baggins— (*All bow.*) — at your service!

Bilbo. Thank you. At yours. (*He bows.*) But now what? We're still stuck here in the dungeon, and if we go out, the guards will grab us and put us right back in! (*Bilbo crosses despondently and sits on one of the barrels.*)

Dwarves (*ad-lib, uneasily*). That's true. He's got a point there, all right. (*and so on*)

Dwalin (*prodding* Balin). Speak to him, Balin.

Balin. Why me?

Dwalin. You're the oldest.

Balin. Uh, Thorin—

Thorin (*warily*). Yes, Balin?

Balin. We were thinking that—umm, maybe it might be best to tell the Elven-Queen about our quest—the treasure and all that.

Dwalin (*putting in*). Maybe if she knew, she might even help us. After all, the dragon has stolen elf treasure, too. They took the Elven crown jewels even!

Thorin (*outraged*). Tell the Queen? And right away she'd ask for a share! Just because you're cowards you want me to ransom you all with *my* treasure! A share? What's to stop her from taking it all?

Gloin. Let's not fight about who gets the treasure until we're out of here.

WORDS TO KNOW

quest (kwĕst) *n.* a journey in search of adventure or to perform a task

Art Note

Conversation with Smaug by J.R.R. Tolkien

Reading the Art What effects do the bats at the top of the painting have? What familiar dragon characteristics does Smaug have? What clues do you see as to the danger the Hobbit faces in his encounter with Smaug?

CUSTOMIZING FOR
Multiple Learning Styles

L **Bodily-Kinesthetic Learners**
While other students observe, have volunteers pantomime the moment Bilbo gets and presents his idea. Students should use body language to communicate to the audience what the words on page 609 communicate. You may wish to have pantomimers rehearse and present their pantomimes before other students have read the text. The audience can then test the effectiveness of the pantomimes by trying to infer what has happened.

Conversation with Smaug (1966), J.R.R. Tolkien. Illustration from *The Hobbit* by J.R.R. Tolkien. Copyright © 1966 J.R.R. Tolkien. Reprinted by permission of Houghton Mifflin Co., all rights reserved.

608   UNIT FIVE   PART 2: RELUCTANT HEROES

608 THE LANGUAGE OF LITERATURE **TEACHER'S EDITION**

Bilbo (*suddenly jumping up, excitedly*). I've got it! (*taps the wine barrel*) And to think they've been here all the time! (*crosses to* Thorin) I've got a plan! You won't like it, but it's our only chance! (*to the others*) Follow me and all keep together. (*The* Dwarves *look at each other blankly.*)

Bofur. We can't see you, Bilbo.

Thorin. Take off your ring.

Bilbo (*slipping off ring*). Sorry.

Bifur. There he is.

Bilbo. Over here! (Dwarves *ascend platform left.*) Balin, guard the door in case anyone comes.

Balin. Right. (*crosses and listens at door*) Not a sound. (*takes up watch, his back against door*)

Bilbo. Now. (*coming down eagerly to* Thorin) As you know, we can't escape through the gates. But there is another way out.

Thorin. There is?

Bilbo. There's a stream under the wine cellar that joins the river further east, and when the wine barrels are empty like these— (*taps one*) —the guards dump them through a trap door just outside here— (*gestures left*) —and they float away.

Bifur. How do you know?

Bilbo. I've watched them. Lots of times. They go bobbing down the river, and the current carries them along to Lake-town. (*excitedly*) And where is Lake-town?

Thorin. At the foot of the Lonely Mountain.

Bilbo (*triumphantly*). Our exact destination.

Thorin. Interesting, but it doesn't help us.

Bilbo. Can't you see? We hide ourselves in the empty barrels, and the elves dump us through the trap door along with the empties. We simply ride down to Lake-town. (*The* Dwarves *hear this with complete dismay.*)

Dwarves (*ad-lib*). No, no. Not me.

Thorin. Bilbo, no! This is madness!

Gloin. We'd be battered to pieces!

Nori. Or drowned like kittens!

Dwalin. Who'll let us out? We'll starve to death nailed up in those things. (*kicks a barrel scornfully*)

Bilbo. No, no! Don't worry! We'll pack the barrels with straw and seal them airtight, and I'll see that everyone gets out.

Thorin. Great! And just how do we breathe?

Bilbo. Air holes.

Bombur. You're not getting *me* into one of those! I won't fit, thank goodness!

Bilbo. Yes, you will, Bombur. We'll shove you in. (Dwarves *all turn away, muttering among themselves.* Bilbo *is annoyed and downcast.*) Oh, very well! Then go back to your cozy cells. I'll lock you all in again, and you can figure out a better plan for escape.

Thorin (*soothingly*). Now, Mr. Baggins, be reasonable.

Bilbo. But I doubt I can ever get hold of the keys again. (Dwarves *groan.*)

Thorin. It seems we have no choice. We'll try your plan. It just might work.

Balin. But there aren't enough barrels.

Bilbo. Most of them are piled out there. (*gestures offstage left*)

Dwalin. I still feel the risk is too great—

Bilbo (*ignoring him*). We'll have to act at once. Time's passing.

Balin (*excitedly*). I hear them. Hurry!

Bilbo. Are they coming?

Balin. Not yet. They're down the corridor. Hear

THE HOBBIT: ACT TWO   609

CUSTOMIZING FOR
Multiple Learning Styles

❶ Musical Learners Invite interested students to make up a tune for the elves' "downriver" chant. "Composers" can teach their tunes to small groups of students to perform for the class.

them singing? (Balin *slightly opens door right.*)

❶ Elves (*chanting offstage right*).
Roll—roll—roll—roll,
Roll-roll-rolling down the hole!
Heave ho! Splash plump!
Down they go, down they bump!
Down the swift dark stream you go
Back to lands you once did know.

Balin. They'll be along for our barrels soon.

Thorin. Line up the barrels. Kili and Fili, bore holes. Gloin, make a list and check every dwarf off as he goes in. Bifur, collect straw from our cells to pad the barrels. Bofur, collect jackets and stuff them with straw to leave in the cells.

Bofur. Whatever for?

Thorin. Make it look as if we're all asleep. They'll finally figure out how we got away, but the longer they think we're still here, the better for us.

Nori (*approvingly*). Pretty smart! (*A scene of great activity follows. Kili and Fili pull tools out of their bags and go from barrel to barrel pretending to bore holes in them while Bifur brings out armfuls of straw and pokes them into the barrels. Gloin, with pad and pencil, checks off the Dwarves as they go into the barrels. Oin has gone off left.*)

Oin (*speaking from offstage*). Fili, Kili, don't forget we've got barrels off here, too.

Fili and **Kili.** In a minute. We're coming.

Bofur (*busily stuffing jackets with straw*). I hate to leave these good jackets behind.

Thorin. Nori, you and Ori start packing dwarves in. Start with Bombur. He'll be the hardest. (*Nori and Ori march the protesting Bombur to a barrel.*)

Bombur. Not me! Let someone else go first!

Thorin. Dwalin, Dori, Oin, you're after Bombur. Line up the rest. Into those barrels fast! Kili and Fili, as soon as you finish boring air holes, head up[20] barrels. Close those outside first.

Kili and **Fili** (*putting aside their drills and picking up hammers*). But who'll head up our barrels?

Bilbo. I'll do it! (*There is a frantic scene of Dwarves hopping into barrels. Some of this supposedly goes on offstage, to make the process faster. Bilbo is everywhere at once. Fili and Kili go out left, and there is a sound of hammering.*)

Balin (*warningly*). I think they're coming. They just said, "That's the last of that lot."

Thorin. Leave the door. Over here, quick. Into your barrel.

Bilbo. Balin, outside. (*Balin goes out left.*) You're next, Thorin.

Thorin. The leader should go last.

Bilbo. No time to argue. Into the barrel, Thorin! (*calling offstage*) Everybody in out there? Hurry!

Kili. Just heading up Balin.

Fili. We're coming!

Thorin. But who'll be last?

(*Kili and Fili enter left and thrust the protesting Thorin into a barrel.*)

Bilbo. I'll be last. Hurry, Kili and Fili. (*They put the barrel head in place. Offstage shouts are heard.*) In with you, Kili and Fili.

Fili. But we can't both fit in one barrel.

Bilbo. Into it. (*Bilbo pushes the protesting pair in and closes the barrel. Suddenly he realizes that there is no one to close his.*) But what

---
23. **head up:** to seal or close up.

610 UNIT FIVE PART 2: RELUCTANT HEROES

Mini-Lesson: Speaking, Listening, and Viewing

BACKGROUND MUSIC Explain to students that background music can help set the mood in a drama. For example, background music can help create suspense or romance. Point out that they most likely have heard background music in movies or in television shows and commercials. Tell students an easy way to test the effectiveness of background music is to turn off the sound briefly while watching television.

Application Assign groups of students one scene each from *The Hobbit*. Have them choose background music for that scene. You may wish to provide students with musical selections from which to choose. Alternatively, have students do their own research, using home collections or the audio-visual section of a local library. If time and resources permit, use the background music that students select for a class production of *The Hobbit*.

610 THE LANGUAGE OF LITERATURE TEACHER'S EDITION

about me? Well, I'll just have to catch a loose barrel and ride on it. (*At the very last he suddenly remembers his journal. He dashes back and grabs it.*) Now into the river! (*holds his nose firmly*)

(*As* Bilbo *seems to leap off into the river, the* Guards *come surging through the door chanting:*)

Guards. Roll—roll—roll—roll—

Scene Three

In front of curtain: Lights come up in front of curtain to reveal Dwalin, Bofur, Bifur, Dori, Ori, Nori, Oin, *and* Gloin *in various stages of exhaustion and saturation.*[21] Thorin *and* Bilbo *are sitting at center stage, back to back. Behind them are three of the wine barrels (fronts, indicated by cardboard props). They contain* Balin, Kili, Fili, *and* Bombur.

Thorin (*groaning*). I've never felt worse than at this moment!

Bilbo (*nudging* Thorin). But are you alive or dead?

Thorin. Achoo!

Bilbo. Are you still in prison or are you free? If you want food and if you want to get on with this silly adventure of yours, you'd better slap your arms and legs and try to help me get the others out while there's a chance! (*stands up*)

Thorin. Uh-huh— (*gets up painfully*) Ooooh! My knees! My elbows! (Thorin *goes over to a barrel and removes the lid.*) It's Balin! Come on, old friend.

(Balin's *head pops out. He pulls some straws from his draggled beard.*)

Balin (*groaning*). Ooooh! I'm too old for this sort of thing.

Bilbo (*removing lid from another barrel*). It's Kili—and Fili! (*Their heads pop out, and then* Kili *and* Fili *crawl out of the barrel.*)

Kili. Aaaa—

Fili. Choo!

Thorin (*removing the lid from the last barrel*). This one's packed solid—must be Bombur.

Bombur (*wailing from inside*). Pull me out!

Thorin. I need help over here. (Bilbo, Bofur, *and* Bifur *go over to barrel. They all reach in and pull.*) Push, Bombur.

Bombur (*still inside*). Oooooh! Ugh!

(Bombur *pops out of the barrel.*)

Bombur. Ah! I hope I never smell the smell of apples again! My barrel was full of it. To smell apples when you can scarcely move and are sick and cold with hunger is torture! I could eat anything in this wide world now for hours on end—but not an apple!

Thorin. Well, that's all of us. It could be worse—and then again, it could be a good deal better.

Bilbo. I'm going into Lake-town for food.

Bombur. Good thinking!

Thorin. Then, we'll make camp and wait for you here. In the morning we can start for the Lonely Mountain to drive the dragon from his cave. (Bilbo *slips his ring on his finger and goes off.*)

Gloin. Maybe he's dead by now. (*There is a tremendous distant, bellowing roar.*)

Dwarves (*ad-lib*). He's alive. That's Smaug. Now our burglar will steal the treasure for us! (*Again the dragon roars.*)

---
21. **saturation:** wetness.

Scene Four

Scene: *The Lonely Mountain, outside the entrance to the dragon's cave. The stage is barren except for a few blackened tree stumps. A few broken mining tools may be lying about at stage right. The mountain is indicated by a 3/4 frame drop,[22] with a practical doorway left of center. Left of the door, the remaining quarter of the drop is scrim[22] gauze so that when lights are brought in front and up behind the scrim portion, you can play the scene in the cave. If this is not possible, travelers[22] may be employed to the same purpose. A scrim, of course, lends more magic to the scene. It is almost sunset, and the sky is reddening in the west.*

At rise of curtain: Bilbo *is discovered busily writing in his journal. He is sitting on the stoop before the cave entrance. Dragon smoke belches from under the entrance. The Dwarves glumly pace around the stage, hands behind their backs.*

Bilbo (*holding script off and reading it*). "And so we have come at last to the Lonely Mountain. What a desolate spot! But Thorin remembers when it was green and fair. According to his map, I am now sitting on the very doorstep of the secret entrance to the dragon's cave. But despite our best efforts, the door remains mysteriously sealed." (*resumes writing silently*)

Thorin (*stopping before the door, shaking his fist passionately*). Come out and get us then! I'd rather face ten thousand of you than stand here doing nothing.

Bilbo (*reading from journal again*). "I don't say so, but our predicament may be a blessing in disguise. I'm not looking forward to burgling old Smaug. No, actually, I prefer just sitting—" (*stops writing and hums pleasantly to himself*)

Gloin. All that treasure in there! Just waiting to be burgled, and *what* is our burglar doing for us?

Thorin (*approaching* Bilbo). Just what *are* you doing, Mr. Baggins?

Bilbo (*who has been humming happily*). Hmmm? You said sitting on the doorstep and thinking would be my job, so I'm sitting and thinking. Come join me. This is certainly the warmest spot on the mountain.

Thorin (*angry*). Mr. Baggins!

Bilbo. That certainly is a fine-looking key Gandalf gave you, Thorin.

Thorin. But there's no keyhole! (*flicks at the key about his neck*)

Bilbo. Let's have another look at your map.

Thorin. Again! What for?

Bilbo. I just thought maybe—

Thorin. Oh, very well. (*Pulls out and opens map.* Bilbo *joins him in scanning it. Droning:*) The runes tell us to stand by the gray stone—we've been doing *that,* all right! And the setting sun by the last light of Durin's Day will—

Thorin and **Bilbo** (*together*). —shine upon the keyhole—

---

22. **3/4 frame drop . . . scrim . . . travelers:** These are all curtains or cloths used for different purposes. A drop is lowered from above the stage to serve as a background. In this case, it is stretched on a frame that is three-fourths as wide as the stage and has a cutout doorway. A scrim is a loosely woven fabric used with the lighting to create a special effect. Travelers are curtains hung from a track and moved onstage from the sides.

WORDS TO KNOW
desolate (dĕs′ə-lĭt) *adj.* lifeless; gloomy
predicament (prĭ-dĭk′ə-mənt) *n.* a situation that is difficult to get out of; problem

Bilbo (*cheerily*). Well, perhaps today is Durin's Day.

Bombur. Wake me when something happens. (*lies down*)

Thorin. Durin's Day! I never heard of it. I've lost track of time altogether . . .

Dwalin. Our beards will grow 'til they hang down the cliff into the valley before anything happens here! (*Suddenly a red ray of sunset light falls upon the cave entrance.*)

Dwarves. Look! The setting sun shines on the door!

Bilbo. This must be the sign!

Thorin. Push! Hard! (*The Dwarves push against the door.*)

Nori. It won't budge!

Bilbo. The keyhole! Look for the keyhole! (*spots it*) Here it is! The key! Quick, Thorin, try your key while the light still shines on the keyhole.

Thorin (*removing the key from around his neck and trying it*). It fits! It fits! (*turns the key*) The door is unlocked.

Dwarves. Hooray!

Thorin (*standing on the stoop and addressing company*). And now is the time for our esteemed Mr. Baggins to perform the service for which he was included in our company.

Now is the time for him to earn his reward—by being first to enter the secret door.

Dwarves. Hear! Hear! Bilbo first!

Bilbo. Well, I don't think I'll refuse. Perhaps I've begun to trust my luck more than I used to.

Gloin. Well, well, look at our burglar now! Is this the same safe fellow who was lost without his pocket hanky?

Thorin. Mr. Baggins, this is your opportunity.

Bilbo. I have no doubt it's an opportunity, but who's coming with me? (*The Dwarves look the other way, embarrassed. They cough self-consciously and shuffle their feet. Bilbo stands to one side.*) Any volunteers?

Thorin. Now, that isn't quite fair of you, Mr. Baggins. You know we would go with you if it would do any good. But the moment the dragon sees us he will kill us. Since he can't see you, you'll be safe.

Bilbo. I'll lend you the ring.

Thorin. But then you'd be seen. No, no, you better wear it. We'll stand by out here.

Bilbo. Hmmmm! In that case, stand by the door. (*slips his ring on*)

Thorin. Good luck, Bilbo, my friend! (*reaches for Bilbo's hand but winds up shaking the air;*

WORDS TO KNOW

esteemed (ĭ-stēmd′) *adj.* highly thought of; respected **esteem** *v.*

613

Literary Concept: DIALOGUE

U Discuss with students how the dialogue between Bilbo and the Elven-Queen helps further develop Bilbo's character. *(Possible responses: Bilbo has come a long way. He takes initiative, acting as a diplomat, to make peace with the Elven-Queen. Bilbo has grown nosy, overconfident, and interfering to come between the Elven-Queen and dwarves in a matter that concerns only these two parties.)*

Critical Thinking: SYNTHESIZING

V Have students compare Thorin's behavior toward Bilbo now with that of the Great Goblin toward his attendants, as described on page 593. *(Possible response: Thorin is behaving in a similar bullying way that tolerates no disagreement.)*

---

tries again and misses) Mr. Baggins?

Bilbo *(clasping* Thorin's *hand).* Here I am, Thorin.

Thorin *(laughing and shaking* Bilbo's *hand).* Oh! Good luck!

(The Elven-Queen, *accompanied by two* Attendants, *rushes on from right. She is followed by a number of her* Elves *armed with bows and arrows.)*

First Attendant. Halt! In the name of the Elven-Queen. *(The* Dwarves *groan as the* Elves *surround them.)*

Elven-Queen *(stepping forward).* So, Thorin Oakenshield, we meet again! Of course I knew I would find you here. Where is the burglar?

Thorin. What burglar?

Elven-Queen. Don't try to deceive me. *He* may be invisible, but the treasure isn't! Well, now that we are all here, we can discuss matters. How shall we divide the treasure?

Thorin. No elf has a claim to the treasure of my people! I will not parley[23] with armed elves.

Elven-Queen. But the wealth of the elves is mingled in Smaug's hoard. Let us discuss that.

Thorin. We will give you nothing! Not a single gold coin. We look on you as foes and thieves!

Elven-Queen. So you claim treasure that is not really yours. Then how are you better than Smaug? Besides, you need my aid.

Bilbo *(stepping up to the* Elven-Queen *and removing his ring).* Have you a better plan than ours, Your Majesty?

Elven-Queen *(startled).* Ah, the burglar has decided to show himself! But you're not a dwarf—what are you?

Bilbo. A Hobbit, ma'am. Allow me to introduce myself. Bilbo Baggins, Esquire, companion to Thorin Oakenshield. At your service. *(bows cordially)*

Thorin *(furious).* Mr. Baggins! Will you please not interfere—

Elven-Queen. A Hobbit? Then maybe you'll listen to reason. Certainly I have a better plan. Dragons have to be *slain.* Then we should share the treasure. Part of it belongs to us. The dragon stole it from us.

Bilbo. Well, slaying dragons is not at all in my line. I was engaged as a burglar. But if part of the treasure belongs to you, I favor giving it to you.

Thorin. I will not share the treasure. I, myself, will slay the dragon.

Elven-Queen. With what?

Thorin. With this! *(draws his battered sword)*

Elven-Queen. You ruined that sword when you struck the troll, not knowing he had turned to stone. Behold the sword of the elves. *(claps her hands)*

(Two Elves *enter carrying a gleaming sword on a purple pillow. They stand before the* Elven-Queen.)

Elven-Queen. This blade was forged to slay Smaug. Agree to give us our rightful share of the treasure and you shall use it.

Thorin. I will not give up so much as one gold piece of the treasure. All of it belongs to me.

Bilbo. But, Thorin, if part of it is really hers—

Thorin *(thrusting him aside).* Silence, traitor!

Balin. Thorin, we know the crown jewels of the elves are in the hoard.

---
23. **parley:** to have a discussion, especially with an enemy.

WORDS TO KNOW
hoard (hôrd) *n.* a supply stored up and hidden for future use

614

Mini-Lesson: Speaking,  Listening, and Viewing

DRAMA Elicit from students that the movements of performers on stage make all the difference in whether a drama comes alive. For example, the highlighted stage directions on page 615 show how the feelings of the Elven-Queen and Thorin change through their movements.

Application Assign groups of students one scene each from *The Hobbit.* Have each group choose roles and a director who blocks out the scene telling performers when, where, and how to move and which position to assume in relation to one another. Have groups perform their scenes while students in the audience view critically. After each scene, allow the audience to give feedback about where different movements or positions would be more effective. Groups can then reconvene to discuss which criticisms they feel are valid.

Finally, students can perform all the scenes in order. You may wish to invite families or another class to view the final performance.

614 THE LANGUAGE OF LITERATURE TEACHER'S EDITION

Thorin. I no longer call you friend, Balin.

Bilbo. It's a bitter thing if our adventure ends this way. I wish Gandalf could help us now!

(Gandalf *enters behind* Bilbo.)

Gandalf (*lifts his staff majestically, with the blue light shining*). Gandalf is here!

Bilbo. Gandalf!

Thorin (*sourly*). Well, I never expected to see you again. I expect you're coming around for a share, too?

Gandalf. You are not cutting a very splendid figure, Thorin. But things may change yet. Instead of destroying each other, you should destroy Smaug together so that Middle Earth can again thrive in peace and plenty. I bring with me certain knowledge that you will need in order to vanquish him. But I will not reveal it unless you and the Elven-Queen agree to join forces. (*The Elven-Queen and Thorin hesitate and then approach one another and clasp hands, at first reluctantly and then with warmth.*)

Dwarves. Hurrah for the wood-elves! (*They toss their hats into the air.*)

Elves. Hurrah for the dwarves! (*They drum with their arrows on their bows.*)

Gandalf. Excellent!

Dwarves (*bowing to* Elves). At your service!

Elves (*returning the bows*). At yours! (*elvish laughter*)

Gandalf. The dragon cannot be wounded except for one spot! He wears a diamond waistcoat[24] that protects him from danger, but there is a bare spot just over his heart.

Thorin (*excited*). Then that's the place to strike.

Gandalf. Quite so. You will only have one chance—if any—and you must use the Elven blade and no other.

Elven-Queen. He shall have it. (*Claps her hands. The* Attendants *offer* Thorin *the sword.*)

Thorin (*taking it*). Many thanks, O Elven-Queen. (*brandishes sword*) Blade! I shall not disgrace you! I shall drive you home to your destiny! (*suddenly realizing*) But how?

Gandalf. Quite simple. Bilbo, you will go in first, wearing your ring. Thorin, you follow, but only as far as the inside of the door, and don't move a muscle or Smaug will see you. Once inside, Bilbo must somehow get Smaug to expose his bare patch.

Bilbo. How?

Gandalf. You'll find a way.

Bilbo. But—

Gandalf (*cutting in*). And when you do, signal to Thorin, who will fall upon Smaug and slay him. Good luck to you both. (Bilbo *slips on his ring and is no longer visible to them.*)

Bilbo. I'm going now, Thorin.

Thorin (*gesturing to* Bilbo). I follow, Mr. Baggins. (Bilbo *steps inside the door, followed by* Thorin.)

(*Lights dim down in front as they come up in the cave behind the scrim. The den is bathed in a golden red light. The walls and ceiling are covered with every kind of treasure: crowns, coats of silver mail, jeweled goblets, shields, etc.* Smaug *lies asleep on a vast pile of precious gems. Bubbling noises and vapors emanate from him.* Bilbo *enters from right. He is dazzled*

---

24. **waistcoat:** a short, vestlike garment with no sleeves or collar.

WORDS TO KNOW

thrive (thrīv) *v.* to grow strong and rich; be successful; do well
vanquish (văng′kwĭsh) *v.* to conquer; defeat
destiny (dĕs′tə-nē) *n.* what will necessarily happen to a person or thing; fate

615

by the light and glittering jewels and rubs his eyes. Suddenly he sees Smaug *and jumps.*)

Smaug (*stirring, in a thundering voice*). Thief! I know you're there. I smell you and I hear your breath. Thought you'd catch me napping, did you? (*Vapors and bubbles increase.*)

Bilbo (*summoning up all his courage*). Oh, no, O Smaug. I did not come to rob you. I only wished to have a look at you and see if you were truly as great as tales say. I did not believe them—

Smaug (*somewhat flattered*). Do you now?

Bilbo. Truly, songs and tales fall far short of the reality! You are the greatest of calamities.[25]

Smaug. Nice manners for a thief and a liar. Come closer so I can eat—I mean, see you.

Bilbo. I don't think that would be wise, O Smaug.

Smaug. Hmmm, you seem familiar with my name, but I don't remember smelling you before. Who are you? Where do you come from?

Bilbo (*trying to sound formidable*). I come from under the hill and over the hills. I am he that walks unseen. I am Barrel-rider and Ringbearer and Luckwearer, and I am here to reclaim the rightful treasure of the King under the Mountain.

Smaug (*snorting and belching smoke*). The King under the Mountain is dead, and I have eaten his people as a wolf eats sheep. I laid low the warriors of old, when I was young and tender. Now I am old and strong! Thief in the shadows!

Bilbo. I am the clue finder. I am he that buries his friends alive and drowns them and draws them alive again from the water. I am Ringwinner and Luckwearer and Barrel-rider!

Smaug (*gloating*). My armor is like tenfold shields, my teeth are swords, my claws spears, the shock of my tail is a thunderbolt, my wings are as a hurricane, and my breath is death!

Bilbo (*in a frightened squeak*). I have always understood that dragons are softer underneath, especially in the region of the, er, chest, but that you are guarded by a diamond waistcoat, if those are real diamonds. I hear they are only fakes.

Smaug (*snapping*). Your information is false and the jewels are real. Look at them, fool. My waistcoat is made entirely of diamonds, which no blade can pierce! (Smaug *rears up and displays the glittering waistcoat. There is a black spot over the heart, bare of diamonds.*)

Bilbo (*calling off*). Now, Thorin!

(Thorin *rushes on from right and plunges his sword into* Smaug's *chest.* Smaug *thrashes about wildly, emitting bubbling noises and thick smoke, then collapses and lies still.*)

Bilbo. Well done, Thorin, well done!

Thorin. What a treasure! (*He looks at it and removes a magnificent golden coat from the wall.*) Mr. Baggins, here is the first payment of your reward! Cast off your old cloak and put on this! It was my grandfather's. (Bilbo *removes his cloak, and* Thorin *helps him into the gold coat.*)

Bilbo. Thank you! My, my, I feel magnificent! But I expect I look rather <u>absurd</u>. How they would laugh back home in the Shire. Still, I wish there was a looking glass handy!

Thorin (*surveying the treasure*). Dividing all this

---

25. **calamities:** disasters; troubles; misfortunes.

WORDS TO KNOW
absurd (əb-sûrd′) *adj.* laughable; ridiculous

616

will be a long task.

Bilbo. I'll miss all that. I must be going home.

Thorin. But yours is a large share. Very large. Wait for it.

Bilbo. How would I get a large share safely back to the Shire, and what would I do with it when I got there? The coat is enough for me.

Thorin. At least take this casket of gold coins. No one can question your right to that. Perhaps you may find good use for it on your return. Things change, and not always for the better.

Bilbo (*accepting the small casket* Thorin *offers*). I thank you, Thorin Oakenshield, and await the day when you rap again on the door of your faithful burglar.

Thorin. And the Queen— (*glances around, and his eyes light on a richly encrusted robe of state*) This robe is not dwarf treasure. (*takes it up*) And here is the ancient Crown of the Elves! (*picks up a jeweled crown*) Help carry them, Bilbo.

Bilbo. Now let us leave this place. (*They leave the cave and join the others. Lights come up again in front.*)

Dwarves and **Elves** (*ad-lib*). Thorin! Mr. Baggins! Hooray!

Thorin. Rejoice, my friends! Smaug is dead!

All. Bravo, Thorin. Bravo, Mr. Baggins!

Thorin (*to the* Elven-Queen). Madam, your robe. (*He puts it over her shoulders. Her ladies adjust it.*) Your crown. (*places it on her head*)

Dwarves and **Elves.** Hail Queen of the Elves!

Elven-Queen. I thank you all. You have grown in stature, Thorin Oakenshield. Dwarves, you have a brave and honorable chief.

Thorin. It was your sword that felled the dragon, Great Queen.

Elven-Queen (*smiling*). But your hand that wielded it!

Gandalf. Excellent! (*crosses right and slips out unnoticed*)

Elven-Queen. I must return to my kingdom. Farewell, and may dwarves and elves ever live in friendship. And you, Bilbo Baggins, I name Elf Friend forever. (*All bow as* Thorin, *holding her hand high, escorts her off right.*)

Bilbo. I, too, must start the long journey home. Farewell, friends. (*smiles at them*) Remember, a certain burglar will always be listening for the sound of a dwarf staff beating on his door! (*He exits right.*)

Dwarves (*waving and laughing*). Good-bye, Mr. Baggins. We shall miss you!

| WORDS TO KNOW | **stature** (stăch′ər) *n.* level of achievement, especially when thought to be worthy of respect |

617

COMPREHENSION CHECK

1. Who is the main character of the selection? (*a Hobbit named Bilbo Baggins*)
2. Why do Bilbo and the dwarves set out together for the Lonely Mountain? (*to regain the dwarves' stolen treasure*)
3. Who is Gandalf? (*a wizard who plans and guides the adventure*)
4. What obstacles do Bilbo and/or the dwarves meet on their journey? (*Possible response: dwarf- and Hobbit-eating trolls; goblins; an evil, menacing creature named Gollum; a forest that sets them at odds with each other; capture by elves; getting into Smaug's cave; and Smaug himself*)
5. What device helps Bilbo escape from Gollum and mastermind the escape from the elves? (*a ring that makes its wearer invisible*)
6. How is Smaug vanquished? (*Possible response: After the dwarves and elves agree to join forces, Gandalf reveals Smaug's vulnerable spot—a bare place over his heart. Bilbo tricks Smaug into exposing the spot, and Thorin quickly attacks with the elven sword.*)

Mini-Lesson Reading Skills/Strategies

REVIEWING WHAT YOU'VE READ Remind students that reviewing what they read can help them remember characters, key events in the plot, and recurring themes. Reviewing can give a new perspective on how the writer develops characters and conflicts. Reviewing also can help students prepare to write papers or take tests.

Application Have partners review *The Hobbit* by completing a graphic organizer, such as the one shown, on external and internal conflicts and their resolution.

External Conflict	*Resolution*
Dwarves against Smaug	The dwarves regain their stolen treasure.

Internal Conflict	*Resolution*
Bilbo against his fears	

THE LANGUAGE OF LITERATURE TEACHER'S EDITION **617**

HISTORICAL INSIGHT

DRAGON FRIENDS AND FOES

Evidence has led researchers to conclude that belief in dragons began with snakes. The word *dragon* comes from the ancient Greek word *drakon,* used to describe any large snake or serpent.

Dragons or dragonlike creatures appear frequently in the ancient myths and legends of Asian and European cultures. In Babylonian legend, the hero Marduk captured the dragon Tiamat, slaying her with a fork of lightning. The Egyptian dragon Apepi, the ruler of darkness, tried to destroy Ra, the god of the sun. The Hydra, a swamp dragon with nine or more heads, viciously battled heroes in several Greek myths. In India, Ananta, an 11-headed dragon, was thought to support the world on its back.

The mythical dragons of the Far East — particularly of China and Japan—are usually wise, friendly creatures who promise good luck and possible wealth. The most powerful group of Chinese dragons was the Shen Lung, whose image was believed to prevent evil spirits from spoiling the new year. Dragons appear on Chinese artifacts dating from the 10th and 11th centuries B.C. The five-clawed dragon (as pictured here) was used as the emblem of Chinese emperors and their families.

In legends of the Western world, dragons are usually portrayed as terrifying, fire-breathing monsters with batlike wings, scaly bodies, and spiky tails. The typical dragon could be found in a distant, desolate place, where it devoured countless people, burned countrysides to cinders, and stole gold and jewels. It made its den in a mountain cave that few dared to approach. It is likely that J.R.R. Tolkien, an expert in medieval literature, had tales such as these in mind when creating his dragon, Smaug.

Dragon, detail of Chinese silk robe. Minneapolis (Minnesota) Institute of Arts.

618 UNIT FIVE PART 2: RELUCTANT HEROES

RESPONDING OPTIONS

FROM PERSONAL RESPONSE TO CRITICAL ANALYSIS

REFLECT
1. Which scene or incident in the play did you find the most exciting? Why?

RETHINK
2. One reader had this comment about the play: "Gandalf planned the whole adventure. He knew everything would come out all right." Tell whether you agree or disagree, and why.

Thematic Link
3. How has this adventure changed Bilbo?
   Consider
   - how he felt about adventure at the beginning of the play

Close Textual Reading
   - his comment that "a certain burglar will always be listening for the sound of a dwarf staff beating on his door!"
   - the feats he accomplishes along the way

4. Based on the events described in *The Hobbit*, do you think you would like to go on a quest? Why or why not?

RELATE
5. A quest is often thought of as something noble—an attempt to right a wrong, such as Bilbo and the dwarves undertook, or an attempt to help others through some effort or mission. Would you consider space missions, deep-sea exploration, and similar activities to be quests? What modern-day quests can you think of?

Multimodal Learning
ANOTHER PATHWAY
Cooperative Learning
Work with a couple of classmates to create a map of the journey. Label every location mentioned in the play, beginning at Bilbo's home, the Shire. Beside each location write a description of the events that occurred and the outcome of those events. Display your map in the classroom.

QUICKWRITES

1. Create a record of the quest for the stolen riches in the form of a **ballad,** a song that describes a famous character or event.

2. Suppose that Gandalf had to advertise for volunteers to regain the treasure from the terrifying Smaug. Write a **newspaper advertisement** for Gandalf.

3. Imagine that Gandalf's wizard supervisor has ordered Gandalf to write a **progress report** on the adventure. Choose a point in the action. Write a report describing what is happening and how well Gandalf thinks the effort is going.

📁 **PORTFOLIO** Save your writing. You may want to use it later as a springboard to a piece for your portfolio.

THE HOBBIT 619

ADVENTURERS WANTED
Do you have an itch to be rich? A hunger for heroism? Join an exciting quest for treasure. Must deal with dwarves, trolls, elves, and a dragon.

From Personal Response to Critical Analysis

1. Responses will vary.
2. Possible responses: Disagree; Gandalf's hurrying back to warn the dwarves and Hobbit when he learned that trolls were on the road shows that he couldn't anticipate the dangers and outcome of the journey. Agree; Gandalf turns up whenever he is really needed in the adventure.
3. Possible response: Bilbo became more confident and more genuinely hospitable. Bilbo's self-image changed from a confirmed homebody to a "burglar."
4. Responses will vary.
5. Responses will vary.

Another Pathway

Cooperative Learning Groups may choose to study the illustrations before they begin and create maps in Tolkien's style. Ensure that each student has a role to play in his or her group; for example, explainer of procedures, options generator (describes several ways to create the map), and integrator (blends group members' ideas into a plan on which all agree).

Rubric

3 Full Accomplishment The map clearly shows the journey, in all its peregrinations, from the Shire to Smaug's cave.

2 Substantial Accomplishment The map shows the journey from start to finish but significant stops along the route (for example, the Elven-Queen's palace) are missing.

1 Little or Partial Accomplishment The map omits more key places than it shows and is difficult to read.

QuickWrites

1. You may wish to bring in a recording of ballads for students to hear before they write their own.
2. Before students begin writing, remind them to consider their audience. They may wish also to reread the "want ad" on page 577 that Gandalf wrote to ensure Bilbo's participation in the quest.
3. Remind students to keep the purpose of the quest and Gandalf's periodic counsel in mind as they write.

The Writer's Craft

Writing a Poem, pp. 86–88
Organizing Details, pp. 217–220

THE LANGUAGE OF LITERATURE TEACHER'S EDITION 619

Literary Links

Ask students to compare Bilbo's adventure with Captain Kidd's. (*Possible responses: Neither Kidd nor Bilbo chose his adventure. Bilbo's adventure enriched his life; Kidd's life ended as a result of his. Bilbo's adventure was part of a humorous fantasy, while Kidd was a real person and his "adventure" ended tragically.*)

Across the Curriculum

Social Studies *In Search of a Vision* Have interested students research the vision quest, a rite of passage among Plains Indians. Students can consult an encyclopedia of Native Americans or a more specialized book such as Joseph Epes Brown's *Animals of the Soul* (Rockport, Mass.: Element Books, 1992).

Social Studies *Hair of Writhing Snakes* Have interested students research the quest of the Greek mythological hero Perseus. Students can write a report in which they contrast and compare this myth to *The Hobbit,* or tell the myth to the class in their own words.

LITERARY CONCEPTS

Dialogue is conversation between characters. A play is made up almost entirely of dialogue, which reveals the plot, the characters' personalities, and the theme. Playwrights rely on dialogue to move along the action and to develop their characters. As they speak, characters often state how they feel about others; however, they usually reveal their own personalities as well. Find a passage from the play that is especially revealing of Bilbo's or another character's personality.

Multimodal Learning

ALTERNATIVE ACTIVITIES

1. Using clay or some other material, make **sculptures** of some of the characters in the play. Refer to the stage directions for descriptions of what the characters look like and what they are wearing.

2. Make a **dramatic recording** of the events of the play. Assign roles and find ways to produce sound effects. You might want to write passages for a narrator to describe the settings of the action in the drama.

CRITIC'S CORNER

The poet W. H. Auden (a student of Tolkien's) wrote, "I suppose readers exist who do not enjoy Heroic Quests, but I have never met them." Auden was fascinated by Tolkien's detailed description of an imaginary world inhabited by hobbits and other creatures in which the forces of good eventually triumphed over those of evil. Based on your impressions of *The Hobbit,* would you be interested in reading other tales of quest and adventure? Why or why not?

ART CONNECTION

The illustration "The Hill: Hobbiton-Across-the-Water" on page 574 is one of many depictions of Middle Earth that J.R.R. Tolkien created. In the process of writing *The Hobbit,* Tolkien made a number of drawings of the settings, characters, and actions.

"The Hill: Hobbiton-Across-the-Water" and the illustration of Smaug in his treasure-filled den (page 608) were used as the front and back dust-jacket illustrations for the first American edition of *The Hobbit,* published in 1938. Some recent editions of *The Hobbit* include others of Tolkien's original illustrations. A collection of his drawings, entitled *Pictures by J.R.R. Tolkien,* was published in 1979.

620   UNIT FIVE   PART 2: RELUCTANT HEROES

Literary Concepts

Students' responses will vary. For example, some students may mention Gandalf's dialogue with Bilbo at the beginning of the selection, which reveals his cunning nature. If students need help in locating examples, you may want to refer them to the specific points in the selection mentioned in the Literary Concept annotations about dialogue.

Alternative Activities

1. You may wish to have students work in small groups. Each group can sculpt a group of characters, such as dwarves or elves, or several main characters, such as Gandalf, Gollum, and Smaug. Allow groups to arrange their completed sculptures in a classroom display.

2. Suggest that students begin by skimming the selection to identify key events. If your school has a visitors' day or open house, you may wish to share a portion of the completed dramatic recording with families or other invited adult guests.

WORDS TO KNOW

EXERCISE A Review the Words to Know in the boxes at the bottom of the selection pages. Then write the vocabulary word that best completes each rhyme. One word appears twice in the same sentence.

1. Bilbo, the Hobbit, thinks something is wrong when his home becomes filled with a loud, noisy _____.
2. The dwarves make him nervous. He's *not* reassured when they tell him their plan, which he thinks is _____.
3. But he goes off with Thorin and all of the rest, off on a dangerous, difficult _____.
4. The trolls get so angry (as each one is beaned) that they fight one another—it's _____ against _____!
5. Bilbo decides he will be a key snatcher, and success at this effort increases his _____.
6. They all get quite seasick from bobbing and rolling, at least they are free (which is very _____).
7. There is danger of death, or at least of great pain, when our heroes sneak into the dragon's _____.
8. A casket of gold becomes Bilbo's reward. There is treasure aplenty in Smaug's secret _____!
9. Bilbo's much cleverer than he first seemed. The dwarves all admire him. He is _____.
10. For the ring that he found helped them all to survive, and the treasure will now surely help them to _____.

EXERCISE B Answer the questions.

1. Is a **conspirator** in a plan of yours someone who works with you, against you, or in spite of you?
2. If you were in a **predicament**, would you be happy, bored, or worried?
3. Which color would a person be most likely to use to make a scene look **desolate**—yellow, gray, or red?
4. Does your **destiny** usually have to do with the past, the present, or the future?
5. If you and your teammates **vanquish** another team, have you won, lost, or tied?

Words to Know

Exercise A
1. throng
2. absurd
3. quest
4. fiend, fiend
5. stature
6. consoling
7. domain
8. hoard
9. esteemed
10. thrive

Exercise B
1. with you
2. worried
3. gray
4. future
5. won

J.R.R. TOLKIEN

Unbeknownst to many of his fans, Tolkien was one of the leading philologists of his time. His passion for languages, spoken and archaic, infuses both *The Hobbit* and the *Ring* trilogy, which *The Hobbit* introduces. The High-elven tongue of Tolkien's stories, for example, derives from Finnish.

Tolkien aimed to give the English people "a mythology of their own." He remarked toward the end of his life, "It is a wonderful thing to be told that I have succeeded, at least with those who have still the undarkened heart and mind."

J.R.R. TOLKIEN

1892–1973

Neither one world nor one career satisfied J.R.R. Tolkien. As a young child, Tolkien made up his own alphabet and language and grew up to become a respected professor of Old English and Middle English. The author of dragon stories at age seven, the adult Tolkien wrote *The Hobbit; or There and Back Again*, a fantasy drawn from the bedtime stories he had made up for his children. The novel, published in 1937, was instantly popular.

The three books that make up the *Lord of the Rings* trilogy, published 17 years after *The Hobbit*, became popular worldwide. Readers of these books found in their pages an entire world—complete with its own languages, races, and histories. Tolkien societies, clubs organized to read and discuss Tolkien's books, were formed, and scholarly studies were written about the trilogy. Tolkien's tales of Middle Earth continue to attract and captivate readers.

OTHER WORKS *The Silmarillion*; The *Lord of the Rings* trilogy: *The Fellowship of the Ring, The Two Towers, The Return of the King*   Extended Reading

WHAT DO YOU THINK?
Reflecting on Theme

Refer students to the activities they did before reading *The Hobbit* in Part 2. Ask students if, now that they have read about Bilbo Baggins, the ideas they explored in any of the activities have changed. Encourage students to revise their monologues, draw another before-and-after picture, or create another board game based on their new thoughts.

OVERVIEW

To gain a deeper understanding of the selections they have read in this unit, students will explore the characteristics of an opinion essay and then create their own essay in this lesson.

Objectives

- To plan an opinion essay by considering such elements as topic, facts, opinions, audience, and organization
- To draft an opinion essay and solicit a response to it
- To revise, edit, and publish an opinion essay
- To reflect on the process of writing an opinion essay

Skills

LITERATURE
- Finding details

WRITING AND LANGUAGE
- Identifying personal opinion
- Selecting an issue
- Gathering support
- Using precise language
- Considering audience
- Drafting a conclusion

GRAMMAR AND USAGE
- Using the active voice

MEDIA LITERACY
- Interpreting photographs
- Reading a survey
- Analyzing a magazine article

CRITICAL THINKING
- Separating fact from opinion

SPEAKING, LISTENING, AND VIEWING
- Conducting a poll
- Holding a debate
- Interviewing your audience
- Reading aloud

Teaching Strategy:
STUMBLING BLOCK

A Students may not understand that in this assignment, they have a dual purpose for writing: to explain an issue and to convince readers to accept their feelings about it. Explore with students how they can use the techniques of definition, problem-solution, and comparing and contrasting to explain and persuade.

CUSTOMIZING FOR
Less-Proficient Writers

B To make sure that inexperienced writers understand the task, invite them to list the characteristics of an opinion essay. Possible responses may include the following:

- Presents a position on an issue the writer feels strongly about
- Uses facts and examples to support that position
- Considers both sides of the issue

WRITING FROM EXPERIENCE

WRITING TO EXPLAIN

Some of the characters you met in Unit Five, "The Pursuit of a Goal," went to great lengths to get what they wanted. Do you agree with what they did? In your opinion, was their reaching the goal worth the price they paid? Writing about a complex issue can help you think about your opinion and figure out why you feel the way you do.

GUIDED ASSIGNMENT

A **Write an Opinion Essay** In this lesson, you'll write an essay explaining and supporting your position on an issue that's important to you.

Photograph

1 What's Your Opinion?

Do you have a strong opinion about something? Do your friends or family members share your feelings? Would writing about your opinions help people to see your side?

The items on these pages present situations you may or may not agree with. In your notebook, describe what the issue is in each example. How do you feel about each situation? Why?

2 What's Important to You?

B People often work toward goals that do not involve material rewards. Pride, good health, or fun may be the payoff.

Connect to Life Do any of the examples on these pages remind you of situations in your own life? Are you or any of your friends going after goals that call for you to give up something? Do you think others would agree with this sacrifice? Do a brief QuickWrite describing your thoughts.

Look for Ideas The following suggestions can help you think of other issues to explore. List your writing ideas in your notebook.

- Search through your journal for issues you feel strongly about.
- Think about people or topics in the news that have caused arguments or discussions between you and your friends.
- Brainstorm a list of things you might try to change if you were president.

622 UNIT FIVE: THE PURSUIT OF A GOAL

PRINT AND MEDIA RESOURCES

UNIT FIVE RESOURCE BOOK
Prewriting, p. 45
Elaboration, p. 46
Peer Response Guide, pp. 47–48
Revising and Editing, p. 49
Student Model, p. 50
Rubric, p. 51

GRAMMAR MINI-LESSONS
Transparencies, p. 17

WRITING MINI-LESSONS
Transparencies, pp. 38, 39, 45, 50

ACCESS FOR STUDENTS ACQUIRING ENGLISH
Reading and Writing Support

FORMAL ASSESSMENT
Guidelines for Writing Assessment

 **LASERLINKS**
Writing Springboard

School Survey

Olympic hopefuls spend 40 hours a week in the gym training, which leaves little time for fun, friends, or a full day in school. Is it worth it?

QUESTION OF THE WEEK:

Have you ever been a winner in an art contest, a band competition, a science fair, or a sporting event? Do you have a ribbon, trophy, medal, or plaque to show as a result?

Some schools in our area have stopped giving out awards. They say they don't want any student to feel better or worse than any other.

The school newspaper staff would like to hear your opinion! Do you think our school should do away with awards, or do you think it's important to reward winners? We'll print the results of this survey in next month's paper.

How do you feel?
(check one) ( ) Award the winners!
( ) Equal treatment for all!
If you like, write us a brief note telling us why you feel the way you do.

Magazine Article

PacificKid Magazine

Don't Skate Here, Dude!

Signs along boardwalks and sidewalks throughout the state have left skateboarders complaining they have no place to go. Boulder Beach city officials explain that skateboarding in public places is not just an annoyance to drivers and pedestrians, but also dangerous to the skateboarders. "And if someone gets hurt, the city will have a lawsuit on its hands," Mayor Jackson is quick to point out.

Since the signs have gone up, many serious sidewalk surfers have moved to vacant lots, turning them into cement playgrounds. Ramps, platforms, and old drainage pipes create courses for those who have mastered the streets, curbs, and even steps of city buildings.

Area business owners are concerned about graffiti, safety, and abusive behavior, and have asked police to crack down on these "parks."

I can see that the business owners might be nervous at first, but I think they should give the kids a chance.

PacificKid has an e-mail address. I wonder if they'd print my opinion if I sent it to them.

LASERLINKS
• WRITING SPRINGBOARD

WRITING COACH

WRITING FROM EXPERIENCE   623

Speaking, Listening, and Viewing: CONDUCTING A POLL

C Ask students to read the school survey and then poll their friends and classmates on the issue presented or on some other issue that interests them. Explain that the issues they feel most strongly about will likely be the ones they can write about most convincingly. Guide students to use the survey and responses as a springboard for ideas on writing topics.

Teaching Strategy: MODELING

D Tell the class that one way to generate topics from a writing model is to create a graphic organizer based on it. Model the process by having students create a chart based on the magazine article on this page. Guide them to isolate the issue presented and then to construct a pro/con chart. Urge students to extend the article by adding their own ideas on the issue. A sample chart is shown here.

| Issue: Skatboarding in vacant lots ||
Pro	Con
quiet	unsafe
doesn't bother people	graffiti
challenging	abusive behavior

WRITING SPRINGBOARD
Dissecting Frogs: One Student's Opinion Listen to the story of one young girl's single-handed fight for the right to choose an alternative to dissecting a frog in biology class.

Writing Prompt Describe a personal goal that was either controversial or required personal sacrifice. Explain why the goal was worth pursuing.

Side B, Frame 24164

THE LANGUAGE OF LITERATURE TEACHER'S EDITION   623

Teaching Strategy:
STUMBLING BLOCK

E Remind students that when they select a topic for a written argument, they must be sure that the topic is open to debate. Caution them not to confuse giving information with debating an issue. Explain that facts are matters of information, not debate. Be sure they understand that an essay becomes persuasive when the writer takes a position concerning the facts. Reinforce this distinction by giving students the following examples:
Fact: Students at South Middle School are required to take physical education.
Argument: Students at South Middle School should not be required to take physical education.

Writing Skill: USING GRAPHIC ORGANIZERS

F After you discuss the freewriting notes on this page, suggest that students use a cluster web to generate ideas for an essay topic. Using a general topic suggested by a volunteer, model how to set up a web by writing the main idea in the center of a sheet of paper and then adding related subtopics around it.

PREWRITING

Finding a Focus

A Thoughtful Opinion Why do you have the opinions you do? Are they based on facts, feelings, or experiences you have had? These pages will help you discover how to learn about other viewpoints and how to use this information to help support your own opinion.

1 Pick an Issue

Do you have an especially strong opinion about one of the topics you listed earlier? You will have an easier time supporting ideas that you really care about. Your topic should also be interesting to other people and have at least two clear sides.

Choose the issue that stands out the most and freewrite for several minutes on the topic. Try listing the key ideas involved, and then state your position in one sentence.

Student's Freewriting Notes

- Kids built a skateboard park because it is now illegal to skate where they normally skated.
- City might tear down park because business owners are worried kids will cause trouble or get hurt.
- I heard it's a pretty safe place (no fights, drugs, or serious injuries).
- At least these kids are out trying to get better at something and not just lying around watching TV.

My opinion: I think the city should help kids keep their park and make it safer.

2 Make It Clear for Yourself

Before you can state your opinion, you have to make sure you understand the issue completely. The following methods may help you find out more about your topic.

Discuss Talk over the issue with classmates or family members to hear their opinions. Listen carefully to ideas that are different from your own.

Test In a small group, challenge each others' opinions to find holes in them. Ask "Why?" and "What's your proof?" You can then strengthen your argument by adding more examples or facts that plug the holes.

Read Some libraries have computerized periodical indexes such as *Infotrac*. By typing in your subject, you'll get a listing of articles from most major magazines and newspapers.

Call an Expert Phone someone who is involved in the issue or knows a lot about it.

624 UNIT FIVE: THE PURSUIT OF A GOAL

 Mini-Lesson Study Skills

PREVIEWING READING Remind students that they must back up their opinion with facts. Tell them that they will find much of the factual support they need in sources such as magazines, newspapers, books, and on-line materials. Then explain that previewing a source can help them read it more efficiently. Explain the technique as follows:
- Skim the material to get an overview of the content. Read the titles and headings. Look at any visual elements, such as charts, pictures, and diagrams.
- Read the first two paragraphs, the last two paragraphs, and the first sentence of each of the intervening paragraphs.

Application Invite students to use this technique to preview the rest of this lesson. Then discuss with students what they learned from their previewing and how they can apply this knowledge to the reading they do for their opinion essay.

624 THE LANGUAGE OF LITERATURE TEACHER'S EDITION

3 Gather Support

When writing an opinion essay, you must not only state your position but back it up. The following types of information can help you support your viewpoint.

- **Facts** are statements that can be proved true. Solid facts, such as statistics and examples, strengthen your case.
- **Opinions** are personal feelings, attitudes, or beliefs. Quoting the opinions of experts can be an effective way to support your ideas. For example, *One skateboarder who has ridden ramps all over the world said this park was "The best by far! It flows!"*
- **Observations** that you or others have made can also be used to support your opinion.

You may want to list under one of these three heads the information you are gathering. See how one student did this in the chart below. (The SkillBuilder offers additional help.)

Student Research Notes

Facts:	Opinions:	Observations:
- Kids worked to clean up area.	- "It's the wrong place for a skateboard park," said one store owner.	- Older kids often help younger kids learn new tricks.
- No rules about using protective gear.	- "The problems are caused by the gangs or other outsiders, not us," said one skateboarder.	- Kids respect one another's skills.
- Park built by kids in Portland, Ore, is now the most successful in the world. At first their city was against it, too.		- Different types of people go there (girls, guys, honor students, kids in college).

4 Think About Your Audience

Will you aim your writing at a certain audience? Will any of them hold a different opinion? Which of your arguments would work best with these readers?

SkillBuilder

CRITICAL THINKING

Separating Fact from Opinion

As you gather support, it's important to recognize the difference between facts and opinions. Although experts' opinions can be valuable, mistaking others' opinions for fact could cause you to misjudge or misunderstand a situation. To identify opinions, ask yourself, Can this statement be proved? The following words and phrases can also help you recognize opinions: *awful, beautiful, best, excellent, nice, interesting, terrible, worst, I feel, I think,* and *in my opinion.*

APPLYING WHAT YOU'VE LEARNED
Before using information, decide whether it is a fact or an opinion. If it is an opinion, be sure to let your readers know.

 WRITING HANDBOOK

For additional help supporting your opinions, see page 796 of the Writing Handbook.

THINK & PLAN

Reflecting on Your Ideas
1. Did your opinion change as you did research? How?
2. Where else might you look for supporting information?
3. What kinds of information will be most meaningful to your audience?

WRITING FROM EXPERIENCE

Research Skill: ACCESSING INFORMATION

G Before students begin to look for support information in the library, have them gather the following basic materials:
- a copy of the assignment and their topic
- a separate notebook to use as a research log
- pens and pencils for note taking
- index cards for note taking
- coins for the library's copying machine
- a library card

CUSTOMIZING FOR
Less-Proficient Writers

H If beginning writers are having a difficult time distinguishing facts from opinions, suggest that they set aside their drafts and study the model research notes on this page. Arrange students in teams to discuss the facts and opinions in the model. Then have them add at least two more facts and two more opinions to the chart.

Writing Skill: IDENTIFYING AUDIENCE

I To help students shape their arguments, suggest that they interview some of the people who will eventually read their essay in order to discover what these readers know about the issue and what opinions they hold on it.

SkillBuilder CRITICAL THINKING

SEPARATING FACT FROM OPINION
Explain that sometimes the difference between facts and opinions is obvious but that at other times, writers intentionally blur the difference. Tell students that when they encounter the latter case, it is essential that they determine the difference between fact and opinion. Give students these guidelines for separating facts from opinions:
- *Look beyond the obvious.* Statements might have the ring of truth but not be facts.
- *Remember that facts sometimes look like opinions and that opinions sometimes look like facts.* Urge students to evaluate and analyze as they read.

Application Arrange students in pairs, and tell the partners to label each other's research findings as facts or opinions. Then have students decide whether each of the following statements is a fact or an opinion:
1. Jogging promotes mental health. *(opinion)*
2. Cotton clothing is more comfortable than polyester clothing. *(opinion)*
3. Wool clothing is warmer than cotton clothing. *(fact)*

THE LANGUAGE OF LITERATURE TEACHER'S EDITION

Writing Skill:
USING THE COMPUTER

J Invite students to write their discovery drafts on a computer. Guide students to copy their work into several documents. Explain that doing so will enable them to try different ways of organizing their material. If students do work on a computer, encourage them to use The Writing Coach, which gives detailed guidelines for the drafting stage.

Writing Skill: PURPOSE

K Guide students to focus on the dual purpose of their writing: to explain an issue and to support their position on it. Suggest that students ask themselves the following questions in order to focus on their purpose as they draft:
- *What effect do I want my writing to have on my readers?*
- *What facts, opinions, examples, and details will convince readers to accept my point of view?*
- *What aspects of this essay will appeal the most to my readers?*

DRAFTING

Pulling It Together

Support for Your Opinion Writing a discovery draft may help you clarify your thoughts about your issue. As you write, you will find your ideas taking shape and maybe even changing. That's fine. Just as you might sway others' opinions with convincing information, your own opinion may be changed as you learn more about an issue.

❶ Write a Discovery Draft

J You may need to refer to your notes as you write to help you back up your opinion. Ask yourself, Why do I believe this is true? Then list the reasons. Use facts, observations, and opinions of experts to support your ideas. Use the SkillBuilder to help you make your writing more precise.

Student's Discovery Draft

K *You might want to start by saying that you read the article in their magazine.*
— JM

Will you give reasons why the Portland park is good? Then tell how ours could work too.
— JM

Dear PacificKid,
I think the skateboarding park that the kids across town built is great! I don't think the city should close it down, because

Put these together →
1. The kids who skate there don't cause any trouble. They go there to have fun and skate. They should be left alone!
2. Kids came together and worked hard to build this. They all pitched in their time and money. (information found in <u>The Boulder Beach Gazette</u>) ←*Add how it is free for others to use*
3̶. Lots of types of people are learning from each other and getting along.
3̶4. If the city tears down the park, where will the kids go? What will they do? *(Might go back to skating in the streets)*
4̶5. Portland, Oregon, has a successful park that was built by kids. Ours can be too. (credit information to <u>The Oregonian</u>)
         ^ *successful*

I think the city officials should go out there and see for themselves what a good place the kids' park is. They wouldn't tear it down, because they'd see how important it is to the kids.

The article mentions safety. Maybe you should talk about injuries.
— JM

626 UNIT FIVE: THE PURSUIT OF A GOAL

WRITING SPRINGBOARD
Teens Talk About Cheating Teens reveal their personal opinions about cheating.

Side B, Frame 27147

Writing Prompt Think about examples of cheating you know about. Write an essay in which you explore one or two incidents of cheating and you give an opinion about the best ways to deal with the situation.

❷ Analyze Your Draft

Did any of your views change as you found out more about your issue? The facts that affected you could also affect your reader. Be sure to include those details in your final draft.

❸ Choose a Form

To help you decide how to present your opinion, think about the best ways to reach your audience. If you want your whole community to read your essay, you might write a letter to the editor of your local newspaper. To reach the students in your school, you might make and distribute pamphlets. Keep your publishing form in mind as you rework your draft.

❹ Rework and Share

Use the following suggestions to make your essay stronger.

Present Your Reasons Effectively One way to organize your essay is to first state your opinion and then order the supporting reasons from the weakest to the strongest, saving your best point for last. Using a different paragraph for each reason will make your essay easy to follow.

Finishing Strong You might end your essay with a recommendation. Asking your audience to think about the issue and come to their own conclusion is another way to finish strong.

The Writing Handbook gives additional tips on organizing persuasive writing on pages 796–797.

PEER RESPONSE

Comments from a peer reader may help you decide how to revise your essay. Invite a classmate to read your draft and respond to the following.

- Restate my opinion in one or two sentences.
- Which parts were most effective? Which were not convincing?
- What other examples would support my opinion?
- What is your own opinion on the issue? How did my writing affect it?

SkillBuilder

 WRITER'S CRAFT

Using Precise Language
As you write your opinion essay, be careful to use words that say exactly what you mean. Avoid vague words like *good, bad, right,* and *wrong*. They may mean different things to different people. Also stay away from words like *huge* and *few*. Be specific whenever possible, giving the actual size, cost, or number. Using precise language will help make your opinion and supporting reasons more convincing.

 WRITING HANDBOOK

For more on using precise language, see page 784 of the Writing Handbook.

APPLYING WHAT YOU'VE LEARNED
Look over your draft and replace vague words or phrases with precise language.

THINK & EVALUATE

Preparing to Revise

1. What do your readers need to know to understand your opinion? Have you presented this information?
2. Will you reorganize your revised draft? How?
3. How can you best get your message to others?

WRITING FROM EXPERIENCE **627**

CUSTOMIZING FOR
Less-Proficient Writers

L Inexperienced writers often have difficulty evaluating their drafts. They find it particularly challenging to evaluate the validity of their arguments. To teach less-proficient writers this skill, pair them with more-accomplished writers and have the partners analyze their drafts. Ask one student to read aloud his or her draft, and have the partner ask "Who says?" after every fact or opinion. Instruct the writer to respond by giving the source, such as "a noted scientist," "a famous musician," or "a well-known government researcher." For an opinion, the response might be "I do."

Writing Skill: PRESENTING REASONS EFFECTIVELY

M Explain to students that when they reason effectively, they increase their chances of convincing their readers to agree with them. Have students use the following guidelines as they rework and share their drafts:
- Be logical: use sound reasoning.
- Establish credibility: show that you are an intelligent person with good sense.
- Tap the reader's emotions: appeal to the reader's values and emotions.

Teaching Strategy: MANAGING THE PAPER LOAD

Ask student writers to attach to their drafts a note in which they ask the question they most want answered about their writing at that point. As you read the drafts, concentrate mainly on the question. Comment on other problems only when they are serious.

SkillBuilder WRITER'S CRAFT

USING PRECISE LANGUAGE Tell students that they can make their language more precise by selecting words that appeal to the five senses: sight, hearing, touch, taste, and smell. Encourage students to locate vague words in their drafts and to replace them with words that appeal to one or more of the senses.

Application Have students work in small groups to underline and replace vague words and phrases in one another's essays.

Additional Suggestions To extend this activity, ask students to bring in newspaper and magazine articles and to work in pairs to isolate examples of precise language. Then have students make charts listing the examples.

Reteaching/Reinforcement
- *Writing Handbook*, anthology p. 786
- *Writing Mini-Lessons* transparencies, pp. 38, 39, 45

 **The Writer's Craft**

Appealing to the Senses, pp. 266–273

THE LANGUAGE OF LITERATURE **TEACHER'S EDITION** **627**

Writing Skill: TONE

N Remind students that tone is especially important in an opinion paper. Be sure students understand that tone is the writer's attitude toward his or her subject matter. For example, the tone can be angry, bitter, sad, or sarcastic. Explain that opinion papers are most persuasive when they have a reasonable tone. Suggest that students choose their words carefully in order to achieve this tone; tell them to avoid words that exaggerate, slant the truth, inflame the issue, or insult the reader. Encourage students to evaluate their tone along with other aspects of their writing and to use the Standards for Evaluation as they revise.

Teaching Strategy: MODELING

O Guide students to compare the final essay on this page with the discovery draft on page 626. Ask students how they know the writer valued the peer comments. Explore with the class how the writer clarified the introduction, added specific reasons, and discussed the issue of injuries. Then have the class compile examples of precise language used in the final essay, such as *Boulder Beach*, *valuable*, *help*, *teach*, *practice*, *making friends*, *four skaters*, *empty lots*, *free*, *professional skateboarder*, *best in the state*, *builders*, and *no serious injuries*.

Students should recognize that the reasons are arranged from least to most important.

REVISING AND PUBLISHING

Adding Final Touches

An Opinion Worth Sharing A well-written opinion paper can influence a reader's beliefs and actions. To make your essay as powerful as possible, take time to make some final revisions.

1 Revise and Edit

Give your draft a rest. Then use the Standards for Evaluation, the Editing Checklist, and the following tips to help you finalize your opinion paper.

- Decide which of your peer readers' suggestions will help you make changes that strengthen your argument.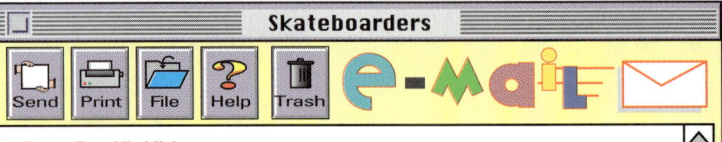
- Have you presented your ideas in the strongest way possible? The SkillBuilder can help you make your writing more powerful.
- Notice how one student states her viewpoint and backs it up with facts, observations, and opinions in the model below.

Student's E-Mail

Skateboarders

Dear PacificKid,

   The article you printed about closing skateboarding parks in Boulder Beach really got my attention. I feel strongly that the city should keep the parks open. If city officials learned the facts, as I have, they'd realize that the parks are valuable for many reasons.

   First, the parks bring out the best in the skaters. Girls and guys from all over the city help one another and teach each other new stunts. The skateboard parks are not just places for kids to go to practice the sport they love. They are places for making friends.

   Second, even though just four skaters spent their time and money turning the empty lots into parks, the parks are free to everyone. According to one professional skateboarder, the parks are some of the best in the state. Our city should thank the builders, not punish them by closing their parks.

   Third, although many people think that skate parks are unsafe, this is just not true. My research shows that there have been no serious injuries at any Boulder Beach skate parks. If they are closed, the kids might go back to skating in the streets, which is dangerous for everyone.

What examples of precise language can you find?

Why do you think the student ordered her reasons the way she did?

628 UNIT FIVE: THE PURSUIT OF A GOAL

Writing Skill: PUBLISHING

 Suggest that students share their writing in the form of a letter to an editor, which they submit to a school or community newspaper. Alternatively, students could present their essay as a speech. Guide interested students to identify a group that might be interested in the issue they have covered and to ask whether they can address that group.

PORTFOLIO

Have students add their opinion essay to their portfolio. Encourage them to reflect on their writing experience, jot down their thoughts in a paragraph, and clip the paragraph to their paper. When students complete the Reflect & Assess activities of Unit 5 (pages 630–631), their paragraphs can serve as a quick reference aid. To spark ideas, have students ask themselves the following questions:

- What did I learn about my beliefs as I wrote the paper?
- Which part of the writing process was the most difficult? Which was the easiest?
- Which comments from peer readers were the most useful?

Standards for Evaluation

Have students review their essay for the following:

Ideas and Content
- states clearly the issue and the writer's opinion
- supports ideas with observations, facts, or expert opinions
- presents ideas logically
- concludes by summing up reasons, making a recommendation, or asking readers to rethink their opinion

Structure and Form
- uses well-organized paragraphs and a clear organization
- includes transitional words and phrases to show relationships among ideas
- uses a variety of sentence structures

Grammar, Usage, and Mechanics
- contains no more than two or three minor errors in grammar and usage
- contains no more than two or three minor errors in spelling, capitalization, and punctuation

---

Student's Campaign

2 Share Your Opinion

Your opinion could take many forms. The materials above show how one student acted on her opinion. She and her friends made pamphlets and buttons to distribute at school, then invited others to join together to help. The following are some additional publishing ideas.

- Hold a class debate between opposing teams.
- Send your essay to friends or selected groups on the Internet.

Standards for Evaluation

An opinion essay
- states clearly the issue and the writer's opinion
- supports ideas with observations, facts, or expert opinions
- presents ideas logically
- concludes by summing up reasons, making a recommendation, or asking readers to rethink their opinion

---

SkillBuilder
GRAMMAR FROM WRITING

Using Active Voice

The **active voice** focuses on the doer of the action: *Kids of all ages built the park.* (Focus is on *kids*.)

The **passive voice** stresses the person or thing being acted upon: *The park was built by kids of all ages.* (Focus is on the *park*.)

Use the active voice to strengthen your position and make readers feel more involved.

GRAMMAR HANDBOOK

For more on using verbs, see page 835 of the Grammar Handbook.

Editing Checklist
- Use precise words and phrases.
- Double-check numbers and statistics for accuracy.
- State ideas in the active voice.

REFLECT & ASSESS

Evaluating Your Experience

1. How did your opinion change or develop as you researched and wrote about your topic?
2. What did you learn about getting other people to see your point?

 PORTFOLIO How did writing this paper help you understand the issue better? Add your answer and essay to your portfolio.

WRITING FROM EXPERIENCE 629

SkillBuilder GRAMMAR FROM WRITING

USING THE ACTIVE VOICE Explain that the voice of a verb shows whether the subject performs the action of the verb or receives the action. Guide students to understand that the active voice is often preferable because it conveys action more directly and immediately. Then tell students that the passive voice is useful in the following cases:

1. When a writer wishes to avoid placing blame
   Passive: A mistake was made.
   Active: You made a mistake.
2. When a writer wishes to focus attention on the action rather than on the performer of the action

   Passive: Oxygen was discovered in 1774.
   Active: Priestly discovered oxygen in 1774.
3. When the performer of the action is unknown
   Passive: The door was broken this afternoon.
   Active: Someone broke the door this afternoon.

Application Have students rewrite each of the following sentences in the active voice:

1. Rocks were brought home from the moon by astronauts.
2. The mouse was stalked by the hungry cat.
3. "The Star-Spangled Banner" was written by Francis Scott Key.

THE LANGUAGE OF LITERATURE TEACHER'S EDITION **629**

UNIT REVIEW

This feature allows students to reflect on what they have learned in Unit Five and to assess how well they understand what they have learned. This feature provides students with multiple opportunities for self-assessment, although you may wish to use some of the activities to informally assess specific skills, such as speaking and listening or cooperative work.

Objectives

- To allow students to reflect on and assess their understanding of theme
- To allow students to reflect on and assess their understanding of literary concepts such as sensory details and style
- To provide students with the opportunity to assess and build their portfolios

REFLECTING ON THEME

OPTION 1

Encourage students to skim their chosen selection and take notes about the character and his or her actions in the story. Students can refer to this information when writing their descriptions. Make sure students describe new situations for their chosen characters that are appropriate for their particular characters.

OPTION 2

Have partners jot down the ways in which each character is encouraged as they skim the selections. You may wish to have partners generate a list of ten tips so that the class has a wide range of alternatives from which to choose when creating the chart.

OPTION 3

You may wish to have groups divide the work by having each student complete a chart for one selection. Tell students to be prepared to support their ratings of characters' attitudes, as interpretations may vary. Encourage students to reflect on their own experiences when writing their essays. Remind students to support their opinions to make their essays as persuasive as possible.

REFLECT & ASSESS

UNIT FIVE: THE PURSUIT OF A GOAL

By reading the selections in this unit, you have seen how goals can be reached or missed and how trying to reach goals can shape people's lives. Now your goal is to complete one or more of the options in each of the following sections. Use the activities to help you reflect on what you've learned.

REFLECTING ON THEME

OPTION 1 Predicting the Future What impact can an early experience have on a person's future? Imagine that ten years have passed in the lives of Elizabeth (in "Flowers and Freckle Cream"), Panchito (in "The Circuit"), and James (in "The Scribe"). Draft a brief description of each character's new situation. Share opinions about how the characters' experiences may have affected their ability to reach their goals.

OPTION 2 Finding Inspiring Thoughts Working with a partner, skim this unit's selections to find ways in which characters encourage themselves or are encouraged by others. Then, with the rest of your classmates, create a chart titled "How to Get What You Want." In it, list ten tips for pursuing goals, based on the experiences of the characters. Copy the chart in your notebook, placing a star by any tip that might apply to pursuing your own goals.

OPTION 3 Comparing Attitudes With a group of classmates, copy the chart shown. Complete the chart, indicating each character's attitudes at the beginning, the middle, and the end of the selection. Use the symbol + to show a positive attitude and the symbol – to show a negative attitude. Then refer to the chart as you draft a persuasive essay about how attitude can affect the ability to achieve a goal.

Attitude Chart			
Character	Beginning	Middle	End
Elizabeth	+		

Self-Assessment: What do you now think is the most important thing to remember about pursuing a goal? How does your idea compare with what you thought before you started working on one of the activities? Answer these questions in your notebook.

REVIEWING LITERARY CONCEPTS

OPTION 1 Noticing Sensory Details Words and phrases that help the reader see, hear, taste, smell, and feel what a writer is describing are called sensory details. Review five of the selections in this unit. Then make a chart, like the one shown, to record details that helped you "experience" the action.

Sensory Details					
Selection	Sight	Sound	Touch	Taste	Smell
"Flowers and Freckle Cream"	"... she had a flawless peaches-and-cream complexion"	"I burst out the door"			

630 UNIT FIVE: THE PURSUIT OF A GOAL

Self-Assessment In order to help students answer the questions, have them review their thoughts and ideas in the notes they took while completing one of the activities above. You may wish to have students organize their thoughts in brief outlines before they begin writing in their notebooks.

OPTION 2 **Looking at Style** As you know, the style of a work of literature is the way it is written. Style involves such elements as sentence length, word choice, use of dialogue, and tone. Look through this unit's selections to find examples of three or four very different styles. Copy this chart in your notebook, and use it to record your examples. Then, with a few classmates, discuss what makes the styles different.

Selection	Example of Style	Description of Style

PORTFOLIO BUILDING

- **QuickWrites** In this unit, some of the QuickWrites assignments asked you to create newspaper accounts of events in selections. If you did these, select the two accounts you're proudest of. What do you think would draw readers into your accounts? How well do the accounts answer the questions *who, what, when, where, why,* and *how?* Write a short note to describe what you like about your work. Then add your accounts and the note to your portfolio.

- **Writing About Literature** You now have written a poem of your own. After rereading your poem, try drawing a picture to go with it. In your picture, try to capture the feelings and actions that you presented in the poem. Attach a copy of the picture to the poem, and place both in your writing portfolio.

- **Writing from Experience** When you wrote your opinion essay, you had a chance to express your views on an issue that you feel strongly about. Make a list of the people that you would like to share your opinion with. Whom would you like to persuade to see your side of the issue? How could you best reach your audience? Include your list with your opinion essay if you decide to keep it in your portfolio.

 Self-Assessment: Besides sensory details and style, the following literary terms were discussed in this unit. With a partner, take turns finding examples (in this unit or in other units of this book) to illustrate each concept. If necessary, look up the terms in the Handbook of Reading Terms and Literary Concepts on page 762.

figurative language
simile
metaphor

- **Personal Choice** Review everything you created while working on this unit—including charts, drawings, writings, and recordings. Pick one piece of work that stands out as your best. Write a note explaining how the writing or activity affected your ideas about pursuing a goal. Attach the note to your choice, and add both to your portfolio.

 Self-Assessment: If the pieces in your portfolio are arranged in chronological order, try arranging them in a different way. You might file your pieces according to how much you like them, according to their themes, or according to the types of writing they represent.

SETTING GOALS

By now you have done a number of Across the Curriculum projects. In completing them, what did you discover to be your greatest strength? In your notebook, describe how that strength can be helpful to you as you work on future projects.

REFLECT & ASSESS **631**

SETTING GOALS

In order to help students answer these questions and set future goals, have them review their work for the Across the Curriculum projects in this unit. Once students have located their greatest strengths, have them consider possible situations in which this particular strength would be valuable.

REVIEWING LITERARY CONCEPTS

OPTION 1

Have students copy the chart into their notebooks. As they review each selection, instruct them to fill in the chart with details from each selection. You may wish to have students compare their charts with a partner, discussing any differences they note in their charts.

OPTION 2

Make sure that students are able to support their thoughts about the writer's style with specific details from each selection. In order to generate discussion among students, have them compare their charts, noting any similarities and differences.

Self-Assessment For terms with which students have difficulty, have them write, in their own words, a definition for each term after checking in the Handbook. In addition to finding examples from the selections, you may wish to have students write their own examples for each of the terms listed.

PORTFOLIO BUILDING

You may wish to help students choose options or modify options for them that best suit the needs you have established for the class. Encourage students to incorporate in their portfolios drafts, in addition to final products, so that they can reflect on and assess their development and progress.

Self-Assessment Have students first make a list of possible ways to organize their portfolios. Then ask them to choose from their lists and organize their portfolios accordingly. You may also wish to have students consider the strengths and weaknesses of the different ways of organizing their work. Suggest that students also review their portfolio work and look at the areas which involved the most revision. Ask students to identify any patterns to their revising processes that might reveal problems or areas in which they need more work.

UNIT SIX

UNIT OVERVIEW

In Unit Six, "Across Time and Place: The Oral Tradition," students will explore folk tales, fables, myths, and legends taken from around the world. The selections of Unit Six are grouped in "links" that correspond thematically to the previous units. The selections may be read separately, or each link may be read with the selections of the corresponding thematic unit.

Links to Unit One: Running Risks
- Wings
- The Red Lion
- Why Monkeys Live in Trees

Links to Unit Two: The Need to Belong
- In the Land of Small Dragon
- The Bamboo Beads
- The Legend of the Hummingbird

Links to Unit Three: A Sense of Fairness
- *Damon and Pythias: A Drama*
- The Three Wishes
- The Disobedient Child

Links to Unit Four: Proving Ground
- Arachne
- Three Strong Women
- The White Buffalo Calf Woman and the Sacred Pipe

Links to Unit Five: The Pursuit of a Goal
- The Living Kuan-yin
- Sister Fox and Brother Coyote
- King Thrushbeard

UNIT SIX

Across Time and Place

The Oral Tradition

"You can learn through the laughter. You can learn through the tears."

— Diane Ferlatte
storyteller

Diane Ferlatte lives in California, where she keeps the ancient traditions of her African ancestors alive through storytelling.

Discussion Questions

Discovering the Oral Tradition
Have students read the quotation on page 632 by storyteller Diane Ferlatte, whose photograph appears on page 633. Then ask the following discussion questions:
1. What do you think Diane Ferlatte means by "the laughter" and "the tears"? *(Possible response: the happiness and sorrow that come into everybody's life)*
2. What might a storyteller learn through the laughter and tears? *(Possible responses: how to tell a story that moves people; how to be in touch with and express her own joys and sorrows)*
3. What stories have you read or seen in movies or television shows that made you laugh or cry? *(Responses will vary.)*
4. What kinds of stories do you think Americans relate to most strongly? *(Some students may say that the stories Americans enjoy vary according to their age, lifestyle, values, and subcultures within the United States.)*

Introducing Storytelling
Use the following activity to help students experience how a story takes shape and changes as it is passed around. Divide the class into four or five groups. Have the first group make up or relate a true story about a childhood experience to tell the second group. Groups may wish to appoint one person as storyteller or take turns telling parts of the story. Have the second group tell the story to the third group and so on until all groups have heard it. Have the last group tell the story to the whole class.

Then have students compare and contrast the story that the last group told and the story that other groups told or heard. Challenge students to make a generalization about what happens to a story as it is passed along orally. *(Possible response: The words change. Details may be added or subtracted. Sometimes the meaning changes, too.)*

Mini-Lesson: Speaking, Listening, and Viewing

STORYTELLING IN THE CLASSROOM
You might wish to modify the classroom to establish an atmosphere that is conducive to storytelling. You may:
- dim the lights
- lower the window shades
- have students sit in a circle on the floor
- provide a box of props for students to use as they tell stories

Students can help create an atmosphere for storytelling by being attentive listeners. Consider having them sit quietly for a moment before beginning a story. Some students might try listening with their eyes closed or try helping the storyteller by adding sound effects.

THE LANGUAGE OF LITERATURE **TEACHER'S EDITION** 633

UNIT SIX
Skills Trace: Links to Units 1–3

ML DENOTES MINI-LESSON IN TEACHER'S EDITION

Selections	Reading Skills and Strategies	Literary Concepts	Writing Opportunities	Speaking, Listening, and Viewing
LINKS TO UNIT ONE Wings The Red Lion Why Monkeys Live in Trees	Recognizing lessons about behavior, PE p. 639 Recognizing humor, PE p. 639 Explain mysteries of nature, PE p. 639 Relating cause and effect, PE p. 639 Connecting, ML TE p. 645	Onomatopoeia, ML TE p. 656	Instruction manual, PE p. 658 Paragraph, ML TE p. 642	Tableau, PE p. 659 Selecting music, ML TE p. 641 Music of the Middle Ages, ML TE p. 650 Drama performance, ML TE p. 651 Create a mural, ML TE p. 654
LINKS TO UNIT TWO In the Land of Small Dragon The Bamboo Beads The Legend of the Hummingbird	Identifying attitudes, PE p. 661 Evaluating, PE p. 661 Recognizing powers, PE p. 661 Classifying, ML TE p. 666	Point of view, ML TE p. 664 Rhythm, ML TE p. 668 Flashback, ML TE p. 671	Brochure, PE p. 680 Script, PE p. 680 Proverbs, PE p. 681 Summary, ML TE p. 664 Dialogue, ML TE p. 674	Dramatize a tale, PE p. 680 Interview, ML TE p. 663 Scientific observation, ML TE p. 665 Reading aloud, ML TE p. 668 Dialect, ML TE p. 670 Choral reading, ML TE p. 677
LINKS TO UNIT THREE Damon and Pythias: A Drama The Three Wishes The Disobedient Child	Recognizing humor, PE p. 683 Identifying supernatural elements, PE p. 683 Recognizing faults, PE p. 683 Cause and effect, ML TE p. 684	Narrator, ML TE p. 687 Conflict, ML TE p. 689	Paragraph, ML TE p. 688 Letter, ML TE p. 695	Make hieroglyphics, PE p. 699 Compare tales, PE p. 699 Construct a stage, PE p. 699 Build a fresco, PE p. 699 Background music, ML TE p. 685 Perform a scene, ML TE p. 686 Sportscast, ML TE p. 694 Critical viewing, ML TE p. 696

Writing	Reading Skills and Strategies	Literary Concepts	Writing Opportunities	Speaking, Listening, and Viewing
WRITING ABOUT LITERATURE Criticism	Evaluating the moral of a story, PE pp. 702–05	Moral, PE pp. 702–703	Rewrite sentences, PE p. 701 Add sentence variety to writing, PE p. 701 Rewrite a paragraph, PE p. 701 Interpretive essay, PE pp. 702–05	Viewing messages, PE p. 707 Interpreting messages, PE p. 707 Discussion, PE p. 707 Evaluating messages, PE p. 707

Grammar, Usage, Mechanics, and Spelling	Multimodal Learning	Research and Study Skills	Vocabulary
Conjunctions, ML TE p. 640 The prefix ex-, ML TE p. 643	Design a game, PE p. 658 Design a labyrinth, PE p. 658 Map the spice routes, PE p. 659 Calligraphy, PE p. 659 Tableau, PE p. 659 Time line, PE p. 659 Time line, ML TE p. 644 Music of the Middle Ages, ML TE p. 650 Drama performance, ML TE p. 651 Create a mural, ML TE p. 654	Research games, PE p. 658 Research the palace at Knossos, PE p. 658 Research the spice routes, PE p. 659 Research the lute, PE p. 659 Skimming, ML TE p. 646 Research music of the Middle Ages, ML TE p. 650	abandon exile gravely maze meager proclaim rival scurry
Compound words and contractions, ML TE p. 673 Subject pronouns, ML TE p. 678	Dramatize a tale, PE p. 680 Create a museum display, PE p. 680 Build a kite, PE p. 681 Interviews, ML TE p. 663 Scientific observation, ML TE p. 665 Reading aloud, ML TE p. 668 Dialect, ML TE p. 670 Choral reading, ML TE p. 677	Research hummingbirds in Aztec and Puerto Rican cultures, PE p. 680 Research bamboo, PE p. 681 Research aerodynamics, PE p. 681 Research kites, PE p. 681 Graphic organizers, ML TE p. 667	curtly hover indolent ravishing taunt
The adverb very, ML TE p. 691 The suffix -ance, ML TE p. 692	Create a picture book, PE p. 698 Construct a stage, PE p. 699 Make hieroglyphics, PE p. 699 Map hurricanes, PE p. 699 Build a fresco, PE p. 699 Background music, ML TE p. 685 Perform a scene, ML TE p.686 Sportscast, ML TE p. 694 Critical viewing, ML TE p. 696	Research pottery making, PE p. 698 Research Greek amphitheaters, PE p. 699 Research hurricanes, PE p. 699 Memorizing, ML TE p. 686	emit mocking repentance subsided tolerate

Grammar, Usage, Mechanics, and Spelling	Multimodal Learning	Research and Study Skills	Media Literacy
Understanding pronouns and their antecedents, PE p. 701 Making compound subjects and verbs agree, PE p. 705 Compound subjects and predicates, PE p. 705	Viewing messages, PE p. 707 Interpreting messages, PE p. 707 Discussion, PE p. 707 Evaluating messages, PE p. 707	Organizing ideas, PE p. 703	Interpreting and evaluating messages, PE pp. 706–07

UNIT SIX
Skills Trace: Links to Units 4–5

ML DENOTES MINI-LESSON IN TEACHER'S EDITION

Selections	Reading Skills and Strategies	Literary Concepts	Writing Opportunities	Speaking, Listening, and Viewing
LINKS TO UNIT FOUR **Arachne** **Three Strong Women** **The White Buffalo Calf Woman and The Sacred Pipe**	Identifying values, PE p. 709 Recognizing virtuous behavior, PE p. 709 Classifying traits, PE p. 709 Cause and effect, ML TE p. 721	Humor, ML TE p. 717 Characterization, ML TE p. 719	Outline a story, PE p. 726	Puppet show, PE p. 726 Wrestling, PE p. 727 Sportscast, ML TE p. 715 Drama, performance, ML TE p. 720
LINKS TO UNIT FIVE **The Living Kuan-yin** **Sister Fox and Brother Coyote** **King Thrushbeard**	Comparing cultures, PE p. 729 Comparing traits, PE p. 729 Recognizing values, PE p. 729 Evaluating ways in which the past is preserved, PE p. 729 Using context clues, ML TE p. 738	Humor, ML TE p. 732 Figurative language, ML TE p. 742 Conflict, ML TE p. 744	Rewrite a paragraph, ML TE p. 733	Storytelling festival, PE p. 746 Mural, PE p. 746 Investigative reporting, ML TE p. 737 Storytelling, ML TE p. 741 Comparing a video with a story, ML TE p. 743

Writing	Reading Skills and Strategies	Literary Concepts	Writing Opportunities	Speaking, Listening, and Viewing
WRITING FROM EXPERIENCE **Writing a Report**			Writing an I-search report, PE pp. 748–55 Drafting, PE pp. 752–53 Outlining, PE p. 753	Interviewing, PE p. 750

633c   UNIT SIX ACROSS TIME AND PLACE: THE ORAL TRADITION

Grammar, Usage, Mechanics, and Spelling	Multimodal Learning	Research and Study Skills	Vocabulary
The prefix *ob-*, ML TE p. 711 Predicate adjectives, ML TE p. 716	Puppet show, PE p. 726 Weaving, PE p. 726 Wrestling, PE p. 727 Trading cards, PE p. 727 Sportscast, ML TE p. 715 Drama performance, ML TE p. 718 Sports media, ML TE p. 720	Research textiles and looms, PE p. 726 Research buffalo, PE p. 727 Research wrestling, PE p. 727 Research gods and goddesses, PE p. 727 Taking objective tests: true/false questions, ML TE p. 712 Research Sumo wrestling, ML TE p. 720	clamber distort distorted erect fate feeble immortal indignantly obscure obstinacy sacred
Subject-verb agreement, ML TE p. 730 The suffixes *-ible/-able*, ML TE p. 736	Storytelling festival, PE p. 746 Mural, PE p. 747 Scrapbook, PE p. 747 Wanted poster, PE p. 747 Investigative reporting, ML TE p. 737 Storyboard or comic strip, ML TE p. 739 Storytelling, ML TE p. 741 Comparing a video with a story, ML TE p. 743	Research money, PE p. 746 Research festivals, PE p. 747 Research minstrels, PE p. 747 Research trickster tales, PE p. 747	compassion destitute dwindled elude extravagantly inadvertently insolent insufferable succulent wily

Grammar, Usage, Mechanics, and Spelling	Multimodal Learning	Research and Study Skills	Media Literacy
	Interviewing, PE p. 750	Using on-line services, PE p. 750 Using source cards, PE p. 751 Taking notes, PE p. 751 Outlining ideas, PE p. 753 Creating a list of sources, PE p. 755 Paraphrasing, ML TE p. 750	Using newspapers, PE p. 750

UNIT SIX
Recommended Resources ENRICHMENT RESEARCH

Recommended Novels and Collections

Misoso
by Verna Aardema

Thematic Links Twelve folk tales from different parts of Africa are collected in this beautifully illustrated volume.

About the Author Verna Aardema (born 1911) has made a name for herself as a reteller of African and Mexican folk tales for English-speaking audiences.

Other Works by Verna Aardema *Sebgugugu the Glutton: A Bantu Tale from Rwanda, Africa; The Vingananee and the Tree Toad: A Liberian Tale*

Flying with the Eagle, Racing with the Bear: Stories from Native North America
retold by Joseph Bruchac

Thematic Links In every story in this collection, a boy makes the transition to manhood. As each character comes from a different tribe, the reader learns the difference between rites of passage in the Inuit, Iroquois, Navajo, and other peoples.

About the Author Joseph Bruchac is an oral storyteller as well as a poet and recorder of written Native-American heritage. His work has appeared in hundreds of anthologies, winning him several notable awards.

Other Works by Joseph Bruchac *Thirteen Moons on Turtle's Back, Keepers of the Earth* (series)

Fafnir
by Bernard Evslin

Thematic Links An account of the mythical shape-changing monster who can transform himself from scorpion to dragon to vampire bat and more.

About the Author Bernard Evslin (1922–1993) was a successful playwright as well as a mythologist. He won numerous awards for his contributions to the field of children's literature.

Other Works by Bernard Evslin *Hercules, Jason and the Argonauts, Hecate*

The Last Tales of Uncle Remus
retold by Julius Lester

Thematic Links In this collection of Uncle Remus Tales, Brer Rabbit meets up with Tiger, Lion, and Fox in escapades of adventure, fun, and trickery.

About the Author Although Julius Lester (born 1939) started out as a singer and social activist, he is now most acclaimed as a storyteller and preserver of African-American history.

Other Works by Julius Lester *More Tales of Uncle Remus, The Knee-High Man and Other Tales, How Many Spots Does a Leopard Have?*

The Golden Carp and Other Tales from Vietnam
by Lynette Dyer Vuong

Thematic Links Fairies and dragon kings spice up these stories from ancient Vietnam.

About the Author Lynette Dyer Vuong (born 1938), a classical scholar, lived for thirteen years in Vietnam where she became interested in Vietnamese legends.

Other Works by Lynette Dyer Vuong *The Brocaded Slipper and Other Vietnamese Tales, A Friend for Carlita*

For Teacher TEACHING LITERATURE

Gates, Henry Louis. *The Signifying Monkey: A Theory of Afro-American Literary Criticism.* New York: Oxford University, 1988.

House, Jeff. "The Modern Quest: Teaching Myths and Folktales ('Make it New Again'; Classics in the Modern Classroom)." *English Journal* 81 (January 1992): 72 (3).

Negro, Janice Del. "The Booklist Interview: Julius Lester." *Booklist* 91 (February 15 1995): 1090 (2).

Scott, Jill E. "Literature Circles in the Middle School Classroom: Developing Reading, Responding, and Responsibility." *Middle School Journal* 26 (November 1994): 37–41.

Yolen, Jane. "An Empress of Thieves (Children's Book Author's Approach to Diverse Cultures)." *The Horn Book Magazine* 70 (November–December 1994): 702 (4).

633e UNIT SIX ACROSS TIME AND PLACE: THE ORAL TRADITION

CROSS-CURRICULAR TEACHING   PROFESSIONAL DEVELOPMENT

Recommended Readings in Cross-Curricular Areas

SOCIAL STUDIES

The Mythology of North America
by John Bierhorst (1985)
North-American myths are explained, showing how some themes also appear in myths of other cultures. Links to *The White Buffalo Calf Woman and the Sacred Pipe.*

Warriors and Gods from Central and South American Mythology
by Douglas Gifford (1983)
Includes index to characters and places, illustrations, maps, and stories from Central and South America. Links to *The Disobedient Child.*

Puerto Rico
by Deborah Kent (1992)
The land, people, history, and culture of Puerto Rico are described. Links to Ricardo E. Alegría's *The Three Wishes* and Pura Belpré's *The Legend of the Hummingbird.*

Cinderella
collected by Judy Sierra (1992)
Versions of *Cinderella* from different cultures are presented; comments, background, and criticism are included. Links to Dang Manh Kha's *In the Land of Small Dragon.*

For Teacher — CROSS-CURRICULAR INSTRUCTION

Beane, James A., ed. *Toward a Coherent Curriculum*. Alexandria, Va.: Association for Supervision and Curriculum Development, 1995.

Henson, Roberta Jeanette. *Collaborative Education Through Writing Across the Curriculum* (PhD Thesis). Ball State University, 1995.

Lounsbury, John H., ed. *Connecting the Curriculum Through Interdisciplinary Instruction.* Columbus, OH: National Middle School Association, 1992.

Nelli, Elizabeth. "Mirror of a People: Folktales and Social Studies." *Social Education* 49 (February 1985): 155–58.

Recommended Media Resources

THE LANGUAGE OF LITERATURE

LASERLINKS
Videodisc, Gr.6
See *LaserLinks Teacher's Source Book*, 60–61.

AUDIO LIBRARY
Tapes
Unit Six: Across Time and Place
Gr. 6, Tape 13: Sides A & B
Gr. 6, Tape 14: Sides A & B
Gr. 6, Tape 15: Sides A & B

WRITING COACH
Writing Coach Software: Writing About Literature: Direct Response; Explanation of an Idea

OUTSIDE RESOURCES

Films/Videos/Film Strips/Audiocassettes
American Storytelling Series. videocassette. New York: The H. W. Wilson Company, 1986. (39 min.)
Ashpet: An American Cinderella. videocassette. Delaplane, VA: Davenport Films, 1989. (45 min.)
A Laughing Matter. 1 film reel. Toronto, Ontario: Triune Films, 1990. (28 min.)
Cinderella. videocassette, Livonia, Mich.: Playhouse Video, 1985. (53 min.)

Internet Resources
Literature and Language Arts Center at http://www.hmco.com/mcdougal/lit/litcent.html

For Teacher — TEACHING WITH TECHNOLOGY

Interface: The Computer Education Quarterly. Mitchell Publishing, Inc. 55 Penny Lane, Ste. 103, Watsonville, CA 95076.

Kinnaman, Daniel E., and Dyrli, Odvard Egil. "Part 2: Developing a Technology-Powered Curriculum (What Every Teacher Needs to Know About Technology)." *Technology & Learning* 15 (February 1995): 46 (6).

Muir, Mike. "Putting Computer Projects at the Heart of the Curriculum (at Skowhegan Middle School)." *Educational Leadership* 51 (April 1994): 30–32.

UNIT SIX

Professional Enrichment

Storytelling

> In every culture, in every corner of the world for millennia, parents have been spinning tales and weaving the narrative web — in Eskimo families in the Arctic Circle, in the jungles of Africa, among Native American tribes, throughout Oceania, and at all points of the compass in between.

Storytelling is basic to every culture, whether it flourished 100,000 years B.C. or is heading into the 21st century A.D.

MARTHA DUPECHER, "THE MAGIC OF STORY"

Remember how much fun it was to listen to a story? Children today are equally delighted to hear a good story, well told. However, storytelling and oral interpretation of written works are very important skills in the adult world as well. People tell stories to interpret and understand literature, to describe key events, to give speeches from manuscripts. Here are some ways you can help your students master this art.

- Guide students to select a story that lends itself to oral interpretation. Any story in Unit Six would be a good choice.
- Have students plan their story carefully. Guide them to think about its incidents, the order in which they occur, and the details that make them memorable.
- Students can begin by identifying the following key story elements: characters (who is involved), setting (when and where the story takes place), and plot (what happens).
- Then readers should isolate the most exciting or important part of the story. This will be the part that receives the most emphasis in the storytelling.
- Allow students sufficient time to rehearse the story before telling it.
- Help students develop an animated delivery. Encourage students to adopt different voices and postures for the different characters. For example, they might try speaking in a high-pitched, squeaky voice for a mouse, or in a low, smooth voice for a lion.
- Students should also decide on a speaking rate and emotional tone that match the selection. For example, students would likely speak about a roller coaster in a fast pace. Remind students that the emotional tone of their voice is created by the rate, pitch, expression, and volume.
- Encourage students to work in pairs to comment on the effectiveness of each other's delivery. Students may also wish to videotape their performances as a rehearsal aid.
- To make the presentation smoother as students learn their stories, they can mark their scripts with key details. Possibilities include highlighting punctuation marks, important ideas and emotions, and the emotional climax.
- Have students arrange a quiet setting for the actual storytelling. The listeners must be able to give the storyteller their complete attention. Avoid settings where television, radio, or other people are competing for attention.
- Remind students to be aware of the attention span of their audience. Children, for example, have a shorter attention span than adults. If the audience is made up primarily of children, you may want to have the storytellers divide the story into segments and tell each segment on a different day or at a different time on the same day.
- When the storytellers have finished, encourage the audience to respond to the presentation. Did they like it? Why or why not? What did they think of individual characters in the story? Would they like to hear other stories by the same author? With the same characters?
- Encourage storytellers to assess their own performance. What would they do differently next time? Why? What would they do the same?

Related Reading

 Detz, Joan. *You Mean I Have to Stand Up and Say Something?* New York: Macmillan LB, 1986.

 Gorog, Judith. *Please Do Not Touch: A Collection of Stories.* New York: Scholastic, 1993. The National Association for the Preservation and Perpetuation of Storytelling (NAPPS), Box 309, Jonesborough, Tennessee 37659.

Soto, Gary. *Baseball in April and Other Stories.* Orlando, Florida: Harcourt, 1990.

Family and Community Involvement

Family

From a Greek myth about the fall of Icarus to a Puerto Rican legend explaining the existence of the hummingbird, all of the selections in Unit Six are part of the oral tradition. By completing some of the following Copymasters for Unit Six activities, your students, their families, and other community members can make important connections outside the classroom as they explore other examples of the oral tradition.

OPTION 1: READ A STORY ALOUD
- **Connection** All of the selections in Unit Six are part of the oral tradition.
- **Activity** *Copymaster, page 1* Students work with family members to read aloud and appreciate a piece of oral literature of their own choosing.

OPTION 2: RECORD A FAMILY STORY
- **Connection** All of the selections in Unit Six are part of the oral tradition.
- **Activity** *Copymaster, page 2* Students work with a family member to tape record or videotape a family member telling a personal story from their family's personal history.

OPTION 3: WRITING YOUR OWN MYTH
- **Connection** Some of the selections in Unit Six, such as "Why Monkeys Live in Trees" and "The Legend of the Hummingbird," offer explanations of the natural world.
- **Activity** *Copymaster, page 3* Students work with a family member to write a short myth or legend that explains an occurrence in the natural world, such as the weather or how a certain animal came to be. A word web is provided to help organize students' thoughts and ideas.

Community

OPTION 1
- **Connection** Many of the selections in Unit Six are Greek myths.
- **Activity** Visit an art museum that features Greek antiquities that depict characters of Greek myths.

OPTION 2
- **Connection** All of the selections in Unit Six represent important cultural aspects of their native countries.
- **Activity** Assign students to bring in and explain objects that represent aspects of their cultural backgrounds.

OPTION 3
- **Connection** One of the selections in Unit Six, "In the Land of Small Dragon," is a Vietnamese version of the Cinderella story.
- **Activity** Encourage students to visit their local library and work with a librarian to research more examples of the Cinderella story from other countries. Students can then read or tell these other versions to the class or to a younger group of students.

OPTION 4
- **Connection** All of the selections in Unit Six are part of the oral tradition.
- **Activity** Invite a storyteller, possibly from your local library, to speak to the class about the importance of storytelling and to give them instruction in telling or reading these kinds of stories aloud.

UNIT SIX
Cooperative Project

Storytelling Guide

Overview

Students will study folklore as a means of preserving the cultural heritage of a group of people.

PROJECT AT A GLANCE
The selections in Unit Six focus on storytelling as the passing on of oral histories and traditions as a means of preserving cultural heritage. For this project, students will examine several folk tales and determine some of the traits they all have in common. They will use this as a starting point for writing a set of guidelines about how folk tales should be told. Groups will compare lists and develop one comprehensive list of common traits. Each group will then write a guide to storytelling based on the list of common characteristics developed by the class.

OBJECTIVES
- To recognize folklore as a means of preserving cultural heritage
- To recognize that all folk tales have certain common elements
- To develop a comprehensive list of those common characteristics
- To write a guide for storytelling based on the list of common characteristics

SUGGESTED GROUP SIZE
3–4 students

MATERIALS
- Paper and writing utensils
- Binders or colored paper for covers

 ## Getting Started

Arranging the Project
Before students begin, alert your school librarian that there will probably be a marked increase in requests for anthologies of folk tales and stories. You might even request that these books be set out for your class to use in the library and ask that they not be checked out during the first part of the project. If another teacher in the school is doing the same project, coordinate your efforts so the books are available to all who need them.

You can make arrangements now for a storyteller to speak to the class. This could be anyone from a well-seasoned library Story Hour teacher to a professional storyteller. Explain the project and ask him or her to explain how to make stories interesting to listeners.

Arranging the Guidebooks
Since this project is student-driven, you will have little preparation to do for the guidebooks. You might gather binders or colored paper for the covers of the completed projects, and if your school has a computer lab, you might want to schedule blocks of time during which students can create their final drafts. The finished guidebooks can be kept in the library or the classroom for a limited time to allow for student perusal.

 ## Creating the Guides

Introducing the Project
Explain that students will be working in small groups to investigate a wide selection of folk tales to determine what elements, characteristics, or traits all or most of them have in common. Groups should keep a running list of these traits, as well as references to brief selections as examples. They should also keep a bibliography of the tales they look at and should be able to point out the elements in each tale. Their final lists will be discussed and narrowed down in class discussion to one final, comprehensive list on which they all agree. This list will be used by each group as a basis for developing a guide to storytelling.

At this point, you can introduce the guest storyteller and allow students to pose questions about the selection of stories, how much acting is involved, what props or costumes might be used, and other techniques storytellers use to keep their audiences enchanted.

Students might also recall and share any favorite stories they remember being told. If possible, they should tell why a particular story made a lasting impression on them, giving credit to the story, the storyteller, or both.

Group Investigations
Divide students into groups of three or four. The groups should begin by assigning tasks and then finding and reading folk tales, keeping a running list of the characteristics evident in each. Group members can compare their lists and finally create one list of the basic similar elements of the tales. Students can then meet as a class and have each group present their list. Ask a volunteer to keep a running list on the chalkboard, eliminating duplicate traits. Allow students to challenge any listing they feel does not belong before designating the list as complete.

Creating a Project Description
You might ask groups to write a description of how they will proceed with the project. They might divide tasks by assigning each member a kind of story, or have each member research stories from one particular culture. Meet with each group to look over the plan and make sure they have a correctly defined goal for the project. As their investigations continue, meet with groups every so often to note their progress. Remind them to keep a bibliography of the tales they have read. Feel free to suggest other stories to round out their selection.

633i UNIT SIX ACROSS TIME AND PLACE: THE ORAL TRADITION

OPTION 1: TELL A TALE Students can take their own advice once the guides are done and tell a story of their choice for the class. Decide if students should read the story aloud, memorize it, or tell it in their own words and with their own interpretation.

OPTION 2: STORY FESTIVAL Students can prepare tales and stories to tell to younger children. If possible, arrange for the class to visit a local day-care center to present their renditions of traditional tales.

OPTION 3: FRACTURED FOLKLORE Students can write and tell parodies of some of the more familiar folk tales. Encourage storytellers to exaggerate, twist, and warp the old standards into something they were never intended to be. Caution them, though, that the audience must be familiar with the original tales in order to understand what is funny about the "new" versions, so they should select widely known tales to parody.

OPTION 4: WHAT'S DIFFERENT? Several television shows—both old and new—include dubbed voice-over narration by the main character. Students can select one of these shows to compare and contrast with a tale told by a storyteller.

While students are engaged in investigative research, don't allow them to lose sight of the forest for the trees. These tales are entertaining as well as enlightening and should be enjoyed as stories and as a part of a culture's heritage.

 Sharing the Guides

When the guides are completed, invite the groups to pass them around the class for inspection. Ask each group to find at least one item among each guide that is new to them or that offers them better insight into storytelling. You might keep the guides in a special place in the classroom for reference, especially if you choose to use one of the options provided above.

 **Assessing the Project**

The following rubric can be used for group or individual assessment.

3 Full Accomplishment Students follow directions and produce a guide that shows, with specific examples, how all (most) stories contain certain elements in common.

2 Substantial Accomplishment Students produce a guide, but it lacks specific examples or clear focus on the elements of the stories.

1 Little or Partial Accomplishment Students' guide is incomplete or does not fulfill the requirements of the assignment.

For the Portfolio
Include a copy of your written assessment of the project in each student's portfolio. You may also include a copy of the group's original plan for carrying out the project.

Note: For other assessment options, see the *Teacher's Guide to Assessment and Portfolio Use.*

Cross-Curricular Options

MUSIC
Ask students to find and record old folk songs, research the age and origins of the songs, and make a presentation to the class.

SOCIAL STUDIES

Have students study the ways folklore reflects the values and attitudes of the originating culture. Then have them compare two versions of the same basic tale in terms of their cultural contexts.

HEALTH AND SAFETY
Students can write a new folk tale about a matter of health or safety. Tales can be set in olden or modern times.

LANGUAGE ARTS
Students can write a one-sentence moral for each tale they read. These can be compared to see how many tales teach the same basic idea.

Resources

The Hungry Woman: Myths and Legends of the Aztecs edited by John Bierhorst includes tales about the creation and destruction of ancient Aztec culture.

The Lotus and the Grail: Legends from East to West retold by Rosemary Harris contains tales from 18 countries.

The Magic Orange Tree and Other Haitian Folktales compiled by Diane Wolkstein offers tales by Haitian storytellers.

The Spring of Butterflies and Other Folktales of China's Minority Peoples by He Liyi includes tales from the Thais, Tibetans, Zhuangs, and Bais.

UNIT SIX
Lesson Planner: Links to Units 1–3

TIME ALLOTMENTS SHOWN ARE APPROXIMATE. DEPENDING ON YOUR GOALS AND THE NEEDS OF YOUR STUDENTS, YOU MAY WISH TO ALLOW MORE OR LESS TIME FOR CERTAIN PORTIONS OF THE LESSON.

Table of Contents	Discussion	Previewing the Selections	Reading the Selections
PART OPENER The Oral Tradition page 632	**30 MINUTES** • Discuss storytellers past and present • Review the history of storytelling		
LINKS TO UNIT ONE Wings page 640 AVERAGE The Red Lion page 649 AVERAGE Why Monkeys Live in Trees page 654 EASY		**10 MINUTES** • GREECE • IRAN • AFRICA	**45 MINUTES** • Introduce vocabulary • Read pp. 640–48 (9 pp.) • Read pp. 649–53 (5 pp.) • Read pp. 654–57 (4 pp.)
LINKS TO UNIT TWO In the Land of Small Dragon page 662 CHALLENGING The Bamboo Beads page 670 AVERAGE The Legend of the Hummingbird page 676 EASY		**10 MINUTES** • VIETNAM • TRINIDAD • PUERTO RICO	**50 MINUTES** • Introduce vocabulary • Read pp. 662–69 (8 pp.) • Read pp. 670–75 (6 pp.) • Read pp. 676–79 (4 pp.)
LINKS TO UNIT THREE Damon and Pythias: A Drama page 684 AVERAGE The Three Wishes page 691 EASY The Disobedient Child page 694 EASY		**10 MINUTES** • GREECE • PUERTO RICO • GUATEMALA	**35 MINUTES** • Introduce vocabulary • Read pp. 684–90 (7 pp.) • Read pp. 691–93 (3 pp.) • Read pp. 694–97 (4 pp.)
Writing WRITING ABOUT LITERATURE Criticism	**Writer's Style** **25 MINUTES**	**Prewriting** **15 MINUTES**	**Drafting and Revising** **75 MINUTES**

Time estimates assume in-class work. You may wish to assign some of these stages as homework.

Responding Options

LITERATURE CONNECTION	CROSS-CURRICULAR CONNECTIONS	CULTURAL CONNECTIONS
	90 MINUTES	
• Design a board game	**SOCIAL STUDIES** • Design a labyrinth **SOCIAL STUDIES** • Map the spice routes	• Try calligraphy • Present a tableau • Create a time line
	90 MINUTES	
• Dramatize a tale	**SOCIAL STUDIES** • Create a museum display **SCIENCE** • Investigate bamboo	• Compare Cinderella tales • Explore flight • Make a kite • Write proverbs
	90 MINUTES	
• Create a picture book	**ART** • Explore pottery making **SOCIAL STUDIES** • Construct a stage	• Make hieroglyphics • Compare tales • Map hurricanes • Build a fresco

Publishing and Reflecting	Grammar in Context	Reading the World
30 MINUTES	5 MINUTES	5 MINUTES

LESSON PLANNER   TEACHER'S EDITION   633I

UNIT SIX

OVERVIEW
Objectives

Through an article and an illustration, students discover the past influences that shaped a modern-day storyteller and her views about why the oral tradition endures.

- To understand and appreciate the richness of oral storytelling
- To apply and practice skills learned in previous selections

CONTEMPORARY CONNECTION "The Cow-Tail Switch," performed here by professional storyteller Diane Ferlatte, is a typical West African folk tale. It is a story that is closely tied to the culture and ancestry of Africa. "Stories come out from the folk," says Ferlatte. "The stories reflect the world in which the people live—their struggles and the conditions of their lives." Ferlatte explains, "The theme of this story shows how important ancestors are in the African culture." She adds, "This story tells us about where Africans come from."

"I tell this story because it has a good message," Ferlatte says. "You are not dead until you are forgotten. Understanding yourself and your family comes from knowing the stories in your life, from your family's stories. The stories you tell come out of who you are and where you're from."

Side B, Frame 35037

STORYTELLERS PAST AND PRESENT

DIANE FERLATTE
A Present-Day Storyteller Speaks

Diane Ferlatte performs stories from the African-American tradition. Like storytellers from ancient times, she uses gestures, props, and facial expressions to engage listeners in the drama of the story.

When I was 10, my parents moved to California, looking for work. Every summer they drove me back to New Orleans. I would complain, "Why won't you take me back to Disneyland?" But my parents knew what they were doing. They took me back to my roots. They took me back to Grandpa and Grandma, to homemade biscuits, singing on the porch, and stories when there was no TV or video. I heard many stories at my grandparents' home. Sitting on the big porch in a swing, that's what we'd do. The old folks would always be talking about family, about fishing, about true stories, about ghost stories, or about something that happened at church. As a little kid, I heard lots of stuff. If I had known I was going to be a storyteller, I sure would have listened more carefully.

My stories come from anywhere and everywhere. Most of the African stories I tell are from West Africa. In the old days, stories served to pass along information. That was part of the job of the *griots* (grē-ōz′) who kept alive the oral tradition of a village or family. They could tell you about your whole family line—where your mother came from, who your father was, what they did. It's important to keep alive the history of where you come from and what you are about.

Stories also told about people's adventures, their fears, their hopes.

634 UNIT SIX: THE ORAL TRADITION

Mini-Lesson: Speaking, Listening, and Viewing

LISTENING TO A STORY Remind students that to enjoy the performance of a storyteller, they must listen carefully. Review with them these elements of being a good listener.

- Be quiet. Don't whisper or talk while the story is being told.
- Watch the storyteller as you listen to him or her. This will keep your attention on the story.

- Don't interrupt if you hear something you don't understand. Wait to see if the next part of the story makes it clear.
- Keep in mind any questions that arise as you listen. After the story has been finished, ask your questions.

Application Have students watch the laserdisc performance of "The Cow-Tail Switch." Afterwards, have them write brief summaries of the story.

634 THE LANGUAGE OF LITERATURE TEACHER'S EDITION

An Ancient Storyteller
For over 500 years the Xhosa (kō´sä) people have lived and shared their stories in southern Africa.

An *umnqwazi* (ŏŏm-ən-kwä´zē), a headdress made of many pieces of cloth, was worn by Xhosa women.

A Xhosa storyteller might begin with a phrase that means "Now for a tale."

The hands are nearly as important as the voice in the telling of a tale, or *ntsomi* (ən-tsō´mē). Hands act out major actions, express emotions, and stress ideas.

Stories were a way of answering questions. That's where a lot of our "why" and "how" stories come from—how the lion got his roar, for example. People were curious. In African cultures, storytelling is not pure narration, or speaking. There is also music and dance and singing and religion connected with storytelling. All the arts are connected.

Stories come from the conditions in which people live. When the Africans came here as slaves, they weren't allowed to speak their own language, to play their drums, even to learn to read or write. But they could still tell their stories. The oral tradition was very strong in the world of the slaves because that was all they had. A lot of African-American stories have humor in them too. Life was so brutal for the slaves they had to laugh to keep from crying.

That's the power of communication, of the oral tradition. Once you hear somebody else's problem, it makes you think, "I'm not alone in this. Somebody else is going through the same thing." When you hear a story, you can see more of a common thread that goes through all of us. With so many cultures in this country today, we need to talk to each other. And the best way to learn about a people and a culture is to know their stories.

LASERLINKS
• CONTEMPORARY CONNECTION

STORYTELLERS **635**

Critical Thinking:
MAKING JUDGMENTS

Have students assess Diane Ferlatte's statement that "the best way to learn about a people and a culture is to know their stories." Then invite volunteers to give examples from their experience of how knowing someone else's life story can make a difference in a personal relationship. *(Possible response: Knowing something about how my parents grew up helped me better understand their values.)*

Linking to Social Studies

The best-known traditional African folk tales feature the spider, hare, or tortoise. Similar folk tales, about these and other characters, arose on different parts of the African continent. With the movement of African peoples, folk tales spread to the Caribbean, Latin America, and North America.

Art Note

Xhosa Storyteller by Hubert Shuptrine

Reading the Art *Study the figure of the ancient storyteller. Why do you think contemporary storytellers might wear traditional dress like that of the Xhosa Storyteller? Are there specific kinds of clothing that a storyteller from your ancestors' cultures might wear? How is it similar to or different from the clothing shown here?*

Mini-Lesson: Speaking, Listening, and Viewing

STORYTELLING Point out that different families have their stories too. You may wish to provide students with an example of a "family folk tale"—a story that is told over and over again in one's own family.

Application Have students work in small groups. Have each group member tell a story either from his or her home cultures or family. Then have the group identify the stories' similarities and differences. If time permits, call on one volunteer from each group to summarize group members' stories for the class.

THE LANGUAGE OF LITERATURE TEACHER'S EDITION **635**

UNIT SIX

TIME LINE
Objectives
- To understand history of oral traditions around the world
- To understand and appreciate types of literature in the oral tradition

---

STRATEGIC READING FOR
Less-Proficient Readers

To help students use the time line, point out that it organizes events in chronological order. Make sure that students understand the difference between B.C. and A.D. Then discuss the following questions:
- Which way do you read the time line to see the events and stories in order from beginning to end? *(Start at the left and read to the right.)*
- Which item on page 63 refers to the end of one civilization and the start of another? *(753 B.C., This item marks the end of the Minoan civilization and the beginning of Rome.)*

Critical Thinking: ANALYZING
Direct students' attention to the photographs of the Sphinx and the Great Wall. Ask what such structures might tell us about the rulers who had these structures built. *(Possible responses: They wanted to show off their importance; they must have been very powerful, commanding the huge labor force that putting up such large monuments requires.)*

LINKING TO HISTORY

The Great Pyramid, resting place of the Pharaoh Khufu, is almost 146 m (480 ft.) high yet was built without cranes, pulleys, or lifting tackle. Even today, archaeologists remain uncertain how the famous pyramid was constructed.

KEEPING THE PAST ALIVE

For nearly as long as words have been spoken, there have been tellers of stories and listeners eager to hear them. When they told stories well, they inspired others to retell the stories. From generation to generation, stories were passed from teller to listener within families, villages, and cultures. The tellers and listeners were taking part in what came to be called the oral tradition. The types of stories in the oral tradition appear in the chart below.

Known as folklore, the stories of the oral tradition continue to be told. Folklore brings the past to life for tellers, listeners, and readers of today. Like thread connecting colorful pieces of cloth, folklore connects people's lives across time and place, revealing our similarities and differences. The time line at the right presents important events of the past in cultures around the world. The folklore in this unit reflects those cultures. By reading it, you can discover for yourself how folklore links people and keeps the past alive.

MYTHS
- attempt to answer basic questions about the world
- are considered truthful by their originators

FOLK TALES
- are told primarily for entertainment
- feature human beings or humanlike animals

COMMON ELEMENTS
- keep the past alive
- teach lessons about human behavior
- reveal the values of the society

FABLES
- are short tales that illustrate morals
- have characters that are animals

LEGENDS
- are considered factual by those who tell them
- may be based on facts
- are usually set in the past

636 UNIT SIX: THE ORAL TRADITION

AFRICA
Why Monkeys Live in Trees 654

. . .

3000–2500 B.C. *First Egyptian pyramid and Great Sphinx of Giza built*

THE AMERICAS
The White Buffalo Calf Woman and the Sacred Pipe 723

Sister Fox and Brother Coyote 735

The Disobedient Child 694

. . .

2750–2000 B.C. *Farmers begin to settle in region between modern-day Mexico and Nicaragua*

Mini-Lesson · Study Skills

INTERPRETING GRAPHICS Point out to students that a time line allows readers to see a sequence of events. Explain that this time line shows the places where stories in this unit originated and historic events that occurred there.

Application Have students work to locate each place shown on the time line on a classroom world map. Call on a volunteer to point out different locations on the map. Classmates at their seats can direct the volunteer to the various locations. As the volunteer points to each location, call on several class members to read aloud the relevant historical information.

636 THE LANGUAGE OF LITERATURE TEACHER'S EDITION

Greece/Rome

Wings 640
Damon and Pythias 684
Arachne 710

. . .

700s B.C. *Destruction of Minoan civilization; First Olympic Games in Greece; Founding of Rome*

Asia

In the Land of Small Dragon 662
Three Strong Women. 715
The Living Kuan-yin 730

. . .

215 B.C. *Reign of Ch'in Shih Huang Ti (The First Emperor); Construction of Great Wall begins; Rise of Buddhist religion in China*

Caribbean

The Three Wishes . . 691
The Bamboo Beads 670
The Legend of the Hummingbird 676

. . .

A.D. 1492 *Carib Indians on various Caribbean islands have first contact with Europeans after the arrival of Christopher Columbus*

LINKING TO HISTORY

Accounts by Julius Caesar and Tacitus describe encounters between Germanic and Celtic tribes and Romans, which occurred from the second to the fifth centuries B.C. In those centuries, the Romans controlled southern and western Europe. Around 50 B.C., Julius Caesar conquered tribes west of the Rhine River in Gaul (modern France). The Romans then tried—and failed—to extend their rule north to the Elbe River in modern Germany.

Literary Concept:
THE ORAL TRADITION

Ask students to review the box diagram on page 636. Have them note the various types of literature in the oral tradition and compare and contrast them. Ask them to describe the similarities and differences among the four types. *(Students may point out the different purposes, characters, or settings in the types. They should be able to point out as similarities the "Common Elements" that all four types of literature serve.)*

The Middle East

The Red Lion. 649

. . .

549 B.C. *Foundations of Persian Empire under Cyrus the Great*

Europe

King Thrushbeard . . 741

. . .

50 B.C. *German tribes practice agriculture and have contact with the Roman Empire*

KEEPING THE PAST ALIVE **637**

Mini-Lesson  Genre Study

ORAL TRADITION Draw on the chalkboard the web shown and use it to explain that myths, folk tales, fables, and legends are all part of the oral tradition. Then summarize the different characteristics of each type.

Application Divide the class into four groups. Assign each group one genre—myth, folk tale, fable, or legend. Have groups brainstorm examples of their genre using stories that they have read or heard. Then have groups make a word web of specific genre characteristics using one of their examples.

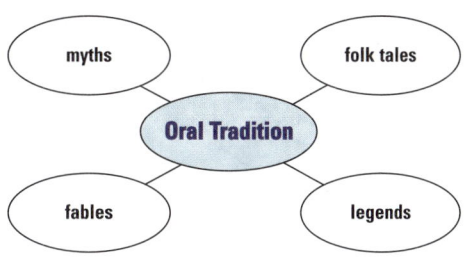

THE LANGUAGE OF LITERATURE TEACHER'S EDITION 637

OVERVIEW

Objectives

- To understand and appreciate two folk tales and a myth about facing danger and overcoming fears
- To appreciate the ancient history and culture of Africa, Persia, and Greece
- To extend understanding of the selection through a variety of multimodal and cross-curricular activities

Reading Pathways

- Select one or several students to read each story aloud to the entire class or to small groups of students. Assign this reading in advance so that the readers can incorporate into their presentations some of the techniques used by professional storytellers. Have the audience listen carefully to the stories without following along in their texts.

- Read the stories aloud to the class, pausing at key points to discuss how elements of the tales inform students about the culture of ancient Africa, Persia, or Greece. Have students compare these cultures with their own. Have students record their responses and observations in their notebooks.

- After students have read the stories once, have them read them again to identify structural elements such as main characters, minor characters, conflict, setting, and plot. Then have students identify similarities and differences between these tales and the selections in the related unit. For example, both "Wings" and "Tuesday of the Other June" (page 75) feature hard-hearted characters. In "Wings," however, Daedalus finally learns wisdom. The Other June does not.

PREVIEWING

LINKS TO UNIT ONE

Running Risks

Activating Prior Knowledge

The selections in Unit One reveal certain challenges that people face in life. Some of those challenges involve making risky choices and accepting what the choices bring. In each of the tales that follow, a character responds to a challenge—and must live with the consequences.

Building Background

AFRICA

Why Monkeys Live in Trees

retold by Julius Lester

In the 1400s B.C., the African kingdom of Kush often included exotic animals such as monkeys in its yearly tribute to Egypt. Most African folk tales have animals as their characters. This folk tale, which recounts Monkey's attempt to outwit the other animals, is a good example of the humorous trickster tales found in most cultures. Told to entertain, "Why Monkeys Live in Trees" is a "why" story that attempts to explain an animal's characteristics.

638   UNIT SIX: THE ORAL TRADITION

PRINT AND MEDIA RESOURCES

UNIT SIX RESOURCE BOOK
Strategic Reading: Literature, p. 4
Vocabulary SkillBuilder, p. 7
Reading SkillBuilder, p. 5
Spelling SkillBuilder, p. 6

GRAMMAR MINI–LESSONS
Transparencies, p. 42

WRITING MINI–LESSONS
Transparencies, p. 29

ACCESS FOR STUDENTS ACQUIRING ENGLISH
Selection Summaries
Reading and Writing Support

TEACHER'S GUIDE TO ASSESSMENT AND PORTFOLIO USE

FORMAL ASSESSMENT
Selection Test, pp. 117–118
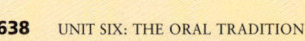 Test Generator

 AUDIO LIBRARY
See Reference Card

 **INTERNET RESOURCES**
McDougal Littell Literature Center at http://www.hmco.com/mcdougal/lit

638   THE LANGUAGE OF LITERATURE   TEACHER'S EDITION

IRAN
The Red Lion
retold by Diane Wolkstein

Building Background
"The Red Lion" comes from the vast Persian empire, which at its height extended from Egypt to the Indus River. Part of the land that was once Persia is modern-day Iran. In ancient Persia, the son of a tribal leader did not automatically inherit his father's rank. In this folk tale, the King of Persia dies, and his son, Prince Azgid (äz'gēd), before he can be crowned, must prove his courage by fighting the Red Lion.

GREECE
Wings
retold by Jane Yolen

Building Background
Many Greek myths focus on individuals and the way they interact with other people. Ancient Greeks placed a great deal of importance on treating others fairly and with kindness. Set mainly on the ancient island of Crete in the Aegean (ĭ-jē'ən) Sea, "Wings" retells the Greek myth of a brilliant inventor named Daedalus (dĕd'l-əs) and his son, Icarus (ĭk'ər-əs). Daedalus is described as clever but not always kind. According to this retelling, "The gods always punish such a man."

Setting a Purpose

AS YOU READ . . .
Discover what lessons about human behavior are taught.

Notice which human weaknesses are seen as humorous.

Find out what mysteries of nature are explained.

See how the consequences of characters' choices unfold.

LINKS TO UNIT ONE 639

SUMMARY

Wings This Greek myth tells about the proud, brilliant inventor Daedalus. After causing the death of his nephew, Daedalus is banished from his home city of Athens. He flees to the island of Crete, where King Minos hires him to build a maze called a labyrinth for the Minotaur, a horrible monster—half bull, half man—who is the queen's son. Daedalus prospers on Crete until he helps Theseus, a fellow Athenian prince, find his way through the labyrinth and slay the Minotaur. King Minos throws Daedalus and his son, Icarus, into a prison tower. Daedalus builds wings of wax and feathers. Under the watchful eyes of the gods, they fly across the sea—until Icarus, foolishly ignoring his father's advice, flies too close to the sun. With his wings melting, Icarus falls into the sea.

The Red Lion When the king of Persia dies, Prince Azgid is supposed to become the next king. But first—like all princes before him—he must battle the Red Lion. His fear of the beast is so great that he runs away. Azgid befriends a shepherd and stays with him in a beautiful valley until the threat of lions drives him away. Next, he joins an Arab camp in the desert, until he is asked to slay a lion to prove his skills in battle. Azgid runs away again. He finds refuge in the palace of an emir, an Arab king. Azgid falls in love with the emir's daughter, Perizide, but faces yet another lion: Boulak, the palace guard, roars to warn Azgid that wherever he goes, a lion will be waiting. The prince hurries home, ready to face the Red Lion. The lion, however, is as tame as a puppy—for he is ferocious only toward those who fear him. Having faced his fear and learned courage, Azgid becomes king and marries Perizide.

Why Monkeys Live in Trees According to this African folk tale, monkeys have lived in trees ever since the day King Gorilla promised a pot of gold to whoever could eat a mound of black dust. Finally only Monkey is left among the contestants. His winning strategy, apparently, is to swallow a mouthful of pepper, rest in some tall grass, then repeat the process. Leopard, astonished by Monkey's success, climbs onto a tree limb to get a better view. What he sees—a hundred monkeys hiding in the tall grass—angers him so much that he jumps down to punish their trickery just as Monkey wins the pot of gold. The only way the monkeys can escape is to climb to the top of the tallest trees, where they still live today.

WORDS TO KNOW

abandon (ə-băn'dən) *n.* a wildness; unrestricted freedom of action (p. 646)
exile (ĕg'sīl') *n.* a person forced to live outside his or her country (p. 642)
gravely (grāv'lē) *adv.* in a very serious manner (p. 644)
maze (māz) *n.* a confusing set of winding pathways through which it is difficult to find one's way (p. 640)
meager (mē'gər) *adj.* of poor quality or inadequate amount (p. 645)
proclaim (prō-klām') *v.* to announce officially (p. 648)
rival (rī'vəl)) *n.* a person who tries to do as well as or better than another (p. 642)
scurry (skûr'ē) *v.* to run quickly; scamper (p. 648)

THE LANGUAGE OF LITERATURE TEACHER'S EDITION **639**

STRATEGIC READING FOR
Less-Proficient Readers

Set a Purpose As students read, they should think about what kind of person Daedalus is and how he adjusts to his new life in Crete.

Use **UNIT SIX RESOURCE BOOK,** pp. 4–5, for guidance in reading the selection.

CUSTOMIZING FOR
Students Acquiring English

- Use **ACCESS FOR STUDENTS ACQUIRING ENGLISH,** *Reading and Writing Support.*
- As some students may not be familiar with Greek history, you may want to provide additional background information about ancient Greek culture and its importance and influence.
- As you guide students through the selection, you may want to use the suggestions in these boxes as well as the suggestions under Strategic Reading for Less-Proficient Readers.

CUSTOMIZING FOR
Gifted and Talented Students

Have students think about how Daedalus changes and how he stays the same. Ask them if Daedalus is less proud when the story ends. Ask how Daedalus' temple to Apollo suggests that Daedalus has changed.

Possible responses:

- Page 646—"On the temple walls Daedalus hung up his beautiful wings as an offering to the bitter wisdom of the gods." Daedalus has learned humility.
- Page 648—"Daedalus was sure he could easily solve the puzzle." Daedalus remains proud. His pride lures him into the trap that King Minos set.

WINGS

retold by Jane Yolen

Once in ancient Greece, when the gods dwelt on a high mountain overseeing the world, there lived a man named Daedalus who was known for the things he made.

He invented the axe, the bevel,[1] and the awl.[2] He built statues that were so lifelike they seemed ready to move. He designed a <u>maze</u> whose winding passages opened one into another as if without beginning, as if without end.

But Daedalus never understood the labyrinth[3] of his own heart. He was clever but he was not always kind. He was full of pride but he did not give others praise. He was a maker—but he was a taker, too.

 The gods always punish such a man.

---
1. **bevel:** tool for measuring and marking angles.
2. **awl:** pointed tool for making holes in materials.
3. **labyrinth** (lăb′ə-rĭnth′): maze.

WORDS TO KNOW
maze (māz) *n.* a confusing set of winding pathways through which it is difficult to find one's way

640

Mini-Lesson Grammar

CONJUNCTIONS Explain to students that a conjunction, such as *and* or *but,* can be used to join whole sentences. Point out that when two sentences are joined, a comma precedes the conjunction, as in the example shown.

Application Have students use a conjunction to join the following sentences.
1. Daedalus leaped out the tower window into the air. Icarus followed. *(Daedalus leaped out the tower window into the air, and Icarus followed.)*

2. Daedalus appreciated King Minos' praise. Daedalus' heart still remained with Athens, his old home. *(Daedalus appreciated King Minos' praise, but Daedalus' heart still remained with Athens, his old home.)*

Reteaching/Reinforcement
- *Grammar Handbook,* anthology p. 853
- *Grammar Mini-Lessons* transparencies, p. 42

 **The Writer's Craft**
What Are Conjunctions? p. 516–517

Conjunctions and Commas

The gods watched Daedalus, and they bided their time.

Daedalus made his way to Sicily, but Icarus perished in the sea.

640 THE LANGUAGE OF LITERATURE **TEACHER'S EDITION**

Illustration Copyright © 1991 Dennis Nolan. From *Wings* by Jane Yolen, reproduced by permission of Harcourt Brace & Company.

WINGS **641**

Literary Note

A Ask students to note the italicized sentences that occur throughout the story. Classical Greek drama contained a chorus, a group of omniscient "narrators" who were not characters in the play. The chorus supplied additional information (which was often prophetic) and gave emotional responses to characters' actions. These italicized sentences that occur throughout the story are similar to the chorus and serve the same purpose.

Mini-Lesson: Speaking, Listening, and Viewing

MUSIC Explain to students that selecting music to accompany an oral reading can help them understand and appreciate the mood and plot of "Wings."

Application Have students select two or three important scenes from the myth. You might encourage students to identify those scenes that convey a clear sense of mood or contain clear dramatic action. Then have students select music that they feel would reinforce the scenes' particular moods or actions. After rehearsing, students should perform oral readings of the scenes, accompanied by the music. Then invite the class to share their ideas on how the music changed their impressions of the scenes' events and descriptions.

THE LANGUAGE OF LITERATURE TEACHER'S EDITION **641**

CUSTOMIZING FOR
Students Acquiring English

1 If students need help understanding the meaning of the phrase *the very elements were his friends*, point out that in the Greek civilization, air, fire, earth, and water were said to be the four elements.

2 Point out that this myth is told in formal language more typical of writing than of speech and give as an example *Crete knew much of Daedalus*. Invite students to give the corresponding informal spoken sentence. *(The people who lived in Crete knew a lot about Daedalus.)*

Critical Thinking:
HYPOTHESIZING

B Have students discuss how Daedalus might have caused his nephew's death. *(Possible response: Perhaps his nephew was helping Daedalus on one of his building projects, and, for the sake of his art, Daedalus took risks with the nephew's safety.)*

Athens was the queen of cities and she had her princes. Daedalus was one. He was a prince and he was an artist, and he was proud of being both.

1 The very elements were his friends, and the people of Athens praised him.

"The gods will love you forever, Daedalus," they cried out to him as he walked through the city streets.

The gods listened and did not like to be told what to do.

A man who hears only praise becomes deaf. A man who sees no rival to his art becomes blind. Though he grew rich and he grew famous in the city, Daedalus also grew lazy and careless. And one day, without thought for the consequences, he caused the death of his young nephew, Prince Talos, who fell from a tall temple.

B Even a prince cannot kill a prince. The king of Athens punished Daedalus by sending him away, away from all he loved: away from the colorful pillars of the temples, away from the noisy, winding streets, away from the bustling shops and stalls, away from his smithy,[4] away from the sound of the dark sea. He would never be allowed to return.

And the gods watched the exile from on high.

Many days and nights Daedalus fled from his past. He crossed strange lands. He crossed strange seas. All he carried with him was a goatskin flask, the clothes on his back, and the knowledge in his hands. All he carried with him was grief that he had caused a child's death and grief that Athens was now dead to him.

He traveled a year and a day until he came at last to the island of Crete,[5] where the powerful King Minos[6] ruled.

The sands of Crete were different from his beloved Athens, the trees in the meadow were different, the flowers and the houses and the little, dark-eyed people were different. Only the birds seemed the same to Daedalus, and the sky—the vast, open, empty road of the sky.

But the gods found nothing below them strange.

2 Daedalus knew nothing of Crete, but Crete knew much of Daedalus, for his reputation had flown on wings before him. King Minos did not care that Daedalus was an exile or that he had been judged guilty of a terrible crime.

"You are the world's greatest builder, Daedalus," King Minos said. "Build me a labyrinth in which to hide a beast."

"A cage would be simpler," said Daedalus.

"This is no ordinary beast," said the king. "This is a monster. This is a prince. His name is Minotaur[7] and he is my wife's own son. He

---

4. **smithy:** workshop of a person who makes or repairs metal objects.
5. **Crete:** island about 200 miles southeast of Athens and the scene of many adventures in Greek literature.
6. **King Minos** (mī′nəs).
7. **Minotaur** (mĭn′ə-tôr′).

| WORDS TO KNOW | **rival** (rī′vəl) *n.* a person who tries to do as well as or better than another |
| | **exile** (ĕg′zīl) *n.* a person forced to live outside his or her country |

642

Mini-Lesson The Writer's Style

MAIN IDEA AND SUPPORTING DETAILS
Help students understand that, throughout the story, Yolen provides details to support the story's main ideas. For example, in the passage highlighted above, she gives supporting details in the form of images that allow readers to picture Daedalus' loss.

Application After Daedalus is exiled, he arrives in Crete. Have students write a paragraph using supporting details to amplify the main idea, "Crete was a strange place to Daedalus."

Reteaching/Reinforcement
• *Writing Mini-Lessons* transparencies, p. 29

Main Idea and Supporting Details, p. 218

---

642 THE LANGUAGE OF LITERATURE TEACHER'S EDITION

has a bull's head but a man's body. He eats human flesh. I cannot kill the queen's child. Even a king cannot kill a prince. And I cannot put him in a cage. But in a maze such as you might build, I could keep him hidden forever."

Daedalus bowed his head, but he smiled at the king's praise. He built a labyrinth for the king with countless corridors and winding ways. He devised such cunning passages that only he knew the secret pathway to its heart—he, and the Minotaur who lived there.

Yet the gods marked the secret way as well.

For many years Daedalus lived on the island of Crete, delighting in the praise he received from king and court. He made hundreds of new things for them. He made dolls with moving parts and a dancing floor inlaid with wood and stone for the princess Ariadne.[8] He made iron gates for the king and queen wrought[9] with cunning designs. He grew fond of the little dark-eyed islanders, and he married a Cretan wife. A son was born to them whom Daedalus named Icarus. The boy was small like his mother, but he had his father's quick, bright ways.

Daedalus taught Icarus many things, yet the one Daedalus valued most was the language of his lost Athens. Though he had a grand house and servants to do his bidding, though he had a wife he loved and a son he adored, Daedalus was not entirely happy. His heart still lay in Athens, the land of his youth, and the words he spoke with his son helped keep the memory of Athens alive.

One night a handsome young man came to Daedalus' house, led by a lovesick Princess Ariadne. The young man spoke with Daedalus in that Athenian tongue.

"I am Theseus,[10] a prince of Athens, where your name is still remembered with praise. It is said that Daedalus was more than a prince, that he had the gods in his hands. Surely such a man has not forgotten Athens."

Daedalus shook his head. "I thought Athens had forgotten me."

"Athens remembers and Athens needs your help, O prince," said Theseus.

"Help? What help can I give Athens, when I am so far from home?"

"Then you do not know . . . ," Theseus began.

"Know what?"

> HE DEVISED SUCH CUNNING PASSAGES THAT ONLY HE KNEW THE SECRET PATHWAY TO ITS HEART.

---

8. **Ariadne** (ăr´ē-ăd´nē): daughter of King Minos.
9. **wrought** (rôt): decorated.
10. **Theseus** (thē´sē-əs): legendary Greek hero.

WINGS **643**

Linking to History

The term *Minoan* derives from several legendary rulers of Crete, one of whom is featured in "Wings." *Minoan* denotes the culture that developed in the Aegean region before the Greeks arrived. Minoan culture reached its zenith around 2000 B.C. Scholars knew nothing about this civilization until the late 19th century, when archaeological discoveries revealed the historical underpinnings of many Greek myths and legends.

STRATEGIC READING FOR Less-Proficient Readers

Ask students to describe Daedalus' personality. *(Possible responses: clever, proud, not always kind)* Making Inferences

- Ask students how Daedalus adjusted to his new home in Crete. *(Possible responses: Well; he made a new life for himself as a successful inventor with a wife and child whom he loved. Not so well; his heart remained in Athens.)* Making Judgments

Set a Purpose Have students read to learn how Daedalus falls out of favor with King Minos.

Mini-Lesson Spelling

THE PREFIX EX- Tell students that the prefix ex- means "out" or "beyond." It is added to word roots.

ex + tra = extra

ex + pect = expect

Application Have students add the prefix ex- to each of these roots.

1. pense *(expense)*
2. pert *(expert)*
3. perience *(experience)*
4. cuse *(excuse)*
5. tent *(extent)*
6. periment *(experiment)*
7. terior *(exterior)*
8. tinguish *(extinguish)*
9. clamation *(exclamation)*
10. ternal *(external)*

Ask students to look for more words that fit this pattern, in their own writing and in things that they read, and to add these words to their personal word lists.

Reteaching/Reinforcement
- Unit Six Resource Book, p. 6

THE LANGUAGE OF LITERATURE TEACHER'S EDITION **643**

Active Reading: EVALUATE

E Ask students why they think Daedalus has built the labyrinth for King Minos. *(Possible response: Daedalus was flattered by the praise of King Minos and he thought no harm would come of it.)*

Active Reading: CONNECT

F Invite students to connect this myth to their own lives. Ask them to describe how they might feel if they were in Daedalus' position. Would they feel relief at the idea of saving the Athenian children? Would they feel any remorse about being responsible for the death of the Minotaur? Would they feel loyalty to King Minos or to their native city of Athens?

STRATEGIC READING FOR
Less-Proficient Readers

G Ask students how Daedalus falls out of favor with King Minos. *(Possible response: He reveals the secret of the maze and helps kill the monster that King Minos' wife had borne.)* **Relating Cause and Effect**

Set a Purpose Have students read to discover Daedalus' plan to escape and the warning he gives to Icarus.

"That every seven years Athens must send a tribute[11] of boys and girls to King Minos. He puts them into the labyrinth you devised, and the monster Minotaur devours them there."

Horrified, Daedalus thought of the bright-eyed boys and girls he had known in Athens. He thought of his own dark-eyed son asleep in his cot. He remembered his nephew, Talos, whose eyes had been closed by death. "How can I help?"

"Only you know the way through the maze," said Theseus. "Show me the way that I may slay the monster."

"I will show you," said Daedalus thoughtfully, "but Princess Ariadne must go as well. The Minotaur is her half-brother. He will not hurt her. She will be able to lead you to him, right into the heart of the maze."

The gods listened to the plan and nodded gravely.

Daedalus drew them a map and gave Princess Ariadne a thread to tie at her waist, that she might unwind it as they went and so find the way back out of the twisting corridors.

Hand in hand, Theseus and Ariadne left, and Daedalus went into his son's room. He looked down at the sleeping boy.

"I am a prince of Athens," he whispered. "I did what must be done."

If Icarus heard his father's voice, he did not stir. He was dreaming still as Ariadne and Theseus threaded their way to the very center of the maze. And before he awakened, they had killed the Minotaur and fled from Crete, taking the boys and girls of Athens with them. They took all hope of Daedalus' safety as well.

Then the gods looked thoughtful and they did not smile.

When King Minos heard that the Minotaur had been slain and Ariadne taken, he guessed that Daedalus had betrayed him, for no one else knew the secret of the maze. He ordered Daedalus thrown into a high prison tower.

"Thus do kings reward traitors!" cried Minos. Then he added, "See that you care for your own son better than you cared for my wife's unfortunate child." He threw Icarus into the tower, too, and slammed the great iron gate shut with his own hand.

The tiny tower room, with its single window overlooking the sea, was Daedalus' home now. Gone was Athens, where he had been a prince; gone was Crete, where he had been a rich man. All he had left was one small room, with a wooden bench and straw pallets[12] on the floor.

Day after day young Icarus stood on the bench and watched through the window as the seabirds dipped and soared over the waves.

"Father!" Icarus called each day. "Come and watch the birds."

But Daedalus would not. Day after day, he leaned against the wall or lay on a pallet

---

11. **tribute:** forced payment.
12. **pallets:** thin mattresses laid directly on the floor.

WORDS TO KNOW
gravely (grāv′lē) *adv.* in a very serious manner

644

Assessment Option

INFORMAL To assess students' understanding of "Wings," have them create a time line, listing in order the events of the story. Encourage them to space out their sequence according to the length of time that occurs between events. For instance, it takes a year and a half for Daedalus to reach Crete but then several years pass before he meets Theseus. Encourage students to look for words or phrases that signal time order of events.

Rubric

3 Full Accomplishment Student creates time line that accurately lists all key events of the selections. Marking of time line demonstrates a good understanding of time lapse between events.

2 Substantial Accomplishment Student creates a time line that lists most key events of the story and markings indicate a general understanding of time lapse between events.

1 Little or Partial Accomplishment Student's time line does not include several key events. Student can not mark time line to indicate time lapse between events.

644 THE LANGUAGE OF LITERATURE TEACHER'S EDITION

bemoaning[13] his fate and cursing the gods who had done this thing to him.

The gods heard his curses and they grew angry.

One bright day Icarus took his father by the hand, leading him to the window.

"Look, Father," he said, pointing to the birds. "See how beautiful their wings are. See how easily they fly."

Just to please the boy, Daedalus looked. Then he clapped his hands to his eyes. "What a fool I have been," he whispered. "What a fool. Minos may have forbidden me sea and land, but he has left me the air. Oh, my son, though the king is ever so great and powerful, he does not rule the sky. It is the gods' own road, and I am a favorite of the gods. To think a child has shown me the way!"

Every day after that, Daedalus and Icarus coaxed the birds to their windows with bread crumbs saved from their meager meals. And every day gulls, gannets, and petrels, cormorants and pelicans, shearwaters and grebes, came to the sill. Daedalus stroked the feeding birds with his clever hands and harvested handfuls of feathers. And Icarus, as if playing a game, grouped the feathers on the floor in order of size, just as his father instructed.

But it was no game. Soon the small piles of feathers became big piles, the big piles, great heaps. Then clever Daedalus, using a needle he had shaped from a bit of bone left over from dinner and thread pulled out of his own shirt, sewed together small feathers, overlapping them with the larger, gently curving them in great arcs. He fastened the ends with molded candle wax and made straps with the leather from their sandals.

At last Icarus understood. "Wings, Father!" he cried, clapping his hands together in delight. "Wings!"

At that the gods laughed, and it was thunder over water.

They made four wings in all, a pair for each of them. Icarus had the smaller pair, for he was still a boy. They practiced for days in the tower, slipping their arms through the straps, raising and lowering the wings, until their arms had grown strong and used to the weight. They hid the wings beneath their pallets whenever the guards came by.

At last they were ready. Daedalus kneeled before his son.

"Your arms are strong now, Icarus," he said, "but do not forget my warning."

---

13. **bemoaning:** complaining about.

> "MINOS MAY HAVE FORBIDDEN ME SEA AND LAND, BUT HE HAS LEFT ME THE AIR."

WORDS TO KNOW
meager (mē′gər) *adj.* of poor quality or inadequate amount

645

Literary Concept:
CHARACTERIZATION

H Ask students what Daedalus' words reveal about his self-understanding. (*Possible response: Daedalus realizes he has been arrogant, proud, and presumptuous about his standing with the gods, but he is still too proud to benefit from this knowledge.*)

Active Reading: EVALUATE

I Have students discuss the gods' reaction to Icarus' delight. (*Possible response: The gods' thunderous laughter implies foreboding and is contemptuous. This does not bode well for the plan's success.*)

Mini-Lesson  Reading Skills/Strategies

ACTIVE READING: CONNECT Remind students that they can increase their understanding of a selection by relating its plot and characters to their own personal experiences.

Application Have students choose a character in "Wings" and record their connections with that character in a chart like the one shown.

Reteaching/Reinforcement
- *Unit Six Resource Book,* p. 5

Character	Experience	Personal Experience
Icarus	Didn't heed his father's warning about flying too high or too low and had a deadly accident.	Didn't heed my mom's warning about being more careful with my bike and it was stolen.

THE LANGUAGE OF LITERATURE **Teacher's Edition** **645**

STRATEGIC READING FOR
Less-Proficient Readers

J Ask students to explain how Daedalus and Icarus plan to escape. *(Daedalus and Icarus create two pairs of wings from bird feathers, thread, wax, and leather. He and Icarus plan to fly away.)*
Summarizing

- What warning does Daedalus give Icarus? *(not to fly too high nor too low)*
Restating

Set a Purpose Have students read to find out the sequence of events through which the conflict between Daedalus and King Minos is resolved.

CUSTOMIZING FOR
Multiple Learning Styles

K Spatial Learners Invite students to make a flip book or draw a storyboard showing Icarus' flight and fall.

Literary Concept:
CHARACTERIZATION

L Ask students what new aspect of the gods' character the italicized words reveal. *(Possible response: The gods are sympathetic as well as jealous. They show sadness that a child has died.)*

The boy nodded solemnly, his dark eyes wide. "I must not fly too low or the water will soak the feathers. I must not fly too high or the sun will melt the wax."

"Remember," his father said. "Remember."

The gods trembled, causing birds to fall through the bright air.

Daedalus climbed onto the sill. The wings made him clumsy but he did not fall. He helped Icarus up.

First the child, then the man, leaped out into the air. They pumped once and then twice with their arms. The wind caught the feathers of the wings and pushed them upward into the Cretan sky.

Wingtip to wingtip they flew, writing the lines of their escape on the air. Some watchers below took them for eagles. Most took them for gods.

As they flew, Daedalus concentrated on long, steady strokes. He remembered earlier days, when the elements had been his friends: fire and water and air. Now, it seemed, they were his friends once more.

But young Icarus had no such memories to steady his wings. He beat them with abandon, glorying in his freedom. He slipped away from his father's careful pattern along a wild stream of wind.

"Icarus, my son—remember!" Daedalus cried out.

But Icarus spiraled higher and higher and higher still. He did not hear his father's voice. He heard only the music of the wind; he heard only the sighing of the gods.

He passed the birds. He passed the clouds. He passed into the realm of the sun. Too late he felt the wax run down his arms; too late he smelled the singe of feathers. Surprised, he hung solid in the air. Then, like a star in nova,[14] he tumbled from the sky, down, down, down into the waiting sea.

And the gods wept bitterly for the child.

"Where are you, my son?" Daedalus called. He circled the water, looking desperately for some sign. All he saw were seven feathers afloat on the sea, spinning into different patterns with each passing wave.

Weeping, he flew away over the dark sea to the isle of Sicily. There he built a temple to the god Apollo, for Apollo stood for life and light, and never grew old but remained a beautiful boy forever. On the temple walls Daedalus hung up his beautiful wings as an offering to the bitter wisdom of the gods.

So Daedalus' story ended—and yet it did not. For in Sicily he was received kindly by King Cocalus,[15] who was well pleased with his skills.

Meanwhile, back in Crete, enraged at his prisoners' escape, King Minos was determined to find and punish them. He proclaimed a great reward for anyone skilled enough to pass

---

14. **a star in nova:** a star that fades away after a period of unusual brilliance.
15. **King Cocalus** (kŏk′ə-ləs).

WORDS TO KNOW
abandon (ə-băn′dən) *n.* a wildness; unrestricted freedom of action
proclaim (prō-klām′) *v.* to announce officially

Mini-Lesson — Study Skills

SKIMMING Remind students that skimming—reading only the most important parts and skipping everything else—is a kind of fast reading that can give them a general idea of what a selection is about. Skimming is also useful for study and review.

Application Have students reread the highlighted text above. Then have them skim the selection and reread an earlier passage that featured the number seven—when it was explained how King Minos fed Athenian children to the Minotaur. Ask students what, if anything, these two passages might have to do with each other. *(Possible response: Seven is a significant symbolic number that ties the two passages together. Daedalus was partly responsible for the deaths of Athenian children every seven years. Now he has in some sense paid for his part in their deaths by losing his own son. Icarus leaves behind seven feathers as he falls to his death.)*

Illustration Copyright © 1991 Dennis Nolan. From *Wings* by Jane Yolen, reproduced by permission of Harcourt Brace & Company.

WINGS **647**

Mini-Lesson  Literary Concepts

REVIEWING TONE Remind students that tone refers to the author's attitude toward his or her subject. The tone may reflect one strong feeling or several emotions. In "Wings," several emotions create a rich and complex tone.

Application Have students work in small groups to locate places in "Wings" that show the writer expressing at least two strong feelings. *(Possible responses: Page 646—"And the gods wept bitterly for the child." Page 645—"'Wings, Father!' he cried, clapping his hands together in delight.")* Have students write a sentence describing the author's tone in their own words. Then ask students to consider how a storyteller might convey the same tone, using his or her voice, facial expressions, and gestures. Encourage students to display their response in a chart of their own design.

THE LANGUAGE OF LITERATURE TEACHER'S EDITION **647**

STRATEGIC READING FOR
Less-Proficient Readers

M Have students describe the sequence of events through which the conflict between Daedalus and King Minos is resolved. *(Possible response: King Minos tries to catch Daedalus by offering a prize for solving a mechanical puzzle; Daedalus falls into the trap by entering and winning the contest, which allows King Minos to trace his whereabouts to Sicily; the king of Sicily fights and kills King Minos to save Daedalus' life.)* **Noting Sequence of Events**

From Personal Response to Critical Analysis

1. How does reading about Icarus' life in the tower prison, and his death in escaping, make you feel toward Icarus and his father Daedalus? Briefly describe your reactions in your notebook. *(Responses will vary.)*

2. What image do you have of King Minos's relationship with Daedalus. *(Possible responses: Daedalus and King Minos were alternately the best of friends and the worst of enemies because they were so much alike. Both were proud. Each saw a reflection of himself in the other.)*

3. What lessons, if any, do you think Daedalus learned? *(Possible responses: He learns that too much pride has its cost. He doesn't learn anything since Minos was able to use Daedalus' pride to trick him.)*

---

a silken thread through the closed spiral of a seashell. He knew that if Daedalus was alive, he could not resist the lure of such a game.

Daedalus was sure he could easily solve the puzzle. He bored a small hole in one end of a shell, moistened it with a bit of honey, then closed up the hole. Fastening a thread to an ant, he put the insect into the shell. The ant <u>scurried</u> through the twisting labyrinth toward the sweet smell, running as easily as Princess Ariadne had run through the maze with the thread unwinding at her waist. When the ant emerged from the other end, it had pulled the silken thread through the spirals of the shell.

Though he used a false name to claim the prize, Daedalus did not fool King Minos. Minos knew the winner was his old enemy. So, with a mighty army, Minos sailed to Sicily to bring Daedalus back.

But King Cocalus would not give up Daedalus to the foreign invaders, and a great battle was fought. With Daedalus' help, King Cocalus was victorious and King Minos was killed. Minos was clever but he was not kind. He had a heart scabbed over with old remembered wounds. ❖

M

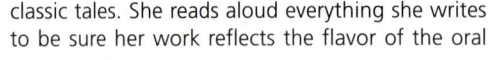

JANE YOLEN

A storyteller, lecturer, and mother of three, Jane Yolen grew up in New York City in a family of writers. Yolen is best known for her folk and fairy tales. She is particularly interested in stories that have been passed from one storyteller to another for hundreds of years. Yolen's style is to give modern twists to familiar stories or to create original stories based on the feel and structure of classic tales. She reads aloud everything she writes to be sure her work reflects the flavor of the oral tradition. *Wings*, her version of the myth of Daedalus and Icarus, won a 1992 Children's Choice award. Yolen is also known for her science fiction and fantasy stories, such as *Dragon's Blood*, the first volume of a three-part fantasy about dragons.

OTHER WORKS *The Girl Who Cried Flowers and Other Tales, Owl Moon, Ring of Earth, Favorite Folktales from Around the World, The Devil's Arithmetic*

1939–

WORDS TO KNOW   **scurry** (skûr′ē) *v.* to run quickly; scamper

648

COMPREHENSION CHECK

1. What made Daedalus famous in Athens? *(the things that he made or invented, including incredibly lifelike statues, the axe, bevel, and awl)*

2. What led to Daedalus' exile from Athens? *(He was blamed for the death of his nephew.)*

3. How did Daedalus help kill the Minotaur? *(Daedalus devised a strategy that allowed Theseus to kill the monster and escape alive.)*

4. What warning did Icarus fail to heed? *(Daedalus' warning not to fly too close to the sun, which would melt the wax on the wing.)*

5. What happens to Icarus? *(He falls to his death when the sun melts the wax on his wings.)*

6. What happens to King Minos? *(He is killed in a battle while trying to recapture Daedalus.)*

THE RED LION

retold by Diane Wolkstein

When the King of Persia[1] died, there was great weeping, for he had been a brave and wise leader. Yet in little more than a month the mourning would be over, and the King's son, Azgid, would be crowned. But before the Prince could be crowned, he would have to prove his courage, just as every Prince before him had done, by fighting the Red Lion.

One day during this time the Vizier[2] went to the young Prince and urged him to prepare himself for the contest. Azgid trembled. He had always been afraid of lions, and the Red Lion was the most <u>ferocious</u> of lions. He decided to run away.

That night, when it was very dark, he crept out of his bedroom, mounted his horse, and rode off. He rode two days and nights. On the morning of the third day he entered a

---

1. **Persia:** ancient empire of southwest Asia.
2. **Vizier** (vĭ-zîr′): in Moslem countries, a high officer in the government.

WORDS TO KNOW — **ferocious** (fə-rō′shəs) *adj.* fierce; savage; violently cruel

---

Multicultural Perspectives

LION HUNTING The male lion is often misrepresented as a fierce man-hunter. In fact, lionesses are the ones who do most of the hunting in the pride, and their prey is other large animals, not humans. Generally, lions will not attack humans unless provoked. However, humans have been hunting lions for centuries to protect their livestock or to show their bravery as hunters. As far back as 1375 B.C., Pharaoh Amenhotep III used a bow and arrows to hunt lions from a chariot. He killed 102 lions this way. Saint Louis rode on horseback to hunt lions during the seventh Crusade. The Masai tribe of East Africa hunted lions on foot.

In ancient times, lions roamed Europe, the Middle East, India, and Africa. There are no longer any lions left in the Middle East (where "The Red Lion" is set) nor in northern Africa. Asian lions are an endangered species; those that remain reside primarily in the Gir forest of India. There are still lions in east and central Africa, mostly on protected reserves.

CUSTOMIZING FOR
Gifted and Talented Students

Have students think about Azgid's strengths as well as his weaknesses, or fears. Ask students what impression Azgid makes on the people he encounters.

Possible responses:

- Page 651—"The shepherd took up his flute and played for the clouds, for the winds, for his sheep, and for the stranger."

- Page 652—"'My men are pleased with your spirit,' [the sheik] said, 'and with your skill at hunting. But there will soon be a battle. My men want to know if they can rely on your strength and courage.'" Azgid impresses the sheik as a skillful rider, hunter, and potential warrior.

- Page 652—"The Emir, who was impressed with Azgid's good manners and fine speech, said to his daughter, 'My child, show this young man our palace and gardens, and be certain he is invited to the entertainment this evening.'" Azgid so impresses the emir that the emir sees him as a potential son-in-law.

Copyright © 1977 Ed Young. Reprinted by permission of McIntosh and Otis, Inc.

650 UNIT SIX: THE ORAL TRADITION

Mini-Lesson: Speaking, Listening, and Viewing

MUSIC Explain to students that music can be used to convey emotions and feeling. In "The Red Lion," the shepherd plays a flute to calm his sheep and Perizide plays a lute to entertain Azgid, who feels his soul lift as he listens.

Application Divide the class into small groups and research music of the Middle East, the region where this story originates. If feasible, encourage some groups to select flute music that the shepherd may have played while other groups look for lute music Perizide might have played. Suggest students check the audio collection of their local library. Have groups play their selections for the class. If Middle Eastern recordings are not readily available, suggest students select and play for the class other suitable wind instruments, such as the pan flute from Ireland.

650 THE LANGUAGE OF LITERATURE TEACHER'S EDITION

grove of trees and heard a sweet melody. Dismounting, he walked quietly until he saw a shepherd sitting in a clearing and playing a flute. All about the shepherd the sheep stood listening.

"God be with you," said the shepherd to the stranger.

"And with you," the Prince replied, "but please do not stop your song."

The shepherd took up his flute and played for the clouds, for the winds, for his sheep, and for the stranger.

When he finished, Azgid spoke: "Surely you are wondering who I am. I wish I could tell you my name. But it is a secret that must stay locked in my heart. I beg you to believe me; I am no enemy. I am an honorable youth who has been forced to flee from his home."

"You are welcome to stay with me," the shepherd answered. "I would be glad of your company, and I can show you a place that will cause you to forget your troubles."

Hour after hour the Prince and the shepherd walked, the Prince leading his horse and the sheep following behind the shepherd. As the sun was setting, they came to the most beautiful valley Azgid had ever seen. It was perfectly quiet, and Azgid and the shepherd sat and gazed in wonder at the hills in front of them. Then suddenly the shepherd jumped up.

"Time to go!" he said.

"But why must we leave so quickly?" asked the Prince. "Can there be any place on earth more lovely?"

"It *is* beautiful," the shepherd agreed. But then he raised his sleeve, revealing a long, cruel red scar. He traced his finger along the scar and said: "Lions! Once I was late returning to the village, and the village gates were closed. This is the result. I do not want it to happen a second time."

"Then return to the village with the sheep,"

the Prince said, "but I cannot stay with you." He mounted his horse and rode north. He rode two days and nights, and on the third morning he came to a desert.

He and his horse were tired and hungry and thirsty. The wind blew sand in the Prince's face, and he was riding with his eyes half-shut when suddenly his horse neighed. Through the streaming sands Azgid saw the tents of an Arab camp. His horse began to prance, but he pulled back on the bridle and continued to ride slowly to show that his was a peaceful visit.

An Arab Sheik[3] greeted him with courtesy. He offered the Prince food and had his horse fed and cared for. After the Prince had eaten, he said to the Sheik: "Forgive me if I do not reveal my name. Because of certain troubles it is a secret that must stay locked in my heart. But I have jewels and precious stones I would gladly give you if you would allow me to remain with you."

"You are our guest," the Sheik replied, and he refused to accept any of the Prince's treasures.

I WISH I COULD TELL YOU MY NAME. BUT IT IS A SECRET THAT MUST STAY LOCKED IN MY HEART.

The following morning the Sheik provided the Prince with a magnificent stallion, and for the next three days the Prince rode with the Sheik and his companions, hunting antelope.

---

3. **Sheik** (shēk): the leader of an Arab family, tribe, or village.

THE RED LION 651

Mini-Lesson: Speaking, Listening, and Viewing

DRAMA PERFORMANCE Tell students that a drama performance is one way of storytelling. Drama, because it involves several people, movement, and sometimes music or dance, provides audiences with a rich, vivid listening and viewing experience.

Application Have students work in small groups to assign roles and create a drama performance of "The Red Lion." Assign each group one scene. Encourage students to incorporate music and sound effects into their performances. Allow groups to perform for the class. If possible, have volunteers videotape the performances for later playback and assessment.

Copyright © 1977 Ed Young. Reprinted by permission of McIntosh and Otis, Inc.

On the third evening the Sheik spoke to the Prince. "My men are pleased with your spirit," he said, "and with your skill at hunting. But there will soon be a battle. My men want to know if they can rely on your strength and courage. To the south lies a range of hills known as the Red Hills. It is lion country. Ride there tomorrow on the stallion. Take your sword and spear, and bring us back the hide of one of these fierce lions to show us we can count on you on the day of battle."

That night, when it was very still, the Prince slipped out of his tent. He stroked the beloved stallion he had ridden and whispered good-bye in his ear. Then he mounted his own horse and rode west.

After two days and nights he came to a country of rolling meadows and green fields. There in the distance he saw a splendid red sandstone palace.

At the gates the Prince took off his ring and asked the guard to present it to the Emir.[4] Immediately the Prince was invited to enter the palace.

As the Prince was explaining his situation to the Emir, Perizide,[5] the Emir's daughter, appeared. The Emir, who was impressed with Azgid's good manners and fine speech, said to his daughter, "My child, show this young man our palace and gardens, and be certain he is invited to the entertainment this evening."

Perizide led the Prince through room after room and then out into the garden. There were flowers and trees of every kind in the garden, and in the middle was an oval-shaped pool filled with rose water. In the water floated one perfect lily. It was perfect and yet not as beautiful as Perizide.

After dinner in the cool evening air, Perizide herself provided the entertainment. She played the lute[6] and sang. As Azgid listened, he felt his soul rising higher and higher. "This is why I have run away," he thought, "so I might find Perizide."

"RRRAAGGGGGH!"

"What was *that*?" cried the Prince, jumping to his feet.

"Oh, that's just our guard Boulak.[7] He's yawning."

"*Yawning*?" repeated the Prince.

"Yes," said Perizide. "He does that when it is late. I will say goodnight now."

After Perizide left, the Emir stood up. "It is late for me, too. Come, I will show you to your bedroom."

They had just begun to climb the staircase when Azgid looked up. His hand froze on the banister. There at the top of the landing was an enormous lion.

"Oh, that's just Boulak," said the Emir. "He's perfectly harmless. He never attacks unless someone is afraid of him."

"Oh, I'm not, ah, quite r-r-ready for, ah, I'm not r-ready for s-s-sleep," faltered[8] the Prince.

"Well, then, come up when you wish," said the Emir. "Yours is the first bedroom on the right."

Azgid backed down the stairs. He backed

---

4. **Emir** (ĭ-mîr´): in Moslem countries, a ruler or prince.
5. **Perizide** (pär´ĭ-zēd´).
6. **lute:** an early stringed instrument, similar to a guitar.
7. **Boulak** (boo´lăk).
8. **faltered:** said in a weak or hesitant way.

652 UNIT SIX: THE ORAL TRADITION

Multicultural Perspectives

PERSIAN MUSIC Two of the most important instruments in Islamic music are the human voice and the lute. Persian music is one form of Islamic music, ancient Persia (like Iran today) having been an Islamic country.

In Persian music the composer and performer are the same. The player improvises on traditional melodies which, like stories in the oral tradition, are passed down from one generation to another.

Solo performances have a strong tradition within Islamic music; performers often play and/or sing a series of independent music sections. Audiences may interject their approval after any of the parts, not necessarily waiting until the conclusion of the performance. Approval may consist of the audience applauding or, more often shouting "*Allah!*" which means "God" and is the root of the Spanish exclamation "*Olé!*"

down the corridor and into the music room and locked the doors. He sat on a chair and waited. Soon he heard the lion padding down the stairs. He heard him claw at the door. The door shook. The lion roared: "RRAAAGGGH!"

Azgid thought the lion would tear down the door and devour him, but he just sat there. He did not try to run away. The lion roared again: "RRAAAAAAGGH!"

Azgid listened. The lion roared a third time. Suddenly the Prince realized that the roars were not threats. They were warnings. They were telling him: Three times you have run away. If you run away again—wherever you may go—a lion will be waiting.

A lion would always be waiting for the Prince until he went home to fight his own lion.

Azgid listened. Boulak did not roar again. Then he heard the lion padding back up the stairs.

Early the next morning the Prince explained that he had to return home at once. He mounted his horse and, thinking only of the Red Lion, rode day and night until he reached his palace.

At the appointed time, Azgid entered the crowded arena. The Emir, Perizide, the Sheik, and the shepherd were all there, seated in the stands. But the Prince did not look up. No, his eyes were on the doors from which the Red Lion would emerge. He waited.

The doors opened. The lion sprang out. Azgid stood firm, his spear in his hand. The lion roared and leapt—right over the head of Azgid. When Azgid whirled around to throw his spear, he saw the Red Lion lying on his back, playfully waving his paws in the air like a happy puppy. Then the lion trotted up to Azgid and affectionately licked his hands.

The Red Lion was tame. Every lion that had ever fought a Prince of Persia had been tame. Only fear would make him ferocious.

And so Azgid was crowned King of Persia. And in due time he married Perizide, and the two lived together happily and ruled their kingdom wisely and well. ❖

DIANE WOLKSTEIN

1942–

An award-winning author and storyteller, Diane Wolkstein was born in New York City. After attending Smith College, she studied pantomime in Paris for a year. From 1968 to 1980, she hosted a weekly radio show, *Stories from Many Lands,* that led one newspaper writer to describe her as "New York City's official storyteller."

Wolkstein's interest in world folklore is reflected in her books and recordings of stories, which range from myths of the Hopi Indians to Biblical stories, from Haitian folk tales to Estonian fairy tales. *The Red Lion: A Tale of Ancient Persia* is based on an old Persian story, probably a Sufi (Moslem) "teaching tale." In addition to writing books for children and young adults, Wolkstein teaches mythology and children's literature and leads storytelling workshops throughout the United States.

OTHER WORKS *The Banza, Esther's Story, Little Mouse's Painting, The Magic Orange Tree and Other Haitian Folk Tales*

WORDS TO KNOW
devour (dĭ-vour′) *v.* to eat up hungrily; swallow up

STRATEGIC READING FOR
Less-Proficient Readers

Set a Purpose Have students note, as they read "Why Monkeys Live in Trees," what test the animals undergo to win a prize.

CUSTOMIZING FOR
Students Acquiring English

1 Point out that the suffix *-ness* is often added to adjectives in order to form nouns; *handsomeness* therefore refers to the leopard's quality of being handsome. If you wish, ask volunteers to form similar nouns from the adjectives *kind, dry, wild,* and *slow.*

2 Point out that *strode* is a past-tense verb and invite students to give the corresponding present-tense form. *(stride)* If they need a hint, write *rode* on the board.

Literary Concept:
CHARACTERIZATION

A Ask students to name Leopard's main character trait. Ask students what the beginning of the folk tale reveals about Leopard. *(Possible response: The folk tale's opening says that gazing at his own reflection is Leopard's favorite activity. This suggests Leopard is vain.)*

Literary Concept: HUMOR

B Have students identify a nonsense word that is used to describe Leopard's journey to the contest. *(north-by-somersault)*

Literary Links

C Have students identify something in the selection "Ghost of the Lagoon" (page 39) that was not what it seemed to be. *(The white ghost of the lagoon was actually a great white shark.)*

WHY MONKEYS LIVE IN TREES

retold by Julius Lester

One day Leopard was looking at his reflection in a pool of water. Looking at himself was Leopard's favorite thing in the world to do. Leopard gazed, wanting to be sure that every hair was straight and that all his spots were where they were supposed to be. This took many hours of looking at his reflection, which Leopard did not mind at all.

Finally he was satisfied that nothing was disturbing his handsomeness, and he turned away from the pool of water. At that exact moment, one of Leopard's children ran up to him.

"Daddy! Daddy! Are you going to be in the contest?"

"What contest?" Leopard wanted to know. If it was a beauty contest, of course he was going to be in it.

"I don't know. Crow the Messenger just flew by. She said that King Gorilla said there was going to be a contest."

Without another word, Leopard set off. He went north-by-northeast, made a right turn at the mulberry bush and traveled east-by-south-by-west until he came to a hole in the ground. He went around in a circle five times and headed north-by-somersault until he came to a big clearing in the middle of the jungle, and that's where King Gorilla was.

King Gorilla sat at one end of the clearing on his throne. Opposite him, at the other side of the clearing, all the animals sat in a semicircle. In the middle, between King Gorilla and the animals, was a huge mound of what looked like black dust.

Leopard looked around with calm dignity. Then he strode regally[1] over to his friend, Lion.

---
1. **strode regally:** walked in a grand manner, like a king or queen.

654 UNIT SIX: THE ORAL TRADITION

Mini-Lesson: Speaking, Listening, and Viewing

ART Explain to students that just as writers plan stories before they begin writing, so artists plan their compositions. Scale, perspective, light and darkness, and color are some elements of artistic composition.

Application Have small groups of students create a mural that represents the events in "Why Monkeys Live in Trees." Remind students to plan their compositions before they begin. Encourage students to attempt a chronological approach to their murals, so that a viewer may see events unfolding as he or she looks from left to right or top to bottom.

Allow students to view murals created in each group. As a class, analyze each composition. Ask students to describe how the murals show the tale unfolding in time.

654 THE LANGUAGE OF LITERATURE TEACHER'S EDITION

Exotic Landscape (1910), Henri Rousseau. Oil on canvas, 51 ¼" × 64". The Norton Simon Foundation, Pasadena, California.

Art Note

Exotic Landscape by Henri Rousseau
Rousseau (1844–1910), today celebrated as a pioneer in modern art, was unappreciated during his lifetime and was buried in a pauper's grave. Rousseau's paintings combine the brilliant colors and decorative patterns of the impressionists with precise detail and highly polished surfaces of his own devising. In addition to subjects from French middle class life, such as wedding parties and patriotic celebrations, Rousseau painted realistic figures in fantastical settings.

Reading the Art *What aspects of this painting look realistic? What aspects do not? How does the painting relate to the selection?*

STRATEGIC READING FOR
Less-Proficient Readers

D Ask students what test the animals undergo to win a prize. *(The animals compete to see who can eat a mound of black dust in one day.)* **Noting Relevant Details**

Set a Purpose Have students read to find out who wins the contest and how.

Active Reading: CLARIFY

E Ask students to name something besides why monkeys live in trees that is explained in this folk tale. *(why chickens don't have ears)*

Active Reading: EVALUATE

F Have students evaluate the attitudes of the animals who are happy because they still have a chance to win the pot of gold, despite having seen the effects of the dust on Hippopotamus. Ask students if the thought of the pot of gold is making the animals greedy and blind to danger.

CUSTOMIZING FOR
Multiple Learning Styles

G **Bodily-Kinesthetic Learners** Students may enjoy pantomiming the reactions of various animals after each has eaten the black pepper. Encourage students to use body language to suggest the movement or characteristic of one of the animals, and have other students guess which animal is being mimed.

"What's that?" he asked, pointing to the mound of black dust.

"Don't know," Lion replied. "King Gorilla said he will give a pot of gold to whoever can eat it in one day. I can eat it in an hour."

Leopard laughed. "I'll eat it in a half hour."

It was Hippopotamus's turn to laugh. "As big as my mouth is, I'll eat that mound in one gulp."

The time came for the contest. King Gorilla had the animals pick numbers to see who would go in what order. To everybody's dismay, Hippopotamus drew Number 1.

Hippopotamus walked over to the mound of black dust. It was bigger than he had thought. It was much too big to eat in one gulp. Nonetheless, Hippopotamus opened his mouth as wide as he could, and that was very wide indeed, and took a mouthful of the black dust.

He started chewing. Suddenly he leaped straight into the air and screamed. He screamed so loudly that it knocked the ears off the chickens, and that's why to this day chickens don't have ears.

Hippopotamus screamed and Hippopotamus yelled. Hippopotamus roared and Hippopotamus bellowed. Then he started sneezing and crying, and tears rolled down his face like he was standing in the shower. Hippopotamus ran to the river and drank as much water as he could, and that was very much, indeed, to cool his mouth and tongue and throat.

The animals didn't understand what had happened to Hippopotamus, but they didn't care. They were happy because they still had a chance to win the pot of gold. Of course, if they had known that the mound of black dust was really a mound of black pepper, maybe they wouldn't have wanted the gold.

Nobody was more happy than Leopard

HIPPOPOTAMUS ROARED AND HIPPOPOTAMUS BELLOWED. THEN HE STARTED SNEEZING AND CRYING.

because he had drawn Number 2. He walked up to the black mound and sniffed at it.

"AAAAAAAAACHOOOOOOO!" Leopard didn't like that, but then he remembered the pot of gold. He opened his mouth wide, took a mouthful and started chewing and swallowing.

Leopard leaped straight into the air, did a back double flip and screamed. He yelled and he roared and he bellowed and, finally, he started sneezing and crying, tears rolling down his face like a waterfall. Leopard ran to the river and washed out his mouth and throat and tongue.

Lion was next, and the same thing happened to him as it did to all the animals. Finally only Monkey remained.

Monkey approached King Gorilla. "I know I can eat all of whatever that is, but after each mouthful, I'll need to lie down in the tall grasses and rest."

King Gorilla said that was okay.

Monkey went to the mound, took a tiny bit of pepper on his tongue, swallowed, and went into the tall grasses. A few minutes later,

656 UNIT SIX: THE ORAL TRADITION

Mini-Lesson ⟡ Literary Concepts

REVIEWING ONOMATOPOEIA Point out to students that the use of words to imitate sounds is called onomatopoeia. Examples include *plop, roar,* and *hiss.* Onomatopoeia is especially useful in storytelling, where the speaker can emphasize the sounds of these words to increase their effect.

Application Have students identify the example of onomatopoeia in the highlighted passage above. Then have students work in groups to brainstorm a list of words they know that imitate sounds and develop a story that incorporates some of these words. Invite groups to share their stories with the class.

656 THE LANGUAGE OF LITERATURE TEACHER'S EDITION

Monkey came out, took a little more, swallowed it, and went into the tall grasses.

Soon the pile was almost gone. The animals were astonished to see Monkey doing what they had not been able to do. Leopard couldn't believe it either. He climbed a tree and stretched out on a sturdy limb to get a better view. From his limb high in the tree Leopard could see into the tall grasses where Monkey went to rest. Wait a minute! Leopard thought something was suddenly wrong with his eyes because he thought he saw a hundred monkeys hiding in the tall grasses.

He rubbed his eyes and looked another look. There wasn't anything wrong with his eyes. There were a hundred monkeys in the tall grasses, and they all looked alike!

Just then, there was the sound of loud applause. King Gorilla announced that Monkey had won the contest and the pot of gold.

Leopard growled a growl so scary that even King Gorilla was frightened. Leopard wasn't thinking about anybody except the monkeys. He took a long and beautiful leap from the tree right smack into the middle of the tall grasses where the monkeys were hiding.

The monkeys ran in all directions. When the other animals saw monkeys running from the grasses, they realized that the monkeys had tricked them, and started chasing them. Even King Gorilla joined in the chase. He wanted his gold back.

The only way the monkeys could escape was to climb to the very tops of the tallest trees where no one else, not even Leopard, could climb.

And that's why monkeys live in trees to this very day. ❖

JULIUS LESTER

1939–

Julius Lester connects his interest in folklore to his father, who was a minister and a good storyteller. Lester says, "As a child, I loved it when my father got together with other ministers on a summer evening, because I knew that I would be treated to stories for as long as I was allowed to stay up, which was never long enough." Lester's work has received numerous awards, including a 1969 Newbery Honor award for *To Be a Slave*. "Why Monkeys Live in Trees" is from the book *How Many Spots Does a Leopard Have?*, which contains tales that reflect both African and Jewish story traditions. Lester currently divides his time between writing and serving as a professor at the University of Massachusetts.

OTHER WORKS *Long Journey Home: Stories from Black History*, *The Tales of Uncle Remus: The Adventures of Brer Rabbit*

STRATEGIC READING FOR
Less-Proficient Readers

H Ask students who won the contest and how he was able to do so. *(Monkey got a number of monkeys to eat a teeny bit of pepper each.)* Making Inferences

CUSTOMIZING FOR
Gifted and Talented Students

Explain to students that folk tales often provide a humorous explanation for natural phenomena. Challenge students to create their own tales to explain why monkeys live in trees or why chickens don't have ears.

From Personal Response to Critical Analysis

1. Which was your favorite character? Explain in your notebook why that character appealed to you. *(Responses will vary.)*
2. Do you think that Monkey should have been allowed to claim the prize? *(Possible responses: Yes, the contest wasn't "fair and square" to begin with. King Gorilla didn't let on that the mound of black dust was pepper. Yes, as long as the monkeys divided the pot of gold among themselves. No, Monkey cheated.)*
3. What visual details, figures of speech, or descriptive passages stayed with you after you heard the story? Share your response with a partner. *(Responses will vary.)*

COMPREHENSION CHECK
1. What did the animals think the objective of King Gorilla's contest was? *(to eat a mound of black dust)*
2. How did King Gorilla trick the contestants? *(He didn't mention that the dust was really pepper.)*
3. Why did Lion, Hippopotamus, and Leopard think that they would win? *(Both Lion and Leopard thought they could eat, in much less time than one day, a mound of black dust; Hippopotamus thought he could swallow a mound of black dust in one gulp.)*
4. What explanation does the folk tale give for why monkeys live in trees? *(Long ago, monkeys tricked the other jungle animals out of a pot of gold. When the animals chased them, the monkeys took refuge in the treetops. They have lived in trees ever since.)*

Literature Connection

Design a Board Game or Video Game
As students develop the game, one student should serve as recorder to write down the steps involved in playing the game. The recorder should read the steps back to the group from time to time, so that they can make sure the game works logically.

Rubric

3 Full Accomplishment The instruction manual clearly and fully explains the rules of the game; the game's design enhances its appeal and strengthens its connection to one of the tales; the game draws significantly and accurately on one of the stories.

2 Substantial Accomplishment The instruction manual does not fully explain the rules of the game; the game's design is not fully exploited to strengthen its connection to one of the tales; or the game does not draw accurately on the story.

1 Little or Partial Accomplishment The instruction manual is unclear, the game's design haphazard, and its connection with one of the tales vague.

RESPONDING OPTIONS

LITERATURE CONNECTION PROJECT 1   Multimodal Activity

Design a Board Game or Video Game
Working in a small group, design a video game or a board game based on one of the tales you've just read. Research popular games to become familiar with the types of graphics and illustrations currently used. Here are some things to consider:

Decide on an appropriate age level to target for the game.

Determine the goal of the game. For example, the goal of a game based on the well-known Cinderella story might be to get Cinderella safely through the trials of the wicked stepsisters to the Prince's ball. Brainstorm details such as which characters will be involved—in this example, Cinderella, the stepsisters and stepmother, the Prince, and the fairy godmother—as well as the rules of the game.

Write a brief instruction manual. The instructions should make it clear to your classmates how the game is played.

Draw sample video screens or a sample game board to show how the game will look. A sample gameboard is shown here.

Add your game to a class display of student-designed games.

SOCIAL STUDIES CONNECTION PROJECT 2   Multimodal Activity

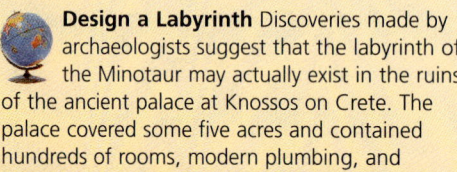

Design a Labyrinth Discoveries made by archaeologists suggest that the labyrinth of the Minotaur may actually exist in the ruins of the ancient palace at Knossos on Crete. The palace covered some five acres and contained hundreds of rooms, modern plumbing, and brilliantly colored frescoes (art painted on fresh, wet plaster). Research the archaeological work that began on Crete in the early 1900s. Use information from your research and details from "Wings" to draw or construct a model of the labyrinth Daedalus built for the Minotaur. Arrange a display of the drawings and models so that students may try to solve the mazes.

658   UNIT SIX: THE ORAL TRADITION

Social Studies Connection

Design a Labyrinth For their research, students can use an on-line or print encyclopedia or a book about Aegean civilization. Begin the activity by having the class brainstorm sources of information and how to procure them. You may wish to suggest students begin their labyrinths by first drawing a correct but twisting path to the center, then embellish the maze with a series of dead-end twists and turns.

Rubric

3 Full Accomplishment Drawings or models show creative use of materials and accurate use of information drawn from independent research and the selection.

2 Substantial Accomplishment Drawings or models show creative use of materials but scanty or occasionally inaccurate use of information drawn from independent research and the selection.

1 Little or Partial Accomplishment Drawings or models are not creative, are frequently inaccurate, and show little independent research.

658 THE LANGUAGE OF LITERATURE TEACHER'S EDITION

Social Studies Connection

Map the Spice Routes Students can research their maps in a print or on-line encyclopedia, an historical atlas, or a book on ancient African history. Encourage students to consult a school or local librarian.

Rubric

3 Full Accomplishment Maps correctly identify spices traded and effectively use arrows, lines, and captions to show the spice trade.

2 Substantial Accomplishment Maps correctly identify spices traded, but arrows, lines, and captions are not used consistently and effectively to show the spice trade.

1 Little or Partial Accomplishment Maps contain inaccurate information and are difficult to read.

SOCIAL STUDIES CONNECTION PROJECT 3 *Multimodal Activity*

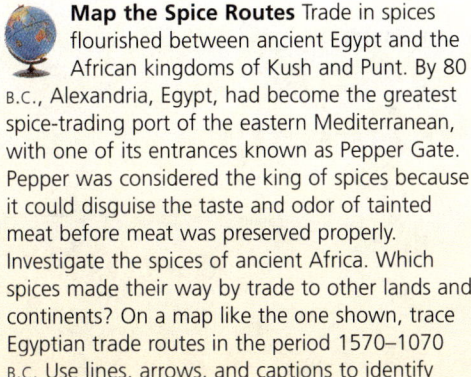

Map the Spice Routes Trade in spices flourished between ancient Egypt and the African kingdoms of Kush and Punt. By 80 B.C., Alexandria, Egypt, had become the greatest spice-trading port of the eastern Mediterranean, with one of its entrances known as Pepper Gate. Pepper was considered the king of spices because it could disguise the taste and odor of tainted meat before meat was preserved properly. Investigate the spices of ancient Africa. Which spices made their way by trade to other lands and continents? On a map like the one shown, trace Egyptian trade routes in the period 1570–1070 B.C. Use lines, arrows, and captions to identify and trace the movement of the various spices traded in ancient Africa.

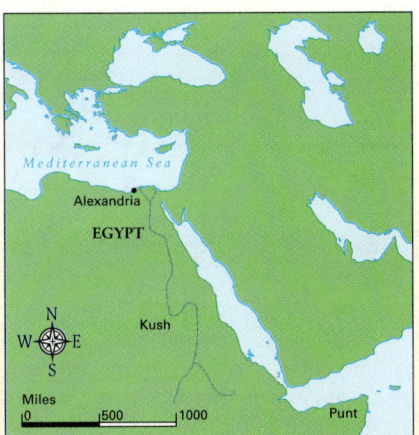

ACROSS CULTURES MINI-PROJECTS *Multimodal Activity*

Try Calligraphy The ancient Persians regarded calligraphy as an art equal to, if not more important than, painting. Experiment with calligraphy, using it to write one of the following items based on "The Red Lion": an announcement of the King's death, an invitation to the contest between Prince Azgid and the Red Lion, a proclamation of Azgid's crowning ceremony, or an announcement of Azgid and Perizide's marriage.

Create a Time Line In "The Red Lion," Perizide entertains Azgid by playing a lute, probably an ancestor of a stringed instrument made from a gourd and played with a bow. Research the lute and design an illustrated time line of its development from ancient times in Babylonia to modern times.

Present a Tableau Design a tableau (tăb′lō′)—a stop-action scene—of the major gods and goddesses of Greek and Roman mythology. Work in pairs to identify a Greek god or goddess and his or her Roman counterpart. For each god or goddess, create a costume and a symbol (for example, a trident for Poseidon) and design a backdrop or setting (for example, for Zeus, a stormy sky with thunderbolts). Then present your tableau to the class, with one partner assuming the role of the Greek god or goddess and the other partner the role of the Roman version. As a class, develop a competition involving identification of the figures portrayed.

Extended Social Studies Reading

> ### MORE ABOUT THE CULTURES
> - *The Kingdom of the Bulls* by Paul Capon
> - *Pompeii* by Ron and Nancy Goor
> - *Digging Up the Bible Lands* by Ronald Harker
> - *Life in Ancient Greece* by Pierre Miguel

PROJECTS **659**

Multicultural Perspectives

Try Calligraphy Students can begin to learn calligraphy by using a book such as *Teach Yourself Calligraphy* by Ellen Korn (New York: William Morrow, 1982). Encourage students to practice their calligraphy before writing one of the items based on "The Red Lion." If possible, provide students with special markers or pens designed for calligraphy.

Present a Tableau Allow students time to research gods and goddesses in the school library. If your school has a costume room, perhaps you could arrange to borrow items for students to use in their costume designs.

Create a Time Line Students can research the lute in a general encyclopedia or an encyclopedia of music. Effective time lines will give accurate dates and all the relevant events that occurred in the development of the lute. You may wish to extend the activity by having students construct a lute of their own. Directions can be found in *Make Mine Music* by Tom Walther (Boston: Little, Brown, 1981).

OVERVIEW

Objectives

- To understand and appreciate a legend and two folk tales that explore the human need to connect with others
- To appreciate the culture and ecology of Puerto Rico and Trinidad
- To extend understanding of the selection through a variety of multimodal and cross-curricular activities

Reading Pathways

- Select one or several students to read each story aloud to the entire class or to small groups of students. Assign this reading in advance so that the readers can incorporate into their presentations some of the techniques used by professional storytellers. Have the audience listen carefully to the stories without following along in their texts.

- Read the stories aloud to the class, pausing at key points to discuss how elements of the stories inform students about the cultures or geographies of Puerto Rico, Vietnam, or Trinidad. Have students compare these cultures to their own.

- After students have read the stories once, have them read them again to identify structural elements such as main characters, minor characters, conflict, setting, and plot. Then have students identify similarities and differences between these stories and the selections in the related unit. For example, both "The Legend of the Hummingbird" and "Aaron's Gift" (page 184) use an animal to treat the same theme, the need to belong.

PREVIEWING

LINKS TO UNIT TWO

The Need to Belong

Activating Prior Knowledge

In Unit Two, the selections explore the conflicting emotions that often occur when an individual is striving to find his or her place in the community. The need to belong is a basic human urge that has been expressed within the folklore of many cultures. The tales you will read next reveal how different people go about meeting this universal need.

Building Background

PUERTO RICO

The Legend of the Hummingbird

retold by Pura Belpré (pōō'rä běl-prā')

Puerto Rico, an island in the Caribbean Sea, is a commonwealth of the United States. The U.S. Congress is responsible for the government of Puerto Rico, but Congress usually allows the Puerto Rican people to make their own decisions. The folklore of Puerto Rico reflects a mixture of cultures, with roots in the Orient, Arabia, Spain, and West Africa. This legend, like other legends, incorporates elements of magic and the supernatural as it explains the origin of the many-colored hummingbird.

660 UNIT SIX: THE ORAL TRADITION

PRINT AND MEDIA RESOURCES

UNIT SIX RESOURCE BOOK
Strategic Reading: Literature, p. 11
Vocabulary SkillBuilder, p. 14
Reading SkillBuilder, p. 12
Spelling SkillBuilder, p. 13

GRAMMAR MINI-LESSONS
Transparencies, p. 10
Copymasters, p. 12

WRITING MINI-LESSONS
Transparencies, p. 48

ACCESS FOR STUDENTS ACQUIRING ENGLISH
Selection Summaries
Reading and Writing Support

FORMAL ASSESSMENT
Selection Test, pp. 119–120
 Test Generator

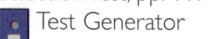 **AUDIO LIBRARY**
See Reference Card

INTERNET RESOURCES
McDougal Littell Literature Center at http://www.hmco.com/mcdougal/lit

660 THE LANGUAGE OF LITERATURE TEACHER'S EDITION

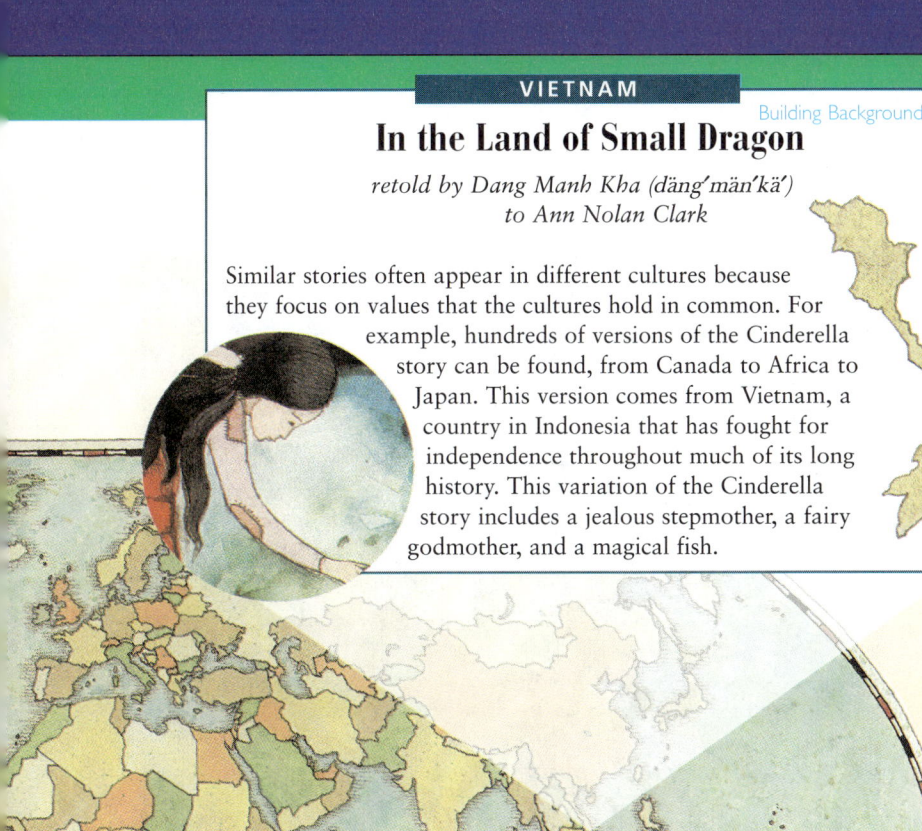

VIETNAM
Building Background

In the Land of Small Dragon

*retold by Dang Manh Kha (däng′män′kä′)
to Ann Nolan Clark*

Similar stories often appear in different cultures because they focus on values that the cultures hold in common. For example, hundreds of versions of the Cinderella story can be found, from Canada to Africa to Japan. This version comes from Vietnam, a country in Indonesia that has fought for independence throughout much of its long history. This variation of the Cinderella story includes a jealous stepmother, a fairy godmother, and a magical fish.

TRINIDAD

Building Background

The Bamboo Beads

by Lynn Joseph

This folk tale comes from Trinidad, a small tropical island off the coast of Venezuela. African, Indian, Spanish, and French influences are reflected in the dialect of Trinidad. The tale features Papa Bois, one of the island's most popular folklore characters. His duty is to protect the trees and animals of the woods, which include the scarlet ibis, the iguana, and such poisonous snakes as the fer-de-lance. However, Papa Bois sometimes chooses to make contact with humans.

Setting a Purpose

AS YOU READ...

See how attitudes regarding power are portrayed.

Evaluate how much humans are allowed to control their own fates.

Notice which powers are connected to gods or other supernatural beings.

LINKS TO UNIT TWO **661**

SUMMARY

In the Land of Small Dragon In a Vietnamese folk tale similar to "Cinderella," the beautiful Tâm is mistreated by her jealous stepmother and her stepsister, Cám. When the girls' father holds a fishing contest to see who will be his Number One Daughter, Cám cheats Tâm out of the title by stealing all but one of her fish. Tâm feels sorry for her little fish and becomes its friend and caretaker—until Cám eats it. A fairy tells the grieving Tâm to bury her fish's bones; later she digs them up and discovers in their place a silk dress and two jeweled shoes. After she loses one shoe in a rice paddy, a bird carries it to the emperor's garden. There the emperor's son picks it up and proclaims that its owner will be his wife. Although Cám's mother does her best to keep Tâm from going with her stepsister to the palace, Tâm does go. The prince easily slips the shoe onto Tâm's foot and declares that she will be his wife.

The Bamboo Beads The Trinidadian narrator of this tale listens as her great-aunt explains the origin of a string of beads she wears. Tantie describes how, as a young girl at the market, she gave bread to a ragged old man with hoofs instead of feet. In return he gave her a piece of string, which she wore as a necklace. Thereafter, colorful bamboo beads began to turn up everywhere, and Tantie added each one to her necklace. Tantie's mother understood that they had come from the forest spirit Papa Bois. When Tantie encountered Papa Bois again at the market, she learned that the beads represented the number of children she would have someday—who turned out actually to be her grandnieces and grandnephews. After telling this story, Tantie entrusts the necklace to her grandniece—the narrator.

The Legend of the Hummingbird This Puerto Rican legend explains how the hummingbird came to be. Alida, the daughter of an Indian chief, falls in love with Taroo, a young man from an enemy tribe. The young lovers meet secretly at a pool surrounded by pomarosa trees. When Alida's father learns of their meetings, he arranges for her to marry someone else. Alida begs the god Yukiyú to spare her from marrying a man she doesn't love, so the god turns her into a delicate red flower. Taroo, knowing nothing of Alida's fate, waits for her by the pool until the moon tells him what has happened. Taroo begs Yukiyú to help him find Alida; the god responds by turning Taroo into a hummingbird. Ever since, the hummingbird flies quickly from flower to flower—especially red ones—looking for his lost love.

WORDS TO KNOW

curtly (kûrt′lē) *adv.* in a way that uses so few words it is either rude or almost rude (p. 668)

hover (hŭv′ər) *v.* to stay fluttering in the air near one place (p. 679)

indolent (ĭn′də-lənt) *adj.* lazy (p. 664)

ravishing (răv′ĭ-shĭng) *adj.* unusually beautiful; delightfully pleasing (p. 668)

taunt (tônt) *v.* to make fun of in a mean way (p. 668)

THE LANGUAGE OF LITERATURE TEACHER'S EDITION **661**

CUSTOMIZING FOR
Students Acquiring English

- Use **ACCESS FOR STUDENTS ACQUIRING ENGLISH**, *Reading and Writing Support.*
- Point out that this story, like "Wings," includes italicized portions set off from the rest of the story. Invite students to compare and contrast the uses of these sections here and in the previous story.
- Some students may not be familiar with the story of Cinderella. Invite volunteers to share their versions of Cinderella with the class. Point out that this selection is one of many versions and that such variation is common in folk tales.
- As you guide students through the selection, you may want to use the suggestions in these boxes as well as the suggestions under Strategic Reading for Less-Proficient Readers.

STRATEGIC READING FOR
Less-Proficient Readers

Set a Purpose As students read the tale, they should think about its similarities to and differences from the story of Cinderella. Have students read to find out about Tấm's relationship with her stepsister and stepmother and what she wants from her father.

Use **UNIT SIX RESOURCE BOOK**, pp. 11–12, for guidance in reading the selection.

Art Note

Reading the Art What adjectives would you use to describe the scene of this painting? Based on this painting, what do you expect the setting of "In the Land of Small Dragon" will be like?

Copyright © 1995 John Wilkinson/Nawrocki Stock Photo, Inc. All rights reserved.

662 UNIT SIX: THE ORAL TRADITION

Multicultural Perspectives

NAMING THE YEARS ON THE CHINESE CALENDAR The Chinese assign an animal, real or mythical, to each year. There are 12 different animals in the cycle, which is sometimes referred to as the Chinese Zodiac. Like a person's astrological sign, a person's birth year is believed to give the person certain characteristics. For example, people born in the Year of the Rooster (or chicken, as it is called in the story) are supposed to be loners who are less adventurous than they appear to be. They are supposed to be most compatible with people born in the year of the Ox, Dragon, or Snake.

The cycle of animals is as follows:

Year	Animal	Year	Animal
1997	Ox	2003	Sheep
1998	Tiger	2004	Monkey
1999	Rabbit	2005	Rooster
2000	Dragon	2006	Dog
2001	Snake	2007	Pig
2002	Horse	2008	Rat

662 THE LANGUAGE OF LITERATURE TEACHER'S EDITION

In the Land of Small Dragon

As told by Dang Manh Kha
to Ann Nolan Clark

1

*Man cannot know the whole world,
But can know his own small part.*

In the Land of Small Dragon,
In the Year of the Chicken,[1]
In a Village of No-Name,
In the bend of the river,
There were many small houses
Tied together by walkways.
Mulberry and apricot,
Pear tree and flowering vine
Dropped their delicate blossoms
On a carpet of new grass.
  In a Village of No-Name
Lived a man and two daughters.
Tâm[2] was the elder daughter;
Her mother died at her birth.

---

1. **Year of the Chicken:** the name of a year in the old Chinese calendar; commonly called Year of the Rooster. Every year in the Chinese calendar has 1 of 12 animal names. For example, 1911 was a Year of the Pig, which next occurred 12 years later, in 1923.
2. **Tâm** (täm).

Mini-Lesson: Speaking, Listening, and Viewing

INTERVIEWS Explain to students that good interviewers bring out interviewees' weaknesses as well as their strengths. Good interviewers elicit information that interviewees may not ordinarily share.

People often agree to be interviewed for publicity. Political candidates use interviews to advance their point of view and to become more recognized by viewers. Effective interviewees are comfortable being in the spotlight. They are friendly, confident, outgoing, and communicative.

Application Select students to portray the stepmother, Cám, and Father. Have other students act as journalists, interviewing the characters about their roles in creating a household in which a child was treated very badly. After the interviews, discuss as a class what information interviewers elicited about the characters and whether the characters managed to skirt uncomfortable questions.

CUSTOMIZING FOR
Gifted and Talented Students

Have students think about Tâm's father. Ask them to infer, as they read, the narrator's attitude toward him.

Possible responses:

- Page 664—"He lived his days in justice, / Standing strong against the wind." Father's sense of justice moves him to treat people, notably the good Tâm and evil Cám, with equal regard.

- In considering the tale as a whole, students may suggest that the narrator portrays Father as putting principles before people. By clinging to his notion of fairness, Father allows an abusive situation to continue.

Literary Concept:
CHARACTERIZATION

A Ask students to interpret the italicized words. How do they apply to Cám? *(Possible response: If a person is bad inside, it shows on his or her face. Cám's ugly face reflects her evil spirit.)*

Critical Thinking: ANALYZING

B Have students identify the things in this passage that come in twos and ones. Ask students what the narrator communicates by giving Cám's mother a single-minded purpose and a heart with a single door. *(Possible response: Disharmony. If Cám's mother could find room in her mind and heart for two daughters, all would be well.)*

Literary Links

C Compare the character of Tâm in this folk tale and that of Selo in "Cricket in the Road" on page 237. *(Possible response: Both Tâm and Selo struggle to meet their need to belong. Both characters' lack of belonging arises, in part, from a blood relationship that excludes them. Cám and Tâm's stepmother are birthmother and daughter. Vern and Amy are brother and sister.)*

A jewel box of gold and jade
Holds only jewels of great price.

Tâm's face was a golden moon,
Her eyes dark as a storm cloud,
Her feet delicate flowers
Stepping lightly on the wind.
No envy lived in her heart,
Nor bitterness in her tears.
Cám[3] was the younger daughter,
Child of Number Two Wife.
Cám's face was long and ugly,
Scowling and discontented,
Frowning in deep displeasure.
<u>Indolent</u>, slow and idle,
Her heart was filled with hatred
For her beautiful sister.

A *An evil heart keeps records*
On the face of its owner.

The father loved both daughters,
One not more than the other.
He did not permit his heart
To call one name more dearly.

He lived his days in justice,
Standing strong against the wind.

Father had a little land,
A house made of mats and clay,
A grove of mulberry trees
Enclosed by growing bamboo,
A garden and rice paddy,[4]
B Two great water buffalo,[5]
A well for drinking water,
And twin fish ponds for the fish.
Cám's mother, Number Two Wife,
Cared only for her own child.
Her mind had only one thought:
What would give pleasure to Cám.

C *Her heart had only one door*
And only Cám could enter.

Number Two Wife was jealous
of Tâm, the elder daughter,
Who was beautiful and good,
So the mother planned revenge
On the good, beautiful child.
To Cám she gave everything,
But nothing but work to Tâm.
Tâm carried water buckets,
Hanging from her bamboo pole.
Tâm carried forest fagots[6]
To burn in the kitchen fire.
Tâm transplanted young rice plants
From seed bed to rice paddy.
Tâm flailed[7] the rice on a rock,
Then she winnowed and gleaned it.[8]
Tâm's body ached with tiredness,
Her heart was heavy and sad.
She said, "Wise Father, listen!
I am your elder daughter;
Therefore why may I not be
Number One Daughter, also?
"A Number One Daughter works,
But she works with dignity.
If I were your Number One
The honor would ease my pain.
As it is, I am a slave,
Without honor or dignity."
Waiting for wisdom to come,
Father was slow to give answer.

---

3. **Cám** (cäm).
4. **rice paddy:** flooded field used for growing rice.
5. **water buffalo:** slow, powerful oxlike animal used for pulling loads.
6. **fagots** (făg′əts): bundles of sticks or twigs; also spelled *faggots*.
7. **flailed:** beat out grain from its husk, or dry outer casing.
8. **winnowed and gleaned it:** separated out the useless parts of the rice and collected the remaining good parts.

WORDS TO KNOW
indolent (ĭn′də-lənt) *adj.* lazy

664

 Mini-Lesson • Literary Concepts

REVIEWING POINT OF VIEW Remind students that point of view refers to how a writer tells a story. This story is told by a narrator, using the third-person point of view. The narrator is outside the story and uses third-person pronouns such as *he, she,* and *they*. In stories told from the first-person point of view, the narrator is a character in the story, and uses first-person pronouns such as *I, me,* and *we*.

Application Have students write a summary of this story using the third-person point of view. Then have them choose a character in the story and rewrite the summary as if that character were telling it.

Point of view
first person
third person

Pronouns
I, me, we, us
he, she, they,
him, her, them

664 THE LANGUAGE OF LITERATURE TEACHER'S EDITION

"Both of my daughters share my heart.
I cannot choose between them.
One of you must earn the right
To be my Number One child."

A man's worth is what he does,
Not what he says he can do.

"Go, Daughters, to the fish pond;
Take your fish baskets with you.
Fish until night moon-mist comes.
Bring your fish catch back to me.
She who brings a full basket
Is my Number One Daughter.
Your work, not my heart, decides
Your place in your father's house."
Tâm listened to her father
And was quick to obey him.
With her basket, she waded
In the mud of the fish pond.
With quick-moving, graceful hands
She caught the quick-darting fish.
Slowly the long hours went by.
Slowly her fish basket filled.
Cám sat on the high, dry bank
Trying to think of some plan,
Her basket empty of fish,
But her mind full of cunning.
"I, wade in that mud?" she thought.
"There must be some better way."
At last she knew what to do
To be Number One Daughter.
"Tâm," she called, "elder sister,
Our father needs a bright flower,
A flower to gladden his heart.
Get it for him, dear sister."
Tâm, the good, gentle sister,
Set her fish basket aside
And ran into the forest
To pick the night-blooming flowers.
Cám crept to Tâm's fish basket,
Emptied it into her own.
Now her fish basket was full.

Illustration Copyright © 1982 Vo-Dinh Mai. From *The Brocaded Slipper and Other Vietnamese Tales* by Lynette Dyer Vuong. Reprinted by permission of HarperCollins Publishers.

Tâm's held only one small fish.
Quickly Cám ran to Father,
Calling, "See my full basket!"
Tâm ran back to the fish pond
With an armload of bright flowers.
"Cám," she called, "what has happened?
What has happened to my fish?"
Slowly Tâm went to Father
Bringing him the flowers and fish.
Father looked at both baskets.
Speaking slowly, he told them,
"The test was a full basket,
Not flowers and one small fish.

IN THE LAND OF SMALL DRAGON **665**

Mini-Lesson: Speaking, Listening, and Viewing

SCIENTIFIC OBSERVATION Explain to students that good readers observe details in a text like a scientist observing a slide under a microscope. Both scientists and readers focus closely on small details in order to develop a better understanding of the whole.

Application Have students create drawings of the Village of No-Name. Drawings can give an aerial view of the village or show a particular scene, such as Father's land. Invite students to present their drawings to the class while observers note the details shown in the drawings.

Active Reading: QUESTION

E Discuss what questions or comments students have as the devious Cám addresses Tãm. You may wish to use the following model to give them ideas of relevant questions:

Think-Aloud Model *I wonder what Cám is up to. I don't trust her. If she is so concerned about Father, why doesn't she sing to him herself?*

CUSTOMIZING FOR
Students Acquiring English

3 Explain that *elder* is a more formal synonym for "older" usually used in writing and that *elder* refers only to people.

4 Call students' attention to *Bitterly she cried for it* and remind them that adverbs in English usually follow the verb, but may precede the verb for literary effect.

---

3 Take your fish, Elder Daughter.
It is much too small to eat.
Cám has earned the right to be
Honorable Number One."

2

Tãm looked at the little fish.
Her heart was filled with pity
At its loneliness and fright.
"Little fish, dear little fish,
I will put you in the well."
At night Tãm brought her rice bowl,
Sharing her food with the fish—
Talked to the thin fish, saying,
"Little fish, come eat with me"—
Stayed at the well at nighttime
With the stars for company.
The fish grew big and trustful.
It grew fat and not afraid.
It knew Tãm's voice and answered,
Swimming to her outstretched hand.
Cám sat in the dark shadows,
Her heart full of jealousy,
Her mind full of wicked thoughts.
Sweetly she called, "Tãm, sister.
Our father is overtired.
E Come sing him a pretty song
That will bring sweet dreams to him."
Quickly Tãm ran to her father,
Singing him a nightbird song.
Cám was hiding near the well,
Watching, waiting and watching.
When she heard Tãm's pretty song
She crept closer to the fish,
Whispering, "Dear little fish,
Come to me! Come eat with me."
The fish came, and greedy Cám
Touched it, caught it and ate it!
Tãm returned. Her fish was gone.
"Little fish, dear little fish,
Come to me! Come eat with me!"
4 Bitterly she cried for it.

666 UNIT SIX: THE ORAL TRADITION

*The stars looked down in pity;
The clouds shed teardrops of rain.*

3

Tãm's tears falling in the well
Made the water rise higher.
And from it rose Nang Tien,
A lovely cloud-dressed fairy.
Her voice was a silver bell

*"Little fish,
dear little fish,
I will put you
in the well."*

Ringing clear in the moonlight.
"My child, why are you crying?"
"My dear little fish is gone!
He does not come when I call."
"Ask Red Rooster to help you.
His hens will find Little Fish."
Soon the hens came in a line
Sadly bringing the fish bones.
Tãm cried, holding the fish bones.
"Your dear fish will not forget.
Place his bones in a clay pot
Safe beneath your sleeping mat.
Those we love never leave us.
Cherished bones keep love alive."
In her treasured clay pot, Tãm
Made a bed of flower petals
For the bones of Little Fish
And put him away with love.
But she did not forget him;

Mini-Lesson Reading Skills/Strategies

CLASSIFYING Remind students that they can remember and review a selection by classifying its various elements, including genre, setting, and theme.

Application Have students classify or identify various elements of "In the Land of Small Dragon" by completing a chart such as the one shown.

Genre	Theme	Conflict	Setting	Main Characters
folk tale	the need to belong	person vs. person: Tãm vs. her stepmother and stepsister	a small village in Vietnam	Tãm, her stepmother, Cám

Reteaching/Reinforcement
• *Unit Six Resource Book*, p. 12

666 THE LANGUAGE OF LITERATURE TEACHER'S EDITION

When the moon was full again,
Tâm, so lonely for her fish,
Dug up the buried clay pot.
Tâm found, instead of fish bones,
A silken dress and two jeweled *hai*.[9]
Her Nang Tien spoke again.
"Your dear little fish loves you.
Clothe yourself in the garments
His love has given you."
Tâm put on the small jeweled *hai*.
They fit like a velvet skin
Made of moonlight and stardust
And the love of Little Fish.
Tâm heard music in her heart
That sent her small feet dancing,
Flitting like two butterflies,
Skimming like two flying birds,
Dancing by the twin fish ponds,
Dancing in the rice paddy.
But the mud in the rice paddy
Kept one jeweled *hai* for its own.
Night Wind brought the *hai* to Tâm.
"What is yours I bring to you."
Water in the well bubbled,
"I will wash your *hai* for you."
Water buffalo came by.
"Dry your *hai* on my sharp horn."
A blackbird flew by singing,
"I know where this *hai* belongs.
In a garden far away
I will take this *hai* for you."

4

What is to be must happen
As day follows after night.

In the Emperor's garden,
Sweet with perfume of roses,
The Emperor's son, the Prince,
Walked alone in the moonlight.
A bird, black against the moon,
Flew along the garden path,
Dropping a star in its flight.
"Look! A star!" exclaimed the Prince.
Carefully he picked it up
And found it was the small jeweled *hai*.
"Only a beautiful maid
Can wear this beautiful *hai*."
The Prince whispered to his heart,
And his heart answered, "Find her."

In truth, beauty seeks goodness:
What is beautiful is good.

The Prince went to his father:
"A bird dropped this at my feet.
Surely it must come as truth,
Good and fair the maid it fits.
Sire,[10] if it is your pleasure
I would take this maid for wife."
The Great Emperor was pleased
With the wishes of his son.
He called his servants to him,
His drummers and his crier,[11]
Proclaiming a Festival
To find one who owned the *hai*.
In the Village of No-Name
The Emperor's subjects heard—
They heard the Royal Command.
There was praise and rejoicing.
They were pleased the Royal Son
Would wed one of their daughters.

5

Father's house was filled with clothes,
Embroidered *áo-dài*[12] and *hai*
Of heavy silks and rich colors.

---

9. **hai** (hī): shoes.
10. **Sire**: title of respect for a superior, in this case, an emperor.
11. **crier**: person who makes public announcements in the streets of a village or town.
12. **embroidered áo-dài** (ou′dī): robes decorated with fancy needlework.

Linking to Science

I Ripe rice consists of a layer of bran surrounding a white endosperm. The layer of bran is enclosed by a brown husk. The most nutritious part of rice is the bran, which contains vitamins E, K, B complex, and protein. Deficiency diseases such as beriberi can be caused by a diet of white rice, from which the nutritious bran has been removed. Brown rice, which contains a layer of bran, is a much more healthful food.

Critical Thinking:
SYNTHESIZING

J Have students identify the animals that have helped Tâm. Ask them how each animal has helped her. *(The fish made Tâm a silken dress and two jeweled hai. A blackbird carried the hai to the Prince's feet. A flock of blackbirds separated the big basket of cleaned and unhusked rice.)*

"Stay at home, you Number Two!"

Father went outside to sit.
Cám and her mother whispered
Their hopes, their dreams and their plans.
Cám, Number One Daughter, asked,
"Mother, will the Prince choose me?"
Mother said, "Of course he will.
You will be the fairest there!
When you curtsy to the Prince
His heart will go out to you."
Tâm, Daughter Number Two, said,
"May I go with you and Cám?"
Cám's mother answered curtly,
"Yes, if you have done this task:
I Separating rice and husks
From one basket into two."
Tâm knew Cám's mother had mixed
The cleaned rice with rice unhusked.
She looked at the big basket
Full to brim with rice and husks.
Separating the cleaned rice
From that of rice unhusked
Would take all harvest moon time,
When the Festival would end.
A cloud passed over the moon.
J Whirring wings outsung the wind.
A flock of blackbirds lighted
On the pile of leaves and grain.
Picking the grain from the leaves,
They dropped clean rice at Tâm's feet. **J**
Tâm could almost not believe
That the endless task was done.
Tâm, the elder daughter, said,
"May I go? May I go, too,
Now that all my work is done?"
Cám taunted, "How could you go?
You have nothing fit to wear."
"If I had a dress to wear
Could I go to the Palace?"
"If wishes were dresses, yes,
But wishes are not dresses."
When Mother left she said,
"Our dear Cám is ravishing.
Stay at home, you Number Two!
Cám will be the one to wed."
Tâm dug up the big clay pot.
The dress and one *hai* were there—
As soft as misty moon clouds,
Delicate as rose perfume.
Tâm washed her face in the well,
Combed her hair by the fish pond.
She smoothed down the silken dress,
Tied one *hai* unto her belt
And, though her feet were bare,
Hurried, scurried, ran and ran.
She ran to the Festival
In the King's Royal Garden.
At the Palace gates the guards
Bowed before her, very low.
Pretty girls stood in a line
With their mothers standing near;
One by one they tried to fit
A foot into a small, jeweled *hai*.
Cám stood beside her mother,
By the gilded[13] throne-room door.

---

13. **gilded:** covered with a thin layer of gold.

WORDS TO KNOW	**curtly** (kûrt′lē) *adv.* in a way that uses so few words it is either rude or almost rude
	taunt (tônt) *v.* to make fun of in a mean way
	ravishing (răv′ĭ-shĭng) *adj.* unusually beautiful; delightfully pleasing

668

Mini-Lesson Literary Concepts

REVIEWING RHYTHM Remind students that rhythm is the pattern of stressed and unstressed syllables in a poem or folk tale. A selection can have a regular or irregular rhythm.

Application Call on students to read aloud different sections of "In the Land of Small Dragon." Have listeners describe the effect of the line breaks on the rhythm. For comparison, read aloud to students one section of the tale, heeding end punctuation but ignoring line breaks. Ask students to compare and contrast the readings.

---

668 THE LANGUAGE OF LITERATURE **TEACHER'S EDITION**

Her face was dark and angry
Like a brooding monsoon[14] wind.
Cám, wiping her tears away,
Sobbed and whimpered and complained,
"My small foot fits his old shoe—
Everything but my big toe."
Tâm stood shyly by the door
Looking in great wonderment
While trumpeters and drummers
Made music for her entrance.
People looked at gentle Tâm.
Everyone was whispering,
"Oh! She is so beautiful!
She must be a Princess fair
From some distant foreign land."
Then the Prince looked up and saw
A lady walking toward him.
Stepping from his Royal Throne,
He quickly went to meet her,
And taking her hand led her
To His Majesty the King.
What is to be must happen
As day happens after night.

Real beauty mirrors goodness.
What is one is the other.

Kneeling, the Prince placed the *hai*
On Tâm's dainty little foot.
Tâm untied the *hai* she wore
And slid her bare foot in it.

Beauty is not painted on.
It is the spirit showing.

The Prince spoke to his father.
"I would take this maid for wife."
His Royal Highness nodded.
"We will have a Wedding feast."
All the birds in all the trees
Sang a song of happiness:
"Tâm, the Number Two Daughter,
Is to be Wife Number One."

What is written in the stars
Cannot be changed or altered.

---

14. **monsoon:** in south Asia, a wind that begins the rainy season.

DANG MANH KHA

Dang Manh Kha was born in Vietnam. After attending St. John's University in Minnesota, he taught school in El Paso, Texas, for four years. In 1975 he worked for the Southeast Asian Resettlement Program to aid Vietnamese refugees. Dang Manh Kha now lives in Tucson, Arizona.

ANN NOLAN CLARK

Born in New Mexico, Ann Nolan Clark (1896–) served for many years as a teacher and writer for the Bureau of Indian Affairs and the U.S. Department of Education in Latin America. Clark has written numerous books about children in various countries, including *The Secret of the Andes*, set in Peru, which won the Newbery Medal in 1952. Clark has said, "All of my books are based upon actual experiences, knowing the people and places I write about, having been there." She lives near Tucson, Arizona.

OTHER WORKS *In My Mother's House, To Stand Against the Wind, Little Navajo Bluebird, Santiago, Tia Maria's Gardens*

IN THE LAND OF SMALL DRAGON **669**

COMPREHENSION CHECK

1. What makes life sad and difficult for Tâm in Father's home? *(Tâm's stepmother loves only her birth daughter, and Tâm's stepsister is deceitful and cruel to her.)*
2. Why does Father hold a fishing contest? *(to answer Tâm's request to be Number One Daughter; Father feels that merit, not birth, must determine who receives that honor)*
3. What is the role of the little fish? *(It is Tâm's friend, Cám's victim, and, finally, Tâm's benefactor.)*
4. How does Tâm block her stepmother's attempt to keep her away from the palace? *(Tâm is helped by a flock of blackbirds, which completes the long task her stepmother set to keep Tâm home. Her task completed, Tâm gets her stepmother's permission to go to the palace, but only if Tâm owns a dress. Unbeknownst to her stepmother, Tâm owns a dress, a beautiful one, that the little fish made.)*
5. What happens to Tâm? *(Because her foot fits the hai, Tâm weds the Prince.)*

STRATEGIC READING FOR
Less-Proficient Readers

K Have students describe the sequence of events through which Tâm escapes her stepmother's clutches. *(Possible response: A raven carries one of Tâm's hai to the Prince. With the Great Emperor's approval, the Prince decides that the owner of the hai will be his wife. Tâm's foot slips into the hai, proving that she is the owner. Tâm is deemed Wife Number One.)* **Noting Sequence of Events**

CUSTOMIZING FOR
Gifted and Talented Students

L Ask students to write a brief essay in response to these final lines of the story. Ask them if they believe a person's fate or destiny is set at birth and cannot be changed. Remind students to support their opinions with examples, either from the story or from their own experiences.

From Personal Response
to Critical Analysis

1. How do you feel toward Father at the end of the tale? Describe your reactions in your notebook. *(Responses will vary.)*
2. Describe the image you have of the Prince. Think about his walking alone in the moonlight, his response upon finding the hai, and his consulting the Great Emperor. *(Possible response: The prince is a romantic young man who shows deference and respect toward his father.)*
3. What message about beauty does this story convey? How does it compare to today's advertising messages about beauty? *(Possible responses: This tale and media advertisements suggest that inner feelings and outer appearance are the same. The tale says beauty isn't painted on, but advertising messages show that a person can become beautiful by buying and using beauty products. The inner spirit is irrelevant.)*

THE LANGUAGE OF LITERATURE **TEACHER'S EDITION** **669**

Art Note

Reading the Art *What activity is taking place in this illustration? Do you think the children are interested in the woman's words? Use details from the illustration to support your answer.*

STRATEGIC READING FOR
Less-Proficient Readers

Set a Purpose Have students read to find out what events lead to Tantie telling a story.

Cultural Note
Trinidad, a small tropical island off the coast of Venezuela, is rich in wildlife. Birds such as the white flamingo and the egret inhabit the Caroni Swamp on the western coast. In the forests (where Papa Bois whittles his bamboo and cares for the trees and beasts), animals such as the agouti, the armadillo, and the iguana—as well as many snakes—make their homes.

The Bamboo Beads
by Lynn Joseph

Illustration Copyright © 1991 Brian Pinkney. Cover from *A Wave in Her Pocket* by Lynn Joseph, reprinted by permission of Clarion Books/Houghton Mifflin Co. All rights reserved.

670 UNIT SIX: THE ORAL TRADITION

Mini-Lesson: Speaking, Listening, and Viewing

DIALECT Explain to students that a dialect is the language spoken by a group of people from a specific region. Point out that the characters in "The Bamboo Beads" speak an island dialect.

Application Invite volunteers to select and read aloud from the story featuring a Trinidad dialect. To help students get a better sense of this dialect, play for them music with lyrics from Trinidad or other West Indian islands.

670 THE LANGUAGE OF LITERATURE **TEACHER'S EDITION**

Last year during the planting season, I helped Mama plant seeds on our hill. "One seed for each of my brothers and sisters," she said, and she covered up seven seeds with dark dirt. Mama's family lives on the other side of the island, so we hardly ever see them.

Each day I watched Mama water the dark mounds of dirt and weed around them. Soon, flowers grew up. They were red as the evening sun. But one day the floods came and swept them to the sea.

"Poor Mama," I said.

"They'll grow again," she replied.

She looked at her gardening gloves hanging on a nail. "If they don't grow back, we'll plant some more." And she smiled.

That night the moon was round and white as my Sunday hat. I told Daddy how Mama's flowers had drowned in the flood rains. He said, "Did I ever show you how *I* count my brothers and sisters?"

"No," I answered.

Then Daddy showed me the fisherman stars. "They point fishermen to the way home," he said. "There are eight of them. I named one each for my brothers and sisters."

"How do you know which is which?" I asked.

Daddy pointed again to the bright stars. "Well, there's Rupert and Hazel, Anthony and Derek, Peter, Janet, and Neil."

"You forgot Auntie Sonia," I said.

Daddy smiled and pointed to a tiny star. "That one's her."

I nodded my head as Daddy moved his finger around, although I couldn't tell which star was who.

After that, Daddy and I looked for the fisherman stars each night. Some nights when the sea breezes blew dark clouds in the sky, we couldn't see them. But Daddy would say, "They'll come back." And he'd smile.

"I wish I had brothers and sisters to plant flowers for or to count stars on," I told Mama and Daddy one day. "I'm tired of having only myself."

"What about all your cousins?" asked Mama.

"You can count them on something," said Daddy.

"What can I count them on?" I wondered.

"Maybe Tantie can help find you something," said Mama. "She's the one who keeps track of all yuh."

So, the next time Tantie came to visit, I said, "Tantie, Mama said you keep track of me and my cousins."

"That's right, chile," said Tantie. "And is plenty of all yuh to keep track of, too."

"I know," I said, "but how you do it? I want something that I can name after each one of my cousins. Something I can count them on. Like Mama has flowers and Daddy has his fisherman stars."

Well, Tantie looked me in the eye for a long time. Then from underneath the neck of her dress she pulled out a brown string full of bright, colorful beads.

"Tantie, where you get those pretty beads from?" I asked.

"These, my dear, is a story by itself, and if you have de time to listen, I'll tell it to you."

I nodded and sat down on the porch swing next to Tantie. As Tantie told her story, I kept trying to push the swing with my foot. But

THE BAMBOO BEADS 671

Literary Concept: SIMILE

A Remind students that a simile is a comparison using *like* or *as*. Ask students to identify the two similes that appear in this passage. (Her mother's flowers "were red as the evening sun"; "the moon was round and white as my Sunday hat.")

CUSTOMIZING FOR
Students Acquiring English

1. Point out that the spelling *chile* for "child" represents Tantie's island accent.

2. Invite students to use context clues to infer what standard English word the spelling *yuh* represents. (you)

STRATEGIC READING FOR
Less-Proficient Readers

B Have students describe the sequence of events that leads to Tantie's telling a story. (Possible response: The narrator watches her mother plant flower seeds for each of her siblings and her father count his siblings by the stars. The narrator, an only child, asks for a way to count her cousins. Her parents suggest that she consult Tantie. In response to the request, Tantie scrutinizes the narrator and begins a story.) **Noting Sequence of Events**

Set a Purpose Have students read to find out what happens after the young Tantie gives bread to a mysterious old man.

Mini-Lesson  Literary Concepts

REVIEWING FLASHBACK Remind students that a flashback is an interruption in a story to present an event that took place before the story began. A flashback can provide information that explains the actions of one or more characters.

Application Have students work in small groups to examine the importance of the flashback in the story. Have one member of the group read aloud the parts of the story that precede and follow the flashback. Then have group members brainstorm a list of questions that they feel need to be answered. Then have a member of the group read the flashback aloud as the rest of the group listens to find out whether the flashback provides the answers to their questions.

CUSTOMIZING FOR
Students Acquiring English

3 Point out that Tantie pronounces "the" as *de*.

4 You may want to point out that single quotation marks are used when quoting direct speech in already quoted material.

Literary Concept:
CHARACTERIZATION

C Although the reader does not realize it at this point in the narrative, this initial meeting between the old man and Tantie is an important one. Have students describe what they learn about Tantie's character from her behavior in this passage. *(Possible response: Tantie's determination not to stare at the man's unusual feet and her instinct to give him food indicate that she is kind, generous, and thoughtful.)*

STRATEGIC READING FOR
Less-Proficient Readers

D Have students explain what happens after Tantie gives bread to a mysterious old man. *(Possible response: The man gives Tantie a string, which she wears as a necklace. Beads pop up all over the place. Tantie strings the beads on her necklace.)* **Noting Relevant Details**

Set a Purpose Have students read to find out what the 33 beads that Tantie acquires represent.

Tantie was too heavy. The swing sat quiet. The only sound was Tantie's voice.

"A long, long time ago," she began, "when I was in my bare feet still, I went to market with a basket of bread and red-currant buns to sell. Market day was de busiest time. There was plenty to see as I set up my little stall and tucked cloths around de bread and buns so de flies wouldn't get them.

"I hadn't sold one thing yet when an old man came up. His clothes were ragged and he didn't have on no shoes. His feet didn't look like no ordinary feet. They looked like cow hooves. I didn't stare, though, because it rude to do that.

"He asked for a piece of bread. Well, I remember Mama telling me that morning to get good prices for de bread, but I was sure Mama hadn't meant from this man too. So, I cut off a hunk of bread, wrapped it in brown paper, and handed it to him. He looked so hungry that I reached for a bun and gave him that too. De man smiled and bowed his head at me. Then he went his way.

"After that I was busy selling bread. De buns went even faster. By afternoon, I had sold them all. Then I saw de old man coming over again. He didn't look so ragged anymore. His hair was combed and he had on a new shirt.

"'I'm sorry,' I said. 'No more bread left.'

"He didn't answer. Instead he handed me something. It was a piece of brown string. It looked like an ordinary old string, but I didn't tell him that.

"'Thank you for de bread, child,' he said. Then he shuffled off and was gone.

"I looked at de string for a while. I could use it to tie up my bread cloths, I thought. Or I could use it as a hair ribbon. But I decided I would put de string around my neck and wear it like a necklace."

"This de same string, Tantie?" I asked, fingering Tantie's bead necklace.

"De very same," she answered.

"Well, that evening, Mama was so proud I had sold all de bread that she gave me a treat. It was a small blue bamboo bead. It was de exact color of Mama's best blue head scarf.

"'Where you get this bead, Mama?' I asked.

"'Found it in de yard,' she replied.

"I wondered how it got there, but it didn't matter. I pulled out my brown string and untied it. Then I slipped de blue bead on and tied it around my neck again. It looked like a real necklace now that it had Mama's bead on it."

"Is this your mama's bead?" I asked, touching a bright blue bead on Tantie's string.

"Yes, that's it, chile," said Tantie.

"And it shines more now than de day I got it.

"Two days later, Daddy found a smooth black bead down by de sea. He brought it home in his pocket.

"'I thought you might like this,' he said, and handed it to me. It sparkled like a black sun. I untied my necklace and slipped it on next to de blue bead. Now my string was beautiful with Mama's and Daddy's bamboo beads on it.

"During de next few days, Mama and Daddy and I kept finding shiny bamboo beads

Then I slipped de blue bead on and tied it around my neck again.

672 UNIT SIX: THE ORAL TRADITION

Multicultural Perspectives

TRINIDAD LANGUAGES The official language of Trinidad is English, but islanders also speak French, Spanish, and Hindi. This mixture of languages reflects Trinidad's history as a colonized island. Christopher Columbus claimed Trinidad for Spain in 1498. The island was then inhabited by the Arawak and Carib tribes. Haitian planters of French ancestry settled in Trinidad and established a profitable sugar cane industry using African slave labor. The British gained possession of the island in 1802. Trinidad, along with the nearby island Tobago, formed a republic in 1962. The Trinidad English that Tantie speaks here is a reflection of these many influences. For instance, her name derives from the French word for aunt, *tante*. *Bois* is a French word for woods, a fitting name for the wood spirit Papa Bois. Words from the Arawak language have also been incorporated into the English language. *Hurricane, tobacco, canoe,* and *hammock* come from the Arawak words *huracan, tobaco, canana,* and *hamaca*.

672 THE LANGUAGE OF LITERATURE **TEACHER'S EDITION**

in de strangest places. I found a red one under de bed. Mama found a green one in de garden, and Daddy found a yellow one in his shoe. Mama and Daddy didn't think nothing of it, but as I added each new bead to my necklace, I got a strange, trembly feeling.

"De next week when I took Mama's bread and currant buns to market, I saw de old man who had given me my string. His clothes were still ragged and he clumped around on his hooves.

"'Hello, mister,' I said when he came over. I wrapped up a chunk of bread and two buns this time and gave them to him. He smiled and shuffled off.

"Again my day of selling flew by. Before lunchtime I had sold everything. Mama hugged me hard when I got home. But then she sat down at de kitchen table and looked serious.

"'What's wrong?' I asked.

Illustration Copyright © 1991 Brian Pinkney. From *A Wave in Her Pocket* by Lynn Joseph, reprinted by permission of Clarion Books/Houghton Mifflin Co. All rights reserved.

"'Look,' she said, pointing to a bowl on the table. I looked inside and there were de most beautiful, shiny bamboo beads I'd ever seen. Lots and lots of them. I put my hand in and touched de smooth wood.

"'Where they come from?' I asked.

"'Don't know,' said Mama. 'They were here when I turned around from de sink this morning. I thought you might know something about them, since you're collecting beads.'

"'No,' I said. 'I don't know about these.'

"Then Mama said, 'Let me see that string of beads around your neck, girl.'

"I showed it to Mama. She looked and looked at de beads and tugged on de string until I thought she'd break it. Then she looked at me and said, 'You've met Papa Bois.'[1]

"'Papa who?'

"'Papa Bois,' she murmured. 'He lives in de

---

1. **Papa Bois** (pä-pä-bwä′) *French:* Father Forest.

THE BAMBOO BEADS **673**

Art Note

Illustration by Brian Pinkney In this illustration done especially for "The Bamboo Beads," artist Brian Pinkney displays a scratchboard technique. A specially prepared surface is covered with black ink. The artist then uses a fine, sharp instrument to scratch the delicate lines of the drawing.

Reading the Art Does this illustration match your ideas about the characters? Why or why not?

Active Reading: PREDICT

E Have students predict where the beads have come from. Which clues and details in the story help them make their predictions?

Literary Note

F Like Papa Bois, Pan—the Greek god of woods, fields, and fertility—was part human and part animal, with not only the hooves but also the horns and ears of a goat. The woodland nymphs regarded Pan as ugly and rejected his attempts to woo them with beautiful music, which he played on his pipes. Like Papa Bois, Pan could provoke fear. The word *panic* is said to derive from the fears of travelers passing through the forest who heard Pan's pipes at night.

Mini-Lesson Spelling

COMPOUND WORDS AND CONTRACTIONS Tell students that when two or more words are connected with no changes, the resulting word is called a compound word. Words joined by a hyphen are another kind of compound word.

When two words are joined and one or more letters are omitted, the result is a contraction. An apostrophe takes the place of the missing letter(s).

Application Have students combine the word parts below, to form compound words and contractions used in the selection.

1. fisher + man
2. some + thing
3. you + are
4. I + am
5. neck + lace
6. my + self
7. do + not
8. thirty + three
9. grand + nieces
10. what + is

Ask students to look for more compound words and contractions, in their own writing and in things that they read, and to add these words to their personal word lists.

Reteaching/Reinforcement
• *Unit Six Resource Book,* p. 13

THE LANGUAGE OF LITERATURE **TEACHER'S EDITION 673**

Literary Concept: FOLK TALE

G Remind students that a folk tale is a story that is handed down, usually by word of mouth, among the people of a region. Like fables, folk tales often teach lessons. Ask students to describe the characteristics of this story that make it a folk tale. (*Possible response: It is being told aloud to another character, it comes from the region of Trinidad, it is about ordinary people, it contains a supernatural being, and it seems to be teaching the value of kindness.*)

CUSTOMIZING FOR
Students Acquiring English

5 Invite French-speaking students to model pronunciation of *Bonjour, vieux Papa* for the class.

CUSTOMIZING FOR
Multiple Learning Styles

H **Linguistic Learners** Have students create a list of words of greeting. Suggest students divide their lists into two columns for formal and informal greetings. You may wish to suggest they add a third column for greetings in other languages. Encourage students to survey their classmates for additional greetings to add to their lists. They can check spellings of any non-English phrases using bilingual dictionaries.

---

forest and protects de trees and forest animals from hunters. He spends his time whittling bamboo beads from fallen bamboo shoots. He's de only one who could make these beads. They're priceless.'

"Mama looked at me and gave me back de necklace. 'Have you met an old man without any feet?' she asked.

"I immediately thought of de old man from de market. 'Yes, Mama, I met him last week at de market. An old man in ragged clothes and no feet. He had cow hooves instead.'

"Mama closed her eyes and nodded her head. 'That's Papa Bois,' she said. 'He can be dangerous. Once he meets someone, he keeps track of them by counting their sins, their blessings, even their teeth, on his whittled beads. You never know with Papa Bois just what he's counting for you. The last time Papa Bois gave someone beads, the beads represented de number of days he had left to live. These beads on de table must be for you. He's counting something for you.'"

"'What?' I whispered, almost too frightened to speak.

"'We won't know till he's ready to say. Were you kind or mean to him?'

"'I gave him some bread to eat because he looked hungry,' I said.

"'Good,' said Mama, and she pulled me into her arms. 'That was very kind. Now you might as well put de beads on de string and wait until Papa Bois comes back and tells you what he's counting.'

"I put de pretty beads on de string. I didn't think they would all fit, but no matter how many I put on, de string never filled up. When every bead was on, I counted thirty-three beads. Then I tied it around my neck once more. It wasn't any heavier than when I wore de string empty.

"As de days passed, Mama, Daddy, and I kept our eyes open for Papa Bois. We thought he might come by any time. I wondered over and over what Papa Bois could be counting on my beads."

"Were you scared, Tantie?" I interrupted.

"A little," she answered. "But I knew I had been kind to Papa Bois, and that was all that mattered.

"De next time I went to market for Mama, she wanted to come with me. I told her Papa Bois might not come to our stall if she was there.

"At the stall I laid de bread and buns out nicely and covered them with cloths. I saw de old man shuffling up to my table.

"'Bonjour, vieux Papa,'[2] I said. Mama had told me that to say hello in French was de polite way to greet Papa Bois. She also said not to look at his feet no matter what.

"'Bonjour,' said de old man.

"'Would you like some bread?' I asked. Papa Bois nodded.

"As I cut him a chunk of bread, I said, 'Thank you for de pretty necklace.'

"'It's for you to wear always,' he said. 'Until you find someone who should wear it instead.'

"Papa Bois's eyes looked kind in his wrinkled face. I decided I go ask him what de beads were for.

"'De beads,' he answered, 'are for all de

> "That was de last time I ever see Papa Bois."

---

2. ***Bonjour, vieux Papa*** (bôn-zhoor′ vyœ′ pä-pä′) *French:* Hello, old Father.

674 UNIT SIX: THE ORAL TRADITION

Mini-Lesson  The Writer's Style

CHOOSING THE RIGHT WORDS Point out to students that author Lynn Joseph chooses language and words that are appropriate for her audience and type of writing. The narrator of "The Bamboo Beads" generally speaks in standard English, language that follows the rules of grammar and usage. Tantie speaks in nonstandard English, which does not. The characters' different ways of speaking give clues about their age and education.

Application Invite students to imagine that the narrator encounters Papa Bois. Have them write a dialogue between the narrator and Tantie, which describes the encounter.

Reteaching/Reinforcement
- *Writing Handbook*, anthology p. 779
- *Writing Mini-Lessons* transparencies, p. 48

The Writer's Craft
Levels of Language, p. 274
Using Dialogue, 278–280

---

674 THE LANGUAGE OF LITERATURE **TEACHER'S EDITION**

little children you'll one day have.'

"'Thirty-three children?' I asked.

"'Yes, they'll be yours, but they won't be yours,' he said mysteriously. But then he smiled a big smile.

"'All right,' I said, and I handed him de bread and buns.

"That was de last time I ever see Papa Bois. Mama said he only comes out of his forest when he's lonely for human company. Otherwise his friends are de deer, de squirrels, and de trees. The first person he meets when he leaves his forest early in de morning is de one who counts. If that person stares at his feet or laughs at him—watch out!"

"But Tantie, what happen to de thirty-three children?" I asked.

"You're one of them," she said. "Ever since your oldest cousin Jarise was born, I been de one helping to take care of all yuh. I have thirty grandnieces and nephews now. That mean three more to come. And all yuh are my children, just like Papa Bois said."

Tantie reached up and unhooked her bamboo bead necklace. Then she laid it in my hands.

"Oh," I said, looking at Tantie's necklace again. "I'd like to be de red bead."

Tantie took the necklace out of my hands and put it around my neck. She tied the string. The necklace felt cool and smooth against my skin.

"I wish I had a mirror," I said.

"It looking beautiful," said Tantie. "And it for you now. You can count your cousins on them beads."

"You're giving this to me, Tantie?" I asked, not believing what I had heard.

"Papa Bois said I go find someone who should wear it."

"Thank you," I said. I ran my fingers over the bamboo smoothness of the beads and admired the pretty colors.

"And since you wear Papa Bois's beads, you can start helping me tell these stories," said Tantie. "I been doing de work alone for too long."

Tantie reached over and adjusted the bead string on my neck.

I looked down at the shiny red bead that was me and smiled and smiled. ❖

LYNN JOSEPH

Lynn Joseph recalls: "When I was a little girl in Trinidad, I could not imagine anywhere else but my beautiful island, with its tall coconut trees, sandy beaches, and happy sounds of steel-band music. I've lived in many other places since then, but I've never forgotten the smells, sounds, and foods of my island." Joseph moved to the United States with her family and graduated from the University of Colorado. She currently lives in New York City. Joseph says she remembers listening to stories like "The Bamboo Beads" when she was growing up.

OTHER WORKS *Coconut Kind of Day: Island Poems, A Wave in Her Pocket, The Mermaid's Twin Sister: More Stories from Trinidad*

THE BAMBOO BEADS **675**

STRATEGIC READING FOR
Less-Proficient Readers

❶ Have students explain what the 33 beads that Tantie acquires represent. *(her grandnieces and grandnephews)*
Restating

From Personal Response to Critical Analysis

1. How did you react to the character of Papa Bois? Briefly describe this reaction in your notebook. *(Responses will vary.)*
2. How might this story have turned out if Tantie had not given bread to Papa Bois? *(Possible responses: The beads might have come to represent not the number of children Tantie would have but the number of days she had to live; Papa Bois might have punished her in some other way for not giving him something to eat.)*
3. In your opinion, does the narrator take after her aunt? Explain why or why not. *(Possible responses: Yes, both are interested in keeping track of their family, both are intrigued by Papa Bois, and both adore the bamboo beads. Not very much; you can tell the narrator has grown up in a different world because she speaks standard English whereas Tantie speaks a dialect.)*
4. How would you describe the ending of the story? Explain. *(Possible responses: Happy. Tantie has found someone to give the necklace to, and the narrator has a way to count her family; Sad. Tantie is getting old. Soon the narrator will take her place.)*

COMPREHENSION CHECK

1. Why does the narrator's mother suggest she talk to Tantie? *(The narrator wants a way to count her cousins, and her mother thinks that Tantie will be able to help.)*
2. What does Tantie give Papa Bois when he appears at her stall? *(a hunk of bread and a bun)*
3. What does Papa Bois tell Tantie the beads signify? *(the "little children" she'll "one day have")*
4. Who are Tantie's children? *(her grandnieces and grandnephews—the narrator and her cousins)*
5. What happens to the bamboo beads? *(Tantie gives the narrator the necklace.)*

THE LANGUAGE OF LITERATURE **TEACHER'S EDITION** **675**

Art Note

Hummingbirds in Thistle by Walter Anderson A prolific artist, Walter Anderson made hundreds of wood block prints and thousands of watercolors. He also illustrated fairy tales and classics. Anderson is best known for his depictions of the flora and fauna of the Gulf Coast, which he captured in lush watercolors.

Reading the Art *How many hummingbirds can you find in the picture? What are the hummingbirds doing? How does the artist convey the hummingbirds' rapid wing movement in this painting?*

STRATEGIC READING FOR
Less-Proficient Readers

Set a Purpose Have students read to find out who the hummingbird is.

Hummingbirds in Thistle (1955), Walter Anderson. Watercolor. Walter Anderson Museum of Art, Ocean Springs, Mississippi, courtesy of the family of Walter Anderson.

676 UNIT SIX: THE ORAL TRADITION

676 THE LANGUAGE OF LITERATURE **TEACHER'S EDITION**

The Legend of the Hummingbird

retold by Pura Belpré

Between the towns of Cayey and Cidra,[1] far up in the hills, there was once a small pool fed by a waterfall that tumbled down the side of the mountain. The pool was surrounded by pomarosa trees,[2] and the Indians used to call it Pomarosa Pool. It was the favorite place of Alida, the daughter of an Indian chief, a man of power and wealth among the people of the hills.

---

1. **Cayey** (kä-yā′) . . . **Cidra** (sē′drä): towns in Puerto Rico.
2. **pomarosa** (pô-mä-rô′sä) **trees**: trees, found in the West Indies, that bear an applelike fruit; also spelled *poma rosa*.

THE LEGEND OF THE HUMMINGBIRD **677**

Linking to Science

A The hummingbird's skeletal structure allows its wings to twist like human wrists. Twisting 22 to 78 times per second, the bird can hover while it drinks from flowers where there is no place to land. As the hummingbird's strong wings beat rapidly, they produce the sound from which its name derives.

CUSTOMIZING FOR
Multiple Learning Styles

B **Spatial or Graphic Learners** Invite students to draw or paint, perhaps in watercolors, the poolside setting of the legend.

Mini-Lesson: Speaking, Listening, and Viewing

CHORAL READING Inform students that a choral reading can make a story sound like music. In a choral reading, groups of readers act as a choir, reading aloud in the same rhythm and loudness or softness.

Application Divide students in small groups for a choral reading. Assign each group a portion of the selection (narrator's passages; words of Alida, Taroo, the moon, and so on). Have each group choose a conductor. Allow groups to practice reading aloud their assignment as a chorus. Then have groups combine their parts in a class choral reading. You may wish to invite families or other classes to attend the choral reading.

THE LANGUAGE OF LITERATURE **TEACHER'S EDITION** **677**

Active Reading: CONNECT

C Ask students whether they have ever been in a situation like Alida's, in which their parents forbade them to be friends with someone they liked. Ask how this made them feel. Ask how they handled the situation with their parents and their friend and what they think Alida might do in this situation.

CUSTOMIZING FOR
Multiple Learning Styles

D **Spatial Learners** Have students close their eyes and visualize Taroo's vigil beside Pomarosa Pool, the moon's speaking to Taroo, and Yukiyú's changing Taroo into a many-colored bird. Invite students to draw or paint their visualizations. Students may wish to make a three-paneled picture (triptych) to show the three different scenes.

One day, when Alida had come to the pool to rest after a long walk, a young Indian came there to pick some fruit from the trees. Alida was surprised, for he was not of her tribe. Yet he said he was no stranger to the pool. This was where he had first seen Alida, and he had often returned since then to pick fruit, hoping to see her again.

And the great god Yukiyú took pity on her and changed her into a delicate red flower.

He told her about himself to make her feel at home. He confessed, with honesty and frankness, that he was a member of the dreaded Carib[3] tribe that had so often attacked the island of Boriquen.[4] As a young boy, he had been left behind after one of those raids, and he had stayed on the island ever since.

Alida listened closely to his story, and the two became friends. They met again in the days that followed, and their friendship grew stronger. Alida admired the young man's courage in living among his enemies. She learned to call him by his Carib name, Taroo, and he called her Alida, just as her own people did. Before long, their friendship had turned into love.

Their meetings by the pool were always brief. Alida was afraid their secret might be discovered, and careful though she was, there came a day when someone saw them and told her father. Alida was forbidden to visit the Pomarosa Pool, and to put an end to her romance with the stranger, her father decided to marry her to a man of his own choosing. Preparations for the wedding started at once.

Alida was torn with grief, and one evening she cried out to her god: "O *Yukiyú*,[5] help me! Kill me or do what you will with me, but do not let me marry this man whom I do not love!"

And the great god Yukiyú took pity on her and changed her into a delicate red flower.

Meanwhile Taroo, knowing nothing of Alida's sorrow, still waited for her by the Pomarosa Pool. Day after day he waited. Sometimes he stayed there until a mantle[6] of stars was spread across the sky.

One night the moon took pity on him. "Taroo," she called from her place high above the stars. "O Taroo, wait no longer for Alida! Your secret was made known, and Alida was to be married to a man of her father's choosing. In her grief she called to her god, Yukiyú; he heard her plea for help and changed her into a red flower."

"Ahee, ahee!" cried Taroo. "O moon, what is the name of the red flower?"

"Only Yukiyú knows that," the moon replied.

---

3. **Carib** (kăr´ĭb): a Native American people of the West Indies.
4. **Boriquen** (bô-rē´kĕn): an early name for Puerto Rico.
5. **Yukiyú** (yōō-kē-yōō´).
6. **mantle**: covering.

678 UNIT SIX: THE ORAL TRADITION

Mini-Lesson Grammar

> **Subject**
> *It was Alida's favorite place.*
> **After Linking Verbs**
> *The red flower was she.*

SUBJECT PRONOUNS Use the example shown to remind students that a pronoun can take the place of a noun. Subject pronouns (*I, you, he, she, it, we,* and *they*) are used as subjects of verbs or after linking verbs.

Application Have students rewrite the sentences, choosing the correct pronoun forms.
1. (<u>She</u>, Her) and (<u>he</u>, him) were changed into a red flower and hummingbird.
2. Yukiyú rescued Alida from a loveless marriage. A compassionate god is (<u>he</u>, him).
3. (<u>We</u>, us) students enjoyed "The Legend of the Hummingbird."

Reteaching/Reinforcement
- *Grammar Handbook,* p. 824–825
- *Grammar Mini-Lessons* copymasters, p. 12, transparencies, p. 10

 **The Writer's Craft**

Using Subject Pronouns, pp. 440–442

678 THE LANGUAGE OF LITERATURE TEACHER'S EDITION

Then Taroo called out: "O Yukiyú, god of my Alida, help me too! Help me to find her!"

And just as the great god had heard Alida's plea, he listened now to Taroo and decided to help him. There by the Pomarosa Pool, before the moon and the silent stars, the great god changed Taroo into a small many-colored bird.

"Fly, Colibrí,[7] and find your love among the flowers," he said.

Off went the Colibrí, flying swiftly, and as he flew, his wings made a sweet humming sound.

In the morning the Indians saw a new bird darting about among the flowers, swift as an arrow and brilliant as a jewel. They heard the humming of its wings, and in amazement they saw it hover in the air over every blossom, kissing the petals of the flowers with its long slender bill. They liked the new bird with the music in its wings, and they called it Hummingbird.

Ever since then the little many-colored bird has hovered over every flower he finds, but returns most often to the flowers that are red. He is still looking, always looking, for the one red flower that will be his lost Alida. He has not found her yet. ❖

---

7. *Colibrí* (kô-lē-brē′).

PURA BELPRÉ

1899–1982

Pura Belpré, author and puppeteer-storyteller, was born in Puerto Rico and came to the United States in the 1920s. Working, beginning in 1921, as the first Hispanic librarian in the New York Public Library, she realized there was no folklore from Puerto Rico and set about expanding Puerto Rican folklore programs. Belpré grew up in a family of storytellers and was fluent in Spanish, English, and French. She incorporated her Spanish ancestry into her puppet shows as well as her books and thus provided young people a way of learning more about the Puerto Rican culture. In 1978 Belpré was honored for her distinguished contribution in Spanish literature by the Bay Area Bilingual Education League and the University of San Francisco.

OTHER WORKS *Juan Bobo and the Queen's Necklace: A Puerto Rican Folk Tale, Dance of the Animals: A Puerto Rican Folk Tale, Once in Puerto Rico*

WORDS TO KNOW
hover (hŭv′ər) *v.* to stay fluttering in the air near one place

---

STRATEGIC READING FOR
Less-Proficient Readers

E Ask students who the hummingbird is. *(Taroo)* Finding the Main Idea

From Personal Response to Critical Analysis

1. What was your favorite element of the legend—its characters, setting, plot, or treatment of the theme "togetherness: a tug of war"? Write your response in your notebook. *(Responses will vary.)*

2. Do you think that Alida should have married the man her father chose? Explain your answer. *(Possible responses: Yes; Alida would ultimately regret betraying her people for a man she loved when she was young. No; Alida had to make her own decision. The great god's helping her shows that Alida was right to flee from a loveless marriage.)*

3. What images or descriptive passages stayed with you after you heard the legend? Write or draw your response in your notebook. *(Responses will vary.)*

COMPREHENSION CHECK
1. Where does the action of the legend take place? *(Beside a small pool, called Pomarosa Pool, which is fed by a waterfall; Pomarosa Pool is located between two hill towns on the island of Boriquen in Puerto Rico.)*
2. Why does Alida's father arrange for her to be married? *(He wants to end her romance with Taroo, who comes from an enemy tribe.)*
3. How do the moon and Yukiyú come to the lovers' aid? *(The moon tells Taroo what has happened to Alida. Yukiyú changes Taroo into a hummingbird and Alida into a flower, which saves Alida from the marriage her father arranged and gives her and Taroo a chance of finding each other again.)*
4. What explanation does the legend give for the hummingbird's drinking nectar? *(The hummingbird is Taroo, "kissing" each flower in hopes of finding his beloved Alida.)*

Literature Connection

Dramatize a Tale As students divide the tasks of preparing the storyboard and drafting the script, they should also assign someone the job of editor, to review the storyboard for accuracy and continuity. The editor should also review the script to make sure it follows the storyboard before the actors begin to learn their lines.

Rubric

3 Full Accomplishment The dramatization grows out of the storyboard. Both depict significant scenes. Dialogue is meaningful and true to character.

2 Substantial Accomplishment The relationship between the storyboard and dramatization is sometimes unclear. Scenes are well played but not always significant enough to merit treatment. Dialogue, while entertaining, shows lapses in understanding of character.

1 Little or Partial Accomplishment Storyboard and dramatization do not reflect careful thought or preparation. The tale would not be intelligible to an audience member who had not heard it already.

RESPONDING OPTIONS

LITERATURE CONNECTION PROJECT 1 — Multimodal Activity

Dramatize a Tale Working in a small group, dramatize one of the tales you've just read. First, organize the plot elements of your adaptation by designing and preparing a storyboard, a series of drawings to illustrate the tale's events. An example of a storyboard for "Why Monkeys Live in Trees" is shown here. Include props, sound effects, and costumes. Next, write a script for a narrator and dialogue for the characters. Then assign roles, rehearse, and perform your adaptation. If equipment is available, you can videotape the performance and share it with another class or a group of parents.

This storyboard shows how the action of a tale unfolds.

SOCIAL STUDIES CONNECTION PROJECT 2 — Multimodal Activity

Create a Museum Display In the 1800s, hummingbirds became important in the trade between Europe and tropical America. In one year alone, a single London dealer imported more than 400,000 hummingbird skins from the West Indies.

Hummingbirds are a familiar feature in legends of Native American cultures. For example, the Aztec war god wears a bracelet of hummingbird feathers, and Puerto Rican natives believe that hummingbird nests cure asthma. With a small group of classmates, explore the role of the hummingbird in the Aztec and Puerto Rican cultures and set up a display on this topic in your classroom. Here are some ideas to pursue:

Writers Use encyclopedias, computer databases, and other reference materials to gather information. Then choose a format, such as an informative brochure or a poster, to include in the display.

Artists Hopi hummingbird kachinas, or spirit dolls, often feature sharp beaks and colored feathers. Use colored pencils or a drawing software program to design a hummingbird kachina. Then work in a group to build a kachina for the display.

Curators Prepare the exhibit space in which to display your group's materials. Write informative cards for the exhibit and act as a museum guide for visitors.

680 UNIT SIX: THE ORAL TRADITION

Social Studies Connection

Create a Museum Display Direct students to the information in their books for tips on gathering information (writers), constructing a kachina (artists), and exhibiting the display (curators).

Rubric

3 Full Accomplishment Students portray the hummingbird in equally compelling writing and art. The display integrates both.

2 Substantial Accomplishment The quality of writing and art is uneven, although the information is interesting. The display does not effectively showcase writers' and artists' work.

1 Little or Partial Accomplishment A viewer would learn little about the hummingbird through viewing the display. Information is poorly organized and kachinas are sloppily constructed.

SCIENCE CONNECTION PROJECT 3 *Multimodal Activity*

 Investigate Bamboo The beads that Papa Bois gave Tantie were whittled from bamboo, a type of huge woody grass that grows in the Eastern and Western Hemispheres. There are about 200 kinds of bamboo, and the plants are used for many purposes. Research the bamboo plant and its uses in Trinidadian and other cultures. Then, as a class, combine your research on a large chart similar to the one shown. Add drawings or pictures to the chart to illustrate some of the products derived from bamboo.

Uses of Bamboo		
Country	Products	Other Uses

ACROSS CULTURES MINI-PROJECTS *Multimodal Activity*

Compare Cinderella Tales Compare "In the Land of Small Dragon" with similar Cinderella-like tales from other cultures, such as China and Germany. Get together with other classmates and take turns sharing your findings. Then arrange a book display of the various picture-book versions of Cinderella you may have found.

Explore Flight Hummingbirds are unique in their ability to fly upside down and in reverse and to hover, as Taroo does in "The Legend of the Hummingbird." Investigate the laws of aerodynamics (âr´ō-dī-năm´ĭks) that explain this ability. Then draw a diagram to demonstrate those laws.

Make a Kite In Asian folklore, dragons were honored. Images of dragons appeared on common objects, including the dragon kites that remain popular in the culture of Vietnam. Find out how kites are constructed. Learn more about kite celebrations in Asian cultures. Then organize a kite day, during which students can build their own kites and display them to their classmates.

Write Proverbs Proverbs, such as those found in "In the Land of Small Dragon," are old and familiar sayings that express a basic truth. For example, you may recognize "A man's worth is what he does, / Not what he says he can do" as "Actions speak louder than words." Write proverbs for "The Bamboo Beads" and "The Legend of the Hummingbird." Compile the class proverbs on a poster.

Extended Social Studies Reading

 MORE ABOUT THE CULTURES
- *The Dorling Kindersley History of the World* by Plantagenet Somerset Fry
- *Exploration and Conquest: The Americas after Columbus* by Betsey and Giulio Maestro
- *The Children's Atlas of Civilizations* by Anthony Mason
- *Street Smart! Cities of the Ancient World* published by Runestone

PROJECTS **681**

Science Connection

Investigate Bamboo For their research, students can use an on-line or print encyclopedia or a specialized book on grasses around the world. Students can do a subject search in a library catalog to locate the latter.

Rubric

3 Full Accomplishment Charts reflect solid research and synthesis of information. Students clearly and imaginatively use words and pictures to show the uses of bamboo.

2 Substantial Accomplishment Charts reflect solid research but little synthesis of information. Students' use of words and pictures varies in clarity and lacks imagination.

1 Little or Partial Accomplishment Charts reflect inadequate research and use of unsynthesized information. Students' use of words and pictures is ineffective.

Multicultural Perspectives

Compare Cinderella Tales Students can use a school or public library to find Cinderella-like tales from other cultures. Effective displays will enable viewers to compare the tales easily.

Explore Flight Gifted students can consult a middle- or high-school physics textbook that explains aerodynamics. Other students might consult a science trade book on forces and motion.

Make a Kite Lead the class in constructing a materials list to help ensure that, on kite day, students have everything they need to construct their kites.

Write Proverbs Additional proverbs for students to consult as models can be found in *Poor Richard's Almanac* by Benjamin Franklin, and the book of Proverbs, in the Bible. Remind students before they begin writing that their proverbs should relate directly to the tales.

THE LANGUAGE OF LITERATURE TEACHER'S EDITION **681**

OVERVIEW

Objectives

- To understand and appreciate a myth, a folk tale, and a fable that tell about characters who are rewarded for kind acts
- To appreciate the history, culture, and geography of ancient Greece, Puerto Rico, and Guatemala
- To extend understanding of the selection through a variety of multimodal and cross-curricular activities

Reading Pathways

- Select one or several students to read each story aloud to the entire class or to small groups of students. Assign this reading in advance so that the readers can incorporate into their presentations some of the techniques used by professional storytellers. Have the audience listen carefully to the stories without following along in their texts.

- Read the stories aloud to the class, pausing at key points to discuss how elements of the stories inform students about the cultures of ancient Greece, Puerto Rico, or Guatemala. Have students compare these cultures to their own.

- After students have read the tales once, they can read them again to identify structural elements such as main characters, minor characters, conflict, setting, and plot. Then have students identify similarities and differences between these tales and the selections in the related unit. For example, both Ibrahima of "Abd al-Rahman Ibrahima" (page 257) and Damon and Pythias extol the value of friendship in resisting injustice.

PREVIEWING

LINKS TO UNIT THREE

A Sense of Fairness

Activating Prior Knowledge
Who is fairest of us all? What is just and what is unjust? These questions were raised in the selections presented in Unit Three. Many folk tales also have explored these issues. Each of the tales you are about to read illustrates a lesson in justice.

Building Background

GUATEMALA

The Disobedient Child

retold by Victor Montejo (môn-tě′hô)

Guatemala is one of the seven countries that form Central America, the narrow land bridge that connects North and South America. One of the first civilizations in the Americas, the Mayan Empire, thrived in Central America from about A.D. 250 to 900. Ancient Mayan culture is reflected in this Guatemalan fable about a boy who disregards warnings. The boy seems unteachable until he is put to the test by someone with super-natural powers.

682 UNIT SIX: THE ORAL TRADITION

PRINT AND MEDIA RESOURCES

UNIT SIX RESOURCE BOOK
Strategic Reading: Literature, p. 17
Vocabulary SkillBuilder, p. 20
Reading SkillBuilder, p. 18
Spelling SkillBuilder, p. 19

GRAMMAR MINI-LESSONS
Transparencies, pp. 12, 40
Copymasters, p. 19

WRITING MINI-LESSONS
Transparencies, p. 34

ACCESS FOR STUDENTS ACQUIRING ENGLISH
Selection Summaries
Reading and Writing Support

FORMAL ASSESSMENT
Selection Test, pp. 121–122
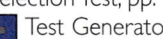 Test Generator

 **AUDIO LIBRARY**
See Reference Card

682 THE LANGUAGE OF LITERATURE TEACHER'S EDITION

GREECE
Building Background

Damon and Pythias: A Drama
retold by Fan Kissen

According to legend, Damon and Pythias lived in the city of Syracuse, on the island of Sicily, in the fourth century B.C. In ancient times, Sicily was a part of the Greek world. Syracuse, one of the most powerful cities in the ancient world, was ruled at that time by a tyrant named Dionysius. Only Damon and Pythias dared to question the king's laws—and lived to talk about it.

PUERTO RICO

The Three Wishes
retold by Ricardo E. Alegría
(ä-lĕ-grē′ä)
Building Background

The island of Puerto Rico—which means "rich port" in Spanish—was named by its Spanish settlers for the abundance of treasures from the fields and forests that were loaded on ships bound for Spain. This Puerto Rican tale takes place in the forest of a distant past. Like many folk tales that involve the granting of wishes, the story illustrates what is most important in life and what brings the greatest happiness.

Setting a Purpose

AS YOU READ . . .

Consider the way humor is used.

Find out which elements of magic and the supernatural are feared or accepted.

Discover what human faults are seen as common to everyone.

LINKS TO UNIT THREE **683**

WORDS TO KNOW

emit (ĭ-mĭt′) *v.* to send out; give forth (p. 696)
mocking (mŏk′ĭng) *adj.* making fun of **mock** *v.* (p. 688)
repentance (rĭ-pĕn′təns) *n.* sorrow for wrongdoing (p. 693)

subside (səb-sīd′) *v.* to become weaker or less active; decrease (p. 697)
tolerate (tŏl′ə-rāt′) *v.* to put up with (p. 695)

SUMMARY

Damon and Pythias Damon and Pythias are best friends who openly criticize Sicily's evil king. When Pythias criticizes the king to his face, he is thrown in prison and sentenced to death. Pythias's only wish is to see his mother and sister before he dies. Damon offers to take his friend's place in prison so that he may travel to see them. Curious to test the limits of their friendship, the king agrees to this arrangement. Pythias makes the trip home safely but is attacked by robbers on his return journey. He arrives just before the execution and finds Damon—who has believed in Pythias throughout his absence—ready to die in his place. The king is so impressed by their faith and friendship that he sets both men free.

The Three Wishes In this Puerto Rican folk tale, a woodsman's wife generously shares her food with a saint disguised as an old man. In return for her kindness, he grants her three wishes. She exclaims, "Oh, if my husband were only here to hear what you say!" The startled woodsman appears and, upon learning that his wife has wasted the first wish, scolds her, saying "May you grow ears of a donkey!" When his wish comes true, the woodsman feels ashamed. His final wish is to regain the happiness that he and his wife shared before she grew donkey ears. Their wish granted, the couple ask God to forgive their greed. The old man then reveals that he was teaching a moral lesson: just as there can be happiness in poverty, there can be unhappiness in riches. He then rewards the repentant couple with a son.

The Disobedient Child This Guatemalan fable tells of a disobedient boy who runs away from home. He takes shelter with an old man, who asks him to cook 13 beans in a pot. When the boy disobeys his instructions, the old man gives him a second chance but forbids him to open a little door in the house. The boy, however, opens the door, finding three capes and three jars, one of which he opens. When huge clouds spring out of the jar, the cold, frightened boy puts on one of the capes. He is then turned into thunder and lifted into the stormy sky. Hearing the thunder, the old man rushes home, rescues the boy, and restores order in the sky. The old man then reveals that he is Qich Mam, a powerful rain spirit. The boy feels guilty and promises Qich Mam never again to disobey his parents—and lives up to his word.

THE LANGUAGE OF LITERATURE TEACHER'S EDITION **683**

Art Note

Roman copy of *Diadoumenos* by Polykleitos (originally created around 440 B.C.)

***Achilles* from a Pompeiian wall painting**

Reading the Art *Compare and contrast the expressions of the two figures. What difference does it make, if any, that one is a sculpture and the other is a wall painting?*

EDITOR'S NOTE *With the permission of the author or copyright holder, the following alterations have been made to the text: The announcer has been deleted from the Cast of Characters and the announcer's only speech has been deleted from the opening of the play.*

CUSTOMIZING FOR
Students Acquiring English

- Use **ACCESS FOR STUDENTS ACQUIRING ENGLISH**, *Reading and Writing Support.*

- Encourage students to take more substantial roles than they have in previous units in this last play in the text. Some may feel more comfortable reading the narrator than one of the characters.

- Students may have difficulty with the formal language of this Greek drama. Encourage students to restate dialogue in their own words to check their understanding of the drama.

- In addition to these boxes, you may want to use the suggestions under Strategic Reading for Less-Proficient Readers.

Top: Detail of statue of Diadoumenos (440 B.C.), unknown artist. Roman copy of Greek original, pentelic marble, The Metropolitan Museum of Art, Fletcher Fund, 1925 (25.78.56). Copyright © The Metropolitan Museum of Art. Bottom: Detail of Chiron the centaur teaching Achilles to play the lyre (first to third century A.D.), Roman fresco from Pompeii, Museo Archeologico Nazionale, Naples, Italy. Photo Copyright © Erich Lessing/Art Resource, New York.

684 UNIT SIX: THE ORAL TRADITION

Mini-Lesson  Reading Skills/Strategies

RELATING CAUSE AND EFFECT Remind students that events are often related by cause and effect. One event causes another event, the effect, to happen. Sometimes the effect of one event then goes on to cause an effect of its own. To help students visualize a cause-and-effect chain of events, have them imagine the action of falling dominoes.

Application Have students link three events in the highlighted passage on pages 685 and 686 in a cause-and-effect relationship. Have students use a chart like the one shown.

Reteaching/Reinforcement
- *Unit Six Resource Book*, p. 18

684 THE LANGUAGE OF LITERATURE **TEACHER'S EDITION**

DAMON AND PYTHIAS: A DRAMA

RETOLD BY FAN KISSEN

CAST OF CHARACTERS

Damon
Pythias
King
Soldier
First Robber
Second Robber
Mother
Narrator
First Voice
Second Voice
Third Voice

(*Sound: Iron door opens and shuts. Key in lock.*)
(*Music: Up full and out.*)

Narrator. Long, long ago there lived on the island of Sicily[1] two young men named Damon and Pythias.[2] They were known far and wide for the strong friendship each had for the other. Their names have come down to our own times to mean true friendship. You may hear it said of two persons:

First Voice. Those two? Why, they're like Damon and Pythias!

Narrator. The king of that country was a cruel tyrant. He made cruel laws, and he showed no mercy toward anyone who broke his laws. Now, you might very well wonder:

Second Voice. Why didn't the people rebel?

Narrator. Well, the people didn't dare rebel because they feared the king's great and powerful army. No one dared say a word against the king or his laws—except Damon and Pythias. One day a soldier overheard Pythias speaking against a new law the king had proclaimed.

Soldier. Ho, there! Who are you that dares to speak so about our king?

Pythias (*unafraid*). I am called Pythias.

Soldier. Don't you know it is a crime to speak against the king or his laws? You are under

---

1. **Sicily** (sĭs′ə-lē): large island off the southern tip of Italy.
2. **Damon** (dā′mən) ... **Pythias** (pĭth′ē-əs).

DAMON AND PYTHIAS **685**

Mini-Lesson: Speaking, Listening, and Viewing

BACKGROUND MUSIC Remind students that background music can enhance the mood in a drama such as *Damon and Pythias*. Background music can be used to heighten suspense, indicate the passage of time, or convey an emotion. In addition, background music can serve as a bridge between scenes.

Application Invite students to select background music to accompany a reading of *Damon and Pythias*. Suggest that students begin by reviewing the text to find places where the stage directions call for music to denote beginnings, endings, or the passage of time. Students may choose to add music in other places as well. In researching and selecting music, students can use the audio resources of a school or local library. You may wish to invite families or other classes to a class reading of the drama with musical accompaniment.

STRATEGIC READING FOR Less-Proficient Readers

B Have students describe Pythias. *(Possible response: brave, honest, intelligent, and forthright)* Making Generalizations

Set a Purpose Have students read to learn the depth of the friendship between Damon and Pythias.

Literary Concept: CHARACTERIZATION

C Have students make inferences about the king's character, based on his behavior in this passage. *(Possible response: The king is cruel and merciless.)*

Active Reading: PREDICT

D Ask students if they think there is anything Damon can do to help save his friend Pythias. *(Possible responses: Damon might appeal to the king for mercy; he might rally support among their mutual friends.)*

---

arrest! Come and tell this opinion of yours to the king's face!

(Music: A few short bars in and out.)

Narrator. When Pythias was brought before the king, he showed no fear. He stood straight and quiet before the throne.

King *(hard, cruel).* So, Pythias! They tell me you do not approve of the laws I make.

Pythias. I am not alone, Your Majesty, in thinking your laws are cruel. But you rule the people with such an iron hand that they dare not complain.

King *(angry).* But you have the daring to complain for them! Have they appointed you their champion?[3]

Pythias. No, Your Majesty. I speak for myself alone. I have no wish to make trouble for anyone. But I am not afraid to tell you that the people are suffering under your rule. They want to have a voice in making the laws for themselves. You do not allow them to speak up for themselves.

King. In other words, you are calling me a tyrant! Well, you shall learn for yourself how a tyrant treats a rebel! Soldier! Throw this man into prison!

Soldier. At once, Your Majesty! Don't try to resist, Pythias!

Pythias. I know better than to try to resist a soldier of the king! And for how long am I to remain in prison, Your Majesty, merely for speaking out for the people?

King *(cruel).* Not for very long, Pythias. Two weeks from today, at noon, you shall be put to death in the public square as an example to anyone else who may dare to question my laws or acts. Off to prison with him, soldier!

(Music: In briefly and out.)

Narrator. When Damon heard that his friend Pythias had been thrown into prison and the severe punishment that was to follow, he was heartbroken. He rushed to the prison and persuaded the guard to let him speak to his friend.

Damon. Oh, Pythias! How terrible to find you here! I wish I could do something to save you!

Pythias. Nothing can save me, Damon, my dear friend. I am prepared to die. But there is one thought that troubles me greatly.

Damon. What is it? I will do anything to help you.

Pythias. I'm worried about what will happen to my mother and my sister when I'm gone.

Damon. I'll take care of them, Pythias, as if they were my own mother and sister.

Pythias. Thank you, Damon. I have money to leave them. But there are other things I must arrange. If only I could go to see them before I die! But they live two days' journey from here, you know.

Damon. I'll go to the king and beg him to give you your freedom for a few days. You'll give your word to return at the end of that time. Everyone in Sicily knows you for a man who has never broken his word.

Pythias. Do you believe for one moment that the king would let me leave this prison, no matter how good my word may have been all my life?

Damon. I'll tell him that I shall take your place in this prison cell. I'll tell him that if you do

---

3. **champion:** one who fights to help or defend a person or group.

686 UNIT SIX: THE ORAL TRADITION

Mini-Lesson Study Skills

MEMORIZING Point out to students that some information is best learned and remembered through memorization. For example, in learning a foreign language students memorize patterns of verb conjugation and vocabulary words. Similarly, by committing lines of a poem or play to memory, students can retain all or part of a selection for years to come.

Application Working in small groups, have students select a short scene of *Damon and Pythias* to memorize. The exchange between the robbers and Pythias, on pages 688 and 689, is one possibility. Give students time to memorize their lines and rehearse. Remind students to include movement and gesture to make their characters come alive. Invite groups to perform for the class.

686 THE LANGUAGE OF LITERATURE TEACHER'S EDITION

not return by the appointed day, he may kill me in your place!

Pythias. No, no, Damon! You must not do such a foolish thing! I cannot—I will not—let you do this! Damon! Damon! Don't go! (*to himself*) Damon, my friend! You may find yourself in a cell beside me!

(*Music: In briefly and out.*)

Damon (*begging*). Your Majesty! I beg of you! Let Pythias go home for a few days to bid farewell to his mother and sister. He gives his word that he will return at your appointed time. Everyone knows that his word can be trusted.

King. In ordinary business affairs—perhaps. But he is now a man under sentence of death. To free him even for a few days would strain his honesty—any man's honesty—too far. Pythias would never return here! I consider him a traitor, but I'm certain he's no fool.

Damon. Your Majesty! I will take his place in the prison until he comes back. If he does not return, then you may take my life in his place.

King (*astonished*). What did you say, Damon?

Damon. I'm so certain of Pythias that I am offering to die in his place if he fails to return on time.

King. I can't believe you mean it!

Damon. I do mean it, Your Majesty.

King. You make me very curious, Damon, so curious that I'm willing to put you and Pythias to the test. This exchange of prisoners will be made. But Pythias must be back two weeks from today, at noon.

Damon. Thank you, Your Majesty!

King. The order with my official seal[4] shall go by your own hand, Damon. But I warn you, if your friend does not return on time, you shall surely die in his place! I shall show no mercy!

(*Music: In briefly and out.*)

Narrator. Pythias did not like the king's bargain with Damon. He did not like to leave his friend in prison with the chance that he might lose his life if something went wrong. But at last Damon persuaded him to leave, and Pythias set out for his home. More than a week went by. The day set for the death sentence drew near. Pythias did not return. Everyone in the city knew of the condition on which the king had permitted Pythias to go home. Everywhere people met, the talk was sure to turn to the two friends.

First Voice. Do you suppose Pythias will come back?

Second Voice. Why should he stick his head under the king's axe once he's escaped?

Third Voice. Still, would an honorable man like Pythias let such a good friend die for him?

First Voice. There's no telling what a man will do when it's a question of his own life against another's.

Second Voice. But if Pythias doesn't come back before the time is up, he will be killing his friend.

Third Voice. Well, there's still a few days' time. I, for one, am certain that Pythias will return in time.

Second Voice. And I am just as certain that he will not. Friendship is friendship, but a man's own life is something stronger, I say!

Narrator. Two days before the time was up, the king himself visited Damon in his prison cell.

---

4. **official seal:** mark or stamp that shows that the order came from the king.

DAMON AND PYTHIAS **687**

Mini-Lesson Literary Concepts

REVIEWING NARRATOR Remind students that a narrator tells a story. A narrator can be a character who takes part in the action of a story or is outside the action. In some plays, the narrator is not seen but is a voice heard from offstage. In other plays, the narrator is seen at the side of the stage. Sometimes the narrator wanders through the action unseen by other characters.

Application In a drama, characters can speak for themselves, so students may wonder why a narrator is needed. Have students review the narrator's speeches and make a list of the functions that this character serves.

Art Note

The Court of Emperor Augustus Roman bas relief (c 1st century B.C.-1st century A.D.)

Reading the Art What expressions do you see on the faces of the crowd? What differences and similarities do you see in people's clothing? What is the role of this crowd? How can you relate this picture to the crowd scenes in Damon and Pythias?

CUSTOMIZING FOR
Multiple Learning Styles

G **Musical Learners** Call on volunteers to demonstrate a mocking tone of voice.

CUSTOMIZING FOR
Students Acquiring English

1. Explain that *meanwhile* means "at the same time."
2. Point out that *Farewell* is a formal and old-fashioned way of saying "good-bye."

Critical Thinking:
MAKING JUDGMENTS

H Ask students to discuss whether they think it was fair of Pythias' mother to plead for him to stay longer. (*Possible responses: It is fair because she loves him and he is about to be executed. It is unfair because his delay could cause Damon's death, and she makes it harder for Pythias to leave.*)

Literary Concept:
CHARACTERIZATION

I Ask students to infer what Pythias' actions in this passage reveal about his character. (*Possible response: Pythias' actions show that he is unselfish. Even when he is facing death, he thinks about others.*)

Detail of Procession of the court of Emperor Augustus (about 13–9 B.C.), unknown Roman artist. Museum of the Ara Pacis, Rome, Nimatallah/Art Resource, New York.

(*Sound: Iron door unlocked and opened.*)

King (*mocking*). You see now, Damon, that you were a fool to make this bargain. Your friend has tricked you! He will not come back here to be killed! He has deserted you!

Damon (*calm and firm*). I have faith in my friend. I know he will return.

King (*mocking*). We shall see!

(*Sound: Iron door shut and locked.*)

Narrator. Meanwhile, when Pythias reached the home of his family, he arranged his business affairs so that his mother and sister would be able to live comfortably for the rest of their years. Then he said a last farewell to them before starting back to the city.

Mother (*in tears*). Pythias, it will take you only two days to get back. Stay another day, I beg you!

Pythias. I dare not stay longer, Mother. Remember, Damon is locked up in my prison cell while I'm gone. Please don't make it harder for me! Farewell! Don't weep for me. My death may help to bring better days for all our people.

Narrator. So Pythias began his return journey in plenty of time. But bad luck struck him on the very first day. At twilight, as he walked along a lonely stretch of woodland, a rough voice called:

First Robber. Not so fast there, young man! Stop!

Pythias (*startled*). Oh! What is it? What do you want?

Second Robber. Your money bags.

Pythias. My money bags? I have only this small bag of coins. I shall need them for some last favors, perhaps, before I die.

WORDS TO KNOW   **mocking** (mŏk´ĭng) *adj.* making fun of   **mock** *v.*

688   THE LANGUAGE OF LITERATURE TEACHER'S EDITION

Mini-Lesson   The Writer's Style

EXAMPLES AS SUPPORTING DETAILS
Point out to students that sometimes the best way to help readers understand a point is to give them an example. In *Damon and Pythias*, author Fan Kissen often uses examples ("He made cruel laws, and he showed no mercy toward anyone who broke his laws") to support main ideas ("The king . . . was a cruel tyrant").

Application Invite students to find examples used to support the Narrator's point on page 688, that "bad luck struck [Pythias] on the very first day."

(*Pythias is robbed, tied up, and abandoned.*) Then have students write a paragraph with the main idea "Damon trusted Pythias with his life." Tell them to use examples from the myth as supporting details.

Reteaching/Reinforcement
- *Writing Handbook*, anthology, p. 784
- *Writing Mini-Lessons* transparencies, p. 34

The Writer's Craft
Developing a Topic, pp. 205–210

STRATEGIC READING FOR

Less-Proficient Readers

J Ask students to characterize the friendship between Damon and Pythias. *(Possible response: They trust each other completely and keep their promises. Damon gives up his freedom for his friend. Pythias leaves his family early to make sure he gets to the city on time.)* **Evaluating**

Set a Purpose Have students read to find out if Pythias gets back in time to save Damon.

Literary Links

K Remind students of the efforts of John Cox to free Ibrahima in "Abd al-Rahman Ibrahima" from *Now Is Your Time!* (page 257). Ask students how the effort is similar to Damon's effort to help Pythias. *(Both are acts of friendship and kindness. Neither task is easy—both Cox and Damon must work hard to convince authorities to agree to their requests.)*

Active Reading: CLARIFY

L Have students discuss the soldier's motivation for cheering. You may wish to use the following model to focus students' thoughts:

Think-Aloud Model *Why does the soldier shout "Long live the king"? Doesn't the soldier realize what a tyrant the king is? Maybe the soldier shouts his support because the army is loyal to the king. Also, this expression is used to introduce a king, so maybe it doesn't reflect the soldier's true thoughts.*

First Robber. What do you mean, before you die? We don't mean to kill you, only to take your money.

Pythias. I'll give you my money, only don't delay me any longer. I am to die by the king's order three days from now. If I don't return to prison on time, my friend must die in my place.

First Robber. A likely story! What man would be fool enough to go back to prison ready to die?

Second Robber. And what man would be fool enough to die for you?

First Robber. We'll take your money, all right. And we'll tie you up while we get away.

Pythias (*begging*). No! No! I must get back to free my friend! (*fade*) I must go back!

Narrator. But the two robbers took Pythias' money, tied him to a tree, and went off as fast as they could. Pythias struggled to free himself. He cried out for help as loud as he could for a long time. But no one traveled through that lonesome woodland after dark. The sun had been up for many hours before he finally managed to free himself from the ropes that had tied him to the tree. He lay on the ground, hardly able to breathe.

(*Music: In briefly and out.*)

Narrator. After a while Pythias got to his feet. Weak and dizzy from hunger and thirst and his struggle to free himself, he set off again. Day and night he traveled without stopping, desperately trying to reach the city in time to save Damon's life.

(*Music: Up and out.*)

Narrator. On the last day, half an hour before noon, Damon's hands were tied behind his back, and he was taken into the public square. The people muttered angrily as Damon was led in by the jailer. Then the king entered and seated himself on a high platform.

(*Sound: Crowd voices in and hold under single voices.*)

Soldier (*loud*). Long live the king!

First Voice (*low*). The longer he lives, the more miserable our lives will be!

DAMON AND PYTHIAS **689**

Mini-Lesson　Literary Concepts

REVIEWING CONFLICT Remind students that the series of events in a story is called the plot. The plot usually centers around a conflict—a problem faced by the main character or characters. For example, in *Damon and Pythias*, Damon faces the possibility of losing his life if Pythias does not return. Remind students that writers use the incidents in a story to develop the conflict and advance the plot.

Application Have students read the passage highlighted above. Ask them why the playwright includes this incident in the drama and how it develops the conflict. If students have difficulty responding, ask them to imagine what would happen if the robbery never took place. *(Possible response: The inclusion of the robbery causes Pythias to lose valuable time. This builds suspense. The audience is wondering whether Pythias will be able to return in time to save Damon. Without the robbery, Pythias would have returned in time to switch places with Damon. Their friendship would not have been tested as strongly.)*

THE LANGUAGE OF LITERATURE TEACHER'S EDITION **689**

CUSTOMIZING FOR
Students Acquiring English

3. Point out that the word *stores* has an unusual meaning here and encourage students to use context clues to infer that it means "supplies."

STRATEGIC READING FOR
Less-Proficient Readers

M Ask students if Pythias arrived in time to save Damon. *(Pythias was just barely in time.)* **Noting Relevant Details**

- How does Pythias' return save Pythias too? *(The King was so impressed by the friendship of these two men that he decided to set them both free.)* **Summarizing**

From Personal Response to Critical Analysis

1. What was the strongest emotion you felt as you read this story? Write about this emotion in your notebook. *(Responses will vary.)*
2. Who do you think is more of a hero—Damon or Pythias? *(Possible responses: Damon, because he volunteered to trade places with Pythias; Pythias, for speaking against the king and for keeping his promise to Damon; both are equally heroic.)*
3. Why do you think the robbers do not believe Pythias' story? *(Possible responses: His story seems too far-fetched; the robbers believe that people will say anything to save their own lives; the robbers cannot even conceive of friends doing something like this for each other because the robbers never would.)*
4. What values does this myth show and support? *(the values of friendship, honor, and trust; the king discovers that the friendship between the two men is more important than his wealth or power.)*

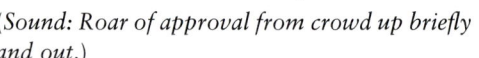

King (*loud, mocking*). Well, Damon, your lifetime is nearly up. Where is your good friend Pythias now?

Damon (*firm*). I have faith in my friend. If he has not returned, I'm certain it is through no fault of his own.

King (*mocking*). The sun is almost overhead. The shadow is almost at the noon mark. And still your friend has not returned to give you back your life!

Damon (*quiet*). I am ready, and happy, to die in his place.

King (*harsh*). And you shall, Damon! Jailer, lead the prisoner to the—

(*Sound: Crowd voices up to a roar, then under.*)

First Voice (*over noise*). Look! It's Pythias!

Second Voice (*over noise*). Pythias has come back!

Pythias (*breathless*). Let me through! Damon!

Damon. Pythias!

Pythias. Thank the gods I'm not too late!

Damon (*quiet, sincere*). I would have died for you gladly, my friend.

Crowd Voices (*loud, demanding*). Set them free! Set them both free!

King (*loud*). People of the city! (*crowd voices out*) Never in all my life have I seen such faith and friendship, such loyalty between men. There are many among you who call me harsh and cruel. But I cannot kill any man who proves such strong and true friendship for another. Damon and Pythias, I set you both free. (*roar of approval from crowd*) I am king. I command a great army. I have stores of gold and precious jewels. But I would give all my money and my power for one friend like Damon or Pythias!

(*Sound: Roar of approval from crowd up briefly and out.*)

(*Music: Up and out.*)

FAN KISSEN

For 17 years, Fan Kissen (1901–1989?) was a radio scriptwriter. In her radio series, *Tales from the Four Winds,* she dramatized world folk tales and legends. Her plays, which are written as radio scripts, always include instructions for music and sound effects. Kissen also has taught elementary school in her hometown of New York City. In addition to writing plays, she writes biographies for young people.

OTHER WORKS *The Crowded House and Other Tales, They Helped Make America, The Straw Ox and Other Plays, The Bag of Fire and Other Plays*

690 UNIT SIX: THE ORAL TRADITION

COMPREHENSION CHECK

1. Why is Pythias arrested? *(He speaks against one of the king's laws.)*
2. What bargain does the king strike with Damon? *(Damon agrees to stay in prison while Pythias visits his family. If Pythias does not return, Damon will be executed in his place.)*
3. What delays Pythias? *(He is robbed and tied up.)*
4. Why does the king free Damon and Pythias? *(Even the ordinarily merciless king cannot kill two people who have such a strong friendship that they are willing to die for each other.)*

CUSTOMIZING FOR
Students Acquiring English

- Many cultures have tales that, like "The Three Wishes," deal with magical wishes. Invite students to share similar stories they know from their home cultures.

STRATEGIC READING FOR
Less-Proficient Readers

Set a Purpose Ask students what they would ask for if they had three wishes. Then have students read to discover the couple's surprising third wish.

CUSTOMIZING FOR
Gifted and Talented Students

As students read the folk tale, they should think about the narrator's understanding of happiness and explain whether they share the narrator's perspective.

Possible responses:

- *Page 693*—"'Until now, you have known happiness together and have never quarreled with each other. Nevertheless the mere knowledge that you could have riches and power has changed you both.'" Happiness consists of a peaceful and loving home.
- *Page 693*—"... the old man said that he would bestow upon them the greatest happiness a married couple can know. Months later, a son was born to them." Happiness in married life is the birth of a child. Students may or may not share the narrator's perspective on happiness.

Copyright © Camille Przewodek.

retold by Ricardo E. Alegría

691

Art Note

Reading the Art *What adjectives would you use to describe this place? Based on this illustration, what do you expect the setting of "The Three Wishes" will be? Is this what you visualize a Puerto Rican village might look like?*

 Mini-Lesson Grammar

THE ADVERB VERY Remind students that an adverb modifies a verb, an adjective, or another adverb. An adverb such as *very*, which modifies an adjective or another adverb, often comes before the word it modifies. Illustrate this with the example shown on the chalkboard.

Application Have students brainstorm phrases that contain the adverb *very* and could be applied to "The Three Wishes." *(Possible responses: very happy, very sorry, very annoyed, very excited, very hungry)* Record each phrase on the board.

Have students use the phrases to write sentences about the folk tale.

Reteaching/Reinforcement
- *Grammar Handbook*, anthology pp. 830–834
- *Grammar Mini-Lessons* copymasters, p. 19, transparencies, pp. 12, 40

 The Writer's Craft

What Are Adverbs? p. 482

They loved each other very much.

The adverb very modifies the adjective much.

THE LANGUAGE OF LITERATURE **TEACHER'S EDITION** **691**

Literary Concept: SETTING

A Have students identify the story's setting—the time and place of the action. Then ask students to explain why this setting is appropriate for a folk tale. *(Possible response: The story is set long ago, in an unspecified forest. The vague setting makes the events of the folk tale seem more believable because readers or listeners can pretend that magical things really are possible.)*

Critical Thinking: SPECULATING

B Ask students to speculate, based on the details they have read thus far, on whether the woman will use her wishes wisely or squander them. *(Possible response: Since the wife has always shared whatever she had, her head will not be turned by her good fortune. She will use her wishes to help others.)*

CUSTOMIZING FOR
Students Acquiring English

1 You may wish to paraphrase *The last word had scarcely left her lips* as "As soon as she said the last word."

Literary Links

C Have students recall the story "User Friendly" (page 277). Ask them to compare the ways these stories illustrate the moral, "Be careful what you wish for." *(In "User Friendly," the boy's father wants him to have a friend, so he gives the boy's computer a personality. This backfires when the computer falls in love with the boy. In this story, the wish backfires when the man accidentally gives his wife donkey ears.)*

A Many years ago, in the days when the saints walked on earth, there lived a woodsman and his wife. They were very poor but very happy in their little house in the forest. Poor as they were, they were always ready to share what little they had with anyone who came to their door. They loved each other very much and were quite content with their life together. Each evening, before eating, they gave thanks to God for their happiness.

One day, while the husband was working far off in the woods, an old man came to the little house and said that he had lost his way in the forest and had eaten nothing for many days. The woodsman's wife had little to eat herself, but, as was her custom, she gave a large portion of it to the old man. After he had eaten everything she gave him, he told the woman that he had been sent by God to test her and that, as a reward for the kindness she and her husband showed to all who came to their house, they would be granted a special grace.[1] This pleased the woman, and she asked what the special grace was.

The old man answered, "Beginning **B** immediately, any three wishes you or your husband may wish will come true."

When she heard these words, the woman was overjoyed and exclaimed, "Oh, if my husband were only here to hear what you say!"

1 The last word had scarcely left her lips when the woodsman appeared in the little house with the ax still in his hands. The first wish had come true.

The woodsman couldn't understand it at all. How did it happen that he, who had been cutting wood in the forest, found himself here in his house? His wife explained it all as she embraced him. The woodsman just stood there, thinking over what his wife had said. He looked at the old man who stood quietly, too, saying nothing.

Suddenly he realized that his wife, without stopping to think, had used one of the three wishes, and he became very annoyed when he remembered all of the useful things she might have asked for with the first wish. For the first time, he became angry with his wife. The desire for riches had turned his head, and he scolded his wife, shouting at her, among other things, "It doesn't seem possible that you could be so stupid! You've wasted one of our wishes, and now we have only two left! May you grow ears of a donkey!"

He had no sooner said the words than his **C** wife's ears began to grow, and they continued to grow until they changed into the pointed, furry ears of a donkey.

When the woman put her hand up and felt them, she knew what had happened and began to cry. Her husband was very ashamed and

> **HE HAD NO SOONER SAID THE WORDS THAN HIS WIFE'S EARS BEGAN TO GROW.**

---
1. **special grace:** gift from God.

692 UNIT SIX: THE ORAL TRADITION

Mini-Lesson  Spelling

THE SUFFIX -ANCE Tell students that the suffix *-ance* is commonly added to complete words to form nouns or adjectives. Write on the chalkboard the example shown. When *-ance* is added to words that end with silent *e*, the final *e* is dropped.

Application Have students combine the word parts below to form nouns and adjectives that end in the suffix *-ance*. Tell them to use at least three of the words in a short paragraph about "The Three Wishes."

1. disturb + ance
2. annoy + ance
3. accept + ance
4. allow + ance
5. insure + ance
6. assist + ance
7. guide + ance
8. acquaint + ance
9. perform + ance
10. avoid + ance

Ask students to look for more words that fit this pattern, in their own writing and in things that they read, and to add these words to their personal word lists.

Reteaching/Reinforcement
- *Unit Six Resource Book,* p. 19

---

repent + ance = repentance

The couple's <u>repentance</u> impressed their mysterious visitor.

sorry, indeed, for what he had done in his temper, and he went to his wife to comfort her.

The old man, who had stood by silently, now came to them and said, "Until now, you have known happiness together and have never quarreled with each other. Nevertheless, the mere knowledge that you could have riches and power has changed you both. Remember, you have only one wish left. What do you want? Riches? Beautiful clothes? Servants? Power?"

The woodsman tightened his arm about his wife, looked at the old man, and said, "We want only the happiness and joy we knew before my wife grew donkey's ears."

No sooner had he said these words than the donkey ears disappeared. The woodsman and his wife fell upon their knees to ask God's forgiveness for having acted, if only for a moment, out of covetousness[2] and greed. Then they gave thanks for all the happiness God had given them.

The old man left, but before going, he told them that they had undergone this test in order to learn that there can be happiness in poverty just as there can be unhappiness in riches. As a reward for their repentance, the old man said that he would bestow upon them the greatest happiness a married couple can know. Months later, a son was born to them. The family lived happily all the rest of their lives. ❖

---

2. **covetousness** (kŭv′ĭ-təs-nəs): a greedy desire for wealth or possessions, especially for something that another person has.

RICARDO E. ALEGRÍA

1921–

Ricardo E. Alegría lives and writes in the city in which he was born—San Juan, Puerto Rico. "The Three Wishes" is taken from Alegría's collection of Puerto Rican folk tales, which is also called *The Three Wishes*. His works are written in Spanish; this story was translated by Elizabeth Culbert. Alegría also is the author of several books and numerous articles on folklore, history, and archaeology. He has taught history at the University of Puerto Rico, and he has served as the director of the Institute of Puerto Rican Culture.

OTHER WORKS *History of the Indians of Puerto Rico*

WORDS TO KNOW
repentance (rĭ-pĕn′təns) *n.* sorrow for wrongdoing

STRATEGIC READING FOR
Less-Proficient Readers

D Ask students to describe the couple's third wish. *(They ask to have the second wish undone, although it would use up their last wish before they could wish for wealth.)* **Restating**

• What does the third wish reveal about the couple? *(It indicates that they value happiness and kindness to others more than power or riches.)* **Drawing Conclusions**

CUSTOMIZING FOR
Students Acquiring English

 Ask students to use context clues to infer the meaning of *bestow*. *(give)*

From Personal Response to Critical Analysis

1. Did you like this story? Jot down your response to it in your notebook. *(Responses will vary.)*
2. Since the husband and wife have always been kind to others and happy with their life, what do you think this experience teaches them about themselves? *(Possible responses: It teaches them that the mere desire for riches corrupts values and destroys happiness; that greed breeds discontent; that they are very fortunate people to know the secret of true happiness.)*
3. What, if anything, do you think the couple would wish for if they could have three more wishes? *(Possible responses: They might not wish for anything at all, having learned their lesson; they might wish for health and happiness for their newborn son; they might wish for more children.)*

COMPREHENSION CHECK
1. What does the wife wish for first? *(She wishes that her husband were present to hear about the three wishes.)*
2. What is the second wish? *(The husband wishes that his wife would grow donkey ears.)*
3. What is their last wish? *(They wish for the happiness they knew before the wife grew donkey ears.)*
4. According to the story, what matters most? *(Possible responses: love, children/family, kindness to others, generosity)*

Art Note

Effigy vessel This hand-painted ceramic vessel, made almost 1,000 years ago, was found in the cave of Balankanché, near Chichén Itzá in Mexico. It was probably used in Maya cave rituals. For the ancient Mayas, caves were the source of rain and fertility and embodied the mysteries of life and death.

Reading the Art What expression does the face have? How can you relate it to the fable of the disobedient boy? What do you suppose the use of color—half blue and half red—on the face might signify?

Linking to Geography

Mountains make up approximately two-thirds of Guatemala's total land area. Many of these mountains are volcanic; however, most of the volcanoes are extinct. Guatemala is vulnerable to earthquakes; many towns have been destroyed along its southern volcanic belt. The devastating earthquake of February 4, 1976, caused 22,778 deaths and measured 7.5 on the Richter scale.

STRATEGIC READING FOR
Less-Proficient Readers

Set a Purpose Invite volunteers to share stories about times when their curiosity caused them trouble. Then have students read to find out the true identity of the man who takes in the runaway child.

Effigy vessel (about A.D. 1000–1250), unknown Mayan artist. Ceramic, painted red, blue, and white, 31.7 cm in height, Museo Nacional de Antropología, Mexico. Photo Copyright © Stuart Rome.

Mini-Lesson: Speaking, Listening, and Viewing

SPORTSCAST Point out to students that they can use a technique from sportscasting to help them summarize the plot of a story. Giving a play-by-play account of the action helps students fix a story in their minds.

Application Have students write and deliver play-by-play "sportscasts" of "The Disobedient Child." If resources permit, allow students to tape-record their broadcasts. You may wish to have students do this activity in small groups.

694 THE LANGUAGE OF LITERATURE TEACHER'S EDITION

THE DISOBEDIENT CHILD

RETOLD BY VICTOR MONTEJO

In old times in *Xaqla'* Jacaltenango[1] there was a very disobedient child who often disappointed his parents. No matter how hard they tried to teach him, he never changed.

One afternoon the boy ran away from home, looking for someone who would tolerate his mischief. Walking through the woods he discovered a lonely little house and ran up to it. On the porch of the straw-covered house sat an old man, smoking peacefully. The boy stood before him without saying hello or any other word of greeting.

When the old man noticed the boy's presence, he stopped smoking and asked him, "Where do you want to go, boy?"

"I am looking for someone who can give me something to eat," the boy answered.

The wise old man, who already knew the boy's story, said, "No one will love you if you continue being so bad."

The boy did not respond except to laugh.

---

1. *Xaqla'* Jacaltenango (chäk-lä′ häk′äl-tĕ-nän′gô): town in the mountains of Guatemala.

WORDS TO KNOW
tolerate (tŏl′ə-rāt′) *v.* to put up with

695

Active Reading: QUESTION

B Discuss what questions or comments students have about the old man's actions at this point. You may wish to use the following model to prompt students' questions:

Think-Aloud Model *I wonder what the old man is up to. Why does he give the boy this strange warning? How could it possibly matter whether the boy puts 13—or 10 or 11 or even 20—beans into the pot? I think the old man is testing the boy to see if the boy will obey his instructions.*

CUSTOMIZING FOR
Students Acquiring English

2 The gesture of hanging one's head in shame is common to many cultures. Ask students to model it and to tell what emotion the boy is feeling.

CUSTOMIZING FOR
Multiple Learning Styles

C Mathematical-Logical Learners
Invite students to diagram a stage set for the scene in which the boy puts on the red cape and is lifted to the sky. Diagrams should include backstage equipment that the scene requires.

Students can consider using ropes and pulleys to lift the boy aloft. They can list needed props and sound effects beneath their diagrams. Allow students to share their diagrams with the class.

A Then the old man smiled and said, "You can stay with me. We will eat together."

B The boy accepted his offer and stayed in the old man's house. On the following day before going to work, the old man told the boy: "You should stay in the house, and the only duty you will have is to put the beans to cook during the afternoon. But listen well. You should only throw thirteen beans in the pot and no more. Do you understand?"

The boy nodded that he understood the directions very well. Later, when the time arrived to cook the beans, the boy put the clay pot on the fire and threw in thirteen beans as he had been directed. But once he had done that, he began to think that thirteen beans weren't very many for such a big pot. So, disobeying his orders, he threw in several more little fistfuls.

When the beans began to boil over the fire, the pot started to fill up, and it filled up until it overflowed. Very surprised, the boy quickly took an empty pot and divided the beans between the two pots. But the beans overflowed the new pot, too. Beans were pouring out of both pots.

When the old man returned home, he found piles of beans, and the two clay pots lay broken on the floor.

"Why did you disobey my orders and cook more than I told you to?" the old man asked angrily.

2 The boy hung his head and said nothing. The old man then gave him instructions for the next day. "Tomorrow you will again cook the beans as I have told you. What's more, I forbid you to open that little door over there. Do you understand?"

The boy indicated that he understood very well.

The next day the old man left the house after warning the boy to take care to do exactly what he had been told. During the afternoon the boy put the beans on the fire to cook. Then he was filled with curiosity. What was behind the little door he had been forbidden to open?

Without any fear, the boy opened the door and discovered in the room three enormous covered water jars. Then he found three capes inside a large trunk. There was one green cape, one yellow cape and one red cape. Not satisfied with these discoveries, the boy took the top off the first water jar to see what it contained.

> **IMMEDIATELY THE WATER JAR BEGAN TO EMIT GREAT CLOUDS THAT QUICKLY HID THE SKY.**

Immediately the water jar began to <u>emit</u> great clouds that quickly hid the sky. Frightened and shivering with cold, the boy opened the trunk and put on the red cape. At that instant a clap of thunder exploded in the house. The boy was turned into thunder and lifted to the sky, where he unleashed a great storm.

When the old man heard the thunder, he guessed that something extraordinary had happened at home, and he hurried in that direction. There he discovered that the forbidden door was open and the top was

WORDS TO KNOW
emit (ĭ-mĭt′) *v.* to send out; give forth

696

Mini-Lesson: Speaking, Listening, and Viewing

CRITICAL VIEWING Inform students that critical viewing sometimes involves comparing and contrasting what they know already and what is shown in a movie, television production, or dramatic performance.

Application Invite students to learn more about some of the best-known fables, those reputedly written by the Greek slave Aesop, by viewing some of the fables in *Aesop's Fable Series* (a collection of 30-minute videos from Golden Book Video). After students watch one or more of the videos, invite them to compare and contrast Aesop's fables and the Guatemalan folk tale they are hearing. Students can work in small groups to create a chart showing how Aesop's fables compare with "The Disobedient Child."

off the jar of clouds, from which churning mists still rose toward the sky. The old man covered the jar and then approached the trunk with the capes. The red cape, the cape of storms, was missing. Quickly the old man put on the green cape and regained control over the sky, calming the great storm. Little by little the storm subsided, and soon the man returned to the house, carrying the unconscious boy in his arms.

A little while later the old man uncapped the same jar, and the clouds which had blackened the sky returned to their resting place, leaving the heavens bright and blue again. When he had done this, the old man capped the jar again and put away the red and green capes.

Through all of this the boy remained stunned and soaked with the rains until the kind old man restored his spirit and brought him back to normal. When the boy was alert again and his fear had left, the old man said, "Your disobedience has almost killed you. You were lucky that I heard the storm and came to help. Otherwise you would have been lost forever among the clouds."

The boy was quiet and the old man continued.

"I am Qich Mam,[2] the first father of all people and founder of *Xaqla'*, he who controls the rain, and waters the community's fields when they are dry. Understand, then, that I wish you no harm and I forgive what you have done. Promise me that in the future you will not disobey your parents."

The boy smiled happily and answered, "I promise, Qich Mam, I promise." Qich Mam patted him gently and said, "Then return to your home and be useful to your parents and to your people."

From that time on the boy behaved differently. He was very grateful for the kindness of the old man who held the secret of the clouds, the rains, the wind and the storms in his hands. ❖

---

2. **Qich Mam** (kēch' mäm'): a thunder spirit of the Mayan people.

VICTOR MONTEJO

Victor Montejo was born and raised in Guatemala and later taught primary school in Jacaltenango, the setting of "The Disobedient Child." Unfortunately, because of the political climate in Guatemala, Montejo was forced to flee to the United States in 1982. Since then, he has published a number of stories, fables, and poems and has worked as a

1952–

writer-in-residence at Bucknell University in Pennsylvania. He has also done doctoral work in anthropology at the University of Connecticut. "The Disobedient Child" is from Montejo's book *The Bird Who Cleans the World*.
OTHER WORKS *Testimony: Death of a Guatemalan Village*

WORDS TO KNOW
subside (səb-sīd') *v.* to become weaker or less active; decrease

697

STRATEGIC READING FOR
Less-Proficient Readers

D Ask students who the old man really is. *(He is Qich Mam, who controls the water and the weather.)* **Noting Relevant Details**

Literary Links

E Ask students how this child and the children in "The Enchanted Raisin" (page 346) learn to be obedient. *(In both stories, disobedience leads to disaster. The boy is almost killed. The children nearly lose their mother.)*

From Personal Response to Critical Analysis

1. What thoughts went through your mind as the boy started to misbehave the second time? Record your thoughts in your notebook. *(Responses will vary.)*
2. Does the boy deserve what happens to him in this story? Why or why not? *(Possible responses: The boy deserves what happens to him because he does not listen to his parents or to the old man; the boy does not deserve what happens to him because he is only a child, and his behavior is not unusual.)*
3. How do you feel about the way Qich Mam treats the boy? *(Possible responses: Qich Mam treats the boy with great patience and kindness and teaches him an important lesson; Qich Mam sets up traps for the boy to lead him to temptation; Qich Mam could have taught the boy without endangering the boy's life.)*
4. Besides disobedience, what qualities does the boy have? *(Possible responses: The boy is also curious, brave, and resourceful; he is stubborn and willful.)*

COMPREHENSION CHECK
1. What directions does the old man give the boy for cooking the beans? *(Cook only 13 beans.)*
2. What does the boy find behind the little door? *(three enormous water jars and a trunk containing three capes)*
3. How does the boy unleash the storm? *(He opens the first water jar and puts on the red cape.)*
4. What does Qich Mam make the boy promise? *(that he will never again disobey his parents)*

THE LANGUAGE OF LITERATURE TEACHER'S EDITION **697**

Literature Connection

Create a Picture Book As students choose a story to use, they should look for scenes that involve action that would work well in a pop-up format. If possible, provide students with examples of simple pop-up books or greeting cards. Have students divide the tasks involved in putting the book together. Roles include artist, writer, and bookbinder.

Rubric

3 Full Accomplishment Students portray the story in pictures that are interesting and intelligible to younger readers. Picture books reflect consideration and adoption of ideas, such as the ones shown here, for retelling the story in a lively manner.

2 Substantial Accomplishment Students portray the story in evocative pictures which, however, do not fully engage or are not readily comprehensible to younger readers. Picture books reflect some, but not thorough, consideration of ideas for retelling the story in a lively manner.

1 Little or Partial Accomplishment Picture books do not reflect consideration of the audience's age level. Books are carelessly and unimaginatively put together.

RESPONDING
OPTIONS

LITERATURE CONNECTION PROJECT 1 *Multimodal Activity*

Create a Picture Book Working with a few classmates, make a picture-book version of one of the stories you've read in this part of the unit to share with a class of younger students. In determining which story to choose, consider the age level of your audience. Then think about these possibilities:

Illustrations Select characters and settings that retell the story. Then use simple drawings, photographs, or pictures from magazines, and present events in chronological order. "Clip art" from a computer program may provide ideas.

Pop-up Choose a character or an event and create a pop-up feature by following the steps shown here. For example, a pop-up feature for "Wings" might show Icarus rising toward the clouds.

Book jacket Design a colorful cover for your book that will make younger readers want to open it.

Share the book with a primary class or with a group of children during a story hour in the library.

ART CONNECTION PROJECT 2 *Multimodal Activity*

Explore Pottery Making Of the cultures represented in these three stories, the ancient Greeks were the first to elevate the making of pottery, one of the oldest human crafts, to an art form. On Crete, the Minoans began using a hand-turned wheel around 2500 B.C. The pottery of the ancient cultures that existed in what is now Puerto Rico and Guatemala reflects the influences of the Arawak, Carib, and Mayan civilizations. The basic steps used in making pottery are almost the same today as they were hundreds of years ago; only the tools have changed.

Explore ancient methods of making pottery, and compare how different cultures practiced the art. Begin by organizing your information in a chart similar to the one shown. Then, for each culture you study, use the information to create illustrations that could be used to make a slide show on pottery as an art form in ancient cultures.

Culture	Date	Materials	Designs

698 UNIT SIX: THE ORAL TRADITION

Art Connection

Explore Pottery Making Students might consult the old but excellent *Pottery of the Ancients* by Helen E. Stiles (New York: Dutton, 1938) to compare and contrast pottery making in ancient cultures. Another source, appropriate for gifted and talented students, is *The World's Master Potters* by Charles P. Woodhouse (Pitman Publishing, 1974).

Rubric

3 Full Accomplishment Charts include accurate and well-organized information. Illustrations incorporate researched information.

2 Substantial Accomplishment Charts give accurate information, but materials and designs do not supply enough information to create detailed illustrations.

1 Little or Partial Accomplishment Charts give skimpy and sometimes inaccurate information. Illustrations do not reflect researched information.

698 THE LANGUAGE OF LITERATURE TEACHER'S EDITION

Social Studies Connection

Construct a Stage Students might consult *Atlas of the Greek World* by Peter Levi (New York: Facts on File, 1982) to see ruins and a diagrammatic reconstruction of a Greek amphitheater. Encourage students to share with one another additional resources that they find.

Rubric

3 Full Accomplishment Dioramas reflect solid research and accurate treatment of a Greek myth.

2 Substantial Accomplishment Dioramas indicate that students have not fully understood research materials. They have, however, accurately rendered the myth with figures representing actors and background painting.

1 Little or Partial Accomplishment Dioramas indicate that students have not researched amphitheaters adequately or carefully studied the myth they chose to portray.

SOCIAL STUDIES CONNECTION PROJECT 3 Multimodal Activity

Construct a Stage The roots of modern drama can be traced to ancient Greece. As early as the fifth century B.C., citizens of Athens gathered at religious festivals in the *agora,* or marketplace, to watch performances of stories about Greek gods or heroes. These early dramas combined religion and history with entertainment.

Create a diorama of a scene from *Damon and Pythias* or another Greek myth. Refer to an encyclopedia or to books about Greece for information on ancient Greek amphitheaters. Some, like the Theater of Epidaurus in Argolis, are still in use today. Use a simple box to create a stage against a painted background, or construct a more elaborate model of an amphitheater. Be sure to include masked figures to represent the actors.

Display your diorama in the classroom.

ACROSS CULTURES MINI-PROJECTS Multimodal Activity

Make Your Own Hieroglyphics Ancient Mayans used hieroglyphics (hī′ər-ə-glĭf′ĭks), a system of writing in which pictures are used to represent meaning or sounds. Research Mayan hieroglyphics, and then make your own copies of the Mayan symbols, using potato or clay prints or some other method. Compare Mayan hieroglyphics with those of ancient Egypt. See if you can communicate with a classmate by using only hieroglyphics.

Compare Tales In "The Three Wishes," a woodsman and his wife are allowed three wishes. What other stories can you recall in which characters are granted wishes? In a small-group discussion, compare and contrast those stories with this Puerto Rican tale. Then present some of the stories to the class.

Map Hurricanes The Caribbean lands of Guatemala and Puerto Rico are subject to hurricanes, tropical storms that are more devastating than the one unleashed by the boy in "The Disobedient Child." The word *hurricane* comes from the name of the Carib god of evil, Juracán. Find out more about the hurricanes that affect these countries, and use a map to chart the typical formation and movement of hurricanes in that region.

Build a Fresco The rooms in Minoan palaces were decorated with colorful frescoes, pictures painted on damp plaster walls. Explore the frescoes of the ancient Greeks, and draw samples to share.

Extended Social Studies Reading

MORE ABOUT THE CULTURES

- *Fired Up! Making Pottery in Ancient Times* by Rivka Gonen
- *The Hispanic Americans* by Milton Meltzer
- *Ancient Greece* by Robert Nicholson
- *Discovering Our Past* by Peter Seymour

PROJECTS **699**

Multicultural Perspectives

Make Your Own Hieroglyphics Students might consult *Hieroglyphs for Fun* by Joseph and Lenore Scott (New York: Van Nostrand, 1974) for information on Egyptian hieroglyphics. Students may need to consult a librarian for materials about Mayan hieroglyphics.

Compare Tales You may wish to provide students with fairy-tale anthologies to spark their memories.

Map Hurricanes Students can find out more about hurricanes and how they move in a book about weather. One source (comprehensive yet challenging for sixth graders) is *Violent Weather: Hurricanes, Tornadoes & Storms* by Stan Gibilisco (Summit, PA: Tab Books, 1984).

Build a Fresco Students can examine color pictures of Minoan frescoes in *Atlas of the Greek World* by Peter Levi (New York: Facts on File, 1982).

OVERVIEW

In the Guided Assignment for this section, students will review the lesson of a folk tale from this unit. By evaluating a piece of literature, students learn to support their opinions with examples. As preparation for this assignment, The Writer's Style will help students understand the effects of writers' varying sentence structure. In Reading the World, students will apply what they learned about evaluating a story to images from movies and television.

Objectives
- To recognize how writers vary sentence structures for different effects
- To add interest to writing by sentence composing
- To organize a review
- To evaluate the lesson of a folk tale
- To evaluate images from television and movies

Skills

LITERATURE
- Identifying different sentence endings

GRAMMAR AND USAGE
- Understanding pronouns and their antecedents
- Making compound subjects and verbs agree

MEDIA LITERACY
- Evaluating movies and television

CRITICAL THINKING
- Making judgments
- Analyzing
- Classifying
- Evaluating the message

SPEAKING, LISTENING, AND VIEWING
- Group collaboration
- Peer discussion
- Group conferencing

Teaching Strategy: MODELING
In the following models, the writers use a variety of sentence structures to add interest to their writing. This technique is used in fiction, poetry, drama, and nonfiction.

A Kha and Clark Possible response: The authors have put phrases in the beginning and middle of the sentence.

B Belpré Possible response: Taroo knows nothing about what has happened to Alida.

WRITING ABOUT LITERATURE

A Lesson Learned

What did you learn from "In the Land of Small Dragon"? What is the moral of "The Three Wishes"? There are many lessons to be learned from folk tales, but not all of the lessons carry the same importance. Each of us must evaluate the lessons we learn and decide which are valuable. On the next few pages, you will

- see how writers and storytellers vary their sentences to hold their readers' interest
- evaluate the lesson in a folk tale
- see how lessons are taught and judged in the real world

The Writer's Style: Sentence Composing Experienced writers vary the way their sentences are arranged. You can add variety to your writing by changing the order of subjects, verbs, and other sentence parts.

Read the Literature

Study the sentences in the following passages and note how the writers added variety.

Literature Models

A Variety in Sentence Beginnings
What have the authors done to add interest to the sentence "Tãm . . . dug up the buried clay pot"?

> When the moon was full again,
> Tãm, so lonely for her fish,
> Dug up the buried clay pot.
> Tãm found, instead of fish bones,
> A silken dress and two jeweled *hai*.
>
> Dang Manh Kha and Ann Nolan Clark
> from "In the Land of Small Dragon"

B Subject-Verb Splits
What information is given between the subject and the verb in the first sentence?

> Meanwhile Taroo, knowing nothing of Alida's sorrow, still waited for her by the Pomarosa Pool. Day after day he waited.
>
> Pura Belpré
> from "The Legend of the Hummingbird"

PRINT AND MEDIA RESOURCES

UNIT SIX RESOURCE BOOK
The Writer's Style, p. 23
Prewriting Guide, p. 24
Elaboration, p. 25
Peer Response Guide, pp. 26–27
Revising and Editing, p. 28
Student Model, p. 29
Rubric, p. 30

ACCESS FOR STUDENTS ACQUIRING ENGLISH
Reading and Writing Support

WRITING MINI-LESSONS
Transparencies, pp. 29, 30

GRAMMAR MINI-LESSONS
Transparencies, pp. 5, 10-11
Copymasters, pp. 5, 15, 16

FORMAL ASSESSMENT
Guidelines for Writing Assessment

Connect to Life

Writers of nonfiction books must take special care not to let their writing become boring. Notice how the writer arranges the sentences in the passage shown below.

Nonfiction Book

> *Nuoc mam,* a brown sauce made from fermented fish, is the trademark of Vietnamese cooking. It is the main ingredient in *nuoc cham,* a dressing and table sauce that the Vietnamese eat with all foods, probably more often than you use ketchup!
>
> Phyllis Shalant
> from *Look What We've Brought You from Vietnam*

Variety in Sentence Endings Notice the definition that the writer has given between the subject and the verb in the first sentence. What interesting note has she included at the end of this passage?

Try Your Hand: Sentence Composing

1. **Unscrambling Sentences** How many ways can you write a complete sentence from each set of scrambled sentence parts? Example: *grew big and trustful / the little fish / loved by T'âm*

   The little fish, loved by T'âm, grew big and trustful.
   Loved by T'âm, the little fish grew big and trustful.

   - mistreated T'âm / Cám / the youngest sister
   - The emperor's son / found the jeweled *hai* / a young Prince

2. **Adding Interest** Add information to each sentence by adding an interesting beginning.
   Example: (*Meeting by the pool every day,*) Alida and Taroo became good friends.

   - . . . his wings made a swift humming sound.
   - . . . he waited by the Pomarosa Pool.
   - . . . he is always looking for red flowers.

3. **Revising Your Writing** Look at some of the other writing you've done so far. Choose a piece that you think needs greater sentence variety. Revise the piece, using what you've learned.

SkillBuilder

C

 GRAMMAR FROM WRITING

Understanding Pronouns and Their Antecedents
In careful sentence composing, sometimes you combine sentences. This means you may have to replace nouns with pronouns. An **antecedent** is the word or words a pronoun stands for. Use a singular pronoun when the antecedent is singular. Use a plural pronoun when the antecedent is plural. Notice the pronouns the authors of "In the Land of Small Dragon" use in this passage:

D

> Pretty girls stood in a line
> With their mothers
>   standing near;
> One by one they tried to fit
> A foot into a small,
>   jeweled hai.

APPLYING WHAT YOU'VE LEARNED
Rewrite this paragraph, using pronouns in place of the words in boldface type.

> I loved **this story** because **this story** was like "Cinderella." T'âm was the main character. T'âm lived with a stepmother and half sister. **T'âm's stepmother and half sister** made T'âm's life miserable.

 GRAMMAR HANDBOOK

For more information on pronouns and their antecedents, see page 826 of the Grammar Handbook.

WRITING ABOUT LITERATURE **701**

Teaching Strategy: USING THE SKILLBUILDER

C To help students understand that they have to take care when they use pronouns, you may want to teach the SkillBuilder on Pronouns and Their Antecedents at this time.

Teaching Strategy: MODELING

D **Shalant** Possible responses: The writer has added a comparison to ketchup. It emphasizes that Vietnamese cooking uses *nuoc mam* a lot.

Try Your Hand

1. Responses will vary. Here are some samples:
   Cám, the youngest sister, mistreated T'âm.
   The youngest sister, Cám, mistreated T'âm.
   The emperor's son, a young prince, found the jeweled *hai.*
   A young prince, the emperor's son, found the jeweled *hai.*
2. Responses will vary. Here are some examples:
   - Faster and faster, his wings made a swift humming sound.
   - Day and night, he waited by the Pomarosa Pool.
   - Until he sees a sign of Alida, he is always looking for red flowers.

 SkillBuilder GRAMMAR FROM WRITING

UNDERSTANDING PRONOUNS AND THEIR ANTECEDENTS Help students identify pronouns by writing this list of common pronouns on the board: *she, him, it, us, they, them, mine, yours, ours, this, that, these, who,* and *which.* Then identify the pronoun and antecedent in the poem: the pronoun *they* and its antecedent *girls.*

Application Possible response:
I loved this story because it was like "Cinderella." T'âm was the main character. T'âm lived with a stepmother and half sister, who made T'âm's life miserable.

Additional Suggestions To help students continue to practice using correct pronouns, have them revise the following by correcting the pronouns.

I thought the stepmother and half sister were cruel. She made T'âm very lonely. When T'âm finally got to try on the slipper, they fit. It was very happy.

Reteaching/Reinforcement
- *Grammar Handbook,* anthology pp. 826–827
- *Grammar Mini-Lessons* copymasters, pp. 15, 16; transparencies, pp. 10–11

 The Writer's Craft
Pronouns and Antecedents, pp. 436–438

THE LANGUAGE OF LITERATURE TEACHER'S EDITION **701**

Critical Thinking:
MAKING JUDGMENTS

E Students may find it difficult to disagree with the moral of a folk tale. Help them make up their own minds by asking them to critically evaluate the lesson of the story. Ask if it is true for everyone. Is it true all of the time? Is it true of you?

Speaking, Listening, and Viewing:
COLLABORATIVE OPPORTUNITY

F Encourage students to work together to discover their reactions to the stories in Unit 6. Pairs or small groups can look through the selections, decide which stories each student likes, and read some favorite passages aloud. Make sure every student is given an opportunity to talk about his or her likes and dislikes in the stories and that they all take notes.

Teaching Strategy: MODELING

G Use the Student's Prewriting Chart as a guide for student charts. Mention that the student has already chosen a story. Then encourage them to go through their own story and jot down its various morals. Then have students think of these morals apart from the story and apply them to situations that may occur in their own lives.

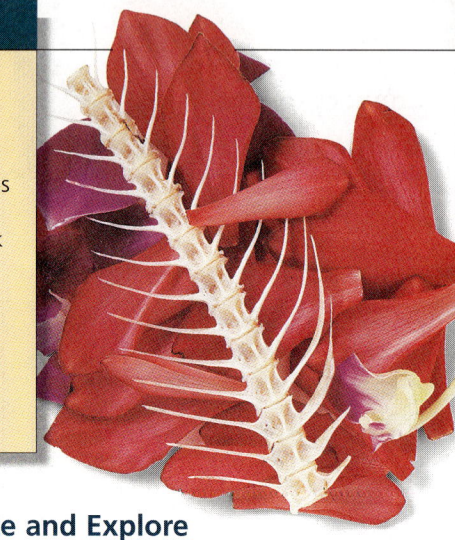

WRITING ABOUT LITERATURE

Criticism

Long ago, people discovered that a story could be a powerful way to teach a lesson. Some stories have lessons that are timeless. Other stories, however, have lost their power over the years. What kinds of lessons do you think are timeless and valuable?

GUIDED ASSIGNMENT

Evaluate the Lesson of a Story In this assignment, you will revisit a folk tale from Unit Six. Then you will write a critical review of the literature, explaining whether you agree or disagree with the moral of the tale.

Student's Prewriting Chart

1 Prewrite and Explore

Think about the stories you read in Unit Six. If you need help remembering, discuss them with classmates. Jot down comments about the ideas the writers present or any questions you have. Then consider the following questions to help you pick a story to write about.

- Which stories do you have strong feelings about, either positive or negative? Why?
- Was there a moral or lesson taught in one of the stories that you agree with or disagree with or are confused about?

FOCUS ON THE LESSON

Based on your answers to the questions above, choose a story to concentrate on. What is the message of this story? A chart like the one on the left can help you think through your notes and figure out what the lesson is.

 Assessment Option

SELF-ASSESSMENT After students have completed the Focus on the Lesson exploration, they can assess their understanding of the moral of their chosen story. Students can ask themselves the following questions:
- Does my story have one or more morals or lessons?
- How well do I understand the moral or lesson?
- Can I apply my moral or lesson to a situation in my own life?
- Can I write more reactions to the moral, or am I ready to go on to freewriting?

702 THE LANGUAGE OF LITERATURE TEACHER'S EDITION

❷ Freewrite to Answer Questions

In some stories, the lesson or moral is not clear. Sometimes a story may have more than one lesson. If this is true of the story you've chosen, try freewriting about your thoughts.

Student's Freewrite

> I think there are a couple of lessons in "In the Land of Small Dragon." The story is about beauty and goodness. But what is the most important message? Tám is the good daughter and Cám is the bad daughter. Tám is beautiful and she also does good things for others. Is "What is beautiful is good" the main lesson? That's not right.

> I think I should tell why I don't like this idea. I could use something from my own life.

> I like the part that says "A man's worth is what he does, / Not what he says he can do." I've heard the saying "Actions speak louder than words." That means the same thing. It says in the story that "real beauty mirrors goodness." I think the most important message is that real beauty comes from being nice to others, not from how a person looks.

> The last sentence is what I should focus on.

❸ Draft and Share

In a review, you must convince readers that you have good reasons for your opinions. Use examples from the story or incidents from personal experience to help support your opinions. Ask yourself these questions as you write your draft:

- What story events support or contradict my opinions?
- How can I organize my review to help my reader understand my opinions better?

 **PEER RESPONSE**

Ask a partner to read and comment on your review.

- Do you agree or disagree with my ideas? Why?
- What parts of my review convinced you or changed your mind about the value of the lesson?
- Where might story events or details help support my review?

SkillBuilder

 WRITER'S CRAFT

Organizing Your Review

A well-organized critical review clearly presents your opinions and allows readers to understand your thinking. As you write your draft, remember that a critical response to literature contains three main parts.

- An introduction gives a brief description of the story. The introduction will help familiarize your reader with the story you are writing about.
- The body contains an in-depth discussion of at least one element of the literature, such as the lesson or moral.
- A conclusion states your opinion about the value of the literature.

APPLYING WHAT YOU'VE LEARNED

Use the guidelines above as you revise your freewriting. Organize your ideas so that you have an introduction, a body, and a conclusion.

 WRITING HANDBOOK

For more information on writing introductions, see page 778 in the Writing Handbook. For information on writing conclusions, see page 786. For information on how to write effective paragraphs, see page 779.

WRITING ABOUT LITERATURE **703**

Writing Skill: POINT OF VIEW

Ⓗ The freewrite provides an opportunity for students to focus further on their story's moral and to sort through the information they have gathered. As they freewrite, students may think of new ideas and new responses, or their responses may change. Tell them to expect this development of their own thinking.

Teaching Strategy:
USING THE SKILLBUILDER

Ⓘ To help students shape their drafts, you may want to teach the SkillBuilder on Organizing Your Review at this time. It describes the three main elements of a critical review and how to present information.

SkillBuilder WRITER'S CRAFT

ORGANIZING YOUR REVIEW Remind students that they need to name the full title and possibly the author or authors of the story in the introduction. They should also focus on one main moral to make their principal point. Encourage them to use evidence from the story to support their opinions.

Application Help students check their own writing. They can work through their freewriting systematically with the help of the list in this SkillBuilder.

Additional Suggestions To help students organize their drafts in more detail, guide them to use paragraphs correctly. The introduction can be one brief paragraph that is separate from the body. The body can be structured around topic sentences. Students write a topic sentence that identifies the element or moral from the story and their opinion about this element. Then they should support their opinion with evidence from the story or from their own lives. The conclusion can contain one or more paragraphs.

Reteaching/Reinforcement
- *Writing Mini-Lessons* transparencies, pp. 29, 30

Creating Paragraphs, pp. 226–229

THE LANGUAGE OF LITERATURE TEACHER'S EDITION **703**

Critical Thinking: ANALYZING

J Explain to students that revising their drafts means making sure that the statements in their drafts accurately reflect what they think about the story. To evaluate and revise their drafts, students should look at sentence variety, check pronouns and antecedents, and consider the organization of the draft.

Teaching Strategy: MODELING

K Discuss with students how this sample meets the Standards for Evaluation on this page. Point out that the first sentence names the story. The second and third sentences summarize the story and identify its main lesson. The fourth sentence, beginning "I agree…," states the writer's opinion. The student's draft offers arguments and ideas from real life to support the opinion. The draft returns to the story to offer further evidence.

Standards for Evaluation

Ideas and Content
- gives title, author, and a brief summary of the literature
- gives supported evaluation of an element of the selection
- includes examples, quotations, and details that support the evaluation
- has a conclusion that clearly summarizes the evaluation

Structure and Form
- uses well-organized paragraphs and a clear organization
- include transitional words and phrases to show relationships among ideas

Grammar, Usage, and Mechanics
- contains no more than two or three minor errors in grammar and usage
- correctly integrates quotations into the text
- contains no more than two or three minor errors in spelling, capitalization, and punctuation

---

WRITING ABOUT LITERATURE

④ Revise and Edit

Now you are ready to revise your draft. Make sure your review contains an introduction, a body, and a conclusion. Consider whether you can find and use additional information to help support your opinions. After you complete your final draft, reflect on what you discovered about yourself or the story from writing a critical review.

Student's Final Draft

Notice that the introduction clearly states the focus of the essay. What is this writer's opinion of the lesson in this tale?

> "In the Land of Small Dragon" teaches several lessons, but one valuable lesson stands out. In this Vietnamese version of "Cinderella," a beautiful peasant girl teaches us that looks aren't as important as how somebody acts. Real beauty comes from goodness, not from how a person looks. I agree strongly with this moral. Important qualities, such as kindness and loyalty, can't be seen. You have to get to know people and observe how they act.

What examples and evidence support the writer's opinion?

> The lesson of this tale is valuable because everybody knows people like Cám and Tâm. Some people who are good-looking are really mean and nobody likes them. Some people are not considered beautiful, but everybody likes them because they treat people nicely and respect others. In the story, Tâm marries the Prince because she is a kind, good person, not simply because she is beautiful.

Standards for Evaluation

A critical review
- identifies the literature by title and author
- gives a brief summary of the literature
- gives a supported evaluation of an element of the story
- states opinions clearly and provides reasons and evidence from the story for those opinions

704 UNIT SIX: THE ORAL TRADITION

Assessment  **Option**

SELF-ASSESSMENT To help students assess their own writing, have them ask themselves the following questions:
- *Do I clearly introduce my topic?*
- *Does my draft have a clear introduction, body, and conclusion?*
- *Does my body group related ideas into paragraphs?*
- *Is my opinion clearly stated?*
- *Can I vary sentence structure to add interest and accuracy to my idea?*

Grammar in Context

Compound Subjects and Predicates Writers often add variety to a sentence by using two or more subjects and verbs. Using compound subjects and verbs can help you avoid short, choppy sentences. When a subject has two or more parts, it is called a **compound subject.**

T'âm went fishing. Cám went fishing.

T'âm and Cám went fishing.

When the predicate has two or more parts, it's called a **compound predicate.**

T'âm put on the hai. T'âm danced in the rice paddy.

T'âm put on the hai and danced in the rice paddy.

When a compound subject or predicate has three or more parts, use commas to separate the parts.

T'âm put on the hai, danced in the rice paddy, and then went fishing.

The writer of the passage below combined verbs to add variety and to make the passage easier to read.

> Important qualities, such as kindness and loyalty, can't be seen. You have to get to know people _{and} You have to observe how they act.

Try Your Hand: Using Compound Subjects and Predicates

From the first group of sentences, create a single sentence with a compound subject. Create a single sentence with a compound predicate from the second group of sentences.

- Alida's favorite place was the Pomarosa Pool. Taroo's favorite place was the Pomarosa Pool.
- Alida admired the young man's courage. Alida learned to respect him.

SkillBuilder

GRAMMAR FROM WRITING

Making Compound Subjects and Verbs Agree

When two or more parts of a compound subject are joined by the conjunction *and*, use the plural form of the verb.

*The Prince and his Father **are** looking for a princess.*

When the parts are joined by *or, either/or,* or *neither/nor,* use the form of the verb that agrees with the subject closest to the verb.

*T'âm's father or stepmother **is** running to the pond.*

*Either Cám or T'âm **has** a chance to become the princess.*

*Neither Cám's meanness nor her lies **change** T'âm.*

APPLYING WHAT YOU'VE LEARNED

Read the paragraph below, correcting any errors in subject-verb agreement. Then rewrite the paragraph in present tense.

The towns of Cayey and Cidra sits far atop the hills. Alida swim and rest by the banks of a beautiful pool. Alida and Taroo fell in love and wants to get married. Neither Alida's father nor the village people wants Alida to marry Taroo.

GRAMMAR HANDBOOK

For more information on subject-verb agreement, see page 815 in the Grammar Handbook.

WRITING ABOUT LITERATURE **705**

CUSTOMIZING FOR
Less-Proficient Writers

L Less-proficient writers may need assistance in identifying places they can use compound subjects or predicates. Guide them to find places where they have repeated words or phrases. The first example given has the repeated verbs and objects *went fishing.* Help students to combine the subjects and predicates using the conjunctions *and* and *or*.

Teaching Strategy:
USING THE SKILLBUILDER

M To help students combine subjects and predicates using correct grammar, you may want to teach the SkillBuilder on Making Compound Subjects and Verbs Agree at this time.

Try Your Hand

- Alida's and Taroo's favorite place was the Pomarosa Pool.
- Alida admired the young man's courage and learned to respect him.

SkillBuilder — GRAMMAR FROM WRITING

MAKING COMPOUND SUBJECTS AND VERBS AGREE Point out to students that the compound subject in the first example is *The Prince and his Father.* In the other examples, guide students to identify the subjects closest to the verbs: *stepmother, T'âm,* and *lies.*

Application Answer:
The towns of Cayey and Cidra sit far atop the hills. Alida swims and rests by the banks of a beautiful pool. Alida and Taroo fall in love and want to get married. Neither Alida's father nor the village people want Alida to marry Taroo.

Additional Suggestions Help students practice compound subject-verb agreement by correcting the verb forms in the following sentences. Help students write in the present tense.

1. The story warm my heart and make me happy. *(warms my heart and makes me happy)*
2. I think it have a strong moral or at least one that some people may want to learn. *(it has a strong moral)*

Reteaching/Reinforcement
- *Grammar Handbook,* anthology pp. 815-816
- *Grammar Mini-Lessons* copymasters, p. 5, transparencies, p. 5

The Writer's Craft
Subject-Verb Agreement, pp. 526–542

THE LANGUAGE OF LITERATURE TEACHER'S EDITION **705**

READING THE WORLD

On pages 702–705, students wrote a critical evaluation of a folk tale. Students also should be aware that other media present morals and teach lessons. On these pages, students will examine how television programs and movies teach lessons.

706 UNIT SIX: THE ORAL TRADITION

706 THE LANGUAGE OF LITERATURE TEACHER'S EDITION

READING THE WORLD

BELIEVE IT OR NOT

Every day we are exposed to morals or lessons on television and in movies. As you learned by reading the folk tales in Unit Six, some lessons are more valuable than others. With so many messages being sent, can you evaluate every one you see or hear?

View Jot down what you know about the shows or movies shown here. Then list other TV shows or movies that these images remind you of.

Interpret Describe what is likely to be going on in each scene. What kinds of lessons do you think are being presented? How valuable are lessons that are presented on TV or in movies?

Discuss In a small group, discuss the kinds of lessons that are often presented in movies or television shows. Then use the SkillBuilder at the right to help you make judgments about the lessons.

CRITICAL THINKING

Evaluating the Message
You know that television shows and movies often present lessons or morals. But how valuable are those lessons to you? Television shows and movies are limited in the way they present information. They can only last a set length of time, sometimes as little as 30 minutes. Just as in written stories, TV shows and movies have to leave out information, which can make them seem predictable. To help you judge the worth of a lesson presented in a TV show, it is useful to ask questions such as these:

- Do people in real life act like the characters on the show?
- Are problems in real life always resolved?
- Do real-life problems always have happy endings, as in many TV shows and movies?

APPLYING WHAT YOU'VE LEARNED
With a partner or a small group discuss specific television shows that presented a message. Talk about your reactions to each show and the value of the message. Describe the reasons behind your opinions.

READING THE WORLD **707**

Critical Thinking: CLASSIFYING

N Students may identify *The Brady Bunch* and *The Cosby Show*. They then may think of other shows that involve family situations or households with children in them. The other image is a common one, and students may identify other movies and advertisements that include the beach or couples at the beach.

Media Literacy: EVALUATING MOVIES AND TELEVISION

O In the scene from *The Brady Bunch*, the oldest daughter seems to be explaining something to the mother. In *The Cosby Show*, the grandfather is explaining something to the granddaughter. In the beach scene, a couple is walking down the beach hand in hand. Guide students to see that the lessons may differ in each. The television shows appear to be lessons in listening. The beach scene may be suggesting that it is romantic and good for couples to spend time together outdoors. Students may have different opinions regarding the value of lessons presented on TV or in movies. Encourage them to explain their thoughts.

Speaking, Listening, and Viewing: GROUP DISCUSSION

P Students can use the examples on this page to discuss the prevalence of images of the family on television. Encourage them to discuss whether the lessons being taught are similar to or different from what occurs in their own families. Invite them to think of lessons that they have been taught that are different from what is taught on television. Guide groups to think of other places where people learn lessons, for instance, at school, with friends, at places of work, and so on.

SkillBuilder — CRITICAL THINKING

EVALUATING THE MESSAGE Students may think that the television shows are realistic because of the characters or settings of the shows. Guide them to think about the action and events in the shows. They will probably agree that television shows are fairly unrealistic. Problems in shows are easily and humorously resolved, whereas problems in real life are rarely so simple. Students may feel that real-life problems do not always have happy endings.

Application Help students to first explain the lessons of the show and how those lessons were presented. Students should be able to do so in enough detail so that members of the group can then understand their reaction.

THE LANGUAGE OF LITERATURE TEACHER'S EDITION **707**

UNIT SIX
Lesson Planner: Links to Units 4–5

TIME ALLOTMENTS SHOWN ARE APPROXIMATE. DEPENDING ON YOUR GOALS AND THE NEEDS OF YOUR STUDENTS, YOU MAY WISH TO ALLOW MORE OR LESS TIME FOR CERTAIN PORTIONS OF THE LESSON.

Table of Contents	Discussion	Previewing the Selections	Reading the Selections
LINKS TO UNIT FOUR **Arachne** page 710 CHALLENGING **Three Strong Women** page 715 AVERAGE **The White Buffalo Calf Woman and the Sacred Pipe** page 723 EASY		**45 MINUTES** • GREECE • JAPAN • UNITED STATES	**45 MINUTES** • Introduce vocabulary • Read pp. 710–14 (5 pp.) • Read pp. 715–22 (8 pp.) • Read pp. 723–25 (3 pp.)
LINKS TO UNIT FIVE **The Living Kuan-yin** page 730 CHALLENGING **Sister Fox and Brother Coyote** page 735 EASY **King Thrushbeard** page 741 CHALLENGING		**35 MINUTES** • CHINA • UNITED STATES • GERMANY	**35 MINUTES** • Introduce vocabulary • Read pp. 730–34 (5 pp.) • Read pp. 735–40 (6 pp.) • Read pp. 741–45 (5 pp.)

Writing	Exploring Topics	Prewriting	Drafting and Revising
WRITING FROM EXPERIENCE **Writing a Report**	**15 MINUTES**	**20 MINUTES**	**75 MINUTES**

Time estimates assume in-class work. You may wish to assign some of these stages as homework.

Responding Options

- LITERATURE CONNECTION
- CROSS-CURRICULAR CONNECTIONS
- CULTURAL CONNECTIONS

90 MINUTES

- Present a puppet show

SCIENCE
- Explore textiles and looms

SOCIAL STUDIES
- Research the buffalo

- Compare/contrast characters
- Demonstrate wrestling
- Design trading cards
- Graph changes in the buffalo

90 MINUTES

- Hold a storytelling festival

SOCIAL STUDIES
- Learn more about money

SOCIAL STUDIES
- Celebrate festivals

- Build on the oral tradition
- Play "What's the Story?"
- Read more about minstrels
- Create a poster

Publishing and Reflecting

25 MINUTES

OVERVIEW

Objectives

- To understand and appreciate a myth, a tall tale, and a legend about characters' tests of strength
- To appreciate the values and customs of ancient Greece, Japan, and the Lakota Sioux
- To extend understanding of the stories through a variety of multimodal and cross-curricular activities

Reading Pathways

- Select one or several students to read each story aloud to the entire class or to small groups of students. Assign this reading in advance so the readers can incorporate into their presentations some of the techniques used by professional storytellers. Have the audience listen carefully to the stories without following along in their texts.

- Read the stories aloud to the class, pausing at key points to discuss how elements of the story inform students about the customs, values, or beliefs of ancient Greece, Japan, or the Lakota Sioux. Have students record their responses and observations in their notebooks.

- After students have read the stories once, they can read them again to identify structural elements such as main character, minor characters, conflict, setting, and plot. Then have students identify similarities and differences between these stories and the selections in Unit 4. For example, students might compare the challenges faced by the main characters of "The White Buffalo Calf Woman and the Sacred Pipe" with "At Last I Kill a Buffalo" (page 457).

PREVIEWING

LINKS TO UNIT FOUR

Proving Ground

Activating Prior Knowledge

In the selections in Unit Four, characters are forced to prove themselves—and in the process reveal some of their strengths and weaknesses. Those with something to prove sometimes go beyond the limits of acceptable behavior. Each tale you're about to read contains a message or lesson on staying within those limits.

Building Background

UNITED STATES

The White Buffalo Calf Woman and the Sacred Pipe

retold by Joseph Bruchac (brōō′chăk′)

The Lakota Sioux are Native Americans who lived on the plains of Nebraska and the Dakotas. Although the Sioux at first relied on agriculture, prolonged warfare with the Ojibwa people eventually forced the Sioux to become hunters and follow buffalo herds across the plains. This Lakota Sioux legend describes the outcome of a fateful meeting between two young men and a holy person called the White Buffalo Calf Woman.

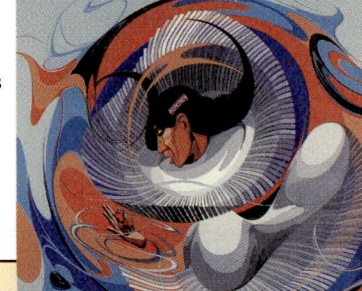

708   UNIT SIX   THE ORAL TRADITION

PRINT AND MEDIA RESOURCES

UNIT SIX RESOURCE BOOK
Strategic Reading: Literature, p. 31
Vocabulary SkillBuilder, p. 34
Reading SkillBuilder, p. 32
Spelling SkillBuilder, p. 33

GRAMMAR MINI-LESSONS
Transparencies, p. 39

WRITING MINI-LESSONS
Transparencies, p. 34

ACCESS FOR STUDENTS ACQUIRING ENGLISH
Selection Summaries
Reading and Writing Support

FORMAL ASSESSMENT
Selection Test, pp. 123–124
 Test Generator

 **AUDIO LIBRARY**
See Reference Card

INTERNET RESOURCES
McDougal Littell Literature Center at http://www.hmco.com/mcdougal/lit

---

708 THE LANGUAGE OF LITERATURE TEACHER'S EDITION

JAPAN

Three Strong Women
retold by Claus Stamm

Building Background

Formed by ancient volcanic eruptions, the islands of Japan stretch about 1,500 miles from north to south. If those islands ran along the eastern coast of the United States, they would stretch from Maine to Florida. Mountains are mentioned often in this Japanese folk tale, perhaps because nearly two-thirds of Japan is covered by them. The character Forever-Mountain finds unexpected challenges on his way to a big wrestling match.

GREECE

Building Background

Arachne
retold by Olivia E. Coolidge

In ancient Greece, the rule of the gods and goddesses was to be unquestioned. Many Greek myths are about characters who do not stay within limits set by the gods or who ignore their warnings. In this myth, a weaver, Arachne, pits herself against Athena, the goddess of wisdom and of all crafts, particularly weaving.

Setting a Purpose

AS YOU READ...

See how the values and customs of the cultures are presented.

Find out what virtuous behavior is and how it is rewarded.

See which traits are admired and respected and which are seen as negative.

LINKS TO UNIT FOUR **709**

WORDS TO KNOW

clamber (klăm′bər) *v.* to climb awkwardly; scramble (p. 716)
distorted (dĭ-stôr′tĭd) *adj.* twisted out of shape
distort *v.* (p. 714)
erect (ĭ-rĕkt′) *adj.* firmly straight in posture; not bending or slumping (p. 713)
fate (fāt) *n.* a final outcome that cannot be avoided (p. 713)
feeble (fē′bəl) *adj.* weak; not strong (p. 718)
immortal (ĭ-môr′tl) *adj.* living or lasting forever (p. 712)

indignantly (ĭn-dĭg′nənt-lē) *adv.* in a way that is angry because of an insult or an attack on one's self-respect (p. 712)
obscure (ŏb-skyŏŏr′) *adj.* not well-known or important (p. 711)
obstinacy (ŏb′stə-nə-sē) *n.* unreasonable stubbornness (p. 713)
sacred (sā′krĭd) *adj.* having to do with religion; holy (p. 724)

SUMMARIES

Arachne The Greek maiden Arachne boasts that her weaving is as beautiful as that of the goddess Athena. An old woman warns her to take back her claim. Arachne refuses, and the old woman reveals herself to be Athena. In the weaving contest that follows, they prove to be equal in skill—but Athena is quicker. Her cloth shows mortals challenging the gods and suffering for it, but Arachne does not listen. She weaves a cloth showing the gods' crimes. The insulted Athena rips the cloth in two and hits Arachne, who is humiliated and tries to hang herself. Before she can do so, Athena turns her into a spider as a reminder to all Greeks never to compete with the gods.

Three Strong Women Forever-Mountain is a famous Japanese wrestler who is very proud of his skill. On his way to wrestle before the emperor, he playfully tickles a small girl. She grabs him and to his shock and shame, the girl—Maru-me—proves to be far stronger than he. She forces him into training as a wrestler at the house of her equally strong mother. Maru-me's "feeble" grandmother, who can actually pull trees out of the ground, becomes Forever-Mountain's wrestling partner. By the end of three months, he too can pull up trees. After marrying Maru-me, Forever-Mountain goes to the emperor's palace and easily wins the wrestling contest. His victory angers the losers, so the emperor orders him to give up wrestling. Forever-Mountain happily returns to Maru-me and takes up farming—although his occasional wrestling matches with Maru-me's grandmother make the earth shake even today.

The White Buffalo Calf Woman and the Sacred Pipe In the time that this Lakota Sioux legend tells of, the tribe has little to eat. Two scouts, hunting for food, encounter a beautiful woman dressed in white buffalo skin. One scout dies after treating her disrespectfully. The White Buffalo Calf Woman gives the other scout a message for his people: "Put up a medicine lodge for me and make it ready. I will come there after four days have passed." The White Buffalo Calf Woman comes as promised and gives the people a sacred pipe; the pipe's three parts symbolize three things: the buffalo people and all other peoples; all trees, plants, and growing things; and Wakan Tanka, the Creator. Soon after the White Buffalo Calf Woman leaves, changing herself into a buffalo. Thereafter, as long as they use the pipe and remember that all things are connected like the parts of the pipe, the people always have buffalo to hunt.

THE LANGUAGE OF LITERATURE TEACHER'S EDITION **709**

CUSTOMIZING FOR
Students Acquiring English

- Use **ACCESS FOR STUDENTS ACQUIRING ENGLISH,** *Reading and Writing Support.*
- Some students may be familiar with the weaving, dying, and embroidery skills Arachne and her father possess. Invite students to describe these skills to their classmates and, if possible, bring in examples of cloth from their home cultures.
- In addition to these boxes, you may want to use the suggestions under Strategic Reading for Less-Proficient Readers.

STRATEGIC READING FOR
Less-Proficient Readers

Set a Purpose Tell students that this myth has two purposes: to illustrate a moral or lesson and to explain the origins of a very common animal. As students read the first part of the myth, have them note the strengths and weaknesses in Arachne's character.

Use **UNIT SIX RESOURCE BOOK,** pp. 31–32, for guidance in reading the selection.

CUSTOMIZING FOR
Gifted and Talented Students

All three of these stories have fantastic or supernatural elements. As students read, they can identify these elements. Ask students to imagine the stories without their fantastic elements. Have them describe how their absence affects the stories. *(Possible responses: In "Arachne," the goddess Athena could be replaced by a human weaver who is more skilled than Arachne. The story would still have an exciting contest, but the outcome would not be as dramatic or interesting. In the other two tales it would be difficult or impossible to eliminate the fantastic elements.)*

Illustration by Arvis Stewart, from *The Macmillan Book of Greek Gods and Heroes* by Alice Low. Copyright © 1985 Macmillan Publishing Company, reprinted with the permission of Simon & Schuster Books for Young Readers, an imprint of Simon & Schuster Children's Publishing Division.

retold by Olivia E. Coolidge

710 UNIT SIX: THE ORAL TRADITION

Multicultural Perspectives

GREEK MYTHOLOGY Greek mythology is an account of the actions of the gods worshipped by the ancient Greeks. There were twelve chief gods and numerous lesser ones. Zeus was the chief god and ruled the gods of the sky who lived on Mount Olympus. Poseidon ruled the seas and rivers; Hades the underworld. The Romans worshipped many of the same gods but called them by different names.

Athena was one of the most important goddesses. She sprang fully grown from the forehead of the god Zeus and was his favorite child. He gave her his main weapon, the thunderbolt, and his shield (called *aegis*). Her major temple, the Parthenon, was in Athens. According to legend, the temple became hers when she won a contest with Poseidon by giving the Athenians the olive tree.

Greek Name	Roman Name	God/Goddess of...
Zeus	Jupiter	Chief god
Poseidon	Neptune	Sea
Athena	Minerva	Wisdom
Aphrodite	Venus	Love
Apollo	Apollo	Sun

710 THE LANGUAGE OF LITERATURE TEACHER'S EDITION

Critical Thinking: SPECULATING

A Tell students that the title of the myth is a clue to what is going to happen to the main character. Invite them to predict the plot of the myth from the title. (*Possible response: The myth will have something to do with spiders because they are called "arachnids."*)

Literary Concept: SENSORY DETAILS

B Have students read the first page of the myth and identify details appealing to sight that the writer uses to describe Arachne's appearance and skill. (*Possible responses: fine, soft thread; high, standing loom; small and pale; dusty brown hair; quick and graceful*)

Active Reading: CONNECT

C Have students think of someone they know who is remarkably talented in the arts or in handicrafts. Ask students if this person is proud and boastful about his or her talents or if the person is modest and unassuming. As students read, they can mentally compare their artist with Arachne, the main character in the myth.

CUSTOMIZING FOR
Multiple Learning Styles

D **Spatial or Graphic Learners** To better understand Arachne's talents, students can find pictures of woven textiles in library books. They may also want to look at diagrams of spinning wheels and looms. Graphic materials that students find can be shared with classmates.

CUSTOMIZING FOR
Students Acquiring English

I Call students' attention to the inversion of subject and predicate in *So soft and even was her thread*. Explain that the writer did this for emphasis and for a musical rhythm.

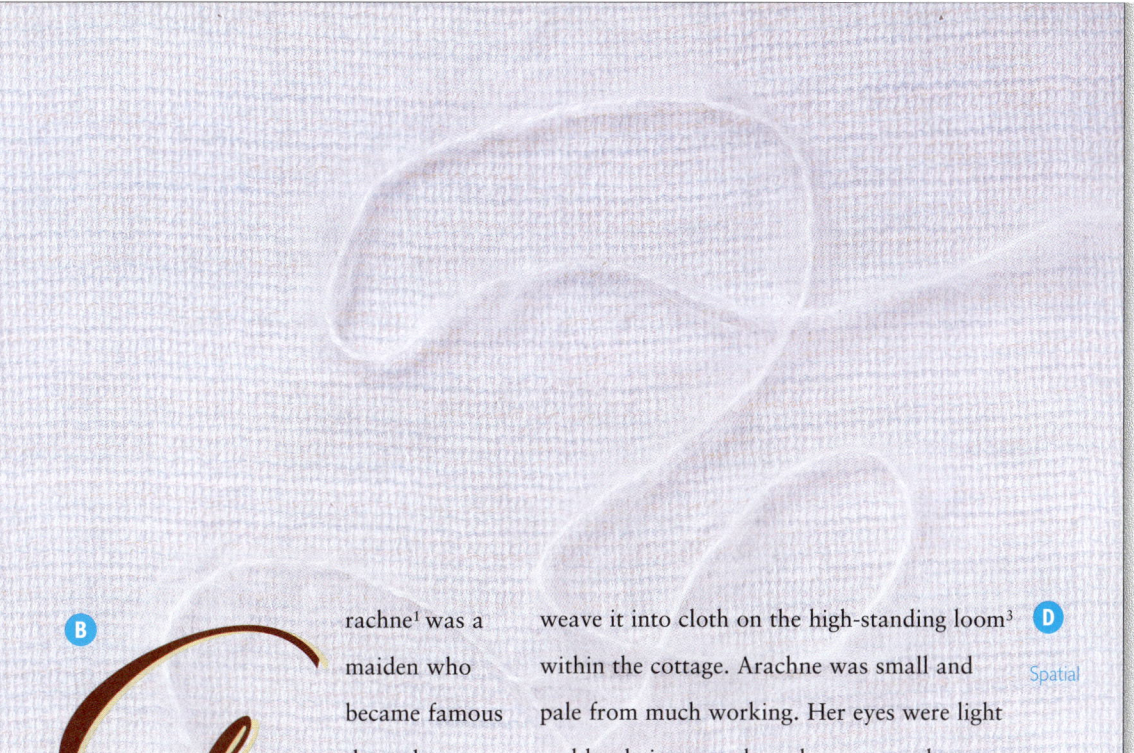

B **A**rachne[1] was a maiden who became famous throughout Greece, though she was neither wellborn[2] nor beautiful and came from no great city. She lived in an <u>obscure</u> little village, and her father was a humble dyer of wool. In this he was very skillful, producing many varied shades, while above all he was famous for the clear, bright scarlet which is made from shellfish and which was the most glorious of all the colors used in **C** ancient Greece. Even more skillful than her father was Arachne. It was her task to spin the fleecy wool into a fine, soft thread and to weave it into cloth on the high-standing loom[3] **D** within the cottage. Arachne was small and pale from much working. Her eyes were light and her hair was a dusty brown, yet she was quick and graceful, and her fingers, roughened as they were, went so fast that it was hard to follow their flickering movements. So soft and **I** even was her thread, so fine her cloth, so gorgeous her embroidery, that soon her products were known all over Greece. No one had ever seen the like of them before.

Spatial

1. Arachne (ə-răk′nē).
2. **wellborn:** of a high social class.
3. **high-standing loom:** a tall frame used to hold threads in a vertical position as other threads are woven through horizontally.

WORDS TO KNOW
obscure (ŏb-skyŏŏr′) *adj.* not well-known or important

Mini-Lesson Spelling

PREFIX OB- Explain to students that the prefix *ob-* means "against" or "in the way of." The spelling of the prefix depends on the root to which it is joined.

Application Write on the chalkboard the examples shown. Have students use one of the spelling words from the box to replace each underlined word or phrase in the following paragraph. Answers are in parentheses.

Arachne was a famous weaver who lived in <u>a small and little-known</u> (*obscure*) village. She <u>complained</u> (*objected*) when people <u>criticized</u> (*opposed*) her. One day as Arachne was <u>busy</u> (*occupied*) at her loom, the goddess Athena decided to teach her a lesson.

Ask students to look for more words that fit this pattern, in their own writing and in things that they read, and to add these words to their personal word lists.

Reteaching/Reinforcement
• *Unit Six Resource Book,* p. 33

---

ob + jected = objected
ob + scure = obscure
oc + cupied = occupied
op + posed = opposed

THE LANGUAGE OF LITERATURE TEACHER'S EDITION **711**

CUSTOMIZING FOR
Students Acquiring English

② Explain that *Arachne was used to being wondered at* means "People often admired Arachne."

Active Reading: EVALUATE

E Ask students what they think of Arachne's pride. *(Possible responses: Her pride is justified, because she is the best weaver anyone has ever seen; her pride is excessive, because her gifts as a weaver are god-given.)*

Critical Thinking:
MAKING JUDGMENTS

F Have students form an opinion of Arachne's character from the information in the myth. *(Possible responses: She isn't very admirable because she is vain, proud, and rude; she is skillful and is justified in her impatience with others.)*

Linking to Science

 **G** At the end of the myth Athena "answers" Arachne by turning her into a spider. Although some spiders weave beautiful webs in order to catch food, there are many others that are not webweavers. For example, trap-door spiders tunnel into the ground and create a corklike lid over the tunnel. Then they lie in wait for passing prey.

At last Arachne's fame became so great that people used to come from far and wide to watch her working. Even the graceful nymphs[4] would steal in from stream or forest and peep shyly through the dark doorway, watching in wonder the white arms of Arachne as she stood at the loom and threw the shuttle[5] from hand to hand between the hanging threads or drew out the long wool, fine as a hair, from the distaff[6] as she sat spinning. "Surely Athena herself must have taught her," people would murmur to one another. "Who else could know the secret of such marvelous skill?"

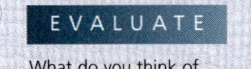
What do you think of Arachne's pride?
Using a Reading Log

Arachne was used to being wondered at, and she was immensely proud of the skill that had brought so many to look on her. Praise was all she lived for, and it displeased her greatly that people should think anyone, even a goddess, could teach her anything. Therefore, when she heard them murmur, she would stop her work and turn round indignantly to say, "With my own ten fingers I gained this skill, and by hard practice from early morning till night. I never had time to stand looking as you people do while another maiden worked. Nor if I had, would I give Athena credit because the girl was more skillful than I. As for Athena's weaving, how could there be finer cloth or more beautiful embroidery than mine? If Athena herself were to come down and compete with me, she could do no better than I."

One day when Arachne turned round with such words, an old woman answered her, a grey old woman, bent and very poor, who stood leaning on a staff and peering at Arachne amid the crowd of onlookers.

"Reckless girl," she said, "how dare you claim to be equal to the immortal gods themselves? I am an old woman and have seen much. Take my advice and ask pardon of Athena for your words. Rest content with your fame of being the best spinner and weaver that mortal eyes have ever beheld."

"Stupid old woman," said Arachne indignantly, "who gave you a right to speak in this way to me? It is easy to see that you were never good for anything in your day, or you would not come here in poverty and rags to gaze at my skill. If Athena resents my words, let her answer them herself. I have challenged

> "STUPID OLD WOMAN," SAID ARACHNE INDIGNANTLY, "WHO GAVE YOU A RIGHT TO SPEAK IN THIS WAY TO ME?"

F
G

---
4. **nymphs** (nĭmfs): in Greek mythology, minor goddesses of nature.
5. **shuttle**: a piece of wood holding the thread that is to be woven horizontally through the vertical threads on a loom.
6. **distaff**: a short rod for holding wool that is to be spun into thread.

WORDS TO KNOW
indignantly (ĭn-dĭg′nənt-lē) *adv.* in a way that is angry, because of an insult or an attack on one's self-respect
immortal (ĭ-môr′tl) *adj.* living or lasting forever

712

Mini-Lesson Study Skills

TAKING OBJECTIVE TESTS: TRUE/FALSE QUESTIONS Remind students that a true/false question asks them to decide if a statement is true or false. The tips listed below may help students with these types of questions.
- If *any* part of the statement is false, the answer is "false."
- Statements that include such words as *all, never, always,* and *none* are often, though not always, false.
- Statements that include such words as *generally, some, most, many,* and *usually* are often, though not always, true.

Application Have students decide whether each statement is true or false.
1. Arachne believed she knew more about weaving than anyone, even a goddess. *(true)*
2. Arachne was lazy and didn't work very hard at her weaving. *(false)*
3. In the myth, Arachne insults an old woman who turns into a spider. *(false)*
4. Athena visits Arachne to teach her to be a better weaver. *(false)*
5. Athena becomes angry at Arachne because Arachne is a faster weaver. *(false)*

712 THE LANGUAGE OF LITERATURE TEACHER'S EDITION

her to a contest, but she, of course, will not come. It is easy for the gods to avoid matching their skill with that of men."

At these words the old woman threw down her staff and stood erect. The wondering onlookers saw her grow tall and fair and stand clad in long robes of dazzling white. They were terribly afraid as they realized that they stood in the presence of Athena. Arachne herself flushed red for a moment, for she had never really believed that the goddess would hear her. Before the group that was gathered there she would not give in; so pressing her pale lips together in obstinacy and pride, she led the goddess to one of the great looms and set herself before the other. Without a word both began to thread the long woolen strands that hung from the rollers and between which the shuttle would move back and forth. Many skeins[7] lay heaped beside them to use, bleached white, and gold, and scarlet, and other shades, varied as the rainbow. Arachne had never thought of giving credit for her success to her father's skill in dyeing, though in actual truth the colors were as remarkable as the cloth itself.

Soon there was no sound in the room but the breathing of the onlookers, the whirring of the shuttles, and the creaking of the wooden frames as each pressed the thread up into place or tightened the pegs by which the whole was held straight. The excited crowd in the doorway began to see that the skill of both in truth was very nearly equal but that, however the cloth might turn out, the goddess was the quicker of the two. A pattern of many pictures was growing on her loom. There was a border of twined branches of the olive, Athena's favorite tree, while in the middle, figures began to appear. As they looked at the glowing colors, the spectators realized that Athena was weaving into her pattern a last warning to Arachne. The central figure was the goddess herself, competing with Poseidon[8] for possession of the city of Athens; but in the four corners were mortals who had tried to strive with gods and pictures of the awful fate that had overtaken them. The goddess ended a little before Arachne and stood back from her marvelous work to see what the maiden was doing.

PREDICT
How do you think the weaving contest will end?
Using a Reading Log

Never before had Arachne been matched against anyone whose skill was equal, or even nearly equal, to her own. As she stole glances from time to time at Athena and saw the goddess working swiftly, calmly, and always a little faster than herself, she became angry instead of frightened, and an evil thought came into her head. Thus, as Athena stepped back a pace to watch Arachne finishing her work, she saw that the maiden had taken for her design a pattern of scenes which showed evil or unworthy actions of the gods, how they had deceived fair maidens, resorted to trickery, and appeared on earth from time to time in the form of poor and humble people. When the goddess saw this insult glowing in bright colors on Arachne's loom, she did not wait while the cloth was judged but stepped

---
7. **skeins** (skānz): rolls of thread or yarn.
8. **Poseidon** (pō-sīd′n): in Greek mythology, the god of the sea.

WORDS TO KNOW
erect (ĭ-rĕkt′) *adj.* firmly straight in posture; not bending or slumping
obstinacy (ŏb′stə-nə-sē) *n.* unreasonable stubbornness
fate (fāt) *n.* a final outcome that cannot be avoided

Mini-Lesson The Writer's Style

ELABORATION Remind students that there are many ways to develop a character. Writers may describe what the character looks like, use dialogue, make comparisons, or relate stories or events.

Application Have students identify both description and dialogue that the writer uses to show Arachne's pride and boastfulness. Suggest that students use a two-column chart to organize their work.

Reteaching/Reinforcement
- *Writing Handbook*, anthology pp. 783–784, 788–789
- *Writing Mini-Lessons* transparencies, p. 34

The Writer's Craft
Developing a Topic, pp. 205–210

Description	Dialogue
"Praise was all she lived for…"	"…how could there be finer cloth or more beautiful embroidery than mine?"

STRATEGIC READING FOR
Less-Proficient Readers

H Ask students how they would describe Arachne's personality. (*Possible responses: arrogant, proud, impatient, rude, conceited*) Making Judgments

Set a Purpose Ask students to continue to read and note the details used to describe the conflict between Arachne and Athena.

CUSTOMIZING FOR
Students Acquiring English

3 Point out that *before*, as used here, means "in the presence of."

4 Point out that *whirring* and *creaking* are two examples of onomatopoeia, words that imitate sounds, in this case, the sound of the looms.

Active Reading: PREDICT

I Ask students how they think the weaving contest will end. (*Possible responses: Arachne will win because of her extraordinary skill; Athena will win because she is a goddess and the greatest weaver of them all.*)

Literary Links

J The myth "Arachne" reflects the theme of Unit 4, "Proving Ground," in which characters go through tests of personal strength in either a public setting or in an inner, private struggle. Have students choose a character from "The Secret of the Wall" (page 389) and compare and contrast that character's struggle with Arachne's. (*Possible response: Serafin discovers he is not as brave as he thought; Arachne discovers her weaving skill will not protect her from Athena's anger.*)

STRATEGIC READING FOR
Less-Proficient Readers

K Ask questions such as the following to help students summarize the end of the myth.

- How does the goddess Athena respond to Arachne's boasts? *(She appears as the old woman, changes into her true form, and then accepts Arachne's challenge to a weaving contest.)* **Relating Cause and Effect**

- What scenes do Athena and Arachne weave? *(Athena: warnings about mortals who had challenged the gods; Arachne: insulting scenes of the gods' unworthy acts)* **Noting Relevant Details**

From Personal Response to Critical Analysis

1. What adjectives would you use to describe Arachne? Write down these adjectives in your notebook. *(Possible responses: skillful, famous, quick, graceful, proud, arrogant, rude, impatient)*

2. What are your impressions of the goddess Athena? *(Possible responses: She is as vain and arrogant as Arachne; she is sincerely trying to help Arachne overcome her excessive pride.)*

3. What does the outcome of the conflict between Athena and Arachne suggest about the relationship between the Greek gods and humans? *(Possible responses: Humans cannot win in contests against the Greek gods; although the Greek gods share many of the same emotions, personality traits, talents, and flaws with humans, the gods have complete power over humans and control their fates.)*

4. Why do you think Arachne is so determined to test her limits? *(Possible responses: She is justly proud of her skill and does not want anyone else to take credit for it; she is overly proud and cannot control herself.)*

---

forward, her grey eyes blazing with anger, and tore Arachne's work across. Then she struck Arachne across the face. Arachne stood there a moment, struggling with anger, fear, and pride. "I will not live under this insult," she cried, and seizing a rope from the wall, she made a noose and would have hanged herself.

The goddess touched the rope and touched the maiden. "Live on, wicked girl," she said. "Live on and spin, both you and your descendants. When men look at you, they may remember that it is not wise to strive with Athena." At that the body of Arachne shriveled up; and her legs grew tiny, spindly, and <u>distorted</u>. There before the eyes of the spectators hung a little dusty brown spider on a slender thread.

All spiders descend from Arachne, and as the Greeks watched them spinning their thread wonderfully fine, they remembered the contest with Athena and thought that it was not right for even the best of men to claim equality with the gods. ❖

OLIVIA E. COOLIDGE

Olivia E. Coolidge (1908–) grew up in England, where her father was a journalist and historian. After completing her studies at Oxford University, Coolidge came to the United States and taught English for several years.

Coolidge has written a number of biographies for young people in which she needed to carefully separate facts from opinions. As Coolidge says, "Facts are the bricks with which a biographer builds. . . . The more facts I have to work with, the freer I am to design my own book." Coolidge carefully researches her subjects and then forms her own opinions.

OTHER WORKS *Greek Myths, Gandhi, The Apprenticeship of Abraham Lincoln, Legends of the North, The Trojan War, Egyptian Adventures, Roman People*

WORDS TO KNOW
distorted (dĭ-stôr′tĭd) *adj.* twisted out of shape **distort** *v.*

714

COMPREHENSION CHECK

1. For what skills is Arachne famous? *(spinning and weaving)*
2. What does the old woman tell Arachne? *(to beg Athena's pardon for excessive pride)*
3. Into whom does the old woman change? *(the goddess Athena)*
4. What scenes does Arachne weave into her cloth? *(the gods' evil or unworthy actions)*
5. What happens to Arachne at the end of the story? *(Athena changes her into a spider.)*

THREE STRONG WOMEN

retold by Claus Stamm

Upper right: Figure of a woman (late 1600s), unknown Japanese artist. Arita ware, Kakiemon porcelain with overglaze polychrome enamel, Edo period, 14¼″ × 5½″, Asian Art Museum of San Francisco, The Avery Brundage Collection (B62 P5+).

715

Art Note

Figure of a Woman This 14 1/4-inch high figure of a woman is made of white porcelain overglazed with polychrome enamel. It dates from the late 17th century and represents a style that became highly prized by European collectors. The woman's outer robe is called a *uchikake* and is decorated with a floral pattern in varying colors.

Reading the Art *What adjectives would you use to describe the woman? How does she compare with the three women in the tall tale?*

CUSTOMIZING FOR
Students Acquiring English

- If possible, invite students from Japanese backgrounds to share information about wrestling in Japanese culture.

STRATEGIC READING FOR
Less-Proficient Readers

Set a Purpose Ask students to read the first page of the tale and note the details used to depict the character of the wrestler Forever-Mountain.

Mini-Lesson: Speaking, Listening, and Viewing

SPORTSCAST Explain to students that an interesting way to summarize and describe the story's action is to turn it into a play-by-play sportscast. Point out that effective announcers convey the action of an event using brief statements that highlight the most exciting elements. The announcer's voice also helps convey the excitement of the sporting contest.

Application Divide the class into small groups. Have each group select one incident where Forever-Mountain wrestles with another character. Tell students to use details from the story to create a play-by-play description of the event. Invite groups to perform their scripts for the class. You may wish to extend the activity by having the "sportscasters" interview other students role-playing the characters. Interviews should recap the event and express wrestlers' feelings about winning or losing.

THE LANGUAGE OF LITERATURE TEACHER'S EDITION **715**

Active Reading: CLARIFY

A Ask students to describe what the wrestler might look like. Then have them look at the prints on pages 720 and 721 to visualize just how large Japanese wrestlers can be. Understanding the great size and strength of the wrestler Forever-Mountain is key to appreciating the humor and irony in the tale.

CUSTOMIZING FOR
Students Acquiring English

I Point out that *zun-zun-zun* imitates the sound the wrestler made when he hummed.

Literary Concept: CHARACTERIZATION

B Ask students if they believe Forever-Mountain is really "far too modest" ever to boast about his strength and skill. *(Possible response: Probably not. He is so impressed with himself that it is unlikely he doesn't brag about it.)*

CUSTOMIZING FOR
Multiple Learning Styles

C **Linguistic Learners** Point out the instances on this page where the writer transliterates nonword sounds Forever-Mountain makes. For humming, the writer uses "zun-zun-zun" and for tickling, "kochokochokocho." Have students write alternates for these types of sounds. For example, humming might be indicated by "da-da da-da" or by "ahmm-hmm-humm."

STRATEGIC READING FOR
Less-Proficient Readers

D Ask students how Forever-Mountain regards himself. *(He is very proud of his skill and strength as a wrestler.)* **Summarizing**

Set a Purpose As students continue to read, they should look for fantastic elements that identify this selection as a tall tale.

There were red and orange trees along the roadside.

The trees along the roadside glowed red and orange.

---

716 THE LANGUAGE OF LITERATURE TEACHER'S EDITION

---

ong ago, in Japan, there lived a famous wrestler, and he was on his way to the capital city to wrestle before the Emperor.

He strode down the road on legs thick as the trunks of small trees. He had been walking for seven hours and could, and probably would, walk for seven more without getting tired.

A

The time was autumn, the sky was a cold, watery blue, the air chilly. In the small, bright sun, the trees along the roadside glowed red and orange. The wrestler hummed to himself, "Zun-zun-zun," in time with the long swing of his legs. Wind blew through his thin brown robe, and he wore no sword at his side. He felt proud that he needed no sword, even in the darkest and loneliest places. The icy air on his body only reminded him that few tailors would have been able to make expensive, warm clothes for a man so broad and tall. He felt much as a wrestler should—strong, healthy, and rather conceited.

I

A soft roar of fast-moving water beyond the trees told him that he was passing above a riverbank. He "zun-zunned" louder; he loved the sound of his voice and wanted it to sound clearly above the rushing water.

He thought, They call me Forever-Mountain because I am such a good strong wrestler—big, too. I'm a fine, brave man and far too modest ever to say so. . . .

B

Just then he saw a girl who must have come up from the river, for she steadied a bucket on her head.

Her hands on the bucket were small, and there was a dimple on each thumb, just below the knuckle. She was a round little girl with red cheeks and a nose like a friendly button. Her eyes looked as though she were thinking of ten thousand funny stories at once. She <u>clambered</u> up onto the road and walked ahead of the wrestler, jolly and bounceful.

> *Her hands on the bucket were small, and there was a dimple on each thumb, just below the knuckle. She was a round little girl with red cheeks and a nose like a friendly button.*

"If I don't tickle that fat girl, I shall regret it all my life," said the wrestler under his breath. "She's sure to go 'squeak' and I shall laugh and laugh. If she drops her bucket, that will be even funnier—and I can always run and fill it again and even carry it home for her."

He tiptoed up and poked her lightly in the ribs with one huge finger.

"Kochokochokocho!" he said, a fine, ticklish sound in Japanese. **C**

The girl gave a satisfying squeal, giggled, and brought one arm down so that the wrestler's hand was caught between it and her body.

"Ho-ho-ho! You've caught me! I can't move at all!" said the wrestler, laughing.

"I know," said the jolly girl.

He felt that it was very good-tempered of her to take a joke so well, and started to pull his hand free. **D**

Somehow, he could not.

He tried again, using a little more strength.

WORDS TO KNOW
clamber (klăm′bər) *v.* to climb awkwardly; scramble

716

Mini-Lesson — Grammar

PREDICATE ADJECTIVES Remind students that an adjective that follows a linking verb is called a predicate adjective. Two or more predicate adjectives may be joined to describe the same subject. Have students compare the two sentences shown.

In both sentences, the adjectives *red* and *orange* modify **trees**. In the first sentence the adjectives come just before the word they modify. In the second sentence, the adjectives follow the linking verb *glowed*.

Application Have students rewrite the following sentences so that the adjectives come just before the boldface word that they modify.
1. Forever-Mountain walked along under a **sky** that was a cold, watery blue.
2. The **wrestler** was proud that he needed no sword.

Reteaching/Reinforcement
- *Grammar Handbook,* anthology p. 852
- *Grammar Mini-Lessons* transparencies, p. 39

 **The Writer's Craft**

Predicate Adjectives, pp. 468–469

Twenty-Second Station, Okabe, Utsu no Yama [Utsu Mountain] (1834), Hiroshige. Color woodcut from *Fifty-Three Stations of the Tokaido*, Print Collection, Miriam and Ira D. Wallach Division of Art, Prints and Photographs, The New York Public Library, Astor, Lenox and Tilden Foundations.

"Now, now—let me go, little girl," he said. "I am a very powerful man. If I pull too hard I might hurt you."

"Pull," said the girl. "I admire powerful men."

She began to walk, and though the wrestler tugged and pulled until his feet dug great furrows in the ground, he had to follow. She couldn't have paid him less attention if he had been a puppy—a small one.

Ten minutes later, still tugging while trudging helplessly after her, he was glad that the road was lonely and no one was there to see.

"Please let me go," he pleaded. "I am the famous wrestler Forever-Mountain. I must go and show my strength before the Emperor"—he burst out weeping from shame and confusion—"and you're hurting my hand!"

The girl steadied the bucket on her head with her free hand and dimpled sympathetically over her shoulder. "You poor, sweet little Forever-Mountain," she said. "Are you tired? Shall I carry you? I can leave the water here and come back for it later."

"I do not want you to carry me. I want you to let me go, and then I want to forget I ever saw you. What do you want with me?" moaned the pitiful wrestler.

"I only want to help you," said the girl, now pulling him steadily up and up a narrow mountain path. "Oh, I am sure you'll have no more trouble than anyone else when you come up against the other wrestlers. You'll win, or else you'll lose, and you won't be too badly hurt either way. But aren't you afraid you might meet a really *strong* man someday?"

Forever-Mountain turned white. He stumbled. He was imagining being laughed at throughout Japan as "Hardly-Ever-Mountain."

She glanced back.

THREE STRONG WOMEN **717**

Art Note

Twenty-Second Station **by Ando Hiroshige** The Japanese artist and print designer Hiroshige (1797–1858) was enormously popular during his own lifetime. This work is one of 55 prints showing stopping places along the Tokaido, a famous road between Kyoto and Tokyo. The road covers a distance of more than 300 miles and, in Hiroshige's day, took more than two weeks to cover on foot. In this print, travelers on the road appear to be walking through a mountain pass.

Reading the Art *How would you describe the mood of the print? What scene or scenes in the tale might the landscape in the print describe?*

Literary Concept: HUMOR

E Ask students to visualize how much bigger the wrestler is in comparison with the "round little girl." Then have them identify places on this page where the size difference is used to create humor. *(Possible responses: the wrestler is pulled along "like a puppy"; he pleads, weeps, and moans; the girl offers to carry him if he is too tired.)*

Critical Thinking: ANALYZING

F Remind students that "Forever-Mountain" is a nickname and not the wrestler's real name. Ask them to give an interpretation of both "Forever-Mountain" and, for comparison, "Hardly-Ever Mountain." *(Possible response: He might have been called Forever-Mountain because the other wrestlers were unable to throw him—he is as unmovable as a mountain. "Hardly-Ever Mountain" might mean the opposite—that he could rarely survive a wrestling contest without being thrown.)*

Mini-Lesson  Literary Concepts

REVIEWING HUMOR Remind students that writers can create humor in many ways. Sources of humor include exaggeration, witty dialogue, amusing descriptions, and impossible situations.

Application Have students contrast the highlighted passages on pages 716 and 717. The first shows a common game adults use to amuse small children. This game is also somewhat patronizing. Ask students how the girl turns the table on the wrestler and why this is humorous.

THE LANGUAGE OF LITERATURE TEACHER'S EDITION **717**

Active Reading: PREDICT

G Ask students to predict what will happen to Forever-Mountain when he gets to the girl's house. Have students create at least two possible plot sequences. You may wish to use the following model to give students ideas of what they might be thinking about:

Think-Aloud Model Since Forever-Mountain doesn't want to go with the girl, he will escape from her house and perhaps get lost in the mountains. Or he may become very impressed with the girl's strength and fall in love with her. Perhaps the girl's mother will dislike the wrestler and order him to leave. He and the girl might run away together.

Literary Concept: PLOT

H Ask students how the cow is used in an unusual way. *(Possible response: The writer uses the cow to exaggerate the mother's strength and to add humor to the story.)* You may wish to tell students that the cow will reappear later in the plot of the tale.

CUSTOMIZING FOR
Multiple Learning Styles

I **Logical-Mathematical Learners** Some students may be confused by the impossible feats of strength in the tale. Remind them that fiction of this type often includes fantastic or incredible events. Ask students to think about the writer's purpose—why does he exaggerate the strength of the three women? *(Possible response: The tale is teaching a lesson about pride, so it is important that Forever-Mountain be humbled by the exaggerated strength of the women.)*

"You see? Tired already," she said. "I'll walk more slowly. Why don't you come along to my mother's house and let us make a strong man of you? The wrestling in the capital isn't due to begin for three months. I know, because Grandmother thought she'd go. You'd be spending all that time in bad company and wasting what little power you have."

"All right. Three months. I'll come along," said the wrestler. He felt he had nothing more to lose. Also, he feared that the girl might become angry if he refused, and place him in the top of a tree until he changed his mind.

"Fine," she said happily. "We are almost there."

She freed his hand. It had become red and a little swollen. "But if you break your promise and run off, I shall have to chase you and carry you back."

Soon they arrived in a small valley. A simple farmhouse with a thatched[1] roof stood in the middle.

"Grandmother is at home, but she is an old lady and she's probably sleeping." The girl shaded her eyes with one hand. "But Mother should be bringing our cow back from the field—oh, there's Mother now!"

She waved. The woman coming around the corner of the house put down the cow she was carrying and waved back.

She smiled and came across the grass, walking with a lively bounce like her daughter's. Well, maybe her bounce was a little more solid, thought the wrestler.

"Excuse me," she said, brushing some cow hair from her dress, and dimpling, also like her daughter. "These mountain paths are full of stones. They hurt the cow's feet. And who is the nice young man you've brought, Maru-me?"

The girl explained. "And we have only three months!" she finished anxiously.

"Well, it's not long enough to do much, but it's not so short a time that we can't do something," said her mother, looking thoughtful. "But he does look terribly feeble. He'll need a lot of good things to eat. Maybe when he gets stronger he can help Grandmother with some of the easy work about the house."

"That will be fine!" said the girl, and she called her grandmother—loudly, for the old lady was a little deaf.

"I'm coming!" came a creaky voice from inside the house, and a little old woman leaning on a stick and looking very sleepy tottered out of the door. As she came towards them, she stumbled over the roots of a great oak tree.

"Heh! My eyes aren't what they used to be. That's the fourth time this month I've stumbled over that tree," she complained and, wrapping her skinny arms about its trunk, pulled it out of the ground.

"Oh, Grandmother! You should have let me pull it up for you," said Maru-me.

"Hm. I hope I didn't hurt my poor old back," muttered the old lady. She called out, "Daughter! Throw that tree away like a good girl, so no one will fall over it. But make sure it doesn't hit anybody."

"You can help Mother with the tree," Maru-me said to Forever-Mountain. "On second thought, you'd better not help. Just watch."

Her mother went to the tree, picked it up in her two hands and threw it. Up went the tree, sailing end over end, growing smaller and smaller as it flew. It landed with a faint crash far up the mountainside.

"Ah, how clumsy," she said. "I meant to throw it *over* the mountain. It's probably

---

1. **thatched:** covered with a plant material, usually straw.

WORDS TO KNOW
feeble (fē´bəl) *adj.* weak; not strong

718

Mini-Lesson: Speaking, Listening, and Viewing

DRAMA PERFORMANCE Explain to students that one way to visualize the events in a story is to try acting them out. The text on this page offers a good opportunity for students to create their own drama performances because it contains so much dialogue.

Application Have students work in groups of four to act out the story from the point Forever-Mountain arrives at the farmhouse until he faints. In preparation for their performance, students should discuss what props they will need, assign roles, and review the characteristics of the characters. After each group has had a chance to act out the scene, you may wish to have students experiment by adding new dialogue to their performances.

718 THE LANGUAGE OF LITERATURE **Teacher's Edition**

blocking the path now, and I'll have to get up early tomorrow to move it."

The wrestler was not listening. He had very quietly fainted.

"Oh! We must put him to bed," said Maru-me.

"Poor, feeble young man," said her mother.

"I hope we can do something for him. Here, let me carry him; he's light," said the grandmother. She slung him over her shoulder and carried him into the house, creaking along with her cane.

The next day they began the work of making Forever-Mountain into what they thought a strong man should be. They gave him the simplest food to eat, and the toughest. Day by day they prepared his rice with less and less water, until no ordinary man could have chewed or digested it.

Every day he was made to do the work of five men, and every evening he wrestled with Grandmother. Maru-me and her mother agreed that Grandmother, being old and feeble, was the least likely to injure him accidentally. They hoped the exercise might be good for the old lady's rheumatism.[2]

He grew stronger and stronger but was hardly aware of it. Grandmother could still throw him easily into the air—and catch him again—without ever changing her sweet old smile.

He quite forgot that outside this valley he was one of the greatest wrestlers in Japan and was called Forever-Mountain. His legs had been like logs; now they were like pillars. His big hands were hard as stones, and when he cracked his knuckles, the sound was like trees splitting on a cold night.

Sometimes he did an exercise that wrestlers do in Japan—raising one foot high above the ground and bringing it down with a crash.

> The next day they began the work of making Forever-Mountain into what they thought a strong man should be. They gave him the simplest food to eat, and the toughest.

Then people in nearby villages looked up at the winter sky and told one another that it was very late in the year for thunder. Soon he could pull up a tree as well as the grandmother. He could even throw one—but only a small distance. One evening, near the end of his third month, he wrestled with Grandmother and held her down for half a minute.

"Heh-heh!" she chortled, and got up, smiling with every wrinkle. "I would never have believed it!"

Maru-me squealed with joy and threw her arms around him—gently, for she was afraid of cracking his ribs.

"Very good, very good! What a strong man," said her mother, who had just come home from the fields, carrying, as usual, the cow. She put the cow down and patted the wrestler on the back.

They agreed that he was now ready to show some *real* strength before the Emperor.

"Take the cow along with you tomorrow when you go," said the mother. "Sell her and

---

2. **rheumatism** (rōō′mə-tĭz′əm): painful condition in which joints and muscles become swollen and stiff.

THREE STRONG WOMEN 719

Mini-Lesson Literary Concepts

CHARACTERIZATION Remind students that the way a writer develops a character's personality is called characterization. Writers develop characters in four basic ways:
- a physical description of the character
- the character's thoughts, speech, and actions
- the thoughts, speech, and actions of other characters
- direct comments on a character's nature

Application Have students create a chart showing the details used in the story to describe the two main characters.

Characters	Details from the story	Physical description of characters
Forever-Mountain		
Maru-me		

CUSTOMIZING FOR
Students Acquiring English

2 Explain that a *souvenir* is an object kept as a reminder or memento of a place or person.

3 Invite students to find three synonyms for *laughed* in this paragraph. You may want to model examples of each type of laughter.

Literary Links

L Have students choose a character from "My Friend Flicka" and compare and contrast that character's struggle with Forever-Mountain's. *(Possible response: Rob McLaughlin discovers that Kennie's love for Flicka is a powerful force; Forever-Mountain decides that his love for Maru-me is more important than his strength and skill as a wrestler.)*

STRATEGIC READING FOR
Less-Proficient Readers

M Ask students to summarize what happens to Forever-Mountain during the three months he spends with the women. *(His strength increases through simple food, hard work, and wrestling with the grandmother.)* Summarizing

- How do his experiences change him? *(At the wrestling match he is quiet and no longer boastful.)* Noting Relevant Details

Set a Purpose Before students read the end of the tale, they should predict what will happen at the wrestling match and whether Forever-Mountain will return to Maru-me. Then have students read to find out if their predictions are correct.

---

buy yourself a belt—a silken belt. Buy the fattest and heaviest one you can find. Wear it when you appear before the Emperor, as a souvenir from us."

"I wouldn't think of taking your only cow. You've already done too much for me. And you'll need her to plough the fields, won't you?"

They burst out laughing. Maru-me squealed; her mother roared. The grandmother cackled so hard and long that she choked and had to be pounded on the back.

"Oh, dear," said the mother, still laughing. "You didn't think we used our cow for anything like *work*! Why, Grandmother here is stronger than five cows!"

"The cow is our pet," Maru-me giggled. "She has lovely brown eyes."

"But it really gets tiresome having to carry her back and forth each day so that she has enough grass to eat," said her mother.

"Then you must let me give you all the prize money that I win," said Forever-Mountain.

"Oh, no! We wouldn't think of it!" said Maru-me. "Because we all like you too much to sell you anything. And it is not proper to accept gifts of money from strangers."

"True," said Forever-Mountain. "I will now ask your mother's and grandmother's permission to marry you. I want to be one of the family."

"Oh! I'll get a wedding dress ready!" said Maru-me.

The mother and grandmother pretended to consider very seriously, but they quickly agreed.

Next morning Forever-Mountain tied his hair up in the topknot[3] that all Japanese wrestlers wear, and got ready to leave. He thanked Maru-me and her mother and bowed very low to the grandmother, since she was the oldest and had been a fine wrestling partner.

Then he picked up the cow in his arms and trudged up the mountain. When he reached the top, he slung the cow over one shoulder and waved good-bye to Maru-me.

At the first town he came to, Forever-Mountain sold the cow. She brought a good price because she was unusually fat from never having worked in her life. With the money, he bought the heaviest silken belt he could find.

When he reached the palace grounds, many of the other wrestlers were already there, sitting about, eating enormous bowls of rice, comparing one another's weight and telling stories. They paid little attention to Forever-Mountain, except to wonder why he had arrived so late this year. Some of them noticed that he had grown very quiet and took no part at all in their boasting.

All the ladies and gentlemen of the court

---
3. **topknot:** a small bunch of hair on the top of the head.

720   UNIT SIX: THE ORAL TRADITION

Mini-Lesson: Speaking,  Listening, and Viewing

SPORTS MEDIA Sumo wrestling is one of Japan's most popular sports; champion wrestlers are highly recognized sports heroes similar to American football, baseball, or basketball stars. Images of Sumo wrestling can be found in a variety of media: television sports coverage, sports magazines, and documentary films and videos. Although Forever-Mountain's size and strength are greatly exaggerated, sumo wrestlers are both large and strong. Explain to students that they can better visualize and understand the story's characters by watching or reading media coverage.

Application Have students work in small groups to find visual examples of Japanese Sumo wrestling. If television, film, or video footage is not readily available, students can research print or on-line resources. Have a multimedia day where groups display and explain how the wrestling visuals have enriched their understanding of "Three Strong Women."

---

720   THE LANGUAGE OF LITERATURE **TEACHER'S EDITION**

Parade Before a Sumo Tournament (1796), Katsukawa Shun'ei. Triptych print, 37.5 cm × 25.5 cm. Copyright © British Museum.

Art Note

Parade Before a Sumo Tournament by Katsukawa Shun'ei The artist Shun'ei (1762–1819) specialized in actor and sumo prints, as in this triptych of the autumn 1796 wrestling tournament. A highlight of the tournament is the parade of wrestlers in their formal aprons, shown in the left and right parts of the work. In the center is the raised ring covered by a traditional shrine roof. The artist has depicted the wrestlers larger than life size to exaggerate their already sizable bulk.

Reading the Art *How does this three-part print help to illustrate the pageantry and importance of the sumo wrestling contests?*

Critical Thinking: ANALYZING

N Have students identify details on this page that show that the wrestling match was an important and rather formal event. *(Possible response: The audience is made up of important people who are elaborately dressed; the Emperor is officiating over the competition.)*

CUSTOMIZING FOR
Multiple Learning Styles

O Spatial or Graphic Learners Have students use the details given on this page to illustrate the scene in the courtyard in which Forever-Mountain competes with the other wrestler. Students can use the drawings on this page and page 720 for inspiration.

---

were waiting in a special courtyard for the wrestling to begin. They wore many robes, one on top of another, heavy with embroidery and gold cloth, and sweat ran down their faces and froze in the winter afternoon. The gentlemen had long swords so weighted with gold and precious stones that they could never have used them, even if they had known how. The court ladies, with their long black hair hanging down behind, had their faces painted dead white, which made them look frightened. They had pulled out their real eyebrows and painted new ones high above the place where eyebrows are supposed to be, and this made them all look as though they were very surprised at something.

Behind a screen sat the Emperor—by himself, because he was too noble for ordinary people to look at. He was a lonely old man with a kind, tired face. He hoped the wrestling would end quickly so that he could go to his room and write poems. **N**

The first two wrestlers chosen to fight were Forever-Mountain and a wrestler who was said to have the biggest stomach in the country. He and Forever-Mountain both threw some salt into the ring. It was understood that this drove away evil spirits.

Then the other wrestler, moving his stomach somewhat out of the way, raised his foot and brought it down with a fearful stamp. He glared fiercely at Forever-Mountain as if to say, "Now *you* stamp, you poor frightened man!" **O**

Forever-Mountain raised his foot. He brought it down.

There was a sound like thunder, the earth

THREE STRONG WOMEN **721**

Mini-Lesson Reading Skills/Strategies

RELATING CAUSE AND EFFECT Remind students that the sequence of events in the plot of a story is often based on cause and effect. The cause may be some action or personality trait of a character. Or it may be one of the events in the story.

Application Have students identify causes and effects in the highlighted passages above. Then have students look for other examples of cause and effect in the story.

Reteaching/Reinforcement
• *Unit Six Resource Book,* p. 32

THE LANGUAGE OF LITERATURE TEACHER'S EDITION **721**

STRATEGIC READING FOR
Less-Proficient Readers

P Ask questions such as the following to help students clarify the end of the tale.

- What happens at the wrestling match in the capital city? *(Forever-Mountain is stronger than everyone else and wins the prize money.)* **Summarizing**
- What does Forever-Mountain decide to do with his life? *(He returns to Maru-me and becomes a farmer.)* **Summarizing**

CUSTOMIZING FOR
Students Acquiring English

4 Ask students to give another word that describes the phrase *the earth shakes.* (earthquake) Make sure that students understand that the final sentence of this story explains the origins of earthquakes.

From Personal Response to Critical Analysis

1. What fault does Forever-Mountain have that sets the plot in motion? *(pride)* In your notebook, describe another instance of how this fault can get someone into difficulty. Use an example from personal experience or from your reading.
2. Compare and contrast Forever-Mountain's opinion of himself with how the three women regard him. *(Possible response: He is conceited about his great strength. They view him as weak and pitiful.)*
3. Describe the theme or moral of this story. *(Possible responses: No matter how strong you think you are, there is always someone who is stronger. Pride and conceit can get you into trouble.)*
4. Do you think Forever-Mountain will make a good husband for Maru-me? *(Possible responses: Yes, he is cheerful, grateful for Maru-me's help, and has learned humility.)*

---

shook, and the other wrestler bounced into the air and out of the ring, as gracefully as any soap bubble.

He picked himself up and bowed to the Emperor's screen.

"The earth god is angry. Possibly there is something the matter with the salt," he said. "I do not think I shall wrestle this season." And he walked out, looking very suspiciously over one shoulder at Forever-Mountain.

Five other wrestlers then and there decided that they were not wrestling this season, either. They all looked annoyed with Forever-Mountain.

From then on, Forever-Mountain brought his foot down lightly. As each wrestler came into the ring, he picked him up very gently, carried him out, and placed him before the Emperor's screen, bowing most courteously every time.

The court ladies' eyebrows went up even higher. The gentlemen looked disturbed and a little afraid. They loved to see fierce, strong men tugging and grunting at each other, but Forever-Mountain was a little too much for them. Only the Emperor was happy behind his screen, for now, with the wrestling over so quickly, he would have that much more time to write his poems. He ordered all the prize money handed over to Forever-Mountain.

"But," he said, "you had better not wrestle anymore." He stuck a finger through his screen and waggled it at the other wrestlers, who were sitting on the ground weeping with disappointment like great fat babies.

Forever-Mountain promised not to wrestle anymore. Everybody looked relieved. The wrestlers sitting on the ground almost smiled.

"I think I shall become a farmer," Forever-Mountain said, and left at once to go back to Maru-me.

Maru-me was waiting for him. When she saw him coming, she ran down the mountain, picked him up, together with the heavy bags of prize money, and carried him halfway up the mountainside. Then she giggled and put him down. The rest of the way she let him carry her.

Forever-Mountain kept his promise to the Emperor and never fought in public again. His name was forgotten in the capital. But up in the mountains, sometimes, the earth shakes and rumbles, and they say that is Forever-Mountain and Maru-me's grandmother practicing wrestling in the hidden valley. ❖

CLAUS STAMM

Claus Stamm, a U.S. citizen, was a Japanese-language specialist for the United States during World War II. Following the war, he attended the Institute of Eastern Studies at Columbia University in New York. Stamm's interest in the Japanese culture led to the 1962 publication of *Three Strong Women*, his retelling, in English, of the Japanese folk tale. He has also published two other books of Japanese tales. In addition, he writes haiku for children and translates them into Japanese. Stamm now lives in Japan.

OTHER WORKS *The Dumplings and the Demons, The Very Special Badgers: A Tale of Magic from Japan*

COMPREHENSION CHECK

1. Where is Forever-Mountain going when he meets Maru-me? *(To the capital city to compete in a wrestling match)*
2. What happens when Forever-Mountain tries to tickle Maru-me? *(She traps his hand with her arm and he can't pull loose.)*
3. Why does Forever-Mountain agree to go home with Maru-me? *(He feels he has nothing more to lose and is afraid she'll be angry and hurt him if he refuses.)*
4. How do the three women train Forever-Mountain? *(They give him simple food, make him work hard, and have him practice wrestling with the grandmother.)*
5. Why does the Emperor tell Forever-Mountain to stop wrestling? *(He is now so strong the competitions are boring.)*

Buffalo Calf Woman, Oscar Howe. U.S. Department of the Interior, Indian Arts and Crafts Board, Sioux Indian Museum and Crafts Center, Rapid City, South Dakota.

THE WHITE BUFFALO CALF WOMAN AND THE SACRED PIPE

RETOLD BY JOSEPH BRUCHAC

Art Note

Buffalo Calf Woman by Oscar Howe
Oscar Howe (1915–) is a Crow artist who often combines familiar objects with abstract forms. In *Buffalo Calf Woman* he has created a whirlpool of abstract patterns. At the center is the head of the mythical Buffalo Calf Woman. This touch of reality in the midst of unreality is intended to focus the eye on the idea of the woman and her place in the swirling world of Native American legend.

Reading the Art *Does this piece differ from what you think of as traditional Native American art? Explain.*

CUSTOMIZING FOR
Students Acquiring English

- Many cultures have legends that, like this one, deal with people that change into animals. Invite students to share similar stories they know from their home cultures.

STRATEGIC READING FOR
Less-Proficient Readers

Set a Purpose Have students read to discover the gift and the teachings the White Buffalo Calf Woman brings to the people.

Multicultural Perspectives

NATIVE AMERICAN RELIGIOUS BELIEFS
Near the end of the legend, the White Buffalo Calf Woman refers to Wakan Tanka, the Creator. The Sioux word *wakan* is the approximate equivalent of the Iroquois word *orenda*, the Algonquian word *manitou*, and the Quechua word *huaca*—all words referring to a supernatural force inherent in nature. Despite tribal differences, most Native Americans have long believed in a unity among the earth's people, animals, and other living things. Furthermore, they believe that each living thing contains a spirit and that spiritual contact can be made between any two living things. Wakan Tanka is understood to represent the sum of all the world's spirits.

CUSTOMIZING FOR
Gifted and Talented Students

Have students use "Arachne," "Three Strong Women," or this legend as a model to write a modern-day tale about a main character who is proud and boastful and then learns a lesson. For example, the main character might be a computer programmer who encounters a mysterious godlike figure on the Internet.

Literary Links

A Have students compare and contrast Ota K'te's experiences in "At Last I Kill a Buffalo" (page 457) with what happens to the two scouts in the legend. *(Possible response: In both stories, the young men are looking for buffalo for food. Ota K'te discovers his inner strength as he resists the temptation to lie. The scout finds that success in hunting buffalo may require heeding the teachings of the White Buffalo Calf Woman.)*

It was a time when there was little food left in the camp and the people were hungry.

Two young men were sent out to scout for game. They went on foot, for this was a time long before the horses, the great Spirit Dogs, were given to the people. The two young men hunted a long time but had no luck. Finally, they climbed to the top of a hill and looked to the west.

"What is that?" said one of the young men.

"I cannot tell, but it is coming toward us," said the other.

And so it was. At first they thought that it was an animal, but as the shape drew closer, they saw it was a woman. She was dressed in white buffalo skin and carried something in her hands. She walked so lightly that it seemed as if she was not walking at all, but floating with her feet barely touching the Earth.

Then the first young man realized that she must be a Holy Person, and his mind filled with good thoughts. But the second young man did not see her that way. He saw her only as a beautiful young woman, and his mind filled with bad thoughts. She was now very close and he reached out to grab her. As soon as he did so, though, there was a sound of lightning, and the young man was covered by a cloud. When it cleared away, there was nothing left of the second young man but a skeleton.

Then the White Buffalo Calf Woman spoke. "Go to your people," she said, holding up the bundle in her hands so that the first young man could see it. "Tell your people that it is a good thing I am bringing. I am bringing a holy thing to your nation, a message from the Buffalo People. Put up a medicine lodge[1] for me and make it ready. I will come there after four days have passed."

The first young man did as he was told. He went back to his people and gave them the message. Then the crier went through the camp and told all the people that something sacred was coming and that all things should be made ready. They built the medicine lodge and made an earth altar which faced the west.

> AT FIRST THEY THOUGHT THAT IT WAS AN ANIMAL, BUT AS THE SHAPE DREW CLOSER, THEY SAW IT WAS A WOMAN.

Four days passed and then the people saw something coming toward them. When it came closer, they saw it was the White Buffalo Calf Woman. In her hands she carried the bundle and a bunch of sacred sage.[2] The people welcomed her into the medicine lodge and gave her the seat of honor. Then she unwrapped the bundle to show them what was inside. It was the Sacred Pipe. As she held it out to them, she told them what it meant.

"The bowl of the Pipe," she said, "is made of the red stone. It represents the flesh and blood of the Buffalo People and all other Peoples. The wooden stem of the Pipe represents all the trees and plants, all the things green and growing on this Earth. The

---

1. **medicine lodge:** a building, hut, or tent used by Native Americans for religious ceremonies.
2. **sage:** an herb having a strong pinelike odor.

WORDS TO KNOW
sacred (sā'krĭd) *adj.* having to do with religion; holy

724

Assessment Option

INFORMAL To assess students' understanding, have them restate in their own words the White Buffalo Calf Woman's teaching.

Rubric

3 Full Accomplishment Students accurately restate the White Buffalo Calf Woman's teaching as described on page 725. Restatements demonstrate students' clear understanding of the story's theme.

2 Substantial Accomplishment Students' restatements demonstrate an understanding of the White Buffalo Calf Woman's teaching, but their restatements overlap too closely with wording of text.

1 Little or Partial Accomplishment Students' responses simply repeat wording of text.

smoke that passes through the Pipe represents the sacred wind, the breath that carries prayers up to Wakan Tanka, the Creator."

When she finished showing them the Pipe, she told the people how to hold it and how to offer it to Earth and Sky and the Four Sacred Directions. She told them many things to remember.

"The Sacred Pipe," said the White Buffalo Calf Woman, "will show you the Good Red Road. Follow it and it will take you in the right direction. Now," she said, "I am going to leave, but you will see me again."

Then she began to walk toward the setting sun. The people watched her as she went, and they saw her stop and roll once on the Earth. When she stood up, she was a black buffalo. Then she went farther and rolled again on the Earth. This time when she stood up, she was a brown buffalo. She went farther and rolled a third time and stood up. Now the people saw that she was a red buffalo. Again she walked farther and for a fourth and final time she rolled upon the Earth. This time she became a white buffalo calf and continued to walk until she disappeared over the horizon.

As soon as the White Buffalo Calf Woman was gone, herds of buffalo were seen all around the camp. The people were able to hunt them, and they gave thanks with the Sacred Pipe for the blessings they had been given. As long as they followed the Good Red Road of the Sacred Pipe and remembered, as the White Buffalo Calf Woman had taught them, that all things were as connected as parts of the Pipe, they lived happily and well. ❖

JOSEPH BRUCHAC

1942–

The poet, novelist, and storyteller Joseph Bruchac began hearing Native American legends as a small child. A descendant of Native Americans, Bruchac says he likes to share stories from Native American traditions because "they have messages, sometimes very subtle, which can help show young people the good paths to follow." Born in the Adirondack Mountains, Bruchac also has drawn upon the legends of those mountains for his stories.

Before becoming a writer and a scholar, Joseph Bruchac taught English and literature in Ghana, West Africa, and creative writing and African-American literature at Skidmore College in New York. Bruchac has received numerous awards for his writing, including a fellowship from the National Endowment for the Arts and a Rockefeller Foundation Humanities Fellowship.

OTHER WORKS *The Wind Eagle and Other Abenaki Folk Stories; Flying with the Eagle, Racing the Great Bear*

Literature Connection

Present a Puppet Show Have students work in "puppet troupes" of five or six students each. Explain that puppet shows should contain as much action as possible, and that students' scripts should have a clear beginning, middle, and end. Scripts may be loose and flexible, allowing students to improvise, or they may clearly dictate dialogue and stage business. Either way, a script should not be considered final until the play has had some run-throughs.

Students may need to research puppet-making techniques. Depending on the available time and materials, students can construct paper-bag, sock, glove, fabric, or rod puppets.

Rubric

3 Full Accomplishment Students' puppet shows accurately reflect the plot, characters, and setting of the chosen selection. Performances are well-rehearsed, show imagination, and are entertaining.

2 Substantial Accomplishment Students' puppet shows reasonably correspond with the plot, characters, and setting of the chosen selection. Performances are fairly smooth and moderately entertaining.

1 Little or Partial Accomplishment Students' puppet shows do not accurately reflect the plot, characters, and/or setting of the chosen selection. Performances are clumsy or incomplete.

RESPONDING OPTIONS

LITERATURE CONNECTION PROJECT 1 Multimodal Activity

Present a Puppet Show Develop a puppet show based on one of the stories you have just read. Form teams to carry out the following tasks: adapting the story into a script; working as puppet makers, costumers, set designers, and stage builders; serving as puppeteers. These suggestions may help:

Writers Identify the characters to be included. Map out the events in the tale in outline form or on storyboards.

Stage builders Make the stage as simple or as complex as time allows. Three different arrangements are shown here.

Puppet makers Research techniques in puppet making. Choose to construct paper-bag, sock, glove, fabric, or stick puppets.

Present your puppet show as part of an arts program at your school or as a performance for a class of first graders or second graders.

Three simple puppet-show stages you can make.

SCIENCE CONNECTION PROJECT 2 Multimodal Activity

Explore Textiles and Looms Two of the three cultures represented in these stories—the ancient Greeks and the Japanese—made use of woven textiles. Both cultures used some version of the loom, a device used to weave thread or yarn into cloth.

Find out more about the textiles and textile-making tools of different civilizations. Visit museums and conduct library research to plan and make your own simple loom, which you might use to weave a piece of cloth. Study the designs and patterns used in textiles of a civilization of your choosing. Then, using colored pencils or construction paper—or even a paint program on a personal computer—draw or make a collage of different examples of the designs and patterns you found.

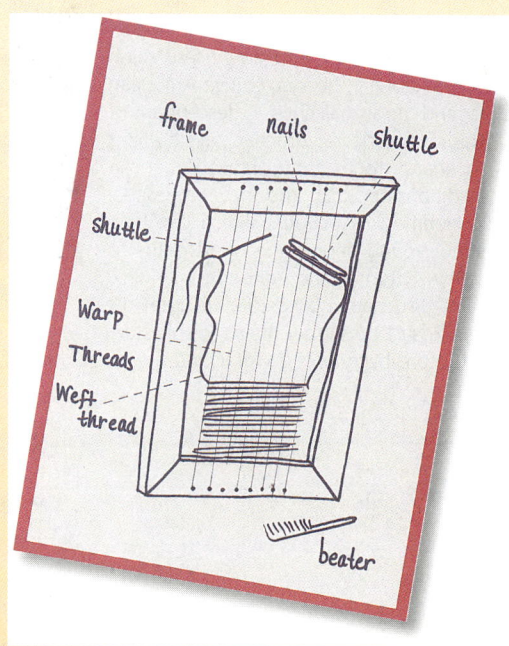

A simple loom you can make yourself

726 UNIT SIX: THE ORAL TRADITION

Science Connection

Explore Textiles and Looms Students will discover that weaving is one of the most ancient crafts, dating back at least 4,000 years. Woven textiles have been made by almost all peoples of the world, so students will have a wide choice of cultures for their example patterns. In addition to the Japanese and Greek cultures depicted in the stories, students might choose designs from Native American, African, or Asian peoples. Each student might look for patterns traditional in his or her own ethnic background.

Rubric

3 Full Accomplishment Students' collages show more than five examples from three or more different cultures. The designs and patterns are annotated with captions showing students' research.

2 Substantial Accomplishment Students' collages show at least three examples from one or two different cultures. The designs and patterns are accurately copied.

1 Little or Partial Accomplishment Students' collages show only one or two examples. The designs and patterns may not be carefully copied.

726 THE LANGUAGE OF LITERATURE TEACHER'S EDITION

Social Studies Connection

Research the Buffalo Students can use nonfiction books, encyclopedias, and on-line reference sources for their research. You may wish to have students work in groups of three or four. Each student does independent research. Groups then share and combine their results.

Students should find that Native Americans used the buffalo herds for food, clothing, bedding, teepees, and tools and utensils made from the bones and horn. Their dependence on the buffalo herds resulted in a nomadic way of life that was threatened and finally destroyed by the white settlers and hunters who hunted the buffalo until they were virtually extinct.

Rubric

3 Full Accomplishment Students' cluster diagrams include a variety of uses for the buffalo and reflect a hierarchy of importance. Their drawings and captions evidence research as well as creativity.

2 Substantial Accomplishment Students' diagrams include several uses for the buffalo. Their drawings and captions are accurate and reflect some research.

1 Little or Partial Accomplishment Students' diagrams include few uses for the buffalo and/or include uses that are not plausible. Their drawings and captions are not accurate and/or do not reflect research.

SOCIAL STUDIES CONNECTION PROJECT 3 Multimodal Activity

Research the Buffalo How important a resource was the American bison, popularly called the buffalo, to the Lakota Sioux and other Native American groups? In a cluster diagram like the one shown, record the ways in which the buffalo was important to Native Americans. Make drawings to illustrate these ways, and write a caption for each drawing. As a class, collect your findings to create a visual encyclopedia.

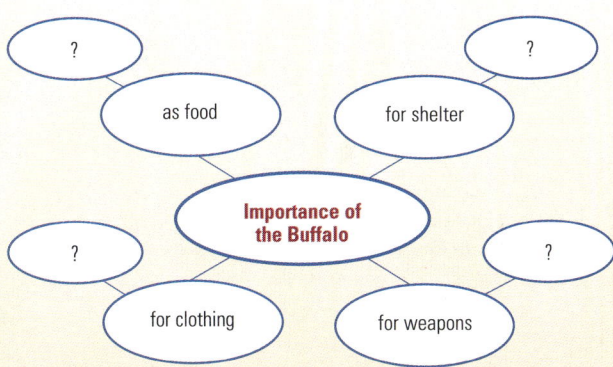

ACROSS CULTURES MINI-PROJECTS Multimodal Activities

Compare and Contrast Characters Use a diagram, like the one shown, to compare and contrast Arachne and Forever-Mountain. Where the ovals overlap, write the qualities that are common to both characters. In the larger section of each oval, write the qualities that are unique to the character.

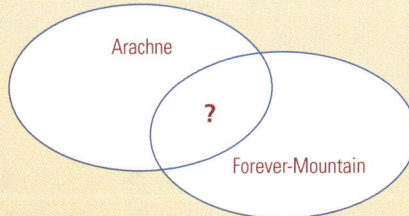

Try Wrestling Wrestling was a popular sport in many ancient cultures, including those of Egypt, Greece, and Japan. The three most common wrestling styles today are Japanese sumo, Greco-Roman, and freestyle. Research any one of the three styles, describe the rules, and demonstrate it for the class.

Design Trading Cards Make trading cards of the Roman gods and goddesses. Find out if the members of this god "family" had different names or abilities in Greek mythology.

Follow the Buffalo Graph the changes in the American buffalo population from 1850, when it was about 20 million, to the present.

Extended Social Studies Reading

MORE ABOUT THE CULTURES

- *A History of Art from 25,000 B.C. to the Present* by Marshall Davidson
- *The Magic Weaver of Rugs: A Tale of the Navajo* by Jerrie Oughton, illustrated by Lisa Desimini
- *The Greek World* by Anton Powell

PROJECTS 727

Multicultural Perspectives

Compare and Contrast Characters Possible responses: Both characters are proud and skillful. Arachne is stubborn and rude; Forever-Mountain is more flexible, willing to learn, and polite.

Try Wrestling Students can use books or videos in their presentations. For instance, both Greco-Roman and freestyle wrestling are Olympic events. Students may find historical footage of past Olympics. Do not allow students to demonstrate wrestling with other class members. All demonstrations should be in pantomime form only.

Design Trading Cards Each god or goddess has a Greek name, a Roman name, and is associated with an activity or idea such as fire, wisdom, hunting, or agriculture. Students' trading cards can show illustrations depicting typical attributes of each deity.

Follow the Buffalo Students should discover that the great buffalo herds were virtually gone by the 1890s, killed off by both Native American and white hunters. In recent years, successful efforts have been made to re-establish small populations of buffalo in their native habitats.

OVERVIEW

Objectives

- To understand and appreciate three folk tales about characters who get what's coming to them
- To appreciate the cultural values of the American Southwest, China, and Germany
- To extend understanding of the stories through a variety of multimodal and cross-curricular activities

Reading Pathways

- Select one or several students to read each folk tale aloud to the entire class or to small groups of students. Assign this reading in advance so the readers can incorporate into their presentations some of the techniques used by professional storytellers. Have the audience listen carefully to the folk tales without following along in their texts.
- Read the folk tales aloud to the class, pausing at key points to discuss how elements of each tale inform students about the customs, values, or beliefs in the American Southwest, China, and Germany. Have students record their responses and observations in their notebooks.
- After students have read the folk tales once, they can read them again to identify structural elements such as main characters, minor characters, conflict, setting, and plot. Then have students identify similarities and differences between these tales and the selections in Unit 5. For example, students might compare and contrast the lives of the main characters in "The Living Kuan-Yin" with "The First Emperor" from *Tomb Robbers* (page 526).

PREVIEWING

LINKS TO UNIT FIVE

The Pursuit of a Goal

Activating Prior Knowledge

The selections in Unit Five explore how an individual's interactions with others can help or hinder that person's efforts to reach a goal. Treating people with kindness and respect is an important theme in folklore. These three selections feature characters who are rewarded or punished because of their actions toward others.

Building Background

UNITED STATES

Sister Fox and Brother Coyote

retold by Robert D. San Souci
(săn sōō'sē)

Tales from the American Southwest reflect a mixture of cultures, including the Hispanic and the Native American. In both cultures, celebrations and communal gatherings are an important way of passing on traditions. In this Mexican-American trickster tale, Sister Fox and her less sensible cousin, Brother Coyote, engage in a contest between brains and physical strength. Sister Fox uses the promise of good food from a fiesta, or festival, to trick her foolish cousin.

728   UNIT SIX   THE ORAL TRADITION

PRINT AND MEDIA RESOURCES

UNIT SIX RESOURCE BOOK
Strategic Reading: Literature, p. 37
Vocabulary SkillBuilder, p. 40
Reading SkillBuilder, p. 38
Spelling SkillBuilder, p. 39

GRAMMAR MINI-LESSONS
Transparencies, p. 3
Copymasters, p. 3

WRITING MINI-LESSONS
Transparencies, p. 29

ACCESS FOR STUDENTS ACQUIRING ENGLISH
Selection Summaries
Reading and Writing Support

FORMAL ASSESSMENT
Selection Test, pp. 125–126
 Test Generator

ALTERNATIVE ASSESSMENT
End-of-Year Integrated Assessment
　　Reader, pp. 31–36
　　Student Response Booklet, pp. 37–50

AUDIO LIBRARY
See Reference Card

728   THE LANGUAGE OF LITERATURE   TEACHER'S EDITION

CHINA

The Living Kuan-yin

*retold by Carol Kendall
and Yao-wen Li (you′wən′ lē′)*

Building Background

China is bounded on every side by mountains, deserts, or ocean. These geographical features have helped to preserve a civilization that dates back nearly 4,000 years. Buddhism, one of the world's major religions, was established in China about 500 B.C. In Buddhism, Kuan-yin (gwän′yĭn′) is the goddess of mercy who works for the salvation of people. This folk tale tells about a man named Chin Po-wan. His generosity gets him into trouble as he journeys to see Kuan-yin and is asked for help by people along the way.

GERMANY

King Thrushbeard

retold by the brothers Grimm

Building Background

This tale was written by the famous brothers Grimm, whose stories continue to be told to children today. In the early 1800s, inspired to capture in writing some of the classic stories that made up early German literature, the brothers collected and recorded stories that had been told orally in Germany for generations. In this story, a proud princess who finds fault with all of her suitors learns through hardship to recognize a person's most valuable qualities.

Setting a Purpose

AS YOU READ . . .

Notice the common threads that appear in different cultures.

Identify traits that vary from one culture to another.

Think about why certain values endure.

Consider ways in which the past is preserved.

LINKS TO UNIT FIVE **729**

SUMMARIES

The Living Kuan-Yin Chin Po-wan travels to the South Sea to get advice from the Living Kuan-yin, a goddess who allows each visitor to ask her three questions. On the way a snake helps Po-wan cross a river, and Po-wan promises to ask the goddess why the snake has not yet become a dragon. Next, Po-wan meets an innkeeper with a mute daughter and promises to ask why. Then Po-wan stays at a rich man's house and promises to ask why the man's plants won't bloom. When Po-wan reaches the Living Kuan-yin, he asks these three questions instead of his own. The goddess tells him the answers. When Po-wan delivers the messages, he becomes a wealthy man again.

Sister Fox and Brother Coyote First, with the promise of chickens, Sister Fox coaxes Brother Coyote into helping her escape from a ranchero's trap—leaving him stuck in her place. The next time they meet, Brother Coyote demands the bread Sister Fox has stolen. She convinces him that it is rooster bait. The coyote is easily fooled, and so he sprinkles bread crumbs—but attracts dogs instead! Brother Coyote next finds Sister Fox beside a pool one night. She talks him into eating a "ball of cheese" in the water, and the greedy coyote dives at the moon's reflection. Finally, Sister Fox persuades Brother Coyote to hide in a thicket of cane plants and wait for a wedding party with food to pass by. "Listen for fireworks," she tells him, then sets fire to the cane. The foolish coyote, mistaking fire for fireworks, meets his final end.

King Thrushbeard A furious king swears to make his too-particular daughter marry the first beggar who comes to his door. Thus, she winds up marrying a type of musician called a minstrel and living with him in extreme poverty. To make ends meet, she unsuccessfully tries weaving baskets and selling pots. Finally, she gets a job as kitchen maid in another king's palace. At the wedding feast of the king's eldest son, she fills her pockets with scraps of food. Suddenly the king's son appears and asks her to dance. To her horror, he is King Thrushbeard—the rejected suitor whose chin she compared to a thrush's beak. She runs away in humiliation but is stopped by Thrushbeard, who explains that he masqueraded as her minstrel husband out of love and to teach her humility. Her lesson well learned, the king's daughter becomes Thrushbeard's wife.

WORDS TO KNOW

compassion (kəm-păsh′ən) *n.* sympathy for the suffering of others; pity (p. 730)
destitute (dĕs′tĭ-tōōt′) *adj.* living in complete poverty; extremely poor (p. 730)
dwindle (dwĭn′dl) *v.* to decrease or shrink (p. 730)
elude (ĭ-lōōd′) *v.* to avoid or escape, especially by means of cleverness or skill (p. 738)
extravagantly (ĭk-străv′ə-gənt-lē) *adv.* excessively; too much (p. 730)

inadvertently (ĭn′əd-vûr′tnt-lē) *adv.* by mistake or without meaning to; not deliberately (p. 732)
insolent (ĭn′sə-lənt) *adj.* rude (p. 745)
insufferable (ĭn-sŭf′ər-ə-bəl) *adj.* hard to put up with; unbearable (p. 736)
succulent (sŭk′yə-lənt) *adj.* tasty; delicious (p. 744)
wily (wī′lē) *adj.* clever and skillful in a tricky way (p. 736)

THE LANGUAGE OF LITERATURE **TEACHER'S EDITION** **729**

CUSTOMIZING FOR
Students Acquiring English

- Use **ACCESS FOR STUDENTS ACQUIRING ENGLISH,** *Reading and Writing Support.*
- In addition to these boxes, you may want to use the suggestions under Strategic Reading for Less-Proficient Readers.

I You may wish to paraphrase *In such wise did he live* as "He lived in such a way" and point out this is formal old-fashioned English.

STRATEGIC READING FOR
Less-Proficient Readers

Set a Purpose Ask students to read the beginning and note details that describe the character of Po-wan and the reasons for his journey.

Use **UNIT SIX RESOURCE BOOK,** pp. 37–38, for guidance in reading the selections.

CUSTOMIZING FOR
Gifted and Talented Students

Have students choose one of the three folk tales to use as a basis for a narrative poem. They might use "The Cremation of Sam McGee" (page 161) or another narrative poem in the text as a model.

Linking To Geography

A On newer maps this province will be spelled "Zhejiang." The location of the South China Sea, Po-wan's destination in the tale, can be found on the east coast of China, north of the island of Taiwan and south of the city of Shanghai.

THE LIVING KUAN-YIN

RETOLD BY
CAROL KENDALL AND YAO-WEN LI

A **E**ven though the family name of Chin means "gold," it does not signify that everyone of that name is rich. Long ago, in the province of Chekiang,[1] however, there was a certain wealthy Chin family of whom it was popularly said that its fortune was as great as its name. It seemed quite fitting, then, when a son was born to the family, that he should be called Po-wan, "Million," for he was certain to be worth a million pieces of gold when he came of age.

With such a happy circumstance of names, Po-wan himself never doubted that he would have a never-ending supply of money chinking through his fingers, and he spent it accordingly —not on himself, but on any unfortunate who came to his attention. He had a deep sense of <u>compassion</u> for anyone in distress of body or spirit: a poor man had only to hold out his hand, and Po-wan poured gold into it; if a <u>destitute</u> widow and her brood of starvelings[2] but lifted sorrowful eyes to his, he provided them with food and lodging and friendship for the rest of their days.

I In such wise did he live that even a million gold pieces were not enough to support him. His resources so <u>dwindled</u> that finally he scarcely had enough food for himself, his clothes flapped threadbare[3] on his wasted frame, and the cold seeped into his bone marrow[4] for lack of a fire. Still he gave away the little money that came to him. **B**

One day, as he scraped out half of his bowl of rice for a beggar even hungrier than he, he began to ponder on his destitute state.

"Why am I so poor?" he wondered. "I have never spent <u>extravagantly</u>. I have never, from the day of my birth, done an evil deed. Why, then, am I, whose very name is A Million Pieces of Gold, no longer able to find even a copper[5] to give this unfortunate creature, and have only a bowl of rice to share with him?" **D**

---

1. **province of Chekiang** (chŭ'kyäng'): a region on the eastern coast of China.
2. **brood of starvelings** (stärv'lĭngz): starving children.
3. **threadbare:** so worn down that the threads show.
4. **marrow:** the soft tissue that fills the middle of most bones.
5. **copper:** a coin of little value.

WORDS TO KNOW
compassion (kəm-pǎsh'ən) *n.* sympathy for the suffering of others; pity
destitute (děs'tǐ-tōōt') *adj.* living in complete poverty; extremely poor
dwindle (dwǐn'dl) *v.* to decrease or shrink
extravagantly (ĭk-străv'ə-gənt-lē) *adv.* excessively; too much

730

Mini-Lesson Grammar

SUBJECT-VERB AGREEMENT Use the examples shown to remind students that a verb must agree in number with its subject. A subject and verb agree in number when they are both singular or both plural. Singular verbs in the present tense usually end in -s or -es. Plural verbs in the present tense do not usually end in -s.

Application Have students write the verb in parentheses that agrees with the subject. The answer is underlined.

1. The fortune of the Chin family (<u>was</u>/were) as great as its name.
2. Unfortunate people in Po-wan's province (<u>ask</u>/asks) him for help.
3. His compassionate feelings (cause/<u>causes</u>) him to (<u>give</u>/gives) away too much money.

Reteaching/Reinforcement
- *Grammar Handbook,* anthology pp. 815–816
- *Grammar Mini-Lessons* copymasters, p. 3, transparencies, p. 3

 **The Writer's Craft**

Subject and Verb Agreement, pp. 528–529

Singular
The family name of Chin <u>means</u> "gold."

Plural
Family names <u>mean</u> various things, such as an occupation.

730 THE LANGUAGE OF LITERATURE TEACHER'S EDITION

Bodhisattva Guanyin (Song Dynasty, 960–1279), unknown Chinese artist. Wood, 30″ × 36″ × 64″, Eugene Fuller Memorial Collection, Seattle (Washington) Art Museum. Photo by Paul Macapia.

THE LIVING KUAN-YIN 731

Multicultural Perspectives

FOLK TALES Many cultures have folk tales, like this one, in which a hero is rewarded for his or her unselfishness. Folk tales are a part of the oral tradition and share the characteristics shown on the word web.

Application Have students copy the web shown. Then have them add details from the tale to their webs.

Active Reading: CONNECT

B Ask students if they have ever met a person who behaves as Po-wan does in these opening scenes. Ask them if they admire his behavior. Then ask if they would stop giving away money to needy people if they were in Po-wan's position.

CUSTOMIZING FOR
Multiple Learning Styles

C Logical-Mathematical Learners
Have students suggest ways that Po-wan could have remained generous without making himself so poor. *(Possible response: He could have made a budget for how much he needed to live and how much he could contribute to needy people.)*

Critical Thinking:
MAKING JUDGMENTS

D Have students give possible answers to Po-wan's question, "Why am I so poor?" *(Possible response: You have overestimated the money you inherited—no one has a "never-ending" supply of money.)*

Art Note

Seated Kuan-yin This 64-inch high wooden statue is a particularly fine example of the artistry of the Sung Dynasty (960–1279). The statue represents the goddess Kuan-yin sitting before a rocky grotto and watching the reflection of the moon in the water.

Reading the Art *What impressions of Kuan-yin does the statue convey? Do you think she will be willing to help Po-wan with his questions?*

Folk Tales
- are told primarily for entertainment
- feature human beings or humanlike animals
- teach lessons about human behavior
- reveal values of society

THE LANGUAGE OF LITERATURE TEACHER'S EDITION 731

Active Reading: CLARIFY

E Ask students what has happened to Po-wan. *(Possible response: Po-wan has given away his fortune to needy, hungry people and become hungry and needy himself.)*

STRATEGIC READING FOR
Less-Proficient Readers

F Ask questions such as the following to check that students understand the story so far.

- How would you describe the character of Po-wan? *(Possible responses: generous, somewhat foolish, a dreamer, not very practical)* Making Judgments

- Why does Po-wan decide to go to the South Sea? *(He has grown poor and uncertain about his future. He wishes to see the Living Kuan-Yin, a goddess who can tell him why he is so poor.)* Summarizing

Set a Purpose Have students read to learn what characters Po-wan meets and what they want from him.

Literary Links

G Have students compare Po-wan to the main character in "The Scribe." Ask students to describe how Po-wan and James's interactions with others affect the characters' personal goals. *(Possible response: Both Po-wan and James are generous and want to help others. Po-wan must survive the dangers of his journey; James must surmount obstacles in his community.)*

CLARIFY
E What has happened to Po-wan?
Using a Reading Log

He thought long about his situation and at last determined to go without delay to the South Sea. Therein, it was told, dwelt the all-merciful goddess, the Living Kuan-yin, who could tell the past and future. He would put his question to her, and she would tell him the answer.

F Soon he had left his home country behind and traveled for many weeks in unfamiliar lands. One day he found his way barred by a wide and furiously flowing river. As he stood first on one foot and then on the other, wondering how he could possibly get across, he heard a commanding voice calling from the top of an overhanging cliff.

"Chin Po-wan!" the voice said. "If you are going to the South Sea, please ask the Living Kuan-yin a question for me!"

The Living Kuan-yin allowed but three questions.

"Yes, yes, of course," Po-wan agreed at once, for he had never in his life refused a request made of him. In any case, the Living Kuan-yin permitted each person who approached her three questions, and he had but one of his own to ask.

Craning his head towards the voice coming from above, he suddenly began to tremble, for the speaker was a gigantic snake with a body as large as a temple column. Po-wan was glad he had agreed so readily to the request.

"Ask her, then," said the snake, "why I am not yet a dragon, even though I have practiced self-denial[6] for more than one thousand years."

"That I will do, and gl-gladly," stammered Po-wan, hoping that the snake would continue to practice self-denial just a bit longer. "But, your . . . your Snakery . . . or your Serpentry, perhaps I should say . . . that is . . . you see, don't you . . . first I must cross this raging river, and I know not how."

"That is no problem at all," said the snake. "I shall carry you across, of course."

"Of course," Po-wan echoed weakly. Overcoming his fear and his reluctance to touch the slippery-slithery scales, Chin Po-wan climbed onto the snake's back and rode across quite safely. Politely, and just a bit hurriedly, he thanked the self-denying serpent and bade him good-bye. Then he continued on his way to the South Sea.

By noon he was very hungry. Fortunately, a nearby inn offered meals at a price he could afford. While waiting for his bowl of rice, he chatted with the innkeeper and told him of the Snake of the Cliff, which the innkeeper knew well and respected, for the serpent always denied bandits the crossing of the river. <u>Inadvertently</u>, during the exchange of stories, Po-wan revealed the purpose of his journey.

G

"Why, then," cried the innkeeper, "let me prevail upon your generosity to ask a word for me." He laid an appealing hand on Po-wan's ragged sleeve. "I have a beautiful daughter," he said, "wonderfully amiable[7] and pleasing of disposition. But although she is in her twentieth year, she has never in all her life

---

6. **self-denial:** the giving up of desires or pleasures.
7. **amiable** (āʹmē-ə-bəl): good-natured and likable.

WORDS TO KNOW
inadvertently (ĭnʹəd-vûrʹtnt-lē) *adv.* by mistake or without meaning to; not deliberately

732

Mini-Lesson **Literary Concepts**

REVIEWING HUMOR Remind students that writers and storytellers have many methods of adding humor to stories. Among these are exaggeration, witty dialogue, amusing descriptions, and wordplay. For example, in the highlighted text above, Po-wan addresses the snake as "your Snakery . . . or your Serpentry," which is a play on the words *your Majesty* or *your Highness*. Po-wan is afraid of the snake, much as a peasant might fear a powerful king.

Application Have students look for other examples of humor in the highlighted text. *(Possible responses: The snake's wish to be a dragon and Po-wan's wish that the snake continue practicing self-denial are funny. It is ironic that the snake is supposed to be giving up his desires, yet he waits for 1,000 years for his wish to come true.)*

---

732 THE LANGUAGE OF LITERATURE TEACHER'S EDITION

Detail of *Beneficent Rain* (Yüan Dynasty, China; about 1300), Chang Yu-ts'ai. Ink on silk, 10⅝" × 106¼", The Metropolitan Museum of Art, gift of Douglas Dillon, 1985 (1985.227.2). Copyright © 1985 The Metropolitan Museum of Art.

uttered a single word. I should be very much obliged if you would ask the Living Kuan-yin why she is unable to speak."

Po-wan, much moved by the innkeeper's plea for his mute daughter, of course promised to do so. For after all, the Living Kuan-yin allowed each person three questions, and he had but one of his own to ask.

Nightfall found him far from any inn, but there were houses in the neighborhood, and he asked for lodging at the largest. The owner, a man obviously of great wealth, was pleased to offer him a bed in a fine chamber but first begged him to partake of a hot meal and good drink. Po-wan ate well, slept soundly, and, much refreshed, was about to depart the following morning when his good host, having learned that Po-wan was journeying to the South Sea, asked if he would be kind enough to put a question for him to the Living Kuan-yin.

"For twenty years," he said, "from the time this house was built, my garden has been cultivated with the utmost care; yet in all those years, not one tree, not one small plant, has bloomed or borne fruit, and because of this, no bird comes to sing, nor bee to gather nectar. I don't like to put you to a bother, Chin Po-wan, but as you are going to the South Sea anyway, perhaps you would not mind seeking out the Living Kuan-yin and asking her why the plants in my garden don't bloom."

"I shall be delighted to put the question to her," said Po-wan. For after all, the Living Kuan-yin allowed each person three questions, and he had but . . .

Traveling onward, Po-wan examined the quandary[8] in which he found himself. The Living Kuan-yin allowed but three questions, and he had somehow, without quite knowing how, accumulated four questions. One of them would have to go unasked, but which? If he left out his own question, his whole journey would have been in vain.[9] If, on the other hand, he left out the question of the snake, or the innkeeper, or the kind host, he would break his promise and betray their faith in him.

PREDICT

Which question will Po-wan leave out?
Using a Reading Log

"A promise should never be made if it cannot be kept," he told himself. "I made the promises and therefore I must keep them. Besides, the journey will not be in vain, for at least some of these problems will be solved by the Living Kuan-yin. Furthermore, assisting others must certainly be counted as a good deed, and the more good deeds abroad in the land, the better for everyone, including me."

At last he came into the presence of the Living Kuan-yin.

---

8. **quandary** (kwŏn′də-rē): confusing situation.
9. **in vain**: useless.

THE LIVING KUAN-YIN 733

Mini-Lesson The Writer's Style

DETAILS IN ORDER OF IMPORTANCE
Remind students that writers use various methods for organizing supporting details. The episodes in this folk tale are organized in chronological order. Some ways of organizing details are shown in the following chart.

Type of Writing	Method
reports, opinion stories, process, directions descriptions persuasive, informative	main idea with supporting details chronological order spatial order order of importance

Application In the highlighted text above, Po-wan gives his reasons for keeping his promises in order of importance. Have students rewrite the paragraph as if Po-wan were convincing himself to *not* keep his promises, again keeping details in order of importance.

Reteaching/Reinforcement
• *Writing Handbook*, anthology p. 785
• *Writing Mini-Lessons* transparencies, p. 29

 **The Writer's Craft**
Organizing Details, pp. 217–221

Art Note

Dragon The mythical dragon has always played an important role in traditional Chinese culture. Chinese emperors used the dragon as their royal symbol. The sinuous body of the imperial dragon allows him to issue orders by moving in all four directions at the same time while still keeping his head fixed in the fifth position, the center. The imperial dragon has five claws to represent these five directions; other dragons have only four.

Reading the Art *Does this dragon seem to you to be threatening? Explain your answer.*

STRATEGIC READING FOR
Less-Proficient Readers

H Ask students what characters Po-wan meets on his journey and what they want him to do. (*He meets a snake, an innkeeper and his daughter, and a wealthy man. They want him to ask Kuan-yin questions for them.*) Noting Relevant Details

Set a Purpose Before students read the end of the tale, they should predict what Po-wan will do and what might happen as a result. Then have them read to check their predictions.

Active Reading: PREDICT

I Ask students which question Po-wan will leave out. (*Any response is valid.*)

CUSTOMIZING FOR
Students Acquiring English

2 Call students' attention to the phrase *on the other hand* and explain that it is used to introduce the opposite side of an argument or debate.

Literary Concept: PLOT

J Have students discuss whether it is possible to predict Kuan-yin's answers from hints or clues earlier in the tale. *(No, the goddess has knowledge no one else possesses.)*

STRATEGIC READING FOR
Less-Proficient Readers

K Ask students to explain what Po-wan decides to do and what happens as a result. *(He asks the three questions for his friends and does not ask his own question. His friends reward him, he becomes rich, and he marries the innkeeper's daughter.)*
Summarizing/Relating Cause and Effect

From Personal Response to Critical Analysis

1. What was your reaction when Po-wan decided to ask the three other questions instead of his own? Write your thoughts in your notebook. *(Responses will vary.)*
2. Besides generosity, what other traits characterize Po-wan? *(Possible responses: He is extremely kind and thoughtful; he seems to be patient and to have a deep sense of responsibility and morality.)*
3. How would you describe the theme of this story, or its message about life? *(Possible response: Generosity and kindness will always be rewarded.)*
4. Do you think Po-wan will remain rich when he returns home? Explain. *(Possible responses: He will not remain rich because nothing has changed in his generous character and he will just give all of his money away again; he might be able to remain rich if he can learn how to balance generosity and supporting himself.)*

First, he asked the serpent's question: "Why is the Snake of the Cliff not yet a dragon, although he has practiced self-denial for more than one thousand years?"

And the Living Kuan-yin answered: "On his head are seven bright pearls. If he removes six of them, he can become a dragon."

Next, Po-wan asked the innkeeper's question: "Why is the innkeeper's daughter unable to speak, although she is in the twentieth year of her life?"

And the Living Kuan-yin answered: "It is her fate to remain mute until she sees the man destined[10] to be her husband."

Last, Po-wan asked the kind host's question: "Why are there never blossoms in the rich man's garden, although it has been carefully cultivated for twenty years?"

J And the Living Kuan-yin answered: "Buried in the garden are seven big jars filled with silver and gold. The flowers will bloom if the owner will rid himself of half the treasure."

Then Chin Po-wan thanked the Living Kuan-yin and bade her good-bye.

On his return journey, he stopped first at the rich man's house to give him the Living Kuan-yin's answer. In gratitude the rich man gave him half the buried treasure.

Next, Po-wan went to the inn. As he approached, the innkeeper's daughter saw him from the window and called out, "Chin Po-wan! Back already! What did the Living Kuan-yin say?"

Upon hearing his daughter speak at long last, the joyful innkeeper gave her in marriage to Chin Po-wan.

Lastly, Po-wan went to the cliffs by the furiously flowing river to tell the snake what the Living Kuan-yin had said. The grateful snake immediately gave him six of the bright pearls and promptly turned into a magnificent dragon, the remaining pearl in his forehead lighting the headland[11] like a great beacon.[12] **K**

And so it was that Chin Po-wan, that generous and good man, was once more worth a million pieces of gold. ❖

---

10. **destined** (dĕs′tĭnd): determined beforehand, as by fate.
11. **headland:** a point of land reaching out into the water.
12. **beacon:** a light for signaling or guiding.

CAROL KENDALL

Carol Kendall (1917–) says the things she likes to do best are writing, reading, studying Chinese, and "climbing to the tops of things."

Kendall is best known for *The Gammage Cup*, a 1960 Newbery Honor Book, which was adapted as an animated film for television in 1987. Kendall now lives in Lawrence, Kansas, where she met Yao-wen Li.

OTHER WORKS *The Firelings, The Wedding of the Rat Family*

YAO-WEN LI

"The Living Kuan-yin" is from *Sweet and Sour*, one of two collections of Chinese folk tales that Yao-wen Li (1924–) has coauthored with Carol Kendall. Born and raised in Canton, China, Li left China in 1947 and has lived in the United States ever since.

A return visit to China in 1973 inspired Li (whose first name means "literary brilliance") to begin collecting traditional Chinese tales.

OTHER WORKS *Cinnamon Moon*

734 UNIT SIX: THE ORAL TRADITION

COMPREHENSION CHECK

1. What is the significance of Chin Po-wan's name? (Chin *means "gold" and* Po-wan *means "million." His name meant he would be worth a million pieces of gold when he came of age.*)
2. What does Po-wan want from the Living Kuan-Yin? *(He wants to know why he is so poor.)*
3. What difficult decision does Po-wan have to make before his interview with the Living Kuan-Yin? *(He must decide whether he should ask his own question instead of one of the three questions he has collected on his journey.)*
4. What do the wealthy man, the innkeeper, and the snake give Po-wan to thank him for asking their questions? *(half a buried treasure; his daughter in marriage; six bright pearls)*
5. At the conclusion of the folk tale, what quality is shared by the snake, the innkeeper, the wealthy man, and Po-wan? *(generosity)*

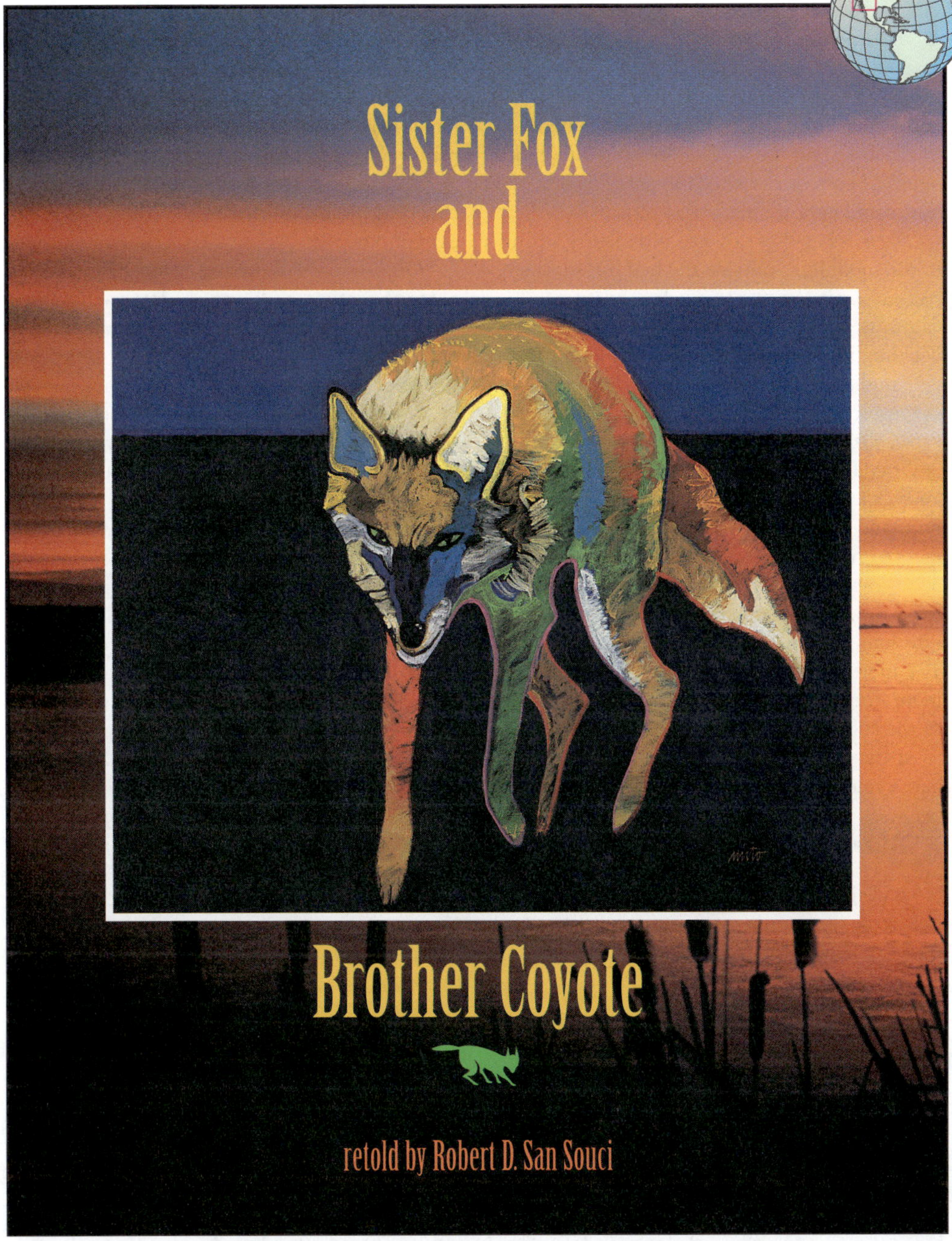

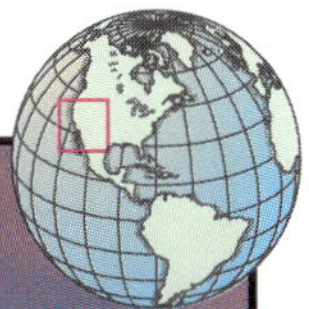

Sister Fox and Brother Coyote

retold by Robert D. San Souci

Inset: Copyright © John Nieto. Courtesy of Bailey Nelson Gallery, Seattle, Washington.

Art Note

Coyote by **John Nieto** Nieto specializes in art of the Southwest with Native-American themes. This coyote is typical of his work—strikingly realistic, but with magical qualities.

Reading the Art *What impressions do you get of this coyote? Compare the animal pictured here with the one described in the folk tale.*

STRATEGIC READING FOR
Less-Proficient Readers

Set a Purpose Ask students to read the beginning of the tale and focus on the relationship between the two main characters.

Multicultural Perspectives

THE COYOTE IN NATIVE AMERICAN CULTURE Native Americans consider the coyote a wise animal and respect it. The numerous coyote tales in Native-American legend usually depict the coyote differently than this tale does. In a Native-American tale the coyote is the character who plans and carries out tricks on other animals rather than the foolish animal described in this story.

Coyote skin was valued by many Native Americans for making quivers to hold arrows. The Coyoteros, a division of the Apaches, may have been given their name because they hunted coyotes for food.

THE LANGUAGE OF LITERATURE TEACHER'S EDITION **735**

Literary Notes

A Students may be familiar with other stories in which a figure of wax or tar is set up to trap an animal character. You may wish to point out that plot elements in folk tales are often borrowed and reused.

Linking to Science

B The coyote, or prairie wolf, is a small wolf with long, thick, tawny fur and a black-tipped bushy tail. It is sometimes called the "barking wolf" because its bark resembles that of a dog. Coyote populations range from Mexico through the west and central United States, Alaska, and southern Canada.

Active Reading: PREDICT

C Have students predict how Sister Fox will escape from the wax figure. You may wish to use the following model to give students ideas of what they might be thinking about:

Think-Aloud Model *Since the story says that Sister Fox is more clever than Brother Coyote, she will probably trick him somehow so that she escapes and he becomes stuck to the wax figure. She might tell him that the figure is valuable so he will want to steal it.*

Literary Concept: AUTHOR'S PURPOSE

D Ask students why the writer uses Spanish words and phrases in the story. (*Possible responses: The Spanish words help to establish the setting of the tale; the Spanish words are a clue to the cultural background of the tale.*)

In the desert country of the Southwest, there was once a very clever fox. She had been stealing a chicken every night from a certain *ranchero*,[1] Don Perez. After having failed many times to trap the sly vixen,[2] the man finally hit upon the idea of creating a manlike figure of soft, sticky wax to guard his hen house and capture her.

When Sister Fox saw the little figure sitting in the moonlight outside the hen house, she paused to size up the stranger. Always cautious, she watched for a long time, finally deciding that the small creature, looking so pale and still, posed no threat to her. Boldly she approached the mannikin[3] and said, "¡Buenas noches, amigo!"[4]

Of course, the little wax figure did not answer back. Several times the fox spoke to him, and always the underlined insufferable person ignored her pleasantries. At last, angered by so much rudeness, Sister Fox grabbed him with her paws. She intended to shake some manners **A** into him. Instead, she found herself stuck fast. The more she struggled to free herself, the more firmly she found her paws and fur wed to the sticky wax.

B At that moment, Brother Coyote, who also had a hunger for the *ranchero*'s chickens, came by.

"¡Hola, amiga!"[5] called the coyote. "¿Qué tal?"[6]

Now the fox and coyote were cousins, but they were also rivals. They often found themselves after the same prize, and each such meeting became a contest between them. Sometimes Brother Coyote won, because he was bigger and stronger. But more often Sister **C** Fox won, because she was clever and knew that brains could often get the better of brawn.[7]

"Hello, dear cousin," replied Sister Fox in her most honeyed voice. "You have come just in time to help me. If you do this, you will also help yourself to a nice fat chicken." She knew only too well that the coyote would more likely help her because of hunger in his belly rather than goodness in his heart.

Licking his chops at the thought of a tasty hen, Brother Coyote asked his cousin, "Please, explain yourself."

"Oh," said the underlined wily fox, "Don Perez has agreed to let me have one chicken each night. This is to thank me for a certain small favor I did for him."

"And what favor is that?" asked the coyote.

"A personal matter. I promised the good *señor*[8] I would not tell. But let us return to my present difficulty. Here I am, come to collect my nightly payment according to my contract with the *ranchero*, and this little creature prevents me. Grab him by the shoulders so that I can pull myself free. Then I will go and get two chickens—one for you—and pass up my dinner tomorrow night."

The greedy coyote was excited at the thought of getting one of the *ranchero*'s celebrated[9] hens without running the risk of being shot. He walked behind the wax figure **D** and grabbed its shoulders with his paws.

Straightaway, Sister Fox pulled free of the wax. "Now you wait here while I get a

---

1. *ranchero* (rän-chĕ′rô) *Spanish*: rancher.
2. **vixen**: a female fox.
3. **mannikin**: a lifelike model of the human body.
4. *¡Buenas noches, amigo!* (bwĕ′näs nô′chĕs ä-mē′gô) *Spanish*: Good evening, friend!
5. *¡Hola, amiga!* (ô′lä ä-mē′gä) *Spanish*: Hello, friend!
6. *¿Qué tal?* (kĕ′ täl′) *Spanish*: What's up?
7. **brawn**: well-developed muscles; physical strength.
8. *señor* (sĕ-nyôr′) *Spanish*: gentleman (also used as a title, like *Mister*).
9. **celebrated**: famous.

WORDS TO KNOW
insufferable (ĭn-sŭf′ər-ə-bəl) *adj.* hard to put up with; unbearable
wily (wī′lē) *adj.* clever and skillful in a tricky way

736

Mini-Lesson ⓉⓂ Spelling

THE SUFFIX -IBLE / -ABLE Explain to students that the suffixes *-ible* and *-able* sound very much the same. The suffix *-ible* is more commonly used with roots than with complete words; *-able* usually follows the hard sound of *c* or *g*. List on the chalkboard the examples shown. Students may need to check words with these suffixes in a dictionary to be sure which spelling to use.

predictable   horrible
remarkable
questionable   impossible

Application Reproduce the following paragraph on an overhead transparency or the chalkboard. Have students copy the paragraph, completing each word with the correct suffix.

It seems remark_____ that Brother Coyote continued to believe Sister Fox's imposs____ stories. One horr_____ outcome after another results from him following her question_____ advice, but he never learns that her tricks are predict_____.

Ask students to look for more words that fit this pattern, in their own writing and in things that they read, and to add these words to their personal word lists.

Reteaching/Reinforcement
• *Unit Six Resource Book*, p. 39

---

736 THE LANGUAGE OF LITERATURE TEACHER'S EDITION

chicken for each of us. Of course, I insist that you take the fatter one!"

So the foolish coyote waited, his paws on the wax figure and his mind on the fat hen that his cousin would soon bring him.

But the only one who came was Don Perez. He had been awakened by the squawking in his hen house when Sister Fox snatched his finest hen and ran off into the night.

When he saw the coyote, he cried, "¡Bandido!"[10] Then he fired his rifle. The shot went amiss and the wax figure exploded, allowing Brother Coyote to escape. But the unhappy creature had bits of wax stuck to his fur for days afterward. He vowed revenge upon Sister Fox for her scheming that had cost him a fine dinner, and—very nearly—his life.

Not long after this, it happened that Sister Fox stole a freshly baked loaf of bread from a house on the edge of town. As she was running away into the desert with her still-warm prize, she met her cousin in a little *arroyo*.[11]

Brother Coyote was still very angry about the business with the wax man. He pounced upon the fox and bared his fangs at her. "Little cousin," he snarled, "if you do not give me that loaf of bread, I will gobble you up on the spot!"

"Oh," said the fox, thinking quickly, "this bread is not to eat. It is to lure the roosters—*¡Hay muchos!*[12] There are so many!—that are kept in a certain *hacienda*[13] I have discovered. Tonight I am going to steal as many as I have crumbs of bread."

"Well," said the gullible coyote, "let me go with you."

"No," said Sister Fox, "those roosters are so fat and lazy that they can barely move. Why should I share the secret with you?"

"Because," said the coyote unpleasantly, "I will devour you if you do *not* let me go with you."

"Well, all right," said the fox, "I will take the bread and run home now. When the moon has set, I will meet you here. ¡Adiós!"[14]

But Brother Coyote slapped a heavy paw

Sister Fox stole a freshly baked loaf of bread from a house on the edge of town.

across her tail. "To be certain that you do not run away, we will stay here together until the moon has set. And I am warning you: If we do not come away with ten times ten fat roosters tonight, you will not see the dawn."

So they lay side by side in the *arroyo* as the moon rose and set. By starlight, Sister Fox led her cousin to a huge wooden gate set in a high adobe wall.

"Here," she whispered.

"Hand over the bread *pronto*,"[15] Brother Coyote ordered.

The fox took a bit of the bread and

---

10. **bandido** (bän-dē'dô) *Spanish:* bandit; thief.
11. **arroyo** (ä-rô'yô) *Spanish:* a gully or large ditch.
12. **¡Hay muchos!** (ī' mōō'chôs) *Spanish:* There are many.
13. **hacienda** (ä-syĕn'dä) *Spanish:* ranch house.
14. **adiós** (ä-dyôs') *Spanish:* goodbye.
15. **pronto** (prôn'tô) *Spanish:* at once; quickly.

SISTER FOX AND BROTHER COYOTE 737

Active Reading: CONNECT

G Ask students to discuss people they have known, read about, or seen in movies that remind them of Sister Fox. Ask students what character traits might be clues that show that this type of trickster is up to no good. *(Possible responses: He or she is a smooth talker, uses flattery, and has some kind of amazing "deal" to sell.)*

Literary Concept: PLOT

H Ask students to compare the plot structure of this tale with that of "The Living Kuan-yin." *(Both stories are composed of episodes, but the scenes are connected chronologically in "The Living Kuan-yin." In this tale, the episodes are independent stories. They could be told in a different order and the plot would still make sense.)*

CUSTOMIZING FOR
Students Acquiring English

2 Point out that *Without a doubt* is a phrase used to introduce information that the speaker considers absolutely true.

> To his surprise, he saw  what seemed to be a huge round cheese just below the surface of the water.

crumbled it into his paw, telling him, "The roosters are just inside this gate. Push open the latch. That will be easy for you because you are bigger and stronger than I am. As soon as you are inside, scatter these bread crumbs and call, 'Here, here, *Señor* Rooster, see what I have brought you.' Then you will get a reward beyond your wildest imagining. Just be sure your greediness does not make you forget your cousin who brought you here."

Eagerly Brother Coyote took the bread crumbs, stood up on his hind legs, and tugged and pushed until he opened the big latch on the gate. Then, slipping through, he began to toss bread crumbs right and left, calling softly, "Here, here, *Señor* Rooster, see what I have for you."

But, once again, his clever cousin had tricked him. The courtyard inside held sleeping dogs, not roosters! In a moment, Brother Coyote, crying "¡Ay! Ay! Ay!" fled through the gate with the hounds snapping at his heels. "Sister Fox!" he howled, but she did not hear. She had long since returned to her lair to finish the loaf of bread and plan more mischief.

As it happened, the coyote <u>eluded</u> the dogs—but not before he had received several painful bites on his flank and left a tuft of his tail in the jaws of the lead hound.

Licking his wounds in his own den, he once again vowed to make his cousin suffer tenfold[16] for the pain and humiliation she had caused him.

Many nights later, he chanced upon Sister Fox as she sat crouched beside a deep pool of water in the foothills near the town.

"Without a doubt, I am going to eat you this time," he growled.

"Well, if it must be so, then it must be so," she said, sounding not in the least worried. "I just hope that when you have swallowed my miserable bones and stringy meat, you still have room for this cheese I am guarding. Behold what a beautiful cheese it is!"

Brother Coyote looked in the direction she was facing. To his surprise, he saw what seemed to be a huge round cheese just below the surface of the water. Of course, it was only the reflection of the full moon, riding high overhead. But the greedy coyote saw only what Sister Fox—and his own stomach—wanted him to see.

"Who left such a fine cheese in the water?" he asked suspiciously.

Sister Fox answered, "The family who lives in the grand *hacienda* not far from here. They are giving a *fiesta*[17] soon. Because the cheese is so big, and the *fiesta* is five days away, they put it in this cool water to keep it from spoiling. I found it quite by accident."

---
16. **tenfold:** ten times as much.
17. ***fiesta*** (fyĕs′tä) *Spanish:* party; celebration.

WORDS TO KNOW
elude (ĭ-lōōd′) *v.* to avoid or escape, especially by means of cleverness or skill

738

Mini-Lesson — Reading Skills/Strategies

USING CONTEXT CLUES Explain to students that readers can pick up clues to the meaning of an unfamiliar word from the words or phrases before or after it. Context clues may define the word, give a synonym or an example, or provide comparisons or contrasts to help a reader infer the meaning. Context clues are particularly helpful when a story includes words in an unfamiliar language.

Application For each Spanish word or phrase, have students explain how context clues could help them infer the meaning.

1. Brother Coyote had a hunger for the *ranchero's* chickens.
2. "I'm in a hurry," said Brother Coyote. "Hand over the bread *pronto*."
3. Nearby was a family who lived in a grand *hacienda*.
4. The lunch included roast chicken, *tortillas*, *frijoles*, and salad.

Reteaching/Reinforcement
• *Unit Six Resource Book*, p. 38

---

738 THE LANGUAGE OF LITERATURE TEACHER'S EDITION

"Well, now you have lost it," said Brother Coyote. "With all that good cheese in easy reach, I will wait and gobble you up another time. ¡Vete![18] Scram!"

"¡Gracias!"[19] called Sister Fox as she scampered away. Then the greedy coyote jumped into the pond to pull out the cheese. But all he got for his efforts was wet fur and a bone-deep chill.

Shivering, his sopping tail dragging in the dust, he returned to his cave to plot a terrible revenge on his cousin.

Their final, fatal meeting came when Brother Coyote chased Sister Fox into a canebrake[20] and cornered her there.

"Now I am going to kill you and eat you, for all the misery you have caused me."

"That is fair," the fox replied. "But, listen! Let me help set things right, so that I can go to heaven with a clear conscience. I had not planned to tell anyone, but I was headed for this very place when you surprised me. You see," she said, lowering her voice to a whisper, "I have learned that a wedding party is coming this way. To reach the church, they must pass through this canebrake. The bride and groom are the children of very wealthy hacendados.[21] Their servants carry chickens to roast, tortillas, frijoles,[22] sweet cakes, and every manner of good thing to eat. Hidden beside the path here, I thought it would be easy to steal the best of what passes by."

"¿De veras?"[23] asked the ever-hungry coyote, wanting to believe her wild story.

"Sí,[24] it is true. Would I dare to tell you a lie," Sister Fox asked, "when you are going to send me to heaven today? San Pedro would not let me through the gate of pearls[25] with a fresh sin on my soul."

"That's true enough," agreed Brother Coyote.

"My only fear," said the fox, "is that the people will take the second path through the canebrake while we are watching this one. I will go and watch the other path. Then we must both listen for fireworks. That will mean the wedding party is coming. Whichever of us hears this must right away go and call the other, so that we will be ready for them."

"¡Bueno!" said the coyote, settling down to watch the path that wound through the

---

18. ¡Vete! (vĕ'tĕ) Spanish: Get out of here!
19. ¡Gracias! (grä'syäs) Spanish: Thank you!
20. canebrake: a dense growth of thick-stemmed grasses or reeds.
21. hacendados (ä-sĕn-dä'dôs) Spanish: landowners; ranchers.
22. tortillas (tôr-tē'yäs), frijoles (frē-hô'lĕs) Spanish: thin, round cakes of corn or wheat bread, and beans.
23. ¿De veras? (dĕ' vĕ'räs) Spanish: Are you telling the truth?
24. sí (sē) Spanish: yes.
25. San Pedro . . . gate of pearls: Some Christians believe that Saint Peter (called San Pedro in Spanish) stands at the gates of heaven and decides who will be allowed to enter.

Critical Thinking:
HYPOTHESIZING

Ask students how, in the episodes with the roosters and the cheese, the coyote could have been more cautious. *(Possible responses: He could have had the fox go to the hacienda and bring back a rooster; he could have made the fox fetch the cheese from the water.)*

STRATEGIC READING FOR
Less-Proficient Readers

Ask students to summarize episodes of the tale in their own words.

- How did Sister Fox trick Brother Coyote with the loaf of bread? *(She convinced him to enter a hacienda guarded by sleeping dogs.)* Summarizing
- How did she trick him about the cheese? *(She told him the reflection of the moon was a ball of cheese, so he jumped in the water to get it.)* Summarizing

Set a Purpose Have students read to find out how the story will end.

Literary Links

Have students compare the plot of this tale with the end of *The Hobbit*. *(Possible response: In both stories a character is killed through a trick. Bilbo tricks the dragon Smaug; Sister Fox tricks Brother Coyote.)*

Assessment ✓ Option

INFORMAL ASSESSMENT To assess students' understanding of the story's plot, have them create a storyboard or comic strip showing one of Sister Fox's tricks and Brother Coyote's response. Encourage students to review the relevant section of the story before they begin drawing.

Rubric
3 Full Accomplishment Student creates a storyboard or comic strip that accurately depicts the cause-and-effect sequence of events. Illustrations reflect the story's humorous tone.

2 Substantial Accomplishment Student creates storyboard or comic strip, accurately illustrating a series of events. The cause-and-effect relationship between panels of storyboard or comic strip may not be clear.

1 Little or Partial Accomplishment Student has difficulty illustrating a coherent sequence of events.

THE LANGUAGE OF LITERATURE TEACHER'S EDITION **739**

STRATEGIC READING FOR
Less-Proficient Readers

L Have students describe the final trick that Sister Fox plays on Brother Coyote. *(She convinces him to hide in a field of sugar cane plants and then sets the field on fire.)* **Summarizing**

CUSTOMIZING FOR
Gifted and Talented Students

M Ask students to write one more episode that might occur in the tale before the final scene. Students may choose to have Sister Fox trick Brother Coyote in another way or to have Brother Coyote finally trick Sister Fox.

From Personal Response to Critical Analysis

1. What adjectives would you use to describe Sister Fox and Brother Coyote. Write down these adjectives in your notebook. *(Possible responses: Sister Fox—wily, tricky, mean, clever, cunning; Brother Coyote—foolish, gullible, trusting, greedy)*
2. What character flaw causes Brother Coyote to fall for Sister Fox's tricks? *(greed)*
3. Which episode in the tale was the most amusing or ridiculous to you? Give reasons for your choice. *(Responses will vary.)*
4. Write a proverb or moral you might use to warn Brother Coyote about Sister Fox's tricks. *(Possible responses: If something seems too good to be true, it probably is. Fool me once, shame on you. Fool me twice, shame on me.)*

---

tall, tinder-dry[26] cane. He kept his ears up to listen for the sound of fireworks or Sister Fox's call.

"¡Adiós!" cried the sly fox, as she slipped out of the canebrake. Soon she returned, carrying in her jaws a burning brand from the kitchen of the *hacienda*. Using this, she set the canebrake on fire. When the blazing cane began to go *Pop! Popple! Pop!* the coyote mistook the sound for the noise of the wedding party's fireworks. He began to dance for joy, thinking of all the good food that he would soon have. He planned to take what he could for himself alone, and then he would punish his cousin.

The nearer the fire came and the louder the crackling and popping grew, the more wildly the coyote leaped and capered.[27] "Ah, here they come, here they come!" he sang.

Too late, the foolish creature discovered that he was dancing not at a wedding, but at a funeral—his own! ❖

---

26. **tinder-dry:** dry as the material used to light a fire.
27. **capered** (kā´pərd): jumped about in a happy, playful way.

ROBERT D. SAN SOUCI

An author of books for both young people and adults, Robert D. San Souci (1946–) has a deep interest in folklore that is reflected in much of his work. When his research into legendary American folk heroes revealed a lack of written accounts of heroines, he was inspired to write *Cut from the Same Cloth*. In that book, from which "Sister Fox and Brother Coyote" is taken, the author celebrates 15 strong-willed women of American folklore. San Souci worked five years on this collection and calls it "a labor of love."

San Souci was born in San Francisco. He worked for several bookstores until 1974, when he became a freelance writer, editor, and consultant. He also writes short stories, book reviews, and theater criticism for newspapers and magazines. San Souci has teamed with his illustrator brother Daniel on several books, including two award winners, *The Legend of Scarface: A Blackfeet Indian Tale* and *Song of Sedna: Sea-Goddess of the North*.

OTHER WORKS *The Talking Eggs, Sukey and the Mermaid, The Tsar's Promise*

---

740 UNIT SIX: THE ORAL TRADITION

COMPREHENSION CHECK

1. Describe the setting of the folk tale. *(Possible response: a rural or farming area in which the people speak Spanish)*
2. How does the rancher Don Perez attempt to catch Sister Fox? *(He puts up a wax figure in the hope she will become stuck to it.)*
3. What goal do Sister Fox and Brother Coyote share in all the episodes in the tale? *(They are looking for food.)*
4. Why might a parent or other older person tell this story to a young child? *(Possible responses: for entertainment; to warn the child against clever and unscrupulous people)*

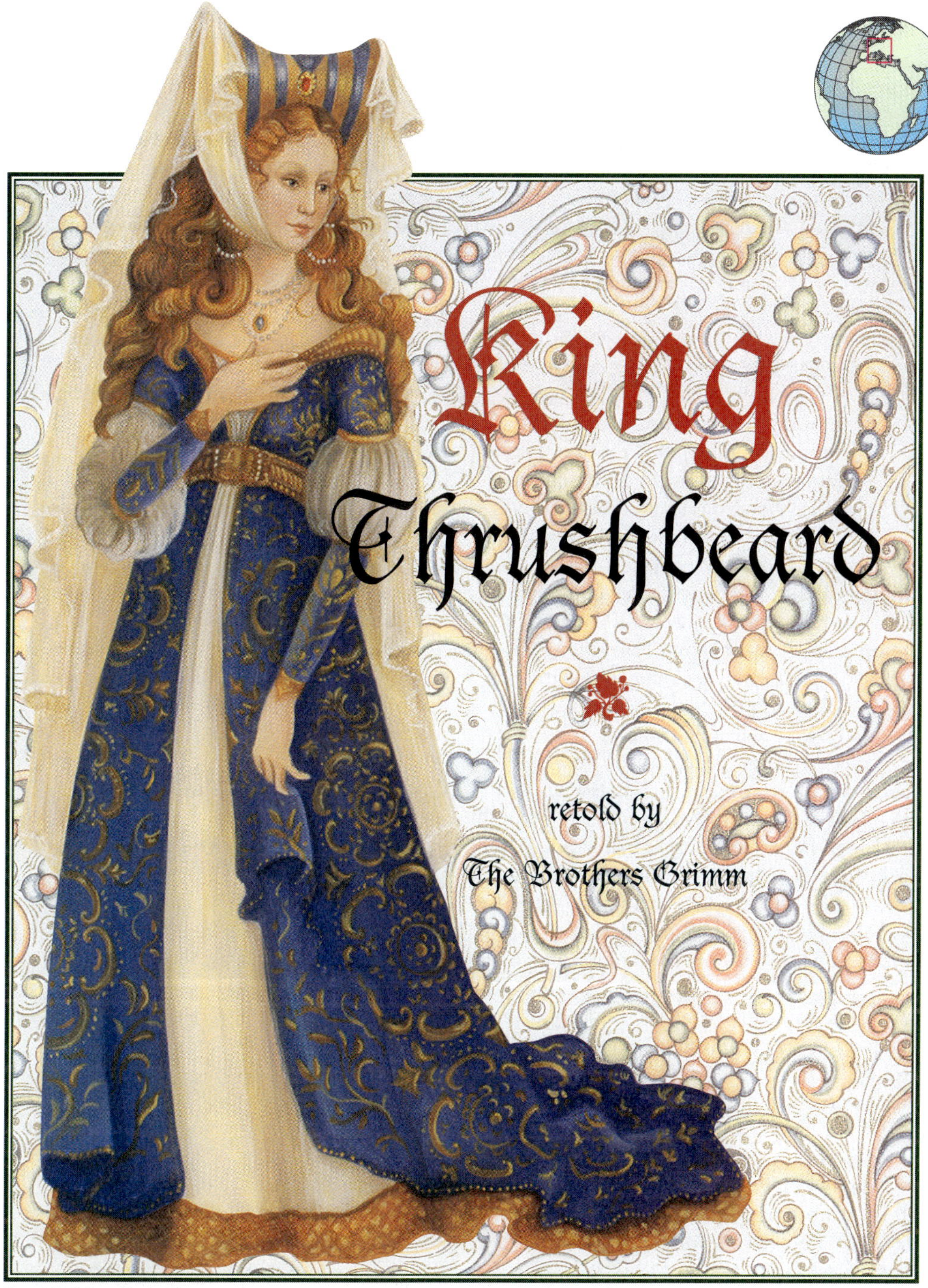

King Thrushbeard

retold by
The Brothers Grimm

Copyright © Joyce Patti.

CUSTOMIZING FOR
Students Acquiring English

Invite students to share with their classmates courtship and marriage customs from their home cultures. Discuss with students whether these customs are still practiced or whether other customs or practices are becoming more popular.

STRATEGIC READING FOR
Less-Proficient Readers

Set a Purpose Tell students that this story is a folk tale with a king's daughter for a main character. Ask them what kinds of plot elements they would expect to find in such a story. As students read the beginning of the tale, they should note how the king's daughter treats her suitors and what this reveals about her character.

Mini-Lesson: Speaking, Listening, and Viewing

STORYTELLING Explain to students that an important part of good storytelling is knowing your audience. Storytellers will revise the story and may alter their performance, depending on their audience.

Application Have students work in small groups of three or four. Tell students to imagine that their group will be presenting "King Thrushbeard" to young children. Have groups decide how they would revise the story to interest this age group.

Ask them what storytelling techniques they might use most effectively. Have a recorder for each group keep track of group decisions. Then ask each group to present and compare their plans.

You may wish to extend this activity by having groups perform a revised version of "King Thrushbeard" for a first- or second-grade audience.

THE LANGUAGE OF LITERATURE TEACHER'S EDITION 741

Active Reading: PREDICT

A Ask students to predict what they think will happen in the story, based on what they know about folk tales. If necessary, have students list the elements of folk tales. (*Possible response: The proud, vain king's daughter will learn a lesson about humility and love.*)

CUSTOMIZING FOR
Students Acquiring English

1 Lead students to understand that a *bill* is a bird's beak and that a *thrush* is a kind of bird.

2 Point out that the sections of the story that are set apart like this one are in rhymed verse.

STRATEGIC READING FOR
Less-Proficient Readers

B Ask students to describe how the king's daughter treats the men who want to marry her. (*She makes fun of them; she rejects them.*) Making Generalizations

- What does her treatment of the men reveal about her character? (*that she is spoiled, vain, cruel, and proud*) Making Inferences

Set a Purpose Have students read to learn what the king's daughter's new life is like.

Literary Concept: CHARACTER

C Ask students to infer what the princess's repeated comment "Alas, poor me..." reveals about her character. If necessary, have students skim the story to find supporting details. (*Possible response: She reveals she is selfish and shallow because she is sorry she didn't marry King Thrushbeard for his possessions.*)

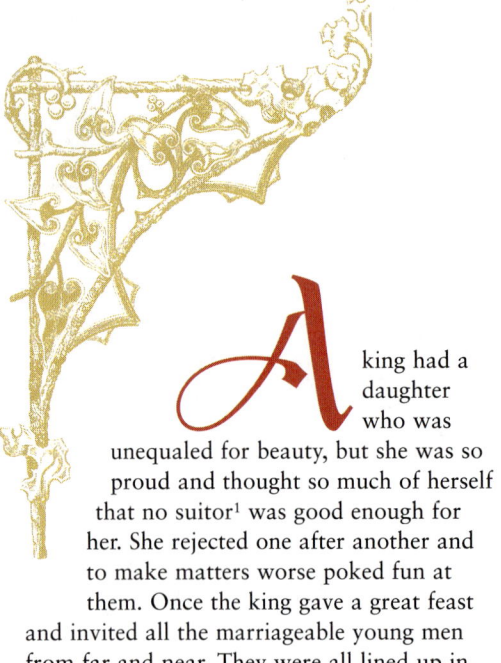

A king had a daughter who was unequaled for beauty, but she was so proud and thought so much of herself that no suitor[1] was good enough for her. She rejected one after another and to make matters worse poked fun at them. Once the king gave a great feast and invited all the marriageable young men from far and near. They were all lined up in the order of their rank: first came the kings, then the dukes, princes, counts, and barons, and last of all the knights. The king's daughter was led down the line, but to each suitor she had some objection. One was too fat and she called him a "wine barrel." The next was too tall: "Tall and skinny, that's a ninny." The third was short: "Short and thick won't do the trick." The fourth was too pale: "As pale as death." The fifth too red: "A turkey." The sixth wasn't straight enough: "Green wood, dried behind the stove." She found some fault with every one of them, but she made the most fun of a kindly king who was standing at the head of the line, and whose chin was slightly crooked. "Heavens above!" she cried. "He's got a chin like a thrush's bill!" And from then on he was known as Thrushbeard.

When the old king saw that his daughter did nothing but make fun of people and rejected all the suitors who had come to the feast, he flew into a rage and swore to make her marry the first beggar who came to his door. A few days later a wandering minstrel[2] came and sang under the window in the hope of earning a few coins. When the king heard him, he said: "Send him up." The minstrel appeared in his ragged, dirty clothes, sang for the king and his daughter, and asked for a gift when he had finished. The king said: "Your singing has pleased me so well that I'll give you my daughter for your wife." The princess was horrified, but the king said: "I swore I'd give you to the first beggar who came by, and I'm going to abide by my oath."

All her pleading was in vain; the priest was called, and she was married to the minstrel then and there. After the ceremony the king said: "Now that you're a beggar woman, I can't have you living in my palace. You can just go away with your husband."

The beggar took her by the hand and led her out of the palace, and she had to go with him on foot. They came to a large forest, and she asked:

"Who does that lovely forest belong to?"
"That forest belongs to King Thrushbeard.
If you'd taken him, you could call it your own."
"Alas, poor me, if I'd only known,
If only I'd taken King Thrushbeard!"

Next they came to a meadow, and she asked:

"Who does that lovely green meadow belong to?"
"That meadow belongs to King Thrushbeard.
If you'd taken him, you could call it your own."
"Alas, poor me, if I'd only known,

---
1. **suitor:** a man seeking to marry a woman.
2. **minstrel** (mĭn′strəl): traveling poet or singer.

742 UNIT SIX: THE ORAL TRADITION

Mini-Lesson • Literary Concepts

REVIEWING FIGURATIVE LANGUAGE
Explain to students that figurative language is writing that extends meaning of words beyond their dictionary meaning. Two examples of figurative language are similes and metaphors. Both are comparisons. A simile makes a comparison using *like, as,* or *resembles*. A metaphor makes a comparison without using these signal words. For example, in the highlighted text above, the king's daughter calls one suitor a "wine barrel." Point out to students that this is a metaphor.

Application Have students identify similes and metaphors in the highlighted passage above. Then have them write one simile and one metaphor to describe the king's daughter.

If only I'd taken King Thrushbeard!"
Then they passed through a big city, and she asked:

"Who does this beautiful city belong to?"
"This city belongs to King Thrushbeard.
If you'd taken him, you could call it your own."
"Alas, poor me, if only I'd known,
If only I'd taken King Thrushbeard!"

"You give me a pain," said the minstrel, "always wishing for another husband. I suppose I'm not good enough for you!" At last they came to a tiny little house, and she said:

"Heavens, this shack is a disgrace!
Who could own such a wretched place?"

> "If you want something done, you'll have to do it for yourself."

The minstrel answered, "It's my house and yours, where we shall live together." The king's daughter had to bend down to get through the low doorway. "Where are the servants?" she asked. "Servants, my foot!" answered the beggar. "If you want something done, you'll have to do it for yourself. And now make a fire and put on water for my supper because I'm dead tired." But the king's daughter didn't know the first thing about fires or cooking, and the beggar had to help her or he wouldn't have had any supper at all. When they had eaten what little there was, they went to bed. But bright and early the next morning he made her get up and clean the house.

They worried along for a few days, but then their provisions were gone, and the man said: "Wife, we can't go on like this, eating and drinking and earning nothing. You'll have to weave baskets." He went out and cut willow withes[3] and brought them home. She began to weave but the hard withes bruised her tender hands. "I see that won't do," said the man. "Try spinning; maybe you'll be better at it." She sat down and tried to spin, but the hard thread soon cut her soft fingers and drew blood. "Well, well!" said the man. "You're no good for any work. I've made a bad bargain. But now I think I'll buy up some earthenware pots and dishes. All you'll have to do is sit in the marketplace and sell them."

"Goodness gracious!" she thought. "If somebody from my father's kingdom goes to the marketplace and sees me sitting there selling pots, how they'll laugh at me!" But there was no help for it; she had to give in or they would have starved.

The first day, all went well: people were glad to buy her wares because she was beautiful; they paid whatever she asked, and some didn't even trouble to take the pots they had paid for. The two of them lived on the proceeds as long as the stock held out, and then the husband

---
3. **withes** (wĭths): tough, bendable twigs.

KING THRUSHBEARD   **743**

Mini-Lesson: Speaking, Listening, and Viewing

COMPARING A VIDEO WITH A STORY
While there are many different video versions of Grimm's fairy tales, actress/producer Shelley Duvall has re-created these tales with unusual beauty, wit, and quality in her series *Faerie Tale Theatre* (Playhouse Video). All the videos in her series star respected contemporary actors and actresses, including Meryl Streep, Robin Williams, and Kevin Kline.

Application Invite students to watch a video of one or more well-known Grimm's fairy tales. Ask them to describe how the version they watched was different from the way they had visualized it. Then discuss how people today might find aspects of these stories strange. For instance, ask if they think members of royalty would be able to disguise themselves as beggars.

bought up a fresh supply of crockery. She took a place at the edge of the market, set out her wares around her and offered them for sale. All of a sudden a drunken hussar[4] came galloping through, upset her pots and smashed them all into a thousand pieces. She began to cry; she was worried sick. "Oh!" she wailed. "What will become of me? What will my husband say!" She ran home and told him what had happened. "What did you expect?" he said. "Setting out earthenware pots at the edge of the market! But stop crying. I can see you're no good for any sensible work. Today I was at our king's palace. I asked if they could use a kitchen maid, and they said they'd take you. They'll give you your meals."

So the king's daughter became a kitchen maid and had to help the cook and do the most disagreeable work. She carried little jars in both her pockets, to take home the leftovers they gave her, and that's what she and her husband lived on.

It so happened that the marriage of the king's eldest son was about to be celebrated. The poor woman went upstairs and stood in the doorway of the great hall, looking on. When the candles were lit and the courtiers[5] began coming in, each more magnificent than the last, and everything was so bright and full of splendor, she was sad at heart. She thought of her miserable life and cursed the pride and arrogance that had brought her so low and made her so poor. Succulent dishes were being carried in and out, and the smell drifted over to her. Now and then a servant tossed her a few scraps, and she put them into her little jars to take home.

> "I can see you're no good for any sensible work."

And then the king's son appeared; he was dressed in silk and velvet and had gold chains around his neck. When he saw the beautiful woman in the doorway, he took her by the hand and asked her to dance with him, but she refused. She was terrified, for she saw it was King Thrushbeard, who had courted her and whom she had laughed at and rejected. She tried to resist, but he drew her into the hall. Then the string that kept her pockets in place snapped, the jars fell to the floor, the soup spilled and the scraps came tumbling out. The courtiers all began to laugh and jeer, and she

---

4. **hussar** (hə-zär′): a cavalry soldier—that is, a soldier who fights on horseback.
5. **courtiers** (kôr′tē-ərz): attendants at a royal palace.

WORDS TO KNOW
succulent (sŭk′yə-lənt) *adj.* tasty; delicious

744

would sooner have been a hundred fathoms[6] under the earth. She bounded through the door and tried to escape, but on the stairs a man caught her and brought her back, and when she looked at him, she saw it was King Thrushbeard again. He spoke kindly to her and said: "Don't be afraid. I am the minstrel you've been living with in that wretched shack; I disguised myself for love of you, and I was also the hussar who rode in and smashed your crockery. I did all that to humble your pride and punish you for the insolent way you laughed at me." Then she wept bitterly and said: "I've been very wicked and I'm not worthy to be your wife." But he said: "Don't cry; the hard days are over; now we shall celebrate our wedding." The maids came and dressed her magnificently, her father arrived with his whole court and congratulated her on her marriage to King Thrushbeard, and it was then that the feast became really joyful. I wish you and I had been there. ❖

---

6. **fathoms** (făth'əmz): units of measurement, each equal to six feet.

JAKOB AND WILHELM GRIMM

1785–1863   1786–1859

The brothers Grimm, born in Hanau, Germany, trained to be lawyers. However, an early exposure to old German romantic poems eventually led them to become interested in the language and literature of the German past. Jakob wrote, "It is high time that these old traditions were collected and rescued before they perish like dew in the hot sun."

Happier collecting local folk tales than practicing law, the brothers began a search for folk tales, particularly ones passed along orally to children, that was to become their lifelong commitment. They were always very close; according to Jakob, "Up to the very end, we worked in two rooms next to each other, always under one roof." *Grimm's Fairy Tales* has remained popular to this day.

OTHER WORKS *German Popular Tales, Grimm's Tales for Young and Old: The Complete Stories*

WORDS TO KNOW

insolent (ĭn'sə-lənt) *adj.* rude

Literature Connection

Hold a Storytelling Festival Choose two volunteers to be the producers and two to be the camera crew. Divide the remaining students into groups of four. In each group, one student will be the storyteller, one will be the publicity agent, and two will be the designers. Explain that each group will be judged on organization, a fair division of work, creativity, and preparation.

Rubric

3 Full Accomplishment Students' stories are well rehearsed and well presented. The flyers, props, and costumes accurately reflect the content of the story and its cultural background.

2 Substantial Accomplishment Students' stories are adequately rehearsed and presented. Flyers are accurate; some props and/or costumes are used.

1 Little or Partial Accomplishment Students' stories are poorly rehearsed. Flyers are incomplete or inaccurate. Few if any props and/or costumes are used.

RESPONDING
OPTIONS

LITERATURE CONNECTION PROJECT 1 Multimodal Activity

Hold a Storytelling Festival Work with your classmates to present a storytelling festival for other classes in your grade or for a group of younger students. First decide which stories from Unit Six and which other tales from world folklore to include. Then, with the class divided into the following groups, prepare the story presentations:

Storytellers Rehearse each story before a mirror or in front of friends. Practice using gestures and tones of voice to make the stories come alive. If necessary, take turns telling some stories so that each person has an opportunity to perform.

Publicity Agents Create flyers to advertise the festival. Design and deliver invitations containing the date, time, and location. Produce illustrated programs to hand out at the festival.

Designers Locate or construct appropriate props, and provide costumes for the storytellers.

Producers Arrange each storyteller in a different location with a sign that announces the story title so that guests can choose among the stories. Producers might also locate audiotapes or videotapes of professional storytellers to set up for viewing in a separate area.

Camera Crew Locate video equipment and videotape the performances to share with other classes.

SOCIAL STUDIES CONNECTION PROJECT 2 Multimodal Activity

Learn More About Money In "The Living Kuan-yin," Chin Po-wan's name foretells the million pieces of gold that will be his—and that he will eventually spend. Throughout history, money has taken various forms, from the salt used in ancient Rome to the seashells once commonly accepted as money in the South Pacific. Research the kinds of objects that served as money in the cultures represented in these stories. Use a chart similar to the one shown to organize your findings.

Culture: _____
Objects used as money:
_____
_____
_____

Country: _____
Objects used as money:
_____
_____
_____

Money Across Cultures

746 UNIT SIX: THE ORAL TRADITION

Social Studies Connection

Learn More About Money Have students do the research independently. Then, in a class discussion, have them share their results. You may wish to add countries so that more types of money are represented. You could divide the class in groups and assign a different continent to each group.

Rubric

3 Full Accomplishment Students' charts are accurate and show a variety of different kinds of money. Dates, where applicable, are included.

2 Substantial Accomplishment Students' charts are fairly accurate and show several kinds of money.

1 Little or Partial Accomplishment Students' charts are not accurate. Research has been done carelessly.

746 THE LANGUAGE OF LITERATURE TEACHER'S EDITION

Social Studies Connection

Celebrate Festivals Prepare 15 index cards or slips of paper, each with one of the stories in Unit 6. Have each student choose a card from a bag to find the culture he or she will research. After the 15 cards have been drawn, replace them in the bag and have students continue until everyone has chosen a story title. Students who have picked the same story title might work together on the research and on painting their portion of the class mural.

Rubric
3 Full Accomplishment Students' mural paintings and captions show careful research and imagination.
2 Substantial Accomplishment Students' mural paintings and captions are accurate.
1 Little or Partial Accomplishment Students' mural paintings are not accurate. Captions, if any, are poorly written.

SOCIAL STUDIES CONNECTION PROJECT 3 Multimodal Activity

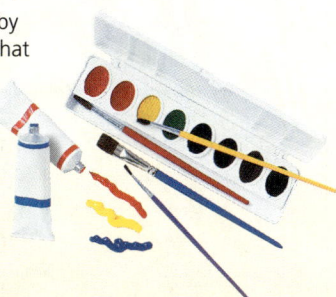

Celebrate Festivals Celebrations, feasts, and festivals are important events in ancient and modern cultures. The ancient Greeks held many celebrations, such as the Olympic games honoring Zeus and the drama festivals honoring Dionysus. Modern Vietnamese continue to celebrate the Dong Ky Fireworks Festival. Identify and research the festivals of the cultures represented in Unit Six. As a class, combine your research by painting a large mural that illustrates these celebrations. Include brief captions that explain the festivals.

ACROSS CULTURES MINI-PROJECTS Multimodal Activities

Build on the Oral Tradition Ask an older family member or friend to share a story that he or she remembers hearing as a child. As he or she tells the story, take notes or use a tape recorder or video camera. With your classmates, gather the written stories in a scrapbook along with photographs of the storytellers. Share the scrapbook with the individuals who told the stories.

Play "What's the Story?" Work with three or four other students to write, on small slips of paper, as many trivia questions about these three stories as you can. For example, one question might be, In which story does a snake play an important role? ("The Living Kuan-yin") Then exchange questions with another team, and see which team can answer the most questions correctly. If time permits, expand the game to include all the selections in this unit.

Read More About Minstrels In the Middle Ages and the Renaissance, minstrels—along with acrobats, puppeteers, and jugglers—wandered through Europe, performing in castles. Find out more about these minstrels and the kind of entertainment they provided. Share your information with the class, playing some recorded examples of the minstrels' music if possible.

Find the Trickster Almost every culture has trickster tales that were passed from one generation to the next through the oral tradition. Find out more about tricksters in world folklore. Then create a "Wanted" poster for your favorite trickster. Include an illustration, a description of the suspect, the charges against the suspect, and the amount of the reward.

Extended Social Studies Reading

MORE ABOUT THE CULTURES

- *The Great Wall of China* by Leonard Everett Fisher
- *See Inside an Ancient Chinese Town* by Penelope Hughes-Stanton
- *Passport to Mexico* by Carmen Irizarry

PROJECTS **747**

Multicultural Perspectives

Build on the Oral Tradition Explain to students that this project differs from collecting oral histories in that they will be recording fiction rather than true anecdotes from a person's life. However, you may wish to have students include some oral history with the stories; for example, the storyteller might add memories of the person who told him or her the story as well as where and when he or she first heard it.

Play "What's the Story?" Before students exchange their trivia questions with another team, they should double-check that each question has just one possible answer.

Read More About Minstrels When doing their research, students can look up *jongleur*, *troubadour*, and *bard* as well as *minstrel*. Explain that they are not looking for *minstrel show*, a different sort of entertainment from what is described in the project.

Find the Trickster Since trickster characters are often animals, suggest that students look in books of animal tales for ideas for trickster characters. Aesop's fables are one source of trickster tales.

THE LANGUAGE OF LITERATURE TEACHER'S EDITION **747**

OVERVIEW

To gain a deeper appreciation of the selections they have read in this unit, students will explore the characteristics of an I-Search report and then create their own report in this lesson.

Objectives

- To plan an I-Search Report by considering such elements as topic, focus, information, and organization
- To draft an I-Search report and solicit a response to it
- To revise, edit, and publish an I-Search report
- To reflect on the process of writing an I-Search report

Skills

LITERATURE
- Analyzing folk tales

WRITING AND LANGUAGE
- Selecting a topic
- Finding a focus
- Taking notes
- Organizing ideas
- Making an outline

GRAMMAR AND USAGE
- Creating a list of sources

MEDIA LITERACY
- Interpreting menus
- Analyzing cultural artifacts
- Studying a newspaper article

SPEAKING, LISTENING, AND VIEWING
- Holding a roundtable
- Reading aloud
- Interviewing

Teaching Strategy: MODELING

A Model how to use a springboard to spark ideas for an I-Search report. First, have a volunteer read the menu aloud. Then provide a think-aloud model to show students how to draw ideas for writing topics from the menu. Use the following sample or one of your own:

Think-Aloud Model *This menu makes me want to find out more about the foods of other countries, such as Germany, Italy, and Korea. I want to discover what foods are popular, what they are called, and how they are prepared.*

Discuss as a class the questions that appear at the bottom of page 748. Encourage students to compare and contrast Japanese culture with the culture of their native country.

WRITING FROM EXPERIENCE

WRITING A REPORT

The stories in Unit Six, "The Oral Tradition," gave you a glimpse of the land, government, culture, and wonderings of people in other countries. Some of the stories may have left you with questions. Through research, you can answer your questions and begin a journey of discovery.

GUIDED ASSIGNMENT
Write an I-Search Report The next few pages will help you write an I-Search report—a report that includes facts about both your topic and your research process.

1 Think About Folk Tales

Which stories from this unit were your favorites? Do they remind you of other folk tales you have read or heard, perhaps from your own or a friend's culture? Would you like to learn about the country a particular folk tale came from? What else would you like to know?

Examining the Stories Think about how the details in the unit's folk tales are related to culture—arts, language, customs, or beliefs. Are these details you would like to explore about a country?

Analyzing the Examples The items on these pages were gathered by a student who became interested in finding out more about Japan after reading "Three Strong Women." What ideas do the items make you want to investigate? What kinds of information could you learn from each item?

Japanese meals sometimes look more like art than like food!

Japanese Menu

Japanese Doll

How would the items on this page compare with similar items from your own culture? In what ways are the two cultures different? How are they the same?

748 UNIT SIX: THE ORAL TRADITION

PRINT AND MEDIA RESOURCES

UNIT SIX RESOURCE BOOK
Prewriting, p. 43
Elaboration, p. 44
Peer Response Guide, pp. 45–46
Revising and Proofreading, p. 47
Student Model, pp. 48–51
Rubric, p. 52

GRAMMAR MINI–LESSONS
Transparencies, pp. 33-34

WRITING MINI–LESSONS
Transparencies, p. 43
Copymasters, pp. 53, 56, 58–60

ACCESS FOR STUDENTS ACQUIRING ENGLISH
Reading and Writing Support

FORMAL ASSESSMENT
Guidelines for Writing Assessment

 LASERLINKS
Writing Springboard

---

748 THE LANGUAGE OF LITERATURE TEACHER'S EDITION

Newspaper Article

The Quake's *Shaken* Lives

KOBE, Japan, Jan. 21—The 1.4 million people who live in this city used to devote themselves to activities such as making steel, building ships, designing computers, running a port and raising children. But at 5:46 a.m. last Tuesday, in one horrifying instant, the fabric of their lives was torn.

The earthquake that rocked western Japan forced hundreds of thousands of people in this sleek city, an important commercial center, to confront scenes of chaos and destruction they never dreamed they would face. Residents of Kobe, who almost universally believed their region to be safe from the quakes that regularly hit many parts of the Japanese archipelago, found themselves heaved into a world of crushed buildings, raging fires and death on an appalling scale.

Paul Blustein, William Branigin, and Shigehiko Togo
from *The Washington Post*

I wonder how often Japan has earthquakes. Probably a lot, since there's a folk tale about them.

Travel Brochure

I heard that some of Japan's mountains are actually volcanoes.

❷ Choose Your Own Topic

Decide on the topic you want to explore—perhaps a country or culture featured in the unit or from your own background. You may even want to research one of the folk tales you read. Take a few minutes to freewrite what you already know about your topic. Then write what you'd like to learn.

- LASERLINKS
- WRITING SPRINGBOARD
- WRITING COACH

WRITING FROM EXPERIENCE   749

WRITING SPRINGBOARD
The Loch Ness Mystery Since 1933, newspapers have reported sightings of a "monster," 40–50 feet long, in a deep loch, or lake in north central Scotland. This short film shows the methods that some scientists are using to investigate this mystery.

Writing Prompt Write an I-Search report based on a topic shrouded in mystery. Use as many resources as you can think of to gather information about the topic. This could include encyclopedia entries, newspaper reports, or stories told by individuals based on their remembrances of an event.

Side B, Frame 28383

Teaching Strategy: MODELING

B Build on the previous activity by having students use the springboards on this page to generate their own writing topics. Arrange students in small groups. Provide each group with stick-on notes on which to write comments and questions about the models. Invite each group to share its reactions with the rest of the class. Discuss how the suggestions can be shaped into writing ideas.

Teaching Strategy: STUMBLING BLOCK

C Students often believe that topics for reports must be commonplace and, thus, dull. Explain that effective topics are anything but dull. Guide students to see that they can draw compelling topics from the models, from their personal experience, and from their reading. In addition, you may wish to encourage students to write a report on an aspect of their own ethnic tradition—for example, folk tales, cuisine, or holiday customs. Students who choose such a topic will often have firsthand information as well as access to people who can give them interesting facts.

THE LANGUAGE OF LITERATURE TEACHER'S EDITION   749

Research Skill:
ACCESSING INFORMATION

D Students often write a more detailed and descriptive report if they find a focus *after* they have done some preliminary research in a general source such as an encyclopedia. Explain to the class that finding a focus often depends on how much information writers gather during the initial research process and how they analyze and evaluate what they have discovered. If possible, allow students class time to locate, read, and analyze a brief encyclopedia article on their proposed topic.

Writing Skill: PURPOSE

E Remind students that there are four basic purposes for writing: to entertain, to persuade, to inform, and to express an opinion. Be sure students understand that writers often combine two or more purposes when they write. For example, informing and persuading are often combined, as are persuading and expressing an opinion. Guide students to set a purpose for their preliminary research and note taking.

CUSTOMIZING FOR
Less-Proficient Writers

F Inexperienced writers may be frustrated by the challenges of finding useful, valid information. Suggest that less-proficient and more-experienced writers work together in pairs as they use the library data base and other on-line sources.

PREWRITING

Researching Your Topic

The "I" in "I-Search" In an I-Search report, the experiences you have while researching are just as important as the information you are gathering. The steps on these pages will help you locate answers to the questions you have and to chart your progress along the way.

❶ Find a Focus

D

You may need to narrow the focus of your topic—for example, you can't cover *everything* about a country in a short report. To help you focus, try reading an encyclopedia article about your topic. Skim the sections to help you find subjects to zero in on.

E **Set a Purpose** Why do you care about your topic? Jot down your purpose for writing. This information can help you focus your research and will be included in your I-Search report.

Make a Research Plan Review your freewriting and list questions you want to answer. Let the list guide your research efforts.

❷ Dig for Information

The research process can uncover information you never thought to ask about. Below are some good sources.

- Check on-line services for information about your topic.
- Newspaper travel sections often describe the culture of a country.
- **F** Your teacher or librarian can help you identify private organizations and government agencies with information about your country.
- Museums provide a great deal of cultural information about countries.
- Neighbors, friends, or family members from the country you're exploring can also provide you with valuable information.

❸ Keep Track of Your Progress

What steps are you taking to find out what you need to know? What are you discovering along the way? To help you keep track of your experiences, you might record your ideas, accomplishments, and questions in an I-Search diary like the one on the opposite page.

750 UNIT SIX: THE ORAL TRADITION

Source cards for a magazine or newspaper article (top), for a book (middle), for an encyclopedia entry (bottom)

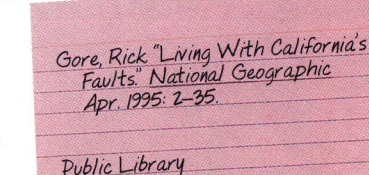

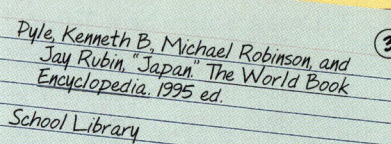

Mini-Lesson Study Skills

PARAPHRASING Suggest that students paraphrase all of the information they collect during the research stage in order to avoid plagiarizing. Provide students with the following steps for writing a paraphrase:

1. *Find the main idea.* Read the passage carefully to find the author's main idea. The main idea is often found in the introduction.
2. *List key details.* Jot down all the details and examples that support the main idea.
3. *Restate ideas in your own words.* Simplify material by replacing difficult words with easier ones.
4. *Edit and revise.* Proofread the paraphrase for errors in spelling, punctuation, capitalization, and grammar.

Remind students to credit all key sources, both quoted and paraphrased.

Application Have students work in small groups to write a paraphrase of the information on this page. Invite each group to share its results.

750 THE LANGUAGE OF LITERATURE TEACHER'S EDITION

4. Create Source Cards

Source cards, like the ones on page 750, can help you keep track of the sources you use in your research. List the publishing information as shown for each book or article on a separate index card, then number each card. The cards will help you create your List of Sources, which you will attach to the end of your report.

5. Take Notes

Many writers record the information they plan to use in their report on index cards like the ones below. Write the main idea of the note at the top of each card, along with the number you assigned the source on its source card. As you take notes, rewrite the information in your own words to avoid plagiarizing, or using other people's words without giving them credit. The SkillBuilder gives more tips on taking notes.

Note Cards

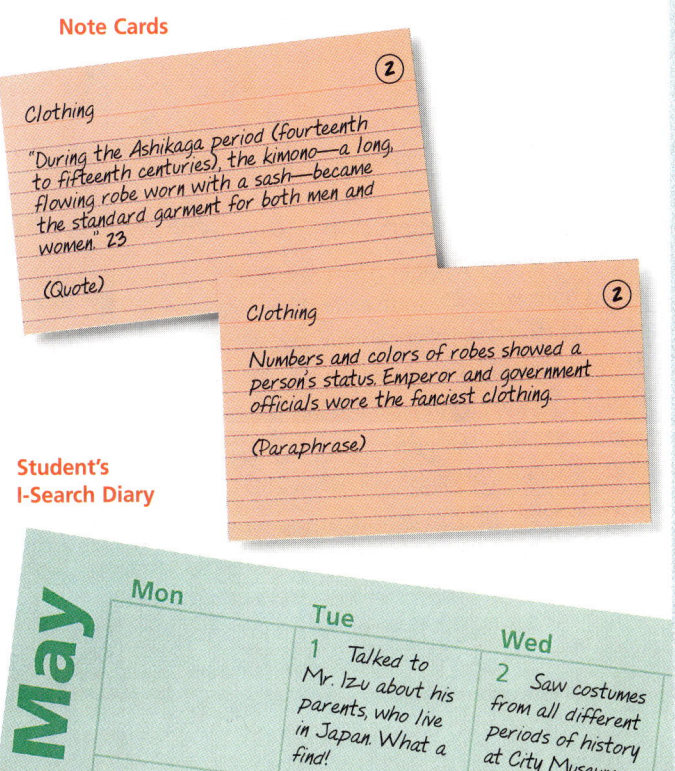

Student's I-Search Diary

SkillBuilder

 RESEARCH SKILLS

Taking Notes

Rewriting information helps you understand what you read. Here are some methods of taking notes on information you find.

Paraphrase Rewrite an author's ideas in your own words. You might list the key points or main ideas of a passage.

Quote If you find statements that are particularly well phrased, and you think you may want to use the exact words, copy the text word for word. Use quotation marks and write the page number of the source on your card.

APPLYING WHAT YOU'VE LEARNED
Try to use these methods of recording information as you take notes on your topic.

 WRITING HANDBOOK

For more information on note cards, see page 798 of the Writing Handbook.

THINK & PLAN

Reflecting on Your Ideas

1. Which questions from your research plan did you have problems with? Which were easily answered?
2. Did you refocus your topic as you researched? How? Why?

WRITING FROM EXPERIENCE **751**

Research Skill: TAKING NOTES

G Tell students that they can save time and space by using abbreviations on their source cards. Share these common abbreviations:

&	and
w/	with
Eng	English
y	why
=	equals
w/o	without
def	definition
re	regarding

Encourage students to use these and other established abbreviations as they create their source cards.

Teaching Strategy: STUMBLING BLOCK

H Knowing when to credit a source is difficult for many students. Explain that plagiarism is presenting someone else's words or ideas as your own. Tell students that they do not need to credit a source that provides general information or "common knowledge." Explore how "common knowledge" depends on the audience—that what is well-known to one audience may be unfamiliar to another. Caution students that they must credit a source that states original ideas.

SkillBuilder RESEARCH SKILLS

TAKING NOTES Most students find extracting information and taking notes very challenging. Some students mistakenly think that changing a few words is the same as paraphrasing. To teach students how to take notes, discuss the note cards on this page. Invite volunteers to point out how the writer expressed the main idea in his or her own words. Provide additional examples by having students work on their own or in small groups to paraphrase the newspaper article on page 749.

Application Suggest that students enter in a computer file the information on their source cards. Explain that using a computer will allow them to organize their notes, easily add information, and call up sources.

Additional Suggestions Tell students that they don't have to worry about grammar and punctuation in their notes but that they must spell the names of people and places correctly.

THE LANGUAGE OF LITERATURE TEACHER'S EDITION **751**

Speaking, Listening, and Viewing: ROUNDTABLE

I The format of an I-Search report provides an ideal opportunity for sharing through a roundtable. Arrange students in small groups around a table or desk, and have them pass around a paper and pencil. Direct each student, in turn, to write an aspect of his or her research process on the paper. Then have one group member read all the responses. Finally, encourage students to compare and contrast their experiences.

Writing Skill: OUTLINING

J Remind students to indent each subdivision of the outline, to capitalize the first word in each line, and to avoid using just a single subheading. Help students create an outline by discussing each aspect of the model on this page.

Teaching Strategy: MODELING

K Invite one volunteer to read the student's rough draft and another to read the peer comments. Ask students whether they agree with the peer reader's comment about the details and purpose. Ask them whether they think it is important to state the purpose, and have them explain why or why not. Then discuss why the peer editor suspects plagiarism and how the passage can be revised to avoid it.

DRAFTING

Sharing Your Experience

A Personal Touch What fascinating information did you learn? Which sources helped you the most, and which let you down? These pages will show you how to set up your report and combine the information you learned with your research experiences, both good and bad.

1 Organize Your Ideas

Before beginning your draft, you might want to sort your cards into groups of similar ideas and then use the groups to create an outline. This outline can help you see where you need more information and what notes don't really fit. The SkillBuilder on page 753 can help you create an outline.

Student's Outline

Introduction (purpose for writing about Japan)

I. Country's Size
   A. Number of islands
   B. Number of people (?)

II. Earthquakes
   A. Why they happen
   B. How many per year

III. Sumo Wrestling
   A. National heroes
   B. ?????

IV. Clothing
   A. Influence of West (?)
   B. Traditional costumes
      1. kimonos
      2. makeup

V. Government
   A. Emperor
   B. How it's like the U.S.

Conclusion (summary)

Student's Rough Draft

Exploring Japan

"Three Strong Women" is a really funny Japanese folk tale that is as enjoyable as a movie. After reading the story, I could picture what everything looked like: the countryside, the clothing, and the makeup the rich people wore. I wondered if I had imagined it right. I was curious if an emperor still ruled the country. I wondered how often Japanese people felt earthquakes. I really wanted to learn more about Japan, but I wasn't too excited about writing a paper on it. — leave this out

The first place I looked was the encyclopedia. I learned that the country of Japan is actually made up of thousands of islands, which form a curve that extends for about 1,200 miles, not just one big one, as I always thought! The encyclopedia article also explained that Japan has about 1,500 earthquakes a year! Most of them are so small they don't cause any damage, but bad ones happen every few years.

I had to find other sources to get more information on the subject I was most curious about: sumo wrestling. — explain this after sumo wrestling

Good details about your purpose and personal experience! A.C.

This doesn't sound like you. Have you paraphrased your source or is this a quote? A.C.

752 UNIT SIX: THE ORAL TRADITION

---

752 THE LANGUAGE OF LITERATURE **TEACHER'S EDITION**

❷ Write a Rough Draft

Let your outline guide you as you write your draft. Refer to your note cards for specific information about your topic, and your I-Search diary for details about your researching experiences. One student's rough draft is shown on the left.

Introduction You might begin by telling why you wanted to learn more about your topic. A brief anecdote or story explaining why you care about the topic is one way to do this.

Body As you present what you learned, explain the steps of your research as well. You might tell where you found information and what you felt like when you did or didn't locate answers to important questions. Focus on the experiences where you learned interesting things or had a strong reaction. Your writing can be personal and informal in this type of a report, but be sure your draft flows logically from one subject to the next.

Conclusion End your I-Search report by summarizing what this personal research experience meant to you. Did you come to a new understanding or appreciation of your topic? How did your feelings or ideas about the topic change?

❸ Rework and Share Your Draft

You chose your topic because it had special meaning for you. Be sure this meaning comes through in your report.

 **PEER RESPONSE**

When you feel ready for feedback, trade drafts with a classmate and ask questions like the following.

- Why do you think I chose to write about this topic?
- Does my report read smoothly from beginning to end? How might I rearrange parts to make it more logical?
- Do you now know more than you did about this topic? Which parts need more explanation?
- Could any part of my research process have been improved? How?

SkillBuilder

 RESEARCH SKILLS

Outlining Your Ideas
An outline like the one on page 752 can make drafting your report easier, because you have a plan to follow. To make an outline, look for main ideas, such as *earthquakes* and *clothing,* in the notes you have taken. List these ideas as headings next to Roman numerals. Then, beneath each main idea, list the details you want to include. Use capital letters for the more general details, then numbers and lowercase letters for finer details.

APPLYING WHAT YOU'VE LEARNED
Try using your note cards to create an outline. You might want to do some follow-up research to fill in any holes.

 WRITING HANDBOOK

For more information on outlining, see page 798 of the Writing Handbook.

RETHINK & EVALUATE

Preparing to Revise

1. Did your outline help you as you wrote your draft? Why or why not?
2. Did you have enough information as you drafted? Did you have too much? What would you change about the way you research next time?

WRITING FROM EXPERIENCE   753

CUSTOMIZING FOR
Less-Proficient Writers

L Suggest that students who are having difficulty writing a rough draft imagine that they are talking to a friend. Guide them to address all their comments to this unseen audience, to help them focus more directly on an audience and a purpose. Provide students with these drafting guidelines:

- Make sure each paragraph focuses on one idea.
- Support the main idea of each paragraph with specific details and examples; try to show instead of tell.
- Delete any information that is not related to the main idea of each paragraph.

Writing Skill:
USING THE COMPUTER

M Encourage students to write their rough draft on a computer. Explain that computer drafting makes reviewing and revising text easier. Explore how writers who draft on a computer are often willing to write freely because they know that it is easy to revise a computer document. Guide students to use The Writing Coach, which provides detailed guidelines for the drafting stage.

 SkillBuilder — **RESEARCH SKILLS**

OUTLINING YOUR IDEAS Explain that there are two main kinds of outlines: topic outlines and sentence outlines. Describe how a topic outline uses parallel words and phrases and how a sentence outline uses parallel sentences. Elicit from students that the model on page 752 is a topic outline because it uses words and phrases rather than sentences. You may also wish to point out that the writer used question marks to show the parts of the outline that were not complete; encourage students to use this technique to flag the parts of their outlines that they have yet to develop.

Application Arrange students in pairs to read each other's outline and suggest revisions.

Additional Suggestions To help students identify parts of their outlines that need additions or deletions, invite them to recast their topic outlines as sentence outlines or vice versa.

THE LANGUAGE OF LITERATURE TEACHER'S EDITION   **753**

Teaching Strategy:
STUMBLING BLOCK

N Students often have difficulty linking related ideas. Suggest that they look for places in their drafts where they can add transitional words or phrases to create stronger unity and coherence. Guide students to select the best transition to add in each instance.

Speaking, Listening and Viewing:
INTERVIEWING

O Since revising and editing techniques vary from writer to writer, students may gain helpful insights by interviewing their classmates about how they approach the revision stage in writing an I-Search report. Have pairs of students interview each other, using the following questions:
- What is your purpose in this report? Where is it stated in the report?
- What information is directly related to the topic? What information is irrelevant and should be omitted?
- What graphic aids can you add? Where will they be the most useful?

Teaching Strategy: MODELING

P Read to the class the model final report. As a class, discuss where the writer found information. Students can look through the text of the report or check the List of Sources to discover that the writer used *The World Book Encyclopedia,* books on Japan, places that teach judo, and a magazine article. Then ask students what other graphics would add more information to the report. They might suggest a map of Japan, for example.

REVISING & PUBLISHING

Pulling It All Together

The Final Product Think about your purpose for writing about your topic. What changes do you need to make to get that purpose across to your readers? Will you add personal experiences, or take out information that's not related? Do you want to include photographs, maps, graphs, or illustrations? Now's your chance to polish your draft.

1 Revise and Edit

The following points will help you finalize your I-Search report.

- Think about which of your peer suggestions you will use to make improvements to your report.
- Be sure you have used your own words or given credit to the proper source if you have included quotes.
- Use the Standards for Evaluation to help you balance information with personal experiences in your report.

2 Prepare Your Final Copy

Use the student model and the SkillBuilder on the opposite page to turn your source cards into a List of Sources. Attach the list to the end of your report.

> Where did this student find information about his topic?
>
> What other graphics might you add to this report to give more information?

754 UNIT SIX: THE ORAL TRADITION

Student's Final Draft

Exploring Japan

Keith Jensen
Mrs. Miller
Room 206
12 May 1997

Jensen 1

Exploring Japan

I read "Three Strong Women," a Japanese folktale that was as good as a movie. I had a picture in my mind of what everything looked like: the countryside, the clothing, and the makeup the rich people wore. I wondered if I had imagined it right. I was curious to know whether an emperor still ruled the country, and why the people did certain things like paint their faces white. I wondered how often Japanese people felt earthquakes, especially since there was a bad one in Kobe, Japan, two years ago.

The first place I looked for information was the encyclopedia, where I found some quick answers. For example, through an article in <u>The World Book</u>

Jensen 2

Encyclopedia, I learned that the country of Japan is actually four big islands and thousands of smaller islands. The four main islands are 1,200 miles long. Over 120 million people live on the islands of Japan!

Next, I went to the library at my school to find out about sumo wrestling. Most of the books about Japan didn't give much information on this sport except to say that almost all Japanese people are big fans. I tried calling places that teach judo to see if they knew where I could find information on the subject. Then my sister showed me an article about sumo wrestlers in a health magazine. It was really helpful. It told how all the wrestlers live and train together. They eat a traditional sumo stew made of rice, fish, and greens. Many wrestlers weigh over 400 pounds!

Jensen 5

List of Sources

Langone, John. In the Shogun's Shadow: Understanding a Changing Japan. Boston: Little, Brown, 1994.

Odijk, Pamela. The Japanese. Englewood Cliffs, N.J.: Silver Burdett, 1991.

Pyle, Kenneth B., Michael Robinson, and Jay Rubin. "Japan." The World Book Encyclopedia. 1995 ed.

Standards for Evaluation

An I-Search report
- shows the writer's strong personal interest in the topic
- presents information from several sources
- includes an account of the writer's research experiences
- concludes with the writer's personal reactions and observations

SkillBuilder

GRAMMAR FROM WRITING

Creating a List of Sources

Include a List of Sources with your I-Search report to show the sources of your information. To create your list, gather only the source cards you actually used in your report and alphabetize them by the authors' last names. The student model at the left shows how to record and punctuate the information on your List of Sources.

GRAMMAR HANDBOOK

For help with creating and editing a List of Sources, see page 842 of the Grammar Handbook and page 798 of the Writing Handbook.

Editing Checklist
- Have you correctly listed and punctuated the information on your List of Sources?
- Have you checked quotes to make sure they are accurate?

REFLECT & ASSESS

Evaluating Your Experience

1. How is an I-Search report different from other writing?
2. What did you learn about yourself from this assignment?

 PORTFOLIO Describe the research skills you used in this assignment. Attach your notes to your report and add them to your portfolio.

WRITING FROM EXPERIENCE 755

SkillBuilder — RESEARCH SKILLS

CREATING A LIST OF SOURCES Point out to students how the sources listed in the model on this page are arranged in alphabetical order by the author's last name. Using the third entry as an example, explain that only the first author's name is inverted when there are multiple authors because it is only this name that is used for alphabetizing. Mention that when there is no author, the entry is alphabetized by the first word of the title, not counting articles. Describe how the titles are underlined. Remind students that the entries are not numbered and that the second and all subsequent lines of each entry are indented.

Application Have students work in pairs to check each other's List of Sources to be sure they conform to the guidelines given here.

Teaching Strategy: MODELING

Q If students are handwriting their papers, remind them to make sure their handwriting distinguishes between capital and lowercase letters. Also remind students to underline or italicize the titles of longer works, such as books, movies, magazines, and newspapers, and to use quotation marks with shorter works, such as short stories, legends, folk tales, articles, and poems. Have volunteers find examples of correctly punctuated sources on the model final draft.

CUSTOMIZING FOR
Students Acquiring English

R Non-native speakers might have difficulty proofreading their reports, especially for spelling, grammar, and usage. Pair them with English-proficient students who can help them locate and correct errors. Suggest that partners use the Standards for Evaluation as they proofread.

PORTFOLIO

Encourage students to add to their portfolio any writing they feel shows their best effort.

Standards for Evaluation

Have students review their report for the following:

Ideas and Content
- shows the writer's strong personal interest in the topic
- presents information from several sources
- includes an account of the writer's research experiences
- concludes with the writer's personal reactions and observations

Structure and Form
- has a logical organization
- gives credit for the ideas and statements of others
- includes a List of Sources and credits sources correctly

Grammar, Usage, and Mechanics
- contains no more than two or three minor errors in grammar and usage
- contains no more than two or three minor errors in spelling, capitalization, and punctuation

THE LANGUAGE OF LITERATURE TEACHER'S EDITION 755

UNIT REVIEW

This feature allows students to reflect on what they have learned in Unit Six and to assess how well they understand what they have learned. This feature provides students with multiple opportunities for self-assessment, although you may wish to use some of the activities to informally assess specific skills such as speaking and listening or cooperative work.

Objectives

- To allow students to reflect on and assess their understanding of theme
- To allow students to reflect on and assess their understanding of the literary concept folklore and its varied cultural expressions
- To provide students with the opportunity to assess and build their portfolios

REFLECTING ON THEME

OPTION 1

Encourage students to review the selections in this unit as well as their notes for these selections in order to generate ideas for appropriate cover illustrations. Suggest students first sketch or outline possible book cover designs. Remind them to use a variety of media: crayons, pencils, paint, and/or photographs.

OPTION 2

Have students complete their charts as they skim each selection. In order to generate discussion among students, have them compare their charts and note the similarities and differences. Make sure students also consider the ways in which each selection can be connected to their own lives today.

OPTION 3

Have partners make a list of heroic qualities as they review the selections in this unit. They can then refer to this information when completing their webs. Encourage students to organize their thoughts and ideas in brief outlines before beginning to write their essays. Remind students to support their choices in their essays with details from the selections.

REFLECT & ASSESS

UNIT SIX: ACROSS TIME AND PLACE: THE ORAL TRADITION

In this unit, you discovered that tales from the past continue to delight, teach, and inspire readers and listeners. To show what you've learned, complete one or more of the options in each of the following sections.

REFLECTING ON THEME

OPTION 1 **Creating a Book Cover** Pretend that the selections in this unit are going to be bound together as a separate book. Design a book cover reflecting as much of the folklore you've read as possible. Include your work in a class exhibit of covers.

Consider . . .
- what cultures are represented in the unit
- which selections have memorable main characters
- what themes or other elements the selections share

OPTION 2 **Watching Behavior** Many characters in this unit have to consider or change their behavior. Use a chart like this one to analyze the actions of four of the characters. In a discussion with your classmates, point out lessons taught in the selections that are still being learned today.

Character	Behavior	Outcome of Behavior	What I Learned

OPTION 3 **Studying Heroes** With a partner, review the folklore you have read, identifying at least five characters who act as heroes. Use a web like this one to list qualities you consider heroic—such as bravery, wisdom, and unselfishness. Choose the character who you think displays the most heroic qualities, and write a brief essay explaining your choice.

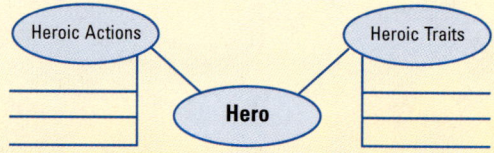

Self-Assessment: What themes—messages about human nature—were present in much of the folklore you've read? What one lesson in the folklore stands out the most for you? What similarities do you see between tales of past heroes and tales about heroes of today? Respond to these questions in your notebook.

REVIEWING LITERARY CONCEPTS

OPTION 1 **Looking at Folklore** This unit has introduced you to different types of folklore. Working with a small group of classmates, choose six selections that you think are most suitable for storytelling. Determine what tones of voice might be used for their characters, as well as what gestures, costumes, and props might be used in telling these selections. In diagrams like the one shown, list at least two storytelling suggestions for each selection. Combine your suggestions with your classmates' in a book of storytelling tips.

Tips for Storytelling — "The Bamboo Beads"
- Use an accented, friendly voice for the narrator
- Dress in brightly colored clothing.

Self-Assessment In order to help students answer the questions, you may wish to have students create Venn diagrams that compare the heroes of the past they read about in this unit with contemporary heroes they know. Suggest that students discuss in their notebooks some of the ways in which the lessons taught by the folklore will impact on their lives in the future.

OPTION 2 **Looking at Cultures** What insights into different cultures did you gain as you read the folklore in this unit? What did you learn about different customs? What similarities and differences between cultures did you see? For at least two pairs of selections in this unit, create Venn diagrams to compare the cultures represented in the selections. Then discuss the similarities and differences between the cultures with a small group of classmates. Present your group's conclusions to the entire class.

Self-Assessment: What do you understand about types of folklore that you didn't realize before completing these activities? What has reading about other cultures revealed to you about your own culture? Answer these questions in your notebook. Also explain why you think the oral tradition continues today.

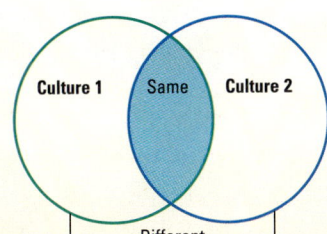

PORTFOLIO BUILDING

- **Connecting to the Literature** Select an example of your work for a Literature Connection that you would like to talk about. Perhaps you wrote a script based on a tale, wrote an instruction manual for a board game, or created a storyboard. In a note, comment on what you enjoyed about creating the work, and explain how the folklore you read inspired you. Add the example and the note to your portfolio.

- **Writing About Literature** Earlier in this unit, you wrote a literary review to explain what you liked and disliked about a story. Imagine that a local bookstore has asked you to design a poster to let people know about the story. What images might you draw to show how you felt about the story? What written information might you include? Attach your ideas and a rough design of the poster to your literary review.

- **Writing from Experience** In writing your I-search report, you had a chance to investigate a topic that is interesting to you. Think about your research process. Where did you find the best information? If you had to do another I-search report, which sources would you return to? Are there other places you might look for information? Include your thoughts with your report if you decide to keep it in your portfolio.

- **Personal Choice** Review all of your work for this unit, including Literature Connections, Social Studies Connections, Art Connections, and Comparing Cultures projects. Select written work or project that you think best captures your response to the folklore you read. Write a note explaining what you learned from the writing or project. Attach the note to the writing or project evaluation, and place both in your portfolio.

Self-Assessment: At this point, your portfolio must be bulging with all of the material you've collected. Which pieces best reflect how you've grown as a writer? Look through your portfolio and identify the pieces that show the greatest development of your writing skills. Clip them together with a note in which you review your portfolio.

SETTING GOALS

As you completed the reading and writing activities in this unit, you probably found certain selections and types of writing that you really liked. Which author's work would you like to find out more about? Which cultures are you curious enough about to continue to explore? Write any goals you have on an index card. Display the card on a bulletin board with those of your classmates.

REFLECT & ASSESS 757

REVIEWING LITERARY CONCEPTS

OPTION 1

Have each small group read through the six selections together and create a list of tones of voice, gestures, costumes, and props that would be suitable to use when reading each story aloud. Students can then refer to these data when completing their diagrams.

OPTION 2

Have students first skim their chosen selections and jot down their thoughts and impressions of the culture represented. Students may wish to create and complete charts that compare and contrast the cultures. They can then refer back to this information when creating their Venn diagrams.

Self-Assessment Encourage students to review the selections in this unit as well as the notes they took while reading these selections to help them answer these questions. Have students list in their notebooks some of the purposes they think the oral tradition serves in their own lives.

PORTFOLIO BUILDING

You may wish to help students choose options or modify options for them that best suit the needs you have established for the class. Have students review any notes they might have attached to previous drafts or to final products as they reflect on and assess their development and progress.

Self-Assessment Students should consider with which kinds of pieces they feel most comfortable and with which pieces they would like to have more practice. Suggest that students review their portfolio work and look at the areas which involved the most revision. Ask students to identify how their writing in these particular areas changed and improved over time.

SETTING GOALS

In order to help students answer these questions and set future goals, have them consider which selections had the greatest impact on them and why they think they were affected by them.

THE LANGUAGE OF LITERATURE TEACHER'S EDITION 757

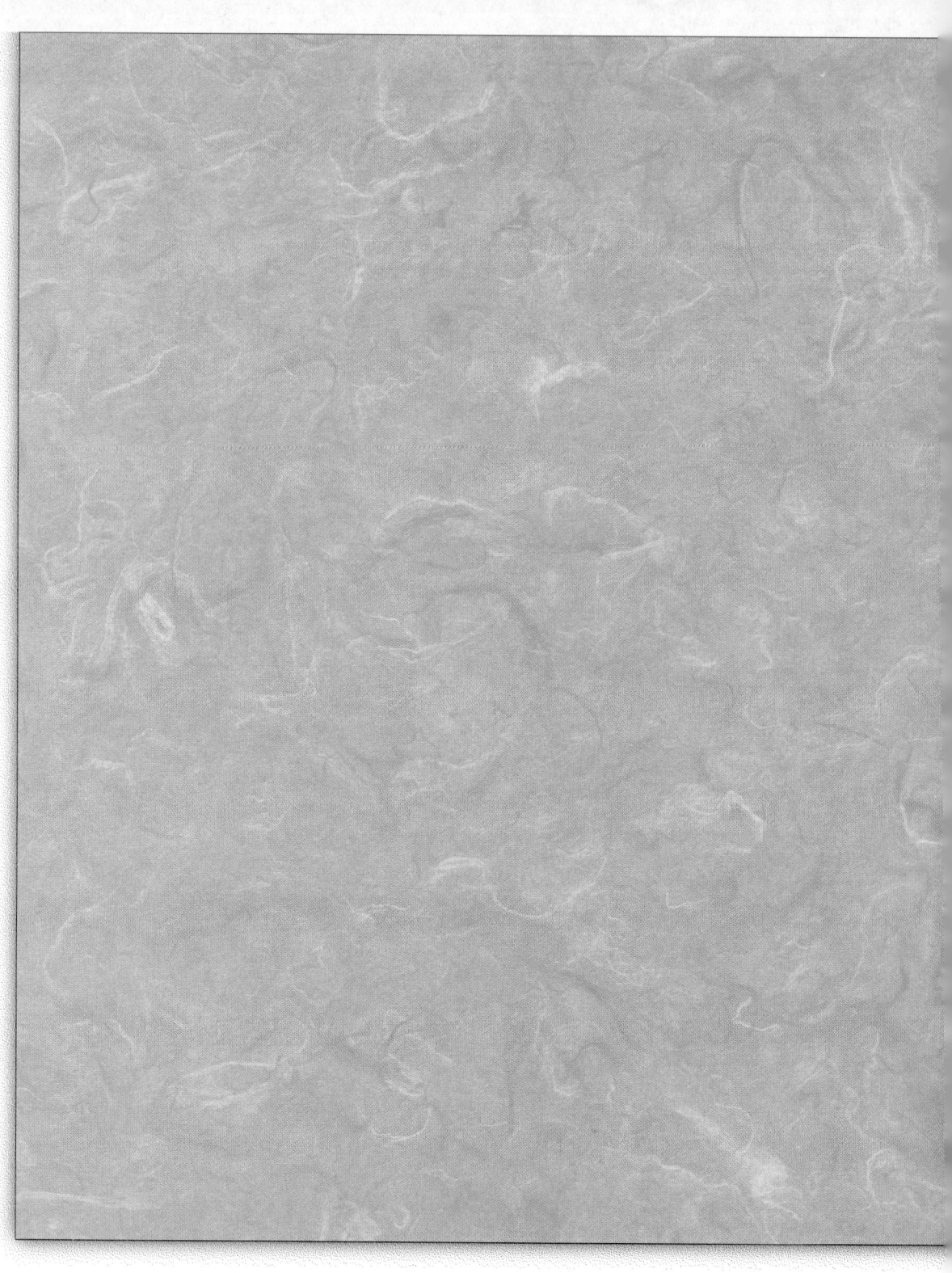

Student Resource Bank

Words to Know Access Guide 760

Literary Handbook
Reading Terms and Literary Concepts 762

Writing Handbook
1 The Writing Process 772
2 Building Blocks of Good Writing 778
3 Narrative Writing 788
4 Explanatory Writing 790
5 Persuasive Writing 796
6 Research Report Writing 798

Multimedia Handbook
1 Getting Information Electronically 802
2 Word Processing 804
3 Using Visuals 807
4 Creating a Multimedia Presentation 809

Grammar Handbook
1 Writing Complete Sentences 812
2 Making Subjects and Verbs Agree 815
3 Using Nouns and Pronouns 822
4 Using Modifiers Effectively 830
5 Using Verbs Correctly 835
6 Correcting Capitalization 839
7 Correcting Punctuation 843
8 Grammar Glossary 852

Words to Know: Access Guide

abandon (646)
absurd (616)
admonishingly (325)
aggression (70)
agility (334)
anxiety (99)
apt (58)
ardent (58)
audacious (220)
audible (415)
banish (26)
bazaar (24)
blissful (492)
bondage (265)
camouflage (67)
chaos (260)
clamber (716)
clamor (401)
clan (24)
client (407)
coexistence (68)
commercial (407)
commitment (408)
compassion (730)
compressed (67)
confirm (421)
confrontation (336)
consequently (294)
console (353)
consolidate (531)
consoling (599)
conspirator (580)
consume (231)
contemporary (331)
contrary (350)
counter (372)
credibility (416)
cunning (324)
curtly (668)
customary (466)
customs (363)
debris (230)
deceit (397)
decree (24)
depleted (33)
deprivation (56)
deprive (217)

descendant (294)
desolate (612)
despair (488)
destiny (615)
destitute (730)
detest (350)
devise (217)
devour (653)
discreet (415)
dislodging (131)
dispense (219)
dissuade (472)
distorted (714)
diverted (421)
domain (593)
dominant (72)
dread (217)
drudgery (331)
dumbfounded (239)
dwindle (730)
dynasty (260)
elegant (71)
elude (738)
embrace (237)
emit (696)
endure (97)
envision (493)
erect (713)
eruption (129)
esteemed (613)
evasive (362)
exceed (231)
exclusive (332)
exile (642)
expedition (44)
exploit (466)
extravagantly (730)
fanatical (495)
fate (713)
feeble (718)
ferocious (649)
fidgety (492)
fiend (583)
frenzied (186)
fume (239)
fumigate (369)
gratification (462)

gravely (644)
grudging (96)
harass (334)
harpoon (41)
hoard (614)
hover (679)
hurtle (69)
illiterate (394)
illuminate (419)
immortal (712)
immortality (530)
inadvertently (732)
indifferent (219)
indignantly (712)
indolent (664)
induce (401)
infinite (232)
inhabitant (260)
insensitive (334)
insignificant (528)
insolent (745)
insufferable (736)
intact (474)
intricate (531)
intrusion (217)
laden (219)
lagoon (41)
lethal (370)
luminous (71)
magnification (68)
maneuver (421)
margin (372)
mascot (188)
maze (640)
meager (645)
menace (121)
menial (57)
mimicking (407)
mocking (688)
monopoly (337)
morosely (392)
mortally (231)
mute (351)
muting (433)
novelty (120)
obscure (711)
obsessed (530)

obstinacy (713)
oceanarium (67)
ominous (365)
peal (238)
phosphorus (45)
pious (218)
plush (332)
pompous (218)
ponder (27)
possess (322)
poverty-stricken (293)
practical (295)
preceding (461)
predator (119)
premise (266)
preservation (532)
prestige (491)
procedure (266)
proclaim (646)
prop (33)
properly (321)
proposition (58)
prosper (266)
pursue (493)
quest (607)
quiver (33)
ravishing (668)
rear (295)
reassure (348)
rebellious (490)
reef (41)
refrain (488)
relentless (33)
repentance (693)
reproduction (531)
resentful (57)
reservation (267)
restore (134)
resume (417)
reunion (152)
revelation (421)
revulsion (399)
rival (642)
rummaging (121)
sacred (724)
salvaging (335)
saunter (391)

savoring (98)	stereotype (172)	tedious (475)	tyranny (57)
scavenging (119)	stoop (187)	tenement (192)	tyrant (532)
scornful (395)	stupendous (416)	thrashing (186)	unique (411)
scurry (648)	stupor (369)	thrive (615)	unparalleled (532)
sedately (99)	subside (697)	throng (578)	vague (489)
sentinel (475)	succulent (744)	tolerate (695)	validate (61)
shrine (128)	sufficient (461)	torrent (238)	vanquish (615)
smirk (33)	sullen (391)	trade (321)	vapor (133)
sodden (367)	surpass (530)	transition (363)	wily (736)
stamina (54)	surveyor (57)	trek (262)	
stature (617)	systematically (472)	tumult (238)	
status (261)	taunt (668)	turmoil (391)	

Pronunciation Key

Symbol	Examples	Symbol	Examples	Symbol	Examples
ă	at, gas	m	man, seem	v	van, save
ā	ape, day	n	night, mitten	w	web, twice
ä	father, barn	ng	sing, anger	y	yard, lawyer
âr	fair, dare	ŏ	odd, not	z	zoo, reason
b	bell, table	ō	open, road, grow	zh	treasure, garage
ch	chin, lunch	ô	awful, bought, horse	ə	awake, even, pencil, pilot, focus
d	dig, bored	oi	coin, boy		
ĕ	egg, ten	o͝o	look, full	ər	perform, letter
ē	evil, see, meal	o͞o	root, glue, through		
f	fall, laugh, phrase	ou	out, cow		**Sounds in Foreign Words**
g	gold, big	p	pig, cap	KH	German ich, auch; Scottish loch
h	hit, inhale	r	rose, star		
hw	white, everywhere	s	sit, face	N	French entre, bon, fin
ĭ	inch, fit	sh	she, mash	œ	French feu, cœur; German schön
ī	idle, my, tried	t	tap, hopped		
îr	dear, here	th	thing, with	ü	French utile, rue; German grün
j	jar, gem, badge	*th*	then, other		
k	keep, cat, luck	ŭ	up, nut		
l	load, rattle	ûr	fur, earn, bird, worm		

Stress Marks

′ This mark indicates that the preceding syllable receives the primary stress. For example, in the word *language,* the first syllable is stressed: lăng′gwĭj.

′ This mark is used only in words in which more than one syllable is stressed. It indicates that the preceding syllable is stressed, but somewhat more weakly than the syllable receiving the primary stress. In the word *literature,* for example, the first syllable receives the primary stress, and the last syllable receives a weaker stress: lĭt′ər-ə-cho͝or′.

Adapted from *The American Heritage Dictionary of the English Language, Third Edition;* Copyright © 1992 by Houghton Mifflin Company. Used with the permission of Houghton Mifflin Company.

Reading Terms and Literary Concepts

Act An act is a major unit of action in a play. *The Hobbit,* for example, has two acts. An act may be divided into smaller sections, called **scenes.**

Alliteration Alliteration is a repetition of consonant sounds at the beginning of words. Poets and songwriters use alliteration to emphasize certain words. Alliteration can also add a musical quality. Note the repetition of the *l* and *r* sound in this line from "The Cremation of Sam McGee":

> In the long, long night, by the lone firelight, while the huskies, round in a ring . . .

Analysis Analysis is a process of breaking something down into its parts so that they can be studied individually. In analyzing a poem, for example, one might look at such elements as form, rhyme, rhythm, figurative language, imagery, mood, and theme.

Anecdote An anecdote is a short, entertaining account of a person or an event. Anecdotes are often included in larger works to amuse or to make a point. In the excerpt from *Woodsong,* Gary Paulsen tells an anecdote about his encounter with a bear to point out that humans must respect the wildness of nature.

Audience The audience of a piece of writing is the particular group of people that the writer is addressing. A writer considers his or her audience when deciding on a subject, a purpose for writing, and a style in which to write.

Author's Purpose An author's purpose is his or her reason for creating a particular work. The purpose may be to entertain, to inform, to express an opinion, or to persuade readers to do or believe something. An author may have more than one purpose for writing, but usually one is the most important.

Autobiography An autobiography is the true story of a person's life, told by that person. Because autobiographies are written about real people and events, they are a form of nonfiction. Autobiographies are normally written from the first-person point of view. The excerpts from *Woodsong* and *The Lost Garden* are examples of autobiography. Shorter autobiographical writings include journals, diaries, and memoirs.

Biography A biography is the true story of a person's life, written by someone else. Biographies are usually written from the third-person point of view. "Matthew Henson at the Top of the World" is an example of biography.

Cast of Characters In the script of a play, a cast of characters is a list of all the characters in the play. It is usually found

762 LITERARY HANDBOOK

at the beginning of the script, and the characters are usually listed in the order they appear. There is a cast of characters at the beginning of *A Shipment of Mute Fate.*

Cause and Effect Two events are related as cause and effect if one brings about, or causes, the other. The event that happens first is the cause; the one that follows is the effect. Writers sometimes signal cause-and-effect relationships with words and phrases such as *because, next, therefore, since, so that,* and *in order that.* This sentence from Woodsong deals with a cause and its effect: "Because we feed processed meat to the dogs, there is always the smell of meat over the kennel."

Character Each person, animal, or imaginary creature in a work of literature is called a character. The most important characters are called **main characters.** Less important characters are called **minor characters.** In "The School Play," Robert is the main character, and Belinda and the other characters are minor characters.

Characterization The ways in which writers create and develop characters' personalities are known as characterization. A writer can develop a character in four basic ways: (1) by physically describing the character, (2) by presenting the character's thoughts, speech, and actions, (3) by presenting the thoughts, speech, and actions of other characters, and (4) by directly commenting on the character's nature.

Chronological Order Chronological order is the order in which events happen in time. In some stories, events are related in chronological order; other stories move forward and backward in time.

Clarifying The process of stopping while reading, to quickly review what has happened and to look for answers to questions, is called clarifying. It helps readers draw conclusions about what is suggested but not directly stated in the writing.

Climax In the plot of a story or play, the climax is the point of greatest interest. At the climax, the outcome of the story becomes clear. The climax of "Tuesday of the Other June," for example, occurs when June T. says "No" to the Other June with such forceful determination that the astonished bully leaves her alone.
See also **Plot.**

Comparison To point out what two or more things have in common is to make a comparison. Writers use comparisons to make ideas and details clearer to readers. In "Eleven," for example, the process of growing older is compared to little wooden dolls that fit together, one inside another.
See also **Metaphor** *and* **Simile.**

Concrete Poetry. *See* **Form.**

Conflict Conflict is a struggle between opposing forces. Almost every story and play is built around a conflict that the main character faces. A conflict may be external or internal. **External conflict** is a struggle between a character and an outside force, such as society, a force of nature, or another character. In the excerpt from *Woodsong,* for example, Gary Paulsen faces an external conflict with a bear. **Internal conflict,** on the other hand, is a struggle within a character's mind. It may occur when the character has to make a difficult decision or deal with opposing feelings. Selo's uncertainty, in "Cricket in the Road," about whether to make up with his friends is an example of internal conflict.
See also **Plot.**

Connecting When readers relate the content of a literary work to what they already know or have experienced, they are making connections.

Connecting helps readers identify with the experiences of the characters. For example, when they read Sandra Cisneros's story "Eleven," readers may remember times when they were embarrassed or falsely accused.

Context Clues Unfamiliar words are often surrounded by context clues—words or phrases that can help readers infer their meaning. A context clue may be a definition, a synonym, an example, or a comparison or contrast.

Contrast To contrast is to point out differences between things. Note how the narrator of "The All-American Slurp" contrasts Chinese and American eating habits in the following sentence: "In fact we didn't use individual plates at all but picked up food from the platters in the middle of the table and brought it directly to our rice bowls."

Couplet A couplet is a rhymed pair of lines in a poem. The poem "Barbara Frietchie" consists entirely of couplets.

Description Description is the process by which a writer creates a picture, in words, of a scene, an event, or a character. To create descriptions, writers choose details carefully—usually details that appeal to readers' senses of sight, sound, smell, touch, and taste. Note the details in this passage from "My Friend Flicka," which describes the view outside Kennie's window:

> The hill opposite the house, covered with arrow-straight jack pines, was sharply etched in the thin air of the eight-thousand-foot altitude. Where it fell away, vivid green grass ran up to meet it; and over range and upland poured the strong Wyoming sunlight that stung everything into burning color.

Dialogue The words that characters speak aloud are called dialogue. Dialogue moves a plot forward and reveals the personalities of the characters. In a play, dialogue is the main way the writer tells the story. The dialogue in fiction is usually set off with quotation marks. No quotation marks are used for the dialogue in plays.

Drama A drama, or play, is a form of literature meant to be performed before an audience. The story is presented through the dialogue and the actions of the characters. The written form of a play is known as a **script.** A script usually includes **dialogue,** a **cast of characters,** and **stage directions** that give specific instructions about performing the play.

Essay An essay is a short work of nonfiction that deals with a single subject. Essays are often found in newspapers and magazines. The purpose of an essay may be to express ideas or feelings, to analyze a topic, to inform, to entertain, or to persuade. "The Mushroom" is an essay that expresses ideas.

Evaluating Evaluating is the process of judging the worth of something or someone. In evaluating a literary work, you might focus on the elements found in that type of work—for example, the plot, setting, characters, and theme of a work of fiction. You can also evaluate a work by comparing and contrasting it with similar works.

External Conflict. See **Conflict.**

Fable A fable is a brief story that teaches a lesson about life. In many fables, the characters are animals that act and speak like human beings. A fable often ends with a moral—a statement that summarizes its lesson. "The Disobedient Child" is an example of a fable.

764 LITERARY HANDBOOK

Fact and Opinion A fact is a statement that can be proved, such as "Mars is the fourth planet from the sun." An opinion, in contrast, is a statement that expresses a person's feelings, such as "Mars is the most beautiful planet." Opinions cannot be proved.

Fantasy Literature that contains at least one fantastic or unreal element is called fantasy. The setting of a work of fantasy might be a totally imaginary world, or it might be a realistic place where very unusual or impossible things happen. "The Enchanted Raisin" is an example of fantasy because it presents a person who turns into a raisin.

Fiction Literature that tells about imaginary people, places, or events is called fiction. In some works of fiction, the entire story is made up; in others, the story is based in part on real people or events. Fiction includes both **short stories** and **novels.** A short story can usually be read in one sitting. Novels are longer and tend to be more complex.

Figurative Language In figurative language, words are used to express more than their dictionary meaning. Figurative language conveys vivid images to the minds of readers. In this passage from "The Circuit," note how the figurative language helps create a picture of working in the fields:

> The sun kept beating down. The buzzing insects, the wet sweat, and the hot dry dust made the afternoon seem to last forever. Finally the mountains around the valley reached out and swallowed the sun.

See also **Metaphor, Personification,** *and* **Simile.**

Folk Tale A folk tale is a simple story that has been passed down from generation to generation by word of mouth. Folk tales are usually about people, animals, or occurrences in nature and are usually set in times long past. Their plots often include supernatural elements, like the talking animals in "Why Monkeys Live in Trees" or the granting of wishes in "The Three Wishes."

Foreshadowing A hint about an event that will occur later in a story is called foreshadowing. An example of foreshadowing occurs in the opening lines of *A Shipment of Mute Fate,* when the main character, Chris, warns the audience that a disturbing event will take place: "But all at once in the midst of those peaceful surroundings, a cold chill gripped me, and I shivered with sudden dread—dread of the thing I was doing, and was about to do!"

Form The form of a poem is the shape the words and lines make on the page. Occasionally, a poet uses the form of a poem to emphasize the poem's meaning. In **concrete poetry,** for example, the poem's shape reflects its subject. Note how the lines in Dorthi Charles's poem "Concrete Cat" resemble the parts of a cat.

Free Verse Poetry without regular patterns of rhyme or rhythm is called free verse. Free verse often sounds like conversation. "Another Mountain" is an example of a poem written in free verse.

Generalization A generalization is a statement about a whole group. Generalizations may be untrue if they are too broad or not based on fact. In "The All-American Slurp," for example, Meg's statement "All Americans slurp" is a generalization. The word *all* in this generalization makes the statement untrue.

Genre Literature is normally divided into four main categories, or genres: **fiction, nonfiction, poetry,** and **drama.**

Haiku Haiku is a traditional form of Japanese poetry. A haiku normally has three lines and describes a single moment, feeling, or thing. In a traditional haiku, the first and third lines contain five syllables each, and the second line contains seven syllables.

Humor The quality that makes something seem funny or amusing is called humor. Writers can create humor by using exaggeration, amusing descriptions, sarcasm, witty dialogue, and other devices. For example, Isaac Bashevis Singer uses Lyzer's ridiculous economies to create humor in "Shrewd Todie and Lyzer the Miser."

Imagery Words and phrases that appeal to readers' senses are referred to as imagery. Writers usually try to describe characters, places, and events in ways that help readers imagine how they look, feel, smell, sound, and taste. Note the imagery in Raymond R. Patterson's haiku "Glory, Glory . . .":

> Across Grandmother's knees
> A kindly sun
> Laid a yellow quilt.

Inference An inference is a logical guess based on evidence. A good reader makes inferences, or draws conclusions, as he or she reads—trying to figure out more than the words say. The evidence may be facts the writer provides, or it may be experiences from the reader's own life. The end of "The Adoption of Albert," for example, requires readers to make an inference about what the coffee contains.

Internal Conflict. See **Conflict.**

Interview An interview is a meeting in which one person asks another about personal matters, professional matters, or both. Interviews may be tape-recorded, filmed, or recorded in writing. The excerpt from *Talking with Artists* is based on an interview.

Legend A legend is a story that is handed down from the past and tells about something that really happened or someone who really lived. Legends often mix fact and fiction. "The White Buffalo Calf Woman and the Sacred Pipe" is an example of a Native American legend.

Main Character. See **Character.**

Main Idea A main idea is a central idea that a writer is trying to get across. It may be the central idea of an entire work or the thought expressed in the topic sentence of a paragraph. (A topic sentence may be found at the beginning, middle, or end of a paragraph.) A writer may need to use several paragraphs to develop a main idea. In one paragraph of "Chinatown," Laurence Yep begins by stating the paragraph's main idea in a topic sentence and, after supporting the idea with examples, concludes with a restatement of it:

> Moreover, my lack of Chinese made me an outsider in Chinatown—sometimes even among my friends. . . . It was as if we belonged to two different worlds.

Memoir. See **Autobiography.**

Metaphor A metaphor is a comparison of two things that have some quality in common. Unlike a simile, a metaphor does not contain a word such as *like, as, than,* or *resembles.* For example, in *A Shipment of Mute Fate,* Chris uses the following metaphor: "Fear was a heavy fog in the lungs of all of us."

766 LITERARY HANDBOOK

Minor Character. *See* **Character.**

Mood A mood is a feeling that a literary work conveys to readers. Writers carefully choose words and phrases to create moods like sadness, excitement, and anger. In "My Friend Flicka," for example, a mood of deep sadness is created when it appears that Flicka will die in the stream.

Myth A myth is a traditional story that explains how something came to be. Some myths explain the origin of the world or of people. Others explain elements of nature or social customs. The characters in myths are often gods and human heroes with supernatural abilities. Because myths have been handed down from one generation to the next for a long time, their original authors are unknown. "Wings" is a retelling of a myth of ancient Greece.

Narrative Writing that tells a story is called a narrative. The events in a narrative may be real or imagined. Narratives that deal with real events include autobiographies and biographies. Fictional narratives include myths, short stories, novels, and narrative poems.

Narrative Poetry Narrative poetry is poetry that tells a story. Like any story, a narrative poem contains a setting, characters, and a plot. It may also contain such elements of poetry as rhyme, rhythm, imagery, and figurative language. "The Walrus and the Carpenter" is an example of a narrative poem.

Narrator A narrator is the teller of a story. Sometimes a story's narrator is a character who takes part in the action; in other cases, the narrator is an outside voice. In "The Scribe," for example, the narrator is James, the main character. "The School Play," in contrast, is narrated by an outside voice.
See also **Point of View.**

Nonfiction Writing that tells about real people, places, and events is called nonfiction. There are two main types of nonfiction. **Informative nonfiction** provides factual information. Newspaper and magazine articles, pamphlets, history and science textbooks, and encyclopedia articles are examples of informative nonfiction. **Literary nonfiction** reads much like fiction, except that the characters, setting, and plot are real rather than imaginary.
See also **Autobiography, Biography,** *and* **Essay.**

Novel A novel is a work of fiction that is longer and more complex than a short story. In a novel, the setting, the plot, and the characters are developed in detail. The plot usually focuses on the actions and personalities of a group of characters.

Onomatopoeia Onomatopoeia is the use of words whose sound suggests their meaning. The words *bang* and *hiss* are examples of onomatopoeia. The onomatopoetic words in "Analysis of Baseball" include *thuds, pow,* and *thwack*.

Personification The giving of human qualities to an animal, object, or idea is known as personification. In "Why Monkeys Live in Trees," the animals are personified, since they act and speak like human beings.

Play. *See* **Drama.**

Plot The series of events in a story is called the story's plot. A plot usually centers around a conflict—a problem faced by the main character. In a typical plot, the action that the characters take to solve the problem builds toward a **climax,** the turning point of the story. At that point, or shortly afterward, the problem is solved and the story ends.

Poetry Poetry is a type of literature in which ideas, images, and feelings are expressed in few words. Poets carefully select words for their sounds and meanings, combining the words in imaginative ways to present feelings, pictures, experiences, and themes vividly. In poetry, the images appeal to readers' senses, as do elements of sound, such as alliteration, rhythm, and rhyme. Most poetry is written in lines, which may be grouped in stanzas.

Point of View Every story is told from a particular point of view, or perspective. Usually, a story is told from either the **first-person** or the third-person point of view. In a story told from the first-person point of view, the narrator is a character in the story and uses pronouns like *I, me,* and *we.* "Eleven" is an example of a story told from the first-person point of view. A story told from the **third-person** point of view has a narrator who is outside the story and uses pronouns such as *he, she,* and *they.* "Aaron's Gift" is told from the third-person point of view.

Predicting Using what you already know to guess what might happen in the future is called predicting. Good readers gather information as they read. They combine that information with their own knowledge and experience to predict what might happen next.

Primary Source The information that writers of nonfiction present comes from various kinds of sources. A primary source conveys direct, first-hand knowledge. "My First Dive with the Dolphins" is a primary source because it is an account of Don C. Reed's own personal experience.
See also **Secondary Source.**

Questioning The process of asking questions when reading is called questioning. As they read, good readers ask questions in an effort to understand characters and events. They then look for answers to their questions.

Radio Play A radio play is a drama that is written specifically to be broadcast over the radio. Because the audience cannot see a radio play, sound effects are used to help listeners imagine the setting and action. The stage directions in the play's script indicate the sound effects. A Shipment of Mute Fate is an example of a radio play.

Repetition Repetition is the use of a sound, word, or phrase more than once. Writers use repetition to bring certain ideas, sounds, or feelings to readers' attention. For example, in the poem "Chang McTang McQuarter Cat," the speaker repeats the words *one part* frequently as he presents the qualities of the cat.
See also **Alliteration** *and* **Rhyme.**

Rhyme Rhyme is a repetition of sounds at the ends of words. In poetry, rhyme that occurs within a line is called **internal rhyme.** Rhyme that occurs at the end of lines is called **end rhyme.** Note both the internal rhymes and the end rhyme in these lines from "The Cremation of Sam McGee":

> Now a promise <u>made</u> is a debt <u>unpaid,</u> and the trail has its own stern <u>code.</u>
> In the days to <u>come,</u> though my lips were <u>dumb,</u> in my heart how I cursed that <u>load.</u>

Rhyme Scheme The pattern of rhymes in a poem is called the poem's rhyme scheme. A rhyme scheme can be described by using a different letter of the alphabet to represent each rhyming sound. Note the rhyme scheme of the first four lines of "The Quarrel":

768 LITERARY HANDBOOK

I quarreled with my brother,	a
I don't know what about,	b
One thing led to another	a
And somehow we fell out.	b

Rhythm The rhythm of a line of poetry is the pattern of stressed and unstressed syllables in the line. When a rhythm is repeated throughout a poem, the poem is said to have a regular beat. Note the regular rhythm in the following lines from "The Walrus and the Carpenter." (The ´ mark indicates a stressed syllable. The ˘ mark indicates an unstressed syllable.)

> The Walrus and the Carpenter
> Were walking close at hand:
> They wept like anything to see
> Such quantities of sand

Scene In a play, a scene is a section that presents events taking place in a single setting. A new scene begins whenever the story calls for a change in time or place. In The Hobbit, for example, each act contains four scenes.

Science Fiction Science fiction is fiction that is based on real or possible scientific developments. Although much science fiction is set in the future, the problems that the characters face may be similar to real problems that people face today. "User Friendly," a story about a computer that has a mind of its own, is an example of science fiction.

Secondary Source The information that writers of nonfiction present comes from various kinds of sources. A secondary source is one that conveys indirect, secondhand knowledge. "Matthew Henson at the Top of the World" is a secondary source, since the information it contains comes from Jim Haskins's reading and research.

See also **Primary Source.**

Sensory Details Words and phrases that help readers see, hear, taste, smell, and feel what a writer is describing are called sensory details. Note the sensory details used to present the fall of Icarus in this passage from "Wings":

> He passed into the realm of the sun. Too late he felt the wax run down his arms; too late he smelled the singe of feathers. Surprised, he hung solid in the air. Then, like a star in nova, he tumbled from the sky, down, down, down into the waiting sea.

See also **Description** and **Imagery.**

Sequence The order in which events occur or ideas are presented is called a sequence. In a narrative, events are usually presented in chronological order—the order in which they happened. A writer may use clue words and phrases—such as then, until, after a while, and finally—to help readers understand the sequence of events.

Setting The setting of a story, poem, or play is the time and place of the action. The time may be past, present, or future. The place may be real or imaginary. In some stories, including many fables, settings may not be clearly defined. In other stories, however, settings play an important part. For example, the desert setting of "Nadia the Willful" plays an important part in the story's action and helps to create its mood.

Setting a Purpose The process of establishing specific reasons to read a work is called setting a purpose. Readers can look at a work's title, headings and subheadings, and illustrations to guess what the work may be about. Then they can use their guesses to guide their reading, discovering whether their ideas match the actual content of the work.

Short Story A short story is a work of fiction that can generally be read in one sitting. Like other works of fiction, short stories contain characters, plots, settings, and themes. The plot of a short story usually involves one main conflict. "The Secret of the Wall" is an example of a short story.

Simile A simile is a comparison of two things that have some quality in common. Unlike a metaphor, a simile contains a word such as *like, as, resembles,* or *than.* Note the simile in this sentence from "The Bamboo Beads": "That night the moon was round and white as my Sunday hat."

Skimming Skimming is the process of reading quickly to get the general idea of a work. It involves reading titles, headings, words in special print, and the first sentence of each paragraph.

Speaker In a poem, the speaker is the voice that talks to the reader—like the narrator in a work of fiction. The speaker is not always the poet, but the speaker may express the feelings of the poet.

Stage Directions In the script of a play, the instructions to the performers, director, and stage crew are called stage directions. They usually appear in italic type and within parentheses. Stage directions provide suggestions about such things as scenery, lighting, music, and sound effects. They may also tell performers how to move and how to speak their lines. Note the stage directions in this passage from *Damon and Pythias.*

Damon (*calm and firm*). I have faith in my friend. I know he will return.

King (*mocking*). We shall see!

(Sound: Iron door shut and locked.)

Stanza A group of lines within a poem is called a stanza. Stanzas are somewhat like paragraphs in stories. "The Walrus and the Carpenter," for example, contains 18 stanzas.

Style A style is a particular way of writing. It involves *how* something is said rather than *what* is said. Word choice, sentence length, tone, imagery, and use of dialogue contribute to a writer's style.

Summarizing Summarizing is telling the main ideas of a piece of writing briefly, in one's own words. When you summarize, you condense a writer's ideas into precise statements, leaving out unimportant details.

Suspense Suspense is a feeling of growing tension and excitement that makes a reader curious about the outcome of a story or an event within a story. In "The Secret of the Wall," for example, suspense is created when Carlos is trapped within the walls of the old house.

Symbol A symbol is a person, a place, or an object that stands for something other than itself. In literature, objects and images may be used to symbolize things that cannot actually be seen, such as ideas or feelings. In "Flowers and Freckle Cream," for example, the tiger lily Elizabeth receives from her grandfather may symbolize the beauty he sees in her freckled appearance.

Theme A theme is a message about life or human nature that is conveyed by a work of literature. Sometimes themes are stated directly, but often readers must figure them out. Any lessons learned by the main character of a story can be clues to a theme. For example, a theme of "The Scribe" might be that helping people is not a simple matter.

Tone The tone of a work conveys the writer's attitude toward his or her subject. A work may have one tone throughout, such as the humorous attitude shown in "The Adoption of Albert." Sometimes, however, the tone may change several times in the course of a work.

Visualizing The process of forming a mental picture based on a written description is called visualizing. Readers use details of sight, sound, touch, taste, and feeling to visualize the characters, settings, and events in works of literature. Mentally picturing writers' descriptions makes reading more enjoyable and memorable.

1 The Writing Process

The writing process consists of four stages: prewriting, drafting, revising and editing, and publishing and reflecting. As the graphic to the right shows, these stages are not steps that you must complete in a set order. Rather, you may return to any one at any time in your writing process, using feedback from your readers along the way.

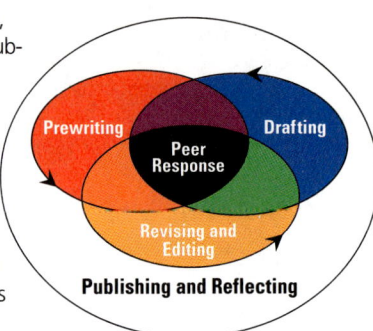

1.1 Prewriting

In the prewriting stage, you explore your ideas and discover what you want to write about.

Choosing a Topic

Ideas for writing can come from just about anywhere: experiences, memories, conversations, dreams, or imaginings. The following techniques can help you to generate ideas for writing and to choose a topic you care about.

Personal Techniques
Make a list of people, places, and activities that have had an effect on you.
Ask who, what, when, where, and why about an important event.
Ask what-if questions about everyday life.
Browse through magazines, newspapers, and on-line bulletin boards for ideas.

Sharing Techniques
With a group, brainstorm a topic by trying to come up with as many ideas as you can. Do not stop to evaluate your ideas for at least five minutes.
With a group, discuss a topic in depth, sharing your questions and ideas.

Writing Techniques
Use a word or picture as a starting point for freewriting.
Freewrite for a short time and then circle the ideas you would like to explore.
Pick a topic and list all the related ideas that occur to you.

Graphic Techniques
Create a time line of memorable events in your life.
Make a cluster diagram of subtopics related to a general topic.

Determining Your Purpose

At some time during your writing process, you need to consider your purpose, or general reason, for writing. For example, your purpose may be one of the following: to express yourself, to entertain, to explain, to describe, to analyze, or to persuade. To clarify your purpose, ask yourself questions like these:

- Why did I choose to write about my topic?
- What aspects of the topic mean the most to me?
- What do I want others to think or feel after they read my writing?

Identifying Your Audience

Knowing who will read your writing can help you clarify your purpose, focus your topic, and choose the details and tone that will best communicate your ideas. As you think about your readers, ask yourself questions like these:

- What do my readers already know about my topic?
- What will they be most interested in?
- What language is most appropriate for this audience?

1.2 Drafting

In the drafting stage, you put your ideas on paper and allow them to develop and change as you write.

There's no right or wrong way to draft. Sometimes you might be adventuresome and just dive right into your writing. At other times, you might draft slowly, planning carefully beforehand. You can combine aspects of these approaches to suit yourself and your writing projects.

 LINK TO LITERATURE

Some of the best ideas for writing can come from your own experiences. Isaac Bashevis Singer, the author of "Shrewd Todie and Lyzer the Miser," on page 319, says, "I prefer to write about the world which I knew, which I know, best. . . . I write about the things where I grew up, and where I feel completely at home."

WRITING HANDBOOK **773**

WRITING TIP

Often what you write in your first draft of a paper may not appear in the final version, but that doesn't mean you have to throw that material away. Keep a folder of drafts or parts of drafts that never became finished papers; you may find an idea in them for future writing projects.

Discovery drafting is a good approach when you've gathered some information on your topic or have a rough idea for writing but are not quite sure how you feel about your subject or what exactly you want to say. You just plunge into your draft and let your ideas lead you where they will. After finishing a discovery draft, you may decide to start another draft, do more prewriting, or revise your first draft.

Planned drafting may work better for reports and other kinds of formal writing. Try thinking through a writing plan or making an outline before you begin drafting. Then, as you write, you can develop your ideas and fill in the details.

1.3 Using Peer Response

The suggestions and comments your peers or classmates make about your writing are called peer response.

Talking with peers about your writing can help you discover what you want to say or how well you have communicated your ideas. You can ask a peer reader for help at any point in the writing process. For example, your peers can help you develop a topic, narrow your focus, discover confusing passages, or organize your writing.

Questions for Your Peer Readers

You can help your peer readers provide you with the most useful kinds of feedback by following these guidelines:

- Tell readers where you are in the writing process. Are you still trying out ideas, or have you completed a draft?
- Ask questions that will help you get specific information about your writing. Open-ended questions that require more than yes-or-no answers are more likely to give you information you can use as you revise.
- Give your readers plenty of time to respond thoughtfully to your writing.
- Encourage your readers to be honest when they respond to your work. It's OK if you don't agree with them—you always get to decide which changes to make.

The chart on the following page explains different peer-response techniques you might use when you're ready to share your work with others.

Technique	When to Use It	Questions to Ask
Sharing	Use this when you are just exploring ideas or when you want to celebrate the completion of a piece of writing by sharing it with another person.	Will you please read or listen to my writing without criticizing it or making suggestions afterward?
Summarizing	Use this when you want to know if your main idea or goals are clear to readers.	What do you think I'm trying to say? What's my main idea?
Telling	Use this to find out which parts of your writing are affecting readers the way you want and which parts are confusing.	What did you think or feel as you read my words? Which passage were you reading when you had that response?
Replying	Use this when you want to get some new ideas to use in your writing.	What are your ideas about my topic? What do you think about what I have said in my piece?
Identifying	Use this when you want to identify the strengths and weaknesses of your writing.	Where do you like the wording? Where can it be improved? Does the organization make sense? What parts were confusing?

Tips for Being a Peer Reader

Remember these guidelines when you act as a peer reader:

- Respect the writer's feelings.
- Make sure you understand what kind of feedback the writer is looking for before you respond, and then limit your comments accordingly.
- Use "I" statements, such as "I like . . .," "I think . . .," and "It would help me if. . . ." Remember that your impressions and opinions may not be the same as someone else's.

1.4 Revising and Editing

In the revising and editing stage, you improve your draft, choose the words that best express your ideas, and proofread for mistakes in spelling, grammar, usage, and punctuation.

WRITING TIP

You may want to ask peer readers questions if their comments are not clear or helpful to you. For example, if a reader says, "This part is confusing," you can probe to find out why. Ask, What are you confused about? What do you think might make it clearer?

> **WRITING TIP**
>
> When you finish a draft, take a break before rereading it. The break will help you distance yourself from your writing and allow you to evaluate it more objectively. You may decide to make several drafts, in which you change direction or even start over, before you're ready to revise and polish a piece of writing.

The changes you make in your writing during this stage usually fall into three categories: revising for ideas, revising for form, and editing to correct mistakes. Use the questions and suggestions that follow to help you assess problems in your draft and determine what kinds of changes would improve it.

Revising for Ideas

- Have I discovered the main idea or focus of my writing? Have I expressed it clearly in my draft?
- Have I accomplished my purpose?
- Do my readers have all the information they need, or would adding more details help?
- Are any of my ideas unnecessary?

Revising for Form and Language

- Is my writing unified? Are all the ideas directly related to my main idea or focus?
- Is my writing organized well? Are the relationships among ideas clear?
- Is my writing coherent? Is the flow of sentences and paragraphs smooth and logical?

Editing to Improve Your Writing

When you are satisfied with your draft, proofread and edit it, correcting any mistakes you might have made in spelling, grammar, usage, and punctuation. You may want to proofread your writing several times, looking for different types of mistakes each time. The following checklist may help you proofread your work.

Proofreading Checklist	
Sentence Structure and Agreement	Are there any run-on sentences or sentence fragments? Do all verbs agree with their subjects? Do all pronouns agree with their antecedents? Are verb tenses correct and consistent?
Forms of Words	Do adverbs and adjectives modify the appropriate words? Are all forms of *be* and other irregular verbs used correctly? Are pronouns used correctly? Are comparative and superlative forms of adjectives correct?
Capitalization, Punctuation, and Spelling	Is any punctuation mark missing or not needed? Are all words spelled correctly? Are all proper nouns and all proper adjectives capitalized?

> **WRITING TIP**
>
> For help with identifying and correcting problems that are listed in the Proofreading Checklist, see the Grammar Handbook, pages 812–851.

776 WRITING HANDBOOK

Use the proofreading symbols shown below to mark your draft with the changes that you need to make. See the Grammar Handbook for models in which these symbols are used.

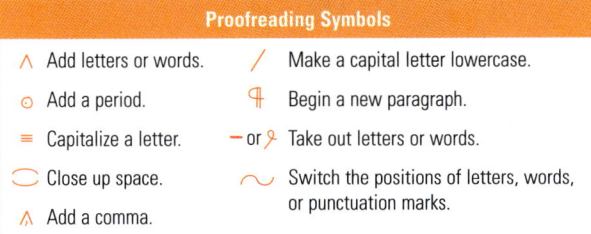

Proofreading Symbols	
∧ Add letters or words.	/ Make a capital letter lowercase.
⊙ Add a period.	¶ Begin a new paragraph.
≡ Capitalize a letter.	— or ℘ Take out letters or words.
⌒ Close up space.	∾ Switch the positions of letters, words, or punctuation marks.
∧ Add a comma.	

1.5 Publishing and Reflecting

After you've completed a writing project, consider sharing it with a wider audience—even when you've produced it for a class assignment. Reflecting on your writing process is another good way to bring closure to a writing project.

Creative Publishing Ideas

Following are some ideas for publishing and sharing your writing.

- Display your writing on a school bulletin board.
- Working with other students in your class, create an anthology, or collection, of stories, poems, plays, and other writing.
- Give a dramatic reading of your work for another class or group.
- Submit your writing to a local newspaper or a magazine that publishes student writing.
- Enter your work in a writing contest.
- Read your work at a school assembly.
- Create a multimedia presentation and share it with classmates.

Reflecting on Your Writing

Think about your writing process and consider whether you'd like to add your writing to your portfolio. You might write yourself a note answering questions like these and attach it to your work:

- What did I learn about myself and my subject?
- Which parts of the writing process did I most and least enjoy?
- As I wrote, what was my biggest problem? How did I solve it?
- What did I learn that I can use the next time I write?

 WRITING TIP

Consider going on-line with your writing by posting it on an electronic bulletin board or sending it to others via e-mail.

Building Blocks of Good Writing

2.1 Introductions

A good introduction catches your reader's interest and often presents the main idea of your writing. To introduce your writing effectively, try one of the following methods.

Share a Fact

Beginning with an interesting fact can make your reader think, I'd like to learn more about that. In the example below, impressive facts about Kodiak bears capture the reader's interest.

> A male Kodiak bear may weigh 1,500 pounds, measure ten feet long, and run 35 miles an hour. Protected within Alaska's Kodiak National Wildlife Refuge, nearly 3,000 of these bears share 100-mile-long Kodiak Island, where they feast on fish, berries, and whale and seal carcasses.

Present a Description

A vivid description sets a mood and brings a scene to life. The description below sets a mood of quiet concentration.

> In the pale morning light, the shadowy track was still. With the soft thump of her feet the only sound, the athlete focused on the race that would take place the next day. Rounding the curve, she locked her eyes on the single floodlight at the far end of the track, her every muscle straining toward it.

Ask a Question

Beginning with a question can make your reader want to read on to find out the answer. Note how the introduction that follows invites the reader to learn more about an unusual sporting event.

WRITING TIP

Writing the introduction does not need to be your first task when you begin a writing project. Instead, start with any part you feel ready to write. Once your ideas come into better focus, you'll probably get a good idea about how to introduce your piece.

778 WRITING HANDBOOK

778 THE LANGUAGE OF LITERATURE **TEACHER'S EDITION**

Why does Danielle Del Ferraro hold a special place in the history of the Soap Box Derby? Since the Derby began in 1934, she has been the only participant ever to win twice. Her success is noteworthy because girls were not allowed to enter the gravity-powered car race until 1970.

Relate an Incident

An engaging story that includes sensory details or dialogue can help catch your reader's attention. The anecdote below leads into a discussion about safety rules for in-line skating.

All dressed in my best clothes, I rushed outside, late for my sister's wedding. I waited impatiently for the light to change at the corner so that I could cross. Then, from out of nowhere an out-of-control in-line skater came hurtling toward me. The result was a head-on collision.

Use Dialogue

Creating fictional dialogue can be an effective way to draw your reader into your piece.

"What's the score?" Seth called across the room.
"Cougars 12, Tigers 6, at the end of the second quarter," Laura responded dejectedly. "What's wrong with our team?"
"Well, the Cougars are only a touchdown ahead," her friend offered encouragingly, "and we still have half the game to go."

WRITING TIP

When writing nonfiction and quoting from a source, be sure the words appear in the same order as they do in the original. For help with punctuation and capitalization in quotations, see page 850 of the Grammar Handbook.

2.2 Paragraphs

A paragraph is made up of sentences that work together to develop an idea or accomplish a purpose. Whether or not it contains a topic sentence stating the main idea, a good paragraph must have both unity and coherence.

Topic Sentences

A topic sentence makes the main idea or purpose of a paragraph clear to your reader. A topic sentence can appear anywhere in a paragraph, but when it is the first sentence, it can capture the reader's attention and clearly suggest what will follow.

> *The most important rule for a beginning photographer is this: check before you click.* Do you know how to operate the camera? Is the film loaded? Is your subject well lighted—with the light source on the subject and not behind it—or will you need a flash? Have you framed your picture carefully? (You don't want a picture of your friend to be missing a head!) Are you holding the camera still? Checking the basics will go a long way toward making your snapshots memorable.

LINK TO LITERATURE

Notice the clear topic sentence at the beginning of page 260 of Walter Dean Myers's "Abd al-Rahman Ibrahima" from *Now Is Your Time!* The opening sentence states that it was a dangerous time in Africa, and the sentences that follow give details to support this idea.

Unity

A paragraph has unity if every sentence in it supports the same main idea or purpose. One way to achieve unity in a paragraph is to state the main idea in a topic sentence and be sure that all the other sentences support that idea, as in the example above. You can create unity in a paragraph without using a topic sentence, however. Decide on a goal for your paragraph and make sure that each sentence supports that goal. Sentences should logically flow from one to the next, as shown in the paragraph below.

> The sun sank into the billowy cushions of clouds. The house, which had been brilliant white in the noonday sun, assumed a pale pink glow. The rocks and even the eerie piñon trees were enveloped in a rosy glow. I sat on the front steps, surveying the transformation and watching the light deepen from rose to mauve to purple to the deepest indigo.

WRITING TIP

When you are revising your writing, be sure to delete any details that do not relate to the main idea of each paragraph. If a paragraph contains two main ideas, you may break it into two separate paragraphs.

Coherence

In a coherent paragraph, details are presented in a clear, sensible order. Notice that the following paragraph is coherent because the changes in the earth are related in chronological order.

Most scientists believe that all of the earth's land once formed one supercontinent. About 200 million years ago, this supercontinent, which scientists have called Pangaea, began to divide into two large masses of land. Laurasia was the northern mass; Gondwanaland was in the south. Since that time the plates on which continents rest have continued to move. The plates move toward each other, away from each other, or past each other.

2.3 Transitions

Transitions are words that show the connections between details, such as relationships in time and space, order of importance, causes and effects, and similarities or differences.

Chronological Order

Some transitions help to clarify the order in which events take place. To arrange details chronologically, as in the example below, use transitional words such as *first, second, always, then, next, later, soon, before, finally, after, earlier, afterward,* and *during.*

During the Revolutionary War, many of the colonists who remained loyal to the British monarchy lost their houses and land by force. *After* the war, almost 80,000 of these Loyalists went to England or emigrated elsewhere.

Spatial Order

Transitional words and phrases such as *across, behind, next to, nearest, lowest, above, below, underneath, on the right,* and *in the middle* can help show where items are located. The following example describes the bleachers from the point of view of a skater.

As I waited, I stared at the bleachers *across* the rink. My family was lined up *in the front* row. *Behind* the group and *to the right* were friends from school, and *next to* my friends were three of my teachers.

LINK TO LITERATURE

In the selection from Anne Terry White's "Tutankhamen" from *Lost Worlds*, on page 470, notice how transitions, such as *nevertheless, in the years that followed,* and *however,* link paragraphs together smoothly.

WRITING HANDBOOK **781**

WRITING TIP

When you begin a sentence with a transition such as *most important, therefore, nevertheless, still,* or *instead,* set the transition off with a comma.

Degree

Transitional words and phrases such as *mainly, strongest, weakest, first, second, most important, least important, worst,* and *best* show degree of importance or rank order of details, as in the model below.

> Why do I read mysteries? *Mainly* because I enjoy the atmosphere of suspense. *Second,* I like meeting characters who are different from anybody I know in real life. *Least important,* but still a reason, is that I enjoy reading about places that interest me.

Compare and Contrast

Words and phrases such as *similarly, likewise, also, like, as, neither . . . nor,* and *either . . . or* show similarity, or likeness, between details. *However, by contrast, yet, but, unlike, instead, whereas,* and *while* show contrast, or difference. Note the use of both types of transitions in the model below.

> Matthew Henson was not recognized as the codiscoverer of the North Pole until 1944, although Robert Peary and he had reached it on April 6, 1909. *By contrast,* the achievement of Roald Amundsen's team, which made it to the South Pole in December 1911, was recognized almost immediately.

Cause and Effect

To show that details are linked in a cause-and-effect relationship, use transitional words and phrases such as *since, because, in order to, so that,* and *as a result.* Transitions in the following example show the relationship between the cotton gin and slavery.

> *Because* Eli Whitney's cotton gin decreased the processing time for cotton, plantation owners in the South planted more cotton. *As a result,* Whitney's labor-saving invention actually led to an increase in slave labor to pick the cotton.

782 WRITING HANDBOOK

2.4 Elaboration

To develop the main idea of a paragraph or a longer piece, you need to provide elaboration, or details, so that your readers aren't left with unanswered questions.

Facts and Statistics

A fact is a statement that can be proved, while a statistic is a fact expressed in numbers. As in the model below, the facts and statistics you use should support the statements you make.

> Women have been part of the United States' military efforts for more than a hundred years. Since the 1860s, more than 11 million women have served in the armed forces. Today approximately 350,000 women are on active or reserve duty in the military.

WRITING TIP

Facts and statistics are especially useful in supporting opinions. Be sure that you double-check in your original sources the accuracy of all facts and statistics you cite.

Sensory Details

By showing how something looks, sounds, smells, tastes, and feels, sensory details like the ones in the model below can help your readers more fully experience your subject.

> Anna Hawk got off her bike and sat beside the muddy road. The rain on her poncho made the only sound, and nothing on the prairie moved. Anna took a sip of warm, sweet cocoa from her thermos bottle.

Incidents

Describing a brief incident can help to explain or develop an idea. The writer of the model below includes an incident to explain the consequences of leaving a child alone.

> Jason left his three-year-old brother Josh alone in the kitchen while he ran upstairs to get his homework. When he returned, Jason found his brother and the kitchen covered with flour. He never finished his homework, but he learned that small children mustn't be left alone.

WRITING HANDBOOK   **783**

Examples

The model below shows how using an example can help support or clarify an idea. A well-chosen example often can be more effective than a lengthy explanation.

> Throughout history, people have used observations about nature to predict the weather. For example, you may have heard that a ring around the moon means rain the next day, or that "a red sky at night is a sailor's delight."

Quotations

Choose quotations that clearly support your points and be sure that you copy each quotation word for word. Always remember to credit the source.

> The narrator of "Thanksgiving in Polynesia" thinks that Polynesian children's lives must be great, and she can't imagine what they would find interesting about her life in Massapequa, New York. She states, "I wonder if when they're in school, they have a unit called 'The Peoples of Massapequa.'"

LINK TO LITERATURE

Notice in the excerpt from *A Long Hard Journey* how the authors Patricia and Fredrick McKissack include a quotation as elaboration on page 332. To explain the environment of a Pullman car, the writers quote a description from an 1867 issue of *Western World* magazine.

2.5 Description

Descriptive writing conveys images and impressions of a person, a place, an event, or a thing.

Descriptive writing appears almost everywhere, from cookbooks to poems. You might use a description to introduce a character in a narrative or to create a strong closing to a persuasive essay. Whatever your purpose and wherever you use description, the following guidelines for good descriptive writing will help you.

Include Plenty of Details

Vivid sensory details help the reader feel like an on-the-scene observer of the subject. The sensory details of the following scene appeal to the senses of sight, sound, touch, and even taste.

> Andrew slumped against the wall outside the gym. His calves ached more than his stomach, empty and tense. He replayed the last minutes of the game—tasting sweat, hearing cheers, feeling the seams of the basketball with his fingers—but he couldn't visualize missing the shot.

Organize Your Details

Details that are presented in a logical order help the reader form a mental picture of the subject. Descriptive details may be organized chronologically, by order of importance, spatially, or by order of impression, as in the model below.

> Mike descended the stairs slowly, so we saw his shoes first—polished to a gleaming black so that they looked almost like patent leather. The satin stripe on each trouser leg told us he was dressed for a formal event. The white bow tie, just below the grin, was the clincher.

Show, Don't Tell

Instead of just telling about a subject in a general way, provide details and quotations that expand and support what you want to say and that enable your readers to share your experience. The following example just tells and doesn't show.

> My little sister was scared by the movie *Snow White*.

The paragraph below uses descriptive details to show how the little girl reacted to the movie.

> Somebody should have warned me about *Snow White*. My little sister, Caroline, liked Sleepy, Doc, Bashful, and the rest. In fact, I had to name them every time they appeared. When the evil queen came back, however, Caroline whimpered. Then she cried very loudly. I still haven't seen the end of the movie.

LINK TO LITERATURE

Note the careful organization of details in "My First Dive with the Dolphins," on page 65. Don C. Reed describes the dive by starting at the surface of the water, noting the sensations during his descent, and finishing with a description of the floor of the oceanarium.

WRITING HANDBOOK **785**

WRITING TIP

Metaphors and similes can help you create more vivid, memorable descriptions. Remember that a metaphor compares things directly (*The burglar was a cat slinking through the alley*), while a simile is a comparison using *like* or *as* (*The drawbridge rose as slowly as a drowsy giant waking up after a long nap*).

Use Precise Language

To create a clear image in your reader's mind, use vivid and precise words. Instead of using general nouns, verbs, and adjectives (*car, walk, tired*), use specific ones (*convertible, shuffle, exhausted*). Notice what happens when vague, general words are replaced with precise words, as in the examples below.

> The dish broke.
> The dish shattered into dozens of tiny pieces.
>
> The wind was strong and caused damage.
> The wind blew fiercely, flattening bushes and flowers.

2.6 Conclusions

A conclusion should leave readers with a strong final impression. Try any of the following approaches for concluding a piece of writing.

Restate the Main Idea

Close by returning to your central idea and stating it in a new way. If possible, link the beginning of your conclusion with the information you have presented, as the model below shows.

> As these examples show, the expansion of nature preserves will protect the wildlife of our state. The preserves allow animals to live in an area that is rarely disrupted by the activities of people. The animals, from the smallest insects to the largest mammals, need to be protected in order for them all to survive.

Ask a Question

Try asking a question that sums up what you have said and gives readers something to think about. The following example from a piece of persuasive writing ends with a question that suggests a course of action.

786   WRITING HANDBOOK

> More and more people are biking to school and work and are riding for exercise. Doesn't it make sense to create safe bike lanes throughout our city?

Make a Recommendation

When you are writing to persuade, you can use your conclusion to tell readers what you want them to do. The conclusion below is from an article on the important role of animal shelters.

> If you want to help animals who are waiting for new homes and to help people find the right pets for them, volunteer your time after school to care for dogs and cats at an animal shelter.

End with the Last Event

If you're telling a story, you may end with the last thing that happens. Here, a story ends with an important moment of understanding.

> Len grinned at me, eager for approval. Suddenly I understood why he had made up all those wild stories about his life.

Generalize About Your Information

The model below concludes by making a specific statement about the importance of the subject.

> At 64, Denise St. Aubyn Hubbard sailed alone across the Atlantic. Bill Pinkney was in his fifties when he sailed around the world by himself. And Tristan Jones, in his sixties and having lost a leg, sailed solo from California to Thailand. Don't ever think courage and the spirit of adventure die with middle age or old age.

LINK TO LITERATURE

In his conclusion of "Chinatown," on page 177, Laurence Yep uses a question that effectively closes his narrative. He asks, "How could I pretend to be somebody else when I didn't even know who I was?"

3 Narrative Writing

Narrative writing tells a story. If you write a story from your imagination, it is called a fictional narrative. A true story is called a nonfictional narrative.

Key Techniques of Narrative Writing

Writing Standards

Good narrative writing
- includes descriptive details and dialogue to develop the characters, setting, and plot
- has a clear beginning, middle, and end
- maintains a consistent tone and point of view
- uses language that is appropriate for the audience
- demonstrates the significance of the events or ideas

Define the Conflict

The conflict of a narrative is the problem that the main character faces. In the example below, the conflict is between a girl and her aunt.

Example
Aunt Jessica knew I didn't want that mean white horse! I'd been begging for a horse to train for almost a year, but I never meant *that* horse.

Clearly Organize the Events

Choose the important events and explain them in an order that is easy to understand. In a fictional narrative, this series of events is the story's plot.

Example
- Aunt Jessica gives me my first horse to train
- he's a horse I don't like; he's stubborn, and when I try to train him nothing works
- I see the horse running in the field; he looks proud and independent
- my aunt asks me if I'd like a different horse to train, but I say no

Depict Characters Vividly

Use vivid details to show your readers what your characters look like, what they say, and what they think.

Example
I forced myself to smile. "Thanks, Aunt Jessica, I know I can train him like you taught me."

788 WRITING HANDBOOK

Organizing Narrative Writing

One way to organize a piece of narrative writing is to arrange the events in chronological order, as shown in Option 1 below.

Option 1   **Example**

Focus on Events	
• Introduce characters and setting	Aunt Jessica gave me my first horse to train.
• Show event 1	He was a horse I didn't like. He was stubborn, and when I tried to train him, nothing worked.
• Show event 2	One day I saw the horse running in the field. Instead of looking stubborn, he looked proud and independent.
• End, perhaps showing the significance of the events	Aunt Jessica offered me another horse to train, and when I said I'd like to keep the one I had, she smiled warmly at me.

You may prefer to focus on characters, especially if a change in character—the way someone thinks, feels, or behaves—is important to the outcome of the story. In that case, try organizing your story according to Option 2. Try Option 3 if you plan to focus on a conflict that a character experiences within himself or herself or with society, nature, or another character.

Option 2

Focus on Character
• Introduce the main character
• Describe the conflict the character faces
• Relate the events and the changes the character goes through as a result of the conflict
• Present the final change or new understanding

Option 3

Focus on Conflict
• Present the characters and setting
• Introduce the conflict
• Describe the events that develop from the initial conflict
• Show the struggle of the main character with the conflict
• Resolve the conflict

Remember: Good narrative writing is organized logically, with clues to help the reader understand the order of events.

> **WRITING TIP**
>
> **Introductions** Try hooking your reader's interest by opening a story with an exciting event. After your introduction, you may need to go back in time and relate the incidents that led up to the exciting event.

WRITING HANDBOOK 789

 Explanatory Writing

 LINK TO LITERATURE

Explanatory writing techniques provide tools for exploring the issues presented by or in literature. The examples on the following pages use explanatory writing techniques to examine Elizabeth Ellis's narrative "Flowers and Freckle Cream," starting on page 519.

Explanatory writing is writing that informs and explains. For example, you can use it to explain how to cook spaghetti, to explore the origins of the universe, or even to compare two different pieces of literature.

Types of Explanatory Writing

Analysis
Analysis explains how something works, how it is defined, or what its parts are.

Example
Unlike the narrator, I believe beauty is made up of a good appearance, self-confidence, and character.

Compare and Contrast
Compare-and-contrast writing explores the similarities and differences between two or more subjects.

Example
The narrator and her grandfather have different standards of beauty.

Cause and Effect
Cause-and-effect writing explains why something happened, why certain conditions exist, or what resulted from an action or a condition.

Example
Because she wears freckle remover in the sun, the narrator's freckles grow darker.

Problem-Solution
Problem-solution writing examines a problem and proposes a solution to it.

Example
Some people, like the narrator, wish they could look like someone else. The best solution is learning to appreciate your appearance as it is.

790 WRITING HANDBOOK

4.1 Compare and Contrast

Compare-and-contrast writing explores the similarities and differences between two or more subjects.

Organizing Compare-and-Contrast Writing

When you compare and contrast, you can organize your information in different ways. Two options are shown below.

Option 1 — **Example**

Feature by Feature
- Feature 1
  - Subject A
  - Subject B
- Feature 2
  - Subject A
  - Subject B

- The characters' standards of beauty
  - The narrator's standard of beauty is based on her cousin's appearance.
  - The grandfather thinks beauty can take many forms.
- The characters' ideas about attaining beauty
  - The narrator thinks she will be beautiful if she loses her freckles.
  - The grandfather thinks she is already beautiful.

Option 2 — **Example**

Subject by Subject
- Subject A
  - Feature 1
  - Feature 2
- Subject B
  - Feature 1
  - Feature 2

- The narrator
  - The narrator's standard of beauty is based on her cousin's appearance.
  - The narrator thinks she will be beautiful if she loses her freckles.
- The grandfather
  - The grandfather thinks beauty can take many forms.
  - The grandfather thinks she is already beautiful.

Writing Standards

Good compare-and-contrast writing

▸ clearly states the subjects being compared and shows how they are alike and different

▸ introduces subjects in an interesting way and gives a reason for the comparison

▸ uses transitions to signal similarities and differences

▸ ends with a conclusion that explains the decision made or that provides a new understanding of the subjects compared

 WRITING TIP

To help your audience understand something that is unfamiliar to them, try comparing and contrasting it with something they already know about.

 WRITING TIP

See page 781 for information on using transitions in your compare-and-contrast writing.

Writing Standards
Good cause-and-effect writing
▸ clearly states the cause-and-effect relationship being examined
▸ shows clear connections between causes and effects
▸ presents causes and effects in a logical order and uses transitional words to indicate order
▸ uses facts, examples, and other details to illustrate each cause and effect

WRITING TIP

You may want to include in your essay a diagram or chart that visually portrays the cause-and-effect relationship explained in your writing.

4.2 Cause and Effect

Cause-and-effect writing explains why something happened, why certain conditions exist, or what resulted from an action or a condition.

Organizing Cause-and-Effect Writing

Your organization will depend on your topic and purpose for writing. If you want to explain the causes of an event like the closing of a factory, you can first state the effect and then examine its causes (Option 1). If your focus is on explaining the effects of an event such as passage of a law, you might start by stating the cause and then proceed to explain the effects (Option 2). If you want to explore a topic such as the disappearance of tropical rain forests or the development of home computers, you might describe a chain of cause-and-effect relationships (Option 3).

Option 1 — **Example**

Effect to Cause
Effect
• Cause 1
• Cause 2
• Cause 3

- The narrator's face becomes covered with dark freckles.
- She doesn't know that freckle remover should never be worn in the sun.
- She applies freckle remover to her face.
- She spends a day hoeing tobacco in the sun.

Option 2

Cause to Effect
Cause
• Effect 1
• Effect 2
• Effect 3

Option 3

Cause-and-Effect Chain
Cause
↓
effect (cause)
↓
effect (cause)
↓
effect (cause)

Remember: Don't assume that a cause-and-effect relationship exists simply because one event follows another. Be sure facts show that the effect couldn't have happened without the cause.

792 WRITING HANDBOOK

4.3 Problem-Solution

Problem-solution writing clearly states a problem, analyzes the problem, and proposes a solution to the problem.

Organizing Problem-Solution Writing

Your organization will depend on the goal of your problem-solution piece, your intended audience, and the specific problem you choose to address. The organizational methods outlined below are effective for different kinds of problem-solution writing.

Option 1

Simple Problem-Solution	Example
Description of problem	Some people, like the narrator, wish they could look like someone else.
Recommended solution	You should learn to appreciate your own unique beauty, as the narrator's grandfather taught her.
Explanation of solution	Learning to like yourself would make you happier than trying to look like someone else.
Conclusion	The story offers a good solution to a common problem.

Option 2

Deciding Between Solutions	Example
Description of problem	Some people, like the narrator, wish they could look like someone else.
Solution A	You can try, as the narrator did, to change the way you look.
• Pros	You might like your new appearance.
• Cons	
Solution B	You can never look like someone else, and you might become frustrated if you try to.
• Pros	
• Cons	
Recommendation	As the narrator did, you can learn to appreciate your appearance because it is unique.

Writing Standards

Good problem-solution writing

▶ gives a clear and concise explanation of the problem and its significance

▶ proposes a workable solution and includes details that explain and support it

▶ concludes by restating the problem

WRITING TIP

Think of possible objections to your solution. You can strengthen your arguments by including possible objections and responding to them in a clear, reasonable way.

Writing Standards
A good analysis
▸ has a strong introduction and conclusion
▸ clearly states the subject and explains its parts
▸ uses a specific organizing structure
▸ uses transitions to connect thoughts
▸ uses language and details appropriate for the audience

4.4 Analysis

In an analysis you try to help your readers understand a subject by explaining how it works, how it is defined, or what its parts are.

The details you include will depend upon the kind of analysis you're writing.

- A **process analysis** should provide background information, such as definitions of terms and a list of needed equipment, and then explain each important step or stage in the process. For example, you might explain the steps to program a VCR or the stages in a plant's growth cycle.
- A **definition** should include the most important characteristics of the subject. To define a rain forest, you might include such characteristics as rainfall, vegetation, and animal life.
- A **parts analysis** should describe each of the parts, groups, or types that make up the subject. For example, you might analyze the parts of the human brain, the groups affected by a new law, or the styles of jazz music.

Organizing Your Analysis

Organize your details in a logical order appropriate for the kind of analysis you're writing. A process analysis is usually organized chronologically, with steps or stages in the order they occur.

Option 1

Process Analysis
- Preview analysis
- Response 1
- Response 2
- Response 3

Example

My response to Elizabeth Ellis's story "Flowers and Freckle Cream" changed when I reread it.

The first time I read the story, I thought the narrator acted like a baby, because she made a big deal about having freckles and wanting to be like her cousin.

The second time, I understood that she bought the freckle remover to feel more comfortable about herself.

In the third reading, I liked the way her grandfather told her to accept herself as beautiful by giving her a tiger lily.

You can organize the details in a definition or a parts analysis in order of importance or impression. Below, qualities in a definition of beauty, are organized from least to most important.

Option 2

Definition

- Introduce term
- General definition
  - Quality 1
  - Quality 2
  - Quality 3

Example

- The narrator of "Flowers and Freckle Cream" sees beauty in terms of appearance.
- I believe beauty consists of a good appearance, self-confidence, and character.
- A good appearance means looking your best. People who exercise and eat right are beautiful.
- Self-confidence draws others to you and is even more important than appearance.
- Good character is beauty's most important quality. People who are kind and help others are beautiful.

The following parts analysis explores the different ideas of beauty in the story "Flowers and Freckle Cream."

Option 3

Parts Analysis

- Introduce subject
- Explain how subject can be broken into parts
  - Part 1
  - Part 2
  - Part 3

Example

- The characters in "Flowers and Freckle Cream" have different ideas about beauty.
- The mother believes her daughter will never attain beauty, the narrator hopes she can, and the grandfather believes she already has.
- The mother says of the narrator, "You can't make a silk purse out of a sow's ear."
- The narrator hopes freckle-remover cream will give her the same flawless complexion as her cousin.
- Her grandfather tells her "there are all kinds of flowers, and they are all beautiful." He leaves a tiger lily, a freckled flower, on her pillow.

WRITING TIP

Introductions You may want to begin with a vivid description of the subject to capture the reader's attention. For example, you might describe why the narrator in "Flowers and Freckle Cream" is jealous of her cousin.

WRITING TIP

Conclusions Try ending an analysis by stating the importance of the subject to the reader. The analysis of the narrative "Flowers and Freckle Cream" could conclude with a statement about the importance of recognizing different kinds of beauty.

WRITING HANDBOOK **795**

Persuasive Writing

Persuasive writing allows you to use the power of language to inform and influence others.

Key Techniques of Persuasive Writing

Writing Standards

Good persuasive writing
- has a strong introduction
- clearly states the issue and the writer's position
- presents ideas logically
- answers opposing viewpoints
- ends with a strong argument or summary or a call for action

State Your Opinion
Taking a stand on an issue and clearly stating your opinion are essential to every piece of persuasive writing you do.

Example
Our city should create bike lanes on all major streets to encourage safety.

Know Your Audience
Knowing who will read your writing will help you decide what information you need to share and what tone you should use to communicate your message. In the example below, the writer has used a formal tone that is appropriate for a petition or a letter to the editor.

Example
We, the undersigned, believe the creation of bike lanes is necessary for public safety.

Support Your Opinion
Using reasons, examples, facts, statistics, and anecdotes to support your opinion will show your audience why you feel the way you do. Below, the writer uses a statistic to support his opinion.

Example
According to the National Safe Kids Campaign, over 50,000 children are injured in bicycle accidents every year, many on major streets.

796 WRITING HANDBOOK

Organizing Persuasive Writing

In persuasive writing, you need to gather information to support your opinions. Here are some ways you can organize that material to convince your audience.

Option 1

Reasons for Your Opinion
Your opinion
- Reason 1
- Reason 2
- Reason 3

Example
- Our city should create bike lanes on all major streets to encourage safety.
- Bicycle accidents often result in serious injuries.
- Bicycle lanes would separate bike traffic from car traffic, making travel safer for everyone.
- Safe bike paths would encourage people to ride bicycles for recreation and transportation.

Depending on the purpose and form of your writing, you may want to show the weaknesses of other opinions as you explain the strengths of your own. Two options for organizing writing that include more than just your side of the issue are shown below.

Option 2

Why Your Opinion Is Stronger

Your opinion
- your reasons

Other opinion
- evidence refuting reasons for other opinion and showing strengths of your opinion

Option 3

Why Another Opinion Is Weaker

Other opinion
- reasons

Your opinion
- reasons supporting your opinion and pointing out the weaknesses of the other side

Remember: Effective persuasion often builds from the weakest argument to the strongest. Keep this in mind when you organize the reasons that support your opinion.

WRITING TIP

Introductions Starting a persuasive piece with a question, a surprising fact, or an anecdote will capture your readers' interest and make them want to keep reading.

WRITING TIP

Conclusions The ending of a persuasive piece is often the part that sticks in a reader's mind. Your conclusion might summarize the two sides of an issue or call for some action.

6 Research Report Writing

In research report writing, you can find answers to questions about a topic you're interested in. Your writing organizes information from various sources and presents it to your readers as a unified and coherent whole.

Writing Standards

Good research report writing
- clearly states the purpose of the report in a thesis statement
- contains only accurate and relevant information
- documents sources correctly
- develops the topic logically
- reflects careful research on the topic

Key Techniques of Research Report Writing

Clarify Your Thesis
Your thesis statement explains to your reader what question your report will answer. In the example below, the writer's thesis statement answers the question "How are stories of dragons from around the world similar and different?"

Example
Folk tales and myths about dragons exist in cultures all over the world, but dragons symbolize good in some cultures and bad in others.

Support Your Ideas
You need to support your ideas with specific details. In the example below, the writer supports the idea that dragon images still exist in cultures today.

Example
During the Chinese New Year, the elaborate dragon dance is used in the celebrations to drive away bad luck and bring people good luck for the coming year.

Document Your Sources
You need to document, or credit, the sources where you find your information. In the example below, the writer paraphrases and documents a passage from David Passes's book about dragons.

Example
In Mordiford, England, people tell the legend of a wyvern, a two-legged dragon with wings. The wyvern terrorized the village until a prisoner named Garston gave his life saving the community from the fire-breathing monster (Passes 30–31).

798 WRITING HANDBOOK

Finding and Evaluating Sources

Begin your research by looking for information on your topic in books, magazines, newspapers, and computer databases. In addition to using your library's card or computer catalog, look up your subject in indexes, such as the *Readers' Guide to Periodical Literature* or the *New York Times Index*. The bibliographies in books that you find during your research may also lead to additional sources. The following checklist will help you evaluate the reliability of the sources you find.

Checklist for Evaluating Your Sources	
Authoritative	Someone who has written several books or articles on your subject or whose work has been published in a well-respected newspaper or journal may be considered an authority.
Up-to-date	Check the publication dates to see if the source reflects the most current research on your subject.
Respected	In general, tabloid newspapers and popular-interest magazines are not reliable sources. If you have questions about whether you are using a respected source, ask your librarian.

 WRITING TIP

Your reading can inspire ideas for research topics. The title of the story "In the Land of Small Dragon," on page 662, might lead you to explore the importance of dragons in Vietnamese traditions as well as in other cultures.

Making Source Cards

For each source you find, record the bibliographic information on a separate index card. You will need this information to give credit to the sources you use in your paper. The samples at the right show how to make source cards for encyclopedia entries, magazine articles, and books. You will use the source number on each card to identify the notes you take during your research.

Taking Notes

As you find material that suits the purpose of your report, record each piece of information on a separate note card. You will probably use all three of the note-taking methods listed on the following page.

WRITING HANDBOOK **799**

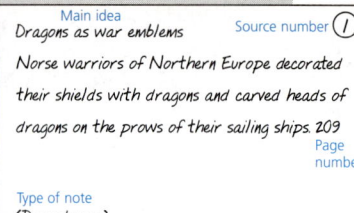

- Paraphrase, or restate in your own words, the main ideas and supporting details from a passage.
- Summarize, or rephrase the original material in fewer words, trying to capture the key ideas.
- Quote, or copy the original text word for word, if you think the author's own words best clarify a particular point. Use quotation marks to signal the beginning and the end of the quotation.

Writing a Thesis Statement

A thesis statement in a research report defines your main idea, or overall purpose, of your report. A clear one-sentence answer to your main question will result in a good thesis statement.

Question: How are stories of dragons from around the world similar and different?

Thesis Statement: Folk tales and myths about dragons exist in cultures all over the world, but dragons symbolize good in some stories and bad in others.

Making an Outline

To organize your report, group your note cards into main ideas and arrange them in a logical order. With your notes, make a topic outline, beginning with a shortened version of your thesis statement. Key ideas are listed after Roman numerals, and sub-points are listed after uppercase letters and Arabic numerals, as in the following example.

> Dragons Around the World
> Introduction—Dragons symbolize good and bad
> I. Origin of dragon stories
> II. Dragon stories around the world
>   A. Asia
>   B. Europe
>   1. Beowulf and the fire dragon
>   2. The Mordiford Wyvern
>   C. North America
> III. Dragon images in cultures today

WRITING TIP

Use the same form for items of the same rank in your outline. For example, if A is a noun, then B and C should be nouns.

800 WRITING HANDBOOK

Documenting Your Sources

When you quote one of your sources or write in your own words information you have found in a source, you need to credit that source, using parenthetical documentation.

Guidelines for Parenthetical Documentation	
Work by One Author	Put the author's last name and the page reference in parentheses: (Passes 19). If you mention the author's name in the sentence, put only the page reference in parentheses: (19).
Work by Two or Three Authors	Put the authors' last names and the page reference in parentheses: (Guise, Gushwa, and Donnelly 99).
Work by More Than Three Authors	Give the first author's last name followed by *et al.* and the page reference: (Park et al. 233).
Work with No Author Given	Give the title or a shortened version and the page reference: ("Dragon" 209).
One of Two or More Works by Same Author	Give the author's last name, the title or a shortened version, and the page reference: (Guccione, "On Dragons' Wings" 71).

 WRITING TIP

Plagiarism Presenting someone else's writing or ideas as your own is plagiarism. To avoid plagiarism, you need to credit sources as noted at the left. However, if a piece of information is common knowledge—information available in several sources—you do not need to credit the source.

Creating a List of Sources Page

At the end of your research report, you need to include a List of Sources page. Any source that you have documented needs to be listed alphabetically by the author's last name. If there is no author, use the editor's last name or the title of the work. Note the guidelines for spacing and punctuation on the model page.

Double-space between all lines
Indent additional lines ½"

Student's last name   Page number

Jensen 14

Center heading

List of Sources

"Dragon." Encyclopaedia Britannica: Micropaedia.

15th ed. 1992.

Passes, David. Dragons: Truth, Myth, and Legend.

New York: Western, 1993.

Tsang, Ka Bo. "The Dragon in Chinese Art." Arts of

Asia Jan.-Feb. 1988: 60-67.

2 spaces after periods

WRITING HANDBOOK 801

MULTIMEDIA HANDBOOK

1 Getting Information Electronically

Electronic resources provide you with a convenient and efficient way to gather information.

1.1 On-line Resources

When you use your computer to communicate with another computer or with another person using a computer, you are working "on-line." On-line resources include commercial information services and information available on the Internet.

Commercial Information Services

You can subscribe to various services that offer information such as the following:

- up-to-date news, weather, and sports reports
- access to encyclopedias, magazines, newspapers, dictionaries, almanacs, and databases (collections of information)
- electronic mail (e-mail) to and from other users
- forums, or ongoing electronic conversations among users interested in a particular topic

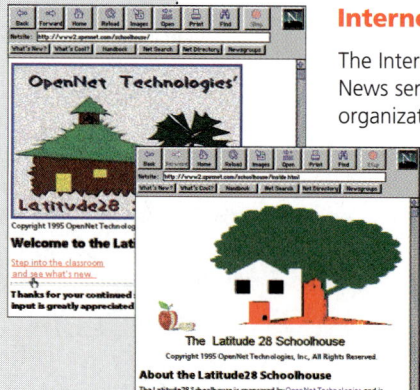

Internet

The Internet is a vast network of computers. News services, libraries, universities, researchers, organizations, and government agencies use the Internet to communicate and to distribute information. The Internet includes two key features:

- **World Wide Web,** which provides you with information on particular subjects and links you to related topics and resources (such as the Web pages shown at the left)
- **Electronic mail** (e-mail), which allows you to communicate with other e-mail users worldwide

802 MULTIMEDIA HANDBOOK

1.2 CD-ROM

A CD-ROM (compact disc–read-only memory) stores data that may include text, sound, photographs, and video.

Almost any kind of information can be found on CD-ROMs, which you can use at the library or purchase, including

- encyclopedias, almanacs, and indexes
- other reference books on a variety of subjects
- news reports from newspapers, magazines, television, or radio
- museum art collections
- back issues of magazines
- literature collections

WHAT YOU'LL NEED

- To access on-line resources, you need a computer with a modem linked to a telephone line. Your school computer lab or resource center may be linked to the Internet or to a commercial information service.
- To use CD-ROMs, you need a computer system with a CD-ROM player.

1.3 Library Computer Services

Many libraries offer computerized catalogs and a variety of other electronic resources.

Computerized Catalogs

You may search for a book in a library by typing the title, author, subject, or key words into a computer terminal. If you enter the title of a book, the screen will display the kind of information shown at right, including the book's call number and whether it is on the shelf or checked out of the library. When a particular work is not available, you may be able to search the catalogs of other libraries.

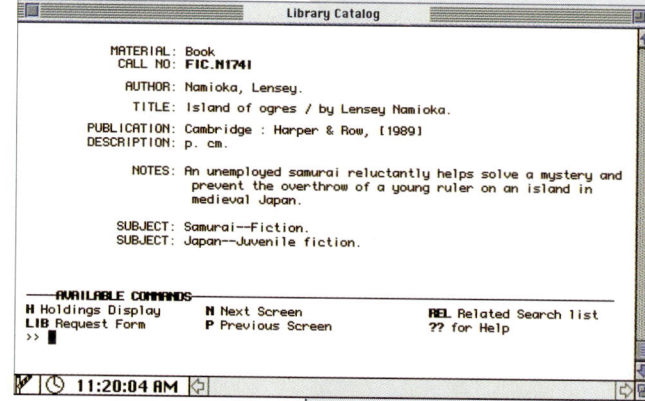

Other Electronic Resources

In addition to computerized catalogs, many libraries offer electronic versions of books or other reference materials. They may also have a variety of indexes on CD-ROM, which allow you to search for magazine or newspaper articles on any topic you choose. Ask your librarian for assistance in using these resources.

② Word Processing

WHAT YOU'LL NEED

- Computer
- Word-processing program
- Printer

Word-processing programs allow you to draft, revise, edit, and format your writing and to produce neat, professional-looking papers. They also allow you to share your writing with others.

2.1 Revising and Editing

Improving the quality of your writing becomes easier when you use a word-processing program to revise and edit.

Revising a Document

Most word-processing programs allow you to make the following kinds of changes:

- add or delete words
- move text from one location in your document to another
- undo a change you have made in the text
- save a document with a new name, allowing you to keep old drafts for reference
- view more than one document at a time, so you can copy text from one document and add it to another

Editing a Document

Many word-processing programs have the following features to help you catch errors and polish your writing:

- The **spell checker** automatically finds misspelled words and suggests possible corrections.
- The **grammar checker** spots possible grammatical errors and suggests ways you might correct them.
- The **thesaurus** suggests synonyms for a word you want to replace.
- The **dictionary** will give you the definitions of words so you can be sure you have used words correctly.
- The **search and replace** feature searches your whole document and corrects every occurrence of something you want to change, such as a misspelled name.

WRITING TIP

Even if you use a spell checker, you should still proofread your draft carefully to make sure you've used the right words. For example, you may have used *there* or *they're* when you meant to use *their*.

804 MULTIMEDIA HANDBOOK

2.2 Formatting Your Work

Format is the layout and appearance of your writing on the page. You may choose your formatting options before or after you write.

Formatting Type

You may want to make changes in the typeface, type size, and type style of the words in your document. For each of these, your word-processing program will most likely have several options to choose from. These options allow you to

- change the typeface to create a different look for the words in your document
- change the type size of the entire document or of just the headings of sections in the paper
- change the type style when necessary; for example, use italics or underline for the titles of books and magazines

Typeface	Size	Style
Geneva	7-point Times	*Italic*
Times	10-point Times	**Bold**
Chicago	12-point Times	Underline
Courier	14-point Times	

Formatting Pages

Not only can you change the way individual words look; you can also change the way they are arranged on the page. Some of the formatting decisions you make will depend on how you plan to use a printout of a draft or on the guidelines of an assignment.

- Set the line spacing, or the amount of space you need between lines of text. Double spacing is commonly used for final drafts.
- Set the margins, or the amount of white space around the edges of your text. A one-inch margin on all sides is commonly used for final drafts.
- Create a header for the top of the page or a footer for the bottom if you want to include such information as your name, the date, or the page number on every page.
- Determine the alignment of your text. The screen at the left shows your options.

WRITING TIP

Keep your format simple. Your goal is to create not only an attractive document but also one that is easy to read. Your readers will have difficulty if you change the type formatting frequently.

TECHNOLOGY TIP

Some word-processing programs or other software packages provide preset templates, or patterns, for writing outlines, memos, letters, newsletters, or invitations. If you use one of these templates, you will not need to adjust the formatting.

2.3 Working Collaboratively

Computers allow you to share your writing electronically. Send a copy of your work to someone via e-mail or put it in someone's drop box if your computer is linked to other computers on a network. Then use the feedback of your peers to help you improve the quality of your writing.

Peer Editing on a Computer

The writer and the reader can both benefit from the convenience of peer editing "on screen," or at the computer.

- Be sure to save your current draft and then make a copy of it for each of your peer readers.
- You might have your peer readers enter their comments in a different typeface or type style from the one you used for your text, as shown in the the example below.
- Ask each of your readers to include his or her initials in the file name.

TECHNOLOGY TIP

Some word-processing programs, such as the Writing Coach software referred to in this book, allow you to leave notes for your peer readers in the side column or in a separate text box. If you wish, leave those areas blank so your readers can write comments or questions.

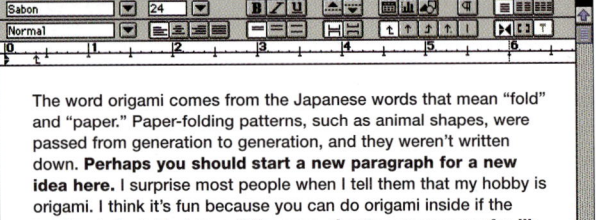

The word origami comes from the Japanese words that mean "fold" and "paper." Paper-folding patterns, such as animal shapes, were passed from generation to generation, and they weren't written down. **Perhaps you should start a new paragraph for a new idea here.** I surprise most people when I tell them that my hobby is origami. I think it's fun because you can do origami inside if the weather is bad. **Explain a little more about your reasons for liking origami. It must be more than just something to do when the weather is bad.** When I first started, I used the colored paper that came with my origami book. Since then, I have used all kinds of paper and have tried wet origami. **What is wet origami? Add some details about it.**

- If your computer allows you to open more than one file at a time, open each reviewer's file and refer to the files as you revise your draft.

Peer Editing on a Printout

Some peer readers prefer to respond to a draft on paper rather than on the computer.

- Double-space or triple-space your document so that your peer editors can make suggestions between the lines.
- Leave extra-wide margins to give your readers room to note their reactions and questions as they read.
- Print out your draft and photocopy it if you want to share it with more than one reader.

806 MULTIMEDIA HANDBOOK

Using Visuals 3

Charts, graphs, diagrams, and pictures often communicate information more effectively than words alone do. Many computer programs allow you to create visuals to use with written text.

3.1 When to Use Visuals

Use visuals in your work to illustrate complex concepts and processes or to make a page look more interesting.

Although you should not expect a visual to do all the work of written text, combining words and pictures or graphics can increase the understanding and enjoyment of your writing. Many computer programs allow you to create and insert graphs, tables, time lines, diagrams, and flow charts into your document. An art program allows you to create border designs for a title page or to draw an unusual character or setting for narrative or descriptive writing. You may also be able to add clip art, or premade pictures, to your document. Clip art can be used to illustrate an idea or concept in your writing or to make your writing more appealing for young readers.

WHAT YOU'LL NEED

- A graphics program to create visuals
- Access to clip-art files from a CD-ROM, a computer disk, or an on-line service

3.2 Kinds of Visuals

The visuals you choose will depend on the type of information you want to present to your readers.

Tables

Tables allow you to arrange facts or numbers into rows and columns so that your reader can compare information more easily. In many word-processing programs, you can create a table by choosing the number of vertical columns and horizontal rows you need and then entering information in each box, as the illustration shows.

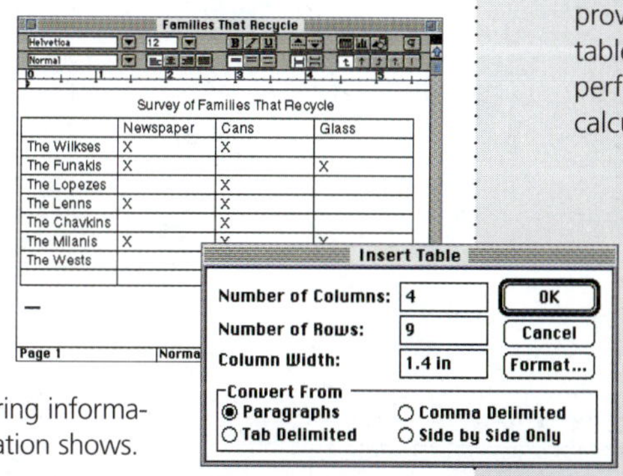

TECHNOLOGY TIP

A spreadsheet program provides you with a preset table for your statistics and performs any necessary calculations.

MULTIMEDIA HANDBOOK 807

TECHNOLOGY TIP

To help your readers easily understand the different parts of a pie chart or bar graph, use a different color or shade of gray for each section.

Graphs and Charts

You can sometimes use a graph or chart to help communicate complex information in a clear visual image. For example, you could use a line graph to show how a trend changes over time, a bar graph to compare statistics, or a pie chart, like the one at the right, to compare percentages. You might want to explore ways of displaying data in more than one visual format before deciding which will work best for you.

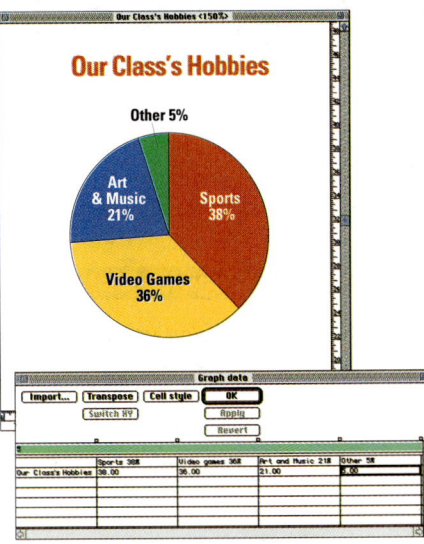

Other Visuals

Art and design programs allow you to create visuals for your writing. Many programs include the following features:

- drawing tools that allow you to draw, color, and shade pictures, such as the drawing below
- clip art that you can copy or change with drawing tools
- page borders that you can use to decorate title pages, invitations, or brochures
- text options that allow you to combine words with your illustrations
- tools for making geometric shapes in flow charts, time lines, and diagrams that show a process or sequence of events

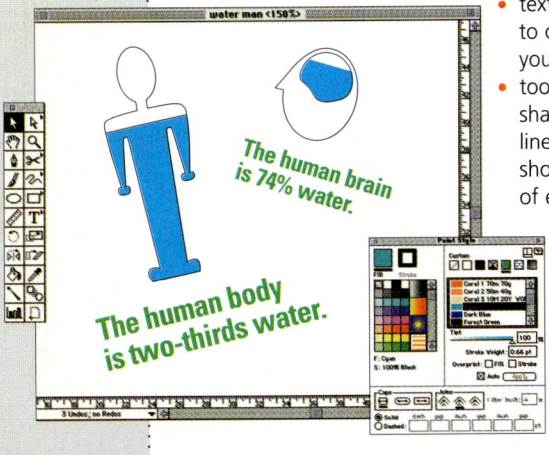

808 MULTIMEDIA HANDBOOK

Creating a Multimedia Presentation 4

A multimedia presentation is a combination of text, sound, and visuals such as photographs, videos, and animation. Your audience reads, hears, and sees your presentation at a computer, following different "paths" you create to lead the user through the information you have gathered.

4.1 Features of Multimedia Programs

To start planning your multimedia presentation, you need to know what options are available to you. You can combine sound, photos, videos, and animation to enhance any text you write about your topic.

Sound

Including sound in your presentation can help your audience understand information in your written text. For example, the user may be able to listen and learn from

- the pronunciation of an unfamiliar or foreign word
- a speech
- a recorded news interview
- a musical selection
- a dramatic reading of a work of literature

Photos and Videos

Photographs and live-action videos can make your subject come alive for the user. Here are some examples:

- videotaped news coverage of a historical event
- videos of music, dance, or theater performances
- charts and diagrams
- photos of an artist's work
- photos or video of a geographical setting that is important to the written text

 WHAT YOU'LL NEED

- Individual programs to create and edit the text, graphics, sound, and videos you will use
- A multimedia authoring program that allows you to combine these elements and create links between the screens

MULTIMEDIA HANDBOOK **809**

TECHNOLOGY TIP

You can download photos, sound, and video from Internet sources onto your computer. This process allows you to add elements to your multimedia presentation that would usually require complex editing equipment.

 TECHNOLOGY TIP

You can now find CD-ROMs with videos of things like wildlife, weather, street scenes, and events, and other CD-ROMs with recordings of famous speeches, musical selections, and dramatic readings.

Animation

Many graphics programs allow you to add animation, or movement, to the visuals in your presentation. Animated figures add to the user's enjoyment and understanding of what you present. You can use animation to illustrate

- what happens in a story
- the steps in a process
- changes in a chart, graph, or diagram
- how your user can explore information in your presentation

4.2 Planning Your Presentation

To create a multimedia presentation, first choose your topic and decide what you want to include. Then plan how you want your user to move through your presentation.

Imagine that you are creating a multimedia presentation about in-line skating. You know that you want to include the following items:

- photo of in-line skaters
- a text history of how in-line skating was developed
- a diagram of an in-line skate
- text on "how to skate" for beginners
- a video of a skating demonstration
- a glossary of in-line skating terms
- an audio description of safety tips

You can choose one of the following ways to organize your presentation:

- step by step with only one path, or order, in which the user can see and hear the information
- a branching path that allows users to make some choices about what they will see and hear, and in what order

A flow chart can help you figure out the path a user can take through your presentation. Each box in the flow chart on the following page represents something about in-line skating for the user to read, see, or hear. The arrows on the flow chart show a branching path the user can follow.

810 MULTIMEDIA HANDBOOK

When boxes branch in more than one direction, it means that the user can choose which item to see or hear first.

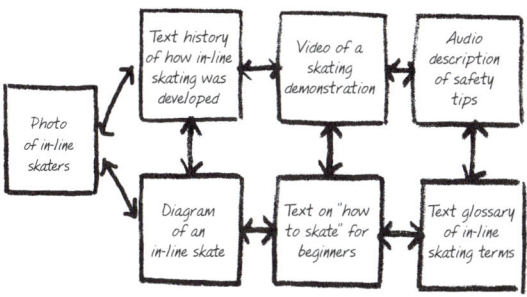

4.3 Guiding Your User

Your user will need directions to follow the path you have planned for your multimedia presentation.

Most multimedia authoring programs allow you to create screens that include text or audio directions that guide the user from one part of your presentation to the next. In the example below, the user can choose between several paths, and directions on the screen explain how to make the choice.

If you need help creating your multimedia presentation, ask your school's technology adviser. You may also be able to get help from your classmates or your software manual.

> **WRITING TIP**
>
> You usually need permission from the person or organization that owns the copyright on materials if you want to copy them. You do not need permission, however, if you are not making money from your presentation, if you use it only for educational purposes, and if you use only a small percentage of the original material.

The user clicks on a button to select any of these options.

Navigational buttons take the user back and forth, one screen at a time.

This screen shows a video of a skating demonstration.

1 Writing Complete Sentences

1.1 Sentence Fragments

A sentence fragment is a group of words that does not express a complete thought. It may be missing a subject, a predicate, or both. A sentence fragment makes you wonder *What is this about?* or *What happened?*

Missing Subject or Predicate

You can correct a sentence fragment by adding the missing subject or predicate to complete the thought.

> "The School Play" is a story about sixth graders who
> *The students*
> put on a play. ∧Rehearse their parts for three weeks.
> *forget their lines.*
> Even then some students.∧

APPLY WHAT YOU'VE LEARNED

Rewrite these sentences, correcting the sentence fragments.

1. "The School Play."
2. Is based on a tragedy of the winter of 1846–1847.
3. Late in October, George and Jacob Donner.
4. Led a party through the Sierra Nevada in California.
5. A terrible snowstorm.
6. Blocked the pass.
7. By April almost half of the 82 members of the original party.
8. Had died of starvation.
9. Some of the survivors.
10. Resorted to eating the corpses of those who had died.

1.1 Sentence Fragments

"The School Play" is based on a tragedy of the winter of 1846–1847. Late in October, George and Jacob Donner led a party through the Sierra Nevada in California. A terrible snowstorm blocked the pass. By April almost half of the 87 members of the original party had died of starvation. Some of the survivors resorted to eating the corpses of those who had died.

1.2 Run-On Sentences

A run-on sentence consists of two or more sentences written incorrectly as one. A run-on sentence occurs because the writer either used no end mark or used a comma instead of a period to end the first complete thought. A run-on sentence may confuse readers because it does not show where one thought ends and the next begins.

Forming Separate Sentences

One way to correct a run-on sentence is to form two separate sentences. Use a period or other end punctuation after the first sentence, and capitalize the first letter of the next sentence.

> *Damon and Pythias* retells an ancient Greek legend this version is in the form of a play. The story is about two great friends each shows his devotion by being willing to die for the other.

Forming Compound Sentences

You can also correct a run-on sentence by rewriting it to form a compound sentence. One way to do this is by using a comma and a coordinating conjunction.

Never join simple sentences with a comma alone, or a run-on sentence will result. You need a comma followed by the conjunction *and, but,* or *or* to hold the sentences together.

> Damon and Pythias lived on the island of Sicily *and* everyone knew what friends they were. Their king was cruel *but* no one dared to criticize him. Pythias spoke against the king *and* the punishment for this offense was death.

LINK TO LITERATURE

In *Damon and Pythias*, on page 684, Fan Kissen writes long sentences that sometimes look like run-ons. These sentences may appear complicated, but they are clear and easy to understand. They present conversation as it usually sounds. Kissen's logical grouping of thoughts, careful use of punctuation, and play format ensure that the reader will understand.

GRAMMAR HANDBOOK

You may use a semicolon to join two ideas that are closely related.

In addition, you can correct a run-on sentence by using a semicolon and a conjunctive adverb. Commonly used conjunctive adverbs are *however, therefore, nevertheless,* and *besides.*

> Pythias had to settle his affairs; he wanted to say goodbye to his mother. Damon took his friend's place for a while Pythias planned to come back; *nevertheless,* Damon would have taken Pythias' punishment; *however,* Pythias returned just in time.

APPLY WHAT YOU'VE LEARNED

Rewrite this paragraph, correcting the run-on sentences in different ways.

1. In *Damon and Pythias* the friendship of two young men helps them face death another story about friends is found in the Bible.
2. David and Jonathan were friends who protected each other they warned each other of danger.
3. Young David was a musician his songs soothed Saul, the king of Israel.
4. Jonathan was the son of Saul he remained David's closest friend throughout his life.
5. David's brave acts made him a national hero Saul became jealous of him.
6. On more than one occasion Jonathan warned David of Saul's plots Saul tried to kill David with a dagger that barely missed its mark.
7. David had opportunities to kill Saul he always refused to do bad things.
8. Such honorable conduct shamed Saul Jonathan defended David even against his own father.

1.2 Run-On Sentences

Answers will vary. See typical answers below.

1. In *Damon and Pythias* the friendship of two young men helps them face death. Another story about friends is found in the Bible.
2. David and Jonathan were friends who protected each other; they warned each other of danger.
3. Young David was a musician, and his songs soothed Saul, the king of Israel.
4. Jonathan was the son of Saul. He remained David's closest friend throughout his life.
5. David's brave acts made him a national hero, and Saul became jealous of him.
6. On more than one occasion Jonathan warned David of Saul's plots; nevertheless, Saul tried to kill David with a dagger that barely missed its mark.
7. David had opportunities to kill Saul, but he always refused to do bad things.
8. Such honorable conduct shamed Saul. Jonathan defended David even against his own father.

Making Subjects and Verbs Agree

2.1 Simple and Compound Subjects

A verb must agree in number with its subject. *Number* refers to whether a word is singular or plural. When a word refers to one thing, it is singular. When a word refers to more than one thing, it is plural.

Agreement with Simple Subjects

Use a singular verb with a singular subject.

When the subject is a singular noun, you use the singular form of the verb. The present-tense singular form of a regular verb usually ends in *-s* or *-es*.

> The selection "Tutankhamen" tell the true story of a famous archaeological discovery.

Use a plural verb with a plural subject.

> Two determined men looks for the tomb of Pharaoh Tutankhamen.

Agreement with Compound Subjects

Use a plural verb with a compound subject whose parts are joined by *and*, regardless of the number of each part.

> Howard Carter and Lord Carnarvon exclaims when they find "wonderful things" in November of 1922.

LINK TO LITERATURE

Notice the agreement of subjects and verbs throughout "Tutankhamen" by Anne Terry White, on page 470. The selection is a historical piece about discoveries made in the 1920s.

REVISING TIP

To find the subject of a sentence, first find the verb. Then ask *who* or *what* the verb refers to. Say the subject and the verb together to see whether they agree.

GRAMMAR HANDBOOK 815

When the parts of a compound subject are joined by *or* or *nor*, make the verb agree in number with the part that is closer to it.

Neither Lord Carnarvon nor the Egyptians knows / where to look for the rich tomb. A frequent problem for archaeologists is that grave robbers or time cause^s great damage.

2.1 Simple and Compound Subjects

1. tells
2. take
3. excites
4. looks
5. seems
6. helps
7. thinks
8. wonder
9. date
10. suggests
11. forms
12. measure
13. produces
14. keeps
15. appears

APPLY WHAT YOU'VE LEARNED

Rewrite the correct form of the verb given in parentheses.

1. "Tutankhamen" (tell, tells) the story of a great archaeological discovery in Egypt.
2. Many wonderful discoveries also (take, takes) place in our part of the world.
3. A recent discovery (excite, excites) archaeologists in Mexico.
4. This great trade center (look, looks) ancient.
5. The city (seems, seem) to have been abandoned suddenly about A.D. 1000.
6. Neither floods nor war (help, helps) city dwellers.
7. One archaeologist (think, thinks) that this city hit its peak in the Classic Period, from A.D. 300 to A.D. 600.
8. S. Jeffrey, K. Wilkerson, and other archaeologists (wonder, wonders) what brought about such growth.
9. Several smaller settlements (date, dates) from about that time.
10. Research (suggest, suggests) that El Pital was a center of trade and culture more complex than that of most other towns.
11. Earth or stone (form, forms) more than a hundred dwellings, ball courts, temples, and long platforms.
12. Some buildings (measure, measures) 130 feet in height.
13. A banana, sugar-cane, or citrus plantation (produces, produce) growth dense enough to hide even these.
14. Either vegetation or flood sediment (keep, keeps) an ancient city hidden.
15. The city of El Tajín (appear, appears) to be more recent than El Pital.

2.2 Pronoun Subjects

When a pronoun is used as a subject, the verb must agree with it in number.

Agreement with Personal Pronouns

When the subject is a singular personal pronoun, use a singular verb. When the subject is a plural personal pronoun, use a plural verb.

Even though *I* and *you* are singular, they take the plural form of the verb.

> I believes that "Abd al-Rahman Ibrahima" is the true story of an enslaved African prince. We likes that story.

When *he, she,* or *it* is the part of the subject closer to the verb in a compound subject containing *or* or *nor*, use a singular verb. When a pronoun is part of a compound subject containing *and*, use a plural verb.

> The other captives and he trusts the slaver. Their past experience makes them trusting. Neither the others nor he prepare_s for treachery.

Agreement with Indefinite Pronouns

When the subject is a singular indefinite pronoun, use the singular form of the verb.

The following are singular indefinite pronouns: *another, either, nobody, anybody, everybody, somebody, no one, anyone, everyone, someone, one, nothing, anything, everything, something, each,* and *neither*.

> During Ibrahima's time with the Irish doctor John Coates Cox, everything go_{es} well. Nothing arouse_s Ibrahima's suspicion about foreigners.

 LINK TO LITERATURE

Notice how the agreement of pronoun subjects with verbs in the excerpt from Walter Dean Myers's *Now Is Your Time!*, on page 257, makes it easy for him to discuss complex events. Correct grammatical constructions give readers a clear view of the incidents the author describes.

GRAMMAR HANDBOOK **817**

When the subject is a plural indefinite pronoun (*both*, *few*, *many*, or *several*), use the plural form of the verb.

Few fears / what they have not been taught to fear. Ibrahima learns from his experience that many deceives / or betrays / others.

The indefinite pronouns *some*, *all*, *any*, *none*, and *most* can be either singular or plural. When the pronoun refers to one thing or part, use a singular verb. When the pronoun refers to more than one thing, use a plural verb.

Of the captives Ibrahima meets, many die on the trip over, and most suffers / on landing. Some of the food seem(s) inedible, and some of the people gets / sick.

2.2 Pronoun Subjects

1. live
2. appear
3. speaks
4. belongs
5. wear
6. raise
7. meet
8. come
9. traces
10. know
11. grow; tend
12. hear
13. speak
14. prosper

APPLY WHAT YOU'VE LEARNED

Write the correct form of the verb given in parentheses.

1. Of the peoples in the world, many (live, lives) in the huge continent of Africa.
2. Some (appear, appears) in the selection "Abd al-Rahman Ibrahima" from *Now Is Your Time!*.
3. Each group has its own culture and customs, and each (speak, speaks) in its own language or dialect.
4. Ibrahima speaks Fulani because he (belong, belongs) to the Fula people.
5. Most of the Fula (wear, wears) their silky hair long.
6. They are a pastoral people, so many (raise, raises) livestock.
7. In the selection, we (meet, meets) the Mandingo, enemies of the Fula.
8. They (come, comes) from West Africa and belong to many independent kingdoms.
9. One (trace, traces) its dynasty back 13 centuries with hardly a break.
10. Africans and we (know, knows) this group as the Kangaba.
11. The Mandingo are an agricultural people; they (grow, grows) grain crops such as millet; and they (tend, tends) cattle.
12. We (hear, hears) of another group, the Songhai, in Myers's account.
13. They (speak, speaks) an independent language.
14. Of the Songhai traders, all (prosper, prospers) from caravan commerce.

818 GRAMMAR HANDBOOK

2.3 Common Agreement Problems

Several other situations can cause problems in subject-verb agreement.

Agreement with Irregular Verbs

Use the singular forms of the irregular verbs *do, be,* and *have* with singular subjects. Use the plural forms of these verbs with plural subjects.

	Do	Be	Have
Singular Subjects	I do you do the car does each does it doesn't	I am/was you are/were Jane is/was she isn't/wasn't either is/was	I have you have Juan hasn't he has anybody has
Plural Subjects	we do cars do they do many don't	we are/were girls are/were they are/were both are/were	we have boys have they haven't few have

The story "The All-American Slurp" do^es a good job of describing our manners. The story has^ examples of Chinese and American mistakes. They are^ is both funny.

Interrupting Words

Be sure the verb agrees with its subject when a word or words come between them.

A word or words that come between the subject and its verb do not affect the number of the verb.

Many of the girls in the group feels embarrassed. A dip of sour cream and onion flakes cause^s a problem for the Lins.

 REVISING TIP

Look carefully at words that come before the verb to find the subject. Remember that the subject may not be the noun or pronoun closest to the verb.

GRAMMAR HANDBOOK **819**

LINK TO LITERATURE

In "The All-American Slurp," on page 6, notice how Lensey Namioka makes subjects and verbs agree in spite of words or phrases that separate them. This skill allows her to add more information to each sentence and to vary the rhythm of the sentences.

Interrupting Phrases

Be certain that the verb agrees with its subject when a phrase comes between them.

The subject of a verb is never found in a prepositional phrase, which may follow the subject and come before the verb.

> The members of the Gleason family offers snacks to the Lins. A cooked vegetable, according to many Chinese people, taste better than a raw one.

Phrases beginning with *including, as well as, along with,* and *in addition to* are not part of the subject.

> The Lins learn that celery, as well as radishes and carrots, count as a finger food. Each guest, including the parents and the children, skip the dip.

The subject of a verb is never found in an appositive, which may follow the subject and come before the verb.

> Meg, daughter of the Gleasons, struggle to eat a traditional Chinese meal. Pot stickers, a Chinese delicacy, is enjoyed by almost everyone.

Inverted Sentences

When the subject comes after the verb, be sure the verb agrees with the subject in number.

A sentence in which the subject follows the verb is called an inverted sentence.

820 GRAMMAR HANDBOOK

From knowing the rules of courtesy come^s confidence. From breaking them, however, comes~ the most fun and laughter.

Questions are usually in inverted form, as are sentences that begin with *here is, here are, there is,* and *there are.* (For example: *Where is the fire? There are people rushing outside.*)

"What kind of food does^{do} you enjoy?" the families might have asked. Why were^{was} each worrying about what to eat? There are~^{is} a good choice of restaurants. Here is~^{are} a few of my favorites.

 REVISING TIP

To check subject-verb agreement in inverted sentences, place the subject before the verb. For example, change *Here is an idea* to *An idea is here.*

APPLY WHAT YOU'VE LEARNED

Write the correct form of each verb given in parentheses.

1. The story "The All-American Slurp" (does, do) readers a favor; it helps us not take ourselves too seriously.
2. Most of us, at some time or another, (has, have) wondered about rules of polite behavior.
3. What (is, are) the right things to do?
4. Dip, including things like sour cream, (was, were) difficult for the Lins.
5. (Does, Do) you handle similar problems in another country as well as the Lins?
6. The difficulties for a traveler (is, are) often greater.
7. Roast gorilla, along with side dishes, (is, are) a delicacy in one African country.
8. A Saudi Arabian (has, have) sheep's eyeballs as a delicacy.
9. (Is, Are) there a gracious way to deal with a disgusting dish? Here (is, are) some ways.
10. Swallowing fast, telling yourself that it "tastes just like chicken," (is, are) a good way.
11. Some, to disguise the form or texture of a food, (slice, slices) the item thinly.
12. Finally, a burp or a belch at the end of a meal, in some places, highly (compliment, compliments) the cook.

2.3 Common Agreement Problems

1. does
2. have
3. are
4. was
5. Do
6. are
7. is
8. has
9. Is; are
10. is
11. slice
12. compliments

GRAMMAR HANDBOOK 821

3 Using Nouns and Pronouns

3.1 Plural and Possessive Nouns

Nouns refer to people, places, things, and ideas. A noun is plural when it refers to more than one person, place, thing, or idea. Possessive nouns show who or what owns something.

Plural Nouns

Follow these guidelines to form noun plurals.

Nouns	To Form Plural	Examples
Most nouns	add -s	eye—eyes
Most nouns that end in s, sh, ch, x, or z	add -es	chorus—choruses bench—benches
Most nouns that end in ay, ey, oy, or uy	add -s	day—days donkey—donkeys
Most nouns that end in a consonant and y	change y to i and add -es	lily—lilies folly—follies
Most nouns that end in o	add -s	piano—pianos radio—radios solo—solos
Some nouns that end in a consonant and o	add -es	mango—mangoes ginkgo—ginkgoes potato—potatoes
Most nouns that end in f or fe	change f to v and add -es or -s	leaf—leaves wife—wives *but* roof—roofs

Some nouns have the same spelling in both singular and plural forms: *deer, moose, shrimp,* and *salmon*. Some nouns have irregular plurals that do not follow any rule: *mice, feet*.

 LINK TO LITERATURE

In "Shrewd Todie and Lyzer the Miser," on page 319, Isaac Bashevis Singer uses vocabulary that may be unfamiliar to the reader. Some examples are *borscht*, referring to a soup made of beets, spinach, or cabbage, and *gulden*, the name of a type of coins. These nouns help capture the flavor of the setting, an old Russian village.

REVISING TIP

The plurals of many musical terms that end in o preceded by a consonant are formed by adding -s. These nouns include *rondos, falsettos,* and *pianos*.

822 GRAMMAR HANDBOOK

In "Shrewd Todie and Lyzer the Miser" Todie has trouble fulfilling his family duties. Firewood and potatoes are very expensive. Loaves of bread are rare.

Possessive Nouns

Follow these guidelines to form possessive nouns.

Nouns	To Form Possessive	Examples
Singular nouns	add apostrophe and -s	team—team's
Plural nouns ending in s	add apostrophe	workers—workers' members—members'
Plural nouns not ending in s	add apostrophe and -s	people—people's men—men's

Because of his children's needs, Todie approaches the rich miser Lyzer for loans. Lyzer's own goat must beg the neighbors for the peelings' of potatoes.

 REVISING TIP

The dictionary usually lists the plural form of a noun if the plural is formed irregularly or if it might be formed in more than one way. Dictionary listings are especially helpful for nouns that end in *o*, *f*, and *fe*.

APPLY WHAT YOU'VE LEARNED

Write the correct noun given in parentheses.

¹Isaac Bashevis (Singers', Singer's) (storys, stories) are known and loved the world over. ²Often set in Russia or Poland, they usually focus on the funny (traits, traites) and problems of the (characters, characters'). ³Most of the (tales, tale's) are simple, yet in 1978 they won Singer a Nobel Prize in literature. ⁴Often the stories have to do with the daily (temptationes, temptations) that everyone faces. ⁵The way (peoples', people's) consciences work is explored. ⁶One might expect (subjects, subject's) such as hating evil and praising good to be heavy or boring. ⁷Instead, the (stories', storie's) plots are usually charming. ⁸Often they are funny, but just as often they catch (readers, readers') off guard. ⁹Some (characters', character's) "flaws" seem to make them more likable. ¹⁰(Other's, Others') virtues, which ought to make us admire the characters, don't appeal to us at all. ¹¹The (truth's, truths) that come out of the stories may seem sad or unfair. ¹²Sometimes, however, the (tales, tale's) are simple and truly heartwarming.

3.1 Plural and Possessive Nouns

1. Singer's; stories
2. traits; characters
3. tales
4. temptations
5. people's
6. subjects
7. stories'
8. readers
9. characters'
10. Others'
11. truths
12. tales

3.2 Pronoun Forms

A personal pronoun is a word that can take the place of a noun or another pronoun. A personal pronoun has three forms: the subject form, the object form, and the possessive form.

Subject Pronouns

Use the subject form of a pronoun when it is the subject of a sentence or the subject of a clause. *I, you, he, she, it, we,* and *they* are subject pronouns.

Using the correct pronoun form is not a problem when the sentence has just one pronoun. Problems can arise, however, when a noun and a pronoun—or two pronouns—are used in a compound subject or compound object. To see whether you are using the correct pronoun form, read the sentence with only one pronoun.

> "The Circuit" tells the story of a boy and his family of migrant workers. The story begins and ends as he and ~~them~~ *they* pack to move on to yet another "home."

Use the subject form of a pronoun when it is a predicate pronoun following a linking verb.

You often hear the object form of a predicate pronoun used in casual conversation (*It is me*). For this reason, the subject form may sound awkward to you, though it is preferred for more-formal writing.

> The boy is the narrator. It is ~~him~~ *he* who helps the readers feel his joy and pain.

Object Pronouns

Use the object form of a pronoun when it is the object of a sentence, the object of a clause, or the object of a preposition. *Me, you, him, her, it, us,* and *them* are object pronouns.

LINK TO LITERATURE

Notice how Francisco Jiménez uses pronouns to avoid repetition of the same nouns and to link ideas in different sentences throughout his short story "The Circuit," on page 545.

REVISING TIP

To check for a correct pronoun, see whether the sentence still makes sense when the subject and the pronoun are reversed. (*It was she. She was it.*)

We share with his family and he [him] the frustration caused by not staying anywhere long. One of the teachers treats he [him] and the other students with kindness.

Possessive Pronouns

Never use an apostrophe in a possessive pronoun. *My, mine, your, yours, his, her, hers, its, our, ours, their,* and *theirs* are possessive pronouns.

Writers often confuse the possessive pronouns *its, your,* and *their* with the contractions *it's, you're,* and *they're.* Remember that the pairs are spelled differently and that they have different meanings.

~~They're~~ [Their] disappointment at putting down roots only to pull them up again touches us. It's as if we, and not ~~them~~ [they], come home to find boxes packed. The sad circuit, or cycle, is our~~'~~s.

APPLY WHAT YOU'VE LEARNED

Write the correct pronoun form given in parentheses.

¹The life of a migrant worker would be hard for you and (I, me). ²(Them, They) and other workers must struggle at low-paying jobs just to survive. ³(They're, Their) working conditions are sometimes intolerable. ⁴Not only must workers settle for extremely low wages, but (they're, their) often unable to find any jobs for half the year. ⁵When (they, them) do, employers provide poor housing for (they, them). ⁶No sick days, holidays, or other benefits are offered their families or (them, they). ⁷You and (I, me) might wonder why anyone would settle for such work. ⁸Many workers come from other countries, however, where (its, it's) even harder to make a living. ⁹Black and Hispanic men, women, and children make up most of the migrant work force; poor whites and (they, them) suffer equally. ¹⁰Some travel with (they're, their) families; others send money home to places such as Haiti and the West Indies. ¹¹Compare (your, you're) life with that of a migrant worker. ¹²At (its, it's) worst it may be easier than what (he, him) or (she, her) must face.

3.2 Pronoun Forms

1. me
2. They
3. Their
4. they're
5. they; them
6. them
7. I
8. it's
9. they
10. their
11. your
12. its; he; she

GRAMMAR HANDBOOK 825

3.3 Pronoun Antecedents

An antecedent is the noun or pronoun to which a personal pronoun refers. The antecedent usually precedes the pronoun.

Pronoun and Antecedent Agreement

A pronoun must agree with its antecedent in
- number—singular or plural
- person—first, second, or third
- gender—masculine, feminine, or neuter

Use a singular pronoun to refer to a singular antecedent; use a plural pronoun to refer to a plural antecedent.

Do not allow interrupting words to determine the number of the personal pronoun.

> In "In the Land of Small Dragon" it is the younger half-sister, not the two older stepsisters, who ~~are~~ *is* unkind to the sweet Cinderella figure, Tâm.

If the antecedent is a noun that could refer to either a male or a female, use *he or she* (*him or her, his or her*), or reword the sentence to avoid the need for a singular pronoun.

> Somebody may wonder who Tâm is. ~~They~~ *He or she* might think she is a princess.
>
> or
>
> ~~Somebody~~ *People* may wonder who Tâm is. They might think she is a princess.

Be sure that the antecedent of a pronoun is clear.

In most cases, do not use a pronoun to refer to an entire idea or clause. Writing is much clearer if the exact reference is given.

LINK TO LITERATURE

"In The Land of Small Dragon," on page 662, was told by Dang Manh Kha to Ann Nolan Clark. The author presents an Asian Cinderella tale in poetic form. Her effective use of pronoun antecedents helps us to keep the characters separate in our minds.

Both this story and the Cinderella tale end happily, and ~~it is~~ *happy endings are* what we hope for.

"Goodness is always rewarded," "Beauty is as beauty does," and "Actions speak louder than words"—all apply *these sayings* in the tale "In the Land of Small Dragon."

Indefinite Pronouns as Antecedents

When a singular indefinite pronoun is the antecedent, use *he or she* (*him or her*, *his or her*), or rewrite the sentence to avoid the need for a singular pronoun.

Each person at the festival rejoiced. ~~They~~ *He or she* shared in the joy of the prince and princess.

or

All who were ~~Everyone~~ at the festival rejoiced. They shared in the joy of the prince and princess.

REVISING TIP

Avoid the indefinite use of *you* and *they*.

~~They say in~~ the story ~~that you should~~ *tells us to* be kind and good to everybody.

Indefinite Pronouns					
Singular	another anybody anyone anything	each either	everybody everyone everything	neither nobody no one nothing one	somebody someone something
Plural	both	few	many	several	
Singular or Plural	all	any	most	none	some

GRAMMAR HANDBOOK **827**

3.3 Pronoun Antecedents

Answers will vary. See typical answers below.

1 A tale like "In the Land of Small Dragon" is found in many countries; it reminds you of Cinderella. 2 Mufaro's Beautiful Daughters is one of these stories. The author drew upon traditional tales from Africa to write it. 3 In this story Nyasha was loved by all, but they usually did not like Nyasha's sister. 4 Nyasha encouraged the snake to live in her garden, where it was very comfortable. 5 Manyara was unkind and rude, and people could not help but see her rudeness. 6 One day a messenger arrived, and he said that the king was looking for a bride. 7 Manyara left on her journey to the king's city before Nyasha, and Nyasha was afraid she would be late. 8 On the way Manyara met an old woman; the woman reminded her to be helpful to anyone she met. 9 Instead, she was often rude to the people she met. 10 Nyasha was kind and courteous, and her kindness was rewarded in the end.

APPLY WHAT YOU'VE LEARNED

Rewrite this paragraph to make the pronoun references clear.

¹A tale like "In the Land of Small Dragon" is found in many countries; they remind you of Cinderella. ²*Mufaro's Beautiful Daughters* is one of these stories. The author drew upon traditional tales from Africa to write them. ³In this story Nyasha was loved by everyone, but they usually did not like her sister. ⁴She encouraged the snake to live in her garden, where it was very comfortable. ⁵Manyara was unkind and rude, and people could not help but see it. ⁶One day a messenger arrived, and they said that the king was looking for a bride. ⁷Manyara left on her journey to the king's city before Nyasha, and she was afraid she would be late. ⁸On the way Manyara met an old woman; she reminded her to be helpful to anyone she met. ⁹Instead, she was often rude to them. ¹⁰Nyasha was kind and courteous, and it was rewarded in the end.

REVISING TIP

Whom should replace *who* in both sentences in the second example:
By whom—object of a preposition
Introduces whom—object of the verb in a clause

3.4 Pronoun Usage

The form that a pronoun takes is always determined by its function within its own clause or sentence.

Who and Whom

Use *who* or *whoever* as the subject of a clause or sentence.

> In "Three Strong Women" a wrestler meets three women whom are much stronger than he.

Use *whom* as the direct or indirect object of a verb or verbal and as the object of a preposition.

People often use *who* for *whom* when speaking informally. However, in written English the pronouns should be used correctly.

> First he meets a young girl by who he is carried up a mountain. Then he learns that her mother and grandmother, who the girl introduces, are just as strong as she is.

828 GRAMMAR HANDBOOK

828 THE LANGUAGE OF LITERATURE TEACHER'S EDITION

In trying to determine the correct pronoun form, ignore interrupters that come between the subject and the verb.

Whom, do you think, needs the most exercise to get into shape? Who would you choose to help move your furniture?
(corrections: Whom → Who; Who → Whom)

Pronouns in Contractions

Do not confuse the contractions *it's*, *they're*, *who's*, and *you're* with possessive pronouns that sound the same—*its*, *their*, *whose*, and *your*.

The story is amusing because its not about traditional Japanese women and strong sumo wrestlers. The characters' roles seem switched, so their funnier.
(corrections: its → it's; their → they're)

APPLY WHAT YOU'VE LEARNED

Write the correct pronoun given in parentheses.

1. In recent years women's bodybuilding has come into (its, it's) own.
2. One reason may be that (its, it's) a challenge.
3. Some women (who, whom) take on this sport start by being concerned about (their, they're) safety.
4. Others, for (who, whom) health is a concern, also find bodybuilding very appealing.
5. (Who, Whom) is more interested in fitness today than the young?
6. People are more aware of (its, it's) importance now than ever before.
7. (Their, They're) finding bodybuilding more enjoyable than aerobics, jogging, or running.
8. Once people thought reducing diets were the only way to lose weight, but now we know (its, it's) more important to exercise.
9. Of all the people you know, (who, whom) do you most look up to?
10. (Who, Whom) do you think is the most fit?

3.4 Pronoun Usage

1. its
2. it's
3. who; their
4. whom
5. Who
6. its
7. They're
8. it's
9. whom
10. Who

 # Using Modifiers Effectively

4.1 Adjective or Adverb?

Use an adjective to modify a noun or a pronoun. Use an adverb to modify a verb, an adjective, or another adverb.

> In "Oh Broom, Get to Work" the author tells interest-*ly*ing about some especially boring visitors to her home. These men usual*ly* were ministers, and they had some peculiarly̶ ways of acting.

Use an adjective after a linking verb to describe the subject.

Remember that in addition to forms of the verb *be*, the following are linking verbs: *become, seem, appear, look, sound, feel, taste, grow,* and *smell*.

> Yo Chan and her sister felt ~~unhappily~~ *unhappy* about the many dull visitors. Only one minister seemed entertainingly.

 REVISING TIP

Always determine first which word is being modified. For example, in the first sentence of the first example, *tells* is the verb being modified, so it takes an adverb, *interestingly*. In the second sentence, *ways* is a noun, so its modifier needs to be an adjective, *peculiar*.

APPLY WHAT YOU'VE LEARNED

Correct the modifiers throughout.

¹In "Oh Broom, Get to Work" Yo Chan's parents are (proud, proudly) graduates of a Christian university in Japan. ²Christianity was brought there by (fearlessly, fearless) missionaries. ³The religion spread (quick, quickly) throughout Japan, beginning, in 1549. ⁴The (stern, sternly) rulers of the nation thought that a Western religion would undermine their power. ⁵In the early 1600s the (nervously, nervous) rulers began to limit the religion. ⁶The number of people practicing Christianity dropped (great, greatly) by 1640. ⁷Missionaries were (reluctant, reluctantly) allowed back into the country in 1873. ⁸After two centuries they found some evidence of Christianity that had survived the (extensive, extensively) persecution.

830 GRAMMAR HANDBOOK

4.1 Adjective or Adverb?

1. proud
2. fearless
3. quickly
4. stern
5. nervous
6. greatly
7. reluctantly
8. extensive

4.2 Comparisons and Negatives

Comparative and Superlative Adjectives

Use the comparative form of an adjective when comparing two things.

Comparative adjectives are formed by adding -er to short adjectives (*small—smaller*) or by using the word *more* with longer adjectives (*horrible—more horrible*).

> "The Adoption of Albert" is an impressive~r~ *a more impressive* story than many I have read. The characters in the story are more funny *funnier* than most.

Use the superlative form when comparing three or more things.

The superlative is formed by adding -est to short adjectives (*tall—tallest*) or by using the word *most* with longer adjectives (*interesting—most interesting*).

> Of the characters, who is the daringest *most*? Who is the most quietest?

REVISING TIP

When comparing something with everything else of its kind, do not leave out the word *other*. (*Andy is quicker than any other player on the team.*)

The comparative and superlative forms of some adjectives are irregular.

Adjective	Comparative	Superlative
good	better	best
well	better	best
bad	worse	worst
ill	worse	worst
little	less *or* lesser	least
much	more	most
many	more	most
far	farther *or* further	farthest *or* furthest

Comparative and Superlative Adverbs

When comparing two actions, use the comparative form of an adverb, adding -er or the word more.

More oftener than not, Aunt Rhoda behaved oddlier [more oddly] than anyone else in her family.

When comparing more than two actions, use the superlative form of an adverb, adding -est or the word most.

Of all the mistakes in the story, the one made by Louis's mother ended humorousliest [most humorously].

Double Negatives

To avoid double negatives, use only one negative word in a clause.

Besides the compounds formed with *no,* the words *barely, hardly,* and *scarcely* also function as negative words.

No one hardly suspected that Albert's parents were searching for him. They couldn't find him nowhere [anywhere].

REVISING TIP

Do not use both *-er* and *more* or *-est* and *most.*

Harry's piranha moves more faster than Jim's. It is the most boldest fish I've ever seen.

APPLY WHAT YOU'VE LEARNED

Correct the mistakes in modifiers used in comparisons.

¹Surely the importantest characters in "The Adoption of Albert" are the earthworms. ²The very tinier earthworms grow only 0.04 inch long. ³The most longest earthworms are 11 feet long. ⁴Earthworms can tell the difference between more easier and more hard work. ⁵After trying to move a leaf that was held down, they switched to a leaf that could be moved more faster. ⁶The earthworm that lasted most longest in captivity lived ten years. ⁷Some earthworms in Great Britain are the beautifullest green. ⁸The more ordinarier red-brown color of common earthworms comes from iron pigment in their blood. ⁹They burrow more deeper in winter or when the soil is dry.

832 GRAMMAR HANDBOOK

4.2 Comparisons and Negatives

1 Surely the most important characters in "The Adoption of Albert" are the earthworms. **2** The tiniest earthworms grow only 0.04 inch long. **3** The longest earthworms are 11 feet long. **4** Earthworms can tell the difference between easier and harder work. **5** After trying to move a leaf that was held down, they switched to a leaf that could be moved faster. **6** The earthworm that lasted longest in captivity lived ten years. **7** Some earthworms in Great Britain are the most beautiful green. **8** The more ordinary red-brown color of common earthworms comes from iron pigment in their blood. **9** They burrow deeper in winter or when the soil is dry.

4.3 Special Problems with Modifiers

The following terms are frequently misused in spoken English, but they should be used correctly in written English.

Them and Those

Them is always a pronoun and never a modifier of a noun. **Those** is a pronoun when it stands alone. It is an adjective when followed by a noun.

> In "Flowers and Freckle Cream" Elizabeth learns that ~~them~~ *those* freckles of hers aren't so bad after all.

Bad and Badly

Always use *bad* as an adjective, whether before a noun or after a linking verb. *Badly* should generally be used to modify an action verb.

> Grandpa saved the day when Elizabeth felt so badly*ly*.
> She acted bad*ly* when she refused to tell anyone what was wrong.

This, That, These, and Those

Whether used as adjectives or as pronouns, *this* and *these* refer to people and things that are nearby, and *that* and *those* refer to people and things that are farther away.

> All day long, Elizabeth worked outdoors in ~~this~~ *that* faraway field. When she came home, she had ~~these~~ *those* hateful freckles on her face.

REVISING TIP

Avoid the use of *here* with *this* and *these*; also, do not use *there* with *that* and *those*.

Why did Elizabeth buy that ~~there~~ freckle cream? Those ~~there~~ products are expensive!

GRAMMAR HANDBOOK 833

Good and Well

Good is always an adjective, never an adverb. Use well as either an adjective or an adverb, depending on the sentence.

When used as an adjective, *well* usually refers to a person's health. As an adverb, *well* modifies an action verb. In the expression "feeling good," *good* refers to being happy or pleased.

> Hoeing tobacco under the hot sun, Elizabeth did her work ~~good~~ *well*. She felt ~~well~~ *good* when she saw all her fine work.

Few and Little, Fewer and Less

Few refers to a number of things that can be counted; little refers to an amount or quantity. Fewer is used when comparing numbers of things; less is used when comparing amounts or quantities.

> Because Elizabeth felt appreciated by Grandpa, having ~~less~~ *fewer* freckles didn't matter. She decided that the ~~fewer~~ *less* she spent on freckle cream, the better.

APPLY WHAT YOU'VE LEARNED

Write the modifier from each pair that fits the meaning of the sentence.

[1] In "Flowers and Freckle Cream" Elizabeth makes one of (them, those) mail-order purchases. [2] In the 1870s big-city department stores decided that mail order was needed (bad, badly) by people on farms. [3] (Less, Fewer) rural people could travel to the city to shop. [4] The stores sent (these, those) customers catalogs. [5] Mail-order merchants did (good, well) by serving farm families. [6] When more people moved to the cities, mail-order business did (bad, badly). [7] Later, (this, that) kind of business was advertised in magazines and on television. [8] Later still, (those, these) merchants began sending catalogs to city dwellers. [9] The merchants also sent catalogs to people who had (few, little) time to shop. [10] Today, cable-television shopping channels work (good, well) to provide the ultimate mail-order experience.

4.3 Special Problems with Modifiers

1. those
2. badly
3. Fewer
4. those
5. well
6. badly
7. that
8. these
9. little
10. well

Using Verbs Correctly 5

5.1 Verb Tenses and Forms

Verb tense shows the time of an action or condition. Writers sometimes cause confusion when they use different verb tenses in describing actions that occur at the same time.

Consistent Use of Tenses

When two or more actions occur at the same time or in sequence, use the same verb tense to describe the actions.

> "The Mushroom" tells about a fungus that starts small and then lived [s/] almost forever. It just got [gets] stronger and stronger all the time.

A shift in tense is necessary when two events occur at different times or out of sequence. The tenses of the verbs should clearly indicate that one action precedes the other.

> Now that the mushroom was [is] a thousand years old, it weighed [s/] 38 tons. But at its birth, a slow, gentle rain helps [ed/] the tiny mushroom spores grow.

Tense	Verb Form
Present	close/closes
Past	closed
Future	will/shall close
Present perfect	have/has closed
Past perfect	had closed
Future perfect	will/shall have closed

LINK TO LITERATURE

Throughout "The Mushroom," page 228, H. M. Hoover uses the past tense and past participles to describe a huge mushroom that lives a very long time. She shifts tense only twice. On page 230 she says, "A sheath of a thousand hyphae is no thicker than a human hair." She says it again on page 233. The shift in tense stands out, emphasizing the fact the author is presenting general information.

REVISING TIP

In telling a story, be careful not to shift tenses so often that the reader has difficulty keeping the sequence of events straight.

Past Tense and the Past Participle

The simple past form of a verb can always stand alone. Always use the past participles of the following irregular verbs when the verbs follow helping verbs.

Present Tense	Past Tense	Past Participle
know	knew	(have, had) known
lay	laid	(have, had) laid
lie	lay	(have, had) lain
ride	rode	(have, had) ridden
rise	rose	(have, had) risen
run	ran	(have, had) run
say	said	(have, had) said
see	saw	(have, had) seen
sing	sang	(have, had) sung
speak	spoke	(have, had) spoken
steal	stole	(have, had) stolen
swim	swam	(have, had) swum
take	took	(have, had) taken
teach	taught	(have, had) taught

Much history ~~have went~~ *had gone* past while the mushroom had been growing. Even though humans paved it over when they built a mall, the fungus ~~have~~ *had* grown too big to die.

APPLY WHAT YOU'VE LEARNED

Write the correct verb for each sentence.

1. In "The Mushroom" we (seen, have seen) an interesting member of the fungus kingdom.
2. Naturalists have (saw, seen) as many as 3,300 kinds of mushrooms.
3. Of those, 2,000 (are, were) nonpoisonous.
4. The inky cap mushroom's gills turn black when it (matures, matured).
5. The indigo lactaria mushroom (is, was) totally blue.
6. Sharp, spiny structures (stick, stuck) out from hedgehog mushroom caps.
7. People have (spoke, spoken) of mushrooms growing 15 inches tall.
8. Humans aren't the only ones to have (took, taken) mushrooms into their diet.
9. People have (saw, seen) red squirrels putting mushrooms on branches to dry.
10. Then, as the people watched, the squirrels (ran, run) off to store the mushrooms.

836 GRAMMAR HANDBOOK

5.1 Verb Tenses and Forms

1. have seen
2. seen
3. are
4. matures
5. is
6. stick
7. spoken
8. taken
9. seen
10. ran

5.2 Commonly Confused Verbs

The following verb pairs are easily confused.

Let and Leave

Let means "to allow or permit." **Leave** means "to depart" or "to allow something to remain where it is."

> "Aaron's Gift" ~~leaves~~ *lets* the reader imagine what to do about a wounded animal. Should you ~~let~~ *leave* it to die?

Lie and Lay

Lie means "to rest in a flat position." **Lay** means "to put or place."

> The pigeon ~~laid~~ *lay* down, almost dead. He ~~lied~~ *laid* his ruffled feathers as close as he could to his body.

Sit and Set

Sit means "to be in a seated position." **Set** means "to put or place."

> Pidge would often ~~set~~ *sit* quietly and look at Aaron. Aaron was glad he'd ~~sat~~ *set* out food to help the bird get well.

Rise and Raise

Rise means "to move upward." **Raise** means "to move something upward."

> Pidge escaped the gang by flying, ~~raising~~ *rising* up quickly. He ~~rose~~ *raised* his healed wing and flapped desperately.

REVISING TIP

If you're uncertain about which verb to use, check to see whether the verb has an object. The verbs *lie*, *sit*, and *rise* never have objects.

GRAMMAR HANDBOOK 837

Learn and Teach

Learn means "to gain knowledge or skill." **Teach** means "to help someone learn."

> Pidge learned[taught] Aaron much about healing and about standing up for a friend.

Here are the principal parts of these troublesome verb pairs.

Present Tense	Past Tense	Past Participle
let	let	(have, had) let
leave	left	(have, had) left
lie	lay	(have, had) lain
lay	laid	(have, had) laid
sit	sat	(have, had) sat
set	set	(have, had) set
rise	rose	(have, had) risen
raise	raised	(have, had) raised
learn	learned	(have, had) learned
teach	taught	(have, had) taught

APPLY WHAT YOU'VE LEARNED

Choose the correct verb from each pair in parentheses.

1. Biologists have (left, let) us know that rock doves are the ancestors of pigeons like the one in "Aaron's Gift."
2. Rock doves like to (sit, set) their nests on cliff ledges, so their descendants thrive in modern cities.
3. People started (raising, rising) rock doves for food around 4500 B.C.
4. (Leave, Let) me tell you that today there are about 285 kinds of pigeons.
5. Pigeons usually are active during the day, but do they ever (lay, lie) down to sleep?
6. Some kinds of pigeons weigh as much as three pounds, so they must be strong fliers to (raise, rise) into the air.
7. When we raised pigeons, they usually (lay, laid) two eggs at a time.
8. Biologists (teach, learn) us that some pigeons use the sounds their feathers make during flight to signal each other.
9. A crowned pigeon has plumage that (raises, rises) up from its head and looks like a peacock's tail.
10. Rats (setting, sitting) in shadowy corners are among a pigeon's enemies.
11. The rats and humans have (learned, taught) pigeons to beware of them.

5.2 Commonly Confused Verbs

1. let
2. set
3. raising
4. Let
5. lie
6. rise
7. laid
8. teach
9. rises
10. sitting
11. taught

Correcting Capitalization

6.1 Proper Nouns and Adjectives

A common noun names a whole class of persons, places, things, or ideas. A proper noun names a particular person, place, thing, or idea. A proper adjective is an adjective formed from a proper noun. All proper nouns and proper adjectives are capitalized.

Names and Personal Titles

Capitalize the name and title of a person.

Also capitalize initials and abbreviations that stand for names and titles. *Captain Greaves, Blackbeard, Sir Henry Morgan, S. Bonnet,* and *Anne Bonny* are capitalized correctly.

> *Gold and Silver, Silver and Gold* tells about captain william kidd, famous as a Pirate. Others besides the Captain included "calico jack" rackham, charles vane, and two women—mary read and jeanne de belleville. Even sir francis drake was a Pirate before the queen knighted him.

Capitalize a word referring to a family relationship when it is used as someone's name (*Uncle Joseph*) but not when it is used to identify a person (*Andrea's aunt*).

> Charlie smith, my Uncle, says he's glad he didn't live in a world with pirates. I disagree with uncle charlie, but my Mother agrees with him.

LINK TO LITERATURE

In the excerpt from *Gold and Silver, Silver and Gold*, on page 430, notice how Alvin Schwartz refers to specific places, people, and things. These precise names help you visualize scenes. More-general words probably would not help you see the story or believe it as easily.

REVISING TIP

Do not capitalize personal titles used as common nouns. (*We met the emperor.*)

GRAMMAR HANDBOOK 839

Languages, Nationalities, Religious Terms

Capitalize the names of languages and nationalities, as well as religious names and terms.

Capitalize words referring to languages and nationalities, such as *Spanish, Norwegian, Turkish, Yiddish,* and *Greek*. Capitalize religious names and terms, such as *Allah, Jehovah, Bible,* and *Koran*.

> Captain kidd took gold from a wrecked french ship, and he stole armenian trading ships owned by the emperor of India. He refused to raid a dutch ship, though.

School Subjects

Capitalize the name of a specific school course (*Choral Music, Physics I, Chemistry 2*). Do not capitalize a general reference to a school subject (*biology, geometry, health*).

> My Social Studies teacher said that next year in history 2 we will learn about the New Orleans pirate Jean Laffite.

Organizations, Institutions

Capitalize the important words in the official names of organizations and institutions (*Parliament, Dutch West India Company*).

Do not capitalize words that refer to kinds of organizations or institutions (*college, hospital, museums*) or a word that refers to specific organization but is not its official name (*to the museum*).

> The smithsonian institution has materials on Captain Kidd. Maybe the new york historical society or another Library does too, since Kidd lived in New York.

REVISING TIP

Do not capitalize minor words in a proper noun that is made up of several words. (*Museum of Modern Art*)

840 GRAMMAR HANDBOOK

Geographical Names, Events, Time Periods

Capitalize geographical names, as well as the names of events, historical periods and documents, holidays, and months and days, but not the names of seasons or directions.

Names	Examples
Continents	North America, Europe, Asia
Bodies of water	Caribbean Sea, Delaware Bay, Hudson River, Indian Ocean
Political units	France, the Netherlands, India, New Jersey
Sections of a country	the Midwest, New England
Public areas	Central Park, Yosemite National Park
Roads and structures	Wall Street, Taj Mahal
Historical events	French and Indian War, Russian Revolution
Documents	Treaty of Westminster, the Constitution
Periods of history	Dark Ages, Enlightenment
Holidays	Fourth of July, Veterans Day
Months and days	November, Monday
Seasons	spring, winter
Directions	east, northwest

> **REVISING TIP**
>
> Do not capitalize a reference that does not use the full name of a place, event, or period. (*Buckingham Palace is the most beautiful palace in the world.*)

Captain Kidd was born in scotland around 1645 and died on may 23, 1701, in london. When he was executed on that late Spring day, he left behind a wife and children on liberty street in new york city.

APPLY WHAT YOU'VE LEARNED

Correct any capitalization errors.

1. *Gold and Silver, Silver and Gold* made me curious about Pirates.
2. Therefore, I found out about buccaneers like barbarossa and henry jennings.
3. Kidd's treasure probably included persian gulf pearls, diamonds from india, and emeralds from south america.
4. My aunt theresa reminded me to check our Village Library for information.
5. I'm glad she's such a helpful Aunt.
6. Maybe the vatican library or the conde museum knows about kidd's life.
7. I could ask the Librarian just how to do this research for my History project.
8. My math II teacher, miss flanders, told me to read about less famous Pirates, like edward low.
9. Finally, uncle charlie said to look into the treaty of paris.
10. He said it outlawed privateering, which was a kind of legal Piracy.

GRAMMAR HANDBOOK **841**

6.1 Proper Nouns and Adjectives

1. *Gold and Silver, Silver and Gold* made me curious about pirates.
2. Therefore, I found out about buccaneers like Barbarossa and Henry Jennings.
3. Kidd's treasure probably included Persian Gulf pearls, diamonds from India, and emeralds from South America.
4. My aunt Theresa reminded me to check our village library for information.
5. I'm glad she's such a helpful aunt.
6. Maybe the Vatican Library or the Conde Museum knows about Kidd's life.
7. I could ask the librarian just how to do this research for my history project.
8. My Math II teacher, Miss Flanders, told me to read about less famous pirates, like Edward Low.
9. Finally, Uncle Charlie said to look into the Treaty of Paris.
10. He said it outlawed privateering, which was a kind of legal piracy.

6.2 Titles of Created Works

Titles follow certain capitalization rules.

Poems, Stories, Articles

Capitalize the first word, the last word, and all other important words in the title of a poem, a story, or an article. Enclose the title in quotation marks.

> Carl Sandburg's poem primer lesson talks about risks you take when you say harsh things. Harsh words hurt people.

Books, Plays, Magazines, Newspapers, Films

Capitalize the first word, the last word, and all other important words in the title of a book, a play or musical, a magazine, a newspaper, or a film. Underline or italicize the title to set it off.

Within a title, don't capitalize articles, conjunctions, and prepositions of fewer than five letters.

> Primer lesson appeared in Sandburg's book complete poems, published in 1950.

REVISING TIP

Underline the titles of books, plays, magazines and newspapers, and movies when they are typed or handwritten. Enclose the titles of poems, short stories, and articles in quotation marks.

APPLY WHAT YOU'VE LEARNED

Rewrite these sentences, correcting the punctuation and capitalization of titles.

1. Sandburg's poem primer lesson is just a tiny part of all the work he did.
2. Most people probably think of him as a poet, especially for his 1914 poem chicago.
3. He also wrote many volumes of historical biography about Lincoln. One set of these was abraham lincoln: the prairie years.
4. I wonder whether the song buffalo gals won't you come out tonight is in his collection called the american songbag.
5. In his early years he worked for the chicago daily news.
6. Critics think Sandburg's poetry was strongly influenced by Walt Whitman's poetry collection leaves of grass.

842 GRAMMAR HANDBOOK

6.2 Titles of Created Works

1. Sandburg's poem "Primer Lesson" is just a tiny part of all the work he did.
2. Most people probably think of him as a poet, especially for his 1914 poem "Chicago."
3. He also wrote many volumes of historical biography about Lincoln. One set of these was *Abraham Lincoln: The Prairie Years.*
4. I wonder whether the song "Buffalo Gals Won't You Come Out Tonight" is in his collection called *The American Songbag.*
5. In his early years he worked for the *Chicago Daily News.*
6. Critics think Sandburg's poetry was strongly influenced by Walt Whitman's poetry collection *Leaves of Grass.*

Correcting Punctuation   7

7.1 Compound Sentences

Punctuation helps organize longer sentences that have several clauses.

Commas in Compound Sentences

Use a comma before the conjunction that joins the clauses of a compound sentence.

> In "Matthew Henson at the Top of the World" Henson got to the North Pole⋏and he worked really hard to make the most of his opportunity.

Semicolons in Compound Sentences

Use a semicolon between the clauses of a compound sentence when no conjunction is used. Use a semicolon before, and a comma after, a conjunctive adverb that joins the clauses of a compound sentence.

Conjunctive adverbs include *therefore, however, nevertheless, consequently,* and *besides.*

> He made the dream of his boyhood come true⋏however⋏ racism interfered with his ambition. The limits placed on African Americans closed doors for him⋏his abilities usually were ignored.

LINK TO LITERATURE

Notice on pages 56 and 57 of "Matthew Henson at the Top of the World" how Jim Haskins uses compound and complex sentences. He combines ideas and merges pieces of information in a way that shows their relation to one another.

REVISING TIP

Even when clauses are connected by a coordinating conjunction, you may use a semicolon between them if one or both clauses contain a comma.

GRAMMAR HANDBOOK **843**

7.1 Compound Sentences

1 "Matthew Henson at the Top of the World" describes the discovery of the North Pole, but the Peary expedition wasn't the first to seek it. **2** The earliest Arctic expedition probably took place in the late 300s b.c.; a Greek explorer, Pytheas, said he found an island six days north of Scotland. **3** People didn't believe him; they thought there was nothing but ice that far north. **4** In the late 1500s people wanted a quick way to the riches of the Orient; therefore, the Englishman Martin Frobisher tried to find a northwest passage through the Arctic. **5** In the 1770s Samuel Hearne was the first European to travel by land to the Arctic Ocean from Hudson Bay, and much exploration followed his journey. **6** In 1926 Richard Byrd and Floyd Bennett made the first flight over the North Pole; the next step was to complete an undersea passage over the pole. **7** A submarine, the *Nautilus*, crossed the North Pole under the icecap in 1958.

APPLY WHAT YOU'VE LEARNED

Rewrite these sentences, adding commas and semicolons where necessary.

1 "Matthew Henson at the Top of the World" describes the discovery of the North Pole but the Peary expedition wasn't the first to seek it. *2* The earliest Arctic expedition probably took place in the late 300s B.C. a Greek explorer, Pytheas, said he found an island six days north of Scotland. *3* People didn't believe him they thought there was nothing but ice that far north. *4* In the late 1500s people wanted a quick way to the riches of the Orient therefore the Englishman Martin Frobisher tried to find a northwest passage through the Arctic. *5* In the 1770s Samuel Hearne was the first European to travel by land to the Arctic Ocean from Hudson Bay and much exploration followed his journey. *6* In 1926 Richard Byrd and Floyd Bennett made the first flight over the North Pole the next step was to complete an undersea passage over the pole. *7* A submarine, the *Nautilus,* crossed the North Pole under the icecap in 1958.

7.2 Elements Set Off in a Sentence

Most elements that are not essential to a sentence are set off by commas to highlight the main idea of the sentence.

Introductory Words

Use a comma to separate an introductory word from the rest of the sentence.

> Definitely⌃ "The First Emperor" gets me thinking about what China was like in the 200s B.C.

Use a comma to separate an introductory phrase from the rest of the sentence.

Use a comma to set off more than one introductory prepositional phrase but not a single prepositional phrase in most cases.

> With its clear images of cruel behavior⌃ this article makes me doubt I could have survived in that world.

844 GRAMMAR HANDBOOK

Interrupters

Use commas to set off a word that interrupts the flow of a sentence.

> What, perchance, would make a king of the smallest, weakest state want to unite all the neighboring states? Was it like, maybe, a kid who is picked on and finally stands up to a bully, except on a larger scale?

Use commas to set off a group of words that interrupts the flow of a sentence.

> The discovery of Ch'in's tomb, including all the soldiers and horses guarding it, has astonished archaeologists.

Nouns of Address

Use a comma to set off a name or noun in direct address at the beginning or end of a sentence.

> If I could talk with Emperor Ch'in, I'd say, "Emperor, why put people in danger for no reason? When you built the Great Wall, all those deaths weren't necessary."

Use commas to set off a noun in direct address in the middle of a sentence.

> Then I'd say, "Maybe you saved lives when you stopped the wars between all those countries. But how many people, Emperor, did you kill because you were scared?"

Appositives

Set off with commas an appositive phrase that is not necessary to the meaning of the sentence.

The following sentence could be understood without the words set off by commas.

> The emperor⌄ a silly person about some things⌄ dug his own grave in more ways than one.

Do not set off with commas an appositive phrase that is necessary to the meaning of the sentence.

The following sentence could not be understood without the words set off by commas.

> Ch'in,⌢ the warrior and unifier,⌢ seems very different from Ch'in,⌢ the shaking-in-his-shoes mouse.

For Clarity

Use commas to prevent misreading or misunderstanding.

> Excavators finally found the tomb of Ch'in that professors had searched for⌄ for a long time.

REVISING TIP

Sometimes if a comma is missing, parts of a sentence can be grouped in more than one way by a reader. A comma separates the parts so that they can be read in only one way.

APPLY WHAT YOU'VE LEARNED

Rewrite these sentences. Add or delete commas where necessary.

¹Ch'in Shih Huang Ti "The First Emperor" sounds like a typical emperor. ²An emperor rules not just one but several countries always staying alert to outside threats. ³Clearly his country is the strongest one. ⁴Usually an emperor holds the empire together by military force. ⁵Empires those vast political machines are formed by war. ⁶Once an empire is established however it reduces the number of wars for a while. ⁷In an empire with strong central control everyone knows who's boss. ⁸Empires can have good effects when for example they force people to exchange languages, art, and technology. ⁹If I could, I'd say to Ch'in, "Tell me Emperor what you accomplished."

846 GRAMMAR HANDBOOK

7.2 Elements Set Off in a Sentence

1 Ch'in Shih Huang Ti, "The First Emperor," sounds like a typical emperor. **2** An emperor rules not just one but several countries, always staying alert to outside threats. **3** Clearly, his country is the strongest one. **4** Usually, an emperor holds the empire together by military force. **5** Empires, those vast political machines, are formed by war. **6** Once an empire is established, however, it reduces the number of wars for a while. **7** In an empire with strong central control, everyone knows who's boss. **8** Empires can have good effects when, for example, they force people to exchange languages, art, and technology. **9** If I could, I'd say to Ch'in, "Tell me, Emperor, what you accomplished."

846 THE LANGUAGE OF LITERATURE TEACHER'S EDITION

7.3 Elements in a Series

Commas should be used to separate three or more items in a series and to separate adjectives preceding a noun.

Subjects, Verbs, Objects, and Other Elements

Use a comma after every item except the last in a series of three or more items.

Subjects, verbs, objects, and other elements often appear in series.

> In *The Hobbit* Bilbo Baggins is rudely dragged from his familiar routine⌃ asked to do more than he thinks he can⌃ and congratulated by his comrades when he does it.

Predicate adjectives also occur in series.

> As the play begins, Bilbo Baggins is fearful⌃ silly⌃ and confused. His dwarf comrades, however, are jolly⌃ boisterous⌃ and rowdy.

Adverbs and prepositional phrases may also occur in series.

> When there's time, Bilbo handles his problems slowly⌃ thoughtfully⌃ and carefully. When he has to, though, he decides on a new course of action with speed⌃ with wit⌃ and with great accuracy.

 REVISING TIP

Note in the example that a comma followed by a conjunction precedes the last element in the series. That comma is always used.

GRAMMAR HANDBOOK **847**

Two or More Adjectives

In many cases when two or more adjectives precede a noun, use a comma after each adjective except the last.

If you can reverse the order of adjectives without changing the meaning or if you can use *and* between them, separate them with commas.

> Bilbo's comrade Dwalin has a long, bushy beard and wears a dark, green hood.

APPLY WHAT YOU'VE LEARNED

Rewrite each sentence, correcting the comma errors.

1. *The Hobbit* was written in 1937 by J.R.R. Tolkien, a novelist scholar and professor.
2. His major fantasy saga, *The Lord of the Rings*, is made up of three parts: *The Fellowship of the Ring The Two Towers* and *The Return of the King*.
3. Tolkien was born in South Africa was raised in England and became a teacher of medieval languages at Oxford in 1925.
4. His fantasy world is dramatic detailed and entertaining.
5. Gollum, a sleazy character in *The Hobbit,* hisses nervously slimily and nastily when he talks to Bilbo, the hero.
6. In *The Lord of the Rings* Frodo, Bilbo's cousin, learns that Bilbo's ring has powers of invisibility of evil and of danger.
7. Industrious and good-natured Bilbo meets the Elven-Queen, who wears elegant, forest green clothing and a simple, oak-leaf crown.

7.4 Dates, Addresses, and Letters

Punctuation in dates, addresses, and letters makes information easy to understand.

Dates

Use a comma between the day of the month and the year. If the date falls in the middle of a sentence, use another comma after the year.

> In "User Friendly" Kevin's computer might greet him with "Today is Monday, April 24, 1996, a nice spring day."

848 GRAMMAR HANDBOOK

7.3 Elements in a Series

1. *The Hobbit* was written in 1937 by J.R.R. Tolkien, a novelist, scholar, and professor.
2. His major fantasy saga, *The Lord of the Rings,* is made up of three parts: *The Fellowship of the Ring, The Two Towers,* and *The Return of the King.*
3. Tolkien was born in South Africa, was raised in England, and became a teacher of medieval languages at Oxford in 1925.
4. His fantasy world is dramatic, detailed, and entertaining.
5. Gollum, a sleazy character in *The Hobbit,* hisses nervously, slimily, and nastily when he talks to Bilbo, the hero.
6. In *The Lord of the Rings* Frodo, Bilbo's cousin, learns that Bilbo's ring has powers of invisibility, of evil, and of danger.
7. Industrious and good-natured Bilbo meets the Elven-Queen, who wears elegant forest green clothing and a simple oak-leaf crown.

848 THE LANGUAGE OF LITERATURE **TEACHER'S EDITION**

Addresses

Use a comma to separate the city and the state in an address or other location. If the city and state fall in the middle of a sentence, use a comma after the state too.

> Kevin's dad has gone to Chicago͜Illinois͜on business for three days. Meanwhile, the computer Kevin calls Louis has developed an outlaw personality.

Parts of a Letter

Use a comma after the greeting and after the closing in a letter.

> If the machine had been a person, its last message might have read as follows:
>
> Dear Kevin͜
> I will always love you.
>
>   Sadly͜
>   Louise

APPLY WHAT YOU'VE LEARNED

Rewrite the following sentences, correcting the comma errors.

1. After reading "User Friendly," I had to write to my friend Darlene in Lima Ohio my old home.
2. Dear Darlene
       The computer named Louis in a story I just read has an "inbuilt logic/growth program" that lets it think and learn like a person. Can computers really do that?
                           Yours truly
                           Markie Malone
3. Darlene told me that computer designers near San Francisco California are working on something called artificial intelligence.
4. On May 8 1996 I decided to write my friend Ernesto about artificial intelligence.
5. Dear Ernesto
       You said your mom designs computers. Could she send me stuff on artificial intelligence?
                           Your friend
                           Markie Malone
6. On May 15 1996 Ernesto and his mom replied that artificial intelligence programs can duplicate some human thinking skills, but not human common sense.

7.4 Dates, Addresses, and Letters

1. After reading "User Friendly," I had to write to my friend Darlene in Lima, Ohio, my old home.
2. Dear Darlene,
   The computer named Louis in a story I just read has an "inbuilt logic/growth program" that lets it think and learn like a person. Can computers really do that?
                   Yours truly,
                   Markie Malone
3. Darlene told me that computer designers near San Francisco, California, are working on something called artificial intelligence.
4. On May 8, 1996, I decided to write my friend Ernesto about artificial intelligence.
5. Dear Ernesto,
   You said your mom designs computers. Could she send me stuff on artificial intelligence?
                   Your friend,
                 Markie Malone
6. On May 15, 1996, Ernesto and his mom replied that artificial intelligence programs can duplicate some human thinking skills, but not human common sense.

7.5 Quotations

Quotation marks let readers know exactly who said what. Incorrectly placed or missing quotation marks cause confusion.

Quotation Marks

Use quotation marks at the beginning and the end of direct quotations and to set off titles of short works.

> In ˅The Red Lion˅ Azgid, prince of Persia, travels in secret, running away from what he's scared of. He keeps saying to people, ˅Forgive me if I do not reveal my name.˅

REVISING TIP

If quoted words form part of a sentence you are writing, you can begin them with a lowercase letter. (*Will Rogers said that everybody "is ignorant, only on different subjects."*)

Capitalize the first word in a direct quotation, especially in a piece of dialogue.

> One person he talks to replies, "you are welcome to stay with me."

End Punctuation

Place periods inside quotation marks. Place question marks and exclamation points inside quotation marks if they belong to the quotation; place them outside if they do not belong to the quotation. Place semicolons outside quotation marks.

> When I read this story, I said to my sister, "I would have been afraid of a lion too"!
>
> "Are you admitting that you're not brave"? she said.
>
> I responded, "Not really;" I added that I had really enjoyed "The Red Lion".

850 GRAMMAR HANDBOOK

Use a comma to end a quotation that is a complete sentence but is followed by explanatory words.

"God be with you͜," said the shepherd to the stranger.

Divided Quotations

Capitalize the first word of the second part of a direct quotation if it begins a new sentence.

"Well, then, come up when you wish," said the emir. "yours is the first bedroom on the right."

Do not capitalize the first word of the second part of a divided quotation if it does not begin a new sentence.

"My men are pleased with your spirit," the prince's host said to him, "nd with your skill at hunting."

> **REVISING TIP**
>
> Should the first word of the second part of a divided quotation be capitalized? Imagine the quotation without the explanatory words. If a capital letter would not be used, then do not use one in the divided quotation. Note that commas always go inside quotation marks.

APPLY WHAT YOU'VE LEARNED

Rewrite these sentences, inserting quotation marks and other appropriate punctuation and correcting capitalization.

1. Gail and Eric were discussing a fable, The Red Lion.
2. Gail said, "to get background, I checked out the new words in the story."
3. "That's just what I did," said Eric. "Because words like *emir, sheik,* and *vizier* looked different. They entered English around 1577."
4. Gail then noted that the dictionary "Comes in handy sometimes."
5. She continued, "The story takes place in Persia, so I checked the encyclopedia. Persia is the old name of Iran"!
6. "The fable," Eric said, "Probably comes from a peaceful time in Persia, the late 1500s to the early 1700s, right"?
7. Gail said, "Well, maybe;" then Eric continued, "Invasions from the west were stopped by some wise treaties."
8. "Except you're forgetting the Arab sheik" muttered Gail.
9. Remember that he and his people were preparing for a battle, she said.

7.5 Quotations

1. Gail and Eric were discussing a fable, "The Red Lion."
2. Gail said, "To get background, I checked out the new words in the story."
3. "That's just what I did," said Eric, "because words like *emir, sheik,* and *vizier* looked different. They entered English around 1577."
4. Gail then noted that the dictionary "comes in handy sometimes."
5. She continued, "The story takes place in Persia, so I checked the encyclopedia. Persia is the old name of Iran!"
6. "The fable," Eric said, "probably comes from a peaceful time in Persia, the late 1500s to the early 1700s, right?"
7. Gail said, "Well, maybe"; then Eric continued, "Invasions from the west were stopped by some wise treaties."
8. "Except you're forgetting the Arab sheik," muttered Gail.
9. "Remember that he and his people were preparing for a battle," she said.

Grammar Glossary

This glossary contains various terms you need to understand when you use the Grammar Handbook. Used as a reference source, this glossary will help you explore grammar concepts and the ways they relate to one another.

Adjective An adjective modifies, or describes, a noun or pronoun. (*sunny* morning, *lucky* me)

A **predicate adjective** follows a linking verb and describes the subject. (The puppy is *lively*.)

A **proper adjective** is formed from a proper noun. (*Canadian* bacon)

The **comparative** form of an adjective compares two things. (*more industrious*, *larger*)

The **superlative** form of an adjective compares three or more things. (*most serious*, *greatest*)

What Adjectives Tell	Examples
How many	*few* songs *many* chances
What kind	*bright* colors *colder* winters
Which one(s)	*this* meeting *those* athletes

Adverb An adverb modifies a verb, an adjective, or another adverb. (Yi-Ming spoke *softly*.)

The **comparative** form of an adverb compares two actions. (*more slyly*, *later*)

The **superlative** form of an adverb compares three or more actions. (*most rapidly*, *soonest*)

What Adverbs Tell	Examples
How	write *carelessly* eat *quickly*
When	*Soon* I'll be home. I'll see you *later*.
Where	They traveled *far*. Put it *someplace*.
To what extent	I am *rather* tired. This is *quite* odd.

Agreement Sentence parts that correspond with one another are said to be in agreement.

In **pronoun-antecedent agreement,** a pronoun and the word it refers to are the same in number, gender, and person. (*Ann* played *her* flute. *We* played *our* drums.)

In **subject-verb agreement,** the subject and the verb in a sentence are the same in number. (*They* act well. *She* acts well.)

Antecedent An antecedent is the noun or pronoun to which a pronoun refers. (If *Leo* hurts *his* leg, *he'll* miss the game. *I* lost *my* pen.)

Appositive An appositive is a noun or phrase that explains one or more words in a sentence. (Lee, *a good artist,* won the prize.)

Article An article is an adjective that makes specific or general references to things. (*the* lamp, *a* bee, *an* onion)

A **definite article** (the word *the*) is used when a noun refers to a specific thing. (*the* anteater)

An **indefinite article** is used with a noun that does not refer to a particular example of a thing. (*a* ribbon, *an* accordion)

Clause A clause is a group of words that contains a verb and its subject. (*we believe*)

A **main (independent) clause** can stand by itself as a sentence.

A **subordinate (dependent) clause** does not express a complete thought and cannot stand by itself as a sentence.

Clause	Example
Main (independent)	The fox hid her young
Subordinate (dependent)	until the hunters were gone.

Collective noun. *See* **Noun.**

Common noun. *See* **Noun.**

Complete predicate The complete predicate of a sentence consists of the main verb plus any words that modify or complete the verb's meaning. (The lantern *showed us the path to the lake.*)

852 GRAMMAR HANDBOOK

852 THE LANGUAGE OF LITERATURE TEACHER'S EDITION

Complete subject The complete subject of a sentence consists of a subject noun or pronoun plus any words that modify or describe it. (*The new red sweater* fits me.)

Complex sentence A complex sentence contains one main clause and one or more subordinate clauses. (*The box came before we left.*)

Compound sentence A compound sentence consists of two or more independent clauses. (*Jo tried calling home, but the line was busy.*)

Compound sentence part A sentence element that consists of two or more subjects, predicates, objects, or other parts is compound. (*Jay* and *Al* agreed. Lou *sang* and *played*. Ann saw *plays* and *movies*.)

Conjunction A conjunction is a word that links other words or groups of words.

   A *coordinating conjunction* connects related words, groups of words, or sentences. (*and, but, or*)

   A *correlative conjunction* is one of a pair of conjunctions that work together to connect sentence parts. (*either . . . or, neither . . . nor*)

   A *subordinating conjunction* introduces a subordinate clause. (*unless, while, if*)

Conjunctive adverb A conjunctive adverb joins the clauses of a compound sentence. (*however, therefore, besides*)

Contraction A contraction is formed by joining two words and substituting an apostrophe for letters left out of one of the words. (*he'll*)

Coordinating conjunction. See **Conjunction.**

Correlative conjunction. See **Conjunction.**

Demonstrative pronoun. See **Pronoun.**

Dependent clause. See **Clause.**

Direct object A direct object receives the action of a verb. (Kim knew the *answer.*)

Double negative A double negative is the incorrect use of two negative words when only one is needed. (We *don't never* come late.)

End mark An end mark is any of the several punctuation marks that can end a sentence. See the chart at the bottom of page 855.

Fragment. See **Sentence fragment.**

Future tense. See **Verb tense.**

Gerund A gerund is a verbal that ends in *-ing* and functions as a noun. (*Swimming* is good exercise.)

Helping verb. See **Verb.**

Indefinite pronoun. See **Pronoun.**

Independent clause. See **Clause.**

Indirect object An indirect object tells to or for whom (sometimes to or for what) something is done. (Ann gave *Barb* a pencil.)

Infinitive An infinitive is a verbal that begins with the word *to* and functions as a noun, an adjective, or an adverb. (I like *to swim*.)

Intensive pronoun. See **Pronoun.**

Interjection An interjection is a word or phrase used to express strong feeling. (*Ugh!*)

Interrogative pronoun. See **Pronoun.**

Inverted sentence An inverted sentence is one in which the subject comes after the verb. (*How is your brother? Here come the clowns.*)

Irregular verb. See **Verb.**

Linking verb. See **Verb.**

Main clause. See **Clause.**

Modifier A modifier makes another word more precise; modifiers most often are adjectives or adverbs. (*tasty* sandwich, smiled *happily*)

Noun A noun names a person, a place, a thing, or an idea. (*Joe, school, flower, freedom*)

   An *abstract noun* names an idea, a quality, or a feeling. (*happiness*)

   A *collective noun* names a group of things. (*band*)

   A *common noun* is the general name of a person, a place, a thing, or an idea. (*friend, office, coat, justice*)

   A *compound noun* contains two or more words. (*steel wool, rainbow, T-square*)

   A *noun of direct address* is the name of a person being directly spoken to. (*Sid,* tell us a story.)

   A *possessive noun* shows who or what owns something. (*Fred's* socks, the *light's* glare)

   A *predicate noun* follows a linking verb and renames the subject. (Marie was the *leader.*)

GRAMMAR HANDBOOK **853**

A ***proper noun*** names a particular person, place, or thing. (*Bill Clinton, Missouri, Grant's Tomb*)

Number A noun, pronoun, or verb is **singular** in number if it refers to just one person, place, thing, or idea; it is **plural** in number if it refers to more than one.

Object of a preposition The object of a preposition is the noun or pronoun after the preposition. (They moved from the old *house*.)

Object of a verb The object of a verb receives the action of the verb. (Gay finished her *work*.)

Participle A participle is often used as part of a verb phrase. (had *seen*) It can also be used as a verbal that functions as an adjective. (the *falling* rocks)

The ***present participle*** is formed by adding *-ing* to the present tense of a verb. (*Singing* merrily, the carolers greeted us.)

The ***past participle*** of a regular verb is formed by adding *-d* or *-ed* to the present tense. The past participles of irregular verbs do not follow this pattern. (*Discouraged*, they looked for the stolen bicycle.)

Past tense. *See* **Verb tense.**

Perfect tenses. *See* **Verb tense.**

Person The person of a pronoun depends on the person to whom it refers.

A ***first-person*** pronoun refers to the person speaking. (*We* sang.)

A ***second-person*** pronoun refers to the person spoken to. (*You* ate.)

A ***third-person*** pronoun refers to some other person(s) or thing(s) being spoken of. (*It* fell.)

Personal pronoun. *See* **Pronoun.**

Phrase A phrase is a group of related words that does not contain a verb and its subject. (*seeing to it*)

Possessive A noun or pronoun that is possessive shows ownership. (*Clare's* pen, *his* plan)

Possessive noun. *See* **Noun.**

Possessive pronoun. *See* **Pronoun.**

Predicate The predicate of a sentence tells what the subject is or does. (Ann *told about her vacation*.)

Predicate adjective. *See* **Adjective.**

Predicate noun. *See* **Noun.**

Predicate pronoun. *See* **Pronoun.**

Preposition A preposition relates a word to another part of the sentence or to the sentence as a whole. (stood *within* the circle)

Prepositional phrase A prepositional phrase consists of a preposition, its object, and the object's modifiers. (leader *of the big band*)

Present tense. *See* **Verb tense.**

Pronoun A pronoun replaces a noun or another pronoun. Some pronouns allow a writer or speaker to avoid repeating a particular noun. Other pronouns let a writer refer to an unknown or unidentified person or thing.

A ***demonstrative pronoun*** singles out one or more persons or things. (*That* is a nice sweater.)

An ***indefinite pronoun*** refers to an unknown or unidentified person or thing. (*Somebody* will help.)

An ***intensive pronoun*** emphasizes a noun or pronoun. (May *herself* set the table.)

An ***interrogative pronoun*** asks a question. (*What* should I do?)

A ***personal pronoun*** refers to the first, second, or third person. (*I* go. *You* see. *He* sings.)

A ***possessive pronoun*** shows ownership. (*Your* answer is right.)

A ***predicate pronoun*** follows a linking verb and renames the subject. (The winner is *she*.)

A ***reflexive pronoun*** reflects an action back on the subject of the sentence. (Rita asked *herself* why.)

A ***relative pronoun*** relates a subordinate clause to the word it modifies in the main clause. (We met the man *who* builds houses.)

Pronoun-antecedent agreement. *See* **Agreement.**

Pronoun forms

The ***subject form of a pronoun*** is used when the pronoun is the subject of a sentence or follows a linking verb as a predicate pronoun. (*We* arrived. The winner was *she*.)

The ***object form of a pronoun*** is used when the pronoun is the direct or indirect object of a verb or verbal or the object of a preposition. (Seeing *him* and his friend, we sent *them* to *her*.)

Proper adjective. *See* **Adjective.**

Proper noun. *See* **Noun.**

Punctuation Punctuation clarifies the structure of sentences. See the chart on the facing page.

Reflexive pronoun. *See* **Pronoun.**

Regular verb. *See* **Verb.**

Relative pronoun. *See* **Pronoun.**

Run-on sentence A run-on sentence consists of two or more sentences written incorrectly as one. (*I ran to the door no one was there.*)

Sentence A sentence expresses a complete thought. The chart on the facing page shows the four kinds of sentences.

854 GRAMMAR HANDBOOK

Kind of Sentence	Example
Declarative (statement)	He helped me.
Exclamatory (strong feeling)	You're home!
Imperative (request, command)	Open the door.
Interrogative (question)	What's wrong?

Sentence fragment A sentence fragment is a group of words that is only part of a sentence. (*When the wind blew, looking at the photo*)

Subject The subject is the part of a sentence that tells whom or what the sentence is about. (*Lee* knitted.)

Subject-verb agreement. *See* **Agreement.**

Subordinate clause. *See* **Clause.**

Verb A verb expresses an action, a condition, or a state of being.

When the subject of a sentence performs the action, the verb is **active.** (Ken *threw* the ball.)

When the subject receives the action or expresses the result of the action, the verb is **passive.** (The box *was opened*.)

A **helping verb** is used with a main verb; together they make up a verb phrase. (*will* ask)

A **linking verb** expresses a state of being or connects the subject with a word or words that describe the subject. (The cocoa *smells* delicious.)

A **main verb** describes action or state of being; it may have one or more helping verbs. (will *do*)

The past tense and past participle of a **regular verb** are formed by adding -d or -ed. (*jump, jumped*)

An **irregular verb** does not follow this pattern. (*speak, spoke, spoken*)

Verbal A verbal is formed from a verb and acts as a noun, an adjective, or an adverb. *See* **Gerund; Infinitive; Participle.**

Verb phrase A verb phrase consists of a main verb and one or more helping verbs. (*might have entertained*)

Verb tense Verb tense shows the time of an action or the time of a state of being.

The **present tense** places an action or condition in the present. (A maid *comes* to the door.)

The **past tense** places an action or condition in the past. (Sid *agreed*.)

The **future tense** places an action or condition in the future. (Rose *will forget*.)

The **present perfect tense** describes an action completed in an indefinite past time or begun in the past and continued in the present. (*has come, have ordered*)

The **past perfect tense** describes one action that happened before another action in the past. (*had announced, had seen*)

The **future perfect tense** describes a future event that will be finished before another future action begins. (*will have baked*)

Punctuation	Uses	Examples
Apostrophe (')	Shows possession	Heather's book the girls' shoes
	Forms a contraction	He'll help. Dad's here.
Colon (:)	Introduces a list or long quotation	these boys: Joseph, Raul, and Sherman
Comma (,)	Separates ideas Separates modifiers Separates items in series	I invited him, but he could not come. the noisy, happy crowd They ate bread, cheese, and fish.
Exclamation point (!)	Ends an exclamatory sentence	What a great time we had!
Hyphen (-)	Joins words in some compound nouns	daughter-in-law, great-grandmother
Period (.)	Ends a declarative sentence Indicates most abbreviations	The fish in the lake were biting. hr. sec. Rd. Mrs. Dec.
Question mark (?)	Ends an interrogative sentence	Where is the library?
Semicolon (;)	Divides some compound sentences Separates items in series that contain commas	The whistle shrieked; the train roared by. Bruce wore a dark, floppy hat; a warm, waterproof jacket; and tough, high boots.

GRAMMAR HANDBOOK **855**

Index of Fine Art

xiv	*Mecklenberg County: High Cotton Mother and Child* (1978), Romare Bearden.
xxi	*Exotic Landscape* (1910), Henri Rousseau.
11	*A Kitchen on the Eve of a Festival*, Zhou Jihe.
16–17	*It's All Relative* (1995), Brad Holland.
22	*Bedouins* (about 1905–06), John Singer Sargent.
25	*La caravane* [The caravan] (1880), Alexandre-Gabriel Decamps.
32	*The Old and the New Year* (1953), Pablo Picasso.
35	*Closing Scene* (1963), David Hockney.
42	*Tahitian Woman and Boy* (1889), Paul Gauguin.
47	*Tahitian Landscape* (1891), Paul Gauguin.
94	*The Gamekeeper's Daughter* (1886), E. A. Walton.
113	*Boy and Dog in a Johnnypump* (1982), Jean-Michel Basquiat.
114	*My Front Yard, Summer* (1941), Georgia O'Keeffe.
118	*Wabana-Wagamuman*, [Bear in the forest] (1989), Tom Uttech.
125	*Cave Canem* [Beware of dog], Roman mosaic.
127	*The Sorceress and the Traveler*, mosaic from Pompeii, House of the Discouri.
131	*Mount Vesuvius in Eruption* (1817), Joseph Mallord William Turner.
148–149	*Swinger in Summer Shade* (1981), Maud Gatewood.
153	*Long Weekend* (1990), Brian Jones.
156	*The Last Picnic* (1993), Brian Jones.
171	*Celebration, Chinatown* (1940), Dong Kingman.
181	Incense wrapper (Edo period, Japan; 17th–18th centuries), attributed to Ogata Korin.
187	*Bobby* (1939), Jack Humphrey.
190	*Backyards, Brooklyn* (1932), Ogden Minton Pleissner.
201	*Snack Bar* (1954), Isabel Bishop.
202–203	*Sunset in Memorium* (1946), Woody Crumbo.
224	*Self-Portrait* (1934), Malvin Gray Johnson.
239	*Schoolboys* (1986), Frané Lessac.
254–255	*Jacob's Ladder* (1958), Jan Müller.
258	*Into Bondage* (1936), Aaron Douglass.
263	*Mecklenberg County: High Cotton Mother and Child* (1978), Romare Bearden.
267	Reliquary figure (1880–1910), Ba Kuba peoples.
274	*Cake Window (Seven Cakes)* (1970–1976), Wayne Thiebaud.
285	*Nervosa* (1980), Ed Paschke.
292	*The Deathless White Pacing Mustang* (1948), Tom Lea.
297	*The Icknield Way* (1912), Spencer Gore.

303	*Centre of the Universe* (1992), Brian Jones.
320	*La cuillerée* [The Spoonful of Milk] (1912), Marc Chagall.
326	*La fête des tabernacles* [The feast of tabernacles] (1916), Marc Chagall.
352	*Alborado de fiesta* [Dawning of a party], Arturo Estrada.
360–361	*Early Morning After the Storm at Sea* (1902), Winslow Homer.
371	*The Nantucket Cat*, Paul Stagg.
386–387	*Out at Third*, Nelson Rosenberg.
396	*Mexican Boy* (1926), Victor Higgins.
399	*Long Day's Shadow* (1994), Marilyn Sunderman.
411	*Paintbox* (1984), Marilyn Groch.
417	*Girl at Piano* (1966), Will Barnet.
420	*Japanese Rain on Canvas* (1972), David Hockney.
424	The goddess Bastet in the form of a cat (about 664–610 B.C.), Egyptian bronze.
426	*Tabitha*, James Lloyd.
429	*Who's the Fairest of Them All?* Frank Paton.
435	*Captain Kidd on Gardiner's Island* (1894), Howard Pyle.
458–459	Buffalo hunter (about 1844), unknown artist.
460	Robe with Mato Tope's exploits (about 1835), Mato Tope.
464	Buffalo hunt (about 1884), New Bear.
467	*Below Zero* (1993), John Axton.
491	*My Children* (1920), W. Herbert Dunton.
494	*New Mexico Spring* (about 1950), Fremont Ellis.
498	*Sweet Talkin' Man* (1982), Gordon Snidow.
501	*In the Valley of the Rosebud* (1992), Ralph E. Oberg.
516–517	*Gathering at Blue Waters* (1989), Floyd E. Newsum, Jr.
521	*Siri* (1970), Andrew Wyeth.
522	*Superb Lilies #2* (1966), Alex Katz.
547	*The Dry Ditch* (1964), Kenneth M. Adams.
548	*Chico* (1974), Hubert Shuptrine.
558	*Afternoon Glare—Main Street* (1991), Carl J. Dalio.
655	*Exotic Landscape* (1910), Henri Rousseau.
676	*Hummingbirds in Thistle* (1955), Walter Anderson.
694	Effigy vessel (about 1000–1250), Mayan artist.
709	Figure of a woman (late 1600s), unknown Japanese artist.
717	*Twenty-Second Station, Okabe, Utsu no Yama (Utsu Mountain)* (1834), Hiroshige.
720–721	*Parade Before a Sumo Tournament* (1796), Katsukawa Shun'ei.
723	*Buffalo Calf Woman*, Oscar Howe.
731	*Bodhisattva Guanyin* (Song Dynasty, 960–1279), unknown Chinese artist.

Index of Skills

Literary Concepts

Alliteration. *See* Poetry.
Anecdote, 221, 762
Audience, 762
Author's purpose, 534, 762
Autobiography, 52, 122, 762
Biography, 52, 63, 269, 762
Caricature, 327
Character, 19, 37, 195, 403, 514, 763
Characterization, 763
Cinderella tales, 681
Climax, 20, 763
Complication, 20
Conflict, 19, 48, 135, 242, 252, 289, 763
    external, 135, 242, 763
    internal, 242, 763
Couplet. *See* Poetry.
Description, 269, 764
Dialogue, 237, 310–11, 327, 357, 620, 763
Drama, 357–58, 764. *See also* Dialogue.
    acts, 358, 762
    cast of characters, 357, 762
    scenes, 358, 769
    script, 764
    stage directions, 357–58, 771
Essay, 52, 235, 764
Exaggeration, 327
Exposition, 19
Fables, 636, 765
Fantasy, 355, 765
Fiction, 19–20, 765
Figurative language, 103, 543, 765
Folklore, 636
Folk tales, 636, 748, 765
Foreshadowing, 765
Form, 223, 543, 765
Free verse. *See* Poetry.
Haiku. *See* Poetry
Historical fiction, 124, 136
Humor, 327, 766
Imagery, 102, 108, 182, 222, 468, 766
Interview, 412, 766. *See also* Speaking, Listening, and Viewing *index*.
Legends, 636, 766
Main idea, 766
Memoir, 178, 179

Metaphor, 103, 543, 767
Mood, 161, 767
Myth, 636, 767
Narration, 275
Narrative, 767
Narrator, 767
Nonfiction, 51–52, 767
    informative, 51
    literary, 51
Novel, 19, 768
Onomatopoeia, 484, 768
Oral tradition, 634–637
Personification, 103, 768
Play. *See* Drama.
Plot, 19–20, 48, 504
Poetry, 102–3, 768
    alliteration, 344
    concrete, 424, 429
    couplet, 344, 764
    form, 102, 765
    free verse, 115, 226, 227, 765
    haiku, 180, 182, 766
    narrative poem, 104, 767
    repetition, 102
    rhyme, 102, 108, 115, 168, 341
    rhyme, end, 168, 769
    rhyme, external, 168, 769
    rhyme, internal, 168, 769
    rhyme scheme, 428, 769
    rhythm, 102, 108, 168, 341, 344, 769
    sound in, 102
    speaker, 110, 770
    tone, 110
    word order in, 109, 341
Poetic language, 341
Point of view, 28, 275, 384, 768
Primary source, 768
Purpose, 73
Quests, 571, 619–20
Radio play, 769
Repetition, 428, 769
Resolution, 20
Rhyme. *See* Poetry.
Scene. *See* Drama.
Sarcasm, 327
Science fiction, 289, 769
Script, 357

Secondary source, 770
Sensory detail, 300, 553, 562, 770. *See also* Imagery, Figurative language.
Setting, 19, 22, 135, 146, 178, 241, 770
Short story, 19, 770
Simile, 103, 226, 543, 770
Sources
    primary, 339
    secondary, 339
Speaker. *See* Poetry.
Stage directions, 771
Story, structure of, 19–20, 328. *See also* Plot.
Suspense, 374, 385, 403, 504, 771
Style, 109, 116, 222, 227, 276, 524, 771
Symbols, 422, 515, 771
Theme, 100, 103, 195, 771
Tone, 159, 439, 771

Reading and Critical Thinking Skills

Advertising, 90–1, 207, 519
Analysis, 762
Appearance. *See* Interpreting appearances.
Audience, 91, 379, 509, 625.
    See also Peer response.
Author's purpose, 344, 534
Brainstorming, 18, 93, 146, 213, 455
Cartoons, 506
Cause and effect, 271, 384, 763, 782, 792
Character
    revelation of, 214
    tests of, 214, 456
Choices and consequences, 318
Choral reading, 537
Chronological order. *See* Organization.
Clarifying. *See* Reading strategies.
Classifying and diagramming. *See also* Classifying and diagramming *in the* Writing Skills *index*.
    cluster diagram, 727
    concept map, 440, 564
    graphs, 385, 480, 486
    problem solving chart, 252, 379
    pyramid graph, 470
    scale of difficulty, 18
    setting dial, 146
    story map, 141, 194, 312, 356, 504
    webs, 21, 117, 147
Comparing and contrasting, 73, 93, 136, 146, 150, 159, 196, 252, 300, 339, 384, 403, 424, 484, 506–11, 514, 535, 681, 698, 699, 763, 764, 727, 782, 791
Conclusions, 213, 511. *See also* Organization.

Conflict resolution. *See* Problem solving.
Connecting, 5, 20, 103, 333, 486, 563, 701, 764
    biographical, 104, 271
    cultural, 151, 215, 291, 319, 359, 405, 414, 480, 486, 519, 545, 727, 747
    geographical, 21, 39, 53, 117, 161, 184, 237, 269
    historical, 30, 93, 124, 170, 257, 268, 329, 341, 389, 430, 457, 470, 526
    literary, 110, 180, 223, 436, 571, 680, 698, 726, 746
    personal, 21, 30, 39, 53, 65, 93, 104, 110, 117, 124, 146, 151, 161, 170, 180, 184, 215, 223, 224, 228, 237, 257, 271, 275, 277, 289, 291, 319, 329, 341, 346, 359, 389, 405, 414, 424, 430, 457, 470, 480, 486, 519, 526, 537, 545, 571, 622
    scientific, 228, 277, 424, 525, 537, 681, 726
    through art, 49, 74, 136, 182, 328, 413, 429, 469, 535, 620, 698
    through reading, 39, 53, 65, 117, 124, 151, 161, 180, 184, 223, 229, 237, 257, 271, 278, 319, 329, 341, 359, 389, 414, 424, 431, 457, 470, 486, 537, 545, 571
    through social studies, 554, 680, 699, 727, 746, 747
    through writing, 21, 30, 93, 110, 170, 194, 215, 291, 346, 405, 480, 519
Context clues, 389, 764
Critical analysis, 28, 37, 63, 73, 100, 108, 113, 115, 122, 135, 159, 168, 178, 182, 194, 221, 223, 235, 241, 268, 275, 289, 300, 327, 339, 344, 355, 373, 402, 412, 422, 425, 428, 439, 468, 481, 484, 503, 524, 534, 543, 553, 619, 794–95
Decision making, 18, 506, 524
Detail. *See* Supporting detail; Sensory detail.
Dialogue, as part of a story, 310–11
Difference, 511
Difficulty, scale of, 18
Domino effect, 318
Drama, strategies for reading, 358, 571
Emotional response, 91
Evaluating. *See* Reading strategies.
Fact, in fiction, 339
Fact vs. opinion, 52, 625, 765. *See also* Opinion.
Fiction, strategies for reading, 20
Folk tales, strategies for reading, 748, 795
Foreign language, use of, 554, 822
Goals
    obstacles to reaching, 518
    setting of, 147, 253, 385, 515, 570
Grammatical links to literature, 813, 815, 817, 820, 822, 824, 826, 835, 839, 843
Graphic organizers, 509. *See also* Classifying and diagramming
Heroism, 570

INDEX OF SKILLS   **859**

Humor, 138, 506
Inference, 245, 414, 766
Interpreting appearances, 212–13, 317, 454–55, 568–69
Introduction, 511. *See also* Organization
Moral lessons, 700–03
    in movies, 707
    in television, 707
Motive, 430
Nonfiction, strategies for reading, 52
Opinion, 622–29. *See also* Fact vs. opinion.
Organization, 52.
    See also Conclusion, Introduction, Main idea, Supporting detail.
    body, 511, 703
    chronological order, 229, 763
    outline, 752–53, 800
    sequence, 770
    transition, 229
Outlines. *See* Organization.
Peer response, 87, 143, 209, 249, 313, 381, 451, 565, 627, 703, 753. *See also* Audience.
Personal response, 28, 37, 48, 63, 73, 84–5, 100, 108, 113, 115, 122, 135, 159, 168, 178, 182, 194, 221, 223, 235, 241, 268, 275, 289, 300, 327, 339, 344, 355, 373, 402, 412, 422, 425, 428, 439, 468, 481, 484, 503, 524, 534, 543, 553, 619.
    See also Connecting.
Plot analysis. *See* Story structure.
Poetic language, 341, 544.
    See also Poetry *in* Literary Terms *index*.
Poetry, strategies for reading, 103–104, 341, 424, 537
Point of view, 28, 159
Predicting. *See* Reading strategies.
Previewing, 20, 52, 103
Problem solving, 252, 256, 318, 431, 793
Purpose, setting a, 457
Questioning. *See* Reading strategies.
Questionnaires, in surveying, 518
Radio play, reading of, 359
Rating scale, 327
Reading aloud, 103, 358, 537
Reading log, 5, 6, 53, 151, 184, 215, 228, 229, 329.
    See also Connecting.
Reading strategies, 6–15, 486, 527. *See also* Connecting *and entries under* Drama, Fiction, Nonfiction, *and* Poetry.
    clarifying, 5, 7–15, 58, 190, 260, 264–65, 434, 486, 732, 763
    evaluating, 5, 7–15, 20, 88, 92, 145, 210, 219, 251, 314, 319, 335, 383, 431, 486, 496, 452, 513, 514, 545, 566, 629, 701, 704, 707, 712, 755, 764
    predicting, 5, 13–14, 20, 52, 117, 120–21, 184, 186, 191, 219, 317, 336, 346, 355, 434, 436, 486, 490,
    713, 733, 768
    questioning, 5, 7–15, 20, 52, 56, 103, 422, 428, 439, 454–55, 468, 484, 486, 497, 503, 527, 768
    reciting, 527
    reviewing, 527
    setting a purpose, 770
    skimming, 770
    summarizing, 257, 771
    surveying, 527
Risk assessment, 92, 146–47
Role models, 256
Scanning. *See* Skimming.
Self-assessment, 146–47, 150, 252–53, 384–85, 514–15, 630–31. *See also* Personal response.
Sensory detail, 484, 503, 562
Signal words, 229
Similarities, 511
Skimming, 470, 527
Story maps. *See* Classifying and diagramming.
Story structure, 253, 328, 346, 440, 571, 635–36
Stylistic analysis. *See* Grammatical links to literature; Word choice.
Summarizing. *See* Reading strategies.
Supporting detail, 53, 206–07, 209, 783–84, 797
Surveying opinion, 388, 518
Synthesizing. *See* Critical analysis.
Technical terms, 359
Theme, 18, 92, 146–47, 150, 214, 256, 318, 384, 388, 456, 518, 570, 700–05,
Transition words, 229, 511. *See also* Signal words.
Visual clues, 213, 317
Visualizing, 20, 39, 103, 180, 276, 771
Webbing. *See* Classifying and diagramming.
Word choice, 84–5, 822

Grammar, Usage, and Mechanics

Addresses. *See* Punctuation.
Adjectives, 830–34, 852
    bad, 833
    comparative, 513, 831, 852
    few, 834
    fewer, 834
    good, 833
    less, 834
    little, 833
    more, 832
    most, 832
    proper, 839
    predicate, 852
    proper, 852
    punctuation of, in series, 847–48

  superlative, 513, 831, 852
  that, 833
  these, 833
  this, 833
  those, 833
Adverbs, 85, 830–34, 852
  badly, 833
  besides, 814, 843
  comparative, 513, 832, 852
  conjunctive, 814, 843, 853
  consequently, 843
  however, 814, 843,
  nevertheless, 814, 843
  punctuation of, in series, 847
  superlative, 513, 832, 852
  therefore, 814, 843
  well, 834
Agreement, 852. *See also* Subject–verb agreement; Pronouns (agreement with antecedents).
Antecedents. *See* Pronouns.
Appositives, 820, 852
  punctuation of, 846
Articles, 852
  definite, 852
  indefinite, 852
Bad and *badly*, 833
Barely, as negative, 832
Capitalization, 116, 839–42
  articles, 842
  books, 842
  events, 841
  films, 842
  geographical names, 841
  institutions, 840
  languages, 840
  magazines, 842
  minor words in proper nouns, 840
  names, 839
  nationalities, 840
  newspapers, 842
  organizations, 840
  plays, 842
  poems, 842
  proper adjectives, 839
  proper nouns, 839
  quotation, 850–51
  religious terms, 840
  school subjects, 840
  stories, 842
  time periods, 841
  titles, 839, 842
Clauses, 852. *See also* Sentences.
  main, 852
  subordinate, 852
Commas. *See* Punctuation.
Comparative forms, 513, 830–31. *See also* Adjectives; Adverbs.
Compound sentences. See Sentences.
Conjunctions, 315, 813, 853
  and, 315, 813
  but, 315, 813
  coordinating, 315, 853
  correlative, 853
  nor, 816
  or, 315, 813, 816
  subordinating, 853
Contractions, 825, 829, 853
Dates. *See* Punctuation.
Double negatives, 832, 853
Few and *little*, 834
Fewer and *less*, 834
Gerunds. *See* Verbals.
Hardly, as negative, 832
Here, with *this* or *these*, 833
Infinitives. *See* Verbals.
Interjection, 853
Interrupting phrases, 820, 845
Interrupting words, 819, 845
Introductory words, 844
Its and *it's*, 825, 829
Learn and *teach*, 838
Let and *leave*, 837
Letters. *See* Punctuation.
Lie and *lay*, 837
Modifiers, 853. *See also* Adjectives, Adverbs.
Musical terms, plurals of, 822
Negatives, 832. *See also* Double negatives.
Nouns, 440, 453, 853
  abstract, 853
  collective, 853
  common, 853
  compound, 853
  direct address, noun of, 845, 853
  irregular plurals, 822–23
  modification of, 830
  plural, 822–23
  possessive, 823, 853
  predicate, 853
  proper, 839
Number, 815–16, 820, 854
  in indefinite pronouns, 817–18
  in irregular verbs, 819
  in personal pronouns, 817
Objects, 453, 824, 854. *See also* Sentences.
  direct, 828, 853
  indirect, 828, 853

of prepositions, 828, 854
punctuation of, in series, 847
Other, use in comparison, 831
Parts of speech, 211, 440, 812–842. *See also* Adjectives, Adverbs, Conjunctions, Nouns, Prepositions, Pronouns, *and* Verbs.
Participles. *See* Verbals.
Person. *See* Pronouns.
Phrases, 854. *See also* Interrupting phrases, Prepositional phrases *and* Verb phrases.
Plural. *See* Number.
Possessives. *See* Nouns (possessive); Pronouns (possessive).
Predicates, 449, 812, 824, 854. *See also* Sentences.
complete, 852
compound, 705
Prepositional phrases, 453, 820, 854
along with, 820
as well as, 820
in addition to, 820
including, 820
punctuation of, in series, 847
Prepositions, 453
Pronouns, 383, 453, 701
agreement with antecedents, 826, 852
all, 818
another, 817
antecedents, 701, 826–27
any, 818
anybody, 817
anyone, 817
anything, 817
as subjects, 817
both, 818
demonstrative, 854
each, 817
either, 817
everybody, 817
everyone, 817
everything, 817
few, 818
first-person, 854
he, 817, 824, 827
her, 824, 827
hers, 825
him, 824, 827
his, 825, 827
I, 817, 824
indefinite, 817–18, 827, 854
intensive, 854
interrogative, 854
it, 817, 824
its, 825
many, 818

me, 824
mine, 825
my, 825
neither, 817
no one, 817
nobody, 817
none, 818
nothing, 817
number in, 826–27
object form, 824, 828, 854
one, 817
our, 825
ours, 825
person of, 854
personal, 817, 826, 854
possessive, 825, 854
predicate, 824, 854
reflexive, 854
relative, 854
second-person, 854
subject forms, 854
several, 818
she, 817, 824, 827
some, 818
somebody, 817
someone, 817
something, 817
subject, 814, 828
their, 825
theirs, 825
them, 824, 833
these, 833
they, 824, 827
this, 833
third-person, 854
those, 833
us, 824
usage of, 828–29
we, 824
who, 828
whoever, 828
whom, 828
you, 817, 814, 827
Punctuation, 116, 843–51, 854–55
addresses, 848
apostrophes, 855
colon, 855
commas, 315, 813, 843–49, 855
dashes, 207
dates, 848
elements in a series, 847
end marks, 813, 850, 853
exclamation point, 855

for clarity, 846
hyphen, 855
letters, 849
of compound sentences, 843
period, 813, 855
question marks, 855
quotation marks, 311, 850
semicolons, 814, 843–44, 855
Quotation, 850–51
    capitalization in, 850–51
    dialogue, 850
    divided quotation, 851
    quoted words, 850
Quotation marks. *See* Punctuation.
Rise and *raise*, 837
Scarcely, as negative, 832
Semicolons. *See* Punctuation.
Sentences, 449, 854. *See also* Objects, Predicates, *and* Subjects.
    complex, 853
    compound, 563, 707, 813, 843, 853
    compound part, 853
    fragments, 211, 812, 855
    inverted, 567, 820–21, 853
    questions, 821
    run-on, 813–14, 854
    subject-verb splits, 700
Singular. *See* Number.
Sit and *set*, 837
Standard English, 237
Subject–verb agreement, 567, 705, 815, 817–18, 819–21
Subjects, 109, 449, 812, 819, 824, 828, 855. *See also* Sentences.
    complete, 853
    compound, 705, 815–16, 817
    finding in sentences, 815, 819
    punctuation of, in series, 847
    simple, 815
Superlative forms, 831–32
Their and *they're*, 825, 829
Them and *those*, 833
There, with *that* or *those*, 833
These and *those*, 833
This and *that*, 833
Verb phrases, 855
Verbals, 855
    gerund, 853
    infinitive, 853
    participle, 854
Verbs, 109, 440, 835–38. *See also* Verbals.
    action, 89, 251
    active voice, 629, 855
    appear, 830
    become, 830
    feel, 830
    future perfect tense, 855
    future tense, 855
    grow, 830
    helping, 855
    irregular, 855
    linking, 89, 824, 830, 855
    look, 830
    main, 855
    modification of, 830
    passive voice, 629, 855
    past participle, 836, 838, 854
    past perfect tense, 855
    past tense, 836, 838, 855
    present participle, 854
    present perfect tense, 855
    present tense, 836, 838, 855
    punctuation of, in series, 847
    regular, 855
    seem, 830
    smell, 830
    sound, 830
    taste, 830
    tense, 145, 835–36, 855
Whose and *who's*, 829
Word order, 109
Your and *you're*, 825, 829

Writing Skills, Modes, and Formats

Action, expression of, 89, 449, 629, 835–36
Alliteration, use of. *See* Sound devices.
Argument. *See* Persuasive writing.
Audience, identification of, 379, 509, 625, 773, 796
Bibliography. *See* Research reports (source lists).
Cause and effect, expression of, 782, 790, 792
Classifying and diagramming. *See also* Graphic organizers; Visuals.
    chart, 18, 53, 65, 73, 92, 93, 110, 179, 182, 194, 221, 229, 237, 241, 252, 253, 300, 327, 329, 344, 384, 389, 405, 414, 422, 469, 514, 515, 524, 553, 571, 727
    cluster diagram, 727, 773
    comparison chart, 508
    concept map, 440, 564
    diagram, 256, 318,
    dial, 146
    flow chart, 290
    graph, 385, 480, 486
    problem-solving chart, 252, 379
    pyramid graph, 470

scale, 18
sequence chart, 450
story map, 141, 194, 312, 356, 504
storyboard, 680
time line, 229, 636–37, 773
Venn diagram, 150, 509
web, 21, 117, 147

Comparing and contrasting, 782, 791. *See also* Explanatory and informative writing.

Conclusion 381, 786–87, 795, 797. *See also* Organization.

Copyright permission, 811

Degree, expression of, 782

Descriptive writing, 84–85, 402, 448–49, 784–86
art guide, 429
as introduction, 778
book-jacket review, 85
character sketch, 28, 226, 244–51
eyewitness account, 135, 235
headline, 373
log, 63, 184, 373, 439, 534
missing-person report, 355
newspaper story, 235, 355, 373, 402
plot summary, 289, 313
profile, 115
science report, 159
sports commentary, 484
summary, 73, 313

Detail, use of, 448–49, 508, 783–784. *See also* Organization.
arrangement of, 785
in descriptive writing, 784–86
in persuasive writing, 796
in research reports, 798–99

Differences, expression of. *See* Transitions.

Documenting sources. *See* Research reports.

Drafting, 142, 248–9, 313, 380–81, 451–52, 703, 752–3, 773–74.
See also Prewriting.

Editing, 88, 144, 210, 250–1, 314, 382–83, 452, 512, 566, 628–29, 704, 754–55, 775–77
correcting punctuation, 776, 843–51
correcting sentence structure, 776
correcting word forms, 776
on word processors, 804, 806
proofreading, 776–777
revising tips, 815, 819, 821, 822, 823, 824, 827, 828, 830, 831, 832, 833, 835, 837, 839, 840, 841, 842, 843, 846, 847, 850, 851

Essays. *See* Explanatory and informative writing; Expressive and personal writing.

Explanatory and informative writing, 622–29, 790–95. *See also* Research reports
analysis, 790, 794–95

budget, 554
comparison, 339, 790–91
decision, judicial, 327
definition, 794
dictionary, 504
e-mail message, 289
evaluation, 553
exhibit catalog, 534
exposition of ideas, 381
guidelines, 214, 503
how-to pamphlet, 518
introduction, 242, 456
legal brief, 440
memo, 28
newsletter, 160
plot analysis, 312–14
prediction, 178, 184, 194, 553
problem–solution essay, 376–83, 790, 793
progress report, 619
questions, 268
report card, 514
review, 37, 412
rules, 221
schedule, 412
supply list, 101
top–ten list, 384
will, 439

Expressive and personal writing
acceptance speech, 63
critical review, 702–5
dedication, 412
diary, 194, 275, 289, 503
epitaph, 534
essay, 37, 86–9, 182, 208–10, 506–12
evaluation, 327
greeting card, 275, 422
journal, 100, 221, 241
legend, 534
letter, 268, 428, 468, 553
letter of complaint, 373
letter of condolence, 168
monologue, 412
motto, 422
note, 524
proverb, 681
speech, 108, 553
tribute, 48

Fact, use of, 778, 783–84. *See also* Detail, use of.

Feeling, expression of, 448–49

Foreign language, use of, 554, 822

Generalizing, 787

Graphic organizers, 509, 773. *See also* Classifying and Diagramming; Visuals.

864 INDEX OF SKILLS

Hooking readers' interest, 789
Humor, 138, 506
Introduction, 381, 778–79, 795, 797. *See also* Organization.
Layout. *See* Word processing.
Narrative and imaginative writing, 138–45, 450–52, 788–89. *See also* Plotting.
   anecdote, 138–45
   as introduction, 779
   characterization, 788–89
   conflict in, 788–89
   dialogue, 178, 241, 311, 543
   event in, 788–89
   narration, 48
   organization of, 789
   personification, 275
   radio play, 374
   scene, 122
   science fiction, 235
   script, 159
   song, 327
   standards for, 788
   story, 428, 450–52
   tall tale, 48
Notebook, 5.
Opinion. *See* Persuasive writing.
Organization, 86–89, 140–44, 208–10, 244–51, 312–14, 380–82, 450–51, 464–65, 506–11, 622–29, 703–5, 752, 778–87, 797
   body, 511, 703
   cause and effect, 792
   chronological order, 229, 781, 794
   coherence, 780
   conclusion, 510, 703, 786–87
   feature-by-feature comparison, 509, 791
   introduction, 511, 703
   main idea, 53, 140, 786
   outlines 752–53, 800
   paragraphs, 143, 779–81
   part and whole, 795
   problem-solution, 793
   spatial order, 781
   subject-by-subject comparison, 509, 791
   supporting detail, 53, 87–8, 140, 209, 783–84, 797
   topic sentences, 780
   transition, 229, 511, 781–82
   unity of purpose, 780
   word order, 109
Outlines. *See* Organization.
Paragraphs. *See* Organization.
Paraphrase. *See* Research reports.
Peer response, 87, 143, 209, 249, 313, 381, 451, 565, 627, 703, 753, 774–75
   identifying, 775
   questions for feedback, 774
   replying, 775
   sharing, 775
   summarizing, 775
   telling, 775
Persuasive writing, 796–97
   advertisement, 339, 524, 619
   advice column, 226
   argument, 327
   award nomination, 115
   credo, 300
   editorial, 73
   opinion, use of, 796–97
   opinion essay, 622–29
   pamphlet, 268
   petition, 383
   proposal, 252
   speech, 402
Plagiarism, 801
Plotting, 450–51
Poetry, 63, 122, 227, 241, 270, 428, 484, 543, 562–66
   ballad, 339, 439, 619
   cinquain, 484
   haiku, 182
   narrative, 28, 168, 300, 468
   rhymed couplets, 344
Point of view, 159
Portfolio building, 4, 147
Precise language, 627–28, 786
Prewriting, 86, 208–09, 246–249, 312–13, 376–79, 450, 508–09, 564, 624–25, 702–03, 749–51, 772–777
   choosing a topic, 86, 138, 140, 208, 246, 312, 376–78, 450, 506, 564, 622, 702, 749, 772
   determining purpose, 773
   discovery draft, 208, 248–49, 380, 510, 565, 626, 703, 774
   focusing response, 86, 140, 247, 378, 510, 624, 702, 750
   freewriting, 86–87, 313, 377, 451, 565, 624, 703, 749, 773
   gathering detail, 140, 625, 750
   note-taking, 141, 246–47, 506, 624–25, 751
Proofreading. *See* Editing.
Publishing your writing, 250–51, 382–83, 628–29, 777. *See also* Word processing.
Questions
   as conclusion, 786
   as introduction, 778
Quotation, 209, 751, 784, 800
Recommendations, 787
Research reports, 748–54, 798–801
   documenting quotation, 801

note-taking for, 751, 799
paraphrasing sources, 751, 798, 800
source cards, 750–51, 799
source lists, 755, 801
sources for, 799
thesis statement, 798, 800
Revising, 88, 144, 210, 250, 314, 381–82, 452, 512, 566, 628, 704, 753–4, 775–77, 815.
See also Editing; Word processing.
Rewriting, exercises in,
capitalization, 841
modifiers, 830, 832
nouns, 823, 829
paragraphs, 814, 828
pronouns, 825, 829
sentences, 812, 842, 846, 848, 849, 851
verbs, 824, 818, 821, 836, 838
Rough draft. See Drafting.
Sensory detail, 247, 562–63, 566, 783
Sentence variety, 87, 249, 700–01
Sequence of action, expression of, 835–36
Setting, 448–49
Similarity, expression of. See Transitions.
Sound devices, 565–66
Sources. See Research reports.
Statistics, use of, 783, 796
Style, 64, 402, 448–49, 524, 562, 700–01
Thesis statement. See Research reports.
Time of action, expression of, 835–36
Topic sentence. See Organization.
Transitions, 511–12
similarities, 511
differences, 511
Visuals, creating and using, 807–08. See also Classifying and diagramming.
charts, 808
clip-art, 807
graphs, 808
spreadsheets, 807
tables, 807
Word choice, 84–85, 143, 524, 563, 627
Word processing, 804–06
dictionary on, 804
formatting pages, 805
formatting type, 805
grammar checker, 804
peer editing on, 806
proofreading on, 804
search and replace, 804
spell checker, 804
templates, 805

thesaurus on, 804
type face, 805
type size, 805
type style, 805
Writing about literature, 84–89, 206–11, 253, 310–15, 385, 448–53, 515, 562–66, 700–05
interpretation, 208–10
personal response, 84–89, 138
researching story background, 748–54
responding as a character, 28, 108, 122, 135, 194, 241, 268, 275, 289, 300, 327, 380, 402, 422, 439, 450–53, 468, 503, 524, 534, 553, 619
responding to a character, 21, 37, 147, 194, 226, 268, 275, 344, 402, 428, 439, 468, 503, 514, 554, 619
responding to action, 289, 312–14
responding to imagery, 108, 182, 300, 422, 535, 773
responding to speaker, 113, 115, 178, 226, 428, 543
responding to theme, 700–5
Writing from experience, 138–45, 244–251, 253, 376–83, 385, 506–513, 515, 622–29, 748–54.
See also Expressive and personal writing.

Vocabulary Skills

Acrostic, 276, 525
Acting out meaning (exercise), 404
Analogy, 328
Antonyms, 137, 404, 536
Computer science, vocabulary in, 278, 290
Context clues, 23, 38, 64, 74, 123, 222, 236, 243, 270, 278, 301, 340, 356, 375, 389, 413, 423, 469, 505, 621
Prefixes, 160, 236
Rhymes, 621
Root words, 160
Suffixes, 160, 236
Synonyms, 101, 137, 196, 356, 536
Word parts, 160
Wordplay, 179, 525

Research and Study Skills

Bibliographies. See Sources.
CD-ROMs, 803
Documentation. See Sources.
Electronic books, 803
Infotrac, 624
Internet, the. See On-line resources.
Library research, 378, 624, 803

picture book, 698
pop-up, 698
portrait, 227
poster, 136, 383
puppets, 356
scrapbook, 747
sculpture, 620
slide show, 251
song, 242, 269, 327, 388
T-shirt, 92
time line, 269, 659
trading cards, 727
travel brochure, 49, 242
trivia, 747
wanted poster, 108, 747
Dramatic presentations, 109, 115, 168, 236, 269, 301, 358, 554, 680. *See also* Stage construction, Stage directions, Stage sets, *and* Story telling.
    dialogue, 345
    dramatic recording, 620
    monologue, 570
    pantomime, 146
    puppet show, 726
    radio play, 359, 373, 374
    Readers Theater, 30, 101, 503
    role playing, 18, 150, 226, 235, 256, 275, 290, 384
    scene, 222
    sports broadcast, 484
    tableau, 146, 659
    talk show, 18, 439, 535
Interviewing, 63, 74, 344, 379, 405–13, 535, 766
Multimedia presentations, 809–11
    animation in, 810
    authoring programs, 809
    copyright permission for, 811
    guiding the user, 811
    photos and video, use of, 809
    sound, use of, 809
Poetry, reading aloud, 223
Props, 212
Public speaking, 30, 256
    debate, 195
    oral report, 169
    soapbox presentation, 383
Role playing. *See* Dramatic presentations.
Sound effects, 359, 373
Speeches. *See* Public speaking.
Spreadsheets. *See* Technology.
Stage construction, 699, 726
Stage directions, 357–58, 571
Stage sets, 212
Story telling, 268, 634–35, 746. *See also* Dramatic presentations.
Technology. *See also* Visuals.
    CD-ROMs, 803, 810
    clip-art, 807
    computers, 277–78, 289–90, 802–11
    electronic-mail, 289, 628, 802
    flow chart, 289
    Internet, 802, 810
    LaserLinks, 21, 29, 30, 36, 39, 50, 65, 74, 93, 101, 104, 109, 110, 117, 123, 124, 139, 161, 169, 170, 179, 184, 228, 236, 237, 359, 377, 389, 404, 413, 424, 440, 457, 469, 470, 486, 505, 526, 544, 554, 635, 623, 749
    on-line interview, 74
    spreadsheets, 807
    video game, 658
    videotaping, 518, 746
    word processing, 804–06
    World Wide Web, 802
Visuals, creation on computers, 807–08

computerized catalogs, 803
New York Times Index, 799
Note-taking, 751, 799
On-line resources
    commercial information services, 802
    electronic mail, 802
    Internet, 802
    World Wide Web, 802
Paraphrasing sources, 751, 800
Periodical indexes, 624, 799
Plagiarism, 801
Quotation, use of, 751, 800
Readers' Guide to Periodical Literature, 799
Research activities
    African kingdoms, 269
    animal teeth, 301
    aurora borealis (northern lights), 169
    bamboo, 681
    bears, 123
    birthday celebrations, 276
    buffalo, 727
    caterpillar, 544
    cats, 429
    Cesar Chavez, 554
    Ch'in Shih Huang Ti, 534
    computers, 290
    coral reefs, 49
    Crete
    deserts, 23
    Donner party, 38
    festivals, 747
    freckles, 525
    geese, 544
    Greek amphitheaters, 699
    hummingbirds, 680
    hurricanes, 699
    lacquer ware, 222
    Mexico, 403
    minstrels, 747
    monetary systems, 403, 746
    mushrooms, 236
    North Pole, 64
    oysters, 109
    pigeons, 195
    pole vaulting, 485
    pottery making, 698
    puppets, 726
    Qin (or Ch'in) dynasty, 535
    sharks, 49
    snakes, 374
    Songhai Empire, 269
    spice routes, 659
    textiles, 726
    Trinidad, 242
    U.S. flag, 345
    volcanoes, 136
    westward movement, 101
    worms, 160
    wrestling, 727
Research plan, 750–51
Research reports, 798–801
Source cards, 750–51, 799
Sources, 750–51, 755. *See also* Paraphrasing sources, Quotation, *and* Source cards.
    documentation of, 798, 801
    evaluation of, 799
    primary, 339
    secondary, 339
Thesis statement, 798, 800

Speaking, Listening, and Viewing

Choral reading, 345, 537
Clip-art. See Technology.
Copyright permission. *See* Multimedia presentations.
Creative response
    advertisement, 289
    animation, 355
    background music, 374
    board game, 570, 658
    book display, 681
    book jacket, 301, 698
    calligraphy, 659
    collage, 116, 179, 428, 726
    comic strip, 37, 160, 256
    costumes, 440
    dance, 49, 227
    diorama, 23, 403, 699
    display, 222, 236, 413
    flipbook, 355
    fresco, 699
    hieroglyphics, 699
    illustration, 48, 74, 109, 169, 269, 276, 698
    jigsaw puzzle, 388
    kite, 681
    labyrinth, 658
    map, 170, 178, 195, 269, 619, 659, 699
    mobile, 146
    model, 136, 440, 469, 535
    mosaic, 136
    mural, 92, 747
    museum display, 680
    musical accompaniment, 116, 403
    photo essay, 251
    photographic display, 554

Index of Titles and Authors

Page numbers that appear in italics refer to biographical information

A
Aaron's Gift, 184
Abd al-Rahman Ibrahima, 257
Adoption of Albert, The, 151
Alegría, Ricardo E., 682, *693*
Alexander, Sue, 21, *29*
All-American Slurp, The, 6
Analysis of Baseball, 480
Ancestors, 267
Angelou, Maya, 110, *116*
Another Mountain, 110
Anthony, Michael, 237, *243*
Arachne, 710
At Last I Kill a Buffalo, 457

B
Balcells, Jacqueline, 346, *356*
Bamboo Beads, The, 670
Barbara Frietchie, 341
Bashō, 180, *183*
Belpré, Pura, 660, *679*
Benét, Rosemary, 99
Benét, Stephen Vincent, 99
Berry, James, 223, *227*
Bethancourt, T. Ernesto, 277, *290*
Bruchac, Joseph, 708, *725*

C
Carroll, Lewis, 104, *109*
Champions, from, 441
Chang McTang McQuarter Cat, 424
Charles, Dorthi, 424, *429*
Chinatown, 170
Chrysalis Diary, 537
Ciardi, John, 424, *429*
Circuit, The, 545

Cisneros, Sandra, 271, *276*
Clark, Ann Nolan, 660, *669*
Clifton, Lucille, *552*
Cohen, Daniel, 526, *536*
Concrete Cat, 424
Coolidge, Olivia E., 708, *714*
Cremation of Sam McGee, The, 161
Cricket in the Road, 237
Crutchfield, Les, 359, *375*
Cummings, Pat, 405, *413*

D
Damon and Pythias: A Drama, 684
Dang Manh Kha, 660, *669*
De Treviño, Elizabeth Borton, 389, *404*
Disobedient Child, The, 694
Dog of Pompeii, The, 124

E
Eleven, 271
Ellis, Elizabeth, 519, *525*
Enchanted Raisin, The, 346
Engle, Paul, 411

F
Farjeon, Eleanor, 240
Field, Rachel, *205*
1st, the, 552
First Emperor, The, 526
Fleischman, Paul, 537, *544*
Flores, Norma Landa, 193
Flower-Fed Buffaloes, The, 467
Flowers and Freckle Cream, 519

G
Ghost of the Lagoon, 39
Gold and Silver, Silver and Gold, from, 430
Gray, Patricia, 571
Grimm, brothers, 728, *745*
Growing Pains, 223

H

Haskins, Jim, 53, *64*
Haven, Susan, 302, *309*
Hobbit, The, 571
Hoover, H. M., 228, *236*
Howitt, Mary, 198
Hunter, Kristin, 555, *561*

I

In the Land of Small Dragon, 662
Issa, 180, *183*
It Seems I Test People, 223

J

Jen, Gish, 414, *423*
Jiménez, Francisco, 545, *554*
Johnson, Dorothy, 93, *101*
Joseph, Lynn, 660, *675*

K

Kendall, Carol, 728, *734*
Kha, Dang Manh, 660, *669*
King Thrushbeard, 741
Kissen, Fan, 682, *690*

L

Legend of the Hummingbird, The, 676
Lester, Julius, 638, *657*
Levoy, Myron, 184, *196*
Li, Yao-Wen, 728, *734*
Life Doesn't Frighten Me, 110
Lindsay, Vachel, 467
Little, Jean, 223, *227*
Littlefield, Bill, 441, *447*
Living Kuan-yin, The, 730
Long Hard Journey, A, from, 329

M

Matthew Henson at the Top of the World, 53
Mazer, Norma Fox, 75, *83*
McKissack, Fredrick, 329, *340*
McKissack, Patricia, 329, *340*
Mean Song, 83
Merriam, Eve, 83
Message from a Caterpillar, 537
Momaday, N. Scott, 202, *204*

Montejo, Victor, 682, *697*
Moore, Lilian, 537, *544*
Mora, Pat, 523
Murano, Shiro, 480, *485*
Mushroom, The, 228
Myers, Walter Dean, 257, *270*
My First Dive with the Dolphins, 65
My Friend Flicka, 486

N

Nadia the Willful, 21
Namioka, Lensey, 6
New World, 202
Night Journey, 338

O

O'Hara, Mary, 486, *505*
Oh Broom, Get to Work, 215
Oyewole, Abiodun, 110, *116*

P

Patterson, Raymond R., 180, *183*
Paulsen, Gary, 117, *123*
Pole Vault, 480
Primer Lesson, 27

Q

Quarrel, The, 240

R

Randall, Dudley, 267
Red Lion, The, 649
Reed, Don C., 65, *74*
Reznikoff, Charles, *201*
Robinson, Barbara, 151, *160*
Roethke, Theodore, 338
Same Song, 523
Sandburg, Carl, 2
San Souci, Robert D., 728, *740*
Saroyan, William, 291, *301*
School Play, The, 30
Schwartz, Alvin, 430, *440*
Scribe, The, 555
Secret of the Wall, The, 389
Service, Robert, 161, *169*
Shipment of Mute Fate, A, 359

870 INDEX OF TITLES AND AUTHORS

Shrewd Todie and Lyzer the Miser, 319
Silverstein, Shel, *197*
Singer, Isaac Bashevis, 319, *328*
Sister Fox and Brother Coyote, 735
Something Told the Wild Geese, 205
Soto, Gary, 30, *38*
Sperry, Armstrong, 39, *50*
Spider and the Fly, The, 198
Stamm, Claus, 708, *722*
Standing Bear, Luther, 457, *469*
Storm, Martin, 359
Street Corner Flight, 193
Summer of the Beautiful White Horse, The, 291
Swenson, May, 480, *485*

T
Talking with Artists, from, 405
Thanksgiving in Polynesia, 302
Three Haiku, 180
Three Strong Women, 715
Three Wishes, The, 691
Tolkien, J.R.R., 571, 618, *621*
Too Soon a Woman, 93
Treviño, Elizabeth Borton de, 389, *404*
Tuesday of the Other June, 75
Tutankhamen, 470
Two girls of twelve or so at a table, 201

U
Uchida, Yoshiko, 215, *222*
Untermeyer, Louis, 124, *137*
User Friendly, 277

W
Walrus and the Carpenter, The, 104
Water Color, 411
Western Wagons, 99
Where the Sidewalk Ends, 197
White, Anne Terry, 470, *479*
White Buffalo Calf Woman and the Sacred Pipe, The, 723
White Umbrella, The, 414
Whittier, John Greenleaf, 341, *345*
Why Monkeys Live in Trees, 654
Wings, 640
Wolkstein, Diane, 638, *653*
Woodsong, from, 117

Y
Yep, Laurence, 170, *179*
Yolen, Jane, 638, *648*

Acknowledgments *(continued)*

Little, Brown and Company: "My First Dive with the Dolphins," from *The Dolphins and Me* by Don C. Reed; Text Copyright © 1989 by Don C. Reed. By permission of Little, Brown and Company.

Elaine Markson Literary Agency, Inc.: "Tuesday of the Other June" by Norma Fox Mazer; Copyright © 1986 by Norma Fox Mazer. By permission of Norma Fox Mazer. All rights reserved.

Marian Reiner: "Mean Song," from *There Is No Rhyme for Silver* by Eve Merriam; Copyright © 1962 by Eve Merriam, renewed 1990 by Eve Merriam. Reprinted by permission of Marian Reiner.

McIntosh and Otis, Inc.: "Too Soon a Woman" by Dorothy Johnson; Copyright 1953 by Dorothy M. Johnson, renewed © 1981 by Dorothy M. Johnson. Reprinted by permission of McIntosh and Otis, Inc.

Brandt & Brandt Literary Agents, Inc.: "Western Wagons" by Rosemary and Stephen Vincent Benét; Copyright 1937 by Stephen Vincent Benét, renewed © 1965 by Thomas C. Benét, Stephanie B. Mahin, Rachel Benét Lewis. Reprinted by permission of Brandt & Brandt Literary Agents, Inc.

Random House, Inc.: "Life Doesn't Frighten Me," from *And Still I Rise* by Maya Angelou; Copyright © 1978 by Maya Angelou. Reprinted by permission of Random House, Inc.

Abiodun Oyewole: "Another Mountain," from *Rooted in the Soil,* first edition. Reprinted by permission of the author.

Macmillan Books for Young Readers: Excerpt from *Woodsong* by Gary Paulsen; Text Copyright © 1990 by Gary Paulsen. Reprinted by permission of Macmillan Books for Younger Readers, an imprint of Simon & Schuster Children's Publishing Division.

Estate of Louis Untermeyer: "The Dog of Pompeii," from *The Donkey of God* by Louis Untermeyer has been published with expressed permission by the Estate of Louis Untermeyer, Norma Anchin Untermeyer, c/o Professional Publishing Services.

Unit Two

HarperCollins Publishers, Inc.: "The Adoption of Albert," from *My Brother Louis Measures Worms* by Barbara Robinson; Copyright © 1988 by Barbara Robinson. "The Quarrel" from *Eleanor Farjeon's Poems for Children*; originally appeared in *Over the Garden Wall* by Eleanor Farjeon; Copyright 1933, renewed © 1961 by Eleanor Farjeon. "Aaron's Gift," from *The Witch of Fourth Street and Other Stories* by Myron Levoy; Text Copyright © 1972 by Myron Levoy. "Where The Sidewalk Ends," from *Where The Sidewalk Ends* by Shel Silverstein; Copyright © 1974 by Evil Eye Music, Inc. Reprinted by permission of HarperCollins Publishers.

Feinman & Krasilovsky: "The Cremation of Sam McGee," from *The Collected Poems of Robert Service* by Robert Service; Copyright 1910 by Dodd Mead & Company. Used by permission of the Estate of Robert Service.

Silver Burdett Press: "Chinatown," from *The Lost Garden* by Laurence Yep; Copyright © 1991 Laurence Yep. Used by permission of Julian Messner, a division of Silver Burdett Press. All rights reserved.

Penguin Books Ltd.: Haiku, "Beautiful, see through holes . . . ," by Kobayashi Issa (p. 123) from *The Penguin Book of Japanese Verse,* translated by Geoffrey Bownas and Anthony Thwaite (Penguin Books, 1964); Copyright © 1964 by Geoffrey Bownas and Anthony Thwaite. By permission of Penguin Books, Ltd.

Raymond R. Patterson: "Glory, Glory," from *26 Ways of Looking at a Black Man and Other Poems* by Raymond R. Patterson; Copyright © 1969 by Raymond R. Patterson. Reprinted by permission of the author.

F. E. Albi: "Street Corner Flight" by Norma Landa Flores, from *Sighs and Songs of Aztlan*; Copyright © 1975 by F. E. Albi and J. G. Nieto. Reprinted by permission of F. E. Albi, editor.

Piccadilly Press, Ltd.: *The Spider and the Fly* by Mary Howitt. First published by Piccadilly Press, Ltd, London 1987. Reprinted by permission of Piccadilly Press, Ltd.

New Directions Publishing Corporation: "Two girls of twelve or so at a table," from *By the Waters of Manhattan* by Charles Reznikoff; Copyright © 1959 by Charles Reznikoff. Reprinted by permission of New Directions Publishing Corporation.

N. Scott Momaday: "New World" by N. Scott Momaday. Reprinted by permission of the author.

Atheneum Books for Young Readers: "Something Told the Wild Geese," from *Poems* by Rachel Field; Copyright 1934 by Macmillan Publishing Company, renewed © 1962 by Arthur S. Pederson. Reprinted with the permission of Atheneum Books for Young Readers, an imprint of Simon & Schuster Children's Publishing Division.

Simon & Schuster: "Oh Broom, Get to Work," from *The Invisible Thread* by Yoshiko Uchida; Copyright © 1991. By permission of the publisher, Julian Messner, a Division of Simon & Schuster.

Harcourt Brace & Company and Penguin Books, Ltd.: "It Seems I Test People," from *When I Dance* by James Berry; Copyright © 1988, renewed 1991 by James Berry. Reprinted by permission of Harcourt Brace & Company and Penguin Books, Ltd.

HarperCollins Publishers, Inc., and Kids Can Press: "Growing Pains," from *Hey World, Here I Am!* by Jean Little; Text Copyright © 1968 by Jean Little. By permission of HarperCollins Publishers and Kids Can Press.

Helen M. Hoover: "The Mushroom," from *The Big Book for Our Planet* by Helen M. Hoover. By permission of Helen M. Hoover.

Andre Deutsch, Ltd.: "Cricket in the Road," from *Cricket in the Road* by Michael Anthony; Copyright © 1973 by Michael Anthony. Reprinted by permission of Andre Deutsch, Ltd., London.

Unit Three

HarperCollins Publishers, Inc.: "Abd al-Rahman Ibrahima," from *Now Is Your Time: The African–American Struggle for Freedom* by Walter Dean Myers; Copyright © 1991 by Walter Dean Myers. Reprinted by permission of HarperCollins Publishers.

Dudley Randall: "Ancestors," from *After the Killing* by Dudley Randall; Copyright © 1973 by Dudley Randall. Reprinted by permission of the author.

Susan Bergholz Literary Services: "Eleven," from *Woman Hollering Creek* by Sandra Cisneros; Copyright © 1991 by Sandra Cisneros. Published by Vintage Books, a division of Random House, Inc., New York and in hardcover by Random House, Inc., New York. Reprinted by permission of Susan Bergholz Literary Services.

Delacorte Press: "User Friendly" by T. Ernesto Bethancourt, from *Connections: Short Stories* edited by Donald R. Gallo; Copyright © 1989 by T. Ernesto Bethancourt. Used by permission of Delacorte Press, a division of Bantam

Doubleday Dell Publishing Group, Inc.

Harcourt Brace & Company and The William Saroyan Foundation: "The Summer of the Beautiful White Horse," from *My Name Is Aram*; Copyright 1938 and renewed © 1966 by William Saroyan. Reprinted by permission of Harcourt Brace & Company and The William Saroyan Foundation.

Delacorte Press: "Thanksgiving in Polynesia" by Susan Haven, from *Funny You Should Ask*, edited by David Gale; Copyright © 1992 by Susan Haven. Used by permission of Delacorte Press, a division of Bantam Doubleday Dell Publishing Group, Inc.

Farrar, Straus & Giroux, Inc.: "Shrewd Todie and Lyzer the Miser," from *Stories for Children* by Isaac Bashevis Singer; Copyright © 1984 by Isaac Bashevis Singer. By permission of Farrar, Straus & Giroux, Inc.

Walker and Company: Excerpt from *A Long Hard Journey: The Story of the Pullman Porter* by Patricia and Fredrick McKissack; Copyright © 1989 by Patricia and Fredrick McKissack. By permission of Walker and Company. All Rights Reserved.

Doubleday: "Night Journey," from *The Collected Poems of Theodore Roethke* by Theodore Roethke; Copyright 1940 by Theodore Roethke. By permission of Doubleday, a division of Bantam Doubleday Dell Publishing Group, Inc.

Latin American Literary Review Press: "The Enchanted Raisin" by Jacqueline Balcells. Reprinted by permission of the publisher, Latin American Review Press, Pittsburgh, Pennsylvania.

CBS Radio and LaVonne Crutchfield: *A Shipment of Mute Fate* by Les Crutchfield; Copyright © 1953 by the Columbia Broadcasting System, Inc. By permission of CBS and the Estate of Les Crutchfield.

Women's Sport and Fitness Magazine: "Sexism and Soccer in Seattle" by Erika Dillman, from *Women's Sport and Fitness* Magazine, April 1995. Reprinted by permission of Women's Sport and Fitness Magazine.

Houghton Mifflin Company: "Threatened and Endangered U.S. Wildlife Species" table from *1993 Information Please Environmental Almanac;* Copyright © 1992 by World Resources Institute. Reprinted by permission of Houghton Mifflin Company. All rights reserved.

Unit Four

Ray Pierre Corsini and Elizabeth Borton de Treviño: "The Secret of the Wall" by Elizabeth Borton de Treviño; Copyright © 1966 by Elizabeth Borton de Treviño. Reprinted by permission of the author and Ray Pierre Corsini, agent for the author.

Jerry Pinkney: "Jerry Pinkney," from *Talking with Artists*, edited by Pat Cummings and published by Bradbury Press. Copyright © 1992 by Jerry Pinkney. Used with permission.

Random House, Inc.: "Water Color," from *Embrace: Selected Love Poems* by Paul Engle; Copyright © 1969 by Paul Engle. By permission of Random House, Inc.

Maxine Groffsky Literary Agency: "The White Umbrella" by Gish Jen. Copyright © 1984 by Gish Jen. First published in *The Yale Review*. Reprinted by permission of the author.

HarperCollins College Publishers: "Concrete Cat," from *An Introduction to Poetry* edited by X. J. Kennedy and Dana Gioia; Copyright © 1994 by X. J. Kennedy and Dana Gioia. By permission of HarperCollins Publishers, Inc.

HarperCollins Publishers: "Chang McTang McQuarter Cat," from *You Read to Me, I'll Read to You* by John Ciardi; Copyright © 1962 by John Ciardi. By permission of HarperCollins Publishers, Inc.

Farrar, Straus & Giroux, Inc.: Excerpt from *Gold and Silver, Silver and Gold* by Alvin Schwartz; Copyright © 1988 by Alvin Schwartz. By permissions of Farrar, Straus & Giroux, Inc.

Little, Brown and Company: "Diana Golden," from *Champions* by Bill Littlefield. Text Copyright © 1993 by Bill Littlefield. By permission of Little, Brown and Company.

Houghton Mifflin Company: "At Last I Kill a Buffalo," from *My Indian Boyhood* by Chief Luther Standing Bear; Copyright 1931 by Chief Luther Standing Bear, renewed © 1959 by May Jones. Reprinted by permission of Houghton Mifflin Company. All rights reserved.

Dutton Children's Books: "The Flower-Fed Buffaloes," from *Going to the Stars* by Vachel Lindsay; Copyright 1926 by D. Appleton & Co., renewed 1954 by Elizabeth C. Lindsay. Used by permission of Dutton Children's Books, a division of Penguin Books, USA.

Random House, Inc.: "Tomb of Tutankh-Amen," from *Lost Worlds* by Anne Terry White; Copyright 1941 by Random House, Inc., renewed © 1969 by Anne Terry White. Reprinted by permission of Random House, Inc.

Poetry Magazine and Constance Urdang: "Pole Vault" by Shiro Murano, translated by Constance Urdang and Satoru Sato; first appeared in *Poetry,* Copyright 1956 by The Modern Poetry Association. Reprinted by permission of the Editor of *Poetry.*

Simon & Schuster Books for Young Readers: "Analysis of Baseball," from *The Complete Poems to Solve* by May Swenson; Copyright © 1993 by The Literary Estate of May Swenson. Reprinted by permission of Simon & Schuster Books for Young Readers, an imprint of Simon & Schuster Children's Publishing Division.

John Hawkins & Associates, Inc.: "My Friend Flicka," by Mary O'Hara, published by *Story Magazine*, 1941; Copyright 1941 by Mary O'Hara. Reprinted by permission of John Hawkins & Associates, Inc.

Unit Five

Elizabeth Ellis: "Flowers and Freckle Cream," by Elizabeth Ellis from *Best-Loved Stories Told at the National Storytelling Festival*. Copyright © by Elizabeth Ellis. Reprinted by permission of Elizabeth Ellis.

Arte Publico Press: "Same Song," from *Borders* (Houston: Arte Publico Press—University of Houston, 1985) by Pat Mora is reprinted with the permission of Arte Publico Press.

Henry Morrison, Inc.: Excerpt from "The First Emperor," from *The Tomb Robbers* by Daniel Cohen, copyright © 1980 by Daniel Cohen. This selection is used by permission of the author and Henry Morrison, Inc., his agents.

Marian Reiner, Literary Agent: "Message from a Caterpillar," from *Little Raccoon and Poems from the Woods* by Lilian Moore; Copyright © 1975 by Lilian Moore. Reprinted by permission of Marian Reiner for the author.

HarperCollins Publishers, Inc.: "Chrysalis Diary," from *Joyful Noise* by Paul Fleischman; Text Copyright © 1988 by Paul Fleischman. Reprinted by permission of HarperCollins Publishers.

Francisco Jiménez: "The Circuit," from *Arizona Quarterly,* Autumn 1973. Reprinted by permission of the author.

BOA Editions Limited: "the 1st," from *Good Woman: Poems and a Memoir 1969–1980* by Lucille Clifton; Copyright © 1987 by Lucille Clifton. Reprinted with the permission of BOA Editions, Ltd., 92 Park Ave., Brockport, NY 14420.

Jane Dystel Literary Management: "The Scribe," from *Guests in the Promised*

Land by Kristin Hunter. Copyright © 1968, 1972, 1973 by Kristin Hunter. Reprinted by permission of the author.

The Dramatic Publishing Company: *The Hobbit,* a dramatization by Patricia Gray; Copyright © 1987 by Patricia Gray, based upon the book by J.R.R. Tolkien. Printed in the United States of America. All Rights Reserved. All inquiries regarding performance rights should be addressed to the Dramatic Publishing Company, 311 Washington St., Woodstock, IL 60098.

Unit Six

Harcourt Brace & Company: Entire text of *Wings* by Jane Yolen; Copyright © 1991 by Jane Yolen. Reprinted by permission of Harcourt Brace & Company.

Rosenstone/Wender: *The Red Lion* by Diane Wolkstein; Copyright © 1977 by Diane Wolkstein. By permission of Rosenstone/Wender.

Scholastic Inc.: "Why Monkeys Live in Trees," from *How Many Spots Does a Leopard Have?* by Julius Lester; Copyright © 1989 by Julius Lester. Reprinted by permission of Scholastic Inc.

Viking Penguin: Excerpt from *In the Land of Small Dragon* as told by Dang Manh Kha to Ann Nolan Clark; Copyright © 1979 by Ann Nolan Clark. Used by permission of Viking Penguin, a division of Penguin Books USA Inc.

Houghton Mifflin Company: "The Bamboo Beads," from *A Wave in Her Pocket* by Lynn Joseph; Copyright ©1991 by Lynn Joseph. "The Legend of Damon and Pythias," from *The Bag of Fire and Other Plays* by Fan Kissen; Copyright © 1964 by Houghton Mifflin Company, renewed © 1993 by John Kissen Heaslip. "Arachne," from *Greek Myths* retold by Olivia E. Coolidge; Copyright 1949, renewed © 1977 by Olivia E. Coolidge. Reprinted by permission of Houghton Mifflin Company. All rights reserved.

Penguin Books USA Inc.: "The Legend of the Hummingbird," from *Once in Puerto Rico* by Pura Belpré; Copyright © 1973 by Pura Belpré. Used by permission of Frederick Warne Books, a division of Penguin Books USA Inc.

Ricardo E. Alegría: "The Three Wishes," from *The Three Wishes: A Collection of Puerto Rican Folktales,* selected and adapted by Ricardo E. Alegría, translated by Elizabeth Culbert; Copyright © 1969 by Ricardo E. Alegría. Reprinted by permission of author.

Curbstone Press: Excerpt from "The Disobedient Child," from *The Bird Who Cleans the World and Other Mayan Fables* by Victor Montejo. Translated by Wallace Kaufman (Curbstone Press, 1991). Reprinted with permission of Curbstone Press.

Dial Books for Young Readers: "Three Strong Women," from *The Woman in the Moon and Other Tales of Forgotten Heroines* by James Riordan; Copyright © 1984 by James Riordan. Used by permission of Dial Books for Young Readers, a division of Penguin Books USA Inc.

Fulcrum Publishing: "The White Buffalo Calf Woman and the Sacred Pipe" by Joseph Bruchac, from *Native American Stories* told by Joseph Bruchac, from *Keepers of the Animals* by Michael J. Caduto and Joseph Bruchac, Fulcrum Publishing, Inc., 350 Indiana St., #350, Golden, CO 80401.

Houghton Mifflin Company and Carol Kendall: "The Living Kuan-yin," from *Sweet and Sour: Tales from China* by Carol Kendall and Yao-Wen Li; Copyright © 1980 by Carol Kendall and Yao-Wen Li. Reprinted by permission of Clarion Books/Houghton Mifflin Company and Carol Kendall. All rights reserved.

Philomel Books: "Sister Fox and Brother Coyote," from *Cut from the Same Cloth* by Robert San Souci; Text Copyright © 1993 by Robert D. San Souci. Reprinted by permission of Philomel Books, a division of the Putnam Publishing Group.

Doubleday: "King Thrushbeard," from *Grimms' Tales for Young and Old* by Jakob and Wilhelm Grimm; Copyright © 1977 by Ralph Manheim. Used by permission of Doubleday, a division of Bantam Doubleday Dell Publishing Group.

The following sections were prepared by **Ligature, Inc., of Chicago, Illinois:** Learning the Language of Literature, Writing About Literature, Writing from Experience, Writing Handbook, Multimedia Handbook, and Grammar Handbook.

Art Credits

Commissioned Art and Photography
2 *top*, 84, 85, 88, 138, 139, 140 *bottom*, 144, 145, 206–210, top 245, 247, 310–315, 378 *top*, 379–381, 509–511, 513, 622, 623, 748, 749 *top right*, 751 *bottom*, 754, 755 Allan Landau. 4–5, 17, 29, 75, 86, 90–91, 109, 111–113, 118–119, 140 *top*, 142, 171, 173, 176, 180, 186, 188, 191, 216, 218, 222, 234, 238, 244 *bottom*, 246, 248–251, 256, 269, 279, 330, 332–336, 347, 351, 354, 356, 373–374, 376–377, 378 *bottom*, 382–383, 386, 388, 403, 406, 412, 415, 422, 433–438, 448–453, 471–472, 506–508, 512, 519–520, 523, 555, 557, 559–560, 562–569, 624–626, 629, 658, 662–663, 670–672, 676–678, 680, 698–705, 710–722, 726, 731, 741, 746, 747, 750, 751 *top*, 752 Sharon Hoogstraten. 29 Paul Dennis. 31 Karen Berntsen. 198–200 Russ Willms. 230-233 Mike Reed. 261–262, 264 Jennifer Carney. 302, 304, 307–308 Clare Hirn. 320–325 Laura Montenegro. 426–427 Barb Rohm. 487, 489, 492, 495, 496, 499 Fran Lee. 506 Josh Neufeld. 577, 580, 588, 594, 599, 600-601, 607, 613, 617 Anne Gavitt. 635 Richard Waldrep.

Maps: 632–633, 636–639, 660–661, 682, 708–709, 728–729 John Sandford. Maps on all Previewing and Responding pages: Robert Voights.

Author Photographs and Portraits
29 Willy Leon. 50 Courtesy of Mrs. Sperry. 74 Marine World Africa USA. 83 George Janoff. 101 Mansfield Library, University of Montana. 109, 345 Stock Montage. 116 UPI/Bettmann. 137 The Library of Congress. 169 Culver Pictures. 179 Photo by K. Yep. 183 *top* Courtesy of New Orleans (Louisiana) Museum of Art; *bottom* Heibonsha, Ltd., Japan. 197, 204, 205, 328, 429, 485, 621 AP/Wide World Photos, Inc. 201, 725 Copyright © Layle Silbert. 222 Copyright © June Finfer, Filmedia, Ltd. 227 Guelph (Ontario) *Daily Mercury.* 276 Rubén Guzmán. 301 National Archives. 375 CBS Photography. 423 Copyright © Jerry Bauer. 554 Courtesy of the University of Santa Clara (California). 561 John I. Lattony. 653 Rachel C. Zucker. 675 Ed Scott. 697 Mel Rosenthal. 745 The Granger Collection, New York.

Miscellaneous Art Credits
xiv *Mecklenberg County: High Cotton Mother and Child* (1978), Romare Bearden. Courtesy of the Estate of Romare Bearden. xix *The Hill: Hobbiton-*

Across-the-Water (1966), J.R.R. Tolkien. Illustration from *The Hobbit* by J.R.R. Tolkien. Copyright © 1966 J.R.R. Tolkien. Reprinted by permission of Houghton Mifflin Co. All rights reserved. **xxi** *Exotic Landscape* (1910), Henri Rousseau. Oil on canvas, $51\frac{1}{4}'' \times 64''$. The Norton Simon Foundation, Pasadena, California. **2** *bottom left* Copyright © Owen Franken/Stock, Boston; *bottom right* Copyright © Richard Hutchings/PhotoEdit. **2–3** *top* Copyright © Lorentz Gullachsen/Tony Stone Images. **3** *top* Copyright © 1990 Arnold Adler/Black Star; **22–23** Copyright © Hugh Sitton/Tony Stone Images. **40–41** Copyright © 1995 Cheryl Cooper. **49** Copyright © Marc Chamberlain/Tony Stone Images. **65** Copyright © François Gohier/Photo Researchers, Inc. **66** Copyright © Bill Wood/Westlight. **66** Copyright © Leland Bobbe/Tony Stone Images. **90** *bottom left* From *The Complete Book of Dog Care: How to Raise a Happy and Healthy Dog* by Ulrich Klever, Copyright © 1989 by Barron's Educational Series, Inc. Reprinted by arrangement with Barron's Educational Series, Inc., Hauppauge, New York. **92** Copyright © R. Walker/H. Armstrong Roberts. **93** The Granger Collection, New York. **124** Copyright © 1995 Everett Johnson/Frozen Images. **125** Doric pillars on Temple of Zeus, Nemea, Peloponnesus, Greece. Copyright © M. Thonig/H. Armstrong Roberts. **136** Detail of *Cave Canem* [Beware of dog], unknown artist. Roman mosaic, Museo Archeologico Nazionale, Naples, Italy, Scala/Art Resource, New York. **138** *right, Calvin and Hobbes* Copyright © 1986 Watterson. Distributed by Universal Press Syndicate. Reprinted with permission. All rights reserved. **151** Copyright © Robert E. Daemmrich/Tony Stone Images. **169** Copyright © Tom Walker/Tony Stone Images. **182** Detail of incense wrapper (Edo period, Japan; 17th–18th centuries) attributed to Ogata Korin. Wrapper mounted on hanging scroll, ink and color on gold-ground paper, 33 cm × 24.1 cm, The Art Institute of Chicago, Russell Tyson Purchase Fund (1966.470). Photo Copyright © 1994 The Art Institute of Chicago. All rights reserved. **193** Copyright © Leland Bobbe/Tony Stone Images. **195** The Bettmann Archive, New York. **212–213** From a production of *Bold Girls* by Rona Munro, produced by Eclipse Theatre Company, Chicago. Scenic design by Ken Puttbach. **228** NASA. **229** The Granger Collection, New York. **242** *left* Copyright © 1982 Tom Hollyman/Photo Researchers; *right* Copyright © Katrina Thomas/Photo Researchers. **244** *bottom left* Courtesy of Hayun Cho; *bottom right* Copyright © Philip Saltonstall. **245** *right* UPI/Bettmann. **247** *center* Courtesy of Lake Bluff Middle School, Lake Bluff, Illinois. **257** *Abd al-Rahman Ibrahima* (1828), Henry Inman. Reproduced from the collections of the Library of Congress. **272** Detail of *Cake Window (Seven Cakes)* (1970–1976), Wayne Thiebaud. Courtesy of Allan Stone Gallery, New York. **277** Archive Photos. **316–317** Copyright © Paul John Miller, all rights reserved. **319** The Bettmann Archive, New York. **328** Detail of *La cuillerée* [The spoonful of milk] (1912), Marc Chagall. Copyright © 1995 Artists Rights Society (ARS), New York/ADAGP, Paris. **329** Copyright © Frank Cezus/Tony Stone Images. **338** Smithsonian Institution, Washington, D.C. Pullman Negative Collection (Neg. # 4586). **342–343** Copyright © Ken Biggs/Tony Stone Images. **359** Copyright © 1995 Classic PIO Partners. **389** Copyright © 1995 Larry Stevens/Nawrocki Stock Photo Inc. All rights reserved. **390** Copyright © Camille Przewodek. **390** Copyright © Les Jorgensen/Photonica. **399** Detail of *Long Day's Shadow* (1994), Marilyn Sunderman. Courtesy of the artist, Sedona, Arizona. **405** Courtesy of Jerry Pinkney. **413** Detail of illustration by Jerry Pinkney. Illustration Copyright © 1994 Jerry Pinkney. From *John Henry* by Julius Lester, used with permission of Dial Books for Young Readers, a division of Penguin

Books USA Inc. **418** *bottom middle* Copyright © Tony Stone Images. **442, 445** Copyright © Joel Rogers/Tony Stone Images. **447** Copyright © Brooks Dodge/Sports File. **454–455** Guy Anderson. **469** Detail of robe with Mato Tope's exploits (about 1835), Mato Tope (Mandan people). Bern (Switzerland) Historical Museum. Copyright © Bern Historical Museum. Photo by Stefan Rebsamen. **477, 479** Copyright © Lee Boltin. **480** Copyright © Dave Cannon/Tony Stone Images. **481** Copyright © David Madison/Tony Stone Images. **487** Detail of *New Mexico Spring* (about 1950), Fremont Ellis. Oil on canvas, 36″ × 30″, The Anschutz Collection, Denver. Photo by James O. Milmoe. **507** *top left, top right* Richard Howard. **528** Chinese characters from *The Spirit of the Chinese Character.* Copyright © 1992 Running Heads Incorporated; *center* Copyright © An Keren/PPS/Photo Researchers, Inc. **535** Copyright © Laurie Platt Winfrey, Inc. **538** Copyright © Bill Ivy/Tony Stone Images. **539, 541–542** Illustrations Copyright © 1988 Eric Beddows. Selection reprinted by permission of Harper Collins Publishers. **540–542** *background* Copyright © Vera R. Storman/Tony Stone Images. **549, 551** Detail of *Chico* (1974), Hubert Shuptrine. Copyright © 1974 Hubert Shuptrine. All rights reserved, used with permission. **550** Detail of *The Dry Ditch* (1964), Kenneth M. Adams. Copyright © Eiteljorg Museum of American Indians and Western Art, Indianapolis, Indiana. **554** AP/Wide World Photos, Inc. **568** *center* Smithsonian Institution, National Museum of American History, Political History Collection (#937204). **570** Copyright © Roger Tully/The Stock Shop. **620** *The Hill: Hobbiton-Across-the-Water* (1966), J.R.R. Tolkien. Illustration from *The Hobbit* by J.R.R. Tolkien. Copyright © 1966 J.R.R. Tolkien. Reprinted by permission of Houghton Mifflin Co. All rights reserved. **622** Copyright © Doug Pensinger/Allsport USA. **626** *top* Copyright © L.L.T. Rhodes/Tony Stone Images; **633–634** Photography by Gordon Lewis. **636** *top* Copyright © Warren Garst/Tony Stone Images; *bottom* Seated figure, Olmec. Stone, 10″. Copyright © Lee Boltin. **637** *top left* Copyright © Ben Nakayama/Tony Stone Images; *top middle* Copyright © Andre Picou/Tony Stone Images; *bottom left and right* The Granger Collection, New York; *bottom middle* Copyright © Tony Stone Images. **639** Detail of illustration, Copyright © 1991 Dennis Nolan. From *Wings* by Jane Yolen, reproduced by permission of Harcourt Brace & Company. **660** Detail of *Hummingbirds in Thistle* (1955), Walter Anderson. Watercolor, Walter Anderson Museum of Art, Ocean Springs, Mississippi, courtesy of the family of Walter Anderson. **661** *top* Detail of illustration, Copyright © 1982 Vo-Dinh Mai. From *The Brocaded Slipper and Other Vietnamese Tales* by Lynette Dyer Vuong, reprinted by permission of HarperCollins Publishers; *bottom* Detail of illustration, Copyright © 1991 Brian Pinkney. Cover of *A Wave in Her Pocket* by Lynn Joseph, reprinted by permission of Clarion Books/Houghton Mifflin Co. All rights reserved. **666** Copyright © 1995 John Wilkinson/Nawrocki Stock Photo, Inc. All rights reserved. **668** Detail of illustration, Copyright © 1982 Vo-Dinh Mai. From *The Brocaded Slipper and Other Vietnamese Tales* by Lynette Dyer Vuong, reprinted by permission of HarperCollins Publishers. **682** Effigy vessel (about A.D. 1000–1250), unknown Mayan artist. Ceramic, painted red, blue, and white, 31.7 cm high, Museo Nacional de Antropología, Mexico. Photo Copyright © Stuart Rome. **683** Copyright © Camille Przewodek. **683** Detail of statue of Diadoumenos, unknown artist. Roman copy of Greek original (440 B.C.), Pentelic marble, The Metropolitan Museum of Art, Fletcher Fund, 1925 (25.78.56). Copyright © The Metropolitan Museum of Art. **706** *background,* Copyright © Cowgirl Stock Photography.

707 *bottom* Copyright © 1982 Warner Bros., Inc. Photo courtesy of the Kobal Collection; *background,* Copyright © Cowgirl Stock Photography; **708** *Buffalo Calf Woman,* Oscar Howe. U.S. Department of the Interior, Indian Arts and Crafts Board, Sioux Indian Museum and Crafts Center, Rapid City, South Dakota. **709** Detail of illustration by Arvis Stewart, from *The Macmillan Book of Greek Gods and Heroes* by Alice Low. Copyright © 1985 Macmillan Publishing Company, reprinted with the permission of Simon & Schuster Books for Young Readers, an imprint of Simon & Schuster Children's Publishing Division. **709** Figure of a woman (late 1600s), unknown Japanese artist. Arita ware, Kakiemon porcelain with overglaze polychrome enamel, $14\frac{1}{4}'' \times 5\frac{1}{2}''$, Asian Art Museum of San Francisco, The Avery Brundage Collection (B62 P5+). **728** Details Copyright © John Nieto. Courtesy of Bailey Nelson Gallery, Seattle, Washington. **729** Copyright © Joyce Patti. **735** Copyright © Jim Stamates/Tony Stone Images. **739** Details Copyright © John Nieto. Courtesy of Bailey Nelson Gallery, Seattle, Washington. **748** *center* Copyright © Felicia Martinez/PhotoEdit. **749** *top left* Copyright © George Mars Cassidy/Tony Stone Images; *center* Copyright © Dallas and John Heaton/Westlight; *bottom left* Copyright © Chris Cole/Tony Stone Images; *bottom right* Copyright © Tony Stone Images. **754** *center* Copyright © Hiroyuki Matsumoto/Black Star. **788** Copyright © Janet Gill/Tony Stone Images. **790** Copyright © Victoria Ross/Southern Stock Photo Agency. **796** Copyright © John Kelly/The Image Bank. **798** Copyright © Christina Rose Mufson/Comstock. **802** Netscape, Netscape Navigator and the Netscape Communications Corporation Logo are trademarks of Netscape Communications Corporation; *center* OpenNet Technologies, Inc. **805–807** Screen shots reprinted with permission from Microsoft Corporation. **808** Used with express permission. Adobe and Adobe Illustrator are trademarks of Adobe Systems Incorporated. **809** Copyright © Lori Adamski Peek/Tony Stone Images. **811** Copyright © Dennis O'Clair/Tony Stone Images.

Teacher Review Panels *(continued)*

Bonnie Garrett, Davis Middle School, Compton School District

Sally Jackson, Madrona Middle School, Torrance Unified School District

Sharon Kerson, Los Angeles Center for Enriched Studies, Los Angeles Unified School District

Gail Kidd, Center Middle School, Azusa School District

Corey Lay, ESL Department Chairperson, Chester Nimitz Middle School, Los Angeles Unified School District

Myra LeBendig, Forshay Learning Center, Los Angeles Unified School District

Dan Manske, Elmhurst Middle School, Oakland Unified School District

Joe Olague, Language Arts Department Chairperson, Alder Middle School, Fontana School District

Pat Salo, 6th Grade Village Leader, Hidden Valley Middle School, Escondido Elementary School District

FLORIDA

Judi Briant, English Department Chairperson, Armwood High School, Hillsborough County School District

Beth Johnson, Polk County English Supervisor, Polk County School District

Sharon Johnston, Learning Resource Specialist, Evans High School, Orange County School District

Eileen Jones, English Department Chairperson, Spanish River High School, Palm Beach County School District

Jan McClure, Winter Park High School Orange County School District

Wanza Murray, English Department Chairperson (retired), Vero Beach Senior High School, Indian River City School District

Shirley Nichols, Language Arts Curriculum Specialist Supervisor, Marion County School District

Debbie Nostro, Ocoee Middle School, Orange County School District

Barbara Quinaz, Assistant Principal, Horace Mann Middle School, Dade County School District

OHIO

Joseph Bako, English Department Chairperson, Carl Shuler Middle School, Cleveland City School District

Deb Delisle, Language Arts Department Chairperson, Ballard Brady Middle School, Orange School District

Ellen Geisler, English/Language Arts Department Chairperson, Mentor Senior High School, Mentor School District

Dr. Mary Gove, English Department Chairperson, Shaw High School, East Cleveland School District

Loraine Hammack, Executive Teacher of the English Department, Beachwood High School, Beachwood City School District

Sue Nelson, Shaw High School, East Cleveland School District

Mary Jane Reed, English Department Chairperson, Solon High School, Solon City School District

Nancy Strauch, English Department Chairperson, Nordonia High School, Nordonia Hills City School District

Ruth Vukovich, Hubbard High School, Hubbard Exempted Village School District

TEXAS

Anita Arnold, English Department Chairperson, Thomas Jefferson High School, San Antonio Independent School District

Gilbert Barraza, J.M. Hanks High School, Ysleta School District

Sandi Capps, Dwight D. Eisenhower High School, Alding Independent School District

Judy Chapman, English Department Chairperson, Lawrence D. Bell High School, Hurst-Euless-Bedford School District

Pat Fox, Grapevine High School, Grapevine-Colley School District

LaVerne Johnson, McAllen Memorial High School, McAllen Independent School District

Donna Matsumura, W.H. Adamson High School, Dallas Independent School District

Ruby Mayes, Waltrip High School, Houston Independent School District

Mary McFarland, Amarillo High School, Amarillo Independent School District

Adrienne Thrasher, A.N. McCallum High School, Austin Independent School District

Manuscript Reviewers *(continued)*

Maryann Lyons, Literacy Specialist, Mentor teacher, San Francisco Unified School District, San Francisco, California

Karis MacDonnell, Ed.D., Dario Middle School, Miami, Florida

Bonnie J. Mansell, Downey Adult School, Downey, California

Martha Mitchell, Memorial Middle School, Orlando, Florida

Nancy Nachman, Landmark High School, Jacksonville, Florida

Karen Williams Perry, English Department Chairperson, Kennedy Jr. High School, Lisle, Illinois

Julia Pferdehirt, free-lance writer, former Special Education teacher, Middleton, Wisconsin

Phyllis Stewart Rude, English Department Head, Mears Jr./Sr. High School, Anchorage, Alaska

Leo Schubert, Bettendorf Middle School, Bettendorf, Iowa

Gertrude H. Vannoy, Curriculum Liaison Specialist, Gifted and Horizon teacher, Meany Middle School, Seattle, Washington

Richard Wagner, Language Arts Curriculum Coordinator, Paradise Valley School District, Phoenix, Arizona

Stephen J. Zadravec, Newmarket Jr./Sr. High School, Newmarket, New Hampshire